D0042048

Great Stories of Suspense

GREAT STORIES
OF SUSPENSE

edited by

ROSS MACDONALD

Alfred A. Knopf / New York / 1974

THIS IS A BORZOI BOOK
PUBLISHED BY ALFRED A. KNOPF, INC.

Copyright © 1974 by Alfred A. Knopf, Inc.

All rights reserved under International and Pan-American Copyright
Conventions. Published in the United States by Alfred A. Knopf, Inc.,
New York, and simultaneously in Canada by Random House of Canada
Limited, Toronto. Distributed by Random House, Inc., New York.

Published by The Reader's Digest Association, Inc., 1993,
by permission of Alfred A. Knopf, Inc.

LIBRARY OF CONGRESS CATALOGING IN PUBLICATION DATA

Macdonald, Ross, Date comp.
Great stories of suspense.
CONTENTS: Collier, J. Wet Saturday. —Fearing, K. The big clock.
—Christie, A. What Mrs. McGillicuddy saw! [etc.]
1. Detective and mystery stories, American.
2. Detective and mystery stories, English. I. Title.
PZI.M146Gr [PS648.D4]   823'.0872   74-7743
ISBN 0-394-49292-7

Manufactured in the United States of America

Grateful acknowledgment is given for permission to reprint previously
published material:

WET SATURDAY, John Collier. Reprinted by permission of Harold
Matson Company, Inc. Originally published in *The New Yorker*. Copyright
1938, 1965 by John Collier.

THE BIG CLOCK, Kenneth Fearing. Reprinted by permission of Russell &
Volkening, Inc. as agents for the Estate of Kenneth Fearing and Xanadu
Publication Limited. Copyright 1946 by Kenneth Fearing and renewed
1974 by Bruce Fearing.

WHAT MRS. MCGILLICUDDY SAW!, Agatha Christie. Reprinted by permission of The Putnam Berkley Publishing Group, Inc. Copyright © 1957
by Agatha Christie Ltd.

THE PAYOFF, Stanley Ellin. Reprinted by permission of Curtis Brown
Ltd. Originally published in *Ellery Queen's Mystery Magazine*. Copyright
© 1971 by Stanley Ellin.

THE BASEMENT ROOM, Graham Greene. Reprinted by permission of Viking Penguin, a division of Penguin Books USA, Inc. and David Higham Associates. From *Collected Stories* by Graham Greene (in the U.K., *Nineteen Stories*, Heinemann). Copyright 1947, renewed 1975 by Graham Greene.

FLY PAPER, Dashiell Hammett. Reprinted by permission of Random House, Inc. From *The Big Knockover: Selected Stories and Short Novels of Dashiell Hammett*. Copyright 1929 and renewed 1957 by Lillian Hellman.

THE FIVE-FORTY-EIGHT, John Cheever. Reprinted by permission of Wylie, Aitken & Stone, Inc. Originally published in *The New Yorker*. Copyright © 1959 by John Cheever.

THE BABY IN THE ICEBOX, James M. Cain. Reprinted by permission of Henry Holt and Company, Inc. From *The Baby in the Icebox and Other Short Fiction* by James M. Cain, edited by Rob Hoopes. Originally appeared in *American Mercury*. Copyright 1933 by James M. Cain, copyright renewed. Copyright © 1981 by Alice M. Piper, the Executrix of the Estate of James M. Cain.

THE COUPLE NEXT DOOR, Margaret Millar. Reprinted by permission of Harold Ober Associates, Inc. Originally appeared in *Ellery Queen's Mystery Magazine*. Copyright 1954 by Mercury Publications, Inc. Copyright renewed 1982 by The Margaret Millar Survivor's Trust u/a 4/12/82.

THE LANDLADY, Roald Dahl. Reprinted by permission of Alfred A. Knopf, Inc. From *Kiss, Kiss* by Roald Dahl. Originally appeared in *The New Yorker*. Copyright © 1959 by Roald Dahl.

THE AMATEUR, Michael Gilbert. Reprinted by permission of Curtis Brown, a division of Curtis Brown Group Ltd., London. Originally published as "The Amateur in Violence" in *Ellery Queen's Mystery Magazine*. Copyright 1934 by Michael Gilbert.

THE TERRAPIN, Patricia Highsmith. Reprinted by permission of the Atlantic Monthly Press. From the book *Eleven*. Originally published in *Ellery Queen's Mystery Magazine*. Copyright © 1962, 1970 and 1990 by Patricia Highsmith.

ENQUIRY, Dick Francis. Reprinted by permission of HarperCollins Publishers, Inc. and John Johnson Ltd. Copyright © 1969 by Dick Francis.

THE FAR SIDE OF THE DOLLAR, Ross Macdonald. Reprinted by permission of Alfred A. Knopf, Inc. Copyright © 1964 by Ross Macdonald.

THE COMFORTS OF HOME, Flannery O'Connor. Reprinted by permission of Farrar, Straus & Giroux, Inc. From *The Complete Stories* by Flannery O'Connor. Copyright © 1960, 1965 by the Estate of Mary Flannery O'Connor.

CONTENTS

INTRODUCTION

Tales of terror and tabu were doubtless told in the firelit caves of our remotest ancestors. Though we pride ourselves on our modern rationality, we still seem to take a peculiar pleasure in the imaginative experience of frightful happenings. Perhaps, like Mithridates sampling his daily poison, we swallow our regular quotas of fictitious fear and danger in order to strengthen our minds against the real thing. Perhaps we need to be reminded that our planet is an uncertain and unsafe place, never completely controlled by the web of civilization that we have spun. Perhaps we like to play dangerous games without risk.

The discovery of startling facts and frightening truths seems to be the central feature of most stories of detection and suspense. The pure detective story is primarily concerned with what has happened, and moves backwards through time in search of an explanation. The pure suspense story is concerned with what is going to happen, and moves forward, often towards catastrophe. Most contemporary crime fiction tends to combine the elements of detection and suspense. This is true of all four of the novels reprinted here: Agatha Christie's *What Mrs. McGillicuddy Saw!*, Kenneth Fearing's *The Big Clock*, Dick Francis's *Enquiry*, and my own *The Far Side of the Dollar*. Each stitches its way backwards and forwards through time in a pattern whose meaning becomes clear and complete just as the novel ends.

These stories develop a growing sense of discrepancy, of something wrong which may lead to something worse. In most pure detective stories, the very worst is averted through the efforts of the principal character, and evil is quelled and punished. But in stories of suspense the worst often occurs, and its fearful truth lights up the world of the story like nocturnal lightning. It may remind us that the world is still largely unknown, not wholly different from the world on which our ancestors looked out through their cave mouths. It may suggest that our own minds have secret places where the dangerous past still lies hidden.

The detective story offers some comfort against the dark, by showing that human reason may be a match for the antihuman forces in the world. In the usual tale of detection the crime of murder is allowed to occur, but the criminal is finally brought to justice. Tales of suspense are often less reassuring. Stanley Ellin's "The Payoff" and John Collier's "Wet Saturday" take away our breath and with it any hope that all will come right in the end. But they exhilarate the mind, teaching us how to deal with the cold fears and the hot impulses that plague us, and redrawing the ancient lines between good and evil.

Readers of crime fiction have long been divided into two main camps. Traditionalists tend to feel that the story of scientific detection is the true original form, and that everything since has been a falling-away. "Detection is, or ought to be, an exact science," as Sherlock Holmes once said to Dr. Watson, "and should be treated in the same cold and unemotional manner. To tinge it with romanticism produces much the same effect as if you worked a love-story or an elopement into the fifth proposition of Euclid." But other readers consider Holmes himself a rather romanticized figure whose cases sometimes fail to come to grips with reality. The contemporary English crime novelist and critic Julian Symons argues for a more serious use of the crime story: "Its author's business will always be to investigate, with all the freedom that the medium permits him, the springs of violence."

But though I rejoice in Mr. Symons's resolve to take the crime story seriously, I feel that the terms of that seriousness are too narrowly stated. To restrict it to the investigation of "the springs of violence" falls into the scientist fallacy, just as Sherlock Holmes's prescription does. Crime fiction is more imaginative than scientific (and this is certainly true of Julian Symons's novels). It is a free form of popular art, and like any other popular art it exists to be enjoyed. Its value lies first in its style and strength as a story, then in its revelation of the shapes and meanings of life in all their subtlety and surprise. It obeys the laws of narrative, which are not derived from either the chemist's laboratory or the psychologist's Rorschach test.

II

The Gothic novel, the root source of much of the fiction collected in this volume, was invented in what we nostalgically call the Age of Enlightenment. One of its foremost practitioners at the end of the eighteenth century was the English novelist Ann Radcliffe. A contemporary reviewer of her *Mysteries of Udolpho* (1794) explains her art as a sophisticated combination of the frightening and the reassuring: "Mysterious terrors are continually exciting in the mind the idea of a supernatural appearance . . . and yet are ingeniously explained by familiar causes; curiosity is kept upon the stretch from page to page."

The author of this review was the poet Coleridge, who in his later poem *Christabel* attempted a Gothic narrative in verse. But Coleridge was unable to finish *Christabel*. It was his American disciple Poe who, a generation later, took hold of the Gothic tradition and remolded it in its major modern forms—the tale of terror and suspense and the detective story.

Poe converted the short tale of terror into an art form which, like his poems, was a personal expression. As D. H. Lawrence wrote in the finest essay ever done on Poe, he was "an adventurer into vaults and cellars and horrible underground passages of the human soul. He sounded the horror and warning of his own doom." We can still use the heritage of guilty knowledge which Poe gave us in his wonderfully various tales. They were and are the foundation of modern suspense fiction in English.

Out of them grew Poe's second major invention in prose fiction, the detective story. I believe he invented it as a means of getting under control the terrible emotional and imaginative dislocations revealed in his tales of horror. His first and most famous detective story, "The Murders in the Rue Morgue," dwells like Mrs. Radcliffe's novels on weird and frightening events which are rationally explained. But the central fact to be accounted for—the body of a girl thrust up a chimney—has a realistic and symbolic force, and the explanation a logical complexity, which together seem peculiarly modern.

One reason for this may be that both Poe's explanation and the detective who provides it, M. Dupin, have been endlessly imitated by later writers. Dupin is a brilliant eccentric whom we see through the eyes of a somewhat less brilliant friend. The two most striking features of his investigative method, his quasi-scientific reliance on physical fact and his apparent ability to read minds by following the association of ideas, were taken up by Conan Doyle and given to Sherlock Holmes.

The line of descent from Poe's Dupin to Sherlock Holmes was not quite direct. Twenty years before Conan Doyle invented his famous character, Wilkie Collins had introduced into his novel *The Moonstone* (1868) an investigator based on an actual English detective, Inspector Whicher of the Constance Kent murder case. Even earlier, in 1860, Collins had produced in *The Woman in White* the first great modern mystery novel. This partly autobiographical "novel of sensation," as it was called, took a dark and knowing look at Victorian society, and particularly at its use and abuse of women.

Collins's great friend Dickens worked rather similar themes into his final novel. *The Mystery of Edwin Drood* (1870) dramatized Victorian England's social and moral schizophrenia in the double life of its central character. He is a cathedral choirmaster who becomes an opium user and possibly the murderer of his nephew Edwin. Though the mystery of the missing Edwin Drood remained unfinished and unsolved at Dickens's death, it leaves an overwhelming impression of a hypocritical society turning its back on its own lower depths, the drug-ridden, prostitute-haunted slums of London.

An even darker vision of Victorian London appears in *The Strange Case of Dr. Jekyll and Mr. Hyde,* which was written some sixteen years after *Edwin Drood* and was probably influenced by it. Though not in the modern sense a work of realism, it is a remarkably explicit and gripping account of a soul being lost by slow degrees and with its own complicity. As the double-minded villain-hero is drawn down through the gradations of crime and despair, the dualisms of the Victorian age are revealed and strangely resolved. The reader is transported to the night streets of a London where a short time later Jack the Ripper roamed and where, a short time after that, Sherlock Holmes and Dr. Watson set off by hansom cab on their errands of justice and mercy.

This late-Victorian hero Holmes, in spite of his scientific and ethical bent, was somewhat restless and ill at ease in his society. He fell prey to black bachelor moods. He played his violin to calm his nerves and, when the fit was on him, took hard drugs. Maurice Richardson has aptly described him as "a *fin-de-siècle* dropout" who later became a member of the establishment. For Holmes was a defender of the status quo, and in this respect Doyle's stories came to represent a falling-away from the deeper, questioning visions of Collins and Dickens. His final message is quietistic: England is safe in the hands of its ruling classes, and anyone who doubts this is a bounder, or possibly a nihilist.

This kind of social and psychological reassurance became a central feature of both the English and the American detective story in what was called, rather hopefully, its Golden Age. It became a formal game, played by rules that were derived from Poe and the Holmes canon rather than from the changing patterns of life. Its world of long weekends in country houses threatened to become as artificial as the medieval courts of love. Even such formidable talents as Dorothy L. Sayers and S. S. Van Dine were sometimes betrayed into self-parody by fantasies of an unreal past and present. Agatha Christie invented in the twenties and developed in the thirties her light, strong tragicomic realism. But it was not until after the Second World War that she did her finest work, represented in this collection by the brilliant and humane novel about what Mrs. McGillicuddy and her friend Miss Marple saw.

III

The First World War and the social changes that followed it had already effected changes in the detective story. The passage from its Golden Age to its Age of Iron started in the United States in the twenties, with what might be called the *Black Mask* revolution. This crime magazine, edited at one time by H. L. Mencken and later by Joseph T. Shaw, encouraged a group of new writers to tell stories about the underworlds of such American cities as New York, San Francisco, Los Angeles, and Miami. Shaw was a demanding editor who enforced on his contributors a swift colloquial style. It was partly inspired by Hemingway's early stories, but also by the discovery by other writers of rich resources in the spoken language. The names of some of these writers were Lester Dent, Paul Cain, George Harmon Coxe, Raymond Chandler, and Dashiell Hammett.

Hammett became their leader, and the most potent imaginative force in the creation of the modern American detective story. His "Continental Op" stories (the finest of which, "Fly Paper," is in the present collection) expanded the social and moral range of the form, and set it talking in a prose which could say almost anything but often chose not to. The Continental Op's essential decency and courage are underplayed, and commonly shown in action, not in talk. Hammett's mature work, particularly in his two great novels *The Glass Key* and *The Maltese Falcon*, has a muted masculine force and a deadpan sincerity which together form a kind of tragic mask.

Though Sam Spade's adventures in *The Maltese Falcon* were based to some extent on Hammett's experiences as a private detective in San Francisco ("I was once falsely accused of perjury and had to perjure myself to escape arrest.") Hammett could see his hero from the outside, without vainglory or romanticism. This marks a sharp break with the Golden Age tradition of the detective as aristocratic superman. Spade is wholly committed to his difficult life, caught in the urban jungle, unable to rise above its tribal customs. He plays for the highest stakes available, a woman he seems to love and a jeweled bird he covets, and loses both. All he holds on to at the end is an obdurate male pride which is more Luciferian than Christian.

Raymond Chandler, who dedicated an early book to Hammett, softened and refined the powerful colloquial mechanisms of Hammett's prose and used it to celebrate a more perfect gentle knight, in the person of Marlowe. The influence of these two writers enlarged the detective story and spread far beyond it, to leave a permanent mark on modern fiction in general. I learned my craft from them, and from their contemporary James M. Cain.

Cain, whose father was an eastern college president and whose mother was an opera singer, grounded his work in the common language and the people who spoke it. He once confessed that he was unable to write convincing fiction until he heard a western roughneck talk. One of the happy consequences was "The Baby in the Icebox." This uproarious story about an escaped tiger walks a difficult and daring line between farce and melodrama. It is humanized by the voice of its narrator, an illiterate man who is capable of honesty and love.

There were parallel and related developments in England, where Graham Greene had begun to use his crime novels to hold a whole society up to view. Greene's serious interest in the inner life of his characters made the superficial elegances of the Golden Age look like peeling gilt. *This Gun for Hire* and *Brighton Rock* were ruthless in the portraiture of their villain-heroes, yet at the same time concerned with the salvation of their souls. *The Confidential Agent,* a beautifully constructed novel about terrible things, shows us a decent man going down to defeat in a lapsed world where the Second World War was being prepared.

The most profoundly moving of Greene's short stories, "The Basement Room," recounts a small boy's introduction to fear and loss. It is illuminated tragically by the author's daring forward-flashes into the later life of the man whom the frightened little boy eventually became. Through Greene's work, English crime literature began to regain its conscience, social and otherwise. It became aware of contemporary movements in psychiatry and anthropology and religion. Without losing its compulsive power to fascinate and thrill—indeed it gained in this power as it became more searching—the story of mystery and crime became a branch of the modern English novel.

IV

One of the most valuable contributions made by those great trail-blazers Greene and Hammett was the gift of freedom they offered to other writers by their example. Without it, our leading contemporary writers might never have dared the bold originality of their mature work. We might never have had Julian Symons's uncompromising explorations of the roots of crime, or Patricia Highsmith's brilliant tragi-comic plots stitching together the fragments of an amoral society. Even a wholly different writer like the exuberantly masculine Dick Francis belongs in the same line of descent, perhaps as close to Hammett as to Greene.

Francis was a leading jockey, indeed he had been the Queen's Jockey, before he took up writing a dozen or so years ago. Most of his novels have to do with horse racing and are full of movement, but running through their leaping action is a realistic understanding of the whole range of English life. *Enquiry,* in the course of telling a breathless story about a jockey robbed of his right to ride, takes a hard look at the English class system and its residual cruelties, from the point of view of a narrator-hero who had started at the bottom and worked his way up. In the works of such writers as these, the transatlantic mystery novel is reaching back towards the strength and depth that Dickens and Wilkie Collins gave it at the start.

Developments in the American mystery field have been equally various and interesting. In 1941, Howard Haycraft had already noticed the abandonment of "rigid formulas in favor of blending the detective elements with the novel of manners and character." The realistic vein opened up by the *Black Mask* writers was enriched by the influence of the ancient classics and modern psychoanalysis. Some of the most original and elegant work to come out of this new meld was done by Margaret Millar (represented here by a short story) and by Kenneth Fearing.

Fearing was a recognized poet who wrote only two suspense novels. The better of these, *The Big Clock* (1946), is about a murder and a manhunt in a New York publishing empire. Narrated with force and speed and wit by several voices, it has lasting value as a record of metropolitan life, both outer and inner. In the nearly twenty years since it was written, its clean, brilliant style has shown no sign of fading. Its suspense still catches continually at the throat, and its jokes are still funny. Fearing's novel, which moves with love and knowledge through New York as G. K. Chesterton's stories moved through London, reminds me of Chesterton's description of the mystery story as "the earliest and only form of popular literature in which is expressed some sense of the poetry of modern life."

I hope these words may be applicable to my own stories. *The Far Side of the Dollar*, an account of an apparent kidnapping, moves through California and the Southwest towards an ending which attempts (as James M. Cain once said of one of his books) to "graze tragedy." The novel belongs not so much to my detective-narrator Archer as to the other people in the book. Archer is a man of action as well as an observer and recorder, but the emphasis is not on his physical exploits. He is less the hero of the novel than its mind, an unwilling judge who is forced to see that a murderer can be his own chief victim.

The present and the preceding generation of writers have been marvelously rich in short suspense fiction which touches the central nerves of modern life. Patricia Highsmith's "The Terrapin" is a deeply realized account of unconscious cruelty and terrible retribution. The stories of those great stylists John Collier and Roald Dahl haunt our minds like memories of our most frightening and self-revealing dreams. Both "Wet Saturday" and "The Landlady" are brief masterpieces, written with the economy of poems. A leading American rival in the art of saying much in little, Stanley Ellin, has told us in the short compass of "The Payoff" nearly everything that we need to know about the irreparable human damage caused by war. Michael Gilbert's "The Amateur" is a story of comparable ferocity, which also notices the continuity between war and crime.

John Cheever and the late Flannery O'Connor are among the greatest American writers of their generation, and probably its two best short story writers. Cheever's "The Five-Forty-Eight" and O'Connor's "The Comforts of Home" are tragicomic stories of guilt and punishment which have the intensity of dramatic poetry, combined with the bite of reality. Each in its way is concerned with the destruction of a man through his attempt to destroy a woman. Indeed all of these stories are about the damage that we do to one another and urge us quietly to change our ways.

But aren't such stories literature rather than suspense fiction? I believe they belong in both categories. The Gothic tradition and the conventions of the crime story that grew out of it have always nourished both popular and serious literature. They are a medium of communication between the popular and the serious, making the former more meaningful, the latter more lively.

A strong popular convention like that of the suspense story is both an artistic and a social heritage. It keeps the forms of the art alive for the writer to use. It trains his readers, endowing both writer and reader with a common vocabulary of structural shapes and narrative possibilities. It becomes a part of the language in which we think and feel, reaching our whole society and helping to hold our civilization together.

Suspense fiction presents a view of modern life as dangerous and flawed but not beyond redemption, a vision in which almost any crime or disaster can be contained and understood. Somehow it helps to take the curse off trouble, perhaps because it is, for both writer and reader, an art form which is also a game of skill. In its highest reaches, where Flannery O'Connor and a few others work their miracles, the reader hardly knows whether to laugh or cry or cheer.

Ross Macdonald

Great Stories of Suspense

WET SATURDAY

by

JOHN COLLIER

It was July. In the large, dull house they were imprisoned by the swish and the gurgle and all the hundred sounds of rain. They were in the drawing room, behind four tall and weeping windows, in a lake of damp and faded chintz.

This house, ill-kept and unprepossessing, was necessary to Mr. Princey, who detested his wife, his daughter, and his hulking son. His life was to walk through the village; touching his hat, not smiling. His cold pleasure was to recapture snapshot memories of the infinitely remote summers of his childhood—coming into the orangery and finding his lost wooden horse, the tunnel in the box hedge, and the little square of light at the end of it. But now all this was threatened—his austere pride of position in the village, his passionate attachment to the house—and all because Millicent, his cloddish daughter Millicent, had done this shocking and incredibly stupid thing. Mr. Princey turned from her in revulsion and spoke to his wife.

"They'd send her to a lunatic asylum," he said. "A criminal-lunatic asylum. We should have to move away. It would be impossible."

His daughter began to shake again. "I'll kill myself," she said.

"Be quiet," said Mr. Princey. "We have very little time. No time for nonsense. I intend to deal with this." He called to his son, who stood looking out of the window. "George, come here. Listen. How far did you get with your medicine before they threw you out as hopeless?"

"You know as well as I do," said George.

"Do you know enough—did they drive enough into your head for you to be able to guess what a competent doctor could tell about such a wound?"

"Well, it's a—it's a knock or blow."

"If a tile fell from the roof? Or a piece of the coping?"

"Well, guv'nor, you see, it's like this—"

"Is it possible?"

"No."

"Why not?"

"Oh, because she hit him several times."

"I can't stand it," said Mrs. Princey.

"You have got to stand it, my dear," said her husband. "And keep that hysterical note out of your voice. It might be overheard. We are talking about the weather. If he fell down the well, George, striking his head several times?"

"I really don't know, guv'nor."

"He'd have had to hit the sides several times in thirty or forty feet, and at the correct angles. No, I'm afraid not. We must go over it all again. Millicent."

"No! No!"

"Millicent, we must go over it all again. Perhaps you have forgotten something. One tiny irrelevant detail may save or ruin us. Particularly you, Millicent. You don't *want* to be put in an asylum, do you? Or be hanged? They might hang you, Millicent. You must stop that shaking. You must keep your voice quiet. We are talking of the weather. Now."

"I can't. I . . . I . . ."

"Be quiet, child. Be quiet." He put his long, cold face very near to his daughter's. He found himself horribly revolted by her. Her features were thick, her jaw heavy, her whole figure repellingly powerful. "Answer me," he said. "You were in the stable?"

"Yes."

"One moment, though. Who knew you were in love with this wretched curate?"

"No one. I've said a—"

"Don't worry," said George. "The whole goddamned village knows. They've been sniggering about it in the Plow for three years past."

"Likely enough," said Mr. Princey. "Likely enough. What filth!" He made as if to wipe something off the backs of his hands. "Well, now, we continue. You were in the stable?"

"Yes."

"You were putting the croquet set into its box?"

"Yes."

"You heard someone crossing the yard?"

"Yes."

"It was Withers?"

"Yes."

"So you called him?"

"Yes."

"Loudly? Did you call him loudly? Could anyone have heard?"

"No, Father. I'm sure not. I didn't call him. He saw me as I went to the door. He just waved his hand and came over."

"How can I find out from you whether there was anyone about? Whether he could have been seen?"

"I'm sure not, Father. I'm quite sure."

"So you both went into the stable?"

"Yes. It was raining hard."

"What did he say?"

"He said 'Hullo, Milly.' And to excuse him coming in the back way, but he'd set out to walk over to Bass Hill."

"Yes."

"And he said, passing the park, he'd seen the house and suddenly thought of me, and he thought he'd just look in for a minute, just to tell me something. He said he was so happy, he wanted me to share it. He'd heard from the Bishop he was to have the vicarage. And it wasn't only that. It meant he could marry. And he began to stutter. And I thought he meant me."

"Don't tell me what you thought. Exactly what he said. Nothing else."

"Well . . . Oh dear!"

"Don't cry! It is a luxury you cannot afford. Tell me."

"He said no. He said it wasn't me. It's Ella Brangwyn-Davies. And he was sorry. And all that. Then he went to go."

"And then?"

"I went mad. He turned his back. I had the winning post of the croquet set in my hand—"

"Did you shout or scream? I mean, as you hit him?"

"No. I'm sure I didn't."

"Did he? Come on! Tell me."

"No, Father."

"And then?"

"I threw it down. I came straight into the house. That's all. I wish I were dead!"

"And you met none of the servants. No one will go into the stable. You see, George, he probably told people he was going to Bass Hill. Certainly no one knows he came here. He might have been attacked in the woods. We must consider every detail . . . A curate, with his head battered in—"

"Don't, Father!" cried Millicent.

"Do you want to be hanged? A curate, with his head battered in, found in the woods. Who'd want to kill Withers?"

There was a tap on the door, which opened immediately. It was little Captain Smollett, who never stood on ceremony. "Who'd kill Withers?" said he. "I would, with pleasure. How d'you do, Mrs. Princey. I walked right in."

"He heard you, Father," moaned Millicent.

"My dear, we can all have our little joke," said her father. "Don't pretend to be shocked. A little theoretical curate-killing, Smollett. In these days we talk nothing but thrillers."

"Parsonicide," said Captain Smollett. "Justifiable parsonicide. Have you heard about Ella Brangwyn-Davies? I shall be laughed at."

"Why?" said Mr. Princey. "Why should you be laughed at?"

"Had a shot in that direction myself," said Smollett, with careful sang-froid. "She half said yes, too. Hadn't you heard? She told most people. Now it'll look as if I got turned down for a white rat in a dog collar."

"Too bad!" said Mr. Princey.

"Fortune of war," said the little captain.

"Sit down," said Mr. Princey. "Mother, Millicent, console Captain Smollett with your best light conversation. George and I have something to look to. We shall be back in a minute or two, Smollett. Come, George."

It was actually five minutes before Mr. Princey and his son returned.

"Excuse me, my dear," said Mr. Princey to his wife. "Smollett, would you care to see something rather interesting? Come out to the stables for a moment."

They went into the stable yard. The buildings were now unused except as old sheds. No one ever went there. Captain Smollett entered, George followed him, Mr. Princey came last. As he closed the door he took up a gun which stood behind it. "Smollett," said he, "we have come out to shoot a rat which George heard squeaking under that tub. Now, you must listen to me very carefully or you will be shot by accident. I mean that."

Smollett looked at him. "Very well," said he. "Go on."

"A very tragic happening has taken place this afternoon," said Mr. Princey. "It will be even more tragic unless it is smoothed over."

"Oh?" said Smollett.

"You heard me ask," said Mr. Princey, "who would kill Withers. You heard Millicent make a comment, an unguarded comment."

"Well?" said Smollett. "What of it?"

"Very little," said Mr. Princey. "Unless you heard that Withers had met a violent end this very afternoon. And that, my dear Smollett, is what you are going to hear."

"Have you killed him?" cried Smollett.

"Millicent has," said Mr. Princey.

"Hell!" said Smollett.

"It *is* Hell," said Mr. Princey. "You would have remembered—and guessed."

"Maybe," said Smollett. "Yes, I suppose I should."

"Therefore," said Mr. Princey, "you constitute a problem."

"Why did she kill him?" said Smollett.

"It is one of these disgusting things," said Mr. Princey. "Pitiable, too. She deluded herself that he was in love with her."

"Oh, of course," said Smollett.

"And he told her about the Brangwyn-Davies girl."

"I see," said Smollett.

"I have no wish," said Mr. Princey, "that she should be proved either a lunatic or a murderess. I could hardly live here after that."

"I suppose not," said Smollett.

"On the other hand," said Mr. Princey, "you know about it."

"Yes," said Smollett. "I am wondering if I could keep my mouth shut. If I promised you—"

"I am wondering if I could believe you," said Mr. Princey.

"If I promised," said Smollett.

"If things went smoothly," said Mr. Princey. "But not if there was any sort of suspicion, any questioning. You would be afraid of being an accessory."

"I don't know," said Smollett.

"I do," said Mr. Princey. "What are we going to do?"

"I can't see anything else," said Smollett. "You'd never be fool enough to do me in. You can't get rid of two corpses."

"I regard it," said Mr. Princey, "as a better risk than the other. It could be an accident. Or you and Withers could both disappear. There are possibilities in that."

"Listen," said Smollett. "You can't—"

"Listen," said Mr. Princey. "There may be a way out. There is a way out, Smollett. You gave me the idea yourself."

"Did I?" said Smollett. "What?"

"You said you would kill Withers," said Mr. Princey. "You have a motive."

"I was joking," said Smollett.

"You are always joking," said Mr. Princey. "People think there must be something behind it. Listen, Smollett, I can't trust you. Therefore you must trust me. Or I will kill you now, in the next minute. I mean that. You can choose between dying and living."

"Go on," said Smollett.

"There is a sewer here," said Mr. Princey, speaking fast and forcefully. "That is where I am going to put Withers. No outsider knows he has come up here this afternoon. No one will ever look for him unless you tell them. You must give me evidence that you have murdered Withers."

"Why?" said Smollett.

"So that I shall be dead sure that you will never open your lips on the matter," said Mr. Princey.

"What evidence?" said Smollett.

"George," said Mr. Princey, "hit him in the face, hard."

"Good god!" said Smollett.

"Again," said Mr. Princey. "Don't bruise your knuckles."

"Oh!" said Smollett.

"I'm sorry," said Mr. Princey. "There must be traces of a struggle between you and Withers. Then it will not be altogether safe for you to go to the police."

"Why don't you take my word?" said Smollett.

"I will when we've finished," said Mr. Princey. "George, get that croquet post. Take your handkerchief to it. As I told you. Smollett, you'll grasp the end of this croquet post. I shall shoot you if you don't."

"Oh, hell," said Smollett. "All right."

"Pull two hairs out of his head, George," said Mr. Princey, "and remember what I told you to do with them. Now, Smollett, you take that bar and raise the big flagstone with the ring in it. Withers is in the next stall. You've got to drag him through and dump him in."

"I won't touch him," said Smollett.

"Stand back, George," said Mr. Princey, raising his gun.

"Wait a minute," cried Smollett. "Wait a minute." He did as he was told.

Mr. Princey wiped his brow. "Look here," said he. "Everything is perfectly safe. Remember, no one knows that Withers came here. Everyone thinks he walked over to Bass Hill. That's five miles of country to search. They'll never look in our sewer. Do you see how safe it is?"

"I suppose it is," said Smollett.

"Now come into the house," said Mr. Princey. "We shall never get that rat."

They went into the house. The maid was bringing tea into the drawing room. "See, my dear," said Mr. Princey to his wife, "we went to the stable to shoot a rat and we found Captain Smollett. Don't be offended, my dear fellow."

"You must have walked up the back drive," said Mrs. Princey.

"Yes. Yes. That was it," said Smollett in some confusion.

"You've cut your lip," said George, handing him a cup of tea.

"I . . . I just knocked it."

"Shall I tell Bridget to bring some iodine?" said Mrs. Princey. The maid looked up, waiting.

"Don't trouble, please," said Smollett. "It's nothing."

"Very well, Bridget," said Mrs. Princey. "That's all."

"Smollett is very kind," said Mr. Princey. "He knows all our trouble. We can rely on him. We have his word."

"Oh, have we, Captain Smollett?" cried Mrs. Princey. "You are good."

"Don't worry, old fellow," Mr. Princey said. "They'll never find anything."

Pretty soon Smollett took his leave. Mrs. Princey pressed his hand very hard. Tears came into her eyes. All three of them watched him go down the drive. Then Mr. Princey spoke very earnestly to his wife for a few minutes and the two of them went upstairs and spoke still more earnestly to Millicent. Soon after, the rain having ceased, Mr. Princey took a stroll round the stable yard.

He came back and went to the telephone. "Put me through to the Bass Hill police station," said he. "Quickly. . . . Hullo, is that the police station? This is Mr. Princey, of Abbott's Laxton. I'm afraid something terrible has happened up here. Can you send someone at once?"

THE BIG CLOCK

by

KENNETH FEARING

George Stroud I

I first met Pauline Delos at one of those substantial parties Earl Janoth liked to give every two or three months, attended by members of the staff, his personal friends, private moguls, and public nobodies, all in haphazard rotation. It was at his home in the East Sixties. Although it was not exactly public, well over a hundred people came and went in the course of two or three hours.

Georgette was with me, and we were introduced at once to Edward Orlin of *Futureways,* and to others in the group who had the familiar mark upon them. Of Pauline Delos, I knew only the name. But although there could not have been anyone in the organization who hadn't heard a great deal about the lady, there were few who had actually seen her, and fewer still who had ever seen her on any occasion when Janoth was also present. She was tall, ice-blonde, and splendid. The eye saw nothing but innocence, to the instincts she was undiluted sex, the brain said here was a perfect hell.

"Earl was asking about you a moment ago," Orlin told me. "Wanted you to meet somebody."

"I was delayed. As a matter of fact, I've just finished a twenty-minute conversation with President McKinley."

Miss Delos looked mildly interested. "Who did you say?" she asked.

"William McKinley. Our twenty-fourth President."

"I know," she said, and smiled. A little. "You probably heard a lot of complaints."

A man I recognized as Emory Mafferson, a tiny little dark fellow who haunted one of the lower floors, *Futureways*, also, I think, spoke up.

"There's a guy with an iron face like McKinley's in the auditing department. If that's who you mean, you bet there were complaints."

"No. I was truly and literally detained in a conversation with Mr. McKinley. At the bar of the Silver Lining."

"He was," said Georgette. "I was, too."

"Yes. And there were no complaints at all. Quite the contrary. He's making out quite well, it seems." I had myself another Manhattan from a passing tray. "He's not under a contract, of course. But working steadily. In addition to being McKinley he's sometimes Justice Holmes, Thomas Edison, Andrew Carnegie, Henry Ward Beecher, or anyone important but dignified. He's been Washington, Lincoln, and Christopher Columbus more times than he can remember."

"I call him a very convenient friend to have," said Delos. "Who is he?"

"His earthly alias is Clyde Norbert Polhemus. For business purposes. I've known him for years, and he's promised to let me be his understudy."

"What's he done?" Orlin asked, with reluctance. "Sounds like he materialized a bunch of ghosts, and can't put them back."

"Radio," I said. "And he can put anyone anywhere."

And that was about all, the first time I met Pauline Delos. The rest of the late afternoon and early evening passed as always in this comfortable little palace, surrounded as it was by the big and little palaces of greater and lesser kingdoms than Janoth Enterprises. Old conversation in new faces. Georgette and I met and talked to the niece of a department store. Of course the niece wanted to conquer new territory. She would inherit several acres of the old territory, anyway. I met a titan in the world of mathematics; he had connected a number of adding machines into a single unit, and this super-calculator was the biggest in the world. It could solve equations unknown to and beyond the grasp of its inventor. I said: "That makes you better than Einstein. When you have your equipment with you."

He looked at me uneasily, and it occurred to me I was a little drunk.

"I'm afraid not. It was a purely mechanical problem, developed for special purposes only."

I told him he might not be the best mathematician on earth but he was certainly the fastest, and then I met a small legal cog in a major political engine. And next Janoth's latest invention in the way of social commentators. And others, all of them pretty damned important people, had they only known it. Some of them unaware they were gentlemen and scholars. Some of them tomorrow's famous fugitives from justice. A sizable sprinkling of lunatics, so plausible they had never been suspected and never would be. Memorable bankrupts of the future, the obscure suicides of ten or twenty years from now. Potentially fabulous murderers. The mothers or fathers of truly great people I would never know.

In short, the big clock was running as usual, and it was time to go home. Sometimes the hands of the clock actually raced, and at other times they hardly moved at all. But that made no difference to the big clock. The hands could move backward, and the time it told would be right just the same. It would still be running as usual, because all other watches have to be set by the big one, which is even more powerful than the calendar, and to which one automatically adjusts his entire life. Compared to this hook-up, the man with the adding machines was still counting on his fingers.

Anyway, it was time I collected Georgette and went home. I always go home. Always. I may sometimes detour, but eventually I get there. Home was 37.4 miles, according to the railroad timetable, but it could be 3,740 miles, and I would still make it. Earl Janoth had emerged from somewhere, and we said good-bye.

There was one thing I always saw, or thought I saw, in Janoth's big, pink, disorderly face, permanently fixed in a faint smile he had forgotten about long ago, his straight and innocent stare that didn't, any more, see the person in front of him at all. He wasn't adjusting himself to the big clock. He didn't even know there was a big clock. The large, gray, convoluted muscle in back of that childlike gaze was digesting something unknown to the ordinary world. That muscle with its long tendons had nearly fastened itself about a conclusion, a conclusion startlingly different from the hearty expression once forged upon the outward face, and left there, abandoned. Some day that conclusion would be reached, the muscle would strike. Probably it had, before. Surely it would, again.

He said how nice Georgette was looking, which was true, how she always reminded him of carnivals and Hallowe'en, the wildest baseball ever pitched in history, and there was as usual a real and extraordinary warmth in the voice, as though this were another, still a third personality.

"I'm sorry an old friend of mine, Major Conklin, had to leave early," he said to me. "He likes what we've been doing recently with *Crimeways*. I told him you were the psychic bloodhound leading us on to new interpretations, and he was interested."

"I'm sorry I missed him."

"Well, Larry recently took over a string of graveyard magazines, and he wants to do something with them. But I don't think a man with your practical experience and precision mentality could advise him. He needs a geomancer."

"It's been a pleasant evening, Earl."

"Hasn't it? Good night."

"Good night."

"Good night."

We made our way down the long room, past an atmospheric disturbance highly political, straight through a group of early settlers whom God would not help tomorrow morning, cautiously around a couple abruptly silent but smiling in helpless rage.

"Where now?" Georgette asked.

"A slight detour. Just for dinner. Then home, of course."

As we got our things, and I waited for Georgette, I saw Pauline Delos, with a party of four, disappearing into the night. Abandoning this planet. As casually as that. But my thought-waves told her to drop in again. Any time.

In the taxi, Georgette said: "George, what's a geomancer?"

"I don't know, George. Earl got it out of the fattest dictionary ever printed, wrote it on his cuff, and now the rest of us know why he's the boss. Remind me to look it up."

George Stroud II

About five weeks later I woke up on a January morning, with my head full of a letter Bob Aspenwell had written me from Haiti. I don't know why this letter came back to me the instant sleep began to go. I had received it days and days before. It was all about the warmth down there, the ease, and above all, the simplicity.

He said it was a Black Republic, and I was grinning in my sleep as I saw Bob and myself plotting a revolt of the whites determined not to be sold down the river into *Crimeways*. Then I really woke up.

Monday morning. On Marble Road. An important Monday.

Roy Cordette and I had scheduled a full staff conference for the April issue, one of those surprise packages good for everyone's ego and imagination. The big clock was running at a leisurely pace, and I was well abreast of it.

But that morning, in front of the mirror in the bathroom, I was certain a tuft of gray on the right temple had stolen at least another quarter-inch march. This renewed a familiar vision, beginning with mortality at one end of the scale, and ending in senile helplessness at the other.

Who's that pathetic, white-haired old guy clipping papers at the desk over there? asked a brisk young voice. But I quickly tuned it out and picked another one: *Who's that distinguished, white-haired, scholarly gentleman going into the directors' room?*

Don't you know who he is? That's George Stroud.

Who's he?

Well, it's a long story. He used to be general manager of this whole railroad. Railroad? Why not something with a farther future? *Airline. He saw this line through its first, pioneer stages. He might have been one of the biggest men in aviation today, only something went wrong. I don't know just what, except that it was a hell of a scandal. Stroud had to go before a Grand Jury, but it was so big it had to be hushed up, and he got off. After that, though, he was through. Now they let him put out the papers and cigars in the board room when there's a meeting. The rest of the time he fills the office inkwells and rearranges the travel leaflets.*

Why do they keep him on at all?

Well, some of the directors feel sentimental about the old fellow, and besides, he has a wife and daughter dependent on him. Hold that copy, boy. This is years and years from now. *Three children, no, I think it's four. Brilliant youngsters, and awfully brave about Stroud. Won't hear a word against him. They think he still runs the whole works around here. And did you ever see the wife? They're the most devoted old couple I ever saw.*

Drying my face, I stared into the glass. I made the dark, bland, somewhat inquisitive features go suddenly hard and still. I said:

"Look here, Roy, we've really got to do something." *About what?* "About getting ourselves some more money." I saw the vague wave of Roy Cordette's thin, long-fingered hand, and discerned his instant retreat into the land of elves, hobgoblins, and double-talk.

I thought, George, you went all over this with Hagen three months ago. There's no doubt about it, you and I are both crowding the limit. And then some.

"What is the limit, do you happen to know?"

The general level throughout the whole organization, I should say, wouldn't you?

"Not for me. I don't exactly crave my job, my contract, or this gilded cage full of gelded birds. I think it's high time we really had a showdown."

Go right ahead. My prayers go with you.

"I said *we*. In a way it involves your own contract as well as mine."

I know. Tell you what, George, why don't the three of us talk this over informally? You and Hagen and myself?

"A good idea." I reached for the phone. "When would be convenient?"

You mean today?

"Why not?"

Well, I'll be pretty busy this afternoon. But all right. If Steve isn't too busy around five.

"A quarter to six in the Silver Lining. After the third round. You know, Jennett-Donohue are planning to add five or six new books. We'll just keep that in mind."

So I heard, but they're on a pretty low level, if you ask me. Besides, it's a year since that rumor went around.

A real voice shattered this imaginary scene.

"George, are you ever coming down? George has to take the school bus, you know."

I called back to Georgette that I was on my way and went back to the bedroom. And when we went into conference with Steve Hagen, then what? A vein began to beat in my forehead. For business purposes he and Janoth were one and the same person, except that in Hagen's slim and sultry form, restlessly through his veins, there flowed some new, freakish, molten virulence.

I combed my hair before the bedroom dresser, and that sprout of gray resumed its ordinary proportions. To hell with Hagen. Why not go to Janoth? Of course.

I laid the comb and brush down on the dresser top, leaned forward on an elbow, and breathed into the mirror: "Cut you the cards, Earl. Low man leaves town in twenty-four hours. High man takes the works."

I put on my tie, my coat, and went downstairs. Georgia looked up thoughtfully from the usual drift of cornflakes surrounding her place at the table. From beneath it came the soft, steady, thump, thump, thump of her feet marking time on a crossbar. A broad beam of sunlight poured in upon the table, drawn close to the window, highlighting the silverware, the percolator, the faces of Georgia and Georgette. Plates reflected more light from a sideboard against one wall, and above it my second favorite painting by Louise Patterson, framed in a strip of walnut, seemed to hang away up in the clouds over the sideboard, the room, and somehow over the house. Another picture by Patterson hung on the opposite wall, and there were two more upstairs.

Georgette's large, glowing, untamed features turned, and her sea-blue eyes swept me with surgical but kindly interest. I said good morning and kissed them both. Georgette called to Nellie that she could bring the eggs and waffles.

"Orange juice," I said, drinking mine. "These oranges just told me they came from Florida."

My daughter gave me a glance of startled faith. "I didn't hear anything," she said.

"You didn't? One of them said they all came from a big ranch near Jacksonville."

Georgia considered this and then waved her spoon, flatly discarding the whole idea. After a full twenty seconds of silence she seemed to remember something, and asked: "What man were you talking to?"

"Me? Man? When? Where?"

"Now. Upstairs. George said you were talking to a man. We heard."

"Oh."

Georgette's voice was neutral, but under the neutrality lay the zest of an innocent bystander waiting to see the first blood in a barroom debate.

"I thought you'd better do your own explaining," she said.

"Well, that man, George. That was me, practicing. Musicians have to do a lot of practicing before they play. Athletes have to train before they race, and actors rehearse before they act." I hurried past Georgette's pointed, unspoken agreement. "And I always run over a few words in the morning before I start talking. May I have the biscuits. Please?"

Georgia weighed this, and forgot about it. She said: "George said you'd tell me a story, George."

"I'll tell you a story, all right. It's about the lonely cornflake." I had her attention now, to the maximum. "It seems that once there was a little girl."

"How old?"

"About five, I think. Or maybe it was seven."

"No, six."

"Six she was. So there was this package of cornflakes—"

"What was her name?"

"Cynthia. So these cornflakes, hundreds of them, they'd all grown up together in the same package, they'd played games and gone to school together, they were all fast friends. Then one day the package was opened and the whole lot were emptied into Cynthia's bowl. And she poured milk and cream and sugar in the bowl, and then she ate one of the flakes. And after a while, this cornflake down in Cynthia's stomach began to wonder when the rest of his friends were going to arrive. But they never did. And the longer he waited, the lonelier he grew. You see, the rest of the cornflakes got only as far as the tablecloth, a lot of them landed on the floor, a few of them on Cynthia's forehead, and some behind her ears."

"And then what?"

"Well, that's all. After a while this cornflake got so lonely he just sat down and cried."

"Then what'd he do?"

"What could he do? Cynthia didn't know how to eat her cornflakes properly, or maybe she wasn't trying, so morning after morning the same thing happened. One cornflake found himself left all alone in Cynthia's stomach."

"Then what?"

"Well, he cried and carried on so bad that every morning she got a bellyache. And she couldn't think why because, after all, she really hadn't eaten anything."

"Then what'd she do?"

"She didn't like it, that's what she did."

Georgia started in on her soft-boiled eggs, which promised to go the way of the cereal. Presently she lowered the handle of the spoon to the table and rested her chin on the tip, brooding and thumping her feet on the crossbar. The coffee in my cup gently rippled, rippled with every thud.

"You always tell that story," she remembered. "Tell me another."

"There's one about the little girl—Cynthia, aged six—the same one—who also had a habit of kicking her feet against the table whenever she ate. Day after day, week in and week out, year after year, she kicked it and kicked it. Then one fine day the table said, 'I'm getting pretty tired of this,' and with that it pulled back its leg and whango, it booted Cynthia clear out of the window. Was she surprised."

This one was a complete success. Georgia's feet pounded in double time, and she upset what was left of her milk.

"Pull your punches, wonder boy," said Georgette, mopping up. A car honked outside the house and she polished Georgia's face with one expert wipe of the bib. "There's the bus, darling. Get your things on."

For about a minute a small meteor ran up and down and around the downstairs rooms, then disappeared, piping. Georgette came back, after a while, for her first cigarette and her second cup of coffee. She said, presently, looking at me through a thin band of smoke: "Would you like to go back to newspaper work, George?"

"God forbid. I never want to see another fire engine as long as I live. Not unless I'm riding on it, steering the back end of a hook-and-ladder truck. The fellow on the back end always steers just the opposite to the guy in the driver's seat. I think."

"That's what I mean."

"What do you mean?"

"You don't like *Crimeways*. You don't really like Janoth Enterprises at all. You'd like to steer in just the opposite direction to all of that."

"You're wrong. Quite wrong. I love that old merry-go-round."

Georgette hesitated, unsure of herself. I could feel the laborious steps her reasoning took before she reached a tentative, spoken conclusion: "I don't believe in square pegs in round holes. The price is too great. Don't you think so, George?" I tried to look puzzled. "I mean, well, really, it seems to me, when I think about it, sometimes, you were much happier, and so was I, when we had the roadhouse. Weren't we? For that matter, it was a lot more fun when you were a race-track detective. Heavens, even the all-night broadcasting job. It was crazy, but I liked it."

I finished my waffle, tracing the same circuit of memories I knew that she, too, was following. Timekeeper on a construction gang, race-track operative, tavern proprietor, newspaper legman, and then rewrite, advertising consultant, and finally—what? Now?

Of all these experiences I didn't know which filled me, in retrospect, with the greater pleasure or the more annoyance. And I knew it was a waste of time to raise such a question even in passing.

Time.

One runs like a mouse up the old, slow pendulum of the big clock, time, scurries around and across its huge hands, strays inside through the intricate wheels and balances and springs of the inner mechanism, searching among the cobwebbed mazes of this machine with all its false exits and dangerous blind alleys and steep runways, natural traps and artificial baits, hunting for the true opening and the real prize.

Then the clock strikes one and it is time to go, to run down the pendulum, to become again a prisoner making once more the same escape.

For of course the clock that measures out the seasons, all gain and loss, the air Georgia breathes, Georgette's strength, the figures shivering on the dials of my own inner instrument board, this gigantic watch that fixes order and establishes the pattern for chaos itself, it has never changed, it will never change, or be changed.

I found I had been looking at nothing. I said: "No. I'm the roundest peg you ever saw."

Georgette pinched out her cigarette, and asked: "Are you driving in?"

I thought of Roy and Hagen and the Silver Lining.

"No. And I may be home late. I'll call you."

"All right, I'll take you to the station. I may go in for a while myself, after lunch."

Finishing my coffee I sped through the headlines of the first three pages of the morning paper and found nothing new. A record-breaking bank robbery in St. Paul, but not for us. While Georgette gave instructions to Nellie I got into my coat and hat, took the car out of the garage, and honked. When Georgette came out I moved over and she took the wheel.

This morning, Marble Road was crisp but not cold, and very bright. Patches of snow from a recent storm still showed on the brown lawns and on the distant hills seen through the crooked black lace of the trees. Away from Marble Road, our community of rising executives, falling promoters, and immovable salesmen, we passed through the venerable but slightly weatherbeaten, huge square boxes of the original citizens. On the edge of the town behind Marble Road lay the bigger estates, scattered through the hills. Lots of gold in them, too. In about three more years, we would stake a claim of several acres there, ourselves.

"I hope I can find the right drapes this afternoon," said Georgette, casually. "Last week I didn't have time. I was in Doctor Dolson's office two solid hours."

"Yes?" Then I understood she had something to say. "How are you and Doc Dolson coming along?"

She spoke without taking her eyes from the road. "He says he thinks it would be all right."

"He thinks? What does that mean?"

"He's sure. As sure can be. Next time I should be all right."

"That's swell." I covered her hand on the wheel. "What have you been keeping it secret for?"

"Well. Do you feel the same?"

"Say, why do you think I've been paying Dolson? Yes. I do."

"I just wondered."

"Well, don't. When, did he say?"

"Any time."

We had reached the station and the 9:08 was just pulling in. I kissed her, one arm across her shoulders, the other arm groping for the handle of the door.

"Any time it is. Get ready not to slip on lots of icy sidewalks."

"Call me," she said, before I closed the door.

I nodded and made for the station. At the stand inside I took another paper and went straight on through. There was plenty of time. I could see an athlete still running, a block away.

The train ride, for me, always began with Business Opportunities, my favorite department in any newspaper, continued with the auction room news and a glance at the sports pages, insurance statistics, and then amusements. Finally, as the train burrowed underground, I prepared myself for the day by turning to the index and reading the gist of the news. If there was something there, I had it by the time the hundreds and thousands of us were intently journeying across the floor of the station's great ant heap, each of us knowing, in spite of the intricate patterns we wove, just where to go, just what to do.

And five minutes later, two blocks away, I arrived at the Janoth Building, looming like an eternal stone deity among a forest of its fellows. It seemed to prefer human sacrifices, of the flesh and of the spirit, over any other token of devotion. Daily, we freely made them.

I turned into the echoing lobby, making mine.

George Stroud III

Janoth Enterprises, filling the top nine floors of the Janoth Building, was by no means the largest of its kind in the United States. Jennett-Donohue formed a larger magazine syndicate; so did Beacon Publications, and Devers & Blair. Yet our organization had its special place, and was far from being the smallest among the many firms publishing fiction and news, covering political, business, and technical affairs.

Newsways was the largest and best-known magazine of our group, a weekly publication of general interest, with a circulation of not quite two million. That was on floor thirty-one. Above it, on the top floor of the building, were the business offices—the advertising, auditing, and circulation departments, with Earl's and Steve Hagen's private headquarters.

Commerce was a business weekly with a circulation of about a quarter of a million, far less than the actual reading public and the influence it had. Associated with it were the four-page daily bulletin, *Trade*, and the hourly wire service, *Commerce Index*. These occupied floor thirty.

The twenty-ninth floor housed a wide assortment of technical newspapers and magazines, most of them published monthly, ranging from *Sportland* to *The Frozen Age* (food products), *The Actuary* (vital statistics), *Frequency* (radio and television), and *Plastic Tomorrow*. There were eleven or twelve of these what's-coming-next and how-to-do-it publications on this floor, none with a large circulation, some of them holdovers from an inspired moment of Earl Janoth's, and possibly now forgotten by him.

The next two floors in descending order held the morgue, the library and general reference rooms, art and photo departments, a small but adequate first-aid room in frequent use, a rest room, the switchboards, and a reception room for general inquiries.

The brains of the organization were to be found, however, on floor twenty-six. It held *Crimeways*, with Roy Cordette as Associate Editor (Room 2618), myself as Executive Editor (2619), Sydney Kislak and Henry Wyckoff, Assistant Editors (2617), and six staff writers in adjoining compartments. In theory we were the nation's police blotter, watchdogs of its purse and conscience, sometimes its morals, its table manners, or anything else that came into our heads. We were diagnosticians of crime; if the FBI had to go to press once a month, that would be us. If the constable of Twin Oaks, Nebraska, had to be a discerning social critic, if the National Council of Protestant Episcopal Bishops had to do a certain amount of legwork, that would be us, too. In short, we were the weather bureau of the national health, recorders of its past and present crimes, forecasters of those in the future. Or so, at one time or another, we had collectively said.

With us on the twenty-sixth floor, also, were four other magazines having similar set-ups: *Homeways* (more than just a journal of housekeeping), *Personalities* (not merely the outstanding success stories of the month), *Fashions* (human, not dress), and *The Sexes* (love affairs, marriages, divorces).

Finally, on the two floors below us, were the long-range research bureaus, the legal department, the organization's public relations staff, office supplies, personnel, and a new phenomenon called *Futureways*, dedicated to planned social evolution, an undertaking that might emerge as a single volume, a new magazine, an after-dinner speech somewhere, or simply disappear suddenly leaving no trace at all. Edward Orlin and Emory Mafferson were both on its staff.

Such was the headquarters of Janoth Enterprises. Bureaus in twenty-one large cities at home and twenty-five abroad fed this nerve-center daily and hourly. It was served by roving correspondents and by master scientists, scholars, technicians in every quarter of the world. It was an empire of intelligence.

Any magazine of the organization could, if necessary, command the help and advice of any channel in it. Or of all of them. *Crimeways* very often did.

We had gone after the missing financier, Paul Isleman, and found him. That one could be credited to me. And we had exercised the legal department, the auditing bureau, and a dozen legmen from our own and other units to disentangle Isleman's involved frauds, while one of our best writers, Bert Finch, had taken a month to make the whole complicated business plain to the general public.

We had found the man who killed Mrs. Frank Sandler, beating the cops by three-tenths of a second. This one, also, could be credited to George Stroud. I had located the guy through our own morgue—with the aid of a staff thrown together for the job.

I went straight through my room into Roy's, stopping only to shed my hat and coat. They were all there in 2618, looking tired but dogged, and vaguely thoughtful. Nat Sperling, a huge, dark, awkward man, went on speaking in a monotonous voice, referring to his notes.

" . . . On a farm about thirty miles outside Reading. The fellow used a shotgun, a revolver, and an ax."

Roy's remote, inquiring gaze flickered away from me back to Sperling. Patiently, he asked: "And?"

"And it was one of those gory, unbelievable massacres that just seem to happen every so often in those out-of-the-way places."

"We have a man in Reading," Roy meditated, out loud. "But what's the point?"

"The score this fellow made," said Nat. "Four people, an entire family. That's really big-scale homicide, no matter where it happens."

Roy sighed and offered a wisp of a comment. "Mere numbers mean nothing. Dozens of people are murdered every day."

"Not four at a clip, by the same man."

Sydney Kislak, perched on a broad window ledge in back of Elliot, sounded a brisk footnote: "Choice of weapons. Three different kinds."

"Well, what was it all about?" Roy equably pursued.

"Jealousy. The woman had promised to run away with the killer, at least he thought she had, and when she brushed him off instead, he shot her, her husband, then he took a gun and an ax to their two—"

Roy murmured absently: "In a thing like that, the big point to consider is the motive. Is it relevant to our book? Is it criminal? And it seems to me this bird just fell in love. It's true that something went wrong, but basically he was driven to his act by love. Now, unless you can show there is something inherently criminal or even anti-social in the mating instinct—" Roy slowly opened and closed the fingers of the hand on the desk before him. "But I think we ought to suggest it to Wheeler for *Sexes.* Or perhaps *Personalities.*"

"*Fashions,*" murmured Sydney.

Roy continued to look expectantly at Nat, across whose candid features had struggled a certain amount of reluctant admiration. He concentrated again on his notes, apparently decided to pass over two or three items, then resumed.

"There's a terrific bank robbery in St. Paul. Over half a million dollars, the biggest bag in history."

"The biggest without benefit of law," Henry Wyckoff amended. "That was last night, wasn't it?"

"Yesterday afternoon. I got the Minneapolis bureau on it, and we already know there was a gang of at least three people, maybe more, working on this single job for more than three years. The thing about this job is that the gang regularly incorporated themselves three years ago, paid income taxes, and paid themselves salaries amounting to $175,000 while they were laying their plans and making preparations for the hold-up. Their funds went through the bank they had in mind, and it's believed they had several full-dress rehearsals before yesterday, right on the spot. A couple of the guards had even been trained, innocently it's believed, to act as their extras. One of them got paid off with a bullet in the leg."

Nat stopped and Roy appeared to gaze through him, a pinch of a frown balancing itself delicately against the curiosity in his blue, tolerant eyes.

"Figures again," he delicately judged. "What is the difference whether it is a half million, half a thousand, or just half a dollar? Three years, three months, or three minutes? Three criminals, or three hundred? What makes it so significant that it must be featured by us?"

"The technical angle, don't you think?" suggested Wyckoff. "Staying within the law while they laid the groundwork. Those rehearsals. Working all that time right through the bank. When you think of it, Roy, why, no bank or business in the world is immune to a gang with sufficient patience, resources, and brains. Here's the last word in criminal technique, matching business methods against business methods. Hell, give enough people enough time and enough money and brains, and eventually they could take Fort Knox."

"Exactly," said Roy. "And is that new? Attack catching up with defense, defense overtaking attack, that is the whole history of crime. We have covered the essential characteristics of this very story, in its various guises, many times before—too many. I can't see much in that for us. We'll give it two or three paragraphs in *Crime Wavelets*. 'Sober, hardworking thugs invest $175,000, three years of toil, to stage a bank robbery. Earn themselves a profit of $325,000, net.' At three men working for three years," he calculated, "that amounts to something over thirty-six thousand a year each. Yes. 'This modest wage, incommensurate with the daring and skill exercised, proves again that crime does not pay— enough.' About like that. Now, can't we get something on a little higher level? We still need three leading articles."

Nat Sperling had no further suggestions to make. I saw it was already 10:45, and with little or nothing done, an early lunch seemed an idle dream. Also, I would have to write off any hope for a conference today with Roy and Hagen. Tony Watson took the ball, speaking in abrupt, nervous rushes and occasionally halting altogether for a moment of pronounced anguish. It seemed to me his neurasthenia could have shown more improvement, if not a complete cure, for the four or five thousand dollars he had spent on psychoanalysis. Still, considering the hazards of our occupation, it could be that without those treatments Tony would today be speechless altogether.

"There's a bulletin by the Welfare Commission," he said, and after we waited for a while he went on, "to be published next month. But we can get copies. I've read it. It's about the criminal abortion racket. Pretty thorough. The commission spent three years investigating. They covered everything, from the small operators to the big, expensive, private s-sanatoriums. Who protects them, why and how. Total estimated number every year, amount of money the industry represents, figures on deaths and prosecutions. Medical effects, pro and con. Causes, results. It's a straight, exhaustive study of the subject. First of its kind. Official, I mean."

Long before Tony had finished, Roy's chin was down upon his chest, and at the close he was making swift notes.

"Do they reach any conclusions? Make any recommendations?" he asked.

"Well, the report gives a complex of causes. Economic reasons are the chief cause of interrupted pregnancies among married women, and among—"

"Never mind that. We'll have to reach our own conclusions. What do they say about old-age assistance?"

"What? Why, nothing, as I recall."

"Never mind, I think we have something. We'll take that bulletin and show what it really means. We'll start by giving the figures for social security survivor benefits. Funeral allowances, in particular, and make the obvious contrasts. Here, on the one hand, is what our government spends every year to bury the dead, while here, at the other end of the scale of life, is what the people spend to prevent birth. Get in touch with the Academy of Medicine and the College of Physicians and Surgeons for a short history of the practice of abortion, and take along a photographer. Maybe they have a collection of primitive and modern instruments. A few pictures ought to be very effective. A short discussion of ancient methods ought to be even more effective."

"Magic was one of them," Bert Finch told Tony.

"Fine," said Roy. "Don't fail to get that in, too. And you might get in touch with the Society of American Morticians for additional figures on what we spend for death, as contrasted with what is spent to prevent life. Call up a half a dozen department stores, ask for figures on what the average expectant mother spends on clothes and equipment up to the date of birth. And don't forget to bring in a good quotation or two from Jonathan Swift on Irish babies."

He looked at Tony, whose meager, freckled features seemed charged with reserve.

"That isn't exactly what I had in mind, Roy. I thought we'd simply dramatize the findings. The commission's findings."

Roy drew a line under the notes on his pad.

"That's what we will be doing, a take-out on the abortion racket. A round-up of the whole subject of inheritance and illegitimacy. But we will be examining it on a higher level, that's all. Just go ahead with the story now, and when the bulletin comes out we'll check through it and draw attention to the real implications of the general picture, at the same time pointing out the survey's omissions. But don't wait for the survey to be released. Can you have a rough draft in, say, two or three weeks?"

Tony Watson's strangled silence indicated that about two thousand dollars' worth of treatments had been shot to hell. Presently, though, he announced: "I can try."

The conference went on, like all those that had gone before, and, unless some tremendous miracle intervened, like many hundreds sure to follow.

Next month Nat Sperling's quadruple-slaying on a lonely farm would become a penthouse shooting in Chicago, Tony's bent for sociological research would produce new parole-board reports, novel insurance statistics, a far-reaching decision of the Supreme Court. Whatever the subject, it scarcely mattered. What did matter was our private and collective virtuosity.

Down the hall, in Sydney's office, there was a window out of which an almost forgotten associate editor had long ago jumped. I occasionally wondered whether he had done so after some conference such as this. Just picked up his notes and walked down the corridor to his own room, opened the window, and then stepped out.

But we were not insane.

We were not children exchanging solemn fantasies in some progressive nursery. Nor were the things we were doing here completely useless.

What we decided in this room, more than a million of our fellow-citizens would read three months from now, and what they read they would accept as final. They might not know they were doing so, they might even briefly dispute our decisions, but still they would follow the reasoning we presented, remember the phrases, the tone of authority, and in the end their crystallized judgments would be ours.

Where our own logic came from, of course, was still another matter. The moving impulse simply arrived, and we, on the face that the giant clock turned to the public, merely registered the correct hour of the standard time.

But being the measure by which so many lives were shaped and guided gave us, sometimes, strange delusions.

At five minutes to twelve, even the tentative schedule lined up for the April book was far too meager. Leon Temple and Roy were engaged in a rather aimless cross-discussion about a radio program that Leon construed as a profound conspiracy against reason, and therefore a cardinal crime, with Roy protesting the program was only a minor nuisance.

"It's on a pretty low level, and why should we give it free advertising?" he demanded. "Like inferior movies and books and plays, it's simply not on our map."

"And like confidence games, and counterfeit money," Leon jibed.

"I know, Leon, but after all—"

"But after all," I intervened, "it's noon, and we've come around to ultimate values, right on the dot."

Roy looked around, smiling. "Well, if you have something, don't let it spoil."

"I think maybe I have," I said. "A little idea that might do everyone a certain amount of good, ourselves included. It's about *Futureways*. We all know something of what they're doing downstairs."

"Those alchemists," said Roy. "Do they know, themselves?"

"I have a strong feeling they've lost their way with Funded Individuals," I began. "We could do a double service by featuring it ourselves, at the same time sending up a trial balloon for them."

I elaborated. In theory, Funded Individuals was something big. The substance of it was the capitalization of gifted people in their younger years for an amount sufficient to rear them under controlled conditions, educate them, and then provide for a substantial investment in some profitable enterprise through which the original indebtedness would be repaid. The original loan, floated as ordinary stocks or bonds, also paid life-insurance premiums guaranteeing the full amount of the issue, and a normal yearly dividend.

Not every one of these incorporated people—Funded Individuals was our registered name for the undertaking—would be uniformly success-ful, of course, however fortunate and talented he might originally be. But the Funded Individuals were operated as a pool, with a single director-ship, and our figures had demonstrated that such a venture would ulti-mately show a tremendous overall profit.

It went without saying that the scheme would mean a great deal to those persons chosen for the pool. Each would be capitalized at some-thing like one million dollars, from the age of seventeen.

I told the staff that the social implications of such a project, carried to its logical conclusions, meant the end of not only poverty, ignorance, disease, and maladjustment, but also inevitably of crime.

"We can suggest a new approach to the whole problem of crime," I concluded. "Crime is no more inherent in society than diphtheria, horse-cars, or black magic. We are accustomed to thinking that crime will cease only in some far-off Utopia. But the conditions for abolishing it are at hand—right now."

The idea was tailored for *Crimeways*, and the staff knew it. Roy said, cautiously: "Well, it does show a perspective of diminishing crime." His thin face was filled with a whole train of afterthoughts. "I see where it could be ours. But what about those people downstairs? And what about the thirty-second floor? It's their material, and they have their own ideas about what to do with it, haven't they?"

I said I didn't think so. Mafferson, Orlin, and half a dozen others downstairs in the research bureau known as *Futureways* had been working on Funded Individuals off and on for nearly a year, with no visible results as yet, and with slight probability there ever would be. I said: "The point is, they don't know whether they want to drop Funded Individuals, or what to do with it if they don't. I think Hagen would welcome any sort of a move. We can give the idea an abbreviated prevue."

" 'Crimeless Tomorrow,' " Roy improvised. " 'Research Shows Why. Finance Shows How.' " He thought for a moment. "But I don't see any pictures, George."

"Graphs."

We let it go at that. That afternoon I cleared the article with Hagen, in a three-minute phone call. Then I had a talk with Ed Orlin, who agreed that Emory Mafferson would be the right man to work with us, and presently Emory put in his appearance.

I knew him only casually. He was not much more than five feet high, and gave the illusion he was taller sitting than standing. He radiated a slight, steady aura of confusion.

After we checked over his new assignment he brought forward a personal matter.

"Say, George."

"Yes?"

"How are you fixed on the staff of *Crimeways?* After we line up Funded Individuals?"

"Why, do you want to join us?"

"Well, I damn near have to. Ed Orlin looked almost happy when he found I was being borrowed up here."

"Don't you get along with Ed?"

"We get along all right, sometimes. But I begin to think he's beginning to think I'm not the *Futureways* type. I know the signs. It's happened before, see."

"You write short stories, don't you?"

Emory appeared to grope for the truth. "Well."

"I understand. It's all right with me, Emory, if you want to come on here. What in hell, by the way, is the *Futureways* type?"

Emory's brown eyes swam around behind thick spectacles like two lost and lonely goldfish. The inner concentration was terrific. "First place, you've got to believe you're shaping something. Destiny, for example. And then you'd better not do anything to attract attention to yourself. It's fatal to come up with a new idea, for instance, and it's also fatal not to have any at all. See what I mean? And above all, it's dangerous to turn in a piece of finished copy. Everything has to be serious, and pending. Understand?"

"No. Just don't try to be the *Crimeways* type, that's all I ask."

We got Emory and Bert Finch teamed for the "Crimeless Tomorrow" feature, and at five o'clock I phoned Georgette to say I'd be home, after all, but Nellie told me Georgette had gone to her sister's in some emergency involving one of Ann's children. She would be home late, might not be home at all. I told Nellie I'd have supper in town.

It was five-thirty when I walked into the Silver Lining, alone. I had a drink and reviewed what I would have said to Roy and Steve Hagen, had they been present to listen. It did not sound as convincing as I had made it sound this morning. Yet there must be a way. I could do something, I had to, and I would.

The bar of the Silver Lining is only twenty feet from the nearest tables. Behind me, at one of them, I heard a woman's voice saying that she really must leave, and then another voice saying they would have to meet again soon. Half turning, I saw the first speaker depart, and then I saw the other woman. It was Pauline Delos. The face, the voice, and the figure registered all at once.

We looked at each other across half the width of the room, and before I had quite placed her I had smiled and nodded. So did she, and in much the same manner.

I picked up my drink and went to her table. Why not?

I said of course she didn't remember me, and she said of course she did.

I said could I buy her a drink. I could.

She was blonde as hell, wearing a lot of black.

"You're the friend of President McKinley," she told me. I admitted it. "And this was where you were talking to him. Is he here tonight?"

I looked all around the room.

I guess she meant Clyde Polhemus, but he wasn't here.

"Not tonight," I said. "How would you like to have dinner with me, instead?"

"I'd love it."

I think we had an apple-brandy sidecar to begin with. It did not seem this was only the second time we had met. All at once a whole lot of things were moving and mixing, as though they had always been there.

George Stroud IV

We were in the Silver Lining for about an hour. We had dinner there, after Pauline made a phone call rearranging some previous plans.

Then we made the studio broadcast of *Rangers of the Sky;* the program itself was one of my favorites, but that was not the main attraction. We could have heard it anywhere, on any set. Quite aside from the appeal of the program, I was fascinated by the work of a new sound-effects man who, I believed, was laying the foundation for a whole new radio technique. This chap could run a sequence of dramatic sound, without voice or music, for as much as five minutes. Sustaining the suspense, and giving it a clear meaning, too. I explained to Pauline, who seemed puzzled but interested, that some day this fellow would do a whole fifteen- or thirty-minute program of sound and nothing but sound, without voice or music of course, a drama with no words, and then radio would have grown up.

After that Pauline made some more phone calls, rearranging some other plans, and I remembered Gil's bar on Third Avenue. It wasn't exactly a bar and it wasn't exactly a night club; perhaps it might have been called a small Coney Island, or just a dive. Or maybe Gil had the right name and description when he called it a museum.

I hadn't been there for a year or two, but when I had been, there was a game Gil played with his friends and customers, and to me it had always seemed completely worth while.

Although most of Gil's was an ordinary greased postage stamp for dancing to any kind of a band, with any kind of entertainment, there was one thing about it that was different. There was a thirty-foot bar, and on a deep shelf in back of it Gil had accumulated and laid out an inexhaustible quantity of junk—there is no other word for it—which he called his "personal museum." It was Gil's claim that everything in the world was there, somewhere, and that the article, whatever it was, had a history closely connected with his own life and doings. The game was to stump him, on one point or the other.

I never had, though all told I certainly had spent many happy hours trying to do so, and lots of money. At the same time, Gil's logic was sometimes strained and his tales not deeply imaginative. There was a recurrent rumor that every time Gil got stuck for something not in stock, he made it a point to go out and get its equivalent, thus keeping abreast of alert students of the game. Furthermore, his ripostes in the forenoon and early afternoon of the day were not on a par with the results achieved later on, when he was drunk.

"Anything?" Pauline asked, surveying the collection.

"Anything at all," I assured her.

We were seated at the bar, which was not very crowded, and Pauline was looking in mild astonishment at the deceptive forest of bric-a-brac facing us. There was even a regular bar mirror behind all that mountain of gadgets, as I knew from personal experience. Shrunken heads, franc notes, mark notes, confederate money, bayonets, flags, a piece of a totem pole, an airplane propeller, some mounted birds and butterflies, rocks and seashells, surgical instruments, postage stamps, ancient newspapers —wherever the eye wandered it saw some other incongruity and slipped rather dazedly on to still more.

Gil came up, beaming, and I saw he was in form. He knew me by sight only. He nodded, and I said: "Gil, the lady wants to play the game."

"Surely," he said. Gil was an affable fifty, I would have guessed, or maybe fifty-five. "What can I show you, Miss?"

I said, "Can you show us a couple of highballs, while she makes up her mind?"

He took our orders and turned to set them up.

"Anything at all?" Pauline asked me. "No matter how ridiculous?"

"Lady, those are Gil's personal memoirs. You wouldn't call a man's life ridiculous, would you?"

"What did he have to do with the assassination of Abraham Lincoln?"

She was looking at the headline of a yellowed, glass-encased newspaper announcing same. Of course, I had once wondered the same thing, and I told her: The paper was a family heirloom; Gil's grandfather had written the headline, when he worked for Horace Greeley.

"Simple," I pointed out. "And don't ask for ladies' hats. He's got Cleopatra's turban back there, and half a dozen other moth-eaten relics that could pass for anything at all."

Gil slid our drinks before us, and gave Pauline his most professional smile.

"I want to see a steamroller," she said.

Gil's beam deepened and he went down the bar, returned with a black and jagged metal cylinder that had once served, if I properly remembered a wild evening, as Christopher Columbus' telescope—a relic certified by the Caribbean natives from whom Gil had personally secured it.

"I can't show you the whole steamroller, ma'am," Gil told Pauline. "Naturally, I haven't room here. Someday I'll have a bigger place, and then I can enlarge my personal museum. But this here is the safety valve from off a steamroller, this is. Go on," he pushed it at her. "It's a very clever arrangement. Look it over."

Pauline accepted the article, without bothering to look at it.

"And this is part of your personal museum?"

"The last time they paved Third Avenue," Gil assured her, "this here steamroller exploded right out in front there. The safety valve, which you have ahold of right there in your hand, came through the window like a bullet. Creased me. As a matter of fact, it left a scar. Look, I'll show you." I knew that scar, and he showed it again. That scar was Gil's biggest asset. "The valve off that steamroller was defective, as you can tell by looking at it. But, as long as it was right here anyway, why, I just left it up in back of the bar where it hit. It was one of the narrowest escapes I ever had."

"Me too," I said. "I was right here when it happened. What'll you have, Gil?"

"Why, I don't mind."

Gil turned and earnestly poured himself a drink, his honest reward for scoring. We lifted our glasses, and Gil jerked his gray, massive head just once. Then he went down the bar to an amateur customer who loudly demanded to see a pink elephant.

Gil patiently showed him the pink elephant, and courteously explained its role in his life.

"I like the museum," said Pauline. "But it must be terrible, sometimes, for Gil. He's seen everything, done everything, gone everywhere, known everyone. What's left for him?"

I muttered that history would be in the making tomorrow, the same as today, and we had another drink on that thought. And then Gil came back and Pauline had another experiment with his memories, and the three of us had another round. And then another.

At one o'clock we were both tired of Gil's life, and I began to think of my own.

I could always create a few more memories, myself. Why not?

There were many reasons why I should not. I weighed them all again, and I tried once more to explain somehow the thing that I knew I was about to do. But they all slipped away from me.

I conjured all sorts of very fancy explanations, besides the simple one, but either the plain or the fancy reasons were good enough; I was not particular on what grounds I behaved foolishly, and even dangerously.

Perhaps I was tired of doing, always, what I ought to do, wearier still of not doing the things that should not be done.

The attractions of the Delos woman multiplied themselves by ten, and then presently they were multiplying by the hundreds. We looked at each other, and that instant was like the white flash of a thrown switch when a new circuit is formed and then the current flows invisibly through another channel.

Why not? I knew the risks and the cost. And still, why not? Maybe the risks and the price were themselves at least some of the reasons why. The cost would be high; it would take some magnificent lying and acting; yet if I were willing to pay that price, why not? And the dangers would be greater still. Of them, I couldn't even begin to guess.

But it would be a very rousing thing to spend an evening with this blonde mystery that certainly ought to be solved. And if I didn't solve it now, I never would. Nobody ever would. It would be something lost forever.

"Well?" she said.

She was smiling, and I realized I had been having an imaginary argument with a shadow of George Stroud standing just in back of the blazing nimbus she had become. It was amazing. All that other Stroud seemed to be saying was: *Why not?* Whatever he meant, I couldn't imagine. Why not what?

I finished a drink I seemed to have in my hand, and said: "I'll have to make a phone call."

"Yes. So will I."

My own phone call was to a nearby semi-residential hotel. The manager had never failed me—I was putting his sons and daughters through school, wasn't I?—and he didn't fail me now. When I returned from the booth, I said: "Shall we go?"

"Let's. Is it far?"

"Not far," I said. "But it's nothing extravagant."

I had no idea, of course, where in that rather sad and partially respectable apartment-hotel we would find ourselves. Pauline took all this for granted, apparently. It gave me a second thought; and the second thought whisked itself away the moment it occurred. Then I hoped she wouldn't say anything about anyone or anything except ourselves.

I needn't have worried. She didn't.

These moments move fast, if they are going to move at all, and with no superfluous nonsense. If they don't move, they die.

Bert Sanders, the manager of the Lexington-Plaza, handed me a note when he gave me the key to a room on the fifth floor. The note said he positively must have the room by noon tomorrow, reservations had been made for it. The room itself, where I found my in-town valise, was all right, a sizable family vault I believed I had lived in once or twice before.

I was a little bit surprised and dismayed to see it was already three o'clock, as I brought out the half bottle of Scotch, the one dressing gown and single pair of slippers, the back number of *Crimeways*—how did that get here?—the three volumes of stories and poetry, the stack of handkerchiefs, pajamas, aspirin tablets comprising most of the contents of the valise. I said: "How would you like some Scotch?"

We both would. Service in the Lexington-Plaza perished at about ten o'clock, so we had our drinks with straight tap water. It was all right. The life we were now living seemed to quicken perceptibly.

I remembered to tell Pauline, lying on the floor with a pillow under her head and looking more magnificent than ever in my pajamas, that our home would no longer be ours after noon. She dreamily told me I needn't worry, it would be all right, and why didn't I go right on explaining about Louise Patterson and the more important trends in modern painting. I saw with some surprise I had a book open in my lap, but I had been talking about something else entirely. And now I couldn't remember what. I dropped the book, and lay down on the floor beside her.

"No more pictures," I said. "Let's solve the mystery."

"What mystery?"

"You."

"I'm a very average person, George. No riddle at all."

I believe I said, "You're the last, final, beautiful, beautiful, ultimate enigma. Maybe you can't be solved."

And I think I looked at our great big gorgeous bed, soft and deep and wide. But it seemed a thousand miles away. I decided it was just too far. But that was all right. It was better than all right. It was perfect. It was just plain perfect.

I found out again why we are on this earth. I think.

And then I woke up and saw myself in that big, wide bed, alone, with a great ringing and hammering and buzzing going on. The phone was closest, so I answered it, and a voice said: "I'm sorry, sir, but Mr. Sanders says you have no reservation for today."

I looked at my watch; 1:30.

"All right."

I believe I moaned and lay back and ate an aspirin tablet that somebody had thoughtfully laid on the table beside the bed, and then after a while I went to the door that was still pounding and buzzing. It was Bert Sanders.

"You all right?" he asked, looking more than a little worried. "You know, I told you I've reserved this suite."

"My God."

"Well, I hate to wake you up, but we have to—"

"All right."

"I don't know exactly when—"

"My God."

"If I'd thought—"

"All right. Where is she?"

"Who? Oh, well, about six o'clock this morning—"

"My God, never mind."

"I thought you'd want to sleep for a few hours, but—"

"All right." I found my trousers and my wallet and I somehow paid off Bert. "I'll be out of here in three minutes. Was there anything, by the way—?"

"Nothing, Mr. Stroud. It's just that this room—"

"Sure. Get my bag out of here, will you?"

He said he would, and after that I got dressed in a hurry, looking around the room for possible notes as I found a clean shirt, washed but did not attempt to shave, poured myself a fraction of an inch that seemed to be left in a bottle of Scotch somehow on hand.

Who was she?

Pauline Delos. Janoth's girl friend. Oh, God. What next?

Where did Georgette think I was? In town, on a job, but coming home a little late. All right. And then?

What was I supposed to be doing at the office today?

I couldn't remember anything important, and that was not so bad.

But about the major problems? Well, there was nothing I could do about them now, if I had been as stupid as all this. Nothing. Well, all right.

I combed my hair, brushed my teeth, put on my tie.

I could tell Georgette, at her sister's in Trenton, that I had to work until three in the morning and didn't want to phone. It would have awakened the whole household. Simple. It had always worked before. It would work this time. Had to.

I closed my valise, left it for Bert in the middle of the room, went downstairs to the barber shop in the lobby. There I got a quick shave, and after that I had a quicker breakfast, and then a split-second drink.

It was three o'clock in the afternoon when I got back to my desk, and there was no one around except Lucille, Roy's and my secretary, listlessly typing in the small room connecting our two offices. She did not appear curious, and I couldn't find any messages on my desk, either, just a lot of inter-office memos and names.

"Anyone phone me, Lucille?" I asked.

"Just those on your pad."

"My home didn't call? Nothing from my wife?"

"No."

So it was all right. So far. Thank God.

I went back to my desk and sat down and took three more aspirin tablets. It was an afternoon like any other afternoon, except for those nerves. But there should be nothing really the matter with them, either. I began to go through the routine items listed by Lucille. Everything was the same as it had always been. Everything was all right. I hadn't done anything. No one had.

George Stroud V

And all of that went off all right. And two months passed. And during those two months, Mafferson and I worked up the data and the groundwork for Funded Individuals, and we also worked up a take-out of bankruptcy for the May issue, and a detailed story about bought-and-sold orphans for the June book.

Then one evening, early in March, I had one of those moods. I reached for the phone, and from our confidential telephone service got the number I wanted. When the number answered I said: "Hello, Pauline. This is your attorney."

"Oh, yes," she said, after a second. "That one."

It was a spring day, I told her, as it was: the first. We fixed it to have cocktails at the Van Barth.

Georgette and Georgia were in Florida, returning in two days. Earl Janoth was in Washington, for at least a couple of hours, and possibly for a week. It was a Friday.

Before leaving that night I stepped into Roy's office and found him conferring with Emory Mafferson and Bert Finch. I gathered that Emory was filled with doubts regarding "Crimeless Tomorrow, Science Shows Why, Finance Shows How."

Emory said: "I can see, on paper, how Funded Individuals works out fine. I can see from the insurance rates and the business statistics that it works out for a few people who happen to be funded, but what I don't see is, what's going to happen if everyone belongs to the corporation pool? See what I'm driving at?"

Roy was being at his confident, patient, understanding best. "That's what it's supposed to lead to," he said. "And I think it's rather nice. Don't you?"

"Let me put it this way, Roy. If a person capitalized at a million dollars actually returns the original investment, plus a profit, then there's going to be a tremendous rush to incorporate still more individuals, for still more profit. And pretty soon, everyone will be in clover except the stockholders. What do they get out of the arrangement?"

Roy's patience took on palpable weight and shape. "Profit," he said.

"Sure, but what can they do with it? What have they got? Just some monetary gain. They don't, themselves, lead perfectly conditioned lives, with a big sum left over to invest in some new, paying enterprise. Seems to me the only people that get it in the neck with this scheme are the subscribers who make the whole thing possible."

Roy said: "You forget that after this has been in operation a few years, funded people will themselves be the first to reinvest their capital in the original pool, so that both groups are always interested parties of the same process."

I decided they were doing well enough without interference from me, and left.

In the bar of the Van Barth I met a beautiful stranger in a rather austere gray and black ensemble that looked like a tailored suit, but wasn't. I hadn't been waiting for more than ten minutes. After we settled on the drink she would have, Pauline said, rather seriously: "I shouldn't be here at all, you know. I have a feeling it's dangerous to know you."

"Me? Dangerous? Kittens a month old get belligerent when they see me coming. Open their eyes for the first time and sharpen up their claws, meowing in anticipation."

She smiled, without humor, and soberly repeated: "You're a dangerous person, George."

I didn't think this was the right note to strike, and so I struck another one. And pretty soon it was all right, and we had another drink, and then after a while we went to Lemoyne's for supper.

I had been living pretty much alone for the last three weeks, since Georgette and Georgia had gone to Florida, and I felt talkative. So I talked. I told her the one about what the whale said to the submarine, why the silents had been the Golden Age of the movies, why Lonny Trout was a fighter's fighter, and then I suggested that we drive up to Albany.

That is what we finally did. I experienced again the pleasure of driving up the heights of the only perfect river in the world, the river that never floods, never dries up, and yet never seems to be the same twice. Albany we reached, by stages, in about three hours.

I had always liked the city, too, which is not as commonplace as it may look to the casual traveler, particularly when the legislature is in session. If there is anything Manhattan has overlooked, it settled here.

After registering under a name I dreamed up with some care and imagination, Mr. and Mrs. Andrew Phelps-Guyon, we went out and spent a couple of hours over food and drink, some entertainment and a few dances on a good, not crowded floor, at a damnably expensive night club. But it was an evening with a definite touch of spring, snatched from the very teeth of the inner works, and exceedingly worth while.

We had breakfast at about noon, and shortly afterwards started a slow drive back to the city, by a different route. It was a different river we followed again, of course, and of course, I fell in love with it all over again; and of course, Pauline helped.

It was late Saturday afternoon when we reached the neighborhood of 58 East, Pauline's apartment building, so early she admitted she had time and lots of it. We went to Gil's. Pauline played the game for about three rounds. I thought Gil was stuck when she asked to see Poe's Raven, but he brought out a stuffed bluebird or something, well advanced in its last molting, and explained it was Poe's original inspiration, personally presented to his close friend, Gil's great-grandfather. And then I remembered it was a long time, all of three months, since I'd explored Antique Row.

That is Third Avenue from about Sixtieth Street all the way down to Forty-second, or thereabouts; there may be bigger, better, more expensive and more authentic shops scattered elsewhere about the city, but the spirit of adventure and rediscovery is not in them, somehow. I once asked, on a tall evening in a Third Avenue shop, for the Pied Piper of Hamlin's pipe. They happened to have it, too. I forget what I did with it, after I bought it for about ten dollars and took it first to the office, where it seemed to have lost its potency, and then home, where somebody broke it and then it disappeared. But it wasn't Third Avenue's fault if I hadn't known how to take care of it properly.

This afternoon Pauline and I dawdled over some not very interesting early New England bedwarmers, spinning wheels converted to floor and table lamps, and the usual commodes disguised as playchairs, bookshelves, and tea carts. All very sound and substantial stuff, reflecting more credit to the ingenuity of the twentieth century than to the imagination of the original craftsmen. It was interesting, some of it, but not exciting.

Then at about half-past seven, with some of the shops closing, we reached a little but simply jam-packed place on Fiftieth Street. Maybe I had been in here before, but I couldn't remember it and neither, seemingly, did the proprietor remember me.

I rummaged about for several minutes without his help, not seeing anything I may have missed before, but I had a fine time answering Pauline's questions. Then after a while somebody else came in and I became increasingly aware of the dialogue going forward at the front of the shop.

"Yes, I have," I heard the dealer say, with some surprise. "But I don't know if they're exactly the type you'd want. Hardly anyone asks for pictures in here, of course. I just put that picture in the window because it happened to be framed. Is that the one you wanted?"

"No. But you have some others, haven't you? Unframed. A friend of mine was in here a couple of weeks ago and said you had."

The customer was a big, monolithic brunette, sloppily dressed and with a face like an arrested cyclone.

"Yes, I have. They're not exactly in perfect condition."

"I don't care," she said. "May I see them?"

The dealer located a roll of canvases on an overhead shelf, and tugged them down. I had drifted down to the front of the shop by now, constituting myself a silent partner in the proceedings. The dealer handed the woman the entire roll, and I practically rested my chin on his left shoulder.

"Look them over," he told the woman.

He turned his head, frowning, and for a fraction of a moment one of his eyes loomed enormously, gazing into one of mine. Mine expressed polite curiosity.

"Where did you get these?" the customer asked.

She unrolled the sheaf of canvases, which were about four by five, some more and some less, and studied the one on top from her reverse viewpoint. It showed a Gloucester clipper under full sail, and it was just like all pictures of clippers, unusual only for a ring of dirt, like an enlarged coffee ring, that wreathed the vessel and several miles of the ocean. To say it was not exactly in perfect condition was plain perjury. The ring, I thought, was about the size of a barrelhead, and that would be about where it came from.

"They were part of a lot," the dealer guardedly told her. The big woman cut loose with a loud, ragged laugh. "Part of a lot of what?" she asked. "Material for an arson? Or is this some of that old WPA stuff they used to wrap up ten-cent store crockery?"

"I don't know where it came from. I told you it wasn't in the best of shape."

She thrust the one on top to the rear, exposing a large bowl of daisies. Nobody said anything at all, this time; I just closed my eyes for a couple of seconds and it went away.

The third canvas was an honest piece of work of the tenement-and-junkyard school; I placed it as of about fifteen years ago; I didn't recognize the signature, but it could have been painted by one of five or six hundred good, professional artists who had done the same scene a little better or a little worse.

"Pretty good," said the shop proprietor. "Colorful. It's real."

The tall, square brunette intently went on to the next one. It was another Gloucester clipper, this one going the other way. It had the same magnificent coffee ring that they all did. And the next one was a basket of kittens. "My Pets," I am sure the nice old lady who painted it had called this one. Anyway, the show was diversified. Clipper artists stuck to clippers, backyard painters did them by the miles, and the nice old lady had certainly done simply hundreds and hundreds of cats. Our gallery had them all.

"I'm afraid you haven't got anything here that would interest me," said the woman.

The man tacitly admitted it, and she resumed the show. Two more pictures passed without comment, and I saw there were only two or three more.

Then she turned up another one, methodically, and I suddenly stopped breathing. It was a Louise Patterson. There was no mistaking the subject, the treatment, the effect. The brothers and sisters of that picture hung on my walls in Marble Road. I had once paid nine hundred dollars for one of them, not much less for the others, all of which I had picked up at regular Patterson shows on Fifty-seventh Street.

The customer had already slipped a tentative finger in back of it to separate it from the next canvas and take it away, when I cleared my throat and casually remarked: "I rather like that."

She looked at me, not very amiably, swung the picture around and held it up before her, at arm's length; it curled at the edges where it wasn't frayed, and it had a few spots of something on it in addition to the trademark of the outsized coffee ring. It was in a frightful condition, no less.

"So do I," she flatly declared. "But it's in one hell of a shape. How much do you want for it?"

The question, ignoring me entirely, was fired at the dealer.

"Why—"

"God, what a mess."

With her second shot she doubtless cut the dealer's intended price in half.

"I wouldn't know how to value it, exactly," he admitted. "But you can have it for ten dollars?"

It was the literal truth that I did not myself know what a Patterson would be worth, today, on the regular market. Nothing fabulous, I knew; but on the other hand, although Patterson hadn't exhibited for years, and for all I knew was dead, it did not seem possible her work had passed into complete eclipse. The things I had picked up for a few hundred had been bargains when I bought them, and later still the artist's canvases had brought much more, though only for a time.

I beamed at the woman. "I spoke first," I said to her, and then to the dealer: "I'll give you fifty for it."

The dealer, who should have stuck to refinished porch furniture, was clearly dazzled and also puzzled. I could tell the exact moment the great electric light went on in his soul: he had something, probably a Rembrandt.

"Well, I don't know," he said. "It's obviously a clever picture. Extremely sound. I was intending to have this lot appraised, when I had the time. This is the first time I've really looked at the lot, myself. I think—"

"It is not a Raphael, Rubens, or Corot," I assured him.

He leaned forward and looked more closely at the picture. The canvas showed two hands, one giving and the other receiving a coin. That was all. It conveyed the whole feeling, meaning, and drama of money. But the proprietor was unwrinkling the bottom right-hand corner of the canvas, where the signature would be rather legibly scrawled. I began to perspire.

"Pat something," he announced, studying it carefully, and the next moment he sounded disappointed. "Oh. Patterson, '32. I ought to know that name, but it's slipped my mind."

I let this transparent perjury die a natural death. The large brunette, built like an old-fashioned kitchen cabinet, didn't say anything either. But she didn't need to. She obviously didn't have fifty dollars. And I had to have that picture.

"It's a very superior work," the dealer began again. "When it's cleaned up, it'll be beautiful."

"I like it," I said. "For fifty bucks."

He said, stalling: "I imagine the fellow who painted it called the picture *Toil*. Something like that."

"I'd call it *Judas*," Pauline spoke up. "No, *The Temptation of Judas*."

"There's only one coin," said the dealer, seriously. "There would have to be thirty." Still stalling, he took the canvases and began to go through those we had not seen. A silo, with a cow in front of it. A nice thing with some children playing in the street. The beach at Coney Island. Depressed at stirring no further interest, he declared, "And that's all I have."

To the brunette, and smiling glassily, I said: "Why don't you take the *Grand Street Children*, for about five dollars? I'll take the *Judas*."

She unchained a whoop of laughter that was not, as far as I could make out, either friendly or hostile. It was just loud.

"No, thanks, I have enough children of my own."

"I'll buy you a frame, we'll fix it here, and you can take it home."

This produced another shriek, followed by a roar.

"Save it for your fifty-dollar masterpiece." This sounded derisive. I asked her, with a bite in it: "Don't you believe it's worth that?"

"A picture that is worth anything at all is certainly worth a lot more than that," she suddenly blazed. "Don't you think so? It is either worth ten dollars or a million times that much." Mentally I agreed with this perfectly reasonable attitude, but the shop proprietor looked as though he did, too. And I had to have that picture. It wasn't my fault I had only sixty odd dollars left after one of the most expensive week ends in history, instead of ten million. "But what do I know about paintings? Nothing. Don't let me interfere. Maybe sometime," there was another bloodcurdling laugh, "I'll have the right kind of wallpaper, and just the right space to match the *Grand Street Children*. Save it for me."

She went away, then, and in the quiet that came back to the little shop I firmly proved I would pay what I said I would and no more, and eventually we went away, too, and I had my prize.

Pauline still had some time, and we stopped in at the cocktail lounge of the Van Barth. I left the canvas in the car, but when we'd ordered our drinks Pauline asked me why on earth I'd bought it, and I described it again, trying to explain. She finally said she liked it well enough, but could not see there was anything extraordinarily powerful about it.

It became evident she was picture-blind. It wasn't her fault; many people are born that way; it is the same as being color-blind or tone-deaf. But I tried to explain what the work of Louise Patterson meant in terms of simplified abstractionism and fresh intensifications of color. Then I argued that the picture must have some feeling for her since she'd surely picked the right title for it.

"How do you know it's right?" she asked.

"I know it. I feel it. It's just what I saw in the picture myself."

On the spur of the moment I decided, and told her, that Judas must have been a born conformist, a naturally common-sense, rubber-stamp sort of fellow who rose far above himself when he became involved with a group of people who were hardly in society, let alone a profitable business.

"Heavens, you make him sound like a saint," Pauline said, smiling and frowning.

I told her very likely he was.

"A man like that, built to fall into line but finding himself always out of step, must have suffered twice the torments of the others. And eventually, the temptation was too much for him. Like many another saint, when he was tempted, he fell. But only briefly."

"Isn't that a little involved?"

"Anyway, it's the name of my picture," I said. "Thanks for your help."

We drank to that, but Pauline upset her cocktail.

I rescued her with my handkerchief for a hectic moment, then left her to finish the job while I called the waiter for more drinks, and he cleared the wet tabletop. After a while we had something to eat, and still more drinks, and a lot more talk.

It was quite dark when we came out of the lounge, and I drove the few blocks to 58 East. Pauline's apartment, which I had never been in, was in one of those austere and permanent pueblos of the Sixties. She asked me to stop away from the entrance, cool as she explained: "I don't think it would be wise for me to go in with a strange overnight bag. Accompanied."

The remark didn't say anything, but it gave me a momentarily uncomfortable measure of the small but nevertheless real risks we were running. I erased that idea and said nothing, but I ran past the building and parked half a block from the lighted, canopied entrance.

There I got out to hand her the light valise she had brought with her to Albany, and for a moment we paused.

"May I phone?" I asked.

"Of course. Please do. But we have to be—well—"

"Of course. It's been wonderful, Pauline. Just about altogether supreme."

She smiled and turned away.

Looking beyond her retreating shoulders I vaguely noticed a limousine pull in at the curb opposite the building's entrance. There was something familiar about the figure and carriage of the man who got out of it. He put his head back into the car to issue instructions to a chauffeur, then turned for a moment in my direction. I saw that it was Earl Janoth.

He noticed Pauline approaching, and I am certain that he looked past her and saw me. But I did not think he could have recognized me; the nearest street lamp was at my back.

And what if he had? He didn't own the woman.

He didn't own me, either.

I stepped into my car and started the motor, and I saw them disappearing together into the lighted entrance.

I didn't feel very happy about this unlucky circumstance, as I drove off, but on the other hand, I didn't see how any irreparable damage could have been done.

I drove back to Gil's. There, it was the usual raucous Saturday night. I had a whole lot of drinks, without much conversation, then I took the car around to my garage and caught the 1:45 for home. It was early, but I wanted to be clear-eyed when Georgette and Georgia got back from Florida in the afternoon. I would return by train, pick them up in the car, and drive them home.

I brought in my own bag, at Marble Road, and of course I didn't forget *The Temptation of St. Judas*. The picture I simply laid down on the dining room table. It would have to be cleaned, repaired, and framed.

I glanced at the Pattersons in the downstairs rooms and at the one upstairs in my study, before I went to bed. The *Temptation* was better than any of them.

It occurred to me that maybe I was becoming one of the outstanding Patterson collectors in the United States. Or anywhere.

But before I went to bed I unpacked my grip, put away the belongings it had contained, then put the grip away, too.

Earl Janoth I

By God, I never had such an evening. I flatter myself that I am never inurbane by impulse only, but these people, supposedly friends of mine, were the limit, and I could have strangled them one by one.

Ralph Beeman, my attorney for fifteen years, showed damned little interest and less sympathy when the question of the wire renewal for *Commerce Index* came up, or was deliberately brought up. The whole bunch of them quite openly discussed the matter, as though I myself were some sort of immaterial pneuma, not quite present at all, and as though I might actually lose the franchise. Really, they weighed alternatives, when I did lose it.

"Ralph and I have something to say about that," I said, heartily, but the mousey bastard didn't turn a hair. He was just plain neutral.

"Oh, certainly. We'll renew no matter whom we have to fight."

To me, it sounded as though he thought the fight was already lost. I gave him a sharp look, but he chose not to understand. It would have been well, had Steve been present. He is immensely alert to such winds and undercurrents as I felt, but could not measure, everywhere around me.

Ten of us were having dinner at John Wayne's, and since he is a smooth but capable political leader, if we were discussing anything at all it should have been politics. But by God, since I came into his home, a festering old incubus dating back at least a hundred years, we hadn't talked about anything except Janoth Enterprises, and what difficulties we were having. But I wasn't having any difficulties. And I wasn't having any of this, either.

Then there was an awkward moment when Hamilton Carr asked me how I had made out in Washington. I had just returned, and I had an uncomfortable feeling that he knew exactly everyone I had seen there and what I was about. Yet it was really nothing. I had thought of broadening the corporate basis of Janoth Enterprises, and my trip to Washington was simply to obtain quick and reliable information on what procedure I might follow to achieve that end and fully observe all SEC regulations.

Ralph Beeman had gone down with me, had not said much while we were there, and I gave him another emphatic thought. But it couldn't be. Or were they all, in fact, in some kind of a conspiracy against me? Voyagers to new continents of reason have been caught offguard before.

But Hamilton Carr was no enemy; at least, I had never thought he was; he was simply my banking adviser. He had always known, to the last dime, what the paper issued by Janoth Enterprises was worth, and who held it. Tonight, he said: "You know, Jennett-Donohue still want either to buy or merge."

I gave him a huge laugh.

"Yes," I said. "So do I. What will they sell for?"

Carr smiled; it was icy dissent. God damn you, I thought, what's up?

There was a blasted foreign person present with a fearful English accent who went by the name of Lady Pearsall, or something equally insignificant, and she told me at great length what was wrong with my magazines. Everything was wrong with them, according to her. But it hadn't crossed her mind that I had gone far out of my way to obtain the very best writers and editors, the broadest and richest minds to be had. I had combed the newspapers, the magazines, the finest universities, and paid the highest salaries in the field, to hire what I knew were the finest bunch of journalists ever gathered together under one roof. She gobbled away extensively, her Adam's apple moving exactly like a scrawny turkey's, but to hear her tell it, I had found my writers in the hospitals, insane asylums, and penitentiaries.

I could smile at everything she had to say, but I didn't feel like smiling at what Carr and Beeman and finally a man by the name of Samuel Lydon had to say.

"You know," he told me, "there may not always be the same demand for superior presentation there has been in the past. I've been getting reports from the distributors." Anyone could. It was public knowledge. "I think you would like me to be quite candid with you, Mr. Janoth."

"Certainly."

"Well, the returns on some of your key magazines have shown strange fluctuations. Out of proportion to those of other publications, I mean." I placed him now. He was executive vice-president of a local distributing organization. "I wondered if there was any definitely known reason?"

This was either colossal ignorance or outrageous effrontery. *If I knew of definite reasons.* I looked at him, but didn't bother to reply.

"Maybe it's that astrology magazine of yours," said Geoffrey Balack, ineffectual, vicious, crude, and thoroughly counterfeit. He was some kind of a columnist. I had hired him once, but his work had not seemed too satisfactory, and when he left to take another job I had thought it was a fortunate change all round. Looking at him now, I couldn't remember whether he'd quit, or whether Steve had fired him. Or possibly I had. Offensively, now, he brushed a hand back over the rather thin hair on his head. "That's one I never understood at all. Why?"

I was still smiling, but it cost me an effort.

"I bought that little book, *Stars,* for its title alone. Today it has nothing to do with astrology. It is almost the sole authority in astrophysics."

"Popular?"

That didn't deserve a reply, either. This was what we had once considered a writer with insight and integrity. And good writers cost money, which I was more than glad to pay.

But they were growing more expensive all the time. Other publishing organizations, even though they were not in the same field at all, were always happy to raid our staff, though they rarely tampered with each other's. The advertising agencies, the motion pictures, radio, we were always losing our really good men elsewhere, at prices that were simply fantastic. A man we had found ourselves, and nursed along until we found just the right way to bring out the best and soundest that was in him, might then casually leave us to write trash for some perfume program, or speeches for a political amplifier. Contract or no contract, and at a figure it would be almost ruinous to the rest of the organization if we thought of meeting.

Either that or they wanted to write books. Or went crazy. Although, God knows, most of them were born that way, and their association with us merely slowed up and postponed the inevitable process for a time.

Well. We still had the finest writers to be had, and the competition only kept us on our toes.

When it came to the point where Jennett-Donohue or Devers & Blair offered twenty-five thousand for a fifteen-thousand-dollar editor, we would go thirty thousand. If radio offered fifty thousand for a man we really had to keep, we'd go to sixty. And when Hollywood began raiding our copy boys and legmen for a million—well, all right. No use being morbid. But sometimes it's impossible not to be.

It was ten o'clock—the earliest moment possible—before I was able to leave. I had enough to worry about, without taking on any extra nonsense from this particular crowd.

It is all a matter of one's inherited nerves and glands. No matter how much one rationalizes, one has either a joyless, negative attitude toward everyone and everything, like these people, and it is purely a matter of the way in which the glands function, or one has a positive and constructive attitude. It is no great credit to me. But neither is it any credit to them.

In the car, I told Bill to drive me home, but halfway there I changed my mind. I told him to drive to Pauline's. Hell, she might even be there. Home was no place to go after an evening squandered among a bunch of imitation cynics, disappointed sentimentalists, and frustrated conspirators.

Without a word Bill spun the wheel and we turned the corner. It reminded me of the way he had always taken my orders, thirty years ago during the hottest part of a circulation war out West, then in the printers' strike upstate. That was why he was with me now. If he wouldn't talk even to me, after thirty odd years, he would never talk to anyone.

When we drew up in front of the place and I got out, I put my head in the window next to him and said: "Go on home, Bill. I'll take a taxi. I don't think I'll need you until tomorrow evening."

He looked at me but said nothing, and eased the car away from the curb.

Earl Janoth II

On the sidewalk I turned to go in, but as I turned, I caught sight of Pauline. She was leaving someone at the next corner. I couldn't see her face, but I recognized her profile, the way she stood and carried herself, and I recognized the hat she had recently helped to design, and the beige coat. As I stood there she started to walk toward me. The man with her I did not recognize at all, though I stared until he turned and stepped into a car, his face still in the shadows.

When Pauline reached me she was smiling and serene, a little warm and a little remote, deliberate as always. I said: "Hello, dear. This is fortunate."

She brushed away an invisible strand of hair, stopped beside me.

"I expected you'd be back yesterday," she said. "Did you have a nice trip, Earl?"

"Fine. Have a pleasant week end?"

"Marvelous. I went riding, swimming, read a grand book, and met some of the most interesting brand-new people."

We had moved into the building by now. I glanced down and saw that she carried an overnight bag.

I could hear though not see somebody moving behind the high screen that partitioned off the apartment switchboard and, as usual, there was no sign of anyone else. Perhaps this isolation was one of the reasons she had liked such a place in the beginning.

There was an automatic elevator, and now it was on the main floor. As I opened the door, then followed her in and pushed the button for five, I nodded toward the street.

"Was he one of them?"

"One of who? Oh, you mean the brand-new people. Yes."

The elevator stopped at five. The inner door slid noiselessly open, and Pauline herself pushed open the outer door. I followed her the dozen or so carpeted steps to 5A. Inside the small four-room apartment there was such silence and so much dead air it did not seem it could have been entered for days.

"What were you doing?" I asked.

"Well, first we went to a terrible place on Third Avenue by the name of Gil's. You'd love it. Personally, I thought it was a bore. But it's some kind of a combination between an old archeology foundation, and a saloon. The weirdest mixture. Then after that we went up and down the street shopping for antiques."

"What kind of antiques?"

"Any kind that we thought might be interesting. Finally, we bought a picture, that is, he did, in a shop about three blocks from here. An awful old thing that just came out of a dust-bin, it looked like, and he practically kidnapped it from another customer, some woman who bid for it, too. Nothing but a couple of hands, by an artist named Patterson."

"A couple of what?"

"Hands, darling. Just hands. It was a picture about Judas, as I understand it. Then after that we went to the Van Barth and had a few drinks, and he brought me home. That's where you came in. Satisfied?"

I watched her open the door of the small closet in the lobby and drop her bag inside of it, then close the door and turn to me again with her shining hair, deep eyes, and perfect, renaissance face.

"Sounds like an interesting afternoon," I said. "Who was this brand-new person?"

"Oh. Just a man. You don't know him. His name is George Chester, in advertising."

Maybe. And my name is George Agropolus. But I'd been around a lot longer than she had, or, for that matter, than her boy friend. I looked at her for a moment, without speaking, and she returned the look, a little too intently. I almost felt sorry for the new satellite she'd just left, whoever he was.

She poured us some brandy from a decanter beside the lounge, and across the top of her glass she crinkled her eyes in the intimate way supposed to fit the texture of any moment. I sipped my own, knowing again that everything in the world was ashes. Cold, and spent, and not quite worth the effort. It was a mood that Steve never had, a mood peculiarly my own. The question crossed my mind whether possibly others, too, experienced the same feeling, at least occasionally, but that could hardly be. I said: "At least, this time it's a man."

Sharply, she said: "Just what do you mean by that?"

"You know what I mean."

"Are you bringing up that thing again? Throwing Alice in my face?" Her voice had the sound of a wasp. Avenue Z was never far beneath the surface, with Pauline. "You never forget Alice, do you?"

I finished the brandy and reached for the decanter, poured myself another drink. Speaking with deliberate slowness, and politely, I said: "No. Do you?"

"Why, you goddamn imitation Napoleon, what in hell do you mean?"

I finished the brandy in one satisfying swallow.

"And you don't forget Joanna, do you?" I said, softly. "And that Berleth woman, and Jane, and that female refugee from Austria. And God knows who else. You can't forget any of them, can you, including the next one."

She seemed to choke, for a speechless moment, then she moved like a springing animal. Something, I believe it was an ashtray, went past my head and smashed against the wall, showering me with fine glass.

"You son of a bitch," she exploded. "You talk. You, of all people. *You.* That's priceless."

Mechanically, I reached for the decanter, splashed brandy into my glass. I fumbled for the stopper, trying to replace it. But I couldn't seem to connect.

"Yes?" I said.

She was on her feet, on the other side of the low table, her face a tangle of rage.

"What about you and Steve Hagen?"

I forgot about the stopper, and simply stared.

"What? What about me? And Steve?"

"Do you think I'm blind? Did I ever see you two together when you weren't camping?"

I felt sick and stunned, with something big and black gathering inside of me. Mechanically, I echoed her: "Camping? With Steve?"

"As if you weren't married to that guy, all your life. And as if I didn't know. Go on, you son of a bitch, try to act surprised."

It wasn't me, any more. It was some giant a hundred feet tall, moving me around, manipulating my hands and arms and even my voice. He straightened my legs, and I found myself standing. I could hardly speak. My voice was a sawtoothed whisper.

"You say this about Steve? The finest man that ever lived? And me?"

"Why, you poor, old carbon copy of that fairy gorilla. Are you so dumb you've lived this long without even knowing it?" Then she suddenly screamed: "Don't. Earl, don't."

I hit her over the head with the decanter and she stumbled back across the room. My voice said: "You can't talk like that. Not about us."

"Don't. Oh, God, Earl, don't. Earl. Earl. Earl."

I had kicked over the table between us, and I moved after her. I hit her again, and she kept talking with that awful voice of hers, and then I hit her twice more.

Then she was lying on the floor, quiet and a little twisted. I said: "There's a limit to this. A man can take just so much."

She didn't reply. She didn't move.

I stood above her for a long, long time. There was no sound at all, except the remote, muffled hum of traffic from the street below. The decanter was still in my hand, and I lifted it, looked at the bottom edge of it faintly smeared, and with a few strands of hair.

"Pauline."

She lay on her back, watching something far away that didn't move. She was pretending to be unconscious.

A fear struck deeper and deeper and deeper, as I stared at her beautiful, bright, slowly bleeding head. Her face had an expression like nothing on earth.

"Oh, God, Pauline. Get up."

I dropped the decanter and placed my hand inside her blouse, over the heart. Nothing. Her face did not change. There was no breath, no pulse, nothing. Only her warmth and faint perfume. I slowly stood up. She was gone.

So all of my life had led to this strange dream.

A darkness and a nausea flooded in upon me, in waves I had never known before. This, this carrion by-product had suddenly become the total of everything. Of everything there had been between us. Of everything I had ever done. This accident.

For it was an accident. God knows. A mad one.

I saw there were stains on my hands, and my shirt front. There were splotches on my trousers, my shoes, and as my eyes roved around the room I saw that there were even spots high on the wall near the lounge where I had first been sitting.

I needed something. Badly. Help and advice.

I moved into the bathroom and washed my hands, sponged my shirt. It came to me that I must be careful. Careful of everything. I closed the taps with my handkerchief. If her boy friend had been here, and left his own fingerprints. If others had. Anyone else. And many others had.

Back in the other room, where Pauline still lay on the carpet, unchanging, I remembered the decanter and the stopper to it. These I both wiped carefully, and the glass. Then I reached for the phone, and at the same time remembered the switchboard downstairs, and drew away.

I let myself out of the apartment, again using my handkerchief as a glove. Pauline had let us in. The final image of her own fingers would be on the knob, the key, the frame.

I listened for a long moment outside the door of 5A. There was no sound throughout the halls, and none from behind that closed door. I knew, with a renewed vertigo of grief and dread, there would never again be life within that apartment. Not for me.

Yet there had been, once, lots of it. All collapsed to the size of a few single moments that were now a deadly, unreal threat.

I moved quietly down the carpeted hall, and down the stairs. From the top of the first floor landing I could just see the partly bald, gray head of the man at the switchboard. He hadn't moved, and if he behaved as usual, he wouldn't.

I went quietly down the last flight of stairs and moved across the lobby carpet to the door. At the door, when I opened it, I looked back. No one was watching, there was no one in sight.

On the street, I walked for several blocks, then at a stand on some corner I took a taxi. I gave the driver an address two blocks from the address I automatically knew I wanted. It was about a mile uptown.

When I got out and presently reached the building it was as quiet as it had been at Pauline's.

There was no automatic elevator, as there was at Pauline's, and I did not want to be seen, not in this condition. I walked up the four flights to the apartment. I rang, suddenly sure there would be no answer.

But there was.

Steve's kindly, wise, compact, slightly leathery face confronted me when the door swung open. He was in slippers and a dressing gown. When he saw me, he held the door wider, and I came in.

He said: "You look like hell. What is it?"

I walked past him and into his living room and sat down in a wide chair. "I have no right to come here. But I didn't know where else to go."

He had followed me into his living room, and he asked, impassively: "What's the matter?"

"God. I don't know. Give me a drink."

Steve gave me a drink. When he said he would ring for some ice, I stopped him.

"Don't bring anyone else in on this," I said. "I've just killed someone."

"Yes?" He waited. "Who?"

"Pauline."

Steve looked at me hard, poured himself a drink, briefly sipped it, still watching me.

"Are you sure?"

This was insane. I suppressed a wild laugh. Instead, I told him, curtly: "I'm sure."

"All right," he said, slowly. "She had it coming to her. You should have killed her three years ago."

I gave him the longest look and the most thought I had ever given him.

There was an edge of iron amusement in his locked face. I knew what was going on in his mind: *She was a tramp, why did you bother with her?* And I know what went on in my mind: *I am about the loneliest person in the world.*

"I came here, Steve," I said, "because this is just about my last stop. I face, well, everything. But I thought—hell, I don't know what I thought. But if there is anything I should do, well, I thought maybe you'd know what that would be."

"She deserved it," Steve quietly repeated. "She was a regular little comic."

"Steve, don't talk like that about Pauline. One of the warmest, most generous women who ever lived."

He finished his drink and casually put down the glass.

"Was she? Why did you kill her?"

"I don't know, I just don't know. From here I go to Ralph Beeman, and then to the cops, and then I guess to prison or even the chair." I finished my drink and put down the glass. "I'm sorry I disturbed you."

Steve gestured. "Don't be a fool," he said. "Forget that prison stuff. What about the organization? Do you know what will happen to it the second you get into serious trouble?"

I looked at my hands. They were clean, but they had undone me. And I knew what would happen to the organization the minute I wasn't there, or became involved in this kind of trouble.

"Yes," I said. "I know. But what can I do?"

"Do you want to fight, or do you want to quit? You aren't the first guy in the world that ever got into a jam. What are you going to do about it? Are you going to put up a battle, or are you going to fold up?"

"If there's any chance at all, I'll take it."

"I wouldn't even know you, if I thought you'd do anything else."

"And of course, it's not only the organization, big as that is. There's my own neck, besides. Naturally, I'd like to save it."

Steve was matter of fact. "Of course. Now, what happened?"

"I can't describe it. I hardly know."

"Try."

"That bitch. Oh, God, Pauline."

"Yes?"

"She said that I, she actually accused both of us, but it's utterly fantastic. I had a few drinks and she must have had several. She said something about us. Can you take it?"

Steve was unmoved. "I know what she said. She would. And then?"

"That's all. I hit her over the head with something. A decanter. Maybe two or three times, maybe ten times. Yes, a decanter. I wiped my fingerprints off of it. She must have been insane, don't you think? To say a thing like that? She's a part-time Liz, Steve, did I ever tell you that?"

"You didn't have to."

"So I killed her. Before I even thought about it. God, I didn't intend anything like it, thirty seconds before. I don't understand it. And the organization is in trouble, real trouble. Did I tell you that?"

"You told me."

"I don't mean about this. I mean Carr and Wayne and—"

"You told me."

"Well, at dinner tonight I was sure of it. And now this. Oh, God."

"If you want to save the whole works you'll have to keep your head. And your nerve. Especially your nerve."

All at once, and for the first time in fifty years, my eyes were filled with tears. It was disgraceful. I could hardly see him. I said: "Don't worry about my nerve."

"That's talking," Steve said, evenly. "And now I want to hear the details. Who saw you go into this place, Pauline's apartment? Where was the doorman, the switchboard man? Who brought you there? Who took you away? I want to know every goddamn thing that happened, what she said to you and what you said to her. What she did and what you did. Where you were this evening, before you went to Pauline's. In the meantime, I'm going to lay out some clean clothes. You have bloodstains on your shirt and your trousers. I'll get rid of them. Meanwhile, go ahead."

"All right," I said, "I was having dinner at the Waynes'. And they couldn't seem to talk about anything else except what a hell of a mess Janoth Enterprises was getting into. God, how they loved my difficulties. They couldn't think or talk about anything else."

"Skip that," said Steve. "Come to the point."

I told him about leaving the Waynes', how Bill had driven me to Pauline's.

"We don't have to worry about Bill," said Steve.

"God," I interrupted. "Do you really think I can get away with this?"

"You told me you wiped your fingerprints off the decanter, didn't you? What else were you thinking of when you did it?"

"That was automatic."

Steve waved the argument away.

"Talk."

I told him the rest of it. How I saw this stranger, leaving Pauline, and how we got into a quarrel in her apartment, and what she had said to me, and what I had said to her, and then what happened, as well as I remembered it.

Finally, Steve said to me: "Well, it looks all right except for one thing."

"What?"

"The fellow who saw you go into the building with Pauline. Nobody else saw you go in. But he did. Who was he?"

"I tell you, I don't know."

"Did he recognize you?"

"I don't know."

"The one guy in the world who saw you go into Pauline's apartment, and you don't know who he was? You don't know whether he knew you, or recognized you?"

"No, no, no. Why, is that important?"

Steve gave me a fathomless glance. He slowly found a cigarette, slowly reached for a match, lit the cigarette. When he blew out the second drag of smoke, still slowly, and thoughtfully blew out the match, and then put the burned match away and exhaled his third lungful, deliberately, he turned and said: "You're damned right it is. I want to hear everything there is to know about that guy." He flicked some ashes into a tray. "Everything. You may not know it, but he's the key to our whole set-up. In fact, Earl, he spells the difference. Just about the whole difference."

Steve Hagen

We went over that evening forward and backward. We put every second of it under a high-powered microscope. Before we finished I knew as much about what happened as though I had been there myself, and that was a lot more than Earl did. This jam was so typical of him that, after the first blow, nothing about it really surprised me.

It was also typical that his simple mind could not wholly grasp how much was at stake and how much he had jeopardized it. Typical, too, that he had no idea how to control the situation. Nor how fast we had to work. Nor how.

Pauline's maid would not return to the apartment until tomorrow evening. There was a good chance the body would not be discovered until then. Then, Earl would be the first person seriously investigated by the police, since his connection with her was common knowledge.

I would have to claim he was with me throughout the dangerous period, and it would have to stick. But Billy would back that.

After leaving the Waynes', Earl had come straight here. Driven by

Billy. Then Billy was given the rest of the night off. That was all right, quite safe.

There would be every evidence of Earl's frequent, former visits to Pauline's apartment, but nothing to prove the last one. Even I had gone there once or twice. She had lots of visitors running in and out, both men and women. But I knew, from Earl's squeamish description, the injuries would rule out a woman.

The cover I had to provide for Earl would be given one hell of a going over. So would I. That couldn't be helped. It was my business, not only Earl's, and since he couldn't be trusted to protect our interests, I would have to do it myself.

Apparently it meant nothing to him, the prospect of going back to a string of garbage-can magazines edited from a due-bill office and paid for with promises, threats, rubber checks, or luck. He didn't even think about it. But I did. Earl's flair for capturing the mind of the reading public was far more valuable than the stuff they cram into banks. Along with this vision, though, he had a lot of whims, scruples, philosophical foibles, a sense of humor that he sometimes used even with me. These served some purpose at business conferences or social gatherings, but not now.

If necessary, if the situation got too hot, if Earl just couldn't take it, I might draw some of the fire myself. I could afford to. One of our men, Emory Mafferson, had phoned me here about the same time Earl was having his damned expensive tantrum. And that alibi was real.

The immediate problem, no matter how I turned it over, always came down to the big question mark of the stranger. No other living person had seen Earl, knowing him to be Earl, after he left that dinner party. For the tenth time, I asked: "There was nothing at all familiar about that person you saw?"

"Nothing. He was in a shadowy part of the street. With the light behind him."

"And you have no idea whether he recognized you?"

"No. But I was standing in the light of the entranceway. If he knew me, he recognized me."

Again I thought this over from every angle. "Or he may sometime recognize you," I concluded. "When he sees your face in the papers, as one of those being questioned. Maybe. And maybe we can take care they aren't good pictures. But I wish I had a line on that headache right now. Something to go on when the story breaks. So that we can always be a jump ahead of everyone, including the cops."

All I knew was that Pauline said the man's name was George Chester. This might even be his true name, though knowing Pauline, that seemed improbable, and the name was not listed in any of the phone books of the five boroughs, nor in any of the books of nearby suburbs. She said he was in advertising. That could mean anything. Nearly everyone was.

They had gone to a place on Third Avenue called Gil's, and for some reason it had seemed like an archeological foundation. This sounded authentic. The place could be located with no difficulty.

They had stopped in at a Third Avenue antique shop, and there the man had bought a picture, bidding for it against some woman who apparently just walked in from the street, as they did. It would not be hard to locate the shop and get more out of the proprietor. The picture was of a couple of hands. Its title, or subject matter, was something about Judas. The artist's name was Patterson. The canvas looked as though it came out of a dustbin. Then they had gone to the cocktail lounge of the Van Barth. It should not be hard to get another line on our character there. He certainly had the picture with him. He may even have checked it.

But the antique shop seemed a surefire bet. There would have been the usual long, pointless talk about the picture. Even if the proprietor did not know either the man or the woman customer, he must have heard enough to offer new leads regarding the clown we wanted. The very fact he had gone into the place, then bought nothing except this thing, something that looked like it belonged in an incinerator, this already gave our bystander an individual profile. I said: "What kind of a person would do that, buy a mess like that in some hole-in-the-wall?"

"I don't know. Hell, I'd do it myself, if I felt like it."

"Well, I wouldn't feel like it. But there's another line. We can surely get a lead on the artist. We'll probably find a few clips in our own morgue. It's possible the man we are looking for is a great admirer of this artist, whoever he is. We can locate Patterson and get the history of this particular picture. Two hands. A cinch. There may be thousands, millions of these canvases around the city, but when you come right down to it, each of them has been seen by somebody besides the genius who painted it, and somebody would be certain to recognize it from a good description. After that, we can trace it along to the present owner."

Earl had by now come out of his first shock. He looked, acted, sounded, and thought more like his natural self. "How are we going to find this man, ahead of the police?" he asked.

"What have we got two thousand people for?"

"Yes, of course. But doesn't that mean—after all—isn't that spreading suspicion just that much farther?"

I had already thought of a way to put the organization in motion without connecting it at all with the death of Pauline.

"No. I know how to avoid that."

He thought that over for a while. Then he said: "Why should you do this? Why do you stick your neck out? This is serious."

I knew him so well I had known, almost to the word, he would say that. "I've done it before, haven't I? And more."

"Yes. I know. But I have a hell of a way of rewarding friendship like that. I merely seem to exact more of it. More risks. More sacrifices."

"Don't worry about me. You're the one who's in danger."

"I hope you're not. But I think you will be, giving me an alibi, and leading the search for this unknown party."

"I won't be leading the search. We want somebody else to do that. I stay in the background." I knew that Earl himself would go right on being our biggest headache. I thought it would be better to take the first hurdle now. "In the first place, I want to disassociate you from this business as far as possible. Don't you agree that's wise?" He nodded, and I slowly added, as an afterthought, "Then, when our comedian is located, we want an entirely different set of people to deal with him."

Earl looked up from the thick, hairy knuckles of the fingers he seemed to be studying. His face had never, even when he was most shaken, lost its jovial appearance. I wondered whether he had seemed to be smiling when he killed the woman, but of course he had been.

The question forming in that slow, unearthly mind of his at last boiled up. "By the way. What happens when we do locate this person?"

"That all depends. When the story breaks, he may go straight to the police. In that case our alibi stands, and our line is this: He says he saw you on the scene. What was he doing there, himself? That makes him as hot as you are. We'll make him even warmer. We already know, for instance, that he spent a large part of the evening with Pauline."

Earl's round, large, staring eyes showed no understanding for a moment, then they came to life. "By God, Steve. I wonder—no. Of course you mean that only to threaten him off."

I said: "Put it this way. If the case goes to trial, and he persists in being a witness, that's the line we'll raise. Your own movements are accounted for, you were with me. But what was he doing there? What about this and that?—all the things we are going to find out about him long in advance. The case against you won't stand up."

Earl knew I had omitted something big, and in his mind he laboriously set out to find what it was. I waited while he thought it over, knowing he couldn't miss. Presently, he said: "All right. But if he doesn't go to the police the minute this breaks? Then what?"

I didn't want him to become even more hysterical, and if that were possible, I didn't want him to be even upset. I said, dispassionately: "If we find him first, we must play it safe."

"Well. What does that mean?"

Elaborately, I explained: "We could have him watched, of course. But we'd never know how much he actually did or did not realize, would we?

And we certainly wouldn't know what he'd do next."

"Well? I can see that."

"Well. What is there to do with a man like that? He's a constant threat to your safety, your position in life, your place in the world. He's a ceaseless menace to your very life. Can you put up with an intolerable situation like that?"

Earl gave me a long, wondering, sick, almost frightened regard.

"I don't like that," he said, harshly. "There has already been one accident. I don't want another one. No. Not if I know what you mean."

"You know what I mean."

"No. I'm still a man."

"Are you? There are millions of dollars involved, all because of your uncontrollable temper and your God-forsaken stupidity. Yours, yours, not mine. Besides being an idiot, are you a coward, too?"

He floundered around for a cigar, got one, and with my help, finally got it going. Then, finally, he sounded a raw croak: "I won't see a man killed in cold blood." And as though he'd read my thoughts he added, "Nor take any part in it, either."

I said, reasonably: "I don't understand you. You know what kind of a world this is. You have always been a solid part of it. You know what anyone in Devers & Blair, Jennett-Donohue, Beacon, anyone above an M.E. in any of those houses would certainly do to you if he could reach out at night and safely push a button—"

"No. I wouldn't, myself. And I don't think they would, either."

He was wrong, of course, but there was no use arguing with a middle-aged child prodigy. I knew that by tomorrow he would see this thing in its true light.

"Well, it needn't come to that. That was just a suggestion. But why are you so worried? You and I have already seen these things happen, and we have helped to commit just about everything else for a lot less money. Why are you so sensitive now?"

He seemed to gag.

"Did we ever before go as far as this?"

"You were never in this spot before. Were you?" Now he looked really ghastly. He couldn't even speak. By God, he would have to be watched like a hawk and nursed every minute. "Let me ask you, Earl, are you ready to retire to a penitentiary and write your memoirs, for the sake of your morals? Or are you ready to grow up and be a man in a man's world, take your full responsibilities along with the rewards?" I liked Earl more than I had ever liked any person on earth except my mother, I really liked him, and I had to get both of us out of this at any cost. "No, we never went this far before. And we will never, if we use our heads, ever have to go this far again."

Earl absently drew at his cigar. "Death by poverty, famine, plague, war, I suppose that is on such a big scale the responsibility rests nowhere, although I personally have always fought against all of these things, in a number of magazines dedicated to wiping out each one of them, separately, and in some cases, in vehicles combating all of them together. But a personal death, the death of a definite individual. That is quite different."

He had reduced himself to the intellectual status of our own writers, a curious thing I had seen happen before. I risked it, and said: "We could take a chance on some simpler way, maybe. But there is more at stake than your private morals, personal philosophy, or individual life. The whole damned organization is at stake. If you're wiped out, so is that. When you go, the entire outfit goes. A flood of factory-manufactured nonsense swamps the market."

Earl stood up and paced slowly across the room. It was a long time before he answered me.

"I can be replaced, Steve. I'm just a cog. A good one, I know, but still only a cog."

This was better. This was more like it. I said, knowing him: "Yes, but when you break, a lot of others break, too. Whenever a big thing like this goes to pieces—and that is what could happen—a hell of a lot of innocent people, their plans, their homes, their dreams and aspirations, the future of their children, all of that can go to pieces with it. Myself, for instance."

He gave me one quick glance. But I had gambled that he was a sucker for the greatest good to the most people. And after a long, long while he spoke, and I knew that at heart he was really sound,

"Well, all right," he said. "I understand, Steve. I guess what has to be, has to be."

George Stroud VI

The awfulness of Monday morning is the world's great common denominator. To the millionaire and the coolie it is the same, because there can be nothing worse.

But I was only fifteen minutes behind the big clock when I sat down to breakfast, commenting that this morning's prunes had grown up very fast from the baby raisins in last night's cake. The table rhythmically shook and vibrated under Georgia's steadily drumming feet. It came to me again that a child drinking milk has the same vacant, contented expression of the well-fed cow who originally gave it. There is a real spiritual kinship there.

It was a fine sunny morning, like real spring, spring for keeps. I was beginning my second cup of coffee, and planning this year's gardening, when Georgette said: "George, have you looked at the paper? There's a dreadful story about a woman we met, I think. At Janoth's."

She waited while I picked up the paper. I didn't have to search. Pauline Delos had been found murdered. It was the leading story on page one.

Not understanding it, and not believing it, I read the headlines twice. But the picture was of Pauline.

The story said her body had been discovered at about noon on Sunday, and her death had been fixed at around ten o'clock on the night before. Saturday. I had left her at about that hour.

"Isn't that the same one?" Georgette asked.

"Yes," I said. "Yes."

She had been beaten to death with a heavy glass decanter. No arrest had been made. Her immediate friends were being questioned; Earl Janoth was one of them, the story went, but the publisher had not seen her for a number of days. He himself had spent the evening dining with acquaintances, and after dinner had spent several hours discussing business matters with an associate.

"A horrible story, isn't it?" said Georgette.

"Yes."

"Aren't you going to finish your coffee? George?"

"Yes?"

"You'd better finish your coffee, and then I'll drive you to the station."

"Yes. All right."

"Is something the matter?"

"No, of course not."

"Well, heavens. Don't look so grim."

I smiled.

"By the way," she went on. "I didn't tell you I liked that new picture you brought home. The one of the two hands. But it's in terrible condition, isn't it?"

"Yes, it is."

"It's another Patterson, isn't it?"

A hundred alarm bells were steadily ringing inside of me.

"Well, perhaps."

"Pity's sake, George, you don't have to be so monosyllabic, do you? Can't you say anything but 'yes,' 'no,' 'perhaps'? Is something the matter?"

"No. Nothing's the matter."

"Where did you get this new canvas?"

"Why, I just picked it up."

I knew quite well I had seen Earl entering that building at ten o'clock on Saturday evening. She was alive when they passed into it. He now claimed he had not seen her for several days. Why? There could be only one answer.

But had he recognized me?

Whether he had or not, where did I stand? To become involved would bring me at once into the fullest and fiercest kind of spotlight. And that meant, to begin with, wrecking Georgette, Georgia, my home, my life.

It would also place me on the scene of the murder. That I did not like at all. Nothing would cover Janoth better.

Yet he almost surely knew someone had at least seen him there. Or did he imagine no one had?

"George?"

"Yes?"

"I asked you if you knew much about this Pauline Delos?"

"Very little."

"Goodness. You certainly aren't very talkative this morning."

I smiled again, swallowed the rest of my coffee, and said: "It is a ghastly business, isn't it?"

Somehow Georgia got packed off to school, and somehow I got down to the station. On the train going into town I read every newspaper, virtually memorizing what was known of the death, but gathering no real additional information.

At the office I went straight to my own room, and the moment I got there my secretary told me Steve Hagen had called and asked that I see him as soon as I got in.

I went at once to the thirty-second floor.

Hagen was a hard, dark little man whose soul had been hit by lightning, which he'd liked. His mother was a bank vault, and his father an International Business Machine. I knew he was almost as loyal to Janoth as to himself.

After we said hello and made about one casual remark, he said he would like me to undertake a special assignment.

"Anything you have on the fire downstairs at the moment," he said, "let it go. This is more important. Have you anything special, at this moment?"

"Nothing." Then because it could not be avoided, plausibly, I said: "By the way, I've just read about the Pauline Delos business. It's pretty damn awful. Have you any idea—?"

Steve's confirmation was short and cold. "Yes, it's bad. I have no idea about it."

"I suppose Earl is, well—"

"He is. But I don't really know any more about it than you do."

He looked around the top of his desk and located some notes. He raked them together, looked them over, and then turned again to me. He paused, in a way that indicated we were now about to go to work.

"We have a job on our hands, not hard but delicate, and it seems you are about the very best man on the staff to direct it." I looked at him, waiting, and he went on. "In essence, the job is this: We want to locate somebody unknown to us. Really, it's a missing person job." He waited again, and when I said nothing, he asked: "Would that be all right with you?"

"Of course. Who is it?"

"We don't know."

"Well?"

He ruffled his notes.

"The person we want went into some Third Avenue bar and grill by the name of Gil's last Saturday afternoon. He was accompanied by a rather striking blonde, also unidentified. They later went to a Third Avenue antique shop. In fact, several of them. But in one of them he bought a picture called *Judas*, or something to that effect. He bought the picture from the dealer, overbidding another customer, a woman who also wanted to buy it. The picture was by an artist named Patterson. According to the morgue," Steve Hagen pushed across a thin heavy-paper envelope from our own files, "this Louise Patterson was fairly well known ten or twelve years ago. You can read up on all that for yourself. But the picture bought by the man we want depicted two hands, I believe, and was in rather bad condition. I don't know what he paid for it. Later, he and the woman with him went to the cocktail lounge of the Van Barth for a few drinks. It is possible he checked the picture there, or he may have had it right with him."

No, I hadn't. I'd left it in the car. Steve stopped, and looked at me. My tongue felt like sandpaper. I asked: "Why do you want this man?"

Steve clasped his hands in back of his neck and gazed off into space, through the wide blank windows of the thirty-second floor. From where we sat, we could see about a hundred miles of New York and New Jersey countryside.

When he again turned to me he was a good self-portrait of candor. Even his voice was a good phonographic reproduction of the slightly confidential friend.

"Frankly, we don't know ourselves."

This went over me like a cold wind.

"You must have some idea. Otherwise, why bother?"

"Yes, we have an idea. But it's nothing definite. We think our party is an important figure, in fact a vital one, in a business and political conspiracy that has reached simply colossal proportions. Our subject is not necessarily a big fellow in his own right, but we have reason to believe he's the payoff man between an industrial syndicate and a political machine, the one man who really knows the entire set-up. We believe we can crack the whole situation, when we find him."

So Earl had gone straight to Hagen. Hagen would then be the business associate who provided the alibi. But what did they want with George Stroud?

It was plain Earl knew he had been seen, and afraid he had been recognized. I could imagine how he would feel.

"Pretty vague, Steve," I said. "Can't you give me more?"

"No. You're right, it is vague. Our information is based entirely on rumors and tips and certain, well, striking coincidences. When we locate our man, then we'll have something definite for the first time."

"What's in it? A story for *Crimeways?*"

Hagen appeared to give that question a good deal of thought. He said, finally, and with apparent reluctance: "I don't think so. I don't know right now what our angle will be when we have it. We might want to give it a big play in one of our books, eventually. Or we might decide to use it in some entirely different way. That's up in the air."

I began to have the shadowy outline of a theory. I tested it.

"Who else is in on this? Should we co-operate with anyone? The cops, for instance?"

Cautiously, and with regret, Steve told me: "Absolutely not. This is our story, exclusively. It must stay that way. You will have to go to other agencies for information, naturally. But you get it only, you don't give it. Is that perfectly clear?"

It was beginning to be. "Quite clear."

"Now, do you think you can knock together a staff, just as large as you want, and locate this person? The only additional information I have is that his name may be George Chester, and he's of average build and height, weight one-forty to one-eighty. It's possible he's in advertising. But your best lead is this place called Gil's, the shop where he bought the picture, and the bar of the Van Barth. And that picture, perhaps the artist. I have a feeling the picture alone might give us the break."

"It shouldn't be impossible," I said.

"We want this guy in a hurry. Can you do it?"

If I didn't, someone else would. It would have to be me.

"I've done it before."

"Yes. That's why you're elected."

"What do I do when I find this person?"

"Nothing." Steve's voice was pleasant, but emphatic. "Just let me know his name, and where he can be found. That's all."

It was like leaning over the ledge of one of these thirty-second floor windows and looking down into the street below. I always had to take just one more look.

"What happens when we locate him? What's the next step?"

"Just leave that to me." Hagen stared at me, coldly and levelly, and I stared back. I saw, in those eyes, there was no room for doubt at all. Janoth knew the danger he was in, Hagen knew it, and for Hagen there was literally no limit. None. Furthermore, this little stick of dynamite was intelligent, and he had his own ways, his private means.

"Now, this assignment has the right-of-way over everything, George. You can raid any magazine, use any bureau, any editor or correspondent, all the resources we have. And you're in charge."

I stood up and scooped together the notes I had taken. The squeeze felt tangible as a vise. My personal life would be destroyed if I ran to the cops. Death if Hagen and his special friends caught up with me.

"All right, Steve," I said. "I take it I have absolute carte blanche."

"You have. Expense, personnel, everything." He waved toward the windows overlooking about ten million people. "Our man is somewhere out there. It's a simple job. Get him."

I looked out of the windows myself. There was a lot of territory out there. A nation within a nation. If I picked the right kind of a staff, twisted the investigation where I could, jammed it where I had to, pushed it hard where it was safe, it might be a very, very, very long time before they found George Stroud.

George Stroud VII

I hated to interrupt work on the coming issues of our own book, and so I decided to draw upon all the others, when needed, as evenly as possible.

But I determined to work Roy into it. Bert Finch, Tony, Nat, Sydney, and the rest of them would never miss either of us. And although I liked Roy personally, I could also count upon him to throw a most complicated monkey-wrench into the simplest mechanism. Leon Temple, too, seemed safe enough. And Edward Orlin of *Futureways*, a plodding, rather wooden esthete, precisely unfitted for the present job. He would be working for George Stroud, in the finest sense.

I told Roy about the new assignment, explained its urgency, and then I put it up to him. I simply had to have someone in charge at the office, constantly. This might be, very likely would be, a round-the-clock job. That meant there would have to be another man to share the responsibility.

Roy was distantly interested, and even impressed. "This takes precedence over everything?"

I nodded.

"All right. I'm in. Where do we start?"

"Let me line up the legmen first. Then we'll see."

Fifteen minutes later I had the nucleus of the staff gathered in my office. In addition to Roy and Leon, there were seven men and two women drawn from other magazines and departments. Edward Orlin, rather huge and dark and fat; Phillip Best of *Newsways*, a small, acrid, wire-haired encyclopedia. The two women, Louella Metcalf and Janet Clark, were included if we needed feminine reserves. Louella, drawn from *The Sexes*, was a tiny, earnest, appealing creature, the most persistent and transparent liar I have ever known. Janet was a very simple, eager, large-boned brunette whose last assignment had been with *Homeways;* she did every job about four times over, eventually doing it very well. Don Klausmeyer of *Personalities* and Mike Felch of *Fashions* had also been conscripted, and one man each from *Commerce, Sportland,* and the auditing department. They would do for a convincing start.

From now on, everything would have to look good. Better than good. Perfect. I gave them a crisp, businesslike explanation.

"You are being asked to take on a unique and rather strange job," I said. "It has to be done quickly, and as quietly as possible. I know you can do it.

"We have been given a blank check as far as the resources of the organization are concerned. If you need help on your particular assignment, help of any sort, you can have it. If it's a routine matter, simply go to the department that can give it. If it's something special, come either to me, or to Roy, here, who will be in charge of the work whenever for some reason I have to be elsewhere myself.

"We are looking for somebody. We don't know much about this person, who he is, where he lives. We don't even know his name. His name may be George Chester, but that is doubtful. It is possible he is in the advertising business, and that will be your job, Harry." I said this to Harry Slater, the fellow from *Commerce*. "You will comb the advertising agencies, clubs, if necessary the advertising departments of first the metropolitan newspapers and magazines, then those farther out. If you have to go that far, you will need a dozen or so more men to help you. You are in complete charge of that line of investigation." Harry's inquiries were safe, and they could also be impressive. I added: "Take as many people as you need. Cross-check with us regularly, for the additional information about our man that will be steadily coming in from all the other avenues we will be exploring at the same time. And that applies to all of you.

"We not only don't know this man's right name or where he lives—and that will be your job, Alvin." This was Alvin Dealey, from the auditing department. "Check all real estate registers in this area, all tax records, public utilities, and all phone books of cities within, say, three or four hundred miles, for George Chester, and any other names we give you. Take as many researchers as you need.

"Now, as I said, we not only don't know this man's name or whereabouts, but we haven't even got any kind of a physical description of him. Just that he is of average height, say five nine to eleven, and average build. Probably between one-forty and one-eighty.

"But there are a few facts we have to go upon. He is an habitué of a place on Third Avenue called Gil's. Here is a description of the place." I gave it, but stayed strictly within the memo as given by Steve Hagen. "This man was in that place, wherever it is, last Saturday afternoon. At that time he was there with a woman we know to be a good-looking blonde. Probably he goes there regularly. That will be your job, Ed. You will find this restaurant, night club, saloon, or whatever it is, and when you do you will stay there until our man comes into it." Ed Orlin's swarthy and rather flabby face betrayed, just for an instant, amazement and incipient distaste.

"On the same evening our subject went into an antique shop, also on Third Avenue. He went into several, but there is one in particular we want, which shouldn't be hard to find. You will find it, Phil. Because the fellow we are looking for bought a picture, unframed, while he was in the place, and he bought it after outbidding another customer, a woman." I did not elaborate by a hairsbreadth beyond Steve's written memo. "The canvas was by an artist named Louise Patterson, it depicted two hands, was in bad condition, and the name of it, or the subject matter, had something to do with Judas. The dealer is certain to remember the incident. You can get an accurate description of our man from him. Perhaps he knows him, and can give us his actual identity.

"Don, here is our file on this Louise Patterson. There is a possibility that this picture can be traced from the artist to the dealer and from him to our unknown. Look up Patterson, or if she's dead, look up her friends. Somebody will remember that canvas, what became of it, may even know who has it now. Find out." I had suddenly the sick and horrid realization I would have to destroy that picture. "Perhaps the man we are looking for is an art collector, even a Patterson enthusiast.

"Leon, I want you and Janet to go to the bar of the Van Barth, where this same blonde went with this same person, on the same evening. At that time he had the picture, and perhaps he checked it. Find out. Question the bartenders, the checkroom attendants for all they can give you regarding the man, and then I guess you'd better stay right there and wait for him to turn up, since he's probably a regular there, as well as Gil's. You may have to be around for several days and if so you will have to be relieved by Louella and Dick Englund."

Leon and Janet looked as though they might not care to be relieved, while Louella and Dick perceptibly brightened. It was almost a pleasure to dispense such largesse. I wished them many a pleasant hour while they awaited my arrival.

"That is about all I have to give you now," I concluded. "Do you all understand your immediate assignments?" Apparently, the lieutenants in charge of the hunt for George Stroud all did, for none of them said anything. "Well, are there any questions?"

Edward Orlin had one. "Why are we looking for this man?"

"All I know about that," I said, "is the fact that he is the intermediary figure in one of the biggest political-industrial steals in history. That is, he is the connecting link, and we need him to establish the fact of this conspiracy. Our man is the payoff man."

Ed Orlin took this information and seemed to retire behind a wall of thought to eat and digest it. Alvin Dealey earnestly asked: "How far can we go in drawing upon the police for information?"

"You can draw upon them, but you are not to tell them anything at all," I said, flatly. "This is our story, in the first place, and we intend to keep it ours. In the second place, I told you there is a political tie-up here. The police machinery we go to may be all right at one end, ours, but we don't know and we have no control over the other end of that machine. Is that clear?"

Alvin nodded. And then the shrewd, rather womanish voice of Phillip Best cut in. "All of these circumstances you have given us concern last Saturday," he said. "That was the night Pauline Delos was killed. Everyone knows what that means. Is there any connection?"

"Not as far as I know, Phil," I said. "This is purely a big-time business scandal that Hagen himself and a few others have been digging into for some time past. Now, it's due to break." I paused for a moment, to let this very thin logic take what hold it could. "As far as I understand it, Earl intends to go through with this story, regardless of the ghastly business last Saturday night."

Phil's small gray eyes bored through his rimless glasses. "I just thought, it's quite a coincidence," he said. I let that pass without even looking at it, and he added: "Am I to make inquiries about the woman who was with the man?"

"You will all have to do that." I had no doubt of what they would discover. Yet even delay seemed in my favor, and I strongly reminded them, "But we are not looking for the woman, or any other outside person. It is the man we want, and only the man."

I let my eyes move slowly over them, estimating their reactions. As far as I could see, they accepted the story. More important, they seemed to give credit to my counterfeit assurance and determination.

"All right," I said. "If there are no more questions, suppose you intellectual tramps get the hell out of here and go to work." As they got up, reviewing the notes they had taken, and stuffed them into their pockets, I added, "And don't fail to report back, either in person or by phone. Soon, and often. Either to Roy or myself."

When they had all gone, except Roy, he got up from his chair beside me at the desk. He walked around in front of it, then crossed to the wall facing it, hands thrust into his pockets. He leaned against the wall, staring at the carpet. Presently, he said: "This is a crazy affair. I can't help feeling that Phil somehow hit the nail on the head. There is a curious connection there, I'm certain, the fact that all of this happened last Saturday."

I waited, with a face made perfectly blank.

"I don't mean it has any connection with that frightful business about Pauline Delos," he went on, thoughtfully. "Of course it hasn't. That would be a little too obvious. But I can't help thinking that something, I don't know what, something happened last week on Friday or Saturday, perhaps while Janoth was in Washington, or certainly a few days before, or even last night, Sunday, that would really explain why we are looking for this mysterious, art-collecting stranger at this moment, and in such a hurry. Don't you think so?"

"Sounds logical," I said.

"Damn right it's logical. It seems to me, we would do well to comb the outstanding news items of the last two weeks, particularly the last five or six days, and see what there is that might concern Janoth. This Jennett-Donohue proposition, for instance. Perhaps they are actually planning to add those new books in our field. That would seriously bother Earl, don't you think?"

Roy was all right. He was doing his level best.

"You may be right. And again it may be something else, far deeper, not quite so apparent. Suppose you follow up that general line? But at the same time, I can't do anything except work from the facts supplied to me."

Actually, I was at work upon a hazy plan that seemed a second line of defense, should it come to that. It amounted to a counterattack. The problem, if the situation got really bad, was this: How to place Janoth at the scene of the killing, through some third, independent witness, or through evidence not related to myself. Somewhere in that fatal detour his car had been noted, he himself had been seen and marked. If I had to fight fire with fire, somehow, surely he could be connected.

But it would never come to that. The gears being shifted, the wheels beginning to move in this hunt for me were big and smooth and infinitely powered, but they were also blind. Blind, clumsy, and unreasoning. "No, you have to work with the data you've been given," Roy admitted. "But I think it would be a good idea if I did follow up my hunch. I'll see if we haven't missed something in recent political developments."

At the same time that I gave him silent encouragement, I became aware of the picture above his head on the wall against which he leaned. It was as though it had suddenly screamed.

Of course. I had forgotten I had placed that Patterson there, two years ago. I had bought it at the Lewis Galleries, the profiles of two faces, showing only the brow, eyes, nose, lips, and chin of each. They confronted each other, distinctly Pattersonian. One of them showed an avaricious, the other a skeptical leer. I believe she had called it *Study in Fury*.

It was such a familiar landmark in my office that to take it away, now, would be fatal. But as I looked at it and then looked away I really began to understand the danger in which I stood. It would have to stay there, though at any moment someone might make a connection. And there must be none, none at all, however slight.

"Yes," I told Roy, automatically, feeling the after-shock in fine points of perspiration all over me. "Why not do that? We may have missed something significant in business changes, as well as politics."

"I think it might simplify matters," he said, and moved away from the wall on which the picture hung. "Janoth was in Washington this week end, remember. Personally, I think there's a tie-up between that and this rush order we've been given."

Thoughtfully, Roy moved away from the wall, crossed the thickly carpeted floor, disappeared through the door leading to his own office.

When he had gone I sat for a long moment, staring at that thing on the wall. I had always liked it before.

But no. It had to stay there.

Edward Orlin

Gil's Tavern looked like just a dive on the outside, and also on the inside. Too bad I couldn't have been assigned to the Van Barth. Well, it couldn't be helped.

It was in the phone book, and not far off, so that part of it was all right. I walked there in twenty minutes.

I took along a copy of *War and Peace*, which I was re-reading, and on the way I saw a new issue of *The Creative Quarterly*, which I bought.

It was a little after one o'clock when I got there, time for lunch, so I had it. The food was awful. But it would go on the expense account, and after I'd eaten I got out my notebook and put it down. Lunch, $1.50. Taxi, $1.00. I thought for a minute, wondering what Stroud would do if he ever came to a dive like this, then I added: Four highballs, $2.00.

After I'd finished my coffee and a slab of pie at least three days old I looked around. It was something dug up by an archeological expedition, all right. There was sawdust in the corners, and a big wreath on the wall in back of me, celebrating a recent banquet, I suppose: CONGRATULA-TIONS TO OUR PAL.

Then I saw the bar at the end of the long room. It was incredible. It looked as though a whole junkyard had been scooped up and dumped there. I saw wheels, swords, shovels, tin cans, bits of paper, flags, pictures, literally hundreds upon hundreds of things, just things.

After I paid for the 85¢ lunch, a gyp, and already I had indigestion, I picked up my Tolstoy and *The Creative Quarterly* and walked down to the bar.

The nearer I came to it the more things I saw, simply thousands of them. I sat down and noticed there was a big fellow about fifty years old, with staring, preoccupied eyes, in back of it. He came down the bar, and I saw that his eyes were looking at me but didn't quite focus. They were like dim electric lights in an empty room. His voice was a wordless grunt.

"A beer," I said. I noticed that he spilled some of it when he put the glass down in front of me. His face really seemed almost ferocious. It was very strange, but none of my business. I had work to do. "Say, what've you got in back of the bar there? Looks like an explosion in a five-and-ten-cent store."

He didn't say anything for a couple of seconds, just looked me over, and now he seemed really sore about something.

"My personal museum," he said, shortly.

So that was what the memo meant. I was in the right place, no doubt about it.

"Quite a collection," I said. "Buy you a drink?"

He had a bottle on the bar by the time I finished speaking. Scotch, and one of the best brands, too. Well, it was a necessary part of the assignment. Made no difference to me; it went on the expense account.

He dropped the first jigger he picked up, left it where it fell, and only finally managed to fill the second one. But he didn't seem drunk. Just nervous.

"Luck," he said. He lifted the glass and the whisky was all gone, in five seconds, less than five seconds, almost in a flash. When he put down the jigger and picked up the bill I laid on the bar he noisily smacked his lips. "First of the day," he said. "That's always the best. Except for the last."

I sipped my beer, and when he laid down the change, he was charging 75¢ for his own Scotch, I said: "So that's your personal museum. What's in it?"

He turned and looked at it and he sounded much better. "Everything. You name it and I've got it. What's more, it's an experience what happened to me or my family."

"Sort of a petrified autobiography, is that it?"

"No, just my personal museum. I been around the world six times, and my folks before me been all over it. Farther than that. Name me one thing I haven't got in that museum, and the drinks are on me."

It was fantastic. I didn't see how I'd ever get any information out of this fellow. He was an idiot.

"All right," I said, humoring him. "Show me a locomotive."

He muttered something that sounded like, "Locomotive? Now, where did that locomotive get to?" Then he reached away over in back of a football helmet, a stuffed bird, a bowl heaped to the brim with foreign coins, and a lot of odds and ends I couldn't even see, and when he turned around he laid a toy railroad engine on the bar. "This here locomotive," he confided, slapping it affectionately and leaning toward me, "was the only toy of mine what got saved out of the famous Third Avenue fire next to the carbarns fifty years ago. Saved it myself. I was six years old. They had nine roasts."

I finished my beer and stared at him, not sure whether he was trying to kid me or whether he was not only half drunk but completely out of his mind besides. If it was supposed to be humor, it was certainly corny, the incredibly childish slapstick stuff that leaves me cold. Why couldn't I have gotten the Van Barth, where I could at least read in peace and comfort, without having to interview a schizophrenic, probably homicidal.

"That's fine," I said.

"Still runs, too," he assured me, and gave the key a twist, put the toy down on the bar, and let it run a few feet. It stopped when it bumped into *The Creative Review*. He actually sounded proud. "See? Still runs."

God, this was simply unbelievable. I might as well be back in the office.

The lunatic gravely put the toy back behind the bar, where I heard its spring motor expend itself, and when he turned around he wordlessly filled up our glasses again, mine with beer and his with Scotch. I was still more surprised when he tossed off his drink, then returned and absently paused in front of me, appearing to wait. For God's sake, did this fellow expect a free drink with every round? Not that it mattered. He had to be humored, I suppose. After I'd paid, and by now he seemed actually friendly, he asked: "Yes, sir. That's one of the best private museums in New York. Anything else you'd care to see?"

"You haven't got a crystal ball, have you?"

"Well, now, as it happens, I have." He brought out a big glass marble from a pile of rubbish surmounted by a crucifix and a shrunken head. "Funny how everybody wants to see that locomotive, or sometimes it's the airplane or the steamroller, and usually they ask to see the crystal ball. Now this here little globe I picked up in Calcutta. I went to a Hindu gypsy what told fortunes, and he seen in the glass that I was in danger of drowning. So I jumped the ship I was on and went on the beach awhile, and not two days passed before that boat went down with all hands. So I says to myself, Holy Smoke, how long's this been going on? I never put much stock in that stuff before, see? So I went back to this fellow, and I says, I'd like to have that there gadget. And he says, in his own language of course, this been in his family for generations after generations and he can't part with it."

This juvenile nonsense went on and on. My God, I thought it would never stop. And I had to look as though I were interested. Finally it got so boring I couldn't stand any more of it. I said: "Well, I wish you'd look into that globe and see if you can locate a friend of mine for me."

"That's a funny thing. When I finally paid the two thousand rupees he wanted, and I took it back to my hotel, I couldn't make the damn thing work. And never could since."

"Never mind," I said. "Have another drink." He put the marble away and drew another beer and poured himself another Scotch. I couldn't see how a fellow like this stayed in business for more than a week.

Before he could put his drink away I went on: "A friend of mine I haven't seen for years comes in here sometimes, and I wonder if you know him. I'd like to see him again. Maybe you know what would be a good time to find him here."

The man's eyes went absolutely blank.

"What's his name?"

"George Chester."

"George Chester." He stared at the far end of the room, apparently thinking, and a little of the mask fell away from him. "That name I don't know. Mostly, I don't know their names, anyway. What's he look like?"

"Oh, medium height and build," I said. "A mutual acquaintance told me he saw him in here late last Saturday afternoon. With a good-looking blonde."

He threw the shot of whisky into his mouth and I don't believe the glass even touched his lips. Didn't this fellow ever take a chaser? He frowned and paused.

"I think I know who you mean. Clean-cut, brown-haired fellow?"

"I guess you could call him that."

"I remember that blonde. She was something for the books. She wanted to see the raven that fellow wrote about, nevermore quoth he. So I let her have a look at it. Yes, they were in here a couple of nights ago, but he don't come around here very often. Four or five years ago he was in here lots, almost every night. Smart, too. Many's the time I used to show him my museum, until me and some hacker had to pick him up and carry him out. One night he wouldn't go home at all, he wanted to sleep right inside the museum. 'Book me the royal suite on your ocean liner, Gil,' he kept saying. We got him home all right. But that was several years ago." He looked at me with sharp interest. "Friend of yours?"

I nodded. "We used to work for the same advertising agency."

He puzzled some more. "I don't think he did then," he decided. "He worked for some newspaper, and before that he and his wife used to run a joint upstate, the same as mine. No museum, of course. Seems to me his name might have been George Chester, at that. I had to garage his car once or twice when he had too much. But he gradually stopped coming in. I don't think he was here more than twice in the last three or four months. But he might come in any time, you never can tell. Very intelligent fellow. What they call eccentric."

"Maybe I could reach him through the blonde."

"Maybe."

"Who is she, do you know?"

This time his whole face went blank. "No idea, sir."

He moved up the bar to serve some customers who had just entered, and I opened *The Creative Review*. There was a promising revaluation of Henry James I would have to read, though I knew the inevitable shortcomings of the man who wrote it. A long article on Tibetan dance ritual that looked quite good.

I finished my beer and went to a phone booth. I called the office and asked for Stroud, but got Cordette instead.

"Where's Stroud?" I asked.

"Out. Who's this?"

"Ed Orlin. I'm at Gil's Tavern."

"Found it, did you? Get the right one?"

"It's the right one, no question. And what a dive."

"Pick up anything?"

"Our man was here last Saturday, all right, and with the blonde."

"Fine. Let's have it."

"There isn't much. The bartender isn't sure of his name, because the guy doesn't come in here any more." I let that sink in, for a moment. I certainly hoped to get called off this drab saloon and that boring imbecile behind the bar. "But he thinks his name may actually be George Chester. He has been described by the bartender, who is either a half-wit or an outright lunatic himself, as very intelligent and eccentric. Believe me, Chester is probably just the opposite."

"Why?"

"It's that kind of a place. Eccentric, yes, but only a moron would come into a dump like this and spend hours talking to the fellow that runs this menagerie."

"Go on."

"The physical description we have does not seem far wrong, but there's nothing to add to it, except that he's brown-haired and clean-cut."

"All right. What else? Any line on the blonde?"

"Nothing."

"That certainly isn't much, is it?"

"Well, wait. Our man is unquestionably a dipsomaniac. Four or five years ago he was in here every night and had to be sent home in a taxi. At that time he was a newspaperman, the bartender believes, and he never heard of him as working for an advertising concern. And before he was a newspaperman he ran a tavern somewhere upstate, with his wife."

"A drunk. Formerly, with his wife, a tavern proprietor. Probably a newspaperman, eccentric, clean-cut in appearance. It isn't much, but it's something. Is that all?"

"That's all. And our baby hasn't been in here more than twice in the last eight or ten months. So what should I do? Come back to the office?"

There was a pause, and I had a moment of hope.

"I think not, Ed. He was in there two days ago, he might not wait so long before he returns. And you can work on the bartender some more. Psychoanalyze him for more details. Have a few drinks with him."

Oh, my God.

"Listen, this fellow is a human blotter."

"All right, get drunk with him, if you have to. But not too drunk. Try some of the other customers. Anyway, stick around until we call you back, or send a relief. What's the address and the phone number?"

I gave them to him.

"All right, Ed. And if you get anything more, call us at once. Remember, this is a hurry-up job."

I hoped so. I went back to the bar, already a little dizzy on the beers. It would be impossible to concentrate on the magazine, which demanded an absolutely clear head. One of the customers was roaring at the bartender, "All right, admit you ain't got it. I ask you, show me a *mot de passe* out of that famous museum, so-called."

"No double-talk allowed. You want to see something, you got to ask for it in plain language."

"That is plain language. Plain, ordinary French. Admit it, and give us a beer. You just ain't got one."

"All right, all right, I'll give you a beer. But what is this here thing? How do you spell it? Only don't ask for nothing in French again. Not in here, see?"

Well, there was a newspaper at the end of the bar, thank God. This morning's, but it could kill a couple of hours.

George Stroud VIII

When they all cleared out of my office on their various assignments, I called in Emory Mafferson. His plump face was in perpetual mourning, his brain was a seething chaos, his brown eyes seemed always trying to escape from behind those heavy glasses, and I don't believe he could see more than ten feet in front of him, but somewhere in Emory I felt there was a solid newspaperman and a lyric investigator.

"How are you coming along with Funded Individuals?" I asked him.

"All right. I've explained it all to Bert, and we're finishing the article together."

"Sure Bert understands it?"

Emory's face took a turn for the worse.

"As well as I do," he finally said. "Maybe better. You know, I can't help feeling there's something sound in back of that idea. It's a new, revolutionary vision in the field of social security."

"Well, what's troubling you?"

"How can you have a revolution without a revolution?"

"Just leave that to Bert Finch. He has your *Futureways* notes, and he can interpret the data as far as you've gone with it. Suppose you let Bert carry on alone from here?"

Emory sighed.

If I understood him, many an afternoon supposedly spent in scholarly research at the library or interviewing some insurance expert had found him instead at Belmont, the Yankee Stadium, possibly home in bed.

"All good things have to come to an end sometime, Emory."

"I suppose so."

I came abruptly to the point. "Right now I have got to work on a special, outside job. At the same time, one of the most sensational murders of the year has occurred, and beyond a doubt it will assume even greater proportions and sometime *Crimeways* will want a big story about it."

"Delos?"

I nodded.

"And I don't want *Crimeways* left at the post. You wanted to go on our regular staff. This can start you off. Suppose you go down to Center Street, Homicide Bureau, and pick up everything you can, as and when it happens. The minute you've got it, phone it to me. I'll be busy with this other assignment, but I want to be up-to-date on the Delos story, every phase of it."

Emory looked more stunned and haggard than ever. Those brown goldfish eyes swam three times around the bowl of his glasses.

"God, you don't expect me to break this thing alone, do you?"

"Of course not. If we wanted to break it, we'd give it a big play, thirty or forty legmen. I just want all the facts ready when the case is broken, by the cops. All you have to do is keep in close touch with developments. And report back to me, and only me, regularly. Got it?"

Emory looked relieved, and said he understood. He got up to go. My private detective force wasn't much bigger standing than sitting, and looked even less impressive.

"What have you got for me to go on?" he asked.

"Nothing. Just what you have, no more."

"Will this be all right with Bert?"

I said I'd arrange that, and sent him on his way. After he'd gone I sat and looked at that Patterson *Study in Fury* on the opposite wall, facing me, and did nothing but think.

The signature was quite visible, and even moving the canvas downward into the lower part of the frame would not obscure it. I did not believe it possible, but there might, also, be others in the Janoth organization who would recognize a Patterson simply from the style.

I could not remove that picture. Even if I changed it for another, the change would be noticed by someone. Maybe not by Roy, the writers, or the reporters, but by someone. Lucille or one of the other girls, somebody else's secretary, some research worker.

If only that picture weren't there. And above all, if only I had never brought home *The Temptation of St. Judas.*

Because Georgette had seen the new picture.

Hagen was certain whoever had bought it could be traced through it. If he thought it necessary, he would insist upon a far more intensive search for it than the one I had, as a safeguard, assigned Don Klausmeyer to undertake. I knew Don would never trace it clear through from the artist to the dealer, let alone to me. But Hagen might at any moment take independent steps; I could think of some, myself, that would be dangerous.

I had better destroy the *Temptation.*

If somebody did his job too well, if Hagen went to work on his own, if some real information got to him before I could short-circuit it, that thing would nail me cold. I must get rid of it.

I put on my hat and went into Roy's office, with two half-formed ideas, to destroy that picture now and to find a means of locating Earl Janoth at 58 East through other witnesses. I could trust no one but myself with either of these jobs.

"I'm going out on a lead, Roy," I told him. "Take over for a while. And by the way, I've assigned somebody to follow the Delos murder. We'll want to handle it in an early issue, don't you think?" He nodded thoughtfully. "I've assigned Mafferson."

He nodded again, dryly and remotely. "I believe Janoth will want it followed, at least," he said. "By the way, I'm having the usual missing-person index prepared."

This was a crisscross of the data that came in, as rapidly as it came, simplified for easy reference. I had myself, at one time or another, helped to simplify it.

Over my shoulder I said, briskly: "That's the stuff."

I went out to the elevators, rode down and crossed the street to the garage. I decided to get the car, drive out to Marble Road, and burn up that business right now.

In the garage, I met Earl Janoth's chauffeur, Billy, coming out of it. He had just brought in Janoth's car. I had ridden in it perhaps a dozen times, and now he nodded, impassively pleasant.

"Hello, Mr. Stroud."

"Hello, Billy."

We passed each other, and I felt suddenly cold and aware. There were two people Janoth trusted without limit, Steve Hagen and Billy, his physical shadow. When and if the missing unknown was located, Billy would be the errand boy sent to execute the final decision. He would be the man. He didn't know it, but I knew it.

Inside the garage an attendant was polishing Janoth's already shining Cadillac. I walked up to him, memorizing the car's license. Somebody else, somewhere, had seen it that night, and Earl, I hoped, and seen them where they were not supposed to be.

"Want your car, Mr. Stroud?"

I said hello and told him I did. I had often stopped for a minute or two with this particular attendant, talking about baseball, horses, whisky, or women.

"Got a little errand to do this afternoon," I said, and then gave him a narrow smile. "I'll bet this bus is giving you plenty of trouble."

I got a knowing grin in return.

"Not exactly trouble," he confided. "But the cops have been giving it a going over. Us too. Was it cleaned since Saturday night? How long was it out Saturday night? Did I notice the gas, the mileage, anything peculiar? Hell, we guys never pay any attention to things like that. Except, of course, we know it wasn't washed, and it wasn't even gassed."

He called to another attendant to bring down my car, and while I waited for it, I asked: "I suppose the cops third degree'd the chauffeur?"

"Sure. A couple of them tackled him again a few minutes ago. But the driver's got nothing to worry about. Neither has Mr. Janoth. They drove to a dinner somewhere and then they drove straight to some other place. Your friend Mr. Hagen's. It checks okay with us. They never garage this car here nights or week ends, so what would we know about it? But I don't mind cops. Only, I don't like that driver. Nothing I could say, exactly. Just, well."

He looked at me and I gave him an invisible signal in return and then my car was brought down.

I got into it and drove off, toward Marble Road. But I hadn't gone more than three blocks before I began to think it all over again, and this time in a different mood.

Why should I destroy that picture? I liked it. It was mine.

Who was the better man, Janoth or myself? I voted for myself. Why should I sacrifice my own property just because of him? Who was he? Only another medium-sized wheel in the big clock.

The big clock didn't like pictures, much. I did. This particular picture it had tossed into the dustbin. I had saved it from oblivion, myself. Why should I throw it back?

There were lots of good pictures that were prevented from being painted at all. If they couldn't be aborted, or lost, then somebody like me was despatched to destroy them.

Just as Billy would be sent to destroy me. And why should I play ball in a deadly set-up like that?

What would it get me to conform?

Newsways, Commerce, Crimeways, Personalities, The Sexes, Fashions, Futureways, the whole organization was full and overrunning with frustrated ex-artists, scientists, farmers, writers, explorers, poets, lawyers, doctors, musicians, all of whom spent their lives conforming, instead. And conforming to what? To a sort of overgrown, aimless, haphazard stenciling apparatus that kept them running to psychoanalysts, sent them to insane asylums, gave them high blood pressure, stomach ulcers, killed them off with cerebral hemorrhages and heart failure, sometimes suicide. Why should I pay still more tribute to this fatal machine? It would be easier and simpler to get squashed stripping its gears than to be crushed helping it along.

To hell with the big gadget. I was a dilettante by profession. A pretty good one, I had always thought. I decided to stay in that business.

I turned down a side street and drove toward 58 East. I could make a compromise. That picture could be put out of circulation, for the present. But it would really be a waste of time to destroy it. That would mean only a brief reprieve, at best. Its destruction was simply not worth the effort.

And I could beat the machine. The super-clock would go on forever, it was too massive to be stopped. But it had no brains, and I did. I could escape from it. Let Janoth, Hagen, and Billy perish in its wheels. They loved it. They liked to suffer. I didn't.

I drove past 58 East, and began to follow the course the other car must have taken going away. Either Janoth had dismissed Billy when he arrived, and returned by taxi, or he had ordered Billy to come back later. In any case, Janoth had dined at the Waynes', according to all accounts, and then, as I knew, he had come to 58 East, and then of course he must have gone directly to Hagen's.

I followed the logical route to Hagen's. I saw two nearby cabstands. Janoth must have used one of them if he had returned by taxi, unless he had found a cruising cab somewhere between the two. He certainly would not have been so stupid as to pick one up near 58 East.

The farthest cabstand was the likeliest. I could begin there, with a photograph of Janoth, then try the nearer, and if necessary I could even check the bigger operators for cruisers picking up fares in the neighborhood on that evening. But that was a tall order for one man to cover.

From Hagen's, timing the drive, I went to the Waynes', then turned around and drove slowly back to 58 East. The route Earl must have followed took about thirty minutes. Allowing another thirty minutes for the fight to develop, that meant Earl was covering up about one hour. This checked with the facts known to me.

Perhaps he had stopped somewhere along the way, but if so, no likely place presented itself.

That gave me only two possible leads, a cab by which Earl may have made his getaway, or possibly some attendant at Pauline's or Hagen's.

It was pretty slim. But something.

I drove back to the office, garaged the car again, and went up to 2619. There was no one there, and no memos. I went straight on into 2618.

Roy, Leon Temple, and Janet Clark were there.

"Any luck?" Roy asked me.

"I don't know," I said.

"Well, we're starting to get some reports." Roy nodded with interest toward the cross-reference chart laid out on a big blackboard covering half of one wall. "Ed Orlin phoned a while ago. He located Gil's with no trouble and definitely placed the man and the woman there. Interesting stuff. I think we're getting somewhere."

"Fine," I said.

I went over to the board, topped with the caption: X.

In the column headed: "Names, Aliases," I read: *George Chester?*

Under "Appearance" it said: *Brown-haired, clean-cut, average height and build.*

I thought, thank you, Ed.

"Frequents": *Antique shops, Van Barth, Gil's. At one time frequented Gil's almost nightly.*

It was true, I had.

"Background": *Advertising? Newspapers? Formerly operated an up-state tavern-resort.*

Too close.

"Habits": *Collects pictures.*

"Character": *Eccentric, impractical. A pronounced drunk.*

This last heading was something that had been added by Roy in the Isleman and Sandler jobs. He imagined he had invented it, and valued it accordingly.

I said, standing beside the word-portrait of myself: "We seem to be getting somewhere."

"That isn't all," Roy told me. "Leon and Janet have just returned from the Van Barth with more. We were discussing it, before putting it on the board."

He looked at Leon, and Leon gave his information in neat, precise, third-person language.

"That's right," he said. "First of all it was established that Chester was in the lounge on Saturday night. He did not check the Judas picture he bought, but he was overheard talking about it with the woman accompanying him. And the woman with him was Pauline Delos."

I registered surprise.

"Are you sure?"

"No doubt about it, George. She was recognized by the waiter, the bartender, and the checkroom girl, from the pictures of her published in today's papers. Delos was in there Saturday night, with a man answering to the description on the board, and they were talking about a picture called *Judas* something-or-other. There can be no doubt about it." He looked at me for a long moment, in which I said nothing, then he finally asked: "I feel that's significant, don't you? Doesn't this alter the whole character of the assignment we are on? Personally, I think it does. Somebody raised the very same question this morning, and now it looks as though he had been right."

I said: "That's logical. Do the police know Delos was in there Saturday night?"

"Of course. Everyone in the place promptly told them."

"Do the police know we are looking for the man with her?"

"No. But they are certainly looking for him, now. We didn't say anything, because we thought this was exclusive with us. But what should we do about it? We're looking for George Chester, and yet this Delos tie-up is terrific, seems to me."

I nodded, and lifted Roy's phone.

"Right," I said. When I had Steve Hagen I barked into the receiver: "Steve? Listen. The woman with our man was Pauline Delos."

The other end of the wire went dead for five, ten, fifteen, twenty seconds.

"Hello, Steve? Are you there? This is George Stroud. We have discovered that the woman who was with the person we want was Pauline Delos. Does this mean something?"

I looked at Roy, Janet, and Leon. They seemed merely expectant, with no second thoughts apparent in their faces. At the other end of the wire I heard what I thought was a faint sigh from Steve Hagen.

"Nothing in particular," he said, carefully. "I knew that she saw this go-between. Perhaps I should have told you. But the fact that she was with him that night does not concern the matter we have in hand. What we want, and what we've got to have, is the name and whereabouts of the man himself. Delos is a blind alley, as far as our investigation is concerned. The murder is one story. This is a different, unrelated one. Is that plain?"

I said I understood him perfectly, and after I broke the connection I repeated the explanation almost verbatim to the three people in the room.

Roy was complacent.

"Yes," he said. "But I said all along this was an issue related to some recent crisis, and now we know damn well it is."

He rose and went over to the blackboard, picked up some chalk. I watched him as he wrote under "Associates": *Pauline Delos*. Where the line crossed "Antique shops," "Gil's," "Van Barth" he repeated the name. Then he began to add a new column.

"At the same time, Leon and Janet brought in something more tangible," he went on. "Tell George about it."

Leon's small and measured voice resumed the report. "When they left the cocktail lounge of the Van Barth, our subject forgot something and left it behind him."

Nothing about me moved except my lips.

"Yes?"

Leon nodded toward Roy's desk and his eyes indicated an envelope. I seemed to float toward it, wondering whether this had all been an extravagant, cold-blooded farce they had put together with Hagen, whether I had actually mislaid or forgotten something that gave me away altogether. But the envelope was blank.

"A handkerchief," I heard Leon say, as from a great distance. "It can probably be traced, because it's obviously expensive, and it has what I believe is an old laundry mark."

Of course. She had borrowed it. When she spilled her cocktail I had used it, then given it to her. And it had been left there.

I turned the envelope over and shook the handkerchief from the unsealed flap. Yes. I could even see, faintly, the old stain.

"I wouldn't touch it, George," said Leon. "We may be able to raise a few fingerprints. It's a very fine, smooth fabric."

So I had to do that. I picked up the handkerchief and unfolded it. And laid it down and spread it out, very carefully and cautiously.

"I imagine it already has plenty," I said. "The waitress's, the cashier's, yours, one more set won't matter." I inspected the familiar square of linen with grave attention. It was one of a lot I had bought at Blanton's & Dent's, about a year ago. And there was the faint, blurred, but recoverable laundry mark on a bit of the hem, several months old, for it must have been put there when I last spent a week in the city and sent some of my things to a midtown laundry. "Yes, I imagine this can be traced."

I refolded the handkerchief, stuffed it back into the envelope. I could now account for the presence of my own fingerprints, but I knew I could not save the handkerchief itself from the mill.

I handed the envelope to Leon.

"Do you want to take this to Sacher & Roberts?" That was the big commercial laboratory we used for such work. "Whatever they find, we'll put another team on it. I suppose Dick and Louella relieved you at the Van Barth?"

"Oh, sure. Our man comes in there once or twice a week, they said."

"We've got the fellow covered at this place called Gil's, and at the Van Barth," Roy pointed out. "He'll come back, and then we've got him."

I nodded, rather thoughtfully. I said: "Certainly. He'll return to one place or the other. Then that will be that."

I don't know how that conference broke up. I think Leon went on to Sacher & Roberts. I believe I left Roy making additional entries on the big progress-board. I told him to eat and get some rest when he'd finished, I would be leaving around seven.

If they actually brought out prints on that handkerchief, we would all have to volunteer our own, mine with the rest. That in itself I had taken care of. But for a long, long time in my own office I sat trying to remember whether my fingerprints could be found anywhere on Pauline's overnight bag. Such a duplication could not be explained away. Hardly.

I forced myself to relive that last day with Pauline. No. I had not touched that grip anywhere except on the handle, and Pauline's final touches had certainly smudged them all out.

Sometime in the afternoon I took a call from Don Klausmeyer.

"Oh, yes, Don," I said. "Any luck with Patterson?"

Don's slow, malicious, pedantic voice told me: "I had a little trouble, but I found her. I've been talking to her for about an hour, going over old catalogues of her shows, looking at her fifth-rate pictures, and trying to keep her four kids out of my hair."

"Okay. Shoot."

"I have turned up one very significant fact. Louise Patterson was the customer who bid, unsuccessfully, for her own picture in the dealer's shop that night. A friend saw her canvas there, told her about it, and it was Patterson's hope that she could buy it back for herself. God knows why."

"I see. Anything else?"

"Do you understand? It was Patterson herself, in the shop that night."

"I get it. And?"

"And she described the man who bought the picture, at great length. Are you ready to take it?"

"Let's have it."

"This is Patterson speaking. Quote. He was a smug, self-satisfied, smart-alecky bastard just like ten million other rubber-stamp sub-executives. He had brown hair, brown eyes, high cheekbones, symmetrical and lean features. His face looked as though he scrubbed and shaved it five times a day. He weighed between one sixty and one sixty-five. Gray tweed suit, dark blue hat and necktie. He knows pictures, says she, and is certainly familiar with the works of L. Patterson, which he doubtless collects, but only for their snob-appeal. Personally, I think the dame overestimates herself. She admits she's been forgotten for the last ten years. But to go on. Our man is a good deal of an exhibitionist. He imagines he is Super-man and that is what he plays at being. The woman with him was beauti-ful if you like Lesbians in standard, Park Avenue models. Unquote. Got it?"

"Yes."

"Does it help?"

"Some," I said.

"I've been poking around the studio-loft she lives in—God what a paradise for rats and termites—looking at acres and acres of pictures. Artistically she's impossible." How would Don know? "But they re-minded me of something I'm sure I've seen somewhere very recently. If I can only remember what it is, maybe I'll have another lead."

He laughed and I echoed him, but I was staring straight at *Study in Fury* on the wall opposite me.

"Maybe you will, but don't worry about it. I'll see you tomorrow."

When he hung up I stared at that picture, without really seeing it, for a long five minutes. Then I took my scribbled notes and went into Roy's empty office and duly entered Don's report on the chart. By now it was crystallizing into a very unpleasant definition of myself indeed. And after that, I took three good, recent photographs of Earl Janoth out of the morgue.

A little past seven o'clock Roy returned. We arranged about relieving each other on the following day and then I went out, feeling I'd had about all I could stand for the time being. But I still had work to do.

At the cabstand I had that afternoon selected as the likeliest, I got my first real break. A good one. A driver identified Janoth as a passenger he'd ridden a little after ten o'clock last Saturday night. The driver was posi-tive. He knew when he'd picked him up, and where, and where he'd put him down. A block from Hagen's.

I knew this might save my neck, as a last desperate resort. But it would not necessarily save my home.

It was around midnight when I reached Marble Road. Georgia and Georgette were asleep.

I found *The Temptation of St. Judas* where I had left it, in a closet downstairs, and in twenty minutes I had it concealed in back of another canvas.

It could be discovered, and easily, if they ever really caught up with me. But if anyone ever got this far, I was finished anyway.

Earl Janoth III

Five days after Steve first organized the search we had enough material concerning that damned phantom to write a long biography of him. We had dates, addresses, his background, a complete verbal description of him, X-rays of every last thought, emotion, and impulse he'd ever had. I knew that blundering weak fool better than his own mother. If I shut my eyes I could actually see him standing in front of me, an imbecilic wisp of a smile on his too good-looking face, I could hear his smooth, studied, disarming voice uttering those round, banal whimsicalities he apparently loved, I could almost reach out and touch him, this horrid wraith who had stumbled into my life from nowhere to bring about Pauline's death and my possible ruin.

Yet we didn't have the man himself. We had nothing.

"Candidly, I think you are holding something back," said George Stroud. He was talking to Steve. I had insisted on being present, though not directly participating, when we re-examined the paralysis that seemed to grip our plans. "And I think that thing, whatever it may be, is the one solid fact we need to wrap up the whole business."

"Stick to the facts," said Steve. "Your imagination is running away with you."

"I think not."

We were in Steve's office, Steve behind his desk, myself a little to one side of it, Stroud facing Steve. The room was filled with sunlight, but to me it looked dim, like the bottom of a pool of water. I don't believe I'd slept more than two hours a night in the last week.

The damned wolves were closing in on me. I'd been questioned by dozens of detectives and members of the district attorney's staff three, four, and sometimes five times a day, every day. At first they'd been polite. Now they weren't bothering much with that any more.

And Wayne knew it. Carr knew it. They all knew it. It was a secret only to the general public. In the downtown district and on Forty-second Street it was open knowledge. Nobody, conspicuously, had phoned or come near me for days. The more tightly the official gang closed in on me, the farther my own crowd drew away. The more they isolated me, the easier it became for the police. I could handle one pack of wolves, but not two.

There was no real evidence against me. Not yet. But neither was there any prospect that the pressure to get it would be relaxed.

I could stand that. But we had to find that damned will-o'-the-wisp, and find him before anyone else did. He was the one serious threat I faced. If the police got to him first, as at any moment they might, and eventually would, I knew exactly what he would say, and what would happen.

It didn't make sense. We had this mountain of data, and yet we were, for all practical purposes, right where we had started.

"All right, let's stick to the facts," Stroud told Steve. "You say this man is the key figure in a political-industrial deal. But we haven't turned up one single political connection, and no business connections worth mentioning. Why not? I say, because there aren't any."

Steve told him sharply: "There are. You simply haven't dug deeply enough to get them. I'm holding nothing back except rumors and suspicions. They'd do you no good at all. In fact, they'd simply throw you off."

Stroud's voice was soft and rather pleasant, but it carried a lot of emphasis.

"I couldn't be thrown off more than I was, when you knew Delos was right in the middle of the situation, but you somehow forgot to tell me so."

This senseless bickering would get us nowhere. I had to intervene.

"What is your own opinion, George?" I asked him. "How do you account for the fact we seem to be going around in circles? It isn't like you to be held up so long on a simple thing like this. What is your honest theory about this business?"

Stroud turned and gave me a long, keen regard. He was what I had always classified as one of those hyper-perceptive people, not good at action but fine at pure logic and theory. He was the sort who could solve a bridge-hand at a glance, down to the last play, but in a simple business deal he would be helpless. The cold fighter's and gambler's nerve that Steve had was completely lacking in him, and he would consider it something foreign or inhuman, if indeed he understood it at all.

After five days of the present job Stroud showed the strain. That was a good thing, because he had to understand this was not merely a routine story.

"Yes, I have a theory," he told me. "I believe the Delos murder and the man we want are so closely connected they are identical. I am forced to reject Steve's idea that one is only accidentally related to the other."

I nodded. It was inevitable, of course. We hadn't selected Stroud to lead the investigation because of his good looks, fancy imagination, or vanity, which was colossal.

I glanced at Steve, trusting he would go on from there more sensibly.

"I follow your reasoning, George," he said. "And I think you are right. But here is something you've overlooked, and we now have to consider.

We know that Pauline had knowledge of this big combination. She helped to fill in the background, fragmentary as it is, of the whole thing. She would naturally follow it up if she could. Suppose she did just that? Suppose somebody caught her doing it? And got to her first. Have you thought of that?"

Stroud paused, remote and deliberate. He was just a little too keen for this.

"If this deal is for such high stakes, and if the other parties have already gone the limit," he said, and stopped for an even longer pause, "then we're in rough company. Our man is either in Mexico and still going south, or he has already been disposed of altogether, in such a way he will never again be found."

"That can't be," Steve told him, sharply. "Here's why. A man like this, eccentric, with a wide and varied circle of acquaintances, married and with at least one child, a responsible position somewhere, would leave a pretty big hole if he suddenly dropped out of circulation. Yet you've been in close touch with the Missing Persons Bureau—since when?"

"Tuesday morning."

"Tuesday. And no one like our man has been reported. His disappearance would certainly leak out somewhere, somehow. It hasn't, and that means he's still around." Stroud nodded, cautiously, and Steve went swiftly to another point. "Now let's look at some of these other leads a little more closely. You're still checking the list of upstate liquor licenses suspended or not renewed with the Board?"

Stroud passed a handkerchief across his perspiring face.

"Yes, but that's a tall order. There are hundreds." Stroud looked down for a moment of abstraction at the handkerchief, then he folded the cloth with great deliberation and thrust it slowly and carefully away. "The list is being fed straight to me. If I get anything, you'll know at once."

It was a strange thing to say. Of course we would.

"You've seen the story *Newsways* ran about this Patterson woman?" Steve asked, and Stroud said he had. "It's too early for results. But our spread is going to put that woman on the map. Somebody is certain to recognize and remember that *Judas* picture from our description of it. Our evaluation of it as 'priceless' is sure to locate it. It's my hunch the picture alone will nail our man to the wall."

Stroud smiled faintly, but said nothing, and then they went on to other lines of investigation involving tax lists, advertising agencies, newspapers, fingerprints on a handkerchief, all of them ending in so much fog and vapor. At length, I heard Steve saying: "Now those bars, art galleries, and so on."

"All covered."

"Exactly. And why hasn't our man shown, by now? To me, that's fantastic. No one suddenly abandons his habitual routine of life. Not without some good reason."

"I've already suggested he has either left the country, or been killed," said Stroud. "Here are some more versions of the same general theory. He may have killed Delos, himself, and in that case he's naturally not making himself conspicuous. Or he knows that he's in fast company, knows the score, and he's gone to ground, right where he is, so that the same thing won't happen to him."

I carefully looked away from Steve, and also away from Stroud. In a curious way Stroud's conclusion was almost perfect. The room was momentarily too quiet.

"You think he may believe himself to be in danger?" Steve presently asked.

"He knows somebody is playing for keeps. Why wouldn't he be worried?"

"And he's keeping pretty well under cover." Steve appeared to be groping toward something. He stared absently at Stroud. "At least, he stays away from all the places where he always went before." Steve was silent for a moment, then he asked: "How many people in the organization, George, know about this particular job?"

Stroud seemed not to understand him.

"Our own?"

"Right here at Janoth Enterprises. How many, at a guess?"

Stroud displayed a thin smile. "Well, with fifty-three people now working on this assignment, I'd say everyone knows about it. The entire two thousand."

"Yes," Steve admitted. "I guess so."

"Why?"

"Nothing. For a second I thought I had something." Steve came back into himself, leaned aggressively forward. "All right, I guess that reports on everything. And it's still nothing."

"Do you think I've missed a bet anywhere?" Stroud demanded.

"Just bear down on it, that's all."

"I shall. Now that we've decided the killing and our particular baby are identical twins, there are a lot more lines we can follow."

"What lines?"

Stroud got up to go. He put a cigarette in his mouth, reflected before lighting it.

"For one thing, I'll have some men cover all the cabstands in the neighborhood of Pauline Delos' apartment. On the night of her death, and a few minutes after it, somebody took a taxi away from that vicinity, and he couldn't help being rather noticeable." He lit his cigarette, drew deeply, casually exhaled. "The driver will remember, and tell us all about him."

My eyes went to Steve, and stayed there. I knew he understood, because he did not, even for a second, glance in my direction.

"I don't follow that, George," he said, in a dead-level voice.

"It's quite simple. Our subject took Pauline to Gil's, to a number of antique shops, and to the Van Barth. Why wouldn't he take her home? Of course he did. Our timing checks with the police timing. He took her home and then he had to leave. No matter what happened there, no matter who killed her, no matter what he saw or what he knew, he had to leave. The first and most obvious line to follow is that he left in a taxi."

I was forced to say, "Perhaps he had his own car."

"Perhaps he did."

"He may have walked," said Steve. "Or taken a bus."

"That's true. But we can't afford to pass up the fact he may have done none of those things. He may have taken a cab. We'll just put a bet on that and hope for the best." Stroud had never lacked confidence in himself, and now it was engraved all over him. He moved toward the door. Standing there, he added, finally: "It's my hunch we'll discover he did take a cab, we'll locate the driver, find out where he went, and that will close our whole assignment."

There was a long and complete silence after he had gone, with Steve intently staring at the door that closed behind him. I thought I was reading his mind. "Yes. You're right."

"About what?"

"We'll close the assignment, all right. We're going to call the whole job off."

"No, we're not. Why should we? I was thinking of something else. About Stroud. I don't like that bastard."

"It's the same thing. I don't want Stroud looking for that taxi."

There was a smoldering anger in Steve that seemed to feed itself, perceptibly mounting.

"That's nothing. You'll never be tied to that. Our staff is good, but not that good. What worries me is what's holding us up? Why is it the only smart idea Stroud can dream up is one we don't like? He's cutting corners somewhere—but where?"

"Pull him off the job. Right now. Before he sends another team out looking for that driver. I hate the way his mind works."

Steve's eyes were shining like an animal's, and as insensate. "We can't drop the inquiry, and there's no point in replacing Stroud. We have to go through with it, and Stroud has to deliver the goods. He has to do it a damn sight quicker, that's all. We started with an inside track, but that advantage we're losing, now, every hour."

I thought of hunters stalking big game, and while they did so, the game closed in on its own prey, and with the circle eventually completing itself, unknown disaster drew near to the hunters. It was a thing ordained. I said: "You don't know the whole situation. There have been a number of informal, really secret board meetings recently, and that dinner last Saturday—"

Steve interrupted, still watching me. "Yes. You told me."

"Well, if this business goes the wrong way, or even drags itself out, that's all they'll need to take some kind of overt action. I'm certain they've been discussing it these last four or five days. If that should happen—well, that's even worse than this."

Steve seemed not to hear. He looked out at me, and upon the whole of life, deeply and steadily as a bronze, inhumanized idol. Surprisingly, he asked: "You haven't been sleeping much, have you?"

"Not since it happened."

He nodded, spoke with persuasive but impersonal finality. "You're going to a hospital. You've got a strep throat. Forget about everything. Doc Reiner is sending you to bed for a couple of days. With no visitors. Except me."

Georgette Stroud

I hadn't seen George when he came home last night. He had worked late, even though it had been Sunday. For that matter, I hadn't seen him any evening during the past week. It was nothing unusual for him to work late, either here or at the office. Some evenings he did not return at all.

But this Monday morning I knew something was different. It was not just another long and tough assignment, though that is what he said it was.

When he came down to breakfast I saw what I had only been feeling, but without knowing it. Now I knew something was altogether unusual, and I forced myself to search for it.

He kissed Georgia and myself and sat down. Always, when he started breakfast, he said something about the first dish he happened to see. Now he began with his grapefruit, and said nothing.

"Tell me a story, George," Georgia presently demanded, as though a perfectly novel idea had just occurred to her.

"Story? Story? What's a story, anyway? Never heard of it."

That was all right, though a little mechanical.

"Go on. George said you would. She promised."

"All right, I'll tell you a story. It's about a little girl named Sophia."

"How old?"

"Six."

Again there was that wrong note. She always had to coax him before he gave her right age.

"So what did she do?"

"Well, this is really about Sophia and her very best friend, another little girl."

"And what was her name?"

"Sonia, as it happens."

"How old?"

"Six."

"So what did they do?"

I saw, for the first time, he must have lost a lot of weight. And when he talked to me, he was not there at all. Normally, he wrapped himself in clouds of confetti, but anyone who knew him at all understood exactly what he meant and just where he could be found. But now he really, really wasn't there. His light evasions weren't light. They were actual evasions. The clouds of confetti were steel doors.

It crossed my mind he had been like this two years ago, during the affair I knew he had with Elizabeth Stoltz. That one I was certain about. And there had been others before that, I had believed then, and more than ever believed now.

A wave of utter unreality swept over me. And I recognized the mood, too well, like the first twinges of a recurrent ailment. It was too hideous to be real. That, that was what made it finally so hideous.

"Well, Sophia never saw her friend Sonia except at certain times. Only when Sophia climbed up on a chair and looked into the mirror to wash her face or comb her hair. Whenever she did that she always found Sonia, of all people, there ahead of her."

"So what did they do then?"

"So then they had long, long talks. 'What's the idea, always getting in my way?' Sophia would ask. 'You go away from here, Sonia, and leave me alone.' "

"So what did Sonia say?"

"Well, that's the strangest thing of all. Sonia never said a word. Not one word. But whatever Sophia did in front of the looking glass, Sonia copied her. Even when Sophia stuck out her tongue and called Sonia an old copycat."

"Then what happened?"

"This went on for a long time, and Sophia was pretty mad, believe me."

Yes, George, Sophia was pretty damn mad. Just how many years, George, did it go on? "But she thought it over, and one day she told Sonia, 'If you don't stop getting in my way every time I come to the mirror, Sonia, why, I'll never get out of your way, either.' "

"So then what?"

"That's just what Sophia did. Every time Sonia, the little girl who never talked, came to the mirror to comb her hair, so did Sophia. And everything Sonia did, Sophia copied her right back."

No. I don't think so. I think they both did something else. They simply went away from each other.

It can't be. I can't go through that horror again.

What is the matter with him? Is he insane? I can't fall over that terrible cliff again.

Can he ever change and grow up? He's been all right since the Stoltz girl. I thought that would be the last, because she had to be the last. There is a limit beyond which nerves cannot be bruised and torn, and still live. If that is what it is, I cannot endure it again.

Is he quite sane? He can't be, to be so blind.

"I have a best friend," Georgia announced.

"I should hope so."

"A new one."

"What do you and your best friend do?"

"We play games. But sometimes she steals my crayons. Her name's Pauline."

"I see. And then what happens?"

It was too pat, like something rehearsed and coming out of a machine, a radio or a phonograph.

The horn of the school bus sounded and Georgia jumped up. I dabbed at her face with my napkin, then followed her into the hall where she rushed for her school bag, contents one drawing pad, one picture book, and the last time I looked into it, a handful of loose beads, some forgotten peanuts, the broken top of a fountain pen.

I stood there for a moment after I kissed her good-bye and she ran down the walk. Perhaps I was wrong.

I had to be wrong. I would be wrong. Until I was forced to be otherwise.

On my way back to the breakfast room I saw the last issue of *Newsways*, and remembered something. I brought it with me.

"George," I said, "you forgot to bring home a *Newsways*."

He went on with his eggs and coffee and said, absently: "It slipped my mind. I'll bring one home tonight without fail. And *Personalities*, just off."

"Never mind the *Newsways*, I bought one yesterday." He looked at me and saw the magazine, and for just an instant there was something strange and drawn in his face I had never seen before, then it was gone so quickly I wasn't sure it had been there at all. "There's something in it I meant to ask you about. Did you read the article about Louise Patterson?"

"Yes, I read it."

"It's grand, isn't it? It's just what you've been saying for years." I quoted a sentence from the article. " 'Homunculus grows to monstrous size, with all the force of a major explosion, by grace of a new talent suddenly shooting meteorlike across the otherwise turgid skies of the contemporary art world. Louise Patterson may view her models through a microscope, but the brush she wields is Gargantuan.' "

"Yes, it's grand. But it is not what I've been saying for years."

"Anyway, they recognize her talent. Don't be so critical, just because they use different words than you would. At least they admit she's a great painter, don't they?"

"That they do."

Something was away off key. The words were meant to be lightly skeptical, but the tone of his voice was simply flat.

"For heaven's sake, George, don't pretend you aren't pleased. You must have seven or eight Pattersons, and now they're all terribly valuable."

"Priceless. I believe that's the *Newsways* term for them." He dropped his napkin and stood up. "I'll have to run. I think I'll drive in as usual, unless you need the car."

"No, of course not. But wait, George. Here's one thing more." I found another paragraph in the same article, and read from it. " 'This week interest of the art world centered in the whereabouts of Patterson's lost masterpiece, her famed *Judas*, admittedly the most highly prized canvas of all among the priceless works that have come from the studio of this artist. Depicting two huge hands exchanging a coin, a consummate study in flaming yellow, red, and tawny brown, this composition was widely known some years ago, then it quietly dropped from view.' And so on."

I looked up from the magazine. George said: "Neat but not gaudy. They make it sound like a rainbow at midnight."

"That's not what I'm driving at. Would you know anything about that picture?"

"Why should I?"

"Didn't I see an unframed picture you brought home, about a week ago, something like that?"

"You sure did, Georgie-porgie. A copy of it."

"Oh, well. What became of it?"

George winked at me, but there was nothing warm in back of it. There was nothing at all. Just something blank.

"Took it to the office, of course. Where do you think those plumbers got such an accurate description of the original?" He patted my shoulder and gave me a quick kiss. "I'll have to step on it. I'll call you this afternoon."

When he'd gone, and I heard the car go down the driveway, I put down the magazine and slowly got up. I went out to Nellie in the kitchen, knowing how it feels to be old, really old.

Emory Mafferson

I'd never known Stroud very well until recently, and for that matter I didn't know him now. Consequently, I couldn't guess how, or whether, he fitted the Janoth pattern.

When he told me not to be the *Crimeways* type, that meant nothing. This was standard counsel on all of our publications, and for all I knew, Stroud was merely another of the many keen, self-centered, ambitious people in the organization who moved from office to office, from alliance to alliance, from one ethical or political fashion to another, never with any real interest in life except to get more money next year than this, and always more than his colleagues did.

Yet I had a feeling Stroud was not that simple. All I knew about him, in fact, was that he considered himself pretty smooth, seemed to value his own wit, and never bought anything we manufactured here.

Neither did I. Until now.

Leon Temple was in Stroud's office when I came in late that Monday morning, asking Stroud to O.K. an order for some money he swore he had to have for this new, hysterical assignment nearly everyone except myself seemed to be working on. From what I gathered, Temple did nothing but loaf around the cocktail lounge of the Van Barth with a nice little wisp of a thing by the name of Janet Clark. Roaming around the office and trying to figure the best approach to Stroud, I felt like an outsider. They were having one long, happy party, while I spent my days in the ancient Homicide Bureau or the crumbling ruins of the District Attorney's office.

When Stroud signed the order for cash and Leon Temple had gone, I went over and lifted myself to the window ledge in back of his desk. He swung his chair around and in the cross-light I saw what I had not noticed before, that the man's face was lined and hard.

"Anything new, Emory?" he asked.

"Well. Yes. Largely routine stuff. But I wanted to talk about something else."

"Shoot."

"Do you know about the strange thing that happened a week ago last Saturday night?"

"The night of the murder?"

"Yes. But this is about Funded Individuals. I met Fred Steichel, M.E. of Jennett-Donohue, that night. Do you know him?"

"I've met him. But I don't know what you are referring to."

"Well, I know Fred pretty well. His wife and mine were classmates, and still see a lot of each other. We met at a dinner, and there was quite a party afterwards. Fred got drunk, and he began to tell me all about Funded Individuals. In fact, he knew as much about it as I did."

Stroud showed no great concern. "No reason why he shouldn't. It isn't a profound secret. Anything like that gets around."

"Sure, in a general way. But this was different. Fred's all right when he's sober, but he's obnoxious when he's drunk, and that night he was deliberately trying to make himself about as unpleasant as possible. It amused him to recite our computations, quote the conclusions we'd reached, and even repeat some of the angles we'd tried out for a while and then abandoned. The point is, he had the exact figures, the precise steps we'd taken, and he had, for instance, a lot of the phrases I'd personally used in my reports. Not just generally correct, but absolutely verbatim. In other words, there was a leak somewhere, and he'd seen the actual research, the reports, and the findings."

"And then?"

"Well, I got pretty sore. It's one thing that Jennett-Donohue hears rumors about what we're doing, but it's another thing if they have access to supposedly confidential records. I mean, what the hell? I just didn't like the way Fred talked about Funded Individuals. As though it's a dead pigeon. According to him, I was wasting my time. It was only a matter of weeks or days before the whole scheme would be shelved. So the more I thought it over, the less I liked it. He didn't get that data just by accident, and his cockiness wasn't based entirely on a few drinks."

Stroud nodded.

"I see. And you thought it's something we ought to know about."

"I did, and I do. I don't pretend to understand it, but it's my baby, I invested a lot of work in it, and it's something more than the run-of-the-mill mirages we put together around here. It fascinates me. There's something about it almost real." Stroud was at least listening with interest, if not agreement, and I pressed the argument. "It's not just another inspirational arrow shot into the air. This is a cash-and-carry business.

And the minute you know there can be a society in which every individual has an actual monetary value of one million dollars, and he's returning dividends on himself, you also know that nobody is going to shoot, starve, or ruin that perfectly sound investment."

Stroud gave me a faint, understanding, but wintry smile.

"I know," he said. "All right, I'll tell Hagen or Earl about this peculiar seepage of our confidential material."

"But that's the point, I already did. That was the strange thing about that Saturday night. I phoned you first, and I couldn't reach you, then I phoned Hagen. He was in, and he agreed with me that it was damn important. He said he would take it up with Earl, and he wanted to see me the first thing Monday morning. Then I didn't hear another word from him."

Stroud leaned back in his chair, studying me, and plainly puzzled. "You called Hagen that night?"

"I had to let somebody know."

"Of course. What time did you call?"

"Almost immediately. I told Steichel I would, and the bastard just laughed."

"Yes, but what time?"

"Well, about ten-thirty. Why?"

"And you talked only to Hagen? You didn't talk to Earl, did you?"

"I didn't talk to him, no. But he must have been there at the time I called. That's where he was that night, you know."

Stroud looked away from me, frowning.

"Yes, I know," he said, in a very tired, distant voice. "But exactly what did Hagen say, do you recall?"

"Not exactly. He told me he would take it up with Earl. That's a double-check on Earl's whereabouts, isn't it? And Hagen said he would see me Monday morning. But on Monday morning I didn't hear from him, I haven't heard from him since, and I began to wonder what happened. I thought maybe he'd relayed the whole matter to you."

"No, I'm sorry, he didn't. But I'll follow it up, of course. I quite agree with you, it's important. And with Hagen." I saw again that wintry smile, this time subzero. "A human life valued at a million paper dollars would make something of a story, wouldn't it? Don't worry, Emory, your dreamchild will not be lost."

He was one of those magnetic bastards I have always admired and liked, and of course envied and hated, and I found myself, stupidly, believing him. I knew it couldn't be true, but I actually believed he was genuinely interested in protecting Funded Individuals, and would find a way, somehow, to give it a full hearing and then, in the end, contrive for it a big, actual trial. I smiled, digging some notes out of my pocket, and said: "Well, that's all I wanted to talk about. Now, here's the latest dope the cops have on the Delos murder. I already told you they know she was out of town from late Friday until the following Saturday afternoon." Stroud gave a half nod, and concentrated his attention. I went on: "Yesterday they found out where she was. She was in Albany, with a man. There was a book of matches found in her apartment, from a night club in Albany that doesn't circulate its matches from coast to coast, only there on the spot, and in the course of a routine check-up with Albany hotels, they found that's where she actually was. Got it?"

He nodded, briefly, waiting and remote and again hard. I said: "The cops know all about this job you're doing here, by the way, and they're convinced the man you are looking for and the man who was with Delos last Friday and Saturday in Albany is one and the same person. Does that help or hinder you any?"

He said: "Go on."

"That's about all. They are sending a man up there this afternoon or tomorrow morning, with a lot of photographs which he will check with the night club, the hotel, and elsewhere. I told you they had the Delos woman's address book. Well, this morning they let me look at it. They've been rounding up pictures of every man mentioned on this extensive list of hers, and most likely the guy that was with her in Albany is one of them. Do you follow me?"

"I follow you."

"They know from the general description of this man, as they got it over the phone from the personnel of the hotel and the club up there, that he most definitely was not Janoth. At the hotel, they were registered as Mr. and Mrs. Andrew Phelps-Guyon, a phoney if there ever was one. Does the name mean anything to you?"

"No."

"Your name was in the woman's address book, by the way."

"Yes," he said. "I knew Pauline Delos."

"Well, that's all."

Stroud seemed to be considering the information I had given him.

"That's fine, Emory," he said, and flashed me a quick, heatless smile. "By the way, is the department looking for a photograph of me?"

"No. They've already got one. Something you once turned in for a license or a passport. The man they are sending upstate has quite a collection. He has fifty or sixty photographs."

"I see."

"I can go along to Albany with this fellow, if you like," I said. "If he doesn't accomplish anything else, I imagine he'll be able to identify the man you've been hunting for, yourself."

"I'm sure he will," he said. "But don't bother. I think that can be done better right here."

George Stroud IX

The two lines of investigation, the organization's and the official one, drew steadily together like invisible pincers. I could feel them closing.

I told myself it was just a tool, a vast machine, and the machine was blind. But I had not fully realized its crushing weight and power. That was insane. The machine cannot be challenged. It both creates and blots out, doing each with glacial impersonality. It measures people in the same way that it measures money, and the growth of trees, the life-span of mosquitoes and morals, the advance of time. And when the hour strikes, on the big clock, that is indeed the hour, the day, the correct time. When it says a man is right, he is right, and when it finds him wrong, he is through, with no appeal. It is as deaf as it is blind.

Of course, I had asked for this.

I returned to the office from a lunch I could not remember having tasted. It had been intended as an interlude to plan for new eventualities and new avenues of escape.

The Janoth Building, covering half of a block, looked into space with five hundred sightless eyes as I turned again, of my own free will, and delivered myself once more to its stone intestines. The interior of this giant God was spick-and-span, restfully lighted, filled with the continuous echo of many feet. A visitor would have thought it nice.

Waiting for me, on my desk, I found the list of nonrenewed licenses for out-of-town taverns, for six years ago. I knew this was the one that would have my own name. That would have to be taken care of later. Right now, I could do nothing but stuff it into the bottom drawer of my desk.

I went into Roy's room and asked him: "Starved?"

"Considerably, considerably."

"The St. Bernards have arrived." He slowly stood up, rolled down the sleeves of his shirt. "Sorry if I kept you waiting. Any developments?"

"Not that I know of, but Hagen wants to see you. Maybe I'd better postpone lunch until you've talked with him."

"All right. But I don't think I'll keep you waiting."

I went upstairs. These conferences had daily become longer, more frequent, and more bitter. It was cold comfort to have a clear understanding of the abyss that Hagen and Janoth, particularly Janoth, saw before them.

For the hundredth time I asked myself why Earl had done this thing.

What could possibly have happened on that night, in that apartment?
God, what a price to pay. But it had happened. And I recognized that
I wasn't really thinking of Janoth, at all, but of myself.

When I stepped into Hagen's office he handed me a note, an envelope,
and a photograph.

"This just came in," he said. "We're giving the picture a half-page cut
in *Newsways,* with a follow-up story."

The note and the envelope were on the stationery of a Fifty-seventh
Street gallery. The photograph, a good, clear 4×6, displayed one wall
of a Louise Patterson exhibition, with five of her canvases clearly reproduced. The note, from the dealer, simply declared the photograph had
been taken at a show nine years ago, and was, as far as known, the only
authentic facsimile of the picture mentioned by *Newsways* as lost.

There could be no mistaking the two hands of my *Judas*. It was right
in the middle. The dealer duly pointed out, however, that its original
proper title was simply: *Study in Fundamentals.*

The canvas at the extreme right, though I recognized none of the
others, was the *Study in Fury* that hung on my wall downstairs.

"This seems to answer the description," I said.

"Beyond any doubt. When we run that, quoting the dealer, I'm certain
we'll uncover the actual picture." Maybe. It was still concealed behind
another canvas on Marble Road. But I knew that if Georgette saw the
follow-up, and she would, my story of finding a copy of it would not hold.
For the photograph would be reproduced as the only known authentic
facsimile. "But I hope to God we have the whole thing cleaned up long
before then." I tensed as he looked at the photograph again, certain he
would recognize the *Fury*. But he didn't. He laid it down, regarded me
with a stare made out of acid. "George, what in hell's wrong? This has
drifted along more than a week."

"It took us three weeks to find Isleman," I said.

"We're not looking for a man missing several months. We're looking
for somebody that vanished a week ago, leaving a trail a mile wide.
Something's the matter. What is it?" But, without waiting for an answer,
he discarded the question, and began to check off our current leads.
"How about those lapsed licenses?"

I said they were still coming in, and I was cross-checking them as fast
as they were received. Methodically, then, we went over all the ground
we had covered before. By now it was hash. I'd done a good job making
it so.

Before leaving I asked about Earl, and learned he was out of the
hospital, after two days. And that was all I learned.

I returned to my office about an hour after I had come upstairs. When
I walked in I found Roy, Leon Temple, and Phil Best. It was apparent,

the second I stepped into the room, there had been a break.

"We've got him," said Leon.

His small and usually colorless face was all lit up. I knew I would never breathe again.

"Where is he?"

"Right here. He came into this building just a little while ago."

"Who is he?"

"We don't know yet. But we've got him." I waited, watching him, and he explained: "I slipped some cash to the staff of the Van Barth, let them know there'd be some more, and they've all been looking around this district in their free hours. One of the porters picked him up and followed him here."

I nodded, feeling as though I'd been kicked in the stomach.

"Nice work," I said. "Where is this porter now?"

"Downstairs. When he phoned me, I told him to watch the elevators and follow the guy if he came out. He hasn't. Now Phil's bringing over the antique dealer, Eddy is bringing a waitress from Gil's, and then we'll have all six banks of elevators completely covered. I've told the special cops what to do when our man tries to leave. They'll grab him and make him identify himself from his first birthday up to now."

"Yes," I said. "I guess that's that." It was as though they had treed an animal, and that, in fact, was just the case. I was the animal. I said: "That's smart stuff, Leon. You used your head."

"Dick and Mike are down on the main floor, helping the fellow from the Van Barth. In about two minutes we'll have every door and exit covered, too."

I suddenly reached for my coat, but didn't go through with it. I couldn't, now, it was too late. Instead, I pulled out some cigarettes, moved around in back of my desk and sat down.

"You're certain it's the right man?" I asked.

But of course there was no question. I had been seen on my way back from lunch. And followed.

"The porter is positive."

"All right," I said. The phone rang and mechanically I answered it. It was Dick, reporting that they now had the elevators fully covered. In addition to the porter, a night bartender at the Van Barth, Gil's waitress, and the dealer had all arrived. "All right," I said again. "Stay with it. You know what to do."

Methodically, Phil Best explained, in his shrewish voice, what was unmistakably plain.

"If he doesn't come out during the afternoon, we're sure to pick him up at five-thirty, when the building empties." I nodded, but my stunned and scattered thoughts were beginning to pull themselves together. "It'll be jammed, as usual, but we can have every inch of the main floor covered."

"He's in the bag," I said. "We can't miss. I'm going to stay right here until we get him. I'll send out for supper, and if necessary I'll sleep upstairs in the restroom on the twenty-seventh floor. Personally, I'm not going to leave this office until we've got it all sewed up. How about the rest of you?"

I wasn't listening to what they replied.

Even Roy would know that if a man came into a building, and didn't go out, he must logically still be inside of it. And this inescapable conclusion must eventually be followed by one and only one logical course of action.

Sooner or later my staff must go through the building, floor by floor and office by office, looking for the only man in it who never went home.

It wouldn't take long, when they did that. The only question was, who would be the first to make the suggestion.

Louise Patterson

This time when I answered the doorbell, which had been ringing steadily for the last four days, I found that tall, thin, romantic squirt, Mr. Klausmeyer, from that awful magazine. It was his third visit, but I didn't mind. He was such a polite, dignified worm, much stuffier than anyone I'd ever met before, he gave my apartment a crazy atmosphere of respectability or something.

"I hope I'm not disturbing you, Mrs. Patterson," he said, making the same mistake he'd made before.

"MISS Patterson," I shrieked, laughing. "You are, but come in. Haven't you caught your murderer yet?"

"We aren't looking for any murderer, Miss Patterson. I have told you the—"

"Save that for *Hokum Fact*'s regular subscribers," I said. "Sit down."

He carefully circled around the four children, where the two younger ones, Pete's and Mike's, were helping the older pair, Ralph's, as they sawed and hammered away at some boards and boxes and wheels, building a wagon, or maybe it was some new kind of scooter. Mr. Klausmeyer carefully hitched up his pants, he would, before sitting down in the big leather chair that had once been a rocker.

"You have us confused with *True Facts,*" he firmly corrected me. "That's another outfit altogether, not in the same field with any of our publications. I'm with Janoth Enterprises. Until recently I was on the staff of *Personalities.*" With wonderful irony he added, "I'm sure you've heard of it. Perhaps you've even read it. But right now I'm working on a special—"

"I know, Mr. Klausmeyer. You wrote that article about me in *Newsways Bunk.*" He looked so mad that if he hadn't come because of his job I'm sure he would have gotten up and gone like a bat out of hell. "Never mind," I said, simply whooping. "I enjoyed it, Mr. Klausmeyer. Really I did. And I appreciated it, too, even if you did get it all cockeyed, and I know you didn't really mean any of those nice things you tried to say about me. I know you're just looking for that murderer. Would you like some muscatel? It's all I have."

I dragged out what was left of a gallon of muscatel and found one of my few remaining good tumblers. It was almost clean.

"No, thank you," he said. "About that article, Miss Patterson—"

"Not even a little?"

"No, really. But regarding the article—"

"It isn't very good," I admitted. "I mean the wine," I explained, then I realized I was simply bellowing, and felt aghast. Mr. Klausmeyer hadn't done anything to me, he looked like the sensitive type who takes everything personally, and the least I could do was to refrain from insulting him. I made up my mind to act exactly like an artist should. I poured myself a glass of the muscatel and urged him, quite gently, "I do wish you'd join me."

"No, thanks. Miss Patterson, I didn't write that article in *Newsways.*"

"Oh, you didn't?"

"No."

"Well, I thought it was a perfectly wonderful story." It came to me that I'd said the wrong thing again, and I simply howled. "I mean, within limits. Please, Mr. Klausmeyer, don't mind me. I'm not used to having my pictures labeled 'costly.' Or was it 'invaluable'? The one the murderer bought for fifty bucks."

Mr. Klausmeyer was mad, I could see, and probably I was boring him besides. I swore I would keep my mouth shut and act reasonably for at least fifteen minutes, no matter what he said, and no matter how I felt. Fifteen minutes. That's not so long.

"I merely supplied some of the information," Mr. Klausmeyer carefully explained. "For instance, I supplied the *Newsways* writer with the description of the *Judas* picture, exactly as you gave it to me."

The son of a bitch.

"God damn it all," I screamed, "where do you get that *Judas* stuff? I told you the name of the picture was *Study in Fundamentals.* What in hell do you mean by giving my own picture some fancy title I never thought of at all? How do you dare, you horrible little worm, how do you dare to throw your idiocy all over my work?"

I looked at him through a haze of rage. He was another picture burner. I could tell it just by looking at his white, stuffy face. Another one of those decent, respectable maniacs who'd like nothing better than to take a butcher knife and slash canvases, slop them with paint, burn them. By God, he looked exactly like Pete. No, Pete's way had been to use them to cover up broken window panes, plug up draughts, and stop leaks in the ceiling. He was more the official type. His method would be to bury them in an authorized warehouse somewhere, destroy the records, and let them stay there forever.

I drank off the muscatel, poured myself some more, and tried to listen to him.

"I did use your own title, I assure you, but there must have been a slip somewhere in the writing and editing. That will be corrected in a story *Newsways* is now running, with a photograph of the *Study in Fundamentals.*"

"I know you, you damned arsonist." His large gray eyes bugged out just the way Ralph's had when he showed me the pile of scraps and ashes and charred fragments, all that was left of five years' work, heaped up in the fireplace. How proud he'd been. You really amount to something, I guess, if you know how to destroy something new and creative. "What do you want now?" I demanded. "Why do you come here?"

I saw that Mr. Klausmeyer was quite pale. I guess if he hadn't been a tame caterpillar doing an errand for *Anything but the News* he would have picked up Elroy's scout hatchet and taken a swing at me.

"We've located the man who bought your picture, Miss Patterson," he said, with great control. "We believe we know where he is, and he'll be found at any moment. We wish you'd come to the office, so that you can identify him. Of course, we'll pay you for your time and trouble. We'll give you a hundred dollars if you can help us. Will you?"

"So you've found the murderer," I said.

With emphatic weariness, Mr. Klausmeyer repeated: "We are not looking for a murderer, Miss Patterson. I assure you, we want this man in some altogether different connection."

"Crap," I said.

"I beg your pardon?"

"Nonsense. Detectives have been around here, asking me the same questions you have. You are both looking for the same man, the one who bought my picture, and murdered that Delos woman. What do you think I am? Apparently you think I'm a complete dope."

"No," Mr. Klausmeyer told me, strongly. "Anything but that. Will you come back to the office with me?"

A hundred dollars was a hundred dollars.

"I don't know why I should help to catch a man with brains enough to like my *Study in Fundamentals*. I haven't got so many admirers I can afford to let any of them go to the electric chair."

Mr. Klausmeyer's face showed that he fully agreed, and it pained him that he couldn't say so.

"But perhaps we can help you reclaim your picture. You wanted to buy it back, didn't you?"

"No. I didn't want to buy it back, I just didn't want it to rot in that black hole of Calcutta."

And I knew no one would ever see that picture again. It was already at the bottom of the East River. The murderer would have to do away with it to save his own hide. He would get rid of anything that connected him with the dead woman.

Yet one more noble little angel of destruction.

I realized this, feeling mad and yet somehow cold. It was no use telling myself that I didn't care. The canvas was not one of my best. And yet I did care. It was hard enough to paint the things, without trying to defend them afterwards from self-appointed censors and jealous lovers and microscopic deities. Like Mr. Klausmeyer.

"All right," I said. "I'll go. But only for the hundred dollars."

Mr. Klausmeyer rose like something popping out of a box. God, he was elegant. When he died they wouldn't have to embalm him. The fluid already ran in his veins.

"Certainly," he said, warmly.

I looked around and found my best hat on the top shelf of the book-cases. Edith, who was four—she was Mike's—scolded me for taking away her bird's nest. I explained the nest would be back in place before night-fall. Leaving, I put the whole trading-post in charge of Ralph junior until further notice. He looked up, and I think he even heard me. Anyway, he understood.

In a taxi, on the way to his office, Mr. Klausmeyer tried to be friendly.

"Splendid children," he told me. "Very bright and healthy. I don't believe you told me much about your husband?"

"I've never been married," I said, again shrieking with laughter, against my will. God, I would learn how to act refined, beginning tomorrow, if it was the last thing I ever did. "They're all LOVE children, Mr. Klausmeyer." He sat so straight and earnest and looking so sophisticated I had to postpone my graduation from kindergarten for at least another minute. And then I had that awful sinking sensation, knowing I'd behaved like a perfect fool. As of course I was. Nobody knew that better than I did. But Mr. Klausmeyer was so perfect, I wondered if he could possibly know it. Probably not. Perfect people never understand much about anything.

"Excuse me, Mr. Klausmeyer, if I confide in you. I've never done it before. There's something about you *Factways* people that seems to invite all kinds of confidences."

I suppose this lie was just too transparent, for he said nothing at all, and a moment later we were getting out of the cab, Mr. Klausmeyer looking just too pleased and preoccupied for words because he would soon be rid of me. God damn him. If I'd been dressed when he arrived, if I'd really wanted to make an impression, I could have had him under my thumb in five seconds. But who wanted to have an angleworm under her thumb?

I was drunk and sedate for the whole three minutes it took us to enter the building and ride up in the elevator. Dignity was a game two could play at. But after I'd used up mine, and we got out of the elevator, I asked: "Just what am I supposed to do, Mr. Klausmeyer? Besides collect a hundred dollars?"

Of course, without meaning to, I'd cut loose with another raucous laugh.

"Don't worry about your hundred dollars," he said, shortly. "The man who bought your picture is somewhere in this building. It is just a question of time, until we locate him. All you have to do is identify him when we do locate him."

I was suddenly awfully sick of Mr. Klausmeyer, the detectives who'd been questioning me, and the whole insane affair. What business was it of mine, all of this? I had just one business in life, to paint pictures. If other people got pleasure out of destroying them, let them; perhaps that was the way they expressed their own creative instincts. They probably referred to the best ones they suppressed or ruined as their outstanding masterpieces.

It was a black thought, and I knew it was not in the right perspective. As Mr. Klausmeyer put his hand on the knob of an office door, and pushed it open, I said: "You must be a dreadfully cynical and sophisticated person, Mr. Klausmeyer. Don't you ever long for a breath of good, clean, wholesome, natural fresh air?"

He gave me a polite, but emotional glare.

"I've always avoided being cynical," he said. "Up until now."

We entered a room filled with a lot of other office angleworms.

"How many children have you got, Mr. Klausmeyer?" I asked, intending to speak in a low voice, but evidently I was yelling, because a lot of people turned around and looked at us.

"Two," he whispered, but it sounded like he was swearing. Then he put on a smile and brought me forward. But as I crossed the room, and looked around it, my attention was abruptly centered upon a picture on the wall. It was one of mine. *Study in Fury*. It was amazing. I could hardly believe it. "George," Mr. Klausmeyer was saying, "this is Miss

Patterson, the artist." It was beautifully framed, too. "Miss Patterson, this is George Stroud, who has charge of our investigation. She's agreed to stay here until we have the man we want. She can give us some help, I believe."

A good-looking angleworm got up in back of a desk and came forward and shook hands with me.

"Miss Patterson," he said. "This is an unexpected pleasure."

I looked at him, and started to bellow, but lost my breath. Something was quite mad. It was the murderer, the very same man who bought the picture in the Third Avenue junkshop.

"How d'you do?" I said. I turned to Mr. Klausmeyer, but Mr. Klausmeyer just looked tired and relieved. I stared back at Mr. Stroud. "Well," I said, uncertainly, "what can I do for you?"

For the fraction of a second we looked at each other with complete realization. I knew who he was, and he knew that I knew. But I couldn't understand it, and I hesitated.

This ordinary, bland, rather debonair and inconsequential person had killed that Delos woman? It didn't seem possible. Where would he get the nerve? What would he know about the terrible, intense moments of life? I must be mistaken. I must have misunderstood the whole situation. But it was the same man. There was no doubt about it.

His eyes were like craters, and I saw that their sockets were hard and drawn and icy cold, in spite of the easy smile he showed. I knew this, and at the same time I knew no one else in the room was capable of knowing it, because they were all like poor Mr. Klausmeyer, perfect.

"It's very kind of you to help us," he said. "I imagine Don explained what we're doing."

"Yes." My knees were suddenly trembling. This was away over my head, all of it. "I know everything, Mr. Stroud. I really do."

"I don't doubt it," he said. "I'm sure you do."

Why didn't somebody do something to break this afternoon nightmare? Of course it was a nightmare. Why didn't somebody admit it was all a stupid joke? What fantastic lie would this Stroud person invent, plausible as all hell, if I chose to identify him here and now?

I gave an automatic, raucous laugh, yanked my hand away from his, and said: "Anyway, I'm glad somebody likes my *Study in Fury.*"

"Yes, I like it very much," said the murderer.

"It's yours?" I squeaked.

"Of course. I like all of your work."

There were about five people in the office, though it seemed more like fifty, and now they all turned to look at the *Fury*. Mr. Klausmeyer said: "I'll be damned. It really is Miss Patterson's picture. Why didn't you tell us, George?"

He shrugged.

"Tell you what? What is there to tell? I liked it, bought it, and there it is. It's been there for a couple of years."

Mr. Klausmeyer looked at the Stroud person with renewed interest, while the rest of them gaped at me as though for the first time convinced I was an artist.

"Would you care for a drink, Miss Patterson?" the murderer invited me. He was actually smiling. But I saw it was not a smile, only the desperate imitation of one.

I swallowed once, with a mouth that was harsh and dry, then I couldn't help the feeble, half-measure of a roar that came out of me. Even as I laughed, I knew I wasn't laughing. It was plain hysteria.

"Where in hell's my *Study in Fundamentals?*" I demanded. "The one your lousy magazine calls *Judas.*"

Stroud was very still and white. The others were only blank. Mr. Klausmeyer said, to Stroud: "I told her we'd try to get the picture back for her." To me, he patiently explained, "I didn't say we had it, Miss Patterson. I meant that we'd automatically find the picture when we found the man."

"Will you?" I said, looking hard at Stroud. "I think more likely it's been destroyed."

Something moved in that rigid face of his, fixed in its casual, counterfeit smile.

"No," he said, at last. "I don't think so, Miss Patterson. I have reason to believe your picture is quite safe." He turned back to his desk and lifted the phone. Holding it, he gave me a hard, uncompromising stare it was impossible for me to misconstrue. "It will be recovered," he told me. "Provided everything else goes off all right. Do you fully understand?"

"Yes," I said. God damn him. He was actually blackmailing me. It was me who should be blackmailing him. In fact, I would. "It damn well better be safe. I understand it's worth thousands and thousands of dollars."

He nodded.

"We think so. Now, what would you like to drink?"

"She likes muscatel," said Mr. Klausmeyer.

"Rye," I yelled. What did I care why he killed her? If the *Fury* was safe, probably the *Fundamentals* was safe, too, and it actually was worth a lot of money—now. And if it wasn't safe, I could always talk up later. Besides, he really did collect my pictures. "Not just one. A whole lot. Order a dozen."

It would take something to stay in the same room with a murderer. And at the same time remember that dignity paid, at least in public.

George Stroud X

Sometime very early I woke on a couch I'd had moved into my office, put on my shoes and necktie, the only clothing I'd removed, and in a mental cloud moved over to my desk.

My watch said a few minutes after eight. Today was the day. I still didn't know how I would meet it. But I knew it was the day. The police would finish the check-up in Albany. Somebody would think of combing the building.

Yesterday should have been the day, and why it wasn't, I would never really know. When that Patterson woman walked in here I should have been through. I knew why she hadn't identified me, the fact that I had not destroyed her picture, and my threat that I still would, if she opened her mouth. Artists are curious. I shuddered when I thought how close I'd come, actually, to getting rid of that canvas. She could still make trouble, any time she felt like it, and maybe she would. She was erratic enough. At about eight in the evening she'd packed herself off. But she might be back. At any moment, for any reason, she might change her mind.

Nobody answered when I pressed the button for a copy boy, and at last I phoned the drugstore downstairs. Eventually I got my sandwich and my quart of black coffee. In Roy's office, Harry Slater and Alvin Dealey were keeping the death watch.

Shortly before nine the rest of the staff began to come in. Leon Temple arrived, and then Roy, Englund, and Don and Eddy reached the office almost simultaneously.

"Why don't you go home?" Roy asked me. "There's nothing you can do now, is there?"

I shook my head. "I'm staying."

"You want to be in at the finish?"

"Right. How's everything downstairs?"

Leon Temple said: "Tighter than a drum. Phil Best has just spelled Mike. We've got the whole night side of the Van Barth down there, and some more special cops. I don't understand it."

This was it. I felt it coming. "What don't you understand?" I asked.

"Why that guy hasn't come out. What the hell. He's here, but where is he?"

"Maybe he left before we threw a line around the place," I said.

"Not a chance."

"He may have simply walked in one door and out the other," I argued. "Perhaps he knew he was being followed."

"No," said Leon. "That porter followed him right to the elevator. He took an express. He could be anywhere above the eighteenth floor. For all we know, he's somewhere up here in our own organization."

"What can we do about it?" Englund asked.

"He'll show," I said.

"I thought time was essential, George," Roy reminded me.

"It is."

"It occurs to me," said Leon, "if he doesn't show—" So it was going to be Leon Temple. I looked at him and waited. "We could take those eyewitnesses, with the building police, and some of our own men, and go through the whole place from top to bottom. We could cover every office. That would settle it. It would take a couple of hours, but we'd know."

I had to appear to consider the idea. It already looked bad that I hadn't suggested it myself. I nodded, and said: "You have something."

"Well, shall we do it?"

If I knew where those eyewitnesses were, if I could be informed of their progress from floor to floor and from suite to suite, there might still be a way. No game is over until the whistle blows.

"Get started," I said. "You handle this, Leon. And I want you to keep me informed of every move. Let me know what floor you start on, which direction you're working, and where you're going next."

"O.K.," he said. "First, we'll get witnesses and cops on every floor above eighteen. They'll cover the stairs, the elevators, and I'll have them be careful to watch people moving from office to office, the mail-chutes, johns, closets—everything." I nodded, but didn't speak. "I think that would be right, don't you?"

God, what a price. Here was the bill, and it had to be paid. Of course this was whining, but I knew no man on earth ever watched his whole life go to bits and pieces, carrying with it the lives of those close to him also down into ashes, without a silent protest. The man who really accepts his fate, really bows without a quiver to the big gamble he has made and lost, that is a lie, a myth. There is no such man, there never has been, never will be.

"All right," I said. "Keep me informed."

"I'd like to take Dick and Eddy and Don. And some more, as soon as they come in."

"Take them."

"And I think those witnesses should be encouraged."

"Pay them. I'll give you a voucher." I signed my name to a cashier's form, leaving the amount blank, and tossed it to Leon. "Good hunting," I said, and I think I created a brief smile.

Pretty soon the office was empty, and then Leon called to say they were going through the eighteenth floor, with all exits closed and all down-elevators being stopped for inspection. There was just one way to go. Up.

I had a half-formed idea that there might be some safety in the very heart of the enemy's territory, Steve's or Earl's offices on the thirty-second floor, and I was trying to hit upon a way to work it when the phone rang and it was Steve himself. His voice was blurred and strained, and somehow bewildered, as he asked me to come up there at once.

In Hagen's office I found, besides Steve, Earl Janoth and our chief attorney, Ralph Beeman, with John Wayne, the organization's biggest stockholder, and four other editors. And then I saw Fred Steichel, M.E. of Jennett-Donohue. All of them looked stunned and slightly embarrassed. Except Steichel, who seemed apologetic, and Earl, who radiated more than his customary assurance. He came forward and heartily shook my hand, and I saw that the self-confidence was, instead, nervous tension mounting to near hysteria.

"George," he said. "This makes me very glad." I don't think he really saw me, though, and I don't believe he saw, actually saw, anyone else in the room as he turned and went on, "I see no reason why we should wait. What I have to say now can be drawn up and issued to the entire staff later, expressing my regret that I could not have the pleasure of speaking to each and every one of them personally." I sat down and looked at the fascinated faces around me. They sensed, as I did, the one and only thing that could be impending. "As you may know, there have been certain differences on our controlling board, as to the editorial policies of Janoth publications. I have consistently worked and fought for free, flexible, creative journalism, not only as I saw it, but as every last member of the staff saw it. I want to say now I think this policy was correct, and I am proud of our record, proud that I have enlisted the services of so much talent." He paused to look at Hagen, who looked at no one as he stonily concentrated upon a scramble of lines and circles on the pad before him. "But the controlling board does not agree that my policies have been for the best interests of the organization. And the recent tragedy, of which you are all aware, has increased the opposition's mistrust of my leadership. Under the circumstances, I cannot blame them. Rather than jeopardize the future of the entire venture, I have consented to step aside, and to permit a merger with the firm of Jennett-Donohue. I hope you will all keep alive the spirit of the old organization in the new one. I hope you will give to Mr. Steichel, your new managing editor, the same loyalty you gave to Steve and myself."

Then the attorney, Beeman, took up the same theme and elaborated upon it, and then Wayne began to talk about Earl's step as being temporary, and that everyone looked to his early return. He was still speaking when the door opened and Leon Temple stepped inside. I went over to him.

"We've drawn a blank so far," he told me. "But just to be sure, I think we should go through both Janoth's and Hagen's offices."

In the second that the door opened and shut, I saw a knot of people in the corridor, a porter from Gil's and a waiter from the Van Barth among them.

"Drop it," I said. "The assignment is killed."

Leon's gaze went slowly around the room, absorbing a scene that might have been posed in some historical museum. His eyes came back to me, and I nodded.

"You mean, send them all away?"

"Send them away. We are having a big change. It is the same as Pompeii."

Back in the room I heard Wayne say to Hagen: "—either the Paris bureau, or the Vienna bureau. I imagine you can have either one, if you want it."

"I'll think it over," Hagen told him.

"The organization comes ahead of everything," Earl was too jovially and confidently reiterating. It was both ghastly and yet heroic. "Whatever happens, that must go on. It is bigger than I am, bigger than any one of us. I won't see it injured or even endangered."

Our new managing editor, Steichel, was the only person who seemed to be on the sidelines. I went over to him.

"Well?" I said.

"I know you want more money," he told me. "But what else do you want?"

I could see he would be no improvement at all. I said: "Emory Mafferson."

I thought that would catch him off balance, and it did.

"What? You actually want Mafferson?"

"We want to bring out Funded Individuals. In cartoon strips. We'll dramatize it in pictures." Doubt and suspicion were still there, in Steichel's eyes, but interest began to kindle. "Nobody reads, any more," I went on. "Pictorial presentation, that's the whole future. Let Emory go ahead with Funded Individuals in a new five-color book on slick paper."

Grudgingly, he said: "I'll have to think that one over. We'll see."

George Stroud XI

The rest of that day went by like a motion picture running wild, sometimes too fast, and again too slow.

I called up Georgette, and made a date to meet her for dinner that evening at the Van Barth. She sounded extra gay, though I couldn't imagine why. I was the only member of the family who knew what it meant to go all the way through life and come out of it alive.

I explained that the last assignment was over, and then she put Georgia on the wire. The conversation proceeded like this:

"Hello? Hello? Is that you, George? This is George."

"Hello, George. This is George."

"Hello."

"Hello."

"Hello? Hello?"

"All right, now we've said hello."

"Hello, George, you have to tell me a story. What's her name?"

"Claudia. And she's at least fifteen years old."

"Six."

"Sixteen."

"Six. Hello? Hello?"

"Hello. Yes, she's six. And here's what she did. One day she started to pick at a loose thread in her handkerchief, and it began to come away, and pretty soon she'd picked her handkerchief until all of it disappeared and before she knew it she was pulling away at some yarn in her sweater, and then her dress, and she kept pulling and pulling and before long she got tangled up with some hair on her head and after that she still kept pulling and pretty soon poor Claudia was just a heap of yarn lying on the floor."

"So then what did she do? Hello?"

"So then she just lay there on the floor and looked up at the chair where she'd been sitting, only of course it was empty by now. And she said, 'Where am I?' "

Success. I got an unbelieving spray of laughter.

"So then what did I do? Hello? Hello?"

"Then you did nothing," I said. "Except you were always careful after that not to pull out any loose threads. Not too far."

"Hello? Is that all?"

"That's all for now."

"Good-bye. Hello?"

"We said hello. Now we're saying good-bye."

"Good-bye, good-bye, good-bye, good-bye."

After that I phoned an agency and got a couple of tickets for a show that evening. And then, on an impulse, I phoned the art dealer who had sent us the photograph of the Louise Patterson exhibit. I told him who I was, and asked: "How much are Pattersons actually worth?"

"That all depends," he said. "Do you want to buy, or have you got one you want to sell?"

"Both. I want a rough evaluation."

"Well. Frankly, nobody knows. I suppose you're referring to that recent article in your *Newsways?*"

"More or less."

"Well. That was an exaggeration, of course. And the market on somebody like Patterson is always fluctuating. But I'd say anything of hers would average two or three thousand. I happen to have a number of canvases of hers, exceptional things, you could buy for around that figure."

"What would the *Judas* bring? I mean the one with the hands. You sent us a photograph of it."

"Well, that's different. It's received a lot of publicity, and I suppose that would be worth a little more. But, unfortunately, I haven't got the picture itself. It is really lost, apparently."

"It isn't lost," I said. "I have it. How much is it worth?"

There was a perceptible wait.

"You actually have it?"

"I have."

"You understand, Mr.—"

"Stroud. George Stroud."

"You understand, Mr. Stroud, I don't buy pictures myself. I simply exhibit pictures, and take a commission from the sales made through my gallery. But if you really have that *Judas* I believe it can be sold for anywhere between five and ten thousand dollars."

I thanked him and dropped the phone.

The big clock ran everywhere, overlooked no one, omitted no one, forgot nothing, remembered nothing, knew nothing. Was nothing, I would have liked to add, but I knew better. It was just about everything. Everything there is.

That afternoon Louise Patterson came roaring into the office, more than a little drunk. I had been expecting her. She wanted to talk to me, and I packed us both off to Gil's.

When we were lined up at the bar at Gil's she said: "What about that picture of mine. What have you done with it?"

"Nothing. I have it at my home. Why should I have done anything with it?"

"You know why," she thundered. "Because it proves you killed Pauline Delos."

Three customers looked around with some interest. So then I had to explain to her that I hadn't, and in guarded language, suppressing most of the details, I outlined the police theory of the case. When I had finished, she said, disappointedly: "So you're really not a murderer, after all?"

"No. I'm sorry."

A cyclone of laughter issued from her. For a moment she couldn't catch her breath. I thought she'd fall off her chair.

"I'm sorry, too, Mr. Stroud. I was being so brave yesterday afternoon in your office, you have no idea. God, what I won't do to save those pictures of mine. The more I saw you the more sinister you looked. Come to think of it, you really are sinister. Aren't you?"

She was quite a woman. I liked her more and more. Yesterday she'd looked like something out of an album, but today she'd evidently taken some pains to put herself together. She was big, and dark, and alive.

Gil ranged down the bar in front of us.

"Evening," he said to both of us, then to me, "Say, a friend of yours was hanging around here for the last week or so, looking for you. He sure wanted to see you. Bad. But he ain't here now. A whole lot of people been looking for you."

"I know," I said. "I've seen them all. Give us a couple of rye highballs, and let the lady play the game."

Then for a while Gil and the Patterson woman worked away at it. She started by asking for a balloon, which was easy, the only toy Gil had saved from the old fire next to the carbarns, and ended by asking for a Raphael, also quite simple, a postcard he'd mailed to his wife from Italy, on a long voyage.

Something like eight drinks later Patterson remembered something, as I'd known she sooner or later would.

"George, there's something I don't understand. Why did they want me to identify you? What was the idea?"

She was more than a little drunk, and I gravely told her: "They wanted to find out who had that picture of yours. It was believed lost. Remember? And it's priceless. Remember that? And naturally, our organization wanted to trace it down."

She stared for a moment of semi-belief, then exploded into another storm of laughter.

"Double-talk. I want the truth. Where's my picture? I want it back. I could have it back the minute you were found, according to Mr. Klausmeyer." The memory of Don seemed to touch off another wave of deafening hilarity. "That angleworm. To hell with him. Well, where is it?"

"Louise," I said.

"It's worth a lot of money, it belongs to me, and I want it. When are you going to give it to me?"

"Louise."

"You're a double-talker. I can spot a guy like you a hundred miles away. You've got a wife, no children, and a house you haven't paid for. Tonight you're slumming, and tomorrow you'll be bragging all over the commuter's special that you know a real artist, the famous Louise Patterson." She slammed a fist on the bar. Gil came back to us and phlegmatically assembled two more drinks. "But to hell with all that. I want my *Study in Fundamentals*. It was promised to me, and it's worth a lot of money. Where is it?"

"You can't have it," I said, bluntly. "It's mine."

She glared, and snarled.

"You bastard, I think you mean it."

"Certainly I mean it. After all, it is mine. I paid for it, didn't I? And it means something to me. That picture is a part of my life. I like it. I want it. I need it."

She was, all at once, moderately amiable.

"Why?"

"Because that particular picture gave me an education. It is continuing to give me an education. Maybe, sometime, it will put me through college." I looked at my watch. If I could get to the Van Barth in ten minutes, I would be approximately on time. "But I'll make a deal with you. I've got that *Fury* in the office, and four other things of yours at home. You can have them all, instead of the *Temptation of St. Judas*, which is not for sale at any price. Not to anyone."

She asked me, wistfully: "Do you really like it so much?"

I didn't have time to explain, and so I simply said: "Yes."

This shut her up, and I somehow got her out of the place. In front of Gil's I put her into a cab, and paid the driver, and gave him her address.

I caught the next taxi that passed. I knew I'd be a few minutes late at the Van Barth. But it didn't seem to matter so much.

The big, silent, invisible clock was moving along as usual. But it had forgotten all about me. Tonight it was looking for someone else. Its arms and levers and steel springs were wound up and poised in search of some other person in the same blind, impersonal way it had been reaching for me on the night before. And it had missed me, somehow. That time. But I had no doubt it would get around to me again. Inevitably. Soon.

I made sure that my notebook was stowed away in an inside pocket. It had Louise's address, and her phone number. I would never call her, of course. It was enough, to be scorched by one serious, near-disaster. All the same, it was a nice, interesting number to have.

My taxi slowed and stopped for a red light. I looked out of the window and saw a newspaper headline on a corner stand.

EARL JANOTH, OUSTED PUBLISHER,
PLUNGES TO DEATH.

WHAT MRS. McGILLICUDDY SAW!

by

AGATHA CHRISTIE

1

Mrs. McGillicuddy panted along the platform in the wake of the porter carrying her suitcase. Mrs. McGillicuddy was short and stout, the porter was tall and free-striding. In addition, Mrs. McGillicuddy was burdened with a large quantity of parcels; the result of a day's Christmas shopping. The race was, therefore, an uneven one, and the porter turned the corner at the end of the platform while Mrs. McGillicuddy was still coming up the straight.

No. 1 platform was not at the moment unduly crowded, since a train had just gone out; but, in the no man's land beyond, a milling crowd was rushing in several directions at once, to and from undergrounds, left-luggage offices, tea rooms, inquiry offices, indicator boards and the two outlets, Arrival and Departure, to the outside world.

Mrs. McGillicuddy and her parcels were buffeted to and fro, but she arrived eventually at the entrance to No. 3 platform, and deposited one parcel at her feet while she searched her bag for the ticket that would enable her to pass the stern, uniformed guardian at the gate.

At that moment, a voice, raucous yet refined, burst into speech over her head.

"The train standing at Platform 3," the voice told her, "is the 4:54 for

Brackhampton, Milchester, Waverton, Carvil Junction, Roxeter and stations to Chadmouth. Passengers for Brackhampton and Milchester travel at the rear of the train. Passengers for Vanequay change at Roxeter." The voice shut itself off with a click, and then reopened conversation by announcing the arrival at Platform 9 of the 4:35 from Birmingham and Wolverhampton.

Mrs. McGillicuddy found her ticket and presented it. The man clipped it, murmured: "On the right—rear portion."

Mrs. McGillicuddy padded up the platform and found her porter, looking bored and staring into space, outside the door of a third-class carriage.

"Here you are, lady."

"I'm traveling first class," said Mrs. McGillicuddy.

"You didn't say so," grumbled the porter. His eye swept her masculine-looking pepper-and-salt tweed coat disparagingly.

Mrs. McGillicuddy, who had said so, did not argue the point. She was sadly out of breath.

The porter retrieved the suitcase and marched with it to the adjoining coach where Mrs. McGillicuddy was installed in solitary splendor. The 4:54 was not much patronized, the first-class clientele preferring either the faster morning express or the 6:40 with dining cars. Mrs. McGillicuddy handed the porter his tip which he received with disappointment, clearly considering it more applicable to third-class than to first-class travel. Mrs. McGillicuddy, though prepared to spend money on comfortable travel after a night journey from the North and a day's feverish shopping, was at no time an extravagant tipper.

She settled herself back on the plush cushions with a sigh and opened a magazine. Five minutes later, whistles blew and the train started. The magazine slipped from Mrs. McGillicuddy's hand, her head dropped sideways, three minutes later she was asleep. She slept for thirty-five minutes and awoke refreshed. Resettling her hat which had slipped askew, she sat up and looked out of the window at what she could see of the flying countryside. It was quite dark now, a dreary, misty December day—Christmas was only five days ahead. London had been dark and dreary; the country was no less so, though occasionally rendered cheerful with its constant clusters of lights as the train flashed through towns and stations.

"Serving last tea now," said an attendant, whisking open the corridor door like a jinni. Mrs. McGillicuddy had already partaken of tea at a large department store. She was for the moment amply nourished. The attendant went on down the corridor uttering his monotonous cry. With a pleased expression, Mrs. McGillicuddy looked up at the rack where her various parcels reposed. The face towels had been excellent value and just what Margaret wanted, the space gun for Robby and the rabbit for Jean were highly satisfactory, and that evening coatee was just the thing she herself wanted, warm but dressy. The pullover for Hector, too . . . her mind dwelt with approval on the soundness of her purchases.

Her satisfied gaze returned to the window, a train traveling in the opposite direction rushed by with a screech, making the windows rattle and causing her to start. The train clattered over points and passed through a station.

Then it began suddenly to slow down, presumably in obedience to a signal. For some minutes it crawled along, then stopped, presently it began to move forward again. Another up train passed them, though with less vehemence than the first one. The train gathered speed again. At that moment another train, also on a down line, swerved inward toward them, for a moment with almost alarming effect. For a time the two trains ran parallel, now one gaining a little, now the other. Mrs. McGillicuddy looked from her window through the windows of the parallel carriages. Most of the blinds were down, but occasionally the occupants of the carriages were visible. The other train was not very full and there were many empty carriages.

At the moment when the two trains gave the illusion of being stationary, a blind in one of the carriages flew up with a snap. Mrs. McGillicuddy looked into the lighted first-class carriage that was only a few feet away.

Then she drew her breath in with a gasp and half rose to her feet.

Standing with his back to the window and to her was a man. His hands were round the throat of a woman who faced him, and he was slowly, remorselessly, strangling her. Her eyes were starting from their sockets, her face was purple and congested. As Mrs. McGillicuddy watched, fascinated, the end came, the body went limp and crumpled in the man's hands.

At the same moment, Mrs. McGillicuddy's train slowed down again and the other began to gain speed. It passed forward and a moment or two later it had vanished from sight.

Almost automatically Mrs. McGillicuddy's hand went up to the communication cord, then paused, irresolute. After all, what use would it be ringing the cord of the train in which she was traveling? The horror of what she had seen at such close quarters and the unusual circumstances made her feel paralyzed. Some immediate action was necessary—but what?

The door of her compartment was drawn back and a ticket collector said, "Ticket, please."

Mrs. McGillicuddy turned to him with vehemence.

"A woman has been strangled," she said. "In a train that has just passed. I saw it."

The ticket collector looked at her doubtfully.

"I beg your pardon, Madam?"

"A man strangled a woman! In a train. I saw it—through there." She pointed to the window.

The ticket collector looked extremely doubtful.

"Strangled?" he said disbelievingly.

"Yes, strangled! I saw it, I tell you. You must do something at once!"

The ticket collector coughed apologetically.

"You don't think, Madam, that you may have had a little nap and—er—" he broke off tactfully.

"I have had a nap, but if you think this was a dream, you're quite wrong. I saw it, I tell you."

The ticket collector's eyes dropped to the open magazine lying on the seat. On the exposed page was a girl being strangled while a man with a revolver threatened the pair from an open doorway.

He said persuasively: "Now don't you think, Madam, that you'd been reading an exciting story, and that you just dropped off, and awaking a little confused—"

Mrs. McGillicuddy interrupted him.

"I saw it," she said. "I was as wide awake as you are. And I looked out of the window into the window of the train alongside, and a man was strangling a woman. And what I want to know is, what are you going to do about it?"

"Well—Madam—"

"You're going to do something, I suppose?"

The ticket collector sighed reluctantly and glanced at his watch.

"We shall be in Brackhampton in exactly seven minutes. I'll report what you've told me. In what direction was the train you mention going?"

"This direction, of course. You don't suppose I'd have been able to see all this if a train had flashed past going in the other direction?"

The ticket collector looked as though he thought Mrs. McGillicuddy was quite capable of seeing anything anywhere as the fancy took her. But he remained polite.

"You can rely on me, Madam," he said. "I will report your statement. Perhaps I might have your name and address—just in case—"

Mrs. McGillicuddy gave him the address where she would be staying for the next few days and her permanent address in Scotland, and he wrote them down. Then he withdrew with the air of a man who has done his duty and dealt successfully with a tiresome member of the traveling public.

Mrs. McGillicuddy remained frowning and vaguely unsatisfied. Would the ticket collector really report her statement? Or had he just been soothing her down? There were, she supposed vaguely, a lot of elderly women traveling around, fully convinced that they had unmasked Communist plots, were in danger of being murdered, saw flying saucers and secret spaceships, and reported murders that had never taken place. If the man dismissed her as one of those . . .

The train was slowing down now, passing over points, and running through the bright lights of a large town.

Mrs. McGillicuddy opened her handbag, pulled out a receipted bill which was all she could find, wrote a rapid note on the back of it with her ball-point pen, put it into a spare envelope that she fortunately happened to have, stuck the envelope down and wrote on it.

The train drew slowly into a crowded platform. The usual ubiquitous voice was intoning:

"The train now arriving at Platform 1 is the 5:38 for Milchester, Waverton, Roxeter and stations to Chadmouth. Passengers for Market Basing take the train now waiting at No. 3 platform. No. 1 Bay for stopping train to Carbury."

Mrs. McGillicuddy looked anxiously along the platform. So many passengers and so few porters. Ah, there was one! She hailed him authoritatively.

"Porter! Please take this at once to the stationmaster's office."

She handed him the envelope and with it a shilling.

Then, with a sigh, she leaned back. Well, she had done what she could. Her mind lingered with an instant's regret on the shilling. Sixpence would really have been enough . . .

Her mind went back to the scene she had witnessed. Horrible, quite horrible. She was a strong-nerved woman, but she shivered. What a strange—what a fantastic thing to happen to her, Elspeth McGillicuddy. If the blind of the carriage had not happened to fly up . . . But that, of course, was Providence.

Providence had willed that she, Elspeth McGillicuddy, should be a witness of the crime. Her lips set grimly.

Voices shouted, whistles blew, doors were banged shut. The 5:38 drew slowly out of Brackhampton Station. An hour and five minutes later it stopped at Milchester.

Mrs. McGillicuddy collected her parcels and her suitcase and got out. She peered up and down the platform. Her mind reiterated its former judgment: not enough porters. Such porters as there were seemed to be engaged with mailbags and luggage vans. Passengers nowadays seemed always expected to carry their own cases. Well, she couldn't carry her suitcase and her umbrella and all her parcels. She would have to wait. In due course she secured a porter.

"Taxi?"

"There will be something to meet me, I expect."

Outside Milchester Station, a taxi driver who had been watching the exit came forward. He spoke in a soft local voice.

"Is it Mrs. McGillicuddy? For St. Mary Mead?"

Mrs. McGillicuddy acknowledged her identity. The porter was recompensed, adequately if not handsomely. The car, with Mrs. McGillicuddy, her suitcase and her parcels, drove off into the night. It was a nine-mile drive. Sitting bolt upright in the car, Mrs. McGillicuddy was unable to relax. Her feelings yearned for expression. At last the taxi drove along the familiar village street and finally drew up at its destination; Mrs. McGillicuddy got out and walked up the brick path to the door. The driver deposited the cases inside as the door was opened by an elderly maid. Mrs. McGillicuddy passed straight through the hall to where, at the open sitting-room door, her hostess awaited her: an elderly, frail old lady.

"Elspeth!"

"Jane!"

They kissed, and without preamble or circumlocution, Mrs. McGillicuddy burst into speech.

"Oh, Jane!" she wailed. "I've just seen a murder!"

2

True to the precepts handed down to her by her mother and grandmother—to wit: that a true lady can neither be shocked nor surprised—Miss Marple merely raised her eyebrows and shook her head, as she said:

"Most distressing for you, Elspeth, and surely most unusual. I think you had better tell me about it at once."

That was exactly what Mrs. McGillicuddy wanted to do. Allowing her hostess to draw her nearer to the fire, she sat down, pulled off her gloves and plunged into a vivid narrative.

Miss Marple listened with close attention. When Mrs. McGillicuddy at last paused for breath, Miss Marple spoke with decision.

"The best thing, I think, my dear, is for you to go upstairs and take off your hat and have a wash. Then we will have supper—during which we will not discuss this at all. After supper we can go into the matter thoroughly and discuss it from every aspect."

Mrs. McGillicuddy concurred with this suggestion. The two ladies had supper, discussing as they ate various aspects of life as lived in the village of St. Mary Mead. Miss Marple commented on the general distrust of the new organist, related the recent scandal about the chemist's wife and touched on the hostility between the schoolmistress and the Village Institute. They then discussed Miss Marple's and Mrs. McGillicuddy's gardens.

"Peonies," said Miss Marple as she rose from table, "are most unaccountable. Either they do—or they don't do. But if they do establish themselves, they are with you for life, so to speak, and really most beautiful varieties nowadays."

They settled themselves by the fire again, and Miss Marple brought out two old Waterford glasses from a corner cupboard, and from another cupboard produced a bottle.

"No coffee tonight for you, Elspeth," she said. "You are already overexcited—and no wonder!—and probably would not sleep. I prescribe a glass of my cowslip wine, and later, perhaps, a cup of camomile tea."

Mrs. McGillicuddy acquiescing in these arrangements, Miss Marple poured out the wine.

"Jane," said Mrs. McGillicuddy, as she took an appreciative sip, "you don't think, do you, that I dreamed it, or imagined it?"

"Certainly not," said Miss Marple with warmth.

Mrs. McGillicuddy heaved a sigh of relief.

"That ticket collector," she said, "he thought so. Quite polite, but all the same—"

"I think, Elspeth, that that was quite natural under the circumstances. It sounded—and indeed was—a most unlikely story. And you were a complete stranger to him. No, I have no doubt at all that you saw what you've told me you saw. It's very extraordinary—but not at all impossible. I recollect myself being interested, when a train ran parallel to one in which I was traveling, to notice what a vivid and intimate picture one got of what was going on in one or two of the carriages. A little girl, I remember once, was playing with a Teddy Bear and suddenly she threw it deliberately at a fat man who was asleep in the corner, and he bounced up and looked most indignant, and the other passengers looked so amused. I saw them all quite vividly. I could have described afterward exactly what they looked like and what they had on."

Mrs. McGillicuddy nodded gratefully.

"That's just how it was."

"The man had his back to you, you say. So you didn't see his face?"

"No."

"And the woman, you can describe her? Young? Old?"

"Youngish. Between thirty and thirty-five, I should think. I couldn't say closer than that."

"Good-looking?"

"That again, I couldn't say. Her face, you see, was all contorted and—"

Miss Marple said quickly:

"Yes, yes, I quite understand. How was she dressed?"

"She had on a fur coat of some kind, a palish fur. No hat. Her hair was blonde."

"And there was nothing distinctive that you can remember about the man?"

Mrs. McGillicuddy took a little time to think carefully before she replied.

"He was tallish—and dark, I think. He had a heavy coat on so that I couldn't judge his build very well." She added despondently, "It's not really very much to go on."

"It's something," said Miss Marple. She paused before saying: "You feel quite sure, in your own mind, that the girl was—dead?"

"She was dead, I'm sure of it. Her tongue came out and—I'd rather not talk about it . . ."

"Of course not. Of course not," said Miss Marple quickly. "We shall know more, I expect, in the morning."

"In the morning?"

"I should imagine it will be in the morning papers. After this man had attacked and killed her, he would have a body on his hands. What would he do? Presumably he would leave the train quickly at the first station —by the way, can you remember if it was a corridor carriage?"

"No, it was not."

"That seems to point to a train that was not going far afield. It would almost certainly stop at Brackhampton. Let us say he leaves the train at Brackhampton, perhaps arranging the body in a corner seat, with the face hidden by the fur collar to delay discovery. Yes—I think that that is what he would do. But of course it will be discovered before very long —and I should imagine that the news of a murdered woman discovered on a train would be almost certain to be in the morning papers. We shall see."

II

But it was not in the morning papers.

Miss Marple and Mrs. McGillicuddy, after making sure of this, finished their breakfast in silence. Both were reflecting.

After breakfast, they took a turn round the garden. But this, usually an absorbing pastime, was today somewhat halfhearted. Miss Marple did indeed call attention to some new and rare species she had acquired for her rock garden but did so in an almost absent-minded manner. And Mrs. McGillicuddy did not, as was customary, counterattack with a list of her own recent acquisitions.

"The garden is not looking at all as it should," said Miss Marple, but still speaking absent-mindedly. "Doctor Haydock has absolutely forbidden me to do any stooping or kneeling—and really, what can you do if you don't stoop or kneel? There's old Edwards, of course—but so opinionated. And all this jobbing gets them into bad habits, lots of cups of tea and so much pottering—not any real work."

"Oh I know," said Mrs. McGillicuddy. "Of course there's no question of my being forbidden to stoop, but really, especially after meals—and having put on weight"—she looked down at her ample proportions—"it does bring on heartburn."

There was a silence and then Mrs. McGillicuddy planted her feet sturdily, stood still and turned on her friend.

"Well?" she said.

It was a small, insignificant word but it acquired full significance from Mrs. McGillicuddy's tone, and Miss Marple understood its meaning perfectly.

"I know," she said.

The two ladies looked at each other.

"I think," said Miss Marple, "we might walk down to the police station and talk to Sergeant Cornish. He's intelligent and patient, and I know him very well and he knows me. I think he'll listen—and pass the information on to the proper quarter."

Accordingly some three quarters of an hour later, Miss Marple and Mrs. McGillicuddy were talking to a fresh-faced, grave man between thirty and forty who listened attentively to what they had to say.

Frank Cornish received Miss Marple with cordiality and even deference. He set chairs for the two ladies and said: "Now, what can we do for you, Miss Marple?"

Miss Marple said: "I would like you, please, to listen to my friend Mrs. McGillicuddy's story."

And Sergeant Cornish had listened. At the close of the recital he remained silent for a moment or two.

Then he said:

"That's a very extraordinary story." His eyes, without seeming to do so, had sized Mrs. McGillicuddy up while she was telling it.

On the whole, he was favorably impressed. A sensible woman, able to tell a story clearly; not, so far as he could judge, an over-imaginative or a hysterical woman. Moreover, Miss Marple, so it seemed, believed in the accuracy of her friend's story and he knew all about Miss Marple. Everybody in St. Mary Mead knew Miss Marple; fluffy and dithery in appearance, but inwardly as sharp and as shrewd as they make them.

He cleared his throat and spoke.

"Of course," he said, "you may have been mistaken—I'm not saying you were, mind—but you may have been. There's a lot of horseplay goes on. It mayn't have been serious or fatal."

"I know what I saw," said Mrs. McGillicuddy grimly.

"And you won't budge from it," thought Frank Cornish, "and I'd say that likely or unlikely, you may be right."

Aloud he said: "You reported it to the railway officials, and you've come and reported it to me. That's the proper procedure and you may rely on me to have inquiries instituted."

He stopped. Miss Marple nodded her head gently, satisfied. Mrs. McGillicuddy was not quite so satisfied, but she did not say anything. Sergeant Cornish addressed Miss Marple, not so much because he wanted her ideas, as because he wanted to hear what she would say.

"Granted the facts are as reported," he said. "What do you think has happened to the body?"

"There seem to be only two possibilities," said Miss Marple without hesitation. "The more likely one, of course, is that the body was left in the train, but that seems improbable now, for it would have been found sometime last night by another traveler or by the railway staff at the train's ultimate destination."

Frank Cornish nodded.

"The only other course open to the murderer would be to push the body out of the train on to the line. It must, I suppose, be still on the track somewhere as yet undiscovered—though that does seem a little unlikely. But there would be, as far as I can see, no other way of dealing with it."

"You read about bodies being put in trunks," said Mrs. McGillicuddy, "but no one travels with trunks nowadays, only suitcases, and you couldn't get a body into a suitcase."

"Yes," said Cornish. "I agree with you both. The body, if there is a body, ought to have been discovered by now, or will be very soon. I'll let you know any developments there are—though I daresay you'll read about them in the papers. There's the possibility, of course, that the woman, though savagely attacked, was not actually dead. She may have been able to leave the train on her own feet."

"Hardly without assistance," said Miss Marple. "And if so, it will have been noticed. A man, supporting a woman whom he says is ill."

"Yes, it will have been noticed," said Cornish. "Or if a woman was found unconscious or ill in a carriage and was removed to a hospital, that, too, will be on record. I think you may rest assured that you'll hear about it all in a very short time."

But that day passed and the next day. On that evening Miss Marple received a note from Sergeant Cornish:

> *In regard to the matter on which you consulted me, full inquiries have been made, with no result. No woman's body has been found. No hospital has administered treatment to a woman such as you describe, and no case of a woman suffering from shock or taken ill, or leaving a station supported by a man has been observed. You may take it that the fullest inquiries have been made. I suggest that your friend may have witnessed a scene such as she described but that it was much less serious than she supposed.*

3

"Less serious? Fiddlesticks!" said Mrs. McGillicuddy. "It was murder!"

She looked defiantly at Miss Marple and Miss Marple looked back at her.

"Go on, Jane," said Mrs. McGillicuddy. "Say it was all a mistake! Say I imagined the whole thing! That's what you think now, isn't it?"

"Anyone can be mistaken," Miss Marple pointed out gently. "Anybody, Elspeth, even you. I think we must bear that in mind. But I still think, you know, that you were most probably not mistaken. You use glasses for reading, but you've got very good far sight—and what you saw impressed you very powerfully. You were definitely suffering from shock when you arrived here."

"It's a thing I shall never forget," said Mrs. McGillicuddy with a shudder. "The trouble is, I don't see what I can do about it!"

"I don't think," said Miss Marple thoughtfully, "that there's anything more you can do about it." (If Mrs. McGillicuddy had been alert to the tones of her friend's voice, she might have noticed a very faint stress laid on the *you*.) "You've reported what you saw—to the railway people and to the police. No, there's nothing more you can do."

"That's a relief, in a way," said Mrs. McGillicuddy, "because, as you know, I'm going out to Ceylon immediately after Christmas to stay with Roderick and I certainly do not want to put that visit off—I've been looking forward to it so much. Though of course I would put it off if I thought it was my duty," she added conscientiously.

"I'm sure you would, Elspeth, but as I say, I consider you've done everything you possibly could do."

"It's up to the police," said Mrs. McGillicuddy. "And if the police choose to be stupid—"

Miss Marple shook her head decisively.

"Oh no," she said, "the police aren't stupid. And that makes it interesting, doesn't it?"

Mrs. McGillicuddy looked at her without comprehension and Miss Marple reaffirmed her judgment of her friend as a woman of excellent principles and no imagination.

"One wants to know," said Miss Marple, "what really happened."

"She was killed."

"Yes, but who killed her, and why, and what happened to her body? Where is it now?"

"That's the business of the police to find out."

"Exactly! And they haven't found out. That means, doesn't it, that the man was clever—very clever. I can't imagine, you know," said Miss Marple knitting her brows, "how he disposed of it. You kill a woman in a fit of passion—it must have been unpremeditated; you'd never choose to kill a woman in such circumstances just a few minutes before running into a big station. No, it must have been a quarrel—jealousy—something of that kind. You strangle her—and there you are, as I say, with a dead body on your hands and on the point of running into a station. What could you do except as I said at first, prop the body up in a corner as though asleep, hiding the face, and then yourself leave the train as quickly as possible. I don't see any other possibility. And yet there must have been one . . ."

Miss Marple lost herself in thought.

Mrs. McGillicuddy spoke to her twice before Miss Marple answered.

"You're getting deaf, Jane."

"Just a little, perhaps. People do not seem to me to enunciate their words as clearly as they used to do. But it wasn't that I didn't hear you. I'm afraid I wasn't paying attention."

"I just asked about the trains to London tomorrow. Would the afternoon be all right? I'm going to Margaret's and she isn't expecting me before teatime."

"I wonder, Elspeth, if you would mind going up by the 12:15? We could have an early lunch."

"Of course and—"

Miss Marple went on, drowning her friend's words:

"And I wonder, too, if Margaret would mind if you didn't arrive for tea —if you arrived about seven, perhaps?"

Mrs. McGillicuddy looked at her friend curiously.

"What's on your mind, Jane?"

"I suggest, Elspeth, that I should travel up to London with you, and that we should travel down again as far as Brackhampton in the train you traveled by the other day. You would then return to London from Brackhampton and I would come on here as you did. I, of course, would pay the fares." Miss Marple stressed this point firmly.

Mrs. McGillicuddy ignored the financial aspect.

"What on earth do you expect, Jane?" she asked. "Another murder?"

"Certainly not," said Miss Marple shocked. "But I confess I should like to see for myself, under your guidance, the—the—really it is most difficult to find the correct term—the terrain of the crime."

So accordingly on the following day Miss Marple and Mrs. McGillicuddy found themselves in two opposite corners of a first-class carriage speeding out of London by the 4:54 from Paddington. Paddington had been even more crowded than on the preceding Friday, as there were now only two days to go before Christmas, but the 4:54 was comparatively peaceful—at any rate in the rear portion.

On this occasion no train drew level with them, or they with another train. At intervals trains flashed past them toward London. On two occasions trains flashed past them the other way going at high speed. At intervals Mrs. McGillicuddy consulted her watch doubtfully.

"It's hard to tell just when—We'd passed through a station I know . . ." But they were continually passing through stations.

"We're due in Brackhampton in five minutes," said Miss Marple.

A ticket collector appeared in the doorway. Miss Marple raised her eyes interrogatively. Mrs. McGillicuddy shook her head. It was not the same ticket collector. He clipped their tickets and passed on, staggering just a little as the train swung round a long curve. It slackened speed as it did so.

"I expect we're coming into Brackhampton," said Mrs. McGillicuddy.

"We're getting into the outskirts, I think," said Miss Marple.

There were lights flashing past outside, buildings, an occasional glimpse of streets and trams. Their speed slackened further. They began crossing points.

"We'll be there in a minute," said Mrs. McGillicuddy, "and I can't really see this journey has been any good at all. Has it suggested anything to you, Jane?"

"I'm afraid not," said Miss Marple in a rather doubtful voice.

"A sad waste of good money," said Mrs. McGillicuddy but with less disapproval than she would have used had she been paying for herself. Miss Marple had been quite adamant on that point.

"All the same," said Miss Marple, "one likes to see with one's own eyes where a thing happened. This train's just a few minutes late. Was yours on time on Friday?"

"I think so. I didn't really notice."

The train drew slowly into the busy length of Brackhampton Station. The loud-speaker announced hoarsely, doors opened and shut, people got in and out, milled up and down the platform. It was a busy, crowded scene.

Easy, thought Miss Marple, for a murderer to merge into that crowd, to leave the station in the midst of that pressing mass of people, or even to select another carriage and go on in the train to wherever its ultimate destination might be. Easy to be one male passenger among many. But not so easy to make a body vanish into thin air. That body must be somewhere.

Mrs. McGillicuddy had descended. She spoke now from the platform, through the open window.

"Now take care of yourself, Jane," she said. "Don't catch a chill. It's a nasty treacherous time of year, and you're not so young as you were."

"I know," said Miss Marple.

"And don't let's worry ourselves any more over all this. We've done what we could."

Miss Marple nodded and said:

"Don't stand about in the cold, Elspeth. Or you'll be the one to catch a chill. Go and get yourself a good hot cup of tea in the refreshment room. You've got time, twelve minutes before your train back to town."

"I think perhaps I will. Good-by, Jane."

"Good-by, Elspeth. A happy Christmas to you. I hope you find Margaret well. Enjoy yourself in Ceylon, and give my love to dear Roderick—if he remembers me at all which I doubt."

"Of course he remembers you—very well. You helped him in some way when he was at school—something to do with money that was disappearing from a locker. He's never forgotten it."

"Oh, that!" said Miss Marple.

Mrs. McGillicuddy turned away, a whistle blew, the train began to move. Miss Marple watched the sturdy thick-set body of her friend recede. Elspeth could go to Ceylon with a clear conscience—she had done her duty and was freed from further obligation.

Miss Marple did not lean back as the train gathered speed. Instead she sat upright and devoted herself seriously to thought. Though in speech Miss Marple was woolly and diffuse, in mind she was clear and sharp. She had a problem to solve, the problem of her own future conduct; and, perhaps strangely, it presented itself to her as it had to Mrs. McGillicuddy, as a question of duty.

Mrs. McGillicuddy had said that they had both done all that they could do. It was true of Mrs. McGillicuddy, but about herself Miss Marple did not feel so sure.

It was a question, sometimes, of using one's special gifts. But perhaps that was conceited. After all, what could she do? Her friend's words came back to her, "You're not so young as you were . . ."

Dispassionately, like a general planning a campaign, or an accountant assessing a business, Miss Marple weighed up and set down in her mind the facts for and against further enterprise. On the credit side were the following:

1) *My long experience of life and human nature.*
2) *Sir Henry Clithering and his nephew (now at Scotland Yard, I believe), who was so very nice in the Little Paddocks case.*
3) *My nephew Raymond's second boy, David, who is, I am almost sure, in British Railways.*
4) *Griselda's boy Leonard who is so very knowledgeable about maps.*

Miss Marple reviewed these assets and approved them. They were all very necessary to reinforce the weaknesses on the debit side—in particular her own bodily weakness.

"It's not," thought Miss Marple, "as though I could go here, there and everywhere, making inquiries and finding out things."

Yes, that was the chief objection, her own age and weakness. Although, for her age, her health was good, yet she was old. And if Doctor Haydock had strictly forbidden her to do practical gardening he would hardly approve of her starting out to track down a murderer. For that, in effect, was what she was planning to do—and it was there that her loophole lay. For if heretofore murder had, so to speak, been forced upon her, in this case it would be that she herself set out deliberately to seek it. And she was not sure that she wanted to do so. She was old—old and tired. She felt at this moment, at the end of a tiring day, a great reluctance to enter upon any project at all. She wanted nothing at all but to reach home and sit by the fire with a nice tray of supper, and go to bed, and potter about the next day just snipping off a few things in the garden, tidying up in a very mild way, without stooping, without exerting herself.

"I'm too old for any more adventures," said Miss Marple to herself, watching absently out of the window the curving line of an embankment.

A curve.

Very faintly something stirred in her mind. Just after the ticket collector had clipped their tickets . . .

It suggested an idea. Only an idea. An entirely different idea. . . .

A little pink flush came into Miss Marple's face. Suddenly she did not feel tired at all!

"I'll write to David tomorrow morning," she said to herself.

And at the same time another valuable asset flashed through her mind.

"Of course. My faithful Florence!"

II

Miss Marple set about her plan of campaign methodically and making due allowance for the Christmas season which was a definitely retarding factor.

She wrote to her great-nephew, David West, combining Christmas wishes with an urgent request for information.

Fortunately she was invited, as on previous years, to the vicarage for Christmas dinner, and here she was able to tackle young Leonard, home for the Christmas season, about maps.

Maps of all kinds were Leonard's passion. The reason for the old lady's inquiry about a large-scale map of a particular area did not rouse his curiousity. He discoursed on maps generally with fluency, and wrote down for her exactly what would suit her purpose best. In fact, he did better. He actually found that he had such a map among his collection and he lent it to her, Miss Marple promising to take great care of it and . return it in due course.

III

"Maps," said his mother, Griselda, who still, although she had a grown-up son, looked strangely young and blooming to be inhabiting the shabby old vicarage. "What does she want with maps? I mean, what does she want them for?"

"I don't know," said young Leonard, "I don't think she said exactly."

"I wonder now . . ." said Griselda. "It seems very fishy to me. At her age the old pet ought to give up that sort of thing."

Leonard asked what sort of thing, and Griselda said elusively:

"Oh, poking her nose into things. Why maps, I wonder?"

In due course Miss Marple received a letter from her great-nephew David West. It ran affectionately:

Dear Aunt Jane,

Now what are you up to? I've got the information you wanted. There are only two trains that can possibly apply—the 4:33 and the 5 o'clock. The former is a slow train and stops at Haling Broadway, Barwell Heath, Brackhampton and then stations to Market Basing. The 5 o'clock is the Welsh express for Cardiff, Newport and Swansea. The former might be overtaken somewhere by the 4:54, although it is due in Brackhampton five minutes earlier and the latter passes the 4:54 just before Brackhampton.

In all this do I smell some village scandal of a fruity character? Did you, returning from a shopping spree in town by the 4:54, observe in a passing

train the mayor's wife being embraced by the sanitary inspector? But why
does it matter which train it was? A weekend at Porthcawl, perhaps? Thank
you for the pullover. Just what I wanted.
   How's the garden? Not very active this time of year, I should imagine.

Yours ever,
David

Miss Marple smiled a little, then considered the information thus presented to her. Mrs. McGillicuddy had said definitely that the carriage had
not been a corridor one. Therefore—not the Swansea express. The 4:33
was indicated.

Also some more traveling seemed unavoidable. Miss Marple sighed,
but made her plans.

She went up to London as before on the 12:15, but this time returned
not by the 4:54, but by the 4:33 as far as Brackhampton. The journey was
uneventful, but she registered certain details. The train was not crowded
—4:33 was before the evening rush hour. Of the first-class carriages only
one had an occupant—a very old gentleman reading the *New Statesman.*
Miss Marple traveled in an empty compartment and at the two stops,
Haling Broadway and Barwell Heath, leaned out of the window to observe passengers entering and leaving the train. A small number of
third-class passengers got in at Haling Broadway. At Barwell Heath several third-class passengers got out. Nobody entered or left a first-class
carriage except the old gentleman carrying his *New Statesman.*

As the train neared Brackhampton, sweeping around a curve of line,
Miss Marple rose to her feet and stood experimentally with her back to
the window over which she had drawn down the blind.

Yes, she decided, the impetus of the sudden curving of the line and the
slackening of speed did throw one off one's balance back against the
window and the blind might, in consequence, very easily fly up. She
peered out into the night. It was lighter than it had been when Mrs.
McGillicuddy had made the same journey—only just dark, but there was
little to see. For observation she must make a daylight journey.

On the next day she went up by the early-morning train, purchased
four linen pillowcases (tut-tutting at the price!) so as to combine investigation with the provision of household necessities, and returned by a
train leaving Paddington at 12:15. Again she was alone in a first-class
carriage. "This taxation," thought Miss Marple, "that's what it is. No one
can afford to travel first class except businessmen in the rush hours. I
suppose because they can charge it to expenses."

About a quarter of an hour before the train was due at Brackhampton,
Miss Marple got out the map with which Leonard had supplied her and
began to observe the countryside. She had studied the map very carefully beforehand, and after noting the name of a station they passed

through, she was soon able to identify where she was just as the train began to slacken for a curve. It was a very considerable curve, indeed. Miss Marple, her nose glued to the window, studied the ground beneath her (the train was running on a fairly high embankment) with close attention. She divided her attention between the country outside and her map until the train finally ran into Brackhampton.

That night she wrote and posted a letter addressed to Miss Florence Hill, 4 Madison Road, Brackhampton. On the following morning, going to the county library, she studied a *Brackhampton Directory and Gazetteer,* and a county history.

Nothing so far had contradicted the very faint and sketchy idea that had come to her. What she had imagined was possible. She would go no farther than that.

But the next step involved action—a good deal of action—the kind of action for which she, herself, was physically unfit. If her theory were to be definitely proved or disproved, she must at this point have help from some other person. The question was—who? Miss Marple reviewed various names and possibilities, rejecting them all with a vexed shake of the head. The intelligent people, on whose intelligence she could rely, were all far too busy. Not only had they all got jobs of varying importance, their leisure hours were usually apportioned long beforehand. The unintelligent who had time on their hands, were simply, Miss Marple decided, no good.

She pondered in growing vexation and perplexity.

Then suddenly her forehead cleared. She ejaculated aloud a name.

"Of course!" said Miss Marple. "Lucy Eyelesbarrow!"

4

The name of Lucy Eyelesbarrow had already made itself felt in certain circles.

Lucy Eyelesbarrow was thirty-two. She had taken a First in mathematics at Oxford, was acknowledged to have a brilliant mind and was confidently expected to take up a distinguished academic career.

But Lucy Eyelesbarrow, in addition to scholarly brilliance, had a core of good, sound common sense. She could not fail to observe that a life of academic distinction was singularly ill rewarded. She had no desire whatever to teach and she took pleasure in contacts with minds much less brilliant than her own. In short, she had a taste for people, all sorts of people—and not the same people the whole time. She also, quite frankly, liked money. To gain money one must exploit shortage.

Lucy Eyelesbarrow hit at once upon a very serious shortage—the shortage of any kind of skilled domestic labor. To the amazement of her friends and fellow scholars, Lucy Eyelesbarrow entered the field of domestic labor.

Her success was immediate and assured. By now, after a lapse of some years, she was known all over the British Isles. It was quite customary for wives to say joyfully to husbands, "It will be all right. I can go with you to the States. *I've got Lucy Eyelesbarrow!*" The point of Lucy Eyelesbarrow was that once she came into a house, all worry, anxiety and hard work went out of it. Lucy Eyelesbarrow did everything, saw to everything, arranged everything. She was unbelievably competent in every conceivable sphere. She looked after elderly parents, accepted the care of young children, nursed the sickly, cooked divinely, got on well with any old crusted servants there might happen to be (there usually weren't), was tactful with impossible people, soothed habitual drunkards, was wonderful with dogs. Best of all she never minded what she did. She scrubbed the kitchen floor, dug in the garden, cleaned up dog messes and carried coals!

One of her rules was never to accept an engagement for any long length of time. A fortnight was her usual period—a month at most under exceptional circumstances. For that fortnight you had to pay the earth! But, during that fortnight, your life was heaven. You could relax completely, go abroad, stay at home, do as you pleased, secure that all was going well on the home front in Lucy Eyelesbarrow's capable hands.

Naturally the demand for her services was enormous. She could have booked herself up if she chose for about three years ahead. She had been offered enormous sums to go as a permanency. But Lucy had no intention of being a permanency, nor would she book herself for more than six months ahead. And within that period, unknown to her clamoring clients, she always kept certain free periods which enabled her either to take a short luxurious holiday (since she spent nothing otherwise and was handsomely paid and kept) or to accept any position at short notice that happened to take her fancy, either by reason of its character, or because she "liked the people." Since she was now at liberty to pick and choose among the vociferous claimants for her services, she went very largely by personal liking. Mere riches would not buy you the services of Lucy Eyelesbarrow. She could pick and choose and she did pick and choose. She enjoyed her life very much and found in it a continual source of entertainment.

Lucy Eyelesbarrow read and reread the letter from Miss Marple. She had made Miss Marple's acquaintance two years ago when her services had been retained by Raymond West, the novelist, to go and look after his old aunt who was recovering from pneumonia. Lucy had accepted the job and had gone down to St. Mary Mead. She had liked Miss Marple very much. As for Miss Marple, once she had caught a glimpse out of her bedroom window of Lucy Eyelesbarrow really trenching for sweet peas in the proper way, she had leaned back on her pillows with a sigh of relief, eaten the tempting little meals that Lucy Eyelesbarrow brought to her, and listened, agreeably surprised, to the tales told by her elderly irascible maidservant of how "I taught that Miss Eyelesbarrow a crochet pattern what she'd never heard of! Proper grateful she was." And had surprised her doctor by the rapidity of her convalescence.

Miss Marple wrote asking if Miss Eyelesbarrow could undertake a certain task for her—rather an unusual one. Perhaps Miss Eyelesbarrow could arrange a meeting at which they could discuss the matter.

Lucy Eyelesbarrow frowned for a moment or two as she considered. She was in reality fully booked up. But the word unusual, and her recollection of Miss Marple's personality, carried the day and she rang up Miss Marple straightaway explaining that she could not come down to St. Mary Mead as she was at the moment working, but that she was free from two to four on the following afternoon and could meet Miss Marple anywhere in London. She suggested her own club, a rather nondescript establishment which had the advantage of having several small, dark writing rooms which were usually empty.

Miss Marple accepted the suggestion and on the following day the meeting took place.

Greetings were exchanged; Lucy Eyelesbarrow led her guest to the gloomiest of the writing rooms, and said: "I'm afraid I'm rather booked up just at present, but perhaps you'll tell me what it is you want me to undertake?"

"It's very simple, really," said Miss Marple. "Unusual, but simple. I want you to find a body."

For a moment the suspicion crossed Lucy's mind that Miss Marple was mentally unhinged, but she rejected the idea. Miss Marple was eminently sane. She meant exactly what she had said.

"What kind of a body?" asked Lucy Eyelesbarrow with admirable composure.

"A woman's body," said Miss Marple. "The body of a woman who was murdered—strangled actually—in a train."

Lucy's eyebrows rose slightly.

"Well, that's certainly unusual. Tell me about it."

Miss Marple told her. Lucy Eyelesbarrow listened attentively, without interrupting. At the end she said:

"It all depends on what your friend saw—or thought she saw—?"

She left the sentence unfinished with a question in it.

"Elspeth McGillicuddy doesn't imagine things," said Miss Marple. "That's why I'm relying on what she said. If it had been Dorothy Cartwright, now, it would have been quite a different matter. Dorothy always has a good story and quite often believes it herself, and there is usually a kind of basis of truth but certainly no more. But Elspeth is the kind of woman who finds it very hard to make herself believe that anything at all extraordinary or out of the way could happen. She's most unsuggestible, rather like granite."

"I see," said Lucy thoughtfully. "Well, let's accept it all. Where do I come in?"

"I was very much impressed by you," said Miss Marple, "and you see I haven't got the physical strength nowadays to get about and do things."

"You want me to make inquiries? That sort of thing? But won't the police have done all that? Or do you think they have been just slack?"

"Oh no," said Miss Marple. "They haven't been slack. It's just that I've got a theory about the woman's body. It's got to be somewhere. If it wasn't found in the train, then it must have been pushed or thrown out of the train—but it hasn't been discovered anywhere on the line. So I traveled down the same way to see if there was anywhere where the body could have been thrown off the train and yet wouldn't have been found on the line—and there was. The railway line makes a big curve before getting into Brackhampton, on the edge of a high embankment. If a body were thrown out there, when the train was leaning at an angle, I think it would pitch right down the embankment."

"But surely it would still be found—even there?"

"Oh yes. It would have to be taken away. But we'll come to that presently. Here's the place—on this map."

Lucy bent to study where Miss Marple's finger pointed.

"It is right in the outskirts of Brackhampton now," said Miss Marple, "but originally it was a country house with extensive park and grounds and it's still there, untouched—ringed round now with building estates and small suburban houses. It's called Rutherford Hall. It was built by a man called Crackenthorpe, a very rich manufacturer, in 1884. The original Crackenthorpe's son, an elderly man, is living there still with, I understand, a daughter. The railway encircles quite half of the property."

"And you want me to do—what?"

Miss Marple replied promptly.

"I want you to get a post there. Everyone is crying out for efficient domestic help. I should not imagine it would be difficult."

"No, I don't suppose it would be difficult."

"I understand that Mr. Crackenthorpe is said locally to be somewhat of a miser. If you accept a low salary, I will make it up to the proper figure which should, I think, be rather more than the current rate."

"Because of the difficulty?"

"Not the difficulty so much as the danger. It might, you know, be dangerous. It's only right to warn you of that."

"I don't know," said Lucy pensively, "that the idea of danger would deter me."

"I didn't think it would," said Miss Marple. "You're not that kind of person."

"I dare say you thought it might even attract me? I've encountered very little danger in my life. But do you really believe it might be dangerous?"

"Somebody," Miss Marple pointed out, "has committed a very successful crime. There has been no hue and cry, no real suspicion. Two elderly ladies have told a rather improbable story, the police have investigated it and found nothing in it. So everything is nice and quiet. I don't think that this somebody, whoever he may be, will care about the matter being raked up—especially if you are successful."

"What do I look for exactly?"

"Any signs along the embankment, a scrap of clothing, broken bushes —that kind of thing."

Lucy nodded.

"And then?"

"I shall be quite close at hand," said Miss Marple. "An old maidservant of mine, my faithful Florence, lives in Brackhampton. She has looked after her old parents for years. They are now both dead, and she takes in lodgers—all most respectable people. She has arranged for me to have rooms with her. She will look after me most devotedly, and I feel I should like to be close at hand. I would suggest that you mention you have an elderly aunt living in the neighborhood, and that you want a post within easy distance of her, and also that you stipulate for a reasonable amount of spare time so that you can go and see her often."

Again Lucy nodded.

"I was going to Taormina the day after tomorrow," she said. "The holiday can wait. But I can only promise three weeks. After that, I am booked up."

"Three weeks should be ample," said Miss Marple. "If we can't find out anything in three weeks, we might as well give up the whole thing as a mare's nest."

Miss Marple departed, and Lucy, after a moment's reflection, rang up a registry office in Brackhampton, the manageress of which she knew very well. She explained her desire for a post in the neighborhood so as to be near her "aunt." After turning down, with a little difficulty and a good deal of ingenuity, several more desirable places, Rutherford Hall was mentioned.

"That sounds exactly what I want," said Lucy firmly.

The registry office rang up Miss Crackenthorpe, Miss Crackenthorpe rang up Lucy.

Two days later Lucy left London en route for Rutherford Hall.

II

Driving her own small car, Lucy Eyelesbarrow turned through an imposing pair of vast iron gates. Just inside them was what had originally been a small lodge which now seemed completely derelict, whether through war damage or merely through neglect, it was difficult to be sure. A long, winding drive led through large gloomy clumps of rhododendrons up to the house. Lucy caught her breath in a slight gasp when she saw the house which was a kind of miniature Windsor Castle. The stone steps in front of the door could have done with attention and the gravel sweep was green with neglected weeds.

She pulled an old-fashioned wrought-iron bell, and its clamor sounded echoing away inside. A slatternly woman, wiping her hands on her apron, opened the door and looked at her suspiciously.

"Expected, aren't you?" she said. "Miss Somethingbarrow, she told me."

"Quite right," said Lucy.

The house was desperately cold inside. Her guide led her along a dark hall and opened a door on the right. Rather to Lucy's surprise, it was quite a pleasant sitting room, with books and chintz-covered chairs.

"I'll tell Her," said the woman, and went away shutting the door after having given Lucy a look of profound disfavor.

After a few minutes the door opened again. From the first moment Lucy decided that she liked Emma Crackenthorpe.

She was a middle-aged woman with no very outstanding characteristics, neither good looking nor plain, sensibly dressed in tweeds and pullover, with dark hair swept back from her forehead, steady hazel eyes and a very pleasant voice.

She said: "Miss Eyelesbarrow?" and held out her hand.

Then she looked doubtful.

"I wonder," she said, "if this post is really what you're looking for? I don't want a housekeeper, you know, to supervise things. I want someone to do the work."

Lucy said that that was what most people needed.

Emma Crackenthorpe said apologetically:

"So many people, you know, seem to think that just a little light dusting will answer the case, but I can do all the light dusting myself."

"I quite understand," said Lucy. "You want cooking and washing up, and housework and stoking the boiler. That's all right. That's what I do. I'm not at all afraid of work."

"It's a big house, I'm afraid, and inconvenient. Of course we only live in a portion of it—my father and myself, that is. He is rather an invalid. We live quite quietly, and there is an Aga stove. I have several brothers, but they are not here very often. Two women come in, a Mrs. Kidder in the morning and Mrs. Hart three days a week, to do brasses and things like that. You have your own car?"

"Yes. It can stand out in the open if there's nowhere to put it. It's used to it."

"Oh, there are any amount of old stables. There's no trouble about that." She frowned a moment, then said, "Eyelesbarrow—rather an unusual name. Some friends of mine were telling me about a Lucy Eyelesbarrow—the Kennedys?"

"Yes. I was with them in North Devon when Mrs. Kennedy was having a baby."

Emma Crackenthorpe smiled.

"I know they said they'd never had such a wonderful time as when you were there seeing to everything. But I had the idea that you were terribly expensive. The sum I mentioned—"

"That's quite all right," said Lucy. "I want particularly, you see, to be near Brackhampton. I have an elderly aunt in a critical state of health and I want to be within easy distance of her. That's why the salary is a secondary consideration. I can't afford to do nothing. If I could be sure of having some time off most days?"

"Oh, of course. Every afternoon, till six, if you like?"

"That seems perfect."

Miss Crackenthorpe hesitated a moment before saying: "My father is elderly and a little—difficult—sometimes. He is very keen on economy, and he says things sometimes that upset people. I wouldn't like—"

Lucy broke in quickly.

"I'm quite used to elderly people of all kinds," she said. "I always manage to get on well with them."

Emma Crackenthorpe looked relieved.

"Trouble with father!" diagnosed Lucy. "I bet he's an old tartar."

She was apportioned a large, gloomy bedroom which a small electric heater did its inadequate best to warm, and was shown round the house, a vast uncomfortable mansion. As they passed a door in the hall a voice roared out:

"That you, Emma? Got the new girl there? Bring her in. I want to look at her."

Emma flushed, glanced at Lucy apologetically.

The two women entered the room. It was richly upholstered in dark velvet, the narrow windows let in very little light, and it was full of heavy mahogany Victorian furniture.

Old Mr. Crackenthorpe was stretched out in an invalid's chair, a silver-headed stick by his side.

He was a big gaunt man, his flesh hanging in loose folds. He had a face rather like a bulldog, with a pugnacious chin. He had thick, dark hair flecked with gray, and small suspicious eyes.

"Let's have a look at you, young lady."

Lucy advanced, composed and smiling.

"There's just one thing you'd better understand straight away. Just because we live in a big house doesn't mean we're rich. We're not rich. We live simply—do you hear?—simply! No good coming here with a lot of highfalutin ideas. Cod's as good a fish as turbot any day and don't you forget it. I don't stand for waste. I live here because my father built the house and I like it. After I'm dead they can sell it up if they want to— and I expect they will want to. No sense of family. This house is well built —it's solid, and we've got our own land round us. Keeps us private. It would bring in a lot for building land but not while I'm alive. You won't get me out of here until you take me out feet first."

He glared at Lucy.

"Your house is your castle," said Lucy.

"Laughing at me?"

"Of course not. I think it's very exciting to have a real country place all surrounded by town."

"Quite so. Can't see another house from here, can you? Fields with cows in them—right in the middle of Brackhampton. You hear the traffic a bit when the wind's that way, but otherwise it's still country."

He added, without pause or change of tone, to his daughter:

"Ring up that damnfool of a doctor. Tell him that last medicine's no good at all."

Lucy and Emma retired. He shouted after them:

"And don't let that damned woman who sniffs dust in here. She's disarranged all my books."

Lucy asked:

"Has Mr. Crackenthorpe been an invalid long?"

Emma said, rather evasively:

"Oh, for years now . . . This is the kitchen."

The kitchen was enormous. A vast kitchen range stood cold and neglected. An Aga stood demurely beside it.

Lucy asked times of meals and inspected the larder. Then she said cheerfully to Emma Crackenthorpe:

"I know everything now. Don't bother. Leave it all to me."

Emma Crackenthorpe heaved a sigh of relief as she went up to bed that night.

"The Kennedys were quite right," she said. "She's wonderful."

Lucy rose at six the next morning. She did the house, prepared vegetables, assembled, cooked and served breakfast. With Mrs. Kidder she made the beds and at eleven o'clock they sat down to strong tea and biscuits in the kitchen. Mollified by the fact that Lucy "had no airs about her" and also by the strength and sweetness of the tea, Mrs. Kidder relaxed into gossip. She was a small, spare woman with a sharp eye and tight lips.

"Regular old skinflint he is. What She has to put up with! All the same, She's not what I call downtrodden. Can hold her own all right when She has to. When the gentlemen come down She sees to it there's something decent to eat."

"The gentlemen?"

"Yes. Big family it was. The eldest, Mr. Edmund, he was killed in the war. Then there's Mr. Cedric, he lives abroad somewhere. He's not married. Paints pictures in foreign parts. Mr. Harold's in the City, lives in London—married an earl's daughter. Then there's Mr. Alfred, he's got a nice way with him, but he's a bit of a black sheep, been in trouble once or twice—and there's Miss Edith's husband, Mr. Bryan, ever so nice he is. She died some years ago, but he's always stayed one of the family. And there's Master Alexander, Miss Edith's little boy. He's at school, comes here for part of the holidays always; Miss Emma's terribly set on him."

Lucy digested all this information, continuing to press tea on her informant. Finally, reluctantly, Mrs. Kidder rose to her feet.

"Seem to have got along a treat we do, this morning," she said wonderingly. "Want me to give you a hand with the potatoes, dear?"

"They're already done."

"Well, you are a one for getting on with things! I might as well be getting along myself as there doesn't seem anything else to do."

Mrs. Kidder departed and Lucy, with time on her hands, scrubbed the kitchen table which she had been longing to do, but which she had put off so as not to offend Mrs. Kidder whose job it properly was. Then she cleaned the silver till it shone radiantly. She cooked lunch, cleared it away, washed up, and at two-thirty was ready to start exploration. She had set out the tea things ready on a tray, with sandwiches and bread and butter covered over with a damp napkin to keep them moist.

She strolled first round the gardens which would be the normal thing to do. The kitchen garden was sketchily cultivated with a few vegetables. The hothouses were in ruins. The paths everywhere were overgrown with weeds. A herbaceous border near the house was the only thing that showed free of weeds and in good condition and Lucy suspected that that had been Emma's hand. The gardener was a very old man, somewhat deaf, who was only making a show of working. Lucy spoke to him pleasantly. He lived in a cottage adjacent to the big stable yard.

Extending out from the stable yard, a back drive led through the park, which was fenced on either side of it, and under a railway arch into a small back lane.

Every few minutes a train thundered along the main line over the railway arch. Lucy watched the trains as they slackened speed going round the sharp curve that encircled the Crackenthorpe property. She passed under the railway arch and out into the lane. It seemed a little-used track. On the one side was the railway embankment, on the other was a high wall which enclosed some tall factory buildings. Lucy followed the lane until it came out into a street of small houses. She could hear a short distance away the busy hum of main-road traffic. She glanced at her watch. A woman came out of a house nearby and Lucy stopped her.

"Excuse me, can you tell me if there is a public telephone near here?"

"Post office just at the corner of the road."

Lucy thanked her and walked along until she came to the post office, which was a combination shop and post office. There was a telephone box at one side. Lucy went into it and made a call. She asked to speak to Miss Marple. A woman's voice spoke in a sharp bark.

"She's resting. And I'm not going to disturb her! She needs her rest—she's an old lady. Who shall I say called?"

"Miss Eyelesbarrow. There's no need to disturb her. Just tell her that I've arrived and everything is going on well and that I'll let her know when I've any news."

She replaced the receiver and made her way back to Rutherford Hall.

5

"I suppose it will be all right if I just practice a few iron shots in the park?" asked Lucy.

"Oh yes, certainly. Are you fond of golf?"

"I'm not much good, but I like to keep in practice. It's a more agreeable form of exercise than just going for a walk."

"Nowhere to walk outside this place," growled Mr. Crackenthorpe. "Nothing but pavements and miserable little bandboxes of houses. Like to get hold of my land and build more of them. But they won't until I'm dead. And I'm not going to die to oblige anybody. I can tell you that! Not to oblige anybody!"

Emma Crackenthorpe said mildly:

"Now, Father."

"I know what they think—and what they're waiting for. All of 'em. Cedric, and that sly fox Harold with his smug face. As for Alfred I wonder he hasn't had a shot at bumping me off himself. Not sure he didn't, at Christmastime. That was a very odd turn I had. Puzzled old Quimper. He asked me a lot of discreet questions."

"Everyone gets these digestive upsets now and again, Father."

"All right, all right, say straight out that I ate too much! That's what you mean. And why did I eat too much? Because there was too much food on the table, far too much. Wasteful and extravagant. And that reminds me—you, young woman. Five potatoes you sent in for lunch—good-sized ones, too. Two potatoes are enough for anybody. So don't send in more than four in future. The extra one was wasted today."

"It wasn't wasted, Mr. Crackenthorpe. I've planned to use it in a Spanish omelet tonight."

"Urgh!" As Lucy went out of the room carrying the coffee tray she heard him say, "Slick young woman, that, always got all the answers. Cooks well, though—and she's a handsome kind of girl."

Lucy Eyelesbarrow took a light iron out of the set of golf clubs she had had the forethought to bring with her and strolled out into the park, climbing over the fencing.

She began playing a series of shots. After five minutes or so, a ball, apparently sliced, pitched on the side of the railway embankment. Lucy went up and began to hunt about for it. She looked back toward the house. It was a long way off and nobody was in the least interested in what she was doing. She continued to hunt for the ball. Now and then she played shots from the embankment down into the grass. During the afternoon she searched about a third of the embankment. Nothing. She played her ball back toward the house.

Then, on the next day, she came upon something. A thornbush growing about halfway up the bank had been snapped off. Bits of it lay scattered about. Lucy examined the tree itself. Impaled on one of the thorns was a torn scrap of fur. It was almost the same color as the wood, a pale brownish color. Lucy looked at it for a moment, then she took a pair of scissors out of her pocket and snipped it carefully in half. The half she had snipped off she put in an envelope which she had in her pocket. She came down the steep slope searching about for anything else. She looked carefully at the rough grass of the field. She thought she could distinguish a kind of track which someone had made walking through the long grass.

But it was very faint—not nearly so clear as her own tracks were. It must have been made some time ago and it was too sketchy for her to be sure that it was not merely imagination on her part.

She began to hunt carefully down in the grass at the foot of the embankment just below the broken thornbush. Presently her search was rewarded. She found a powder compact, a small cheap enameled affair. She wrapped it in her handkerchief and put it in her pocket. She searched on but did not find anything more.

On the following afternoon, she got into her car and went to see her invalid aunt. Emma Crackenthorpe said kindly, "Don't hurry back. We shan't want you until dinnertime."

"Thank you, but I shall be back at six by the latest."

No. 4, Madison Road was a small drab house in a small drab street. It had very clean Nottingham lace curtains, a shining white doorstep and a well-polished brass door-handle. The door was opened by a tall, grim-looking woman, dressed in black with a large knob of iron-gray hair.

She eyed Lucy in suspicious appraisal as she showed her in to Miss Marple.

Miss Marple was occupying the back sitting room which looked out on to a small, tidy square of garden. It was aggressively clean with a lot of mats and doilies, a great many china ornaments, a rather big Jacobean suite and two ferns in pots. Miss Marple was sitting in a big chair by the fire busily engaged in crocheting.

Lucy came in and shut the door. She sat down in the chair facing Miss Marple.

"Well!" she said, "it looks as though you were right."

She produced her findings and gave the details of their discovery.

A faint flush of achievement came into Miss Marple's cheeks.

"Perhaps one ought not to feel so," she said, "but it is rather gratifying to form a theory and get proof that it is correct!"

She fingered the small tuft of fur. "Elspeth said the woman was wearing a light-colored fur coat. I suppose the compact was in the pocket of the coat and fell out as the body rolled down the slope. It doesn't seem distinctive in any way, but it may help. You didn't take all the fur?"

"No, I left half of it on the thornbush."

Miss Marple nodded approval.

"Quite right. You are very intelligent, my dear. The police will want to check exactly."

"You are going to the police—with these things?"

"Well—not quite yet. . . ." Miss Marple considered. "It would be better, I think, to find the body first. Don't you?"

"Yes, but isn't that rather a tall order? I mean, granting that your estimate is correct. The murderer pushed the body out of the train, then presumably got out himself at Brackhampton and at some time—probably that same night—came along and removed the body. But what happened after that? He may have taken it anywhere."

"Not anywhere," said Miss Marple. "I don't think you've followed the thing to its logical conclusion, my dear Miss Eyelesbarrow."

"Do call me Lucy. Why not anywhere?"

"Because, if so, he might much more easily have killed the girl in some lonely spot and driven the body away from there. You haven't appreciated—"

Lucy interrupted.

"Are you saying—do you mean—that this was a premeditated crime?"

"I didn't think so at first," said Miss Marple. "One wouldn't—naturally. It seemed like a quarrel and a man losing control and strangling the girl and then being faced with the problem of disposing of his victim—a problem which he had to solve within a very few minutes. But it really is too much of a coincidence that he should kill the girl in a fit of passion, and then look out of the window and find the train was going round a curve exactly at a spot where he could tip the body out, and where he could be sure of finding his way later and removing it! If he'd just thrown her out there by chance, he'd have done no more about it, and the body would, long before now, have been found."

She paused. Lucy stared at her.

"You know," said Miss Marple thoughtfully, "it's really quite a clever way to have planned a crime—and I think it was very carefully planned. There's something so anonymous about a train. If he'd killed her in the place where she lived or was staying, somebody might have noticed him come or go. Or if he'd driven her out into the country somewhere, someone might have noticed the car and its number and make. But a train is full of strangers coming and going. In a non-corridor carriage, alone with her, it was quite easy—especially if you realize that he knew exactly what he was going to do next. He knew—he must have known —all about Rutherford Hall—its geographical position, I mean, its queer isolation: an island bounded by railway lines."

"It is exactly like that," said Lucy. "It's an anachronism out of the past. Bustling urban life goes on all around it, but doesn't touch it. The tradespeople deliver in the mornings and that's all."

"So we assume, as you said, that the murderer comes to Rutherford Hall that night. It is already dark when the body falls and no one is likely to discover it before the next day."

"No, indeed."

"The murderer would come—how? In a car? Which way?"

Lucy considered.

"There's a rough lane, alongside a factory wall. He'd probably come that way, turn in under the railway arch and along the back drive. Then he could climb the fence, go along at the foot of the embankment, find the body, and carry it back to the car."

"And then," continued Miss Marple, "he took it to some place he had already chosen beforehand. This was all thought out, you know. And I don't think, as I say, that he would take it away from Rutherford Hall, or if so, not very far. The obvious thing, I suppose, would be to bury it somewhere?" She looked inquiringly at Lucy.

"I suppose so," said Lucy considering. "But it wouldn't be quite as easy as it sounds."

Miss Marple agreed.

"He couldn't bury it in the park. Too hard work and very noticeable. Somewhere where the earth was turned already?"

"The kitchen garden, perhaps, but that's very close to the gardener's cottage. He's old and deaf—but still it might be risky."

"Is there a dog?"

"No."

"Then in a shed, perhaps, or an outhouse?"

"That would be simpler and quicker. There are a lot of unused old buildings: broken down pigsties, harness rooms, workshops that nobody ever goes near. Or he might perhaps have thrust it into a clump of rhododendrons or shrubs somewhere."

Miss Marple nodded.

"Yes, I think that's much more probable."

There was a knock on the door and the grim Florence came in with a tray.

"Nice for you to have a visitor," she said to Miss Marple, "I've made you my special scones you used to like."

"Florence always made the most delicious teacakes," said Miss Marple.

Florence, gratified, creased her features into a totally unexpected smile and left the room.

"I think, my dear," said Miss Marple, "we won't talk any more about murder during tea. Such an unpleasant subject!"

II

After tea Lucy rose.

"I'll be getting back," she said. "As I've already told you, there's no one actually living at Rutherford Hall who could be the man we're looking for. There's only an old man and a middle-aged woman, and an old, deaf gardener."

"I didn't say he was actually living there," said Miss Marple. "All I mean is that he's someone who knows Rutherford Hall very well. But we can go into that after you've found the body."

"You seem to assume quite confidently that I shall find it," said Lucy. "I don't feel nearly so optimistic."

"I'm sure you will succeed, my dear Lucy. You are such an efficient person."

"In some ways, but I haven't had any experience in looking for bodies."

"I'm sure all it needs is a little common sense," said Miss Marple encouragingly.

Lucy looked at her, then laughed. Miss Marple smiled back at her.

Lucy set to work systematically the next afternoon.

She poked round outhouses, prodded the briars which wreathed the old pigsties, and was peering into the boiler room under the greenhouse when she heard a dry cough and turned to find old Hillman, the gardener, looking at her disapprovingly.

"You be careful you don't get a nasty fall, Miss," he warned her. "Them steps isn't safe, and you was up in the loft just now and the floor there ain't safe neither."

Lucy was careful to display no embarrassment.

"I expect you think I'm very nosy," she said cheerfully. "I was just wondering if something couldn't be made out of this place—growing mushrooms for the market, that sort of thing. Everything seems to have been let go terribly."

"That's the master, that is. Won't spend a penny. Ought to have two men and a boy here, I ought, to keep the place proper, but won't hear of it, he won't. Had all I could do to make him get a motor mower. Wanted me to mow all that front grass by hand, he did."

"But if the place could be made to pay—with some repairs?"

"Won't get a place like this to pay—too far gone. And he wouldn't care about that, anyway. Only cares about saving. Knows well enough what'll happen after he's gone—the young gentlemen'll sell up as fast as they can. Only waiting for him to pop off, they are. Going to come into a tidy lot of money when he dies, so I've heard."

"I suppose he's a very rich man?" said Lucy.

"Crackenthorpe's Fancies, that's what they are. The old gentleman started it, Mr. Crackenthorpe's father. A sharp one he was, by all accounts. Made his fortune and built this place. Hard as nails, they say, and never forgot an injury. But with all that, he was openhanded. Nothing of the miser about him. Disappointed in both his sons, so the story goes. Give 'em an education and brought 'em up to be gentlemen—Oxford and all. But they were too much of gentlemen to want to go into the business. The younger one married an actress and then smashed himself up in a car accident when he'd been drinking. The elder one, our one here, his father never fancied so much. Abroad a lot, he was, bought a lot of heathen statues and had them sent home. Wasn't so close with his money when he was young—come on him more in middle age, it did. No, they never did hit it off, him and his father, so I've heard."

Lucy digested this information with an air of polite interest. The old man leaned against the wall and prepared to go on with his saga. He much preferred talking to doing any work.

"Died afore the war, the old gentleman did. Terrible temper he had. Didn't do to give him any sauce, he wouldn't stand for it."

"And after he died, this Mr. Crackenthorpe came and lived here?"

"Him and his family, yes. Nigh to grown up they was by then."

"But surely— Oh, I see, you mean the 1914 war."

"No, I don't. Died in 1928, that's what I mean."

Lucy supposed that 1928 qualified as "before the war" though it was not the way she would have described it herself.

She said: "Well, I expect you'll be wanting to go on with your work. You mustn't let me keep you."

"Ar," said old Hillman without enthusiasm, "not much you can do this time of day. Light's too bad."

Lucy went back to the house, pausing to investigate a likely looking copse of birch and azalea on her way.

She found Emma Crackenthorpe standing in the hall reading a letter. The afternoon post had just been delivered.

"My nephew will be here tomorrow—with a school friend. Alexander's room is the one over the porch. The one next to it will do for James Stoddart-West. They'll use the bathroom just opposite."

"Yes, Miss Crackenthorpe. I'll see the rooms are prepared."

"They'll arrive in the morning before lunch." She hesitated. "I expect they'll be hungry."

"I bet they will," said Lucy. "Roast beef, do you think? And perhaps treacle tart?"

"Alexander's very fond of treacle tart."

The two boys arrived on the following morning. They both had well-brushed hair, suspiciously angelic faces, and perfect manners. Alexander Eastley had fair hair and blue eyes, Stoddart-West was dark and spectacled.

They discoursed gravely during lunch on events in the sporting world, with occasional references to the latest space fiction. Their manner was that of elderly professors discussing paleolithic implements. In comparison with them, Lucy felt quite young.

The sirloin of beef vanished in no time and every crumb of the treacle tart was consumed.

Mr. Crackenthorpe grumbled: "You two will eat me out of house and home."

Alexander gave him a blue-eyed reproving glance.

"We'll have bread and cheese if you can't afford meat, Grandfather."

"Afford it? I can afford it. I don't like waste."

"We haven't wasted any, sir," said Stoddart-West, looking down at his plate which bore clear testimony of that fact.

"You boys both eat twice as much as I do."

"We're at the body-building stage," Alexander explained. "We need a big intake of proteins."

The old man grunted.

As the two boys left the table, Lucy heard Alexander say apologetically to his friend:

"You mustn't pay any attention to my grandfather. He's on a diet or something and that makes him rather peculiar. He's terribly mean, too. I think it must be a complex of some kind."

Stoddart-West said comprehendingly:

"I had an aunt who kept thinking she was going bankrupt. Really, she had oodles of money. Pathological, the doctor said. Have you got that football, Alex?"

After she had cleared away and washed up lunch, Lucy went out. She could hear the boys calling out in the distance on the lawn. She herself went in the opposite direction, down the front drive and from there she struck across to some clumped masses of rhododendron bushes. She began to hunt carefully, holding back the leaves and peering inside. She moved from clump to clump systematically, and was raking inside with a golf club when the polite voice of Alexander Eastley made her start.

"Are you looking for something, Miss Eyelesbarrow?"

"A golf ball," said Lucy promptly. "Several golf balls, in fact. I've been practicing golf shots most afternoons and I've lost quite a lot of balls. I thought that today I really must find some of them."

"We'll help you," said Alexander obligingly.

"That's very kind of you. I thought you were playing football."

"One can't go on playing footer," explained Stoddart-West. "One gets too hot. Do you play a lot of golf?"

"I'm quite fond of it. I don't get much opportunity."

"I suppose you don't. You do the cooking here, don't you?"

"Yes."

"Did you cook the lunch today?"

"Yes. Was it all right?"

"Simply wizard," said Alexander. "We get awful meat at school, all dried up. I love beef that's pink and juicy inside. That treacle tart was pretty smashing, too."

"You must tell me what things you like best."

"Could we have apple meringue one day? It's my favorite thing."

"Of course."

Alexander sighed happily.

"There's a clock golf set under the stairs," he said. "We could fix it up on the lawn and do some putting. What about it, Stodders?"

"Good oh!" said Stoddart-West.

"He isn't really Australian," explained Alexander courteously. "But he's practicing talking that way in case his people take him out to see the Test Match next year."

Encouraged by Lucy, they went off to get the clock golf set. Later, as she returned to the house, she found them setting it out on the lawn and arguing about the position of the numbers.

"We don't want it like a clock," said Stoddart-West. "That's kid stuff. We want to make a course of it. Long holes and short ones. It's a pity the numbers are so rusty. You can hardly see them."

"They need a lick of white paint," said Lucy. "You might get some tomorrow and paint them."

"Good idea." Alexander's face lighted up. "I say, I believe there are some old pots of paint in the Long Barn—left there by the painters. Shall we see?"

"What's the Long Barn?" asked Lucy.

Alexander pointed to a long, stone building a little way from the house near the back drive.

"It's quite old," he said. "Grandfather calls it a Leak Barn and says it's Elizabethan, but that's just swank. It belonged to the farm that was here originally. My great-grandfather pulled it down and built this awful house instead."

He added: "A lot of grandfather's collection is in the barn. Things he had sent home from abroad when he was a young man. Most of them are pretty frightful, too. The Long Barn is used sometimes for whist drives and things like that. Women's Institute stuff. And Conservative Sales of Work. Come and see it."

Lucy accompanied them willingly.

There was a big oak, nail-studded door to the barn.

Alexander raised his hand and detached a key on a nail just under some ivy to the right hand of the top of the door. He turned it in the lock, pushed the door open and they went in.

At a first glance Lucy felt that she was in a singularly bad museum. The heads of two Roman emperors in marble glared at her out of bulging eyeballs, there was a huge sarcophagus of a decadent Greco-Roman period, a simpering Venus stood on a pedestal clutching her falling draperies. Besides these works of art, there were a couple of trestle tables, some stacked-up chairs, and sundry oddments such as a rusted hand mower, two buckets, a couple of moth-eaten car seats, and a green-painted, iron garden seat that had lost a leg.

"I think I saw the paint over here," said Alexander vaguely. He went to a corner and pulled aside a tattered curtain that shut it off.

They found a couple of paint pots and brushes; the latter dry and stiff.

"You really need some turpentine," said Lucy.

They could not, however, find any. The boys suggested bicycling off to get some, and Lucy urged them to do so. Painting the clock golf numbers would keep them amused for some time, she thought.

The boys went off, leaving her in the barn.

"This really could do with a clear up," she had murmured.

"I shouldn't bother," Alexander advised her. "It gets cleaned up if it's going to be used for anything, but it's practically never used this time of year."

"Do I hang the key up outside the door again? Is that where it's kept?"

"Yes. There's nothing to pinch here, you see. Nobody would want those awful marble things and anyway they weigh a ton."

Lucy agreed with him. She could hardly admire old Mr. Crackenthorpe's taste in art. He seemed to have an unerring instinct for selecting the worst specimen of any period.

She stood looking round her after the boys had gone. Her eyes came to rest on the sarcophagus and stayed there.

That sarcophagus. . . .

The air in the barn was faintly musty as though unaired for a long time. She went over to the sarcophagus. It had a heavy, close-fitting lid. Lucy looked at it speculatively.

Then she left the barn, went to the kitchen, found a heavy crowbar and returned.

It was not an easy task but Lucy toiled doggedly.

Slowly the lid began to rise, pried up by the crowbar.

It rose sufficiently for Lucy to see what was inside.

6

A few minutes later Lucy, rather pale, left the barn, locked the door and put the key back on the nail.

She went rapidly to the stables, got out her car and drove down the back drive. She stopped at the post office at the end of the road. She went into the telephone box, put in the money and dialed.

"I want to speak to Miss Marple."

"She's resting, Miss. It's Miss Eyelesbarrow, isn't it?"

"Yes."

"I'm not going to disturb her and that's flat, Miss. She's an old lady and she needs her rest."

"You must disturb her. It's urgent."

"I'm not—"

"Please do what I say at once."

When she chose, Lucy's voice could be as incisive as steel. Florence knew authority when she heard it.

Presently Miss Marple's voice spoke.

"Yes, Lucy?"

Lucy drew a deep breath.

"You were quite right," she said. "I've found it."

"A woman's body?"

"Yes. A woman in a fur coat. It's in a stone sarcophagus in a kind of Barn-*cum*-Museum near the house. What do you want me to do? I ought to inform the police, I think."

"Yes. You must inform the police. At once."

"But what about the rest of it? About you? The first thing they'll want to know is why I was prying up a lid that weighs tons for apparently no reason. Do you want me to invent a reason? I can."

"No. I think, you know," said Miss Marple in her gentle serious voice, "that the only thing to do is to tell the exact truth."

"About you?"

"About everything."

A sudden grin split the whiteness of Lucy's face.

"That will be quite simple for me," she said. "But I imagine they'll find it quite hard to believe!"

She rang off, waited a moment and then rang and got the police station.

"I have just discovered a dead body in a sarcophagus in the Long Barn at Rutherford Hall."

"What's that?"

Lucy repeated her statement and anticipating the next question gave her name.

She drove back, put the car away and entered the house.

She paused in the hall for a moment, thinking.

Then she gave a brief sharp nod of the head and went to the library where Miss Crackenthorpe was sitting helping her father to do the *Times* crossword.

"Can I speak to you a moment, Miss Crackenthorpe?"

Emma looked up, a shade of apprehension on her face. The apprehension was, Lucy thought, purely domestic. In such words do useful household staff announce their imminent departure.

"Well, speak up, girl, speak up," said old Mr. Crackenthorpe irritably.

Lucy said to Emma, "I'd like to speak to you alone, please."

"Nonsense," said Mr. Crackenthorpe. "You say straight out here what you've got to say."

"Just a moment, Father." Emma rose and went toward the door.

"All nonsense. It can wait," said the old man angrily.

"I'm afraid it can't wait," said Lucy.

Mr. Crackenthorpe said, "What impertinence!"

Emma came out into the hall. Lucy followed her and shut the door behind them.

"Yes?" said Emma, "what is it? If you think there's too much to do with the boys here, I can help you and—"

"It's not that at all," said Lucy. "I didn't want to speak before your father because I understand he is an invalid and it might give him a shock. You see, I've just discovered the body of a murdered woman in that big sarcophagus in the Long Barn."

Emma Crackenthorpe stared at her.

"In the sarcophagus? A murdered woman? It's impossible!"

"I'm afraid it's quite true. I've rung up the police. They will be here at any minute."

A slight flush came into Emma's cheek.

"You should have told me first—before notifying the police."

"I'm sorry," said Lucy.

"I didn't hear you ring up—" Emma's glance went to the telephone on the hall table.

"I rang up from the post office just down the road."

"But how extraordinary—why not from here?"

Lucy thought quickly.

"I was afraid the boys might be about—might hear—if I rang up from the hall here."

"I see . . . Yes—I see. They are coming—the police, I mean?"

"They're here now," said Lucy, as with a squeal of brakes a car drew up at the front door and the bell pealed through the house.

II

"I'm sorry, very sorry—to have asked this of you," said Inspector Bacon.

His hand under her arm, he led Emma Crackenthorpe out of the barn. Emma's face was very pale; she looked sick, but she walked firmly erect.

"I'm quite sure that I've never seen the woman before in my life."

"We're very grateful to you, Miss Crackenthorpe. That's all I wanted to know. Perhaps you'd like to lie down?"

"I must go to my father. I telephoned to Doctor Quimper as soon as I heard about this and he is with him now."

Doctor Quimper came out of the library as they crossed the hall. He was a tall, genial man, with a casual, offhand, cynical manner that his patients found very stimulating.

He and the Inspector nodded to each other.

"Miss Crackenthorpe has performed an unpleasant task very bravely," said Bacon.

"Well done, Emma," said the doctor, patting her on the shoulder. "You can take things. I've always known that. Your father's all right. Just go in and have a word with him, and then go into the dining room and get yourself a glass of brandy. That's a prescription."

Emma smiled at him gratefully and went into the library.

"That woman's the salt of the earth," said the doctor looking after her. "A thousand pities she's never married. The penalty of being the only female in a family of men. The other sister got clear, married at seventeen, I believe. This one's quite a handsome woman, really. She'd have been a success as a wife and mother."

"Too devoted to her father, I suppose," said Inspector Bacon.

"She's not really as devoted as all that—but she's got the instinct some women have to make their men folk happy. She sees that her father likes being an invalid, so she lets him be an invalid. She's the same with her brothers. Cedric feels he's a good painter, what's-his-name, Harold, knows how much she relies on his sound judgment—she lets Alfred shock her with his stories of his clever deals. Oh yes, she's a clever woman— no fool. Well, do you want me for anything? Want me to have a look at your corpse now Johnstone has done with it" (Johnstone was the police surgeon) "and see if it happens to be one of my medical mistakes?"

"I'd like you to have a look, yes, Doctor. We want to get her identified. I suppose it's impossible for old Mr. Crackenthorpe? Too much of a strain?"

"Strain? Fiddlesticks. He'd never forgive you or me if you didn't let him have a peep. He's all agog. Most exciting thing that's happened to him for fifteen years or so—and it won't cost him anything!"

"There's nothing really much wrong with him, then?"

"He's seventy-two," said the doctor. "That's all, really, that's the matter with him. He has odd rheumatic twinges—who doesn't? So he calls it arthritis. He has palpitations after meals—as well he may—he puts them down to 'heart.' But he can always do anything he wants to do! I've plenty of patients like that. The ones who are really ill usually insist desperately that they're perfectly well. Come on, let's go and see this body of yours. Unpleasant, I suppose?"

"Johnstone estimates she's been dead between a fortnight and three weeks."

"Quite unpleasant, then."

The doctor stood by the sarcophagus and looked down with frank curiosity, professionally unmoved by what he had named the "unpleasantness."

"Never seen her before. No patient of mine. I don't remember ever seeing her about in Brackhampton. She must have been quite good-looking once—hm— Somebody had it in for her all right."

They went out again into the air. Doctor Quimper glanced up at the building.

"Found in the—what do they call it?—the Long Barn—in a sarcophagus! Fantastic! Who found her?"

"Miss Lucy Eyelesbarrow."

"Oh, the latest lady help? What was she doing, poking about in sarcophagi?"

"That," said Inspector Bacon grimly, "is just what I am going to ask her. Now, about Mr. Crackenthorpe. Will you—?"

"I'll bring him along."

Mr. Crackenthorpe, muffled in scarves, came walking at a brisk pace, the doctor beside him.

"Disgraceful," he said. "Absolutely disgraceful! I brought back that sarcophagus from Florence in—let me see—it must have been in 1908—or was it 1909?"

"Steady now," the doctor warned him. "This isn't going to be nice, you know."

"No matter how ill I am, I've got to do my duty, haven't I?"

A very brief visit inside the Long Barn was, however, quite long enough. Mr. Crackenthorpe shuffled out into the air again with remarkable speed.

"Never saw her before in my life!" he said. "What's it mean? Absolutely disgraceful. It wasn't Florence—I remember now—it was Naples. A very fine specimen. And some fool of a woman has to come and get herself killed in it!"

He clutched at the folds of his overcoat on the left side.

"Too much for me . . . My heart . . . Where's Emma? Doctor. . . ."

Doctor Quimper took his arm.

"You'll be all right," he said. "I prescribe a little stimulant. Brandy."

They went back together toward the house.

"Sir. Please, sir."

Inspector Bacon turned. Two boys had arrived, breathless, on bicycles. Their faces were full of eager pleading.

"Please, sir, can we see the body?"

"No, you can't," said Inspector Bacon.

"Oh sir, please, sir. You never know. We might know who she was. Oh please, sir, do be a sport. It's not fair. Here's a murder, right in our own barn. It's the sort of chance that might never happen again. Do be a sport, sir."

"Who are you two?"

"I'm Alexander Eastley and this is my friend James Stoddart-West."

"Have you ever seen a blonde woman wearing a light-colored, dyed squirrel coat anywhere about the place?"

"Well—I can't remember exactly," said Alexander astutely. "If I were to have a look—"

"Take 'em in, Sanders," said Inspector Bacon to the constable who was standing by the barn door. "One's only young once!"

"Oh sir, thank you, sir." Both boys were vociferous. "It's very kind of you, sir."

Bacon turned away toward the house.

"And now," he said to himself grimly, "for Miss Lucy Eyelesbarrow!"

III

After leading the police to the Long Barn and giving a brief account of her actions, Lucy had retired into the background, but she was under no illusion that the police had finished with her.

She was preparing potatoes for chips that evening when word was brought to her that Inspector Bacon required her presence. Putting aside the large bowl of cold water and salt in which the chips were reposing, Lucy followed the policeman to where the Inspector awaited her. She sat down and awaited his questions composedly.

She gave her name, her address in London, and added of her own accord:

"I will give you some names and addresses of reference if you want to know all about me."

The names were very good ones. An Admiral of the Fleet, the provost of an Oxford college and a Dame of the British Empire. In spite of himself Inspector Bacon was impressed.

"Now, Miss Eyelesbarrow, you went into the Long Barn to find some paint—is that right? And after having found the paint you got a crowbar, forced up the lid of this sarcophagus and found the body. What were you looking for in the sarcophagus?"

"I was looking for a body," said Lucy.

"You were looking for a body—and you found one! Doesn't that seem to you a very extraordinary story?"

"Oh yes, it is an extraordinary story. Perhaps you will let me explain it to you."

"I certainly think you had better do so."

Lucy gave him a precise recital of the events which had led up to her sensational discovery.

The Inspector summed it up in an outraged voice.

"You were engaged by an elderly lady to obtain a post here and to search the house and grounds for a dead body? Is that right?"

"Yes."

"Who is this elderly lady?"

"Miss Jane Marple. She is at present living at 4 Madison Road."

The Inspector wrote it down.

"You expect me to believe this story?"

Lucy said gently:

"Not, perhaps, until after you have interviewed Miss Marple and got her confirmation of it."

"I shall interview her all right. She must be cracked."

Lucy forbore to point out that to be proved right is not really a proof of mental incapacity. Instead she said:

"What are you proposing to tell Miss Crackenthorpe? About me, I mean?"

"Why do you ask?"

"Well, as far as Miss Marple is concerned I've done my job. I've found the body she wanted found. But I'm still engaged by Miss Crackenthorpe, and there are two hungry boys in the house and probably some more of the family will soon be coming down after all this upset. She needs domestic help. If you go and tell her that I only took this post in order to hunt for dead bodies she'll probably throw me out. Otherwise I can get on with my job and be useful."

The Inspector looked hard at her.

"I'm not saying anything to anyone at present," he said. "I haven't verified your statement yet. For all I know you may be making the whole thing up."

Lucy rose.

"Thank you. Then I'll go back to the kitchen and get on with things."

7

"We'd better have the Yard in on it; is that what you think, Bacon?"

The Chief Constable looked inquiringly at Inspector Bacon. The Inspector was a big solid man—his expression was that of one utterly disgusted with humanity.

"The woman wasn't a local, sir," he said. "There's some reason to believe—from her underclothing—that she might have been a foreigner. Of course," added Inspector Bacon hastily, "I'm not letting on about that yet awhile. We're keeping it up our sleeves until after the inquest."

The Chief Constable nodded.

"The inquest will be purely formal, I suppose?"

"Yes, sir. I've seen the coroner."

"And it's fixed for—when?"

"Tomorrow. I understand the other members of the Crackenthorpe family will be here for it. There's just a chance one of them might be able to identify her. They'll all be here."

He consulted a list he held in his hand.

"Harold Crackenthorpe, he's something in the City—quite an important figure, I understand. Alfred—don't quite know what he does. Cedric—that's the one who lives abroad. Paints!" The Inspector invested the word with its full quota of sinister significance. The Chief Constable smiled into his mustache.

"No reason, is there, to believe the Crackenthorpe family are connected with the crime in any way?" he asked.

"Not apart from the fact that the body was found on the premises," said Inspector Bacon. "And of course it's just possible that this artist member of the family might be able to identify her. What beats me is this extraordinary rigmarole about the train."

"Ah yes. You've been to see this old lady, this—er"—he glanced at the memorandum lying on his desk—"Miss Marple?"

"Yes, sir. And she's quite set and definite about the whole thing. Whether she's barmy or not, I don't know, but she sticks to her story—about what her friend saw and all the rest of it. As far as all that goes, I dare say it's just make believe—sort of thing old ladies do make up, like seeing flying saucers at the bottom of the garden, and Russian agents in the lending library. But it seems quite clear that she did engage this young woman, the lady help, and told her to look for a body—which the girl did."

"And found one," observed the Chief Constable. "Well, it's all a very remarkable story. Marple, Miss Jane Marple—the name seems familiar somehow. . . . Anyway, I'll get on to the Yard. I think you're right about its not being a local case—though we won't advertize the fact just yet. For the moment we'll tell the press as little as possible."

II

The inquest was a purely formal affair. No one came forward to identify the dead woman. Lucy was called to give evidence of finding the body and medical evidence was given as to the cause of death—strangulation. The proceedings were then adjourned.

It was a cold, blustery day when the Crackenthorpe family came out of the hall where the inquest had been held. There were five of them all told: Emma, Cedric, Harold, Alfred and Bryan Eastley, the husband of the dead daughter Edith. There was also Mr. Wimborne, the senior partner of the firm of solicitors who dealt with the Crackenthorpes' legal affairs. He had come down specially from London at great inconvenience to attend the inquest. They all stood for a moment on the pavement, shivering. Quite a crowd had assembled; the piquant details of the "Body in the Sarcophagus" had been fully reported in both the London and the local press.

A murmur went round: "That's them . . ."

Emma said sharply: "Let's get away."

The big hired Daimler drew up to the curb. Emma got in and motioned to Lucy. Mr. Wimborne, Cedric and Harold followed. Bryan Eastley said: "I'll take Alfred with me in my little bus." The chauffeur shut the door and the Daimler prepared to roll away.

"Oh, stop!" cried Emma. "There are the boys!"

The boys, in spite of aggrieved protests, had been left behind at Rutherford Hall, but they now appeared grinning from ear to ear.

"We came on our bicycles," said Stoddart-West. "The policeman was very kind and let us in at the back of the hall. I hope you don't mind, Miss Crackenthorpe," he added politely.

"She doesn't mind," said Cedric, answering for his sister. "You're only young once. Your first inquest, I expect?"

"It was rather disappointing," said Alexander. "All over so soon."

"We can't stay here talking," said Harold irritably. "There's quite a crowd. And all those men with cameras."

At a sign from him, the chauffeur pulled away from the curb. The boys waved cheerfully.

"All over so soon!" said Cedric. "That's what they think, the young innocents! It's just beginning."

"It's all very unfortunate. Most unfortunate," said Harold. "I suppose—"

He looked at Mr. Wimborne, who compressed his thin lips and shook his head with distaste.

"I hope," he said sententiously, "that the whole matter will soon be cleared up satisfactorily. The police are very efficient. However, the whole thing, as Harold says, has been most unfortunate."

He looked, as he spoke, at Lucy, and there was distinct disapproval in his glance. "If it had not been for this young woman," his eyes seemed to say, "poking about where she had no business to be, none of this would have happened."

This sentiment, or one closely resembling it, was voiced by Harold Crackenthorpe.

"By the way—er—Miss er—er Eyelesbarrow, just what made you go looking in that sarcophagus?"

Lucy had already wondered just when this thought would occur to one of the family. She had known that the police would ask it first thing; what surprised her was that it seemed to have occurred to no one else until this moment.

Cedric, Emma, Harold and Mr. Wimborne all looked at her.

Her reply, for what it was worth, had naturally been prepared for some time.

"Really," she said in a hesitating voice, "I hardly know. . . . I did feel that the whole place needed a thorough clearing out and cleaning. And there was"—she hesitated—"a very peculiar and disagreeable smell—"

She had counted accurately on the immediate shrinking of everyone from the unpleasantness of this idea.

Mr. Wimborne murmured: "Yes, yes, of course . . . about three weeks the police surgeon said. I think, you know, we must all try and not let our minds dwell on this thing." He smiled encouragingly at Emma who had turned very pale. "Remember," he said, "this wretched young woman was nothing to do with any of us."

"Ah, but you can't be so sure of that, can you?" said Cedric.

Lucy Eyelesbarrow looked at him with some interest. She had already been intrigued by the rather startling differences between the three brothers. Cedric was a big man with a weather-beaten, rugged face, unkempt dark hair and a jocund manner. He had arrived from the airport unshaven, and though he had shaved in preparation for the inquest, he was still wearing the clothes in which he had arrived and which seemed to be the only ones he had: old gray-flannel trousers and a patched and rather threadbare baggy jacket. He looked the stage Bohemian to the life and proud of it.

His brother Harold, on the contrary, was the perfect picture of a city gentleman and a director of important companies. He was tall with a neat, erect carriage, had dark hair going slightly bald on the temples, a small black mustache, and was impeccably dressed in a dark, well-cut suit and a pearl-gray tie. He looked what he was, a shrewd and successful businessman.

He now said stiffly:

"Really, Cedric, that seems a most uncalled-for remark."

"Don't see why. She was in our barn after all. What did she come there for?"

Mr. Wimborne coughed and said:

"Possibly some—er—assignation. I understand that it was a matter of local knowledge that the key was kept outside on a nail."

His tone indicated outrage at the carelessness of such procedure. So clearly marked was this that Emma spoke apologetically.

"It started during the war. For the air-raid wardens. There was a little spirit stove and they made themselves hot cocoa. And afterward, since there was really nothing there anybody could have wanted to take, we went on leaving the key hanging up. It was convenient for the Women's Institute people. If we'd kept it in the house it might have been awkward —when there was no one at home to give it them when they wanted it to get the place ready. With only daily women and no resident servants . . ."

Her voice tailed away. She had spoken mechanically, giving a wordy explanation without interest, as though her mind was elsewhere.

Cedric gave her a quick, puzzled glance.

"You're worried, Sis. What's up?"

Harold spoke with exasperation:

"Really, Cedric, can you ask?"

"Yes, I do ask. Granted a strange young woman has got herself killed in the barn at Rutherford Hall (sounds like a Victorian melodrama) and granted it gave Emma a shock at the time—but Emma's always been a sensible girl—I don't see why she goes on being worried now. Dash it, one gets used to everything."

"Murder takes a little more getting used to by some people than it may in your case," said Harold acidly. "I dare say murders are two a penny in Majorca and—"

"Iviza, not Majorca."

"It's the same thing."

"Not at all—it's quite a different island."

Harold went on talking:

"My point is that though murder may be an everyday commonplace to you, living among hot-blooded Latin people, nevertheless in England we take such things seriously." He added with increasing irritation, "And really, Cedric, to appear at a public inquest in those clothes—"

"What's wrong with my clothes? They're comfortable."

"They're unsuitable."

"Well, anyway, they're the only clothes I've got with me. I didn't pack my wardrobe trunk when I came rushing home to stand in with the family over this business. I'm a painter and painters like to be comfortable in their clothes."

"So you're still trying to paint?"

"Look here, Harold, when you say trying to paint—"

Mr. Wimborne cleared his throat in an authoritative manner.

"This discussion is unprofitable," he said reprovingly. "I hope, my dear Emma, that you will tell me if there is any further way in which I can be of service to you before I return to town?"

The reproof had its effect. Emma Crackenthorpe said quickly:

"It was most kind of you to come down."

"Not at all. It was advisable that someone should be at the inquest to watch the proceedings on behalf of the family. I have arranged for an interview with the Inspector at the house. I have no doubt that, distressing as all this has been, the situation will soon be clarified. In my own mind, there seems little doubt as to what occurred. As Emma has told us, the key of the Long Barn was known locally to hang outside the door. It seems highly probable that the place was used in the winter months as a place of assignation by local couples. No doubt there was a quarrel and some young man lost control of himself. Horrified at what he had done, his eye lit on the sarcophagus and he realized that it would make an excellent place of concealment."

Lucy thought to herself, "Yes, it sounds most plausible. That's just what one might think."

Cedric said, "You say a local couple—but nobody's been able to identify the girl locally."

"It's early days yet. No doubt we shall get an identification before long. And it is possible, of course, that the man in question was a local resident, but that the girl came from elsewhere, perhaps from some other part of Brackhampton. Brackhampton's a big place—it's grown enormously in the last twenty years."

"If I were a girl coming to meet my young man, I'd not stand for being taken to a freezing-cold barn miles from anywhere," Cedric objected. "I'd stand out for a nice bit of cuddle in the cinema, wouldn't you, Miss Eyelesbarrow?"

"Do we need to go into all this?" Harold demanded plaintively.

And with the voicing of the question the car drew up before the front door of Rutherford Hall and they all got out.

8

On entering the library Mr. Wimborne blinked a little as his shrewd old eyes went past Inspector Bacon, whom he had already met, to the fair-haired, good-looking man beyond him.

Inspector Bacon performed introductions.

"This is Detective Inspector Craddock of New Scotland Yard," he said.

"New Scotland Yard—hm." Mr. Wimborne's eyebrows rose.

Dermot Craddock, who had a pleasant manner, went easily into speech.

"We have been called in on the case, Mr. Wimborne," he said. "As you are representing the Crackenthorpe family, I feel it is only fair that we should give you a little confidential information."

Nobody could make a better show of presenting a very small portion of the truth and implying that it was the whole truth than young Inspector Craddock.

"Inspector Bacon will agree, I am sure," he added, glancing at his colleague.

Inspector Bacon agreed with all due solemnity and not at all as though the whole matter were prearranged.

"It's like this," said Craddock. "We have reason to believe, from information that has come into our possession, that the dead woman is not a native of these parts, that she actually traveled down here from London and that she had recently come from abroad. Probably—though we are not sure of that—from France."

Mr. Wimborne again raised his eyebrows.

"Indeed," he said. "Indeed?"

"That being the case," explained Inspector Bacon, "the Chief Constable felt that the Yard was better fitted to investigate the matter."

"I can only hope," said Mr. Wimborne, "that the case will be solved quickly. As you can no doubt appreciate, the whole business has been a source of much distress to the family. Although not personally concerned in any way, they are—"

He paused for a bare second, but Inspector Craddock filled the gap quickly.

"It's not a pleasant thing to find a murdered woman on your property. I couldn't agree with you more. Now I should like to have a brief interview with the various members of the family—"

"I really cannot see—"

"What they can tell me? Probably nothing of interest—but one never knows. I dare say I can get most of the information I want from you, sir. Information about this house and the family."

"And what can that possibly have to do with an unknown young woman coming from abroad and getting herself killed here?"

"Well, that's rather the point," said Craddock. "Why did she come here? Had she once had some connection with this house? Had she been, for instance, a servant here at one time? A lady's maid, for instance. Or did she come here to meet a former occupant of Rutherford Hall—"

Mr. Wimborne said coldly that Rutherford Hall had been occupied by the Crackenthorpes ever since Josiah Crackenthorpe built it in 1884.

"That's interesting in itself," said Craddock. "If you'd just give me a brief outline of the family history—"

Mr. Wimborne shrugged his shoulders.

"There is very little to tell. Josiah Crackenthorpe was a manufacturer of sweet and savory biscuits, relishes, pickles, etc. He accumulated a vast fortune. He built this house. Luther Crackenthorpe, his eldest son, lives here now."

"Any other sons?"

"One other son, Henry, who was killed in a motor accident in 1911."

"And the present Mr. Crackenthorpe has never thought of selling the house?"

"He is unable to do so," said the lawyer dryly. "By the terms of his father's will."

"Perhaps you'll tell me about the will?"

"Why should I?"

Inspector Craddock smiled.

"Because I can look it up myself if I want to at Somerset House."

Against his will, Mr. Wimborne gave a crabbed little smile.

"Quite right, Inspector. I was merely protesting that the information you ask for is quite irrelevant. As to Josiah Crackenthorpe's will, there is no mystery about it. He left his very considerable fortune in trust, the income from it to be paid to his son Luther for life, and after Luther's death the capital to be divided equally among Luther's children, Edmund, Cedric, Harold, Alfred, Emma and Edith. Edmund was killed in the war and Edith died four years ago, so that on Luther Crackenthorpe's decease the money will be divided among Cedric, Harold, Alfred, Emma and Edith's son Alexander Eastley."

"And the house?"

"That will go to Luther Crackenthorpe's eldest surviving son or his issue."

"Was Edmund Crackenthorpe married?"

"No."

"So the property will actually go—?"

"To the next son—Cedric."

"Mr. Luther Crackenthorpe himself cannot dispose of it?"

"No."

"And he has no control of the capital."

"No."

"Isn't that rather unusual? I suppose," said Inspector Craddock shrewdly, "that his father didn't like him."

"You suppose correctly," said Mr. Wimborne. "Old Josiah was disappointed that his eldest son showed no interest in the family business—or indeed in business of any kind. Luther spent his time traveling abroad and collecting *objets d'art*. Old Josiah was very unsympathetic to that kind of thing. So he left his money in trust for the next generation."

"But in the meantime the next generation have no income except what they make or what their father allows them, and their father has considerable capital but no power of disposal of it."

"Exactly. And what all this has to do with the murder of an unknown young woman of foreign origin I cannot imagine!"

"It doesn't seem to have anything to do with it," Inspector Craddock agreed promptly. "I just wanted to ascertain all the facts."

Mr. Wimborne looked at him sharply; then, seemingly satisfied with the result of his scrutiny, rose to his feet.

"I am proposing now to return to London," he said. "Unless there is anything further you wish to know?"

He looked from one man to the other.

"No, thank you, sir."

The sound of the gong rose fortissimo from the hall outside.

"Dear me," said Mr. Wimborne. "One of the boys, I think, must be performing."

Inspector Craddock raised his voice to be heard above the clamor, as he said:

"We'll leave the family to have lunch in peace, but Inspector Bacon and I would like to return after it—say at 2:15—and have a short interview with every member of the family."

"You think that is necessary?"

"Well—" Craddock shrugged his shoulders. "It's just an off chance. Somebody might remember something that would give us a clue to the woman's identity."

"I doubt it, Inspector. I doubt it very much. But I wish you good luck. As I said just now, the sooner this distasteful business is cleared up, the better for everybody."

Shaking his head, he went slowly out of the room.

II

Lucy had gone straight to the kitchen on getting back from the inquest, and was busy with preparations for lunch when Bryan Eastley put his head in.

"Can I give you a hand in any way?" he asked. "I'm handy about the house."

Lucy gave him a quick, slightly preoccupied glance. Bryan had arrived at the inquest direct in his small M.G. car and she had not as yet had much time to size him up.

What she saw was likeable enough. Eastley was an amiable-looking young man of thirty-odd with brown hair, rather plaintive blue eyes and an enormous fair mustache.

"The boys aren't back yet," he said, coming in and sitting on the end of the kitchen table. "It will take 'em another twenty minutes on their bikes."

Lucy smiled.

"They were certainly determined not to miss anything."

"Can't blame them. I mean to say—first inquest in their young lives and right in the family, so to speak."

"Do you mind getting off the table, Mr. Eastley? I want to put the baking dish down there."

Bryan obeyed.

"I say, that fat's corking hot. What are you going to put in it?"

"Yorkshire pudding."

"Good old Yorkshire. Roast beef of old England, is that the menu for today?"

"Yes."

"The funeral baked meats, in fact. Smells good," he sniffed appreciatively. "Do you mind my gassing away?"

"If you came in to help I'd rather you helped." She drew another pan from the oven. "Here—turn all these potatoes over so that they brown on the other side."

Bryan obeyed with alacrity.

"Have all these things been fizzling away in here while we've been at the inquest? Supposing they'd been all burned up."

"Most improbable. There's a regulating number on the oven."

"Kind of electric brain, eh what? Is that right?"

Lucy threw a swift look in his direction.

"Quite right. Now put the pan in the oven. Here, take the cloth. On the second shelf—I want the top one for the Yorkshire pudding."

Bryan obeyed, but not without uttering a shrill yelp.

"Burn yourself?"

"Just a bit. It doesn't matter. What a dangerous game cooking is!"

"I suppose you never do your own cooking?"

"As a matter of fact I do—quite often. But not this sort of thing. I can boil an egg, if I don't forget to look at the clock. And I can do eggs and bacon. And I can put a steak under the grill or open a tin of soup. I've got one of those little electric whatnots in my flat."

"You live in London?"

"If you call it living—yes."

His tone was despondent. He watched Lucy shoot in the dish with the Yorkshire pudding mixture.

"This is awfully jolly," he said, and sighed.

Her immediate preoccupations over, Lucy looked at him with more attention.

"What is—this kitchen?"

"Yes—reminds me of our kitchen at home—when I was a boy."

It struck Lucy that there was something strangely forlorn about Bryan Eastley. Looking closely at him, she realized that he was older than she had at first thought. He must be close on forty. It seemed difficult to think of him as Alexander's father. He reminded her of innumerable young pilots she had known during the war when she had been at the impressionable age of fourteen. She had gone on and grown up into a postwar world—but she felt as though Bryan had not gone on but had been overtaken in the passage of years. His next words confirmed this. He had subsided on to the kitchen table again.

"It's a difficult sort of world," he said, "isn't it? To get your bearings in, I mean. You see, one hasn't been trained for it."

Lucy recalled what she had heard from Emma.

"You were a fighter pilot, weren't you?" she said. "You've got a D.F.C."

"That's the sort of thing that puts you wrong. You've got a decoration and so people try to make it easy for you. Give you a job and all that. Very decent of them. But they're all white-collar jobs, and one simply isn't any good at that sort of thing. Sitting at a desk getting tangled up in figures. I've had ideas of my own, you know, tried out a wheeze or two. But you can't get the backing. Can't get the chaps to come in and put down the money. If I had a bit of capital—"

He brooded.

"You didn't know Edie, did you? My wife. No, of course you didn't. She was quite different from all this lot. Younger, for one thing. She was in the Air Force. She always said her old man was an Ebenezer Scrooge. He is, you know. Mean as hell over money. And it's not as though he could take it with him. It's got to be divided up when he dies. Edie's share will go to Alexander, of course. He won't be able to touch the capital until he's twenty-one, though."

"I'm sorry, but will you get off the table again. I want to dish up and make gravy."

At that moment Alexander and Stoddart-West arrived with rosy faces and very much out of breath.

"Hello, Bryan," said Alexander kindly to his father. "So this is where you've got to. I say, what a smashing piece of beef. Is there Yorkshire pudding?"

"Yes, there is."

"We have awful Yorkshire pudding at school—all damp and limp."

"Get out of my way," said Lucy. "I want to make the gravy."

"Make lots of gravy. Can we have two sauceboats full?"

"Yes."

"Good oh!" said Stoddart-West, pronouncing the words carefully.

"I don't like it pale," said Alexander anxiously.

"It won't be pale."

"She's a smashing cook," said Alexander to his father.

Lucy had a momentary impression that their roles were reversed. Alexander spoke like a kindly father to his son.

"Can we help you, Miss Eyelesbarrow?" asked Stoddart-West politely.

"Yes, you can. Alexander, go and sound the gong. James, will you carry this tray into the dining room? And will you take the joint in, Mr. Eastley? I'll bring the potatoes and the Yorkshire pudding."

"There's a Scotland Yard man here," said Alexander. "Do you think he will have lunch with us?"

"That depends on what your aunt arranges."

"I don't suppose Aunt Emma would mind. She's very hospitable. But I suppose Uncle Harold wouldn't like it. He's being very sticky over this murder." Alexander went out through the door with the tray, adding a little additional information over his shoulder. "Mr. Wimborne's in the library with the Scotland Yard men now. But he isn't staying to lunch. He said he had to get back to London. Come on, Stodders. Oh, he's gone to do the gong."

At that moment the gong took charge. Stoddart-West was an artist; he gave it everything he had and all further conversation was inhibited.

Bryan carried in the joint, Lucy followed with the vegetables—returned to the kitchen to get the two brimming sauceboats of gravy.

Mr. Wimborne was standing in the hall putting on his gloves as Emma came quickly down the stairs.

"Are you really sure you won't stop for lunch, Mr. Wimborne? It's all ready."

"No. I've an important appointment in London. There is a restaurant car on the train."

"It was very good of you to come down," said Emma gratefully.

The two police officers emerged from the library.

Mr. Wimborne took Emma's hand in his.

"There's nothing to worry about, my dear," he said. "This is Detective Inspector Craddock from New Scotland Yard who has come down to take charge of the case. He is coming back at 2:15 to ask you for any facts that may assist him in his inquiry. But as I say, you have nothing to worry about." He looked toward Craddock. "I may repeat to Miss Crackenthorpe what you have told me?"

"Certainly, sir."

"Inspector Craddock has just told me that this almost certainly was not a local crime. The murdered woman is thought to have come from London and was probably a foreigner."

Emma Crackenthorpe said sharply, "A foreigner. Was she French?"

Mr. Wimborne had clearly meant his statement to be consoling. He looked slightly taken aback. Dermot Craddock's glance went quickly from him to Emma's face.

He wondered why she had leaped to the conclusion that the murdered woman was French, and why that thought disturbed her so much.

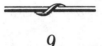

9

The only people who really did justice to Lucy's excellent lunch were the two boys and Cedric Crackenthorpe, who appeared completely unaffected by the circumstances which had caused him to return to England. He seemed, indeed, to regard the whole thing as a rather good joke of a macabre nature.

This attitude, Lucy noted, was most unpalatable to his brother Harold. Harold seemed to take the murder as a kind of personal insult to the Crackenthorpe family and so great was his sense of outrage that he ate hardly any lunch. Emma looked worried and unhappy and also ate very little. Alfred seemed lost in a train of thought of his own and spoke very little. He was a good-looking man with a thin, dark face and eyes set rather too close together.

After lunch the police officers returned and politely asked if they could have a few words with Mr. Cedric Crackenthorpe.

Inspector Craddock was very pleasant and friendly.

"Sit down, Mr. Crackenthorpe. I understand you have just come back from the Balearics? You live out there?"

"Have done for the last six years. In Iviza. Suits me better than this dreary country."

"You get a good deal more sunshine than we do, I expect," said Inspector Craddock agreeably. "You were home not so very long ago, I understand—for Christmas, to be exact. What made it necessary for you to come back again so soon?"

Cedric grinned.

"Got a wire from Emma—my sister. We've never had a murder on the premises before. Didn't want to miss anything—so along I came."

"You are interested in criminology?"

"Oh, we needn't put it in such highbrow terms! I just like murders. Whodunnits and all that! With a whodunnit parked right on the family doorstep, it seemed the chance of a lifetime. Besides I thought poor old Em might need a spot of help—managing the old man and the police and all the rest of it."

"I see. It appealed to your sporting instincts and also to your family feelings. I've no doubt your sister will be very grateful to you—although her two other brothers have also come to be with her."

"But not to cheer and comfort," Cedric told him. "Harold is terrifically put out. It's not at all the thing for a city magnate to be mixed up with the murder of a questionable female."

Craddock's eyebrows rose gently.

"Was she—a questionable female?"

"Well, you're the authority on that point. Going by the facts, it seemed to me likely."

"I thought perhaps you might have been able to make a guess at who she was?"

"Come now, Inspector, you already know—or your colleagues will tell you—that I haven't been able to identify her."

"I said a guess, Mr. Crackenthorpe. You might never have seen the woman before, but you might have been able to make a guess at who she was—or who she might have been?"

Cedric shook his head.

"You're barking up the wrong tree. I've absolutely no idea. You're suggesting, I suppose, that she may have come to the Long Barn to keep an assignation with one of us? But we none of us live here—the only people in the house were a woman and an old man. You don't seriously believe that she came here to keep a date with my revered Pop?"

"Our point is—Inspector Bacon agrees with me—that the woman may once have had some association with this house. It may have been a considerable number of years ago. Cast your mind back, Mr. Crackenthorpe—"

Cedric thought a moment or two, then shook his head.

"We've had foreign help from time to time, like most people, but I can't think of any likely possibility. Better ask the others. They'd know more than I would."

"We shall do that, of course."

Craddock leaned back in his chair and went on:

"As you have heard at the inquest, the medical evidence cannot fix the time of death very accurately. Longer than two weeks, less than four—which brings it somewhere around Christmastime. You have told me you came home for Christmas. When did you arrive in England and when did you leave?"

Cedric reflected.

"Let me see . . . I flew. Got here on the Saturday before Christmas—that would be the twenty-first."

"You flew straight from Majorca?"

"Yes. Left at five in the morning and got here midday."

"And you left?"

"I flew back on the following Friday, the twenty-seventh."

"Thank you."

Cedric grinned.

"Leaves me well within the limit, unfortunately. But really, Inspector, strangling young women is not my favorite form of Christmas fun."

"I hope not, Mr. Crackenthorpe."

Inspector Bacon merely looked disapproving.

"There would be a remarkable absence of peace and good will about such an action, don't you agree?"

Cedric addressed this question to Inspector Bacon, who merely grunted. Inspector Craddock said politely:

"Well, thank you, Mr. Crackenthorpe. That will be all."

"And what do you think of him?" Craddock asked as Cedric shut the door behind him.

Bacon grunted again.

"Cocky enough for anything," he said. "I don't care for the type, myself. A loose living lot, these artists, and very likely to be mixed up with a disreputable class of women."

Craddock smiled.

"I don't like the way he dresses, either," went on Bacon. "No respect —going to an inquest like that. Dirtiest pair of trousers I've seen in a long while. And did you see his tie? Looked as though it was made of colored string. If you ask me, he's the kind that would easily strangle a woman and make no bones about it."

"Well, he didn't strangle this one—if he didn't leave Majorca until the twenty-first. And that's a thing we can verify easily enough."

Bacon threw him a sharp glance.

"I notice that you're not tipping your hand yet about the actual date of the crime."

"No, we'll keep that dark for the present. I always like to have something up my sleeve in the early stages."

Bacon nodded in full agreement.

"Spring it on 'em when the time comes," he said. "That's the best plan."

"And now," said Craddock, "we'll see what our correct City gentleman has to say about it all."

Harold Crackenthorpe, thin-lipped, had very little to say about it. It was most distasteful—a very unfortunate incident. The newspapers, he was afraid— Reporters, he understood, had already been asking for interviews. All that sort of thing . . . Most regrettable . . .

Harold's staccato unfinished sentences ended. He leaned back in his chair with the expression of a man confronted with a very bad smell.

The Inspector's probing produced no result. No, he had no idea who the woman was or could be. Yes, he had been at Rutherford Hall for Christmas. He had been unable to come down until Christmas Eve, but had stayed on over the following weekend.

"That's that, then," said Inspector Craddock, without pressing his questions further. He had already made up his mind that Harold Crackenthorpe was not going to be helpful.

He passed on to Alfred, who came into the room with a nonchalance that seemed just a trifle overdone.

Craddock looked at Alfred Crackenthorpe with a faint feeling of recognition. Surely he had seen this particular member of the family somewhere before. Or had it been his picture in the paper? There was something discreditable attached to the memory. He asked Alfred his occupation and Alfred's answer was vague.

"I'm in insurance at the moment. Until recently I've been interested in putting a new type of talking machine on the market. Quite revolutionary. I did very well out of that, as a matter of fact."

Inspector Craddock looked appreciative, and no one could have had the least idea that he was noticing the superficially smart appearance of Alfred's suit and gauging correctly the low price it had cost. Cedric's clothes had been disreputable, almost threadbare, but they had been originally of good cut and excellent material. Here there was a cheap smartness that told its own tale. Craddock passed pleasantly on to his routine questions. Alfred seemed interested, even slightly amused.

"It's quite an idea, that the woman might once have had a job here. Not as a lady's maid; I doubt if my sister has ever had such a thing. I don't think anyone has nowadays. But of course there is a good deal of foreign domestic labor floating about. We've had Poles, and a temperamental

German or two. As Emma definitely didn't recognize the woman, I think that washes your idea out, Inspector. Emma's got a very good memory for a face. No, if the woman came from London . . . What gives you the idea she came from London, by the way?"

He slipped the question in quite casually, but his eyes were sharp and interested.

Inspector Craddock smiled and shook his head.

Alfred looked at him keenly.

"Not telling, eh? Return ticket in her coat pocket, perhaps, is that it?"

"It could be, Mr. Crackenthorpe."

"Well, granting she came from London, perhaps the chap she came to meet had the idea that the Long Barn would be a nice place to do a quiet murder. He knows the setup here, evidently. I should go looking for him if I were you, Inspector."

"We are," said Inspector Craddock, and made the two little words sound quiet and confident.

He thanked Alfred and dismissed him.

"You know," he said to Bacon, "I've seen that chap somewhere before. . . ."

Inspector Bacon gave his verdict.

"Sharp customer," he said. "So sharp that he cuts himself sometimes."

II

"I don't suppose you want to see me," said Bryan Eastley apologetically, coming into the room and hesitating by the door. "I don't exactly belong to the family."

"Let me see, you are Mr. Bryan Eastley, the husband of Miss Edith Crackenthorpe, who died four years ago?"

"That's right."

"Well, it's very kind of you, Mr. Eastley, especially if you know something that you think could assist us in some way?"

"But I don't. Wish I did. Whole thing seems so ruddy peculiar, doesn't it? Coming along and meeting some fellow in that drafty old barn in the middle of winter. Wouldn't be my cup of tea!"

"It is certainly very perplexing," Inspector Craddock agreed.

"Is it true that she was a foreigner? Word seems to have got round to that effect."

"Does that fact suggest anything to you?" The Inspector looked at him sharply, but Bryan seemed amiably vacuous.

"No, it doesn't, as a matter of fact."

"Maybe she was French," said Inspector Bacon, with dark suspicion.

Bryan was roused to slight animation. A look of interest came into his blue eyes, and he tugged at his big, fair mustache.

"Really? Gay Paree?" He shook his head. "On the whole, it seems to make it even more unlikely, doesn't it? Messing about in the barn, I mean. You haven't had any other sarcophagus murders, have you? One of these fellows with an urge—or a complex? Thinks he's Caligula or someone like that?"

Inspector Craddock did not even trouble to reject this speculation. Instead, he asked in a casual manner:

"Nobody in the family got any French connections, or—or—relationships that you know of?"

Bryan said that the Crackenthorpes weren't a very gay lot.

"Harold's respectably married," he said. "Fish-faced woman, some impoverished peer's daughter. Don't think Alfred cares about women much—spends his life going in for shady deals which usually go wrong in the end. I dare say Cedric's got a few Spanish señoritas jumping through hoops for him in Iviza. Women rather fall for Cedric. Doesn't always shave and looks as though he never washes. Don't see why that should be attractive to women, but apparently it is—I say, I'm not being very helpful, am I?"

He grinned at them.

"Better get young Alexander on the job. He and James Stoddart-West are out hunting for clues in a big way. Bet you they turn up something."

Inspector Craddock said he hoped they would. Then he thanked Bryan Eastley and said he would like to speak to Miss Emma Crackenthorpe.

III

Inspector Craddock looked with more attention at Emma Crackenthorpe than he had done previously. He was still wondering about the expression that he had surprised on her face before lunch.

A quiet woman. Not stupid. Not brilliant, either. One of those comfortable, pleasant women whom men were inclined to take for granted, and who had the art of making a house into a home, giving it an atmosphere of restfulness and quiet harmony. Such, he thought, was Emma Crackenthorpe.

Women such as this were often underrated. Behind their quiet exterior they had force of character, they were to be reckoned with. Perhaps, Craddock thought, the clue to the mystery of the dead woman in the sarcophagus was hidden away in the recesses of Emma's mind.

While these thoughts were passing through his head, Craddock was asking various unimportant questions.

"I don't suppose there is much that you haven't already told Inspector Bacon," he said. "So I needn't worry you with many questions."

"Please ask me anything you like."

"As Mr. Wimborne told you, we have reached the conclusion that the dead woman was not native of these parts. That may be a relief to you —Mr. Wimborne seemed to think it would be—but it makes it really more difficult for us. She's less easily identified."

"But didn't she have anything? A handbag? Papers?"

Craddock shook his head.

"No handbag, nothing in her pockets."

"You've no idea of her name—of where she came from—anything at all?"

Craddock thought to himself: She wants to know—she's very anxious to know—who the woman is. Has she felt like that all along, I wonder? Bacon didn't give me that impression—and he's a shrewd man. . . .

"We know nothing about her," he said. "That's why we hoped one of you could help us. Are you sure you can't? Even if you didn't recognize her, can you think of anyone she might be?"

He thought, but perhaps he imagined it, that there was a very slight pause before she answered.

"I've absolutely no idea," she said.

Imperceptibly, Inspector Craddock's manner changed. It was hardly noticeable except as a slight hardness in his voice.

"When Mr. Wimborne told you that the woman was a foreigner, why did you assume that she was French?"

Emma was not disconcerted. Her eyebrows rose slightly.

"Did I? Yes, I believe I did. I don't really know why, except that one always tends to think foreigners are French until one finds out what nationality they really are. Most foreigners in this country are French, aren't they?"

"Oh, I really wouldn't say that was so, Miss Crackenthorpe. Not nowadays. We have so many nationalities over here. Italians, Germans, Austrians, all the Scandinavian countries."

"Yes, I suppose you're right."

"You didn't have some special reason for thinking that this woman was likely to be French?"

She didn't hurry to deny it. She just thought a moment and then shook her head almost regretfully.

"No," she said. "I really don't think so."

Her glance met his placidly, without flinching.

Craddock looked toward Inspector Bacon. The latter leaned forward and presented a small, enamel powder compact.

"Do you recognize this, Miss Crackenthorpe?"

She took it and examined it.

"No. It's certainly not mine."

"You've no idea to whom it belonged?"

"No."

"Then I don't think we need worry you any more—for the present."

"Thank you."

She smiled briefly at them, got up, and left the room. Again he may have imagined it, but Craddock thought she moved rather quickly, as though a certain relief hurried her.

"Think she knows anything?" asked Bacon.

Inspector Craddock said ruefully:

"At a certain stage one is inclined to think everyone knows a little more than they are willing to tell you."

"They usually do, too," said Bacon out of the depth of his experience. "Only," he added, "it quite often isn't anything to do with the business in hand. It's some family peccadillo or some silly scrape that people are afraid is going to be dragged into the open."

"Yes, I know. Well, at least—"

But whatever Inspector Craddock had been about to say never got said, for the door was flung open and old Mr. Crackenthorpe shuffled in, in a high state of indignation.

"A pretty pass," he said. "Things have come to a pretty pass when Scotland Yard comes down and doesn't have the courtesy to talk to the head of the family first! Who's the master of this house, I'd like to know? Answer me that? Who's master here?"

"You are, of course, Mr. Crackenthorpe," said Craddock soothingly and rising as he spoke. "But we understood that you had already told Inspector Bacon all you knew, and that your health not being good, we must not make too many demands upon it. Doctor Quimper said—"

"I dare say. I dare say. I'm not a strong man. As for Doctor Quimper, he's a regular old woman—perfectly good doctor, understands my case —but inclined to wrap me up in cotton wool. Got a bee in his bonnet about food. Went on at me Christmastime when I had a bit of a turn. What did I eat? When? Who cooked it? Who served it? Fuss, fuss, fuss! But though I may have indifferent health, I'm well enough to give you all the help that's in my power. Murder in my own house, or at any rate in my own barn! Interesting building, that. Elizabethan. Local architect says not—but the fellow doesn't know what he's talking about. Not a day later than 1580—but that's not what we're talking about. What do you want to know? What's your present theory?"

"It's a little too early for theories, Mr. Crackenthorpe. We are still trying to find out who the woman was."

"Foreigner, you say?"

"We think so."

"Enemy agent?"

"Unlikely, I should say."

"You'd say! You'd say! They're everywhere, these people. Infiltrating! Why the Home Office lets them in beats me. Spying on industrial secrets, I'd bet. That's what she was doing."

"In Brackhampton?"

"Factories everywhere. One outside my own back gate."

Craddock shot an inquiring glance at Bacon who responded.

"Metal Boxes."

"How do you know that's what they're really making? Can't swallow all these fellows tell you. All right, if she wasn't a spy, who do you think she was? Think she was mixed up with one of my precious sons? It would be Alfred, if so. Not Harold, he's too careful. And Cedric doesn't condescend to live in this country. All right, then, she was Alfred's bit of skirt. And some violent fellow followed her down here, thinking she was coming to meet him, and did her in. How's that?"

Inspector Craddock said diplomatically that it was certainly a theory. But Mr. Alfred Crackenthorpe, he said, had not recognized her.

"Pah! Afraid, that's all! Alfred always was a coward. But he's a liar, remember, always was! Lie himself black in the face. None of my sons are any good. Crowd of vultures, waiting for me to die, that's their real occupation in life." He chuckled. "And they can wait. I won't die to oblige them! Well, if that's all I can do for you . . . I'm tired. Got to rest."

He shuffled out again.

"Alfred's bit of skirt?" said Bacon questioningly. "In my opinion the old man just made that up." He paused, hesitated. "I think, personally, Alfred's quite all right—perhaps a shifty customer in some ways, but not our present cup of tea. Mind you, I did just wonder about that Air Force chap."

"Bryan Eastley?"

"Yes. I've run into one or two of his type. They're what you might call adrift in the world—had danger and death and excitement too early in life. Now they find it tame. Tame and unsatisfactory. In a way, we've given them a raw deal. Though I don't really know what we could do about it. But there they are, all past and no future, so to speak. And they're the kind that don't mind taking chances. The ordinary fellow plays safe by instinct, it's not so much morality as prudence. But these fellows aren't afraid—playing safe isn't really in their vocabulary. If Eastley were mixed up with a woman and wanted to kill her—" He stopped, threw out a hand hopelessly. "But why should he want to kill her? And if you do kill a woman, why plant her in your father-in-law's sarcophagus? No, if you ask me, none of this lot had anything to do with the murder.

If they had, they wouldn't have gone to all the trouble of planting the body on their own back doorstep, so to speak."

Craddock agreed that that hardly made sense.

"Anything more you want to do here?"

Craddock said there wasn't.

Bacon suggested coming back to Brackhampton and having a cup of tea, but Inspector Craddock said that he was going to call on an old acquaintance.

10

Miss Marple, sitting erect against a background of china dogs and presents from Margate, smiled approvingly at Inspector Dermot Craddock.

"I'm so glad," she said, "that you have been assigned to the case. I hoped you would be."

"When I got your letter," said Craddock, "I took it straight to the Assistant Commissioner. As it happened he had just heard from the Brackhampton people calling us in. They seemed to think it wasn't a local crime. The A.C. was very interested in what I had to tell him about you. He'd heard about you, I gather, from my uncle."

"Dear Sir Henry," murmured Miss Marple affectionately.

"He got me to tell him all about the Little Paddocks business. Do you want to hear what he said next?"

"Please tell me if it is not a breach of confidence."

"He said, 'Well, as this seems a completely cockeyed business, all thought up by a couple of old ladies who've turned out, against all probability, to be right, and since you already know one of these old ladies, I'm sending you down on the case.' So here I am! And now, my dear Miss Marple, where do we go from here? This is not, as you probably appreciate, an official visit. I haven't got my henchmen with me. I thought you and I might take down our back hair together first."

Miss Marple smiled at him.

"I'm sure," she said, "that no one who only knows you officially would ever guess that you could be so human, and better-looking than ever—don't blush. Now what, exactly, have you been told so far?"

"I've got everything, I think. Your friend Mrs. McGillicuddy's original statement to the police at St. Mary Mead, confirmation of her statement by the ticket collector and also the note to the stationmaster at Brack-hampton. I may say that all the proper inquiries were made by the people concerned—the railway people and the police. But there's no doubt that you outsmarted them all by a most fantastic process of guess-work."

"Not guesswork," said Miss Marple. "And I had a great advantage. I knew Elspeth McGillicuddy. Nobody else did. There was no obvious confirmation of her story, and if there was no question of any woman being reported missing, then quite naturally they would think it was just an elderly lady imagining things—as elderly ladies often do, but not Elspeth McGillicuddy."

"Not Elspeth McGillicuddy," agreed the Inspector. "I'm looking for-ward to meeting her, you know. I wish she hadn't gone to Ceylon. We're arranging for her to be interviewed there, by the way."

"My own process of reasoning was not really original," said Miss Mar-ple. "It's all in Mark Twain. The boy who found the horse. I just imagined where I would go if I were a horse and I went there and there was the horse."

"You imagined what you'd do if you were a cruel and cold-blooded murderer?" said Craddock, looking thoughtfully at Miss Marple's pink and white elderly fragility. "Really, your mind—"

"Like a sink, my nephew Raymond used to say," Miss Marple agreed, nodding her head briskly. "But as I always told him, sinks are necessary domestic equipment and actually very hygienic."

"Can you go a little further still, put yourself in the murderer's place, and tell me just where he is now?"

Miss Marple sighed.

"I wish I could. I've no idea—no idea at all. But he must be someone who has lived in, or knows all about Rutherford Hall."

"I agree. But that opens up a very wide field. Quite a succession of daily women have worked there. There's the Women's Institute, and the air-raid wardens before them. They all know the Long Barn and the sarcoph-agus and where the key was kept. The whole setup there is widely known locally. Anybody living roundabout might hit on it as a good spot for his purpose."

"Yes, indeed. I quite understand your difficulties."

Craddock said: "We'll never get anywhere until we identify the body."

"And that, too, may be difficult?"

"Oh, we'll get there—in the end. We're checking up on all the re-ported disappearances of a woman of that age and appearance. There's no one outstanding who fits the bill. The Medical Officer puts her down as about thirty-five, healthy, probably a married woman, has had at least one child. Her fur coat is a cheap one, purchased at a London store. Hundreds of such coats were sold in the last three months, about sixty per cent of them to blonde women. No salesgirl can recognize the photograph of the dead woman, or is likely to if the purchase were made just before Christmas. Her other clothes seem mainly of foreign manufacture, mostly purchased in Paris. There are no English laundry marks. We've communicated with Paris and they are checking up there for us. Sooner or later, of course, someone will come forward with a missing relative or lodger. It's just a matter of time."

"The compact wasn't any help?"

"Unfortunately, no. It's a type sold by the hundred in the rue de Rivoli, quite cheap. By the way, you ought to have turned that over to the police at once, you know, or rather Miss Eyelesbarrow should have done so."

Miss Marple shook her head.

"But at that moment there wasn't any question of a crime having been committed," she pointed out. "If a young lady, practicing golf shots, picks up an old compact of no particular value in the long grass, surely she doesn't rush straight off to the police with it?" Miss Marple paused, and then added firmly: "I thought it much wiser to find the body first."

Inspector Craddock was tickled.

"You don't seem to have ever had any doubts but that it would be found?"

"I was sure it would. Lucy Eyelesbarrow is a most efficient and intelligent person."

"I'll say she is! She scares the life out of me, she's so devastatingly efficient. No man will ever dare marry that girl."

"Now you know, I wouldn't say that. It would have to be a special type of man, of course." Miss Marple brooded on this thought a moment. "How is she getting on at Rutherford Hall?"

"They're completely dependent upon her as far as I can see. Eating out of her hand—literally as you might say. By the way, they know nothing about her connection with you. We've kept that dark."

"She has no connection now with me. She has done what I asked her to do."

"So she could hand in her notice and go if she wanted to?"

"Yes."

"But she stays on. Why?"

"She has not mentioned her reasons to me. She is a very intelligent girl. I suspect that she has become interested."

"In the problem? Or in the family?"

"It may be," said Miss Marple, "that it is rather difficult to separate the two."

Craddock looked hard at her.

"Have you got anything particular in mind?"

"Oh no—oh, dear me, no."

"I think you have."

Miss Marple shook her head.

Dermot Craddock sighed. "So all I can do is to 'prosecute my inquiries'—to put it in jargon. A policeman's life is a dull one!"

"You'll get results, I'm sure."

"Any ideas for me? More inspired guesswork?"

"I was thinking of things like theatrical companies," said Miss Marple rather vaguely. "Touring from place to place and perhaps not many home ties. One of those young women would be much less likely to be missed."

"Yes. Perhaps you've got something there. We'll pay special attention to that angle." He added, "What are you smiling about?"

"I was just thinking," said Miss Marple, "of Elspeth McGillicuddy's face when she hears we've found a body!"

II

"Well!" said Mrs. McGillicuddy. "Well!"

Words failed her. She looked across at the nicely spoken, pleasant young man who had called upon her with official credentials and then down at the photographs that he had handed her.

"That's her all right," she said. "Yes, that's her. Poor soul. Well, I must say I'm glad you've found her body. Nobody believed a word I said! The police or the railway people or anyone else. It's very galling not to be believed. At any rate, nobody could say I didn't do all I possibly could."

The nice young man made sympathetic and appreciative noises.

"Where did you say the body was found?"

"In a barn at a house called Rutherford Hall, just outside Brackhampton."

"Never heard of it. How did it get there, I wonder?"

The young man did not reply.

"Jane Marple found it, I suppose. Trust Jane."

"The body," said the young man, referring to some notes, "was found by a Miss Lucy Eyelesbarrow."

"Never heard of her either," said Mrs. McGillicuddy. "I still think Jane Marple had something to do with it."

"Anyway, Mrs. McGillicuddy, you definitely identify this picture as that of the woman whom you saw in a train?"

"Being strangled by a man. Yes, I do."

"Now, can you describe this man?"

"He was a tall man," said Mrs. McGillicuddy.

"Yes?"

"And dark."

"Yes?"

"That's all I can tell you," said Mrs. McGillicuddy. "He had his back to me. I didn't see his face."

"Would you be able to recognize him if you saw him?"

"Of course I shouldn't! He had his back to me. I never saw his face."

"You've no idea at all as to his age?"

Mrs. McGillicuddy considered.

"No—not really—I mean, I don't know. He wasn't, I'm almost sure, very young. His shoulders looked—well, set, if you know what I mean." The young man nodded. "Thirty and upward, I can't get closer than that. I wasn't really looking at him, you see. It was her—with those hands round her throat and her face—all blue. . . . You know, sometimes I dream of it even now."

"It must have been a very distressing experience," said the young man sympathetically.

He closed his notebook and said, "When are you returning to England?"

"Not for another three weeks. It isn't necessary, is it, for me?"

He quickly reassured her.

"Oh no. There's nothing you could do at present. Of course, if we make an arrest . . ."

It was left like that.

The mail brought a letter from Miss Marple to her friend. The writing was spiky and spidery and heavily underlined. Long practice made it easy for Mrs. McGillicuddy to decipher. Miss Marple wrote à very full account to her friend who devoured every word with great satisfaction.

She and Jane had shown them all right!

11

"I simply can't make you out," said Cedric Crackenthorpe.

He eased himself down on the decaying wall of a long-derelict pigsty and stared at Lucy Eyelesbarrow.

"What can't you make out?"

"What you're doing here."

"I'm earning my living."

"As a skivvy?" he spoke disparagingly.

"You're out of date," said Lucy. "Skivvy, indeed! I'm a household help, a professional domestician, or an answer to prayer, mainly the latter."

"You can't like all the things you have to do—cooking and making beds and whirring about with a Hoover cleaner and sinking your arms up to the elbows in greasy water."

Lucy laughed.

"Not the details, perhaps, but cooking satisfies my creative instincts, and there's something in me that really revels in clearing up mess."

"I live in a permanent mess," said Cedric. "I like it," he added defiantly.

"You look as though you did."

"My cottage in Iviza is run on simple straightforward lines. Three plates, two cups and saucers, a bed, a table and a couple of chairs. There's dust everywhere and smears of paint and chips of stone—I sculpt as well as paint—and nobody's allowed to touch a thing. I won't have a woman near the place."

"Not in any capacity?"

"Just what do you mean by that?"

"I was assuming that a man of such artistic tastes presumably had some kind of love life."

"My love life, as you call it, is my own business," said Cedric with dignity. "What I won't have is a woman in her tidying-up, interfering, bossing capacity!"

"How I'd love to have a go at your cottage," said Lucy. "It would be a challenge!"

"You won't get the opportunity."

"I suppose not."

Some bricks fell out of the pigsty. Cedric turned his head and looked into its nettle-ridden depths.

"Dear old Madge," he said. "I remember her well. A sow of most endearing disposition and a prolific mother. Seventeen in the last litter, I remember. We used to come here on fine afternoons and scratch Madge's back with a stick. She loved it."

"Why has this whole place been allowed to get into the state it's in? It can't only be the war?"

"You'd like to tidy this up, too, I suppose? What an interfering female you are. I quite see now why you would be the person to discover a body! You couldn't even leave a Greco-Roman sarcophagus alone." He paused and then went on. "No, it's not only the war. It's my father. What do you think of him, by the way?"

"I haven't had much time for thinking."

"Don't evade the issue. He's as mean as hell and in my opinion a bit crazy as well. Of course he hates all of us, except perhaps Emma. That's because of my grandfather's will."

Lucy looked inquiring.

"My grandfather was the man who mada-da-monitch. With the Crunchies and the Cracker Jacks and the Cozy Crisps. All the afternoon-tea delicacies, and then, being farsighted, he switched on very early to cheesies and canapés so that now we cash in on cocktail parties in a big way. Well, the time came when father intimated that he had a soul above Crunchies. He traveled in Italy and the Balkans and Greece and dabbled in art. My grandfather was peeved. He decided my father was no man of business and a rather poor judge of art (quite right in both cases), so left all his money in trust for his grandchildren. Father had the income for life, but he couldn't touch the capital. Do you know what he did? He stopped spending money. He came here and began to save. I'd say that by now he's accumulated nearly as big a fortune as my grandfather left. And in the meantime all of us, Harold, myself, Alfred and Emma haven't got a penny of grandfather's money. I'm a stony-broke painter. Harold went into business and is now a prominent man in the City—he's the one with the money-making touch, though I've heard rumors that he's in Queer Street lately. Alfred. Well, Alfred is usually known in the privacy of the family as Flash Alf."

"Why?"

"What a lot of things you want to know! The answer is that Alf is the black sheep of the family. He's not actually been to prison yet, but he's been very near it. He was in the Ministry of Supply during the war, but left it rather abruptly under questionable circumstances. And after that there were some dubious deals in tinned fruits, and trouble over eggs. Nothing in a big way—just a few doubtful deals on the side."

"Isn't it rather unwise to tell strangers all these things?"

"Why? Are you a police spy?"

"I might be."

"I don't think so. You were here slaving away before the police began to take an interest in us. I should say—"

He broke off as his sister Emma came through the door of the kitchen garden.

"Hullo, Em? You're looking very perturbed about something."

"I am. I want to talk to you, Cedric."

"I must get back to the house," said Lucy, tactfully.

"Don't go," said Cedric. "Murder has made you practically one of the family."

"I've got a lot to do," said Lucy. "I only came out to get some parsley."

She beat a rapid retreat to the kitchen garden. Cedric's eyes followed her.

"Good-looking girl," he said. "Who is she really?"

"Oh, she's quite well known," said Emma. "She's made a specialty of this kind of thing. But never mind Lucy Eyelesbarrow, Cedric. I'm terribly worried. Apparently the police think that this girl was a foreigner, perhaps French. Cedric, you don't think that she could possibly be—Martine?"

II

For a moment or two Cedric stared at her as though uncomprehending.

"Martine? But who on earth—oh, you mean Martine?"

"Yes. Do you think—"

"Why on earth should it be Martine?"

"Well, her sending that telegram was odd when you come to think of it. It must have been roughly about the same time. Do you think that she may, after all, have come down here and . . ."

"Nonsense. Why should Martine come down here and find her way into the Long Barn? What for? It seems wildly unlikely to me."

"You don't think, perhaps, that I ought to tell Inspector Bacon, or the other one?"

"Tell him what?"

"Well—about Martine. About her letter."

"Now don't you go complicating things, Sis, by bringing up a lot of irrelevant stuff that has nothing to do with all this. I was never very convinced about that letter from Martine, anyway."

"I was."

"You've always been good at believing impossible things before breakfast, old girl. My advice to you is, sit tight and keep your mouth shut. It's up to the police to identify their precious corpse. And I bet Harold would say the same."

"Oh, I know Harold would. And Alfred, also. But I'm worried, Cedric, I really am worried. I don't know what I ought to do."

"Nothing," said Cedric promptly. "You keep your mouth shut, Emma. Never go halfway to meet trouble, that's my motto."

Emma Crackenthorpe sighed. She went slowly back to the house, uneasy in her mind.

As she came into the drive, Doctor Quimper emerged from the house and opened the door of his battered Austin car. He paused when he saw her; then, leaving the car, he came toward her.

"Well, Emma," he said. "Your father's in splendid shape. Murder suits him. It's given him an interest in life. I must recommend it for more of my patients."

Emma smiled mechanically. Doctor Quimper was always quick to notice reactions.

"Anything particular the matter?" he asked.

Emma looked up at him. She had come to rely a lot on the kindliness and sympathy of the doctor. He had become a friend on whom to lean, not only a medical attendant. His calculated brusqueness did not deceive her; she knew the kindness that lay behind it.

"I am worried, yes," she admitted.

"Care to tell me? Don't, if you don't want to."

"I'd like to tell you. Some of it you know already. The point is I don't know what to do."

"I should say your judgment was usually most reliable. What's the trouble?"

"You remember—or perhaps you don't—what I once told you about my brother—the one who was killed in the war?"

"You mean about his having married, or wanting to marry, a French girl? Something of that kind?"

"Yes. Almost immediately after I got that letter, he was killed. We never heard anything of or about the girl. All we knew, actually, was her Christian name. We always expected her to write or to turn up, but she didn't. We never heard anything—until about a month ago, just before Christmas."

"I remember. You got a letter, didn't you?"

"Yes. Saying she was in England and would like to come and see us. It was all arranged and then, at the last minute, she sent a wire that she had to return unexpectedly to France."

"Well?"

"The police think that this woman who was killed—was French."

"They do, do they? She looked more of an English type to me, but one can't really judge. What's worrying you, then, is that just possibly the dead woman might be your brother's girl?"

"Yes."

"I think it's most unlikely," said Doctor Quimper, adding: "But all the same, I understand what you feel."

"I'm wondering if I ought not to tell the police about—about it all. Cedric and the others say it's quite unnecessary. What do you think?"

"Hm." Doctor Quimper pursed up his lips. He was silent for a moment or two, deep in thought. Then he said, almost unwillingly, "It's much simpler, of course, if you say nothing. I can understand what your brothers feel about it. All the same—"

"Yes?"

Quimper looked at her. His eyes had an affectionate twinkle in them.

"I'd go ahead and tell 'em," he said. "You'll go on worrying if you don't. I know you."

Emma flushed a little.

"Perhaps I'm foolish."

"You do what you want to do, my dear, and let the rest of the family go hang! I'd back your judgment against the lot of them any day."

12

"Girl! You, girl! Come in here."

Lucy turned her head, surprised. Old Mr. Crackenthorpe was beckoning to her fiercely from just inside a door.

"You want me, Mr. Crackenthorpe?"

"Don't talk so much. Come in here."

Lucy obeyed the imperative finger. Old Mr. Crackenthorpe took hold of her arm and pulled her inside the door and shut it.

"Want to show you something," he said.

Lucy looked round her. They were in a small room evidently designed to be used as a study, but equally evidently not used as such for a very long time. There were piles of dusty papers on the desk and cobwebs festooned from the corners of the ceiling. The air smelled damp and musty.

"Do you want me to clean this room?" she asked.

Old Mr. Crackenthorpe shook his head fiercely.

"No, you don't! I keep this room locked up. Emma would like to fiddle about in here, but I don't let her. It's my room. See these stones? They're geological specimens."

Lucy looked at a collection of twelve or fourteen lumps of rock, some polished and some rough.

"Lovely," she said kindly. "Most interesting."

"You're quite right. They are interesting. You're an intelligent girl. I don't show them to everybody. I'll show you some more things."

"It's very kind of you, but I ought really to get on with what I was doing. With six people in the house—"

"Eating me out of house and home. That's all they do when they come down here! Eat. They don't offer to pay for what they eat, either. Leeches! All waiting for me to die. Well, I'm not going to die just yet— I'm not going to die to please them. I'm a lot stronger than even Emma knows."

"I'm sure you are."

"I'm not so old, either. She makes out I'm an old man, treats me as an old man. You don't think I'm old, do you?"

"Of course not," said Lucy.

"Sensible girl. Take a look at this."

He indicated a large, faded chart which hung on the wall. It was, Lucy saw, a genealogical tree; some of it done so finely that one would have had to have a magnifying glass to read the names. The remote forebears, however, were written in large, proud capitals with crowns over the names.

"Descended from kings," said Mr. Crackenthorpe. "My mother's family tree, that is, not my father's. He was a vulgarian! Common old man! Didn't like me. I was a cut above him always. Took after my mother's side. Had a natural feeling for art and classical sculpture—he couldn't see anything in it, silly old fool. Don't remember my mother—died when I was two. Last of her family. They were sold up and she married my father. But you look there—Edward the Confessor—Ethelred the Unready—whole lot of them. And that was before the Normans came. Before the Normans—that's something, isn't it?"

"It is indeed."

"Now I'll show you something else." He guided her across the room to an enormous piece of dark oak furniture. Lucy was rather uneasily conscious of the strength of the fingers clutching her arm. There certainly seemed nothing feeble about old Mr. Crackenthorpe today. "See this? Came out of Lushington—that was my mother's people's place. Elizabethan, this is. Takes four men to move it. You don't know what I keep inside it, do you? Like me to show you?"

"Do show me," said Lucy politely.

"Curious, aren't you? All women are curious." He took a key from his pocket and unlocked the door of the lower cupboard. From this he took out a surprisingly new-looking cash box. This, again, he unlocked.

"Take a look here, my dear. Know what these are?"

He lifted out a small, paper-wrapped cylinder and pulled away the paper from one end. Gold coins trickled out into his palm.

"Look at these, young lady. Look at 'em, hold 'em, touch 'em. Know what they are? Bet you don't! You're too young. Sovereigns—that's what they are. Good, golden sovereigns. What we used before all these dirty bits of paper came into fashion. Worth a lot more than silly pieces of paper. Collected them a long time back. I've got other things in this box, too. Lots of things put away in here. All ready for the future. Emma doesn't know. Nobody knows. It's our secret, see, girl? D'you know why I'm telling you and showing you?"

"Why?"

"Because I don't want you to think I'm a played-out, sick old man. Lots of life in the old dog yet. My wife's been dead a long time. Always objecting to everything, she was. Didn't like the names I gave the children—good Saxon names. No interest in that family tree. I never paid any attention to what she said, though, and she was a poor-spirited creature—always gave in. Now you're a spirited filly—a very nice filly, indeed. I'll give you some advice. Don't throw yourself away on a young man. Young men are fools! You want to take care of your future. You wait—" His fingers pressed into Lucy's arm. He leaned to her ear. "I don't say more than that. Wait. Those silly fools think I'm going to die soon. I'm not. Shouldn't be surprised if I outlived the lot of them. And then we'll see! Oh yes, then we'll see. Harold's got no children. Cedric and Alfred aren't married. Emma—Emma will never marry now. She's a bit sweet on Quimper, but Quimper will never think of marrying Emma. There's Alexander, of course. Yes, there's Alexander. But, you know, I'm fond of Alexander. Yes, that's awkward. I'm fond of Alexander."

He paused for a moment, frowning, then said:

"Well, girl, what about it? What about it, eh?"

"Miss Eyelesbarrow . . ."

Emma's voice came faintly through the closed study door. Lucy seized gratefully at the opportunity.

"Miss Crackenthorpe's calling me. I must go. Thank you so much for all you have shown me."

"Don't forget . . . our secret . . ."

"I won't forget," said Lucy and hurried out into the hall, not quite certain as to whether she had or had not just received a conditional proposal of marriage.

II

Dermot Craddock sat at his desk in his room at New Scotland Yard. He was slumped sideways in an easy attitude and was talking into the telephone receiver, which he held with one elbow propped up on the table. He was speaking in French, a language in which he was tolerably proficient.

"It was only an idea, you understand," he said.

"But decidedly it is an idea," said the voice at the other end, from the Prefecture in Paris. "Already I have set inquiries in motion in those circles. My agent reports that he has two or three promising lines of inquiry. Unless there is some family life or a lover, these women drop out of circulation very easily and no one troubles about them. They have gone on tour, or there is some new man—it is no one's business to ask. It is a pity that the photograph you sent me is so difficult for anyone to recognize. Strangulation, it does not improve the appearance. Still, that cannot be helped. I go now to study the latest reports of my agents on this matter. There will be, perhaps, something. *Au revoir, mon cher.*"

As Craddock reiterated the farewell politely, a slip of paper was placed before him on the desk. It read:

> *Miss Emma Crackenthorpe*
> *To see Detective Inspector Craddock.*
> *Rutherford Hall case.*

He replaced the receiver and said to the police constable:
"Bring Miss Crackenthorpe up."

As he waited, he leaned back in his chair, thinking.

So he had not been mistaken; there was something that Emma Crackenthorpe knew—not much, perhaps, but something. And she had decided to tell him.

He rose to his feet as she was shown in, shook hands, settled her in a chair and offered her a cigarette which she refused. Then there was a momentary pause. She was trying, he decided, to find just the words she wanted. He leaned forward.

"You have come to tell me something, Miss Crackenthorpe? Can I help you? You've been worried about something, haven't you? Some little thing, perhaps, that you feel probably has nothing to do with the case, but on the other hand just might be related to it. You've come here to tell me about it, haven't you? It's to do, perhaps, with the identity of the dead woman. You think you know who she was?"

"No, no, not quite that. I think really it's most unlikely. But—"

"But there is some possibility that worries you. You'd better tell me about it, because we may be able to set your mind at rest."

Emma took a moment or two before speaking. Then she said:

"You have seen three of my brothers. I had another brother, Edmund, who was killed in the war. Shortly before he was killed, he wrote to me from France."

She opened her handbag and took out a worn and faded letter. She read from it:

"I hope this won't be a shock to you, Emmie, but I'm getting married —to a French girl. It's all been very sudden, but I know you'll be fond of Martine and look after her if anything happens to me. Will write you all the details in my next, by which time I shall be a married man! Break it gently to the old man, won't you? He'll probably go up in smoke."

Inspector Craddock held out a hand. Emma hesitated, then put the letter into it. She went on, speaking rapidly.

"Two days after receiving this letter, we had a telegram saying Edmund was missing, believed killed. Later he was definitely reported killed. It was just before Dunkirk and a time of great confusion. There was no Army record, as far as I could find out, of his having been married, but as I say, it was a confused time. I never heard anything from the girl. I tried, after the war, to make some inquiries, but I only knew her Christian name and that part of France had been occupied by the Germans and it was difficult to find out anything, without knowing the girl's surname and more about her. In the end I assumed that the marriage had never taken place and that the girl had probably married someone else before the end of the war, or might possibly herself have been killed."

Inspector Craddock nodded. Emma went on.

"Imagine my surprise to receive a letter, just about a month ago, signed *Martine Crackenthorpe.*"

"You have it?"

Emma took it from her bag and handed it to him. Craddock read it with interest. It was written in a slanting French hand, an educated hand.

> *Dear Mademoiselle,*
>
> *I hope it will not be a shock to you to get this letter. I do not even know if your brother Edmund told you that we were married. He said he was going to do so. He was killed only a few days after our marriage, and at the same time the Germans occupied our village. After the war ended, I decided that I would not write to you or approach you, though Edmund had told me to do so. But by then I had made a new life for myself, and it was not necessary. But now things have changed. For my son's sake I write this letter. He is your brother's son, you see, and I can no longer give him the advantages he ought to have. I am coming to England early next week. Will you let me know if I can come and see you? My address for letters is 126 Elvers Crescent, N. 10. I hope again this will not be the great shock to you.*
>
> *I remain with assurance of my excellent sentiments,*
>
> *Martine Crackenthorpe*

Craddock was silent for a moment or two. He reread the letter carefully before handing it back.

"What did you do on receipt of this letter, Miss Crackenthorpe?"

"My brother-in-law, Bryan Eastley, happened to be staying with me at the time and I talked to him about it. Then I rang up my brother Harold in London and consulted him about it. Harold was rather skeptical about the whole thing and advised extreme caution. We must, he said, go carefully into this woman's credentials."

Emma paused and then went on:

"That, of course, was only common sense and I quite agreed. But if this girl—woman—was really the Martine about whom Edmund had written to me, I felt that we must make her welcome. I wrote to the address she gave in her letter, inviting her to come down to Rutherford Hall and meet us. A few days later I received a telegram from London— *Very sorry forced to return to France unexpectedly. Martine.* There was no further letter or news of any kind."

"All this took place, when?"

Emma frowned.

"It was shortly before Christmas. I know, because I wanted to suggest her spending Christmas with us. But my father would not hear of it, so I suggested she should come down the weekend after Christmas while the family would still be there. I think the wire saying she was returning to France came actually a few days before Christmas."

"And you believe that this woman whose body was found in the sarcophagus might be this Martine?"

"No, of course I don't. But when you said she was probably a foreigner, well, I couldn't help wondering . . . if perhaps—"

Her voice died away.

Craddock spoke quickly and reassuringly.

"You did quite right to tell me about this. We'll look into it. I should say there is probably little doubt that the woman who wrote to you actually did go back to France and is there now, alive and well. On the other hand, there is a certain coincidence of dates, as you yourself have been clever enough to realize. As you heard at the inquest, the woman's death, according to the police surgeon's evidence, must have occurred about three to four weeks ago. Now don't worry, Miss Crackenthorpe, just leave it to us." He added casually, "You consulted Mr. Harold Crackenthorpe. What about your father and your other brothers?"

"I had to tell my father, of course. He got very worked up," she smiled faintly. "He was convinced it was a put-up thing to get money out of us. My father gets very excited about money. He believes, or pretends to believe, that he is a very poor man and that he must save every penny he can. I believe elderly people do get obsessions of that kind sometimes. It's not true, of course; he has a very large income and doesn't actually spend a quarter of it, or used not to until these days of high income tax. Certainly he has a large amount of savings put by." She paused and then went on. "I told my other two brothers also. Alfred seemed to consider it rather a joke, though he, too, thought it was almost certainly an imposture. Cedric just wasn't interested. He's inclined to be self-centered. Our idea was that the family would receive Martine, and that our lawyer, Mr. Wimborne, should also be asked to be present."

"What did Mr. Wimborne think about the matter?"

"We hadn't got as far as discussing the matter with him. We were on the point of doing so when Martine's telegram arrived."

"You have taken no further steps?"

"Yes. I wrote to the address in London with *Please forward* on the envelope, but I have had no reply of any kind."

"Rather a curious business. Hm . . ."

He looked at her sharply.

"What do you yourself think about it?"

"I don't know what to think."

"What were your reactions at the time? Did you think the letter was genuine, or did you agree with your father and brothers? What about your brother-in-law, by the way, what did he think?"

"Oh, Bryan thought that the letter was genuine."

"And you?"

"I wasn't sure."

"And what were your feelings about it, supposing that this girl really was your brother Edmund's widow?"

Emma's face softened.

"I was very fond of Edmund. He was my favorite brother. The letter seemed to me exactly the sort of letter that a girl like Martine would write under the circumstances. The course of events she described were entirely natural. I assumed that by the time the war ended she had either married again or was with some man who was protecting her and the child. Then, perhaps, this man had died or left her, and it then seemed right to her to apply to Edmund's family, as he himself had wanted her to do. The letter seemed genuine and natural to me, but of course, Harold pointed out that if it was written by an impostor, it would be written by some woman who had known Martine and who was in possession of all the facts, and so could write a thoroughly plausible letter. I had to admit the justice of that, but all the same—"

She stopped.

"You wanted it to be true?" said Craddock gently.

She looked at him gratefully.

"Yes, I wanted it to be true. I would be so glad if Edmund had left a son."

Craddock nodded.

"As you say, the letter, on the face of it, sounds genuine enough. What is surprising is the sequel; Martine Crackenthorpe's abrupt departure for Paris and the fact that you have never heard from her since. You had replied kindly to her, were prepared to welcome her. Why, even if she had to return to France, did she not write again? That is, presuming her to be the genuine article. If she were an impostor, of course, it's easier to explain. I thought perhaps that you might have consulted Mr. Wimborne, and that he might have instituted inquiries which alarmed the woman. That, you tell me, is not so. But it's still possible that one or other of your brothers may have done something of the kind. It's possible that this Martine may have had a background that would not stand investigation. She may have assumed that she would be dealing only with Edmund's affectionate sister, not with hardheaded, suspicious businessmen. She may have hoped to get sums of money out of you for the child—hardly a child now, a boy presumably of fifteen or sixteen—without many questions being asked. But instead she found she was going to run up against something quite different. After all, I should imagine that serious legal aspects would arise. If Edmund Crackenthorpe left a son, born in wedlock, he would be one of the heirs to your grandfather's estate?"

Emma nodded.

"Moreover, from what I have been told, he would in due course inherit Rutherford Hall and the land round it, very valuable building land, probably, by now."

Emma looked slightly startled.

"Yes, I hadn't thought of that."

"Well, I shouldn't worry," said Inspector Craddock. "You did quite right to come and tell me. I shall make inquiries, but it seems to me highly probable that there is no connection between the woman who wrote the letter—and who was probably trying to cash in on a swindle—and the woman whose body was found in the sarcophagus."

Emma rose with a sigh of relief.

"I'm so glad I've told you. You've been very kind."

Craddock accompanied her to the door.

Then he rang for Detective Sergeant Wetherall.

"Bob, I've got a job for you. Go to 126 Elvers Crescent, N. 10. Take photographs of the Rutherford Hall woman with you. See what you can find out about a woman calling herself Mrs. Crackenthorpe—Mrs. Martine Crackenthorpe—who was either living there or calling for letters there, between the dates of, say the fifteenth to the end of December."

"Right, sir."

Craddock busied himself with various other matters that were waiting attention on his desk. In the afternoon he went to see a theatrical agent who was a friend of his. His inquiries were not fruitful.

Later in the day when he returned to his office he found a wire from Paris on his desk.

PARTICULARS GIVEN BY YOU MIGHT APPLY TO ANNA STRAVINSKA OF BALLET MARITSKI. SUGGEST YOU COME OVER. DESSIN, PREFECTURE.

Craddock heaved a big sigh of relief and his brow cleared.

At last! So much, he thought, for the Martine Crackenthorpe hare. He decided to take the night ferry to Paris.

13

"It's so very kind of you to have asked me to take tea with you," said Miss Marple to Emma Crackenthorpe.

Miss Marple was looking particularly woolly and fluffy, a picture of a sweet old lady. She beamed as she looked round her: at Harold Crackenthorpe in his well-cut dark suit, at Alfred handing her sandwiches with a charming smile, at Cedric standing by the mantelpiece in a ragged tweed jacket, scowling at the rest of his family.

"We are very pleased that you could come," said Emma politely.

There was no hint of the scene which had taken place after lunch that day when Emma had exclaimed: "Dear me, I quite forgot. I told Miss Eyelesbarrow that she could bring her old aunt to tea today."

"Put her off," said Harold brusquely. "We've still got a lot to talk about. We don't want strangers here."

"Let her have tea in the kitchen or somewhere with the girl," said Alfred.

"Oh no, I couldn't do that," said Emma firmly. "That would be very rude."

"Oh, let her come," said Cedric. "We can draw her out a little about the wonderful Lucy. I should like to know more about that girl, I must say. I'm not sure that I trust her. Too smart by half."

"She's very well connected and quite genuine," said Harold. "I've made it my business to find out. One wanted to be sure. Poking about and finding the body the way she did . . ."

"If we only knew who this damned woman was," said Alfred.

Harold added angrily, "I must say, Emma, that I think you were out of your senses, going and suggesting to the police that the dead woman might be Edmund's French girl friend. It will make them convinced that she came here, and that probably one or other of us killed her."

"Oh no, Harold. Don't exaggerate."

"Harold's quite right," said Alfred. "Whatever possessed you, I don't know. I've a feeling I'm being followed everywhere I go by plain-clothes men."

"I told her not to do it," said Cedric. "Then Quimper backed her up."

"It's no business of his," said Harold angrily. "Let him stick to pills and powders and national health."

"Oh, do stop quarreling," said Emma wearily. "I'm really glad this old Miss What's-her-name is coming to tea. It will do us all good to have a stranger here and be prevented from going over and over the same things again and again. I must go and tidy myself up a little."

She left the room.

"This Lucy Eyelesbarrow," said Harold and stopped. "As Cedric says, it is odd that she should nose about in the barn and go opening up a sarcophagus—really a Herculean task. Perhaps we ought to take steps. Her attitude, I thought, was rather antagonistic at lunch."

"Leave her to me," said Alfred. "I'll soon find out if she's up to anything."

"I mean, why open up that sarcophagus?"

"Perhaps she isn't really Lucy Eyelesbarrow at all," suggested Cedric.

"But what would be the point—" Harold looked thoroughly upset. "Oh damn!"

They looked at each other with worried faces.

"And here's this pestilential old woman coming to tea. Just when we want to think."

"We'll talk things over this evening," said Alfred. "In the meantime, we'll pump the old aunt about Lucy."

So Miss Marple had duly been fetched by Lucy and installed by the fire, and she was now smiling up at Alfred as he handed her sandwiches with the approval she always showed toward a good-looking man.

"Thank you so much. May I ask—? Oh, egg and sardine, yes that will be very nice. I'm afraid I'm always rather greedy over my tea. As one gets on, you know—and of course, at night only a very light meal—I have to be careful. I shall be ninety next year. Yes, indeed."

"Eighty-seven," said Lucy.

"No, dear, ninety. You young people don't know best about everything." Miss Marple spoke with a faint acidity. Then she turned to her hostess once more. "What a beautiful house you have. And so many beautiful things in it. Those bronzes, now, they remind me of some my father bought at the Paris Exhibition. Really, your grandfather did? In the classical style, aren't they? Very handsome. How delightful for you having your brothers with you. So often families are scattered—India, though I suppose that is all done with now, and Africa—the West Coast, such a bad climate."

"Two of my brothers live in London."

"That is very nice for you."

"But my brother Cedric is a painter and lives in Iviza, one of the Balearic Islands."

"Painters are so fond of islands, are they not?" said Miss Marple. "Chopin—that was Majorca, was it not? but he was a musician. It is Gauguin I am thinking of. A sad life; misspent, one feels. I myself never really care for paintings of native women, and although I know he is very much admired, I have never cared for that lurid mustard color. One really feels quite bilious looking at his pictures."

She eyed Cedric with a slightly disapproving air.

"Tell us about Lucy as a child, Miss Marple," said Cedric.

She smiled up at him delightedly.

"Lucy was always so clever," she said. "Yes, you were, dear. Now don't interrupt. Quite remarkable at arithmetic. Why, I remember when the butcher overcharged me for topside of beef—"

Miss Marple launched full steam ahead into reminiscences of Lucy's childhood and from there to experiences of her own in village life.

The stream of reminiscence was interrupted by the entry of Bryan and the boys, rather wet and dirty as a result of an enthusiastic search for clues. Tea was brought in and with it came Doctor Quimper who raised his eyebrows slightly as he looked round after acknowledging his introduction to the old lady.

"Hope your father's not under the weather, Emma?"

"Oh no—that is, he was just a little tired this afternoon."

"Avoiding visitors, I expect," said Miss Marple with a roguish smile. "How well I remember my own dear father. 'Got a lot of old pussies coming?' he would say to my mother. 'Send my tea into the study.' Very naughty about it, he was."

"Please don't think—" began Emma, but Cedric cut in.

"It's always tea in the study when his dear sons come down. Psychologically to be expected, eh, Doctor?"

Doctor Quimper, who was devouring sandwiches and coffee cake with the frank appreciation of a man who has usually too little time to spend on his meals, said:

"Psychology's all right if it's left to the psychologists. Trouble is, everyone is an amateur psychologist nowadays. My patients tell me exactly what complexes and neuroses they're suffering from, without giving me a chance to tell them. Thanks, Emma, I will have another cup. No time for lunch today."

"A doctor's life, I always think, is so noble and self-sacrificing," said Miss Marple.

"You can't know many doctors," said Doctor Quimper. "Leeches they used to be called and leeches they often are! At any rate we do get paid nowadays, the state sees to that. No sending in of bills that you know won't ever be met. Trouble is that all one's patients are determined to get everything they can 'out of the government,' and as a result if little Jenny coughs twice in the night, or little Tommy eats a couple of green apples, out the poor doctor has to come in the middle of the night. Oh well! Glorious cake, Emma. What a cook you are!"

"Not mine. Miss Eyelesbarrow's."

"You make 'em just as good," said Quimper loyally.

"Will you come and see Father?"

She rose and the doctor followed her. Miss Marple watched them leave the room.

"Miss Crackenthorpe is a very devoted daughter, I see," she said.

"Can't imagine how she sticks the old man, myself," said the outspoken Cedric.

"She has a very comfortable home here, and Father is very much attached to her," said Harold quickly.

"Em's all right," said Cedric. "Born to be an old maid."

There was a faint twinkle in Miss Marple's eye as she said:

"Oh, do you think so?"

Harold said quickly:

"My brother didn't use the term old maid in any derogatory sense, Miss Marple."

"Oh, I wasn't offended," said Miss Marple. "I just wondered if he was right. I shouldn't say myself that Miss Crackenthorpe would be an old maid. She's the type, I think, that's quite likely to marry late in life, and make a success of it."

"Not very likely living here," said Cedric. "Never sees anybody she could marry."

Miss Marple's twinkle became more pronounced than ever.

"There are always clergymen and doctors."

Her eyes, gentle and mischievous, went from one to another.

It was clear that she had suggested to them something that they had never thought of and which they did not find overpleasing.

Miss Marple rose to her feet, dropping as she did so, several little woolly scarves and her bag.

The three brothers were most attentive picking things up.

"So kind of you," fluted Miss Marple. "Oh yes, and my little blue muffler. Yes, as I say, so kind to ask me here. I've been picturing, you know, just what your home was like, so that I can visualize dear Lucy working here."

"Perfect home conditions, with murder thrown in," said Cedric.

"Cedric!" Harold's voice was angry.

Miss Marple smiled up at Cedric.

"Do you know who you remind me of? Young Thomas Eade, our bank manager's son. Always out to shock people. It didn't do in banking circles, of course, so he went to the West Indies. He came home when his father died and inherited quite a lot of money. So nice for him. He was always better at spending money than making it."

II

Lucy took Miss Marple home. On her way back a figure stepped out of the darkness and stood in the glare of the headlights just as she was about to turn into the back lane. He held up his hand and Lucy recognized Alfred Crackenthorpe.

"That's better," he observed, as he got in. "Brrr, it's cold! I fancied I'd like a nice bracing walk. I didn't. Taken the old lady home all right?"

"Yes. She enjoyed herself very much."

"One could see that. Funny what a taste old ladies have for any kind of society, however dull. And really, nothing could be duller than Rutherford Hall. Two days here is about as much as I can stand. How do you manage to stick it out, Lucy? Don't mind if I call you Lucy, do you?"

"Not at all. I don't find it dull. Of course with me it's not a permanency."

"I've been watching you. You're a smart girl, Lucy. Too smart to waste yourself cooking and cleaning."

"Thank you, but I prefer cooking and cleaning to the office desk."

"So would I. But there are other ways of living. You could be a free lance."

"I am."

"Not this way. I mean, working for yourself, pitting your wits against—"

"Against what?"

"The powers that be! All the silly pettifogging rules and regulations that hamper us all nowadays. The interesting thing is there's always a way round them if you're smart enough to find it. And you're smart. Come now, does the idea appeal to you?"

"Possibly."

Lucy maneuvered the car into the stable yard.

"Not going to commit yourself?"

"I'd have to hear more."

"Frankly, my dear girl, I could use you. You've got the sort of manner that's invaluable, creates confidence."

"Do you want me to help you sell gold bricks?"

"Nothing so risky. Just a little bypassing of the law—no more." His hand slipped up her arm. "You're a damned attractive girl, Lucy. I'd like you as a partner."

"I'm flattered."

"Meaning, nothing doing? Think about it. Think of the fun, the pleasure you'd get out of outwitting all the sobersides. The trouble is, one needs capital."

"I'm afraid I haven't got any."

"Oh, it wasn't a touch! I'll be laying my hands on some before long. My revered Papa can't live forever, mean old brute. When he pops off, I lay my hands on some real money. What about it, Lucy?"

"What are the terms?"

"Marriage if you fancy it. Women seem to, no matter how advanced and self-supporting they are. Besides, married women can't be made to give evidence against their husbands."

"Not so flattering!"

"Come off it, Lucy. Don't you realize I've fallen for you?"

Rather to her surprise Lucy was aware of a queer fascination. There was a quality of charm about Alfred, perhaps due to sheer animal magnetism. She laughed and slipped from his encircling arm.

"This is no time for dalliance. There's dinner to think about."

"So there is, Lucy, and you're a lovely cook. What's for dinner?"

"Wait and see! You're as bad as the boys!"

They entered the house and Lucy hurried to the kitchen. She was rather surprised to be interrupted in her preparations by Harold Crackenthorpe.

"Miss Eyelesbarrow, can I speak to you about something?"

"Would later do, Mr. Crackenthorpe? I'm rather behindhand."

"Certainly. Certainly. After dinner?"

"Yes, that will do."

Dinner was duly served and appreciated. Lucy finished washing up and came out into the hall to find Harold Crackenthorpe waiting for her.

"Yes, Mr. Crackenthorpe?"

"Shall we come in here?" He opened the door of the drawing room and led the way. He shut the door behind her.

"I shall be leaving early in the morning," he explained, "but I want to tell you how struck I have been by your ability."

"Thank you," said Lucy feeling a little surprised.

"I feel that your talents are wasted here—definitely wasted."

"Do you? I don't."

At any rate, he can't ask me to marry him, thought Lucy. He's got a wife already.

"I suggest that having very kindly seen us through this lamentable crisis, you call upon me in London. If you will ring up and make an appointment, I will leave instructions with my secretary. The truth is that we could use someone of your outstanding ability in the firm. We could discuss fully in what field your talents would be most ably employed. I can offer you, Miss Eyelesbarrow, a very good salary indeed with brilliant prospects. I think you will be agreeably surprised."

His smile was magnanimous.

Lucy said demurely, "Thank you, Mr. Crackenthorpe, I'll think about it."

"Don't wait too long. These opportunities should not be missed by a young woman anxious to make her way in the world."

Again his teeth flashed.

"Good night, Miss Eyelesbarrow, sleep well."

"Well," said Lucy to herself, "well. . . . This is all very interesting."

On her way up to bed, Lucy encountered Cedric on the stairs.

"Look here, Lucy, there's something I want to say to you."

"Do you want me to marry you and come to Iviza and look after you?"

Cedric looked very much taken aback and slightly alarmed.

"I never thought of such a thing."

"Sorry. My mistake."

"I just wanted to know if you've a timetable in the house?"

"Is that all? There's one on the hall table."

"You know," said Cedric, reprovingly, "you shouldn't go about thinking everyone wants to marry you. You're quite a good-looking girl but not as good-looking as all that. There's a name for that sort of thing. It grows on you and you get worse. Actually you're the last girl in the world I should care to marry. The last girl."

"Indeed?" said Lucy. "You needn't rub it in. Perhaps you'd prefer me as a stepmother?"

"What's that?" Cedric stared at her, stupefied.

"You heard me," said Lucy, and went into her room and shut the door.

14

Dermot Craddock was fraternizing with Armand Dessin of the Paris Prefecture. The two men had met on one or two occasions and got on well together. Since Craddock spoke French fluently, most of their conversation was conducted in that language.

"It is an idea only," Dessin warned him. "I have a picture here of the corps de ballet. That is she, the fourth from the left. It says anything to you, yes?"

Inspector Craddock said that actually it didn't. A strangled young woman is not easy to recognize, and in this picture all the young women concerned were heavily made up and were wearing extravagant bird headdresses.

"It could be," he said. "I can't go further than that. Who was she? What do you know about her?"

"Almost less than nothing," said the other cheerfully. "She was not important, you see. And the Ballet Maritski—it is not important, either. It plays in suburban theaters and goes on tour. It has no real names, no stars, no famous ballerinas. But I will take you to see Madame Joliet who runs it."

Madame Joliet was a brisk businesslike Frenchwoman with a shrewd eye, a small mustache and a good deal of adipose tissue.

"Me, I do not like the police!" She scowled at them, without camouflaging her dislike of the visit. "Always, if they can, they make me embarrassments."

"No, no, Madame, you must not say that," said Dessin who was a tall, thin, melancholy looking man. "When have I ever caused you embarrassments?"

"Over that little fool who drank the carbolic acid," said Madame Joliet promptly. "And all because she has fallen in love with the *chef d'orchestre,* who does not care for women and has other tastes. Over that you made the big brou ha ha! Which is not good for my beautiful ballet."

"On the contrary, big box-office business," said Dessin. "And that was three years ago. You should not bear malice. Now about this girl, Anna Stravinska."

"Well, what about her?"

"Is she Russian?" asked Inspector Craddock.

"No, indeed. You mean, because of her name? But they all call themselves names like that, these girls. She was not important, she did not dance well, she was not particularly good-looking. *Elle etait assez bien, c'est tout.* She danced well enough for the corps de ballet, but no solos."

"Was she French?"

"Perhaps. She had a French passport. But she told me once that she had an English husband."

"She told you that she had an English husband? Alive or dead?"

Madame Joliet shrugged her shoulders.

"Dead, or he had left her. How should I know which? These girls—there is always some trouble with men."

"When did you last see her?"

"I take my company to London for six weeks. We play at Torquay, at Bournemouth, at Eastbourne, at somewhere else I forget and at Hammersmith. Then we come back to France, but Anna, she does not come. She sends a message only that she leaves the company, that she goes to live with her husband's family, some nonsense of that kind. I did not think it is true, myself. I think it more likely that she has met a man, you understand."

Inspector Craddock nodded. He perceived that that was what Madame Joliet would invariably think.

"And it is no loss to me. I do not care. I can get girls just as good and better to come and dance, so I shrug the shoulders and do not think of it any more. Why should I? They are all the same, these girls, mad about men."

"What date was this?"

"When we return to France? It was—yes—the Sunday before Christmas. And Anna she leaves two, or is it three, days before that? I cannot remember exactly. But the end of the week at Hammersmith we have to dance without her, and it means rearranging things. It was very naughty of her, but these girls—the moment they meet a man they are all the same. Only I say to everybody, 'Zut, I do not take her back, that one!' "

"Very annoying for you."

"Ah! me—I do not care. No doubt she passes the Christmas holiday with some man she has picked up. It is not my affair. I can find other girls —girls who will leap at the chance of dancing in the Ballet Maritski and who can dance as well or better than Anna."

Madame Joliet paused and then asked with a sudden gleam of interest, "Why do you want to find her? Has she come into money?"

"On the contrary," said Inspector Craddock politely. "We think she may have been murdered."

Madame Joliet relapsed into indifference.

"*Ça se peut!* It happens. Ah well! She was a good Catholic. She went to Mass on Sundays, and no doubt to confession."

"Did she ever speak to you, Madame, of a son?"

"A son? Do you mean she had a child? That, now, I should consider most unlikely. These girls, all—all of them—know a useful address to which to go. M. Dessin knows that as well as I do."

"She may have had a child before she adopted a stage life," said Craddock. "During the war, for instance."

"*Ah! dans la guerre.* That is always possible. But if so, I know nothing about it."

"Who among the other girls were her closest friends?"

"I can give you two or three names, but she was not very intimate with anyone."

They could get nothing else useful from Madame Joliet.

Shown the compact, she said Anna had one of that kind, but so had most of the other girls. Anna had perhaps bought a fur coat in London, she did not know. "Me, I occupy myself with the rehearsals, with the stage lighting, with all the difficulties of my business. I have not time to notice what my artists wear."

After Madame Joliet, they interviewed the girls whose names she had given them. One or two of them had known Anna fairly well, but they all said that she had not been one to talk much about herself, and that when she did, it was, so one girl said, mostly lies.

"She liked to pretend things—stories about having been the mistress of a grand duke or of a great English financier or how she worked for the Resistance in the war, even a story about being a film star in Hollywood."

Another girl said:

"I think that really she had had a very tame bourgeoise existence. She liked to be in ballet because she thought it was romantic, but she was not a good dancer. You understand that if she were to say, 'My father was a draper in Amiens,' that would not be romantic! So instead she made up things."

"Even in London," said the first girl, "she threw out hints about a very rich man who was going to take her on a cruise round the world, because she reminded him of his dead daughter who had died in a car accident. *Quelle blague!*"

"She told me she was going to stay with a rich lord in Scotland," said the second girl. "She said she would shoot the deer there."

None of this was helpful. All that seemed to emerge from it was that Anna Stravinska was a proficient liar. She was certainly not shooting deer with a peer in Scotland, and it seemed equally unlikely that she was on the sundeck of a liner cruising round the world. But neither was there any real reason to believe that her body had been found in a sarcophagus at Rutherford Hall. The identification by the girls and Madame Joliet was very uncertain and hesitating. It looked something like Anna, they all agreed. But really! All swollen up—it might be anybody!

The only fact that was established was that, on December 19, Anna Stravinska had decided not to return to France, and that on the twentieth of December a woman resembling her in appearance had traveled to Brackhampton by the 4:54 train and had been strangled.

If the woman in the sarcophagus was not Anna Stravinska, where was Anna now?

To that, Madame Joliet's answer was simple and inevitable:

"With a man!"

And it was probably the correct answer, Craddock reflected ruefully.

One other possibility had to be considered, raised by the casual remark that Anna had once referred to having an English husband.

Had that husband been Edmund Crackenthorpe?

It seemed unlikely, considering the word picture of Anna that had been given him by those who knew her. What was much more probable was that Anna had at one time known the girl Martine sufficiently intimately to be acquainted with the necessary details. It might have been Anna who wrote that letter to Emma Crackenthorpe and, if so, Anna would have been quite likely to have taken fright at any question of an investigation. Perhaps she had even thought it prudent to sever her connection with the Ballet Maritski. Again, where was she now?

And again, inevitably, Madame Joliet's answer seemed the most likely. With a man.

II

Before leaving Paris, Craddock discussed with Dessin the question of the woman named Martine. Dessin was inclined to agree with his English colleague that the matter had probably no connection with the woman found in the sarcophagus. All the same, he agreed, the matter ought to be investigated.

He assured Craddock that the Sûreté would do their best to discover if there actually was any record of a marriage between Lieutenant Edmund Crackenthorpe of the 4th Southshire Regiment and a French girl whose Christian name was Martine. Time: just prior to the fall of Dunkirk.

He warned Craddock, however, that a definite answer was doubtful. The area in question had not only been occupied by the Germans at almost exactly that time, but subsequently that part of France had suffered severe war damage at the time of the invasion. Many buildings and records had been destroyed.

"But rest assured, my dear colleague, we shall do our best."

With this, he and Craddock took leave of each other.

III

On Craddock's return Sergeant Wetherall was waiting to report with gloomy relish:

"Accommodation address, sir—that's what 126 Elvers Crescent is. Quite respectable and all that."

"Any identifications?"

"No. Nobody could recognize the photograph as that of a woman who had called for letters, but I don't think they would anyway. It's a month ago, very near, and a good many people use the place. It's actually a boardinghouse for students."

"She might have stayed there under another name."

"If so, they didn't recognize her as the original of the photograph." He added:

"We circularized the hotels—nobody registering as Martine Cracken-thorpe anywhere. On receipt of your call from Paris, we checked up on Anna Stravinska. She was registered with other members of the company in a cheap hotel off Brook Green—mostly theatricals there. She cleared out on the night of Thursday the nineteenth after the show. No further record."

Craddock nodded. He suggested a line of further inquiries, though he had little hope of success from them.

After some thought, he rang up Wimborne, Henderson and Carstairs and asked for an appointment with Mr. Wimborne.

In due course, he was ushered into a particularly airless room where Mr. Wimborne was sitting behind a large old-fashioned desk covered with bundles of dusty-looking papers. Various deed boxes labeled *Sir John ffouldes, dec. Lady Derrin, George Rowbotham, Esq.*, ornamented the walls; whether as relics of a bygone era or as part of present-day legal affairs, the Inspector did not know.

Mr. Wimborne eyed his visitor with the polite wariness characteristic of a family lawyer toward the police.

"What can I do for you, Inspector?"

"This letter." Craddock pushed Martine's letter across the table. Mr. Wimborne touched it with a distasteful finger but did not pick it up. His color rose very slightly and his lips tightened.

"Quite so," he said, "quite so! I received a letter from Miss Emma Crackenthorpe yesterday morning, informing me of her visit to Scotland Yard and of—ah—all the circumstances. I may say that I am at a loss to understand—quite at a loss—why I was not consulted about this letter at the time of its arrival! Most extraordinary! I should have been informed immediately."

Inspector Craddock repeated soothingly such platitudes as seemed best calculated to reduce Mr. Wimborne to an amenable frame of mind.

"I'd no idea that there was ever any question of Edmund's having married," said Mr. Wimborne in an injured voice.

Inspector Craddock said that he supposed, in wartime . . . and left it to trail away vaguely.

"Wartime!" snapped Mr. Wimborne with waspish acerbity. "Yes, in-deed, we were in Lincoln's Inn Fields at the outbreak of war and there was a direct hit on the house next door, and a great number of our records were destroyed. Not the really important documents, of course; they had been removed to the country for safety. But it caused a great deal of confusion. Of course, the Crackenthorpe business was in my father's hands at that time. He died six years ago. I dare say he may have been told about this so-called marriage of Edmund's, but on the face of it, it looks as though that marriage, even if contemplated, never took place, and so, no doubt my father did not consider the story of any importance. I must say, all this sounds very fishy to me. This coming forward, after all these years, and claiming a marriage and a legitimate son. Very fishy, indeed. What proofs had she got, I'd like to know?"

"Just so," said Craddock. "What would her position or her son's position be?"

"The idea was, I suppose, that she would get the Crackenthorpes to provide for her and for the boy."

"Yes, but I meant, what would she and the son be entitled to, legally speaking, if she could prove her claim?"

"Oh, I see." Mr. Wimborne picked up his spectacles which he had laid aside in his irritation, and put them on, staring through them at Inspector Craddock with shrewd attention. "Well, at the moment, nothing. But if she could prove that the boy was the son of Edmund Crackenthorpe, born in lawful wedlock, then the boy would be entitled to his share of Josiah Crackenthorpe's trust, on the death of Luther Crackenthorpe. More than that, he'd inherit Rutherford Hall, since he's the son of the eldest son."

"Would anyone want to inherit the house?"

"To live in? I should say, certainly not. But that estate, my dear Inspector, is worth a considerable amount of money. Very considerable. Land for industrial and building purposes. Land which is now in the heart of Brackhampton. Oh yes, a very considerable inheritance."

"If Luther Crackenthorpe dies, I believe you told me that Cedric gets it?"

"He inherits the real estate, yes, as the eldest surviving son."

"Cedric Crackenthorpe, I have been given to understand, is not interested in money?"

Mr. Wimborne gave Craddock a cold stare.

"Indeed? I am inclined, myself, to take statements of such a nature with what I might term a grain of salt. There are doubtless certain unworldly people who are indifferent to money. I myself have never met one."

Mr. Wimborne obviously derived a certain satisfaction from this remark.

Inspector Craddock hastened to take advantage of this ray of sunshine.

"Harold and Alfred Crackenthorpe," he ventured, "seem to have been a good deal upset by the arrival of this letter?"

"Well they might be," said Mr. Wimborne. "Well they might be."

"It would reduce their eventual inheritance?"

"Certainly. Edmund Crackenthorpe's son—always presuming there is a son—would be entitled to a fifth share of the trust money."

"That doesn't really seem a very serious loss?"

Mr. Wimborne gave him a shrewd glance.

"It is a totally inadequate motive for murder, if that is what you mean."

"But I suppose they're both pretty hard up," Craddock murmured.

He sustained Mr. Wimborne's sharp glance with perfect impassivity.

"Oh! So the police have been making inquiries? Yes, Alfred is almost incessantly in low water. Occasionally he is very flush of money for a short time, but it soon goes. Harold, as you seem to have discovered, is at present somewhat precariously situated."

"In spite of his appearance of financial prosperity?"

"Façade. All façade! Half these City concerns don't even know if they're solvent or not. Balance sheets can be made to look all right to the inexpert eye. But when the assets that are listed aren't really assets—when those assets are trembling on the brink of a crash—where are you?"

"Where, presumably, Harold Crackenthorpe is, in bad need of money."

"Well, he wouldn't have got it by strangling his late brother's widow," said Mr. Wimborne. "And nobody's murdered Luther Crackenthorpe, which is the only murder that would do the family any good. So really, Inspector, I don't quite see where your ideas are leading you."

The worst of it was, Inspector Craddock thought, that he wasn't very sure himself.

15

Inspector Craddock had made an appointment with Harold Crackenthorpe at his office, and he and Sergeant Wetherall arrived there punctually. The office was on the fourth floor of a big block of City offices. Inside everything showed prosperity and the acme of modern business taste.

A neat young woman took his name, spoke in a discreet murmur through a telephone, and then rising, showed them into Harold Crackenthorpe's own private office.

Harold was sitting behind a large leather-topped desk and was looking as impeccable and self-confident as ever. If, as the Inspector's private knowledge led him to surmise, he was close upon Queer Street, no trace of it showed.

He looked up with a frank, welcoming interest.

"Good morning, Inspector Craddock. I hope this means that you have some definite news for us at last."

"Hardly that, I am afraid, Mr. Crackenthorpe. It's just a few more questions I'd like to ask."

"More questions? Surely by now we have answered everything imaginable."

"I dare say it feels like that to you, Mr. Crackenthorpe, but it's just a question of our regular routine."

"Well, what is it this time?" He spoke impatiently.

"I should be glad if you could tell me exactly what you were doing on the afternoon and evening of December the twentieth last, say between the hours of three p.m. and midnight."

Harold Crackenthorpe went an angry shade of plum red.

"That seems to be a most extraordinary question to ask me. What does it mean, I should like to know?"

Craddock smiled gently.

"It just means that I should like to know where you were between the hours of three p.m. and midnight on Friday, December the twentieth."

"Why?"

"It would help to narrow things down."

"Narrow them down? You have extra information, then?"

"We hope that we're getting a little closer, sir."

"I'm not at all sure that I ought to answer your question. Not, that is, without having my solicitor present."

"That, of course, is entirely up to you," said Craddock. "You are not bound to answer any questions and you have a perfect right to have a solicitor present before you do so."

"You are not—let me be quite clear—er—warning me in anyway?"

"Oh no, sir." Inspector Craddock looked properly shocked. "Nothing of that kind. The questions I am asking you I am asking of several other people as well. There's nothing directly personal about this. It's just a matter of necessary eliminations."

"Well, of course, I'm anxious to assist in any way I can. Let me see now. Such a thing isn't easy to answer offhand, but we're very systematic here. Miss Ellis, I expect, can help."

He spoke briefly into one of the telephones on his desk and almost immediately a streamlined young woman in a well-cut black suit entered with a notebook.

"My secretary, Miss Ellis, Inspector Craddock. Now, Miss Ellis, the Inspector would like to know what I was doing on the afternoon and evening of—what was the date?"

"Friday, December the twentieth."

"Friday, December the twentieth. I expect you will have some record."

"Oh yes." Miss Ellis left the room, returned with an office memorandum calendar and turned the pages.

"You were in the office on the morning of December the twentieth. You had a conference with Mr. Goldie about the Cromartie merger, you lunched with Lord Forthville at the Berkeley—"

"Ah, it was that day, yes."

"You returned to the office at about three o'clock and dictated half a dozen letters. You then left to attend Sotheby's sale rooms where you were interested in some rare manuscripts which were coming up for sale that day. You did not return to the office again, but I have a note to remind you that you were attending the Catering Club dinner that evening." She looked up interrogatively.

"Thank you, Miss Ellis."

Miss Ellis glided from the room.

"That is all quite clear in my mind," said Harold. "I went to Sotheby's that afternoon but the items I wanted there went for far too high a price. I had tea in a small place in Jermyn Street—Russell's, I think it is called. I dropped into a News Theatre for about half an hour or so, then went home. I live at 43 Cardigan Gardens. The Catering Club dinner took place at seven-thirty at Caterers' Hall, and after it I returned home to bed. I think that should answer your questions?"

"That's all very clear, Mr. Crackenthorpe. What time was it when you returned home to dress?"

"I don't think I can remember exactly. Soon after six, I should think."

"And after the dinner?"

"It was, I think, half-past eleven when I got home."

"Did your manservant let you in? Or perhaps Lady Alice Crackenthorpe?"

"My wife, Lady Alice, is abroad in the South of France and has been since early in December. I let myself in with my latchkey."

"So there is no one who can vouch for your returning home when you say you did?"

Harold gave him a cold stare.

"I dare say the servants heard me come in. I have a man and wife. But really, Inspector—"

"Please, Mr. Crackenthorpe, I know these questions are annoying, but I have nearly finished. Do you own a car?"

"Yes, a Humber Hawk."

"You drive it yourself?"

"Yes. I don't use it much except at weekends. Driving in London is quite impossible nowadays."

"I presume you use it when you go down to see your father and sister at Brackhampton?"

"Not unless I am going to stay there for some length of time. If I just go down for the night, as, for instance, to the inquest the other day, I always go by train. There is an excellent train service and it is far quicker than going by car. The car my sister hires meets me at the station."

"Where do you keep your car?"

"I rent a garage in the mews behind Cardigan Gardens. Any more questions?"

"I think that's all for now," said Inspector Craddock smiling and rising. "I'm very sorry for having to bother you."

When they were outside, Sergeant Wetherall, a man who lived in a state of dark suspicion of all and sundry, remarked meaningly:

"He didn't like those questions—didn't like them at all. Put out, he was."

"If you have not committed a murder, it naturally annoys you if it seems someone thinks that you have," said Inspector Craddock mildly. "It would particularly annoy an ultrarespectable man like Harold Crackenthorpe. There's nothing in that. What we've got to find out now is if anyone actually saw Harold Crackenthorpe at the sale that afternoon, and the same applies to the teashop place. He could easily have traveled by the 4:54, pushed the woman out of the train and caught a train back to London in time to appear at the dinner. In the same way he could have driven his car down that night, moved the body to the sarcophagus and driven back again. Make inquiries in the mews."

"Yes, sir. Do you think that's what he did do?"

"How do I know?" asked Inspector Craddock. "He's a tall, dark man. He could have been on that train and he's got a connection with Rutherford Hall. He's a possible suspect in this case. Now for brother Alfred."

II

Alfred Crackenthorpe had a flat in West Hampstead, in a big modern building of slightly jerry-built type with a large courtyard in which the owners of flats parked their cars with a certain lack of consideration for others.

The flat was of the modern built-in type, evidently rented furnished. It had a long plywood table that let down from the wall, a divan bed and various chairs of improbable proportions.

Alfred Crackenthorpe met them with engaging friendliness but was, the Inspector thought, nervous.

"I'm intrigued," he said. "Can I offer you a drink, Inspector Crad-dock?" He held up various bottles invitingly.

"No, thank you, Mr. Crackenthorpe."

"As bad as that?" He laughed at his own little joke, then asked what it was all about.

Inspector Craddock said his little piece.

"What was I doing on the afternoon and evening of December the twentieth? How should I know? Why, that's—what?—over three weeks ago."

"Your brother Harold has been able to tell us very exactly."

"Brother Harold, perhaps. Not brother Alfred." He added with a touch of something, envious malice possibly: "Harold is the successful member of the family—busy, useful, fully employed, a time for everything and everything at that time. Even if he were to commit a murder, shall we say? it would be carefully timed and exact."

"Any particular reason for using that example?"

"Oh no—it just came into my mind as a supreme absurdity."

"Now about yourself."

Alfred spread out his hands.

"It's as I tell you, I've no memory for times or places. If you were to say Christmas Day now, then I should be able to answer you—there's a peg to hang it on. I know where I was Christmas Day. We spend that with my father at Brackhampton. I really don't know why. He grumbles at the expense of having us, and would grumble that we never came near him if we didn't come. We really do it to please my sister."

"And you did it this year?"

"Yes."

"But unfortunately your father was taken ill, was he not?"

Craddock was pursuing a side line deliberately, led by the kind of instinct that often came to him in his profession.

"He was taken ill. Living like a sparrow in the glorious cause of economy, sudden full eating and drinking had its effect."

"That was all it was, was it?"

"Of course. What else?"

"I gathered that his doctor was—worried."

"Oh, that old fool Quimper," Alfred spoke quickly and scornfully. "It's no use listening to him, Inspector. He's an alarmist of the worst kind."

"Indeed? He seemed a rather sensible kind of man to me."

"He's a complete fool. Father's not really an invalid, there's nothing wrong with his heart, but he takes in Quimper completely. Naturally, when father really felt ill, he made a terrific fuss, and had Quimper going and coming, asking questions, going into everything he'd eaten and drunk. The whole thing was ridiculous!" Alfred spoke with unusual heat.

Craddock was silent for a moment or two, rather effectively. Alfred fidgeted, shot him a quick glance and then said petulantly:

"Well, what is all this? Why do you want to know where I was on a particular Friday, three or four weeks ago?"

"So you do remember that it was a Friday?"

"I thought you said so."

"Perhaps I did," said Inspector Craddock. "At any rate, Friday the twentieth is the day I am asking about."

"Why?"

"A routine inquiry."

"That's nonsense. Have you found out something more about this woman? About where she came from?"

"Our information is not yet complete."

Alfred gave him a sharp glance.

"I hope you're not being led aside by this wild theory of Emma's that she might have been my brother Edmund's widow. That's complete nonsense."

"This Martine did not at any time apply to you?"

"To me? Good Lord, no. That would have been a laugh."

"She would be more likely, you think, to go to your brother Harold?"

"Much more likely. His name's frequently in the papers. He's well off. Trying a touch there wouldn't surprise me. Not that she'd have got anything. Harold's as tightfisted as the old man himself. Emma, of course, is the softhearted one of the family, and she was Edmund's favorite sister. All the same, Emma isn't credulous. She was quite alive to the possibility of this woman being phony. She had it all laid on for the entire family to be there—and a hardheaded solicitor as well."

"Very wise," said Craddock. "Was there a definite date fixed for this meeting?"

"It was to be soon after Christmas. The weekend of the twenty-seventh—" He stopped.

"Ah," said Craddock pleasantly. "So I see some dates have a meaning to you."

"I've told you no definite date was fixed."

"But you talked about it—when?"

"I really can't remember."

"And you can't tell me what you yourself were doing on Friday, December the twentieth?"

"Sorry, my mind's an absolute blank."

"You don't keep an engagement book?"

"Can't stand the things."

"The Friday before Christmas—it shouldn't be too difficult."

"I played golf one day with a likely prospect." Alfred shook his head.

"No, that was the week before. I probably just mooched around. I spend a lot of my time doing that. I find one's business gets done in bars more than anywhere else."

"Perhaps the people here, or some of your friends, may be able to help?"

"Maybe. I'll ask them. Do what I can."

Alfred seemed more sure of himself now.

"I can't tell you what I was doing that day," he said, "but I can tell you what I wasn't doing. I wasn't murdering anyone in the Long Barn."

"Why should you say that, Mr. Crackenthorpe?"

"Come now, my dear Inspector. You're investigating this murder, aren't you? And when you begin to ask 'Where were you on such and such a day at such and such a time?' you're narrowing down things. I'd very much like to know why you've hit on Friday the twentieth between —what?—lunchtime and midnight? It couldn't be medical evidence, not after all this time. Did somebody see the deceased sneaking into the barn that afternoon? She went in and she never came out, etc.? Is that it?"

The sharp, black eyes were watching him narrowly, but Inspector Craddock was far too old a hand to react to that sort of thing.

"I'm afraid we'll have to let you guess about that," he said pleasantly.

"The police are so secretive."

"Not only the police. I think, Mr. Crackenthorpe, you could remember what you were doing on that Friday if you tried. Of course, you may have reasons for not wishing to remember—"

"You won't catch me that way, Inspector. It's very suspicious, of course, very suspicious, indeed, that I can't remember, but there it is! Wait a minute now! I went to Leeds that week, stayed at a hotel close to the town hall—can't remember its name, but you'd find it easily enough. That might have been on the Friday."

"We'll check up," said the Inspector unemotionally.

He rose: "I'm sorry you couldn't have been more co-operative, Mr. Crackenthorpe."

"Most unfortunate for me! There's Cedric with a safe alibi in Iviza, and Harold, no doubt, checked with business appointments and public dinners every hour, and here am I with no alibi at all. Very sad. And all so silly. I've already told you I don't murder people. And why should I murder an unknown woman anyway? What for? Even if the corpse is the corpse of Edmund's widow, why should any of us wish to do away with her? Now if she'd been married to Harold in the war and had suddenly reappeared, then it might have been awkward for the respectable Harold—bigamy and all that. But Edmund! Why, we'd all have enjoyed making Father stump up a bit to give her an allowance and send the boy to a decent school. Father would have been wild, but he couldn't in decency refuse to do something. Won't you have a drink before you go, Inspector? Sure? Too bad I haven't been able to help you."

III

"Sir, listen, do you know what?"

Inspector Craddock looked at his excited sergeant.

"Yes, Wetherall, what is it?"

"I've placed him, sir. That chap. All the time I was trying to fix it and suddenly it came. He was mixed up in that tinned-food business with Dicky Rogers. Never got anything on him—too cagey for that. And he's been in with one or more of the Soho lot. Watches and that Italian sovereign business."

Of course! Craddock realized now why Alfred's face had seemed vaguely familiar from the first. It had all been small-time stuff, never anything that could be proved. Alfred had always been on the outskirts of the racket with a plausible, innocent reason for having been mixed up in it at all. But the police had been quite sure that a small, steady profit came his way.

"That throws rather a light on things," Craddock said.

"Think he done it?"

"I shouldn't have said he was the type to do murder. But it explains other things—the reason why he couldn't come up with an alibi."

"Yes, that looks bad for him."

"Not really," said Craddock. "It's quite a clever line, just to say firmly you can't remember. Lots of people can't remember what they did and where they were even a week ago. It's especially useful if you don't particularly want to call attention to the way you spend your time—interesting rendezvous at lorry pullups with the Dicky Rogers crowd, for instance."

"So you think he's all right?"

"I'm not prepared to think anyone's all right just yet," said Inspector Craddock. "You've got to work on it, Wetherall."

Back at his desk, Craddock sat frowning, and making little notes on the pad in front of him.

Murderer (he wrote). . . . *A tall, dark man!!!*

Victim?. . . . *Could have been Martine, Edmund Crackenthorpe's girl friend or widow.*

 or

 Could have been Anna Stravinska. Went out of circulation at appropriate time, right age and appearance, clothing, etc. No connection with Rutherford Hall as far as is known.

Could be Harold's first wife! Bigamy!
"   "   "   *mistress. Blackmail?!*
If connection with Alfred, might be blackmailer had knowledge
that could have sent him to jail?
If Cedric—might have had connection with him abroad—Paris?
Balearics?
                    or
Victim could be Anna S. posing as Martine
                    or
Victim is unknown woman killed by unknown murderer!

"And most probably the latter," said Craddock aloud.

He reflected gloomily on the situation. You couldn't get far with a case until you had the motive. All the motives suggested so far seemed either inadequate or farfetched.

Now if only it had been the murder of old Mr. Crackenthorpe. Plenty of motive there.

Something stirred in his memory.

He made further notes on his pad.

Ask Dr. Q. about Christmas illness.
Cedric—alibi.
Consult Miss M. for latest gossip.

16

When Craddock got to 4 Madison Road he found Lucy Eyelesbarrow with Miss Marple.

He hesitated for a moment on his plan of campaign and then decided that Lucy Eyelesbarrow might prove a valuable ally.

After greetings, he solemnly drew out his notecase, extracted three pound notes, added three shillings and pushed them across the table to Miss Marple.

"What's this, Inspector?"

"Consultation fee. You're a consultant—on murder! Pulse, temperature, local reactions, possible deep-seated cause of said murder. I'm just the poor harassed local G.P."

Miss Marple looked at him and twinkled. He grinned at her. Lucy Eyelesbarrow gave a faint gasp and then laughed.

"Why, Inspector Craddock, you're human after all."

"Oh well, I'm not strictly on duty this afternoon."

"I told you we had met before," said Miss Marple to Lucy. "Sir Henry Clithering is his godfather, a very old friend of mine."

"Would you like to hear, Miss Eyelesbarrow, what my godfather said about her, the first time we met? He described her as just the finest detective God ever made—natural genius cultivated in a suitable soil. He told me never to despise the"—Dermot Craddock paused for a moment to seek for a synonym for "old pussies"—"er—elderly ladies. He said they could usually tell you what might have happened, what ought to have happened and even what actually did happen! And," he said, "they can tell you why it happened!" He added that "this particular—er—elderly lady was at the top of the class."

"Well!" said Lucy, "that seems to be a testimonial all right."

Miss Marple was pink and confused and looked unusually dithery.

"Dear Sir Henry," she murmured. "Always so kind. Really I'm not at all clever, just, perhaps, a slight knowledge of human nature—living, you know, in a village."

She added, with more composure:

"Of course, I am somewhat handicapped, by not actually being on the spot. It is so helpful, I always feel, when people remind you of other people, because types are alike everywhere and that is such a valuable guide."

Lucy looked a little puzzled, but Craddock nodded comprehendingly.

"But you've been to tea there, haven't you?" he said.

"Yes, indeed. Most pleasant. I was a little disappointed that I didn't see old Mr. Crackenthorpe, but one can't have everything."

"Do you feel that if you saw the person who had done the murder, you'd know?" asked Lucy.

"Oh, I wouldn't say that, dear. One is always inclined to guess, and guessing would be very wrong when it is a question of anything as serious as murder. All one can do is to observe the people concerned, or who might have been concerned, and see of whom they remind you."

"Like Cedric and the bank manager?"

Miss Marple corrected her.

"The bank manager's son, dear. Mr. Eade himself was far more like Mr. Harold, a very conservative man, but perhaps a little too fond of money —the sort of man, too, who would go a long way to avoid scandal."

Craddock smiled and said:

"And Alfred?"

"Jenkins at the garage," Miss Marple replied promptly. "He didn't exactly appropriate tools, but he used to exchange a broken or inferior jack for a good one. And I believe he wasn't very honest over batteries, though I don't understand these things very well. I know Raymond left off dealing with him and went to the garage on the Milchester road. As for Emma," continued Miss Marple thoughtfully, "she reminds me very much of Geraldine Webb—always very quiet, almost dowdy—and bullied a good deal by her elderly mother. Quite a surprise to everybody when the mother died unexpectedly and Geraldine came into a nice sum of money and went and had her hair cut and permed and went off on a cruise and came back married to a very nice barrister. They had two children."

The parallel was clear enough. Lucy said, rather uneasily: "Do you think you ought to have said what you did about Emma marrying? It seemed to upset the brothers."

Miss Marple nodded.

"Yes," she said. "So like men, quite unable to see what's going on under their eyes. I don't believe you noticed yourself."

"No," admitted Lucy. "I never thought of anything of that kind. They both seemed to me—"

"So old?" said Miss Marple smiling a little. "But Doctor Quimper isn't much over forty, I should say, though he's going gray on the temples, and it's obvious that he's longing for some kind of home life; and Emma Crackenthorpe is under forty, not too old to marry and have a family. The doctor's wife died quite young having a baby, so I have heard."

"I believe she did. Emma said something about it one day."

"He must be lonely," said Miss Marple. "A busy hard-working doctor needs a wife, someone sympathetic, not too young."

"Listen, darling," said Lucy. "Are we investigating crime, or are we matchmaking?"

Miss Marple twinkled.

"I'm afraid I am rather romantic. Because I am an old maid, perhaps. You know, dear Lucy, that as far as I am concerned, you have fulfilled your contract. If you really want a holiday abroad before taking up your next engagement, you would have time still for a short trip."

"And leave Rutherford Hall? Never! I'm the complete sleuth by now. Almost as bad as the boys. They spend their entire time looking for clues. They looked all through the dustbins yesterday. Most unsavory, and they hadn't really the faintest idea what they were looking for. If they come to you in triumph, Inspector Craddock, bearing a torn scrap of paper with *Martine—if you value your life keep away from the Long Barn!* on it, you'll know that I've taken pity on them and concealed it in the pigsty!"

"Why the pigsty, dear?" asked Miss Marple with interest. "Do they keep pigs?"

"Oh no, not nowadays. It's just that I go there sometimes."

For some reason Lucy blushed. Miss Marple looked at her with increased interest.

"Who's at the house now?" asked Craddock.

"Cedric's there, and Bryan's down for the weekend. Harold and Alfred are coming down tomorrow. They rang up this morning. I somehow got the impression that you had been putting the cat among the pigeons, Inspector Craddock."

Craddock smiled.

"I shook them up a little. Asked them to account for their movements on Friday, December the twentieth."

"And could they?"

"Harold could. Alfred couldn't or wouldn't."

"I think alibis must be terribly difficult," said Lucy. "Times and places and dates. They must be hard to check up on, too."

"It takes time and patience, but we manage." He glanced at his watch. "I'll be coming along to Rutherford Hall presently to have a word with Cedric, but I want to get hold of Doctor Quimper first."

"You'll be just about right. He has his surgery at six and he's usually finished about half-past. I must get back and deal with dinner."

"I'd like your opinion on one thing, Miss Eyelesbarrow. What's the family view about this Martine business, among themselves?"

Lucy replied promptly.

"They're all furious with Emma for going to you about it, and with Doctor Quimper who, it seemed, encouraged her to do so. Harold and Alfred think it was a try on and not genuine. Emma isn't sure. Cedric thinks it was phony, too, but he doesn't take it as seriously as the other two. Bryan, on the other hand, seems quite sure that it's genuine."

"Why, I wonder?"

"Well, Bryan's rather like that. Just accepts things at their face value. He thinks it was Edmund's wife, or rather widow, and that she had suddenly to go back to France, but that they'll hear from her again sometime. The fact that she hasn't written or anything up to now, seems to him to be quite natural because he never writes letters himself. Bryan's rather sweet. Just like a dog that wants to be taken for a walk."

"And do you take him for a walk, dear?" asked Miss Marple. "To the pigsties, perhaps?"

Lucy shot a keen glance at her.

"So many gentlemen in the house, coming and going," mused Miss Marple.

When Miss Marple uttered the word "gentlemen" she always gave it its full Victorian flavor—an echo from an era actually before her own time. You were conscious at once of dashing, full-blooded (and probably whiskered) males, sometimes wicked, but always gallant.

"You're such a handsome girl," pursued Miss Marple appraising Lucy. "I expect they pay you a good deal of attention, don't they?"

Lucy flushed slightly. Scrappy remembrances passed across her mind.

Cedric leaning against the pigsty wall. Bryan sitting disconsolately on the kitchen table. Alfred's fingers touching hers as he helped her collect the coffee cups.

"Gentlemen," said Miss Marple, in the tone of one speaking of some alien and dangerous species, "are all very much alike in some ways— even if they are quite old . . ."

"Darling," cried Lucy. "A hundred years ago you would certainly have been burned as a witch!"

And she told her story of old Mr. Crackenthorpe's conditional proposal of marriage.

"In fact," said Lucy, "they've all made what you might call advances to me, in a way. Harold's was very correct; an advantageous financial position in the City. I don't think it's my attractive appearance; they must think I know something."

She laughed.

But Inspector Craddock did not laugh.

"Be careful," he said. "They might murder you instead of making advances to you."

"I suppose it might be simpler," Lucy agreed.

Then she gave a slight shiver.

"One forgets," she said. "The boys have been having such fun that one almost thought of it all as a game. But it's not a game."

"No," said Miss Marple. "Murder isn't a game."

She was silent for a moment or two before she said:

"Don't the boys go back to school soon?"

"Yes, next week. They go tomorrow to James Stoddart-West's home for the last few days of the holidays."

"I'm glad of that," said Miss Marple gravely. "I shouldn't like anything to happen while they're there."

"You mean to old Mr. Crackenthorpe. Do you think he's going to be murdered next?"

"Oh no!" said Miss Marple. "He'll be all right. I meant to the boys."

"To the boys?"

"Well, to Alexander."

"But surely—"

"Hunting about, you know, looking for clues. Boys love that sort of thing, but it might be very dangerous."

Craddock looked at her thoughtfully.

"You're not prepared to believe, are you, Miss Marple, that it's a case of an unknown woman murdered by an unknown man? You tie it up definitely with Rutherford Hall?"

"I think there's a definite connection, yes."

"All we know about the murderer is that he's a tall, dark man. That's what your friend says and all she can say. There are three tall, dark men at Rutherford Hall. On the day of the inquest, you know, I came out to see the three brothers standing waiting on the pavement for the car to drive up. They had their backs to me and it was astonishing how, in their heavy overcoats, they looked all alike. *Three tall, dark men.* And yet, actually, they're all three quite different types." He sighed. "It makes it very difficult."

"I wonder," murmured Miss Marple. "I have been wondering whether it might perhaps be all much simpler than we suppose. Murders so often are quite simple, with an obvious rather sordid motive . . ."

"Do you believe in the mysterious Martine, Miss Marple?"

"I'm quite ready to believe that Edmund Crackenthorpe either married, or meant to marry, a girl called Martine. Emma Crackenthorpe showed you his letter, I understand, and from what I've seen of her and from what Lucy tells me, I should say Emma Crackenthorpe is quite incapable of making up a thing of that kind. Indeed, why should she?"

"So granted Martine," said Craddock thoughtfully, "there is a motive of a kind. Martine's reappearance with a son would diminish the Crackenthorpe inheritance, though hardly to a point, one would think, to activate murder. They're all very hard up."

"Even Harold?" Lucy demanded incredulously.

"Even the prosperous-looking Harold Crackenthorpe is not the sober and conservative financier he appears to be. He's been plunging heavily and mixing himself up in some rather undesirable ventures. A large sum of money, soon, might avoid a crash."

"But if so—" said Lucy and stopped.

"Yes, Miss Eyelesbarrow—"

"I know, dear," said Miss Marple. "The wrong murder, that's what you mean."

"Yes. Martine's death wouldn't do Harold, or any of the others, any good. Not until—"

"Not until Luther Crackenthorpe died. Exactly. That occurred to me. And Mr. Crackenthorpe, senior, I gather from his doctor, is in much better life than any outsider would imagine."

"He'll last for years," said Lucy. Then she frowned.

"Yes?" Craddock spoke encouragingly.

"He was rather ill at Christmastime," said Lucy. "He said the doctor made a lot of fuss about it. 'Anyone would have thought I'd been poisoned by the fuss he made.' That's what he said."

She looked inquiringly at Craddock.

"Yes," said Craddock. "That's really what I want to ask Doctor Quimper about."

"Well, I must go," said Lucy. "Heavens, it's late."

Miss Marple put down her knitting and picked up the *Times* with a half-done crossword puzzle.

"I wish I had a dictionary here," she murmured. "Tontine and Tokay —I always mix those two words up. One, I believe, is a Hungarian wine."

"That's Tokay," said Lucy looking back from the door. "But one's a five-letter word and one's a seven. What's the clue?"

"Oh, it wasn't in the crossword," said Miss Marple vaguely. "It was in my head."

Inspector Craddock looked at her very hard. Then he said good-by and went.

17

Craddock had to wait a few minutes while Quimper finished his evening surgery, and then the doctor came to him. He looked tired and depressed.

He offered Craddock a drink and when the latter accepted he mixed one for himself as well.

"Poor devils," he said as he sank down in a worn easy chair. "So scared and so stupid—no sense. Had a painful case this evening. Woman who ought to have come to me a year ago. If she'd come then, she might have been operated on successfully. Now it's too late. Makes me mad. The truth is people are an extraordinary mixture of heroism and cowardice. She's been suffering agony and borne it without a word, just because she was too scared to come and find out that what she feared might be true. At the other end of the scale are the people who come and waste my time because they've got a dangerous swelling causing them agony on their little finger which they think may be cancer and which turns out to be a common or garden chilblain! Well, don't mind me. I've blown off steam now. What did you want to see me about?"

"First, I've got you to thank, I believe, for advising Miss Crackenthorpe to come to me with the letter that purported to be from her brother's widow."

"Oh, that? Anything in it? I didn't exactly advise her to come. She wanted to. She was worried. All the dear little brothers were trying to hold her back, of course."

"Why should they?"

The doctor shrugged his shoulders.

"Afraid the lady might be proved genuine, I suppose."

"Do you think the letter was genuine?"

"No idea. Never actually saw it. I should say it was someone who knew the facts, just trying to make a touch. Hoping to work on Emma's feelings. They were dead wrong, there. Emma's no fool. She wouldn't take an unknown sister-in-law to her bosom without asking a few practical questions first."

He added with some curiosity, "But why ask my views? I've got nothing to do with it."

"I really came to ask you something quite different, but I don't quite know how to put it."

Doctor Quimper looked interested.

"I understand that not long ago—at Christmastime I think it was—Mr. Crackenthorpe had rather a bad turn of illness."

He saw a change at once in the doctor's face. It hardened.

"Yes."

"I gather a gastric disturbance of some kind?"

"Yes."

"This is difficult. Mr. Crackenthorpe was boasting of his health, saying he intended to outlive most of his family. He referred to you—you'll excuse me, Doctor—"

"Oh, don't mind me. I'm not sensitive as to what my patients say about me!"

"He spoke of you as an old fuss pot." Quimper smiled. "He said you had asked him all sorts of questions, not only as to what he had eaten, but as to who prepared it and served it."

The doctor was not smiling now. His face was hard again.

"Go on."

"He used some such phrase as 'talked as though he believed someone had poisoned me.'"

There was a pause.

"Had you any suspicion of that kind?"

Quimper did not answer at once. He got up and walked up and down. Finally he wheeled round on Craddock.

"What the devil do you expect me to say? Do you think a doctor can go about flinging accusations of poisoning here and there without any real evidence?"

"I'd just like to know, off the record, if that idea did enter your head?"

Doctor Quimper said evasively, "Old Crackenthorpe leads a fairly frugal life. When the family comes down, Emma steps up the food. Result —a nasty attack of gastroenteritis. The symptoms were consistent with that diagnosis."

Craddock persisted.

"I see. You were quite satisfied? You were not at all—shall we say—puzzled?"

"All right. All right. Yes, I was Yours Truly Puzzled! Does that please you?"

"It interests me," said Craddock. "What actually did you suspect, or fear?"

"Gastric cases vary, of course, but there were certain indications that would have been, shall we say, more consistent with arsenical poisoning than with plain gastroenteritis. Mind you, the two things are very much alike. Better men than myself have failed to recognize arsenical poisoning and have given a certificate in all good faith."

"And what was the result of your inquiries?"

"It seemed that what I suspected could not possibly be true. Mr. Crackenthorpe assured me that he had had similar attacks before I attended him, and from the same cause, he said. They had always taken place when there was too much rich food about."

"Which was when the house was full? With the family? Or guests?"

"Yes. That seemed reasonable enough. But frankly, Craddock, I wasn't happy. I went so far as to write to old Doctor Morris. He was my senior partner and retired soon after I joined him. Crackenthorpe was his patient originally. I asked about these earlier attacks that the old man had had."

"And what response did you get?"

Quimper grinned.

"I got a flea in the ear. I was more or less told not to be a damned fool. Well—" he shrugged his shoulders. "Presumably I was a damned fool."

"I wonder." Craddock was thoughtful.

Then he decided to speak frankly.

"Throwing discretion aside, Doctor, there are people who stand to benefit pretty considerably from Luther Crackenthorpe's death." The doctor nodded. "He's an old man and a hale and hearty one. He may live to be ninety-odd?"

"Easily. He spends his life taking care of himself, and his constitution is sound."

"And his sons and daughters are all getting on, and they are all feeling the pinch?"

"You leave Emma out of it. She's no poisoner. These attacks only happen when the others are there, not when she and he are alone."

"An elementary precaution if she's the one," the Inspector thought, but was careful not to say so aloud.

He paused, choosing his words carefully.

"Surely—I'm ignorant in these matters—but supposing just as a hypothesis that arsenic was administered, hasn't Crackenthorpe been very lucky not to succumb?"

"Now there," said the doctor, "you have got something odd. It is exactly that fact that leads me to believe that I have been, as old Morris puts it, a damned fool. You see, it's obviously not a case of small doses of arsenic administered regularly, which is what you might call the classic method of arsenic poisoning. Crackenthorpe has never had any chronic gastric trouble. In a way, that's what makes these sudden violent attacks seem unlikely. So, assuming they are not due to natural causes, it looks as though the poisoner is muffing it every time, which hardly makes sense."

"Giving an inadequate dose, you mean?"

"Yes. On the other hand, Crackenthorpe's got a strong constitution and what might do in another man doesn't do him in. There's always personal idiosyncrasy to be reckoned with. But you'd think that by now, the poisoner—unless he's unusually timid—would have stepped up the dose. Why hasn't he?

"That is," he added, "if there is a poisoner which there probably isn't! Probably all my ruddy imagination from start to finish."

"It's an odd problem," the Inspector agreed. "It doesn't seem to make sense."

II

"Inspector Craddock!"

The eager whisper made the Inspector jump.

He had been just on the point of ringing the front-doorbell.

Alexander and his friend Stoddart-West emerged cautiously from the shadows.

"We heard your car and we wanted to get hold of you."

"Well, let's come inside." Craddock's hand went out to the doorbell again, but Alexander pulled at his coat with the eagerness of a pawing dog.

"We've found a clue," he breathed.

"Yes, we've found a clue," Stoddart-West echoed.

"Damn that girl," thought Craddock unamiably.

"Splendid," he said in perfunctory manner. "Let's go inside the house and look at it."

"No." Alexander was insistent. "Someone's sure to interrupt. Come to the harness room. We'll guide you."

Somewhat unwillingly, Craddock allowed himself to be guided round the corner of the house and along to the stable yard. Stoddart-West pushed open a heavy door, stretched up, and turned on a rather feeble electric light. The harness room, once the acme of Victorian spit and polish, was now the sad repository of everything that no one wanted. Broken garden chairs, rusted old garden implements, a vast decrepit mowing machine, rusted spring mattresses, hammocks and disintegrated tennis nets.

"We come here a good deal," said Alexander. "One can really be private here."

There were certain tokens of occupancy about. The decayed mattresses had been piled up to make a kind of divan, there was an old rusted table on which reposed a large tin of chocolate biscuits, there was a hoard of apples, a tin of toffee and a jigsaw puzzle.

"It really is a clue, sir," said Stoddart-West eagerly, his eyes gleaming behind his spectacles. "We found it this afternoon."

"We've been hunting for days. In the bushes—"

"And inside hollow trees."

"And we went all through the ashbins."

"There were some jolly interesting things there, as a matter of fact."

"And then we went into the boiler house—"

"Old Hillman keeps a great galvanized tub there full of waste paper."

"For when the boiler goes out and he wants to start it again."

"Any odd paper that's blowing about. He picks it up and shoves it in there."

"And that's where we found it."

"Found *what?*" Craddock interrupted the duet.

"The clue. Careful, Stodders, get your gloves on."

Importantly, Stoddart-West, in the best detective-story tradition, drew on a pair of rather dirty gloves and took from his pocket a Kodak photographic folder. From this he extracted in his gloved fingers with the utmost care a soiled and crumpled envelope which he handed importantly to the Inspector.

Both boys held their breath in excitement.

Craddock took it with due solemnity. He liked the boys and he was ready to enter into the spirit of the thing.

The letter had been through the post; there was no enclosure inside, it was just a torn envelope addressed to Mrs. Martine Crackenthorpe, 126 Elvers Crescent, N. 10.

"You see?" said Alexander breathlessly. "It shows she was here—Uncle Edmund's French wife, I mean—the one there's all the fuss about. She must have actually been here and dropped it somewhere. So it looks, doesn't it?"

Stoddart-West broke in, "It looks as though she was the one who got murdered—I mean, don't you think, sir, that it simply must have been her in the sarcophagus?"

They waited anxiously.

Craddock played up. "Possible, very possible," he said.

"This is important, isn't it?"

"You'll test it for fingerprints, won't you, sir?"

"Of course," said Craddock.

Stoddart-West gave a deep sigh.

"Smashing luck for us, wasn't it?" he said. "On our last day, too."

"Last day?"

"Yes," said Alexander. "I'm going to Stodders' place tomorrow for the last few days of the holidays. Stodders' people have got a smashing house —Queen Anne, isn't it?"

"William and Mary," said Stoddart-West.

"I thought your mother said—"

"Mum's French. She doesn't really know about English architecture."

"But your father said it was built—"

Craddock was examining the envelope.

Clever of Lucy Eyelesbarrow. How had she managed to fake the postmark? He peered closely, but the light was too feeble. Great fun for the boys, of course, but rather awkward for him. Lucy, drat her, hadn't considered that angle. If this were genuine, it would enforce a course of action. There—

Beside him a learned architectural argument was being hotly pursued. He was deaf to it.

"Come on boys," he said, "we'll go into the house. You've been very helpful."

18

Craddock was escorted by the boys through the back door into the house. This was, it seemed, their common mode of entrance. The kitchen was bright and cheerful. Lucy, in a large, white apron was rolling out pastry. Leaning against the dresser, watching her with a kind of doglike attention, was Bryan Eastley. With one hand he tugged at his large fair mustache.

"Hello, Dad," said Alexander kindly. "You out here again?"

"I like it out here," said Bryan, and added: "Miss Eyelesbarrow doesn't mind."

"Oh, I don't mind," said Lucy. "Good evening, Inspector Craddock."

"Coming to detect in the kitchen?" asked Bryan with interest.

"Not exactly. Mr. Cedric Crackenthorpe is still here, isn't he?"

"Oh yes, Cedric's here. Do you want him?"

"I'd like a word with him, yes, please."

"I'll go and see if he's in," said Bryan. "He may have gone round to the local pub."

He unpropped himself from the dresser.

"Thank you so much," said Lucy to him. "My hands are all over flour or I'd go."

"What are you making?" asked Stoddart-West anxiously.

"Peach flan."

"Good oh," said Stoddart-West.

"Is it nearly suppertime?" asked Alexander.

"No."

"Gosh! I'm terribly hungry."

"There's the end of the ginger cake in the larder."

The boys made a concerted rush and collided in the door.

"They're just like locusts," said Lucy.

"My congratulations to you," said Craddock.

"What on, exactly?"

"Your ingenuity, over this!"

"Over what?"

Craddock indicated the folder containing the letter.

"Very nicely done," he said.

"What are you talking about?"

"This, my dear girl, this." He half drew it out.

She stared at him uncomprehendingly.

Craddock felt suddenly dizzy.

"Didn't you fake this clue and put it in the boiler room for the boys to find? Quick—tell me."

"I haven't the faintest idea what you're talking about," said Lucy. "Do you mean that—"

Craddock slipped the folder quickly back in his pocket as Bryan returned.

"Cedric's in the library," he said. "Go on in."

He resumed his place on the dresser. Inspector Craddock went to the library.

II

Cedric Crackenthorpe seemed delighted to see the Inspector.

"Doing a spot more sleuthing down here?" he asked. "Got any farther?"

"I think I can say we are a little farther on, Mr. Crackenthorpe."

"Found out who the corpse was?"

"We've not got a definite identification, but we have a fairly shrewd idea."

"Good for you."

"Arising out of our latest information, we want to get a few statements. I'm starting with you, Mr. Crackenthorpe, as you're on the spot."

"I shan't be much longer. I'm going back to Iviza in a day or two."

"Then I seem to be just in time."

"Go ahead."

"I should like a detailed account, please, of exactly where you were and what you were doing on Friday, December the twentieth."

Cedric shot a quick glance at him. Then he leaned back, yawned, assumed an air of great nonchalance and appeared to be lost in the effort of remembrance.

"Well, as I've already told you, I was in Iviza. Trouble is, one day there is so like another. Painting in the morning, siesta from three p.m. to five. Perhaps a spot of sketching if the light's suitable. Then an *apéritif,* sometimes with the mayor, sometimes with the doctor, at the café in the plaza. After that some kind of a scratch meal. Most of the evening in Scotty's Bar with some of my lower-class friends. Will that do you?"

"I'd rather have the truth, Mr. Crackenthorpe."

Cedric sat up.

"That's a most offensive remark, Inspector."

"Do you think so? You told me, Mr. Crackenthorpe, that you left Iviza on December the twenty-first and arrived in England that same day?"

"So I did. Em! Hi, Em!"

Emma Crackenthorpe came through the adjoining door from the small morning room. She looked inquiringly from Cedric to the Inspector.

"Look here, Em. I arrived here for Christmas on the Saturday before, didn't I? Came straight from the airport?"

"Yes," said Emma wonderingly. "You got here about lunchtime."

"There you are," said Cedric to the Inspector.

"You must think us very foolish, Mr. Crackenthorpe," said Craddock pleasantly. "We can check on these things, you know. I think, if you'll show me your passport—"

He paused expectantly.

"Can't find the damned thing," said Cedric. "Was looking for it this morning. Wanted to send it to Cook's."

"I think you could find it, Mr. Crackenthorpe. But it's not actually necessary. The records show that you actually entered this country on the evening of December the nineteenth. Perhaps you will now account to me for your movements between that time until lunchtime on December the twenty-first when you arrived here."

Cedric looked very cross indeed.

"That's the hell of life nowadays," he said angrily. "All this red tape and form filling. That's what comes of a bureaucratic state. Can't go where you like and do as you please any more! Somebody's always asking questions. What's all this fuss about the twentieth, anyway? What's special about the twentieth?"

"It happens to be the day we believe the murder was committed. You can refuse to answer, of course, but—"

"Who says I refuse to answer? Give a chap time. And you were vague enough about the date of the murder at the inquest. What's turned up new since then?"

Craddock did not reply.

Cedric said, with a sidelong glance at Emma, "Shall we go into the other room?"

Emma said quickly: "I'll leave you." At the door, she paused and turned.

"This is serious, you know, Cedric. If the twentieth was the day of the murder, then you must tell Inspector Craddock exactly what you were doing."

She went through into the next room and closed the door behind her.

"Good old Em," said Cedric. "Well, here goes! Yes, I left Iviza on the nineteenth all right. Planned to break the journey in Paris and spend a couple of days routing up some old friends on the Left Bank. But as a matter of fact, there was a very attractive woman on the plane. Quite a dish. To put it plainly, she and I got off together. She was on her way to the States, had to spend a couple of nights in London to see about some business or other. We got to London on the nineteenth. We stayed at the Kingsway Palace in case your spies haven't found that out yet! Called myself John Brown—never does to use your own name on these occasions."

"And on the twentieth?"

Cedric made a grimace.

"Morning pretty well occupied by a terrific hangover."

"And the afternoon. From three o'clock onward?"

"Let me see. Well, I mooned about, as you might say. Went into the National Gallery—that's respectable enough. Saw a film. *Rowenna of the Range*. I've always had a passion for Westerns. This was a corker. . . . Then a drink or two in the bar and a bit of a sleep in my room, and out about ten o'clock with the girl friend and a round of various hot spots. Can't even remember most of their names—Jumping Frog was one, I think. She knew 'em all. Got pretty well plastered and, to tell you the truth, don't remember much more till I woke up the next morning with an even worse hangover. Girl friend hopped off to catch her plane and I poured cold water over my head, got a chemist to give me a devil's brew, and then started off for this place, pretending I'd just arrived at Heathrow. No need to upset Emma, I thought. You know what women are, always hurt if you don't come straight home. I had to borrow money from her to pay the taxi. I was completely cleaned out. No use asking the old man. He'd never cough up. Mean old brute. Well, Inspector, satisfied?"

"Can any of this be substantiated, Mr. Crackenthorpe? Say, between three p.m. and seven p.m."

"Most unlikely, I should think," said Cedric cheerfully. "National Gallery where the attendants look at you with lackluster eyes and a crowded picture house. No, not likely."

Emma re-entered. She held a small engagement book in her hand.

"You want to know what everyone was doing on December the twentieth, is that right, Inspector Craddock?"

"Well—er—yes, Miss Crackenthorpe."

"I have just been looking in my engagement book. On the twentieth I went into Brackhampton to attend a meeting of the Church Restoration Fund. That finished about a quarter to one and I lunched with Lady Adington and Miss Bartlett, who was also on the committee, at the Cadena Café. After lunch I did some shopping, stores for Christmas and also Christmas presents. I went to Greenford's and Lyall and Swift's, Boot's, and probably several other shops. I had tea about a quarter to five in the Shamrock Tea Rooms and then went to the station to meet Bryan who was coming by train. I got home about six o'clock and found my father in a very bad temper. I had left lunch ready for him, but Mrs. Hart who was to come in in the afternoon and give him his tea had not arrived. He was so angry that he had shut himself in his room and would not let me in or speak to me. He does not like my going out in the afternoon, but I make a point of doing so now and then."

"You're probably wise. Thank you, Miss Crackenthorpe."

He could hardly tell her that as she was a woman, height five-foot seven, her movements that afternoon were of no great importance. Instead he said: "Your other two brothers came down later, I understand?"

"Alfred came down late on Saturday evening. He tells me he tried to ring me on the telephone the afternoon I was out, but my father, if he is upset, will never answer the telephone. My brother Harold did not come down until Christmas Eve."

"Thank you, Miss Crackenthorpe."

"I suppose I mustn't ask"—she hesitated—"what has come up new that prompts these inquiries?"

Craddock took the folder from his pocket. Using the tips of his fingers, he extracted the envelope.

"Don't touch it, please, but do you recognize this?"

"But—" Emma stared at him, bewildered. "That's my handwriting. That's the letter I wrote to Martine."

"I thought it might be."

"But how did you get it? Did she—? Have you found her—?"

"It would seem possible that we have—found her. This empty envelope was found here."

"In the house?"

"In the grounds."

"Then, she did come here! She— You mean, it was Martine, there in the sarcophagus?"

"It would seem very likely, Miss Crackenthorpe," said Craddock gently.

It seemed even more likely when he got back to town. A message was awaiting him from Armand Dessin.

"One of the girl friends has had a postcard from Anna Stravinska. Apparently the cruise story was true! She has reached Jamaica and is having, in your phrase, a wonderful time!"

Craddock crumpled up the message and threw it into the wastepaper basket.

III

"I must say," said Alexander, sitting up in bed, thoughtfully consuming a chocolate bar, "that this has been the most smashing day ever. Actually finding a real clue!"

His voice was awed.

"In fact the whole holidays have been smashing," he added happily. "I don't suppose such a thing will ever happen again."

"I hope it won't happen again to me," said Lucy who was on her knees packing Alexander's clothes into a suitcase. "Do you want all this space fiction with you?"

"Not those two top ones. I've read them. The football and my football boots and the gum boots can go separately."

"What difficult things you boys do travel with."

"It won't matter. They're sending the Rolls for us. They've got a smashing Rolls. They've got one of the new Mercedes Benz, too."

"They must be rich."

"Rolling! Jolly nice, too. All the same, I rather wish we weren't leaving here. Another body might turn up."

"I sincerely hope not."

"Well, it often does in books. I mean somebody who's seen something or heard something gets done in, too. It might be you," he added, unrolling a second chocolate bar.

"Thank you!"

"I don't want it to be you," Alexander assured her. "I like you very much and so does Stodders. We think you're out of this world as a cook. Absolutely lovely grub. You're very sensible, too."

This last was clearly an expression of high approval. Lucy took it as such and said: "Thank you. But I don't intend to get killed just to please you."

"Well, you'd better be careful, then," Alexander told her.

He paused to consume more nourishment and then said in a slightly offhand voice:

"If Dad turns up from time to time, you'll look after him, won't you?"

"Yes, of course," said Lucy, a little surprised.

"The trouble with Dad is," Alexander informed her, "that London life doesn't suit him. He gets in, you know, with quite the wrong type of women." He shook his head in a worried manner.

"I'm very fond of him," he added, "but he needs someone to look after him. He drifts about and gets in with the wrong people. It's a great pity Mum died when she did. Bryan needs a proper home life."

He looked solemnly at Lucy and reached out for another chocolate bar.

"Not a fourth one, Alexander," Lucy pleaded. "You'll be sick."

"Oh, I don't think so. I ate six running once and I wasn't. I'm not the bilious type." He paused and then said, "Bryan likes you, you know."

"That's very nice of him."

"He's a bit of an ass in some ways," said Bryan's son, "but he was a jolly good fighter pilot. He's awfully brave. And he's awfully good-natured."

He paused. Then, averting his eyes to the ceiling, he said rather self-consciously:

"I think really, you know, it would be a good thing if he married again. Somebody decent. I shouldn't, myself, mind at all having a stepmother —not, I mean, if she was a decent sort. . . ."

With a sense of shock Lucy realized that there was a definite point in Alexander's conversation.

"All this stepmother bosh," went on Alexander, still addressing the ceiling, "is really quite out of date. Lots of chaps Stodders and I know have stepmothers—divorce and all that—and they get on quite well together. Depends on the stepmother, of course. And, of course, it does make a bit of confusion taking you out and on Sports Day and all that— I mean if there are two sets of parents, though again it helps if you want to cash in!" He paused, confronted with the problems of modern life. "It's nicest to have your own home and your own parents, but if your mother's dead—well, you see what I mean? If she's a decent sort," said Alexander for the third time.

Lucy felt touched.

"I think you're very sensible, Alexander," she said. "We must try and find a nice wife for your father."

"Yes," said Alexander noncommittally.

He added in an offhand manner, "I thought I'd just mention it. Bryan likes you very much. He told me so."

"Really," thought Lucy to herself. "There's too much matchmaking round here. First Miss Marple and now Alexander!"

For some reason or other, pigsties came into her mind. . . .

She stood up.

"Good night, Alexander. There will be only your washing things and pajamas to put in in the morning. Good night."

"Good night," said Alexander. He slid down in bed, laid his head on the pillow, closed his eyes, giving a perfect picture of a sleeping angel, and was immediately asleep.

19

"Not what you'd call conclusive," said Sergeant Wetherall with his usual gloom.

Craddock was reading through the report on Harold Crackenthorpe's alibi for December 20th.

He had been noticed at Sotheby's about 3:30, but was thought to have left shortly after that. His photograph had not been recognized at Russell's teashop, but as they did a busy trade there at teatime and he was not a habitué, that was hardly surprising. His manservant confirmed that he had returned to Cardigan Gardens to dress for his dinner party at a quarter to seven—rather late, since the dinner was at 7:30, and Mr. Crackenthorpe had been somewhat irritable in consequence. Did not remember hearing him come in that evening, but as it was some time ago could not remember accurately and, in any case, he frequently did not hear Mr. Crackenthorpe come in. He and his wife liked to retire early whenever they could. The garage in the mews where Harold kept his car was a private lockup that he rented and there was no one to notice who came or went or any reason to remember one evening in particular.

"All negative," said Craddock, with a sigh.

"He was at the Caterers' dinner all right, but left rather early before the end of the speeches."

"What about the railway stations?"

But there was nothing there, either at Brackhampton or at Paddington. It was nearly four weeks ago, and it was highly unlikely that anything would have been remembered.

Craddock sighed and stretched out his hand for the data on Cedric. That again was negative, though a taxi driver had made a doubtful recognition of having taken a fare to Paddington that day some time in the afternoon "what looked something like that bloke. Dirty trousers and a shock of hair. Cussed and swore a bit because fares had gone up since he was last in England." He identified the day because a horse called Crawler had won the 2:30 and he'd had a tidy bit on. Just after dropping the gent, he'd heard it on the radio in his cab and had gone home forthwith to celebrate.

"Thank God for racing," said Craddock, and put the report aside.

"And here's Alfred," said Sergeant Wetherall.

Some nuance in his voice made Craddock look up sharply. Wetherall had the pleased appearance of a man who has kept a tidbit until the end.

In the main the check was unsatisfactory. Alfred lived alone in his flat and came and went at unspecified times. His neighbors were not the inquisitive kind and were in any case office workers who were out all day. But toward the end of the report, Wetherall's large finger indicated the final paragraph.

Sergeant Leakie, assigned to a case of thefts from lorries had been at the Load of Bricks, a lorry pullup on the Waddington-Brackhampton Road, keeping certain lorry drivers under observation. He had noticed, at an adjoining table, Chick Evans, one of the Dicky Rogers mob. With him had been Alfred Crackenthorpe, whom he knew by sight, having seen him give evidence in the Dicky Rogers case. He'd wondered what they were cooking up together. Time: 9:30 p.m., Friday, December 20th. Alfred Crackenthorpe had boarded a bus a few minutes later, going in the direction of Brackhampton. William Baker, ticket collector at Brackhampton Station, had clipped ticket of gentleman whom he recognized by sight as one of Miss Crackenthorpe's brothers, just before departure of 11:55 train for Paddington. Remembers day as there had been story of some batty old lady who swore she had seen somebody murdered in a train that afternoon.

"Alfred?" said Craddock as he laid the report down. "Alfred? I wonder."

"Puts him right on the spot, there," Wetherall pointed out.

Craddock nodded. Yes, Alfred could have traveled down by the 4:33

to Brackhampton, committing murder on the way. Then he could have gone out by bus to the Load of Bricks. He could have left there at 9:30 and would have had plenty of time to go to Rutherford Hall, move the body from the embankment to the sarcophagus and get into Brackhampton in time to catch the 11:55 back to London. One of the Dicky Rogers gang might even have helped him move the body, though Craddock doubted this. An unpleasant lot, but not killers.

"Alfred?" he repeated speculatively.

II

At Rutherford Hall there had been a gathering of the Crackenthorpe family. Harold and Alfred had come down from London and very soon voices were raised and tempers were running high.

On her own initiative, Lucy mixed cocktails in a jug with ice and took them toward the library. The voices sounded clearly in the hall, and indicated that a good deal of acrimony was being directed toward Emma.

"Entirely your fault, Emma." Harold's deep-bass voice rang out angrily. "How you could be so shortsighted and foolish beats me. If you hadn't taken that letter to Scotland Yard and started all this—"

Alfred's higher-pitched voice said: "You must have been out of your senses!"

"Now don't bully her," said Cedric. "What's done is done. Much more fishy if they'd identified the woman as the missing Martine and we'd all kept mum about having heard from her."

"It's all very well for you, Cedric," said Harold angrily. "You were out of the country on the twentieth which seems to be the day they are inquiring about. But it's very embarrassing for Alfred and myself. Fortunately I can remember where I was that afternoon and what I was doing."

"I bet you can," said Alfred. "If you'd arranged a murder, Harold, you'd arrange your alibi very carefully, I'm sure."

"I gather you are not so fortunate," said Harold coldly.

"That depends," said Alfred. "Anything's better than presenting a cast-iron alibi to the police if it isn't really cast iron. They're so clever at breaking these things down."

"If you are insinuating that I killed the woman—"

"Oh, do stop, all of you," cried Emma. "Of course none of you killed the woman."

"And just for your information, I wasn't out of England on the twentieth," said Cedric. "And the police are wise to it! So we're all under suspicion."

"If it hadn't been for Emma—"

"Oh, don't begin again, Harold," cried Emma.

Doctor Quimper came out of the study where he had been closeted with old Mr. Crackenthorpe. His eye fell on the jug in Lucy's hand.

"What's this? A celebration?"

"More in the nature of oil on troubled waters. They're at it hammer and tongs in there."

"Recriminations?"

"Mostly abusing Emma."

Doctor Quimper's eyebrows rose.

"Indeed?" He took the jug from Lucy's hand, opened the library door and went in.

"Good evening."

"Ah, Doctor Quimper, I should like a word with you." It was Harold's voice, raised and irritable. "I should like to know what you meant by interfering in a private and family matter, and telling my sister to go to Scotland Yard about it."

Doctor Quimper said calmly, "Miss Crackenthorpe asked my advice. I gave it to her. In my opinion she did perfectly right."

"You dare to say—"

"Girl!"

It was old Mr. Crackenthorpe's familiar salutation. He was peering out of the study door just behind Lucy.

Lucy turned rather reluctantly.

"Yes, Mr. Crackenthorpe?"

"What are you giving us for dinner tonight? I want curry. You make a very good curry. It's ages since we've had curry."

"The boys don't care much for curry, you see."

"The boys, the boys—what do the boys matter? I'm the one who matters. And anyway, the boys have gone—good riddance. I want a nice hot curry, do you hear?"

"All right, Mr. Crackenthorpe, you shall have it."

"That's right. You're a good girl, Lucy. You look after me, and I'll look after you."

Lucy went back to the kitchen. Abandoning the fricassee of chicken which she had planned, she began to assemble the preparations for curry. The front door banged and from the window she saw Doctor Quimper stride angrily from the house to his car and drive away.

Lucy sighed. She missed the boys. And in a way she missed Bryan, too.

Oh well! She sat down and began to peel mushrooms.

At any rate she'd give the family a rattling good dinner.

Feed the brutes!

III

It was 3:00 a.m. when Doctor Quimper drove his car into the garage, closed the doors and came in pulling the front door behind him rather wearily. Well, Mrs. Josh Simpkins had a fine, healthy pair of twins to add to her present family of eight. Mr. Simpkins had expressed no elation over the arrival. "Twins," he had said gloomily. "What's the good of them? Quads now, they're good for something. All sorts of things you get sent, and the press comes round and there's pictures in the paper, and they do say as Her Majesty sends you a telegram. But what's twins except two mouths to feed instead of one? Never been twins in our family, nor in the missus's either. Don't seem fair, somehow."

Doctor Quimper walked upstairs to his bedroom and started throwing off his clothes. He glanced at his watch. Five minutes past three. It had proved an unexpectedly tricky business bringing those twins into the world, but all had gone well. He yawned. He was tired, very tired. He looked appreciatively at his bed.

Then the telephone rang.

Doctor Quimper swore and picked up the receiver.

"Doctor Quimper?"

"Speaking."

"This is Lucy Eyelesbarrow from Rutherford Hall. I think you'd better come over. Everybody seems to have been taken ill."

"Taken ill? How? What symptoms?"

Lucy detailed them.

"I'll be over straightaway. In the meantime—" He gave her short, sharp instructions.

Then he quickly resumed his clothes, flung a few extra things into his emergency bag, and hurried down to his car.

IV

It was some three hours later when the doctor and Lucy, both of them somewhat exhausted, sat down by the kitchen table to drink large cups of black coffee.

"Ha." Doctor Quimper drained his cup, set it down with a clatter on the saucer. "I needed that. Now, Miss Eyelesbarrow, let's get down to brass tacks."

Lucy looked at him. The lines of fatigue showed clearly on his face, making him look older than his forty-four years; the dark hair on his temples was flecked with gray; and there were lines under his eyes.

"As far as I can judge," said the doctor, "they'll be all right now. But how come? That's what I want to know. Who cooked the dinner?"

"I did," said Lucy.

"And what was it? In detail."

"Mushroom soup. Curried chicken and rice. Sillabubs. A savory of chicken livers in bacon."

"*Canapés Diane,*" said Doctor Quimper unexpectedly.

Lucy smiled faintly.

"Yes, *Canapés Diane.*"

"All right, let's go through it. Mushroom soup, out of a tin, I suppose?"

"Certainly not. I made it."

"You made it. Out of what?"

"Half a pound of mushrooms, chicken stock, milk, a *roux* of butter and flour, and lemon juice."

"Ah. And one's supposed to say 'It must have been the mushrooms.' "

"It wasn't the mushrooms. I had some of the soup myself and I'm quite all right."

"Yes, you're quite all right. I hadn't forgotten that."

Lucy flushed.

"If you mean—"

"I don't mean. You're a highly intelligent girl. You'd be groaning upstairs, too, if I'd meant what you thought I meant. Anyway, I know all about you. I've taken the trouble to find out."

"Why on earth did you do that?"

Doctor Quimper's lips were set in a grim line.

"Because I'm making it my business to find out about the people who come here and settle themselves in. You're a bona fide young woman who does this particular job for a livelihood, and you seem never to have had any contact with the Crackenthorpe family previous to coming here. So you're not a girl friend of either Cedric, Harold or Alfred, helping them to do a bit of dirty work."

"Do you really think?"

"I think quite a lot of things," said Quimper. "But I have to be careful. That's the worst of being a doctor. Now, let's get on. Curried chicken. Did you have some of that?"

"No. When you've cooked a curry, you've dined off the smell, I find. I tasted it, of course. I had soup and some sillabub."

"How did you serve the sillabub?"

"In individual glasses."

"Now then, how much of all this is cleared up?"

"If you mean washing up, everything was washed up and put away."

Doctor Quimper groaned.

"There's such a thing as being overzealous," he said.

"Yes, I can see that as things have turned out, but there it is, I'm afraid."

"What do you have still?"

"There's some of the curry left in a bowl in the larder. I was planning to use it as a basis for mulligatawny soup this evening. There's some mushroom soup left, too. No sillabub and none of the savory."

"I'll take the curry and the soup. What about chutney? Did they have chutney with it?"

"Yes. In one of those stone jars."

"I'll have some of that, too."

He rose: "I'll go up and have a look at them again. After that, can you hold the fort until morning? Keep an eye on them all? I can have a nurse round, with full instructions, by eight o'clock."

"I wish you'd tell me straight out. Do you think it's food poisoning—or—or, well, poisoning."

"I've told you already. Doctors can't think, they have to be sure. If there's a positive result from these food specimens I can go ahead. Other-wise—"

"Otherwise?" Lucy repeated.

Doctor Quimper laid a hand on her shoulder.

"Look after two people in particular," he said. "Look after Emma. I'm not going to have anything happen to Emma . . ."

There was emotion in his voice that could not be disguised. "She's not even begun to live yet," he said. "And you know, people like Emma Crackenthorpe are the salt of the earth. Emma—well, Emma means a lot to me. I've never told her so but I shall. Look after Emma."

"You bet I will," said Lucy.

"And look after the old man. I can't say that he's ever been my favorite patient but he is my patient and I'm damned if I'm going to let him be hustled out of the world because one or other of his unpleasant sons—or all three of them, maybe—want him out of the way so that they can handle his money."

He threw her a sudden quizzical glance.

"There," he said. "I've opened my mouth too wide. But keep your eyes skinned, there's a good girl and, incidentally, keep your mouth shut."

V

Inspector Bacon was looking upset.

"Arsenic?" he said. "Arsenic?"

"Yes. It was in the curry. Here's the rest of the curry, for your fellow to have a go at. I've only done a very rough test on a little of it, but the result was quite definite."

"So there's a poisoner at work?"

"It would seem so," said Doctor Quimper dryly.

"And they're all affected, you say, except that Miss Eyelesbarrow."

"Except Miss Eyelesbarrow."

"Looks a bit fishy for her."

"What motive could she possibly have?"

"Might be barmy," suggested Bacon. "Seem all right, they do, sometimes, and yet all the time they're right off their rocker, so to speak."

"Miss Eyelesbarrow isn't off her rocker. Speaking as a medical man, Miss Eyelesbarrow is as sane as you or I. If Miss Eyelesbarrow is feeding the family arsenic in their curry, she's doing it for a reason. Moreover, being a highly intelligent young woman, she'd be careful not to be the only one unaffected. What she'd do, what any intelligent poisoner would do, would be to eat a very little of the poisoned curry, and then exaggerate the symptoms."

"And then you wouldn't be able to tell?"

"That she'd had less than the others? Probably not. People don't all react alike to poisons anyway; the same amount will upset some people more than others. Of course," added Doctor Quimper cheerfully, "once the patient's dead, you can estimate fairly closely how much was taken."

"Then it might be—" Inspector Bacon paused to consolidate his ideas. "It might be that there's one of the family now who's making more fuss than he need, someone who you might say is mucking in with the rest so as to avoid arousing suspicion? How's that?"

"The idea has already occurred to me. That's why I'm reporting to you. It's in your hands now. I've got a nurse on the job that I can trust, but she can't be everywhere at once. In my opinion, nobody's had enough to cause death."

"Made a mistake, the poisoner did?"

"No. It seems to me more likely that the idea was to put enough in the curry to cause signs of food poisoning, for which probably the mushrooms would be blamed. People are always obsessed with the idea of mushroom poisoning. Then one person would probably take a turn for the worse and die."

"Because he'd been given a second dose?"

The doctor nodded.

"That's why I'm reporting to you at once, and why I've put a special nurse on the job."

"She knows about the arsenic?"

"Of course. She knows and so does Miss Eyelesbarrow. You know your own job best, of course, but if I were you, I'd get out there and make it quite clear to them all that they're suffering from arsenic poisoning. That will probably put the fear of the Lord into our murderer and he won't dare to carry out his plan. He's probably been banking on the food-poisoning theory."

The telephone rang on the Inspector's desk. He picked it up and said:

"O.K. Put her through." He said to Quimper, "It's your nurse on the phone. Yes, hullo—speaking . . . What's that? Serious relapse . . . Yes . . . Doctor Quimper's with me now . . . If you'd like a word with him—"

He handed the receiver to the doctor.

"Quimper speaking . . . I see . . . Yes . . . Quite right. . . . Yes, carry on with that. We'll be along."

He put the receiver down and turned to Bacon.

"Who is it?"

"It's Alfred," said Doctor Quimper. "And he's dead."

20

Over the telephone, Craddock's voice came in sharp disbelief.

"Alfred?" he said. "Alfred?"

Inspector Bacon, shifting the telephone receiver a little, said: "You didn't expect that?"

"No, indeed. As a matter of fact, I'd just got him taped for the murderer!"

"I heard about him being spotted by the ticket collector. Looked bad for him all right. Yes, looked as though we'd got our man."

"Well," said Craddock flatly, "we were wrong."

There was a moment's silence. Then Craddock asked:

"There was a nurse in charge. How did she come to slip up?"

"Can't blame her. Miss Eyelesbarrow was all in and went to get a bit of sleep. The nurse had got five patients on her hands: the old man, Emma, Cedric, Harold and Alfred. She couldn't be everywhere at once. It seems old Mr. Crackenthorpe started creating in a big way. Said he was dying. She went in, got him soothed down, came back again and took Alfred in some tea with glucose. He drank it and that was that."

"Arsenic again?"

"Seems so. Of course it could have been a relapse, but Quimper doesn't think so and Johnstone agrees."

"I suppose," said Craddock, doubtfully, "that Alfred was meant to be the victim?"

Bacon sounded interested. "You mean that whereas Alfred's death wouldn't do anyone a penn'orth of good, the old man's death would benefit the lot of them? I suppose it might have been a mistake; somebody *might* have thought the tea was intended for the old man."

"Are they sure that that's the way the stuff was administered?"

"No, of course they aren't sure. The nurse, like a good nurse, washed up the whole contraption. Cups, spoons, teapot—everything. But it seems the only feasible method."

"Meaning?" said Craddock thoughtfully, "that one of the patients wasn't as ill as the others. Saw his chance and doped the cup."

"Well, there won't be any more funny business," said Inspector Bacon grimly. "We've got two nurses on the job now, to say nothing of Miss Eyelesbarrow, and I've got a couple of men there, too. You coming down?"

"As fast as I can make it!"

II

Lucy Eyelesbarrow came across the hall to meet Inspector Craddock. She looked pale and drawn.

"You've been having a bad time of it," said Craddock.

"It's been like one long ghastly nightmare," said Lucy. "I really thought last night that they were all dying."

"About this curry—"

"It was the curry?"

"Yes, very nicely laced with arsenic. Quite the Borgia touch."

"If that's true," said Lucy. "It must—it's got to be—one of the family."

"No other possibility?"

"No, you see I only started making that damned curry quite late, after six o'clock, because Mr. Crackenthorpe specially asked for curry. And I had to open a new tin of curry powder, so that couldn't have been tampered with. I suppose curry would disguise the taste?"

"Arsenic hasn't any taste," said Craddock absently. "Now—opportunity. Which of them had the chance to tamper with the curry while it was cooking?"

Lucy considered.

"Actually," she said, "anyone could have sneaked into the kitchen while I was laying the table in the dining room."

"I see. Now who was there in the house? Old Mr. Crackenthorpe, Emma, Cedric—"

"Harold and Alfred. They'd come down from London in the afternoon. Oh, and Bryan, Bryan Eastley. But he left just before dinner. He had to meet a man in Brackhampton."

Craddock said thoughtfully, "It ties up with the old man's illness at Christmas. Quimper suspected that that was arsenic. Did they all seem equally ill last night?"

Lucy considered. "I think old Mr. Crackenthorpe seemed the worst. Doctor Quimper had to work like a maniac on him. He's a jolly good doctor, I will say. Cedric made far the most fuss. Of course, strong, healthy people always do."

"What about Emma?"

"She has been pretty bad."

"Why Alfred I wonder?" said Craddock.

"I know," said Lucy. "I suppose it was meant to be Alfred?"

"Funny, I asked that too!"

"It seems, somehow, so pointless."

"If I could only get at the motive for all this business," said Craddock. "It doesn't seem to tie up. The strangled woman in the sarcophagus was Edmund Crackenthorpe's widow, Martine. Let's assume that. It's pretty well proved by now. There must be a connection between that and the deliberate poisoning of Alfred. It's all here, in the family somewhere. Even saying one of them's mad doesn't help."

"Not really," Lucy agreed.

"Well, look after yourself," said Craddock warningly. "There's a poisoner in this house, remember, and one of your patients upstairs probably isn't as ill as he pretends to be."

Lucy went upstairs again slowly after Craddock's departure. An imperious voice, somewhat weakened by illness, called to her as she passed old Mr. Crackenthorpe's room.

"Girl, girl, is that you? Come here."

Lucy entered the room. Mr. Crackenthorpe was lying in bed well propped up with pillows. For a sick man he was looking, Lucy thought, remarkably cheerful.

"The house is full of damned hospital nurses," complained Mr. Crackenthorpe. "Rustling about, making themselves important, taking my temperature, not giving me what I want to eat—a pretty penny all that must be costing. Tell Emma to send 'em away. You could look after me quite well."

"Everybody's been taken ill, Mr. Crackenthorpe," said Lucy. "I can't look after everybody, you know."

"Mushrooms," said Mr. Crackenthorpe. "Damned dangerous things, mushrooms. It was that soup we had last night. You made it," he added accusingly.

"The mushrooms were quite all right, Mr. Crackenthorpe."

"I'm not blaming you, girl, I'm not blaming you. It's happened before. One blasted fungus slips in and does it. Nobody can tell. I know you're a good girl. You wouldn't do it on purpose. How's Emma?"

"Feeling rather better this afternoon."

"Ah. And Harold?"

"He's better too."

"What's this about Alfred having kicked the bucket?"

"Nobody's supposed to have told you that, Mr. Crackenthorpe."

Mr. Crackenthorpe laughed, a high, whinnying laugh of intense amusement. "I hear things," he said. "Can't keep things from the old man. They try to. So Alfred's dead, is he? He won't sponge on me any more, and he won't get any of the money either. They've all been waiting for me to die, you know; Alfred in particular. Now he's dead. I call that rather a good joke."

"That's not very kind of you, Mr. Crackenthorpe," said Lucy severely.

Mr. Crackenthorpe laughed again. "I'll outlive them all," he crowed. "You see if I don't, my girl. You see if I don't."

Lucy went to her room, took out her dictionary and looked up the word *tontine*. She closed the book thoughtfully and stared ahead of her.

III

"Don't see why you want to come to me," said Doctor Morris, irritably.

"You've known the Crackenthorpe family a long time," said Inspector Craddock.

"Yes, yes, I knew all the Crackenthorpes. I remember old Josiah Crackenthorpe. He was a hard nut—shrewd man, though. Made a lot of money." He shifted his aged form in his chair and peered under bushy eyebrows at Inspector Craddock. "So you've been listening to that young fool, Quimper," he said. "These zealous young doctors! Always getting ideas in their heads. Got it into his head that somebody was trying to poison Luther Crackenthorpe. Nonsense! Melodrama! Of course, he had gastric attacks. I treated him for them. Didn't happen very often, nothing peculiar about them."

"Doctor Quimper," said Craddock, "seemed to think there was."

"Doesn't do for a doctor to go thinking. After all, I should hope I could recognize arsenical poisoning when I saw it."

"Quite a lot of well-known doctors haven't noticed it," Craddock pointed out. "There was"—he drew upon his memory—"the Greenbarrow case, Mrs. Reney, Charles Leeds, three people in the Westbury family, all buried nicely and tidily without the doctors who attended them having the least suspicion. Those doctors were all good, reputable men."

"All right, all right," said Doctor Morris, "you're saying that I could have made a mistake. Well, I don't think I did." He paused a minute and then said, "Who did Quimper think was doing it, if it was being done?"

"He didn't know," said Craddock. "He was worried. After all, you know," he added, "there's a great deal of money there."

"Yes, yes, I know, which they'll get when Luther Crackenthorpe dies. And they want it pretty badly. That is true enough, but it doesn't follow that they'd kill the old man to get it."

"Not necessarily," agreed Inspector Craddock.

"Anyway," said Doctor Morris, "my principle is not to go about suspecting things without due cause. Due cause," he repeated. "I'll admit that what you've just told me has shaken me up a bit. Arsenic on a big scale, apparently, but I still don't see why you come to me. All I can tell you is that I didn't suspect it. Maybe I should have. Maybe I should have taken those gastric attacks of Luther Crackenthorpe's much more seriously. But you've got a long way beyond that now."

Craddock agreed. "What I really need," he said, "is to know a little more about the Crackenthorpe family. Is there any queer mental strain in them, a kink of any kind?"

The eyes under the bushy eyebrows looked at him sharply. "Yes, I can see your thoughts might run that way. Well, old Josiah was sane enough. Hard as nails, very much all there. His wife was neurotic, had a tendency to melancholia. Came of an inbred family. She died soon after Luther was born. I'd say, you know, that Luther inherited a certain—well—instability from her. He was commonplace enough as a young man, but he was always at loggerheads with his father. His father was disappointed in him and I think he resented that and brooded on it, and in the end got a kind of obsession about it. He carried that on into his own married life. You'll notice, if you talk to him at all, that he's got a hearty dislike for all his own sons. His daughters he was fond of. Both Emma and Edie, the one who died."

"Why does he dislike the sons so much?" asked Craddock.

"You'll have to go to one of these new-fashioned psychiatrists to find that out. I'd just say that Luther has never felt very adequate as a man himself, and that he bitterly resents his financial position. He has possession of an income but no power of appointment of capital. If he had the power to disinherit his sons he probably wouldn't dislike them as much. Being powerless in that respect gives him a feeling of humiliation."

"That's why he's so pleased at the idea of outliving them all?" said Inspector Craddock.

"Possibly. It is the root, too, of his parsimony, I think. I should say that he's managed to save a considerable sum out of his large income, mostly, of course, before taxation rose to its present giddy heights."

A new idea struck Inspector Craddock. "I suppose he's left his savings by will to someone? That he can do."

"Oh, yes, though God knows who he has left it to. Maybe to Emma, but I should rather doubt it. She'll get her share of the old man's money. Maybe to Alexander, the grandson."

"He's fond of him, is he?" said Craddock.

"Used to be. Of course he was his daughter's child, not a son's child. That may have made a difference. And he had quite an affection for Bryan Eastley, Edie's husband. Of course I don't know Bryan well; it's some years since I've seen any of the family. But it struck me that he was going to be very much at a loose end after the war. He's got those qualities that you need in wartime: courage, dash and a tendency to let the future take care of itself. But I don't think he's got any stability. He'll probably turn into a drifter."

"As far as you know there's no peculiar kink in any of the younger generation?"

"Cedric's an eccentric type, one of those natural rebels. I wouldn't say he was perfectly normal, but you might say, who is? Harold's fairly orthodox, not what I call a very pleasant character, coldhearted, eye to the main chance. Alfred's got a touch of the delinquent about him. He's a wrong 'un, always was. Saw him taking money out of a missionary box once that they used to keep in the hall. That type of thing. Ah well, the poor fellow's dead, I suppose I shouldn't be talking against him."

"What about—" Craddock hesitated. "Emma Crackenthorpe?"

"Nice girl, quiet, one doesn't always know what she's thinking. Has her own plans and her own ideas but she keeps them to herself. She's more character than you might think from her general manner and appearance."

"You knew Edmund, I suppose, the son who was killed in France?"

"Yes. He was the best of the bunch, I'd say. Goodhearted, gay, a nice boy."

"Did you ever hear that he was going to marry or had married a French girl just before he was killed?"

Doctor Morris frowned. "It seems as though I remember something about it," he said, "but it's a long time ago."

"Quite early on in the war, wasn't it?"

"Yes. Ah well, I daresay he'd have lived to regret it if he had married a foreign wife."

"There's some reason to believe that he did do just that," said Craddock.

In a few brief sentences he gave an account of recent happenings.

"I remember seeing something in the papers about a woman found in a sarcophagus. So it was at Rutherford Hall."

"And there's reason to believe that the woman was Edmund Crackenthorpe's widow."

"Well, well, that seems extraordinary. More like a novel than real life. But who'd want to kill the poor thing—I mean, how does it tie up with arsenical poisoning in the Crackenthorpe family?"

"In one of two ways," said Craddock, "but they are both very farfetched. Somebody perhaps is greedy and wants the whole of Josiah Crackenthorpe's fortune."

"Damn fool if he does," said Doctor Morris. "He'll only have to pay the most stupendous taxes on the income from it."

21

"Nasty things, mushrooms," said Mrs. Kidder.

Mrs. Kidder had made the same remark about ten times in the last few days. Lucy did not reply.

"Never touch 'em myself," said Mrs. Kidder, "much too dangerous. It's a merciful Providence as there's only been one death. The whole lot might have gone and you too, Miss. A wonderful escape you've had."

"It wasn't the mushrooms," said Lucy. "They were perfectly all right."

"Don't you believe it," said Mrs. Kidder. "Dangerous they are, mushrooms. One toadstool in among the lot and you've had it.

"Funny," went on Mrs. Kidder, among the rattle of plates and dishes in the sink, "how things seem to come all together, as it were. My sister's eldest had measles and our Ernie fell down and broke 'is arm, and my 'usband came out all over with boils. All in the same week! You'd hardly believe it, would you. It's been the same thing here," went on Mrs. Kidder. "First that nasty murder and now Mr. Alfred dead with mushroom poisoning. Who'll be the next, I'd like to know?"

Lucy felt rather uncomfortably that she would like to know, too.

"My husband, he doesn't like me coming here now," said Mrs. Kidder, "thinks it's unlucky, but what I say is I've known Miss Crackenthorpe a long time now and she's a nice lady and she depends on me. And I couldn't leave poor Miss Eyelesbarrow, I said, not to do everything herself in the house. Pretty hard it is on you, Miss, all these trays."

Lucy was forced to agree that life did seem to consist very largely of trays at the moment. She was at the moment arranging trays to take to the various invalids.

"As for them nurses, they never do a hand's turn," said Mrs. Kidder. "All they want is pots and pots of tea made strong. And meals prepared. Wore out, that's what I am." She spoke in a tone of great satisfaction, though actually she had done very little more than her normal morning's work.

Lucy said solemnly, "You never spare yourself, Mrs. Kidder."

Mrs. Kidder looked pleased. Lucy picked up the first of the trays and started off up the stairs.

"What's this?" said Mr. Crackenthorpe disapprovingly.

"Beef tea and baked custard," said Lucy.

"Take it away," said Mr. Crackenthorpe. "I won't touch that sort of stuff. I told that nurse I wanted a beefsteak."

"Doctor Quimper thinks you ought not to have beefsteak just yet," said Lucy.

Mr. Crackenthorpe snorted. "I'm practically well again. I'm getting up tomorrow. How are the others?"

"Mr. Harold's much better," said Lucy. "He's going back to London tomorrow."

"Good riddance," said Mr. Crackenthorpe. "What about Cedric? Any hope that he's going back to his island tomorrow?"

"He won't be going just yet."

"Pity. What's Emma doing? Why doesn't she come and see me?"

"She's still in bed, Mr. Crackenthorpe."

"Women always coddle themselves," said Mr. Crackenthorpe, "but you're a good, strong girl," he added approvingly. "Run about all day, don't you?"

"I get plenty of exercise," said Lucy.

Old Mr. Crackenthorpe nodded his head approvingly. "You're a good, strong girl," he said, "and don't think I've forgotten what I talked to you about before. One of these days you'll see what you'll see. Emma isn't always going to have things her own way. And don't listen to the others when they tell you I'm a mean old man. I'm careful of my money. I've got a nice little packet put by and I know who I'm going to spend it on when the time comes." He leered at her affectionately.

Lucy went rather quickly out of the room, avoiding his clutching hand.

The next tray was taken in to Emma.

"Oh, thank you, Lucy. I'm really feeling quite myself again by now. I'm hungry, and that's a good sign, isn't it? My dear," went on Emma as Lucy settled the tray on her knees, "I'm really feeling very upset about your aunt. You haven't had any time to go and see her, I suppose?"

"No, I haven't, as a matter of fact."

"I'm afraid she must be missing you."

"Oh, don't worry, Miss Crackenthorpe. She understands what a terrible time we've been through."

"Have you rung her up?"

"No, I haven't just lately."

"Well, do. Ring her up every day. It makes such a difference to old people to get news."

"You're very kind," said Lucy. Her conscience smote her a little as she went down to fetch the next tray. The complications of illness in the house had kept her thoroughly absorbed and she had had no time to think of anything else. She decided that she would ring Miss Marple up as soon as she had taken Cedric his meal.

There was only one nurse in the house now and she passed Lucy on the landing, exchanging greetings.

Cedric, looking incredibly tidied up and neat, was sitting up in bed writing busily on sheets of paper.

"Hullo, Lucy," he said, "what hell brew have you got for me today? I wish you'd get rid of that god-awful nurse, she's simply too arch for words. Calls me 'we' for some reason. 'And how are we this morning? Have we slept well? Oh dear, we're very naughty, throwing off the bedclothes like that.'" He imitated the refined accents of the nurse in a high falsetto voice.

"You seem very cheerful," said Lucy. "What are you busy with?"

"Plans," said Cedric. "Plans for what to do with this place when the old man pops off. It's a jolly good bit of land here, you know. I can't make up my mind whether I'd like to develop some of it myself, or whether I'll sell it in lots all in one go. Very valuable for industrial purposes. The house will do for a nursing home or a school. I'm not sure I shan't sell half the land and use the money to do something rather outrageous with the other half. What do you think?"

"You haven't got it yet," said Lucy, dryly.

"I shall have it, though," said Cedric. "It's not divided up like the other stuff. I get it outright. And if I sell it for a good fat price the money will be capital, not income, so I shan't have to pay taxes on it. Money to burn. Think of it."

"I always understood you rather despised money," said Lucy.

"Of course I despise money when I haven't got any," said Cedric. "It's the only dignified thing to do. What a lovely girl you are, Lucy, or do I just think so because I haven't seen any good-looking women for a long time?"

"I expect that's it," said Lucy.

"Still busy tidying everyone and everything up?"

"Somebody seems to have been tidying you up," said Lucy, looking at him.

"That's that damned nurse," said Cedric with feeling. "Have they had the inquest on Alfred yet? What happened?"

"It was adjourned," said Lucy.

"Police being cagey. This mass poisoning does give one a bit of a turn, doesn't it? Mentally, I mean. I'm not referring to more obvious aspects," he added. "Better look after yourself, my girl."

"I do," said Lucy.

"Has young Alexander gone back to school yet?"

"I think he's still with the Stoddart-Wests. I think it's the day after tomorrow that school begins."

Before getting her own lunch Lucy went to the telephone and rang up Miss Marple.

"I'm so terribly sorry I haven't been able to come over, but I've really been very busy."

"Of course, my dear, of course. Besides there's nothing that can be done just now. We just have to wait."

"Yes, but what are we waiting for?"

"Elspeth McGillicuddy ought to be home very soon now," said Miss Marple. "I wrote to her to fly home at once. I said it was her duty. So don't worry too much, my dear." Her voice was kindly and reassuring.

"You don't think—" Lucy began, but stopped.

"That there will be any more deaths? Oh, I hope not, my dear. But one never knows, does one? When anyone is really wicked, I mean. And I think there is great wickedness here."

"Or madness," said Lucy.

"Of course I know that is the modern way of looking at things. I don't agree myself."

Lucy rang off, went into the kitchen and picked up her tray of lunch. Mrs. Kidder had divested herself of her apron and was about to leave.

"You'll be all right, Miss, I hope?" she asked solicitously.

"Of course I shall be all right," snapped Lucy.

She took her tray not into the big, gloomy dining room but into the small study. She was just finishing the meal when the door opened and Bryan Eastley came in.

"Hello," said Lucy, "this is very unexpected."

"I suppose it is," said Bryan. "How is everybody?"

"Oh, much better. Harold's going back to London tomorrow."

"What do you think about it all? Was it really arsenic?"

"It was arsenic all right," said Lucy.

"It hasn't been in the papers yet."

"No, I think the police are keeping it up their sleeves for the moment."

"Somebody must have a pretty good down on the family," said Bryan. "Who's likely to have sneaked in and tampered with the food?"

"I suppose I'm the most likely person, really," said Lucy.

Bryan looked at her anxiously. "But you didn't, did you?" he asked. He sounded slightly shocked.

"No. I didn't," said Lucy.

Nobody could have tampered with the curry. She had made it alone in the kitchen and brought it to table, and the only person who could have tampered with it was one of the five people who sat down to the meal.

"I mean, why should you?" said Bryan. "They're nothing to you, are they? I say," he added, "I hope you don't mind my coming back here like this?"

"No, no, of course I don't. Have you come to stay?"

"Well, I'd like to, if it wouldn't be an awful bore to you."

"No. No, we can manage."

"You see, I'm out of a job at the moment and I—well, I get rather fed up. Are you really sure you don't mind?"

"Oh, I'm not the person to mind, anyway. It's Emma."

"Oh, Emma's all right," said Bryan. "Emma's always been very nice to me. In her own way, you know. She keeps things to herself a lot, in fact she's rather a dark horse, old Emma. This living here and looking after the old man would get most people down. Pity she never married. Too late now, I suppose."

"I don't think it's too late at all," said Lucy.

"Well—" Bryan considered. "A clergyman perhaps," he said hopefully. "She'd be useful in the parish and tactful with the Mothers' Union. I do mean the Mothers' Union, don't I? Not that I know what it really is, but you come across it sometimes in books. And she'd wear a hat in church on Sundays," he added.

"Doesn't sound much of a prospect to me," said Lucy, rising and picking up the tray.

"I'll do that," said Bryan, taking the tray from her. They went into the kitchen together. "Shall I help you wash up? I do like this kitchen," he added. "In fact, I know it isn't the sort of thing that people do like nowadays, but I like this whole house. Shocking taste, I suppose, but there it is. You could land a plane quite easily in the park," he added with enthusiasm.

He picked up a glass cloth and began to wipe the spoons and forks.

"Seems a waste, it coming to Cedric," he remarked. "First thing he'll do is to sell the whole thing and go beaking off abroad again. Can't see, myself, why England isn't good enough for anybody. Harold wouldn't want this house either, and of course it's much too big for Emma. Now if only it came to Alexander, he and I would be as happy together here as a couple of sandboys. Of course it would be nice to have a woman about the house." He looked thoughtfully at Lucy. "Oh, well, what's the good of talking? If Alexander were to get this place it would mean a whole lot of them would have to die first, and that's not really likely, is it? Though from what I've seen of the old boy he might easily live to be a hundred, just to annoy them all. I don't suppose he was much cut up by Alfred's death, was he?"

Lucy said shortly, "No, he wasn't."

"Cantankerous old devil," said Bryan Eastley cheerfully.

22

"Dreadful, the things people go about saying," said Mrs. Kidder. "I don't listen, mind you, more than I can help. But you'd hardly believe it." She waited hopefully.

"Yes, I suppose so," said Lucy.

"About that body that was found in the Long Barn," went on Mrs. Kidder, moving crablike backward on her hands and knees, as she scrubbed the kitchen floor, "saying as how she'd been Mr. Edmund's fancy piece during the war, and how she come over here and a jealous husband followed her and did her in. It is a likely thing as a foreigner would do, but it wouldn't be likely after all these years, would it?"

"It sounds most unlikely to me."

"But there's worse things than that, they say," said Mrs. Kidder. "Say anything, people will. You'd be surprised. There's those that say Mr. Harold married somewhere abroad and that she come over and found out he'd committed bigamy with that Lady Alice, and that she was going to bring 'im to court and that he met her down here and did her in and hid her body in the sarcoffus. Did you ever!"

"Shocking," said Lucy vaguely, her mind elsewhere.

"Of course I don't listen," said Mrs. Kidder virtuously, "I wouldn't put no stock in such tales myself. It beats me how people think up such things, let alone say them. All I hope is none of it gets to Miss Emma's ears. It might upset her and I shouldn't like that. She's a very nice lady, Miss Emma is, and I've not heard a word against her, not a word. And of course Mr. Alfred being dead nobody says anything against him now.

Not even that it's a judgment, which they well might do. But it's awful, Miss, isn't it, the wicked talk there is."

Mrs. Kidder spoke with immense enjoyment.

"It must be quite painful for you to listen to it," said Lucy.

"Oh, it is," said Mrs. Kidder. "It is, indeed. I says to my husband, I says, 'However can they?' "

The bell rang.

"There's the doctor, Miss. Will you let 'im in, or shall I?"

"I'll go," said Lucy.

But it was not the doctor. On the doorstep stood a tall, elegant woman in a mink coat. Drawn up to the gravel sweep was a purring Rolls with a chauffeur at the wheel.

"Can I see Miss Emma Crackenthorpe, please?"

It was an attractive voice, the R's slightly blurred. The woman was attractive, too. About thirty-five, with dark hair and expensively and beautifully made up.

"I'm sorry," said Lucy, "Miss Crackenthorpe is ill in bed and can't see anyone."

"I know she has been ill, yes, but it is very important that I should see her."

"I'm afraid," Lucy began.

The visitor interrupted her. "I think you are Miss Eyelesbarrow, are you not?" She smiled, an attractive smile. "My son has spoken of you, so I know. I am Lady Stoddart-West and Alexander is staying with me now."

"Oh, I see," said Lucy.

"And it is really important that I should see Miss Crackenthorpe," continued the other. "I know all about her illness and I assure you this is not just a social call. It is because of something that the boys have said to me—that my son has said to me. It is, I think, a matter of grave importance and I would like to speak to Miss Crackenthorpe about it. Please, will you ask her?"

"Come in." Lucy ushered her visitor into the hall and into the drawing room. Then she said, "I'll go up and ask Miss Crackenthorpe."

She went upstairs, knocked on Emma's door and entered.

"Lady Stoddart-West is here," she said. "She wants to see you very particularly."

"Lady Stoddart-West?" Emma looked surprised. A look of alarm came into her face. "There's nothing wrong, is there, with the boys—with Alexander?"

"No, no," Lucy reassured her. "I'm sure the boys are all right. It seems to be something the boys have told her or said to her."

"Oh. Well—" Emma hesitated. "Perhaps I ought to see her. Do I look all right, Lucy?"

"You look very nice," said Lucy.

Emma was sitting up in bed, a soft, pink shawl was round her shoulders and brought out the faint rose-pink of her cheeks. Her dark hair had been neatly brushed and combed by the nurse. Lucy had placed a bowl of autumn leaves on the dressing table the day before. Her room looked attractive and quite unlike a sickroom.

"I'm really quite well enough to get up," said Emma. "Doctor Quimper said I could tomorrow."

"You look really quite yourself again," said Lucy. "Shall I bring Lady Stoddart-West up?"

"Yes, do."

Lucy went downstairs again. "Will you come up to Miss Crackenthorpe's room?"

She escorted the visitor upstairs, opened the door for her to pass in and then shut it. Lady Stoddart-West approached the bed with outstretched hand.

"Miss Crackenthorpe? I really do apologize for breaking in on you like this. I have seen you, I think, at the sports at the school."

"Yes," said Emma, "I remember you quite well. Do sit down."

In the chair conveniently placed by the bed, Lady Stoddart-West sat down. She said in a quiet low voice,

"You must think it very strange of me coming here like this, but I have a reason. I think it is an important reason. You see, the boys have been telling me things. You can understand that they were very excited about the murder that happened here. I confess I did not like it at the time. I was nervous. I wanted to bring James home at once. But my husband laughed. He said that obviously it was a murder that had nothing to do with the house and the family and he said that from what he remembered from his boyhood, and from James's letters, both he and Alexander were enjoying themselves so wildly that it would be sheer cruelty to bring them back. So I gave in and agreed that they should stay on until the time arranged for James to bring Alexander back with him."

Emma said: "You think we ought to have sent your son home earlier?"

"No, no, that is not what I mean at all. Oh, it is difficult for me, this! But what I have to say must be said. You see, they have picked up a good deal, the boys. They told me that this woman—the murdered woman—that the police have an idea that she may be a French girl whom your eldest brother, who was killed in the war, knew in France. That is so?"

"It is a possibility," said Emma, her voice breaking slightly, "that we are forced to consider. It may have been so."

"There is some reason for believing that the body is that of this girl, this Martine?"

"I have told you, it is a possibility."

"But why—why should they think that she was this Martine? Did she have letters on her—papers?"

"No. Nothing of that kind. But you see I had had a letter from this Martine."

"You had had a letter from *Martine?*"

"Yes. A letter telling me she was in England and would like to come and see me. I invited her down here, but got a telegram saying she was going back to France. Perhaps she did go back to France. We do not know. But since then an envelope was found here addressed to her. That seems to show that she had come down here. But I really don't see—" She broke off.

Lady Stoddart-West broke in quickly,

"You really do not see what concern it is of mine? That is very true. I should not, in your place. But when I heard this, or rather, a garbled account of this, I had to come to make sure it was really so, because, if it is—"

"Yes?" said Emma.

"Then I must tell you something that I had never intended to tell you. You see, *I am Martine.*"

Emma stared at her guest as though she could hardly take in the sense of her words.

"You!" she said. "You are Martine?"

The other nodded vigorously. "But yes. It surprises you, I am sure, but it is true. I met your brother Edmund in the first days of the war. He was indeed billeted at our house. Well, you know the rest. We fell in love. We intended to be married, and then there was the retreat to Dunkirk, Edmund was reported missing. Later he was reported killed. I will not speak to you of that time. It was long ago and it is over. But I will say to you that I loved your brother very much.

"Then came the grim realities of war. The Germans occupied France. I became a worker for the Resistance. I was one of those who was assigned to pass Englishmen through France to England. It was in that way that I met my present husband. He was an Air Force officer, parachuted into France to do special work. When the war ended we were married. I considered once or twice whether I should write to you or come and see you but I decided against it. It could do no good, I thought, to rake up old memories. I had a new life and I had no wish to recall the old." She paused and then said, "But it gave me, I will tell you, a strange pleasure when I found that my son James's greatest friend at his school was a boy whom I found to be Edmund's nephew. Alexander, I may say, is very like Edmund, as I dare say you yourself appreciate. It seemed to me a very happy state of affairs that James and Alexander should be such friends."

She leaned forward and placed her hand on Emma's arm. "But you see, dear Emma, do you not, that when I heard this story about the murder, about this dead woman being suspected to be the Martine that Edmund had known, that I had to come and tell you the truth. Either you or I must inform the police of the fact. Whoever the dead woman is, she is not Martine."

"I can hardly take it in," said Emma, "that you, you should be the Martine that dear Edmund wrote to me about." She sighed, shaking her head, then she frowned perplexedly. "But I don't understand. Was it you, then, who wrote to me?"

Lady Stoddart-West shook a vigorous head. "No, no, of course I did not write to you."

"Then—" Emma stopped.

"Then there was someone pretending to be Martine who wanted perhaps to get money out of you? That is what it must have been. But who can it be?"

Emma said slowly: "I suppose there were people at the time who knew?"

The other shrugged her shoulders. "Probably, yes. But there was no one intimate with me, no one very close to me. I have never spoken of it since I came to England. And why wait all this time? It is curious, very curious."

Emma said, "I don't understand it. We will have to see what Inspector Craddock has to say." She looked with suddenly softened eyes at her visitor. "I'm so glad to know you at last, my dear."

"And I you. Edmund spoke of you very often. He was very fond of you. I am happy in my new life, but all the same, I do not quite forget."

Emma leaned back and heaved a deep sigh. "It's a terrible relief," she said. "As long as we feared that the dead woman might be Martine, it seemed to be tied up with the family. But now, oh, it's an absolute load off my back. I don't know who the poor soul was but she can't have had anything to do with us!"

23

The streamlined secretary brought Harold Crackenthorpe his usual afternoon cup of tea.

"Thanks, Miss Ellis, I shall be going home early today."

"I'm sure you ought really not to have come at all, Mr. Crackenthorpe," said Miss Ellis. "You look quite pulled down still."

"I'm all right," said Harold Crackenthorpe, but he did feel pulled down. No doubt about it, he'd had a very nasty turn. Ah well, that was over.

Extraordinary, he thought broodingly, that Alfred should have succumbed and the old man should have come through. After all, what was he?—seventy-three, seventy-four? Been an invalid for years. If there was one person you'd have thought would have been taken off, it would have been the old man. But no. It had to be Alfred. Alfred who, as far as Harold knew, was a healthy, wiry sort of chap. Nothing much the matter with him.

He leaned back in his chair sighing. That girl was right. He didn't feel up to things yet, but he had wanted to come down to the office. Wanted to get the hang of how affairs were going. Touch and go, that's what it was! Touch and go. All this—he looked round him—the richly appointed office, the pale gleaming wood, the expensive modern chairs, it all looked prosperous enough, and a good thing, too! That's where Alfred had always gone wrong. If you looked prosperous, people thought you were prosperous. There were no rumors going around as yet about his financial stability. All the same, the crash couldn't be delayed very long. Now if only his father had passed out instead of Alfred, as surely, surely he ought to have done. Practically seemed to thrive on arsenic! Yes, if his father had succumbed: well, there wouldn't have been anything to worry about.

Still, the great thing was not to seem worried. A prosperous appearance. Not like poor old Alfred who always looked seedy and shiftless, who looked in fact exactly what he was. One of those small-time speculators, never going all out boldly for the big money. In with a shady crowd here, doing a doubtful deal there, never quite rendering himself liable to prosecution but going very near the edge. And where had it got him? Short periods of affluence and then back to seediness and shabbiness once more. No broad outlook about Alfred. Taken all in all, you couldn't say Alfred was much loss. He'd never been particularly fond of Alfred and with Alfred out of the way the money that was coming to him from that old curmudgeon, his grandfather, would be sensibly increased, divided not into five shares but into four shares. Very much better.

Harold's face brightened a little. He rose, took his hat and coat and left the office. Better take it easy for a day or two. He wasn't feeling too strong yet. His car was waiting below and very soon he was weaving through the London traffic to his house.

Darwin, his manservant, opened the door.

"Her Ladyship has just arrived, sir," he said.

For a moment Harold stared at him. Alice! Good Heavens, was it today that Alice was coming home? He'd forgotten all about it. Good thing

Darwin had warned him. It wouldn't have looked so good if he'd gone upstairs and looked too astonished at seeing her. Not that it really mattered, he supposed. Neither Alice nor he had many illusions about the feeling they had for each other. Perhaps Alice was fond of him; he didn't know.

All in all Alice was a great disappointment to him. He hadn't been in love with her, of course, but though a plain woman she was quite a pleasant one. And her family and connections had undoubtedly been useful. Not perhaps as useful as they might have been, because in marrying Alice he had been considering the position of hypothetical children. Nice relations for his boys to have. But there hadn't been any boys, or girls either, and all that had remained had been him and Alice growing older together without much to say to each other and with no particular pleasure in each other's company.

She stayed away a good deal with relations and usually went to the Riviera in the winter. It suited her and it didn't worry him.

He went upstairs now into the drawing room and greeted her punctiliously.

"So you're back, my dear. Sorry I couldn't meet you, but I was held up in the City. I got back as early as I could. How was San Raphael?"

Alice told him how San Raphael was. She was a thin woman with sandy-colored hair, a well-arched nose and vague, hazel eyes. She talked in a well-bred, monotonous and rather depressing voice. It had been a good journey back, the Channel a little rough. The customs, as usual, very trying at Dover.

"You should come by air," said Harold, as he always did. "So much simpler."

"I dare say, but I don't really like air travel. I never have. Makes me nervous."

"Saves a lot of time," said Harold.

Lady Alice Crackenthorpe did not answer. It was possible that her problem in life was not to save time but to occupy it. She inquired politely after her husband's health.

"Emma's telegram quite alarmed me," she said. "You were all taken ill, I understand."

"Yes, yes," said Harold.

"I read in the paper the other day," said Alice, "of forty people in a hotel going down with food poisoning at the same time. All this refrigeration is dangerous, I think. People keep things too long in them."

"Possibly," said Harold. Should he, or should he not mention arsenic? Somehow, looking at Alice, he felt himself quite unable to do so. In Alice's world, he felt, there was no place for poisoning by arsenic. It was a thing you read about in the papers. It didn't happen to you or your own family.

But it had happened in the Crackenthorpe family. . . .

He went up to his room and lay down for an hour or two before dressing for dinner. At dinner, tête-à-tête with his wife, the conversation ran on much the same lines. Desultory, polite. The mention of acquaintances and friends at San Raphael.

"There's a parcel for you on the hall table, a small one," Alice said.

"Is there? I didn't notice it."

"It's an extraordinary thing but somebody was telling me about a murdered woman having been found in a barn or something like that. She said it was at Rutherford Hall. I suppose it must be some other Rutherford Hall."

"No," said Harold, "no, it isn't. It was in our barn, as a matter of fact."

"Really, Harold! A murdered woman in the barn at Rutherford Hall, and you never told me anything about it."

"Well, there hasn't been much time, really," said Harold, "and it was all rather unpleasant. Nothing to do with us, of course. The press milled round a good deal. Of course we had to deal with the police and all that sort of thing."

"Very unpleasant," said Alice. "Did they find out who did it?" she added, with rather perfunctory interest.

"Not yet," said Harold.

"What sort of a woman was she?"

"Nobody knows. French apparently."

"Oh, French," said Alice, and allowing for the difference in class, her tone was not unlike that of Inspector Bacon. "Very annoying for you all," she agreed.

They went out from the dining room and crossed into the small study where they usually sat when they were alone. Harold was feeling quite exhausted by now. I'll go up to bed early, he thought.

He picked up the small parcel from the hall table, about which his wife had spoken to him. It was a small neatly waxed parcel, done up with meticulous exactness. Harold ripped it open as he came to sit down in his usual chair by the fire.

Inside was a small tablet box bearing the label, *"Two to be taken nightly."* With it was a small piece of paper with the chemist's heading in Brackhampton. *"Sent by request of Doctor Quimper"* was written on it.

Harold Crackenthorpe frowned. He opened the box and looked at the tablets. Yes, they seemed to be the same tablets he had been having. But surely, surely Quimper had said that he needn't take any more? "You won't want them now." That's what Quimper had said.

"What is it, dear?" said Alice. "You look worried."

"Oh, it's just some tablets. I've been taking them at night. But I rather thought the doctor said don't take any more."

His wife said placidly, "He probably said don't forget to take them."

"He may have done, I suppose," said Harold doubtfully.

He looked across at her. She was watching him. Just for a moment or two he wondered—he didn't often wonder about Alice—exactly what she was thinking. That mild gaze of hers told him nothing. Her eyes were like windows in an empty house. What did Alice think about him, feel about him? Had she been in love with him once? He supposed she had. Or did she marry him because she thought he was doing well in the City and she was tired of her own impecunious existence? Well, on the whole, she'd done quite well out of it. She'd got a car and a house in London, she could travel abroad when she felt like it and get herself expensive clothes, though goodness knows they never looked like anything on Alice. Yes, on the whole, she'd done pretty well. He wondered if she thought so. She wasn't really fond of him, of course, but then he wasn't really fond of her. They had nothing in common, nothing to talk about, no memories to share. If there had been children, but there hadn't been any children. Odd that there were no children in the family except young Edie's boy. Young Edie. She'd been a silly girl, making that foolish, hasty wartime marriage. Well, he'd given her good advice.

He'd said, "It's all very well, these dashing young pilots, glamour, courage, all that, but he'll be no good in peacetime, you know. Probably be barely able to support you."

And Edie had said, what did it matter? She loved Bryan and Bryan loved her, and he'd probably be killed quite soon. Why shouldn't they have some happiness? What was the good of looking to the future when they might all be bombed any minute. And after all, Edie had said, the future doesn't really matter because some day there'll be all grandfather's money.

Harold squirmed uneasily in his chair. Really, that will of his grandfather's had been iniquitous! Keeping them all dangling on a string. The will hadn't pleased anybody. It didn't please the grandchildren and it made their father quite livid. The old boy was absolutely determined not to die. That's what made him take so much care of himself. But he'd have to die soon. Surely, surely he'd have to die soon. Otherwise— All Harold's worries swept over him once more, making him feel sick and tired and giddy.

Alice was still watching him, he noticed. Those pale, thoughtful eyes, they made him uneasy somehow.

"I think I shall go to bed," he said. "It's been my first day out in the City."

"Yes," said Alice, "I think that's a good idea. I'm sure the doctor told you to take things easily at first."

"Doctors always tell you that," said Harold.

"And don't forget to take your tablets, dear," said Alice. She picked up the box and handed it to him.

He said good night and went upstairs. Yes, he needed the tablets. It would have been a mistake to leave them off too soon. He took two of them and swallowed them with a glass of water.

24

"Nobody could have made more of a muck of it than I seem to have done," said Dermot Craddock gloomily.

He sat, his long legs stretched out, looking somehow incongruous in faithful Florence's somewhat overfurnished parlor. He was thoroughly tired, upset and dispirited.

Miss Marple made soft, soothing noises of dissent. "No, no, you've done very good work, my dear boy. Very good work, indeed."

"I've done very good work, have I? I've let a whole family be poisoned, Alfred Crackenthorpe's dead and now Harold's dead, too. What the hell's going on there? That's what I should like to know."

"Poisoned tablets," said Miss Marple thoughtfully.

"Yes. Devilishly cunning, really. They looked just like the tablets that he'd been having. There was a printed slip sent in with them *'by Doctor Quimper's instructions.'* Well, Quimper never ordered them. There were chemist's labels used. The chemist knew nothing about it, either. No. That box of tablets came from Rutherford Hall."

"Do you actually know it came from Rutherford Hall?"

"Yes. We've had a thorough checkup. Actually it's the box that held the sedative tablets prescribed for Emma."

"Oh, I see. For Emma . . ."

"Yes. It's got her fingerprints on it and the fingerprints of both the nurses and the fingerprints of the chemist who made it up. Nobody else's, naturally. The person who sent them was careful."

"And the sedative tablets were removed and something else substituted?"

"Yes. That of course is the devil with tablets. One tablet looks exactly like another."

"You are so right," agreed Miss Marple. "I remember so very well in my young days, the black mixture and the brown mixture—the cough mixture that was—and the white mixture, and Doctor So-and-So's pink mixture. People didn't mix those up nearly as much. In fact, you know, in my village in St. Mary Mead we still like that kind of medicine. It's a bottle they always want, not tablets. What were the tablets?" she asked.

"Aconite. They were the kind of tablets that are usually kept in a poison bottle, diluted one in a hundred for outside application."

"And so Harold took them and died," Miss Marple said thoughtfully. Dermot Craddock uttered something like a groan.

"You mustn't mind my letting off steam to you," he said. "Tell it all to Aunt Jane; that's how I feel!"

"That's very, very nice of you," said Miss Marple, "and I do appreciate it. As Sir Henry's godson I feel toward you quite differently from the way I should feel to any ordinary detective inspector."

Dermot Craddock gave her a fleeting grin. "But the fact remains that I've made the most ghastly mess of things all along the line," he said. "The Chief Constable down here calls in Scotland Yard, and what do they get? They get me making a prize ass of myself!"

"No, no," said Miss Marple.

"Yes, yes. I don't know who poisoned Alfred, I don't know who poisoned Harold, and to cap it all I haven't the least idea now who the original murdered woman was! This Martine business seemed a perfectly safe bet. The whole thing seemed to tie up. And now what happens? The real Martine shows up and turns out, most improbably, to be the wife of Sir Robert Stoddart-West. So who's the woman in the barn now? Goodness knows. First I go all out on the idea she's Anna Stravinska, and then she's out of it."

He was arrested by Miss Marple giving one of her small, peculiarly significant coughs.

"But is she?" she murmured.

Craddock stared at her. "Well, that postcard from Jamaica."

"Yes," said Miss Marple, "but that isn't really evidence, is it? I mean, anyone can get a postcard sent from almost anywhere, I suppose. I remember Mrs. Brierly, such a very bad nervous breakdown. Finally they said she ought to go to the mental hospital for observation, and she was so worried about the children knowing about it and so she wrote about fourteen postcards and arranged that they should be posted from different places abroad, and told them that Mummie was going abroad on a holiday." She added, looking at Dermot Craddock, "You see what I mean."

"Yes, of course," said Craddock, staring at her. "Naturally we'd have checked that postcard if it hadn't been for the Martine business fitting the bill so well."

"So convenient," murmured Miss Marple.

"It tied up," said Craddock. "After all there's the letter Emma received signed Martine Crackenthorpe. Lady Stoddart-West didn't send that, but somebody did. Somebody who was going to pretend to be Martine, and who was going to cash in, if possible, on being Martine. You can't deny that."

"No, no."

"And then, the envelope of the letter Emma wrote to her with the London address on it. Found at Rutherford Hall, showing she'd actually been there."

"But the murdered woman hadn't been there!" Miss Marple pointed out. "Not in the sense you mean. She only came to Rutherford Hall after she was dead. Pushed out of a train on to the railway embankment."

"Oh—yes."

"What the envelope really proves is that the murderer was there. Presumably he took that envelope off her with her other papers and things, and then dropped it by mistake—or—I wonder now, was it a mistake? Surely Inspector Bacon, and your men too, made a thorough search of the place, didn't they, and didn't find it. It only turned up later in the boiler house."

"That's understandable," said Craddock. "The old gardener chap used to spear up any odd stuff that was blowing about and shove it in there."

"Where it was very convenient for the boys to find," said Miss Marple thoughtfully.

"You think we were meant to find it?"

"Well, I just wonder. After all it would be fairly easy to know where the boys were going to look next, or even to suggest to them . . . Yes, I do wonder. It stopped you thinking about Anna Stravinska any more, didn't it?"

Craddock said, "And you think it really may be her all the time?"

"I think someone may have got alarmed when you started making inquiries about her, that's all. I think somebody didn't want those inquiries made."

"Let's hold on to the basic fact that someone was going to impersonate Martine," said Craddock. "And then for some reason didn't. Why?"

"That's a very interesting question," said Miss Marple.

"Somebody sent a wire saying Martine was going back to France, then arranged to travel down with the girl and kill her on the way. You agree so far?"

"Not exactly," said Miss Marple. "I don't think, really, you're making it simple enough."

"Simple!" exclaimed Craddock. "You're mixing me up," he complained.

Miss Marple said in a distressed voice that she wouldn't think of doing anything like that.

"Come, tell me," said Craddock, "do you or do you not think you know who the murdered woman was?"

Miss Marple sighed. "It's so difficult," she said, "to put it the right way. I mean, I don't know *who* she was, but at the same time I'm fairly sure who she *was*, if you know what I mean."

Craddock threw up his head. "Know what you mean? I haven't the faintest idea." He looked out through the window. "There's your Lucy Eyelesbarrow coming to see you," he said. "Well, I'll be off. My *amour propre* is very low this afternoon and having a young woman coming in, radiant with efficiency and success, is more than I can bear."

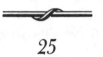

25

"I looked up *tontine* in the dictionary," said Lucy.

The first greetings were over and now Lucy was wandering rather aimlessly round the room, touching a china dog here, an antimacassar there, the plastic work box in the window.

"I thought you probably would," said Miss Marple equably.

Lucy spoke slowly, quoting the words. "Lorenzo Tonti, Italian banker, originator, 1653, of a form of annuity in which the shares of subscribers who die are added to the profit shares of the survivors." She paused. "That's it, isn't it? That fits well enough, and you were thinking of it even then before the last two deaths."

She took up once more her restless, almost aimless prowl round the room. Miss Marple sat watching her. This was a very different Lucy Eyelesbarrow from the one she knew.

"I suppose it was asking for it really," said Lucy. "A will of that kind, ending so that if there was only one survivor left he'd get the lot. And yet, there was quite a lot of money, wasn't there? You'd think it would be enough shared out—" She paused, the words tailing off.

"The trouble is," said Miss Marple, "that people are greedy. Some people. That's so often, you know, how things start. You don't start with murder, with wanting to do murder or even thinking of it. You just start by being greedy, by wanting more than you're going to have." She laid her knitting down on her knee and stared ahead of her into space. "That's how I came across Inspector Craddock first, you know. A case in the country. Near Medenham Spa. That began the same way, just a weak amiable character who wanted a great deal of money. Money that that person wasn't entitled to, but there seemed an easy way to get it. Not murder then. Just something so easy and simple that it hardly seemed wrong. That's how things begin. But it ended with three murders."

"Just like this," said Lucy. "We've had three murders now. The woman who impersonated Martine and who would have been able to claim a share for her son, and then Alfred, and then Harold. And now it only leaves two, doesn't it?"

"You mean," said Miss Marple, "there are only Cedric and Emma left?"

"Not Emma. Emma isn't a tall, dark man. No. I mean Cedric and Bryan Eastley. I never thought of Bryan because he's fair. He's got a great, fair mustache and blue eyes, but you see—the other day.—" She paused.

"Yes, go on," said Miss Marple. "Tell me. Something has upset you very badly, hasn't it?"

"It was when Lady Stoddart-West was going away. She had said good-by and then suddenly turned to me just as she was getting into the car and asked: 'Who was that tall, dark man who was standing on the terrace as I came in?'

"I couldn't imagine who she meant at first, because Cedric was still laid up. So I said, rather puzzled, 'You don't mean Bryan Eastley?' and she said, 'Of course, that's who it was, Squadron Leader Eastley. He was hidden in our loft once in France during the Resistance. I remembered the way he stood, and the set of his shoulders,' and she said, 'I should like to meet him again,' but we couldn't find him."

Miss Marple said nothing, just waited.

"And then," said Lucy, "later I looked at him . . . He was standing with his back to me and I saw what I ought to have seen before. That even when a man's fair, his hair looks dark because he plasters it down with stuff. Bryan's hair is a sort of medium brown, I suppose, but it can look dark. So, you see, it might have been Bryan that your friend saw in the train. It might. . . ."

"Yes," said Miss Marple. "I had thought of that."

"I suppose you think of everything!" said Lucy bitterly.

"Well, dear, one has to really."

"But I can't see what Bryan would get out of it. I mean, the money would come to Alexander, not to him. I suppose it would make an easier life, they could have a bit more luxury, but he wouldn't be able to tap the capital for his schemes, or anything like that."

"But if anything happened to Alexander before he was twenty-one, then Bryan would get the money as his father and next of kin," Miss Marple pointed out.

Lucy cast a look of horror at her.

"He'd never do that. No father would ever do that just—just to get the money."

Miss Marple sighed. "People do, my dear. It's very sad and very terrible, but they do.

"People do very terrible things," Miss Marple continued. "I know a woman who poisoned three of her children just for a little bit of insurance money. And then there was an old woman, quite a nice old woman apparently, who poisoned her son when he came home on leave. Then there was that old Mrs. Stanwich. That case was in the paper. I dare say you read about it. Her daughter died and her son, and then she said she was poisoned herself. There was poison in some gruel, but it came out, you know, that she'd put it there herself. She was just planning to poison the last daughter. That wasn't exactly for money. She was jealous of them for being younger than she was and alive, and she was afraid—it's a terrible thing to say but it's true—they would enjoy themselves after she was gone. She'd always kept a very tight hold on the purse strings. Yes, of course she was a little peculiar, as they say, but I never see myself that that's any real excuse. I mean you can be a little peculiar in so many different ways. Sometimes you just go about giving all your possessions away and writing checks on bank accounts that don't exist, just so as to benefit people. It shows, you see, that behind being peculiar you have quite a nice disposition. But of course if you're peculiar and behind it you have a bad disposition, well, there you are. Now, does that help you at all, my dear Lucy?"

"Does what help me?" asked Lucy, bewildered.

"What I've been telling you," said Miss Marple. She added gently, "You mustn't worry, you know. You really mustn't worry. Elspeth McGillicuddy will be here any day now."

"I don't see what that has to do with it."

"No, dear, perhaps not. But I think it's important myself."

"I can't help worrying," said Lucy. "You see I've got interested in the family."

"I know, dear, it's very difficult for you because you are quite strongly attracted to both of them, aren't you, in very different ways."

"What do you mean?" said Lucy. Her tone was sharp.

"I was talking about the two sons of the house," said Miss Marple. "Or rather the son and the son-in-law. It's fortunate that the two more unpleasant members of the family have died and the two more attractive ones are left. I can see that Cedric Crackenthorpe is very attractive. He is inclined to make himself out worse than he is and has a provocative way with him."

"He makes me fighting mad sometimes," said Lucy.

"Yes," said Miss Marple, "and you enjoy that, don't you? You're a girl with a lot of spirit and you enjoy a battle. Yes, I can see where that attraction lies. And then Mr. Eastley is a rather plaintive type, rather like an unhappy little boy. That of course is attractive, too."

"And one of them's a murderer," said Lucy bitterly, "and it may be either of them. There's nothing to choose between them really. There's Cedric, not caring a bit about his brother Alfred's death or about Harold's. He just sits back looking thoroughly pleased making plans for what he'll do with Rutherford Hall, and he keeps saying that it'll need a lot of money to develop it in the way he wants to do. Of course I know he's the sort of person who exaggerates his own callousness and all that. But that could be a cover, too. I mean everyone says that you're more callous than you really are. But you mightn't be. You might be even more callous than you seem!"

"Dear, dear Lucy, I'm so sorry about all this."

"And then Bryan," went on Lucy. "It's extraordinary, but Bryan really seems to want to live there. He thinks he and Alexander would find it awfully jolly and he's full of schemes."

"He's always full of schemes of one kind or another, isn't he?"

"Yes, I think he is. They all sound rather wonderful, but I've got an uneasy feeling that they'd never really work. I mean, they're not practical. The idea sounds all right, but I don't think he ever considers the actual working difficulties."

"They are up in the air, so to speak?"

"Yes, in more ways than one. I mean they are usually literally up in the air. They are all air schemes. Perhaps a really good fighter pilot never does quite come down to earth again. . . ."

She added: "And he likes Rutherford Hall so much because it reminds him of the big rambling Victorian house he lived in when he was a child."

"I see," said Miss Marple thoughtfully. "Yes, I see."

Then, with a quick sideways glance at Lucy, she said with a kind of verbal pounce, "But that isn't all of it, is it, dear? There's something else."

"Oh yes, there's something else. Just something that I didn't realize until just a couple of days ago. Bryan was actually on that train."

"On the 4:33 from Paddington?"

"Yes. You see Emma thought she was required to account for her movements on December the twentieth and she went over it all very carefully—a committee meeting in the morning and then shopping in the afternoon and tea at the Green Shamrock, and then, she said, she went to meet Bryan at the station. I worked out when she'd had tea and the time, and the train she met must have been the 4:33. So I asked Bryan, quite casually, and he said, Yes, it was, and added that his car had had a bump and was being repaired and so he had to come down by train —an awful bore, he said, he hates trains. He seemed quite natural about it all. It may be quite all right, but I wish, somehow, he hadn't been on that train. . . ."

"Actually on the train," said Miss Marple thoughtfully.

"It doesn't really prove anything. The awful thing is all this suspicion. Not to know. And perhaps we never shall know!"

"Of course we shall know, dear," said Miss Marple briskly. "I mean, all this isn't going to stop just at this point. The one thing I do know about murderers is that they can never let well alone. Or perhaps one should say, ill alone. At any rate," said Miss Marple with finality, "they can't once they've done a second murder. Now don't get too upset, Lucy. The police are doing all they can, and looking after everybody, and the great thing is that Elspeth McGillicuddy will be here very soon now!"

26

"Now, Elspeth, you're quite clear as to what I want you to do?"

"I'm clear enough," said Mrs. McGillicuddy, "but what I say to you is, Jane, that it seems very odd."

"It's not odd at all," said Miss Marple.

"Well, I think so. To arrive at the house and to ask almost immediately whether I can—er—go upstairs."

"It's very cold weather," Miss Marple pointed out, "and after all, you might have eaten something that disagreed with you and—er—have to ask to go upstairs. I mean, these things happen. I remember poor Louisa Felby came to see me once and she had to ask to go upstairs five times during one little half hour. That," added Miss Marple parenthetically, "was a bad Cornish pasty."

"If you'd just tell me what you're driving at, Jane," said Mrs. McGillicuddy.

"That's just what I don't want to do," said Miss Marple.

"How irritating you are, Jane. First you make me come all the way back to England before I need—"

"I'm sorry about that," said Miss Marple, "but I couldn't do anything else. Someone, you see, may be killed at any moment. Oh, I know they're all on their guard and the police are taking all the precautions they can, but there's always the outside chance that the murderer might be too clever for them. So you see, Elspeth, it was your duty to come back. After all, you and I were brought up to do our duty, weren't we?"

"We certainly were," said Mrs. McGillicuddy, "no laxness in our young days."

"So that's quite all right," said Miss Marple. "And that's the taxi now," she added, as a faint hoot was heard outside the house.

Mrs. McGillicuddy donned her heavy pepper-and-salt coat and Miss Marple wrapped herself up with a good many shawls and scarves. Then the two ladies got into the taxi and were driven to Rutherford Hall.

II

"Who can this be driving up?" Emma asked, looking out of the window, as the taxi swept past it. "I do believe it's Lucy's old aunt."

"What a bore," said Cedric.

He was lying back in a long chair looking at *Country Life* with his feet reposing on the side of the mantelpiece.

"Tell her you're not at home."

"When you say tell her I'm not at home, do you mean that I should go out and say so? Or that I should tell Lucy to tell her aunt so?"

"Hadn't thought of that," said Cedric. "I suppose I was thinking of our butler-and-footman days, if we ever had them. I seem to remember a footman before the war. He had an affair with the kitchen maid and there was a terrific rumpus about it. Isn't there one of those old hags about the place cleaning?"

But at that moment the door was opened by Mrs. Hart, whose afternoon it was for cleaning the brasses, and Miss Marple came in, very fluttery, in a whirl of shawls and scarves, with a tall, uncompromising figure behind her.

"I do hope," said Miss Marple, taking Emma's hand, "that we are not intruding. But you see, I'm going home the day after tomorrow, and I couldn't bear not to come over and see you and say good-by and thank you again for your goodness to Lucy. Oh, I forgot. May I introduce my friend, Mrs. McGillicuddy, who is staying with me?"

"How d'you do," said Mrs. McGillicuddy, looking at Emma with complete attention and then shifting her gaze to Cedric, who had now risen to his feet. Lucy entered the room at this moment.

"Aunt Jane, I had no idea . . ."

"I had to come and say good-by to Miss Crackenthorpe," said Miss Marple, turning to her, "who has been so very, very kind to you, Lucy."

"It's Lucy who's been very kind to us," said Emma.

"Yes, indeed," said Cedric. "We've worked her like a galley slave. Waiting on the sick room, running up and down the stairs, cooking little invalid messes . . ."

Miss Marple broke in. "I was so very, very sorry to hear of your illness. I do hope you're quite recovered now, Miss Crackenthorpe?"

"Oh, we're quite well again now," said Emma.

"Lucy told me you were all very ill. So dangerous, isn't it, food poisoning? Mushrooms, I understand."

"The cause remains rather mysterious," said Emma.

"Don't you believe it," said Cedric. "I bet you've heard the rumors that are flying round, Miss—er—"

"Marple," said Miss Marple.

"Well, as I say, I bet you've heard the rumors that are flying round. Nothing like arsenic for raising a little flutter in the neighborhood."

"Cedric," said Emma, "I wish you wouldn't. You know Inspector Craddock said . . ."

"Bah," said Cedric, "everybody knows. Even you've heard something, haven't you?" He turned to Miss Marple and Mrs. McGillicuddy.

"I myself," said Mrs. McGillicuddy, "have only just returned from abroad. The day before yesterday," she added.

"Ah, well, you're not up in our local scandal then," said Cedric. "Arsenic in the curry, that's what it was. Lucy's aunt knows all about it, I bet."

"Well," said Miss Marple, "I did just hear—I mean, it was just a hint, but of course I didn't want to embarrass you in any way, Miss Crackenthorpe."

"You must pay no attention to my brother," said Emma. "He just likes making people uncomfortable." She gave him an affectionate smile as she spoke.

The door opened and Mr. Crackenthorpe came in, tapping angrily with his stick.

"Where's tea?" he said. "Why isn't tea ready? You! Girl!" he addressed Lucy, "why haven't you brought tea in?"

"It's just ready, Mr. Crackenthorpe. I'm bringing it in now. I was just getting the table ready."

Lucy went out of the room again and Mr. Crackenthorpe was introduced to Miss Marple and Mrs. McGillicuddy.

"Like my meals on time," said Mr. Crackenthorpe. "Punctuality and economy. Those are my watchwords."

"Very necessary, I'm sure," said Miss Marple, "especially in these times with taxation and everything."

Mr. Crackenthorpe snorted. "Taxation! Don't talk to me of those robbers. A miserable pauper, that's what I am. And it's going to get worse, not better. You wait, my boy," he addressed Cedric, "when you get this place ten to one the Socialists will have it off you and turn it into a Welfare Center or something. And take all your income to keep it up with!"

Lucy reappeared with a tea tray, Bryan Eastley following her carrying a tray of sandwiches, bread and butter and cake.

"What's this? What's this?" Mr. Crackenthorpe inspected the tray. "Frosted cake? We having a party today? Nobody told me about it."

A faint flush came into Emma's face.

"Doctor Quimper's coming to tea, Father. It's his birthday today and—"

"Birthday?" snorted the old man, "what's he doing with a birthday? Birthdays are only for children. I never count my birthdays and I won't let anyone else celebrate them either."

"Much cheaper," agreed Cedric. "You save the price of candles on your cake."

"That's enough from you, boy," said Mr. Crackenthorpe.

Miss Marple was shaking hands with Bryan Eastley. "I've heard about you, of course," she said, "from Lucy. Dear me, you remind me so much of someone I used to know at St. Mary Mead. That's the village where I've lived for so many years, you know. Ronnie Wells, the solicitor's son. Couldn't seem to settle somehow when he went into his father's business. He went out to East Africa and started a series of cargo boats on the lakes out there. Victoria Nyanza, or is it Albert I mean? Anyway, I'm sorry to say that it wasn't a success, and he lost all his capital. Most unfortunate! Not any relation of yours, I suppose? The likeness is so great."

"No," said Bryan, "I don't think I've any relations called Wells."

"He was engaged to a very nice girl," said Miss Marple. "Very sensible. She tried to dissuade him, but he wouldn't listen to her. He was wrong of course. Women have a lot of sense, you know, when it comes to money matters. Not high finance, of course. No woman can hope to understand that, my dear father said. But every day matters. . . . What a delightful view you have from this window," she added, making her way across and looking out.

Emma joined her.

"Such an expanse of parkland! How picturesque the cattle look against the trees. One would never dream that one was in the middle of a town."

"We're rather an anachronism, I think," said Emma. "If the windows were open now you'd hear far off the noise of the traffic."

"Oh, of course," said Miss Marple, "there's noise everywhere, isn't there? Even in St. Mary Mead. We're now quite close to an airfield, you know, and really the way those jet planes fly over. Most frightening. Two panes in my little greenhouse broken the other day. Going through the sound barrier, or so I understand, though what it means I never have known."

"It's quite simple, really," said Bryan, approaching amiably. "You see, it's like this."

Miss Marple dropped her handbag and Bryan politely picked it up. At

the same moment Mrs. McGillicuddy approached Emma and murmured, in an anguished voice, and the anguish was quite genuine, since
Mrs. McGillicuddy deeply disliked the task which she was now performing:

"I wonder, could I go upstairs for a moment?"

"Of course," said Emma.

"I'll take you," said Lucy.

Lucy and Mrs. McGillicuddy left the room together.

"Very cold, driving today," said Miss Marple in a vaguely explanatory
manner.

"About the sound barrier," said Bryan, "you see, it's like this— Oh,
hello, there's Quimper."

The doctor drove up in his car. He came in rubbing his hands and
looking very cold.

"Going to snow," he said, "that's my guess. Hello, Emma, how are you?
Good lord, what's all this?"

"We made you a birthday cake," said Emma. "D'you remember? You
told me today was your birthday."

"I didn't expect all this," said Quimper. "You know it's years—why, it
must be, yes, sixteen years—since anyone's remembered my birthday."
He looked almost uncomfortably touched.

"Do you know Miss Marple?" Emma introduced him.

"Oh yes," said Miss Marple, "I met Doctor Quimper here before and
he came and saw me when I had a very nasty chill the other day and he
was most kind."

"All right again now, I hope?" said the doctor.

Miss Marple assured him that she was quite all right now.

"You haven't been to see me lately, Quimper," said Mr. Crackenthorpe. "I might be dying for all the notice you take of me!"

"I don't see you dying yet awhile," said Doctor Quimper.

"I don't mean to," said Mr. Crackenthorpe. "Come on, let's have tea.
What're we waiting for?"

"Oh, please," said Miss Marple, "don't wait for my friend. She would
be most upset if you did."

They sat down and started tea. Miss Marple accepted a piece of bread
and butter first, and then went on to a sandwich.

"Are they—?" She hesitated.

"Fish," said Bryan. "I helped make 'em."

Mr. Crackenthorpe gave a cackle of laughter.

"Poisoned fishpaste," he said. "That's what they are. Eat 'em at your
peril."

"Please, Father!"

"You've got to be careful what you eat in this house," said Mr. Crackenthorpe to Miss Marple. "Two of my sons have been murdered like flies. Who's doing it—that's what I want to know."

"Don't let him put you off," said Cedric, handing the plate once more to Miss Marple. "A touch of arsenic improves the complexion, they say, so long as you don't have too much."

"Eat one yourself, boy," said old Mr. Crackenthorpe.

"Want me to be official taster?" said Cedric. "Here goes."

He took a sandwich and put it whole into his mouth. Miss Marple gave a gentle, ladylike little laugh and took a sandwich. She took a bite and said:

"I do think it's so brave of you all to make these jokes. Yes, really, I think it's very brave indeed. I do admire bravery so much."

She gave a sudden gasp and began to choke. "A fish bone," she gasped out, "in my throat."

Quimper rose quickly. He went across to her, moved her backwards toward the window and told her to open her mouth. He pulled out a case from his pocket, selecting some forceps from it. With quick professional skill he peered down the old lady's throat. At that moment the door opened and Mrs. McGillicuddy, followed by Lucy, came in. Mrs. McGillicuddy gave a sudden gasp as her eyes fell on the tableau in front of her: Miss Marple leaning back and the doctor holding her throat and tilting up her head.

"But that's him," cried Mrs. McGillicuddy. "That's the man in the train. . . ."

With incredible swiftness Miss Marple slipped from the doctor's grasp and came toward her friend.

"I thought you'd recognize him, Elspeth!" she said. "No. Don't say another word." She turned triumphantly round to Doctor Quimper. "You didn't know, did you, Doctor, when you strangled that woman in the train, that somebody actually saw you do it? It was my friend here. Mrs. McGillicuddy. She saw you. Do you understand? *Saw you with her own eyes.* She was in another train that was running parallel with yours."

"What the hell—" Doctor Quimper made a quick step toward Mrs. McGillicuddy but again, swiftly, Miss Marple was between him and her.

"Yes," said Miss Marple. "She saw you, and she recognizes you, and she'll swear to it in court. It's not often, I believe," went on Miss Marple in her gentle plaintive voice, "that anyone actually sees a murder committed. It's usually circumstantial evidence of course. But in this case the conditions were very unusual. There was actually an eye witness to murder."

"You devilish old hag," said Doctor Quimper. He lunged forward at Miss Marple but this time it was Cedric who caught him by the shoulder.

"So you're the murdering devil, are you?" said Cedric as he swung him round. "I never liked you and I always thought you were a wrong 'un, but Lord knows, I never suspected you."

Bryan Eastley came quickly to Cedric's assistance. Inspector Craddock and Inspector Bacon entered the room from the farther door.

"Doctor Quimper," said Bacon, "I must caution you that . . ."

"You can take your caution to hell," said Doctor Quimper. "Do you think anyone's going to believe what a couple of batty old women say? Who's ever heard of all this rigmarole about a train!"

Miss Marple said, "Elspeth McGillicuddy reported the murder to the police at once on the twentieth of December and gave a description of the man."

Doctor Quimper gave a sudden heave of the shoulders. "If ever a man had the devil's own luck," said Doctor Quimper.

"But—" said Mrs. McGillicuddy.

"Be quiet, Elspeth," said Miss Marple.

"Why should I want to murder a perfectly strange woman?" said Doctor Quimper.

"She wasn't a strange woman," said Inspector Craddock. "She was your wife."

27

"So you see," said Miss Marple, "it really turned out to be, as I began to suspect, very, very simple. The simplest kind of crime. So many men seem to murder their wives."

Mrs. McGillicuddy looked at Miss Marple and Inspector Craddock. "I'd be obliged," she said, "if you'd put me a little more up to date."

"He saw a chance, you see," said Miss Marple, "of marrying a rich wife, Emma Crackenthorpe. Only he couldn't marry her because he had a wife already. They'd been separated for years but she wouldn't divorce him. That fitted in very well with what Inspector Craddock told me of this girl who called herself Anna Stravinska. She had an English husband, so she told one of her friends, and it was also said she was a very devout Catholic. Doctor Quimper couldn't risk marrying Emma bigamously, so he decided, being a very ruthless and cold-blooded man, that he would get rid of his wife. The idea of murdering her in the train and later putting her body in the sarcophagus in the barn was really rather a clever one. He meant it to tie up, you see, with the Crackenthorpe family. Before that he'd written a letter to Emma which purported to be from the girl Martine whom Edmund Crackenthorpe had talked of marrying. Emma had told Doctor Quimper all about her brother, you see. Then, when the moment arose he encouraged her to go to the police with the story. He wanted the dead woman identified as Martine. I think he may have heard that inquiries were being made by the Paris police about Anna Stravinska, and so he arranged to have a postcard come from her from Jamaica.

"It was easy for him to arrange to meet his wife in London, to tell her that he hoped to be reconciled with her and that he would like her to come down and 'meet his family.' We won't talk about the next part of it, which is very unpleasant to think about. Of course he was a greedy man. When he thought about taxation, and how much it cuts into income, he began thinking that it would be nice to have a good deal more capital. Perhaps he'd already thought of that before he decided to murder his wife. Anyway he started spreading rumors that someone was trying to poison old Mr. Crackenthorpe so as to get the ground prepared, and then he ended by administering arsenic to the family. Not too much, of course, for he didn't want old Mr. Crackenthorpe to die."

"But I still don't see how he managed," said Craddock. "He wasn't in the house when the curry was being prepared."

"Oh, but there wasn't any arsenic in the curry then," said Miss Marple. "He added it to the curry afterward when he took it away to be tested. He probably put the arsenic in the cocktail jug earlier. Then of course it was quite easy for him in his role of medical attendant, to poison off Alfred Crackenthorpe and also to send the tablets to Harold in London, having safeguarded himself by telling Harold that he wouldn't need any more tablets. Everything he did was bold and audacious and cruel and greedy, and I am really very, very glad," finished Miss Marple, looking as fierce as a fluffy old lady can look, "that they haven't abolished capital punishment yet because I do feel that if there is anyone who ought to hang, it's Doctor Quimper."

"Hear, hear," said Inspector Craddock.

"It occurred to me, you know," continued Miss Marple, "that even if you only see anybody from the back view, so to speak, nevertheless a back view is characteristic. I thought that if Elspeth were to see Doctor Quimper in exactly the same position as she'd seen the man in the train, that is, with his back to her bent over a woman whom he was holding by the throat, then I was almost sure she would recognize him, or would make some kind of startled exclamation. That is why I had to lay my little plan with Lucy's kind assistance."

"I must say," said Mrs. McGillicuddy, "it gave me quite a turn. I said

'That's him' before I could stop myself. And yet, you know, I hadn't actually seen the man's face and . . ."

"I was terribly afraid that you were going to say so, Elspeth," said Miss Marple.

"I was," said Mrs. McGillicuddy. "I was going to say that of course I hadn't seen his face."

"That," said Miss Marple, "would have been quite fatal! You see, dear, he thought you really did recognize him. I mean, he couldn't know that you hadn't seen his face."

"A good thing I held my tongue then," said Mrs. McGillicuddy.

"I wasn't going to let you say another word," said Miss Marple.

Craddock laughed suddenly. "You two!" he said. "You're a marvelous pair. What next, Miss Marple? What's the happy ending? What happens to poor Emma Crackenthorpe, for instance?"

"She'll get over the doctor, of course," said Miss Marple, "and I dare say if her father were to die—and I don't think he's quite so robust as he thinks he is—that she'd go on a cruise or perhaps stay abroad like Geraldine Webb, and I dare say something might come of it. A nicer man than Doctor Quimper, I hope."

"What about Lucy Eyelesbarrow? Wedding bells there, too?"

"Perhaps," said Miss Marple. "I shouldn't wonder."

"Which of 'em is she going to choose?" said Dermot Craddock.

"Don't you know?" said Miss Marple.

"No, I don't," said Craddock. "Do you?"

"Oh yes, I think so," said Miss Marple.

And she twinkled at him.

THE PAYOFF

by

STANLEY ELLIN

The four men aboard *Belinda II* watched the Coast Guard helicopter racketing its way southward on patrol along the Miami Beach shoreline.

"Handy little gadget," Broderick said, and Yates, echoing the boss man as usual, said, "Very handy."

"Depends," Del said sourly. He glanced at Chappie, who said nothing.

Broderick and Yates were in their middle forties, both of them big and hefty, with paunches showing under their yachting jackets. Chappie and Del were in their early twenties, flat-bellied in swim trunks.

Broderick, glassy-eyed with bourbon, squinted at his watch. "Thirty-five minutes. Last time was thirty-three. Let's call it an even half hour to be on the safe side." He looked Chappie up and down. "You sure that's enough time for you?"

Chappie said, "It's enough," and went back to whetting the blade of his clasp knife on the stone Broderick had turned up in the galley. The blade was four inches long, Bowie-shaped.

Broderick, one hand on the wheel, steadied *Belinda II*, keeping her bow toward the swells riding inshore, her motor almost idling. "You absolutely sure?"

Del said angrily, "You heard him, didn't you? What the hell you want to keep picking on him about it?"

"Because we are cutting down on the excuse quotient," Yates said. He was as stoned as Broderick, his face even more flaming red with wind-burn and Jim Beam. "Because we do not want to hear afterward how you couldn't do it because that chopper didn't allow enough time. Or any other excuse."

"Well, you won't be hearing no excuses," Del said, and Chappie snapped the knife shut and said to him, "Cool it, man. Just get that baby boat over here."

As Del hauled the dinghy alongside *Belinda II* by its line, Chappie shoved the knife into a plastic sandwich-bag, rolled up the bag, and thrust it into the waistband of his trunks. The outboard motor had already been clamped to the sternboard of the dinghy. Del stepped down into the dinghy, took his place at the motor. Chappie dropped down into the bow of the dinghy, untied its line, pushed off from *Belinda II*. Broderick joined Yates at the rail of the cabin cruiser, both of them watching with the same tight little smiles. Broderick cupped his hands to his mouth and yelled over the noise of the outboard, "Twenty-eight minutes left."

They were about two miles away from the towering line of hotels and high-rises along the shore. The sunlight was scorching, but a cool gusting breeze made it bearable. Del centered the bow of the dinghy on the big hotel dead ahead, the Royal Oceanic, tried to keep the boat from yawing and chopping too badly as it moved landward. He eyed Chappie who squatted there on the bow seat, rocking with the motion, his face empty.

"Suppose the layout's changed over there from the way Broderick told it," Del said. He pointed his chin at the hotel.

"Changed how?"

"Rooms, halls, you know what I mean. That was a couple of years ago he stayed there. They could have tore down things, built up things, so it's all changed around now."

"You worry too much," Chappie said.

"Because I just don't like this kind of a deal, man. We wouldn't even be in it if that big-mouth Broderick wasn't a mess of bad vibrations. Now ain't that the truth?"

"Nothing but," Chappie said.

"You see." Del solemnly shook his head. "Man, it sure is different from yesterday. I mean like up Palm Beach way when they said come on along and they'd give us a hitch right to Freeport. Fact is, I kind of took to them first look."

"Only way to find out about people is move in with them," Chappie said.

They were getting close to shore now. The swells the dinghy had been riding were taking shape as combers that crested and broke on the narrow, dirty-looking strip of sand fronting the hotel. Some people were standing in the surf. One of them shaded his eyes to look at the dinghy.

Del swung it around, bow pointing seaward, and cut the motor. He stood up to gauge the distance to the beach.

"Maybe a hundred yards," he said. "Just remember the low profile, man."

"You, too," Chappie said. He slid overboard, ducked underwater, came up shaking the hair out of his eyes. He rested a hand on the edge of the dinghy. "Don't let it look like you're waiting here. Take a ride for yourself. Then when you're back here, fool around with the motor."

He went deep under the boat, swam hard, and when he bobbed to the surface on the crest of a wave he turned and saw the dinghy wheeling away northward. He let the next wave carry him half the remaining distance to the beach. When he got to his feet he found the water only up to his waist. Off-balance, he was thrown forward on his hands and knees by a following wave. As he pitched forward, he felt the plastic bag with the knife in it slither down his thigh. He clutched at it, missed it, and came up with a handful of slimy, oil-soaked seaweed instead. He flung the seaweed aside. Then he saw the bag, open now, the knife showing through it, come to roost on the tide line up ahead. None of the bathers around him seemed to take any special notice as he got to the bag fast, poured the water out of it, wrapped it tight around the knife again, and shoved it back into his waistband.

He stood for a few seconds looking seaward. *Belinda II*, a small white patch on the horizon, got even smaller as it ran out into the Gulf Stream. Overhead there was no helicopter in sight. Nobody to take in the scene and connect the cabin cruiser with its dinghy or the dinghy with the passenger it had just landed.

He turned, crossed the strip of beach to the walled-in sun deck of the hotel. A broad flight of concrete steps led to the sun deck. A life-guard type in white ducks and a T-shirt marked *Royal Oceanic* stood at the head of the steps, his arms folded on his chest, his eyes on the beach. As Chappie passed by, the eyes swiveled toward him, flicked over him, then went back to surveying the beach.

Lounges in long neat rows took up most of the sun deck. The rest was taken up by a big swimming pool, its deep end toward the beach, its shallow end not far from the rear entrance to the hotel. A lot of the lounges were occupied; the pool was almost empty. Chappie strolled toward the pool, stepped up on the edge of it.

"Hey, you!"

Chappie froze there. He glanced over his shoulder and saw the life-guard type walking toward him, aiming a finger at him. "You," the man said. "What goes on?" The finger aimed downward now at Chappie's feet. "Bring all that sand up from the beach, mister, you ought to know enough to take a shower before you get in the pool." He nodded toward what looked like a phone booth with canvas walls. "Shower's right over there."

Chappie slowly released his breath. Thumb in the waistband of his trunks, hand covering the bulge of the knife in the waistband, he went over to the shower booth, stepped inside, braced himself against the shock of cold water jetting down on him.

When he walked out of the booth the life-guard type gave him á nod and a smile, and he nodded and smiled in return. Then he went into the pool feetfirst, keeping a grip on the knife in his belt until he picked up his swimming stroke. He covered almost the whole length of the pool under water, hoisted himself out at the shallow end. It was only a few steps from there to the hotel entrance. Inside the entrance he was in an arcade, a coffee shop on one side, a souvenir shop on the other. After the searing glare of sunlight outside, the arcade seemed like a cool, damp, unlit cave, but by the time he had walked past the coffee shop he was used to the lighting. A door beyond the shop was marked *Men's Sauna*, and there was a steady traffic coming and going through it.

Chappie went in and entered a long and wide corridor, narrower corridors branching off from it on both sides. It was hot and close here, the air growing steadily hotter and more humid as he walked along counting, and when he turned into the fourth corridor on the left a smell of sweat became unpleasantly noticeable. The walls in this section were all white tile, and each door along the way had a lettered plate on it: *Steam Room, Dry Heat, Showers, Personnel, Service.* The door to the service room was wide-open, kept in place by a rubber doorstop. As he passed it, Chappie took quick notice of the shelves of towels and sheets there. Almost out of sight in a corner of the room, someone was hauling towels from a shelf.

When he reached the end of the corridor, Chappie leaned against the wall, bent down as if to examine an ankle, his eyes sidelong on the open door of the service room. Then a boy in sandals and swim trunks emerged from the room with a bundle of towels under his arm. As soon as he was out of sight around a corner, Chappie went into the service room and helped himself to an armful of towels. He carried them back to the end of the corridor which ran into a short hallway that crossed it like the head of a capital T.

The doors in this hallway were numbered. Chappie carefully pushed open Number One an inch and looked inside. The room was small and windowless, its only furnishings a rubbing table and a shelf on the wall with a row of bottles and jars on it. On the table a big man with the build of a football linebacker was getting a rubdown from a masseur.

Chappie left the door as it was and tried the next room. It was empty. The third room, however, was occupied. A man wearing dark goggles lay stretched out on his back on the rubbing table, a cigar clamped between his teeth and pointing up at the ceiling, a sunlamp brilliantly lighting his naked body. A white-haired man, skinny and wrinkled, his face and body tanned a leathery brown. Clearly visible in the glare of the sunlamp was a tattoo on one scrawny forearm, done in garish colors. A coiled rattle-snake, and circling it in bold print the words *Don't Tread On Me*.

Chappie looked over his shoulder. There was no hotel staff man in sight, only some customers walking around in sandals and bathsheets. He got a good grip on the bundle of towels under his arm and went into the room. It reeked of cigar smoke and was hot enough to make him break into a sweat as he stood there closing the door softly behind him. He could feel the beads of sweat starting to trickle down his forehead and chest.

The click of the door lock roused the man. Without turning his head he said, "Benny?"

"No, sir," Chappie said. He moved toward the table. "But he sent me in to check up."

"Check up?" the man said. "What the hell's he trying to do, fix up everybody in the place with a handout?"

"No, sir. But he said you're not to get too much of that lamp on your front and more on your back."

As Chappie walked over to the table, his toes struck something on the floor beside it. A plastic ashtray with cigar ash in it. More cigar ash was scattered on the floor around it. Chappie stacked his armful of towels on the foot of the rubbing table and picked up the ashtray, the clasp knife digging into his groin as he did so. He said, "If you don't mind, sir," and took the cigar from between the man's teeth and deposited it in the ashtray. He put the ashtray back on the floor, pushing it far under the table.

The lenses in the goggles were so dark that Chappie couldn't see the man's eyes through them as he leaned forward over him. The man's head was resting on a folded towel. Chappie lifted the head barely enough to slide the towel out, and found the towel soaked through with sweat. He dropped it on the floor and gently set the man's head down again. "Want me to help you turn over, sir?"

The goggles fixed on him. "You new around here, boy?"

"Yes, sir."

"I thought so. Well, if you know what's good for you you'll help me turn over so nice and easy I don't feel a twinge. Damn bursitis is killing me. So very nice and easy, you hear?"

"Yes, sir."

The man grunted and groaned as he was arranged on his belly. Then he raised his head a little. "What the hell are you saving those towels for? This thing is like an ironing board."

"Yes, sir," said Chappie.

He took a towel from the pile, folded it and slid it under the man's head. The man rested his head on it. "All right," he said, "now beat it."

Chappie glanced at the closed door. Then he came up on his toes like a bullfighter preparing to plant his *pics*, both arms raised, left elbow out as if warding off an attack. His right hand flashed down expertly, all his strength behind it, and the edge of the palm drove into the nape of the man's neck like an ax blade. The leathery old body jerked violently, the legs snapping backward from the knees, then falling to the table again, one leg shivering. Chappie came up on his toes again, struck again. The leg stopped shivering. The body settled down into the table like a tub of fresh dough poured on it. One stringy arm slipped off the table and dangled there, its fingers half curled.

Chappie pulled the plastic bag from his waistband, took the knife out of it, opened the blade. He pulled the goggles high up on the man's forehead to give himself room, then slashed off the man's ear with one stroke of the knife. There was no welling of blood, just an ooze of it along the line of the wound. He cleaned the knife blade hastily with a fresh towel from the pile, snapped it shut, and put the knife and ear into the plastic bag.

Coming out of the arcade into glaring daylight he was blinded by the sun and almost bumped into a couple of people as he made his way to the pool. He swam fast to the deep end, giving the diving boards there a wide berth, but as he neared the ladder at the deep end there was a sudden loud splash in his face, a blow on the side of the head that pulled him up short.

It was a girl who had jumped off the side of the pool and was now treading water face to face with him. She was about 16 or 17, her long straight hair in strings down her face. She pulled some of the strings aside and said worriedly, "Honest, I didn't mean that. Are you all right?"

"Sure," Chappie said. He rested his hands on her shoulders and she let them stay there. She seemed to like it.

Chappie saw that some of the people standing on the edge of the pool were looking down at them. He released the girl and went up the ladder. "Hey," the girl called after him, "are you staying here at the hotel?" but he didn't answer or look back.

The life-guard type was still at the head of the stairway to the beach. Chappie slowed down to a casual walk going past the man and down the steps. He took his time crossing the narrow strip of beach and looked out over the pale green water. The dinghy was rocking up and down beyond the line of breakers, its motor pulled up horizontal, Del pretending to fiddle with it. *Belinda II* was barely in sight on the horizon. She seemed to be stationary now, but it was hard to judge from that distance. Chappie looked up. No helicopter showing anywhere.

He waded into the surf, went under a couple of lines of breakers, and swam to the dinghy. As he hauled himself into the bow, Del dropped the motor back into the water, got it snarling into life with a quick flick of the cord. The dinghy aimed for *Belinda II*, bouncing hard, and Chappie said, "Don't make it look like a getaway, man. Cut it down."

Del eased up on the throttle. He looked at Chappie. "You do it?"

"I did it."

"No sweat?"

"No. He looked about ready to go anyhow. And you can swim right up to that door there. You don't even have to walk in front of people." Chappie spat overboard to get the taste of salt water out of his mouth. "There's some massage artist name of Benny who is in for a big surprise pretty soon. Maybe even got it already." He had to smile at the thought.

Del said, "All the same, man, you ain't getting near enough bread for this kind of a deal. And that Broderick is loaded. I mean loaded."

"All I want is what's coming to me. If I wanted more I would have told him so."

"Sure enough. But you know how much that Yates said that *Belinda* boat cost? Forty thousand. And that Caddie of theirs up in Palm Beach. Man, that heap had everything in it but a Coke machine."

"What about it? All they are is a couple of fat old men with a lot of money. You want to trade around with them, just remember that the fat and the old goes along with the money."

Del shook his head. "Then it's no trade, man. What happens after Freeport? You don't figure to come back with them two, do you?"

"Hell, no. I figure we do some of those islands around there. Then maybe Mexico. Acapulco. How does that grab you?"

"Any place as long as it ain't Danang or like that grabs me just fine." Del looked up over his shoulder. "And talking about that—" The Coast Guard helicopter was in sight again, loudly making its northward run along the coast. "Man, it makes me sick to even hear the sound of them things now," Del said. "I can feel that pack breaking my back all over again."

"Full field pack," Chappie said. "Stuffed full of those delicious C-rations."

When they pulled alongside *Belinda II*, Broderick was at the wheel of the cruiser, Yates was at the rail watching them. Yates took the line Chappie handed up to him and made it fast to *Belinda II*. "Well, well," he said, "look who's home again. And with a tale to tell, I'm sure, about what went wrong and why."

Chappie disregarded him. He went aboard the cruiser, and Del, after tilting the outboard motor out of the water, followed him. Broderick looked them over.

"Not even breathing hard," he said. "A couple of real tough ones."

Chappie went over to the card table where Broderick and Yates played gin when someone else was at the wheel. He pulled the plastic bag from under his waistband, turned it upside down, and let the knife and the ear fall out on the table. The ear was putty-colored now, its severed edge a gummy red and brown where the ooze of blood had clotted.

The little smile on Broderick's face disappeared. He released the wheel and walked over to the table, eyes fixed on it. Del immediately grabbed the wheel and steadied it. He said to Broderick, "What the hell you looking so surprised at, man? He told you he could do it, didn't he? And bring back all the proof you wanted, didn't he?"

Broderick stood staring at the table. Then he stared at Chappie the same intent way, wiping a hand slowly back and forth over his mouth. Finally he said in a thick voice, "You really killed somebody? I mean, killed him?"

Chappie nodded at the table. "You think he just lay there and asked me to cut that off him?"

"But who was he? My God, you couldn't even know who he was!"

"I'm in no rush," Chappie said. "I can wait to find out when we see the papers over in Freeport tomorrow. But I'm not waiting until then for the payoff." He held out his hand and wiggled the fingers invitingly. "Right now's the time."

"Payoff?" said Broderick.

"Man, you said it was your ten dollars to my dime I couldn't do it. So I did it. Now it's payoff time."

Broderick said in anguish, "But I swear to God I never meant you to go through with it. I never expected you to. It was just talk, that's all. You knew it was just talk. You must have known it."

"You told him the layout there," Del said. "You told him where to look for somebody he could waste. You were the one scared about that chopper spotting us coming back here. Man, don't you start crawfishing now."

"Now look," Broderick said, then stopped short, shaking his head at his own thoughts.

Yates walked over to him fast, caught hold of his wrist. "Listen to me, Brod. I'm talking to you as your lawyer. You give him any money now, you are really in this up to your neck. And you're not taking them to the Bahamas or anywhere else out of the country. We can make it to Key Largo before dark and they'll haul out right there."

Chappie shrugged. "Freeport, Key Largo, whatever makes you happy." He picked up the knife from the table, opened its blade, held it up, admiring the way the sunlight ran up and down the blade. Then he leveled the knife at Broderick's belly. "But first I collect everything that's coming to me."

Broderick looked down at the knife, looked up at Chappie's face. Behind him at the wheel, Del said, "There's two of us, man," and Broderick pulled his wrist free of Yates's grip on it, shoved his hand into his hip pocket. He came up with a wad of bills in a big gold clip. He drew a ten-dollar bill from the clip and held it out to Chappie. "For ten lousy dollars," he said unbelievingly.

Chappie took the bill, studied it front and back as if making sure it was honest money. Then he slowly tore it in half, held the two halves high and released them to the breeze. They fluttered over the jackstaff at the stern of *Belinda II* and landed in her wake not far behind the trailing dinghy.

"That was the nothing part of the deal," Chappie said. "Now how about the real payoff?"

"The real payoff?" Broderick said.

"Mister, you told me that if I pulled it off you'd come right out and say you didn't know what it was all about. You told me you'd look me straight in the eye and say there's just as good men in Nam right now as that chicken company you were with in Korea. Just as good and maybe a lot better. Now say it."

Broderick said between his teeth, "If your idea of a good man—"

Chappie reached out and lightly prodded Broderick's yachting jacket with the point of the knife. "Say it."

Broderick said it. Then he suddenly wheeled and lurched into the cabin, Yates close on his heels. Through the open door Chappie watched them pour out oversized drinks.

"Key Largo's the place," he said to Del at the wheel, and as *Belinda II* swung southward, picking up speed as she went, Chappie stood there, his lip curled, watching the two men in the cabin gulping down their Jim Beam until Yates took notice of him and slammed the cabin door shut as hard as he could.

THE BASEMENT ROOM

by

GRAHAM GREENE

1

When the front door had shut the two of them out and the butler Baines had turned back into the dark and heavy hall, Philip began to live. He stood in front of the nursery door, listening until he heard the engine of the taxi die out along the street. His parents were safely gone for a fortnight's holiday; he was "between nurses," one dismissed and the other not arrived; he was alone in the great Belgravia house with Baines and Mrs. Baines.

He could go anywhere, even through the green baize door to the pantry or down the stairs to the basement living-room. He felt a happy stranger in his home because he could go into any room and all the rooms were empty.

You could only guess who had once occupied them: the rack of pipes in the smoking-room beside the elephant tusks, the carved wood tobacco jar; in the bedroom the pink hangings and the pale perfumes and three-quarter finished jars of cream which Mrs. Baines had not yet cleared away for her own use; the high glaze on the never-opened piano in the drawing-room, the china clock, the silly little tables and the silver. But here Mrs. Baines was already busy, pulling down the curtains, covering the chairs in dust-sheets.

"Be off out of here, Master Philip," and she looked at him with her peevish eyes, while she moved round, getting everything in order, meticulous and loveless and doing her duty.

Philip Lane went downstairs and pushed at the baize door; he looked into the pantry, but Baines was not there, then he set foot for the first time on the stairs to the basement. Again he had the sense: this is life. All his seven nursery years vibrated with the strange, the new experience. His crowded brain was like a city which feels the earth tremble at a distant earthquake shock. He was apprehensive, but he was happier than he had ever been. Everything was more important than before.

Baines was reading a newspaper in his shirt-sleeves. He said, "Come in, Phil, and make yourself at home. Wait a moment and I'll do the honours," and going to a white cleaned cupboard he brought out a bottle of ginger-beer and half a Dundee cake. "Half past eleven in the morning," Baines said. "It's opening time, my boy," and he cut the cake and poured out the ginger-beer. He was more genial than Philip had ever known him, more at his ease, a man in his own home.

"Shall I call Mrs. Baines?" Philip asked, and he was glad when Baines said no. She was busy. She liked to be busy, so why interfere with her pleasure?

"A spot of drink at half-past eleven," Baines said, pouring himself out a glass of ginger-beer, "gives an appetite for chop and does no man any harm."

"A chop?" Philip asked.

"Old Coasters," Baines said, "they call all food chop."

"But it's not a chop?"

"Well, it might be, you know, if cooked with palm oil. And then some paw-paw to follow."

Philip looked out of the basement window at the dry stone yard, the ash-can and the legs going up and down beyond the railings.

"Was it hot there?"

"Ah, you never felt such heat. Not a nice heat, mind, like you get in the park on a day like this. Wet," Baines said, "corruption." He cut himself a slice of cake. "Smelling of rot," Baines said, rolling his eyes round the small basement room, from clean cupboard to clean cupboard, the sense of bareness, of nowhere to hide a man's secrets. With an air of regret for something lost he took a long draught of ginger-beer.

"Why did father live out there?"

"It was his job," Baines said, "same as this is mine now. And it was mine then too. It was a man's job. You wouldn't believe it now, but I've had forty niggers under me, doing what I told them to."

"Why did you leave?"

"I married Mrs. Baines."

Philip took the slice of Dundee cake in his hand and munched it round the room. He felt very old, independent and judicial; he was aware that Baines was talking to him as man to man. He never called him Master Philip as Mrs. Baines did, who was servile when she was not authoritative.

Baines had seen the world; he had seen beyond the railings. He sat there over his ginger pop with the resigned dignity of an exile; Baines didn't complain; he had chosen his fate, and if his fate was Mrs. Baines he had only himself to blame.

But today—the house was almost empty and Mrs. Baines was upstairs and there was nothing to do—he allowed himself a little acidity.

"I'd go back tomorrow if I had the chance."

"Did you ever shoot a nigger?"

"I never had any call to shoot," Baines said. "Of course I carried a gun. But you didn't need to treat them bad. That just made them stupid. Why," Baines said, bowing his thin grey hair with embarrassment over the ginger pop, "I loved some of those damned niggers. I couldn't help loving them. There they'd be laughing, holding hands; they liked to touch each other; it made them feel fine to know the other fellow was around. It didn't mean anything we could understand; two of them would go about all day without loosing hold, grown men; but it wasn't love; it didn't mean anything we could understand."

"Eating between meals," Mrs. Baines said. "What would your mother say, Master Philip?"

She came down the steep stairs to the basement, her hands full of pots of cream and salve, tubes of grease and paste. "You oughtn't to encourage him, Baines," she said, sitting down in a wicker armchair and screwing up her small ill-humoured eyes at the Coty lipstick, Pond's cream, the Leichner rouge and Cyclax powder and Elizabeth Arden astringent.

She threw them one by one into the wastepaper basket. She saved only the cold cream. "Telling the boy stories," she said. "Go along to the nursery, Master Philip, while I get lunch."

Philip climbed the stairs to the baize door. He heard Mrs. Baines's voice like the voice in a nightmare when the small Price light has guttered in the saucer and the curtains move; it was sharp and shrill and full of malice, louder than people ought to speak, exposed.

"Sick to death of your ways, Baines, spoiling the boy. Time you did some work about the house," but he couldn't hear what Baines said in reply. He pushed open the baize door, came up like a small earth animal in his grey flannel shorts into a wash of sunlight on a parquet floor, the gleam of mirrors dusted and polished and beautified by Mrs. Baines.

Something broke downstairs, and Philip sadly mounted the stairs to the nursery. He pitied Baines; it occurred to him how happily they could live together in the empty house if Mrs. Baines were called away. He didn't want to play with his Meccano sets; he wouldn't take out his train or his soldiers; he sat at the table with his chin on his hands: this is life; and suddenly he felt responsible for Baines, as if he were the master of the house and Baines an ageing servant who deserved to be cared for. There was not much one could do; he decided at least to be good.

He was not surprised when Mrs. Baines was agreeable at lunch; he was used to her changes. Now it was "another helping of meat, Master Philip," or "Master Philip, a little more of this nice pudding." It was a pudding he liked, Queen's pudding with a perfect meringue, but he wouldn't eat a second helping lest she might count that a victory. She was the kind of woman who thought that any injustice could be counter-balanced by something good to eat.

She was sour, but she liked making sweet things; one never had to complain of a lack of jam or plums; she ate well herself and added soft sugar to the meringue and the strawberry jam. The half-light through the basement window set the motes moving above her pale hair like dust as she sifted the sugar, and Baines crouched over his plate saying nothing.

Again Philip felt responsibility. Baines had looked forward to this, and Baines was disappointed: everything was being spoilt. The sensation of disappointment was one which Philip could share; he could understand better than anyone this grief, something hoped for not happening, some-thing promised not fulfilled, something exciting which turned dull. "Baines," he said, "will you take me for a walk this afternoon?"

"No," Mrs. Baines said, "no. That he won't. Not with all the silver to clean."

"There's a fortnight to do it in," Baines said.

"Work first, pleasure afterwards."

Mrs. Baines helped herself to some more meringue.

Baines put down his spoon and fork and pushed his plate away. "Blast," he said.

"Temper," Mrs. Baines said, "temper. Don't you go breaking any more things, Baines, and I won't have you swearing in front of the boy. Master Philip, if you've finished you can get down."

She skinned the rest of the meringue off the pudding.

"I want to go for a walk," Philip said.

"You'll go and have a rest."

"I want to go for a walk."

"Master Philip," Mrs. Baines said. She got up from the table, leaving her meringue unfinished, and came towards him, thin, menacing, dusty in the basement room. "Master Philip, you just do as you're told." She took him by the arm and squeezed it; she watched him with a joyless passionate glitter and above her head the feet of typists trudged back to the Victoria offices after the lunch interval.

"Why shouldn't I go for a walk?"

But he weakened; he was scared and ashamed of being scared. This was life; a strange passion he couldn't understand moving in the basement room. He saw a small pile of broken glass swept into a corner by the wastepaper basket. He looked at Baines for help and only intercepted hate; the sad hopeless hate of something behind bars.

"Why shouldn't I?" he repeated.

"Master Philip," Mrs. Baines said, "you've got to do as you're told. You mustn't think just because your father's away there's nobody here to—"

"You wouldn't dare," Philip cried, and was startled by Baines's low interjection:

"There's nothing she wouldn't dare."

"I hate you," Philip said to Mrs. Baines. He pulled away from her and ran to the door, but she was there before him; she was old, but she was quick.

"Master Philip," she said, "you'll say you're sorry." She stood in front of the door quivering with excitement. "What would your father do if he heard you say that?"

She put a hand out to seize him, dry and white with constant soda, the nails cut to the quick, but he backed away and put the table between them, and suddenly to his surprise she smiled; she became again as servile as she had been arrogant. "Get along with you, Master Philip," she said with glee, "I see I'm going to have my hands full till your father and mother come back."

She left the door unguarded and when he passed her she slapped him playfully. "I've got too much to do today to trouble about you. I haven't covered half the chairs," and suddenly even the upper part of the house became unbearable to him as he thought of Mrs. Baines moving around shrouding the sofas, laying out the dust-sheets.

So he wouldn't go upstairs to get his cap but walked straight out across the shining hall into the street, and again, as he looked this way and looked that way, it was life he was in the middle of.

2

The pink sugar cakes in the window on a paper doily, the ham, the slab of mauve sausage, the wasps driving like small torpedoes across the pane caught Philip's attention. His feet were tired by pavements; he had been afraid to cross the road, had simply walked first in one direction, then in the other. He was nearly home now; the square was at the end of the street; this was a shabby outpost of Pimlico, and he smudged the pane with his nose looking for sweets, and saw between the cakes and ham a different Baines. He hardly recognized the bulbous eyes, the bald forehead. This was a happy, bold and buccaneering Baines, even though it was, when you looked closer, a desperate Baines.

Philip had never seen the girl, but he remembered Baines had a niece. She was thin and drawn, and she wore a white mackintosh; she meant nothing to Philip; she belonged to a world about which he knew nothing at all. He couldn't make up stories about her, as he could make them up about withered Sir Hubert Reed, the Permanent Secretary, about Mrs. Wince-Dudley who came up once a year from Penstanley in Suffolk with a green umbrella and an enormous black handbag, as he could make them up about the upper servants in all the houses where he went to tea and games. She just didn't belong. He thought of mermaids and Undine, but she didn't belong there either, nor to the adventures of Emil, nor to the Bastables. She sat there looking at an iced pink cake in the detachment and mystery of the completely disinherited, looking at the half-used pots of powder which Baines had set out on the marble-topped table between them.

Baines was urging, hoping, entreating, commanding, and the girl looked at the tea and the china pots and cried. Baines passed his handkerchief across the table, but she wouldn't wipe her eyes; she screwed it in her palm and let the tears run down, wouldn't do anything, wouldn't speak, would only put up a silent resistance to what she dreaded and wanted and refused to listen to at any price. The two brains battled over the tea-cups loving each other, and there came to Philip outside, beyond the ham and wasps and dusty Pimlico pane, a confused indication of the struggle.

He was inquisitive and he didn't understand and he wanted to know. He went and stood in the doorway to see better, he was less sheltered than he had ever been; other people's lives for the first time touched and pressed and moulded. He would never escape that scene. In a week he had forgotten it, but it conditioned his career, the long austerity of his life; when he was dying, rich and alone, it was said that he asked: "Who is she?"

Baines had won; he was cocky and the girl was happy. She wiped her face, she opened a pot of powder, and their fingers touched across the table. It occurred to Philip that it might be amusing to imitate Mrs. Baines's voice and to call "Baines" to him from the door.

His voice shrivelled them; you couldn't describe it in any other way, it made them smaller, they weren't together any more. Baines was the first to recover and trace the voice, but that didn't make things as they were. The sawdust was spilled out of the afternoon; nothing you did could mend it, and Philip was scared. "I didn't mean . . ." He wanted to say that he loved Baines, that he had only wanted to laugh at Mrs. Baines. But he had discovered you couldn't laugh at Mrs. Baines. She wasn't Sir Hubert Reed, who used steel nibs and carried a pen-wiper in his pocket; she wasn't Mrs. Wince-Dudley; she was darkness when the night-light went out in a draught; she was the frozen blocks of earth he had seen one winter in a graveyard when someone said, "They need an electric drill"; she was the flowers gone bad and smelling in the little closet room at Penstanley. There was nothing to laugh about. You had to endure her when she was there and forget about her quickly when she was away, suppress the thought of her, ram it down deep.

Baines said, "It's only Phil," beckoned him in and gave him the pink iced cake the girl hadn't eaten, but the afternoon was broken, the cake was like dry bread in the throat. The girl left them at once: she even forgot to take the powder. Like a blunt icicle in her white mackintosh she stood in the doorway with her back to them, then melted into the afternoon.

"Who is she?" Philip asked. "Is she your niece?"

"Oh, yes," Baines said, "that's who she is; she's my niece," and poured the last drops of water on to the coarse black leaves in the teapot.

"May as well have another cup," Baines said.

"The cup that cheers," he said hopelessly, watching the bitter black fluid drain out of the spout.

"Have a glass of ginger pop, Phil?"

"I'm sorry. I'm sorry, Baines."

"It's not your fault, Phil. Why, I could really believe it wasn't you at all, but her. She creeps in everywhere." He fished two leaves out of his cup and laid them on the back of his hand, a thin soft flake and a hard stalk. He beat them with his hand: "Today," and the stalk detached itself, "tomorrow, Wednesday, Thursday, Friday, Saturday, Sunday," but the flake wouldn't come, stayed where it was, drying under his blows, with a resistance you wouldn't believe it to possess. "The tough one wins," Baines said.

He got up and paid the bill and out they went into the street. Baines said, "I don't ask you to say what isn't true. But you needn't actually *tell* Mrs. Baines you met us here."

"Of course not," Philip said, and catching something of Sir Hubert Reed's manner, "I understand, Baines." But he didn't understand a thing; he was caught up in other people's darkness.

"It was stupid," Baines said. "So near home, but I hadn't time to think, you see. I'd got to see her."

"Of course, Baines."

"I haven't time to spare," Baines said. "I'm not young. I've got to see that she's all right."

"Of course you have, Baines."

"Mrs. Baines will get it out of you if she can."

"You can trust me, Baines," Philip said in a dry important Reed voice; and then, "Look out. She's at the window watching." And there indeed she was, looking up at them, between the lace curtains, from the basement room, speculating. "Need we go in, Baines?" Philip asked, cold lying heavy on his stomach like too much pudding; he clutched Baines's arm.

"Careful," Baines said softly, "careful."

"But need we go in, Baines? It's early. Take me for a walk in the park."

"Better not."

"But I'm frightened, Baines."

"You haven't any cause," Baines said. "Nothing's going to hurt you. You just run along upstairs to the nursery. I'll go down by the area and talk to Mrs. Baines." But he stood hesitating at the top of the stone steps pretending not to see her, where she watched between the curtains. "In at the front door, Phil, and up the stairs."

Philip didn't linger in the hall; he ran, slithering on the parquet Mrs. Baines had polished, to the stairs. Through the drawing-room doorway on the first floor he saw the draped chairs; even the china clock on the mantel was covered like a canary's cage. As he passed, it chimed the hour, muffled and secret under the duster. On the nursery table he found his supper laid out: a glass of milk and a piece of bread and butter, a sweet biscuit, and a little cold Queen's pudding without the meringue. He had no appetite; he strained his ears for Mrs. Baines's coming, for the sound of voices, but the basement held its secrets; the green baize door shut off that world. He drank the milk and ate the biscuit, but he didn't touch the rest, and presently he could hear the soft precise footfalls of Mrs. Baines on the stairs: she was a good servant, she walked softly; she was a determined woman, she walked precisely.

But she wasn't angry when she came in; she was ingratiating as she opened the night nursery door—"Did you have a good walk, Master Philip?"—pulled down the blinds, laid out his pyjamas, came back to clear his supper. "I'm glad Baines found you. Your mother wouldn't have liked your being out alone." She examined the tray. "Not much appetite, have you, Master Philip? Why don't you try a little of this nice pudding? I'll bring you up some more jam for it."

"No, no, thank you, Mrs. Baines," Philip said.

"You ought to eat more," Mrs. Baines said. She sniffed round the room like a dog. "You didn't take any pots out of the wastepaper basket in the kitchen, did you, Master Philip?"

"No," Philip said.

"Of course you wouldn't. I just wanted to make sure." She patted his shoulder and her fingers flashed to his lapel; she picked off a tiny crumb of pink sugar. "Oh, Master Philip," she said, "that's why you haven't any appetite. You've been buying sweet cakes. That's not what your pocket money's for."

"But I didn't," Philip said, "I didn't."

She tasted the sugar with the tip of her tongue.

"Don't tell lies to me, Master Philip. I won't stand for it any more than your father would."

"I didn't, I didn't," Philip said. "They gave it me. I mean Baines," but she had pounced on the word "they." She had got what she wanted; there was no doubt about that, even when you didn't know what it was she wanted. Philip was angry and miserable and disappointed because he hadn't kept Baines's secret. Baines oughtn't to have trusted him; grown-up people should keep their own secrets, and yet here was Mrs. Baines immediately entrusting him with another.

"Let me tickle your palm and see if you can keep a secret." But he put his hand behind him; he wouldn't be touched. "It's a secret between us, Master Philip, that I know all about them. I suppose she was having tea with him," she speculated.

"Why shouldn't she?" he asked, the responsibility for Baines weighing on his spirit, the idea that he had got to keep her secret when he hadn't kept Baines's making him miserable with the unfairness of life. "She was nice."

"She was nice, was she?" Mrs. Baines said in a bitter voice he wasn't used to.

"And she's his niece."

"So that's what he said," Mrs. Baines struck softly back at him like the clock under the duster. She tried to be jocular. "The old scoundrel. Don't you tell him I know, Master Philip." She stood very still between the table and the door, thinking very hard, planning something. "Promise you won't tell. I'll give you that Meccano set, Master Philip . . ."

He turned his back on her; he wouldn't promise, but he wouldn't tell. He would have nothing to do with their secrets, the responsibilities they were determined to lay on him. He was only anxious to forget. He had received already a larger dose of life than he had bargained for, and he was scared. "A 2A Meccano set, Master Philip." He never opened his Meccano set again, never built anything, never created anything, died the old dilettante, sixty years later with nothing to show rather than preserve the memory of Mrs. Baines's malicious voice saying good night, her soft determined footfalls on the stairs to the basement, going down, going down.

3

The sun poured in between the curtains and Baines was beating a tattoo on the water-can. "Glory, glory," Baines said. He sat down on the end of the bed and said, "I beg to announce that Mrs. Baines has been called away. Her mother's dying. She won't be back till tomorrow."

"Why did you wake me up so early?" Philip complained. He watched Baines with uneasiness; he wasn't going to be drawn in; he'd learnt his lesson. It wasn't right for a man of Baines's age to be so merry. It made a grown person human in the same way that you were human. For if a grown-up could behave so childishly, you were liable to find yourself in their world. It was enough that it came at you in dreams: the witch at the corner, the man with a knife. So "It's very early," he whined, even though he loved Baines, even though he couldn't help being glad that Baines was happy. He was divided by the fear and the attraction of life.

"I want to make this a long day," Baines said. "This is the best time." He pulled the curtains back. "It's a bit misty. The cat's been out all night. There she is, sniffing round the area. They haven't taken in any milk at 59. Emma's shaking out the mats at 63." He said, "This was what I used to think about on the Coast: somebody shaking mats and the cat coming home. I can see it today," Baines said, "just as if I was still in Africa. Most days you don't notice what you've got. It's a good life if you don't weaken." He put a penny on the washstand. "When you've dressed, Phil, run and get a *Mail* from the barrow at the corner. I'll be cooking the sausages."

"Sausages?"

"Sausages," Baines said. "We're going to celebrate today." He celebrated at breakfast, restless, cracking jokes, unaccountably merry and nervous. It was going to be a long, long day, he kept on coming back to that: for years he had waited for a long day, he had sweated in the damp Coast heat, changed shirts, gone down with fever, lain between the blankets and sweated, all in the hope of this long day, that cat sniffing round the area, a bit of mist, the mats beaten at 63. He propped the *Mail* in front of the coffee-pot and read pieces aloud. He said, "Cora Down's been married for the fourth time." He was amused, but it wasn't his idea of a long day. His long day was the Park, watching the riders in the Row, seeing Sir Arthur Stillwater pass beyond the rails ("He dined with us once in Bo; up from Freetown; he was governor there"), lunch at the Corner

House for Philip's sake (he'd have preferred himself a glass of stout and some oysters at the York bar), the Zoo, the long bus ride home in the last summer light: the leaves in the Green Park were beginning to turn and the motors nuzzled out of Berkeley Street with the low sun gently glowing on their windscreens. Baines envied no one, not Cora Down, or Sir Arthur Stillwater, or Lord Sandale, who came out on to the steps of the Army and Navy and then went back again—he hadn't anything to do and might as well look at another paper. "I said don't let me see you touch that black again." Baines had led a man's life; everyone on top of the bus pricked his ears when he told Philip all about it.

"Would you have shot him?" Philip asked, and Baines put his head back and tilted his dark respectable manservant's hat to a better angle as the bus swerved round the Artillery Memorial.

"I wouldn't have thought twice about it. I'd have shot to kill," he boasted, and the bowed figure went by, the steel helmet, the heavy cloak, the down-turned rifle and the folded hands.

"Have you got the revolver?"

"Of course I've got it," Baines said. "Don't I need it with all the burglaries there've been?" This was the Baines whom Philip loved: not Baines singing and carefree, but Baines responsible, Baines behind barriers, living his man's life.

All the buses streamed out from Victoria like a convoy of aeroplanes to bring Baines home with honour. "Forty blacks under me," and there waiting near the area steps was the proper reward, love at lighting-up time.

"It's your niece," Philip said, recognizing the white mackintosh, but not the happy sleepy face. She frightened him like an unlucky number; he nearly told Baines what Mrs. Baines had said; but he didn't want to bother, he wanted to leave things alone.

"Why, so it is," Baines said. "I shouldn't wonder if she was going to have a bit of supper with us." But, he said, they'd play a game, pretend they didn't know her, slip down the area steps, "and here," Baines said, "we are," lay the table, put out the cold sausages, a bottle of beer, a bottle of ginger pop, a flagon of harvest burgundy. "Everyone his own drink," Baines said. "Run upstairs, Phil, and see if there's been a post."

Philip didn't like the empty house at dusk before the lights went on. He hurried. He wanted to be back with Baines. The hall lay there in quiet and shadow prepared to show him something he didn't want to see. Some letters rustled down and someone knocked. "Open in the name of the Republic." The tumbrils rolled, the head bobbed in the bloody basket. Knock, knock, and the postman's footsteps going away. Philip gathered the letters. The slit in the door was like the grating in a jeweller's window. He remembered the policeman he had seen peer through. He had said to his nurse, "What's he doing?" and when she said, "He's seeing if everything's all right," his brain immediately filled with images of all that might be wrong. He ran to the baize door and the stairs. The girl was already there and Baines was kissing her. She leant breathless against the dresser.

"Here's Emmy, Phil."

"There's a letter for you, Baines."

"Emmy," Baines said, "it's from her." But he wouldn't open it. "You bet she's coming back."

"We'll have supper, anyway," Emmy said. "She can't harm that."

"You don't know her," Baines said. "Nothing's safe. Damn it," he said, "I was a man once," and he opened the letter.

"Can I start?" Philip asked, but Baines didn't hear; he presented in his stillness an example of the importance grown-up people attached to the written word: you had to write your thanks, not wait and speak them, as if letters couldn't lie. But Philip knew better than that, sprawling his thanks across a page to Aunt Alice who had given him a teddy bear he was too old for. Letters could lie all right, but they made the lie permanent. They lay as evidence against you: they made you meaner than the spoken word.

"She's not coming back till tomorrow night," Baines said. He opened the bottles, he pulled up the chairs, he kissed Emmy again against the dresser.

"You oughtn't to," Emmy said, "with the boy here."

"He's got to learn," Baines said, "like the rest of us," and he helped Philip to three sausages. He only took one himself; he said he wasn't hungry, but when Emmy said she wasn't hungry either he stood over her and made her eat. He was timid and rough with her and made her drink the harvest burgundy because he said she needed building up; he wouldn't take no for an answer, but when he touched her his hands were light and clumsy too, as if he was afraid to damage something delicate and didn't know how to handle anything so light.

"This is better than milk and biscuits, eh?"

"Yes," Philip said, but he was scared, scared for Baines as much as for himself. He couldn't help wondering at every bite, at every draught of the ginger pop, what Mrs. Baines would say if she ever learnt of this meal; he couldn't imagine it, there was a depth of bitterness and rage in Mrs. Baines you couldn't sound. He said, "She won't be coming back tonight?" but you could tell by the way they immediately understood him that she wasn't really away at all; she was there in the basement with them, driving them to longer drinks and louder talk, biding her time for the right cutting word. Baines wasn't really happy; he was only watching happiness from close to instead of from far away.

"No," he said, "she'll not be back till late tomorrow." He couldn't keep his eyes off happiness. He'd played around as much as other men; he kept on reverting to the Coast as if to excuse himself for his innocence. He wouldn't have been so innocent if he'd lived his life in London, so innocent when it came to tenderness. "If it was you, Emmy," he said, looking at the white dresser, the scrubbed chairs, "this'd be like a home." Already the room was not quite so harsh; there was a little dust in corners, the silver needed a final polish, the morning's paper lay untidily on a chair. "You'd better go to bed, Phil; it's been a long day."

They didn't leave him to find his own way up through the dark shrouded house; they went with him, turning on lights, touching each other's fingers on the switches. Floor after floor they drove the night back. They spoke softly among the covered chairs. They watched him undress, they didn't make him wash or clean his teeth, they saw him into bed and lit his night-light and left his door ajar. He could hear their voices on the stairs, friendly like the guests he heard at dinner-parties when they moved down the hall, saying good night. They belonged; wherever they were they made a home. He heard a door open and a clock strike, he heard their voices for a long while, so that he felt they were not far away and he was safe. The voices didn't dwindle, they simply went out, and he could be sure that they were still somewhere not far from him, silent together in one of the many empty rooms, growing sleepy together as he grew sleepy after the long day.

He just had time to sigh faintly with satisfaction, because this too perhaps had been life, before he slept and the inevitable terrors of sleep came round him: a man with a tricolour hat beat at the door on His Majesty's service, a bleeding head lay on the kitchen table in a basket, and the Siberian wolves crept closer. He was bound hand and foot and couldn't move; they leapt round him breathing heavily; he opened his eyes and Mrs. Baines was there, her grey untidy hair in threads over his face, her black hat askew. A loose hairpin fell on the pillow and one musty thread brushed his mouth. "Where are they?" she whispered. "Where are they?"

4

Philip watched her in terror. Mrs. Baines was out of breath as if she had been searching all the empty rooms, looking under loose covers.

With her untidy grey hair and her black dress buttoned to her throat, her gloves of black cotton, she was so like the witches of his dreams that he didn't dare to speak. There was a stale smell in her breath.

"She's here," Mrs. Baines said, "you can't deny she's here." Her face was simultaneously marked with cruelty and misery; she wanted to "do things" to people, but she suffered all the time. It would have done her good to scream, but she daren't do that: it would warn them. She came ingratiatingly back to the bed where Philip lay rigid on his back and whispered, "I haven't forgotten the Meccano set. You shall have it tomorrow, Master Philip. We've got secrets together, haven't we? Just tell me where they are."

He couldn't speak. Fear held him as firmly as any nightmare. She said, "Tell Mrs. Baines, Master Philip. You love your Mrs. Baines, don't you?" That was too much; he couldn't speak, but he could move his mouth in terrified denial, wince away from her dusty image.

She whispered, coming closer to him, "Such deceit. I'll tell your father. I'll settle with you myself when I've found them. You'll smart; I'll see you smart." Then immediately she was still, listening. A board had creaked on the floor below, and a moment later, while she stooped listening above his bed, there came the whispers of two people who were happy and sleepy together after a long day. The night-light stood beside the mirror and Mrs. Baines could see there her own reflection, misery and cruelty wavering in the glass, age and dust and nothing to hope for. She sobbed without tears, a dry, breathless sound, but her cruelty was a kind of pride which kept her going; it was her best quality, she would have been merely pitiable without it. She went out of the door on tiptoe, feeling her way across the landing, going so softly down the stairs that no one behind a shut door could hear her. Then there was complete silence again; Philip could move; he raised his knees; he sat up in bed; he wanted to die. It wasn't fair, the walls were down again between his world and theirs, but this time it was something worse than merriment that the grown people made him share; a passion moved in the house he recognized but could not understand.

It wasn't fair, but he owed Baines everything: the Zoo, the ginger pop, the bus ride home. Even the supper called to his loyalty. But he was frightened; he was touching something he touched in dreams; the bleeding head, the wolves, the knock, knock, knock. Life fell on him with savagery, and you couldn't blame him if he never faced it again in sixty years. He got out of bed. Carefully from habit he put on his bedroom slippers and tiptoed to the door: it wasn't quite dark on the landing below because the curtains had been taken down for the cleaners and the light from the street washed in through the tall windows. Mrs. Baines had her hand on the glass door-knob; she was very carefully turning it; he screamed: "Baines, Baines."

Mrs. Baines turned and saw him cowering in his pyjamas by the banisters; he was helpless, more helpless even than Baines, and cruelty grew at the sight of him and drove her up the stairs. The nightmare was on him again and he couldn't move; he hadn't any more courage left, he couldn't even scream.

But the first cry brought Baines out of the best spare bedroom and he moved quicker than Mrs. Baines. She hadn't reached the top of the stairs before he'd caught her round the waist. She drove her black cotton gloves at his face and he bit her hand. He hadn't time to think, he fought her like a stranger, but she fought back with knowledgeable hate. She was going to teach them all and it didn't really matter whom she began with; they had all deceived her; but the old image in the glass was by her side, telling her she must be dignified, she wasn't young enough to yield her dignity; she could beat his face, but she mustn't bite; she could push, but she mustn't kick.

Age and dust and nothing to hope for were her handicaps. She went over the banisters in a flurry of black clothes and fell into the hall; she lay before the front door like a sack of coals which should have gone down the area into the basement. Philip saw; Emmy saw; she sat down suddenly in the doorway of the best spare bedroom with her eyes open as if she were too tired to stand any longer. Baines went slowly down into the hall.

It wasn't hard for Philip to escape; they'd forgotten him completely. He went down the back, the servants' stairs, because Mrs. Baines was in the hall. He didn't understand what she was doing lying there; like the pictures in a book no one had read to him, the things he didn't understand terrified him. The whole house had been turned over to the grown-up world; he wasn't safe in the night nursery; their passions had flooded in. The only thing he could do was to get away, by the back stairs, and up through the area, and never come back. He didn't think of the cold, of the need for food and sleep; for an hour it would seem quite possible to escape from people for ever.

He was wearing pyjamas and bedroom slippers when he came up into the square, but there was no one to see him. It was that hour of the evening in a residential district when everyone is at the theatre or at home. He climbed over the iron railings into the little garden: the plane-trees spread their large pale palms between him and the sky. It might have been an illimitable forest into which he had escaped. He crouched behind a trunk and the wolves retreated; it seemed to him between the little iron seat and the tree-trunk that no one would ever find him again. A kind of embittered happiness and self-pity made him cry; he was lost; there wouldn't be any more secrets to keep; he surrendered responsibility once and for all. Let grown-up people keep to their world and he would keep to his, safe in the small garden between the plane-trees.

Presently the door of 48 opened and Baines looked this way and that; then he signalled with his hand and Emmy came; it was as if they were only just in time for a train, they hadn't a chance of saying good-bye. She went quickly by like a face at a window swept past the platform, pale and unhappy and not wanting to go. Baines went in again and shut the door; the light was lit in the basement, and a policeman walked round the square, looking into the areas. You could tell how many families were at home by the lights behind the first-floor curtains.

Philip explored the garden: it didn't take long: a twenty-yard square of bushes and plane-trees, two iron seats and a gravel path, a padlocked gate at either end, a scuffle of old leaves. But he couldn't stay: something stirred in the bushes and two illuminated eyes peered out at him like a Serbian wolf, and he thought how terrible it would be if Mrs. Baines found him there. He'd have no time to climb the railings; she'd seize him from behind.

He left the square at the unfashionable end and was immediately among the fish-and-chip shops, the little stationers selling *Bagatelle*, among the accommodation addresses and the dingy hotels with open doors. There were few people about because the pubs were open, but a blowsy woman carrying a parcel called out to him across the street and the commissionaire outside a cinema would have stopped him if he hadn't crossed the road. He went deeper: you could go farther and lose yourself more completely here than among the plane-trees. On the fringe of the square he was in danger of being stopped and taken back: it was obvious where he belonged; but as he went deeper he lost the marks of his origin. It was a warm night: any child in those free-living parts might be expected to play truant from bed. He found a kind of camaraderie even among grown-up people; he might have been a neighbour's child as he went quickly by, but they weren't going to tell on him, they'd been young once themselves. He picked up a protective coating of dust from the pavements, of smuts from the trains which passed along the backs in a spray of fire. Once he was caught in a knot of children running away from something or somebody, laughing as they ran; he was whirled with them round a turning and abandoned, with a sticky fruit-drop in his hand.

He couldn't have been more lost, but he hadn't the stamina to keep on. At first he feared that someone would stop him; after an hour he hoped that someone would. He couldn't find his way back, and in any case he was afraid of arriving home alone; he was afraid of Mrs. Baines, more afraid than he had ever been. Baines was his friend, but something had happened which gave Mrs. Baines all the power. He began to loiter on purpose to be noticed, but no one noticed him. Families were having a last breather on the doorsteps, the refuse bins had been put out and bits of cabbage stalks soiled his slippers. The air was full of voices, but he was cut off; these people were strangers and would always now be strangers; they were marked by Mrs. Baines and he shied away from them into a deep class-conciousness. He had been afraid of policemen, but now he wanted one to take him home; even Mrs. Baines could do nothing against a policeman. He sidled past a constable who was directing traffic, but he was too busy to pay him any attention. Philip sat down against a wall and cried.

It hadn't occurred to him that that was the easiest way, that all you had to do was to surrender, to show you were beaten and accept kindness. . . . It was lavished on him at once by two women and a pawnbroker. Another policeman appeared, a young man with a sharp incredulous face. He looked as if he noted everything he saw in pocket-books and drew conclusions. A woman offered to see Philip home, but he didn't trust her: she wasn't a match for Mrs. Baines immobile in the hall. He wouldn't give his address; he said he was afraid to go home. He had his way; he got his protection. "I'll take him to the station," the policeman said, and holding him awkwardly by the hand (he wasn't married; he had his career to make) he led him round the corner, up the stone stairs into the little bare over-heated room where Justice lived.

5

Justice waited behind a wooden counter on a high stool; it wore a heavy moustache; it was kindly and had six children ("three of them nippers like yourself"); it wasn't really interested in Philip, but it pretended to be, it wrote the address down and sent a constable to fetch a glass of milk. But the young constable was interested; he had a nose for things.

"Your home's on the telephone, I suppose," Justice said. "We'll ring them up and say you are safe. They'll fetch you very soon. What's your name, sonny?"

"Philip."

"Your other name?"

"I haven't got another name." He didn't want to be fetched; he wanted to be taken home by someone who would impress even Mrs. Baines. The constable watched him, watched the way he drank the milk, watched him when he winced away from questions.

"What made you run away? Playing truant, eh?"

"I don't know."

"You oughtn't to do it, young fellow. Think how anxious your father and mother will be."

"They are away."

"Well, your nurse."

"I haven't got one."

"Who looks after you, then?" The question went home. Philip saw Mrs. Baines coming up the stairs at him, the heap of black cotton in the hall. He began to cry.

"Now, now, now," the sergeant said. He didn't know what to do; he wished his wife were with him; even a policewoman might have been useful.

"Don't you think it's funny," the constable said, "that there hasn't been an inquiry?"

"They think he's tucked up in bed."

"You are scared, aren't you?" the constable said. "What scared you?"

"I don't know."

"Somebody hurt you?"

"No."

"He's had bad dreams," the sergeant said. "Thought the house was on fire, I expect. I've brought up six of them. Rose is due back. She'll take him home."

"I want to go home with you," Philip said; he tried to smile at the constable, but the deceit was immature and unsuccessful.

"I'd better go," the constable said. "There may be something wrong."

"Nonsense," the sergeant said. "It's a woman's job. Tact is what you need. Here's Rose. Pull up your stockings, Rose. You're a disgrace to the Force. I've got a job of work for you." Rose shambled in: black cotton stockings drooping over her boots, a gawky Girl Guide manner, a hoarse hostile voice. "More tarts, I suppose."

"No, you've got to see this young man home." She looked at him owlishly.

"I won't go with her," Philip said. He began to cry again. "I don't like her."

"More of that womanly charm, Rose," the sergeant said. The telephone rang on his desk. He lifted the receiver. "What? What's that?" he said. "Number 48? You've got a doctor?" He put his hand over the telephone mouth. "No wonder this nipper wasn't reported," he said. "They've been too busy. An accident. Woman slipped on the stairs."

"Serious?" the constable asked. The sergeant mouthed at him; you didn't mention the word death before a child (didn't he know? he had six of them), you made noises in the throat, you grimaced, a complicated shorthand for a word of only five letters anyway.

"You'd better go, after all," he said, "and make a report. The doctor's there."

Rose shambled from the stove; pink apply-dapply cheeks, loose stockings. She stuck her hands behind her. Her large morgue-like mouth was full of blackened teeth. "You told me to take him and now just because something interesting . . . I don't expect justice from a man . . ."

"Who's at the house?" the constable asked.

"The butler."

"You don't think," the constable said, "he saw . . ."

"Trust me," the sergeant said. "I've brought up six. I know 'em through and through. You can't teach me anything about children."

"He seemed scared about something."

"Dreams," the sergeant said.

"What name?"

"Baines."

"This Mr. Baines," the constable said to Philip, "you like him, eh? He's good to you?" They were trying to get something out of him; he was suspicious of the whole roomful of them; he said "yes" without conviction because he was afraid at any moment of more responsibilities, more secrets.

"And Mrs. Baines?"

"Yes."

They consulted together by the desk. Rose was hoarsely aggrieved; she was like a female impersonator, she bore her womanhood with an unnatural emphasis even while she scorned it in her creased stockings and her weather-exposed face. The charcoal shifted in the stove; the room was over-heated in the mild late summer evening. A notice on the wall described a body found in the Thames, or rather the body's clothes: wool vest, wool pants, wool shirt with blue stripes, size ten boots, blue serge suit worn at the elbows, fifteen and a half celluloid collar. They couldn't find anything to say about the body, except its measurements, it was just an ordinary body.

"Come along," the constable said. He was interested, he was glad to be going, but he couldn't help being embarrassed by his company, a small boy in pyjamas. His nose smelt something, he didn't know what, but he smarted at the sight of the amusement they caused: the pubs had closed and the streets were full again of men making as long a day of it as they could. He hurried through the less frequented streets, chose the darker pavements, wouldn't loiter, and Philip wanted more and more to loiter, pulling at his hand, dragging with his feet. He dreaded the sight of Mrs. Baines waiting in the hall: he knew now that she was dead. The sergeant's mouthing had conveyed that; but she wasn't buried, she wasn't out of sight; he was going to see a dead person in the hall when the door opened.

The light was on in the basement, and to his relief the constable made for the area steps. Perhaps he wouldn't have to see Mrs. Baines at all. The constable knocked on the door because it was too dark to see the bell, and Baines answered. He stood there in the doorway of the neat bright basement room and you could see the sad complacent plausible sentence he had prepared wither at the sight of Philip; he hadn't expected Philip to return like that in the policeman's company. He had to begin thinking all over again; he wasn't a deceptive man. If it hadn't been for Emmy he would have been quite ready to let the truth lead him where it would.

"Mr. Baines?" the constable asked.

He nodded; he hadn't found the right words; he was daunted by the shrewd knowing face, the sudden appearance of Philip there.

"This little boy from here?"

"Yes," Baines said. Philip could tell that there was a message he was trying to convey, but he shut his mind to it. He loved Baines, but Baines had involved him in secrets, in fears he didn't understand. That was what happened when you loved—you got involved; and Philip extricated himself from life, from love, from Baines.

"The doctor's here," Baines said. He nodded at the door, moistened his mouth, kept his eyes on Philip, begging for something like a dog you can't understand. "There's nothing to be done. She slipped on these stone basement stairs. I was in here. I heard her fall." He wouldn't look at the notebook, at the constable's spidery writing which got a terrible lot on one page.

"Did the boy see anything?"

"He can't have done. I thought he was in bed. Hadn't he better go up? It's a shocking thing. O," Baines said, losing control, "it's a shocking thing for a child."

"She's through there?" the constable asked.

"I haven't moved her an inch," Baines said.

"He'd better then—"

"Go up the area and through the hall," Baines said, and again he begged dumbly like a dog: one more secret, keep this secret, do this for old Baines, he won't ask another.

"Come along," the constable said. "I'll see you up to bed. You're a gentleman. You must come in the proper way through the front door like the master should. Or will you go along with him, Mr. Baines, while I see the doctor?"

"Yes," Baines said, "I'll go." He came across the room to Philip, begging, begging, all the way with his old soft stupid expression: this is Baines, the old Coaster; what about a palm-oil chop, eh?; a man's life;

forty niggers; never used a gun; I tell you I couldn't help loving them; it wasn't what we call love, nothing we could understand. The messages flickered out from the last posts at the border, imploring, beseeching, reminding: this is your old friend Baines; what about an elevenses; a glass of ginger pop won't do you any harm; sausages; a long day. But the wires were cut, the messages just faded out into the vacancy of the scrubbed room in which there had never been a place where a man could hide his secrets.

"Come along, Phil, it's bedtime. We'll just go up the steps . . ." Tap, tap, tap, at the telegraph; you may get through, you can't tell, somebody may mend the right wire. "And in at the front door."

"No," Philip said, "no. I won't go. You can't make me go. I'll fight. I won't see her."

The constable turned on them quickly. "What's that? Why won't you go?"

"She's in the hall," Philip said. "I know she's in the hall. And she's dead. I won't see her."

"You moved her then?" the constable said to Baines. "All the way down here? You've been lying, eh? That means you had to tidy up. . . . Were you alone?"

"Emmy," Philip said, "Emmy." He wasn't going to keep any more secrets: he was going to finish once and for all with everything, with Baines and Mrs. Baines and the grown-up life beyond him. "It was all Emmy's fault," he protested with a quaver which reminded Baines that after all he was only a child; it had been hopeless to expect help there; he was a child; he didn't understand what it all meant; he couldn't read this shorthand of terror; he'd had a long day and he was tired out. You could see him dropping asleep where he stood against the dresser, dropping back into the comfortable nursery peace. You couldn't blame him. When he woke in the morning, he'd hardly remember a thing.

"Out with it," the constable said, addressing Baines with professional ferocity, "who is she?" just as the old man sixty years later startled his secretary, his only watcher, asking, "Who is she? Who is she?" dropping lower and lower into death, passing on the way perhaps the image of Baines: Baines hopeless, Baines letting his head drop, Baines "coming clean."

FLY PAPER

by

DASHIELL HAMMETT

It was a wandering daughter job.

The Hambletons had been for several generations a wealthy and decently prominent New York family. There was nothing in the Hambleton history to account for Sue, the youngest member of the clan. She grew out of childhood with a kink that made her dislike the polished side of life, like the rough. By the time she was twenty-one, in 1926, she definitely preferred Tenth Avenue to Fifth, grifters to bankers, and Hymie the Riveter to the Honorable Cecil Window, who had asked her to marry him.

The Hambletons tried to make Sue behave, but it was too late for that. She was legally of age. When she finally told them to go to hell and walked out on them there wasn't much they could do about it. Her father, Major Waldo Hambleton, had given up all the hopes he ever had of salvaging her, but he didn't want her to run into any grief that could be avoided. So he came into the Continental Detective Agency's New York office and asked to have an eye kept on her.

Hymie the Riveter was a Philadelphia racketeer who had moved north to the big city, carrying a Thompson submachine gun wrapped in blue-checkered oil cloth, after a disagreement with his partners. New York wasn't so good a field as Philadelphia for machine gun work. The Thompson lay idle for a year or so while Hymie made expenses with an automatic, preying on small-time crap games in Harlem.

Three or four months after Sue went to live with Hymie he made what looked like a promising connection with the first of the crew that came into New York from Chicago to organize the city on the western scale. But the boys from Chi didn't want Hymie; they wanted the Thompson. When he showed it to them, as the big item in his application for employment, they shot holes in the top of Hymie's head and went away with the gun.

Sue Hambleton buried Hymie, had a couple of lonely weeks in which she hocked a ring to eat, and then got a job as hostess in a speakeasy run by a Greek named Vassos.

One of Vassos' customers was Babe McCloor, two hundred and fifty pounds of hard Scotch-Irish-Indian bone and muscle, a black-haired, blue-eyed, swarthy giant who was resting up after doing a fifteen-year hitch in Leavenworth for ruining most of the smaller post offices between New Orleans and Omaha. Babe was keeping himself in drinking money while he rested by playing with pedestrians in dark streets.

Babe liked Sue. Vassos liked Sue. Sue liked Babe. Vassos didn't like that. Jealousy spoiled the Greek's judgment. He kept the speakeasy door locked one night when Babe wanted to come in. Babe came in, bringing pieces of the door with him. Vassos got his gun out, but couldn't shake Sue off his arm. He stopped trying when Babe hit him with the part of the door that had the brass knob on it. Babe and Sue went away from Vassos' together.

Up to that time the New York office had managed to keep in touch with Sue. She hadn't been kept under constant surveillance. Her father hadn't wanted that. It was simply a matter of sending a man around every week or so to see that she was still alive, to pick up whatever information he could from her friends and neighbors, without, of course, letting her know she was being tabbed. All that had been easy enough, but when she and Babe went away after wrecking the gin mill, they dropped completely out of sight.

After turning the city upside-down, the New York office sent a journal on the job to the other Continental branches throughout the country, giving the information above and enclosing photographs and descriptions of Sue and her new playmate. That was late in 1927.

We had enough copies of the photographs to go around, and for the next month or so whoever had a little idle time on his hands spent it looking through San Francisco and Oakland for the missing pair. We didn't find them. Operatives in other cities, doing the same thing, had the same luck.

Then, nearly a year later, a telegram came to us from the New York office. Decoded, it read:

> Major Hambleton today received telegram from daughter in San Francisco quote Please wire me thousand dollars care apartment two hundred six number six hundred one Eddis Street stop I will come home if you will let me stop Please tell me if I can come but please please wire money anyway unquote Hambleton authorizes payment of money to her immediately stop Detail competent operative to call on her with money and to arrange for her return home stop If possible have man and woman operative accompany her here stop Hambleton wiring her stop Report immediately by wire.

The Old Man gave me the telegram and a check, saying, "You know the situation. You'll know how to handle it."

I pretended I agreed with him, went down to the bank, swapped the check for a bundle of bills of several sizes, caught a streetcar, and went up to 601 Eddis Street, a fairly large apartment building on the corner of Larkin.

The name on Apartment 206's vestibule mail box was J.M. Wales.

I pushed 206's button. When the locked door buzzed off I went into the building, past the elevator to the stairs, and up a flight. 206 was just around the corner from the stairs.

The apartment door was opened by a tall, slim man of thirty-something in neat dark clothes. He had narrow dark eyes set in a long pale face. There was some gray in the dark hair brushed flat to his scalp.

"Miss Hambleton," I said.

"Uh—what about her?" His voice was smooth, but not too smooth to be agreeable.

"I'd like to see her."

His upper eyelids came down a little and the brows over them came a little closer together. He asked, "Is it—?" and stopped, watching me steadily.

I didn't say anything. Presently he finished his question, "Something to do with a telegram?"

"Yeah."

His long face brightened immediately. He asked, "You're from her father?"

"Yeah."

He stepped back and swung the door wide open, saying, "Come in. Major Hambleton's wire came to her only a few minutes ago. He said someone would call."

We went through a small passageway into a sunny living room that was cheaply furnished, but neat and clean enough.

"Sit down," the man said, pointing at a brown rocking chair.

I sat down. He sat on the burlap-covered sofa facing me. I looked around the room. I didn't see anything to show that a woman was living there.

He rubbed the long bridge of his nose with a longer forefinger and asked slowly, "You brought the money?"

I said I'd feel more like talking with her there.

He looked at the finger with which he had been rubbing his nose, and then up at me, saying softly, "But I'm her friend."

I said, "Yeah?" to that.

"Yes," he repeated. He frowned slightly, drawing back the corners of his thin-lipped mouth. "I've only asked whether you've brought the money."

I didn't say anything.

"The point is," he said quite reasonably, "that if you brought the money she doesn't expect you to hand it over to anybody except her. If you didn't bring it she doesn't want to see you. I don't think her mind can be changed about that. That's why I asked if you had brought it."

"I brought it."

He looked doubtfully at me. I showed him the money I had got from the bank. He jumped up briskly from the sofa.

"I'll have her here in a minute or two," he said over his shoulder as his long legs moved him toward the door. At the door he stopped to ask, "Do you know her? Or shall I have her bring means of identifying herself?"

"That would be best," I told him.

He went out, leaving the corridor door open.

In five minutes he was back with a slender blonde girl of twenty-three in pale green silk. The looseness of her small mouth and the puffiness around her blue eyes weren't yet pronounced enough to spoil her prettiness.

I stood up.

"This is Miss Hambleton," he said.

She gave me a swift glance and then lowered her eyes again, nervously playing with the strap of a handbag she held.

"You can identify yourself?" I asked.

"Sure," the man said. "Show them to him, Sue."

She opened the bag, brought out some papers and things, and held them up for me to take.

"Sit down, sit down," the man said as I took them.

They sat on the sofa. I sat in the rocking chair again and examined the things she had given me. There were two letters addressed to Sue Hambleton here, her father's telegram welcoming her home, a couple of receipted department store bills, an automobile driver's license, and a savings account pass book that showed a balance of less than ten dollars.

By the time I had finished my examination the girl's embarrassment was gone. She looked levelly at me, as did the man beside her. I felt in my pocket, found my copy of the photograph New York had sent us at the beginning of the hunt, and looked from it to her.

"Your mouth could have shrunk, maybe," I said, "but how could your nose have got that much longer?"

"If you don't like my nose," she said, "how'd you like to go to hell?" Her face had turned red.

"That's not the point. It's a swell nose, but it's not Sue's." I held the photograph out to her. "See for yourself."

She glared at the photograph and then at the man.

"What a smart guy you are," she told him.

He was watching me with dark eyes that had a brittle shine to them between narrow-drawn eyelids. He kept on watching me while he spoke to her out the side of his mouth, crisply. "Pipe down."

She piped down. He sat and watched me. I sat and watched him. A clock ticked seconds away behind me. His eyes began shifting their focus from one of my eyes to the other. The girl sighed.

He said in a low voice, "Well?"

I said, "You're in a hole."

"What can you make out of it?" he asked casually.

"Conspiracy to defraud."

The girl jumped up and hit one of his shoulders angrily with the back of a hand, crying, "What a smart guy you are, to get me in a jam like this. It was going to be duck soup—yeh! Eggs in the coffee—yeh! Now look at you. You haven't even got guts enough to tell this guy to go chase himself." She spun around to face me, pushing her red face down at me —I was still sitting in the rocker—snarling, "Well, what are you waiting for? Waiting to be kissed goodby? We don't owe you anything, do we? We didn't get any of your lousy money, did we? Outside, then. Take the air. Dangle."

"Stop it, sister," I growled. "You'll bust something."

The man said, "For God's sake stop that bawling, Peggy, and give somebody else a chance." He addressed me, "Well, what do you want?"

"How'd you get into this?" I asked.

He spoke quickly, eagerly, "A fellow named Kenny gave me that stuff and told me about this Sue Hambleton, and her old man having plenty. I thought I'd give it a whirl. I figured the old man would either wire the dough right off the reel or wouldn't send it at all. I didn't figure on this send-a-man stuff. Then when his wire came, saying he was sending a man to see her, I ought to have dropped it.

"But hell! Here was a man coming with a grand in cash. That was too good to let go of without a try. It looked like there still might be a chance of copping, so I got Peggy to do Sue for me. If the man was coming today, it was a cinch he belonged out here on the Coast, and it was an even bet he wouldn't know Sue, would only have a description of her. From what Kenny had told me about her, I knew Peggy would come pretty close to fitting her description. I still don't see how you got that photograph. I only wired the old man yesterday. I mailed a couple of letters to Sue, here, yesterday, so we'd have them with the other identification stuff to get the money from the telegraph company on."

"Kenny gave you the old man's address?"

"Sure he did."

"Did he give you Sue's?"

"No."

"How'd Kenny get hold of the stuff?"

"He didn't say."

"Where's Kenny now?"

"I don't know. He was on his way east, with something else on the fire, and couldn't fool with this. That's why he passed it on to me."

"Big-hearted Kenny," I said. "You know Sue Hambleton?"

"No," emphatically. "I'd never even heard of her till Kenny told me."

"I don't like this Kenny," I said, "though without him your story's got some good points. Could you tell it leaving him out?"

He shook his head slowly from side to side, saying, "It wouldn't be the way it happened."

"That's too bad. Conspiracies to defraud don't mean as much to me as finding Sue. I might have made a deal with you."

He shook his head again, but his eyes were thoughtful, and his lower lip moved up to overlap the upper a little.

The girl had stepped back so she could see both of us as we talked, turning her face, which showed she didn't like us, from one to the other as we spoke our pieces. Now she fastened her gaze on the man, and her eyes were growing angry again.

I got up on my feet, telling him, "Suit yourself. But if you want to play it that way I'll have to take you both in."

He smiled with indrawn lips and stood up.

The girl thrust herself in between us, facing him.

"This is a swell time to be dummying up," she spit at him. "Pop off, you lightweight, or I will. You're crazy if you think I'm going to take the fall with you."

"Shut up," he said in his throat.

"Shut me up," she cried.

He tried to, with both hands. I reached over her shoulders and caught one of his wrists, knocked the other hand up.

She slid out from between us and ran around behind me, screaming, "Joe does know her. He got the things from her. She's at the St. Martin on O'Farrell Street—her and Babe McCloor."

While I listened to this I had to pull my head aside to let Joe's right hook miss me, had got his left arm twisted behind him, had turned my hip to catch his knee, and had got the palm of my left hand under his chin. I was ready to give his chin the Japanese tilt when he stopped wrestling and grunted, "Let me tell it."

"Hop to it," I consented, taking my hands away from him and stepping back.

He rubbed the wrist I had wrenched, scowling past me at the girl. He called her four unlovely names, the mildest of which was "a dumb twist," and told her, "He was bluffing about throwing us in the can. You don't think old man Hambleton's hunting for newspaper space, do you?" That wasn't a bad guess.

He sat on the sofa again, still rubbing his wrist. The girl stayed on the other side of the room, laughing at him through her teeth.

I said, "All right, roll it out, one of you."

"You've got it all," he muttered. "I glaumed that stuff last week when I was visiting Babe, knowing the story and hating to see a promising layout like that go to waste."

"What's Babe doing now?" I asked.

"I don't know."

"Is he still puffing them?"

"I don't know."

"Like hell you don't."

"I don't," he insisted. "If you know Babe you know you can't get anything out of him about what he's doing."

"How long have he and Sue been here?"

"About six months that I know of."

"Who's he mobbed up with?"

"I don't know. Any time Babe works with a mob he picks them up on the road and leaves them on the road."

"How's he fixed?"

"I don't know. There's always enough grub and liquor in the joint."

Half an hour of this convinced me that I wasn't going to get much information about my people here.

I went to the phone in the passageway and called the Agency. The boy on the switchboard told me MacMan was in the operative's room. I asked to have him sent up to me, and went back to the living room. Joe and Peggy took their heads apart when I came in.

MacMan arrived in less than ten minutes. I let him in and told him, "This fellow says his name's Joe Wales, and the girl's supposed to be

Peggy Carroll who lives upstairs in 421. We've got them cold for conspiracy to defraud, but I've made a deal with them. I'm going out to look
at it now. Stay here with them, in this room. Nobody goes in or out, and
nobody but you gets to the phone. There's a fire escape in front of the
window. The window's locked now. I'd keep it that way. If the deal turns
out O.K., we'll let them go, but if they cut up on you while I'm gone
there's no reason why you can't knock them around as much as you
want."

MacMan nodded his hard round head and pulled a chair out between
them and the door. I picked up my hat.

Joe Wales called, "Hey, you're not going to uncover me to Babe, are
you? That's got to be part of the deal."

"Not unless I have to."

"I'd just as leave stand the rap," he said. "I'd be safer in jail."

"I'll give you the best break I can," I promise, "but you'll have to take
what's dealt you."

Walking over to the St. Martin—only half a dozen blocks from Wales's
place—I decided to go up against McCloor and the girl as a Continental
op who suspected Babe of being in on a branch bank stick-up in Alameda
the previous week. He hadn't been in on it—if the bank people had
described half-correctly the men who had robbed them—so it wasn't
likely my supposed suspicions would frighten him much. Clearing himself, he might give me some information I could use. The chief thing I
wanted, of course, was a look at the girl, so I could report to her father
that I had seen her. There was no reason for supposing that she and Babe
knew her father was trying to keep an eye on her. Babe had a record.
It was natural enough for sleuths to drop in now and then and try to hang
something on him.

The St. Martin was a small three-story apartment house of red brick
between two taller hotels. The vestibule register showed, R. K. McCloor,
313, as Wales and Peggy had told me.

I pushed the bell button. Nothing happened. Nothing happened any
of the four times I pushed it. I pushed the button labeled *Manager.*

The door clicked open. I went indoors. A beefy woman in a pink-
striped cotton dress that needed pressing stood in an apartment doorway
just inside the street door.

"Some people named McCloor live here?" I asked.

"Three-thirteen," she said.

"Been living here long?"

She pursed her fat mouth, looked intently at me, hesitated, but finally
said, "Since last June."

"What do you know about them?"

She balked at that, raising her chin and her eyebrows.

I gave her my card. That was safe enough; it fit in with the pretext I intended using upstairs.

Her face, when she raised it from reading the card, was oily with curiosity.

"Come in here," she said in a husky whisper, backing through the doorway.

I followed her into her apartment. We sat on a Chesterfield and she whispered, "What is it?"

"Maybe nothing." I kept my voice low, playing up to her theatricals. "He's done time for safe burglary. I'm trying to get a line on him now, on the off chance that he might have been tied up in a recent job. I don't know that he was. He may be going straight for all I know." I took his photograph—front and profile, taken at Leavenworth—out of my pocket. "This him?"

She seized it eagerly, nodded, said, "Yes, that's him, all right," turned it over to read the description on the back, and repeated, "Yes, that's him, all right."

"His wife is here with him?" I asked.

She nodded vigorously.

"I don't know her," I said. "What sort of looking girl is she?"

She described a girl who could have been Sue Hambleton. I couldn't show Sue's picture; that would have uncovered me if she and Babe heard about it.

I asked the woman what she knew about the McCloors. What she knew wasn't a great deal: paid their rent on time, kept irregular hours, had occasional drinking parties, quarreled a lot.

"Think they're in now?" I asked. "I got no answer on the bell."

"I don't know," she whispered. "I haven't seen either of them since night before last, when they had a fight."

"Much of a fight?"

"Not much worse than usual."

"Could you find out if they're in?" I asked.

She looked at me out of the ends of her eyes.

"I'm not going to make any trouble for you," I assured her. "But if they've blown I'd like to know it, and I reckon you would too."

"All right, I'll find out." She got up, patting a pocket in which keys jingled. "You wait here."

"I'll go as far as the third floor with you," I said, "and wait out of sight there."

"All right," she said reluctantly.

On the third floor, I remained by the elevator. She disappeared around a corner of the dim corridor, and presently a muffled electric bell rang.

It rang three times. I heard her keys jingle and one of them grate in a lock. The lock clicked. I heard the doorknob rattle as she turned it.

Then a long moment of silence was ended by a scream that filled the corridor from wall to wall.

I jumped for the corner, swung around it, saw an open door ahead, went through it, and slammed the door shut behind me.

The scream had stopped.

I was in a small dark vestibule with three doors beside the one I had come through. One door was shut. One opened into a bathroom. I went to the other.

The fat manager stood just inside it, her round back to me. I pushed past her and saw what she was looking at.

Sue Hambleton, in pale yellow pajamas trimmed with black lace, was lying across the bed. She lay on her back. Her arms were stretched out over her head. One leg was bent under her, one stretched out so that its bare foot rested on the floor. That bare foot was whiter than a live foot could be. Her face was white as her foot, except for a mottled swollen area from the right eyebrow to the right cheek-bone and dark bruises on her throat.

"Phone the police," I told the woman, and began poking into corners, closets and drawers.

It was late afternoon when I returned to the Agency. I asked the file clerk to see if we had anything on Joe Wales and Peggy Carroll, and then went into the Old Man's office.

He put down some reports he had been reading, gave me a nodded invitation to sit down, and asked, "You've seen her?"

"Yeah. She's dead."

The Old Man said, "Indeed," as if I had said it was raining, and smiled with polite attentiveness while I told him about it—from the time I had rung Wales's bell until I had joined the fat manager in the dead girl's apartment.

"She had been knocked around some, was bruised on the face and neck," I wound up. "But that didn't kill her."

"You think she was murdered?" he asked, still smiling gently.

"I don't know. Doc Jordan says he thinks it could have been arsenic. He's hunting for it in her now. We found a funny thing in the joint. Some thick sheets of dark gray paper were stuck in a book—*The Count of Monte Cristo*—wrapped in a month-old newspaper and wedged into a dark corner between the stove and the kitchen wall."

"Ah, arsenical fly paper," the Old Man murmured. "The Maybrick-Seddons trick. Mashed in water, four to six grains of arsenic can be soaked out of a sheet—enough to kill two people."

I nodded, saying, "I worked on one in Louisville in 1916. The mulatto janitor saw McCloor leaving at half-past nine yesterday morning. She was probably dead before that. Nobody's seen him since. Earlier in the morning the people in the next apartment had heard them talking, her groaning. But they had too many fights for the neighbors to pay much attention to that. The landlady told me they had a fight the night before that. The police are hunting for him."

"Did you tell the police who she was?"

"No. What do we do on that angle? We can't tell them about Wales without telling them all."

"I dare say the whole thing will have to come out," he said thoughtfully. "I'll wire New York."

I went out of his office. The file clerk gave me a couple of newspaper clippings. The first told me that fifteen months ago Joseph Wales, alias Holy Joe, had been arrested on the complaint of a farmer named Toomey that he had been taken for twenty-five hundred dollars on a phony "business opportunity" by Wales and three other men. The second clipping said the case had been dropped when Toomey failed to appear against Wales in court—bought off in the customary manner by the return of part or all of his money. That was all our files held on Wales, and they had nothing on Peggy Carroll.

MacMan opened the door for me when I returned to Wales's apartment.

"Anything doing?" I asked him.

"Nothing—except they've been belly-aching a lot." Wales came forward, asking eagerly, "Satisfied now?"

The girl stood by the window, looking at me with anxious eyes.

I didn't say anything.

"Did you find her?" Wales asked, frowning. "She was where I told you?"

"Yeah," I said.

"Well, then." Part of his frown went away. "That lets Peggy and me out, doesn't—" He broke off, ran his tongue over his lower lip, put a hand to his chin, asked sharply, "You didn't give them the tip-off on me, did you?"

I shook my head, no.

He took his hand from his chin and asked irritably, "What's the matter with you, then? What are you looking like that for?"

Behind him the girl spoke bitterly. "I knew damned well it would be like this," she said. "I knew damned well we weren't going to get out of it. Oh, what a smart guy you are!"

"Take Peggy into the kitchen, and shut both doors," I told MacMan. "Holy Joe and I are going to have a real heart-to-heart talk."

The girl went out willingly, but when MacMan was closing the door she put her head in again to tell Wales, "I hope he busts you in the nose if you try to hold out on him."

MacMan shut the door.

"Your playmate seems to think you know something," I said.

Wales scowled at the door and grumbled, "She's more help to me than a broken leg." He turned his face to me, trying to make it look frank and friendly. "What do you want? I came clean with you before. What's the matter now?"

"What do you guess?"

He pulled his lips in between his teeth. "What do you want to make me guess for?" he demanded. "I'm willing to play ball with you. But what can I do if you won't tell me what you want? I can't see inside your head."

"You'd get a kick out of it if you could."

He shook his head wearily and walked back to the sofa, sitting down bent forward, his hands together between his knees. "All right," he sighed. "Take your time about asking me. I'll wait for you."

I went over and stood in front of him. I took his chin between my left thumb and fingers, raising his head and bending my own down until our noses were almost touching. I said, "Where you stumbled, Joe, was in sending the telegram right after the murder."

"He's dead?" It popped out before his eyes had even had time to grow round and wide.

The question threw me off balance. I had to wrestle with my forehead to keep it from wrinkling, and I put too much calmness in my voice when I asked, "Is who dead?"

"Who? How do I know? Who do you mean?"

"Who did you think I meant?" I insisted.

"How do I know? Oh, all right! Old man Hambleton, Sue's father."

"That's right," I said, and took my hand away from his chin.

"And he was murdered, you say?" He hadn't moved his face an inch from the position into which I had lifted it. "How?"

"Arsenic fly paper."

"Arsenic fly paper." He looked thoughtful. "That's a funny one."

"Yeah, very funny. Where'd you go about buying some if you wanted it?"

"Buying it? I don't know. I haven't seen any since I was a kid. Nobody uses fly paper here in San Francisco anyway. There aren't enough flies."

"Somebody used some here," I said, "on Sue."

"Sue?" He jumped so that the sofa squeaked under him.

"Yeah. Murdered yesterday morning—arsenical fly paper."

"Both of them?" he asked incredulously.

"Both of who?"

"Her and her father."

"Yeah."

He put his chin far down on his chest and rubbed the back of one hand with the palm of the other. "Then I am in a hole," he said slowly.

"That's what," I cheerfully agreed. "Want to try talking yourself out of it?"

"Let me think."

I let him think, listening to the tick of the clock while he thought. Thinking brought drops of sweat out on his gray-white face. Presently he sat up straight, wiping his face with a fancily colored handkerchief. "I'll talk," he said. "I've got to talk now. Sue was getting ready to ditch Babe. She and I were going away. She— Here, I'll show you."

He put his hand in his pocket and held out a folded sheet of thick note paper to me. I took it and read:

Dear Joe:—
    I can't stand this much longer—we've simply got to go soon. Babe beat me again tonight. Please, if you really love me, let's make it soon.
                                       Sue

The handwriting was a nervous woman's, tall, angular, and piled up.

"That's why I made the play for Hambleton's grand," he said. "I've been shatting on my uppers for a couple of months, and when that letter came yesterday I just had to raise dough somehow to get her away. She wouldn't have stood for tapping her father though, so I tried to swing it without her knowing."

"When did you see her last?"

"Day before yesterday, the day she mailed that letter. Only I saw her in the afternoon—she was here—and she wrote it that night."

"Babe suspect what you were up to?"

"We didn't think he did. I don't know. He was jealous as hell all the time, whether he had any reason to be or not."

"How much reason did he have?"

Wales looked me straight in the eye and said, "Sue was a good kid."

I said, "Well, she's been murdered."

He didn't say anything.

Day was darkening into evening. I went to the door and pressed the light button. I didn't lose sight of Holy Joe Wales while I was doing it.

As I took my finger away from the button, something clicked at the window. The click was loud and sharp.

I looked at the window.

A man crouched there on the fire escape, looking in through the glass and lace curtain. He was a thick-featured dark man whose size identified him as Babe McCloor. The muzzle of a big black automatic was touching the glass in front of him. He had tapped the glass with it to catch our attention.

He had our attention.

There wasn't anything for me to do just then. I stood there and looked at him. I couldn't tell whether he was looking at me or at Wales. I could see him clearly enough, but the lace curtain spoiled my view of details like that. I imagined he wasn't neglecting either of us, and I didn't imagine the lace curtain hid much from him. He was closer to the curtain than we, and I had turned on the room's lights.

Wales, sitting dead-still on the sofa, was looking at McCloor. Wales's face wore a peculiar, stiffly sullen expression. His eyes were sullen. He wasn't breathing.

McCloor flicked the nose of his pistol against the pane, and a triangular piece of glass fell out, tinkling apart on the floor. It didn't, I was afraid, make enough noise to alarm MacMan in the kitchen. There were two closed doors between here and there.

Wales looked at the broken pane and closed his eyes. He closed them slowly, little by little, exactly as if he were falling asleep. He kept his stiffly sullen blank face turned straight to the window.

McCloor shot him three times.

The bullets knocked Wales down on the sofa, back against the wall. Wales's eyes popped open, bulging. His lips crawled back over his teeth, leaving them naked to the gums. His tongue came out. Then his head fell down and he didn't move any more.

When McCloor jumped away from the window I jumped to it. While I was pushing the curtain aside, unlocking the window and raising it, I heard his feet land on the cement paving below.

MacMan flung the door open and came in, the girl at his heels.

"Take care of this," I ordered as I scrambled over the sill. "McCloor shot him."

Wales's apartment was on the second floor. The fire escape ended there with a counter-weighted iron ladder that a man's weight would swing down into a cement-paved court.

I went down as Babe McCloor had gone, swinging down on the ladder till within dropping distance of the court, and then letting go.

There was only one street exit to the court. I took it.

A startled looking, smallish man was standing in the middle of the sidewalk close to the court, gaping at me as I dashed out.

I caught his arm, shook it. "A big guy running." Maybe I yelled. "Where?"

He tried to say something, couldn't, and waved his arm at billboards standing across the front of a vacant lot on the other side of the street.

I forgot to say, "Thank you," in my hurry to get over there.

I got behind the billboards by crawling under them instead of going to either end, where there were openings. The lot was large enough and weedy enough to give cover to anybody who wanted to lie down and bushwhack a pursuer—even anybody as large as Babe McCloor.

While I considered that, I heard a dog barking at one corner of the lot. He could have been barking at a man who had run by. I ran to that corner of the lot. The dog was in a board-fenced backyard, at the corner of a narrow alley that ran from the lot to a street.

I chinned myself on the board fence, saw a wire-haired terrier alone in the yard, and ran down the alley while he was charging my part of the fence.

I put my gun back into my pocket before I left the alley for the street.

A small touring car was parked at the curb in front of a cigar store some fifteen feet from the alley. A policeman was talking to a slim dark-faced man in the cigar store doorway.

"The big fellow that come out of the alley a minute ago," I said. "Which way did he go?"

The policeman looked dumb. The slim man nodded his head down the street, said, "Down that way," and went on with his conversation.

I said, "Thanks," and went on down to the corner. There was a taxi phone there and two idle taxis. A block and a half below, a streetcar was going away. "Did the big fellow who came down here a minute ago take a taxi or the streetcar?" I asked the two taxi chauffeurs who were leaning against one of the taxis.

The rattier-looking one said, "He didn't take a taxi."

I said, "I'll take one. Catch that streetcar for me."

The streetcar was three blocks away before we got going. The street wasn't clear enough for me to see who got on and off it. We caught it when it stopped at Market Street.

"Follow along," I told the driver as I jumped out.

On the rear platform of the streetcar I looked through the glass. There were only eight or ten people aboard.

"There was a great big fellow got on at Hyde Street," I said to the conductor. "Where'd he get off?"

The conductor looked at the silver dollar I was turning over in my fingers and remembered that the big man got off at Taylor Street. That won the silver dollar.

I dropped off as the streetcar turned into Market Street. The taxi, close behind, slowed down, and its door swung open. "Sixth and Mission," I said as I hopped in.

McCloor could have gone in any direction from Taylor Street. I had to guess. The best guess seemed to be that he would make for the other side of Market Street.

It was fairly dark by now. We had to go down to Fifth Street to get off Market, then over to Mission, and back up to Sixth. We got to Sixth Street without seeing McCloor. I couldn't see him on Sixth Street—either way from the crossing.

"On up to Ninth," I ordered, and while we rode told the driver what kind of man I was looking for.

We arrived at Ninth Street. No McCloor. I cursed and pushed my brains around.

The big man was a yegg. San Francisco was on fire for him. The yegg instinct would be to use a rattler to get away from trouble. The freight yards were in this end of town. Maybe he would be shifty enough to lie low instead of trying to powder. In that case, he probably hadn't crossed Market Street at all. If he stuck, there would still be a chance of picking him up tomorrow. If he was high-tailing, it was catch him now or not at all.

"Down to Harrison," I told the driver.

We went down to Harrison Street, and down Harrison to Third, up Bryant to Eighth, down Brannan to Third again, and over to Townsend —and we didn't see Babe McCloor.

"That's tough, that is," the driver sympathized as we stopped across the street from the Southern Pacific passenger station.

"I'm going over and look around in the station," I said. "Keep your eyes open while I'm gone."

When I told the copper in the station my trouble he introduced me to a couple of plain-clothes men who had been planted there to watch for McCloor. That had been done after Sue Hambleton's body was found. The shooting of Holy Joe Wales was news to them.

I went outside again and found my taxi in front of the door, its horn working overtime, but too asthmatically to be heard indoors. The ratty driver was excited.

"A guy like you said come up out of King Street just now and swung on a Number 16 car as it pulled away," he said.

"Going which way?"

"Thataway," pointing southeast.

"Catch him," I said, jumping in.

The streetcar was out of sight around a bend in Third Street two blocks below. When we rounded the bend, the streetcar was slowing up, four blocks ahead. It hadn't slowed up very much when a man leaned far out and stepped off. He was a tall man, but didn't look tall on account of his shoulder spread. He didn't check his momentum, but used it to carry him across the sidewalk and out of sight.

We stopped where the man had left the car.

I gave the driver too much money and told him, "Go back to Town-

send Street and tell the copper in the station that I've chased Babe
McCloor into the S. P. yards."

I thought I was moving silently down between two strings of box cars,
but I had gone less than twenty feet when a light flashed in my face and
a sharp voice ordered, "Stand still, you."

I stood still. Men came from between cars. One of them spoke my
name, adding, "What are you doing here? Lost?" It was Harry Pebble,
a police detective.

I stopped holding my breath and said, "Hello, Harry. Looking for
Babe?"

"Yes. We've been going over the rattlers."

"He's here. I just tailed him in from the street."

Pebble swore and snapped the light off.

"Watch, Harry," I advised. "Don't play with him. He's packing plenty
of gun and he's cut down one boy tonight."

"I'll play with him," Pebble promised, and told one of the men with
him to go over and warn those on the other side of the yard that McCloor
was in, and then to ring for reinforcements.

"We'll just sit on the edge and hold him in till they come," he said.

That seemed a sensible way to play it. We spread out and waited. Once
Pebble and I turned back a lanky bum who tried to slip into the yard
between us, and one of the men below us picked up a shivering kid who
was trying to slip out. Otherwise nothing happened until Lieutenant
Duff arrived with a couple of carloads of coppers.

Most of our force went into a cordon around the yard. The rest of us
went through the yard in small groups, working it over car by car. We
picked up a few hoboes that Pebble and his men had missed earlier, but
we didn't find McCloor.

We didn't find any trace of him until somebody stumbled over a railroad bum huddled in the shadow of a gondola. It took a couple of minutes
to bring him to, and he couldn't talk then. His jaw was broken. But when
we asked if McCloor had slugged him, he nodded, and when we asked
in which direction McCloor had been headed, he moved a feeble hand
to the east.

We went over and searched the Santa Fe yards.

We didn't find McCloor.

I rode up to the Hall of Justice with Duff. MacMan was in the captain
of detectives' office with three or four police sleuths.

"Wales die?" I asked.

"Yep."

"Say anything before he went?"

"He was gone before you were through the window."

"You held on to the girl?"

"She's here."

"She say anything?"

"We were waiting for you before we tapped her," Detective-Sergeant O'Gar said, "not knowing the angle on her."

"Let's have her in. I haven't had any dinner yet. How about the autopsy on Sue Hambleton?"

"Chronic arsenic poisoning."

"Chronic? That means it was fed to her little by little, and not in a lump?"

"Uh-huh. From what he found in her kidneys, intestines, liver, stomach and blood, Jordan figures there was less than a grain of it in her. That wouldn't be enough to knock her off. But he says he found arsenic in the tips of her hair, and she'd have to be given some at least a month ago for it to have worked out that far."

"Any chance that it wasn't arsenic that killed her?"

"Not unless Jordan's a bum doctor."

A policewoman came in with Peggy Carroll.

The blonde girl was tired. Her eyelids, mouth corners and body drooped, and when I pushed a chair out toward her she sagged down in it.

O'Gar ducked his grizzled bullet head at me.

"Now, Peggy," I said, "tell us where you fit into this mess."

"I don't fit into it." She didn't look up. Her voice was tired. "Joe dragged me into it. He told you."

"You his girl?"

"If you want to call it that," she admitted.

"You jealous?"

"What," she asked, looking up at me, her face puzzled, "has that got to do with it?"

"Sue Hambleton was getting ready to go away with him when she was murdered."

The girl sat up straight in the chair and said deliberately, "I swear to God I didn't know she was murdered."

"But you did know she was dead," I said positively.

"I didn't," she replied just as positively.

I nudged O'Gar with my elbow. He pushed his undershot jaw at her and barked, "What are you trying to give us? You knew she was dead. How could you kill her without knowing it?"

While she looked at him I waved the others in. They crowded close around her and took up the chorus of the sergeant's song. She was barked, roared, and snarled at plenty in the next few minutes.

The instant she stopped trying to talk back to them I cut in again. "Wait," I said, very earnestly. "Maybe she didn't kill her."

"The hell she didn't," O'Gar stormed, holding the center of the stage so the others could move away from the girl without their retreat seeming too artificial. "Do you mean to tell me this baby—"

"I didn't say she didn't," I remonstrated. "I said maybe she didn't."

"Then who did?"

I passed the question to the girl. "Who did?"

"Babe," she said immediately.

O'Gar snorted to make her think he didn't believe her.

I asked, as if I were honestly perplexed, "How do you know that if you didn't know she was dead?"

"It stands to reason he did," she said. "Anybody can see that. He found out she was going away with Joe, so he killed her and then came to Joe's and killed him. That's just exactly what Babe would do when he found it out."

"Yeah? How long have *you* known they were going away together?"

"Since they decided to. Joe told me a month or two ago."

"And you didn't mind?"

"You've got this all wrong," she said. "Of course I didn't mind. I was being cut in on it. You know her father had the bees. That's what Joe was after. She didn't mean anything to him but an in to the old man's pockets. And I was to get my dib. And you needn't think I was crazy enough about Joe or anybody else to step off in the air for them. Babe got next and fixed the pair of them. That's a cinch."

"Yeah? How do you figure Babe would kill her?"

"That guy? You don't think he'd—"

"I mean, how would he go about killing her?"

"Oh!" She shrugged. "With his hands, likely as not."

"Once he'd made up his mind to do it, he'd do it quick and violent?" I suggested.

"That would be Babe," she agreed.

"But you can't see him slow-poisoning her—spreading it out over a month?"

Worry came into the girl's blue eyes. She put her lower lip between her teeth, then said slowly, "No, I can't see him doing it that way. Not Babe."

"Who can you see doing it that way?"

She opened her eyes wide, asking, "You mean Joe?"

I didn't say anything.

"Joe might have," she said persuasively. "God only knows what he'd want to do it for, why he'd want to get rid of the kind of meal ticket she was going to be. But you couldn't always guess what he was getting at.

He pulled plenty of dumb ones. He was too slick without being smart. If he was going to kill her, though, that would be about the way he'd go about it."

"Were he and Babe friendly?"

"No."

"Did he go to Babe's much?"

"Not at all that I know about. He was too leery of Babe to take a chance on being caught there. That's why I moved upstairs, so Sue could come over to our place to see him."

"Then how could Joe have hidden the fly paper he poisoned her with in her apartment?"

"Fly paper!" Her bewilderment seemed honest enough.

"Show it to her," I told O'Gar.

He got a sheet from the desk and held it close to the girl's face.

She stared at it for a moment and then jumped up and grabbed my arm with both hands.

"I didn't know what it was," she said excitedly. "Joe had some a couple of months ago. He was looking at it when I came in. I asked him what it was for, and he smiled that wisenheimer smile of his and said, 'You make angels out of it,' and wrapped it up again and put it in his pocket. I didn't pay much attention to him; he was always fooling with some kind of tricks that were supposed to make him wealthy, but never did."

"Ever see it again?"

"No."

"Did you know Sue very well?"

"I didn't know her at all. I never even saw her. I used to keep out of the way so I wouldn't gum Joe's play with her."

"But you know Babe?"

"Yes, I've been on a couple of parties where he was. That's all I know him."

"Who killed Sue?"

"Joe," she said. "Didn't he have that paper you say she was killed with?"

"Why did he kill her?"

"I don't know. He pulled some awful dumb tricks sometimes."

"You didn't kill her?"

"No, no, no!"

I jerked the corner of my mouth at O'Gar.

"You're a liar," he bawled, shaking the fly paper in her face. "You killed her." The rest of the team closed in, throwing accusations at her. They kept it up until she was groggy and the policewoman was beginning to look worried.

Then I said angrily, "All right. Throw her in a cell and let her think it over." To her, "You know what you told Joe this afternoon: this is no time to dummy up. Do a lot of thinking tonight."

"Honest to God I didn't kill her," she said.

I turned my back to her. The policewoman took her away.

"Ho-hum," O'Gar yawned. "We gave her a pretty good ride at that, for a short one."

"Not bad," I agreed. "If anybody else looked likely, I'd say she didn't kill Sue. But if she's telling the truth, then Holy Joe did it. And why should he poison the goose that was going to lay nice yellow eggs for him? And how and why did he cache the poison in their apartment? Babe had the motive, but damned if he looks like a slow-poisoner to me. You can't tell, though; he and Holy Joe could even have been working together on it."

"Could," Duff said. "But it takes a lot of imagination to get that one down. Anyway you twist it, Peggy's our best bet so far. Go up against her again, hard, in the morning?"

"Yeah," I said. "And we've got to find Babe."

The others had had dinner. MacMan and I went out and got ours. When we returned to the detective bureau an hour later it was practically deserted of the regular operatives.

"All gone to Pier 42 on a tip that McCloor's there," Steve Ward told us.

"How long ago?"

"Ten minutes."

MacMan and I got a taxi and set out for Pier 42. We didn't get to Pier 42.

On First Street, half a block from the Embarcadero, the taxi suddenly shrieked and slid to a halt.

"What—?" I began, and saw a man standing in front of the machine. He was a big man with a big gun. "Babe," I grunted, and put my hand on MacMan's arm to keep him from getting his gun out.

"Take me to—" McCloor was saying to the frightened driver when he saw us. He came around to my side and pulled the door open, holding the gun on us.

He had no hat. His hair was wet, plastered to his head. Little streams of water trickled down from it. His clothes were dripping wet.

He looked surprised at us and ordered, "Get out."

As we got out he growled at the driver, "What the hell you got your flag up for if you had fares?"

The driver wasn't there. He had hopped out the other side and was scooting away down the street. McCloor cursed him and poked his gun at me, growling, "Go on, beat it."

Apparently he hadn't recognized me. The light here wasn't good, and I had a hat on now. He had seen me for only a few seconds in Wales's room.

I stepped aside. MacMan moved to the other side.

McCloor took a backward step to keep us from getting him between us and started an angry word.

MacMan threw himself on McCloor's gun arm.

I socked McCloor's jaw with my fist. I might just as well have hit somebody else for all it seemed to bother him.

He swept me out of his way and pasted MacMan in the mouth. Mac-Man fell back till the taxi stopped him, spit out a tooth, and came back for more.

I was trying to climb up McCloor's left side.

MacMan came in on his right, failed to dodge a chop of the gun, caught it square on the top of the noodle, and went down hard. He stayed down.

I kicked McCloor's ankle, but couldn't get his foot from under him. I rammed my right fist into the small of his back and got a left-handful of his wet hair, swinging on it. He shook his head, dragging me off my feet.

He punched me in the side and I could feel my ribs and guts flattening together like leaves in a book.

I swung my fist against the back of his neck. That bothered him. He made a rumbling noise down in his chest, crunched my shoulder in his left hand, and chopped at me with the gun in his right.

I kicked him somewhere and punched his neck again.

Down the street, at the Embarcadero, a police whistle was blowing. Men were running up First Street toward us.

McCloor snorted like a locomotive and threw me away from him. I didn't want to go. I tried to hang on. He threw me away from him and ran up the street.

I scrambled up and ran after him, dragging my gun out.

At the first corner he stopped to squirt metal at me—three shots. I squirted one at him. None of the four connected.

He disappeared around the corner. I swung wide around it, to make him miss if he were flattened to the wall waiting for me. He wasn't. He was a hundred feet ahead, going into a space between two warehouses. I went in after him, and out after him at the other end, making better time with my hundred and ninety pounds than he was making with his two-fifty.

He crossed a street, turning up, away from the waterfront. There was a light on the corner. When I came into its glare he wheeled and leveled his gun at me. I didn't hear it click, but I knew it had when he threw it at me. The gun went past with a couple of feet to spare and raised hell against a door behind me.

McCloor turned and ran up the street. I ran up the street after him.

I put a bullet past him to let the others know where we were. At the next corner he started to turn to the left, changed his mind, and went straight on.

I sprinted, cutting the distance between us to forty or fifty feet, and yelped, "Stop or I'll drop you."

He jumped sidewise into a narrow alley.

I passed it on the jump, saw he wasn't waiting for me, and went in. Enough light came in from the street to let us see each other and our surroundings. The alley was blind—walled on each side and at the other end by tall concrete buildings with steel-shuttered windows and doors.

McCloor faced me, less than twenty feet away. His jaw stuck out. His arms curved down free of his sides. His shoulders were bunched.

"Put them up," I ordered, holding my gun level.

"Get out of my way, little man," he grumbled, taking a stiff-legged step toward me. "I'll eat you up."

"Keep coming," I said, "and I'll put you down."

"Try it." He took another step, crouching a little. "I can still get to you *with* slugs in me."

"Not where I'll put them." I was wordy, trying to talk him into waiting till the others came up. I didn't want to have to kill him. We could have done that from the taxi. "I'm no Annie Oakley, but if I can't pop your kneecaps with two shots at this distance, you're welcome to me. And if you think smashed kneecaps are a lot of fun, give it a whirl."

"Hell with that," he said and charged.

I shot his right knee.

He lurched toward me.

I shot his left knee.

He tumbled down.

"You would have it," I complained.

He twisted around, and with his arms pushed himself into a sitting position facing me.

"I didn't think you had sense enough to do it," he said through his teeth.

I talked to McCloor in the hospital. He lay on his back in bed with a couple of pillows slanting his head up. The skin was pale and tight around his mouth and eyes, but there was nothing else to show he was in pain.

"You sure devastated me, bo," he said when I came in.

"Sorry," I said, "but—"

"I ain't beefing. I asked for it."

"Why'd you kill Holy Joe?" I asked, off-hand, as I pulled a chair up beside the bed.

"Uh-uh—you're tooting the wrong ringer."

I laughed and told him I was the man in the room with Joe when it happened.

McCloor grinned and said, "I thought I'd seen you somewheres before.

So that's where it was. I didn't pay no attention to your mug, just so your hands didn't move."

"Why'd you kill him?"

He pursed his lips, screwed up his eyes at me, thought something over, and said, "He killed a broad I knew."

"He killed Sue Hambleton?" I asked.

He studied my face a while before he replied, "Yep."

"How do you figure that out?"

"Hell," he said, "I don't have to. Sue told me. Give me a butt."

I gave him a cigarette, held a lighter under it, and objected. "That doesn't exactly fit in with other things I know. Just what happened and what did she say? You might start back with the night you gave her the goog."

He looked thoughtful, letting smoke sneak slowly out of his nose, then said, "I hadn't ought to hit her in the eye, that's a fact. But, see, she had been out all afternoon and wouldn't tell me where she'd been, and we had a row about it. What's this—Thursday morning? That was Monday, then. After the row I went out and spent the night in a dump over on Army Street. I got home about seven the next morning. Sue was sick as hell, but she wouldn't let me get a croaker for her. That was kind of funny, because she was scared stiff."

McCloor scratched his head meditatively and suddenly drew in a great lungful of smoke, practically eating up the rest of the cigarette. He let the smoke leak out of mouth and nose together, looking dully through the cloud at me. Then he said brusquely, "Well, she went under. But before she went she told me she'd been poisoned by Holy Joe."

"She say how he'd given it to her?"

McCloor shook his head.

"I'd been asking her what was the matter, and not getting anything out of her. Then she starts whining that she's poisoned. 'I'm poisoned, Babe,' she whines. 'Arsenic. That damned Holy Joe,' she says. Then she won't say anything else, and it's not a hell of a while after that that she kicks off."

"Yeah? Then what'd you do?"

"I went gunning for Holy Joe. I knew him but didn't know where he jungled up, and didn't find out till yesterday. You was there when I came. You know about that. I had picked up a boiler and parked it over on Turk Street, for the getaway. When I got back to it, there was a copper standing close to it. I figured he might have spotted it as a hot one and was waiting to see who came for it, so I let it alone, and caught a streetcar instead, and cut for the yards. Down there I ran into a whole flock of hammer and saws and had to go overboard in China Basin, swimming up to a pier, being ranked again by a watchman there, swimming off to another, and finally getting through the line only to run into another bad break. I wouldn't of flagged that taxi if the *For Hire* flag hadn't been up."

"You knew Sue was planning to take a run-out on you with Joe?"

"I don't know it yet," he said. "I knew damned well she was cheating on me, but I didn't know who with."

"What would you have done if you had known that?" I asked.

"Me?" He grinned wolfishly. "Just what I did."

"Killed the pair of them," I said.

He rubbed his lower lip with a thumb and asked calmly, "You think I killed Sue?"

"You did."

"Serves me right," he said. "I must be getting simple in my old age. What the hell am I doing barbering with a lousy dick? That never got nobody nothing but grief. Well, you might just as well take it on the heel and toe now, my lad. I'm through spitting."

And he was. I couldn't get another word out of him.

The Old Man sat listening to me, tapping his desk lightly with the point of a long yellow pencil, staring past me with mild blue rimless-spectacled eyes. When I had brought my story up to date, he asked pleasantly, "How is MacMan?"

"He lost two teeth, but his skull wasn't cracked. He'll be out in a couple of days."

The Old Man nodded and asked, "What remains to be done?"

"Nothing. We can put Peggy Carroll on the mat again, but it's not likely we'll squeeze much more out of her. Outside of that, the returns are pretty well all in."

"And what do you make of it?"

I squirmed in my chair and said, "Suicide."

The Old Man smiled at me, politely but skeptically.

"I don't like it either," I grumbled. "And I'm not ready to write in a report yet. But that's the only total that what we've got will add up to. That fly paper was hidden behind the kitchen stove. Nobody would be crazy enough to try to hide something from a woman in her own kitchen like that. But the woman might hide it there.

"According to Peggy, Holy Joe had the fly paper. If Sue hid it, she got it from him. For what? They were planning to go away together, and were only waiting till Joe, who was on the nut, raised enough dough. Maybe they were afraid of Babe, and had the poison there to slip him if he tumbled to their plan before they went. Maybe they meant to slip it to him before they went anyway.

"When I started talking to Holy Joe about murder, he thought Babe was the one who had been bumped off. He was surprised, maybe, but as if he was surprised that it had happened so soon. He was more surprised when he heard that Sue had died too, but even then he wasn't so surprised as when he saw McCloor alive at the window.

"She died cursing Holy Joe, and she knew she was poisoned, and she wouldn't let McCloor get a doctor. Can't that mean that she had turned against Joe, and had taken the poison herself instead of feeding it to Babe? The poison was hidden from Babe. But even if he found it, I can't figure him as a poisoner. He's too rough. Unless he caught her trying to poison him and made her swallow the stuff. But that doesn't account for the month-old arsenic in her hair."

"Does your suicide hypothesis take care of that?" the Old Man asked.

"It could," I said. "Don't be kicking holes in my theory. It's got enough as it stands. But, if she committed suicide this time, there's no reason why she couldn't have tried it once before—say after a quarrel with Joe a month ago—and failed to bring it off. That would have put the arsenic in her. There's no real proof that she took any between a month ago and day before yesterday."

"No real proof," the Old Man protested mildly, "except the autopsy's finding—chronic poisoning."

I was never one to let experts' guesses stand in my way. I said, "They base that on the small amount of arsenic they found in her remains—less than a fatal dose. And the amount they find in your stomach after you're dead depends on how much you vomit before you die."

The Old Man smiled benevolently at me and asked, "But you're not, you say, ready to write this theory into a report? Meanwhile what do you propose doing?"

"If there's nothing else on tap, I'm going home, fumigate my brains with Fatimas, and try to get this thing straightened out in my head. I think I'll get a copy of *The Count of Monte Cristo* and run through it. I haven't read it since I was a kid. It looks like the book was wrapped up with the fly paper to make a bundle large enough to wedge tightly between the wall and stove, so it wouldn't fall down. But there might be something in the book. I'll see anyway."

"I did that last night," the Old Man murmured.

I asked, "And?"

He took a book from his desk drawer, opened it where a slip of paper marked a place, and held it out to me, one pink finger marking a paragraph.

"Suppose you were to take a milligramme of this poison the first day, two milligrammes the second day, and so on. Well, at the end of ten days you would have taken a centigramme: at the end of twenty days, increasing another milligramme, you would have taken three hundred centigrammes; that is to say, a dose you would support without inconvenience, and which would be very dangerous for any other person who had not taken the same precautions as yourself. Well, then, at the end of the month, when drinking water from the same carafe, you would kill the person who had drunk this water, without your perceiving otherwise than from slight inconvenience that there was any poisonous substance mingled with the water."

"That does it," I said. "That does it. They were afraid to go away without killing Babe, too certain he'd come after them. She tried to make herself immune from arsenic poisoning by getting her body accustomed to it, taking steadily increasing doses, so when she slipped the big shot in Babe's food she could eat it with him without danger. She'd be taken sick, but wouldn't die, and the police couldn't hang his death on her because she too had eaten the poisoned food.

"That clicks. After the row Monday night, when she wrote Joe the note urging him to make the getaway soon, she tried to hurry up her immunity, and increased her preparatory doses too quickly, took too large a shot. That's why she cursed Joe at the end; it was his plan."

"Possibly she overdosed herself in an attempt to speed it along," the Old Man agreed, "but not necessarily. There are people who can cultivate an ability to take large doses of arsenic without trouble, but it seems to be a sort of natural gift with them, a matter of some constitutional peculiarity. Ordinarily, anyone who tried it would do what Sue Hambleton did—slowly poison themselves until the cumulative effect was strong enough to cause death."

Babe McCloor was hanged, for killing Holy Joe Wales, six months later.

THE FIVE-FORTY-EIGHT

by

JOHN CHEEVER

When Blake stepped out of the elevator, he saw her. A few people, mostly men waiting for girls, stood in the lobby watching the elevator doors. She was among them. As he saw her, her face took on a look of such loathing and purpose that he realized she had been waiting for him. He did not approach her. She had no legitimate business with him. They had nothing to say. He turned and walked toward the glass doors at the end of the lobby, feeling that faint guilt and bewilderment we experience when we bypass some old friend or classmate who seems threadbare, or sick, or miserable in some other way. It was five-eighteen by the clock in the Western Union office. He could catch the express. As he waited his turn at the revolving doors, he saw that it was still raining. It had been raining all day, and he noticed now how much louder the rain made the noises of the street. Outside, he started walking briskly east toward Madison Avenue. Traffic was tied up, and horns were blowing urgently on a crosstown street in the distance. The sidewalk was crowded. He wondered what she had hoped to gain by a glimpse of him coming out of the office building at the end of the day. Then he wondered if she was following him.

Walking in the city, we seldom turn and look back. The habit restrained Blake. He listened for a minute—foolishly—as he walked, as if he could distinguish her footsteps from the worlds of sound in the city at the end of a rainy day. Then he noticed, ahead of him on the other side of the street, a break in the wall of buildings. Something had been torn down; something was being put up, but the steel structure had only just risen above the sidewalk fence and daylight poured through the gap. Blake stopped opposite here and looked into a store window. It was a decorator's or an auctioneer's. The window was arranged like a room in which people live and entertain their friends. There were cups on the coffee table, magazines to read, and flowers in the vases, but the flowers were dead and the cups were empty and the guests had not come. In the plate glass, Blake saw a clear reflection of himself and the crowds that were passing, like shadows, at his back. Then he saw her image—so close to him that it shocked him. She was standing only a foot or two behind him. He could have turned then and asked her what she wanted, but instead of recognizing her, he shied away abruptly from the reflection of her contorted face and went along the street. She might be meaning to do him harm—she might be meaning to kill him.

The suddenness with which he moved when he saw the reflection of her face tipped the water out of his hatbrim in such a way that some of it ran down his neck. It felt unpleasantly like the sweat of fear. Then the cold water falling into his face and onto his bare hands, the rancid smell of the wet gutters and paving, the knowledge that his feet were beginning to get wet and that he might catch cold—all the common discomforts of walking in the rain—seemed to heighten the menace of his pursuer and to give him a morbid consciousness of his own physicalness and of the ease with which he could be hurt. He could see ahead of him the corner of Madison Avenue, where the lights were brighter. He felt that if he could get to Madison Avenue he would be all right. At the corner, there was a bakery shop with two entrances, and he went in by the door on the crosstown street, bought a coffee ring, like any other commuter, and went out the Madison Avenue door. As he started down Madison Avenue, he saw her waiting for him by a hut where newspapers were sold.

She was not clever. She would be easy to shake. He could get into a taxi by one door and leave by the other. He could speak to a policeman. He could run—although he was afraid that if he did run, it might precipitate the violence he now felt sure she had planned. He was approaching a part of the city that he knew well and where the maze of street-level and underground passages, elevator banks, and crowded lobbies made it easy for a man to lose a pursuer. The thought of this, and a whiff of sugary warmth from the coffee ring, cheered him. It was absurd to imagine being harmed on a crowded street. She was foolish, misled, lonely perhaps—that was all it could amount to. He was an insignificant man, and there was no point in anyone's following him from his office to the station. He knew no secrets of any consequence. The reports in his brief case had no bearing on war, peace, the dope traffic, the hydrogen bomb, or any of the other international skulduggeries that he associated with pursuers, men in trench coats, and wet sidewalks. Then he saw ahead of him the door of a men's bar. Oh, it was so simple!

He ordered a Gibson and shouldered his way in between two other men at the bar, so that if she should be watching from the window she would lose sight of him. The place was crowded with commuters putting down a drink before the ride home. They had brought in on their clothes —on their shoes and umbrellas—the rancid smell of the wet dusk outside, but Blake began to relax as soon as he tasted his Gibson and looked around at the common, mostly not-young faces that surrounded him and that were worried, if they were worried at all, about tax rates and who would be put in charge of merchandising. He tried to remember her name—Miss Dent, Miss Bent, Miss Lent—and he was surprised to find that he could not remember it, although he was proud of the retentiveness and reach of his memory and it had only been six months ago.

Personnel had sent her up one afternoon—he was looking for a secretary. He saw a dark woman—in her twenties, perhaps—who was slender and shy. Her dress was simple, her figure was not much, one of her stockings was crooked, but her voice was soft and he had been willing to try her out. After she had been working for him a few days, she told him that she had been in the hospital for eight months and that it had been hard after this for her to find work, and she wanted to thank him for giving her a chance. Her hair was dark, her eyes were dark; she left with him a pleasant impression of darkness. As he got to know her better, he felt that she was oversensitive and, as a consequence, lonely. Once, when she was speaking to him of what she imagined his life to be—full of friendships, money, and a large and loving family—he had thought he recognized a peculiar feeling of deprivation. She seemed to imagine the lives of the rest of the world to be more brilliant than they were. Once, she had put a rose on his desk, and he had dropped it into the wastebasket. "I don't like roses," he told her.

She had been competent, punctual, and a good typist, and he had found only one thing in her that he could object to—her handwriting. He could not associate the crudeness of her handwriting with her appearance. He would have expected her to write a rounded backhand, and in her writing there were intermittent traces of this, mixed with clumsy printing. Her writing gave him the feeling that she had been the victim of some inner—some emotional—conflict that had in its violence broken the continuity of the lines she was able to make on paper. When she had been working for him three weeks—no longer—they stayed late one night and he offered, after work, to buy her a drink. "If you really want a drink," she said, "I have some whiskey at my place."

She lived in a room that seemed to him like a closet. There were suit boxes and hatboxes piled in a corner, and although the room seemed hardly big enough to hold the bed, the dresser, and the chair he sat in, there was an upright piano against one wall, with a book of Beethoven sonatas on the rack. She gave him a drink and said that she was going to put on something more comfortable. He urged her to; that was, after all, what he had come for. If he had had any qualms, they would have been practical. Her diffidence, the feeling of deprivation in her point of view, promised to protect him from any consequences. Most of the many women he had known had been picked for their lack of self-esteem.

When he put on his clothes again, an hour or so later, she was weeping. He felt too contented and warm and sleepy to worry much about her tears. As he was dressing, he noticed on the dresser a note she had written to a cleaning woman. The only light came from the bathroom—the door was ajar—and in this half light the hideously scrawled letters again seemed entirely wrong for her, and as if they must be the handwriting of some other and very gross woman. The next day, he did what he felt was the only sensible thing. When she was out for lunch, he called personnel and asked them to fire her. Then he took the afternoon off. A few days later, she came to the office, asking to see him. He told the switchboard girl not to let her in. He had not seen her again until this evening.

Blake drank a second Gibson and saw by the clock that he had missed the express. He would get the local—the five-forty-eight. When he left the bar the sky was still light; it was still raining. He looked carefully up and down the street and saw that the poor woman had gone. Once or twice, he looked over his shoulder, walking to the station, but he seemed to be safe. He was still not quite himself, he realized, because he had left his coffee ring at the bar, and he was not a man who forgot things. This lapse of memory pained him.

He bought a paper. The local was only half full when he boarded it, and he got a seat on the river side and took off his raincoat. He was a slender man with brown hair—undistinguished in every way, unless you could have divined in his pallor or his gray eyes his unpleasant tastes. He dressed—like the rest of us—as if he admitted the existence of sumptuary laws. His raincoat was the pale buff color of a mushroom. His hat was dark brown; so was his suit. Except for the few bright threads in his necktie, there was a scrupulous lack of color in his clothing that seemed protective.

He looked around the car for neighbors. Mrs. Compton was several seats in front of him, to the right. She smiled, but her smile was fleeting. It died swiftly and horribly. Mr. Watkins was directly in front of Blake. Mr. Watkins needed a haircut, and he had broken the sumptuary laws; he was wearing a corduroy jacket. He and Blake had quarreled, so they did not speak.

The swift death of Mrs. Compton's smile did not affect Blake at all. The Comptons lived in the house next to the Blakes, and Mrs. Compton had never understood the importance of minding her own business. Louise Blake took her troubles to Mrs. Compton, Blake knew, and instead of discouraging her crying jags, Mrs. Compton had come to imagine herself a sort of confessor and had developed a lively curiosity about the Blakes' intimate affairs. She had probably been given an account of their most recent quarrel. Blake had come home one night, overworked and tired, and had found that Louise had done nothing about getting supper. He had gone into the kitchen, followed by Louise, and he had pointed out to her that the date was the fifth. He had drawn a circle around the date on the kitchen calendar. "One week is the twelfth," he had said. "Two weeks will be the nineteenth." He drew a circle around the nineteenth. "I'm not going to speak to you for two weeks," he had said. "That will be the nineteenth." She had wept, she had protested, but it had been eight or ten years since she had been able to touch him with her entreaties. Louise had got old. Now the lines in her face were ineradicable, and when she clapped her glasses onto her nose to read the evening paper she looked to him like an unpleasant stranger. The physical charms that had been her only attraction were gone. It had been nine years since Blake had built a bookshelf in the doorway that connected their rooms and had fitted into the bookshelf wooden doors that could be locked, since he did not want the children to see his books. But their prolonged estrangement didn't seem remarkable to Blake. He had quarreled with his wife, but so did every other man born of woman. It was human nature. In any place where you can hear their voices—a hotel courtyard, an air shaft, a street on a summer evening—you will hear harsh words.

The hard feeling between Blake and Mr. Watkins also had to do with Blake's family, but it was not as serious or as troublesome as what lay behind Mrs. Compton's fleeting smile. The Watkinses rented. Mr. Watkins broke the sumptuary laws day after day—he once went to the eight-fourteen in a pair of sandals—and he made his living as a commercial artist. Blake's oldest son—Charlie was fourteen—had made friends with the Watkins boy. He had spent a lot of time in the sloppy rented house where the Watkinses lived. The friendship had affected his manners and his neatness. Then he had begun to take some meals with the Watkinses, and to spend Saturday nights there. When he had moved most of his possessions over to the Watkinses' and had begun to spend more than half his nights there, Blake had been forced to act. He had spoken not to Charlie but to Mr. Watkins, and had, of necessity, said a number of things that must have sounded critical. Mr. Watkins' long and dirty hair and his corduroy jacket reassured Blake that he had been in the right.

But Mrs. Compton's dying smile and Mr. Watkins' dirty hair did not lessen the pleasure Blake took in setting himself in an uncomfortable seat on the five-forty-eight deep underground. The coach was old and smelled oddly like a bomb shelter in which whole families had spent the night. The light that spread from the ceiling down onto their heads and shoulders was dim. The filth on the window glass was streaked with rain from some other journey, and clouds of rank pipe and cigarette smoke had begun to rise from behind each newspaper, but it was a scene that meant to Blake that he was on a safe path, and after his brush with danger he even felt a little warmth toward Mrs. Compton and Mr. Watkins.

The train traveled up from underground into the weak daylight, and the slums and the city reminded Blake vaguely of the woman who had followed him. To avoid speculation or remorse about her, he turned his attention to the evening paper. Out of the corner of his eye he could see the landscape. It was industrial and, at that hour, sad. There were machine sheds and warehouses, and above these he saw a break in the clouds—a piece of yellow light. "Mr. Blake," someone said. He looked up. It was she. She was standing there holding one hand on the back of the seat to steady herself in the swaying coach. He remembered her name then—Miss Dent. "Hello, Miss Dent," he said.

"Do you mind if I sit here?"

"I guess not."

"Thank you. It's very kind of you. I don't like to inconvenience you like this. I don't want to . . ." He had been frightened when he looked up and saw her, but her timid voice rapidly reassured him. He shifted his hams —that futile and reflexive gesture of hospitality—and she sat down. She sighed. He smelled her wet clothing. She wore a formless black hat with a cheap crest stitched onto it. Her coat was thin cloth, he saw, and she wore gloves and carried a large pocketbook.

"Are you living out in this direction now, Miss Dent?"

"No."

She opened her purse and reached for her handkerchief. She had begun to cry. He turned his head to see if anyone in the car was looking, but no one was. He had sat beside a thousand passengers on the evening train. He had noticed their clothes, the holes in their gloves; and if they fell asleep and mumbled he had wondered what their worries were. He had classified almost all of them briefly before he buried his nose in the paper. He had marked them as rich, poor, brilliant or dull, neighbors or strangers, but not one of the thousand had ever wept. When she opened her purse, he remembered her perfume. It had clung to his skin the night he went to her place for a drink.

"I've been very sick," she said. "This is the first time I've been out of bed in two weeks. I've been terribly sick."

"I'm sorry that you've been sick, Miss Dent," he said in a voice loud enough to be heard by Mr. Watkins and Mrs. Compton. "Where are you working now?"

"What?"

"Where are you working now?"

"Oh, don't make me laugh," she said softly.

"I don't understand."

"You poisoned their minds."

He straightened his back and braced his shoulders. These wrenching movements expressed a brief—and hopeless—longing to be in some other place. She meant trouble. He took a breath. He looked with deep feeling at the half-filled, half-lighted coach to affirm his sense of actuality, of a world in which there was not very much bad trouble after all. He was conscious of her heavy breathing and the smell of her rain-soaked coat. The train stopped. A nun and a man in overalls got off. When it started again, Blake put on his hat and reached for his raincoat.

"Where are you going?" she said.

"I'm going up to the next car."

"Oh, no," she said. "No, no, no." She put her white face so close to his ear that he could feel her warm breath on his cheek. "Don't do that," she whispered. "Don't try and escape me. I have a pistol and I'll have to kill you and I don't want to. All I want to do is to talk with you. Don't move or I'll kill you. Don't, don't, don't!"

Blake sat back abruptly in his seat. If he had wanted to stand and shout for help, he would not have been able to. His tongue had swelled to twice its size, and when he tried to move it, it stuck horribly to the roof of his mouth. His legs were limp. All he could think of to do then was to wait for his heart to stop its hysterical beating, so that he could judge the extent of his danger. She was sitting a little sidewise, and in her pocketbook was the pistol, aimed at his belly.

"You understand me now, don't you?" she said. "You understand that I'm serious?" He tried to speak but he was still mute. He nodded his head. "Now we'll sit quietly for a little while," she said. "I got so excited that my thoughts are all confused. We'll sit quietly for a little while, until I can get my thoughts in order again."

Help would come, Blake thought. It was only a question of minutes. Someone, noticing the look on his face or her peculiar posture, would stop and interfere, and it would all be over. All he had to do was to wait

until someone noticed his predicament. Out of the window he saw the
river and the sky. The rain clouds were rolling down like a shutter, and
while he watched, a streak of orange light on the horizon became brilliant. Its brilliance spread—he could see it move—across the waves until
it raked the banks of the river with a dim firelight. Then it was put out.
Help would come in a minute, he thought. Help would come before they
stopped again; but the train stopped, there were some comings and
goings, and Blake still lived on, at the mercy of the woman beside him.
The possibility that help might not come was one that he could not face.
The possibility that his predicament was not noticeable, that Mrs. Compton would guess that he was taking a poor relation out to dinner at Shady
Hill, was something he would think about later. Then the saliva came
back into his mouth and he was able to speak.

"Miss Dent?"

"Yes."

"What do you want?"

"I want to talk with you."

"You can come to my office."

"Oh, no. I went there every day for two weeks."

"You could make an appointment."

"No," she said. "I think we can talk here. I wrote you a letter but I've
been too sick to go out and mail it. I've put down all my thoughts. I like
to travel. I like trains. One of my troubles has always been that I could
never afford to travel. I suppose you see this scenery every night and
don't notice it any more, but it's nice for someone who's been in bed a
long time. They say that He's not in the river and the hills but I think
He is. 'Where shall wisdom be found,' it says. 'And where is the place of
understanding? . . . The depth saith, It is not in me: and the sea saith, It
is not with me. . . . Destruction and death say, We have heard the fame
thereof with our ears.'

"Oh, I know what you're thinking," she said. "You're thinking that I'm
crazy, and I have been very sick again but I'm going to be better. It's
going to make me better to talk with you. I was in the hospital all the time
before I came to work for you but they never tried to cure me, they only
wanted to take away my self-respect. I haven't had any work now for
three months. Even if I did have to kill you, they wouldn't be able to do
anything to me except put me back in the hospital, so you see I'm not
afraid. But let's sit quietly for a little while longer. I have to be calm."

The train continued its halting progress up the bank of the river, and
Blake tried to force himself to make some plans for escape, but the
immediate threat to his life made this difficult, and instead of planning
sensibly, he thought of the many ways in which he could have avoided
her in the first place. As soon as he had felt these regrets, he realized their

futility. It was like regretting his lack of suspicion when she first mentioned her months in the hospital. It was like regretting his failure to have been warned by her shyness, her diffidence, and the handwriting that looked like the marks of a claw. There was no way now of rectifying his mistakes, and he felt—for perhaps the first time in his mature life—the full force of regret. Out of the window, he saw some men fishing on the nearly dark river, and then a ramshackle boat club that seemed to have been nailed together out of scraps of wood that had been washed up on the shore.

Mr. Watkins had fallen asleep. He was snoring. Mrs. Compton read her paper. The train creaked, slowed, and halted infirmly at another station. Blake could see the southbound platform, where a few passengers were waiting to go into the city. There was a workman with a lunch pail, a dressed-up woman, and a man with a suitcase. They stood apart from one another. Some advertisements were posted on the wall behind them. There was a picture of a couple drinking a toast in wine, a picture of a Cat's Paw rubber heel, and a picture of a Hawaiian dancer. Their cheerful intent seemed to go no farther than the puddles of water on the platform and to expire there. The platform and the people on it looked lonely. The train drew away from the station into the scattered lights of a slum and then into the darkness of the country and the river.

"I want you to read my letter before we get to Shady Hill," she said. "It's on the seat. Pick it up. I would have mailed it to you, but I've been too sick to go out. I haven't gone out for two weeks. I haven't had any work for three months. I haven't spoken to anybody but the landlady. Please read my letter."

He picked up the letter from the seat where she had put it. The cheap paper felt abhorrent and filthy to his fingers. It was folded and refolded. "Dear Husband," she had written, in that crazy, wandering hand, "they say that human love leads us to divine love, but is this true? I dream about you every night. I have such terrible desires. I have always had a gift for dreams. I dreamed on Tuesday of a volcano erupting with blood. When I was in the hospital they said they wanted to cure me but they only wanted to take away my self-respect. They only wanted me to dream about sewing and basketwork but I protected my gift for dreams. I'm clairvoyant. I can tell when the telephone is going to ring. I've never had a true friend in my whole life. . . ."

The train stopped again. There was another platform, another picture of the couple drinking a toast, the rubber heel, and the Hawaiian dancer. Suddenly she pressed her face close to Blake's again and whispered in his ear. "I know what you're thinking. I can see it in your face. You're thinking you can get away from me in Shady Hill, aren't you? Oh, I've been planning this for weeks. It's all I've had to think about. I won't harm you if you'll let me talk. I've been thinking about devils. I mean if there are devils in the world, if there are people in the world who represent evil, is it our duty to exterminate them? I know that you always prey on weak people. I can tell. Oh, sometimes I think that I ought to kill you. Sometimes I think you're the only obstacle between me and my happiness. Sometimes . . ."

She touched Blake with the pistol. He felt the muzzle against his belly. The bullet, at that distance, would make a small hole where it entered, but it would rip out of his back a place as big as a soccer ball. He remembered the unburied dead he had seen in the war. The memory came in a rush: entrails, eyes, shattered bone, ordure, and other filth.

"All I've ever wanted in life is a little love," she said. She lightened the pressure of the gun. Mr. Watkins still slept. Mrs. Compton was sitting calmly with her hands folded in her lap. The coach rocked gently, and the coats and mushroom-colored raincoats that hung between the windows swayed a little as the car moved. Blake's elbow was on the window sill and his left shoe was on the guard above the steampipe. The car smelled like some dismal classroom. The passengers seemed asleep and apart, and Blake felt that he might never escape the smell of heat and wet clothing and the dimness of the light. He tried to summon the calculated self-deceptions with which he sometimes cheered himself, but he was left without any energy for hope of self-deception.

The conductor put his head in the door and said, "Shady Hill, next, Shady Hill."

"Now," she said. "Now you get out ahead of me."

Mr. Watkins waked suddenly, put on his coat and hat, and smiled at Mrs. Compton, who was gathering her parcels to her in a series of maternal gestures. They went to the door. Blake joined them, but neither of them spoke to him or seemed to notice the woman at his back. The conductor threw open the door, and Blake saw on the platform of the next car a few other neighbors who had missed the express, waiting patiently and tiredly in the wan light for their trip to end. He raised his head to see through the open door the abandoned mansion outside of town, a NO TRESPASSING sign nailed to a tree, and then the oil tanks. The concrete abutments of the bridge passed, so close to the open door that he could have touched them. Then he saw the first of the lampposts on the northbound platform, the sign SHADY HILL in black and gold, and the little lawn and flower bed kept up by the Improvement Association, and then the cab stand and a corner of the old-fashioned depot. It was raining again; it was pouring. He could hear the splash of water and see the lights reflected in puddles and in the shining pavement, and the idle sound of splashing and dripping formed in his mind a conception of shelter, so light and strange that it seemed to belong to a time of his life that he could not remember.

He went down the steps with her at his back. A dozen or so cars were waiting by the station with their motors running. A few people got off from each of the other coaches; he recognized most of them, but none of them offered to give him a ride. They walked separately or in pairs— purposefully out of the rain to the shelter of the platform, where the car horns called to them. It was time to go home, time for a drink, time for love, time for supper, and he could see the lights on the hill—lights by which children were being bathed, meat cooked, dishes washed—shining in the rain. One by one, the cars picked up the heads of families, until there were only four left. Two of the stranded passengers drove off in the only taxi the village had. "I'm sorry, darling," a woman said tenderly to her husband when she drove up a few minutes later. "All our clocks are slow." The last man looked at his watch, looked at the rain, and then walked off into it, and Blake saw him go as if they had some reason to say good-by—not as we say good-by to friends after a party but as we say good-by when we are faced with an inexorable and unwanted parting of the spirit and the heart. The man's footsteps sounded as he crossed the parking lot to the sidewalk, and then they were lost. In the station, a telephone began to ring. The ringing was loud, plaintive, evenly spaced, and unanswered. Someone wanted to know about the next train to Albany, but Mr. Flanagan, the stationmaster, had gone home an hour ago. He had turned on all his lights before he went away. They burned in the empty waiting room. They burned, tin-shaded, at intervals up and down the platform and with the peculiar sadness of dim and purposeless light. They lighted the Hawaiian dancer, the couple drinking a toast, the rubber heel.

"I've never been here before," she said. "I thought it would look different. I didn't think it would look so shabby. Let's get out of the light. Go over there."

His legs felt sore. All his strength was gone. "Go on," she said.

North of the station there were a freight house and a coalyard and an inlet where the butcher and the baker and the man who ran the service station moored the dinghies from which they fished on Sundays, sunk now to the gunwales with the rain. As he walked toward the freight house, he saw a movement on the ground and heard a scraping sound, and then he saw a rat take its head out of a paper bag and regard him. The rat seized the bag in its teeth and dragged it into a culvert.

"Stop," she said. "Turn around. Oh, I ought to feel sorry for you. Look at your poor face. But you don't know what I've been through. I'm afraid to go out in the daylight. I'm afraid the blue sky will fall down on me. I'm like poor Chicken-Licken. I only feel like myself when it begins to get dark. But still and all I'm better than you. I still have good dreams sometimes. I dream about picnics and Heaven and the brotherhood of man, and about castles in the moonlight and a river with willow trees all along the edge of it and foreign cities, and after all I know more about love than you."

He heard from off the dark river the drone of an outboard motor, a sound that drew slowly behind it across the dark water such a burden of clear, sweet memories of gone summers and gone pleasures that it made his flesh crawl, and he thought of dark in the mountains and the children singing. "They never wanted to cure me," she said. "They . . ." The noise of a train coming down from the north drowned out her voice, but she went on talking. The noise filled his ears, and the windows where people ate, drank, slept, and read flew past. When the train had passed beyond the bridge, the noise grew distant, and he heard her screaming at him, *"Kneel down!* Kneel down! Do what I say. *Kneel down!"*

He got to his knees. He bent his head. "There," she said. "You see, if you do what I say, I won't harm you, because I really don't want to harm you, I want to help you, but when I see your face it sometimes seems to me that I can't help you. Sometimes it seems to me that if I were good and loving and sane—oh, much better than I am—sometimes it seems to me that if I were all these things and young and beautiful, too, and if I called to show you the right way, you wouldn't heed me. Oh, I'm better than you, I'm better than you, and I shouldn't waste my time or spoil my life like this. Put your face in the dirt. *Put your face in the dirt!* Do what I say. Put your face in the dirt."

He fell forward in the filth. The coal skinned his face. He stretched out on the ground, weeping. "Now I feel better," she said. "Now I can wash my hands of you, I can wash my hands of all this, because you see there is some kindness, some saneness in me that I can find again and use. I can wash my hands." Then he heard her footsteps go away from him, over the rubble. He heard the clearer and more distant sound they made on the hard surface of the platform. He heard them diminish. He raised his head. He saw her climb the stairs of the wooden footbridge and cross it and go down to the other platform, where her figure in the dim light looked small, common, and harmless. He raised himself out of the dust —warily at first, until he saw by her attitude, her looks, that she had forgotten him; that she had completed what she had wanted to do, and that he was safe. He got to his feet and picked up his hat from the ground where it had fallen and walked home.

THE STRANGE CASE OF DR. JEKYLL AND MR. HYDE

by

ROBERT LOUIS STEVENSON

Story of the Door

Mr. Utterson the lawyer was a man of a rugged countenance, that was never lighted by a smile; cold, scanty and embarrassed in discourse; backward in sentiment; lean, long, dusty, dreary, and yet somehow lovable. At friendly meetings, and when the wine was to his taste, something eminently human beaconed from his eye; something indeed which never found its way into his talk, but which spoke not only in these silent symbols of the after-dinner face, but more often and loudly in the acts of his life. He was austere with himself; drank gin when he was alone, to mortify a taste for vintages; and though he enjoyed the theatre, had not crossed the doors of one for twenty years. But he had an approved tolerance for others; sometimes wondering, almost with envy, at the high pressure of spirits involved in their misdeeds; and in any extremity inclined to help rather than to reprove. "I incline to Cain's heresy," he used to say quaintly: "I let my brother go to the devil in his own way." In this character, it was frequently his fortune to be the last reputable acquaintance and the last good influence in the lives of down-going men. And to such as these, so long as they came about his chambers, he never marked a shade of change in his demeanour.

No doubt the feat was easy to Mr. Utterson; for he was undemonstrative at the best, and even his friendships seemed to be founded in a similar catholicity of good-nature. It is the mark of a modest man to accept his friendly circle ready made from the hands of opportunity; and that was the lawyer's way. His friends were those of his own blood, or those whom he had known the longest; his affections, like ivy, were the growth of time, they implied no aptness in the object. Hence, no doubt, the bond that united him to Mr. Richard Enfield, his distant kinsman, the well-known man about town. It was a nut to crack for many, what these two could see in each other, or what subject they could find in common. It was reported by those who encountered them in their Sunday walks, that they said nothing, looked singularly dull, and would hail with obvious relief the appearance of a friend. For all that, the two men put the greatest store by these excursions, counted them the chief jewel of each week, and not only set aside occasions of pleasure, but even resisted the calls of business, that they might enjoy them uninterrupted.

It chanced on one of these rambles that their way led them down a by-street in a busy quarter of London. The street was small and what is called quiet, but it drove a thriving trade on the week-days. The inhabitants were all doing well, it seemed, and all emulously hoping to do better still, and laying out the surplus of their gains in coquetry; so that the shop fronts stood along that thoroughfare with an air of invitation, like rows of smiling saleswomen. Even on Sunday, when it veiled its more florid charms and lay comparatively empty of passage, the street shone out in contrast to its dingy neighbourhood, like a fire in a forest; and with its freshly painted shutters, well-polished brasses, and general cleanliness and gaiety of note, instantly caught and pleased the eye of the passenger.

Two doors from one corner, on the left hand going east, the line was broken by the entry of a court; and just at that point, a certain sinister block of building thrust forward its gable on the street. It was two storeys high; showed no window, nothing but a door on the lower storey and a blind forehead of discoloured wall on the upper; and bore in every feature the marks of prolonged and sordid negligence. The door, which was equipped with neither bell nor knocker, was blistered and distained. Tramps slouched into the recess and struck matches on the panels; children kept shop upon the steps; the schoolboy had tried his knife on the mouldings; and for close on a generation, no one had appeared to drive away these random visitors or to repair their ravages.

Mr. Enfield and the lawyer were on the other side of the by-street; but when they came abreast of the entry, the former lifted up his cane and pointed.

"Did you ever remark that door?" he asked; and when his companion had replied in the affirmative, "It is connected in my mind," added he, "with a very odd story."

"Indeed!" said Mr. Utterson, with a slight change of voice, "and what was that?"

"Well, it was this way," returned Mr. Enfield: "I was coming home from some place at the end of the world, about three o'clock of a black winter morning, and my way lay through a part of town where there was literally nothing to be seen but lamps. Street after street, and all the folks asleep—street after street, all lighted up as if for a procession, and all as empty as a church—till at last I got into that state of mind when a man listens and listens and begins to long for the sight of a policeman. All at once, I saw two figures: one a little man who was stumping along eastwards at a good walk, and the other a girl of maybe eight or ten who was running as hard as she was able down a cross street. Well, sir, the two ran into one another naturally enough at the corner; and then came the horrible part of the thing; for the man trampled calmly over the child's body and left her screaming on the ground. It sounds nothing to hear, but it was hellish to see. It wasn't like a man; it was like some damned Juggernaut. I gave a view halloa, took to my heels, collared my gentleman, and brought him back to where there was already quite a group about the screaming child. He was perfectly cool and made no resistance, but gave me one look, so ugly that it brought out the sweat on me like running. The people who had turned out were the girl's own family; and pretty soon the doctor, for whom she had been sent, put in his appearance. Well, the child was not much the worse, more frightened, according to the Sawbones; and there you might have supposed would be an end to it. But there was one curious circumstance. I had taken a loathing to my gentleman at first sight. So had the child's family, which was only natural. But the doctor's case was what struck me. He was the usual cut and dry apothecary, of no particular age and colour, with a strong Edinburgh accent, and about as emotional as a bagpipe. Well, sir, he was like the rest of us; every time he looked at my prisoner, I saw that Sawbones turned sick and white with the desire to kill him. I knew what was in his mind, just as he knew what was in mine; and killing being out of the question, we did the next best. We told the man we could and would make such a scandal out of this, as should make his name stink from one end of London to the other. If he had any friends or any credit, we undertook that he should lose them. And all the time, as we were pitching it in red hot, we were keeping the women off him as best we could, for they were as wild as harpies. I never saw a circle of such hateful faces; and there was the man in the middle, with a kind of black, sneering coolness—frightened too, I could see that—but carrying it off, sir, really like Satan. 'If you choose to make capital out of this accident,' said he, 'I am naturally helpless. No gentleman but wishes to avoid a scene,' says he. 'Name your figure.' Well, we screwed him up to a hundred pounds for the child's family; he would have clearly liked to stick out; but there was something about the lot of us that meant mischief, and at last he struck. The next thing was to get the money; and where do you think he carried us but to that place with the door?—whipped out a key, went in, and presently came back with the matter of ten pounds in gold and a cheque for the balance on Coutt's, drawn payable to bearer, and signed with a name that I can't mention, though it's one of the points of my story, but it was a name at least very well known and often printed. The figure was stiff; but the signature was good for more than that, if it was only genuine. I took the liberty of pointing out to my gentleman that the whole business looked apocryphal; and that a man does not, in real life, walk into a cellar door at four in the morning and come out of it with another man's cheque for close upon a hundred pounds. But he was quite easy and sneering. 'Set your mind at rest,' says he; 'I will stay with you till the banks open, and cash the cheque myself.' So we all set off, the doctor, and the child's father, and our friend and myself, and passed the rest of the night in my chambers; and next day, when we had break-fasted, went in a body to the bank. I gave in the cheque myself, and said I had every reason to believe it was a forgery. Not a bit of it. The cheque was genuine."

"Tut-tut!" said Mr. Utterson.

"I see you feel as I do," said Mr. Enfield. "Yes, it's a bad story. For my man was a fellow that nobody could have to do with, a really damnable man; and the person that drew the cheque is the very pink of the proprie-ties, celebrated too, and (what makes it worse) one of your fellows who do what they call good. Black mail, I suppose; an honest man paying through the nose for some of the capers of his youth. Black Mail House is what I call that place with the door, in consequence. Though even that, you know, is far from explaining all," he added; and with the words fell into a vein of musing.

From this he was recalled by Mr. Utterson asking rather suddenly: "And you don't know if the drawer of the cheque lives there?"

"A likely place, isn't it?" returned Mr. Enfield. "But I happen to have noticed his address; he lives in some square or other."

"And you never asked about—the place with the door?" said Mr. Utter-son.

"No, sir: I had a delicacy," was the reply. "I feel very strongly about putting questions; it partakes too much of the style of the day of judg-ment. You start a question, and it's like starting a stone. You sit quietly on the top of a hill; and away the stone goes, starting others; and pres-ently some bland old bird (the last you would have thought of) is knocked on the head in his own back garden, and the family have to change their name. No, sir, I make it a rule of mine: the more it looks like Queer Street, the less I ask."

"A very good rule, too," said the lawyer.

"But I have studied the place for myself," continued Mr. Enfield. "It seems scarcely a house. There is no other door, and nobody goes in or out of that one, but, once in a great while, the gentleman of my adventure. There are three windows looking on the court on the first floor; none below; the windows are always shut, but they're clean. And then there is a chimney, which is generally smoking; so somebody must live there. And yet it's not so sure; for the buildings are so packed together about that court, that it's hard to say where one ends and another begins."

The pair walked on again for a while in silence; and then—"Enfield," said Mr. Utterson, "that's a good rule of yours."

"Yes, I think it is," returned Enfield.

"But for all that," continued the lawyer, "there's one point I want to ask: I want to ask the name of that man who walked over the child."

"Well," said Mr. Enfield, "I can't see what harm it would do. It was a man of the name of Hyde."

"Hm," said Mr. Utterson. "What sort of a man is he to see?"

"He is not easy to describe. There is something wrong with his appearance; something displeasing, something downright detestable. I never saw a man I so disliked, and yet I scarce know why. He must be deformed somewhere; he gives a strong feeling of deformity, although I couldn't specify the point. He's an extraordinary looking man, and yet I really can name nothing out of the way. No, sir; I can make no hand of it; I can't describe him. And it's not want of memory; for I declare I can see him this moment."

Mr. Utterson again walked some way in silence, and obviously under a weight of consideration. "You are sure he used a key?" he inquired at last.

"My dear sir . . ." began Enfield, surprised out of himself.

"Yes, I know," said Utterson; "I know it must seem strange. The fact is, if I do not ask you the name of the other party, it is because I know it already. You see, Richard, your tale has gone home. If you have been inexact in any point, you had better correct it."

"I think you might have warned me," returned the other, with a touch of sullenness. "But I have been pedantically exact, as you call it. The fellow had a key; and, what's more, he has it still. I saw him use it, not a week ago."

Mr. Utterson sighed deeply, but said never a word; and the young man presently resumed. "Here's another lesson to say nothing," said he. "I am ashamed of my long tongue. Let us make a bargain never to refer to this again."

"With all my heart," said the lawyer. "I shake hands on that, Richard."

Search for Mr. Hyde

That evening Mr. Utterson came home to his bachelor house in sombre spirits, and sat down to dinner without relish. It was his custom of a Sunday, when this meal was over, to sit close by the fire, a volume of some dry divinity on his reading desk, until the clock of the neighbouring church rang out the hour of twelve, when he would go soberly and gratefully to bed. On this night, however, as soon as the cloth was taken away, he took up a candle and went into his business room. There he opened his safe, took from the most private part of it a document endorsed on the envelope as Dr. Jekyll's Will, and sat down with a clouded brow to study its contents. The will was holograph; for Mr. Utterson, though he took charge of it now that it was made, had refused to lend the least assistance in the making of it; it provided not only that, in case of the decease of Henry Jekyll, M.D., D.C.L., LL.D., F.R.S., etc., all his possessions were to pass into the hands of his "friend and benefactor Edward Hyde"; but that in case of Dr. Jekyll's "disappearance or unexplained absence for any period exceeding three calendar months," the said Edward Hyde should step into the said Henry Jekyll's shoes without further delay, and free from any burthen or obligation, beyond the payment of a few small sums to the members of the doctor's household. This document had long been the lawyer's eyesore. It offended him both as a lawyer and as a lover of the sane and customary sides of life, to whom the fanciful was the immodest. And hitherto it was his ignorance of Mr. Hyde that had swelled his indignation; now, by a sudden turn, it was his knowledge. It was already bad enough when the name was but a name of which he could learn no more. It was worse when it began to be clothed upon with detestable attributes; and out of the shifting, insubstantial mists that had so long baffled his eye, there leaped up the sudden, definite presentment of a fiend.

"I thought it was madness," he said, as he replaced the obnoxious paper in the safe; "and now I begin to fear it is disgrace."

With that he blew out his candle, put on a great coat, and set forth in the direction of Cavendish Square, that citadel of medicine, where his friend, the great Dr. Lanyon, had his house and received his crowding patients. "If anyone knows, it will be Lanyon," he had thought.

The solemn butler knew and welcomed him; he was subjected to no stage of delay, but ushered direct from the door to the dining-room, where Dr. Lanyon sat alone over his wine. This was a hearty, healthy, dapper, red-faced gentleman, with a shock of hair prematurely white, and a boisterous and decided manner. At sight of Mr. Utterson, he sprang up from his chair and welcomed him with both hands. The geniality, as was the way of the man, was somewhat theatrical to the eye; but it reposed on genuine feeling. For these two were old friends, old mates both at school and college, both thorough respecters of themselves and of each other, and, what does not always follow, men who thoroughly enjoyed each other's company.

After a little rambling talk, the lawyer led up to the subject which so disagreeably preoccupied his mind.

"I suppose, Lanyon," said he, "you and I must be the two oldest friends that Henry Jekyll has?"

"I wish the friends were younger," chuckled Dr. Lanyon. "But I suppose we are. And what of that? I see little of him now."

"Indeed!" said Utterson. "I thought you had a bond of common interest."

"We had," was the reply. "But it is more than ten years since Henry Jekyll became too fanciful for me. He began to go wrong, wrong in mind; and though, of course, I continue to take an interest in him for old sake's sake as they say, I see and I have seen devilish little of the man. Such unscientific balderdash," added the doctor, flushing suddenly purple, "would have estranged Damon and Pythias."

This little spirit of temper was somewhat of a relief to Mr. Utterson. "They have only differed on some point of science," he thought; and being a man of no scientific passions (except in the matter of conveyancing) he even added: "It is nothing worse than that!" He gave his friend a few seconds to recover his composure, and then approached the question he had come to put.

"Did you ever come across a *protégé* of his—one Hyde?" he asked.

"Hyde?" repeated Lanyon. "No. Never heard of him. Since my time."

That was the amount of information that the lawyer carried back with him to the great, dark bed on which he tossed to and fro, until the small hours of the morning began to grow large. It was a night of little ease to his toiling mind, toiling in mere darkness and besieged by questions.

Six o'clock struck on the bells of the church that was so conveniently near to Mr. Utterson's dwelling, and still he was digging at the problem. Hitherto it had touched him on the intellectual side alone; but now his imagination was also engaged, or rather enslaved; and as he lay and tossed in the gross darkness of the night and the curtained room, Mr. Enfield's tale went by before his mind in a scroll of lighted pictures. He would be aware of the great field of lamps of a nocturnal city; then of the figure of a man walking swiftly; then of a child running from the doctor's; and then these met, and that human Juggernaut trod the child down and passed on regardless of her screams. Or else he would see a room in a rich house, where his friend lay asleep, dreaming and smiling at his dreams; and then the door of that room would be opened, the curtains of the bed plucked apart, the sleeper recalled, and, lo! there would stand by his side a figure to whom power was given, and even at that dead hour, he must rise and do its bidding. The figure in these two phases haunted the lawyer all night; and if at any time he dozed over, it was but to see it glide more stealthily through sleeping houses, or move the more swiftly and still the more swiftly, even to dizziness, through wider labyrinths of lamp-lighted city, and at every street corner crush a child and leave her screaming. And still the figure had no face by which he might know it; even in his dreams, it had no face, or one that baffled him and melted before his eyes; and thus it was that there sprang up and grew apace in the lawyer's mind a singularly strong, almost an inordinate, curiosity to behold the features of the real Mr. Hyde. If he could but once set eyes on him, he thought the mystery would lighten and perhaps roll altogether away, as was the habit of mysterious things when well examined. He might see a reason for his friend's strange preference or bondage (call it which you please), and even for the startling clauses of the will. And at least it would be a face worth seeing: the face of a man who was without bowels of mercy: a face which had but to show itself to raise up, in the mind of the unimpressionable Enfield, a spirit of enduring hatred.

From that time forward, Mr. Utterson began to haunt the door in the by-street of shops. In the morning before office hours, at noon when business was plenty and time scarce, at night under the face of the fogged city moon, by all lights and at all hours of solitude or concourse, the lawyer was to be found on his chosen post.

"If he be Mr. Hyde," he had thought, "I shall be Mr. Seek."

And at last his patience was rewarded. It was a fine dry night; frost in the air; the streets as clean as a ballroom floor; the lamps, unshaken by any wind, drawing a regular pattern of light and shadow. By ten o'clock, when the shops were closed, the by-street was very solitary, and, in spite of the low growl of London from all round, very silent. Small sounds carried far; domestic sounds out of the houses were clearly audible on either side of the roadway; and the rumor of the approach of any passenger preceded him by a long time. Mr. Utterson had been some minutes at his post when he was aware of an odd, light footstep drawing near. In the course of his nightly patrols he had long grown accustomed to the quaint effect with which the footfalls of a single person, while he is still a great way off, suddenly spring out distinct from the vast hum and clatter of the city. Yet his attention had never before been so sharply and decisively arrested; and it was with a strong, superstitious prevision of success that he withdrew into the entry of the court.

The steps drew swiftly nearer, and swelled out suddenly louder as they turned the end of the street. The lawyer, looking forth from the entry, could soon see what manner of man he had to deal with. He was small, and very plainly dressed; and the look of him, even at that distance, went somehow strongly against the watcher's inclination. But he made straight for the door, crossing the roadway to save time; and as he came, he drew a key from his pocket, like one approaching home.

Mr. Utterson stepped out and touched him on the shoulder as he passed. "Mr. Hyde, I think?"

Mr. Hyde shrank back with a hissing intake of the breath. But his fear was only momentary; and though he did not look the lawyer in the face, he answered coolly enough: "That is my name. What do you want?"

"I see you are going in," returned the lawyer. "I am an old friend of Dr. Jekyll's—Mr. Utterson, of Gaunt Street—you must have heard my name; and meeting you so conveniently, I thought you might admit me."

"You will not find Dr. Jekyll; he is from home," replied Mr. Hyde, blowing in the key. And then suddenly, but still without looking up, "How did you know me?" he asked.

"On your side," said Mr. Utterson, "will you do me a favour?"

"With pleasure," replied the other. "What shall it be?"

"Will you let me see your face?" asked the lawyer.

Mr. Hyde appeared to hesitate; and then, as if upon some sudden reflection, fronted about with an air of defiance; and the pair stared at each other pretty fixedly for a few seconds. "Now I shall know you again," said Mr. Utterson. "It may be useful."

"Yes," returned Mr. Hyde, "it is as well we have met; and *à propos*, you should have my address." And he gave a number of a street in Soho.

"Good God!" thought Mr. Utterson, "can he too have been thinking of the will?" But he kept his feelings to himself, and only grunted in acknowledgment of the address.

"And now," said the other, "how did you know me?"

"By description," was the reply.

"Whose description?"

"We have common friends," said Mr. Utterson.

"Common friends!" echoed Mr. Hyde, a little hoarsely. "Who are they?"

"Jekyll, for instance," said the lawyer.

"He never told you," cried Mr. Hyde, with a flush of anger. "I did not think you would have lied."

"Come," said Mr. Utterson, "that is not fitting language."

The other snarled aloud into a savage laugh; and the next moment, with extraordinary quickness, he had unlocked the door and disappeared into the house.

The lawyer stood awhile when Mr. Hyde had left him, the picture of disquietude. Then he began slowly to mount the street, pausing every step or two, and putting his hand to his brow like a man in mental perplexity. The problem he was thus debating as he walked was one of a class that is rarely solved. Mr. Hyde was pale and dwarfish; he gave an impression of deformity without any nameable malformation, he had a displeasing smile, he had borne himself to the lawyer with a sort of murderous mixture of timidity and boldness, and he spoke with a husky, whispering and somewhat broken voice—all these were points against him; but not all of these together could explain the hitherto unknown disgust, loathing and fear with which Mr. Utterson regarded him. "There must be something else," said the perplexed gentleman. "There *is* something more, if I could find a name for it. God bless me, the man seems hardly human! Something troglodytic, shall we say? or can it be the old story of Dr. Fell? or is it the mere radiance of a foul soul that thus transpires through, and transfigures, its clay continent? The last, I think; for, O my poor old Harry Jekyll, if ever I read Satan's signature upon a face, it is on that of your new friend."

Round the corner from the by-street there was a square of ancient, handsome houses, now for the most part decayed from their high estate, and let in flats and chambers to all sorts and conditions of men: map-engravers, architects, shady lawyers, and the agents of obscure enterprises. One house, however, second from the corner, was still occupied entire; and at the door of this, which bore a great air of wealth and comfort, though it was now plunged in darkness except for the fan-light, Mr. Utterson stopped and knocked. A well-dressed, elderly servant opened the door.

"Is Dr. Jekyll at home, Poole?" asked the lawyer.

"I will see, Mr. Utterson," said Poole, admitting the visitor, as he spoke, into a large, low-roofed, comfortable hall, paved with flags, warmed (after the fashion of a country house) by a bright, open fire, and furnished with costly cabinets of oak. "Will you wait here by the fire, sir? or shall I give you a light in the dining-room?"

"Here, thank you," said the lawyer; and he drew near and leaned on the tall fender. This hall, in which he was now left alone, was a pet fancy of his friend the doctor's; and Utterson himself was wont to speak of it as the pleasantest room in London. But to-night there was a shudder in his blood; the face of Hyde sat heavy on his memory; he felt (what was rare with him) a nausea and distaste of life; and in the gloom of his spirits, he seemed to read a menace in the flickering of the firelight on the polished cabinets and the uneasy starting of the shadow on the roof. He was ashamed of his relief, when Poole presently returned to announce that Dr. Jekyll was gone out.

"I saw Mr. Hyde go in by the old dissecting room door, Poole," he said. "Is that right, when Dr. Jekyll is from home?"

"Quite right, Mr. Utterson, sir," replied the servant. "Mr. Hyde has a key."

"Your master seems to repose a great deal of trust in that young man, Poole," resumed the other, musingly.

"Yes, sir, he do, indeed," said Poole. "We have all orders to obey him."

"I do not think I ever met Mr. Hyde?" asked Utterson.

"O dear no, sir. He never *dines* here," replied the butler. "Indeed, we see very little of him on this side of the house; he mostly comes and goes by the laboratory."

"Well, good-night, Poole."

"Good-night, Mr. Utterson."

And the lawyer set out homeward with a very heavy heart. "Poor Harry Jekyll," he thought, "my mind misgives me he is in deep waters! He was wild when he was young; a long while ago, to be sure; but in the law of God, there is no statute of limitations. Ah, it must be that; the ghost of some old sin, the cancer of some concealed disgrace; punishment coming, *pede claudo*, years after memory has forgotten and self-love condoned the fault." And the lawyer, scared by the thought, brooded awhile on his own past, groping in all the corners of memory, lest by chance some Jack-in-the-Box of an old iniquity should leap to light there. His past was fairly blameless; few men could read the rolls of their life with less apprehension; yet he was humbled to the dust by the many ill things he had done, and raised up again into a sober and fearful gratitude by the many that he had come so near to doing, yet avoided. And then by a return on his former subject, he conceived a spark of hope. "This Master Hyde, if he were studied," thought he, "must have secrets of his own: black secrets, by the look of him; secrets compared to which poor Jekyll's worst would be like sunshine. Things cannot continue as they are. It turns me cold to think of this creature stealing like a thief to Harry's bedside; poor Harry, what a wakening! And the danger of it! for if this Hyde suspects the existence of the will, he may grow impatient to inherit. Ah, I must put my shoulder to the wheel—if Jekyll will but let me," he added, "if Jekyll will only let me." For once more he saw before his mind's eye, as clear as a transparency, the strange clauses of the will.

Dr. Jekyll Was Quite at Ease

A fortnight later, by excellent good fortune, the doctor gave one of his pleasant dinners to some five or six old cronies, all intelligent reputable men, and all judges of good wine; and Mr. Utterson so contrived that he remained behind after the others had departed. This was no new arrangement, but a thing that had befallen many scores of times. Where Utterson was liked, he was liked well. Hosts loved to detain the dry lawyer, when the light-hearted and the loose-tongued had already their foot on the threshold; they liked to sit awhile in his unobtrusive company, practising for solitude, sobering their minds in the man's rich silence, after the expense and strain of gaiety. To this rule, Dr. Jekyll was no exception; and as he now sat on the opposite side of the fire—a large, well-made, smooth-faced man of fifty, with something of a slyish cast perhaps, but every mark of capacity and kindness—you could see by his looks that he cherished for Mr. Utterson a sincere and warm affection.

"I have been wanting to speak to you, Jekyll," began the latter. "You know that will of yours?"

A close observer might have gathered that the topic was distasteful; but the doctor carried it off gaily. "My poor Utterson," said he, "you are unfortunate in such a client. I never saw a man so distressed as you were by my will; unless it were that hide-bound pedant, Lanyon, at what he called my scientific heresies. O, I know he's a good fellow—you needn't frown—an excellent fellow, and I always mean to see more of him; but a hide-bound pedant for all that; an ignorant blatant pedant. I was never more disappointed in any man than Lanyon."

"You know I never approved of it," pursued Utterson, ruthlessly disregarding the fresh topic.

"My will? Yes, certainly, I know that," said the doctor, a trifle sharply. "You have told me so."

"Well, I tell you so again," continued the lawyer. "I have been learning something of young Hyde."

The large handsome face of Dr. Jekyll grew pale to the very lips, and there came a blackness about his eyes. "I do not care to hear more," said he. "This is a matter I thought we had agreed to drop."

"What I heard was abominable," said Utterson.

"It can make no change. You do not understand my position," returned the doctor, with a certain incoherency of manner. "I am painfully situated, Utterson; my position is a very strange one—a very strange one. It is one of those affairs that cannot be mended by talking."

"Jekyll," said Utterson, "you know me: I am a man to be trusted. Make a clean breast of this in confidence; and I make no doubt I can get you out of it."

"My good Utterson," said the doctor, "this is very good of you, this is downright good of you, and I cannot find words to thank you in. I believe you fully; I would trust you before any man alive, ay, before myself, if I could make the choice; but indeed it isn't what you fancy; it is not so bad as that; and just to put your good heart at rest, I will tell you one thing: the moment I choose, I can be rid of Mr. Hyde. I give you my hand upon that; and I thank you again and again; and I will just add one little word, Utterson, that I'm sure you'll take in good part: this is a private matter, and I beg of you to let it sleep."

Utterson reflected a little, looking in the fire.

"I have no doubt you are perfectly right," he said at last, getting to his feet.

"Well, but since we have touched upon this business, and for the last time I hope," continued the doctor, "there is one point I should like you to understand. I have really a very great interest in poor Hyde. I know you have seen him; he told me so; and I fear he was rude. But I do sincerely take a great, a very great interest in that young man; and if I am taken away, Utterson, I wish you to promise me that you will bear with him and get his rights for him. I think you would, if you knew all; and it would be a weight off my mind if you would promise."

"I can't pretend that I shall ever like him," said the lawyer.

"I don't ask that," pleaded Jekyll, laying his hand upon the other's arm; "I only ask for justice; I only ask you to help him for my sake, when I am no longer here."

Utterson heaved an irrepressible sigh. "Well," said he, "I promise."

The Carew Murder Case

Nearly a year later, in the month of October, 18—, London was startled by a crime of singular ferocity, and rendered all the more notable by the high position of the victim. The details were few and startling. A maid-servant living alone in a house not far from the river, had gone upstairs to bed about eleven. Although a fog rolled over the city in the small hours, the early part of the night was cloudless, and the lane, which the maid's window overlooked, was brilliantly lit by the full moon. It seems she was romantically given; for she sat down upon her box, which stood immediately under the window, and fell into a dream of musing. Never (she used to say, with streaming tears, when she narrated that experience), never had she felt more at peace with all men or thought more kindly of the world. And as she so sat she became aware of an aged and beautiful gentleman with white hair, drawing near along the lane; and advancing to meet him, another and very small gentleman, to whom at first she paid less attention. When they had come within speech (which was just under the maid's eyes) the older man bowed and accosted the other with a very pretty manner of politeness. It did not seem as if the subject of his address were of great importance; indeed, from his pointing, it sometimes appeared as if he were only inquiring his way; but the moon shone on his face as he spoke, and the girl was pleased to watch it, it seemed to breathe such an innocent and old-world kindness of disposition, yet with something high too, as of a well-founded self-content. Presently her eye wandered to the other, and she was surprised to recognize in him a certain Mr. Hyde, who had once visited her master, and for whom she had conceived a dislike. He had in his hand a heavy cane, with which he was trifling; but he answered never a word, and seemed to listen with an ill-contained impatience. And then all of a sudden he broke out in a great flame of anger, stamping with his foot, brandishing the cane, and carrying on (as the maid described it) like a madman. The old gentleman took a step back, with the air of one very much surprised and a trifle hurt; and at that Mr. Hyde broke out of all bounds, and clubbed him to the earth. And next moment, with ape-like fury, he was trampling his victim under foot, and hailing down a storm of blows, under which the bones were audibly shattered and the body jumped upon the roadway. At the horror of these sights and sounds, the maid fainted.

It was two o'clock when she came to herself and called for the police. The murderer was gone long ago; but there lay his victim in the middle of the lane, incredibly mangled. The stick with which the deed had been done, although it was of some rare and very tough and heavy wood, had broken in the middle under the stress of this insensate cruelty; and one splintered half had rolled in the neighbouring gutter—the other, without doubt, had been carried away by the murderer. A purse and a gold watch were found upon the victim; but no cards or papers, except a sealed and stamped envelope, which he had been probably carrying to the post, and which bore the name and address of Mr. Utterson.

This was brought to the lawyer the next morning before he was out of bed; and he had no sooner seen it and been told the circumstances, than he shot out a solemn lip. "I shall say nothing till I have seen the body," said he; "this may be very serious. Have the kindness to wait while I dress." And with the same grave countenance he hurried through his breakfast and drove to the police station, whither the body had been carried. As soon as he came into the cell, he nodded.

"Yes," said he, "I recognize him. I am sorry to say that this is Sir Danvers Carew."

"Good God, sir," exclaimed the officer, "is it possible?" And the next moment his eye lighted up with professional ambition. "This will make a deal of noise," he said. "And perhaps you can help us to the man." And he briefly narrated what the maid had seen, and showed the broken stick.

Mr. Utterson had already quailed at the name of Hyde; but when the stick was laid before him, he could doubt no longer: broken and battered as it was, he recognized it for one that he had himself presented many years before to Henry Jekyll.

"Is this Mr. Hyde a person of small stature?" he inquired.

"Particularly small and particularly wicked-looking, is what the maid calls him," said the officer.

Mr. Utterson reflected; and then, raising his head, "If you will come with me in my cab," he said, "I think I can take you to his house."

It was by this time about nine in the morning, and the first fog of the season. A great chocolate-coloured pall lowered over heaven, but the wind was continually charging and routing these embattled vapours; so that as the cab crawled from street to street, Mr. Utterson beheld a marvellous number of degrees and hues of twilight; for here it would be dark like the back-end of evening; and there would be a glow of a rich, lurid brown, like the light of some strange conflagration; and here, for a moment, the fog would be quite broken up, and a haggard shaft of daylight would glance in between the swirling wreaths. The dismal quarter of Soho seen under these changing glimpses, with its muddy ways, and slatternly passengers, and its lamps, which had never been extinguished or had been kindled afresh to combat this mournful reinvasion of darkness, seemed, in the lawyer's eyes, like a district of some city in a nightmare. The thoughts of his mind, besides, were of the gloomiest dye; and when he glanced at the companion of his drive, he was conscious of some touch of that terror of the law and the law's officers, which may at times assail the most honest.

As the cab drew up before the address indicated, the fog lifted a little and showed him a dingy street, a gin palace, a low French eating-house, a shop for the retail of penny numbers and twopenny salads, many ragged children huddled in the doorways, and many women of many different nationalities passing out, key in hand, to have a morning glass;

and the next moment the fog settled down again upon that part, as brown as umber, and cut him off from his blackguardly surroundings. This was the home of Henry Jekyll's favourite; of a man who was heir to a quarter of a million sterling.

An ivory-faced and silvery-haired old woman opened the door. She had an evil face, smoothed by hypocrisy; but her manners were excellent. Yes, she said, this was Mr. Hyde's, but he was not at home; he had been in that night very late, but had gone away again in less than an hour: there was nothing strange in that; his habits were very irregular, and he was often absent; for instance, it was nearly two months since she had seen him till yesterday.

"Very well, then, we wish to see his rooms," said the lawyer; and when the woman began to declare it was impossible, "I had better tell you who this person is," he added. "This is Inspector Newcomen, of Scotland Yard."

A flash of odious joy appeared upon the woman's face. "Ah!" said she, "he is in trouble! What has he done?"

Mr. Utterson and the inspector exchanged glances. "He don't seem a very popular character," observed the latter. "And now, my good woman, just let me and this gentleman have a look about us."

In the whole extent of the house, which but for the old woman remained otherwise empty, Mr. Hyde had only used a couple of rooms; but these were furnished with luxury and good taste. A closet was filled with wine; the plate was of silver, the napery elegant; a good picture hung upon the walls, a gift (as Utterson supposed) from Henry Jekyll, who was much of a connoisseur; and the carpets were of many piles and agreeable in colour. At this moment, however, the rooms bore every mark of having been recently and hurriedly ransacked; clothes lay about the floor, with their pockets inside out; lockfast drawers stood open; and on the hearth there lay a pile of grey ashes, as though many papers had been burned. From these embers the inspector disinterred the butt end of a green cheque book, which had resisted the action of the fire; the other half of the stick was found behind the door; and as this clinched his suspicions, the officer declared himself delighted. A visit to the bank, where several thousand pounds were found to be lying to the murderer's credit, completed his gratification.

"You may depend upon it, sir," he told Mr. Utterson: "I have him in my hand. He must have lost his head, or he never would have left the stick, or, above all, burned the cheque book. Why, money's life to the man. We have nothing to do but wait for him at the bank, and get out the handbills."

This last, however, was not so easy of accomplishment; for Mr. Hyde had numbered few familiars—even the master of the servant-maid had only seen him twice; his family could nowhere be traced; he had never been photographed; and the few who could describe him differed widely, as common observers will. Only on one point were they agreed; and that was the haunting sense of unexpressed deformity with which the fugitive impressed his beholders.

Incident of the Letter

It was late in the afternoon, when Mr. Utterson found his way to Dr. Jekyll's door, where he was at once admitted by Poole, and carried down by the kitchen offices and across a yard which had once been a garden, to the building which was indifferently known as the laboratory or the dissecting rooms. The doctor had bought the house from the heirs of a celebrated surgeon; and his own tastes being rather chemical than anatomical, had changed the destination of the block at the bottom of the garden. It was the first time that the lawyer had been received in that part of his friend's quarters; and he eyed the dingy windowless structure with curiosity, and gazed round with a distasteful sense of strangeness as he crossed the theatre, once crowded with eager students and now lying gaunt and silent, the tables laden with chemical apparatus, the floor strewn with crates and littered with packing straw, and the light falling dimly through the foggy cupola. At the further end, a flight of stairs mounted to a door covered with red baize; and through this, Mr. Utterson was at last received into the doctor's cabinet. It was a large room, fitted round with glass presses, furnished, among other things, with a cheval-glass and a business table, and looking out upon the court by three dusty windows barred with iron. The fire burned in the grate; a lamp was set lighted on the chimney shelf, for even in the houses the fog began to lie thickly; and there, close up to the warmth, sat Dr. Jekyll, looking deadly sick. He did not rise to meet his visitor, but held out a cold hand, and bade him welcome in a changed voice.

"And now," said Mr. Utterson, as soon as Poole had left them, "you have heard the news?"

The doctor shuddered. "They were crying it in the square," he said. "I heard them in my dining-room."

"One word," said the lawyer. "Carew was my client, but so are you; and I want to know what I am doing. You have not been mad enough to hide this fellow?"

"Utterson, I swear to God," cried the doctor, "I swear to God I will never set eyes on him again. I bind my honour to you that I am done with him in this world. It is all at an end. And indeed he does not want my help; you do not know him as I do; he is safe, he is quite safe; mark my words, he will never more be heard of."

The lawyer listened gloomily; he did not like his friend's feverish manner. "You seem pretty sure of him," said he; "and for your sake, I hope you may be right. If it came to a trial, your name might appear."

"I am quite sure of him," replied Jekyll; "I have grounds for certainty that I cannot share with any one. But there is one thing on which you may advise me. I have—I have received a letter; and I am at a loss whether I should show it to the police. I should like to leave it in your hands, Utterson; you would judge wisely, I am sure; I have so great a trust in you."

"You fear, I suppose, that it might lead to his detection?" asked the lawyer.

"No," said the other. "I cannot say that I care what becomes of Hyde; I am quite done with him. I was thinking of my own character, which this hateful business has rather exposed."

Utterson ruminated awhile; he was surprised at his friend's selfishness, and yet relieved by it. "Well," said he, at last, "let me see the letter."

The letter was written in an odd, upright hand, and signed "Edward Hyde"; and it signified, briefly enough, that the writer's benefactor, Dr. Jekyll, whom he had long so unworthily repaid for a thousand generosities, need labour under no alarm for his safety, as he had means of escape on which he placed a sure dependence. The lawyer liked this letter well enough: it put a better colour on the intimacy than he had looked for; and he blamed himself for some of his past suspicions.

"Have you the envelope?" he asked.

"I burned it," replied Jekyll, "before I thought what I was about. But it bore no postmark. The note was handed in."

"Shall I keep this and sleep upon it?" asked Utterson.

"I wish you to judge for me entirely," was the reply. "I have lost confidence in myself."

"Well, I shall consider," returned the lawyer. "And now one word more: it was Hyde who dictated the terms in your will about that disappearance?"

The doctor seemed seized with a qualm of faintness; he shut his mouth tight and nodded.

"I knew it," said Utterson. "He meant to murder you. You have had a fine escape."

"I have had what is far more to the purpose," returned the doctor solemnly: "I have had a lesson—O God, Utterson, what a lesson I have had!" And he covered his face for a moment with his hands.

On his way out, the lawyer stopped and had a word or two with Poole. "By the by," said he, "there was a letter handed in to-day: what was the messenger like?" But Poole was positive nothing had come except by post; "and only circulars by that," he added.

This news sent off the visitor with his fears renewed. Plainly the letter had come by the laboratory door; possibly, indeed, it had been written in the cabinet; and, if that were so, it must be differently judged, and handled with the more caution. The news-boys, as he went, were crying themselves hoarse along the footways: "Special edition. Shocking murder of an M.P." That was the funeral oration of one friend and client; and he could not help a certain apprehension lest the good name of another should be sucked down in the eddy of the scandal. It was, at least, a ticklish decision that he had to make; and, self-reliant as he was by habit, he began to cherish a longing for advice. It was not to be had directly; but perhaps, he thought, it might be fished for.

Presently after, he sat on one side of his own hearth, with Mr. Guest, his head clerk, upon the other, and midway between, at a nicely calculated distance from the fire, a bottle of a particular old wine that had long dwelt unsunned in the foundations of his house. The fog still slept on the wing above the drowned city, where the lamps glimmered like carbuncles; and through the muffle and smother of these fallen clouds, the procession of the town's life was still rolling in through the great arteries with a sound as of a mighty wind. But the room was gay with firelight. In the bottle the acids were long ago resolved; the imperial dye had softened with time, as the colour grows richer in stained windows; and the glow of hot autumn afternoons on hillside vineyards was ready to be set free and to disperse the fogs of London. Insensibly the lawyer melted. There was no man from whom he kept fewer secrets than Mr. Guest; and he was not always sure that he kept as many as he meant. Guest had often been on business to the doctor's, he knew Poole; he could scarce have failed to hear of Mr. Hyde's familiarity about the house; he might draw conclusions: was it not as well, then, that he should see a letter which put that mystery to rights? and, above all, since Guest, being a great student and critic of handwriting, would consider the step natural and obliging? The clerk, besides, was a man of counsel; he would scarce read so strange a document without dropping a remark; and by that remark Mr. Utterson might shape his future course.

"This is a sad business about Sir Danvers," he said.

"Yes, sir, indeed. It has elicited a great deal of public feeling," returned Guest. "The man, of course, was mad."

"I should like to hear your views on that," replied Utterson. "I have a document here in his handwriting; it is between ourselves, for I scarce know what to do about it; it is an ugly business at the best. But there it is; quite in your way: a murderer's autograph."

Guest's eyes brightened, and he sat down at once and studied it with passion. "No, sir," he said; "not mad; but it is an odd hand."

"And by all accounts a very odd writer," added the lawyer.

Just then the servant entered with a note.

"Is that from Dr. Jekyll, sir?" inquired the clerk. "I thought I knew the writing. Anything private, Mr. Utterson?"

"Only an invitation to dinner. Why? Do you want to see it?"

"One moment. I thank you, sir;" and the clerk laid the two sheets of paper alongside and sedulously compared their contents. "Thank you, sir," he said at last, returning both; "it's a very interesting autograph."

There was a pause, during which Mr. Utterson struggled with himself. "Why did you compare them, Guest?" he inquired suddenly.

"Well, sir," returned the clerk, "there's a rather singular resemblance; the two hands are in many points identical: only differently sloped."

"Rather quaint," said Utterson.

"It is, as you say, rather quaint," returned Guest.

"I wouldn't speak of this note, you know," said the master.

"No, sir," said the clerk. "I understand."

But no sooner was Mr. Utterson alone that night, than he locked the note into his safe, where it reposed from that time forward. "What!" he thought. "Henry Jekyll forge for a murderer!" And his blood ran cold in his veins.

Remarkable Incident of Dr. Lanyon

Time ran on; thousands of pounds were offered in reward, for the death of Sir Danvers was resented as a public injury; but Mr. Hyde had disappeared out of the ken of the police as though he had never existed. Much of his past was unearthed, indeed, and all disreputable: tales came out of the man's cruelty, at once so callous and violent, of his vile life, of his strange associates, of the hatred that seemed to have surrounded his career; but of his present whereabouts, not a whisper. From the time he had left the house in Soho on the morning of the murder, he was simply blotted out; and gradually, as time drew on, Mr. Utterson began to recover from the hotness of his alarm, and to grow more at quiet with himself. The death of Sir Danvers was, to his way of thinking, more than paid for by the disappearance of Mr. Hyde. Now that that evil influence had been withdrawn, a new life began for Dr. Jekyll. He came out of his seclusion, renewed relations with his friends, became once more their familiar guest and entertainer; and whilst he had always been known for charities, he was now no less distinguished for religion. He was busy, he was much in the open air, he did good; his face seemed to open and brighten, as if with an inward consciousness of service; and for more than two months, the doctor was at peace.

On the 8th of January Utterson had dined at the doctor's with a small party; Lanyon had been there; and the face of the host had looked from one to the other as in the old days when the trio were inseparable friends. On the 12th, and again on the 14th, the door was shut against the lawyer. "The doctor was confined to the house," Poole said, "and saw no one." On the 15th he tried again, and was again refused; and having now been used for the last two months to see his friend almost daily, he found this return of solitude to weigh upon his spirits. The fifth night, he had in Guest to dine with him; and the sixth, he betook himself to Dr. Lanyon's.

There at least he was not denied admittance; but when he came in, he was shocked at the change which had taken place in the doctor's appearance. He had his death-warrant written legibly upon his face. The rosy man had grown pale; his flesh had fallen away; he was visibly balder and older; and yet it was not so much these tokens of a swift physical decay that arrested the lawyer's notice, as a look in the eye and quality of manner that seemed to testify to some deep-seated terror of the mind. It was unlikely that the doctor should fear death; and yet that was what Utterson was tempted to suspect. "Yes," he thought; "he is a doctor, he must know his own state and that his days are counted; and the knowledge is more than he can bear." And yet when Utterson remarked on his ill looks, it was with an air of great firmness that Lanyon declared himself a doomed man.

"I have had a shock," he said, "and I shall never recover. It is a question of weeks. Well, life has been pleasant; I liked it; yes, sir, I used to like it. I sometimes think if we knew all, we should be more glad to get away."

"Jekyll is ill, too," observed Utterson. "Have you seen him?"

But Lanyon's face changed, and he held up a trembling hand. "I wish to see or hear no more of Dr. Jekyll," he said, in a loud, unsteady voice. "I am quite done with that person; and I beg that you will spare me any allusion to one whom I regard as dead."

"Tut, tut!" said Mr. Utterson; and then, after a considerable pause, "Can't I do anything?" he inquired. "We are three very old friends, Lanyon; we shall not live to make others."

"Nothing can be done," returned Lanyon: "ask himself."

"He will not see me," said the lawyer.

"I am not surprised at that," was the reply. "Some day, Utterson, after I am dead, you may perhaps come to learn the right and wrong of this. I cannot tell you. And in the meantime, if you can sit and talk with me of other things, for God's sake, stay and do so; but if you cannot keep clear of this accursed topic, then in God's name, go, for I cannot bear it."

As soon as he got home, Utterson sat down and wrote to Jekyll, complaining of his exclusion from the house, and asking the cause of this unhappy break with Lanyon; and the next day brought him a long answer, often very pathetically worded, and sometimes darkly mysterious in drift. The quarrel with Lanyon was incurable. "I do not blame our old friend," Jekyll wrote, "but I share his view that we must never meet. I mean from henceforth to lead a life of extreme seclusion; you must not be surprised, nor must you doubt my friendship, if my door is often shut even to you. You must suffer me to go my own dark way. I have brought on myself a punishment and a danger that I cannot name. If I am the chief of sinners, I am the chief of sufferers also. I could not think that this earth contained a place for sufferings and terrors so unmanning; and you can do but one thing, Utterson, to lighten this destiny, and that is to respect my silence." Utterson was amazed; the dark influence of Hyde had been withdrawn, the doctor had returned to his old tasks and amities; a week ago, the prospect had smiled with every promise of a cheerful and an honoured age; and now in a moment, friendship and peace of mind and the whole tenor of his life were wrecked. So great and unprepared a change pointed to madness; but in view of Lanyon's manner and words, there must lie for it some deeper ground.

A week afterwards Dr. Lanyon took to his bed, and in something less than a fortnight he was dead. The night after the funeral, at which he had been sadly affected, Utterson locked the door of his business room, and sitting there by the light of a melancholy candle, drew out and set before him an envelope addressed by the hand and sealed with the seal of his dead friend. "PRIVATE: for the hands of J. G. Utterson ALONE, and in case of his predecease *to be destroyed unread,*" so it was emphatically superscribed; and the lawyer dreaded to behold the contents. "I have buried one friend to-day," he thought: "what if this should cost me another?" And then he condemned the fear as a disloyalty, and broke the seal. Within there was another enclosure, likewise sealed, and marked upon the cover as "not to be opened till the death or disappearance of Dr. Henry Jekyll." Utterson could not trust his eyes. Yes, it was disappearance; here again, as in the mad will, which he had long ago restored to its author, here again were the idea of a disappearance and the name of Henry Jekyll bracketed. But in the will, that idea had sprung from the sinister suggestion of the man Hyde; it was set there with a purpose all too plain and horrible. Written by the hand of Lanyon, what should it mean? A great curiosity came to the trustee, to disregard the prohibition, and dive at once to the bottom of these mysteries; but professional honour and faith to his dead friend were stringent obligations; and the packet slept in the inmost corner of his private safe.

It is one thing to mortify curiosity, another to conquer it; and it may be doubted if, from that day forth, Utterson desired the society of his surviving friend with the same eagerness. He thought of him kindly; but his thoughts were disquieted and fearful. He went to call, indeed; but he was perhaps relieved to be denied admittance; perhaps, in his heart, he preferred to speak with Poole upon the doorstep, and surrounded by the air and sounds of the open city, rather than to be admitted into that house of voluntary bondage, and to sit and speak with its inscrutable recluse. Poole had, indeed, no very pleasant news to communicate. The doctor, it appeared, now more than ever confined himself to the cabinet over the laboratory, where he would sometimes even sleep: he was out of spirits, he had grown very silent, he did not read; it seemed as if he had something on his mind. Utterson became so used to the unvarying character of these reports, that he fell off little by little in the frequency of his visits.

Incident at the Window

It chanced on Sunday, when Mr. Utterson was on his usual walk with Mr. Enfield, that their way lay once again through the by-street; and that when they came in front of the door, both stopped to gaze on it.

"Well," said Enfield, "that story's at an end, at least. We shall never see more of Mr. Hyde."

"I hope not," said Utterson. "Did I ever tell you that I once saw him, and shared your feeling of repulsion?"

"It was impossible to do the one without the other," returned Enfield. "And, by the way, what an ass you must have thought me, not to know that this was a back way to Dr. Jekyll's! It was partly your own fault that I found it out, even when I did."

"So you found it out, did you?" said Utterson. "But if that be so, we may step into the court and take a look at the windows. To tell you the truth, I am uneasy about poor Jekyll; and even outside, I feel as if the presence of a friend might do him good."

The court was very cool and a little damp, and full of premature twilight, although the sky, high up overhead, was still bright with sunset. The middle one of the three windows was half way open; and sitting close beside it, taking the air with an infinite sadness of mien, like some disconsolate prisoner, Utterson saw Dr. Jekyll.

"What! Jekyll!" he cried. "I trust you are better."

"I am very low, Utterson," replied the doctor drearily; "very low. It will not last long, thank God."

"You stay too much indoors," said the lawyer. "You should be out, whipping up the circulation, like Mr. Enfield and me. (This is my cousin —Mr. Enfield—Dr. Jekyll.) Come now; get your hat, and take a quick turn with us."

"You are very good," sighed the other. "I should like to very much; but no, no, no; it is quite impossible; I dare not. But indeed, Utterson, I am very glad to see you; this is really a great pleasure. I would ask you and Mr. Enfield up, but the place is really not fit."

"Why then," said the lawyer, good-naturedly, "the best thing we can do is to stay down here, and speak with you from where we are."

"That is just what I was about to venture to propose," returned the doctor, with a smile. But the words were hardly uttered, before the smile was struck out of his face and succeeded by an expression of such abject terror and despair, as froze the very blood of the two gentlemen below. They saw it but for a glimpse, for the window was instantly thrust down; but that glimpse had been sufficient, and they turned and left the court without a word. In silence, too, they traversed the by-street; and it was not until they had come into a neighbouring thoroughfare, where even upon a Sunday there were still some stirrings of life, that Mr. Utterson at last turned and looked at his companion. They were both pale; and there was an answering horror in their eyes.

"God forgive us! God forgive us!" said Mr. Utterson.

But Mr. Enfield only nodded his head very seriously, and walked on once more in silence.

The Last Night

Mr. Utterson was sitting by his fireside one evening after dinner, when he was surprised to receive a visit from Poole.

"Bless me, Poole, what brings you here?" he cried; and then, taking a second look at him, "What ails you?" he added; "is the doctor ill?"

"Mr. Utterson," said the man, "there is something wrong."

"Take a seat, and here is a glass of wine for you," said the lawyer. "Now, take your time, and tell me plainly what you want."

"You know the doctor's ways, sir," replied Poole, "and how he shuts himself up. Well, he's shut up again in the cabinet; and I don't like it, sir —I wish I may die if I like it. Mr. Utterson, sir, I'm afraid."

"Now, my good man," said the lawyer, "be explicit. What are you afraid of?"

"I've been afraid for about a week," returned Poole, doggedly disregarding the question; "and I can bear it no more."

The man's appearance amply bore out his words; his manner was altered for the worse: and except for the moment when he had first announced his terror, he had not once looked the lawyer in the face. Even now, he sat with the glass of wine untasted on his knee, and his eyes directed to a corner of the floor. "I can bear it no more," he repeated.

"Come," said the lawyer, "I see you have some good reason, Poole; I see there is something seriously amiss. Try to tell me what it is."

"I think there's been foul play," said Poole, hoarsely.

"Foul play!" cried the lawyer, a good deal frightened, and rather inclined to be irritated in consequence. "What foul play? What does the man mean?"

"I daren't say, sir," was the answer; "but will you come along with me and see for yourself?"

Mr. Utterson's only answer was to rise and get his hat and great coat; but he observed with wonder the greatness of the relief that appeared upon the butler's face, and perhaps with no less, that the wine was still untasted when he set it down to follow.

It was a wild, cold, seasonable night of March, with a pale moon, lying on her back as though the wind had tilted her, and a flying wrack of the most diaphanous and lawny texture. The wind made talking difficult, and flecked the blood into the face. It seemed to have swept the streets unusually bare of passengers, besides; for Mr. Utterson thought he had never seen that part of London so deserted. He could have wished it otherwise; never in his life had he been conscious of so sharp a wish to see and touch his fellow-creatures; for, struggle as he might, there was borne in upon his mind a crushing anticipation of calamity. The square, when they got there, was all full of wind and dust, and the thin trees in the garden were lashing themselves along the railing. Poole, who had kept all the way a pace or two ahead, now pulled up in the middle of the pavement, and in spite of the biting weather, took off his hat and mopped his brow with a red pocket-handkerchief. But for all the hurry of his coming, these were not the dews of exertion that he wiped away, but the moisture of some strangling anguish; for his face was white, and his voice, when he spoke, harsh and broken.

"Well, sir," he said, "here we are, and God grant there be nothing wrong."

"Amen, Poole," said the lawyer.

Thereupon the servant knocked in a very guarded manner; the door was opened on the chain; and a voice asked from within, "Is that you, Poole?"

"It's all right," said Poole. "Open the door."

The hall, when they entered it, was brightly lighted up; the fire was built high; and about the hearth the whole of the servants, men and women, stood huddled together like a flock of sheep. At the sight of Mr. Utterson, the housemaid broke into hysterical whimpering; and the cook, crying out, "Bless God! it's Mr. Utterson," ran forward as if to take him in her arms.

"What, what? Are you all here?" said the lawyer, peevishly. "Very irregular, very unseemly; your master would be far from pleased."

"They're all afraid," said Poole.

Blank silence followed, no one protesting; only the maid lifted up her voice, and now wept loudly.

"Hold your tongue!" Poole said to her, with a ferocity of accent that testified to his own jangled nerves; and indeed when the girl had so suddenly raised the note of her lamentation, they had all started and turned towards the inner door with faces of dreadful expectation. "And now," continued the butler, addressing the knife-boy, "reach me a candle, and we'll get this through hands at once." And then he begged Mr. Utterson to follow him, and led the way to the back garden.

"Now, sir," said he, "you come as gently as you can. I want you to hear, and I don't want you to be heard. And see here, sir, if by any chance he was to ask you in, don't go."

Mr. Utterson's nerves, at this unlooked-for termination, gave a jerk that nearly threw him from his balance; but he re-collected his courage, and followed the butler into the laboratory building and through the surgical theatre, with its lumber of crates and bottles, to the foot of the stair. Here Poole motioned him to stand on one side and listen; while he himself, setting down the candle and making a great and obvious call on his resolution, mounted the steps, and knocked with a somewhat uncertain hand on the red baize of the cabinet door.

"Mr. Utterson, sir, asking to see you," he called; and even as he did so, once more violently signed to the lawyer to give ear.

A voice answered from within: "Tell him I cannot see anyone," it said, complainingly.

"Thank you, sir," said Poole, with a note of something like triumph in his voice; and taking up his candle, he led Mr. Utterson back across the yard and into the great kitchen, where the fire was out and the beetles were leaping on the floor.

"Sir," he said, looking Mr. Utterson in the eyes, "was that my master's voice?"

"It seems much changed," replied the lawyer, very pale, but giving look for look.

"Changed? Well, yes, I think so," said the butler. "Have I been twenty years in this man's house, to be deceived about his voice? No, sir; master's made away with; he was made away with, eight days ago, when we heard him cry out upon the name of God; and *who's* in there instead of him, and *why* it stays there, is a thing that cries to Heaven, Mr. Utterson!"

"This is a very strange tale, Poole; this is rather a wild tale, my man," said Mr. Utterson, biting his finger. "Suppose it were as you suppose, supposing Dr. Jekyll to have been—well, murdered, what could induce the murderer to stay? That won't hold water; it doesn't commend itself to reason."

"Well, Mr. Utterson, you are a hard man to satisfy, but I'll do it yet," said Poole. "All this last week (you must know) him, or it, or whatever it is that lives in that cabinet, has been crying night and day for some sort of medicine and cannot get it to his mind. It was sometimes his way— the master's, that is—to write his orders on a sheet of paper and throw it on the stair. We've had nothing else this week back; nothing but papers, and a closed door, and the very meals left there to be smuggled in when nobody was looking. Well, sir, every day, ay, and twice and thrice in the same day, there have been orders and complaints, and I have been sent flying to all the wholesale chemists in town. Every time I brought the stuff back, there would be another paper telling me to return it, because it was not pure, and another order to a different firm. This drug is wanted bitter bad, sir, whatever for."

"Have you any of these papers?" asked Mr. Utterson.

Poole felt in his pocket and handed out a crumpled note, which the lawyer, bending nearer to the candle, carefully examined. Its contents ran thus: "Dr. Jekyll presents his compliments to Messrs. Maw. He assures them that their last sample is impure and quite useless for his present purpose. In the year 18—, Dr. J. purchased a somewhat large quantity from Messrs. M. He now begs them to search with the most sedulous care, and should any of the same quality be left, to forward it to him at once. Expense is no consideration. The importance of this to Dr. J. can hardly be exaggerated." So far the letter had run composedly enough; but here, with a sudden splutter of the pen, the writer's emotion had broken loose. "For God's sake," he had added, "find me some of the old."

"This is a strange note," said Mr. Utterson; and then sharply, "How do you come to have it open?"

"The man at Maw's was main angry, sir, and he threw it back to me like so much dirt," returned Poole.

"This is unquestionably the doctor's hand, do you know?" resumed the lawyer.

"I thought it looked like it," said the servant, rather sulkily; and then, with another voice, "But what matters hand of write?" he said. "I've seen him!"

"Seen him?" repeated Mr. Utterson. "Well?"

"That's it!" said Poole. "It was this way. I came suddenly into the theatre from the garden. It seems he had slipped out to look for this drug, or whatever it is; for the cabinet door was open, and there he was at the far end of the room, digging among the crates. He looked up when I came in, gave a kind of cry, and whipped upstairs into the cabinet. It was but for one minute that I saw him, but the hair stood upon my head like quills. Sir, if that was my master, why had he a mask upon his face? If it was my master, why did he cry out like a rat, and run from me? I have served him long enough. And then . . ." the man paused, and passed his hand over his face.

"These are all very strange circumstances," said Mr. Utterson, "but I think I begin to see daylight. Your master, Poole, is plainly seized with one of those maladies that both torture and deform the sufferer; hence, for aught I know, the alteration of his voice; hence the mask and his avoidance of his friends; hence his eagerness to find this drug, by means of which the poor soul retains some hope of ultimate recovery—God grant that he be not deceived! There is my explanation; it is sad enough, Poole, ay, and appalling to consider; but it is plain and natural, hangs well together, and delivers us from all exorbitant alarms."

"Sir," said the butler, turning to a sort of mottled pallor, "that thing was not my master, and there's the truth. My master"—here he looked round him, and began to whisper—"is a tall fine build of a man, and this was more of a dwarf." Utterson attempted to protest. "O, sir," cried Poole, "do you think I do not know my master after twenty years? do you think I do not know where his head comes to in the cabinet door, where I saw him every morning of my life? No, sir, that thing in the mask was never Dr. Jekyll—God knows what it was, but it was never Dr. Jekyll; and it is the belief of my heart that there was murder done."

"Poole," replied the lawyer, "if you say that, it will become my duty to make certain. Much as I desire to spare your master's feelings, much as I am puzzled by this note, which seems to prove him to be still alive, I shall consider it my duty to break in that door."

"Ah, Mr. Utterson, that's talking!" cried the butler.

"And now comes the second question," resumed Utterson: "Who is going to do it?"

"Why, you and me, sir," was the undaunted reply.

"That is very well said," returned the lawyer; "and whatever comes of it, I shall make it my business to see you are no loser."

"There is an axe in the theatre," continued Poole; "and you might take the kitchen poker for yourself."

The lawyer took that rude but weighty instrument into his hand, and balanced it. "Do you know, Poole," he said, looking up, "that you and I are about to place ourselves in a position of some peril?"

"You may say so, sir, indeed," returned the butler.

"It is well, then, that we should be frank," said the other. "We both think more than we have said; let us make a clean breast. This masked figure that you saw, did you recognize it?"

"Well, sir, it went so quick, and the creature was so doubled up, that I could hardly swear to that," was the answer. "But if you mean, was it Mr. Hyde?—why, yes, I think it was! You see, it was much of the same bigness; and it had the same quick light way with it; and then who else could have got in by the laboratory door? You have not forgot, sir, that at the time of the murder he had still the key with him? But that's not all. I don't know, Mr. Utterson, if ever you met this Mr. Hyde?"

"Yes," said the lawyer, "I once spoke with him."

"Then you must know, as well as the rest of us, that there was something queer about that gentleman—something that gave a man a turn—I don't know rightly how to say it, sir, beyond this: that you felt it in your marrow—kind of cold and thin."

"I own I felt something of what you describe," said Mr. Utterson.

"Quite so, sir," returned Poole. "Well, when that masked thing like a monkey jumped from among the chemicals and whipped into the cabinet, it went down my spine like ice. O, I know it's not evidence, Mr. Utterson; I'm book-learned enough for that; but a man has his feelings; and I give you my bible-word it was Mr. Hyde!"

"Ay, ay," said the lawyer. "My fears incline to the same point. Evil, I fear, founded—evil was sure to come—of that connection. Ay, truly, I believe you; I believe poor Harry is killed; and I believe his murderer (for what purpose, God alone can tell) is still lurking in his victim's room. Well, let our name be vengeance. Call Bradshaw."

The footman came at the summons, very white and nervous.

"Pull yourself together, Bradshaw," said the lawyer. "This suspense, I know, is telling upon all of you; but it is now our intention to make an end of it. Poole, here, and I are going to force our way into the cabinet. If all is well, my shoulders are broad enough to bear the blame. Meanwhile, lest anything should really be amiss, or any malefactor seek to escape by the back, you and the boy must go round the corner with a pair of good sticks, and take your post at the laboratory door. We give you ten minutes to get to your stations."

As Bradshaw left, the lawyer looked at his watch. "And now, Poole, let us get to ours," he said; and taking the poker under his arm, he led the way into the yard. The scud had banked over the moon, and it was now quite dark. The wind, which only broke in puffs and draughts into that deep well of building, tossed the light of the candle to and fro about their steps, until they came into the shelter of the theatre, where they sat down silently to wait. London hummed solemnly all round; but nearer at hand, the stillness was only broken by the sound of a footfall moving to and fro along the cabinet floor.

"So it will walk all day, sir," whispered Poole; "ay, and the better part of the night. Only when a new sample comes from the chemist, there's a bit of a break. Ah, it's an ill conscience that's such an enemy to rest! Ah, sir, there's blood foully shed in every step of it! But hark again, a little closer—put your heart in your ears, Mr. Utterson, and tell me, is that the doctor's foot?"

The steps fell lightly and oddly, with a certain swing, for all they went so slowly; it was different indeed from the heavy creaking tread of Henry Jekyll. Utterson sighed. "Is there never anything else?" he asked.

Poole nodded. "Once," he said. "Once I heard it weeping!"

"Weeping? how that?" said the lawyer, conscious of a sudden chill of horror.

"Weeping like a woman or a lost soul," said the butler. "I came away with that upon my heart, that I could have wept too."

But now the ten minutes drew to an end. Poole disinterred the axe from under a stack of packing straw; the candle was set upon the nearest table to light them to the attack; and they drew near with bated breath to where that patient foot was still going up and down, up and down in the quiet of the night.

"Jekyll," cried Utterson, with a loud voice, "I demand to see you." He paused a moment, but there came no reply. "I give you fair warning, our suspicions are aroused, and I must and shall see you," he resumed; "if not by fair means, then by foul—if not of your consent, then by brute force!"

"Utterson," said the voice, "for God's sake, have mercy!"

"Ah, that's not Jekyll's voice—it's Hyde's!" cried Utterson. "Down with the door, Poole!"

Poole swung the axe over his shoulder; the blow shook the building, and the red baize door leaped against the lock and hinges. A dismal screech, as of mere animal terror, rang from the cabinet. Up went the axe again, and again the panels crashed and the frame bounded; four times the blow fell; but the wood was tough and the fittings were of excellent workmanship; and it was not until the fifth, that the lock burst in sunder, and the wreck of the door fell inwards on the carpet.

The besiegers, appalled by their own riot and the stillness that had succeeded, stood back a little and peered in. There lay the cabinet before their eyes in the quiet lamp-light, a good fire glowing and chattering on the hearth, the kettle singing its thin strain, a drawer or two open, papers neatly set forth on the business table, and nearer the fire, the things laid out for tea: the quietest room, you would have said, and, but for the glazed presses full of chemicals, the most commonplace that night in London.

Right in the midst there lay the body of a man sorely contorted and still twitching. They drew near on tiptoe, turned it on his back, and beheld the face of Edward Hyde. He was dressed in clothes far too large for him, clothes of the doctor's bigness; the cords of his face still moved with a semblance of life, but life was quite gone; and by the crushed phial in the hand and the strong smell of kernels that hung upon the air, Utterson knew that he was looking on the body of a self-destroyer.

"We have come too late," he said sternly, "whether to save or punish. Hyde is gone to his account; and it only remains for us to find the body of your master."

The far greater proportion of the building was occupied by the theatre, which filled almost the whole ground storey, and was lighted from above, and by the cabinet, which formed an upper storey at one end and looked upon the court. A corridor joined the theatre to the door on the by-street; and with this, the cabinet communicated separately by a second flight of stairs. There were besides a few dark closets and a spacious cellar. All these they now thoroughly examined. Each closet needed but a glance, for all were empty, and all, by the dust that fell from their doors, had stood long unopened. The cellar, indeed, was filled with crazy lumber, mostly dating from the times of the surgeon who was Jekyll's predecessor; but even as they opened the door, they were advertised of the uselessness of further search, by the fall of a perfect mat of cobweb which had for years sealed up the entrance. Nowhere was there any trace of Henry Jekyll, dead or alive.

Poole stamped on the flags of the corridor. "He must be buried here," he said, hearkening to the sound.

"Or he may have fled," said Utterson, and he turned to examine the door in the by-street. It was locked; and lying near by on the flags, they found the key, already stained with rust.

"This does not look like use," observed the lawyer.

"Use!" echoed Poole. "Do you not see, sir, it is broken? much as if a man had stamped on it."

"Ah," continued Utterson, "and the fractures, too, are rusty." The two men looked at each other with a scare. "This is beyond me, Poole," said the lawyer. "Let us go back to the cabinet."

They mounted the stair in silence, and still, with an occasional awe-struck glance at the dead body, proceeded more thoroughly to examine the contents of the cabinet. At one table there were traces of chemical work, various measured heaps of some white salt being laid on glass saucers, as though for an experiment in which the unhappy man had been prevented.

"That is the same drug that I was always bringing him," said Poole; and even as he spoke, the kettle with a startling noise boiled over.

This brought them to the fireside, where the easy chair was drawn cosily up, and the tea things stood ready to the sitter's elbow, the very sugar in the cup. There were several books on a shelf; one lay beside the tea things open, and Utterson was amazed to find a copy of a pious work, for which Jekyll had several times expressed a great esteem, annotated, in his own hand, with startling blasphemies.

Next, in the course of their review of the chamber, the searchers came to the cheval-glass, into whose depth they looked with an involuntary horror. But it was so turned as to show them nothing but the rosy glow playing on the roof, the fire sparkling in a hundred repetitions along the glazed front of the presses, and their own pale and fearful countenances stooping to look in.

"This glass has seen some strange things, sir," whispered Poole.

"And surely none stranger than itself," echoed the lawyer, in the same tone. "For what did Jekyll"—he caught himself up at the word with a start, and then conquering the weakness: "what could Jekyll want with it?" he said.

"You may say that!" said Poole.

Next they turned to the business table. On the desk among the neat array of papers, a large envelope was uppermost, and bore, in the doctor's hand, the name of Mr. Utterson. The lawyer unsealed it, and several enclosures fell to the floor. The first was a will drawn in the same eccentric terms as the one which he had returned six months before, to serve as a testament in case of death and as a deed of gift in case of disappearance; but in place of the name of Edward Hyde, the lawyer, with indescribable amazement, read the name of Gabriel John Utterson. He looked at Poole, and then back at the papers, and last of all at the dead malefactor stretched upon the carpet.

"My head goes round," he said. "He has been all these days in possession; he had no cause to like me; he must have raged to see himself displaced; and he has not destroyed this document."

He caught the next paper; it was a brief note in the doctor's hand, and dated at the top. "O Poole!" the lawyer cried, "he was alive and here this day. He cannot have been disposed of in so short a space; he must be still alive, he must have fled! And then, why fled? and how? and in that case can we venture to declare this suicide? O, we must be careful. I foresee that we may yet involve your master in some dire catastrophe."

"Why don't you read it, sir?" asked Poole.

"Because I fear," replied the lawyer, solemnly. "God grant I have no cause for it!" And with that he brought the paper to his eye, and read as follows:

My dear Utterson,

When this shall fall into your hands, I shall have disappeared, under what circumstances I have not the penetration to foresee; but my instincts and all the circumstances of my nameless situation tell me that the end is sure and must be early. Go then, and first read the narrative which Lanyon warned me he was to place in your hands; and if you care to hear more, turn to the confession of

Your unworthy and unhappy friend,
Henry Jekyll.

"There was a third enclosure?" asked Utterson.

"Here, sir," said Poole, and gave into his hands a considerable packet sealed in several places.

The lawyer put it in his pocket. "I would say nothing of this paper. If your master has fled or is dead, we may at least save his credit. It is now ten; I must go home and read these documents in quiet; but I shall be back before midnight, when we shall send for the police."

They went out, locking the door of the theatre behind them; and Utterson, once more leaving the servants gathered about the fire in the hall, trudged back to his office to read the two narratives in which this mystery was now to be explained.

Dr. Lanyon's Narrative

On the ninth ot January, now four days ago, I received by the evening delivery a registered envelope, addressed in the hand of my colleague and old school-companion, Henry Jekyll. I was a good deal surprised by this; for we were by no means in the habit of correspondence; I had seen the man, dined with him, indeed, the night before; and I could imagine nothing in our intercourse that should justify the formality of registration. The contents increased my wonder; for this is how the letter ran:

10th December, 18—

Dear Lanyon,

You are one of my oldest friends; and although we may have differed at times on scientific questions, I cannot remember, at least on my side, any break in our affection. There was never a day when, if you had said to me,

"Jekyll, my life, my honour, my reason, depend upon you," I would not have sacrificed my fortune or my left hand to help you. Lanyon, my life, my honour, my reason, are all at your mercy; if you fail me to-night, I am lost. You might suppose, after this preface, that I am going to ask you for something dishonourable to grant. Judge for yourself.

I want you to postpone all other engagements for to-night—ay, even if you were summoned to the bedside of an emperor; to take a cab, unless your carriage should be actually at the door; and, with this letter in your hand for consultation, to drive straight to my house. Poole, my butler, has his orders; you will find him waiting your arrival with a locksmith. The door of my cabinet is then to be forced; and you are to go in alone; to open the glazed press (letter E) on the left hand, breaking the lock if it be shut; and to draw out, with all its contents as they stand, *the fourth drawer from the top or (which is the same thing) the third from the bottom. In my extreme distress of mind, I have a morbid fear of misdirecting you; but even if I am in error, you may know the right drawer by its contents: some powders, a phial, and a paper book. This drawer I beg of you to carry back with you to Cavendish Square exactly as it stands.*

That is the first part of the service: now for the second. You should be back, if you set out at once on the receipt of this, long before midnight; but I will leave you that amount of margin, not only in the fear of one of those obstacles that can neither be prevented nor foreseen, but because an hour when your servants are in bed is to be preferred for what will then remain to do. At midnight, then, I have to ask you to be alone in your consulting room, to admit with your own hand into the house a man who will present himself in my name, and to place in his hands the drawer that you will have brought with you from my cabinet. Then you will have played your part, and earned my gratitude completely. Five minutes afterwards, if you insist upon an explanation, you will have understood that these arrangements are of capital importance; and that by the neglect of one of them, fantastic as they must appear, you might have charged your conscience with my death or the shipwreck of my reason.

Confident as I am that you will not trifle with this appeal, my heart sinks and my hand trembles at the bare thought of such a possibility. Think of me at this hour, in a strange place, labouring under a blackness of distress that no fancy can exaggerate, and yet well aware that, if you will but punctually serve me, my troubles will roll away like a story that is told. Serve me, my dear Lanyon, and save

Your friend,

H.J.

P.S.—I had already sealed this up when a fresh terror struck upon my soul. It is possible that the post office may fail me, and this letter not come into your hands until tomorrow morning. In that case, dear Lanyon, do my errand when it shall be most convenient for you in the course of the day; and once more expect my messenger at midnight. It may then already be too late; and if that night passes without event, you will know that you have seen the last of Henry Jekyll.

Upon the reading of this letter, I made sure my colleague was insane; but till that was proved beyond the possibility of doubt, I felt bound to do as he requested. The less I understood of this farrago, the less I was in a position to judge of its importance; and an appeal so worded could not be set aside without a grave responsibility. I rose accordingly from table, got into a hansom, and drove straight to Jekyll's house. The butler was awaiting my arrival; he had received by the same post as mine a registered letter of instruction, and had sent at once for a locksmith and a carpenter. The tradesmen came while we were yet speaking; and we moved in a body to old Dr. Denman's surgical theatre, from which (as you are doubtless aware) Jekyll's private cabinet is most conveniently entered. The door was very strong, the lock excellent; the carpenter avowed he would have great trouble, and have to do much damage, if force were to be used; and the locksmith was near despair. But this last was a handy fellow, and after two hours' work, the door stood open. The press marked E was unlocked; and I took out the drawer, had it filled up with straw and tied in a sheet, and returned with it to Cavendish Square.

Here I proceeded to examine its contents. The powders were neatly enough made up, but not with the nicety of the dispensing chemist; so that it was plain they were of Jekyll's private manufacture; and when I opened one of the wrappers, I found what seemed to me a simple crystalline salt of a white colour. The phial, to which I next turned my attention, might have been about half full of a blood-red liquor, which was highly pungent to the sense of smell, and seemed to me to contain phosphorus and some volatile ether. At the other ingredients I could make no guess. The book was an ordinary version book, and contained little but a series of dates. These covered a period of many years; but I observed that the entries ceased nearly a year ago, and quite abruptly. Here and there a brief remark was appended to a date, usually no more than a single word: "double" occurring perhaps six times in a total of several hundred entries; and once very early in the list, and followed by several marks of exclamation, "total failure! ! !" All this, though it whetted my curiosity, told me little that was definite. Here were a phial of some tincture, a paper of some salt, and the record of a series of experiments that had led (like too many of Jekyll's investigations) to no end of practical usefulness. How could the presence of these articles in my house affect either the honour, the sanity, or the life of my flighty colleague? If his messenger could go to one place, why could he not go to another? And even granting some impediment, why was this gentleman to be received by me in secret? The more I reflected, the more convinced I grew that I was dealing with a case of cerebral disease; and though I dismissed my servants to bed, I loaded an old revolver, that I might be found in some posture of self-defence.

Twelve o'clock had scarce rung out over London, ere the knocker sounded very gently on the door. I went myself at the summons, and found a small man crouching against the pillars of the portico.

"Are you come from Dr. Jekyll?" I asked.

He told me "yes" by a constrained gesture; and when I had bidden him enter, he did not obey me without a searching backward glance into the darkness of the square. There was a policeman not far off, advancing with his bull's-eye open; and at the sight, I thought my visitor started and made greater haste.

These particulars struck me, I confess, disagreeably; and as I followed him into the bright light of the consulting room, I kept my hand ready on my weapon. Here, at last, I had a chance of clearly seeing him. I had never set eyes on him before, so much was certain. He was small, as I have said; I was struck besides with the shocking expression of his face, with his remarkable combination of great muscular activity and great apparent debility of constitution, and—last but not least—with the odd, subjective disturbance caused by his neighbourhood. This bore some resemblance to incipient rigor, and was accompanied by a marked sinking of the pulse. At the time, I set it down to some idiosyncratic, personal distaste, and merely wondered at the acuteness of the symptoms; but I have since had reason to believe the cause to lie ·much deeper in the nature of man, and to turn on some nobler hinge than the principle of hatred.

This person (who had thus, from the first moment of his entrance, struck in me what I can only describe as a disgustful curiosity) was dressed in a fashion that would have made an ordinary person laughable; his clothes, that is to say, although they were of rich and sober fabric, were enormously too large for him in every measurement—the trousers hanging on his legs and rolled up to keep them from the ground, the waist of the coat below his haunches, and the collar sprawling wide upon his shoulders. Strange to relate, this ludicrous accoutrement was far from moving me to laughter. Rather, as there was something abnormal and misbegotten in the very essence of the creature that now faced me— something seizing, surprising and revolting—this fresh disparity seemed but to fit in with and to reinforce it; so that to my interest in the man's nature and character, there was added a curiosity as to his origin, his life, his fortune and status in the world.

These observations, though they have taken so great a space to be set down in, were yet the work of a few seconds. My visitor was, indeed, on fire with sombre excitement.

"Have you got it?" he cried. "Have you got it?" And so lively was his impatience that he even laid his hand upon my arm and sought to shake me.

I put him back, conscious at his touch of a certain icy pang along my blood. "Come, sir," said I. "You forget that I have not yet the pleasure of your acquaintance. Be seated, if you please." And I showed him an example, and sat down myself in my customary seat and with as fair an imitation of my ordinary manner to a patient, as the lateness of the hour, the nature of my pre-occupations, and the horror I had of my visitor, would suffer me to muster.

"I beg your pardon, Dr. Lanyon," he replied, civilly enough. "What you say is very well founded; and my impatience has shown its heels to my politeness. I come here at the instance of your colleague, Dr. Henry Jekyll, on a piece of business of some moment; and I understood . . ." he paused and put his hand to his throat, and I could see, in spite of his collected manner, that he was wrestling against the approaches of the hysteria—"I understood, a drawer . . ."

But here I took pity on my visitor's suspense, and some perhaps on my own growing curiosity.

"There it is, sir," said I, pointing to the drawer, where it lay on the floor behind a table, and still covered with the sheet.

He sprang to it, and then paused, and laid his hand upon his heart; I could hear his teeth grate with the convulsive action of his jaws; and his face was so ghastly to see that I grew alarmed both for his life and reason.

"Compose yourself," said I.

He turned a dreadful smile to me, and, as if with the decision of despair, plucked away the sheet. At sight of the contents, he uttered one loud sob of such immense relief that I sat petrified. And the next moment, in a voice that was already fairly well under control, "Have you a graduated glass?" he asked.

I rose from my place with something of an effort, and gave him what he asked.

He thanked me with a smiling nod, measured out a few minims of the red tincture and added one of the powders. The mixture, which was at first of a reddish hue, began, in proportion as the crystals melted, to brighten in colour, to effervesce audibly, and to throw off small fumes of vapour. Suddenly, and at the same moment, the ebullition ceased, and the compound changed to a dark purple, which faded again more slowly to a watery green. My visitor, who had watched these metamorphoses with a keen eye, smiled, set down the glass upon the table, and then turned and looked upon me with an air of scrutiny.

"And now," said he, "to settle what remains. Will you be wise? will you be guided? will you suffer me to take this glass in my hand, and to go forth from your house without further parley? or has the greed of curiosity too much command of you? Think before you answer, for it shall be done as you decide. As you decide, you shall be left as you were before, and neither richer nor wiser, unless the sense of service rendered to a man in mortal distress may be counted as a kind of riches of the soul. Or, if you shall so prefer to choose, a new province of knowledge and new avenues to fame and power shall be laid open to you, here, in this room, upon the instant; and your sight shall be blasted by a prodigy to stagger the unbelief of Satan."

"Sir," said I, affecting a coolness that I was far from truly possessing, "you speak enigmas, and you will perhaps not wonder that I hear you with no very strong impression of belief. But I have gone too far in the way of inexplicable services to pause before I see the end."

"It is well," replied my visitor. "Lanyon, you remember your vows: what follows is under the seal of our profession. And now, you who have so long been bound to the most narrow and material views, you who have denied the virtue of transcendental medicine, you who have derided your superiors—behold!"

He put the glass to his lips, and drank at one gulp. A cry followed; he reeled, staggered, clutched at the table and held on, staring with injected eyes, gasping with open mouth; and as I looked there came, I thought, a change—he seemed to swell—his face became suddenly black and the features seemed to melt and alter—and the next moment I had sprung to my feet and leaped back against the wall, my arm raised to shield me from that prodigy, my mind submerged in terror.

"O God!" I screamed, and "O God!" again and again; for there before my eyes—pale and shaken, and half fainting, and groping before him with his hands, like a man restored from death—there stood Henry Jekyll!

What he told me in the next hour I cannot bring my mind to set on paper. I saw what I saw, I heard what I heard, and my soul sickened at it; and yet, now when that sight has faded from my eyes, I ask myself if I believe it, and I cannot answer. My life is shaken to its roots; sleep has left me; the deadliest terror sits by me at all hours of the day and night; I feel that my days are numbered, and that I must die; and yet I shall die incredulous. As for the moral turpitude that man unveiled to me, even with tears of penitence, I cannot, even in memory, dwell on it without a start of horror. I will say but one thing, Utterson, and that (if you can bring your mind to credit it) will be more than enough. The creature who crept into my house that night was, on Jekyll's own confession, known by the name of Hyde and hunted for in every corner of the land as the murderer of Carew.

Hastie Lanyon.

Henry Jekyll's Full Statement of the Case

I was born in the year 18— to a large fortune, endowed besides with excellent parts, inclined by nature to industry, fond of the respect of the wise and good among my fellow-men, and thus, as might have been supposed, with every guarantee of an honourable and distinguished future. And indeed, the worst of my faults was a certain impatient gaiety of disposition, such as has made the happiness of many, but such as I found it hard to reconcile with my imperious desire to carry my head high, and wear a more than commonly grave countenance before the public. Hence it came about that I concealed my pleasures; and that when I reached years of reflection, and began to look round me, and take stock of my progress and position in the world, I stood already committed to a profound duplicity of life. Many a man would have even blazoned such irregularities as I was guilty of; but from the high views that I had set before me, I regarded and hid them with an almost morbid sense of shame. It was thus rather the exacting nature of my aspirations, than any particular degradation in my faults, that made me what I was, and, with even a deeper trench than in the majority of men, severed in me those provinces of good and ill which divide and compound man's dual nature. In this case, I was driven to reflect deeply and inveterately on that hard law of life, which lies at the root of religion, and is one of the most plentiful springs of distress. Though so profound a double-dealer, I was in no sense a hypocrite; both sides of me were in dead earnest; I was no more myself when I laid aside restraint and plunged in shame, than when I laboured, in the eye of day, at the furtherance of knowledge or the relief of sorrow and suffering. And it chanced that the direction of my scientific studies, which led wholly towards the mystic and the transcendental, reacted and shed a strong light on this consciousness of the perennial war among my members. With every day, and from both sides of my intelligence, the moral and the intellectual, I thus drew steadily nearer to that truth, by whose partial discovery I have been doomed to such a dreadful shipwreck: that man is not truly one, but truly two. I say two, because the state of my own knowledge does not pass beyond that point. Others will follow, others will outstrip me on the same lines; and I hazard the guess that man will be ultimately known for a mere polity of multifarious, incongruous and independent denizens. I, for my part, from the nature of my life, advanced infallibly in one direction, and in one direction only. It was on the moral side, and in my own person, that I learned to recognize the thorough and primitive duality of man; I saw that, of the two natures that contended in the field of my consciousness, even if I could rightly be said to be either, it was only because I was radically both; and from an early date, even before the course of my scientific discoveries had begun to suggest the most naked possibility of such a miracle, I had learned to dwell with pleasure, as a beloved daydream, on the thought of the separation of these elements. If each, I told myself, could but be housed in separate identities, life would be relieved of all that was unbearable; the unjust might go his way, delivered from the aspirations and remorse of his more upright twin; and the just could walk steadfastly and securely on his upward path, doing the good things in which he found his pleasure, and no longer exposed to disgrace and penitence by the hands of his extraneous evil. It was the curse of mankind that these incongruous faggots were thus bound together—that in the agonized womb of consciousness, these polar twins should be continuously struggling. How, then, were they dissociated?

I was so far in my reflections, when, as I have said, a side light began to shine upon the subject from the laboratory table. I began to perceive more deeply than it has ever yet been stated, the trembling immateriality, the mist-like transience, of this seemingly so solid body in which we walk attired. Certain agents I found to have the power to shake and to pluck back that fleshly vestment, even as a wind might toss the curtains of a pavilion. For two good reasons, I will not enter deeply into this scientific branch of my confession. First, because I have been made to learn that the doom and burthen of our life is bound for ever on man's shoulders; and when the attempt is made to cast it off, it but returns upon us with more unfamiliar and more awful pressure. Second, because, as my narrative will make, alas! too evident, my discoveries were incomplete. Enough, then, that I not only recognized my natural body from the mere aura and effulgence of certain of the powers that made up my spirit, but managed to compound a drug by which these powers should be dethroned from their supremacy, and a second form and countenance substituted, none the less natural to me because they were the expression, and bore the stamp, of lower elements in my soul.

I hesitated long before I put this theory to the test of practice. I knew well that I risked death; for any drug that so potently controlled and shook the very fortress of identity, might by the least scruple of an overdose or at the least inopportunity in the moment of exhibition, utterly blot out that immaterial tabernacle which I looked to it to change. But the temptation of a discovery so singular and profound, at last overcame the suggestions of alarm. I had long since prepared my tincture; I purchased at once, from a firm of wholesale chemists, a large quantity of a particular salt, which I knew, from my experiments, to be the last ingredient required; and, late one accursed night, I compounded the elements, watched them boil and smoke together in the glass and when the ebullition had subsided, with a strong glow of courage, drank off the potion.

The most racking pangs succeeded: a grinding in the bones, deadly nausea, and a horror of the spirit that cannot be exceeded at the hour of birth or death. Then these agonies began swiftly to subside, and I came to myself as if out of a great sickness. There was something strange in my sensations, something indescribably new, and, from its very novelty, incredibly sweet. I felt younger, lighter, happier in body; within I was conscious of a heady recklessness, a current of disordered sensual images running like a mill race in my fancy, a solution of the bonds of obligation, an unknown but not an innocent freedom of the soul. I knew myself, at the first breath of this new life, to be more wicked, tenfold more wicked, sold a slave to my original evil; and the thought, in that moment, braced and delighted me like wine. I stretched out my hands, exulting in the freshness of these sensations; and in the act, I was suddenly aware that I had lost in stature.

There was no mirror, at that date, in my room; that which stands beside me as I write was brought there later on, and for the very purpose of those transformations. The night, however, was far gone into the morning—the morning, black as it was, was nearly ripe for the conception of the day—the inmates of my house were locked in the most rigorous hours of slumber; and I determined, flushed as I was with hope and triumph, to venture in my new shape as far as to my bedroom. I crossed the yard, wherein the constellations looked down upon me, I could have thought, with wonder, the first creature of that sort that their unsleeping vigilance had yet disclosed to them; I stole through the corridors, a stranger in my own house; and coming to my room, I saw for the first time the appearance of Edward Hyde.

I must here speak by theory alone, saying not that which I know, but that which I suppose to be most probable. The evil side of my nature, to which I had now transferred the stamping efficacy, was less robust and less developed than the good which I had just deposed. Again, in the course of my life, which had been, after all, nine-tenths a life of effort, virtue and control, it had been much less exercised and much less exhausted. And hence, as I think, it came about that Edward Hyde was so much smaller, slighter, and younger than Henry Jekyll. Even as good shone upon the countenance of the one, evil was written broadly and plainly on the face of the other. Evil besides (which I must still believe to be the lethal side of man) had left on that body an imprint of deformity and decay. And yet when I looked upon that ugly idol in the glass, I was conscious of no repugnance, rather of a leap of welcome. This, too, was myself. It seemed natural and human. In my eyes it bore a livelier image of the spirit, it seemed more express and single, than the imperfect and divided countenance I had been hitherto accustomed to call mine. And in so far I was doubtless right. I have observed that when I wore the semblance of Edward Hyde, none could come near to me at first without a visible misgiving of the flesh. This, as I take it, was because all human beings, as we meet them, are commingled out of good and evil; and Edward Hyde, alone, in the ranks of mankind, was pure evil.

I lingered but a moment at the mirror: the second and conclusive experiment had yet to be attempted; it yet remained to be seen if I had lost my identity beyond redemption and must flee before daylight from a house that was no longer mine: and hurrying back to my cabinet, I once more prepared and drank the cup, once more suffered the pangs of dissolution, and came to myself once more with the character, the stature, and the face of Henry Jekyll.

That night I had come to the fatal cross roads. Had I approached my discovery in a more noble spirit, had I risked the experiment while under the empire of generous or pious aspirations, all must have been otherwise, and from these agonies of death and birth I had come forth an angel instead of a fiend. The drug had no discriminating action; it was neither diabolical nor divine; it but shook the doors of the prison-house of my disposition; and, like the captive of Philippi, that which stood within ran forth. At that time my virtue slumbered; my evil, kept awake by ambition, was alert and swift to seize the occasion; and the thing that was projected was Edward Hyde. Hence, although I had now two characters as well as two appearances, one was wholly evil, and the other was still the old Henry Jekyll, that incongruous compound of whose reformation and improvement I had already learned to despair. The movement was thus wholly toward the worse.

Even at that time, I had not yet conquered my aversion to the dryness of a life to study, I would still be merrily disposed at times; and as my pleasures were (to say the least) undignified, and I was not only well known and highly considered, but growing towards the elderly man, this incoherency of my life was daily growing more unwelcome. It was on this side that my new power tempted me until I fell in slavery. I had but to drink the cup, to doff at once the body of the noted professor, and to assume, like a thick cloak, that of Edward Hyde. I smiled at the notion; it seemed to me at the time to be humorous; and I made my preparations with the most studious care. I took and furnished that house in Soho, to which Hyde was tracked by the police; and engaged as housekeeper a creature whom I well knew to be silent and unscrupulous. On the other side, I announced to my servants that a Mr. Hyde (whom I described) was to have full liberty and power about my house in the square; and, to parry mishaps, I even called and made myself a familiar object, in my second character. I next drew up that will to which you so much objected; so that if anything befell me in the person of Dr. Jekyll, I could enter on that of Edward Hyde without pecuniary loss. And thus fortified, as I supposed, on every side, I began to profit by the strange immunities of my position.

Men have before hired bravos to transact their crimes, while their own person and reputation sat under shelter. I was the first that ever did so for his pleasures. I was the first that could thus plod in the public eye with a load of genial respectability, and in a moment, like a school-boy, strip off these lendings and spring headlong into the sea of liberty. But for me, in my impenetrable mantle, the safety was complete. Think of it—I did not even exist! Let me but escape into my laboratory door, give me but a second or two to mix and swallow the draught that I had always standing ready; and, whatever he had done, Edward Hyde would pass away like the stain of breath upon a mirror; and there in his stead, quietly at home, trimming the midnight lamp in his study, a man who could afford to laugh at suspicion, would be Henry Jekyll.

The pleasures which I made haste to seek in my disguise were, as I have said, undignified; I would scarce use a harder term. But in the hands of Edward Hyde, they soon began to turn towards the monstrous. When I would come back from these excursions, I was often plunged into a kind of wonder at my vicarious depravity. This familiar that I called out of my own soul, and sent forth alone to do this good pleasure, was a being inherently malign and villainous; his every act and thought centred on self; drinking pleasure with bestial avidity from any degree of torture to another; relentless like a man of stone. Henry Jekyll stood at times aghast before the acts of Edward Hyde; but the situation was apart from ordinary laws, and insidiously relaxed the grasp of conscience. It was Hyde, after all, and Hyde alone, that was guilty. Jekyll was no worse; he woke again to his good qualities seemingly unimpaired; he would even make haste, where it was impossible, to undo the evil by Hyde, and thus his conscience slumbered.

Into the details of the infamy at which I thus connived (for even now I can scarce grant that I committed it) I have no design of entering; I mean but to point out the warnings and the successive steps with which my chastisement approached. I met with one accident which, as it brought on no consequence, I shall no more than mention. An act of cruelty to a child aroused against me the anger of a passer-by, whom I recognized the other day in the person of your kinsman; the doctor and the child's family joined him; there were moments when I feared for my life; and at last, in order to pacify their too just resentment, Edward Hyde had to bring them to the door, and pay them in a cheque drawn in the name of Henry Jekyll. But this danger was easily eliminated from the future, by opening an account at another bank in the name of Edward Hyde himself; and when, by sloping my own hand backwards, I had supplied my double with a signature, I thought I sat beyond the reach of fate.

Some two months before the murder of Sir Danvers, I had been out for one of my adventures, had returned at a late hour, and woke the next day in bed with somewhat odd sensations. It was in vain I looked about me; in vain I saw the decent furniture and tall proportions of my room in the square; in vain that I recognized the pattern of the bed curtains and the design of the mahogany frame; something still kept insisting that I was not where I was, that I had not wakened where I seemed to be, but in the little room in Soho where I was accustomed to sleep in the body of Edward Hyde. I smiled to myself, and, in my psychological way, began lazily to inquire into the elements of this illusion, occasionally, even as I did so, dropping back into a comfortable morning doze. I was still so engaged when, in one of my more wakeful moments, my eye fell upon my hand. Now, the hand of Henry Jekyll (as you have often remarked) was professional in shape and size; it was large, firm, white and comely. But the hand which I now saw, clearly enough, in the yellow light of a mid-London morning, lying half shut on the bedclothes, was lean, corded, knuckly, of a dusky pallor, and thickly shaded with a swart growth of hair. It was the hand of Edward Hyde.

I must have stared upon it for near half a minute, sunk as I was in the mere stupidity of wonder, before terror woke up in my breast as sudden and startling as the crash of cymbals; and bounding from my bed, I rushed to the mirror. At the sight that met my eyes, my blood was changed into something exquisitely thin and icy. Yes, I had gone to bed Henry Jekyll, I had awakened Edward Hyde. How was this to be explained? I asked myself; and then, with another bound of terror—how was it to be remedied? It was well on in the morning; the servants were up; all my drugs were in the cabinet—a long journey, down two pair of stairs, through the back passage, across the open court and through the anatomical theatre, from where I was then standing horror-struck. It might indeed be possible to cover my face; but of what use was that, when I was unable to conceal the alteration of my stature? And then, with an overpowering sweetness of relief, it came back upon my mind that the servants were already used to the coming and going of my second self. I had soon dressed, as well as I was able, in clothes of my own size; had soon passed through the house, where Bradshaw stared and drew back at seeing Mr. Hyde at such an hour and in such a strange array; and ten minutes later, Dr. Jekyll had returned to his own shape, and was sitting down, with a darkened brow, to make a feint of breakfasting.

Small indeed was my appetite. This inexplicable incident, this reversal of my previous experience, seemed, like the Babylonian finger on the wall, to be spelling out the letters of my judgment; and I began to reflect more seriously than ever before on the issues and possibilities of my double existence. That part of me which I had the power of projecting had lately been much exercised and nourished; it had seemed to me of late as though the body of Edward Hyde had grown in stature, as though (when I wore that form) I were conscious of a more generous tide of blood; and I began to spy a danger that, if this were much prolonged, the balance of my nature might be permanently overthrown, the power of voluntary change be forfeited, and the character of Edward Hyde become irrevocably mine. The power of the drug had not been always equally displayed. Once, very early in my career, it had totally failed me; since than I had been obliged on more than one occasion to double, and once, with infinite risk of death, to treble the amount; and these rare uncertainties had cast hitherto the sole shadow on my contentment. Now, however, and in the light of that morning's accident, I was led to remark that whereas, in the beginning, the difficulty had been to throw off the body of Jekyll, it had of late gradually but decidedly transferred itself to the other side. All things therefore seemed to point to this: that I was slowly losing hold of my original and better self, and becoming slowly incorporated with my second and worse.

Between these two, I now felt I had to choose. My two natures had memory in common, but all other faculties were most unequally shared between them. Jekyll (who was composite) now with the most sensitive apprehensions, now with a greedy gusto, projected and shared in the pleasures and adventures of Hyde; but Hyde was indifferent to Jekyll, or but remembered him as the mountain bandit remembers the cavern in which he conceals himself from pursuit. Jekyll had more than a father's interest; Hyde had more than a son's indifference. To cast in my lot with Jekyll was to die to those appetites which I had long secretly indulged and had of late begun to pamper. To cast it in with Hyde was to die to a thousand interests and aspirations, and to become, at a blow and for ever, despised and friendless. The bargain might appear unequal; but there was still another consideration in the scale; for while Jekyll would suffer smartingly in the fires of abstinence, Hyde would not be even conscious of all that he had lost. Strange as my circumstances were, the terms of this debate are as old and commonplace as man; much the same inducements and alarms cast the die for any tempted and trembling sinner; and it fell out with me, as it falls with so vast a majority of my fellows, that I chose the better part, and was found wanting in the strength to keep to it.

Yes, I preferred the elderly and discontented doctor, surrounded by friends, and cherishing honest hopes; and bade a resolute farewell to the liberty, the comparative youth, the light step, leaping pulses and secret pleasures, that I had enjoyed in the disguise of Hyde. I made this choice perhaps with some unconscious reservation, for I neither gave up the house in Soho, nor destroyed the clothes of Edward Hyde, which still lay ready in my cabinet. For two months, however, I was true to my determination; for two months I led a life of such severity as I had never before attained to, and enjoyed the compensations of an approving conscience. But time began at last to obliterate the freshness of my alarm; the praises of conscience began to grow into a thing of course; I began to be tortured with throes and longings, as of Hyde struggling after freedom; and at last, in an hour of moral weakness, I once again compounded and swallowed the transforming draught.

I do not suppose that when a drunkard reasons with himself upon his vice, he is one out of five hundred times affected by the dangers that he runs through his brutish physical insensibility; neither had I, long as I had considered my position, made enough allowance for the complete moral insensibility and insensate readiness to evil, which were the leading characters of Edward Hyde. Yet it was by these that I was punished. My devil had been long caged, he came out roaring. I was conscious, even when I took the draught, of a more unbridled, a more furious propensity to ill. It must have been this, I suppose, that stirred in my soul that tempest of impatience with which I listened to the civilities of my unhappy victim; I declare at least, before God, no man morally sane could have been guilty of that crime upon so pitiful a provocation; and that I struck in no more reasonable spirit than that in which a sick child may break a plaything. But I had voluntarily stripped myself of all those balancing instincts by which even the worst of us continues to walk with some degree of steadiness among temptations; and in my case, to be tempted, however slightly, was to fall.

Instantly the spirit of hell awoke in me and raged. With a transport of glee, I mauled the unresisting body, tasting delight from every blow; and it was not till weariness had begun to succeed that I was suddenly, in the top fit of my delirium, struck through the heart by a cold thrill of terror. A mist dispersed; I saw my life to be forfeit; and fled from the scene of these excesses, at once glorying and trembling, my lust of evil gratified and stimulated, my love of life screwed to the topmost peg. I ran to the house in Soho, and (to make assurance doubly sure) destroyed my papers; thence I set out through the lamplit streets, in the same divided ecstasy of mind, gloating on my crime, lightheadedly devising others in the future, and yet still hastening and still hearkening in my wake for the steps of the avenger. Hyde had a song upon his lips as he compounded the draught, and as he drank it pledged the dead man. The pangs of transformation had not done tearing him, before Henry Jekyll, with streaming tears of gratitude and remorse, had fallen upon his knees and lifted his clasped hands to God. The veil of self-indulgence was rent from head to foot, I saw my life as a whole: I followed it up from the days of childhood, when I had walked with my father's hand, and through the self-denying toils of my professional life, to arrive again and again, with the same sense of unreality, at the damned horrors of the evening. I could have screamed aloud; I sought with tears and prayers to smother down the crowd of hideous images and sounds with which my memory swarmed against me; and still, between the petitions, the ugly face of my iniquity stared into my soul. As the acuteness of this remorse began to die away, it was succeeded by a sense of joy. The problem of my conduct was solved. Hyde was thenceforth impossible; whether I would or not, I was now confined to the better part of my existence; and oh, how I rejoiced to think it! with what willing humility I embraced anew the restrictions of natural life! with what sincere renunciation I locked the door by which I had so often gone and come, and ground the key under my heel!

The next day came the news that the murder had been overlooked, that the guilt of Hyde was patent to the world, and that the victim was a man high in public estimation. It was not only a crime, it had been a tragic folly. I think I was glad to know it; I think I was glad to have my better impulses thus buttressed and guarded by the terrors of the scaffold. Jekyll was now my city of refuge; let but Hyde peep out an instant, and the hands of all men would be raised to take and slay him.

I resolved in my future conduct to redeem the past; and I can say with honesty that my resolve was fruitful of some good. You know yourself how earnestly in the last months of last year I laboured to relieve suffering; you know that much was done for others, and that the days passed quietly, almost happily for myself. Nor can I truly say that I wearied of this beneficent and innocent life; I think instead that I daily enjoyed it more completely; but I was still cursed with my duality of purpose; and as the first edge of my penitence wore off, the lower side of me, so long indulged, so recently chained down, began to growl for licence. Not that I dreamed of resuscitating Hyde; the bare idea of that would startle me to frenzy: no, it was in my own person that I was once more tempted to trifle with my conscience; and it was as an ordinary secret sinner that I at last fell before the assaults of temptation.

There comes an end to all things; the most capacious measure is filled at last; and this brief condescension to my evil finally destroyed the balance of my soul. And yet I was not alarmed; the fall seemed natural, like a return to the old days before I had made my discovery. It was a fine, clear January day, wet under foot where the frost had melted, but cloudless overhead; and the Regent's Park was full of winter chirrupings and sweet with spring odours. I sat in the sun on a bench; the animal within me licking the chops of memory; the spiritual side a little drowsed, promising subsequent penitence, but not yet moved to begin. After all, I reflected, I was like my neighbours; and then I smiled, comparing myself with other men, comparing my active goodwill with the lazy cruelty of their neglect. And at the very moment of that vainglorious thought, a qualm came over me, a horrid nausea and the most deadly shuddering. These passed away, and left me faint; and then as in its turn the faintness subsided, I began to be aware of a change in the temper of my thoughts, a greater boldness, a contempt of danger, a solution of the bonds of obligation. I looked down; my clothes hung formlessly on my shrunken limbs; the hand that lay on my knee was corded and hairy. I was once more Edward Hyde. A moment before I had been safe of all men's respect, wealthy, beloved—the cloth laying for me in the dining-room at home; and now I was the common quarry of mankind, hunted, houseless, a known murderer, thrall to the gallows.

My reason wavered, but it did not fail me utterly. I have more than once observed that, in my second character, my faculties seemed sharpened to a point and my spirits more tensely elastic; thus it came about that, where Jekyll perhaps might have succumbed, Hyde rose to the importance of the moment. My drugs were in one of the presses of my cabinet: how was I to reach them? That was the problem that (crushing my temples in my hands) I set myself to solve. The laboratory door I had closed. If I sought to enter by the house, my own servants would consign me to the gallows. I saw I must employ another hand, and thought of Lanyon. How was he to be reached? how persuaded? Supposing that I escaped capture in the streets, how was I to make my way into his presence? and how should I, an unknown and displeasing visitor, prevail on the famous physician to rifle the study of his colleague, Dr. Jekyll? Then I remembered that of my original character, one part remained to me: I could write my own hand; and once I had conceived that kindling spark, the way that I must follow became lighted up from end to end.

Thereupon, I arranged my clothes as best I could, and summoning a passing hansom, drove to an hotel in Portland Street, the name of which I chanced to remember. At my appearance (which was indeed comical enough, however tragic a fate these garments covered) the driver could not conceal his mirth. I gnashed my teeth upon him with a gust of devilish fury and the smile withered from his face—happily for him—yet more happily for myself, for in another instant I had certainly dragged him from his perch. At the inn, as I entered, I looked about me with so black a countenance as made the attendants tremble; not a look did they exchange in my presence; but obsequiously took my orders, led me to a private room, and brought me wherewithal to write. Hyde in danger of his life was a creature new to me: shaken with inordinate anger, strung to the pitch of murder, lusting to inflict pain. Yet the creature was astute; mastered his fury with a great effort of the will; composed his two important letters, one to Lanyon and one to Poole; and, that he might receive actual evidence of their being posted, sent them out with directions that they should be registered.

Thenceforward, he sat all day over the fire in the private room, gnawing his nails; there he dined, sitting alone with his fears, the waiter visibly quailing before his eye; and thence, when the night was fully come, he set forth in the corner of a closed cab, and was driven to and fro about the streets of the city. He, I say—I cannot say I. That child of Hell had nothing human; nothing lived in him but fear and hatred. And when at last, thinking the driver had begun to grow suspicious, he discharged the cab and ventured on foot, attired in his misfitting clothes, an object marked out for observation, into the midst of the nocturnal passengers, these two base passions raged within him like a tempest. He walked fast, hunted by his fears, chattering to himself, skulking through the less frequented thoroughfares, counting the minutes that still divided him from midnight. Once a woman spoke to him, offering, I think, a box of lights. He smote her in the face, and she fled.

When I came to myself at Lanyon's, the horror of my old friend perhaps affected me somewhat: I do not know; it was at least but a drop in the sea to the abhorrence with which I looked back upon these hours. A change had come over me. It was no longer the fear of the gallows, it was the horror of being Hyde that racked me. I received Lanyon's condemnation partly in a dream; it was partly in a dream that I came home to my own house and got into bed. I slept after the prostration of the day, with a stringent and profound slumber which not even the nightmare that wrung me could avail to break. I awoke in the morning, shaken, weakened, but refreshed. I still hated and feared the thought of the brute that slept within me, and I had not of course forgotten the appalling dangers of the day before; but I was once more at home, in my own house and close to my drugs; and gratitude for my escape shone so strong in my soul that it almost rivalled the brightness of hope.

I was stepping leisurely across the court after breakfast, drinking the chill of the air with pleasure, when I was seized again with those indescribable sensations that heralded the change; and I had but the time to gain the shelter of my cabinet, before I was once again raging and freezing with the passions of Hyde. It took on this occasion a double dose to recall me to myself; and, alas! six hours after, as I sat looking sadly in the fire, the pangs returned, and the drug had to be readministered. In short, from that day forth it seemed only by a great effort as of gymnastics, and only under the immediate stimulation of the drug, that I was able to wear the countenance of Jekyll. At all hours of the day and night I would be taken with the premonitory shudder; above all, if I slept or even dozed for a moment in my chair, it was always as Hyde that I awakened. Under the strain of this continually impending doom and by the sleeplessness to which I now condemned myself, ay, even beyond what I had thought possible to man, I became, in my own person, a creature eaten up and emptied by fever, languidly weak both in body and mind, and solely occupied by one thought: the horror of my other self. But when I slept or when the virtue of the medicine wore off, I would leap almost without transition (for the pangs of transformation grew daily less marked) into the possession of a fancy brimming with images of terror, a soul boiling with causeless hatreds, and a body that seemed not strong enough to contain the raging energies of life. The powers of Hyde seemed to have grown with the sickliness of Jekyll. And certainly the hate that now divided them was equal on each side. With Jekyll, it was a thing of vital instinct. He had now seen the full deformity of that creature that shared with him some of the phenomena of consciousness, and was co-heir with him to death: and beyond these links of community, which in themselves made the most poignant part of his distress, he thought of Hyde, for all his energy of life, as of something not only hellish but inorganic. This was the shocking thing; that the slime of the pit seemed to utter cries and voices; that the amorphous dust gesticulated and sinned; that what was dead, and had no shape, should usurp the offices of life. And this again, that that insurgent horror was knit to him closer than a wife, closer than an eye; lay caged in his flesh, where he heard it mutter and felt it struggle to be born; and at every hour of weakness, and in the confidence of slumber, prevailed against him, and deposed him out of life. The hatred of Hyde for Jekyll was of a different order. His terror of the gallows drove him continually to commit temporary suicide, and return to his subordinate station of a part instead of a person; but he loathed the necessity, he loathed the despondency into which Jekyll was now fallen, and he resented the dislike with which he was himself regarded. Hence the apelike tricks that he would play me, scrawling in my own hand blasphemies on the pages of my books, burning the letters and destroying the portrait of my father; and indeed, had it not been for his fear of death, he would long ago have ruined himself in order to involve me in the ruin. But his love of life is wonderful; I go further: I, who sicken and freeze at the mere thought of him, when I recall the abjection and passion of this attachment, and when I know how he fears my power to cut him off by suicide, I find it in my heart to pity him.

It is useless, and the time awfully fails me, to prolong this description;

no one has ever suffered such torments, let that suffice; and yet even to these, habit brought—no, not alleviation—but a certain callousness of soul, a certain acquiescence of despair; and my punishment might have gone on for years, but for the last calamity which has now befallen, and which has finally severed me from my own face and nature. My provision of the salt, which had never been renewed since the date of the first experiment, began to run low. I sent out for a fresh supply, and mixed the draught; the ebullition followed, and the first change of colour, not the second; I drank it, and it was without efficiency. You will learn from Poole how I have had London ransacked; it was in vain; and I am now persuaded that my first supply was impure, and that it was that unknown impurity which lent efficacy to the draught.

About a week has passed, and I am now finishing this statement under the influence of the last of the old powders. This, then, is the last time, short of a miracle, that Henry Jekyll can think his own thoughts or see his own face (now how sadly altered!) in the glass. Nor must I delay too long to bring my writing to an end; for if my narrative has hitherto escaped destruction, it has been by a combination of great prudence and great good luck. Should the throes of change take me in the act of writing it, Hyde will tear it in pieces; but if some time shall have elapsed after I have laid it by, his wonderful selfishness and circumscription to the moment will probably save it once again from the action of his apelike spite. And indeed the doom that is closing on us both has already changed and crushed him. Half an hour from now, when I shall again and for ever reindue that hated personality, I know how I shall sit shuddering and weeping in my chair, or continue, with the most strained and fearstruck ecstasy of listening, to pace up and down this room (my last earthly refuge) and give ear to every sound of menace. Will Hyde die upon the scaffold? or will he find the courage to release himself at the last moment? God knows; I am careless; this is my true hour of death, and what is to follow concerns another than myself. Here, then, as I lay down the pen, and proceed to seal up my confession, I bring the life of that unhappy Henry Jekyll to an end.

THE BABY IN
THE ICEBOX

by

JAMES M. CAIN

Of course there was plenty pieces in the paper about what happened out at the place last Summer, but they got it all mixed up, so I will now put down how it really was, and specially the beginning of it, so you will see it is not no lies in it.

Because when a guy and his wife begin to play leapfrog with a tiger, like you might say, and the papers put in about that part and not none of the stuff that started it off, and then one day say X marks the spot and next day say it wasn't really no murder but don't tell you what it was, why I don't blame people if they figure there was something funny about it or maybe that somebody ought to be locked up in the booby-hatch. But there wasn't no booby-hatch to this, nothing but plain onriness and a dirty rat getting it in the neck where he had it coming to him, as you will see when I get the first part explained right.

Things first began to go sour between Duke and Lura when they put the cats in. They didn't need no cats. They had a combination auto camp, filling-station, and lunchroom out in the country a ways, and they got along all right. Duke run the filling-station, and got me in to help him, and Lura took care of the lunchroom and shacks. But Duke wasn't satisfied. Before he got this place he had raised rabbits, and one time he had bees, and another time canary birds, and nothing would suit him now but to put in some cats to draw trade. Maybe you think that's funny, but out here in California they got every kind of a farm there is, from kangaroos to alligators, and it was just about the idea that a guy like Duke would think up. So he begun building a cage, and one day he showed up with a truckload of wildcats.

I wasn't there when they unloaded them. It was two or three cars waiting and I had to gas them up. But soon as I got a chance I went back there to look things over. And believe me, they wasn't pretty. The guy that sold Duke the cats had went away about five minutes before, and Duke was standing outside the cage and he had a stick of wood in his hand with blood on it. Inside was a dead cat. The rest of them was on a shelf, that had been built for them to jump on, and every one of them was snarling at Duke.

I don't know if you ever saw a wildcat, but they are about twice as big as a house cat, brindle gray, with tufted ears and a bobbed tail. When they set and look at you they look like a owl, but they wasn't setting and looking now. They was marching around, coughing and spitting, their eyes shooting red and green fire, and it was an ugly sight, specially with that bloody dead one down on the ground. Duke was pale, and the breath was whistling through his nose, and it didn't take no doctor to see he was scared to death.

"You better bury that cat," he says to me. "I'll take care of the cars."

I looked through the wire and he grabbed me. "Look out!" he says. "They'd kill you in a minute."

"In that case," I says, "how do I get the cat out?"

"You have to get a stick," he says, and shoves off.

I was pretty sore, but I begun looking around for a stick. I found one, but when I got back to the cage Lura was there. "How did that happen?" she says.

"I don't know," I says, "but I can tell you this much: If there's any more of them to be buried around here, you can get somebody else to do it. My job is to fix flats, and I'm not going to be no cat undertaker."

She didn't have nothing to say to that. She just stood there while I was trying the stick, and I could hear her toe snapping up and down in the sand, and from that I knowed she was choking it back, what she really thought, and didn't think no more of this here cat idea than I did.

The stick was too short. "My," she says, pretty disagreeable, "that looks terrible. You can't bring people out here with a thing like that in there."

"All right," I snapped back. "Find me a stick."

She didn't make no move to find no stick. She put her hand on the gate. "Hold on," I says. "Them things are nothing to monkey with."

"Huh," she says. "All they look like to me is a bunch of cats."

There was a kennel back of the cage, with a drop door on it, where they was supposed to go at night. How you got them back there was bait them with food, but I didn't know that then. I yelled at them, to drive them back in there, but nothing happened. All they done was yell back. Lura listened to me a while, and then she give a kind of gasp like she couldn't stand it no longer, opened the gate, and went in.

Now believe me, that next was a bad five minutes, because she wasn't hard to look at, and I hated to think of her getting mauled up by them babies. But a guy would of had to of been blind if it didn't show him that she had a way with cats. First thing she done, when she got in, she stood still, didn't make no sudden motions or nothing, and begun to talk to them. Not no special talk. Just "Pretty pussy, what's the matter, what they been doing to you?"—like that. Then she went over to them.

They slid off, on their bellies, to another part of the shelf. But she kept after them, and got her hand on one, and stroked him on the back. Then she got a-hold of another one, and pretty soon she had give them all a pat. Then she turned around, picked up the dead cat by one leg, and come out with him. I put him on the wheelbarrow and buried him.

Now, why was it that Lura kept it from Duke how easy she had got the cat out and even about being in the cage at all? I think it was just because she didn't have the heart to show him up to hisself how silly he looked. Anyway, at supper that night, she never said a word. Duke, he was nervous and excited and told all about how the cats had jumped at him and how he had to bean one to save his life, and then he give a long spiel about cats and how fear is the only thing they understand, so you would of thought he was Martin Johnson just back from the jungle or something.

But it seemed to me the dishes was making quite a noise that night, clattering around on the table, and that was funny, because one thing you could say for Lura was: she was quiet and easy to be around. So when Duke, just like it was nothing at all, asks me by the way how did I get the cat out, I heared my mouth saying, "With a stick," and not nothing more. A little bird flies around and tells you, at a time like that. Lura let it pass. Never said a word. And if you ask me, Duke never did find out how easy she could handle the cats, and that ain't only guesswork, but on account of something that happened a little while afterward, when we got the mountain-lion.

A mountain-lion is a cougar, only out here they call them a mountain-lion. Well, one afternoon about five o'clock this one of ours squat down on her hunkers and set up the worst squalling you ever listen to. She kept it up all night, so you wanted to go out and shoot her, and next morning at breakfast Duke come running in and says come on out and look what happened. So we went out there, and there in the cage with her was the prettiest he mountain-lion you ever seen in your life. He was big, probably weighed a hundred and fifty pounds, and his coat was a pearl gray so glossy it looked like a pair of new gloves, and he had a spot of white on his throat. Sometimes they have white.

"He come down from the hills when he heard her call last night," says Duke, "and he got in there somehow. Ain't it funny? When they hear that note nothing can stop them."

"Yeah," I says. "It's love."

"That's it," says Duke. "Well, we'll be having some little ones soon. Cheaper'n buying them."

After he had went off to town to buy the stuff for the day, Lura sat down to the table with me. "Nice of you," I says, "to let Romeo in last night."

"Romeo?" she says.

"Yes, Romeo. That's going to be papa of twins soon, out in the lion cage."

"Oh," she says, "didn't he get in there himself?"

"He did not. If she couldn't get out, how could he get in?"

All she give me at that time was a dead pan. Didn't know nothing about it at all. Fact of the matter, she made me a little sore. But after she brung me my second cup of coffee she kind of smiled. "Well?" she says. "You wouldn't keep two loving hearts apart, would you?"

So things was, like you might say, a little gritty, but they got a whole lot worse when Duke come home with Rajah, the tiger. Because by that time, he had told so many lies that he begun to believe them hisself, and put on all the airs of a big animal-trainer. When people come out on Sundays, he would take a black-snake whip and go in with the mountain-lions and wildcats, and snap it at them, and they would snarl and yowl, and Duke acted like he was doing something. Before he went in, he would let the people see him strapping on a big six-shooter, and Lura got sorer by the week.

For one thing, he looked so silly. She couldn't see nothing to going in with the cats, and specially couldn't see no sense in going in with a whip, a six-shooter, and a ten-gallon hat like them cow people wears. And for another thing, it was bad for business. In the beginning, when Lura would take the customers' kids out and make out the cat had their finger, they loved it, and they loved it still more when the little mountain-lions come and they had spots and would push up their ears to be scratched. But when Duke started that stuff with the whip it scared them to death, and even the fathers and mothers was nervous, because there was the gun and they didn't know what would happen next. So business begun to fall off.

And then one afternoon he put down a couple of drinks and figured it was time for him to go in there with Rajah. Now it had took Lura one minute to tame Rajah. She was in there sweeping out his cage one morning when Duke was away, and when he started sliding around on his belly he got a bucket of water in the face, and that was that. From then on he was her cat. But what happened when Duke tried to tame him was awful. The first I knew what he was up to was when he made a speech to the people from the mountain-lion cage telling them not to go away yet, there was more to come. And when he come out he headed over to the tiger.

"What's the big idea?" I says. "What you up to now?"

"I'm going in with that tiger," he says. "It's got to be done, and I might as well do it now."

"Why has it got to be done?" I says.

He looked at me like as though he pitied me.

"I guess there's a few things about cats you don't know yet," he says. "You got a tiger on your hands, you got to let him know who's boss, that's all."

"Yeah?" I says. "And who *is* boss?"

"You see that?" he says, and cocks his finger at his face.

"See what?" I says.

"The human eye," he says. "The human eye, that's all. A cat's afraid of it. And if you know your business, you'll keep him afraid of it. That's all I'll use, the human eye. But of course, just for protection, I've got these too."

"Listen, sweetheart," I says to him. "If you give me a choice between the human eye and a Bengal tiger, which one *I* got the most fear of, you're going to see a guy getting a shiner every time. If I was you, I'd lay off that cat."

He didn't say nothing: hitched up his holster, and went in. He didn't even get a chance to unlimber his whip. That tiger, soon as he saw him, begun to move around in a way that made your blood run cold. He didn't make for Duke first, you understand. He slid over, and in a second he was between Duke and the gate. That's one thing about a tiger you better not forget if you ever meet one. He can't work examples in arithmetic, but when it comes to the kind of brains that mean meat, he's the brightest boy in the class and then some. He's born knowing more about cutting off a retreat than you'll ever know, and his legs do it for him, just automatic, so his jaws will be free for the main business of the meeting.

Duke backed away, and his face was awful to see. He was straining every muscle to keep his mouth from sliding down in his collar. His left hand fingered the whip a little, and his right pawed around, like he had some idea of drawing the gun. But the tiger didn't give him time to make up his mind what his idea was, if any.

He would slide a few feet on his belly, then get up and trot a step or two, then slide on his belly again. He didn't make no noise, you understand. He wasn't telling Duke, Please go away: he meant to kill him, and a killer don't generally make no more fuss than he has to. So for a few seconds you could even hear Duke's feet sliding over the floor. But all of a sudden a kid begun to whimper, and I come to my senses. I run around to the back of the cage, because that was where the tiger was crowding him, and I yelled at him.

"Duke!" I says. "In his kennel! Quick!"

He didn't seem to hear me. He was still backing, and the tiger was still coming. A woman screamed. The tiger's head went down, he crouched on the ground, and tightened every muscle. I knew what that meant. Everybody knew what it meant, and specially Duke knew what it meant. He made a funny sound in his throat, turned, and ran.

That was when the tiger sprung. Duke had no idea where he was going, but when he turned he fell through the trap door and I snapped it down. The tiger hit it so hard I thought it would split. One of Duke's legs was out, and the tiger was on it in a flash, but all he got on that grab was the sole of Duke's shoe. Duke got his leg in somehow and I jammed the door down tight.

It was a sweet time at supper that night. Lura didn't see this here, because she was busy in the lunchroom when it happened, but them people had talked on their way out, and she knowed all about it. What she said was plenty. And Duke, what do you think he done? He passed it off like it wasn't nothing at all. "Just one of them things you got to expect," he says. And then he let on he knowed what he was doing all the time, and the only lucky part of it was that he didn't have to shoot a valuable animal like Rajah was. "Keep cool, that's the main thing," he says. "A thing like that can happen now and then, but never let a animal see you excited."

I heard him, and I couldn't believe my ears, but when I looked at Lura I jumped. I think I told you she wasn't hard to look at. She was a kind of medium size, with a shape that would make a guy leave his happy home, sunburned all over, and high cheekbones that give her eyes a funny slant. But her eyes was narrowed down to slits, looking at Duke, and they shot green where the light hit them, and it come over me all of a sudden that she looked so much like Rajah, when he was closing in on Duke in the afternoon, that she could of been his twin sister.

Next off, Duke got it in his head he was such a big cat man now that he had to go up in the hills and do some trapping. Bring in his own stuff, he called it.

I didn't pay much attention to it at the time. Of course, he never brought in no stuff, except a couple of raccoons that he probably bought down the road for $2, but Duke was the kind of a guy that every once in a while has to sit on a rock and fish, so when he loaded up the flivver and blew, it wasn't nothing you would get excited about. Maybe I didn't really care what he was up to, because it was pretty nice, running the place with Lura with him out of the way, and I didn't ask no questions. But it was more to it than cats or 'coons or fish, and Lura knowed it, even if I didn't.

Anyhow, it was while he was away on one of them trips of his that Wild Bill Smith the Texas Tornado showed up. Bill was a snake-doctor. He had a truck, with his picture painted on it, and two or three boxes of old rattlesnakes with their teeth pulled out, and he sold snake-oil that would cure what ailed you, and a Indian herb medicine that would do the same. He was a fake, but he was big and brown and had white teeth, and I guess he really wasn't no bad guy. The first I seen of him was when he drove up in his truck, and told me to gas him up and look at his tires. He had a bum differential that made a funny rattle, but he said never mind and went over to the lunchroom.

He was there a long time, and I thought I better let him know his car was ready. When I went over there, he was setting on a stool with a sheepish look on his face, rubbing his hand. He had a snake ring on one finger, with two red eyes, and on the back of his hand was red streaks. I knew what that meant. He had started something and Lura had fixed him. She had a pretty arm, but a grip like iron, that she said come from milking cows when she was a kid. What she done when a guy got fresh was take hold of his hand and squeeze it so the bones cracked, and he generally changed his mind.

She handed him his check without a word, and I told him what he owed on the car, and he paid up and left.

"So you settled his hash, hey?" I says to her.

"If there's one thing gets on my nerves," she says, "it's a man that starts something the minute he gets in the door."

"Why didn't you yell for me?"

"Oh, I didn't need no help."

But the next day he was back, and after I filled up his car I went over to see how he was behaving. He was setting at one of the tables this time, and Lura was standing beside him. I saw her jerk her hand away quick, and he give me the bright grin a man has when he's got something he wants to cover up. He was all teeth.

"Nice day," he says. "Great weather you have in this country."

"So I hear," I says. "Your car's ready."

"What I owe you?" he says.

"Dollar twenty."

He counted it out and left.

"Listen," says Lura: "we weren't doing anything when you come in.

He was just reading my hand. He's a snake doctor, and knows about the zodiac."

"Oh, wasn't we?" I says. "Well, wasn't we nice!"

"What's it to you?" she says.

"Nothing," I snapped at her. I was pretty sore.

"He says I was born under the sign of Yin," she says. You would of thought it was a piece of news fit to put in the paper.

"And who is Yin?" I says.

"It's Chinese for tiger," she says.

"Then bite yourself off a piece of raw meat," I says, and slammed out of there. We didn't have no nice time running the joint *that* day.

Next morning he was back. I kept away from the lunchroom, but I took a stroll, and seen them back there with the tiger. We had hauled a tree in there by that time, for Rajah to sharpen his claws on, and she was setting on that. The tiger had his head in her lap, and Wild Bill was looking through the wire. He couldn't even draw his breath. I didn't go near enough to hear what they was saying. I went back to the car and begin blowing the horn.

He was back quite a few times after that, in between while Duke was away. Then one night I heard a truck drive up. I knowed that truck by its rattle. And it was daylight before I heard it go away.

Couple weeks after that, Duke come running over to me at the filling-station. "Shake hands with me," he says. "I'm going to be a father."

"Gee," I says, "that's great!"

But I took good care he wasn't around when I mentioned it to Lura.

"Congratulations," I says. "Letting Romeos into the place seems to be about the best thing you do."

"What do you mean?" she says.

"Nothing," I says. "Only I heard him drive up that night. Look like to me the moon was under the sign of Cupid. Well, it's nice if you can get away with it."

"Oh," she says.

"Yeah," I says. "A fine double cross you thought up. I didn't know they tried that any more."

She set and looked at me, and then her mouth begin to twitch and her eyes filled with tears. She tried to snuffle them up but it didn't work. "It's not any double cross," she says. "That night, I never went out there. And I never let anybody in. I was supposed to go away with him that night, but—"

She broke off and begin to cry. I took her in my arms. "But then you found this out?" I says. "Is that it?" She nodded her head. It's awful to have a pretty woman in your arms that's crying over somebody else.

From then on, it was terrible. Lura would go along two or three days pretty nice, trying to like Duke again on account of the baby coming, but then would come a day when she looked like some kind of a hex, with her eyes all sunk in so you could hardly see them at all, and not a word out of her.

Them bad days, anyhow when Duke wasn't around, she would spend with the tiger. She would set and watch him sleep, or maybe play with him, and he seemed to like it as much as she did. He was young when we got him, and mangy and thin, so you could see his slats. But now he was about six year old, and had been fed good, so he had got his growth and his coat was nice, and I think he was the biggest tiger I ever seen. A tiger, when he is really big, is a lot bigger than a lion, and sometimes when Rajah would be rubbing around Lura, he looked more like a mule than a cat.

His shoulders come up above her waist, and his head was so big it would cover both her legs when he put it in her lap. When his tail would go sliding past her it looked like some kind of a constrictor snake. His teeth were something to make you lie awake nights. A tiger has the biggest teeth of any cat, and Rajah's must have been four inches long, curved like a cavalry sword, and ivory white. They were the most murderous-looking fangs I ever set eyes on.

When Lura went to the hospital it was a hurry call, and she didn't even have time to get her clothes together. Next day Duke had to pack her bag, and he was strutting around, because it was a boy, and Lura had named him Ron. But when he come out with the bag, he didn't have much of a strut.

"Look what I found," he says to me, and fishes something out of his pocket. It was the snake ring.

"Well?" I says. "They sell them in any dime store."

"H'm," he says, and kind of weighed the ring in his hand. That afternoon, when he come back, he says, "Ten-cent store, hey? I took it to a jeweler today, and he offered me two hundred dollars for it."

"You ought to sold it," I says. "Maybe save you bad luck."

Duke went away again right after Lura come back, and for a little while things was all right. She was crazy about the little boy, and I thought he was pretty cute myself, and we got along fine. But then Duke come back and at lunch one day he made a crack about the ring. Lura didn't say nothing, but he kept at it, and pretty soon she wheeled on him.

"All right," she says. "There was another man around here, and I loved him. He give me that ring, and it meant that he and I belonged to each other. But I didn't go with him, and you know why I didn't. For Ron's sake, I've tried to love you again, and maybe I can yet, God knows. A woman can do some funny things if she tries. But that's where we're at now. That's right where we're at. And if you don't like it, you better say what you're going to do."

"When was this?" says Duke.

"It was quite a while ago. I told you I give him up, and I give him up for keeps."

"It was just before you knowed about Ron, wasn't it?" he says.

"Hey," I cut in. "That's no way to talk."

"Just what I thought," he says, not paying no attention to me. "Ron. That's a funny name for a kid. I thought it was funny, right off when I heard it. Ron. Ron. That's a laugh, ain't it?"

"That's a lie," she says. "That's a lie, every bit of it. And it's not the only lie you've been getting away with around here. Or think you have. Trapping up in the hills, hey? And what do you trap?"

But she looked at me, and choked it back. I begun to see that the cats wasn't the only things that had been gumming it up.

"All right," she wound up. "Say what you're going to do. Go on. Say it!"

But he didn't.

"Ron," he cackles, "that's a hot one," and walks out.

Next day was Saturday, and he acted funny all day. He wouldn't speak to me or Lura, and once or twice I heard him mumbling to himself. Right after supper he says to me, "How are we on oil?"

"All right," I says. "The truck was around yesterday."

"You better drive in and get some," he says. "I don't think we got enough."

"Enough?" I says. "We got enough for two weeks."

"Tomorrow is Sunday," he says, "and there'll be a big call for it. Bring out a hundred gallon and tell them to put it on the account."

By that time, I would give in to one of his nutty ideas rather than have an argument with him, and besides, I never tumbled that he was up to anything. So I wasn't there for what happened next, but I got it out of Lura later, so here is how it was:

Lura didn't pay much attention to the argument about the oil, but washed up the supper dishes, and then went in the bedroom to make sure everything was all right with the baby. When she come out she left the door open, so she could hear if he cried. The bedroom was off the sitting-room, because these here California houses don't have but one floor, and all the rooms connect. Then she lit the fire, because it was cool, and sat there watching it burn. Duke come in, walked around, and then went out back. "Close the door," she says to him. "I'll be right back," he says.

So she sat looking at the fire, she didn't know how long, maybe five minutes, maybe ten minutes. But pretty soon she felt the house shake. She thought maybe it was a earthquake, and looked at the pictures, but they was all hanging straight. Then she felt the house shake again. She listened, but it wasn't no truck outside that would cause it, and it wouldn't be no State road blasting or nothing like that at that time of night. Then she felt it shake again, and this time it shook in a regular movement, one, two, three, four, like that. And then all of a sudden she knew what it was, why Duke had acted so funny all day, why he had sent me off for the gas, why he had left the door open, and all the rest of it. There was five hundred pounds of cat walking through the house, and Duke had turned him loose to kill her.

She turned around, and Rajah was looking at her, not five foot away. She didn't do nothing for a minute, just set there thinking what a boob Duke was to figure on the tiger doing his dirty work for him, when all the time she could handle him easy as a kitten, only Duke didn't know it. Then she spoke. She expected Rajah to come and put his head in her lap, but he didn't. He stood there and growled, and his ears flattened back. That scared her, and she thought of the baby. I told you a tiger has that kind of brains. It no sooner went through her head about the baby than Rajah knowed she wanted to get to that door, and he was over there before she could get out of the chair.

He was snarling in a regular roar now, but he hadn't got a whiff of the baby yet, and he was still facing Lura. She could see he meant business. She reached in the fireplace, grabbed a stick that was burning bright, and walked him down with it. A tiger is afraid of fire, and she shoved it right in his eyes. He backed past the door, and she slid in the bedroom. But he was right after her, and she had to hold the stick at him with one hand and grab the baby with the other.

But she couldn't get out. He had her cornered, and he was kicking up such a awful fuss she knowed the stick wouldn't stop him long. So she dropped it, grabbed up the baby's covers, and threw them at his head. They went wild, but they saved her just the same. A tiger, if you throw something at him with a human smell, will generally jump on it and bite at it before he does anything else, and that's what he done now. He jumped so hard the rug went out from under him, and while he was scrambling to his feet she shot past him with the baby and pulled the door shut after her.

She run in my room, got a blanket, wrapped the baby in it, and run out to the electric icebox. It was the only thing around the place that was steel. Soon as she opened the door she knowed why she couldn't do nothing with Rajah. His meat was in there, Duke hadn't fed him. She pulled the meat out, shoved the baby in, cut off the current, and closed the door. Then she picked up the meat and went around outside of the house to the window of the bedroom. She could see Rajah in there, biting at the top of the door, where a crack of light showed through. He reached to the ceiling. She took a grip on the meat and drove at the screen with it. It give way, and the meat went through. He was on it before it hit the floor.

Next thing was to give him time to eat. She figured she could handle him once he got something in his belly. She went back to the sitting-room. And in there, kind of peering around, was Duke. He had his gun strapped on, and one look at his face was all she needed to know she hadn't made no mistake about why the tiger was loose.

"Oh," he says, kind of foolish, and then walked back and closed the door. "I meant to come back sooner, but I couldn't help looking at the night. You got no idea how beautiful it is. Stars is bright as anything."

"Yeah," she says. "I noticed."

"Beautiful," he says. "Beautiful."

"Was you expecting burglars or something?" she says, looking at the gun.

"Oh, that," he says. "No. Cats been kicking up a fuss. I put it on, case I have to go back there. Always like to have it handy."

"The tiger," she says. "I thought I heard him, myself."

"Loud," says Duke. "Awful loud."

He waited. She waited. She wasn't going to give him the satisfaction of opening up first. But just then there come a growl from the bedroom, and the sound of bones cracking. A tiger acts awful sore when he eats. "What's that?" says Duke.

"I wonder," says Lura. She was hell-bent on making him spill it first.

They both looked at each other, and then there was more growls, and more sound of cracking bones. "You better go in there," says Duke, soft and easy, with the sweat standing out on his forehead and his eyes shining bright as marbles. "Something might be happening to Ron."

"Do you know what I think it is?" says Lura.

"What's that?" says Duke. His breath was whistling through his nose like it always done when he got excited.

"I think it's that tiger you sent in here to kill me," says Lura. "So you could bring in that woman you been running around with for over a year. That redhead that raises rabbit fryers on the Ventura road. That cat you been trapping!"

"And stead of getting you he got Ron," says Duke. "Little Ron! Oh my, ain't that tough? Go in there, why don't you? Ain't you got no mother love? Why don't you call up his pappy, get him in there? What's the matter? Is he afraid of a cat?"

Lura laughed at him. "All right," she says. "Now you go." With that she took hold of him. He tried to draw the gun, but she crumpled up his hand like a piece of wet paper and the gun fell on the floor. She bent him back on the table and beat his face in for him. Then she picked him up, dragged him to the front door, and threw him out. He run off a little ways. She come back and saw the gun. She picked it up, went to the door again, and threw it after him. "And take that peashooter with you," she says.

That was where she made her big mistake. When she turned to go back in the house, he shot, and that was the last she knew for a while.

Now, for what happened next, it wasn't nobody there, only Duke and the tiger, but after them State cops got done fitting it all together, combing the ruins and all, it wasn't no trouble to tell how it was, anyway most of it, and here's how they figured it out:

Soon as Duke seen Lura fall, right there in front of the house, he knowed he was up against it. So the first thing he done was to run to where she was and put the gun in her hand, to make it look like she had shot herself. That was where he made *his* big mistake, because if he had kept the gun he might of had a chance. Then he went inside to telephone, and what he said was, soon as he got hold of the State police:

"For God's sake come out here quick. My wife has went crazy and throwed the baby to the tiger and shot herself and I'm all alone in the house with him and—*Oh, my God, here he comes!*"

Now, that last was something he didn't figure on saying. So far as he knowed, the tiger was in the room, having a nice meal off his son, so everything was hotsy-totsy. But what he didn't know was that that piece of burning firewood that Lura had dropped had set the room on fire and on account of that the tiger had got out. How did he get out? We never did quite figure that out. But this is how I figure it, and one man's guess is good as another's:

The fire started near the window, we knew that much. That was where Lura dropped the stick, right next to the cradle, and that was where a guy coming down the road in a car first seen the flames. And what I think is that soon as the tiger got his eye off the meat and seen the fire, he begun to scramble away from it, just wild. And when a wild tiger hits a beaverboard wall, he goes through, that's all. While Duke was telephoning, Rajah come through the wall like a clown through a hoop, and the first thing he seen was Duke, at the telephone, and Duke wasn't no friend, not to Rajah he wasn't.

Anyway, that's how things was when I got there, with the oil. The State cops was a little ahead of me, and I met the ambulance with Lura in it, coming down the road seventy mile an hour, but just figured there had been a crash up the road, and didn't know nothing about it having Lura in it. And when I drove up, there was plenty to look at all right. The house was in flames, and the police was trying to get in, but couldn't get nowheres near it on account of the heat, and about a hundred cars parked all around, with people looking, and a gasoline pumper cruising up and down the road, trying to find a water connection somewheres they could screw their hose to.

But inside the house was the terrible part. You could hear Duke screaming, and in between Duke was the tiger. And both of them was screams of fear, but I think the tiger was worse. It is a awful thing to hear a animal letting out a sound like that. It kept up about five minutes after I got there, and then all of a sudden you couldn't hear nothing but the tiger. And then in a minute that stopped.

There was nothing to do about the fire. In a half hour the whole place was gone, and they was combing the ruins for Duke. Well, they found him. And in his head was four holes, two on each side, deep. We measured them fangs of the tiger. They just fit.

Soon as I could I run to the hospital. They had got the bullet out by that time, and Lura was laying in bed all bandaged around the head, but there was a guard over her, on account of what Duke said over the telephone. He was a State cop. I sat down with him, and he didn't like it none. Neither did I. I knowed there was something funny about it, but what broke your heart was Lura, coming out of the ether. She would groan and mutter and try to say something so hard it would make your head ache. After a while I got up and went in the hall. But then I see the State cop shoot out of the room and line down the hall as fast as he could go. At last she had said it. The baby was in the electric icebox. They found him there, still asleep and just about ready for his milk. The fire had blacked up the outside, but inside it was as cool and nice as a new bathtub.

Well, that was about all. They cleared Lura, soon as she told her story, and the baby in the icebox proved it. Soon as she got out of the hospital she got a offer from the movies, but stead of taking it she come out to the place and her and I run it for a while, anyway the filling-station end, sleeping in the shacks and getting along nice. But one night I heard a rattle from a bum differential, and I never even bothered to show up for breakfast the next morning.

I often wish I had. Maybe she left me a note.

THE COUPLE NEXT DOOR

by

MARGARET MILLAR

It was by accident that they lived next door to each other, but by design that they became neighbors—Mr. Sands, who had retired to California after a life of crime investigation, and the Rackhams, Charles and Alma. Rackham was a big, innocent-looking man in his fifties. Except for the accumulation of a great deal of money, nothing much had ever happened to Rackham, and he liked to listen to Sands talk, while Alma sat with her knitting, plump and contented, unimpressed by any tale that had no direct bearing on her own life. She was half Rackham's age, but the fullness of her figure, and her air of having withdrawn from life quietly and without fuss, gave her the stamp of middle-age.

Two or three times a week Sands crossed the concrete driveway, skirted the eugenia hedge, and pressed the Rackhams' door chime. He stayed for tea or for dinner, to play gin or Scrabble, or just to talk. "That reminds me of a case I had in Toronto," Sands would say, and Rackham would produce martinis and an expression of intense interest, and Alma would smile tolerantly, as if she didn't really believe a single thing Sands, or anyone else, ever said.

They made good neighbors: the Rackhams, Charles younger than his years, and Alma older than hers, and Sands who could be any age at all . . .

It was the last evening of August and through the open window of Sands' study came the scent of jasmine and the sound of a woman's harsh, wild weeping.

He thought at first that the Rackhams had a guest, a woman on a crying jag, perhaps, after a quarrel with her husband.

He went out into the front yard to listen, and Rackham came around the corner of the eugenia hedge, dressed in a bathrobe.

He said, sounding very surprised, "Alma's crying."

"I heard."

"I asked her to stop. I begged her. She won't tell me what's the matter."

"Women have cried before."

"Not Alma." Rackham stood on the damp grass, shivering, his forehead streaked with sweat. "What do you think we should do about it?"

The *I* had become *we*, because they were good neighbors, and along with the games and the dinners and the scent of jasmine, they shared the sound of a woman's grief.

"Perhaps you could talk to her," Rackham said.

"I'll try."

"I don't think there is anything physically the matter with her. We both had a check-up at the Tracy clinic last week. George Tracy is a good friend of mine—he'd have told me if there was anything wrong."

"I'm sure he would."

"If anything ever happened to Alma I'd kill myself."

Alma was crouched in a corner of the davenport in the living room, weeping rhythmically, methodically, as if she had accumulated a hoard of tears and must now spend them all in one night. Her fair skin was blotched with patches of red, like strawberry birthmarks, and her eyelids were blistered from the heat of her tears. She looked like a stranger to Sands, who had never seen her display any emotion stronger than lady-like distress over a broken teacup or an overdone roast.

Rackham went over and stroked her hair. "Alma, dear. What is the matter?"

"Nothing . . . nothing . . ."

"Mr. Sands is here, Alma. I thought he might be able—we might be able—"

But no one was able. With a long shuddering sob, Alma got up and lurched across the room, hiding her blotched face with her hands. They heard her stumble up the stairs.

Sands said, "I'd better be going."

"No, please don't. I—the fact is, I'm scared. I'm scared stiff. Alma's always been so quiet."

"I know that."

"You don't suppose—there's no chance she's losing her mind?"

If they had not been good neighbors Sands might have remarked that Alma had little mind to lose. As it was, he said cautiously, "She might have had bad news, family trouble of some kind."

"She has no family except me."

"If you're worried, perhaps you'd better call your doctor."

"I think I will."

George Tracy arrived within half an hour, a slight, fair-haired man in his early thirties, with a smooth unhurried manner that imparted confidence. He talked slowly, moved slowly, as if there was all the time in the world to minister to desperate women.

Rackham chafed with impatience while Tracy removed his coat, placed it carefully across the back of the chair, and discussed the weather with Sands.

"It's a beautiful evening," Tracy said, and Alma's moans sliding down the stairs distorted his words, altered their meaning: *a terrible evening, an awful evening.* "There's a touch of fall in the air. You live in these parts, Mr. Sands?"

"Next door."

"For heaven's sake, George," Rackham said, "will you hurry up? For all you know, Alma might be dying."

"That I doubt. People don't die as easily as you might imagine. She's in her room?"

"Yes. Now will you *please*—"

"Take it easy, old man."

Tracy picked up his medical bag and went towards the stairs, leisurely, benign.

"He's always like that." Rackham turned to Sands scowling. "Exasperating son-of-a-gun. You can bet that if he had a wife in Alma's condition he'd be taking those steps three at a time."

"Who knows?—perhaps he has."

"*I* know," Rackham said crisply. "He's not even married. Never had time for it, he told me. He doesn't look it but he's very ambitious."

"Most doctors are."

"Tracy is, anyway."

Rackham mixed a pitcher of martinis, and the two men sat in front of the unlit fire, waiting and listening. The noises from upstairs gradually ceased, and pretty soon the doctor came down again.

Rackham rushed across the room to meet him. "How is she?"

"Sleeping. I gave her a hypo."

"Did you talk to her? Did you ask her what was the matter?"

"She was in no condition to answer questions."

"Did you find anything wrong with her?"

"Not physically. She's a healthy young woman."

"Not *physically*. Does that mean—?"

"Take it easy, old man."

Rackham was too concerned with Alma to notice Tracy's choice of words, but Sands noticed, and wondered if it had been conscious or unconscious: Alma's a healthy young woman . . . Take it easy, old man.

"If she's still depressed in the morning," Tracy said, "bring her down to the clinic with you when you come in for your X-rays. We have a good neurologist on our staff." He reached for his coat and hat. "By the way, I hope you followed the instructions."

Rackham looked at him stupidly. "What instructions?"

"Before we can take specific X-rays, certain medication is necessary."

"I don't know what you're talking about."

"I made it very clear to Alma," Tracy said, sounding annoyed. "You were to take one ounce of sodium phosphate after dinner tonight, and report to the X-ray department at 8 o'clock tomorrow morning without breakfast."

"She didn't tell me."

"Oh."

"It must have slipped her mind."

"Yes. Obviously. Well, it's too late now." He put on his coat, moving quickly for the first time, as if he were in a rush to get away. The change made Sands curious. He wondered why Tracy was suddenly so anxious to leave, and whether there was any connection between Alma's hysteria and her lapse of memory about Rackham's X-rays. He looked at Rackham and guessed, from his pallor and his worried eyes, that Rackham had already made a connection in his mind.

"I understood," Rackham said carefully, "that I was all through at the clinic. My heart, lungs, metabolism—everything fit as a fiddle."

"People," Tracy said, "are not fiddles. Their tone doesn't improve with age. I will make another appointment for you and send you specific instructions by mail. Is that all right with you?"

"I guess it will have to be."

"Well, good night, Mr. Sands, pleasant meeting you." And to Rackham, "Good night, old man."

When he had gone, Rackham leaned against the wall, breathing hard. Sweat crawled down the sides of his face like worms and hid in the collar of his bathrobe. "You'll have to forgive me, Sands. I feel—I'm not feeling very well."

"Is there anything I can do?"

"Yes," Rackham said. "Turn back the clock."

"Beyond my powers, I'm afraid."

"Yes . . . Yes, I'm afraid."

"Good night, Rackham." *Good night, old man.*

"Good night, Sands." *Good night old man to you, too.*

Sands shuffled across the concrete driveway, his head bent. It was a dark night, with no moon at all.

From his study Sands could see the lighted windows of Rackham's bedroom. Rackham's shadow moved back and forth behind the blinds as if seeking escape from the very light that gave it existence. Back and forth, in search of nirvana.

Sands read until far into the night. It was one of the solaces of growing old—if the hours were numbered, at least fewer of them need be wasted in sleep. When he went to bed, Rackham's bedroom light was still on.

They had become good neighbors by design; now, also by design, they became strangers. Whose design it was, Alma's or Rackham's, Sands didn't know.

There was no definite break, no unpleasantness. But the eugenia hedge seemed to have grown taller and thicker, and the concrete driveway a mile wide. He saw the Rackhams occasionally; they waved or smiled or said, "Lovely weather," over the backyard fence. But Rackham's smile was thin and painful, Alma waved with a leaden arm, and neither of them cared about the weather. They stayed indoors most of the time, and when they did come out they were always together, arm in arm, walking slowly and in step. It was impossible to tell whose step led, and whose followed.

At the end of the first week in September, Sands met Alma by accident in a drug store downtown. It was the first time since the night of the doctor's visit that he'd seen either of the Rackhams alone.

She was waiting at the prescription counter wearing a flowery print dress that emphasized the fullness of her figure and the bovine expression of her face. A drug-store length away, she looked like a rather dull, badly dressed young woman with a passion for starchy foods, and it was hard to understand what Rackham had seen in her. But then Rackham had never stood a drug-store length away from Alma; he saw her only in close-up, the surprising, intense blue of her eyes, and the color and texture of her skin, like whipped cream. Sands wondered whether it was her skin and eyes, or her quality of serenity which had appealed most to Rackham, who was quick and nervous and excitable.

She said, placidly, "Why, hello there."

"Hello, Alma."

"Lovely weather, isn't it?"

"Yes. . . . How is Charles?"

"You must come over for dinner one of these nights."

"I'd like to."

"Next week, perhaps. I'll give you a call—I must run now, Charles is waiting for me. See you next week."

But she did not run, she walked; and Charles was not waiting for her, he was waiting for Sands. He had let himself into Sands' house and was pacing the floor of the study, smoking a cigarette. His color was bad, and he had lost weight, but he seemed to have acquired an inner calm. Sands could not tell whether it was the calm of a man who had come to an important decision, or that of a man who had reached the end of his rope and had stopped struggling.

They shook hands, firmly, pressing the past week back into shape.

Rackham said, "Nice to see you again, old man."

"I've been here all along."

"Yes. Yes, I know. . . . I had things to do, a lot of thinking to do."

"Sit down. I'll make you a drink."

"No, thanks. Alma will be home shortly, I must be there."

Like a Siamese twin, Sands thought, *separated by a miracle, but returning voluntarily to the fusion—because the fusion was in a vital organ.*

"I understand," Sands said.

Rackham shook his head. "No one can understand, really, but you come very close sometimes, Sands. Very close." His cheeks flushed, like a boy's. "I'm not good at words or expressing my emotions, but I wanted to thank you before we leave, and tell you how much Alma and I have enjoyed your companionship."

"You're taking a trip?"

"Yes. Quite a long one."

"When are you leaving?"

"Today."

"You must let me see you off at the station."

"No, no," Rackham said quickly. "I couldn't think of it. I hate last-minute depot farewells. That's why I came over this afternoon to say goodbye."

"Tell me something of your plans."

"I would if I had any. Everything is rather indefinite. I'm not sure where we'll end up."

"I'd like to hear from you now and then."

"Oh, you'll hear from me, of course." Rackham turned away with an impatient twitch of his shoulders as if he was anxious to leave, anxious to start the trip right now before anything happened to prevent it.

"I'll miss you both," Sands said. "We've had a lot of laughs together."

Rackham scowled out of the window. "Please, no farewell speeches. They might shake my decision. My mind is already made up, I want no second thoughts."

"Very well."

"I must go now. Alma will be wondering—"

"I saw Alma earlier this afternoon," Sands said.

"Oh?"

"She invited me for dinner next week."

Outside the open window two hummingbirds fought and fussed, darting with crazy accuracy in and out of the bougainvillaea vine.

"Alma," Rackham said carefully, "can be very forgetful sometimes."

"Not that forgetful. She doesn't know about this trip you've planned, does she? . . . Does she, Rackham?"

"I wanted it to be a surprise. She's always had a desire to see the world. She's still young enough to believe that one place is different from any other place. . . . You and I know better."

"Do we?"

"Goodbye, Sands."

At the front door they shook hands again, and Rackham again promised to write, and Sands promised to answer his letters. Then Rackham crossed the lawn and the concrete driveway, head bent, shoulders hunched. He didn't look back as he turned the corner of the eugenia hedge.

Sands went over to his desk, looked up a number in the telephone directory, and dialed.

A girl's voice answered, "Tracy clinic, X-ray department."

"This is Charles Rackham," Sands said.

"Yes, Mr. Rackham."

"I'm leaving town unexpectedly. If you'll tell me the amount of my bill I'll send you a check before I go."

"The bill hasn't gone through, but the standard price for a lower gastrointestinal is twenty-five dollars."

"Let's see, I had that done on the—"

"The fifth. Yesterday."

"But my original appointment was for the first, wasn't it?"

The girl gave a does-it-really-matter sigh. "Just a moment, sir, and I'll check." Half a minute later she was back on the line.

"We have no record of an appointment for you on the first, sir."

"You're sure of that?"

"Even without the record book, I'd be sure. The first was a Monday. We do only gall bladders on Monday."

"Oh. Thank you."

Sands went out and got into his car. Before he pulled away from the curb he looked over at Rackham's house and saw Rackham pacing up and down the veranda, waiting for Alma.

The Tracy clinic was less impressive than Sands had expected, a converted two-story stucco house with a red tile roof. Some of the tiles were broken and the whole building needed paint, but the furnishings inside were smart and expensive.

At the reception desk a nurse wearing a crew cut and a professional smile told Sands that Dr. Tracy was booked solid for the entire afternoon. The only chance of seeing him was to sit in the second-floor waiting room and catch him between patients.

Sands went upstairs and took a chair in a little alcove at the end of the hall, near Tracy's door. He sat with his face half hidden behind an open magazine. After a while the door of Tracy's office opened and over the top of his magazine Sands saw a woman silhouetted in the door frame—a plump, fair-haired young woman in a flowery print dress.

Tracy followed her into the hall and the two of them stood looking at each other in silence. Then Alma turned and walked away, passing Sands without seeing him because her eyes were blind with tears.

Sands stood up. "Dr. Tracy?"

Tracy turned sharply, surprise and annoyance pinching the corners of his mouth. "Well? Oh, it's Mr. Sands."

"May I see you a moment?"

"I have quite a full schedule this afternoon."

"This is an emergency."

"Very well. Come in."

They sat facing each other across Tracy's desk.

"You look pretty fit," Tracy said with a wry smile, "for an emergency case."

"The emergency is not mine. It may be yours."

"If it's mine, I'll handle it alone, without the help of a poli— I'll handle it myself."

Sands leaned forward. "Alma has told you, then, that I used to be a policeman."

"She mentioned it in passing."

"I saw Alma leave a few minutes ago. . . . She'd be quite a nice-looking woman if she learned to dress properly."

"Clothes are not important in a woman," Tracy said, with a slight flush. "Besides, I don't care to discuss my patients."

"Alma is a patient of yours?"

"Yes."

"Since the night Rackham called you when she was having hysterics?"

"Before then."

Sands got up, went to the window, and looked down at the street.

People were passing, children were playing on the sidewalk, the sun shone, the palm trees rustled with wind—everything outside seemed normal and human and real. By contrast, the shape of the idea that was forming in the back of his mind was so grotesque and ugly that he wanted to run out of the office, to join the normal people passing on the street below. But he knew he could not escape by running. The idea would follow him, pursue him until he turned around and faced it.

It moved inside his brain like a vast wheel, and in the middle of the wheel, impassive, immobile, was Alma.

Tracy's harsh voice interrupted the turning of the wheel. "Did you come here to inspect my view, Mr. Sands?"

"Let's say, instead, your viewpoint."

"I'm a busy man. You're wasting my time."

"No. I'm giving you time."

"To do what?"

"Think things over."

"If you don't leave my office immediately, I'll have you thrown out." Tracy glanced at the telephone but he didn't reach for it, and there was no conviction in his voice.

"Perhaps you shouldn't have let me in. Why did you?"

"I thought you might make a fuss if I didn't."

"Fusses aren't in my line." Sands turned from the window. "Liars are, though."

"What are you implying?"

"I've thought a great deal about that night you came to the Rackhams' house. In retrospect, the whole thing appeared too pat, too contrived: Alma had hysterics and you were called in to treat her. Natural enough, so far."

Tracy stirred but didn't speak.

"The interesting part came later. You mentioned casually to Rackham that he had an appointment for some X-rays to be taken the following day, September the first. It was assumed that Alma had forgotten to tell him. Only Alma *hadn't* forgotten. There was nothing to forget. I checked with your X-ray department half an hour ago. They have no record of any appointment for Rackham on September the first."

"Records get lost."

"This record wasn't lost. It never existed. You lied to Rackham. The lie itself wasn't important, it was the *kind* of lie. I could have understood a lie of vanity, or one to avoid punishment or to gain profit. But this seemed such a silly, senseless, little lie. It worried me. I began to wonder about Alma's part in the scene that night. Her crying was most unusual for a woman of Alma's inert nature. What if her crying was also a lie? And what was to be gained by it?"

"Nothing," Tracy said wearily. "Nothing was gained."

"But something was *intended*—and I think I know what it was. The scene was played to worry Rackham, to set him up for an even bigger scene. If that next scene has already been played, I am wasting my time here. Has it?"

"You have a vivid imagination."

"No. The plan was yours—I only figured it out."

"Very poor figuring, Mr. Sands." But Tracy's face was gray, as if mold had grown over his skin.

"I wish it were. I had become quite fond of the Rackhams."

He looked down at the street again, seeing nothing but the wheel turning inside his head. Alma was no longer in the middle of the wheel, passive and immobile; she was revolving with the others—Alma and Tracy and Rackham, turning as the wheel turned, clinging to its perimeter.

Alma, devoted wife, a little on the dull side. . . . What sudden passion of hate or love had made her capable of such consummate deceit? Sands imagined the scene the morning after Tracy's visit to the house. Rackham, worried and exhausted after a sleepless night: *"Are you feeling better now, Alma?"*

"Yes."

"What made you cry like that?"

"I was worried."

"About me?"

"Yes."

"Why didn't you tell me about my X-ray appointment?"

"I couldn't. I was frightened. I was afraid they would discover something serious the matter with you."

"Did Tracy give you any reason to think that?"

"He mentioned something about a blockage. Oh, Charles, I'm scared! If anything ever happened to you, I'd die. I couldn't live without you!"

For an emotional and sensitive man like Rackham, it was a perfect set-up: his devoted wife was frightened to the point of hysterics, his good friend and physician had given her reason to be frightened. Rackham was ready for the next step. . . .

"According to the records in your X-ray department," Sands said, "Rackham had a lower gastrointestinal X-ray yesterday morning. What was the result?"

"Medical ethics forbid me to—"

"You can't hide behind a wall of medical ethics that's already full of holes. What was the result?"

There was a long silence before Tracy spoke. "Nothing."

"You found nothing the matter with him?"

"That's right."

"Have you told Rackham that?"

"He came in earlier this afternoon, alone."

"Why alone?"

"I didn't want Alma to hear what I had to say."

"Very considerate of you."

"No, it was not considerate," Tracy said dully. "I had decided to back out of our—our agreement—and I didn't want her to know just yet."

"The agreement was to lie to Rackham, convince him that he had a fatal disease?"

"Yes."

"Did you?"

"No. I showed him the X-rays, I made it clear that there was nothing wrong with him. . . . I tried. I tried my best. It was no use."

"What do you mean?"

"He wouldn't believe me! He thought I was trying to keep the real truth from him." Tracy drew in his breath, sharply. "It's funny, isn't it? —after days of indecision and torment I made up my mind to do the right thing. But it was too late. Alma had played her role too well. She's the only one Rackham will believe."

The telephone on Tracy's desk began to ring but he made no move to answer it, and pretty soon the ringing stopped and the room was quiet again.

Sands said, "Have you asked Alma to tell him the truth?"

"Yes, just before you came in."

"She refused?"

Tracy didn't answer.

"She wants him to think he is fatally ill?"

"I—yes."

"In the hope that he'll kill himself, perhaps?"

Once again Tracy was silent. But no reply was necessary.

"I think Alma miscalculated," Sands said quietly. "Instead of planning suicide, Rackham is planning a trip. But before he leaves, he's going to hear the truth—from you and from Alma." Sands went towards the door. "Come on, Tracy. You have a house call to make."

"No. I can't." Tracy grasped the desk with both hands, like a child resisting the physical force of removal by a parent. "I won't go."

"You have to."

"No! Rackham will ruin me if he finds out. That's how this whole thing started. We were afraid, Alma and I, afraid of what Rackham would do if she asked him for a divorce. He's crazy in love with her, he's obsessed!"

"And so are you?"

"Not the way he is. Alma and I both want the same things—a little peace, a little quiet together. We are alike in many ways."

"That I can believe," Sands said grimly. "You wanted the same things, a little peace, a little quiet—and a little of Rackham's money?"

"The money was secondary."

"A very close second. How did you plan on getting it?"

Tracy shook his head from side to side, like an animal in pain. "You keep referring to plans, ideas, schemes. We didn't start out with plans or schemes. We just fell in love. We've been in love for nearly a year, not daring to do anything about it because I knew how Rackham would react if we told him. I have worked hard to build up this clinic; Rackham could destroy it, and me, within a month."

"That's a chance you'll have to take. Come on, Tracy."

Sands opened the door and the two men walked down the hall, slowly and in step, as if they were handcuffed together.

A nurse in uniform met them at the top of the stairs. "Dr. Tracy, are you ready for your next—?"

"Cancel all my appointments, Miss Leroy."

"But that's imposs—"

"I have a very important house call to make."

"Will it take long?"

"I don't know."

The two men went down the stairs, past the reception desk, and out into the summer afternoon. Before he got into Sands' car, Tracy looked back at the clinic, as if he never expected to see it again.

Sands turned on the ignition and the car sprang forward like an eager pup.

After a time Tracy said, "Of all the people in the world who could have been at the Rackhams' that night, it had to be an ex-policeman."

"It's lucky for you that I was there."

"Lucky." Tracy let out a harsh little laugh. "What's lucky about financial ruin?"

"It's better than some other kinds of ruin. If your plan had gone through, you could never have felt like a decent man again."

"You think I will anyway?"

"Perhaps, as the years go by."

"The years." Tracy turned, with a sigh. "What are you going to tell Rackham?"

"Nothing. You will tell him yourself."

"I can't. You don't understand, I'm quite fond of Rackham, and so is Alma. We—it's hard to explain."

"Even harder to understand." Sands thought back to all the times he had seen the Rackhams together and envied their companionship, their mutual devotion. Never, by the slightest glance or gesture of impatience or slip of the tongue, had Alma indicated that she was passionately in love with another man. He recalled the games of Scrabble, the dinners, the endless conversations with Rackham, while Alma sat with her knitting, her face reposeful, content. Rackham would ask, "Don't you want to play too, Alma?" And she would reply, "No, thank you, dear, I'm quite happy with my thoughts."

Alma, happy with her thoughts of violent delights and violent ends.

Sands said, "Alma is equally in love with you?"

"Yes." He sounded absolutely convinced. "No matter what Rackham says or does, we intend to have each other."

"I see."

"I wish you did."

The blinds of the Rackham house were closed against the sun. Sands led the way up the veranda steps and pressed the door chime, while Tracy stood, stony-faced and erect, like a bill collector or a process server.

Sands could hear the chimes pealing inside the house and feel their vibrations beating under his feet.

He said, "They may have gone already."

"Gone where?"

"Rackham wouldn't tell me. He just said he was planning the trip as a surprise for Alma."

"He can't take her away! He can't force her to leave if she doesn't want to go!"

Sands pressed the door chime again, and called out, "Rackham? Alma?" But there was no response.

He wiped the sudden moisture off his forehead with his coat sleeve. "I'm going in."

"I'm coming with you."

"No."

The door was unlocked. He stepped into the empty hall and shouted up the staircase, "Alma? Rackham? Are you there?"

The echo of his own voice teased him from the dim corners.

Tracy had come into the hall. "They've left, then?"

"Perhaps not. They might have just gone out for a drive. It's a nice day for a drive."

"Is it?"

"Go around to the back and see if their car's in the garage."

When Tracy had gone, Sands closed the door behind him and shot the bolt. He stood for a moment listening to Tracy's nervous footsteps on the concrete driveway. Then he turned and walked slowly into the living room, knowing the car would be in the garage, no matter how nice a day it was for a drive.

The drapes were pulled tight across the windows and the room was cool and dark, but alive with images and noisy with the past:

"I wanted to thank you before we leave, Sands."

"You're taking a trip?"

"Yes, quite a long one."

"When are you leaving?"

"Today."

"You must let me see you off at the station. . . ."

But no station had been necessary for Rackham's trip. He lay in front of the fireplace in a pool of blood, and beside him was his companion on the journey, her left arm curving around his waist.

Rackham had kept his promise to write. The note was on the mantel, addressed not to Sands, but to Tracy.

Dear George:
   You did your best to foil me but I got the truth from Alma. She could never hide anything from me; we are too close to each other. This is the easiest way out. I am sorry that I must take Alma along, but she told me so often that she could not live without me. I cannot leave her behind to grieve.
   Think of us now and then, and try not to judge me too harshly.
                                                            Charles Rackham

Sands put the note back on the mantel. He stood quietly, his heart pierced by the final splinter of irony: before Rackham had used the gun on himself, he had lain down on the floor beside Alma and placed her dead arm lovingly around his waist.

From outside came the sound of Tracy's footsteps returning along the driveway, and then the pounding of his fists on the front door.

"Sands, I'm locked out. Open the door. Let me in! Sands, do you hear me? Open this door!"

Sands went and opened the door.

THE LANDLADY

by

ROALD DAHL

Billy Weaver had travelled down from London on the slow afternoon train, with a change at Swindon on the way, and by the time he got to Bath it was about nine o'clock in the evening and the moon was coming up out of a clear starry sky over the houses opposite the station entrance. But the air was deadly cold and the wind was like a flat blade of ice on his cheeks.

"Excuse me," he said, "but is there a fairly cheap hotel not too far away from here?"

"Try The Bell and Dragon," the porter answered, pointing down the road. "They might take you in. It's about a quarter of a mile along on the other side."

Billy thanked him and picked up his suitcase and set out to walk the quarter-mile to The Bell and Dragon. He had never been to Bath before. He didn't know anyone who lived there. But Mr. Greenslade at the Head Office in London had told him it was a splendid city. "Find your own lodgings," he had said, "and then go along and report to the Branch Manager as soon as you've got yourself settled."

Billy was seventeen years old. He was wearing a new navy-blue over-coat, a new brown trilby hat, and a new brown suit, and he was feeling fine. He walked briskly down the street. He was trying to do everything briskly these days. Briskness, he had decided, was *the* one common characteristic of all successful businessmen. The big shots up at Head Office were absolutely fantastically brisk all the time. They were amazing.

There were no shops on this wide street that he was walking along, only a line of tall houses on each side, all of them identical. They had porches and pillars and four or five steps going up to their front doors, and it was obvious that once upon a time they had been very swanky residences. But now, even in the darkness, he could see that the paint was peeling from the woodwork on their doors and windows, and that the handsome white façades were cracked and blotchy from neglect.

Suddenly, in a downstairs window that was brilliantly illuminated by a street-lamp not six yards away, Billy caught sight of a printed notice propped up against the glass in one of the upper panes. It said BED AND BREAKFAST. There was a vase of yellow chrysanthemums, tall and beautiful, standing just underneath the notice.

He stopped walking. He moved a bit closer. Green curtains (some sort of velvety material) were hanging down on either side of the window. The chrysanthemums looked wonderful beside them. He went right up and peered through the glass into the room, and the first thing he saw was a bright fire burning in the hearth. On the carpet in front of the fire, a pretty little dachshund was curled up asleep with its nose tucked into its belly. The room itself, so far as he could see in the half-darkness, was filled with pleasant furniture. There was a baby-grand piano and a big sofa and several plump armchairs; and in one corner he spotted a large parrot in a cage. Animals were usually a good sign in a place like this, Billy told himself; and all in all, it looked to him as though it would be a pretty decent house to stay in. Certainly it would be more comfortable than The Bell and Dragon.

On the other hand, a pub would be more congenial than a boarding-house. There would be beer and darts in the evenings, and lots of people to talk to, and it would probably be a good bit cheaper, too. He had stayed a couple of nights in a pub once before and he had liked it. He had never stayed in any boarding-houses, and, to be perfectly honest, he was a tiny bit frightened of them. The name itself conjured up images of watery cabbage, rapacious landladies, and a powerful smell of kippers in the living-room.

After dithering about like this in the cold for two or three minutes, Billy decided that he would walk on and take a look at The Bell and Dragon before making up his mind. He turned to go.

And now a queer thing happened to him. He was in the act of stepping back and turning away from the window when all at once his eye was caught and held in the most peculiar manner by the small notice that was there. BED AND BREAKFAST, it said. BED AND BREAKFAST, BED AND BREAKFAST, BED AND BREAKFAST. Each word was like a large black eye staring at him through the glass, holding him, compelling him, forcing him to stay where he was and not to walk away from that house, and the next thing he knew, he was actually moving across from the window to the front door of the house, climbing the steps that led up to it, and reaching for the bell.

He pressed the bell. Far away in a back room he heard it ringing, and then *at once*—it must have been at once because he hadn't even had time to take his finger from the bell-button—the door swung open and a woman was standing there.

Normally you ring the bell and you have at least a half-minute's wait before the door opens. But this dame was like a jack-in-the-box. He pressed the bell—and out she popped! It made him jump.

She was about forty-five or fifty years old, and the moment she saw him, she gave him a warm welcoming smile.

"*Please* come in," she said pleasantly. She stepped aside, holding the door wide open, and Billy found himself automatically starting forward. The compulsion or, more accurately, the desire to follow after her into that house was extraordinarily strong.

"I saw the notice in the window," he said, holding himself back.

"Yes, I know."

"I was wondering about a room."

"It's *all* ready for you, my dear," she said. She had a round pink face and very gentle blue eyes.

"I was on my way to The Bell and Dragon," Billy told her. "But the notice in your window just happened to catch my eye."

"My dear boy," she said, "why don't you come in out of the cold?"

"How much do you charge?"

"Five and sixpence a night, including breakfast."

It was fantastically cheap. It was less than half of what he had been willing to pay.

"If that is too much," she added, "then perhaps I can reduce it just a tiny bit. Do you desire an egg for breakfast? Eggs are expensive at the moment. It would be sixpence less without the egg."

"Five and sixpence is fine," he answered. "I should like very much to stay here."

"I knew you would. Do come in."

She seemed terribly nice. She looked exactly like the mother of one's best school-friend welcoming one into the house to stay for the Christmas holidays. Billy took off his hat, and stepped over the threshold.

"Just hang it there," she said, "and let me help you with your coat."

There were no other hats or coats in the hall. There were no umbrellas, no walking-sticks—nothing.

"We have it *all* to ourselves," she said, smiling at him over her shoulder as she led the way upstairs. "You see, it isn't very often I have the pleasure of taking a visitor into my little nest."

The old girl is slightly dotty, Billy told himself. But at five and sixpence a night, who gives a damn about that? "I should've thought you'd be simply swamped with applicants," he said politely.

"Oh, I am, my dear, I am, of course I am. But the trouble is that I'm inclined to be just a teeny weeny bit choosy and particular—if you see what I mean."

"Ah, yes."

"But I'm always ready. Everything is always ready day and night in this house just on the off-chance that an acceptable young gentleman will come along. And it is such a pleasure, my dear, such a very great pleasure when now and again I open the door and I see someone standing there who is just *exactly* right." She was halfway up the stairs, and she paused with one hand on the stair-rail, turning her head and smiling down at him with pale lips. "Like you," she added, and her blue eyes travelled slowly all the way down the length of Billy's body, to his feet, and then up again.

On the second-floor landing she said to him, "This floor is mine."

They climbed up another flight. "And this one is *all* yours," she said. "Here's your room. I do hope you'll like it." She took him into a small but charming front bedroom, switching on the light as she went in.

"The morning sun comes right in the window, Mr. Perkins. It *is* Mr. Perkins, isn't it?"

"No," he said. "It's Weaver."

"Mr. Weaver. How nice. I've put a water-bottle between the sheets to air them out, Mr. Weaver. It's such a comfort to have a hot water-bottle in a strange bed with clean sheets, don't you agree? And you may light the gas fire at any time if you feel chilly."

"Thank you," Billy said. "Thank you ever so much." He noticed that the bedspread had been taken off the bed, and that the bedclothes had been neatly turned back on one side, all ready for someone to get in.

"I'm so glad you appeared," she said, looking earnestly into his face. "I was beginning to get worried."

"That's all right," Billy answered brightly. "You mustn't worry about me." He put his suitcase on the chair and started to open it.

"And what about supper, my dear? Did you manage to get anything to eat before you came here?"

"I'm not a bit hungry, thank you," he said. "I think I'll just go to bed as soon as possible because tomorrow I've got to get up rather early and report to the office."

"Very well, then. I'll leave you now so that you can unpack. But before you go to bed, would you be kind enough to pop into the sitting-room on the ground floor and sign the book? Everyone has to do that because it's the law of the land, and we don't want to go breaking any laws at *this* stage in the proceedings, do we?" She gave him a little wave of the hand and went quickly out of the room and closed the door.

Now, the fact that his landlady appeared to be slightly off her rocker didn't worry Billy in the least. After all, she not only was harmless—there was no question about that—but she was also quite obviously a kind and generous soul. He guessed that she had probably lost a son in the war, or something like that, and had never gotten over it.

So a few minutes later, after unpacking his suitcase and washing his hands, he trotted downstairs to the ground floor and entered the living-room. His landlady wasn't there, but the fire was glowing in the hearth, and the little dachshund was still sleeping soundly in front of it. The room was wonderfully warm and cosy. I'm a lucky fellow, he thought, rubbing his hands. This is a bit of all right.

He found the guest-book lying open on the piano, so he took out his pen and wrote down his name and address. There were only two other entries above his on the page, and, as one always does with guest-books, he started to read them. One was a Christopher Mulholland from Cardiff. The other was Gregory W. Temple from Bristol.

That's funny, he thought suddenly. Christopher Mulholland. It rings a bell.

Now where on earth had he heard that rather unusual name before?

Was it a boy at school? No. Was it one of his sister's numerous young men, perhaps, or a friend of his father's? No, no, it wasn't any of those. He glanced down again at the book.

> Christopher Mulholland   *231 Cathedral Road, Cardiff*
> Gregory W. Temple   *27 Sycamore Drive, Bristol*

As a matter of fact, now he came to think of it, he wasn't at all sure that the second name didn't have almost as much of a familiar ring about it as the first.

"Gregory Temple?" he said aloud, searching his memory. "Christopher Mulholland? . . ."

"Such charming boys," a voice behind him answered, and he turned and saw his landlady sailing into the room with a large silver tea-tray in her hands. She was holding it well out in front of her, and rather high up, as though the tray were a pair of reins on a frisky horse.

"They sound somehow familiar," he said.

"They do? How interesting."

"I'm almost positive I've heard those names before somewhere. Isn't that odd? Maybe it was in the newspapers. They weren't famous in any way, were they? I mean famous cricketers or footballers or something like that?"

"Famous," she said, setting the tea-tray down on the low table in front of the sofa. "Oh no, I don't think they were famous. But they were incredibly handsome, both of them, I can promise you that. They were tall and young and handsome, my dear, just exactly like you."

Once more, Billy glanced down at the book. "Look here," he said, noticing the dates. "This last entry is over two years old."

"It is?"

"Yes, indeed. And Christopher Mulholland's is nearly a year before that—more than *three years* ago."

"Dear me," she said, shaking her head and heaving a dainty little sigh. "I would never have thought it. How times does fly away from us all, doesn't it, Mr. Wilkins?"

"It's Weaver," Billy said. "W-e-a-v-e-r."

"Oh, of course it is!" she cried, sitting down on the sofa. "How silly of me. I do apologize. In one ear and out the other, that's me, Mr. Weaver."

"You know something?" Billy said. "Something that's really quite extraordinary about all this?"

"No, dear, I don't."

"Well, you see, both of these names—Mulholland and Temple—I not only seem to remember each one of them separately, so to speak, but somehow or other, in some peculiar way, they both appear to be sort of connected together as well. As though they were both famous for the same sort of thing, if you see what I mean—like . . . well . . . like Dempsey and Tunney, for example, or Churchill and Roosevelt."

"How amusing," she said. "But come over here now, dear, and sit down beside me on the sofa and I'll give you a nice cup of tea and a ginger biscuit before you go to bed."

"You really shouldn't bother," Billy said. "I didn't mean you to do anything like that." He stood by the piano, watching her as she fussed about with the cups and saucers. He noticed that she had small, white, quickly moving hands, and red finger-nails.

"I'm almost positive it was in the newspapers I saw them," Billy said. "I'll think of it in a second. I'm sure I will."

There is nothing more tantalizing than a thing like this that lingers just outside the borders of one's memory. He hated to give up.

"Now wait a minute," he said. "Wait just a minute. Mulholland . . . Christopher Mulholland . . . wasn't *that* the name of the Eton schoolboy who was on a walking-tour through the West Country, and then all of a sudden . . ."

"Milk?" she said. "And sugar?"

"Yes, please. And then all of a sudden . . ."

"Eton schoolboy?" she said. "Oh no, my dear, that can't possibly be right because *my* Mr. Mulholland was certainly not an Eton schoolboy when he came to me. He was a Cambridge undergraduate. Come over here now and sit next to me and warm yourself in front of this lovely fire. Come on. Your tea's all ready for you." She patted the empty place beside her on the sofa, and she sat there smiling at Billy and waiting for him to come over.

He crossed the room slowly, and sat down on the edge of the sofa. She placed his teacup on the table in front of him.

"*There* we are," she said. "How nice and cosy this is, isn't it?"

Billy started sipping his tea. She did the same. For half a minute or so, neither of them spoke. But Billy knew that she was looking at him. Her body was half turned toward him, and he could feel her eyes resting on his face, watching him over the rim of her teacup. Now and again, he caught a whiff of a peculiar smell that seemed to emanate directly from her person. It was not in the least unpleasant, and it reminded him—well, he wasn't quite sure what it reminded him of. Pickled walnuts? New leather? Or was it the corridors of a hospital?

At length, she said, "Mr. Mulholland was a great one for his tea. Never in my life have I seen anyone drink as much tea as dear, sweet Mr. Mulholland."

"I suppose he left fairly recently," Billy said. He was still puzzling his head about the two names. He was positive now that he had seen them in the newspapers—in the headlines.

"Left?" she said, arching her brows. "But my dear boy, he never left. He's still here. Mr. Temple is also here. They're on the fourth floor, both of them together."

Billy set his cup down slowly on the table and stared at his landlady. She smiled back at him, and then she put out one of her white hands and patted him comfortingly on the knee. "How old are you, my dear?" she asked.

"Seventeen."

"Seventeen!" she cried. "Oh, it's the perfect age! Mr. Mulholland was also seventeen. But I think he was a trifle shorter than you are; in fact I'm sure he was, and his teeth weren't *quite* so white. You have the most beautiful teeth, Mr. Weaver, did you know that?"

"They're not as good as they look," Billy said. "They've got simply masses of fillings in them at the back."

"Mr. Temple, of course, was a little older," she said, ignoring his remark. "He was actually twenty-eight. And yet I never would have guessed it if he hadn't told me, never in my whole life. There wasn't a *blemish* on his body."

"A what?" Billy said.

"His skin was *just* like a baby's."

There was a pause. Billy picked up his teacup and took another sip of his tea, then he set it down again gently in its saucer. He waited for her to say something else, but she seemed to have lapsed into another of her silences. He sat there staring straight ahead of him into the far corner of the room, biting his lower lip.

"That parrot," he said at last. "You know something? It had me completely fooled when I first saw it through the window. I could have sworn it was alive."

"Alas, no longer."

"It's most terribly clever the way it's been done," he said. "It doesn't look in the least bit dead. Who did it?"

"I did."

"*You* did?"

"Of course," she said. "And have you met my little Basil as well?" She nodded toward the dachshund curled up so comfortably in front of the fire. Billy looked at it. And suddenly he realized that this animal had all the time been just as silent and motionless as the parrot. He put out a hand and touched it gently on the top of its back. The back was hard and cold, and when he pushed the hair to one side with his fingers, he could see the skin underneath, greyish-black and dry and perfectly preserved.

"Good gracious me," he said. "How absolutely fascinating." He turned away from the dog and stared with deep admiration at the little woman beside him on the sofa. "It must be most awfully difficult to do a thing like that."

"Not in the least," she said. "I stuff *all* my little pets myself when they pass away. Will you have another cup of tea?"

"No, thank you," Billy said. The tea tasted faintly of bitter almonds, and he didn't much care for it.

"You did sign the book, didn't you?"

"Oh, yes."

"That's good. Because later on, if I happen to forget what you were called, then I could always come down here and look it up. I still do that almost every day with Mr. Mulholland and Mr. . . . Mr. . . . ."

"Temple," Billy said. "Gregory Temple. Excuse my asking, but haven't there been *any* other guests here except them in the last two or three years?"

Holding her teacup high in one hand, inclining her head slightly to the left, she looked up at him out of the corners of her eyes and gave him another gentle little smile.

"No, my dear," she said. "Only you."

THE AMATEUR

by

MICHAEL GILBERT

We were talking about violence. "Some people," I said, "are afraid of people and some people are afraid of things."

Chief Inspector Hazlerigg gave this remark more consideration than it seemed to merit and then said: "Illustration, please."

"Well, some people are afraid of employers and some of razors."

"I don't think that sort of fear is a constant," said Hazlerigg. "It changes as you grow older, you know—or get more experienced. I haven't much occasion for bodily violence in my present job." (He was one of the chief inspectors on the cab rank at Scotland Yard.) "When I was a young constable the customers I chiefly disliked were drunken women. Nowadays—well, perhaps I should look at it the other way round. Perhaps I could describe the sort of man whom *I* should hate to have after *me.*"

In the pause that followed I tried hard to visualize what precise mixture of thug and entrepreneur would terrify the red-faced, gray-eyed, bulky, equitable man sitting beside me.

"He'd be English," said Hazlerigg at last, "Anglo-Saxon anyway, getting on for middle age and a first-class businessman. He would have had some former experience of lethal weapons—as an infantry soldier, perhaps, in one of the World Wars. But definitely an amateur—an amateur in violence. He would believe passionately in the justice of what he was doing—but without ever allowing the fanatic to rule the businessman.

"Now that's a type I should hate to have after me! He's unstoppable."

"Is that a portrait from life?" I said.

"Yes," said Hazlerigg slowly. "Yes, it's a portrait from life. It all happened a good time ago—in the early thirties, when I was a junior inspector. Even now, you'll have to be very careful about names, you know, because if the real truth came out—however, judge for yourself."

Inspector Hazlerigg first met Mr. Collet (*the* Collets, the shipping people—this one was the third of the dynasty) in his managing director's mahogany-lined office. Hazlerigg was there by appointment. He had arrived at the building in a plain van and had been introduced via the goods entrance, but once inside he had been treated with every consideration.

Even during the few minutes which had elapsed before he could be brought face to face with Mr. Collet, Hazlerigg had managed to collect a few impressions. Small things, from the way the commissionaire and the messenger spoke about him, and more still from the way his secretary spoke *to* him: that they liked him and liked working for him; that they knew something was wrong and were sorry.

They didn't, of course, know exactly what the trouble was. Hazlerigg did.

Kidnaping—the extorting of money by kidnaping—is a filthy thing. Fortunately, it does not seem to come very easily to the English criminal. But there was a little wave of it that year.

Mr. Collet had an only child, a boy of nine. On the afternoon of the previous day he had been out with his aunt, Mr. Collet's sister, in the park. A car had overtaken them on an empty stretch. A man had got out, pitched the boy into the back of the car, and driven off. As simple as that.

"So far as we know," said Hazlerigg, "there's just the one crowd. I'll be quite frank. We know very little about them. But there have been four cases already, and the features have been too much alike for coincidence."

"Such as—?" said Mr. Collet. His voice and his hands, Hazlerigg noticed, were under control. He couldn't see the eyes. Mr. Collet was wearing heavy sunglasses.

"Well—they don't ask for too much to start with, that's one thing. The first demand has always been quite modest. The idea being that a man will be more likely to go on paying once he has started."

"Right so far," said Mr. Collet. "They asked for only five thousand pounds— They could have had it this morning—if I'd thought it would do any good."

"Then there's also their method of collecting. It's disarming. They employ known crooks. I don't know what they pay them—just enough to make it worth their while to take the risk. These crooks are strictly carriers only. We could arrest them at the moment they contact you without getting any nearer to the real organizers."

"The Piccadilly side of Green Park, at two o'clock tomorrow," said Mr. Collet. "I got the rendezvous quite openly over the telephone. Could they be followed?"

"That's where the organization really starts," said Hazlerigg. "Every move after that is worked out—and when you come to think about it the cards are very heavily stacked in their favor. All they've got to do is to hand the money on. There are a hundred ways of doing it. They might pass it over in a crowd in an underground train or a bus in the rush hour, or they might be picked up by car and driven somewhere fast, or they might hand it over in a cinema. They might get rid of the money the same day, or they might wait a week."

"Yes," said Mr. Collet, "a little organization and that part shouldn't be too difficult. Any other peculiarities about this crowd?"

He said this as a businessman might inquire about a firm with whom he was going to trade.

Hazlerigg hesitated. What he was going to say had to be said some time. It might as well be said now.

"Yes, sir," he said. "There's this to consider. However much the victim pays—however often he pays—however promptly he pays—he doesn't get the child back. You've given us the best chance so far by coming to us immediately." Mr. Collet said nothing. "You know Roger Barstow— he lost his little girl—Zilla was her name. He paid nine times. More than £100,000—until he had no more left and said so. Next morning they found Zilla; in the swill bin at the back of his house."

There was another silence. Hazlerigg saw the whites of the knuckle-bones start up for a moment on one of Mr. Collet's thin brown hands. At last he got to his feet and said: "Thank you, Inspector. I have your contact number. I'll get hold of you as soon as I—as soon as anything happens."

As he walked to the door he took off his glasses for the first time and Hazlerigg saw in his eyes that he had got his ally. It had been a risk, but it had come off.

Mr. Collet was going to fight.

When the door had closed behind the chief inspector Mr. Collet thought for a few moments and then rang the bell and asked for Mr. Stevens.

Mr. Stevens, who was a month or two short of fifteen, was the head of the Collet messenger service, and a perfectly natural organizer. He spent a good deal of his time organizing the messenger boys of the firm into a sort of trade union, and he had already engineered two beautifully timed strikes, the second of which had called for Mr. Collet's personal intervention.

It says a good deal for both parties that when Mr. Collet sent for him and asked for his help, young Stevens listened carefully to what he had to say and promised him the fullest assistance of himself and his organization.

"No film stuff," said Mr. Collet. "These men are real crooks. They're dangerous. And they're wide awake. They expect to be followed. We're going to do this on business lines."

That was Wednesday. At four o'clock on Thursday afternoon Inspector Hazlerigg again visited Archangel Street, taking the same precautions. Mr. Collet was at his desk. "You've got something for me...." It was more a statement than a question.

"Before I answer that," said Mr. Collet, "I want something from you. I want your promise that you won't act on my information without my permission."

Hazlerigg said: "All right. I can't promise not to go on with such steps as I'm already taking. But I promise not to use your information until you say so. What do you know?"

"I know the names of most of the men concerned," said Mr. Collet. "I know where my son is—I know where these people are hiding."

When Hazlerigg had recovered his breath he said: "Perhaps you'll explain."

"I thought a good deal," said Mr. Collet, "about what you told me—about the sort of people we were dealing with. Particularly about the men who would make contact with me and carry back the money. It was obvious that they weren't afraid of violence. They weren't even, basically, afraid of being arrested. That was part of the risk. They certainly weren't open to any sort of persuasion. If they observed the routine, which had no doubt been carefully laid down for them, they would take the money from me and get it back to their employers, without giving us any chance of following them. Their position seemed to be pretty well impregnable. In the circumstances it seemed—do you play bridge, Inspector?"

"Badly," said Hazlerigg. "But I'm very fond of it."

"Then you understand the Vienna Coup."

"In theory—though I could never work it. It's a sort of squeeze. You start by playing away one of your winning aces, isn't that it?"

"Exactly," said Mr. Collet. "You give—or appear to give—your opponents an unexpected gift. And like all unexpected gifts it throws them off balance and upsets their defense. I decided to do the same. To be precise, I gave them five thousand pounds *more* than they asked for. I

met these men—there were two of them as I told you—by appointment
in Green Park. I simply opened my brief-case and put a brown paper
packet into their hands. They opened it quickly, and as they were doing
so I said: 'Ten thousand pounds in one-pound notes—that's right, isn't it?'
I could almost see it hit them. To give them time to cover up I said:
'When do I see my boy?' The elder of the two men said: 'You'll be seeing
him soon. We'll ring you tomorrow.' Then they pushed off. I could see
them starting to argue."

Mr. Collet paused. Inspector Hazlerigg, who was still trying to work
out the angles, said nothing.

"The way I figured it out," said Mr. Collet, "they'd have all their plans
made for handing on five thousand pounds to their employers. So I gave
them ten thousand. That meant five thousand for themselves if they kept
quiet about it, and played it right. But I'd put all the notes in one packet,
you see. They had to be divided out. Then they had to split the extra five
thousand among themselves—they were both in on it. Above all, they
had to get somewhere safe and somewhere quiet and talk it out. You see
what that meant. Their original plan—the careful one laid down for them
by the bosses—had to be scrapped.

"They had to make another plan, and make it rather quickly. It would
be something simple. They'd either go to one of their own houses, or a
safe friend's house—and it would probably be somewhere with a telephone—because they'd have to invent some sort of story for the bosses
to explain why they'd abandoned the original plan. That last bit was only
surmise, but it was a fair business risk."

"Yes," said Hazlerigg. "I see. You still had to follow them, though."

"Not me," said Mr. Collet. "It was the boys who did that. The streets
round the park were full of them. They're a sort of car-watching club—
you see them anywhere in the streets of London if you look. They collect
car numbers. Boy of mine called Stevens ran it. He's a born organizer.
I went straight back to the office. Fifteen minutes later I got a call. Just
an address, near King's Cross.

"I passed it on to a friend of mine—he's quite a senior official, so I won't
give you his name. Inside five minutes he had the line from that house
tapped. He was just in time to collect the outgoing call. That was that.
It was to a house in Essex. Here's the address." He pushed a slip of paper
across. "That's the name."

"Just like that," said Hazlerigg. "Simple. Scotland Yard has been trying
to do it for six months."

"I had more at stake than you."

"Yes," said Hazlerigg. "What happens now?"

"Now," said Mr. Collet, "We sit back and wait."

*   *   *

Continuing the story, Hazlerigg said to me: "I think that was one of the bravest and coolest things I ever saw a man do. He was quite right, of course. The people we were dealing with moved by instinct—that sort of deadly instinct which those people get who sleep with one finger on the trigger.

"When their messengers reported the change of plan—I don't know what sort of story they put up—their bristles must have been on end. These people can smell when something's wrong. They're so used to double-crossing other people that they get a sort of second sight about it themselves. If we'd rushed them then, we should never have got the boy alive. So we waited. We had a man watch the house—it was a big, rather lonely house, between Pitsea and Rayleigh on the north of the Thames."

And, meanwhile, Mr. Collet sat in his mahogany-lined office and transacted the business of his firm. On the fourth morning he got a letter, in a painstaking, schoolboy script.

> *Dear Father,*
> *I am to write this to you. You are to pay five thousand pounds more. They will telephone you how to pay. I am quite well. It is quite a nice house. It is quite a nice room. The sun wakes me in the early morning.*
> *Love from David*
> *P.S. Please be quick.*

Mr. Andrews, senior partner in the firm of Andrews and Mackay, house agents of Pitsea, summed up his visitor at one glance which took in the silk tie, the pigskin brief-case and the hood of the chauffeur-driven Daimler standing outside the office, and said in his most deferential voice: "Certainly, Mr.—er—Robinson. Anything we can do to help you. It's not everybody's idea of a house, but if you're looking for something quiet and secluded—"

"I understand that it's occupied at the moment," said Mr. Robinson.

"Temporarily," agreed Mr. Andrews. "But you could have possession. The owner let it on short notice to a syndicate of men who are interested in a new color process. They needed the big grounds—the quiet, you understand, the freedom from interruption. The only difficulty which occurs to me is that you will not be able to inspect the house today. By the terms of our arrangement we have to give at least forty-eight hours' notice."

Mr. Robinson thought for a moment and then said: "Have you such a thing as a plan of the house?"

"Why certainly," said Mr. Andrews. "We had a very careful survey made when the house was put up for sale. Here you are—on two floors only, you see."

"Only one bedroom," said Mr. Robinson, "looks due east?"

"Why, yes." Mr. Andrews was hardened to the vagaries of clients.

" 'The sun wakes me in the early morning,' " said Mr. Robinson softly.

"I beg your pardon?"

"Nothing," said Mr. Robinson. "Nothing. Thinking aloud. A bad habit. Would it be asking too much if I borrowed these plans for a day?"

"Why, of course," said Mr. Andrews. "Keep them for as long as you like."

Four o'clock of a perfect summer afternoon. It was so silent that the clack of a scythe blade on a stone sounded clear across the valley where the big gray house dozed in the sun.

As the double chime of the half-hour sounded from Rayleigh Church a figure appeared on the dusty road. It was a man, in postman's uniform, wheeling a bicycle.

The woman in the lodge answered the bell and unlocked one of the big gates, without comment. Then she returned to her back room, picked up the house telephone, and said: "All right. It's only the postman."

It was a mistake which might have cost her very dearly.

As Mr. Collet wheeled his borrowed machine slowly up the long drive he was thinking about the bulky sack which rested on the saddle and balanced there with difficulty. He knew that some very sharp eyes would be watching his approach. It couldn't be helped though. He had been able to see no better method of getting this particular apparatus up to the house.

He propped his bicycle against the pillar of the front door, lifted the sack down, keeping the mouth of it gathered in his left hand, and rang the bell. So far, so good.

The door was opened by a man in corduroys and a tweed jacket. He might have been a gardener or a gamekeeper. Mr. Collet, looking at his eyes, knew better.

"Don't shout," he said. The gun in his hand was an argument.

For a moment the man stared. Then he jumped to one side and started to open his mouth.

Even for an indifferent shot three yards is not a long range. The big bullet lifted the man back onto his heels like a punch under the heart and crumpled him onto the floor.

In the deep silence which followed the roar of the gun, Mr. Collet raced for the stairs. The heavy sack was against him but he made good time.

At the top he turned left with the sureness of a man who knows his mind and made for the room at the end of the corridor.

He saw that it was padlocked.

He put the muzzle of his gun as near to the padlock as he dared and pulled the trigger.

The jump of the gun threw the bullet up into the door jamb, missing the padlock altogether. He took a lower aim and tried again. Once, twice, again. The padlock buckled.

Mr. Collet kicked the door open and went in.

The boy was half sitting, half kneeling in one corner. Mr. Collet grinned at him with a good deal more confidence than he felt and said: "Stand out of the way, son. The curtain's going up for the last act."

As he spoke he was piling together mattresses, bedclothes, a rug, and a couple of small chairs into a barricade. When he had done this he opened the sack, pulled out the curious-looking instrument from inside it, laid it beside his homemade parapet, and started working on it.

"Get into that far corner, son," said Mr. Collet. "And you might keep an eye on the window, just in case it occurs to the gentry to run a ladder up. Keep your head down, though. Here they come."

Joe Keller had tortured children and had killed for pleasure as well as for profit, but he was not physically a coward.

As he watched his henchman twitching on the hall floor, with the indifference of a man who has seen many men die, he was already working out his plan of attack.

"Take a long ladder," he said to one man, "and run it up to the window. Not the bedroom window—be your age. Put it against the landing window, this end. You can see the bedroom door from there, can't you? If it's shut, wait. If it's open, start shooting into the room—aim high. We'll go in together along the floor."

"He'll pick us off as we come."

"Not if Hoppy keeps him pinned down," said Keller. "Besides, I reckon he doesn't know much about guns. It took him four shots to knock off that lock, didn't it? Any more arguments?"

Half a mile away, at points round the lip of the valley, four police cars had started up their engines at the sound of the first shot.

Hazlerigg was lying full length on the roof of one of them, a pair of long binoculars in his hands.

The Essex Superintendent looked up at him.

"I made that five shots," he said. "Do we start?"

"No, sir," said Hazlerigg. "You remember the signal we arranged."

"Do you think he can do his stuff?" The Superintendent sounded worried.

"He hasn't done badly so far," said Hazlerigg shortly, and silence settled down once more.

It was the driver of their car who saw it first, and gave a shout. From one of the first-floor windows of the house, unmistakable and ominous, a cloud of black and sooty smoke rolled upward.

The four cars started forward as one.

In that long upstairs passage things had gone according to plan—at first. Covered by a fusillade from the window, Joe Keller and his two assistants had inched their way forward on elbows and knees, their guns ahead of them.

At the end of the passage stood the door, open and inviting. The outer end of Mr. Collet's barricade came into sight as they advanced, but it was offset from the doorway, and Mr. Collet himself was still invisible.

Five yards to go.

Then, as the three men bunched for the final jump, it came out to meet them. A great red and yellow river of flame, overmantled with black smoke, burning and hissing and dripping with oil. As they turned to fly, it caught them . . .

"There was nothing very much for us to do when we did get there," said Inspector Hazlerigg. "We had to get Mr. Collet and the boy out of the window—the passage floor was red-hot. We caught one man in the garden. His nerve was gone—he seemed glad to give himself up.

"As for the other three—an infantry flame thrower is not a discriminating sort of weapon, particularly at close quarters. There was just about enough left of them—well—say just about enough of the three of them to fill the swill bin where they found little Zilla Barstow. No, never tangle with a wholehearted amateur."

THE TERRAPIN

by

PATRICIA HIGHSMITH

Victor heard the elevator door open, his mother's quick footsteps in the hall, and he flipped his book shut. He shoved it under the sofa pillow out of sight, and winced as he heard it slip between sofa and wall to the floor with a thud. Her key was in the lock.

"Hello, Vee-ector-r!" she cried, raising one arm in the air. Her other arm circled a brown paper bag, her hand held a cluster of little bags. "I have been to my publisher and to the market and also to the fish market," she told him. "Why aren't you out playing? It's a lovely, lovely day!"

"I was out," he said. "For a little while. I got cold."

"Ugh!" She was unloading the grocery bag in the tiny kitchen off the foyer. "You are seeck, you know that? In the month of October, you are cold? I see all kinds of children playing on the sidewalk. Even, I think, that boy you like. What's his name?"

"I don't know," Victor said. His mother wasn't really listening anyway. He pushed his hands into the pockets of his short, too small shorts, making them tighter than ever, and walked aimlessly around the living-room, looking down at his heavy, scuffed shoes. At least his mother had to buy him shoes that fit him, and he rather liked these shoes, because they had the thickest soles of any he had ever owned, and they had heavy toes that rose up a little, like mountain climbers' shoes. Victor paused at the window and looked straight out at a toast-coloured apartment building across Third Avenue. He and his mother lived on the eighteenth floor, next to the top floor where the penthouses were. The building across the street was even taller than this one. Victor had liked their Riverside Drive apartment better. He had liked the school he had gone to there better. Here they laughed at his clothes. In the other school, they had finally got tired of laughing at them.

"You don't want to go out?" asked his mother, coming into the living-room, wiping her hands briskly on a paper bag. She sniffed her palms. "Ugh! That stee-enk!"

"No, Mama," Victor said patiently.

"Today is Saturday."

"I know."

"Can you say the days of the week?"

"Of course."

"Say them."

"I don't want to say them. I know them." His eyes began to sting around the edges with tears. "I've known them for years. Years and years. Kids five years old can say the days of the week."

But his mother was not listening. She was bending over the drawing-table in the corner of the room. She had worked late on something last night. On his sofa bed in the opposite corner of the room, Victor had not been able to sleep until two in the morning, when his mother had gone to bed on the studio couch.

"Come here, Veector. Did you see this?"

Victor came on dragging feet, hands still in his pockets. No, he hadn't even glanced at her drawing-board this morning, hadn't wanted to.

"This is Pedro, the little donkey. I invented him last night. What do you think? And this is Miguel, the little Mexican boy who rides him. They ride and ride all over Mexico, and Miguel thinks they are lost, but Pedro knows the way home all the time, and . . ."

Victor did not listen. He deliberately shut his ears in a way he had learned to do from many years of practice, but boredom, frustration—he knew the word frustration, had read all about it—clamped his shoulders, weighted like a stone in his body, pressed hatred and tears up to his eyes, as if a volcano were churning in him. He had hoped his mother might take a hint from his saying that he was cold in his silly short shorts. He had hoped his mother might remember what he had told her, that the fellow he had wanted to get acquainted with downstairs, a fellow who looked about his own age, eleven, had laughed at his short pants on Monday afternoon. *They make you wear your kid brother's pants or something?* Victor had drifted away, mortified. What if the fellow knew he didn't even own any longer pants, not even a pair of knickers, much less *long* pants, even blue jeans! His mother, for some cock-eyed reason, wanted him to look "French," and made him wear short shorts and stockings that came to just below his knees, and dopey shirts with round collars. His mother wanted him to stay about six years old, for ever, all his life. She liked to test out her drawings on him. *Veector is my sounding board,* she sometimes said to her friends. *I show my drawings to Veector and I know if children will like them.* Often Victor said he liked stories that he did not like, or drawings that he was indifferent to, because he felt sorry for his mother and because it put her in a better mood if he said he liked them. He was quite tired now of children's book illustrations, if he had ever in his life liked them—he really couldn't remember—and now he had two favourites: Howard Pyle's illustrations in some of Robert Louis Stevenson's books and Cruikshank's in Dickens'. It was too bad, Victor thought, that he was absolutely the last person of whom his mother should have asked an opinion, because he simply *hated* children's illustrations. And it was a wonder his mother didn't see this, because she hadn't sold any illustrations for books for years and years, not since *Wimple-Dimple*, a book whose jacket was all torn and turning yellow now from age, which sat in the centre of the bookshelf in a little cleared spot, propped up against the back of the bookcase so everyone could see it. Victor had been seven years old when that book was printed. His mother liked to tell people and remind him, too, that he had told her what he had wanted to see her draw, had watched her make every drawing, had shown his opinion by laughing or not, and that she had been absolutely guided by him. Victor doubted this very much, because first of all the story was somebody else's and had been written before his mother did the drawings, and her drawings had had to follow the story, naturally. Since then, his mother had done only a few illustrations now and then for magazines for children, how to make paper pumpkins and black paper cats for Hallowe'en and things like that, though she took her portfolio around to publishers all the time. Their income came from his father, who was a wealthy businessman in France, an exporter of perfumes. His mother said he was very wealthy and very handsome. But he married again, he never wrote, and Victor had no interest in him, didn't even care if he never saw a picture of him, and he never had. His father was French with some Polish, and his mother was Hungarian with some French. The word Hungarian made Victor think of gypsies, but when he had asked his mother once, she had said emphatically that she hadn't any gypsy blood, and she had been annoyed that Victor brought the question up.

And now she was sounding him out again, poking him in the ribs to make him wake up, as she repeated:

"Listen to me! Which do you like better, Veector? 'In all Mexico there was no bur-r-ro as wise as Miguel's Pedro,' or 'Miguel's Pedro was the wisest bur-r-ro in all Mexico'?"

"I think—I like it the first way better."

"Which way is that?" demanded his mother, thumping her palm down on the illustration.

Victor tried to remember the wording, but realized he was only staring at the pencil smudges, the thumbprints on the edge of his mother's illustration board. The coloured drawing in the centre did not interest him at all. He was not-thinking. This was a frequent, familiar sensation to him now, there was something exciting and important about not-thinking, Victor felt, and he thought one day he would find something about it—perhaps under another name—in the Public Library or in the psychology books around the house that he browsed in when his mother was out.

"Veec-tor! What are you doing?"

"Nothing, Mama!"

"That is exactly it! Nothing! Can you not even *think?*"

A warm shame spread through him. It was as if his mother read his thoughts about not-thinking. "I am thinking," he protested. "I'm think-ing about *not*-thinking." His tone was defiant. What could she do about it, after all?

"About what?" Her black, curly head tilted, her mascaraed eyes nar-rowed at him.

"Not-thinking."

His mother put her jewelled hands on her hips. "Do you know, Veec-tor, you are a little bit strange in the head?" She nodded. "You are seeck. Psychologically seeck. And retarded, do you know that? You have the behaviour of a leetle boy five years old," she said slowly and weightily. "It is just as well you spend your Saturdays indoors. Who knows if you would not walk in front of a car, eh? But that is why I love you, little Veector." She put her arm around his shoulders, pulled him against her and for an instant Victor's nose pressed into her large, soft bosom. She was wearing her flesh-coloured dress, the one you could see through a little where her breast stretched it out.

Victor jerked his head away in a confusion of emotions. He did not know if he wanted to laugh or cry.

His mother was laughing gaily, her head back. "Seeck you are! Look at you! My lee-tle boy still, lee-tle short pants—Ha! Ha!"

Now the tears showed in his eyes, he supposed, and his mother acted as if she were enjoying it! Victor turned his head away so she would not see his eyes. Then suddenly he faced her. "Do you think I like these pants? *You* like them, not me, so why do you have to make fun of them?"

"A lee-tle boy who's crying!" she went on, laughing.

Victor made a dash for the bathroom, then swerved away and dived on to the sofa, his face toward the pillows. He shut his eyes tight and opened his mouth, crying but not-crying in a way he had learned through practice also. With his mouth open, his throat tight, not breathing for nearly a minute, he could somehow get the satisfaction of crying, screaming even, without anybody knowing it. He pushed his nose, his open mouth, his teeth, against the tomato-red sofa pillow, and though his mother's voice went on in a lazily mocking tone, and her laughter went on, he imagined that it was getting fainter and more distant from him. He imagined, rigid in every muscle, that he was suffering the absolute worst that any human being could suffer. He imagined that he was dying. But he did not think of death as an escape, only as a concentrated and a painful incident. This was the climax of his not-crying. Then he breathed again, and his mother's voice intruded:

"Did you hear me?—*Did you hear me?* Mrs. Badzerkian is coming for tea. I want you to wash your face and put on a clean shirt. I want you to recite something for her. Now what are you going to recite?"

"In winter when I go to bed," said Victor. She was making him memorize every poem in *A Child's Garden of Verses*. He had said the first one that came into his head, and now there was an argument, because he had recited that one the last time. "I said it, because I couldn't think of any other one right off the bat!" Victor shouted.

"Don't yell at me!" his mother cried, storming across the room at him. She slapped his face before he knew what was happening.

He was up on one elbow on the sofa, on his back, his long, knobby-kneed legs splayed out in front of him. All right, he thought, if that's the way it is, that's the way it is. He looked at her with loathing. He would not show the slap had hurt, that it still stung. No more tears for today, he swore, no more even not-crying. He would finish the day, go through the tea, like a stone, like a soldier, not wincing. His mother paced around the room, turning one of her rings round and round, glancing at him from time to time, looking quickly away from him. But his eyes were steady on her. He was not afraid. She could even slap him again and he wouldn't care.

At last, she announced that she was going to wash her hair, and she went into the bathroom.

Victor got up from the sofa and wandered across the room. He wished he had a room of his own to go to. In the apartment on Riverside Drive, there had been three rooms, a living-room and his and his mother's rooms. When she was in the living-room, he had been able to go into his bedroom and vice versa, but here . . . They were going to tear down the old building they had lived in on Riverside Drive. It was not a pleasant thing for Victor to think about. Suddenly remembering the book that had fallen, he pulled out the sofa and reached for it. It was Menninger's *The Human Mind*, full of fascinating case histories of people. Victor put it back on the bookshelf between an astrology book and *How to Draw*. His mother did not like him to read psychology books, but Victor loved them, especially ones with case histories in them. The people in the case histories did what they wanted to do. They were natural. Nobody bossed them. At the local branch library, he spent hours browsing through the psychology shelves. They were in the adults' section, but the librarian did not mind his sitting at the tables there, because he was quiet.

Victor went into the kitchen and got a glass of water. As he was standing there drinking it, he heard a scratching noise coming from one of the paper bags on the counter. A mouse, he thought, but when he moved a couple of the bags, he didn't see any mouse. The scratching was coming from inside one of the bags. Gingerly, he opened the bag with his fingers, and waited for something to jump out. Looking in, he saw a white paper carton. He pulled it out slowly. Its bottom was damp. It opened like a pastry box. Victor jumped in surprise. It was a turtle on its back, a live turtle. It was wriggling its legs in the air, trying to turn over. Victor moistened his lips, and frowning with concentration, took the turtle by its sides with both hands, turned him over and let him down gently into the box again. The turtle drew in its feet then, and its head stretched up a little and it looked straight at him. Victor smiled. Why hadn't his mother told him she'd brought him a present? A live turtle. Victor's eyes glazed with anticipation as he thought of taking the turtle down, maybe with a leash around its neck, to show the fellow who'd laughed at his short pants. He might change his mind about being friends with him, if he found he owned a turtle.

"Hey, Mama! Mama!" Victor yelled at the bathroom door. "You brought me a tur-rtle?"

"A what?" The water shut off.

"A turtle! In the kitchen!" Victor had been jumping up and down in the hall. He stopped.

His mother had hesitated, too. The water came on again, and she said in a shrill tone, "C'est une terrapène! Pour un ragoût!"

Victor understood, and a small chill went over him because his mother had spoken in French. His mother addressed him in French when she was giving an order that had to be obeyed, or when she anticipated resistance from him. So the terrapin was for a stew. Victor nodded to himself with a stunned resignation, and went back to the kitchen. For a stew. Well, the terrapin was not long for this world, as they say. What did the terrapin like to eat? Lettuce? Raw bacon? Boiled potato? Victor peered into the refrigerator.

He held a piece of lettuce near the terrapin's horny mouth. The terrapin did not open its mouth, but it looked at him. Victor held the lettuce near the two little dots of its nostrils, but if the terrapin smelled it, it showed no interest. Victor looked under the sink and pulled out a large wash pan. He put two inches of water into it. Then he gently dumped the terrapin into the pan. The terrapin paddled for a few seconds, as if it had to swim, then finding that its stomach sat on the bottom of the pan, it stopped, and drew its feet in. Victor got down on his knees and studied the terrapin's face. Its upper lip overhung the lower, giving it a rather stubborn and unfriendly expression, but its eyes—they were bright and shining. Victor smiled when he looked hard at them.

"Okay, monsieur terrapène," he said, "just tell me what you'd like to eat and we'll get it for you!— Maybe some tuna?"

They had had tuna fish salad yesterday for dinner, and there was a small bowl of it left over. Victor got a little chunk of it in his fingers and presented it to the terrapin. The terrapin was not interested. Victor looked around the kitchen, wondering, then seeing the sunlight on the floor of the living-room, he picked up the pan and carried it to the living-room and set it down so the sunlight would fall on the terrapin's back. All turtles liked sunlight, Victor thought. He lay down on the floor on his side, propped up on an elbow. The terrapin stared at him for a moment, then very slowly and with an air of forethought and caution, put out its legs and advanced, found the circular boundary of the pan, and moved to the right, half its body out of the shallow water. It wanted out, and Victor took it in one hand, by the sides, and said:

"You can come out and have a little walk."

He smiled as the terrapin started to disappear under the sofa. He caught it easily, because it moved so slowly. When he put it down on the carpet, it was quite still, as if it had withdrawn a little to think what it should do next, where it should go. It was a brownish green. Looking at it, Victor thought of river bottoms, of river water flowing. Or maybe oceans. Where did terrapins come from? He jumped up and went to the dictionary on the bookshelf. The dictionary had a picture of a terrapin, but it was a dull, black and white drawing, not so pretty as the live one. He learned nothing except that the name was of Algonquian origin, that the terrapin lived in fresh or brackish water, and that it was edible. Edible. Well, that was bad luck, Victor thought. But he was not going to eat any terrapène tonight. It would be all for his mother, that ragoût, and even if she slapped him and made him learn an extra two or three poems, he would not eat any terrapin tonight.

His mother came out of the bathroom. "What are you doing there?— Veector?"

Victor put the dictionary back on the shelf. His mother had seen the pan. "I'm looking at the terrapin," he said, then realized the terrapin had disappeared. He got down on hands and knees and looked under the sofa.

"Don't put him on the furniture. He makes spots," said his mother. She was standing in the foyer, rubbing her hair vigorously with a towel.

Victor found the terrapin between the wastebasket and the wall. He put him back in the pan.

"Have you changed your shirt?" asked his mother.

Victor changed his shirt, and then at his mother's order sat down on the sofa with *A Child's Garden of Verses* and tackled another poem, a brand new one for Mrs. Badzerkian. He learned two lines at a time, reading it aloud in a soft voice to himself, then repeating it, then putting two, four and six lines together, until he had the whole thing. He recited it to the terrapin. Then Victor asked his mother if he could play with the terrapin in the bathtub.

"No! And get your shirt all splashed?"

"I can put on my other shirt."

"No! It's nearly four o'clock now. Get that pan out of the living-room!"

Victor carried the pan back to the kitchen. His mother took the terrapin quite fearlessly out of the pan, put it back into the white paper box, closed its lid, and stuck the box in the refrigerator. Victor jumped a little as the refrigerator door slammed. It would be awfully cold in there for the terrapin. But then, he supposed, fresh or brackish water was cold now and then, too.

"Veector, cut the lemon," said his mother. She was preparing the big round tray with cups and saucers. The water was boiling in the kettle.

Mrs. Badzerkian was prompt as usual, and his mother poured the tea as soon as she had deposited her coat and pocketbook on the foyer chair and sat down. Mrs. Badzerkian smelled of cloves. She had a small, straight mouth and a thin moustache on her upper lip which fascinated Victor, as he had never seen one on a woman before, not one at such short range, anyway. He never had mentioned Mrs. Badzerkian's moustache to his mother, knowing it was considered ugly, but in a strange way, her moustache was the thing he liked best about her. The rest of her was dull, uninteresting, and vaguely unfriendly. She always pretended to listen carefully to his poetry recitals, but he felt that she fidgeted, thought of other things while he spoke, and was glad when it was over. Today, Victor recited very well and without any hesitation, standing in the middle of the living-room floor and facing the two women, who were then having their second cups of tea.

"Très bien," said his mother. "Now you may have a cookie."

Victor chose from the plate a small round cookie with a drop of orange goo in its centre. He kept his knees close together when he sat down. He always felt Mrs. Badzerkian looked at his knees and with distaste. He often wished she would make some remark to his mother about his being old enough for long pants, but she never had, at least not within his hearing. Victor learned from his mother's conversation with Mrs. Badzerkian that the Lorentzes were coming for dinner tomorrow evening. It was probably for them that the terrapin stew was going to be made. Victor was glad that he would have the terrapin one more day to play with. Tomorrow morning, he thought, he would ask his mother if he could take the terrapin down on the sidewalk for a while, either on a leash or in the paper box, if his mother insisted.

"—like a chi-ild!" his mother was saying, laughing, with a glance at him, and Mrs. Badzerkian smiled shrewdly at him with her small, tight mouth.

Victor had been excused, and was sitting across the room with a book on the studio couch. His mother was telling Mrs. Badzerkian how he had played with the terrapin. Victor frowned down at his book, pretending not to hear. His mother did not like him to open his mouth to her or her guests once he had been excused. But now she was calling him her "lee-tle ba-aby Veec-tor . . ."

He stood up with his finger in the place in his book. "I don't see why it's childish to look at a terrapin!" he said, flushing with sudden anger. "They are very interesting animals, they—"

His mother interrupted him with a laugh, but at once the laugh disappeared and she said sternly, "Veector, I thought I had excused you. Isn't that correct?"

He hesitated, seeing in a flash the scene that was going to take place when Mrs. Badzerkian had left. "Yes, Mama. I'm sorry," he said. Then he sat down and bent over his book again. Twenty minutes later, Mrs. Badzerkian left. His mother scolded him for being rude, but it was not a five- or ten-minute scolding of the kind he had expected. It lasted hardly two minutes. She had forgotten to buy heavy cream, and she wanted Victor to go downstairs and get some. Victor put on his grey woollen jacket and went out. He always felt embarrassed and conspicuous in the jacket, because it came just a little bit below his short pants, and he looked as if he had nothing on underneath the coat.

Victor looked around for Frank on the sidewalk, but he didn't see him. He crossed Third Avenue and went to a delicatessen in the big building that he could see from the living-room window. On his way back, he saw Frank walking along the sidewalk, bouncing a ball. Now Victor went right up to him.

"Hey," Victor said. "I've got a terrapin upstairs."

"A what?" Frank caught the ball and stopped.

"A terrapin. You know, like a turtle. I'll bring him down tomorrow morning and show you, if you're around. He's pretty big."

"Yeah?—why don't you bring him down now?"

"Because we're gonna eat now," said Victor. "See you." He went into his building. He felt he had achieved something. Frank had looked really interested. Victor wished he could bring the terrapin down now, but his mother never liked him to go out after dark, and it was practically dark now.

When Victor got upstairs, his mother was still in the kitchen. Eggs were boiling and she had put a big pot of water on a back burner. "You took him out again!" Victor said, seeing the terrapin's box on the counter.

"Yes, I prepare the stew tonight," said his mother. "That is why I need the cream."

Victor looked at her. "You're going to— You have to kill it tonight?"

"Yes, my little one. Tonight." She jiggled the pot of eggs.

"Mama, can I take him downstairs to show Frank?" Victor asked quickly. "Just for five minutes, Mama. Frank's down there now."

"Who is Frank?"

"He's that fellow you asked me about today. The blond fellow we always see. Please, Mama."

His mother's black eyebrows frowned. "Take the terrapène downstairs? Certainly not. Don't be absurd, my baby! The terrapène is not a toy!"

Victor tried to think of some other lever of persuasion. He had not removed his coat. "You wanted me to get acquainted with Frank—"

"Yes. What has that got to do with a terrapin?"

The water on the back burner began to boil.

"You see, I promised him I'd—" Victor watched his mother lift the terrapin from the box, and as she dropped it into the boiling water, his mouth fell open. *"Mama!"*

"What is this? What is this noise?"

Victor, open-mouthed, stared at the terrapin whose legs were now racing against the steep sides of the pot. The terrapin's mouth opened, its eyes looked directly at Victor for an instant, its head arched back in torture, the open mouth sank beneath the seething water—and that was the end. Victor blinked. It was dead. He came closer, saw the four legs and the tail stretched out in the water, its head. He looked at his mother.

She was drying her hands on a towel. She glanced at him, then said, "Ugh!" She smelled her hands, then hung the towel back.

"Did you have to kill him like that?"

"How else? The same way you kill a lobster. Don't you know that? It doesn't hurt them."

He stared at her. When she started to touch him, he stepped back. He thought of the terrapin's wide open mouth, and his eyes suddenly flooded with tears. Maybe the terrapin had been screaming and it hadn't been heard over the bubbling of the water. The terrapin had looked at him, wanting him to pull him out, and he hadn't moved to help him. His mother had tricked him, done it so fast, he couldn't save him. He stepped back again. "No, don't touch me!"

His mother slapped his face, hard and quickly.

Victor set his jaw. Then he about-faced and went to the closet and threw his jacket on to a hanger and hung it up. He went into the living-room and fell down on the sofa. He was not crying now, but his mouth opened against the sofa pillow. Then he remembered the terrapin's mouth and he closed his lips. The terrapin had suffered, otherwise it would not have moved its legs fast to get out. Then he wept, soundlessly as the terrapin, his mouth open. He put both hands over his face, so as not to wet the sofa. After a long while, he got up. In the kitchen, his mother was humming, and every few minutes he heard her quick, firm steps as she went about her work. Victor had set his teeth again. He walked slowly to the kitchen doorway.

The terrapin was out on the wooden chopping board, and his mother, after a glance at him, still humming, took a knife and bore down on its blade, cutting off the terrapin's little nails. Victor half closed his eyes, but he watched steadily. The nails, with bits of skin attached to them, his mother scooped off the board into her palm and dumped into the gar-bage bag. Then she turned the terrapin on to its back and with the same sharp, pointed knife, she began to cut away the pale bottom shell. The terrapin's neck was bent sideways. Victor wanted to look away, but still he stared. Now the terrapin's insides were all exposed, red and white and greenish. Victor did not listen to what his mother was saying, about cooking terrapins in Europe, before he was born. Her voice was gentle and soothing, not at all like what she was doing.

"All right, don't look at me like that!" she suddenly threw at him, stomping her foot. "What's the matter with you? Are you crazy? Yes, I think so! You are seeck, you know that?"

Victor could not touch any of his supper, and his mother could not force him to, even though she shook him by the shoulders and threatened to slap him. They had creamed chipped beef on toast. Victor did not say a word. He felt very remote from his mother, even when she screamed right into his face. He felt very odd, the way he did sometimes when he was sick at his stomach, but he was not sick at his stomach. When they went to bed, he felt afraid of the dark. He saw the terrapin's face very large, its mouth open, its eyes wide and full of pain. Victor wished he could walk out the window and float, go anywhere he wanted to, disap-pear, yet be everywhere. He imagined his mother's hands on his shoul-ders, jerking him back, if he tried to step out the window. He hated his mother.

He got up and went quietly into the kitchen. The kitchen was absolutely dark, as there was no window, but he put his hand accurately on the knife rack and felt gently for the knife he wanted. He thought of the terrapin, in little pieces now, all mixed up in the sauce of cream and egg yolks and sherry in the pot in the refrigerator.

His mother's cry was not silent; it seemed to tear his ears off. His second blow was in her body, and then he stabbed her throat again. Only tiredness made him stop, and by then people were trying to bump the door in. Victor at last walked to the door, pulled the chain bolt back, and opened it for them.

He was taken to a large, old building full of nurses and doctors. Victor was very quiet and did everything he was asked to do, and answered the questions they put to him, but only those questions, and since they didn't ask him anything about a terrapin, he did not bring it up.

ENQUIRY

by

DICK FRANCIS

Part One: February

I

Yesterday I lost my licence.

To a professional steeplechase jockey, losing his licence and being warned off Newmarket Heath is like being chucked off the medical register, only more so.

Barred from race riding, barred from racecourses. Barred, moreover, from racing stables. Which poses me quite a problem, as I live in one.

No livelihood and maybe no home.

Last night was a right so-and-so, and I prefer to forget those grisly sleepless hours. Shock and bewilderment, the feeling that it couldn't have happened, it was all a mistake . . . this lasted until after midnight. And at least the disbelieving stage had had some built-in comfort. The full thudding realization which followed had none at all. My life was lying around like the untidy bits of a smashed teacup, and I was altogether out of glue and rivets.

This morning I got up and percolated some coffee and looked out of the window at the lads bustling around in the yard and mounting and cloppeting away up the road to the Downs, and I got my first real taste of being an outcast.

Fred didn't bellow up at my window as he usually did, "Going to stay there all day, then?"

This time, I was.

None of the lads looked up . . . they more or less kept their eyes studiously right down. They were quiet, too. Dead quiet. I watched Bouncing Bernie heave his ten stone seven on to the gelding I'd been riding lately, and there was something apologetic about the way he lowered his fat bum into the saddle.

And he, too, kept his eyes down.

Tomorrow, I guessed, they'd be themselves again. Tomorrow they'd be curious and ask questions. I understood that they weren't despising me. They were sympathetic. Probably too sympathetic for their own comfort. And embarrassed: that too. And instinctively delicate about looking too soon at the face of total disaster.

When they'd gone I drank my coffee slowly and wondered what to do next. A nasty, very nasty, feeling of emptiness and loss.

The papers had been stuck as usual through my letterbox. I wondered what the boy had thought, knowing what he was delivering. I shrugged. Might as well read what they'd said, the Goddamned pressmen, God bless them.

The *Sporting Life,* short on news, had given us the headlines and the full treatment.

"Cranfield and Hughes Disqualified."

There was a picture of Cranfield at the top of the page, and halfway down one of me, all smiles, taken the day I won the Hennessy Gold Cup. Some little sub-editor letting his irony loose, I thought sourly, and printing the most cheerful picture he could dig out of the files.

The close-printed inches north and south of my happy face were unrelieved gloom.

> *"The Stewards said they were not satisfied with my explanation," Cranfield said. "They have withdrawn my licence. I have no further comment to make."*

Hughes, it was reported, had said almost exactly the same. Hughes, if I remembered correctly, had in fact said nothing whatsoever. Hughes had been too stunned to put one word collectedly after another, and if he had said anything at all it would have been unprintable.

I didn't read all of it. I'd read it all before, about the other people. For "Cranfield and Hughes" one could substitute any other trainer and jockey who had been warned off. The newspaper reports on these occasions were always the same; totally uninformed. As a racing Enquiry was a private trial the ruling authorities were not obliged to open the proceedings to the public or the Press, and as they were not obliged to, they never did. In fact like many another inward-looking concern they seemed to be permanently engaged in trying to stop too many people from finding out what was really going on.

The *Daily Witness* was equally fog-bound, except that Daddy Leeman had suffered his usual rush of purple prose to the head. According to him:

> *Kelly Hughes, until now a leading contender for this season's jump-jockeys' crown, and fifth on the list last year, was sentenced to an indefinite suspension of his licence. Hughes, thirty, left the hearing ten minutes after Cranfield. Looking pale and grim, he confirmed that he had lost his licence, and added, "I have no further comment."*

They had remarkable ears, those pressmen.

I put down the paper with a sigh and went into the bedroom to exchange my dressing-gown for trousers and a jersey, and after that I made my bed, and after that I sat on it, staring into space. I had nothing else to do. I had nothing to do for as far ahead as the eye could see. Unfortunately I also had nothing to think about except the Enquiry.

Put baldly, I had lost my licence for losing a race. More precisely, I had ridden a red-hot favourite into second place in the Lemonfizz Crystal Cup at Oxford in the last week of January, and the winner had been an unconsidered outsider. This would have been merely unfortunate, had it not been that both horses were trained by Dexter Cranfield.

The finishing order at the winning post had been greeted with roars of disgust from the stands, and I had been booed all the way to the unsaddling enclosure. Dexter Cranfield had looked worried more than delighted to have taken first and second places in one of the season's big sponsored steeplechases, and the Stewards of the meeting had called us both in to explain. They were not, they announced, satisfied with the explanations. They would refer the matter to the Disciplinary Committee of the Jockey Club.

The Disciplinary Committee, two weeks later, were equally sceptical that the freak result had been an accident. Deliberate fraud on the betting public, they said. Disgraceful, dishonest, disgusting, they said. Racing must keep its good name clean. Not the first time that either of you have been suspected. Severe penalties must be inflicted, as a deterrent to others.

Off, they said. Warned off. And good riddance.

It wouldn't have happened in America, I thought in depression. There, all runners from one stable, or one owner, for that matter, were covered by a bet on any of them. So if the stable's outsider won instead of its favourite, the backers still collected their money. High time the same system crossed the Atlantic. Correction, more than high time; long, long overdue.

The truth of the matter was that Squelch, my red-hot favourite, had been dying under me all the way up the straight, and it was in the miracle class that I'd finished as close as second, and not fifth or sixth. If he hadn't carried so many people's shirts, in fact, I wouldn't have exhausted him as I had. That it had been Cranfield's other runner Cherry Pie who had passed me ten yards from the finish was just the worst sort of luck.

Armed by innocence, and with reason to believe that even if the Oxford Stewards had been swayed by the crowd's hostile reception, the Disciplinary Committee were going to consider the matter in an atmosphere of cool common-sense, I had gone to the Enquiry without a twinge of apprehension.

The atmosphere was cool, all right. Glacial. Their own common-sense was taken for granted by the Stewards. They didn't appear to think that either Cranfield or I had any.

The first faint indication that the sky was about to fall came when they read out a list of nine previous races in which I had ridden a beaten favourite for Cranfield. In six of them, another of Cranfield's runners had won. Cranfield had also had other runners in the other three.

"That means," said Lord Gowery, "that this case before us is by no means the first. It has happened again and again. These results seem to have been unnoticed in the past, but this time you have clearly overstepped the mark."

I must have stood there looking stupid with my mouth falling open in astonishment, and the trouble was that they obviously thought I was astonished at how much they had dug up to prove my guilt.

"Some of those races were years ago," I protested. "Six or seven, some of them."

"What difference does that make?" asked Lord Gowery. "They happened."

"That sort of thing happens to every trainer now and then," Cranfield said hotly. "You must know it does."

Lord Gowery gave him an emotionless stare. It stirred some primeval reaction in my glands, and I could feel the ripple of goose pimples up my spine. He really believes, I thought wildly, he really believes us guilty. It was only then that I realized we had to make a fight of it; and it was already far too late.

I said to Cranfield, "We should have had that lawyer," and he gave me an almost frightened glance of agreement.

Shortly before the Lemonfizz the Jockey Club had finally thrown an old autocratic tradition out of the twentieth century and agreed that people in danger of losing their livelihood could be legally represented at their trials, if they wished. The concession was so new that there was no accepted custom to be guided by. One or two people had been acquitted with lawyers' help who would presumably have been acquitted anyway; and if an accused person engaged a lawyer to defend him, he had in all cases to pay the fees himself. The Jockey Club did not award costs to anyone they accused, whether or not he managed to prove himself innocent.

At first Cranfield had agreed with me that we should find a lawyer, though both of us had been annoyed at having to shell out. Then Cranfield had by chance met at a party the newly elected Disciplinary Steward who was a friend of his, and had reported to me afterwards, "There's no need for us to go to the expense of a lawyer. Monty Midgely told me in confidence that the Disciplinary Committee think the Oxford Stewards were off their heads reporting us, that he knows the Lemonfizz result was just one of those things, and not to worry, the Enquiry will only be a formality. Ten minutes or so, and it will be over."

That assurance had been good enough for both of us. We hadn't even seen any cause for alarm when three or four days later Colonel Sir Montague Midgely had turned yellow with jaundice and taken to his bed, and it had been announced that one of the Committee, Lord Gowery, would deputize for him in any Enquiries which might be held in the next few weeks.

Monty Midgely's liver had a lot to answer for. Whatever he had intended, it now seemed all too appallingly clear that Gowery didn't agree.

The Enquiry was held in a large lavishly furnished room in the Portman Square headquarters of the Jockey Club. Four Stewards sat in comfortable armchairs along one side of a polished table with a pile of papers in front of each of them, and a shorthand writer was stationed at a smaller table a little to their right. When Cranfield and I went into the room the shorthand writer was fussing with a tape-recorder, unwinding a lead from the machine which stood on his own table and trailing it across the floor towards the Stewards. He set up a microphone on a stand in front of Lord Gowery, switched it on, blew into it a couple of times, went back to his machine, flicked a few switches, and announced that everything was in order.

Behind the Stewards, across a few yards of plushy dark red carpet, were several more armchairs. Their occupants included the three Stewards who had been unconvinced at Oxford, the Clerk of the Course, the Handicapper who had allotted the Lemonfizz weights, and a pair of Stipendiary Stewards, officials paid by the Jockey Club and acting at meetings as an odd mixture of messenger boys for the Stewards and the industry's private police. It was they who, if they thought there had been an infringement of the rules, brought it to the notice of the Stewards of the meeting concerned, and advised them to hold an Enquiry.

As in any other job, some Stipendiaries were reasonable men and some were not. The Stipe who had been acting at Oxford on Lemonfizz day was notoriously the most difficult of them all.

Cranfield and I were to sit facing the Stewards' table, but several feet from it. For us, too, there were the same luxurious armchairs. Very civilized. Not a hatchet in sight. We sat down, and Cranfield casually crossed his legs, looking confident and relaxed.

We were far from soul-mates, Cranfield and I. He had inherited a fortune from his father, an ex-soap manufacturer who had somehow failed to acquire a coveted peerage in spite of donating madly to every fashionable cause in sight, and the combination of wealth and disappointed social ambition had turned Cranfield *fils* into a roaring snob. To him, since he employed me, I was a servant; and he didn't know how to treat servants.

He was, however, a pretty good trainer. Better still, he had rich friends who could afford good horses. I had ridden for him semi-regularly for nearly eight years, and although at first I had resented his snobbish little ways, I had eventually grown up enough to find them amusing. We operated strictly as a business team, even after all that time. Not a flicker of friendship. He would have been outraged at the very idea, and I didn't like him enough to think it a pity.

He was twenty years older than me, a tallish, thin Anglo-Saxon type with thin fine mousy hair, greyish-blue eyes with short fair lashes, a well-developed straight nose, and aggressively perfect teeth. His bone structure was of the type acceptable to the social circle in which he tried to move, but the lines his outlook on life had etched in his skin were a warning to anyone looking for tolerance or generosity. Cranfield was mean-minded by habit and open-handed only to those who could lug him upwards. In all his dealings with those he considered his inferiors he left behind a turbulent wake of dislike and resentment. He was charming to his friends, polite in public to his wife, and his three teenage children echoed his delusions of superiority with pitiful faithfulness.

Cranfield had remarked to me some days before the Enquiry that the Oxford Stewards were all good chaps and that two of them had personally apologized to him for having to send the case on to the Disciplinary Committee. I nodded without answering. Cranfield must have known as well as I did that all three of the Oxford Stewards had been elected for social reasons only; that one of them couldn't read a number board at five paces, that another had inherited his late uncle's string of racehorses but not his expert knowledge, and that the third had been heard to ask his trainer which his own horse was, during the course of a race. Not one of the three could read a race at anything approaching the standard of a racecourse commentator. Good chaps they might well be, but as judges, frightening.

"We will show the film of the race," Lord Gowery said.

They showed it, projecting from the back of the room on to a screen on the wall behind Cranfield and me. We turned our armchairs round to watch it. The Stipendiary Steward from Oxford, a fat pompous bully, stood by the screen, pointing out Squelch with a long baton.

"This is the horse in question," he said, as the horses lined up for the start. I reflected mildly that if the Stewards knew their job they would have seen the film several times already, and would know which was Squelch without needing to have him pointed out.

The Stipe more or less indicated Squelch all the way round. It was an unremarkable race, run to a well-tried pattern: hold back at the start, letting someone else make the pace; ease forwards to fourth place and settle there for two miles or more; move smoothly to the front coming towards the second last fence, and press on home regardless. If the horse liked that sort of race, and if he were good enough, he would win.

Squelch hated to be ridden any other way. Squelch was, on his day, good enough. It just hadn't been his day.

The film showed Squelch taking the lead coming into the second last fence. He rolled a bit on landing, a sure sign of tiredness. I'd had to pick him up and urge him into the last, and it was obvious on the film. Away from the last, towards the winning post, he'd floundered about beneath me, and if I hadn't been ruthless he'd have slowed to a trot. Cherry Pie, at the finish, came up surprisingly fast and passed him as if he'd been standing still.

The film flicked off abruptly and someone put the lights on again. I thought that the film was conclusive and that that would be the end of it.

"You didn't use your whip," Lord Gowery said accusingly.

"No, sir," I agreed. "Squelch shies away from the whip. He has to be ridden with the hands."

"You were making no effort to ride him out."

"Indeed I was, sir. He was dead tired, you can see on the film."

"All I can see on the film is that you were making absolutely no effort to win. You were sitting there with your arms still, making no effort whatsoever."

I stared at him. "Squelch isn't an easy horse to ride, sir. He'll always do his best but only if he isn't upset. He has to be ridden quietly. He stops if he's hit. He'll only respond to being squeezed, and to small flicks on the reins, and to his jockey's voice."

"That's quite right," said Cranfield piously. "I always give Hughes orders not to treat the horse roughly."

As if he hadn't heard a word, Lord Gowery said, "Hughes didn't pick up his whip."

He looked enquiringly at the two Stewards flanking him, as if to collect their opinions. The one on his left, a youngish man who had ridden as an amateur, nodded non-committally. The other one was asleep.

I suspected Gowery kicked him under the table. He woke up with a jerk, said, "Eh? Yes, definitely," and eyed me suspiciously.

It's a farce, I thought incredulously. The whole thing's a bloody farce.

Gowery nodded, satisfied. "Hughes never picked up his whip."

The fat bullying Stipe was oozing smugness. "I am sure you will find this next film relevant, sir."

"Quite," agreed Gowery. "Show it now."

"Which film is this?" Cranfield enquired.

Gowery said, "This film shows Squelch winning at Reading on January 3rd."

Cranfield reflected. "I was not at Reading on that day."

"No," agreed Gowery. "We understand you went to the Worcester meeting instead." He made it sound suspicious instead of perfectly normal. Cranfield had run a hot young hurdler at Worcester and had wanted to see how he shaped. Squelch, the established star, needed no supervision.

The lights went out again. The Stipe used his baton to point out Kelly Hughes riding a race in Squelch's distinctive colours of black and white chevrons and a black cap. Not at all the same sort of race as the Lemonfizz Crystal Cup. I'd gone to the front early to give myself a clear view of the fences, pulled back to about third place for a breather at midway, and forced to the front again only after the last fence, swinging my whip energetically down the horse's shoulder and urging him vigorously with my arms.

The film stopped, the lights went on, and there was a heavy accusing silence. Cranfield turned towards me, frowning.

"You will agree," said Gowery ironically, "that you used your whip, Hughes."

"Yes, sir," I said. "Which race did you say that was?"

"The last race at Reading," he said irritably. "Don't pretend you don't know."

"I agree that the film you've just shown was the last race at Reading, sir. But Squelch didn't run in the last race at Reading. The horse in that film was Wanderlust. He belongs to Mr. Kessel, like Squelch does, so the colours are the same, and both horses are by the same sire, which accounts for them looking similar, but the horse you've just shown is Wanderlust. Who does, as you saw, respond well if you wave a whip at him."

There was dead silence. It was Cranfield who broke it, clearing his throat.

"Hughes is quite right. That is Wanderlust."

He hadn't realized it, I thought in amusement, until I'd pointed it out.

It's all too easy for people to believe what they're told.

There was a certain amount of hurried whispering going on. I didn't help them. They could sort it out for themselves.

Eventually Lord Gowery said, "Has anyone got a form book?" and an official near the door went out to fetch one. Gowery opened it and took a long look at the Reading results.

"It seems," he said heavily, "that we have the wrong film. Squelch ran in the sixth race at Reading, which is of course usually the last. However, it now appears that on that day there were seven races, the Novice Chase having been divided and run in two halves, at the beginning and end of the day. Wanderlust won the *seventh* race. A perfectly understandable mix-up, I am afraid."

I didn't think I would help my cause by saying that I thought it a disgraceful mix-up, if not criminal.

"Could we now, sir," I asked politely, "see the right film? The one that Squelch won."

Lord Gowery cleared his throat. "I don't, er, think we have it here. However," he recovered fast, "we don't need it. It is immaterial. We are not considering the Reading result, but that at Oxford."

I gasped. I was truly astounded. "But sir, if you watch Squelch's race, you will see that I rode him at Reading exactly as I did at Oxford, without using the whip."

"That is beside the point, Hughes, because Squelch may not have needed the whip at Reading, but at Oxford he did."

"Sir, it *is* the point," I protested. "I rode Squelch at Oxford in exactly the same manner as when he won at Reading, only at Oxford he tired."

Lord Gowery absolutely ignored this. Instead he looked left and right to his Stewards alongside and remarked, "We must waste no more time. We have three or four witnesses to call before lunch."

The sleepy eldest Steward nodded and looked at his watch. The younger one nodded and avoided meeting my eyes. I knew him quite well from his amateur jockey days, and had often ridden against him. We had all been pleased when he had been made a Steward, because he knew at first-hand the sort of odd circumstances which cropped up in racing to make a fool of the brightest, and we had thought that he would always put forward or explain our point of view. From his downcast semi-apologetic face I now gathered that we had hoped too much. He had not so far contributed one single word to the proceedings, and he looked, though it seemed extraordinary, intimidated.

As plain Andrew Tring he had been lighthearted, amusing, and almost reckless over fences. His recently inherited baronetcy and his even more recently acquired Stewardship seemed on the present showing to have hammered him into the ground.

Of Lord Plimborne, the elderly sleepyhead, I knew very little except his name. He seemed to be in his seventies and there was a faint tremble about many of his movements as if old age were shaking at his foundations and would soon have him down. He had not, I thought, clearly heard or understood more than a quarter of what had been said.

An Enquiry was usually conducted by three Stewards, but on this day there were four. The fourth, who sat on the left of Andrew Tring, was not, as far as I knew, even on the Disciplinary Committee, let alone a Disciplinary Steward. But he had in front of him a pile of notes as large if not larger than the others, and he was following every word with sharp hot eyes. Exactly where his involvement lay I couldn't work out, but there was no doubt that Wykeham, second Baron Ferth, cared about the outcome.

He alone of the four seemed really disturbed that they should have shown the wrong film, and he said quietly but forcefully enough for it to carry across to Cranfield and me, "I did advise against showing the Reading race, if you remember."

Gowery gave him an icelance of a look which would have slaughtered thinner-skinned men, but against Ferth's inner furnace it melted impotently.

"You agreed to say nothing," Gowery said in the same piercing undertone. "I would be obliged if you would keep to that."

Cranfield had stirred beside me in astonishment, and now, thinking about it on the following day, the venomous little exchange seemed even more incredible. What, I now wondered, had Ferth been doing there, where he didn't really belong and was clearly not appreciated.

The telephone bell broke up my thoughts. I went into the sitting-room to answer it and found it was a jockey colleague ringing up to commiserate. He himself, he reminded me, had had his licence suspended for a while three or four years back, and he knew how I must be feeling.

"It's good of you, Jim, to take the trouble."

"No trouble, mate. Stick together, and all that. How did it go?"

"Lousy," I said. "They didn't listen to a word either Cranfield or I said. They'd made up their minds we were guilty before we ever went there."

Jim Enders laughed. "I'm not surprised. You know what happened to me?"

"No. What?"

"Well, when they gave me my licence back, they'd called the Enquiry for the Tuesday, see, and then for some reason they had to postpone it until the Thursday afternoon. So along I went on Thursday afternoon and they hummed and hahed and warned me as to my future conduct and kept me in suspense for a bit before they said I could have my licence back. Well, I thought I might as well collect a Racing Calendar and take it home with me, to keep abreast of the times and all that, so, anyway, I collected my Racing Calendar which is published at twelve o'clock on Thursdays, twelve o'clock mind you, and I opened it, and what is the first thing I see but the notice saying my licence has been restored. So how about *that?* They'd published the result of that meeting two hours before it had even begun."

"I don't believe it," I said.

"Quite true," he said. "Mind you, that time they were giving my licence back, not taking it away. But even so, it shows they'd made up their minds. I've always wondered why they bothered to hold that second Enquiry at all. Waste of everyone's time, mate."

"It's incredible," I said. But I did believe him: which before my own Enquiry I would not have done.

"When are they giving you your licence back?" Jim asked.

"They didn't say."

"Didn't they tell you when you could apply?"

"No."

Jim shoved one very rude word down the wires. "And that's another thing, mate, you want to pick your moment right when you *do* apply."

"How do you mean?"

"When I applied for mine, on the dot of when they told me I could, they said the only Steward who had authority to give it back had gone on a cruise to Madeira and I would have to wait until he turned up again."

II

When the horses came back from second exercise at midday my cousin Tony stomped up the stairs and trod muck and straw into my carpet. It was his stable, not Cranfield's, that I lived in. He had thirty boxes, thirty-two horses, one house, one wife, four children, and an overdraft. Ten more boxes were being built, the fifth child was four months off, and the overdraft was turning puce. I lived alone in the flat over the yard and rode everything which came along.

All very normal. And, in the three years since we had moved in, increasingly successful. My suspension meant that Tony and the owners were going to have to find another jockey.

He flopped down gloomily in a green velvet armchair.

"You all right?"

"Yes," I said.

"Give me a drink, for God's sake."

I poured half a cupful of J and B into a chunky tumbler.

"Ice?"

"As it is."

I handed him the glass and he made inroads. Restoration began to take place.

Our mothers had been Welsh girls, sisters. Mine had married a local boy, so that I had come out wholly Celt, shortish, dark, compact. My aunt had hightailed off with a six-foot-four languid blond giant from Wyoming who had endowed Tony with most of his physique and double his brain. Out of USAF uniform, Tony's father had reverted to ranch-hand, not ranch owner, as he had led his in-laws to believe, and he'd considered it more important for his only child to get to ride well than to acquire any of that there fancy book learning.

Tony therefore played truant for years with enthusiasm, and had never regretted it. I met him for the first time when he was twenty-five, when his pa's heart had packed up and he had escorted his sincerely weeping mum back to Wales. In the seven years since then he had acquired with some speed an English wife, a semi-English accent, an unimpassioned knowledge of English racing, a job as assistant trainer, and a stable of his own. And also, somewhere along the way, an unquenchable English thirst. For Scotch.

He said, looking down at the diminished drink, "What are you going to do?"

"I don't know, exactly."

"Will you go back home?"

"Not to live," I said. "I've come too far."

He raised his head a little and looked round the room, smiling. Plain white walls, thick brown carpet, velvet chairs in two or three greens, antique furniture, pink and orange striped curtains, heavy and rich. "I'll say you have," he agreed. "A big long way from Coedlant Farm, boyo."

"No farther than your prairie."

He shook his head. "I still have grass roots. You've pulled yours up."

Penetrating fellow, Tony. An extraordinary mixture of raw intelligence and straws in the hair. He was right; I'd shaken the straws out of mine. We got on very well.

"I want to talk to someone who has been to a recent Enquiry," I said, abruptly.

"You want to just put it behind you and forget it," he advised. "No percentage in comparing hysterectomies."

I laughed, which was truly something in the circumstances. "Not on a pain for pain basis," I explained. "It's just that I want to know if what happened yesterday was . . . well, unusual. The procedure, that is. The form of the thing. Quite apart from the fact that most of the evidence was rigged."

"Is that what you were mumbling about on the way home? Those few words you uttered in a wilderness of silence?"

"Those," I said, "were mostly 'they didn't believe a word we said.' "

"So who rigged what?"

"That's the question."

He held out his empty glass and I poured some more into it.

"Are you serious?"

"Yes. Starting from point A, which is that I rode Squelch to win, we arrive at point B, which is that the Stewards are convinced I didn't. Along the way were three or four little birdies all twittering their heads off and lying in their bloody teeth."

"I detect," he said, "that something is stirring in yesterday's ruins."

"What ruins?"

"You."

"Oh."

"You should drink more," he said. "Make an effort. Start now."

"I'll think about it."

"Do that." He wallowed to his feet. "Time for lunch. Time to go back to the little nestlings with their mouths wide open for worms."

"Is it worms, today?"

"God knows. Poppy said to come, if you want."

I shook my head.

"You must eat," he protested.

"Yes."

He looked at me consideringly. "I guess," he said, "that you'll manage." He put down his empty glass. "We're here, you know, if you want anything. Company. Food. Dancing girls. Trifles like that."

I nodded my thanks, and he clomped away down the stairs. He hadn't mentioned his horses, their races, or the other jockeys he would have to engage. He hadn't said that my staying in the flat would be an embarrassment to him.

I didn't know what to do about that. The flat was my home. My only home. Designed, converted, furnished by me. I liked it, and didn't want to leave.

I wandered into the bedroom.

A double bed, but pillows for one.

On the dressing chest, in a silver frame, a photograph of Rosalind. We had been married for two years when she went to spend a routine weekend with her parents. I'd been busy riding five races at Market Rasen on the Saturday, and a policeman had come into the weighing-room at the end of the afternoon and told me unemotionally that my father-in-law had set off with his wife and mine to visit friends and had misjudged his overtaking distance in heavy rain and had driven head on into a lorry and killed all three of them instantly.

It was four years since it had happened. Quite often I could no longer remember her voice. Other times she seemed to be in the next room. I had loved her passionately, but she no longer hurt. Four years was a long time.

I wished she had been there, with her tempestuous nature and fierce loyalty, so that I could have told her about the Enquiry, and shared the wretchedness, and been comforted.

That Enquiry . . .

Gowery's first witness had been the jockey who had finished third in the Lemonfizz, two or three lengths behind Squelch. About twenty, round faced and immature, Master Charlie West was a boy with a lot of natural talent but too little self-discipline. He had a great opinion of himself, and was in danger of throwing away his future through an apparent belief that rules only applied to everyone else.

The grandeur of Portman Square and the trappings of the Enquiry seemed to have subdued him. He came into the room nervously and stood where he was told, at one end of the Stewards' table: on their left, and to our right. He looked down at the table and raised his eyes only once or twice during his whole testimony. He didn't look across to Cranfield and me at all.

Gowery asked him if he remembered the race.

"Yes, sir." It was a low mumble, barely audible.

"Speak up," said Gowery irritably.

The shorthand writer came across from his table and moved the microphone so that it was nearer Charlie West. Charlie West cleared his throat.

"What happened during the race?"

"Well, sir . . . Shall I start from the beginning, sir?"

"There's no need for unnecessary detail, West," Gowery said impatiently. "Just tell us what happened on the far side of the course on the second circuit."

"I see, sir. Well . . . Kelly, that is, I mean, Hughes, sir . . . Hughes . . . Well . . . Like . . ."

"West, come to the point." Gowery's voice would have left a lazer standing. A heavy flush showed in patches on Charlie West's neck. He swallowed.

"Round the far side, sir, where the stands go out of sight, like, for a few seconds, well, there, sir . . . Hughes gives this hefty pull back on the reins, sir . . ."

"And what did he say, West?"

"He said, sir, 'OK. Brakes on, chaps.' Sir."

Gowery said meaningfully, though everyone had heard the first time and a pin would have crashed on the Wilton, "Repeat that, please, West."

"Hughes, sir, said, 'OK. Brakes on, chaps.'"

"And what did you take him to mean by that, West?"

"Well sir, that he wasn't trying, like. He always says that when he's pulling one back and not trying."

"Always?"

"Well, something like that, sir."

There was a considerable silence.

Gowery said formally, "Mr. Cranfield . . . Hughes . . . You may ask this witness questions, if you wish."

I got slowly to my feet.

"Are you seriously saying," I asked bitterly, "that at any time during the Lemonfizz Cup I pulled Squelch back and said 'OK, brakes on, chaps'? "

He nodded. He had begun to sweat.

"Please answer aloud." I said.

"Yes. You said it."

"I did not."

"I heard you."

"You couldn't have done."

"I heard you."

I was silent. I simply had no idea what to say next. It was too like a playground exchange: you did, I didn't, you did, I didn't . . .

I sat down. All the Stewards and all the officials ranked behind them were looking at me. I could see that all, to a man, believed West.

"Hughes, are you in the habit of using this phrase?" Gowery's voice was dry acid.

"No, sir."

"Have you *ever* used it?"

"Not in the Lemonfizz Cup, sir."

"I said, Hughes, have you *ever* used it?"

To lie or not to lie . . . "Yes, sir, I have used it, once or twice. But not on Squelch in the Lemonfizz Cup."

"It is sufficient that you said it at all, Hughes. We will draw our own conclusions as to *when* you said it."

He shuffled one paper to the bottom of his pack and picked up another. Consulting it with the unseeing token glance of those who know their subject by heart, he continued, "And now, West, tell us what Hughes did after he had said these words."

"Sir, he pulled his horse back, sir."

"How do you know this?" The question was a formality. He asked with the tone of one already aware of the answer.

"I was just beside Hughes, sir, when he said that about brakes. Then he sort of hunched his shoulders, sir, and give a pull, sir, and, well, then he was behind me, having dropped out, like."

Cranfield said angrily, "But he finished in front of you."

"Yes, sir." Charlie West flicked his eyes upwards to Lord Gowery, and spoke only to him. "My old horse couldn't act on the going, sir, and Hughes came past me again going into the second last, like."

"And how did Squelch jump that fence?"

"Easy, sir. Met it just right. Stood back proper, sir."

"Hughes maintains that Squelch was extremely tired at that point."

Charlie West left a small pause. Finally he said, "I don't know about that, sir. I thought as how Squelch would win, myself, sir. I still think as how he ought to have won, sir, being the horse he is, sir."

Gowery glanced left and right, to make sure that his colleagues had taken the point. "From your position during the last stages of the race, West, could you see whether or not Hughes was making every effort to win?"

"Well he didn't look like it, sir, which was surprising, like."

"Surprising?"

"Yes, sir. See, Hughes is such an artist at it, sir."

"An artist at what?"

"Well, at riding what looks from the stands one hell of a finish, sir, while all the time he's smothering it like mad."

"Hughes is in the habit of not riding to win?"

Charlie West worked it out. "Yes, sir."

"Thank you, West," Lord Gowery said with insincere politeness. "You may go and sit over there at the back of the room."

Charlie West made a rabbit's scurry towards the row of chairs reserved for those who had finished giving evidence. Cranfield turned fiercely to me and said, "Why didn't you deny it more vehemently, for God's sake? Why the Hell didn't you insist he was making the whole thing up?"

"Do you think they'd believe me?"

He looked uneasily at the accusing ranks opposite, and found his answer in their implacable stares. All the same, he stood up and did his best.

"Lord Gowery, the film of the Lemonfizz Cup does not bear out West's accusation. At no point does Hughes pull back his horse."

I lifted my hand too late to stop him. Gowery's and Lord Ferth's intent faces both registered satisfaction. They knew as well as I did that what West had said was borne out on the film. Sensing that Squelch was going to run out of steam, I'd given him a short breather a mile from home, and this normal everyday little act was now wide open to misinterpretation.

Cranfield looked down at me, surprised by my reaction.

"I gave him a breather," I said apologetically. "It shows."

He sat down heavily, frowning in worry.

Gowery was saying to an official, "Show in Mr. Newtonnards," as if Cranfield hadn't spoken. There was a pause before Mr. Newtonnards, whoever he was, materialized. Lord Gowery was looking slightly over his left shoulder, towards the door, giving me the benefit of his patrician profile. I realized with almost a sense of shock that I knew nothing about him as a person, and that he most probably knew nothing about me. He had been, to me, a figure of authority with a capital A. I hadn't questioned his right to rule over me. I had assumed naïvely that he would do so with integrity, wisdom, and justice.

So much for illusions. He was leading his witnesses in a way that would make the Old Bailey reel. He heard truth in Charlie West's lies and lies in my truth. He was prosecutor as well as judge, and was only admitting evidence if it fitted his case.

He was dispersing the accepting awe I had held him in like candyfloss in a thunderstorm, and I could feel an unforgiving cynicism growing in its stead. Also I was ashamed of my former state of trust. With the sort of education I'd had, I ought to have known better.

Mr. Newtonnards emerged from the waiting-room and made his way to the witnesses' end of the Stewards' table, sporting a red rosebud in his lapel and carrying a large blue ledger. Unlike Charlie West he was confident, not nervous. Seeing that everyone else was seated he looked around for a chair for himself, and not finding one, asked.

After a fractional pause Gowery nodded, and the official-of-all-work near the door pushed one forwards. Mr. Newtonnards deposited into it his well-cared-for pearl-grey-suited bulk.

"Who is he?" I said to Cranfield. Cranfield shook his head and didn't answer, but he knew, because his air of worry had if anything deepened.

Andrew Tring flipped through his pile of papers, found what he was looking for, and drew it out. Lord Plimborne had his eyes shut again. I was beginning to expect that; and in any case I could see that it didn't matter, since the power lay somewhere between Gowery and Ferth, and Andy Tring and Plimborne were so much window-dressing.

Lord Gowery too picked up a paper, and again I had the impression that he knew its contents by heart.

"Mr. Newtonnards?"

"Yes, my lord." He had a faint cockney accent overlaid by years of cigars and champagne. Mid-fifties, I guessed; no fool, knew the world, and had friends in show business. Not too far out: Mr. Newtonnards, it transpired, was a bookmaker.

Gowery said, "Mr. Newtonnards, will you be so good as to tell about a certain bet you struck on the afternoon of the Lemonfizz Cup?"

"Yes, my lord. I was standing on my pitch in Tattersall's when this customer come up and asked me for five tenners on Cherry Pie." He stopped there, as if that was all he thought necessary.

Gowery did some prompting. "Please describe this man, and also tell us what you did about his request."

"Describe him? Let's see, then. He was nothing special. A biggish man in a fawn coat, wearing a brown trilby and carrying race glasses over his shoulder. Middle-aged, I suppose. Perhaps he had a moustache. Can't remember, really."

The description fitted half the men on the racecourse.

"He asked me what price I'd give him about Cherry Pie," Newton-nards went on. "I didn't have any price chalked on my board, seeing Cherry Pie was such an outsider. I offered him tens, but he said it wasn't enough, and he looked like moving off down the line. Well . . ." Newton-nards waved an expressive pudgy hand ". . . business wasn't too brisk, so I offered him a hundred to six. Couldn't say fairer than that now, could I, seeing as there were only eight runners in the race? Worst decision I made in a long time." Gloom mixed with stoicism settled on his well-covered features.

"So when Cherry Pie won, you paid out?"

"That's right. He put down fifty smackers; I paid him nine hundred."

"Nine hundred pounds?"

"That's right, my lord," Newtonnards confirmed easily, "nine hundred pounds."

"And we may see the record of this bet?"

"Certainly." He opened the big blue ledger at a marked page. "On the left, my lord, just over halfway down. Marked with a red cross. Nine hundred and fifty, ticket number nine seven two."

The ledger was passed along the Stewards' table. Plimborne woke up for the occasion and all four of them peered at the page. The ledger returned to Newtonnards, who shut it and let it lie in front of him.

"Wasn't that a very large bet on an outsider?" Gowery asked.

"Yes it was, my lord. But then, there are a lot of mugs about. Except, of course, that once in a while they go and win."

"So you had no qualms about risking such a large amount?"

"Not really, my lord. Not with Squelch in the race. And anyway, I laid a bit of it off. A quarter of it, in fact, at thirty-threes. So my actual losses were in the region of four hundred and eighty-seven pounds ten. Then I took three hundred and two-ten on Squelch and the others, which left a net loss on the race of one eight five."

Cranfield and I received a glare in which every unit of the one eight five rankled.

Gowery said, "We are not enquiring into how much you lost Mr. Newtonnards, but into the identity of the client who won nine hundred pounds on Cherry Pie."

I shivered. If West could lie, so could others.

"As I said in my statement, my lord, I don't know his name. When he came up to me I thought I knew him from somewhere, but you see a lot of folks in my game, so I didn't think much of it. You know. So it wasn't until after I paid him off. After the last race, in fact. Not until I was driving home. Then it came to me, and I went spare, I can tell you."

"Please explain more clearly," Gowery said patiently. The patience of a cat at a mousehole. Anticipation making the waiting sweet.

"It wasn't him, so much, as who I saw him talking to. Standing by the parade ring rails before the first race. Don't know why I should remember it, but I do."

"And who did you see this client talking to?"

"Him." He jerked his head in our direction. "Mr. Cranfield."

Cranfield was immediately on his feet.

"Are you suggesting that I advised this client of yours to back Cherry Pie?" His voice shook with indignation.

"No, Mr. Cranfield," said Gowery like the North Wind, "the suggestion is that the client was acting on your behalf and that it was you yourself that backed Cherry Pie."

"That's an absolute lie."

His hot denial fell on a lot of cold ears.

"Where is this mysterious man?" he demanded. "This unidentified, unidentifiable nobody? How can you possibly trump up such a story and present it as serious evidence? It is ridiculous. Utterly, utterly ridiculous."

"The bet was struck," Gowery said plonkingly, pointing to the ledger.

"And I saw you talking to the client," confirmed Newtonnards.

Cranfield's fury left him gasping for words, and in the end he too sat down again, finding like me nothing to say that could dent the preconceptions ranged against us.

"Mr. Newtonnards," I said, "would you know this client again?"

He hesitated only a fraction. "Yes, I would."

"Have you seen him at the races since Lemonfizz day?"

"No. I haven't."

"If you see him again, will you point him out to Lord Gowery?"

"If Lord Gowery's at the races." Several of the back ranks of officials smiled at this, but Newtonnards, to give him his due, did not.

I couldn't think of anything else to ask him, and I knew I had made no headway at all. It was infuriating. By our own choice we had thrust ourselves back into the bad old days when people accused at racing trials were not allowed a legal defendant. If they didn't know how to defend themselves: if they didn't know what sort of questions to ask or in what form to ask them, that was just too bad. Just their hard luck. But this wasn't hard luck. This was our own stupid fault. A lawyer would have been able to rip Newtonnards' testimony to bits, but neither Cranfield nor I knew how.

Cranfield tried. He was back on his feet.

"Far from backing Cherry Pie, I backed Squelch. You can check up with my own bookmaker."

Gowery simply didn't reply. Cranfield repeated it.

Gowery said, "Yes, yes. No doubt you did. It is quite beside the point."

Cranfield sat down again with his mouth hanging open. I knew exactly how he felt. Not so much banging the head against a brick wall as being actively attacked by a cliff.

They waved Newtonnards away and he ambled easily off to take his place beside Charlie West. What he had said stayed behind him, stuck fast in the officials' minds. Not one of them had asked for corroboration. Not one had suggested that there might have been a loophole in identity. The belief was written plain on their faces: if someone had backed Cherry Pie to win nine hundred pounds, it must have been Cranfield.

Gowery hadn't finished. With a calm satisfaction he picked up another paper and said, "Mr. Cranfield, I have here an affidavit from a Mrs. Joan Jones, who handled the five-pound selling window on the Totalizator in the paddock on Lemonfizz Cup day, that she sold ten win-only tickets for horse number eight to a man in a fawn raincoat, middle-aged, wearing a trilby. I also have here a similar testimony from a Mr. Leonard Roberts, who was paying out at the five-pound window in the same building, on the same occasion. Both of these Tote employees remember the client well, as these were almost the only five-pound tickets sold on Cherry Pie, and certainly the only large block. The Tote paid out to this man more than eleven hundred pounds in cash. Mr. Roberts advised him not to carry so much on his person, but the man declined to take his advice."

There was another accusing silence. Cranfield looked totally non-plussed and came up with nothing to say. This time, I tried for him. "Sir, did this man back any other horses in the race, on the Tote? Did he back all, or two or three or four, and just hit the jackpot by accident?"

"There was no accident about this, Hughes."

"But did he, in fact, back any other horses?"

Dead silence.

"Surely you asked?" I said reasonably.

Whether anyone had asked or not, Gowery didn't know. All he knew was what was on the affidavit. He gave me a stony stare, and said, "No one puts fifty pounds on an outsider without good grounds for believing it will win."

"But sir . . ."

"However," he said, "we will find out." He wrote a note on the bottom of one of the affidavits. "It seems to me extremely unlikely. But we will have the question asked."

There was no suggestion that he would wait for the answer before giving his judgement. And in fact he did not.

III

I wandered aimlessly round the flat, lost and restless. Reheated the coffee. Drank it. Tried to write to my parents, and gave it up after half a page. Tried to make some sort of decision about my future, and couldn't.

Felt too battered. Too pulped. Too crushed.

Yet I had done nothing.

Nothing.

Late afternoon. The lads were bustling round the yard setting the horses fair for the night, and whistling and calling to each other as usual. I kept away from the windows and eventually went back to the bedroom and lay down on the bed. The day began to fade. The dusk closed in.

After Newtonnards they had called Tommy Timpson, who had ridden Cherry Pie.

Tommy Timpson "did his two" for Cranfield and rode such of the stable's second strings as Cranfield cared to give him. Cranfield rang the changes on three jockeys: me, Chris Smith (at present taking his time over a fractured skull) and Tommy. Tommy got the crumbs and deserved better. Like many trainers, Cranfield couldn't spot talent when it was under his nose, and it wasn't until several small local trainers had asked for his services that Cranfield woke up to the fact that he had a useful emerging rider in his own yard.

Raw, nineteen years old, a stutterer, Tommy was at his worst at the Enquiry. He looked as scared as a two-year-old colt at his first starting gate, and although he couldn't help being jittery it was worse than useless for Cranfield and me.

Lord Gowery made no attempt to put him at ease but simply asked questions and let him get on with the answers as best he could.

"What orders did Mr. Cranfield give you before the race? How did he tell you to ride Cherry Pie? Did he instruct you to ride to win?"

Tommy stuttered and stumbled and said Mr. Cranfield had told him to keep just behind Squelch all the way round and try to pass him after the last fence.

Cranfield said indignantly, "That's what he *did.* Not what I told him to do."

Gowery listened, turned his head to Tommy, and said again, "Will you tell us what instructions Mr. Cranfield gave you *before* the race? Please think carefully."

Tommy swallowed, gave Cranfield an agonized glance, and tried again. "M . . . M . . . M . . . Mr. Cranfield s . . . s . . . said to take my p . . . p . . . pace from S . . . S . . . Squelch and s . . . s . . . stay with him as long as I c . . . c . . . could."

"And did he tell you to win?"

"He s . . . s . . . said of course g . . . go . . . go on and w . . . w . . . win if you c . . . c . . . can, sir."

These were impeccable instructions. Only the most suspicious or biased mind could have read any villainy into them. If these Stewards' minds were not suspicious and biased, snow would fall in the Sahara.

"Did you hear Mr. Cranfield giving Hughes instructions as to how he should ride Squelch?"

"N . . . No, sir. M . . . Mr. Cranfield did . . . didn't g . . . give Hughes any orders at all, sir."

"Why not?"

Tommy ducked it and said he didn't know. Cranfield remarked furiously that Hughes had ridden the horse twenty times and knew what was needed.

"Or you had discussed it with him privately, beforehand?"

Cranfield had no explosive answer to that because of course we *had* discussed it beforehand. In general terms. In an assessment of the opposition. As a matter of general strategy.

"I discussed the race with him, yes. But I gave him no specific orders."

"So according to you," Lord Gowery said, "you intended both of your jockeys to try to win?"

"Yes. I did. My horses are always doing their best."

Gowery shook his head. "Your statement is not borne out by the facts."

"Are you calling me a liar?" Cranfield demanded.

Gowery didn't answer. But yes, he was.

They shooed a willing Tommy Timpson away and Cranfield went on simmering at boiling point beside me. For myself, I was growing cold, and no amount of central heating could stop it. I thought we must now have heard everything, but I was wrong. They had saved the worst until last, building up the pyramid of damning statements until they could put the final cap on it and stand back and admire their four-square structure, their solid, unanswerable edifice of guilt.

The worst, at first, had looked so harmless. A quiet slender man in his early thirties, endowed with an utterly forgettable face. After twenty-four hours I couldn't recall his features or remember his voice, and yet I couldn't think about him without shaking with sick impotent fury.

His name was David Oakley. His business, enquiry agent. His address, Birmingham.

He stood without fidgeting at the end of the Stewards' table holding a spiral-bound notebook which he consulted continually, and from beginning to end not a shade of emotion affected his face or his behaviour or even his eyes.

"Acting upon instructions, I paid a visit to the flat of Kelly Hughes, jockey, of Corrie House training stables, Corrie, Berkshire, two days after the Lemonfizz Crystal Cup."

I sat up with a jerk and opened my mouth to deny it, but before I could say a word he went smoothly on.

"Mr. Hughes was not there, but the door was open, so I went in to wait for him. While I was there I made certain observations." He paused.

Cranfield said to me, "What is all this about?"

"I don't know. I've never seen him before."

Gowery steamrollered on. "You found certain objects."

"Yes, my lord."

Gowery sorted out three large envelopes, and passed one each to Tring and Plimborne. Ferth was before them. He had removed the contents from a similar envelope as soon as Oakley had appeared, and was now, I saw, watching me with what I took to be contempt.

The envelopes each held a photograph.

Oakley said, "The photograph is of objects I found on a chest of drawers in Hughes' bedroom."

Andy Tring looked, looked again, and raised a horrified face, meeting my eyes accidentally and for the first and only time. He glanced away hurriedly, embarrassed and disgusted.

"I want to see that photograph," I said hoarsely.

"Certainly." Lord Gowery turned his copy round and pushed it across the table. I got up, walked the three dividing steps, and looked down at it.

For several seconds I couldn't take it in, and when I did, I was breathless with disbelief. The photograph had been taken from above the dressing chest, and was sparkling clear. There was the edge of the silver frame and half of Rosalind's face, and from under the frame, as if it had been used as a paperweight, protruded a sheet of paper dated the day after the Lemonfizz Cup. There were three words written on it, and two initials.

As agreed. Thanks. D.C.

Slanted across the bottom of the paper, and spread out like a pack of cards, were a large number of ten-pound notes.

I looked up, and met Lord Gowery's eyes, and almost flinched away from the utter certainty I read there.

"It's a fake," I said. My voice sounded odd. "It's a complete fake."

"What is it?" Cranfield said from behind me, and in his voice too everyone could hear the awareness of disaster.

I picked up the photograph and took it across to him, and I couldn't feel my feet on the carpet. When he had grasped what it meant he stood up slowly and in a low biting voice said formally, "My lords, if you believe this, you will believe anything."

It had not the slightest effect.

Gowery said merely, "That is your handwriting, I believe."

Cranfield shook his head. "I didn't write it."

"Please be so good as to write those exact words on this sheet of paper." Gowery pushed a plain piece of paper across the table, and after a second Cranfield went across and wrote on it. Everyone knew that the two samples would look the same, and they did. Gowery passed the sheet of paper significantly to the other Stewards, and they all compared and nodded.

"It's a fake," I said again. "I never had a letter like that."

Gowery ignored me. To Oakley he said, "Please tell us where you found the money."

Oakley unnecessarily consulted his notebook. "The money was folded inside this note, fastened with a rubber band, and both were tucked behind the photo of Hughes's girlfriend, which you see in the picture."

"It's not true," I said. I might as well not have bothered. No one listened.

"You counted the money, I believe?"

"Yes, my lord. There was five hundred pounds."

"There was no money," I protested. Useless. "And anyway," I added desperately, "why would I take five hundred for losing the race when I would get about as much as that for winning?"

I thought for a moment that I might have scored a hit. Might have made them pause. A pipe dream. There was an answer to that, too.

"We understand from Mr. Kessel, Squelch's owner," Gowery said flatly, "that he pays you ten per cent of the winning stake money through official channels by cheque. This means that all presents received by you from Mr. Kessel are taxed; and we understand that as you pay a high rate of tax your ten per cent from Mr. Kessel would have in effect amounted to half, or less than half, of five hundred pounds."

They seemed to have enquired into my affairs down to the last penny. Dug around in all directions. Certainly I had never tried to hide anything, but this behind-my-back tin-opening made me feel naked. Also, revolted. Also, finally, hopeless. And it wasn't until then that I realized I had been subconsciously clinging to a fairytale faith that it would all finally come all right, that because I was telling the truth I was bound to be believed in the end.

I stared across at Lord Gowery, and he looked briefly back. His face was expressionless, his manner entirely calm. He had reached his conclusions and nothing could overthrow them.

Lord Ferth, beside him, was less bolted down, but a great deal of his earlier heat seemed to have evaporated. The power he had generated no longer troubled Gowery at all, and all I could interpret from his expression was some kind of resigned acceptance.

There was little left to be said. Lord Gowery briefly summed up the evidence against us. The list of former races. The non-use of the whip. The testimony of Charlie West. The bets struck on Cherry Pie. The riding orders given in private. The photographic proof of a pay off from Cranfield to Hughes.

"There can be no doubt that this was a most flagrant fraud on the racing public . . . No alternative but to suspend your licences . . . And you, Dexter Cranfield, and you, Kelly Hughes, will be warned off Newmarket Heath until further notice."

Cranfield, pale and shaking, said, "I protest that this has not been a fair hearing. Neither Hughes nor I are guilty. The sentence is outrageous."

No response from Lord Gowery. Lord Ferth, however, spoke for the second time in the proceedings.

"Hughes?"

"I rode Squelch to win," I said. "The witnesses were lying."

Gowery shook his head impatiently. "The Enquiry is closed. You may go."

Cranfield and I both hesitated, still unable to accept that that was all. But the official near the door opened it, and all the ranks opposite began to talk quietly to each other and ignore us, and in the end we walked out. Stiff legged. Feeling as if my head were a floating football and my body a chunk of ice. Unreal.

There were several people in the waiting-room outside, but I didn't see them clearly. Cranfield, tight lipped, strode away from me, straight across the room and out of the far door, shaking off a hand or two laid on his sleeve. Dazed, I started to follow him, but was less purposeful, and was effectively stopped by a large man who planted himself in my way.

I looked at him vaguely. Mr. Kessel. The owner of Squelch.

"Well?" he said challengingly.

"They didn't believe us. We've both been warned off."

He hissed a sharp breath out between his teeth. "After what I've been hearing, I'm not surprised. And I'll tell you this, Hughes, even if you get your licence back, you won't be riding for me again."

I looked at him blankly and didn't answer. It seemed a small thing after what had already happened. He had been talking to the witnesses, in the waiting-room. They would convince anyone, it seemed. Some owners were unpredictable anyway, even in normal times. One day they had all the faith in the world in their jockey, and the next day, none at all. Faith with slender foundations. Mr. Kessel had forgotten all the races I had won for him because of the one I had lost.

I turned blindly away from his hostility and found a more welcome hand on my arm. Tony, who had driven up with me instead of seeing his horses work.

"Come on," he said. "Let's get out of here."

I nodded and went down with him in the lift, out into the hall, and towards the front door. Outside there we could see a bunch of newspaper reporters waylaying Cranfield with their notebooks at the ready, and I stopped dead at the sight.

"Let's wait till they've gone," I said.

"They won't go. Not before they've chewed you up too."

We waited, hesitating, and a voice called behind me, "Hughes."

I didn't turn round. I felt I owed no one the slightest politeness. The footsteps came up behind me and he finally came to a halt in front.

Lord Ferth. Looking tired.

"Hughes. Tell me. Why in God's name did you do it?"

I looked at him stonily.

"I didn't."

He shook his head. "All the evidence . . ."

"You tell me," I said, rudely, "why decent men like Stewards so easily believe a lot of lies."

I turned away from him, too. Twitched my head at Tony and made for the front door. To hell with the Press. To hell with the Stewards and Mr. Kessel. And with everything to do with racing. The upsurge of fury took me out of the building and fifty yards along the pavement in Portman Square and only evaporated into grinding misery when we had climbed into the taxi Tony whistled for.

Tony thumped up the stairs to the darkened flat. I heard him calling.

"Are you there, Kelly?"

I unrolled myself from the bed, stood up, stretched, went out into the sitting-room and switched on the lights. He was standing in the far doorway, blinking, his hands full of tray.

"Poppy insisted," he explained.

He put the tray down on the table and lifted off the covering cloth. She'd sent hot chicken pie, a tomato, and about half a pound of Brie.

"She says you haven't eaten for two days."

"I suppose not."

"Get on with it, then." He made an instinctive line for the whisky bottle and poured generously into two tumblers.

"And here. For once, drink this."

I took the glass and a mouthful and felt the fire trickle down inside my chest. The first taste was always the best. Tony tossed his off and ordered himself a refill.

I ate the pie, the tomato, and the cheese. Hunger, I hadn't consciously felt, rolled contentedly over and slept.

"Can you stay a bit?" I asked.

"Natch."

"I'd like to tell you about the Enquiry."

"Shoot," he said with satisfaction. "I've been waiting."

I told him all that had happened, almost word for word. Every detail had been cut razor sharp into my memory in the way that only happens in disasters.

Tony's astonishment was plain. "You were framed!"

"That's right."

"But surely no one can get away with that?"

"Someone seems to be doing all right."

"But was there *nothing* you could say to prove . . ."

"I couldn't think of anything yesterday, which is all that matters. It's always easy to think of all the smart clever things one *could* have said, afterwards, when it's too late."

"What would you have said, then?"

"I suppose for a start I should have asked who had given that so-called enquiry agent instructions to search my flat. Acting on instructions, he said. Well, *whose* instructions? I didn't think of asking, yesterday. Now I can see that it could be the whole answer."

"You assumed the Stewards had instructed him?"

"I suppose so. I didn't really think. Most of the time I was so shattered that I couldn't think clearly at all."

"Maybe it *was* the Stewards."

"Well, no. I suppose it's barely possible they might have sent an investigator, though when you look at it in cold blood it wouldn't really seem likely, but it's a tear drop to the Atlantic that they wouldn't have supplied him with five hundred quid and a forged note and told him to photograph them somewhere distinctive in my flat. But that's what he did. Who instructed him?"

"Even if you'd asked, he wouldn't have said."

"I guess not. But at least it might have made the Stewards think a bit too."

Tony shook his head. "He would still have said he found the money behind Rosalind's picture. His word against yours. Nothing different."

He looked gloomily into his glass. I looked gloomily into mine.

"That bloody little Charlie West," I said. "Someone got at him, too."

"I presume you didn't in fact say 'Brakes on, chaps'?"

"I did say it, you see. Not in the Lemonfizz, of course, but a couple of weeks before, in that frightful novice 'chase at Oxford, the day they abandoned the last two races because it was snowing. I was hitting every fence on that deadly bad jumper that old Almond hadn't bothered to school properly, and half the other runners were just as green, and a whole bunch of us had got left about twenty lengths behind the four who were any use, and sleet was falling, and I didn't relish ending up with a broken bone at nought degrees centigrade, so as we were handily out of sight of the stands at that point I shouted 'OK, brakes on, chaps,' and a whole lot of us eased up thankfully and finished the race a good deal slower than we could have done. It didn't affect the result, of course. But there you are. I did say it. What's more, Charlie West heard me. He just shifted it from one race to another."

"The bastard."

"I agree."

"Maybe no one got at him. Maybe he just thought he'd get a few more rides if you were out of the way."

I considered it and shook my head. "I wouldn't have thought he was *that* much of a bastard."

"You never know." Tony finished his drink and absent-mindedly replaced it. "What about the bookmaker?"

"Newtonnards? I don't know. Same thing, I suppose. Someone has it in for Cranfield too. Both of us, it was. The Stewards couldn't possibly have warned off one of us without the other. We were knitted together so neatly."

"It makes me livid," Tony said violently. "It's wicked."

I nodded. "There was something else, too, about that Enquiry. Some undercurrent, running strong. At least, it was strong at the beginning. Something between Lord Gowery and Lord Ferth. And then Andy Tring, he was sitting there looking like a wilted lettuce." I shook my head in puzzlement. "It was like a couple of heavy animals lurking in the undergrowth, shaping up to fight each other. You couldn't see them, but there was a sort of quiver in the air. At least, that's how it seemed at one point . . ."

"Stewards are men," Tony said with bubble-bursting matter-of-factness. "Show me any organization which doesn't have some sort of power struggle going on under its gentlemanly surface. All you caught was a whiff of the old brimstone. State of nature. Nothing to do with whether you and Cranfield were guilty or not."

He half convinced me. He polished off the rest of the whisky and told me not to forget to get some more.

Money. That was another thing. As from yesterday I had no income. The Welfare State didn't pay unemployment benefits to the self-employed, as all jockeys remembered every snow-bound winter.

"I'm going to find out," I said abruptly.

"Find out what?"

"Who framed us."

"Up the Marines," Tony said unsteadily. "Over the top, boys. Up and at 'em." He picked up the empty bottle and looked at it regretfully. "Time for bed, I guess. If you need any help with the campaign, count on my Welsh blood to the last clot."

He made an unswerving line to the door, turned, and gave me a grimace of friendship worth having.

"Don't fall down the stairs," I said.

Part Two: March

IV

Roberta Cranfield looked magnificent in my sitting-room. I came back from buying whisky in the village and found her gracefully draped all over my restored Chippendale. The green velvet supported a lot of leg and a deep purple size-ten wool dress, and her thick long hair the colour of dead beech leaves clashed dramatically with the curtains. Under the hair she had white skin, incredible eyebrows, amber eyes, photogenic cheekbones and a petulant mouth.

She was nineteen, and I didn't like her.

"Good morning," I said.

"Your door was open."

"It's a habit I'll have to break."

I peeled the tissue wrapping off the bottle and put it with the two chunky glasses on the small silver tray I had once won in a race sponsored by some sweet manufacturers. Troy weight, twenty-four ounces: but ruined by the inscription, K. HUGHES, WINNING JOCKEY, STARCHOCS SILVER STEEPLECHASE. Starchocs indeed. And I never ate chocolates. Couldn't afford to, from the weight point of view.

She flapped her hand from a relaxed wrist, indicating the room.

"This is all pretty lush."

I wondered what she had come for. I said, "Would you like some coffee?"

"Coffee and cannabis."

"You'll have to go somewhere else."

"You're very prickly."

"As a cactus," I agreed.

She gave me a half-minute unblinking stare with her liquid eyes. Then she said, "I only said cannabis to jolt you."

"I'm not jolted."

"No. I can see that. Waste of effort."

"Coffee, then?"

"Yes."

I went into the kitchen and fixed up the percolator. The kitchen was white and brown and copper and yellow. The colours pleased me. Colours gave me the sort of mental food I imagined others got from music. I disliked too much music, loathed the type of stuff you couldn't escape in restaurants and airliners, didn't own a record-player, and much preferred silence.

She followed me in from the sitting-room and looked around her with mild surprise.

"Do all jockeys live like this?"

"Naturally."

"I don't believe it."

She peered into the pine-fronted cupboard I'd taken the coffee from. "Do you cook for yourself?"

"Mostly."

"*Recherché* things like *shashlik?*" An undercurrent of mockery.

"Steaks."

I poured the bubbling coffee into two mugs and offered her cream and sugar. She took the cream, generously, but not the sugar, and perched on a yellow-topped stool. Her copper hair fitted the kitchen, too.

"You seem to be taking it all right," she said.

"What?"

"Being warned off."

I didn't answer.

"A cactus," she said, "isn't in the same class."

She drank the coffee slowly, in separate mouthfuls, watching me thoughtfully over the mug's rim. I watched her back. Nearly my height, utterly self-possessed, as cool as the stratosphere. I had seen her grow from a demanding child into a selfish fourteen-year-old, and from there into a difficult-to-please debutante and from there to a glossy imitation model girl heavily tinged with boredom. Over the eight years I had ridden for her father we had met briefly and spoken seldom, usually in parade rings and outside the weighing-room, and on the occasions when she did speak to me she seemed to be aiming just over the top of my head.

"You're making it difficult," she said.

"For you to say why you came?"

She nodded. "I thought I knew you. Now it seems I don't."

"What did you expect?"

"Well . . . Father said you came from a farm cottage with pigs running in and out of the door."

"Father exaggerates."

She lifted her chin to ward off the familiarity, a gesture I'd seen a hundred times in her and her brothers. A gesture copied from her parents.

"Hens," I said, "not pigs."

She gave me an up-stage stare. I smiled at her faintly and refused to be reduced to the ranks. I watched the wheels tick over while she worked out how to approach a cactus, and gradually the chin came down.

"Actual hens?"

Not bad at all. I could feel my own smile grow genuine.

"Now and then."

"You don't look like . . . I mean . . ."

"I know exactly what you mean," I agreed. "And it's high time you got rid of those chains."

"Chains? What are you talking about?"

"The fetters in your mind. The iron bars in your soul."

"My mind is all right."

"You must be joking. It's chock-a-block with ideas half a century out of date."

"I didn't come here to . . ." she began explosively, and then stopped.

"You didn't come here to be insulted," I said ironically.

"Well, as you put it in that well-worn hackneyed phrase, no, I didn't. But I wasn't going to say that."

"What did you come for?"

She hesitated. "I wanted you to help me."

"To do what?"

"To . . . to *cope* with Father."

I was surprised, first that Father needed coping with, and second that she needed help to do it.

"What sort of help?"

"He's . . . he's so *shattered.*" Unexpectedly there were tears standing in her eyes. They embarrassed and angered her, and she blinked furiously so that I shouldn't see. I admired the tears but not her reason for trying to hide them.

"Here are you," she said in a rush, "walking about as cool as you please and buying whisky and making coffee as if no screaming avalanche had poured out on you and smothered your life and made every thought an absolute bloody Hell, and maybe you don't understand how anyone in that state needs help, and come to that I don't understand why *you* don't need help, but anyway, Father *does.*"

"Not from me," I said mildly. "He doesn't think enough of me to give it any value."

She opened her mouth angrily and shut it again and took two deep controlling breaths. "And it looks as though he's right."

"Ouch," I said ruefully. "What sort of help, then?"

"I want you to come and talk to him."

My talking to Cranfield seemed likely to be as therapeutic as applying itching powder to a baby. However, she hadn't left me much room for kidding myself that fruitlessness was a good reason for not trying.

"When?"

"Now . . . Unless you have anything else to do."

"No," I said carefully. "I haven't."

She made a face and an odd little gesture with her hands. "Will you come now, then . . . please?"

She herself seemed surprised about the real supplication in that "please." I imagined that she had come expecting to instruct, not to ask.

"All right."

"Great." She was suddenly very cool, very employer's daughter again. She put her coffee mug on the draining board and started towards the door. "You had better follow me, in your car. It's no good me taking you, you'll need your own car to come back in."

"That is so," I agreed.

She looked at me suspiciously, but decided not to pursue it. "My coat is in your bedroom."

"I'll fetch it for you."

"Thank you."

I walked across the sitting-room and into the bedroom. Her coat was lying on my bed in a heap. Black and white fur, in stripes going round. I picked it up and turned, and found she had followed me.

"Thank you so much." She presented her back to me and put her arms in the coat-putting-on position. On went the coat. She swivelled slowly, buttoning up the front with shiny black saucers. "This flat really is fantastic. Who is your decorator?"

"Chap called Kelly Hughes."

She raised her eyebrows. "I know the professional touch when I see it."

"Thank you."

She raised the chin. "Oh well, if you won't say . . ."

"I would say. I did say. I did the flat myself. I've been whitewashing pigsties since I was six."

She wasn't quite sure whether to be amused or offended, and evaded it by changing the subject.

"That picture . . . that's your wife, isn't it?"

I nodded.

"I remember her," she said. "She was always so sweet to me. She seemed to know what I was feeling. I was really awfully sorry when she was killed."

I looked at her in surprise. The people Rosalind had been sweetest to had invariably been unhappy. She had had a knack of sensing it, and of giving succour without being asked. I would not have thought of Roberta Cranfield as being unhappy, though I supposed from twelve to fifteen, when she had known Rosalind, she could have had her troubles.

"She wasn't bad, as wives go," I said flippantly, and Miss Cranfield disapproved of that, too.

We left the flat and this time I locked the door, though such horses as I'd had had already bolted. Roberta had parked her Sunbeam Alpine behind the stables and across the doors of the garage where I kept my Lotus. She backed and turned her car with aggressive poise, and I left a leisurely interval before I followed her through the gates, to avoid a competition all the eighteen miles to her home.

Cranfield lived in an early Victorian house in a hamlet four miles out of Lambourn. A country gentleman's residence, estate agents would have called it: built before the Industrial Revolution had invaded Berkshire and equally impervious to the social revolution a hundred years later. Elegant, charming, timeless, it was a house I liked very much. Pity about the occupants.

I drove up the back drive as usual and parked alongside the stable yard. A horsebox was standing there with its ramp down, and one of the lads was leading a horse into it. Archie, the head lad, who had been helping, came across as soon as I climbed out of the car.

"This is a God awful bloody business," he said. "It's wicked, that's what it is. Downright bloody wicked."

"The horses are going?"

"Some owners have sent boxes already. All of them will be gone by the day after tomorrow." His weather-beaten face was a mixture of fury, frustration, and anxiety. "All the lads have got the sack. Even me. And the missus and I have just taken a mortgage on one of the new houses up the road. Chalet bungalow, just what she'd always set her heart on. Worked for years, she has, saving for it. Now she won't stop crying. We moved in only a month ago, see? How do you think we're going to keep up the payments? Took every pound we had, what with the deposit and the solicitors, and curtains and all. Nice little place, too, she's got it looking real nice. And it isn't as if the Guvnor really fiddled the blasted race. That Cherry Pie, anyone could see with half an eye he was going to be good some day. I mean, if the Guvnor had done it, like, somehow all this wouldn't be so bad. I mean, if he deserved it, well serve him right, and I'd try and get a bit of compensation from him because we're going to have a right job selling the house again, I'll tell you, because there's still two of them empty, they weren't so easy to sell in the first place, being so far out of Lambourn . . . I'll tell you straight, I wish to God we'd never moved out of the Guvnor's cottage, dark and damp though it may be . . . George," he suddenly shouted at a lad swearing and tugging at a reluctant animal, "don't take it out on the horse, it isn't *his* fault . . ." He bustled across the yard and took the horse himself, immediately quietening it and leading it without trouble into the horsebox.

He was an excellent head lad, better than most, and a lot of Cranfield's success was his doing. If he sold his house and got settled in another job, Cranfield wouldn't get him back. The training licence might not be lost for ever, but the stable's main prop would be.

I watched another lad lead a horse round to the waiting box. He too looked worried. His wife, I knew, was on the point of producing their first child.

Some of the lads wouldn't care, of course. There were plenty of jobs going in racing stables, and one lot of digs was much the same as another. But they too would not come back. Nor would most of the horses, nor many of the owners. The stable wasn't being suspended for a few months. It was being smashed.

Sick and seething with other people's fury as well as my own, I walked down the short stretch of drive to the house. Roberta's Alpine was parked outside the front door and she was standing beside it looking cross.

"So there you are. I thought you'd ratted."

"I parked down by the yard."

"I can't bear to go down there. Nor can Father. In fact, he won't move out of his dressing-room. You'll have to come upstairs to see him."

She led the way through the front door and across thirty square yards of Persian rug. When we had reached the foot of the stairs the door of the library was flung open and Mrs. Cranfield came through it. Mrs. Cranfield always flung doors open, rather as if she suspected something reprehensible was going on behind them and she was intent on catching the sinners in the act. She was a plain woman who wore no make-up and dressed in droopy woollies. To me she had never talked about anything except horses, and I didn't know whether she could. Her father was an Irish baron, which may have accounted for the marriage.

"My father-in-law, Lord Coolihan . . ." Cranfield was wont to say: and he was wont to say it far too often. I wondered whether, after Gowery, he was the tiniest bit discontented with the aristocracy.

"Ah, there you are, Hughes," Mrs. Cranfield said. "Roberta told me she was going to fetch you. Though what good you can do I cannot understand. After all, it was you who got us into the mess."

"I what?"

"If you'd ridden a better race on Squelch, none of this would have happened."

I bit back six answers and said nothing. If you were hurt enough you lashed out at the nearest object. Mrs. Cranfield continued to lash.

"Dexter was thoroughly shocked to hear that you had been in the habit of deliberately losing races."

"So was I," I said dryly.

Roberta moved impatiently. "Mother, do stop it. Come along, Hughes. This way."

I didn't move. She went up three steps, paused, and looked back. "Come on, what are you waiting for?"

I shrugged. Whatever I was waiting for, I wouldn't get it in that house. I followed her up the stairs, along a wide passage, and into her father's dressing-room.

There was too much heavy mahogany furniture of a later period than the house, a faded plum-coloured carpet, faded plum plush curtains, and a bed with an Indian cover.

On one side of the bed sat Dexter Cranfield, his back bent into a bow and his shoulders hunched round his ears. His hands rolled loosely on his knees, fingers curling, and he was staring immovably at the floor.

"He sits like that for hours," Roberta said on a breath beside me. And, looking at him, I understood why she had needed help.

"Father," she said, going over and touching his shoulder. "Kelly Hughes is here."

Cranfield said, "Tell him to go and shoot himself."

She saw the twitch in my face, and from her expression thought that I minded, that I believed Cranfield too thought me the cause of all his troubles. On the whole I decided not to crystallize her fears by saying I thought Cranfield had said shoot because shoot was in his mind.

"Hop it," I said, and jerked my head towards the door.

The chin went up like a reflex. Then she looked at the husk of her father, and back to me, whom she'd been to some trouble to bring, and most of the starch dissolved.

"All right. I'll be down in the library. Don't go without . . . telling me."

I shook my head, and she went collectedly out of the room, shutting the door behind her.

I walked to the window and looked at the view. Small fields trickling down into the valley. Trees all bent one way by the wind off the Downs. A row of pylons, a cluster of council-house roofs. Not a horse in sight. The dressing-room was on the opposite side of the house to the stables.

"Have you a gun?" I asked.

No answer from the bed. I went over and sat down beside him. "Where is it?"

His eyes slid a fraction in my direction and then back. He had been looking past me. I got up and went to the table beside his bed, but there was nothing lethal on it, and nothing in the drawer.

I found it behind the high mahogany bedhead. A finely wrought Purdey more suitable for pheasants. Both barrels were loaded. I unloaded them.

"Very messy," I remarked. "Very inconsiderate. And anyway, you didn't mean to do it."

I wasn't at all sure about that, but there was no harm in trying to convince him.

"What are you doing here?" he said indifferently.

"Telling you to snap out of it. There's work to be done."

"Don't speak to me like that."

"How, then?"

His head came up a little, just like Roberta's. If I made him angry, he'd be halfway back to his normal self. And I could go home.

"It's useless sitting up here sulking. It won't achieve anything at all."

"*Sulking?*" He was annoyed, but not enough.

"Someone took our toys away. Very unfair. But nothing to be gained by grizzling in corners."

"*Toys* . . . You're talking nonsense."

"Toys, licences, what's the difference. The things we prized most. Someone's snatched them away. Tricked us out of them. And nobody except us can get them back. Nobody else will bother."

"We can apply," he said without conviction.

"Oh, we can apply. In six months' time, I suppose. But there's no guarantee we'd get them. The only sensible thing to do is to start fighting back right now and find out who fixed us. Who, and why. And after that I'll wring his bloody neck."

He was still staring at the floor, still hunched. He couldn't even look me in the face yet, let alone the world. If he hadn't been such a climbing snob, I thought uncharitably, his present troubles wouldn't have produced such a complete cave-in. He was on the verge of literally not being able to bear the public disgrace of being warned off.

Well, I wasn't so sure I much cared for it myself. It was all very well knowing that one was not guilty, and even having one's closest friends believe it, but one could hardly walk around everywhere wearing a notice proclaiming "I am innocent. I never done it. It were all a stinking frame-up."

"It's not so bad for you," he said.

"That's perfectly true." I paused. "I came in through the yard."

He made a low sound of protest.

"Archie seems to be seeing to everything himself. And he's worried about his house."

Cranfield made a waving movement of his hand as much as to ask how did I think he could be bothered with Archie's problems on top of his own.

"It wouldn't hurt you to pay Archie's mortgage for a bit."

"*What?*" That finally reached him. His head came up at least six inches.

"It's only a few pounds a week. Peanuts to you. Life or death to him. And if you lose him, you'll never get so many winners again."

"You . . . you . . ." He spluttered. But he still didn't look up.

"A trainer is as good as his lads."

"That's stupid."

"You've got good lads just now. You've chucked out the duds, the rough and lazy ones. It takes time to weed out and build up a good team, but you can't get a high ratio of winners without one. You might get your licence back but you won't get these lads back and it'll take years for the stable to recover. If it ever does. And I hear you have already given them all the sack."

"What else was there to do?"

"You could try keeping them on for a month."

His head came up a little more. "You haven't the slightest idea what that would cost me. The wages come to more than four hundred pounds a week."

"There must still be quite a lot to come in training fees. Owners seldom pay in advance. You won't have to dig very deep into your own pocket. Not for a month, anyway, and it might not take as long as that."

"What might not?"

"Getting our licences back."

"Don't be so bloody ridiculous."

"I mean it. What is it worth to you? Four weeks' wages for your lads? Would you pay that much if there was a chance you'd be back in racing in a month? The owners would send their horses back, if it was as quick as that. Particularly if you tell them you confidently expect to be back in business almost immediately."

"They wouldn't believe it."

"They'd be uncertain. That should be enough."

"There isn't a chance of getting back."

"Oh yes there damn well is," I said forcefully. "But only if you're willing to take it. Tell the lads you're keeping them on for a bit. Especially Archie. Go down to the yard and tell them now."

"*Now.*"

"Of course," I said impatiently. "Probably half of them have already read the Situations Vacant columns and written to other trainers."

"There isn't any point." He seemed sunk in fresh gloom. "It's all hopeless. And it couldn't have happened, it simply could *not* have happened at a worse time. Edwin Byler was going to send me his horses. It was all fixed up. Now of course he's telephoned to say it's all off, his horses are staying where they are, at Jack Roxford's."

To train Edwin Byler's horses was to be presented with a pot of gold. He was a North country businessman who had made a million or two out of mail order, and had used a little of it to fulfil a long held ambition to own the best string of steeplechasers in Britain. Four of his present horses had in turn cost more than anyone had paid before. When he wanted, he bid. He only wanted the best, and he had bought enough of them to put him for the two previous seasons at the top of the Winning Owners' list. To have been going to train Edwin Byler's horses, and now not to be going to, was a refined cruelty to pile on top of everything else.

To have been going to *ride* Edwin Byler's horses . . . as I would no doubt have done . . . that too was a thrust where it hurt.

"There's all the more point, then," I said. "What more do you want in the way of incentive? You're throwing away without a struggle not only what you've got but what you might have . . . Why in the Hell don't you get off your bed and behave like a gentleman and show some spirit?"

"Hughes!" He was outraged. But he still sat. He still wouldn't look at me.

I paused, considering him. Then, slowly, I said, "All right, then. I'll tell you why you won't. You won't because . . . to some degree . . . you are in fact guilty. You made sure Squelch wouldn't win. And you backed Cherry Pie."

That got him. Not just his head up, but up, trembling, onto his feet.

V

"How dare you?"

"Frankly, just now I'd dare practically anything."

"You said we were framed."

"So we were."

Some of his alarm subsided. I stoked it up again.

"You handed us away on a plate."

He swallowed, his eyes flicking from side to side, looking everywhere except at me.

"I don't know what you mean."

"Don't be so weak," I said impatiently. "I rode Squelch, remember? Was he his usual self? He was not."

"If you're suggesting," he began explosively, "that I doped . . ."

"Oh of course not. Anyway, they tested him, didn't they? Negative result. Naturally. No trainer needs to dope a horse he doesn't want to win. It's like swatting a fly with a bull-dozer. There are much more subtle methods. Undetectable. Even innocent. Maybe you should be kinder to yourself and admit that you quite innocently stopped Squelch. Maybe you even did it subconsciously, wanting Cherry Pie to win."

"Bull," he said.

"The mind plays tricks," I said. "People often believe they are doing something for one good reason, while they are subconsciously doing it for another."

"Twaddle."

"The trouble comes sometimes when the real reason rears its ugly head and slaps you in the kisser."

"Shut up." His teeth and jaw were clenched tight.

I drew a deep breath. I'd been guessing, partly. And I'd guessed right.

I said, "You gave Squelch too much work too soon before the race. He lost the Lemonfizz on the gallops at home."

He looked at me at last. His eyes were dark, as if the pupils had expanded to take up all the iris. There was a desperate sort of hopelessness in his expression.

"It wouldn't have been so bad," I said, "if you had admitted it to yourself. Because then you would never have risked not engaging a lawyer to defend us."

"I didn't mean to over-train Squelch," he said wretchedly. "I didn't realize it until afterwards. I did back him, just as I said at the Enquiry."

I nodded. "I imagined you must have done. But you backed Cherry Pie as well."

He explained quite simply, without any of his usual superiority, "Trainers are often caught out, as you know, when one of their horses suddenly develops his true form. Well, I thought Cherry Pie might just be one of those. So I backed him, on the off chance."

Some off chance. Fifty pounds with Newtonnards and fifty pounds on the Tote. Gross profit, two thousand.

"How much did you have on Squelch?"

"Two hundred and fifty."

"Whew," I said. "Was that your usual sort of bet?"

"He was odds on . . . I suppose a hundred is my most usual bet."

I had come to the key question, and I wasn't sure I wanted to ask it, let alone have to judge whether the answer was true. However . . .

"Why," I said matter-of-factly, "didn't you back Cherry Pie with your own usual bookmaker?"

He answered without effort, "Because I didn't want Kessel knowing I'd backed Cherry Pie, if he won instead of Squelch. Kessel's a funny man, he takes everything personally, he'd as like as not have whisked Squelch away . . ." He trailed off, remembering afresh that Squelch was indeed being whisked.

"Why should Kessel have known?"

"Eh? Oh, because he bets with my bookmaker too, and the pair of them are as thick as thieves."

Fair enough.

"Well, who was the middle-aged man who put the bets on for you?"

"Just a friend. There's no need to involve him. I want to keep him out of it."

"Could Newtonnards have seen you talking to him by the parade ring before the first race?"

"Yes," he said with depression. "I did talk to him. I gave him the money to bet with."

And he still hadn't seen any danger signals. Had taken Monty Midgely's assurance at its face value. Hadn't revealed the danger to me. I could have throttled him.

"What did you do with the winnings?"

"They're in the safe downstairs."

"And you haven't been able to admit to anyone that you've got them."

"No."

I thought back. "You lied about it at the Enquiry."

"What else was there to do?"

By then, what indeed. Telling the truth hadn't done much for me.

"Let's see, then." I moved over to the window again, sorting things out. "Cherry Pie won on his merits. You backed him because he looked like coming into form rather suddenly. Squelch had had four hard races in two months, and a possibly over-zealous training gallop. These are the straight facts."

"Yes . . . I suppose so."

"No trainer should lose his licence because he didn't tell the world he might just possibly have a flier. I never see why the people who put in all the work shouldn't have the first dip into the well."

Owners, too, were entitled. Cherry Pie's owner, however, had died three weeks before the Lemonfizz, and Cherry Pie had run for the executors. Someone was going to have a fine time deciding his precise value at the moment of his owner's death.

"It means, anyway, that you do have a fighting fund," I pointed out.

"There's no point in fighting."

"You," I said exasperatedly, "are so soft that you'd make a marshmallow look like granite."

His mouth slowly opened. Before that morning I had never given him anything but politeness. He was looking at me as if he'd really noticed me, and it occurred to me that if we did indeed get our licences back he would remember that I'd seen him in pieces, and maybe find me uncomfortable to have around. He paid me a retainer, but only on an annual contract. Easy enough to chuck me out, and retain someone else. Expediently, and not too pleased with myself for it, I took the worst crags out of my tone.

"I presume," I said, "that you do want your licence back?"

"There isn't a chance."

"If you'll keep the lads for a month, I'll get it back for you."

Defeatism still showed in every sagging muscle, and he didn't answer.

I shrugged. "Well, I'm going to try. And if I give you your licence back on a plate it will be just too bad if Archie and the lads have gone." I walked towards the door and put my hand on the knob. "I'll let you know how I get on."

Twisted the knob. Opened the door.

"Wait," he said.

I turned round. A vestige of starch had returned, mostly in the shape of the reappearance of the mean lines round his mouth. Not so good.

"I don't believe you can do it. But as you're so cocksure, I'll make a bargain with you. I'll pay the lads for two weeks. If you want me to keep them on for another two weeks after that, you can pay them yourself."

Charming. He'd made two thousand pounds out of Cherry Pie and had over-trained Squelch and was the direct cause of my being warned off. I stamped on a violent inner tremble of anger and gave him a cold answer.

"Very well. I agree to that. But you must make a bargain with me too. A bargain that you'll keep your mouth tight shut about your guilt feelings. I don't want to be sabotaged by you hairshirting it all over the place and confessing your theoretical sins at awkward moments."

"I am unlikely to do that," he said stiffly.

I wasn't so sure. "I want your word on it," I said.

He drew himself up, offended. It at least had the effect of straightening his backbone.

"You have it."

"Fine." I held the door open for him. "Let's go down to the yard, then."

He still hesitated, but finally made up his mind to it, and went before me through the door and down the stairs.

Roberta and her mother were standing in the hall, looking as if they were waiting for news at a pithead after a disaster. They watched the reappearance of the head of the family in mixture of relief and apprehension, and Mrs. Cranfield said tentatively, "Dexter? . . ."

He answered irritably, as if he saw no cause for anxiety in his having shut himself away with a shotgun for thirty-six hours, "We're going down to the yard."

"Great," said Roberta practically smothering any tendency to emotion from her mother, "I'll come too."

Archie hurried to meet us and launched into a detailed account of which horses had gone and which were about to go next. Cranfield hardly listened and certainly didn't take it in. He waited for a gap in the flow, and when he'd waited long enough, impatiently interrupted.

"Yes, yes, Archie, I'm sure you have everything in hand. That is not what I've come down for, however. I want you to tell the lads at once that their notice to leave is withdrawn for one month."

Archie looked at me, not entirely understanding.

"The sack," I said, "is postponed. Pending attempts to get wrongs righted."

"Mine too?"

"Absolutely," I agreed. "Especially, in fact."

"Hughes thinks there is a chance we can prove ourselves innocent and recover our licences," Cranfield said formally, his own disbelief showing like two heads. "In order to help me keep the stable together while he makes enquiries, Hughes has agreed to contribute one half towards your wages for one month." I looked at him sharply. That was not at all what I had agreed. He showed no sign of acknowledging his reinterpretation (to put it charitably) of the offer I had accepted, and went authoritatively on. "Therefore, as your present week's notice still has five days to run, none of you will be required to leave here for five weeks. In fact," he added grudgingly, "I would be obliged if you would all stay."

Archie said to me, "You really mean it?" and I watched the hope suddenly spring up in his face and thought that maybe it wasn't only my own chance of a future that was worth eight hundred quid.

"That's right," I agreed. "As long as you don't all spend the month busily fixing up to go somewhere else at the end of it."

"What do you take us for?" Archie protested.

"Cynics," I said, and Archie actually laughed.

I left Cranfield and Archie talking together with most of the desperation evaporating from both of them, and walked away to my aerodynamic burnt-orange car. I didn't hear Roberta following me until she spoke in my ear as I opened the door.

"Can you really do it?" she said.

"Do what?"

"Get your licences back."

"It's going to cost me too much not to. So I guess I'll have to or . . ."

"Or what?"

I smiled. "Or die in the attempt."

It took me an hour to cross into Gloucestershire and almost half as long to sort out the geography of the village of Downfield, which mostly seemed to consist of culs-de-sac.

The cottage I eventually found after six misdirections from local inhabitants was old but not beautiful, well painted but in dreary colours, and a good deal more trustworthy than its owner.

When Mrs. Charlie West saw who it was, she tried to shut the front door in my face. I put out a hand that was used to dealing with strong horses and pulled her by the wrist, so that if she slammed the door she would be squashing her own arm.

She screeched loudly. An inner door at the back of the hall opened all of six inches, and Charlie's round face appeared through the crack. A distinct lack of confidence was discernible in that area.

"He's hurting me," Mrs. West shouted.

"I want to talk to you," I said to Charlie over her shoulder.

Charlie West was less than willing. Abandoning his teenage wife, long straight hair, Dusty Springfield eyelashes, beige lipstick and all, he retreated a pace and quite firmly shut his door. Mrs. West put up a loud and energetic defence to my attempt to establish further contact with Master Charlie, and I went through the hall fending off her toes and fists.

Charlie had wedged a chair under the door handle.

I shouted through the wood. "Much as you deserve it, I haven't come here to beat you up. Come out and talk."

No response of any sort. I rattled the door. Repeated my request. No results. With Mrs. West still stabbing around like an agitated hornet I went out of the front door and round the outside to try to talk to him through the window. The window was open, and the sitting-room inside was empty.

I turned round in time to see Charlie's distant backview disappearing across a field and into the next parish. Mrs. West saw him too, and gave a nasty smile.

"So there," she said triumphantly.

"Yes," I said. "I'm sure you must be very proud of him."

The smile wobbled. I walked back down their garden path, climbed into the car, and drove away.

Round one slightly farcically to the opposition.

Two miles away from the village I stopped the car in a farm gateway and thought it over. Charlie West had been a great deal more scared of me than I would have supposed, even allowing for the fact that I was a couple of sizes bigger and a fair amount stronger. Maybe Charlie was as much afraid of my fury as of my fists. He almost seemed to have been expecting that I would attempt some sort of retaliation, and certainly after what he had done, he had a right to. All the same, he still represented my quickest and easiest route to who, if not to why.

After a while I started up again and drove on into the nearest town. Remembered I hadn't eaten all day, put away some rather good cold beef at three-thirty in a home-made café geared more to cake and scones, dozed in the car, waited until dark, and finally drove back again to Charlie's village.

There were lights on in several rooms of his cottage. The Wests were at home. I turned the car and re-tracked about a hundred yards, stopping half on and half off a grassy verge. Climbed out. Stood up.

Plan of attack: vague. I had had some idea of ringing the front-door bell, disappearing and waiting for either Charlie or his dolly wife to take one incautious step outside to investigate. Instead, unexpected allies materialized in the shape of one small boy and one large dog.

The boy had a torch, and was talking to his dog, who paused to dirty up the roadside five yards ahead.

"What the hell d'you think you were at, you bloody great nit, scoffing our mum's stewing steak? Gor blimey, mate, don't you ever learn nothing? Tomorrow's dinner gone down your useless big gullet and our dad will give us both a belting this time I shouldn't wonder, not just you, you senseless rotten idiot. Time you knew the bloody difference between me mum's stewing steak and dog meat, it is straight, though come to think of it there isn't all that difference, 'specially as maybe your eyes don't look at things the same. Do they? I damn well wish you could talk, mate."

I clicked shut the door of the car and startled him, and he swung round with the torch searching wildly. The beam caught me and steadied on my face.

The boy said, "You come near me and I'll set my dog on you." The dog, however, was still squatting and showed no enthusiasm.

"I'll stay right here, then," I said amicably, leaning back against the car. "I only want to know who lives in that cottage over there, where the lights are."

"How do I know? We only come to live here the day before yesterday."

"Great . . . I mean, that must be great for you, moving."

"Yeah. Sure. You stay there, then. I'm going now." He beckoned to the dog. The dog was still busy.

"How would it be if you could offer your mum the price of the stewing steak? Maybe she wouldn't tell your dad, then, and neither you nor the dog would get a belting."

"Our mum says we mustn't talk to strange men."

"Hm. Well, never mind then. Off you go."

"I'll go when I'm ready," he said belligerently. A natural born rebel. About nine years old, I guessed.

"What would I have to do for it?" he said, after a pause.

"Nothing much. Just ring the front-door bell of that cottage and tell whoever answers that you can't stop your dog eating the crocuses they've got growing all along the front there. Then when they come out to see, just nip off home as fast as your dog can stagger."

It appealed to him. "Steak probably cost a good bit," he said.

"Probably." I dug into my pocket and came up with a small fistful of pennies and silver. "This should leave a bit over."

"He doesn't really have to eat the crocuses, does he?"

"No."

"OK then." Once his mind was made up he was jaunty and efficient.

He shoveled my small change into his pocket, marched up to Charlie's front door, and told Mrs. West, who cautiously answered it, that she was losing her crocuses. She scolded him all the way down the path, and while she was bending down to search for the damage, my accomplice quietly vanished. Before Mrs. West exactly realized she had been misled I had stepped briskly through her front door and shut her out of her own house.

When I opened the sitting-room door Charlie said, without lifting his eyes from a racing paper, "It wasn't him again, then."

"Yes," I said, "it was."

Charlie's immature face crumpled into a revolting state of fear and Mrs. West leaned on the door bell. I shut the sitting-room door behind me to cut out some of the din.

"What are you so afraid of?" I said loudly.

"Well . . . you . . ."

"And so you damn well ought to be," I agreed. I took a step towards him and he shrank back into his armchair. He was brave enough on a horse, which made this abject cringing all the more unexpected, and all the more unpleasant. I took another step. He fought his way into the upholstery.

Mrs. West gave the door bell a rest.

"Why did you do it?" I said.

He shook his head dumbly, and pulled his feet up on to the chair seat in the classic womb position. Wishful regression to the first and only place where the world couldn't reach him.

"Charlie, I came here for some answers, and you're going to give them to me."

Mrs. West's furious face appeared at the window and she started rapping hard enough to break the glass. With one eye on her husband to prevent him making another bolt for it, I stepped over and undid the latch.

"Get out of here," she shouted. "Go on, get out."

"You get in. Through here, I'm not opening the door."

"I'll fetch the police."

"Do what you like. I only want to talk to your worm of a husband. Get in or stay out, but shut up."

She did anything but. Once she was in the room it took another twenty minutes of fruitless slanging before I could ask Charlie a single question without her loud voice obliterating any chance of an answer.

Charlie himself tired of it first and told her to stop, but at least her belligerence had given him a breathing space. He put his feet down on the floor again and said it was no use asking those questions, he didn't know the answers.

"You must do. Unless you told those lies about me out of sheer personal spite."

"No."

"Then why?"

"I'm not telling you."

"Then I'll tell you something, you little louse. I'm going to find out who put you up to it. I'm going to stir everything up until I find out, and then I'm going to raise such a stink about being framed that sulphur will smell like sweet peas by comparison, and you, Master Charlie West, *you* will find yourself without a licence, not me, and even if you get it back you'll never live down the contempt everyone will feel for you."

"Don't you talk to my Charlie like that!"

"Your Charlie is a vicious little liar who would sell you too for fifty pounds."

"It wasn't fifty," she snapped triumphantly. "It was five hundred."

Charlie yelled at her and I came as near to hitting him as the distance between my clenched teeth. Five hundred pounds. He'd lied my licence away for a handout that would have insulted a tout.

"That does it," I said. "And now you tell me who paid you."

The girl wife started to look as frightened as Charlie, and it didn't occur to me then that my anger had flooded through that little room like a tidal wave.

Charlie stuttered, "I d . . . d . . . don't know."

I took a pace towards him and he scrambled out of his chair and took refuge behind it.

"K . . . k . . . keep away from me. I don't know. I don't know."

"That isn't good enough."

"He really doesn't know," the girl wailed. "He really doesn't."

"He does," I repeated furiously.

The girl began to cry. Charlie seemed to be on the verge of copying her.

"I never saw . . . never saw the bloke. He telephoned."

"And how did he pay you?"

"In two . . . in two packages. In one-pound notes. A hundred of them came the day before the Enquiry, and I was to get . . ." His voice trailed away.

"You were to get the other four hundred if I was warned off?"

He nodded, a fractional jerk. His head was tucked into his shoulders, as if to avoid a blow.

"And have you?"

"What?"

"Have you had it yet? The other four hundred?"

His eyes widened, and he spoke in jerks. "No . . . but . . . of course . . . it . . . will . . . come."

"Of course it won't," I said brutally. "You stupid treacherous little ninny." My voice sounded thick, and each word came out separately and loaded with fury.

Both of the Wests were trembling, and the girl's eye make-up was beginning to run down her cheeks.

"What did he sound like, this man on the telephone?"

"Just . . . just a man," Charlie said.

"And did it occur to you to ask *why* he wanted me warned off?"

"I said . . . you hadn't done anything to harm me . . . and he said . . . you never know . . . supposing one day he does . . ."

Charlie shrank still farther under my astounded glare.

"Anyway . . . five hundred quid . . . I don't earn as much as you, you know." For the first time there was a tinge of spite in his voice, and I knew that in truth jealousy had been a factor, that he hadn't in fact done it entirely for the money. He'd got his kicks, too.

"You're only twenty," I said. "What exactly do you expect?"

But Charlie expected everything, always, to be run entirely for the best interests of Charlie West.

I said, "And you'll be wise to spend that money carefully, because, believe me, it's going to be the most expensive hundred quid you've ever earned."

"Kelly . . ." He was halfway to entreaty. Jealous, greedy, dishonest, and afraid. I felt not the remotest flicker of compassion for him, only a widening anger that the motives behind his lies were so small.

"And when you lose your licence for this, and I'll see that you do, you'll have plenty of time to understand that it *serves you right.*"

The raw revenge in my voice made a desert of their little home. They both stood there dumbly with wide miserable eyes, too broken up to raise another word. The girl's beige mouth hung slackly open, mascara halfway to her chin, long hair straggling in wisps across her face and round her shoulders. She looked sixteen. A child. So did Charlie. The worst vandals are always childish.

I turned away from them and walked out of their cottage, and my anger changed into immense depression on the drive home.

VI

At two o'clock in the morning the rage I'd unleashed on the Wests looked worse and worse.

To start with, it had achieved nothing helpful. I'd known before I went there that Charlie must have had a reason for lying about me at the Enquiry. I now knew the reason to be five hundred pounds. Marvellous. A useless scrap of information out of a blizzard of emotion.

Lash out when you're hurt . . . I'd done that, all right. Poured out on them the roaring bitterness I'd smothered under a civilized front ever since Monday.

Nor had I given Charlie any reason to do me any good in future. Very much the reverse. He wasn't going to be contrite and eager to make amends. When he'd recovered himself he'd be sullen and vindictive.

I'd been taught the pattern over and over. Country A plays an isolated shabby trick. Country B is outraged and exacts revenge. Country A is forced to express apologies and meekly back down, but thoroughly resents it. Country A now holds a permanent grudge, and harms Country B whenever possible. One of the classic variations in the history of politics and aggression. Also applicable to individuals.

To have known about the pitfalls and jumped in regardless was a mite galling. It just showed how easily good sense lost out to anger. It also showed me that I wasn't going to get results that way. A crash course in detection would have been handy. Failing that, I'd have to start taking stock of things coolly, instead of charging straight off again towards the easiest looking target, and making another mess of it.

Cool stock-taking . . .

Charlie West hadn't wanted to see me because he had a guilty conscience. It followed that everyone else who had a guilty conscience wouldn't want to see me. Even if they didn't actually spring off across the fields, they would all do their best to avoid my reaching them. I was going to have to become adept—and fast—at entering their lives when their backs were turned.

If Charlie West didn't know who had paid him, and I believed that he didn't, it followed that perhaps no one else who had lied knew who had persuaded them to. Perhaps it had all been done on the telephone. Long-distance leverage. Impersonal and undiscoverable.

Perhaps I had set myself an impossible task and I should give up the whole idea and emigrate to Australia.

Except that they had racing in Australia, and I wouldn't be able to go. The banishment covered the world. Warned off. Warned off.

Oh God.

All right, so maybe I did let the self-pity catch up with me for a while. But I was privately alone in my bed in the dark, and I'd jeered myself out of it by morning.

Looking about as ragged as I felt, I got up at six and pointed the Lotus's smooth nose towards London, NW7, Mill Hill.

Since I could see no one at the races I had to catch them at home, and in the case of George Newtonnards, bookmaker, home proved to be a sprawling pink-washed ranch-type bungalow in a prosperous suburban road. At eight-thirty AM I hoped to find him at breakfast, but in fact he was opening his garage door when I arrived. I parked squarely across the entrance to his drive, which was hardly likely to make me popular, and he came striding down towards me to tell me to move.

I climbed out of the car. When he saw who it was, he stopped dead. I walked up the drive to meet him, shivering a little in the raw east wind and regretting I wasn't snug inside a fur-collared jacket like his.

"What are you doing here?" he said sharply.

"I would be very grateful if you would just tell me one or two things . . ."

"I haven't time." He was easy, self-assured, dealing with a small-sized nuisance. "And nothing I can say will help you. Move your car, please."

"Certainly . . . Could you tell me how it was that you came to be asked to give evidence against Mr. Cranfield?"

"How it was? . . ." He looked slightly surprised. "I received an official letter, requiring me to attend."

"Well, why? I mean, how did the Stewards know about Mr. Cranfield's bet on Cherry Pie? Did you write and tell them?"

He gave me a cool stare. "I hear," he said, "that you are maintaining you were framed."

"News travels."

A faint smile. "News always travels—towards me. An accurate information service is the basis of good bookmaking."

"How did the Stewards know about Mr. Cranfield's bet?"

"Mm. Well, yes, that I don't know."

"Who, besides you, knew that you believed that Cranfield had backed Cherry Pie?"

"He did back him."

"Well, who besides you knew that he had?"

"I haven't time for this."

"I'll be happy to move my car . . . in a minute or two."

His annoyed glare gradually softened round the edges into a half-amused acceptance. A very smooth civilized man, George Newtonnards.

"Very well. I told a few of the lads . . . other bookmakers, that is. I was angry about it, see? Letting myself be taken to the cleaners like that. Me, at my age, I should know better. So maybe one of them passed on the word to the Stewards, knowing the Enquiry was coming up. But no, I didn't do it myself."

"Could you guess which one might have done? I mean, do you know of anyone who has a grudge against Cranfield?"

"Can't think of one." He shrugged. "No more than against any other trainer who tries it on."

"Tries it on?" I echoed, surprised. "But he doesn't."

"Oh yeah?"

"I ride them," I protested. "I should know."

"Yes," he said sarcastically. "You should. Don't come the naïve bit with me, chum. Your friend Chris Smith, him with the cracked skull, he's a proper artist at strangulation, wouldn't you say? Same as you are. A fine pair, the two of you."

"You believe I pulled Squelch, then?"

"Stands to reason."

"All the same, I didn't."

"Tell it to the Marines." A thought struck him. "I don't know any bookmakers who have a grudge against Cranfield, but I sure know one who has a grudge against *you*. A whopping great life-sized grudge. One time, he was almost coming after you with a chopper. You got in his way proper, mate, you did indeed."

"How? And who?"

"You and Chris Smith, you were riding two for Cranfield . . . about six months ago. It was . . . right at the beginning of the season anyway . . . in a novice 'chase at Fontwell. Remember? There was a big holiday crowd in from the South Coast because it was a bit chilly that day for lying on the beach . . . anyway, there was a big crowd all primed with holiday money . . . and there were you and Chris Smith on these two horses, and the public fancying both of them, and Pelican Jobberson asked you which was off, and you said you hadn't an earthly on yours, so he rakes in the cash on you and doesn't bother to balance his book, and then you go and ride a hell of a finish and win by a neck, when you could have lost instead without the slightest trouble. Pelican went spare and swore he'd be even with you when he got the chance."

"I believed what I told him," I said. "It was that horse's first attempt over fences. No one could have predicted he'd have been good enough to win."

"Then why did you?"

"The owner wanted to, if possible."

"Did he bet on it?"

"The owner? No. It was a woman. She never bets much. She just likes to see her horses win."

"Pelican swore you'd backed it yourself, and put him off so that you could get a better price."

"You bookmakers are too suspicious for your own good."

"Hard experience proves us right."

"Well, he's wrong this time," I insisted. "This bird friend of yours. If he asked me . . . and I don't remember him asking . . . then I told him the truth. And anyway, any bookmaker who asks jockeys questions like that is asking for trouble. Jockeys are the worst tipsters in the world."

"Some aren't," he said flatly. "Some are good at it."

I skipped that. "Is he still angry after all these months? And if so, would he be angry enough not just to tell the Stewards that Cranfield backed Cherry Pie, but to bribe other people to invent lies about us?"

His eyes narrowed while he thought about it. He pursed his mouth, undecided. "You'd better ask him yourself."

"Thanks." Hardly an easy question.

"Move your car now?" he suggested.

"Yes." I walked two steps towards it, then stopped and turned back. "Mr. Newtonnards, if you see the man who put the money on for Mr. Cranfield, will you find out who he is . . . and let me know?"

"Why don't you ask Cranfield?"

"He said he didn't want to involve him."

"But you do?"

"I suppose I'm grasping at anything," I said. "But yes, I think I do."

"Why don't you just quieten down and take it?" he said reasonably. "All this thrashing about . . . you got copped. So, you got copped. Fair enough. Sit it out, then. You'll get your licence back, eventually."

"Thank you for your advice," I said politely, and went and moved my car out of his gateway.

It was Thursday. I should have been going to Warwick to ride in four races. Instead, I drove aimlessly back round the North Circular Road wondering whether or not to pay a call on David Oakley, enquiry agent and imaginative photographer. If Charlie West didn't know who had framed me, it seemed possible that Oakley might be the only one who did. But even if he did, he was highly unlikely to tell me. There seemed no point in confronting him, and yet nothing could be gained if I made no attempt.

In the end I stopped at a telephone box and found his number via enquiries.

A girl answered. "Mr. Oakley isn't in yet."

"Can I make an appointment?"

She asked me what about.

"A divorce."

She said Mr. Oakley could see me at 11:30, and asked me my name.

"Charles Crisp."

"Very well, Mr. Crisp. Mr. Oakley will be expecting you."

I doubted it. On the other hand, he, like Charlie West, might in general be expecting some form of protest.

From the North Circular Road I drove ninety miles up the M1 Motorway to Birmingham and found Oakley's office above a bicycle and radio shop half a mile from the town centre.

His street door, shabby black, bore a neat small nameplate stating, simply, "Oakley." There were two keyholes, Yale and Chubb, and a discreetly situated peephole. I tried the handle of this apparent fortress, and the door opened easily under my touch. Inside, there was a narrow passage with pale blue walls leading to an uncarpeted staircase stretching upwards.

I walked up, my feet sounding loud on the boards. At the top there was a small landing with another shabby black door, again and similarly fortified. On this door, another neat notice said, "Please ring." There was a bell push. I gave it three seconds' work.

The door was opened by a tall strong-looking girl dressed in a dark coloured leather trouser-suit. Under the jacket she wore a black sweater, and under the trouser legs, black leather boots. Black eyes returned my scrutiny, black hair held back by a tortoiseshell band fell straight to her shoulders before curving inwards. She seemed at first sight to be about twenty-four, but there were already wrinkle lines round her eyes, and the deadness in their expression indicated too much familiarity with dirty washing.

"I have an appointment," I said. "Crisp."

"Come in." She opened the door wider and left it for me to close.

I followed her into the room, a small square office furnished with a desk, typewriter, telephone, and four tall filing cabinets. On the far side of the room there was another door. Not black; modern flat hardboard, painted grey. More keyholes. I eyed them thoughtfully.

The girl opened the door, said through it, "It's Mr. Crisp," and stood back for me to pass her.

"Thank you," I said. Took three steps forwards, and shut myself in with David Oakley.

His office was not a great deal larger than the anteroom, and no thrift had been spared with the furniture. There was dim brown linoleum, a bentwood coat stand, a small cheap armchair facing a grey metal desk, and over the grimy window, in place of curtains, a tough-looking fixed frame covered with chicken wire. Outside the window there were the heavy bars and supports of a fire escape. The Birmingham sun, doing its best against odds, struggled through and fell in wrinkled honeycomb shadows on the surface of an ancient safe. In the wall on my right, another door, firmly closed. With yet more keyholes.

Behind the desk in a swivel chair sat the proprietor of all this glory, the totally unmemorable Mr. Oakley. Youngish. Slender. Mouse-coloured hair. And this time, sunglasses.

"Sit down, Mr. Crisp," he said. Accentless voice, entirely emotionless, as before. "Divorce, I believe? Give me the details of your requirements, and we can arrive at a fee." He looked at his watch. "I can give you just ten minutes, I'm afraid. Shall we get on?"

He hadn't recognized me. I thought I might as well take advantage of it.

"I understand you would be prepared to fake some evidence for me . . . photographs?"

He began to nod, and then grew exceptionally still. The unrevealing dark glasses were motionless. The pale straight mouth didn't twitch. The hand lying on the desk remained loose and relaxed.

Finally he said, without any change of inflection, "Get out."

"How much do you charge for faking evidence?"

"Get out."

I smiled. "I'd like to know how much I was worth."

"Dust," he said. His foot moved under the desk.

"I'll pay you in gold dust, if you'll tell me who gave you the job."

He considered it. Then he said, "No."

The door to the outer office opened quietly behind me.

Oakley said calmly, "This is not a Mr. Crisp, Didi. This is a Mr. Kelly Hughes. Mr. Hughes will be leaving."

"Mr. Hughes is not ready," I said.

"I think Mr. Hughes will find he is," she said.

I looked at her over my shoulder. She was carrying a large black-looking pistol with a very large black-looking silencer. The whole works were pointing steadily my way.

"How dramatic," I said. "Can you readily dispose of bodies in the centre of Birmingham?"

"Yes," Oakley said.

"For a fee, of course, usually," Didi added.

I struggled not to believe them, and lost. All the same . . .

"Should you decide after all to sell the information I need, you know where to find me." I relaxed against the back of the chair.

"I may have a liking for gold dust," he said calmly. "But I am not a fool."

"Opinions differ," I remarked lightly.

There was no reaction. "It is not in my interest that you should prove you were . . . shall we say . . . set up."

"I understand that. Eventually, however, you will wish that you hadn't helped to do it."

He said smoothly, "A number of other people have said much the same, though few, I must confess, as quietly as you."

It occurred to me suddenly that he must be quite used to the sort of enraged onslaught I'd thrown at the Wests, and that perhaps that was why his office . . . Didi caught my wandering glance and cynically nodded.

"That's right. Too many people tried to smash the place up. So we keep the damage to a minimum."

"How wise."

"I'm afraid I really do have another appointment now," Oakley said. "So if you'll excuse me? . . ."

I stood up. There was nothing to stay for.

"It surprises me," I remarked, "that you're not in jail."

"I am clever," he said matter-of-factly. "My clients are satisfied, and people like you . . . impotent."

"Someone will kill you, one day."

"Will you?"

I shook my head. "Not worth it."

"Exactly," he said calmly. "The jobs I accept are never what the victims would actually kill me for. I really am not a fool."

"No," I said.

I walked across to the door and Didi made room for me to pass. She put the pistol down on her desk in the outer office and switched off a red bulb which glowed brightly in a small switchboard.

"Emergency signal?" I enquired. "Under his desk."

"You could say so."

"Is that gun loaded?"

Her eyebrows rose. "Naturally."

"I see." I opened the outer door. She walked over to close it behind me as I went towards the stairs.

"Nice to have met you, Mr. Hughes," she said unemotionally. "Don't come back."

I walked along to my car in some depression. From none of the three damaging witnesses at the Enquiry had I got any change at all, and what David Oakley had said about me being impotent looked all too true.

There seemed to be no way of proving that he had simply brought with him the money he had photographed in my flat. No one at Corrie had seen him come or go: Tony had asked all the lads, and none of them had seen him. And Oakley would have found it easy enough to be unobserved. He had only had to arrive early, while everyone was out riding on the Downs at morning exercise. From seven-thirty to eight-thirty the stable yard would be deserted. Letting himself in through my unlocked door, setting up his props, loosing off a flash or two, and quietly retreating . . . The whole process would have taken him no more than ten minutes.

It was possible he had kept a record of his shady transactions. Possible, not probable. He might need to keep some hold over his clients, to prevent their later denouncing him in fits of resurgent civil conscience. If he did keep such records, it might account for the multiplicity of locks. Or maybe the locks were simply to discourage people from breaking in to search for records, as they were certainly discouraging me.

Would Oakley, I wondered, have done what Charlie West had done, and produced his lying testimony for a voice on the telephone? On the whole, I decided not. Oakley had brains where Charlie had vanity, and Oakley would not involve himself without his clients up tight too. Oakley had to know who had done the engineering.

But stealing that information . . . or beating it out of him . . . or tricking him into giving it . . . as well as buying it from him . . . every course looked as hopeless as the next. I could only ride horses. I couldn't pick locks, fights, or pockets. Certainly not Oakley's.

Oakley and Didi. They were old at the game. They'd invented the rules. Oakley and Didi were senior league.

How did anyone get in touch with Oakley, if they needed his brand of service?

He could scarcely advertise.

Someone had to know about him.

I thought it over for a while, sitting in my car in the car park wondering what to do next. There was only one person I knew who could put his finger on the pulse of Birmingham if he wanted to, and the likelihood was that in my present circumstances he wouldn't want to.

However . . .

I started the car, threaded away through the one-way streets, and found a slot in the crowded park behind the Great Stag Hotel. Inside, the ritual of Business Lunch was warming up, the atmosphere thickening nicely with the smell of alcohol, the resonance of fruity voices, the haze of cigars. The Great Stag Hotel attracted almost exclusively a certain grade of wary, prosperous, level-headed businessmen needing a soft background for hard options, and it attracted them because the landlord, Teddy Dewar, was the sort of man himself.

I found him in the bar, talking to two others almost indistinguishable from him in their dark grey suits, white shirts, neat maroon ties, seventeen-inch necks, and thirty-eight-inch waists.

A faint glaze came over his professionally noncommittal expression when he caught sight of me over their shoulders. A warned-off jockey didn't rate too high with him. Lowered the tone of the place, no doubt.

I edged through to the bar on one side of him and ordered whisky.

"I'd be grateful for a word with you," I said.

He turned his head a fraction in my direction, and without looking at me directly answered, "Very well. In a few minutes."

No warmth in the words. No ducking of the unwelcome situation, either. He went on talking to the two men about the dicky state of oil shares, and eventually smoothly disengaged himself and turned to me.

"Well, Kelly . . ." His eyes were cool and distant, waiting to see what I wanted before showing any real feeling.

"Will you lunch with me?" I made it casual.

His surprise was controlled. "I thought . . ."

"I may be banned," I said, "but I still eat."

He studied my face. "You mind."

"What do you expect . . . ? I'm sorry it shows."

He said neutrally, "There's a muscle in your jaw . . . Very well: if you don't mind going in straight-away."

We sat against the wall at an inconspicuous table and chose beef cut from a roast on a trolley. While he ate his eyes checked the running of the dining-room, missing nothing. I waited until he was satisfied that all was well and then came briefly to the point.

"Do you know anything about a man called David Oakley? He's an enquiry agent. Operates from an office about half a mile from here."

"David Oakley? I can't say I've ever heard of him."

"He manufactured some evidence which swung things against me at the Stewards' Enquiry on Monday."

"Manufactured?" There was delicate doubt in his voice.

"Oh yes," I sighed. "I suppose it sounds corny, but I really was not guilty as charged. But someone made sure it looked like it." I told him about the photograph of money in my bedroom.

"And you never had this money?"

"I did not. And the note supposed to be from Cranfield was a forgery. But how could we prove it?"

He thought it over.

"You can't."

"Exactly," I agreed.

"This David Oakley who took the photograph . . . I suppose you got no joy from him."

"No joy is right."

"I don't understand precisely why you've come to me." He finished his beef and laid his knife and fork tidily together. Waiters appeared like genii to clear the table and bring coffee. He waited still noncommittally while I paid the bill.

"I expect it is too much to ask," I said finally. "After all, I've only stayed here three or four times, I have no claim on you personally for friendship or help . . . and yet, there's no one else I know who could even begin to do what you could . . . if you will."

"What?" he said succinctly.

"I want to know how people are steered towards David Oakley, if they want some evidence faked. He as good as told me he is quite accustomed to do it. Well . . . how does he get his clients? Who recommends him? I thought that among all the people you know, you might think of some- one who could perhaps pretend he wanted a job done . . . or pretend he had a friend who wanted a job done . . . and throw out feelers, and see if anyone finally recommended Oakley. And if so, who."

He considered it. "Because if you found one contact you might work back from there to another . . . and eventually perhaps to a name which meant something to you? . . ."

"I suppose it sounds feeble," I said resignedly.

"It's a very outside chance," he agreed. There was a long pause. Then he added, "All the same, I do know of someone who might agree to try." He smiled briefly, for the first time.

"That's . . ." I swallowed. "That's marvellous."

"Can't promise results."

VII

Tony came clomping up my stairs on Friday morning after first exercise and poured half an inch of Scotch into the coffee I gave him. He drank the scalding mixture and shuddered as the liquor bit.

"God," he said. "It's cold on the Downs."

"Rather you than me," I said.

"Liar," he said amicably. "It must feel odd to you, not riding."

"Yes."

He sprawled in the green armchair. "Poppy's got the morning ickies again. I'll be glad when this lousy pregnancy is over. She's been ill half the time."

"Poor Poppy."

"Yeah . . . Anyway, what it means is that we ain't going to that dance tonight. She says she can't face it."

"Dance? . . ."

"The Jockeys' Fund dance. You know. You've got the tickets on your mantel over there."

"Oh . . . yes. I'd forgotten about it. We were going together."

"That's right. But now, as I was saying, you'll have to go without us."

"I'm not going at all."

"I thought you might not." He sighed and drank deeply. "Where did you get to yesterday?"

"I called on people who didn't want to see me."

"Any results?"

"Not many." I told him briefly about Newtonnards and David Oakley, and about the hour I'd spent with Andrew Tring.

It was because the road home from Birmingham led near his village that I'd thought of Andrew Tring, and my first instinct anyway was to shy away from even the thought of him. Certainly visiting one of the Stewards who had helped to warn him off was not regulation behaviour for a disbarred jockey. If I hadn't been fairly strongly annoyed with him I would have driven straight on.

He was disgusted with me for calling. He opened the door of his prosperous sprawling old manor house himself and had no chance of saying he was out.

"Kelly! What are you doing here?"

"Asking you for some explanation."

"I've nothing to say to you."

"You have indeed."

He frowned. Natural good manners were only just preventing him from retreating and shutting the door in my face. "Come in then. Just for a few minutes."

"Thank you," I said without irony, and followed him into a nearby small room lined with books and containing a vast desk, three deep armchairs and a colour television set.

"Now," he said, shutting the door and not offering the armchairs, "why have you come?"

He was four years older than me, and about the same size. Still as trim as when he rode races, still outwardly the same man. Only the casual, long-established changing-room friendliness seemed to have withered somewhere along the upward path from amateurship to Authority.

"Andy," I said, "do you really and honestly believe that that Squelch race was rigged?"

"You were warned off," he said coldly.

"That's far from being the same thing as guilty."

"I don't agree."

"Then you're stupid," I said bluntly. "As well as scared out of your tiny wits."

"That's enough, Kelly. I don't have to listen to this." He opened the door again and waited for me to leave. I didn't. Short of throwing me out bodily he was going to have to put up with me a little longer. He gave me a furious stare and shut the door again.

I said more reasonably, "I'm sorry. Really, I'm sorry. It's just that you rode against me for at least five years . . . I'd have thought you wouldn't so easily believe I'd deliberately lose a race. I've never yet lost a race I could win."

He was silent. He knew that I didn't throw races. Anyone who rode regularly knew who would and who wouldn't and in spite of what Charlie West had said at the Enquiry, I was not an artist at stopping one because I hadn't given it the practice.

"There was that money," he said at last. He sounded disillusioned and discouraged.

"I never had it. Oakley took it with him into my flat and photographed it there. All that so-called evidence, the whole bloody Enquiry in fact, was as genuine as a lead sixpence."

He gave me a long doubtful look. Then he said, "There's nothing I can do about it."

"What are you afraid of?"

"Stop saying I'm afraid," he said irritably. "I'm not afraid. I just can't do anything about it, even if what you say is true."

"It is true . . . and maybe you don't think you are afraid, but that's definitely the impression you give. Or maybe . . . are you simply overawed? The new boy among the old powerful prefects. Is that it? Afraid of putting a foot wrong with them?"

"Kelly!" he protested; but it was the protest of a touched nerve.

I said unkindly, "You're a gutless disappointment," and took a step towards his door. He didn't move to open it for me. Instead he put up a hand to stop me, looking as angry as he had every right to.

"That's not fair. Just because I can't help you . . ."

"You could have done. At the Enquiry."

"You don't understand."

"I do indeed. You found it easier to believe me guilty than to tell Gowery you had any doubts."

"It wasn't as easy as you think."

"Thanks," I said ironically.

"I don't mean . . ." He shook his head impatiently. "I mean, it wasn't all as simple as you make out. When Gowery asked me to sit with him at the Enquiry I believed it was only going to be a formality, that both you and Cranfield had run the Lemonfizz genuinely and were surprised yourselves by the result. Colonel Midgely told me it was ridiculous having to hold the Enquiry at all, really. I never expected to be caught up in having to warn you off."

"Did you say," I said, "that Lord Gowery asked you to sit with him?"

"Of course. That's the normal procedure. The Stewards sitting at an Enquiry aren't picked out of a hat . . ."

"There isn't any sort of rota?"

"No. The Disciplinary Steward asks two colleagues to officiate with him . . . and that's what put me on the spot, if you must know, because I didn't want to say no to Lord Gowery . . ." He stopped.

"Go on," I urged without heat. "Why not?"

"Well because . . ." He hesitated, then said slowly, "I suppose in a way I owe it to you . . . I'm sorry, Kelly, desperately sorry, I do know you don't usually rig races . . . I'm in an odd position with Gowery and it's vitally important I keep in with him."

I stifled my indignation. Andrew Tring's eyes were looking inward and from his expression he didn't very much like what he could see.

"He owns the freehold of the land just north of Manchester where our main pottery is." Andrew Tring's family fortunes were based not on fine porcelain but on smashable teacups for institutions. His products were dropped by washers-up in schools and hospitals from Waterloo to Hong Kong, and the pieces in the world's dustbins were his perennial licence to print money.

He said, "There's been some redevelopment round there and that land is suddenly worth about a quarter of a million. And our lease runs out in three years . . . We have been negotiating a new one, but the old one was for ninety-nine years and no one is keen to renew for that long . . . The ground rent is in any case going to be raised considerably, but if Gowery changes his mind and wants to sell that land for development, there's nothing we can do about it. We only own the buildings . . . We'd lose the entire factory if he didn't renew the lease . . . And we can only make cups and saucers so cheaply because our overheads are small . . . If we have to build or rent a new factory our prices will be less competitive and our world trade figures will slump. Gowery himself has the final say as to whether our lease will be renewed or not, and on what terms . . . so you see, Kelly, it's not that I'm afraid of him . . . there's so much more at stake . . . and he's always a man to hold it against you if you argue with him."

He stopped and looked at me gloomily. I looked gloomily back. The facts of life stared us stonily in the face.

"So that's that," I agreed. "You are quite right. You can't help me. You couldn't, right from the start. I'm glad you explained . . ." I smiled at him twistedly, facing another dead end, the last of a profitless day.

"I'm sorry, Kelly . . ."

"Sure," I said.

Tony finished his fortified breakfast and said, "So there wasn't anything sinister in Andy Tring's lily-livered bit on Monday."

"It depends what you call sinister. But no, I suppose not."

"What's left, then?"

"Damn all," I said in depression.

"You can't give up," he protested.

"Oh no. But I've learned one thing in learning nothing, and that is that I'm getting nowhere because I'm me. First thing Monday morning I'm going to hire me my own David Oakley."

"Attaboy," he said. He stood up. "Time for second lot, I hear." Down in the yard the lads were bringing out the horses, their hooves scrunching hollowly on the packed gravel.

"How are they doing?" I asked.

"Oh . . . so so. I sure hate having to put up other jocks. Given me a bellyful of the whole game, this business has."

When he'd gone down to ride I cleaned up my already clean flat and made some more coffee. The day stretched emptily ahead. So did the next day and the one after that, and every day for an indefinite age.

Ten minutes of this prospect was enough. I searched around and found another straw to cling to: telephoned to a man I knew slightly at the BBC. A cool secretary said he was out, and to try again at eleven.

I tried again at eleven. Still out. I tried at twelve. He was in then, but sounded as if he wished he weren't.

"Not Kelly Hughes, the . . ." His voice trailed off while he failed to find a tactful way of putting it.

"That's right."

"Well . . . er . . . I don't think . . ."

"I don't want anything much," I assured him resignedly. "I just want to know the name of the outfit who make the films of races. The camera patrol people."

"Oh." He sounded relieved. "That's the Racecourse Technical Services. Run by the Levy Board. They've a virtual monopoly, though there's one other small firm operating sometimes under licence. Then there are the television companies, of course. Did you want any particular race? Oh . . . the Lemonfizz Crystal Cup, I suppose."

"No," I said. "The meeting at Reading two weeks earlier."

"Reading . . . Reading . . . Let's see, then. Which lot would that be?" He hummed a few out-of-tune bars while he thought it over. "I should think . . . yes, definitely the small firm, the Cannot Lie people. Cannot Lie, Ltd. Offices at Woking, Surrey. Do you want their number?"

"Yes please."

He read it to me.

"Thank you very much," I said.

"Any time . . . er . . . well . . . I mean . . ."

"I know what you mean," I agreed. "But thanks anyway."

I put down the receiver with a grimace. It was still no fun being everyone's idea of a villain.

The BBC man's reaction made me decide that the telephone might get me nil results from the Cannot Lie brigade. Maybe they couldn't lie, but they would certainly evade. And anyway, I had the whole day to waste.

The Cannot Lie office was a rung or two up the luxury ladder from David Oakley's, which wasn't saying a great deal. A large rather bare room on the second floor of an Edwardian house in a side street. A rickety lift large enough for one slim man or two starving children. A well-worn desk with a well-worn blonde painting her toenails on top of it.

"Yes?" she said, when I walked in.

She had lilac panties on, with lace. She made no move to prevent me seeing a lot of them.

"No one in?" I asked.

"Only us chickens," she agreed. She had a South London accent and the smart back-chatting intelligence that often goes with it. "Which do you want, the old man or our Alfie?"

"You'll do nicely," I said.

"Ta." She took it as her due, with a practised come-on-so-far-but-no-further smile. One foot was finished. She stretched out her leg and wiggled it up and down to help with the drying.

"Going to a dance tonight," she explained. "In me peep-toes."

I didn't think anyone would concentrate on the toes. Apart from the legs she had a sharp pointed little bosom under a white cotton sweater and a bright pink patent leather belt clasping a bikini-sized waist. Her body looked about twenty years old. Her face looked as if she'd spent the last six of them hopping.

"Paint the other one," I suggested.

"You're not in a hurry?"

"I'm enjoying the scenery."

She gave a knowing giggle and started on the other foot. The view was even more hair-raising than before. She watched me watching, and enjoyed it.

"What's your name?" I asked.

"Carol. What's yours?"

"Kelly."

"From the Isle of Man?"

"No. The land of our fathers."

She gave me a bright glance. "You catch on quick, don't you?"

I wished I did. I said regretfully, "How long do you keep ordinary routine race films?"

"Huh? For ever, I suppose." She changed mental gear effortlessly, carrying straight on with her uninhibited painting. "We haven't destroyed any so far, that's to say. 'Course, we've only been in the racing business eighteen months. No telling what they'll do when the big storeroom's full. We're up to the eyebrows in all the others with films of motor races, golf matches, three-day events, any old things like that."

"Where's the big storeroom?"

"Through there." She waved the small pink enamelling brush in the general direction of a scratched once-cream door. "Want to see?"

"If you don't mind."

"Go right ahead."

She had finished the second foot. The show was over. With a sigh I removed my gaze and walked over to the door in question. There was only a round hole where most doors have a handle. I pushed against the wood and the door swung inwards into another large high room, furnished this time with rows of free standing bookshelves, like a public library. The shelves, however, were of bare functional wood, and there was no covering on the planked floor.

Well over half the shelves were empty. On the others were rows of short wide box files, their backs labelled with neat typed strips explaining what was to be found within. Each box proved to contain all the films from one day's racing, and they were all efficiently arranged in chronological order. I pulled out the box for the day I rode Squelch and Wanderlust at Reading, and looked inside. There were six round cans of sixteen-millimetre film, numbered one to six, and space enough for another one, number seven.

I took the box out to Carol. She was still sitting on top of the desk, dangling the drying toes and reading through a woman's magazine.

"What have you found then?"

"Do you lend these films to anyone who wants them?"

"Hire, not lend. Sure."

"Who to?"

"Anyone who asks. Usually it's the owners of the horses. Often they want prints made to keep, so we make them."

"Do the Stewards often want them?"

"Stewards? Well, see, if there's any doubt about a race the Stewards see the film on the racecourse. That van the old man and our Alfie's got develops it on the spot as soon as it's collected from the cameras."

"But sometimes they send for them afterwards?"

"Sometimes, yeah. When they want to compare the running of some horse or other." Her legs suddenly stopped swinging. She put down the magazine and gave me a straight stare.

"Kelly . . . Kelly *Hughes?*"

I didn't answer.

"Hey, you're not a bit like I thought." She put her blond head on one side, assessing me. "None of those sports writers ever said anything about you being smashing looking and dead sexy."

I laughed. I had a crooked nose and a scar down one cheek from where a horse's hoof had cut my face open, and among jockeys I was an also-ran as a bird-attracter.

"It's your eyes," she said. "Dark and sort of smiley and sad and a bit withdrawn. Give me the happy shivers, your eyes do."

"You read all that in a magazine," I said.

"I never!" But she laughed.

"Who asked for the film that's missing from the box?" I said. "And what exactly did they ask for?"

She sighed exaggeratedly and edged herself off the desk into a pair of bright pink sandals.

"Which film is that?" She looked at the box and its reference number, and did a Marilyn Monroe sway over to a filing cabinet against the wall. "Here we are. One official letter from the Stewards' secretary saying please send film of last race at Reading . . ."

I took the letter from her and read it myself. The words were quite clear: "the last race at Reading." Not the sixth race. The last race. And there had been seven races. It hadn't been Carol or the Cannot Lie Co. who had made the mistake.

"So you sent it?"

"Of course. Off to the authorities, as per instructions." She put the letter back in the files. "Did you in, did it?"

"Not that film, no."

"Alfie and the old man say you must have made a packet out of the Lemonfizz, to lose your licence over it."

"Do you think so too?"

"Stands to reason. Everyone thinks so."

"Man in the street?"

"Him too."

"Not a cent."

"You're a nit, then," she said frankly. "Whatever did you do it for?"

"I didn't."

"Oh yeah?" She gave me a knowing wink. "I suppose you have to say that, don't you?"

"Well," I said, handing her the Reading box to put back in the store-room. "Thanks anyway." I gave her half a smile and went away across the expanse of mottled linoleum to the door out.

I drove home slowly, trying to think. Not a very profitable exercise. Brains seemed to have deteriorated into a mushy blankness.

There were several letters for me in the mailbox on my front door, including one from my parents. I unfolded it walking up the stairs, feeling as usual a million miles away from them on every level.

My mother had written the first half in her round regular handwriting on one side of a large piece of lined paper. As usual there wasn't a full stop to be seen. She punctuated entirely with commas.

Dear Kelly,

Thanks for your note, we got it yesterday, we don't like reading about you in the papers, I know you said you hadn't done it, son, but no smoke without fire is what Mrs. Jones the post office says, and it is not nice for us what people are saying about you round here, all the airs and graces they say you are and pride goes before a fall and all that, well the pullets have started laying at last, we are painting your old room for Auntie Myfanwy who is coming to live here her arthritis is too bad for those stairs she has, well Kelly, I wish I could say we want you to come home but your Da is that angry and

now Auntie Myfanwy needs the room anyway, well son, we never wanted
you to go for a jockey, there was that nice job at the Townhall in Tenby you
could have had, I don't like to say it but you have disgraced us, son, there's
horrid it is going into the village now, everyone whispering, your loving
Mother.

I took a deep breath and turned the page over to receive the blast from
my father. His writing was much like my mother's as they had learned
from the same teacher, but he had pressed so hard with his ballpoint that
he had almost dug through the paper.

Kelly,
 You're a damned disgrace boy. It's soft saying you didn't do it. They
wouldn't of warned you off if you didn't do it. Not lords and such. They
know what's right. You're lucky you're not here I would give you a proper
belting. After all that scrimping your Ma did to let you go off to the Univer-
sity. And people said you would get too ladidah to speak to us, they were
right. Still, this is worse, being a cheat. Don't you come back here, your Ma's
that upset, what with that cat Mrs. Jones saying things. It would be best to
say don't send us any more money into the bank. I asked the manager but
he said only you can cancel a banker's order so you'd better do it. Your Ma
says it's as bad as you being in prison, the disgrace and all.

He hadn't signed it. He wouldn't know how to, we had so little affection for each other. He had despised me from childhood for my liking
school, and had mocked me unmercifully all the way to college. He
showed his jolly side only to my two older brothers, who had had what
he considered a healthy contempt for education: one of them had gone
into the Merchant Navy and the other lived next door and worked
alongside my father for the farmer who owned the cottages.

When in the end I had turned my back on all the years of learning and
taken to racing my family had again all disapproved of me, though I
guessed they would have been pleased enough if I'd chosen it all along.
I'd wasted the country's money, my father said; I wouldn't have been
given all those grants if they'd known that as soon as I was out I'd go
racing. That was probably true. It was also true that since I'd been racing
I'd paid enough in taxes to send several other farm boys through college
on grants.

I put my parents' letter under Rosalind's photograph. Even she had
been unable to reach their approval, because they thought I should have
married a nice girl from my own sort of background, not the student
daughter of a colonel.

They had rigid minds. It was doubtful now if they would ever be
pleased with me, whatever I did. And if I got my licence back, as like as
not they would think I had somehow cheated again.

You couldn't take aspirins for that sort of pain. It stayed there, sticking
in like knives. Trying to escape it I went into the kitchen, to see if there

was anything to eat. A tin of sardines, one egg, the dried-up remains of some Port-Salut.

Wrinkling my nose at that lot I transferred to the sittingroom and looked at the television programmes.

Nothing I wanted to see.

I slouched in the green velvet armchair and watched the evening slowly fade the colours into subtle greys. A certain amount of peace edged its way past the dragging gloom of the last four days. I wondered almost academically whether I would get my licence back before or after I stopped wincing at the way people looked at me, or spoke to me, or wrote about me. Probably the easiest course would be to stay out of sight, hiding myself away.

Like I was hiding away at that minute, by not going to the Jockeys' Fund dance.

The tickets were on the mantel. Tickets for Tony and Poppy, and for me and the partner I hadn't got around to inviting. Tickets which were not going to be used, which I had paid twelve fund-raising guineas for.

I sat in the dark for half an hour thinking about the people who would be at the Jockeys' Fund dance.

Then I put on my black tie and went to it.

VIII

I went prepared to be stared at.

I was stared at.

Also pointed out and commented on. Discreetly, however, for the most part. And only two people decisively turned their backs.

The Jockeys' Fund dance glittered as usual with titles, diamonds, champagne, and talent. Later it might curl round the edges into spilled drinks, glassy eyes, raddled make-up, and slurring voices, but the gloss wouldn't entirely disappear. It never did. The Jockeys' Fund dance was one of the great social events of the steeplechasing year.

I handed over my ticket and walked along the wide passage to where the lights were low, the music hot, and the air thick with smoke and scent. The opulent ballroom of the Royal Country Hotel, along the road from Ascot racecourse.

Around the dancing area there were numbers of large circular tables with chairs for ten or twelve round each, most of them occupied already. According to the chart in the hall, at table number thirty-two I would find the places reserved for Tony and me, if in fact they were still reserved. I gave up looking for table thirty-two less than halfway down the room because whenever I moved a new battery of curious eyes swivelled my way. A lot of people raised a hello but none of them could hide their slightly shocked surprise. It was every bit as bad as I'd feared.

A voice behind me said incredulously, "Hughes!"

I knew the voice. I turned round with an equal sense of the unexpected. Roberta Cranfield. Wearing a honey-coloured silk dress with the top smothered in pearls and gold thread and her copper hair drawn high with a trickle of ringlets down the back of her neck.

"You look beautiful," I said.

Her mouth opened. "Hughes!"

"Is your father here?"

"No," she said disgustedly. "He wouldn't face it. Nor would Mother. I came with a party of neighbours but I can't say I was enjoying it much until you turned up."

"Why not?"

"You must be joking. Just look around. At a rough guess fifty people are rubber-necking at you. Doesn't it make you cringe inside? Anyway, I've had quite enough of it myself this evening, and I didn't even *see* the damned race, let alone get myself warned off." She stopped. "Come and dance with me. If we're hoisting the flag we may as well do it thoroughly."

"On one condition," I said.

"What's that?"

"You stop calling me Hughes."

"What?"

"Cranfield, I'm tired of being called Hughes."

"Oh!" It had obviously never occurred to her. "Then . . . Kelly . . . how about dancing?"

"Enchanted, Roberta."

She gave me an uncertain look. "I still feel I don't know you."

"You never bothered."

"Nor have you."

That jolted me. It was true. I'd disliked the idea of her. And I didn't really know her at all.

"How do you do?" I said politely. "Come and dance."

We shuffled around in one of those affairs which look like formalized jungle rituals, swaying in rhythm but never touching. Her face was quite calm, remotely smiling. From her composure one would have guessed her to be entirely at ease, not the target of turned heads, assessing glances, half-hidden whispers.

"I don't know how you do it," she said.

"Do what?"

"Look so . . . so matter of fact."

"I was thinking exactly the same about you."

She smiled, eyes crinkling and teeth gleaming, and incredibly in the circumstances she looked happy.

We stuck it for a good ten minutes. Then she said we would go back to her table, and made straight off to it without waiting for me to agree. I didn't think her party would be pleased to have me join them, and half of them weren't.

"Sit down and have a drink, my dear fellow," drawled her host, reaching for a champagne bottle with a languid hand. "And tell me all about the bring-back-Cranfield campaign. Roberta tells me you are working on a spot of reinstatement."

"I haven't managed it yet," I said deprecatingly.

"My dear chap . . ." He gave me an inspecting stare down his nose. He'd been in the Guards, I thought. So many ex-Guards officers looked at the world down the sides of their noses: it came of wearing those blinding hats. He was blond, in his forties, not unfriendly. Roberta called him Bobbie.

The woman the other side of him leaned over and drooped a heavy pink satin bosom perilously near her brimming glass.

"Do tell me," she said, giving me a thorough gaze from heavily made-up eyes, "what made you come?"

"Natural cussedness," I said pleasantly.

"Oh." She looked taken aback. "How extraordinary."

"Joined to the fact that there was no reason why I shouldn't."

"And are you enjoying it?" Bobbie said. "I mean to say, my dear chap, you are somewhat in the position of a rather messily struck-off doctor turning up four days later at the British Medical Association's grandest function."

I smiled. "Quite a parallel."

"Don't needle him, Bobbie," Roberta protested.

Bobbie removed his stare from me and gave it to her instead. "My dear Roberta, this cookie needs no little girls rushing to his defence. He's as tough as old oak."

A disapproving elderly man on the far side of the pink bosom said under his breath, "Thick skinned, you mean."

Bobbie heard, and shook his head. "Vertebral," he said. "Different altogether." He stood up. "Roberta, my dear girl, would you care to dance?"

I stood up with him.

"No need to go, my dear chap. Stay. Finish your drink."

"You are most kind," I said truthfully. "But I really came tonight to have a word with one or two people . . . If you'll excuse me, I'll try to find them."

He gave me an odd formal little inclination of the head, halfway to a bow. "Come back later, if you'd care to."

"Thank you," I said, "very much."

He took Roberta away to dance and I went up the stairs to the balcony which encircled the room. There were tables all round up there too, but in places one could get a good clear view of most people below. I spent some length of time identifying them from the tops of their heads.

There must have been about six hundred there, of whom I knew personally about a quarter. Owners, trainers, jockeys, Stewards, pressmen, two or three of the bigger bookmakers, starters, judges, Clerks of Courses, and all the others, all with their wives and friends and chattering guests.

Kessel was there, hosting a party of twelve almost exactly beneath where I stood. I wondered if his anger had cooled since Monday, and decided if possible not to put it to the test. He had reputedly sent Squelch off to Pat Nikita, a trainer who was a bitter rival of Cranfield's, which had been rubbing it in a bit. The report looked likely to be true, as Pat Nikita was among the party below me.

Cranfield and Nikita regularly claimed each other's horses in selling races and were apt to bid each other up spitefully at auctions. It was a public joke. So in choosing Nikita as his trainer, Kessel was unmistakably announcing worldwide that he believed Cranfield and I had stopped his horse. Hardly likely to help convince that we hadn't.

At one of the most prominent tables, near the dancing space, sat Lord Ferth, talking earnestly to a large lady in pale blue ostrich feathers. All the other chairs round the table were askew and unoccupied, but while I watched the music changed to a latin rhythm, and most of the party drifted back. I knew one or two of them slightly, but not well. The man I was chiefly looking for was not among them.

Two tables away from Lord Ferth sat Edwin Byler, gravely beckoning to the waiter to fill his guests' glasses, too proud of his home-made wealth to lift the bottle himself. His cuddly little wife on the far side of the table was loaded with half the stock of Hatton Garden and was rather touchingly revelling in it.

Not to be going to ride Edwin Byler's string of super horses . . . The wry thrust of regret went deeper than I liked.

There was a rustle behind me and the smell of Roberta's fresh flower scent. I turned towards her.

"Kelly? . . ."

She really looked extraordinarily beautiful.

"Kelly . . . Bobbie suggested that you should take me in to supper."

"That's generous of him."

"He seems to approve of you. He said . . ." She stopped abruptly. "Well, never mind what he said."

We went down the stairs and through an archway to the supper room.

The light there was of a heartier wattage. It didn't do any damage to
Roberta.

Along one wall stretched a buffet table laden with aspic-shining cold
meats and oozing cream gateaux. Roberta said she had dined at Bobbie's
before coming on to the dance and wasn't hungry, but we both collected
some salmon and sat down at one of the twenty or so small tables clus-
tered into half of the room.

Six feet away sat three fellow jockeys resting their elbows among a
debris of empty plates and coffee cups.

"Kelly!" one of them exclaimed in a broad northern voice. "My God.
Kelly. Come over here, you old so and so. Bring the talent with you."

The talent's chin began its familiar upward tilt.

"Concentrate on the character, not the accent," I said.

She gave me a raw look of surprise, but when I stood up and picked
up her plate, she came with me. They made room for us, admired Roberta's appearance, and didn't refer to anyone being warned off. Their girls,
they explained, were powdering their noses, and when the noses reappeared, immaculate, they all smiled goodbye and went back to the ballroom.

"They were kind." She sounded surprised.

"They would be."

She fiddled with her fork, not looking at me. "You said the other day
that my mind was in chains. Was that what you meant . . . that I'm
inclined to judge people by their voices . . . and that it's wrong?"

"Eton's bred its rogues," I said. "Yes."

"Cactus. You're all prickles."

"Original sin exists," I said mildly. "So does original virtue. They both
crop up regardless. No respecters of birth."

"Where did you go to school?"

"In Wales."

"You haven't a Welsh accent. You haven't any accent at all. And that's
odd really, considering you are only . . ." Her voice trailed away and she
looked aghast at her self-betrayal. "Oh dear . . . I'm sorry."

"It's not surprising," I pointed out. "Considering your father. And
anyway, in my own way I'm just as bad. I smothered my Welsh accent
quite deliberately. I used to practise in secret, while I was still at school,
copying the BBC news' announcers. I wanted to be a Civil Servant, and
I was ambitious, and I knew I wouldn't get far if I sounded like the son
of a Welsh farm labourer. So in time this became my natural way of
talking. And my parents despise me for it."

"Parents!" she said despairingly. "Why can we never escape them?
Whatever we are, it is because of *them*. I want to be *me.*" She looked
astonished at herself. "I've never felt like this before. I don't understand . . ."

"Well I do," I said, smiling. "Only it happens to most people around fifteen or sixteen. Rebellion, it's called."

"You're mocking me." But the chin stayed down.

"No."

We finished the salmon and drank coffee. A large, loudly chattering party collected food from the buffet and pushed the two tables next to us together so that they could all sit at one. They were well away on a tide of alcohol and bonhomie, loosened and expansive. I watched them idly. I knew four of them, two trainers, one wife, one owner.

One of the trainers caught sight of me and literally dropped his knife.

"That's Kelly Hughes," he said disbelievingly. The whole party turned round and stared. Roberta drew a breath in distress. I sat without moving.

"What are you doing here?"

"Drinking coffee," I said politely.

His eyes narrowed. Trevor Norse was not amused. I sighed inwardly. It was never good to antagonize trainers, it simply meant one less possible source of income: but I'd ridden for Trevor Norse several times already, and knew that it was practically impossible to please him anyway.

A heavy man, six feet plus, labouring under the misapprehension that size could substitute for ability. He was much better with owners than with horses, tireless at cultivating the one and lazy with the other.

His brainless wife said brightly, "I hear you're paying Dexter's lads' wages, because you're sure you'll get your licence back in a day or two."

"What's all that?" Norse said sharply. "Where did you hear all that nonsense?"

"Everyone's talking about it, darling," she said protestingly.

"Who's everyone?"

She giggled weakly. "I heard it in the ladies, if you must know. But it's quite true, I'm sure it is. Dexter's lads told Daphne's lads in the local pub, and Daphne told Miriam, and Miriam was telling us in the ladies . . ."

"Is it true?" Norse demanded.

"Well, more or less," I agreed.

"Good Lord."

"Miriam said Kelly Hughes says he and Dexter were framed, and that he's finding out who did it." Mrs. Norse giggled at me. "My *dear*, isn't it all such fun."

"Great," I said dryly. I stood up, and Roberta also.

"Do you know Roberta Cranfield?" I said formally, and they all exclaimed over her, and she scattered on them a bright artificial smile, and we went back and tried another dance.

It wasn't altogether a great idea because we were stopped halfway round by Daddy Leeman of the *Daily Witness* who raked me over with avid eyes and yelled above music was it true I was claiming I'd been framed. He had a piercing voice. All the nearby couples turned and stared. Some of them raised sceptical eyebrows at each other.

"I really can't stand a great deal more of this," Roberta said in my ear. "How can you? Why don't you go home now?"

"I'm sorry," I said contritely. "You've been splendid. I'll take you back to Bobbie."

"But you? . . ."

"I haven't done what I came for. I'll stay a bit longer."

She compressed her mouth and started to dance again. "All right. So will I."

We danced without smiling.

"Do you want a tombola ticket?" I asked.

"No." She was astonished.

"You might as well. I want to go down that end of the room."

"Whatever for?"

"Looking for someone. Haven't been down that end at all."

"Oh. All right, then."

She stepped off the polished wood on to the thick dark carpet, and threaded her way to the clear aisle which led down to the gaily decorated tombola stall at the far end of the ballroom.

I looked for the man I wanted, but I didn't see him. I met too many other eyes, most of which hastily looked away.

"I hate them," Roberta said fiercely. "I hate people."

I bought her four tickets. Three of them were blanks. The fourth had a number which fitted a bottle of vodka.

"I don't like it much," she said, holding it dubiously.

"Nor do I."

"I'll give it to the first person who's nice to you."

"You might have to drink it yourself."

We went slowly back down the aisle, not talking.

A thin woman sprang up from her chair as we approached her table and in spite of the embarrassed holding-back clutches of her party managed to force her way out into our path. We couldn't pass her without pushing. We stopped.

"You're Roberta Cranfield, aren't you?" she said. She had a strong-boned face, no lipstick, angry eyes, and stiffly-regimented greying hair. She looked as if she'd had far too much to drink.

"Excuse us," I said gently, trying to go past.

"Oh no you don't," she said. "Not until I've had my say."

"Grace!" wailed a man across the table. I looked at him more closely. Edwin Byler's trainer, Jack Roxford. "Grace, dear, leave it. Sit down, dear," he said.

Grace dear had no such intentions. Grace dear's feelings were far too strong.

"Your father's got exactly what he deserves, my lass, and I can tell you I'm glad about it. Glad." She thrust her face towards Roberta's, glaring like a mad woman. Roberta looked down her nose at her, which I would have found as infuriating as Grace did.

"I'd dance on his grave," she said furiously. "That I would."

"Why?" I said flatly.

She didn't look at me. She said to Roberta, "He's a bloody snob, your father. A bloody snob. And he's got what he deserved. So there. You tell him that."

"Excuse me," Roberta said coldly, and tried to go forwards.

"Oh no you don't." Grace clutched at her arm. Roberta shook her hand off angrily. "Your bloody snob of a father was trying to get Edwin Byler's horses away from us. Did you know that? Did you know that? All those grand ways of his. Thought Edwin would do better in a bigger stable, did he? Oh, I heard what he said. Trying to persuade Edwin he needed a grand top-drawer trainer now, not poor little folk like us, who've won just rows of races for him. Well, I could have laughed my head off when I heard he'd been had up. I'll tell you. Serves him right, I said. What a laugh."

"Grace," said Jack Roxford despairingly. "I'm sorry, Miss Cranfield. She isn't really like this."

He looked acutely embarrassed. I thought that probably Grace Roxford was all too often like this. He had the haunted expression of the for-ever apologizing husband.

"Cheer up then, Mrs. Roxford," I said loudly. "You've got what you want. You're laughing. So why the fury?"

"Eh?" She twisted her head round at me, staggering a fraction. "As for you, Kelly Hughes, you just asked for what you got, and don't give me any of that crap we've been hearing this evening that you were framed, because you know bloody well you weren't. People like you and Cranfield, you think you can get away with murder, people like you. But there's justice somewhere in this world sometimes and you won't forget that in a hurry, will you now, Mr. Clever Dick."

One of the women of the party stood up and tried to persuade her to quieten down, as every ear for six tables around was stretched in her direction. She was oblivious to them. I wasn't.

Roberta said under her breath, "Oh God."

"So you go home and tell your bloody snob of a father," Grace said to her, "that it's a great big laugh him being found out. That's what it is, a great big laugh."

The acutely embarrassed woman friend pulled her arm, and Grace swung angrily round from us to her. We took the brief opportunity and edged away round her back, and as we retreated we could hear her shouting after us, her words indistinct above the music except for "laugh" and "bloody snob."

"She's *awful*," Roberta said.

"Not much help to poor old Jack," I agreed.

"I do hate scenes. They're so messy."

"Do you think all strong emotions are messy?"

"That's not the same thing," she said. "You can have strong emotions without making scenes. Scenes are disgusting."

I sighed. "That one was."

"Yes."

She was walking, I noticed, with her neck stretched very tall, the classic signal to anyone watching that she was not responsible or bowed down or amused at being involved in noise and nastiness. Rosalind, I reflected nostalgically, would probably have sympathetically agreed with dear disturbed Grace, led her off to some quiet mollifying corner, and reappeared with her eating out of her hand. Rosalind had been tempestuous herself and understood uncontrollable feelings.

Unfortunately, at the end of the aisle we almost literally bumped into Kessel, who came in for the murderous glance from Roberta which had been earned by dear Grace. Kessel naturally misinterpreted her expression and spat first.

"You can tell your father that I had been thinking for some time of sending my horses to Pat Nikita, and that this business has made me regret that I didn't do it a long time ago. Pat has always wanted to train for me. I stayed with your father out of a mistaken sense of loyalty, and just look how he repaid me."

"Father has won a great many races for you," Roberta said coldly. "And if Squelch had been good enough to win the Lemonfizz Cup, he would have done."

Kessel's mouth sneered. It didn't suit him.

"As for you, Hughes, it's a disgrace you being here tonight and I cannot think why you were allowed in. And don't think you can fool me by spreading rumours that you are innocent and on the point of proving it. That's all piffle, and you know it, and if you have any ideas you can reinstate yourself with me that way, you are very much mistaken."

He turned his back on us and bristled off, pausing triumphantly to pat Nikita on the shoulder, and looking back to make sure we had noticed. Very small of him.

"There goes Squelch," I said resignedly.

"He'll soon be apologizing and sending him back," she said, with certainty.

"Not a hope. Kessel's not the humble-pie kind. And Pat Nikita will never let go of that horse. Not to see him go back to your father. He'd break him down first."

"Why are people so jealous of each other," she exclaimed.

"Born in them," I said. "And almost universal."

"You have a very poor opinion of human nature." She disapproved.

"An objective opinion. There's as much good as bad."

"You can't be objective about being warned off," she protested.

"Er . . . no," I conceded. "How about a drink?"

She looked instinctively towards Bobbie's table, and I shook my head. "In the bar."

"Oh . . . still looking for someone?"

"That's right. We haven't tried the bar yet."

"Is there going to be another scene?"

"I shouldn't think so."

"All right, then."

We made our way slowly through the crowd. By then the fact that we were there must have been known to almost everyone in the place. Certainly the heads no longer turned in open surprise, but the eyes did, sliding into corners, giving us a surreptitious once-over, probing and hurtful. Roberta held herself almost defiantly straight.

The bar was heavily populated, with cigar smoke lying in a haze over the well-groomed heads and the noise level doing justice to a discotheque. Almost at once through a narrow gap in the cluster I saw him, standing against the far wall, talking vehemently. He turned his head suddenly and looked straight at me, meeting my eyes briefly before the groups between us shifted and closed the line of sight. In those two seconds, however, I had seen his mouth tighten and his whole face compress into annoyance; and he had known I was at the dance, because there was no surprise.

"You've seen him," Roberta said.

"Yes."

"Well . . . who is it?"

"Lord Gowery."

She gasped. "Oh no, Kelly."

"I want to talk to him."

"It can't do any good."

"You never know."

"Annoying Lord Gowery is the last, positively the last way of getting your licence back. Surely you can see that?"

"Yes . . . he's not going to be kind, I don't think. So would you mind very much if I took you back to Bobbie first?"

She looked troubled. "You won't say anything silly? It's Father's licence as well, remember."

"I'll bear it in mind," I said flippantly. She gave me a sharp suspicious glance, but turned easily enough to go back to Bobbie.

Almost immediately outside the bar we were stopped by Jack Roxford, who was hurrying towards us through the throng.

"Kelly," he said, half panting with the exertion. "I just wanted to catch you . . . to say how sorry I am that Grace went off the deep end like that. She's not herself, poor girl . . . Miss Cranfield, I do apologize."

Roberta unbent a little. "That's all right, Mr. Roxford."

"I wouldn't like you to believe that what Grace said . . . all those things about your father . . . is what I think too." He looked from her to me, and back again, the hesitant worry furrowing his forehead. A slight, unaggressive man of about forty-five; bald crown, nervous eyes, permanently worried expression. He was a reasonably good trainer but not enough of a man of the world to have achieved much personal stature. To me, though I had never ridden for him, he had always been friendly, but his restless anxiety-state made him tiring to be with.

"Kelly," he said, "if it's really true that you were both framed, I do sincerely hope that you get your licences back. I mean, I know there's a risk that Edwin will take his horses to your father, Miss Cranfield, but he did tell me this evening that he won't do so now, even if he could . . . But please believe me, I hold no dreadful grudge against either of you, like poor Grace . . . I do hope you'll forgive her."

"Of course, Mr. Roxford," said Roberta, entirely placated. "Please don't give it another thought. And oh!" she added impulsively, "I think you've earned this!" and into his astonished hands she thrust the bottle of vodka.

IX

When I went back towards the bar I found Lord Gowery had come out of it. He was standing shoulder to shoulder with Lord Ferth, both of them watching me walk towards them with faces like thunder.

I stopped four feet away, and waited.

"Hughes," said Lord Gowery for openers, "you shouldn't be here."

"My lord," I said politely. "This isn't Newmarket Heath."

It went down badly. They were both affronted. They closed their ranks.

"Insolence will get you nowhere," Lord Ferth said, and Lord Gowery added, "You'll never get your licence back, if you behave like this."

I said without heat, "Does justice depend on good manners?"

They looked as if they couldn't believe their ears. From their point of view I was cutting my own throat, though I had always myself doubted that excessive meekness got licences restored any quicker than they would have been without it. Meekness in the accused brought out leniency in some judges, but severity in others. To achieve a minimum sentence, the guilty should always bone up on the character of their judge, a sound maxim which I hadn't had the sense to see applied even more to the innocent.

"I would have thought some sense of shame would have kept you away," Lord Ferth said.

"It took a bit of an effort to come," I agreed.

His eyes narrowed and opened again quickly.

Gowery said, "As to spreading these rumours . . . I say categorically that you are not only not on the point of being given your licence back, but that your suspension will be all the longer in consequence of your present behaviour."

I gave him a level stare and Lord Ferth opened his mouth and shut it again.

"It is no rumour that Mr. Cranfield and I are not guilty," I said at length. "It is no rumour that two at least of the witnesses were lying. These are facts."

"Nonsense," Gowery said vehemently.

"What you believe, sir," I said, "doesn't alter the truth."

"You are doing yourself no good, Hughes." Under his heavy authoritative exterior he was exceedingly angry. All I needed was a bore hole and I'd get a gusher.

I said, "Would you be good enough to tell me who suggested to you or the other Stewards that you should seek out and question Mr. Newton-nards?"

There was the tiniest shift in his eyes. Enough for me to be certain. "Certainly not."

"Then will you tell me upon whose instructions the enquiry agent David Oakley visited my flat?"

"I will not." His voice was loud, and for the first time, alarmed.

Ferth looked in growing doubt from one of us to the other.

"What is all this about?" he said.

"Mr. Cranfield and I were indeed wrongly warned off," I said. "Someone sent David Oakley to my flat to fake that photograph. And I believe Lord Gowery knows who it was."

"I most certainly do not," he said furiously. "Do you want to be sued for slander?"

"I have not slandered you, sir."

"You said . . ."

"I said you knew who sent David Oakley. I did not say that you knew the photograph was a fake."

"And it wasn't," he insisted fiercely.

"Well," I said. "It was."

There was a loaded, glaring silence. Then Lord Gowery said heavily, "I'm not going to listen to this," and turned on his heel and dived back into the bar.

Lord Ferth, looking troubled, took a step after him.

I said, "My lord, may I talk to you?" And he stopped and turned back to me and said, "Yes, I think you'd better."

He gestured towards the supper room next door and we went through the archway into the brighter light. Nearly everyone had eaten and gone. The buffet table bore shambled remains and all but two of the small tables were unoccupied. He sat down at one of these and pointed to the chair opposite. I took it, facing him.

"Now," he said. "Explain."

I spoke in a flat calm voice, because emotion was going to repel him where reason might get through. "My lord, if you could look at the Enquiry from my point of view for a minute, it is quite simple. I know that I never had any five hundred pounds or any note from Mr. Cranfield, therefore I am obviously aware that David Oakley was lying. It's unbelievable that the Stewards should have sent him, since the evidence he produced was faked. So someone else did. I thought Lord Gowery might know who. So I asked him."

"He said he didn't know."

"I don't altogether believe him."

"Hughes, that's preposterous."

"Are you intending to say, sir, that men in power positions are infallibly truthful?"

He looked at me without expression in a lengthening silence. Finally he said, as Roberta had done, "Where did you go to school?"

In the usual course of things I kept dead quiet about the type of education I'd had because it was not likely to endear me to either owners or trainers. Still, there was a time for everything, so I told him.

"Coedlant Primary, Tenby Grammar, and LSE."

"LSE . . . you don't mean . . . the London School of Economics?" He looked astonished.

"Yes."

"My God . . ."

I watched while he thought it over. "What did you read there?"

"Politics, philosophy, and economics."

"Then what on earth made you become a jockey?"

"It was almost an accident," I said. "I didn't plan it. When I'd finished my final exams I was mentally tired, so I thought I'd take a sort of paid holiday working on the land . . . I knew how to do that, my father's a farm-hand. I worked at harvesting for a farmer in Devon and every morning I used to ride his 'chasers out at exercise, because I'd ridden most of my life, you see. He had a permit, and he was dead keen. And then his brother, who raced them for him, broke his shoulder at one of the early Devon meetings, and he put me up instead, and almost at once I started winning . . . and then it took hold of me . . . so I didn't get around to being a Civil Servant, as I'd always vaguely intended, and . . . well . . . I've never regretted it."

"Not even now?" he said with irony.

I shook my head. "Not even now."

"Hughes . . ." His face crinkled dubiously. "I don't know what to think. At first I was sure you were not the type to have stopped Squelch deliberately . . . and then there was all that damning evidence. Charlie West saying you had definitely pulled back . . ."

I looked down at the table. I didn't after all want an eye for an eye, when it came to the point.

"Charlie was mistaken," I said. "He got two races muddled up. I did pull back in another race at about that time . . . riding a novice 'chaser with no chance, well back in the field. I wanted to give it a good schooling race. That was what Charlie remembered."

He said doubtfully, "It didn't sound like it."

"No," I agreed. "I've had it out with Charlie since. He might be prepared to admit now that he was talking about the wrong race. If you will ask the Oxford Stewards, you'll find that Charlie said nothing to them directly after the Lemonfizz, when they made their first enquiries, about me not trying. He only said it later, at the Enquiry in Portman Square." Because in between some beguiling seducer had offered him five hundred pounds for the service.

"I see." He frowned. "And what was it that you asked Lord Gowery about Newtonnards?"

"Newtonnards didn't volunteer the information to the Stewards about Mr. Cranfield backing Cherry Pie, but he did tell several bookmaker colleagues. Someone told the Stewards. I wanted to know who."

"Are you suggesting that it was the same person who sent Oakley to your flat?"

"It might be. But not necessarily." I hesitated, looking at him doubtfully.

"What is it?" he said.

"Sir, I don't want to offend you, but would you mind telling me why you sat in at the Enquiry? Why there were four of you instead of three, when Lord Gowery, if you'll forgive me saying so, was obviously not too pleased at the arrangement."

His lips tightened. "You're being uncommonly tactful all of a sudden."

"Yes, sir."

He looked at me steadily. A tall thin man with high cheekbones, strong black hair, hot fiery eyes. A man whose force of character reached out and hit you, so that you'd never forget meeting him. The best ally in the whole 'chasing set up, if I could only reach him.

"I cannot give you my reasons for attending," he said with some reproof.

"Then you had some . . . reservations . . . about how the Enquiry would be conducted?"

"I didn't say that," he protested. But he had meant it.

"Lord Gowery chose Andrew Tring to sit with him at the hearing, and Andrew Tring wants a very big concession from him just now. And he chose Lord Plimborne as the third Steward, and Lord Plimborne continually fell asleep."

"Do you realize what you're saying?" He was truly shocked.

"I want to know how Lord Gowery acquired all that evidence against us. I want to know why the Stewards' Secretaries sent for the wrong film. I want to know why Lord Gowery was so biased, so deaf to our denials, so determined to warn us off."

"That's slanderous . . ."

"I want you to ask him," I finished flatly.

He simply stared.

I said, "He might tell you. He might just possibly tell you. But he'd never in a million years tell *me.*"

"Hughes . . . You surely don't expect . . ."

"That wasn't a straight trial, and he knows it. I'm just asking you to tackle him with it, to see if he will explain."

"You are talking about a much respected man," he said coldly.

"Yes, sir. He's a baron, a rich man, a Steward of long standing. I know all that."

"And you *still* maintain? . . ."

"Yes."

His hot eyes brooded. "He'll have you in Court for this."

"Only if I'm wrong."

"I can't possibly do it," he said, with decision.

"And please, if you have one, use a tape-recorder."

"I told you . . ."

"Yes, sir, I know you did."

He got up from the table, paused as if about to say something, changed his mind, and as I stood up also, turned abruptly and walked sharply away. When he had gone I found that my hands were trembling, and I followed him slowly out of the supper room feeling a battered wreck.

I had either resurrected our licences or driven the nails into them, and only time would tell which.

*   *   *

Bobbie said, "Have a drink, my dear fellow. You look as though you've been clobbered by a steamroller."

I took a mouthful of champagne and thanked him, and watched Roberta swing her body to a compelling rhythm with someone else. The ringlets bounced against her neck. I wondered without disparagement how long it had taken her to pin them on.

"Not the best of evenings for you, old pal," Bobbie observed.

"You never know."

He raised his eyebrows, drawling down his nose, "Mission accomplished?"

"A fuse lit, rather."

He lifted his glass. "To a successful detonation."

"You are most kind," I said formally.

The music changed gear and Roberta's partner brought her back to the table.

I stood up. "I came to say goodbye," I said. "I'll be going now."

"Oh not yet," she exclaimed. "The worst is over. No one's staring any more. Have some fun."

"Dance with the dear girl," Bobbie said, and Roberta put out a long arm and pulled mine, and so I went and danced with her.

"Lord Gowery didn't eat you then?"

"He's scrunching the bones at this minute."

"Kelly! If you've done any damage . . ."

"No omelettes without smashing eggs, love."

The chin went up. I grinned. She brought it down again. Getting quite human, Miss Cranfield.

After a while the hot rhythm changed to a slow smooch, and couples around us went into clinches. Bodies to bodies, heads to heads, eyes shut, swaying in the dimming light. Roberta eyed them coolly and prickled when I put my arms up to gather her in. She danced very straight, with four inches of air between us. Not human enough.

We ambled around in that frigid fashion through three separate wodges of glutinous music. She didn't come any closer, and I did nothing to persuade her, but equally she seemed to be in no hurry to break it up. Composed, cool, off-puttingly gracious, she looked as flawless in the small hours as she had when I'd arrived.

"I'm glad you were here," I said.

She moved her head in surprise. "It hasn't been exactly the best Jockeys' Fund dance of my life . . . but I'm glad I came."

"Next year this will be all over, and everyone will have forgotten."

"I'll dance with you again next year," she said.

"It's a pact."

She smiled, and just for a second a stray beam of light shimmered on some expression in her eyes which I didn't understand.

She was aware of it. She turned her head away, and then detached herself altogether, and gestured that she wanted to go back to the table. I delivered her to Bobbie, and she sat down immediately and began powdering a non-shiny nose.

"Goodnight," I said to Bobbie. "And thank you."

"My dear fellow. Any time."

"Goodnight, Roberta."

She looked up. Nothing in the eyes. Her voice was collected. "Goodnight, Kelly."

I lowered myself into the low-slung burnt-orange car in the park and drove away thinking about her. Roberta Cranfield. Not my idea of a cuddly bed mate. Too cold, too controlled, too proud. And it didn't go with that copper hair, all that rigidity. Or maybe she was only rigid to me because I was a farm labourer's son. Only that, and only a jockey . . . and her father had taught her that jockeys were the lower classes, dear, and don't get your fingers dirty . . .

Kelly, I said to myself, you've a fair-sized chip on your shoulder, old son. Maybe she does think like that, but why should it bother you? And even if she does, she spent most of the evening with you . . . although she was really quite careful not to touch you too much. Well . . . maybe that was because so many people were watching . . . and maybe it was simply that she didn't like the thought of it.

I was on the short cut home that led round the south of Reading, streaking down deserted back roads, going fast for no reason except that speed had become a habit. This car was easily the best I'd ever had, the only one I had felt proud of. Mechanically a masterpiece and with looks to match. Even thirty thousand miles in the past year hadn't dulled the pleasure I got from driving it. Its only fault was that like so many other sports cars it had a totally inefficient heater, which in spite of coaxing and overhauls stubbornly refused to do more than demist the windscreen and raise my toes one degree above frostbite. If kicked, it retaliated with a smell of exhaust.

I had gone to the dance without a coat, and the night was frosty. I shivered and switched on the heater to maximum. As usual, damn all.

There was a radio in the car, which I seldom listened to, and a spare crash helmet, and my five-pound racing saddle which I'd been going to take to Wetherby races.

Depression flooded back. Fierce though the evening had been, in many ways I had forgotten for a while the dreariness of being banned. It could be a long slog now, after what I had said to the Lords Gowery and Ferth. A very long slog indeed. Cranfield wouldn't like the gamble. I wasn't too sure that I could face telling him, if it didn't come off.

Lord Ferth . . . would he or wouldn't he? He'd be torn between loyalty to an equal and a concept of justice. I didn't know him well, enough to be sure which would win. And maybe anyway he would shut everything I'd said clean out of his mind, as too far-fetched and preposterous to bother about.

Bobbie had been great, I thought. I wondered who he was. Maybe one day I'd ask Roberta.

Mrs. Roxford . . . poor dear Grace. What a life Jack must lead . . . Hope he liked vodka . . .

I took an unexpectedly sharp bend far too fast. The wheels screeched when I wrenched the nose round and the car went weaving and skidding for a hundred yards before I had it in control again. I put my foot gingerly back on the accelerator and still had in my mind's eye the solid trunks of the row of trees I had just missed by centimetres.

God, I thought, how could I be so careless. It rocked me. I was a careful driver, even if fast, and I'd never had an accident. I could feel myself sweating. It was something to sweat about.

How stupid I was, thinking about the dance, not concentrating on driving, and going too fast for these small roads. I rubbed my forehead, which felt tense and tight, and kept my speed down to forty.

Roberta had looked beautiful . . . keep your mind on the road, Kelly, for God's sake . . . Usually I drove semi-automatically without having to concentrate every yard of the way. I found myself going slower still, because both my reactions and my thoughts were growing sluggish. I'd drunk a total of about half a glass of champagne all evening, so it couldn't be that.

I was simply going to sleep.

I stopped the car, got out, and stamped about to wake myself up. People who went to sleep at the wheels of sports cars on the way home from dances were not a good risk.

Too many sleepless nights, grinding over my sorry state. Insulting the lions seemed to have released the worst of that. I felt I could now fall unconscious for a month.

I considered sleeping there and then, in the car. But the car was cold and couldn't be heated. I would drive on, I decided, and stop for good if I felt really dozy again. The fresh air had done the trick; I was wide awake and irritated with myself.

The beam of my headlights on the cats' eyes down the empty road was soon hypnotic. I switched on the radio to see if that would hold my attention, but it was all soft and sweet late-night music. Lullaby. I switched it off.

Pity I didn't smoke. That would have helped.

It was a star-clear night with a bright full moon. Ice crystals sparkled like diamond dust on the grass verges, now that I'd left the wooded part behind. Beautiful but unwelcome, because a hard frost would mean no racing tomorrow at Sandown . . . With a jerk I realized that that didn't matter to me any more.

I glanced at the speedometer. Forty. It seemed very fast. I slowed down still further to thirty-five, and nodded owlishly to myself. Anyone would be safe at thirty-five.

The tightness across my forehead slowly developed into a headache. Never mind, only an hour to home, then sleep . . . sleep . . . sleep . . .

It's no good, I thought fuzzily. I'll have to stop and black out for a bit, even if I do wake up freezing, or I'll black out without stopping first, and that will be that.

The next layby, or something like that . . .

I began looking, forgot what I was looking for, took my foot still farther off the accelerator and reckoned that thirty miles an hour was quite safe. Maybe twenty five . . . would be better.

A little farther on there were some sudden bumps in the road surface and my foot slipped off the accelerator altogether. The engine stalled. Car stopped.

Oh well, I thought. That settles it. Ought to move over to the side though. Couldn't see the side. Very odd.

The headache was pressing on my temples, and now that the engine had stopped I could hear a faint ringing in my ears.

Never mind. Never mind. Best to go to sleep. Leave the lights on . . . no one came along that road much . . . not at two in the morning . . . but have to leave the lights on just in case.

Ought to pull in to the side.

Ought to . . .

Too much trouble. Couldn't move my arms properly, anyway, so couldn't possibly do it.

Deep deep in my head a tiny instinct switched itself to emergency.

Something was wrong. Something was indistinctly but appallingly wrong.

Sleep. Must sleep.

Get out, the flickering instinct said. Get out of the car.

Ridiculous.

Get out of the car.

Unwillingly, because it was such an effort, I struggled weakly with the handle. The door swung open. I put one leg out and tried to pull myself up, and was swept by a wave of dizziness. My head was throbbing. This wasn't . . . it couldn't be . . . just ordinary sleep.

Get out of the car . . .

My arms and legs belonged to someone else. They had me on my feet . . . I was standing up . . . didn't remember how I got there. But I was out.

Out.

Now what?

I took three tottering steps towards the back of the car and leant against the rear wing. Funny, I thought, the moonlight wasn't so bright any more.

The earth was trembling.

Stupid. Quite stupid. The earth didn't tremble.

Trembling. And the air was wailing. And the moon was falling on me. Come down from the sky and rushing towards me . . .

Not the moon. A great roaring wailing monster with a blinding moon eye. A monster making the earth tremble. A monster racing to gobble me up, huge and dark and faster than the wind and unimaginably terrifying . . .

I didn't move. Couldn't.

The one-thirty mail express from Paddington to Plymouth ploughed into my sturdy little car and carried its crumpled remains half a mile down the track.

X

I didn't know what had happened. Didn't understand. There was a tremendous noise of tearing metal and a hundred-mile-an-hour whirl of ninety-ton diesel engine one inch away from me, and a thudding catapulting scrunch which lifted me up like a rag doll and toppled me somersaulting through the air in a kaleidoscopic black arc.

My head crashed against a concrete post. The rest of my body felt mangled beyond repair. There were rainbows in my brain, blue, purple, flaming pink, with diamond-bright pin stars. Interesting while it lasted. Didn't last very long. Dissolved into an embracing inferno in which colours got lost in pain.

Up the line the train had screeched to a stop. Lights and voices were coming back that way.

The earth was cold, hard, and damp. A warm stream ran down my face. I knew it was blood. Didn't care much. Couldn't think properly, either. And didn't really want to.

More lights. Lots of lights. Lots of people. Voices.

A voice I knew.

"Roberta, my dear girl, don't look."

"It's Kelly!" she said. Shock. Wicked, unforgettable shock. "It's Kelly." The second time, despair.

"Come away, my dear girl."

She didn't go. She was kneeling beside me. I could smell her scent, and feel her hand on my hair. I was lying on my side, face down. After a while I could see a segment of honey silk dress. There was blood on it.

I said, "You're ruining . . . your dress."

"It doesn't matter."

It helped somehow to have her there. I was grateful that she had stayed. I wanted to tell her that. I tried . . . and meant . . . to say "Roberta." What in fact I said was . . . "Rosalind."

"Oh, Kelly . . ." Her voice held a mixture of pity and distress.

I thought groggily that she would go away, now that I'd made such a silly mistake, but she stayed, saying small things like, "You'll be all right soon," and sometimes not talking at all, but just being there. I didn't know why I wanted her to stay. I remembered that I didn't even like the girl.

All the people who arrive after accidents duly arrived. Police with blue flashing lights. Ambulance waking the neighbourhood with its siren. Bobbie took Roberta away, telling her there was no more she could do. The ambulance men scooped me unceremoniously on to a stretcher and if I thought them rough it was only because every movement brought a scream up as far as my teeth and heaven knows whether any of them got any farther.

By the time I reached the hospital the mists had cleared. I knew what had happened to my car. I knew that I wasn't dying. I knew that Bobbie and Roberta had taken the back-roads detour like I had, and had reached the level crossing not long after me.

What I didn't understand was how I had come to stop on the railway. That crossing had drop-down-fringe gates, and they hadn't been shut.

A young dark-haired doctor with tired dark-ringed eyes came to look at me, talking to the ambulance men.

"He'd just come from a dance," they said. "The police want a blood test."

"Drunk?" said the doctor.

The ambulance men shrugged. They thought it possible.

"No," I said. "It wasn't drink. At least . . ."

They didn't pay much attention. The young doctor stooped over my lower half, feeling the damage with slender gentle fingers. "That hurts? Yes." He parted my hair, looking at my head. "Nothing much up there. More blood than damage." He stood back. "We'll get your pelvis X-rayed. And that leg. Can't tell what's what until after that."

A nurse tried to take my shoes off. I said very loudly, "Don't."

She jumped. The doctor signed to her to stop. "We'll do it under an anaesthetic. Just leave him for now."

She came instead and wiped my forehead.

"Sorry," she said.

The doctor took my pulse. "Why ever did you stop on a level crossing?" he said conversationally. "Silly thing to do."

"I felt . . . sleepy. Had a headache." It didn't sound very sensible.

"Had a bit to drink?"

"Almost nothing."

"At a dance?" He sounded sceptical.

"Really," I said weakly. "I didn't."

He put my hand down. I was still wearing my dinner jacket, though someone had taken off my tie. There were bright scarlet blotches down my white shirt and an unmendable tear down the right side of my black trousers.

I shut my eyes. Didn't do much good. The screaming pain showed no signs of giving up. It had localized into my right side from armpit to toes, with repercussions up and down my spine. I'd broken a good many bones racing, but this was much worse. Much. It was impossible.

"It won't be long now," the doctor said comfortingly. "We'll have you under."

"The train didn't hit me," I said. "I got out of the car . . . I was leaning against the back of it . . . the train hit the car . . . not me."

I felt sick. How long? . . .

"If it had hit you, you wouldn't be here."

"I suppose not . . . I had this thumping headache . . . needed air . . ." Why couldn't I pass out, I thought. People always passed out, when it became unbearable. Or so I'd always believed.

"Have you still got the headache?" he asked clinically.

"It's gone off a bit. Just sore now." My mouth was dry. Always like that, after injuries. The least of my troubles.

Two porters came to wheel me away, and I protested more than was stoical about the jolts. I felt grey. Looked at my hands. They were quite surprisingly red.

X-ray department. Very smooth, very quick. Didn't try to move me except for cutting the zip out of my trousers. Quite enough.

"Sorry," they said.

"Do you work all night?" I asked.

They smiled. On duty, if called.

"Thanks," I said.

Another journey. People in green overalls and white masks, making soothing remarks. Could I face taking my coat off? No? Never mind then.

Needle into vein in back of hand. Marvellous. Oblivion rolled through me in grey and black and I greeted it with a sob of welcome.

The world shuffled back in the usual way, bit by uncomfortable bit, with a middle-aged nurse patting my hand and telling me to wake up dear, it was all over.

I had to admit that my wildest fears were not realized. I still had two legs. One I could move. The other had plaster on. Inside the plaster it gently ached. The scream had died to a whisper. I sighed with relief.

What was the time? Five o'clock, dear.

Where was I? In the recovery ward, dear. Now go to sleep again and when you wake up you'll be feeling much better, you'll see.

I did as she said, and she was quite right.

Mid-morning, a doctor came. Not the same one as the night before. Older, heavier, but just as tired looking.

"You had a lucky escape," he said.

"Yes, I did."

"Luckier than you imagine. We took a blood test. Actually we took two blood tests. The first one for alcohol. With practically negative results. Now this interested us, because who except a drunk would stop a car on a level crossing and get out and lean against it? The casualty doctor told us you swore you hadn't been drinking and that anyway you seemed sober enough to him . . . but that you'd had a bad headache which was now better . . . We gave you a bit of thought, and we looked at those very bright scarlet stains on your shirt . . . and tested your blood again . . . and there it was!" He paused triumphantly.

"What?"

"Carboxyhaemoglobin."

"What?"

"Carbon monoxide, my dear chap. Carbon-monoxide poisoning. Explains everything, don't you see?"

"Oh . . . but I thought . . . with carbon monoxide . . . one simply blacked out."

"It depends. If you got a large dose all at once that would happen, like it does to people who get stuck in snow drifts and leave their engines running. But a trickle, that would affect you more slowly. But it would all be the same in the end, of course. The haemoglobin in the red corpuscles has a greater affinity for carbon monoxide than for oxygen, so it mops up any carbon monoxide you breathe in, and oxygen is disregarded. If the level of carbon monoxide in your blood builds up gradually . . . you get gradual symptoms. Very insidious they are too. The trouble is that it seems that when people feel sleepy they light a cigarette to keep themselves awake, and tobacco smoke itself introduces significant quantities of carbon monoxide into the body, so the cigarette may be the final knock out. Er . . . do you smoke?"

"No." And to think I'd regretted it.

"Just as well. You obviously had quite a dangerous concentration of CO in any case."

"I must have been driving for half an hour . . . maybe forty minutes. I don't really know."

"It's a wonder you stopped safely at all. Much more likely to have crashed into something."

"I nearly did . . . on a corner."

He nodded. "Didn't you smell exhaust fumes?"

"I didn't notice. I had too much on my mind. And the heater burps out exhaust smells sometimes. So I wouldn't take much heed, if it wasn't strong." I looked down at myself under the sheets. "What's the damage?"

"Not much now," he said cheerfully. "You were lucky there too. You had multiple dislocations . . . hip, knee, and ankle. Never seen all three before. Very interesting. We reduced them all successfully. No crushing or fractures, no severed tendons. We don't even think there will be a recurring tendency to dislocate. One or two frayed ligaments round your knee, that's all."

"It's a miracle."

"Interesting case, yes. Unique sort of accident, of course. No direct force involved. We think it might have been air impact . . . that it sort of blew or stretched you apart. Like being on the rack; eh?" He chuckled. "We put plaster on your knee and ankle, to give them a chance to settle, but it can come off in three or four weeks. We don't want you to put weight on your hip yet, either. You can have some physiotherapy. But take it easy for a while when you leave here. There was a lot of spasm in the muscles, and all your ligaments and so on were badly stretched. Give everything time to subside properly before you run a mile." He smiled, which turned halfway through into a yawn. He smothered it apologetically. "It's been a long night . . ."

"Yes," I said.

I went home on Tuesday afternoon in an ambulance with a pair of crutches and instructions to spend most of my time horizontal.

Poppy was still sick. Tony followed my slow progress up the stairs apologizing that she couldn't manage to have me stay, the kids were exhausting her to distraction.

"I'm fine on my own."

He saw me into the bedroom, where I lay down in my clothes on top of the bedspread, as per instructions. Then he made for the whisky and refreshed himself after my labours.

"Do you want anything? I'll fetch you some food, later."

"Thanks," I said. "Could you bring the telephone in here?"

He brought it in and plugged the lead into the socket beside my bed. "OK?"

"Fine," I said.

"That's it, then." He tossed off his drink quickly and made for the door, showing far more haste than usual and edging away from me as though embarrassed.

"Is anything wrong?" I said.

He jumped. "No. Absolutely nothing. Got to get the kids their tea before evening stables. See you later, pal. With the odd crust." He smiled sketchily and disappeared.

I shrugged. Whatever it was that was wrong, he would tell me in time, if he wanted to.

I picked up the telephone and dialled the number of the local garage. Its best mechanic answered.

"Mr. Hughes . . . I heard . . . Your beautiful car." He commiserated genuinely for half a minute.

"Yes," I said. "Look, Derek, is there any way that exhaust gas could get into the car through the heater?"

He was affronted. "Not the way I looked after it. Certainly not."

"I apparently breathed in great dollops of carbon monoxide," I said.

"Not through the heater . . . I can't understand it." He paused, thinking. "They take special care not to let that happen, see? At the design stage. You could only get exhaust gas through the heater if there was a loose or worn gasket on the exhaust manifold *and* a crack or break in the heater tubing *and* a tube connecting the two together, and you can take it from me, Mr. Hughes, there was nothing at all like that on your car. Maintained perfect, it is."

"The heater does sometimes smell of exhaust. If you remember, I did mention it, sometime ago."

"I gave the whole system a thorough check then, too. There wasn't a thing wrong. Only thing I could think of was the exhaust might have eddied forwards from the back of the car when you slowed down, sort of, and got whirled in through the fresh-air intake, the one down beside the heater."

"Could you possibly go and look at my car? At what's left of it? . . ."

"There's a good bit to do here," he said dubiously.

"The police have given me the name of the garage where it is now. Apparently all the bits have to stay there until the insurance people have seen them. But you know the car . . . it would be easier for you to spot anything different with it from when you last serviced it. Could you go?"

"D'you mean," he paused. "You don't mean . . . there might be something . . . well . . . *wrong* with it?"

"I don't know," I said. "But I'd like to find out."

"It would cost you," he said warningly. "It would be working hours."

"Never mind. If you can go, it will be worth it."

"Hang on, then." He departed to consult. Came back. "Yes, all right. The Guvnor says I can go first thing in the morning.

"That's great," I said. "Call me when you get back."

"It couldn't have been a gasket," he said suddenly.

"Why not?"

"You'd have heard it. Very noisy. Unless you had the radio on?"

"No."

"You'd have heard a blown gasket," he said positively. "But there again, if the exhaust was being somehow fed straight into the heater . . . perhaps not. The heater would damp the noise, same as a silencer . . . but I don't see how it could have happened. Well . . . all I can do is take a look."

I would have liked to have gone with him. I put down the receiver and looked gloomily at my right leg. The neat plaster casing stretched from well up my thigh down to the base of my toes, which were currently invisible inside a white hospital theatre sock. A pair of Tony's slacks, though too long by six inches, had slid up easily enough over the plaster, decently hiding it, and as far as looks went, things were passable.

I sighed. The plaster was a bore. They'd designed it somehow so that I found sitting in a chair uncomfortable. Standing and lying down were both better. It wasn't going to stay on a minute longer than I could help, either. The muscles inside it were doing themselves no good in immobility. They would be getting flabby, unfit, wasting away. It would be just too ironic if I got my licence back and was too feeble to ride.

Tony came back at eight with half a chicken. He didn't want to stay, not even for a drink.

"Can you manage?" he said.

"Sure. No trouble."

"Your leg doesn't hurt, does it?"

"Not a flicker," I said. "Can't feel a thing."

"That's all right then." He was relieved; wouldn't look at me squarely; went away.

Next morning, Roberta Cranfield came.

"Kelly?" she called. "Are you in?"

"In the bedroom."

She walked across the sitting-room and stopped in the doorway. Wearing the black-and-white striped fur coat, hanging open. Underneath it, black pants and a stagnant pond-coloured sweater.

"Hullo," she said. "I've brought you some food. Shall I put it in the kitchen?"

"That's pretty good of you."

She looked me over. I was lying, dressed, on top of the bedspread, reading the morning paper. "You look comfortable enough."

"I am. Just bored. Er . . . not now you've come, of course."

"Of course," she agreed. "Shall I make some coffee?"

"Yes, do."

She brought it back in mugs, shed her fur, and sat loose limbed in my bedroom armchair.

"You look a bit better today," she observed.

"Can you get that blood off your dress?"

She shrugged. "I chucked it at the cleaners. They're trying."

"I'm sorry about that . . ."

"Think nothing of it." She sipped her coffee. "I rang the hospital on Saturday. They said you were OK."

"Thanks."

"Why on earth did you stop on the railway?"

"I didn't know it was the railway, until too late."

"But how did you get there, anyway, with the gates down?"

"The gates weren't down."

"They were when we came along," she said. "There were all those lights and people shouting and screaming and we got out of the car to see what it was all about, and someone said the train had hit a car . . . and then I saw you, lying spark out with your face all covered in blood, about ten feet up the line. Nasty. Very nasty. It was, really."

"I'm sorry . . . I'd had a couple of lungfuls of carbon monoxide. What you might call diminished responsibility."

She grinned. "You're some moron."

The gates must have shut after I'd stopped on the line. I hadn't heard them or seen them. I must, I supposed, have been more affected by the gas than I remembered.

"I called you Rosalind," I said apologetically.

"I know." She made a face. "Did you think I was her?"

"No . . . It just came out. I meant to say Roberta."

She unrolled herself from the chair, took a few steps, and stood looking at Rosalind's picture. "She'd have been glad . . . knowing she still came first with you after all this time."

The telephone rang sharply beside me and interrupted my surprise. I picked up the receiver.

"Is that Kelly Hughes?" The voice was cultivated, authoritative, loaded indefinably with power. "This is Wykeham Ferth speaking. I read about your accident in the papers . . . a report this morning says you are now home. I hope . . . you are well?"

"Yes, thank you, my lord."

It was ridiculous, the way my heart had bumped. Sweating palms, too.

"Are you in shape to come to London?"

"I'm . . . I've got plaster on my leg . . . I can't sit in a car very easily, I'm afraid."

"Hm." A pause. "Very well. I will drive down to Corrie instead. It's Harringay's old place, isn't it?"

"That's right. I live in a flat over the yard. If you walk into the yard from the drive, you'll see a green door with a brass letter box in the far corner. It won't be locked. There are some stairs inside. I live up there."

"Right," he said briskly. "This afternoon? Good. Expect me at . . . er . . . four o'clock. Right?"

"Sir . . ." I began.

"Not now, Hughes. This afternoon."

I put the receiver down slowly. Six hours' suspense. Damn him.

"What an absolutely heartless letter," Roberta exclaimed.

I looked at her. She was holding the letter from my parents, which had been under Rosalind's photograph.

"I dare say I shouldn't have been so nosey as to read it," she said unrepentantly.

"I dare say not."

"How *can* they be so beastly?"

"They're not really."

"This sort of thing always happens when you get one bright son in a family of twits," she said disgustedly.

"Not always. Some bright sons handle things better than others."

"Stop clobbering yourself."

"Yes, ma'am."

"Are you going to stop sending them money?"

"No. All they can do about that is not spend it . . . or give it to the local cats' and dogs' home."

"At least they had the decency to see they couldn't take your money *and* call you names."

"Rigidly moral man, my father," I said. "Honest to the last farthing. Honest for its own sake. He taught me a lot that I'm grateful for."

"And that's why this business hurts him so much?"

"Yes."

"I've never . . . Well, I know you'll despise me for saying it . . . but I've never thought about people like your father before as . . . well . . . *people.*"

"If you're not careful," I said, "those chains will drop right off."

She turned away and put the letter back under Rosalind's picture.

"Which university did you go to?"

"London. Starved in a garret on a grant. Great stuff."

"I wish . . . how odd . . . I wish I'd trained for something. Learned a job."

"It's hardly too late," I said, smiling.

"I'm nearly twenty. I didn't bother much at school with exams . . . no one made us. Then I went to Switzerland for a year, to a finishing school . . . and since then I've just lived at home . . . What a waste!"

"The daughters of the rich are always at a disadvantage," I said solemnly.

"Sarcastic beast."

She sat down again in the armchair and told me that her father really seemed to have snapped out of it at last, and had finally accepted a dinner invitation the night before. All the lads had stayed on. They spent most of their time playing cards and football, as the only horses left in the yard were four half-broken two-year-olds and three old 'chasers recovering from injuries. Most of the owners had promised to bring their horses back at once, if Cranfield had his licence restored in the next few weeks.

"What's really upsetting Father now is hope. With the big Cheltenham meeting only a fortnight away, he's biting his nails about whether he'll get Breadwinner back in time for him to run in his name in the Gold Cup."

"Pity Breadwinner isn't entered in the Grand National. That would give us a bit more leeway."

"Would your leg be right in time for the Gold Cup?"

"If I had my licence, I'd saw the plaster off myself."

"Are you any nearer . . . with the licences?"

"Don't know."

She sighed. "It was a great dream while it lasted. And you won't be able to do much about it now."

She stood up and came over and picked up the crutches which were lying beside the bed. They were black tubular metal with elbow supports and hand grips.

"These are much better than those old fashioned under-the-shoulder affairs," she said. She fitted the crutches round her arms and swung around the room a bit with one foot off the floor. "Pretty hard on your hands, though."

She looked unselfconscious and intent. I watched her. I remembered the revelation it had been in my childhood when I first wondered what it was like to be someone else.

Into this calm sea Tony appeared with a wretched face and a folded paper in his hand.

"Hi," he said, seeing Roberta. A very gloomy greeting.

He sat down in the armchair and looked at Roberta standing balanced on the crutches with one knee bent. His thoughts were not where his eyes were.

"What is it, then?" I said. "Out with it."

"This letter . . . came yesterday," he said heavily.

"It was obvious last night that something was the matter."

"I couldn't show it to you then, not straight out of hospital. And I don't know what to do, Kelly pal, sure enough I don't."

"Let's see, then."

He handed me the paper worriedly. I opened it up. A brief letter from the racing authorities. Bang bang, both barrels.

Dear Sir,

It has been brought to our attention that a person warned off Newmarket Heath is living as a tenant in your stable yard. This is contrary to the regulations, and you should remedy the situation as soon as possible. It is perhaps not necessary to warn you that your own training licence might have to be reviewed if you should fail to take the steps suggested.

"Sods," Tony said forcefully. "Bloody sods."

XI

Derek from the garage came while Roberta was clearing away the lunch she had stayed to cook. When he rang the door bell she went downstairs to let him in.

He walked hesitatingly across the sitting-room looking behind him to see if his shoes were leaving dirty marks and out of habit wiped his hands down his trousers before taking the one I held out to him.

"Sit down," I suggested. He looked doubtfully at the khaki velvet armchair, but in the end lowered himself gingerly into it. He looked perfectly clean. No grease, no filthy overalls, just ordinary slacks and sports jacket. He wasn't used to it.

"You all right?" he said.

"Absolutely."

"If you'd been in that car . . ." He looked sick at what he was thinking, and his vivid imagination was one of the things which made him a reliable mechanic. He didn't want death on his conscience. Young, fair haired, diffident, he kept most of his brains in his fingertips and outside of cars used the upstairs lot sparingly.

"You've never seen nothing like it," he said. "You wouldn't know it was a car, you wouldn't straight. It's all in little bits . . . I mean, like, bits of metal that don't look as if they were ever part of anything. Honestly. It's like twisted shreds of stuff." He swallowed. "They've got it collected up in tin baths."

"The engine too?"

"Yeah. Smashed into fragments. Still, I had a look. Took me a long time, though, because everything is all jumbled up, and honest you can't tell what anything used to be. I mean, I didn't think it was a bit of exhaust manifold that I'd picked up, not at first, because it wasn't any shape that you'd think of."

"You found something?"

"Here." He fished in his trouser pocket. "This is what it was all like. This is a bit of the exhaust manifold. Cast iron, that is, you see, so of course it was brittle, sort of, and it had shattered into bits. I mean, it wasn't sort of crumpled up like all the aluminium and so on. It wasn't bent, see, it was just in bits."

"Yes, I do see," I said. The anxious lines on his forehead dissolved when he saw that he had managed to tell me what he meant. He came over and put the small black jagged-edged lump into my hands. Heavy for its size. About three inches long. Asymmetrically curved. Part of the side wall of a huge tube.

"As far as I can make out, see," Derek said, pointing, "it came from about where the manifold narrows down to the exhaust pipe, but really it might be anywhere. There were quite a few bits of manifold, when I looked, but I couldn't see the bit that fits into this, and I dare say it's still rusting away somewhere along the railway line. Anyway, see this bit here . . ." He pointed a stubby finger at a round dent in part of one edge. "That's one side of a hole that was bored in the manifold wall. Now don't get me wrong, there's quite a few holes might have been drilled through the wall. I mean, some people have exhaust-gas temperature gauges stuck into the manifold . . . and other gauges too. Things like that. Only, see, there weren't no gauges in your manifold, now, were there?"

"You tell me," I said.

"There weren't, then. Now you couldn't really say what the hole was for, not for certain you couldn't. But as far as I know, there weren't any holes in your manifold last time I did the service."

I fingered the little semi-circular dent. No more than a quarter of an inch across.

"However did you spot something so small?" I asked.

"Dunno, really. Mind you, I was there a good couple of hours, picking through those tubs. Did it methodical, like. Since you were paying for it and all."

"Is it a big job . . . drilling a hole this size through an exhaust manifold. Would it take long?"

"Half a minute, I should think."

"With an electric drill?" I asked.

"Oh yeah, sure. If you did it with a hand drill, then it would take five minutes. Say nearer eight or ten, to be on the safe side."

"How many people carry drills around in their tool kits?"

"That, see, it depends on the chap. Now some of them carry all sorts of stuff in their cars. Proper work benches, some of them. And then others, the tool kit stays strapped up fresh from the factory until the car's dropping to bits."

"People do carry drills, then?"

"Oh yeah, sure. Quite a lot do. Hand drills, of course. You wouldn't have much call for an electric drill, not in a tool kit, not unless you did a lot of repairs, like, say on racing cars."

He went and sat down again. Carefully, as before.

"If someone drilled a hole this size through the manifold, what would happen?"

"Well, honestly, nothing much. You'd get exhaust gas out through the engine, and you'd hear a good lot of noise, and you might smell it in the car, but it would sort of blow away, see, it wouldn't come in through the heater. To do that, like I said before, you'd have to put some tubing into the hole there and then stick the other end of the tubing into the heater. Mind you that would be pretty easy, you wouldn't need a drill. Some heater tubes are really only cardboard."

"Rubber tubing from one end to the other?" I suggested.

He shook his head. "No. Have to be metal. Exhaust gas, that's very hot. It'd melt anything but metal."

"Do you think anyone could do all that on the spur of the moment?"

He put his head on one side, considering. "Oh sure, yeah. If he'd got a drill. Like, say the first other thing he needs is some tubing. Well, he's only got to look around for that. Lots lying about, if you look. The other day, I used a bit of a kiddy's old cycle frame, just the job it was. Right, you get the tube ready first and then you fit a drill nearest the right size, to match. And Bob's your uncle."

"How long, from start to finish?"

"Fixing the manifold to the heater? Say, from scratch, including maybe having to cast around for a bit of tube, well, at the outside half an hour. A quarter, if you had something all ready handy. Only the drilling would take any time, see? The rest would be like stealing candy from a baby."

Roberta appeared in the doorway shrugging herself into the stripy coat. Derek stood up awkwardly and didn't know where to put his hands. She smiled at him sweetly and unseeingly and said to me, "Is there anything else you want, Kelly?"

"No. Thank you very much."

"Think nothing of it. I'll see . . . I might come over again tomorrow."

"Fine," I said.

"Right."

She nodded, smiled temperately, and made her usual poised exit. Derek's comment approached, "Cor."

"I suppose you didn't see any likely pieces of tube in the wreckage?" I asked.

"Huh?" He tore his eyes away with an effort from the direction

Roberta had gone. "No, like it was real bad. Lots of bits, you couldn't have told what they were. I never seen anything like it. Sure, I seen crashes, stands to reason. Different, this was." He shivered.

"Did you have any difficulty with being allowed to search?"

"No, none. They didn't seem all that interested in what I did. Just said to help myself. 'Course, I told them it was my car, like. I mean, that I looked after it. Mind you, they were right casual about it, anyway, because when I came away they were letting this other chap have a good look too."

"Which other chap?"

"Some fellow. Said he was an insurance man, but he didn't have a notebook."

I felt like saying Huh? too. I said, "Notebook?"

"Yeah, sure, insurance men, they're always crawling round our place looking at wrecks and never one without a notebook. Write down every blessed detail, they do. But this other chap, looking at your car, he didn't have any notebook."

"What did he look like?"

He thought.

"That's difficult, see. He didn't look like anything, really. Medium, sort of. Not young and not old really either. A nobody sort of person, really."

"Did he wear sunglasses?"

"No. He had a hat on, but I don't know if he had ordinary glasses. I can't actually remember. I didn't notice that much."

"Was he looking through the wreckage as if he knew what he wanted?"

"Uh . . . don't know, really. Strikes me he was a bit flummoxed, like, finding it was all in such small bits."

"He didn't have a girl with him?"

"Nope." He brightened. "He came in a Volkswagen, an oldish grey one."

"Thousands of those about," I said.

"Oh yeah, sure. Er . . . was this chap important?"

"Only if he was looking for what you found."

He worked it out.

"Cripes," he said.

Lord Ferth arrived twenty minutes after he'd said, which meant that I'd been hopping round the flat on my crutches for half an hour, unable to keep still.

He stood in the doorway into the sitting-room holding a briefcase and bowler hat in one hand and unbuttoning his short fawn overcoat with the other.

"Well, Hughes," he said. "Good afternoon."

"Good afternoon, my lord."

He came right in, shut the door behind him, and put his hat and case on the oak chest beside him.

"How's the leg?"

"Stagnating," I said. "Can I get you some tea . . . coffee . . . or a drink?"

"Nothing just now . . ." He laid his coat on the chest and picked up the briefcase again, looking round him with the air of surprise I was used to in visitors. I offered him the green armchair with a small table beside it. He asked where I was going to sit.

"I'll stand," I said. "Sitting's difficult."

"But you don't stand all day!"

"No. Lie on my bed, mostly."

"Then we'll talk in your bedroom."

We went through the door at the end of the sitting-room and this time he murmured aloud.

"Whose flat is this?" he asked.

"Mine."

He glanced at my face, hearing the dryness in my voice. "You resent surprise?"

"It amuses me."

"Hughes . . . it's a pity you didn't join the Civil Service. You'd have gone all the way."

I laughed. "There's still time . . . Do they take in warned-off jockeys at the Administrative Grade?"

"So you can joke about it?"

"It's taken nine days. But yes, just about."

He gave me a long straight assessing look, and there was a subtle shift somewhere in both his manner to me and in basic approach, and when I shortly understood what it was I was shaken, because he was taking me on level terms, level in power and understanding and experience: and I wasn't level.

Few men in his position would have thought that this course was viable, let alone chosen it. I understood the compliment. He saw, too, that I did, and I knew later that had there not been this fundamental change of ground, this cancellation of the Steward-jockey relationship, he would not have said to me all that he did. It wouldn't have happened if he hadn't been in my flat.

He sat down in the khaki velvet armchair, putting the briefcase carefully on the floor beside him. I took the weight off my crutches and let the bed springs have a go.

"I went to see Lord Gowery," he said neutrally. "And I can see no reason not to tell you straight away that you and Dexter Cranfield will have your warning off rescinded within the next few days."

"Do you mean it?" I exclaimed. I tried to sit up. The plaster inter-vened.

Lord Ferth smiled. "As I see it, there is no alternative. There will be a quiet notice to that effect in next week's Calendar."

"That is, of course," I said, "all you need to tell me."

He looked at me levelly. "True. But not all you want to know."

"No."

"No one has a better right . . . and yet you will have to use your discretion about whether you tell Dexter Cranfield."

"All right."

He sighed, reached down to open the briefcase, and pulled out a neat little tape-recorder.

"I did try to ignore your suggestion. Succeeded, too, for a while. How-ever . . ." He paused, his fingers hovering over the controls. "This conver-sation took place late on Monday afternoon, in the sitting-room of Lord Gowery's flat near Sloane Square. We were alone . . . you will see that we were alone. He knew, though, that I was making a recording." He still hesitated. "Compassion. That's what you need. I believe you have it."

"Don't con me," I said.

He grimaced. "Very well."

The recording began with the self-conscious platitudes customary in front of microphones, especially when no one wants to take the first dive into the deep end. Lord Ferth had leapt, eventually.

"Norman, I explained why we must take a good look at this Enquiry."

"Hughes is being ridiculous. Not only ridiculous, but downright slan-derous. I don't understand why you should take him seriously." Gowery sounded impatient.

"We have to, even if only to shut him up." Lord Ferth looked across the room, his hot eyes gleaming ironically. The recording ploughed on, his voice like honey. "You know perfectly well, Norman, that it will be better all round if we can show there is nothing whatever in these allegations he is spreading around. Then we can emphatically confirm the suspension and squash all the rumours."

Subtle stuff. Lord Gowery's voice grew easier, assured now that Ferth was still an ally. As perhaps he was. "I do assure you Wykeham, that if I had not sincerely believed that Hughes and Dexter Cranfield were guilty, I would not have warned them off."

There was something odd about that. Both Ferth and Gowery had thought so too, as there were several seconds of silence on the tape.

"But you do still believe it?" Ferth said eventually.

"Of course." He was emphatic. "Of course I do." Much too emphatic.

"Then . . . er . . . taking one of Hughes' questions first . . . How did it come about that Newtonnards was called to the Enquiry?"

"I was informed that Cranfield had backed Cherry Pie with him."

"Yes . . . but who informed you?"

Gowery didn't reply.

Ferth's voice came next, with absolutely no pressure in it.

"Um . . . Have you any idea how we managed to show the wrong film of Hughes racing at Reading?"

Gowery was on much surer ground. "My fault, I'm afraid. I asked the Secretaries to write off for the film of the last race. Didn't realize there were seven races. Careless of me, I'll admit. But of course, as it was the wrong film, it was irrelevant to the case."

"Er . . ." said Lord Ferth. But he hadn't yet been ready to argue. He cleared his throat and said, "I suppose you thought it would be relevant to see how Hughes had ridden Squelch last time out."

After another long pause Gowery said, "Yes."

"But in the event we didn't show it."

"No."

"Would we have shown it if, after having sent for it, we found that the Reading race bore out entirely Hughes' assertion that he rode Squelch in the Lemonfizz in exactly the same way as he always did?"

More silence. Then he said quietly, "Yes," and he sounded very troubled.

"Hughes asked at the Enquiry that we should show the right film," Ferth said.

"I'm sure he didn't."

"I've been reading the transcript. Norman, I've been reading and re-reading that transcript all weekend and frankly, that is why I'm here. Hughes did in fact suggest that we should show the right film, presumably because he knew it would support his case . . ."

"Hughes was guilty!" Gowery broke in vehemently. "Hughes was guilty. I had no option but to warn him off."

Lord Ferth pressed the stop button on the tape-recorder.

"Tell me," he said, "what you think of that last statement?"

"I think," I said slowly, "that he did believe it. Both from that statement and from what I remember of the Enquiry. His certainty that day shook me. He believed me guilty so strongly that he was stone deaf to anything which looked even remotely likely to assault his opinion."

"That was your impression?"

"Overpowering," I said.

Lord Ferth took his lower lip between his teeth and shook his head, but I gathered it was at the general situation, not at me. He pressed the start button again. His voice came through, precise, carefully without emotion, gentle as Vaseline.

"Norman, about the composition of the Enquiry . . . the members of the Disciplinary Committee who sat with you . . . What guided you to choose Andrew Tring and old Plimborne?"

"What guided me?" He sounded astonished at the question. "I haven't any idea."

"I wish you'd cast back."

"I can't see that it has any relevance . . . but let's see . . . I suppose I had Tring in my mind anyway, as I'm in the middle of some business negotiations with him. And Plimborne . . . well, I just saw him snoozing away in the Club. I was talking to him later in the lobby, and I asked him just on the spur of the moment to sit with me. I don't see the point of your asking."

"Never mind. It doesn't matter. Now . . . about Charlie West. I can see that of course you would call the rider of the third horse to give evidence. And it is clear from the transcript that you knew what the evidence would be. However, at the preliminary enquiry at Oxford, West said nothing at all about Hughes having pulled his horse back. I've consulted all three of the Oxford Stewards this morning. They confirm that West did not suggest it at the time. He asserted it, however, at the Enquiry, and you knew what he was going to say, so . . . er . . . how did you know?"

More silence.

Ferth's voice went on a shade anxiously. "Norman, if you instructed a Stipendiary Steward to interview West privately and question him further, for heaven's sake say so. These jockeys stick together. It is perfectly reasonable to believe that West wouldn't speak up against Hughes to begin with, but might do so if pressed with questions. Did you send a Stipendiary?"

Gowery said faintly, "No."

"Then how did you know what West was going to say?"

Gowery didn't answer. He said instead, "I did instruct a Stipendiary to look up all the races in which Cranfield had run two horses and compile me a list of all the occasions when the lesser-backed had won. And as you know, it is the accepted practice to bring up everything in a jockey's past history at an Enquiry. It was a perfectly normal procedure."

"I'm not saying it wasn't," Ferth's voice said, puzzled.

Ferth stopped the recorder and raised his eyebrows at me.

"What d'you make of *that?*"

"He's grabbing for a rock in a quicksand."

He sighed, pressed the starter again and Gowery's voice came back.

"It was all there in black and white . . . It was quite true . . . they'd been doing it again and again."

"What do you mean, it was quite true? Did someone *tell* you they'd been doing it again and again?"

More silence. Gowery's rock was crumbling.

Again Ferth didn't press him. Instead he said in the same unaccusing way, "How about David Oakley?"

"Who?"

"David Oakley. The enquiry agent who photographed the money in Hughes' flat. Who suggested that he should go there?"

No answer.

Ferth said with the first faint note of insistence, "Norman, you really must give some explanation. Can't you see that all this silence just won't do? We *have* to have some answers if we are going to squash Hughes' rumours."

Gowery reacted with defence in his voice. "The evidence against Cranfield and Hughes was collected. What does it matter who collected it?"

"It matters because Hughes asserts that much of it was false."

"No," he said fiercely. "It was not false."

"Norman," Ferth said, "is that what you believe . . . or what you *want* to believe?"

"Oh . . ." Gowery's exclamation was more of anguish than surprise. I looked sharply across at Ferth. His dark eyes were steady on my face. His voice went on, softer again. Persuasive.

"Norman, was there any reason why you *wanted* Cranfield and Hughes warned off?"

"No." Half a shout. Definitely a lie.

"Any reason why you should go so far as to manufacture evidence against them, if none existed?"

"Wykeham!" He was outraged. "How can you say that! You are suggesting . . . You are suggesting . . . something so dishonourable . . ."

Ferth pressed the stop button. "Well?" he said challengingly.

"That was genuine," I said. "He didn't manufacture it himself. But then I never thought he did. I just wanted to know where he got it from."

Ferth nodded. Pressed the start again.

His voice. "My dear Norman, you lay yourself open to such suggestions if you will not say how you came by all the evidence. Do you not see? If you will not explain how you came by it, you cannot be too surprised if you are thought to have procured it yourself."

"The evidence was genuine!" he asserted. A rearguard action.

"You are still trying to convince yourself that it was."

"No! It was."

"Then where did it come from?"

Gowery's back was against the wall. I could see from the remembered emotion twisting Ferth's face that this had been a saddening and perhaps embarrassing moment.

"I was sent," said Gowery with difficulty, "a package. It contained

. . . various statements . . . and six copies of the photograph taken in Hughes' flat."

"Who sent it to you?"

Gowery's voice was very low. "I don't know."

"You don't know?" Ferth was incredulous. "You warned two men off on the strength of it, and you don't know where it came from?"

A miserable assenting silence.

"You just accepted all that so-called evidence on its face value?"

"It was all true." He clung to it.

"Have you still got that package?"

"Yes."

"I'd like to see it." A touch of iron in Ferth's voice.

Gowery hadn't argued. There were sounds of moving about, a drawer opening and closing, a rustling of papers.

"I see," Ferth said slowly. "These papers do, in fact, look very convincing."

"Then you see why I acted on them," Gowery said eagerly, with a little too much relief.

"I can see why you should consider doing so . . . after making a careful check."

"I did check."

"To what extent?"

"Well . . . the package only came four days before the Enquiry. On the Thursday before. I had the Secretaries send out the summonses to Newtonnards, Oakley, and West immediately. They were asked to confirm by telegram that they would be attending, and they all did so. Newtonnards was asked to bring his records for the Lemonfizz Cup. And then of course I asked a Stipendiary to ask the Totalizator people if anyone had backed Cherry Pie substantially, and he collected those affidavits . . . the ones we produced at the Enquiry. There was absolutely no doubt whatsoever that Cranfield had backed Cherry Pie. He lied about it at the Enquiry. That made it quite conclusive. He was entirely guilty, and there was no reason why I should not warn him off."

Ferth stopped the recorder. "What do you say to that?" he asked.

I shrugged. "Cranfield did back Cherry Pie. He was stupid to deny it, but admitting it was, as he saw it, cutting his own throat. He told me that he backed him—through this unidentified friend—with Newtonnards an on the Tote, and not with his normal bookmaker, because he didn't want Kessel to know, as Kessel and the bookmaker are tattleswapping buddies. He in fact put a hundred pounds on Cherry Pie because he thought the horse might be warming up to give everyone a surprise. He also put two hundred and fifty pounds on Squelch, because reason suggested that *he* would win. And where is the villainy in that?"

Ferth looked at me levelly. "You didn't know he had backed Cherry Pie, not at the Enquiry."

"I tackled him with it afterwards. It had struck me by then that that had to be true, however hard he had denied it. Newtonnards might have lied or altered his books, but no one can argue against Tote tickets."

"That was one of the things which convinced me too," he admitted.

He started the recorder. He himself was speaking and now there was a distinct flavour in his voice of cross examination. The whole interview moved suddenly into the shape of an Enquiry of its own. "This photograph . . . didn't it seem at all odd to you?"

"Why should it?" Gowery said sharply.

"Didn't you ask yourself how it came to be taken?"

"No."

"Hughes says Oakley took the money and the note with him and simply photographed them in his flat."

"No."

"How can you be sure?" Ferth pounced on him.

"No!" Gowery said again. There was a rising note in his voice, the sound of pressure approaching blow-up.

"Who sent Oakley to Hughes' flat?"

"I've told you, I don't know."

"But you're sure that is a genuine photograph?"

"Yes. Yes it is."

"You are sure beyond doubt?" Ferth insisted.

"Yes!" The voice was high, the anxiety plain, the panic growing. Into this screwed up moment Ferth dropped one intense word, like a bomb.

"Why?"

XII

The tape ran on for nearly a minute. When Gowery finally answered his voice was quite different. Low, broken up, distressed to the soul.

"It had . . . to be true. I said at first . . . I couldn't warn them off if they weren't guilty . . . and then the package came . . . and it was such a relief . . . they really were guilty . . . I could warn them off . . . and everything would be all right."

My mouth opened. Ferth watched me steadily, his eyes narrowed with the pity of it.

Gowery went on compulsively. Once started, he needed to confess.

"If I tell you . . . from the beginning . . . perhaps you will understand. It began the day after I was appointed to substitute for the Disciplinary Steward at the Cranfield-Hughes Enquiry. It's ironic to think of it now, but I was quite pleased to be going to do it . . . and then . . . and then . . ." He paused and took an effortful control of his voice. "Then, I had a telephone call." Another pause. "This man said . . . said . . . I must warn Cranfield off." He cleared his throat. "I told him I would do no such thing, unless Cranfield was guilty. Then he said . . . then he said . . . that he knew things about me . . . and he would tell everyone . . . if I didn't warn Cranfield off. I told him I couldn't warn him off if he wasn't guilty . . . and you see I didn't think he *was* guilty. I mean, racehorses are so unpredictable, and I saw the Lemonfizz myself and although after that crowd demonstration it was obvious the Stewards would have Cranfield and Hughes in, I was surprised when they referred it to the Disciplinary Committee . . . I thought that there must have been circumstances that I didn't know of . . . and then I was asked to take the Enquiry . . . and I had an open mind . . . I told the man on the telephone that no threats could move me from giving Cranfield a fair judgement."

Less jelly in his voice while he remembered that first strength. It didn't last.

"He said . . . in that case . . . I could expect . . . after the Enquiry . . . if Cranfield got off . . . that my life wouldn't be worth living . . . I would have to resign from the Jockey Club . . . and everyone would know . . . And I said again that I would not warn Cranfield off unless I was convinced of his guilt, and that I would not be blackmailed, and I put down the receiver and cut him off."

"And then," Ferth suggested, "you began to worry?"

"Yes." Little more than a whisper.

"What exactly did he threaten to publish?"

"I can't . . . can't tell you. Not criminal . . . not a matter for the police . . . but . . ."

"But enough to ruin you socially?"

"Yes . . . I'm afraid so . . . yes, completely."

"But you stuck to your guns?"

"I was desperately worried . . . I couldn't . . . how could I? . . . take away Cranfield's livelihood just to save myself . . . It would have been dishonourable . . . and I couldn't see myself living with it . . . and in any case I couldn't just warn him off, just like that, if there was no proof he was guilty . . . So I did worry . . . couldn't sleep . . . or eat . . ."

"Why didn't you ask to be relieved of the Enquiry?"

"Because he told me . . . if I backed out . . . it would count the same with him as letting Cranfield off . . . so I had to go on, just in case some proof turned up."

"Which it did," Ferth said drily. "Conveniently."

"Oh . . . " Again the anguish. "I didn't realize . . . I didn't indeed . . . that it might have been the blackmailer who had sent the package. I didn't wonder very much who had sent it. It was release . . . that's all

I could see . . . it was a heaven-sent release from the most unbearable . . . I didn't question . . . I just believed it . . . believed it absolutely . . . and I was so grateful . . . so grateful . . ."

Four days before the Enquiry, that package had come. He must have been sweating for a whole week, taking a long bleak look at the wilderness. Send a St. Bernard to a dying mountaineer and he's unlikely to ask for the dog licence.

"When did you begin to doubt?" Ferth said calmly.

"Not until afterwards. Not for days. It was Hughes . . . at the dance. You told me he was insisting he'd been framed and was going to find out who . . . and then he asked me directly who had sent Oakley to his flat . . . and it . . . Wykeham, it was *terrible*. I realized . . . what I'd done. Inside, I did know . . . but I couldn't admit to it myself . . . I shut it away . . . they *had* to be guilty . . ."

There was another long silence. Then Gowery said, "You'll see to it . . . that they get their licences back?"

"Yes," Ferth said.

"I'll resign . . ." He sounded desolate.

"From the Disciplinary Committee, I agree," Ferth said reasonably. "As to the rest . . . we will see."

"Do you think the . . . the blackmailer . . . will tell . . . everyone . . . anyway, when Cranfield has his licence back?"

"He would have nothing to gain."

"No, but . . ."

"There are laws to protect you."

"They couldn't."

"What does he in fact have over you?"

"I . . . I . . . oh God." The tape stopped abruptly, cutting off words that were disintegrating into gulps.

Ferth said, "I switched it off. He was breaking down. One couldn't record that."

"No."

"He told me what it was he was being blackmailed about. I think I am prepared to tell you also, although he would hate it if he knew. But you only."

"Only," I said. "I won't repeat it."

"He told me . . ." His nose wrinkled in distaste. "He told me that he has . . . he suffers from . . . unacceptable sexual appetites. Not homosexual. Perhaps that would have been better . . . simpler . . . he wouldn't nowadays have been much reviled for that. No. He says he belongs to a sort of club where people like him can gratify themselves fairly harmlessly, as they are all there because they enjoy . . . in varying forms . . . the same thing." He stopped. He was embarrassed.

"Which is what?" I said matter-of-factly.

He said, as if putting a good yard of clean air between himself and the world, "Flagellation."

"That old thing!" I said.

"What?"

"The English disease. Shades of Fanny Hill. Sex tangled up with self-inflicted pain, like nuns with their little disciplines and sober citizens paying a pound a lash to be whipped."

"Kelly!"

"You must have read their coy little advertisements? 'Correction given.' That's what it's all about. More widespread than most people imagine. Starts with husbands spanking their wives regularly before they bed them, and carries right on up to the parties where they all dress up in leather and have a right old orgy. I don't actually understand why anyone should get fixated on leather or rubber or hair, or on those instead of anything else. Why not coal, for instance . . . or silk? But they do, apparently."

"In this case . . . leather."

"Boots and whips and naked bosoms?"

Ferth shook his head in disbelief. "You take it so coolly."

"Live and let live," I said. "If that's what they feel compelled to do . . . why stop them? As he said, they're not harming anyone, if they're in a club where everyone else is the same."

"But for a Steward," he protested. "A member of the Disciplinary Committee!"

"Gives you pause," I agreed.

He looked horrified. "But there would be nothing sexual in his judgement on racing matters."

"Of course not. Nothing on earth as unsexual as racing."

"But one can see . . . he would be finished in the racing world, if this got out. Even I . . . I cannot think of him now without this . . . this perversion . . . coming into my mind. It would be the same with everyone. One can't respect him any more. One can't like him."

"Difficult," I agreed.

"It's . . . horrible." In his voice, all the revulsion of the normal for the deviation. Most racing men were normal. The deviation would be cast out. Ferth felt it. Gowery knew it. And so did someone else . . .

"Don't they wear masks, at this club?" I asked.

Ferth looked surprised. "Why, yes, they do. I asked him who could know about him . . . in order to blackmail him . . . and he said he didn't know, they all wore masks. Hoods, actually, was the word he used. Hoods . . . and aprons . . ." He was revolted.

"All leather?"

He nodded. "How can they?"

"They do less harm than the ones who go out and rape small children."

"I'm glad I . . ." he said passionately.

"Me too," I said. "But it's just luck." Gowery had been unlucky, in more ways than one. "Someone may have seen him going in, or leaving afterwards."

"That's what he thinks. But he says he doesn't know the real names of any of his fellow members. They all call each other by fanciful made-up names, apparently."

"There must be a secretary . . . with a list of members?"

Ferth shook his head. "I asked him that. He said he'd never given his own name to anyone there. It wasn't expected. There's no annual subscription, just ten pounds in cash every time he attends. He says he goes about once a month, on average."

"How many other members are there?"

"He didn't know the total number. He says there are never fewer than ten, and sometimes thirty or thirty-five. More men than women, usually. The club isn't open every day; only Mondays and Thursdays."

"Where is it?"

"In London. He wouldn't tell me exactly where."

"He wants . . . needs . . . to keep on going," I said.

"You don't think he will!"

"After a while. Yes."

"Oh no . . ."

"Who introduced him to the club, do you know?"

"He said it couldn't be the person who introduced him to the club. She was a prostitute . . . he'd never told her his real name."

"But she understood his needs."

He sighed. "It would seem so."

"Some of those girls make more money out of whipping men than sleeping with them."

"How on earth do you know?"

"I had digs once in the next room to one. She told me."

"Good Lord." He looked as if he'd turned over a stone and found creepy-crawlies underneath. He had plainly no inkling of what it was like to *be* a creepy-crawly. His loss.

"Anyway," he said slowly, "you will understand why he accepted that package at its face value."

"And why he chose Lord Plimborne and Andy Tring."

Lord Ferth nodded. "At the end, when he'd recovered a little, he understood that he'd chosen them for the reasons you said, but he believed at the time that they were impulsive choices. And he is now, as you would expect, a very worried and troubled man."

"Was he," I asked, "responsible for this?"

I held out to him the letter Tony had received from the Stewards'
Secretaries. He stood up, came to take it, and read its brief contents with
exasperation.

"I don't know," he said explosively. "I really don't know. When did this
arrive?"

"Tuesday. Postmarked noon on Monday."

"Before I saw him . . . He didn't mention it."

"Could you find out if it was his doing?"

"Do you mean . . . it will be all the more impossible to forgive him?"

"No. Nothing like that. I was just wondering if it was our little framer-
blackmailer at work again. See those words 'It has been brought to our
attention'? . . . What I'd like to know is who brought it."

"I'll find out," he agreed positively. "That shouldn't be difficult. And
of course, disregard the letter. There won't be any question now of your
having to move."

"How are you going to work it? Giving our licences back. How are you
going to explain it?"

He raised his eyebrows. "We never have to give reasons for our decisions."

I smothered a laugh. The system had its uses.

Lord Ferth sat down in the chair again and put the letter in his briefcase. Then he packed up the tape-recorder and tucked that away too.
Then with an air of delicately choosing his words he said, "A scandal of
this sort would do racing a great deal of harm."

"So you want me to take my licence back and shut up?"

"Er . . . yes."

"And not chase after the blackmailer, in case he blows the gaffe?"

"Exactly." He was relieved that I understood.

"No." I said.

"Why not?" Persuasion in his voice.

"Because he tried to kill me."

"*What?*"

I showed him the chunk of exhaust manifold, and explained. "Someone
at the dance," I said. "That means that our blackmailer is one of about
six hundred people, and from there it shouldn't be too hard. You can
more or less rule out the women, because few of them would drill
through cast iron wearing an evening dress. Much too conspicuous, if
anyone saw them. That leaves three hundred men."

"Someone who knew your car," he said. "Surely that would narrow it
down considerably."

"It might not. Anyone could have seen me getting out of it at the races.
It was a noticeable car, I'm afraid. But I arrived late at the dance. The
car was parked right at the back."

"Have you . . . " He cleared his throat. "Are the police involved in this?"

"If you mean are they at present investigating an attempted murder, then no, they are not. If you mean, am I going to ask them to investigate, etc., then I haven't decided."

"Once you start the police on something, you can't stop them."

"On the other hand if I don't start them the blackmailer might have another go at me, with just a fraction of an inch more success. Which would be quite enough."

"Um." He thought it over. "But if you made it clear to everyone now that you are not any longer trying to find out who framed you . . . he might not try again."

I said curiously, "Do you really think it would be best for racing if we just leave this blackmailing murderer romping around free?"

"Better than a full-blown scandal."

The voice of Establishment diplomacy.

"And if he doesn't follow your line of reasoning . . . and he does kill me . . . how would that do for a scandal?"

He didn't answer. Just looked at me levelly with the hot eyes.

"All right, then," I said. "No police."

"Thank you."

"Us, though. We'll have to do it ourselves. Find him and deal with him."

"How do you mean?"

"I'll find him. You deal with him."

"To your satisfaction, I suppose," he said ironically.

"Absolutely."

"And Lord Gowery?"

"He's yours entirely. I shan't tell Dexter Cranfield anything at all."

"Very well." He stood up, and I struggled off the bed on to the crutches.

"Just one thing," I said. "Could you arrange to have that package of Lord Gowery's sent to me here?"

"I have it with me." Without hesitation he took a large Manila envelope out of the briefcase and put it on the bed. "You'll understand how he fell on it with relief."

"Things being as they were," I agreed. He walked across the sitting-room to the way out, stopping by the chest to put on his coat.

"Can Cranfield tell his owners to shovel their horses back?" I said. "The sooner the better, you see, if they're to come back in time for Cheltenham."

"Give me until tomorrow morning. There are several other people who must know first."

"All right."

He held out his hand. I transferred the right crutch to the left, and shook it.

He said, "Perhaps one day soon . . . when this is over . . . you will dine with me?"

"I'd like to," I said.

"Good." He picked up his bowler and his briefcase, swept a last considering glance round my flat, nodded to me as if finalizing a decision, and quietly went away.

I telephoned to the orthopod who regularly patched me up after falls. "I want this plaster off."

He went into a long spiel of which the gist was two or three more weeks.

"Monday," I said.

"I'll give you up."

"Tuesday I start getting it off with a chisel."

I always slept in shirt-and-shorts pyjamas, which had come in very handy in the present circs. Bedtime that day I struggled into a lime-green and white checked lot I had bought in an off moment at Liverpool the year before with my mind more on the imminent Grand National than on what they would do to my yellow complexion at six on a winter's morning.

Tony had gloomily brought me some casseroled beef and had stayed to celebrate when I told him I wouldn't have to leave. I was out of whisky again in consequence.

When he'd gone I went to bed and read the pages which had sent me to limbo. And they were, indeed, convincing. Neatly typed, well set out, written in authoritative language. Not at first, second, or even third sight the product of malevolence. Emotionless. Cool. Damaging.

"Charles Richard West is prepared to testify that during the course of the race, and in particular at a spot six furlongs from the winning post on the second circuit, he heard Hughes say that he (Hughes) was about to ease his horse so that it should be in no subsequent position to win. Hughes' precise words were, 'OK. Brakes on, chaps.' "

The four other sheets were equally brief, equally to the point. One said that through an intermediary Dexter Cranfield had backed Cherry Pie with Newtonnards. The second pointed out that an investigation of the past form would show that on several other occasions Cranfield's second string had beaten his favourite. The third suggested watching the discrepancies in Hughes' riding in the Lemonfizz and in the last race at Reading . . . and there it was in black and white, "the last race at Reading." Gowery hadn't questioned it or checked; had simply sent for the last race at Reading. If he had shown it privately to Plimborne and Tring only, and not to me as well, no one might ever have realized it was the wrong race. This deliberate piece of misleading had in fact gone astray, but only just. And the rest hadn't. Page four stated categorically that Cranfield had bribed Hughes not to win, and photographic evidence to prove it was hereby attached.

There was also a short covering note of explanation.

"These few facts have come to my notice. They should clearly be laid before the appropriate authorities, and I am therefore sending them to you, sir, as Steward in command of the forthcoming Enquiry."

The typewriting itself was unremarkable, the paper medium-quality quarto. The paper clip holding the sheets together was sold by the hundred million, and the buff envelope in which they'd been sent cost a penny or two in any stationer's in the country.

There were two copies only of the photograph. On the back, no identifications.

I slid them all back into the envelope, and put it in the drawer of the table beside my bed. Switched out the light. Lay thinking of riding races again with a swelling feeling of relief and excitement. Wondered how poor old Gowery was making out, going fifteen rounds with his conscience. Thought of Archie and his mortgage . . . Kessel having to admit he'd been wrong . . . Roberta stepping off her dignity . . . the blackmailer biting his nails in apprehension . . . sweet dreams every one . . . slid into the first easy sleep since the Enquiry.

I woke with a jolt, knowing I'd heard a sound which had no business to be there.

A pen-sized flashlight was flickering round the inside of one of the top drawers of the dressing chest. A dark shape blocked off half of its beam as an arm went into the drawer to feel around. Cautious. Very quiet, now.

I lay watching through slit-shut eyes, wondering how close I was this time to the pearly gates. Inconveniently my pulse started bashing against my eardrums as fear stirred up the adrenals, and inside the plaster all the hairs on my leg fought to stand on end.

Trying to keep my breathing even and make no rustle with the sheets I very cautiously slid one arm over the side of the bed and reached down to the floor for a crutch. Any weapon handy was better than none.

No crutches.

I felt around, knowing exactly where I'd laid them beside me, feeling nothing but carpet under my fingers.

The flashlight moved out of the drawer and swung in a small arc while the second top drawer was opened, making the same tiny crack as it loosened which had woken me with the other. The scrap of light shone fractionally on my two crutches propped up against the wall by the door.

I drew the arm very slowly back into bed and lay still. If he'd meant just to kill me, he would have done it by now: and whatever he intended I had little chance of avoiding. The plaster felt like a ton, chaining me immobile.

A clammy crawling feeling all over my skin. Jaw tight clenched with tension. Dryness in the mouth. Head feeling as if it were swelling. I lay and tried to beat the physical sensations, tried to will them away.

No noticeable success.

He finished with the drawers. The flashlight swung over the khaki chair and steadied on the polished oak chest behind it, against the wall. He moved over there soundlessly and lifted the lid. I almost cried out to him not to, it would wake me. The lid always creaked loudly. I really didn't want him to wake me, it was much too dangerous.

The lid creaked sharply. He stopped dead with it six inches up. Lowered it back into place. It creaked even louder.

He stood there, considering. Then there were quick soft steps on the carpet, a hand fastening in my hair and yanking my head back, and the flashlight beam full in my eyes.

"Right, mate. You're awake. So you'll answer some questions."

I knew the voice. I shut my eyes against the light and spoke in as bored a drawl as I could manage.

"Mr. Oakley, I presume?"

"Clever, Mr. Hughes."

He let go of my hair and stripped the bedclothes off with one flick. The flashlight swung away and fell on top of them. I felt his grip on my neck and the front of my shirt as he wrenched me off the bed and on to the floor. I fell with a crash.

"That's for starters," he said.

XIII

He was fast, to give him his due. Also strong and ruthless and used to this sort of thing.

"Where is it?" he said.

"What?"

"A chunk of metal with a hole in it."

"I don't know what you're talking about."

He swung his arm and hit me with something hard and knobbly. When it followed through to the tiny light I could see what it was. One of my own crutches. Delightful.

I tried to disentangle my legs and roll over and stand up. He shone the light on me to watch. When I was half up he knocked me down again.

"Where is it?"

"I told you . . ."

"We both know, chum, that you have this chunk of metal. I want it. I have a customer for it. And you're going to hand it over like a good little warned-off crook."

"Go scratch yourself."

I rolled fast and almost missed the next swipe. It landed on the plaster. Some flakes came off. Less work for Tuesday.

"You haven't a hope," he said. "Face facts."

The facts were that if I yelled for help only the horses would hear. Pity.

I considered giving him the chunk of metal with the hole in it. Correction, half a hole. He didn't know it was only half a hole. I wondered whether I should tell him. Perhaps he'd be only half as savage.

"Who wants it?" I said.

"Be your age." He swung the crutch.

Contact.

I cursed.

"Save yourself, chum. Don't be stupid."

"What is this chunk of metal?"

"Just hand it over."

"I don't know what you're looking for."

"Chunk of metal with a hole in it."

"What chunk of metal?"

"Look, chum, what does it matter what chunk of metal? The one you've got."

"I haven't."

"Stop playing games." He swung the crutch. I grunted. "Hand it over."

"I haven't . . . got . . . any chunk of metal."

"Look chum, my instructions are as clear as glass. You've got some lump of metal and I've come to fetch it. Understand? Simple. So save yourself, you stupid crumb."

"What is he paying for it?"

"You still offering more?"

"Worth a try."

"So you said before. But nothing doing."

"Pity."

"Where's the chunk?. . ."

I didn't answer, heard the crutch coming, rolled at the right instant, and heard it thud on the carpet, roughly where my nose had been.

The little flashlight sought me out. He didn't miss the second time, but it was only my arm, not my face.

"Didn't you ask what it was?" I said.

"None of your bloody business. You just tell me" . . . bash . . . "where" . . . bash . . ."it is."

I'd had about enough. Too much, in fact. And I'd found out all I was likely to, except how far he was prepared to go, which was information I could do without.

I'd been trying to roll towards the door. Finally made it near enough. Stretched backwards over my head and felt my fingers curl round the bottom of the other crutch still propped against the wall.

The rubber knob came into my hand, and with one scything movement I swept the business end round viciously at knee level.

It caught him square and unexpected on the back of the legs just as he himself was in mid swing, and he overbalanced and crashed down half on top of me. I reached out and caught something, part of his coat, and gripped and pulled, and tried to swing my plaster leg over his body to hold him down.

He wasn't having any. We scrambled around on the floor, him trying to get up and me trying to stop him, both of us scratching and punching and gouging in a thoroughly unsportsmanlike manner. The flashlight had fallen away across the far side of the room and shone only on the wall. Not enough light to be much good. Too much for total evasion of his efficient fists.

The bedside table fell over with a crash and the lamp smashed. Oakley somehow reached into the ruins and picked up a piece of glass, and I just saw the light shimmer on it as he slashed it towards my eyes. I dodged it by a millimetre in the last half-second.

"You bugger," I said bitterly.

We were both gasping for breath. I loosed the grip I had on his coat in order to have both hands free to deal with the glass, and as soon as he felt me leave go he was heaving himself back on to his feet.

"Now," he said, panting heavily, "where bloody is it?"

I didn't answer. He'd got hold of a crutch again. Back to square one. On the thigh, that time.

I was lying on the other crutch. The elbow supports were digging into my back. I twisted my arm underneath me and pulled out the crutch, hand-swung it at him just as he was having a second go. The crutches met and crashed together in the air. I held on to mine for dear life and rolled towards the bed.

"Give . . . up . . ." he said.

"Get . . . stuffed."

I made it to the bed and lay in the angle between it and the floor. He couldn't get a good swing at me there. I turned the crutch round, and held it by the elbow and hand grips with both of my own. To hit me where I was lying he had to come nearer.

He came. His dark shadow was above me, exaggerated by the dim torchlight. He leant over, swinging. I shoved the stick end of the crutch hard upwards. It went into him solidly and he screeched sharply. The crutch he had been swinging dropped harmlessly on top of me as he reeled away, clutching at his groin.

"I'll . . . kill you . . . for that . . ." His voice was high with pain. He groaned, hugging himself.

"Serves . . . you . . . right," I said breathlessly.

I pulled myself across the floor, dragging the plaster, aiming for the telephone which had crashed on to the floor with the little table. Found the receiver. Pulled the cord. The telephone bumped over the carpet into my hand.

Put my finger on the button. Small ting. Dialling tone. Found the numbers. Three . . . nine . . . one . . .

"Yeah?" Tony's voice, thick with sleep.

Dead careless, I was. Didn't hear a thing. The crutch swung wickedly down on the back of my head and I fell over the telephone and never told him to gallop to the rescue.

I woke where Oakley had left me, still lying on the floor over the telephone, the receiver half in and half out of my hand.

It was daylight, just. Grey and raw and raining. I was stiff. Cold. Had a headache.

Remembered bit by bit what had happened. Set about scraping myself off the carpet.

First stop, back on to the bed, accompanied by bedclothes. Lay there feeling terrible and looking at the mess he had made of my room.

After he'd knocked me out, he had nothing to be quiet about. Everything had been pulled out of the closet and drawers and flung on the floor. Everything smashable was smashed. The sleeves of some of my suits were ripped and lying in tatters. Rosalind's picture had been torn into four pieces and the silver frame twisted and snapped. It had been revenge more than a search. A bad loser, David Oakley.

What I could see of the sitting-room through the open door seemed to have received the same treatment.

I lay and ached in most places you could think of.

Didn't look to see if Oakley had found the piece of manifold because I knew he wouldn't have. Thought about him coming, and about what he'd said.

Thought about Cranfield.

Thought about Gowery.

Once I got the plaster off and could move about again, it shouldn't take me too long now to dig out the enemy. A bit of leg work. Needed two legs.

Oakley would shortly be reporting no success from the night's work.

I wondered if he would be sent to try again. Didn't like that idea particularly.

I shifted on the bed, trying to get comfortable. I'd been concussed twice in five days once before, and got over it. I'd been kicked along the ground by a large field of hurdlers, which had been a lot worse than the crutches. I'd broken enough bones to stock a cemetery and this time they were all whole. But all the same I felt sicker than after racing falls, and in the end realized my unease was revulsion against being hurt by another man. Horses, hard ground, even express trains, were impersonal. Oakley had been a different type of invasion. The amount you were mentally affected by a pain always depended on how you got it.

I felt terrible. Had no energy at all to get up and tidy the mess.

Shut my eyes to blot it out. Blotted myself out, too. Went to sleep.

A voice said above my head, "Won't you ever learn to keep your door shut?"

I smiled feebly. "Not if you're coming through it."

"Finding you flat out is becoming a habit."

"Try to break it."

I opened my eyes. Broad daylight. Still raining.

Roberta was standing a foot from the bed wearing a blinding yellow raincoat covered in trickling drops. The copper hair was tied up in a pony tail and she was looking around her with disgust.

"Do you realize it's half past ten?" she said.

"No."

"Do you always drop your clothes all over the place when you go to bed?"

"Only on Wednesdays."

"Coffee?" she said abruptly, looking down at me.

"Yes, please."

She picked her way through the mess to the door, and then across the sitting-room until she was out of sight. I rubbed my hand over my chin. Bristly. And there was a tender lump on the back of my skull and a sore patch all down one side of my jaw, where I hadn't dodged fast enough. Bruises in other places set up a morning chorus. I didn't listen.

She came back minus the raincoat and carrying two steaming mugs which she put carefully on the floor. Then she picked up the bedside table and transferred the mugs to its top.

The drawer had fallen out of the table, and the envelope had fallen out of the drawer. But Oakley hadn't apparently looked into it: hadn't known it was there to find.

Roberta picked up the scattered crutches and brought them over to the bed.

"Thanks," I said.

"You take it very calmly."

"I've seen it before," I pointed out.

"And you just went to sleep?"

"Opted out," I agreed.

She looked more closely at my face and rolled my head over on the pillow. I winced. She took her hand away.

"Did you get the same treatment as the flat?"

"More or less."

"What for?"

"For being stubborn."

"Do you mean," she said incredulously, "that you could have avoided all this . . . and didn't?"

"If there's a good reason for backing down, you back down. If there isn't, you don't."

"And all this . . . isn't a good enough reason?"

"No."

"You're crazy," she said.

"You're so right," I sighed, pushed myself up a bit, and reached for the coffee.

"Have you called the police?" she asked.

I shook my head. "Not their quarrel."

"Who did it, then?"

I smiled at her. "Your father and I have got our licences back."

"What?"

"It'll be official some time today."

"Does Father know? How did it happen? Did you do it?"

"No, he doesn't know yet. Ring him up. Tell him to get on to all the owners. It'll be confirmed in the papers soon, either today's evening editions, or tomorrow's dailies."

She picked the telephone off the floor and sat on the edge of my bed, and telephoned to her father with real joy and sparkling eyes. He wouldn't believe it at first.

"Kelly says it's true," she said.

He argued again, and she handed the telephone to me.

"You tell him."

Cranfield said, "Who told you?"

"Lord Ferth."

"Did he say why?"

"No," I lied. "Just that the sentences had been reviewed . . . and reversed. We're back, as from today. The official notice will be in next week's Calendar."

"No explanation at all?" he insisted.

"They don't have to give one," I pointed out.

"All the same . . ."

"Who cares why?" I said. "The fact that we're back . . . that's all that matters."

"Did you find out who framed us?"

"No."

"Will you go on trying?"

"I might do," I said. "We'll see."

He had lost interest in that. He bounded into a stream of plans for the horses, once they were back. "And it will give me great pleasure to tell Henry Kessel . . ."

"I'd like to see his face," I agreed. But Pat Nikita would never part with Squelch, nor with Kessel, now. If Cranfield thought Kessel would come crawling apologetically back, he didn't know his man. "Concentrate on getting Breadwinner back," I suggested. "I'll be fit to ride in the Gold Cup."

"Old Strepson promised Breadwinner would come back at once . . . and Pound Postage of his . . . that's entered in the National, don't forget."

"I haven't," I assured him, "forgotten."

He ran down eventually and disconnected, and I could imagine him sitting at the other end still wondering whether to trust me.

Roberta stood up with a spring, as if the news had filled her with energy.

"Shall I tidy up for you?"

"I'd love some help."

She bent down and picked up Rosalind's torn picture.

"They didn't have to do that," she said in disgust.

"I'll get the bits stuck together and re-photographed."

"You'd hate to lose her . . ."

I didn't answer at once. She looked at me curiously, her eyes dark with some unreadable expression.

"I lost her," I said slowly. "Rosalind . . . Roberta . . . you are so unalike."

She turned away abruptly and put the pieces on the chest of drawers where they had always stood.

"Who wants to be a carbon copy?" she said, and her voice was high and cracking. "Get dressed . . . while I start on the sitting-room." She disappeared fast and shut the door behind her.

I lay there looking at it.

Roberta Cranfield. I'd never liked her.

Roberta Cranfield. I couldn't bear it . . . I was beginning to love her.

She stayed most of the day, helping me clear up the mess.

Oakley had left little to chance: the bathroom and kitchen both looked as if they'd been gutted by a whirlwind. He'd searched everywhere a good enquiry agent could think of, including in the lavatory cistern and the refrigerator; and everywhere he'd searched he'd left his trail of damage.

After midday, which was punctuated by some scrambled eggs, the telephone started ringing. Was it true, asked the *Daily Witness* in the shape of Daddy Leeman, that Cranfield and I? . . . "Check with the Jockey Club," I said.

The other papers had checked first. "May we have your comments?" they asked.

"Thrilled to bits," I said gravely. "You can quote me."

A lot of real chums rang to congratulate, and a lot of pseudo chums rang to say they'd never believed me guilty anyway.

For most of the afternoon I lay flat on the sitting-room floor with my head on a cushion talking down the telephone while Roberta stepped around and over me nonchalantly, putting everything back into place.

Finally she dusted her hands off on the seat of her black pants, and said she thought that that would do. The flat looked almost as good as ever. I agreed gratefully that it would do very well.

"Would you consider coming down to my level?" I asked.

She said calmly, "Are you speaking literally, metaphorically, intellectually, financially, or socially?"

"I was suggesting you might sit on the floor."

"In that case," she said collectedly, "yes." And she sank gracefully into a cross-legged sprawl.

I couldn't help grinning. She grinned companionably back.

"I was scared stiff of you when I came here last week," she said.

"You were *what?*"

"You always seemed so aloof. Unapproachable."

"Are we talking about me . . . or you?"

"You, of course," she said in surprise. "You always made me nervous. I always get sort of . . . strung up . . . when I'm nervous. Put on a bit of an act, to hide it, I suppose."

"I see," I said slowly.

"You're still a pretty good cactus, if you want to know . . . but . . . well, you see people differently when they've been bleeding all over your best dress and looking pretty vulnerable . . ."

I began to say that in that case I would be prepared to bleed on her any time she liked, but the telephone interrupted me at halfway. And it was old Strepson, settling down for a long cosy chat about Breadwinner and Pound Postage.

Roberta wrinkled her nose and got to her feet.

"Don't go," I said, with my hand over the mouthpiece.

"Must. I'm late already."

"Wait." I said. But she shook her head, fetched the yellow raincoat from the bath, where she'd put it, and edged herself into it.

" 'Bye," she said.

"Wait . . ."

She waved briefly and let herself out of the door. I struggled up on to my feet, and said, "Sir . . . could you hold on a minute . . ." into the telephone, and hopped without the crutches over to the window. She looked up when I opened it. She was standing in the yard, tying on a headscarf. The rain had eased to drizzle.

"Will you come tomorrow?" I shouted down.

"Can't tomorrow. Got to go to London."

"Saturday?"

"Do you want me to?"

"Yes."

"I'll try, then."

"Please come."

"Oh . . ." She suddenly smiled in a way I'd never seen before. "All right."

Careless I might be about locking my front door, but in truth I left little about worth stealing. Five hundred pounds would never have been lying around on my chest of drawers for enquiry agents to photograph.

When I'd converted the flat from an old hay loft I'd built in more than mod cons. Behind the cabinet in the kitchen which housed things like fly killer and soap powder, and tucked into a crafty piece of brickwork, lay a maximum security safe. It was operated not by keys or combinations, but by electronics. The manufacturers had handed over the safe itself and also the tiny ultrasonic transmitter which sent out the special series of radio waves which alone would release the lock mechanism, and I'd installed them myself: the safe in the wall and the transmitter in a false bottom to the cabinet. Even if anyone found the transmitter, they had still to find the safe and to know the sequence of frequencies which unlocked it.

A right touch of the Open Sesame. I'd always liked gadgets.

Inside the safe there were, besides money and some racing trophies, several pieces of antique silver, three paintings by Houthuesen, two Chelsea figures, a Meissen cup and saucer, a Louis XIV snuff box, and four uncut diamonds totalling twenty-eight carats. My retirement pension, all wrapped in green baize and appreciating nicely. Retirement for a steeple-chase jockey could lurk in the very next fall; and the ripe age of forty, if one lasted that long, was about the limit.

There was also a valueless lump of cast iron, with a semi-circular dent in it. To these various treasures I added the envelope which Ferth had given me, because it wouldn't help if I lost that either.

Bolting my front door meant a hazardous trip down the stairs, and another in the morning to open it. I decided it could stay unlocked as usual. Wedged a chair under the door into my sitting-room instead.

During the evening I telephoned to Newtonnards in his pink washed house in Mill Hill.

"Hallo," he said. "You've got your licence back then. Talk of the meeting it was at Wincanton today, soon as the Press Association chaps heard about it."

"Yes, it's great news."

"What made their lordships change their minds?"

"I've no idea . . . Look, I wondered if you'd seen that man again yet, the one who backed Cherry Pie with you."

"Funny thing," he said, "but I saw him today. Just after I'd heard you were back in favour, though, so I didn't think you'd be interested any more."

"Did you by any chance find out who he is?"

"I did, as a matter of fact. More to satisfy my own curiosity, really. He's the Honourable Peter Foxcroft. Mean anything to you?"

"He's a brother of Lord Middleburg."

"Yeah. So I'm told."

I laughed inwardly. Nothing sinister about Cranfield refusing to name his mysterious pal. Just another bit of ladder climbing. He might be one rung up being in a position to use the Hon. P. Foxcroft as a runner, but he would certainly be five rungs down involving him in a messy Enquiry.

"There's one other thing . . ." I hesitated. "Would you . . . could you . . . do me a considerable favour?"

"Depends on what it is." He sounded cautious but not truculent. A smooth, experienced character.

"I can't offer much in return."

He chuckled. "Warning me not to expect tip offs when you're on a hot number?"

"Something like that," I admitted.

"OK then. You want something for strictly nothing. Just as well to know where we are. So shoot."

"Can you remember who you told about Cranfield backing Cherry Pie?"

"Before the Enquiry, you mean?"

"Yes. Those bookmaker colleagues you mentioned."

"Well . . ." he sounded doubtful.

"If you can," I said, "could you ask *them* who *they* told?"

"Phew." He half breathed, half whistled down the receiver. "That's some favour."

"I'm sorry. Just forget it."

"Hang on, hang on, I didn't say I wouldn't do it. It's a bit of a tall order, though, expecting them to remember."

"I know. Very long shot. But I still want to know who told the Stewards about the bet with you."

"You've got your licence back. Why don't you let it rest?"

"Would you?"

He sighed. "I don't know. All right then, I'll see what I can do. No promises, mind. Oh, and by the way, it can be just as useful to know when one of your mounts is *not* fit or likely to win. If you take my meaning."

"I take it," I said smiling. "It's a deal."

I put down the receiver reflecting that only a minority of bookmakers were villains, and that most of them were more generous than they got credit for. The whole tribe were reviled for the image of the few. Like students.

XIV

Oakley didn't come. No one came. I took the chair from under the door knob to let the world in with the morning. Not much of the world accepted the invitation.

Made some coffee. Tony came while I was standing in the kitchen drinking it and put whisky into a mug of it for himself by way of breakfast. He'd been out with one lot of horses at exercise and was waiting to go out with the other, and spent the interval discussing their prospects as if nothing had ever happened. For him the warning off was past history, forgotten. His creed was that of newspapers; today is important, tomorrow more so, but yesterday is nothing.

He finished the coffee and left, clapping me cheerfully on the shoulder and setting up a protest from an Oakley bruise. I spent most of the rest of the day lying flat on my bed, answering the telephone, staring at the ceiling, letting Nature get on with repairing a few ravages, and thinking.

Another quiet night. I had two names in my mind, juggling them. Two to work on. Better than three hundred. But both could be wrong.

Saturday morning the postman brought the letters right upstairs, as he'd been doing since the era of plaster. I thanked him, sorted through them, dropped a crutch, and had the usual awkward fumble picking it up. When I opened one of the letters I dropped both the crutches again in surprise.

Left the crutches on the floor. Leant against the wall and read.

Dear Kelly Hughes,
I have seen in the papers that you have had your licence restored, so perhaps this information will be too late to be of any use to you. I am

sending it anyway because the friend who collected it is considerably out of pocket over it, and would be glad if you could reimburse him. I append also his list of expenses.

As you will see he went to a good deal of trouble over this, though to be fair he also told me that he had enjoyed doing it. I hope it is what you wanted.

Sincerely,
Teddy Dewar

Great Stag Hotel, Birmingham

Clipped behind the letter were several other sheets of varying sizes. The top one was a schematic presentation of names which looked at first glance like an inverted family tree. There were clumps of three or four names inside two-inch circles. The circles led via arrows to other circles below and sometimes beside them, but the eye was led downwards continually until all the arrows had converged to three circles, and then to two, and finally to one. And the single name in the bottom circle was David Oakley.

Behind the page was an explanatory note.

I knew one contact, the J. L. Jones underlined in the third row of circles. From him I worked in all directions, checking people who knew of David Oakley. Each clump of people heard about him from one of the people in the next clump. Everyone on the page, I guarantee, has heard either directly or indirectly that Oakley is the man to go to if one is in trouble. I posed as a man in trouble, as you suggested, and nearly all that I talked to either mentioned him of their own accord, or agreed when I brought him up as a possibility.

I only hope that one at least of these names has some significance for you, as I'm afraid the expenses were rather high. Most of the investigation was conducted in pubs or hotels, and it was sometimes necessary to get the contact tight before he would divulge.

Faithfully,
B. R. S. Timieson

The expense list was high enough to make me whistle. I turned back to the circled names, and read them carefully through.

Looking for one of two.

One was there.

Perhaps I should have rejoiced. Perhaps I should have been angry. Instead, I felt sad.

I doubled the expenses and wrote out a cheque with an accompanying note:

"This is really magnificent. Cannot thank you enough. One of the names has great significance, well worth all your perseverance. My eternal thanks."

I wrote also a grateful letter to Teddy Dewar saying the information couldn't have been better timed, and enclosing the envelope for his friend Timieson.

As I was sticking on the stamp the telephone rang. I hopped over to it and lifted the receiver.

George Newtonnards.

"Spent all last evening on the blower. Astronomical phone bill I'm going to have."

"Send me the account," I said resignedly.

"Better wait to see if I've got results," he suggested. "Got a pencil handy?"

"Just a sec." I fetched a writing pad and ballpoint. "OK. Go ahead."

"Right then. First, here are the chaps *I* told." He dictated five names. "The last one, Pelican Jobberson, is the one who holds a fierce grudge against you for that bum steer you gave him, but as it happens he didn't tell the Stewards or anyone else because he went off to Casablanca the next day for a holiday. Well . . . here are the people Harry Ingram told . . ." He read out three names. "And these are the people Herbie Subbing told . . ." Four names. "These are the people Dimmie Ovens told . . ." Five names. "And Clobber Mackintosh, he really spread it around . . ." Eight names. "That's all they can remember. They wouldn't swear there was no one else. And of course, all those people they've mentioned could have passed the info on to someone else . . . I mean, things like this spread out in ripples."

"Thanks anyway," I said sincerely. "Thank you very much indeed for taking so much trouble."

"Has it been any help?"

"Oh yes, I think so. I'll let you know, some time."

"And don't forget. The obvious non-winner . . . give me the wink."

"I'll do that," I promised. "If you'll risk it, after Pelican Jobberson's experience."

"He's got no sense," he said. "But I have."

He rang off, and I studied his list of names. Several were familiar and belonged to well-known racing people: the bookmakers' clients, I supposed. None of the names were the same as those on Timieson's list of Oakley contacts, but there was something . . .

For ten minutes I stood looking at the paper wondering what was hovering around the edge of consciousness, and finally, with a thud, the association clicked.

One of the men Herbie Subbing had told was the brother-in-law of the person I had found among the Oakley contacts.

I thought for a while, and then opened the newspaper and studied the programme for the day's racing, which was at Reading. Then I telephoned to Lord Ferth at his London house, and reached him via a plummy-voiced manservant.

"Well, Kelly? . . ." There was something left of Wednesday's relationship. Not all, but something.

"Sir," I said, "are you going to Reading races?"

"Yes, I am."

"I haven't yet had any official notice of my licence being restored . . . Will it be all right for me to turn up there? I would particularly like to talk to you."

"I'll make sure you have no difficulty, if it's important." There was a faint question in his tone, which I answered.

"I know," I said, "who engineered things."

"Ah . . . Yes. Then come. Unless the journey would be too uncomfortable for you? I could, you know, come on to Corrie after the races. I have no engagements tonight."

"You're very thoughtful. But I think our engineer will be at the races too . . . or at least there's a very good chance of it."

"As you like," he agreed. "I'll look out for you."

Tony had two runners at the meeting and I could ask him to take me. But there was also Roberta . . . she was coming over, probably, and she too might take me. I smiled wryly to myself. She might take me anywhere. Roberta Cranfield. Of all people.

As if by telepathy the telephone rang, and it was Roberta herself on the other end. She sounded breathless and worried.

"Kelly! I can't come just yet. In fact . . ." The words came in a rush. "Can you come over here?"

"What's the matter?"

"Well . . . I don't really know if *anything's* the matter . . . seriously, that is. But Grace Roxford has turned up here."

"Dear Grace?"

"Yes . . . look, Kelly, she's just sitting in her car outside the house sort of glaring at it. Honestly, she looks a bit mad. We don't know quite what to do. Mother wants to call the police, but, I mean, one *can't* . . . Supposing the poor woman has come to apologize or something, and is just screwing herself up?"

"She's still sitting in the car?"

"Yes. I can see her from here. Can you come? I mean . . . Mother's useless and you know how dear Grace feels about *me* . . . She looks pretty odd, Kelly." Definite alarm in her voice.

"Where's your father?"

"Out on the gallops with Breadwinner. He won't be back for about an hour."

"All right then. I'll get Tony or someone to drive me over. As soon as I can."

"That's great," she said with relief. "I'll try and stall her till you come."

It would take half an hour to get there. More, probably. By then dear
Grace might not still be sitting in her car . . .

I dialled three nine one.

"Tony," I said urgently. "Can you drop everything instantly and drive
me to Cranfield's? Grace Roxford has turned up there and I don't like the
sound of it."

"I've got to go to Reading," he protested.

"You can go on from Cranfield's when we've sorted Grace out . . . and
anyway, I want to go to Reading too, to talk to Lord Ferth. So be a pal,
Tony. Please."

"Oh all right. If you want it that much. Give me five minutes."

He took ten. I spent some of them telephoning to Jack Roxford. He was
surprised I should be calling him.

"Look, Jack," I said, "I'm sorry to be upsetting you like this, but have
you any idea where your wife has gone?"

"Grace?" More surprise, but also anxiety. "Down to the village, she
said."

The village in question was roughly forty miles from Cranfield's house.

"She must have gone some time ago," I said.

"I suppose so . . . what's all this about?" The worry was sharp in his
voice.

"Roberta Cranfield has just telephoned to say that your wife is outside
their house, just sitting in her car."

"Oh God," he said. "She can't be."

"I'm afraid she is."

"Oh *no* . . ." he wailed. "She seemed better this morning . . . quite her
old self . . . it seemed safe to let her go and do the shopping . . . she's been
so upset, you see . . . and then you and Dexter got your licences back
. . . it's affected her . . . it's all been so awful for her."

"I'm just going over there to see if I can help," I said. "But . . . can you
come down and collect her?"

"Oh *yes,*" he said. "I'll start at once. Oh poor dear Grace . . . Take care
of her, till I come."

"Yes," I said reassuringly, and disconnected.

I made it without mishap down the stairs and found Tony had com-
mandeered Poppy's estate car for the journey. The back seat lay flat so
that I could lie instead of sit, and there were even cushions for my
shoulders and head.

"Poppy's idea," Tony said briefly, helping me climb in through the rear
door. "Great girl."

"She sure is," I said gratefully, hauling in the crutches behind me.
"Lose no time, now, friend."

"You sound worried." He shut the doors, switched on and drove away
with minimum waste of time.

"I am, rather. Grace Roxford is unbalanced."

"But surely not dangerous?"

"I hope not."

I must have sounded doubtful because Tony's foot went heavily down on the accelerator. "Hold on to something," he said. We rocked round corners. I couldn't find any good anchorage: had to wedge my useful foot against the rear door and push myself off the swaying walls with my hands.

"OK?" he shouted.

"Uh . . . yes," I said breathlessly.

"Good bit of road just coming up." We left all the other traffic at a standstill. "Tell me if you see any cops."

We saw no cops. Tony covered the eighteen miles through Berkshire in twenty-three minutes. We jerked to a stop outside Cranfield's house, and the first thing I saw was that there was no one in the small grey Volkswagen standing near the front door.

Tony opened the back of the car with a crash and unceremoniously tugged me out.

"She's probably sitting down cosily having a quiet cup of tea," he said.

She wasn't.

Tony rang the front-door bell and after a lengthy interval Mrs. Cranfield herself opened it.

Not her usual swift wide-opening fling. She looked at us through a nervous six inches.

"Hughes. What are you doing here? Go away."

"Roberta asked me to come. To see Grace Roxford."

"Mrs. Roxford is no longer here." Mrs. Cranfield's voice was as strung up as her behaviour.

"Isn't that her car?" I pointed to the Volkswagen.

"No," she said sharply.

"Whose is it, then?"

"The gardener's. Now, Hughes, go away at once. Go away."

"Very well," I said, shrugging. And she instantly shut the door.

"Help me back into the car," I said to Tony.

"Surely you're not just *going?*"

"Don't argue," I said. "Get me into the car, drive away out through the gates, then go round and come back in through the stable entrance."

"That's better." He shuffled me in, threw in the crutches, slammed the door and hustled round to the driving seat.

"Don't rush so," I said. "Scratch your head a bit. Look disgusted."

"You think she's watching?" He didn't start the car: looked at me over his shoulder.

"I think Mrs. Cranfield would never this side of doomsday allow her gardener to park outside her front door. Mrs. Cranfield was doing her best to ask for help."

"Which means," he added slowly, "that Grace Roxford is very dangerous indeed."

I nodded with a dry mouth. "Drive away, now."

He went slowly. Rolled round into the back drive, accelerated along that, and stopped with a jerk beside the stables. Yet again he helped me out.

"There's a telephone in the small office in the yard," I said. "Next to the tackroom. Look up in the classified directory and find a local doctor. Tell him to come smartish. Then wait here until Dexter Cranfield comes back with the horses, and stop him going into the house."

"Kelly, couldn't you be exaggerating? . . . I'll never be able to stop Cranfield."

"Tell him no one ever believes anything tragic will happen until it has."

He looked at me for two seconds, then wheeled away into the yard.

I peg-legged up the back drive and tried the back door. Open. It would be. For Cranfield to walk easily through it. And to what?

I went silently along into the main hall, and listened. There was no sound in the house.

Tried the library first, juggling the crutches to get a good grip on the door handle, sweating lest I should drop one with a crash. Turned the handle, pressed the door quietly inwards.

The library was uninhabited. A large clock on the mantel ticked loudly. Out of time with my heart.

I left the door open. Went slowly, silently towards the small sitting-room beside the front door. Again the meticulously careful drill with the handle. If they'd seen me come, they would most probably be in this room.

The door swung inwards. Well oiled. No creaks. I saw the worn chintz covers on the armchairs, the elderly rugs, the debris of living, scattered newspapers, a pair of spectacles on some letters, a headscarf and a flower basket. No people.

On the other side of the hall there were the double doors into the large formal drawing-room, and at the back, beyond the staircase, the doors to the dining-room and to Dexter Cranfield's own study, where he kept his racing books and did all his paper work.

I swung across to the study, and opened the door. It was quiet in there. Dust slowly gravitated. Nothing else moved.

That left only the two large rooms downstairs, and the whole of upstairs. I looked at the long broad flight uneasily. Wished it were an escalator.

The dining-room was empty. I shifted back through the hall to the double doors of the drawing-room. Went through the crutch routine with more difficulty, because if I were going in there I would need both doors open, and to open both doors took both hands. I managed it in the end by hooking both crutches over my left arm like walking sticks, and standing on one leg.

The doors parted and I pushed them wide. The quarter-acre of drawing-room contained chairs of gold brocade upholstery, a pale cream Chinese carpet and long soft blue curtains. A delicate, elegant, class-concious room designed for Cranfield's glossiest aspirations.

Everything in there was motionless. A tableau.

I hitched the crutches into place, and walked forwards. Stopped after a very few paces. Stopped because I had to.

Mrs. Cranfield was there. And Roberta. And Grace Roxford. Mrs. Cranfield was standing by the fireplace, hanging on to the shoulder-high mantel as if needing support. Roberta sat upright in an armless wooden chair set out of its usual place in a large clear area of carpet. Behind her and slightly to one side, and with one hand firmly grasping Roberta's shoulder, stood Grace Roxford.

Grace Roxford held the sort of knife used by fishmongers. Nearly a foot long, razor sharp, with a point like a needle. She was resting the lethal end of it against Roberta's neck.

"Kelly!" Roberta said. Her voice was high and a trifle wavery, but the relief in it was overwhelming. I feared it might be misplaced.

Grace Roxford had a bright colour over her taut cheekbones and a piercing glitter in her eyes. Her body was rigid with tension. The hand holding the knife trembled in uneven spasms. She was as unstable as wet gelignite; but she still knew what she was doing.

"You went away, Kelly Hughes," she said. "You went away."

"Yes, Grace," I agreed. "But I came back to talk to Roberta."

"You come another step," she said, "and I'll cut her throat."

Mrs. Cranfield drew a breath like a sob, but Roberta's expression didn't change. Grace had made that threat already. Several times, probably. Especially when Tony and I had arrived at the front door.

She was desperately determined. Neither I nor the Cranfields had room to doubt that she wouldn't do as she said. And I was twenty feet away from her and a cripple besides.

"What do you want, Grace?" I said, as calmly as possible.

"Want? Want?" Her eyes flickered. She seemed to be trying to remember what she wanted. Then her rage sharpened on me like twin darts, and her purpose came flooding back.

"Dexter Cranfield . . . bloody snob . . . I'll see he doesn't get those horses . . . I'm going to kill him, see, kill him . . . then he can't get them, can he? No . . . he can't."

Again there was no surprise in either Roberta or her mother. Grace had told them already what she'd come for.

"Grace, killing Mr. Cranfield won't help your husband."

"Yes. Yes. Yes. Yes." She nodded sharply between each yes, and the knife jumped against Roberta's neck. Roberta shut her eyes for a while and swayed on the chair.

I said, "How do you hope to kill him, Grace?"

She laughed. It got out of control at halfway and ended in a maniacal high-pitched giggle. "He'll come here, won't he? He'll come here and stand beside me, because he'll do just what I say, won't he? Won't he?"

I looked at the steel blade beside Roberta's pearly skin and knew that he would indeed do as she said. As I would.

"And then, see," she said, "I'll just stick the knife into *him,* not into her. See? See?"

"I see," I said.

She nodded extravagantly and her hand shook.

"And then what?" I asked.

"Then what?" She looked puzzled. She hadn't got any further than killing Cranfield. Beyond that lay only darkness and confusion. Her vision didn't extend to consequences.

"Edwin Byler could send his horses to someone else," I said.

"No. No. Only Dexter Cranfield. Only him. Telling him he ought to have a more snobbish trainer. Taking him away from us. I'm going to kill him. Then he can't have those horses." The words tumbled out in a vehement monotone, all the more frightening for being clearly automatic. These were thoughts she'd had in her head for a very long time.

"It would have been all right, of course," I said slowly. "If Mr. Cranfield hadn't got his licence back."

"Yes!" It was a bitterly angry shriek.

"I got it back for him," I said.

"They just gave it back. They just gave it back. They shouldn't have done that. They shouldn't."

"They didn't just give it back," I said. "They gave it back because I made them."

"You couldn't . . ."

"I told everyone I was going to. And I did."

"No. No. No."

"Yes," I said flatly.

Her expression slowly changed, and highly frightening it was too. I waited while it sank into her disorganized brain that if Byler sent his horses to Cranfield after all it was me alone she had to thank for it. I watched the intention to kill widen to embrace me too. The semi-cautious restraint in her manner towards me was transforming itself into a vicious glare of hate.

I swallowed. I said again, "If I hadn't made the Stewards give Mr. Cranfield's licence back, he would still be warned off."

Roberta said in horror, "No, Kelly. Don't. Don't do it."

"Shut up," I said. "Me or your father . . . which has more chance? And run, when you can."

Grace wasn't listening. Grace was grasping the essentials and deciding on a course of action.

There was a lot of white showing round her eyes.

"I'll kill you," she said. "I'll kill you."

I stood still. I waited. The seconds stretched like centuries.

"Come here" she said. "Come here, or I'll cut her throat."

XV

I took myself crutch by crutch towards her. When I was halfway there Mrs. Cranfield gave a moaning sigh and fainted, falling awkwardly on the rug and scattering the brass fire irons with a nerve-shattering crash.

Grace jumped. The knife snicked into Roberta's skin and she cried out. I stood half unbalanced, freezing into immobility, trying to will Grace not to disintegrate into panic, not to go over the edge, not to lose the last tiny grip she had on her reason. She wasn't far off stabbing everything in sight.

"Sit still," I said to Roberta with dreadful urgency and she gave me a terrified look and did her best not to move. She was trembling violently. I had never thought I could pray. I prayed.

Grace was moving her head in sharp birdlike jerks. The knife was still against Roberta's neck. Grace's other hand still grasped Roberta's shoulder. A thread of blood trickled down Roberta's skin and was blotted up in a scarlet patch by her white jersey.

No one went to help Roberta's mother. I didn't even dare to look at her, because it meant turning my eyes away from Grace.

"Come here," Grace said. "Come here."

Her voice was husky, little more than a loud whisper. And although she was watching me come with unswerving murder in her eyes, I was inexpressibly thankful that she could still speak at all, still think, still hold a purpose.

During the last few steps I wondered how I was going to dodge, since I couldn't jump, couldn't bend my knees, and hadn't even my hands free. A bit late to start worrying. I took the last step short so that she would have to move to reach me and at the same time eased my elbow out of the right-hand crutch.

She was almost too fast. She struck at me instantly, in a flashing thrust directed at my throat, and although I managed to twist the two inches needed to avoid it, the hissing knife came close enough, through the collar of my coat. I brought my right arm up and across, crashing a crutch against her as she prepared to try again.

Out of the corner of my eye I saw Roberta wrench herself out of Grace's clutching grasp, and half stumble, half fall as she got away from the chair.

"Kill you," Grace said. The words were distorted. The meaning clear. She had no thought of self-defence. No thought at all, as far as I could see. Just one single burning obsessive intention.

I brought up the left-hand crutch like a pole to push her away. She dived round it and tried to plunge her knife through my ribs, and in throwing myself away from that I over-balanced and half fell down, and she was standing over me with her arm raised like a priest at a human sacrifice.

I dropped one crutch altogether. Useless warding off a knife with a bare hand. I tried to shove the other crutch round into her face, but got it tangled up against an armchair.

Grace brought her arm down. I fell right to the floor as soon as I saw her move and the knife followed me harmlessly, all the impetus gone by the time it reached me. Another tear in my coat.

She came down on her knees beside me, her arm going up again.

From nowhere my lost crutch whistled through the air and smashed into the hand which held the knife. Grace hissed like a snake and dropped it, and it fell point down in to my plaster. She twisted round to see who had hit her and spread out her hands towards the crutch that Roberta was aiming at her again.

She caught hold of it and tugged. I wriggled round on the floor, stretched until I had my fingers round the handle of the knife, and threw it as hard as I could towards the open door into the hall.

Grace was too much for Roberta. Too much for me. She was appallingly, insanely, strong. I heaved myself up on to my left knee and clasped my arms tight round her chest from behind, trying to pin her arms down to her sides. She shook me around like a sack of feathers, struggling to get to her feet.

She managed it, lifting me with her, plaster and all. She knew where I'd thrown the knife. She started to go that way, dragging me with her still fastened to her back like a leech.

"Get that knife and run to the stables," I gasped to Roberta. A girl in a million. She simply ran and picked up the knife and went on running, out into the hall and out of the house.

Grace started yelling unintelligibly and began trying to unclamp the fingers I had laced together over her thin breastbone. I hung on for everyone's dear life, and when she couldn't dislodge them she began pinching wherever she could reach with fierce hurting spite.

The hair which she usually wore screwed into a fold up the back of her neck had come undone and was falling into my face. I could see less and less of what was going on. I knew only that she was still headed towards the doorway, still unimaginably violent, and mumbling now in a continuous flow of senseless words interspersed with sudden shrieks.

She reached the doorway and started trying to get free of me by crashing me against the jamb. She had a hard job of it, but she managed it in the end, and when she felt my weight fall off her she turned in a flash, sticking out her hands with rigid fingers towards my neck.

Her face was a dark congested crimson. Her eyes were stretched wide in a stark screaming stare. Her lips were drawn back in a tight line from her teeth.

I had never in all my life seen anything so terrifying. Hadn't imagined a human could look like that, had never visualized homicidal madness.

She would certainly have killed me if it hadn't been for Tony, because her strength made a joke of mine. He came tearing into the hall from the kitchen and brought her down with a rugger tackle about the knees, and I fell too, on top of her, because she was trying to tear my throat out in handfuls, and she didn't leave go.

It took all Tony could do, all Archie could do, all three other lads could do to unlatch her from me and hold her down on the floor. They sat on her arms and legs and chest and head, and she threshed about convulsively underneath them.

Roberta had tears streaming down her face and I hadn't any breath left to tell her to cheer up, there was no more danger, no more . . . no more . . . I leant weakly against the wall and thought it would be too damned silly to pass out now. Took three deep breaths instead. Everything steadied again, reluctantly.

Tony said, "There's a doctor on his way. Don't think he's expecting this, though."

"He'll know what to do."

"Mother!" exclaimed Roberta suddenly. "I'd forgotten about her." She hurried past me into the drawing-room and I heard her mother's voice rising in a disturbed, disorientated question.

Grace was crying out, but her voice sounded like seagulls and nothing she said made sense. One of the lads said sympathetically, "Poor thing, oughtn't we to let her get up?" and Tony answered fiercely, "Only under a tiger net."

"She doesn't know what's happening," I said wearily. "She can't control what she does. So don't for God's sake let go of her."

Except for Tony's resolute six foot they all sat on her gingerly and twice she nearly had them off. Finally and at long last the front-door bell rang, and I hopped across the hall to answer it.

It was the local doctor, looking tentative, wondering no doubt if it were a hoax. But he took one look at Grace and was opening his case while he came across the hall. Into her arm he pushed a hypodermic needle and soon the convulsive threshing slackened, and the high-pitched crying dulled to murmurs and in the end to silence.

The five men slowly stood up and stepped away from her, and she lay there looking shrunk and crumpled, her greying hair falling in streaks away from her flaccidly relaxing face. It seemed incredible that such thin limbs, such a meagre body, could have put out such strength. We all stood looking down at her with more awe than pity, watching while the last twitches shook her and she sank into unconscious peace.

Half an hour later Grace still lay on the floor in the hall, but with a pillow under her head and a rug keeping her warm.

Dexter Cranfield had come back from watching the horses work and walked unprepared into the aftermath of drama. His wife's semi-hysterical explanations hadn't helped him much.

Roberta told him that Grace had come to kill him because he had his licence back and that she was the cause of his losing it in the first place, and he stamped around in a fury which I gathered was mostly because the source of our troubles was a woman. He basically didn't like women. She should have been locked up years ago, he said. Spiteful, petty minded, scheming, interfering . . . just like a woman, he said. I listened to him gravely and concluded he had suffered from a bossy nanny.

The doctor had done some intensive telephoning, and presently an ambulance arrived with two compassionate-looking men and a good deal of special equipment. The front door stood wide open and the prospect of Grace's imminent departure was a relief to everyone.

Into this active bustling scene drove Jack Roxford.

He scrambled out of his car, took a horrified look at the ambulance, and ploughed in through the front door. When he saw Grace lying there with the ambulance men preparing to lift her on to a stretcher, he went down on his knees beside her.

"Grace, dear . . ." He looked at her more closely. She was still unconscious, very pale now, looking wizened and sixty. "Grace, dear!" There was anguish in his voice. "What's the matter with her?"

The doctor started to break it to him. Cranfield interrupted the gentle words and said brutally, "She's raving mad. She came here trying to kill me and she could have killed my wife and daughter. It's absolutely disgraceful that she should have been running around free in that state. I'm going to see my solicitors about it."

Jack Roxford only heard the first part. His eyes went to the cut on Roberta's neck and the blood-stain on her jersey, and he put his hand over his mouth and looked sick.

"Grace," he said. "Oh, Grace . . ."

There was no doubt he loved her. He leant over her, stroking the hair away from her forehead, murmuring to her, and when he finally looked up there were tears in his eyes and on his cheeks.

"She'll be all right, won't she?"

The doctor shifted uncomfortably and said one would have to see, only time would tell, there were marvellous treatments nowadays . . .

The ambulance men loaded her gently on to the stretcher and picked it up.

"Let me go with her," Jack Roxford said. "Where are you taking her? Let me go with her."

One of the ambulance men told him the name of the hospital and advised him not to come.

"Better try this evening, sir. No use you waiting all day, now, is it?" And the doctor added that Grace would be unconscious for some time yet and under heavy sedation after that, and it was true, it would be better if Roxford didn't go with her.

The uniformed men carried Grace out into the sunshine and loaded her into the ambulance, and we all followed them out into the drive. Jack Roxford stood there looking utterly forlorn as they shut the doors, consulted finally with the doctor, and with the minimum of fuss, drove away.

Roberta touched his arm. "Can't I get you a drink, Mr. Roxford?"

He looked at her vaguely, and then his whole face crumpled and he couldn't speak.

"Don't, Mr. Roxford," Roberta said with pity. "She isn't in any pain, or anything."

He shook his head. Roberta put her arm across his shoulders and steered him back into the house.

"Now what?" Tony said. "I've really got to get to Reading, pal. Those runners of mine have to be declared for the second race."

I looked at my watch. "You could spare another quarter of an hour. I think we should take Jack Roxford with us. He's got a runner too, incidentally, though I imagine he doesn't much care about that . . . Except that it's one of Edwin Byler's. But he's not fit to drive anywhere himself, and the races would help to keep him from brooding too much about Grace."

"Yeah. A possible idea," Tony grinned.

"Go into the house and see if you can persuade him to let you take him."

"OK." He went off amiably, and I passed the time swinging around the drive on my crutches and peering into the cars parked there. I'd be needing a new one . . . probably choose the same again, though.

I leant against Tony's car and thought about Grace. She'd left on me a fair legacy of bruises from her pinches to add to the crop grown by Oakley. Also my coat would cost a fortune at the invisible menders, and my throat felt like a well-developed case of septic tonsils. I looked gloomily down at my plastered leg. The dangers of detection seemed to be twice as high as steeplechasing. With luck, I thought with a sigh, I could now go back to the usual but less frequent form of battery.

Tony came out of the house with Roberta and Jack Roxford. Jack looked dazed, and let Tony help him into the front of the estate car as if his thoughts were miles away. As indeed they probably were.

I scrunched across the gravel towards Roberta.

"Is your neck all right?" I asked.

"Is yours?"

I investigated her cut more closely. It wasn't deep. Little more than an inch long.

"There won't be much of a scar," I said.

"No," she agreed.

Her face was close to mine. Her eyes were amber with dark flecks.

"Stay here," she said abruptly. "You don't have to go to the races."

"I've an appointment with Lord Ferth . . . Best to get this business thoroughly wrapped up."

"I suppose so." She looked suddenly very tired. She'd had a wearing Saturday morning.

"If you've nothing better to do," I suggested, "would you come over tomorrow . . . and cook me some lunch?"

A small smile tugged at her mouth and wrinkled her eyes.

"I fell hopelessly in love with you," she said, "when I was twelve."

"And then it wore off?"

"Yes."

"Pity," I said.

Her smile broadened.

"Who is Bobbie?" I asked.

"Bobbie? Oh . . . he's Lord Iceland's son."

"He would be."

She laughed. "Father wants me to marry him."

"That figures."

"But Father is going to be disappointed."

"Good," I said.

"Kelly," yelled Tony. "Come on, for Hell's sakes, or I'll be late."

"Goodbye," she said calmly. "See you tomorrow."

Tony drove to Reading races with due care and attention and Jack Roxford sat sunk in gloomy silence from start to finish. When we stopped in the car park he stepped out of the car and walked dazedly away towards the entrance without a word of thanks or explanation.

Tony watched him go and clicked his tongue. "That woman isn't worth it."

"She is, to him," I said.

Tony hurried off to declare his horses, and I went more slowly through the gate looking out for Lord Ferth.

It felt extraordinary being back on a racecourse. Like being let out of prison. The same people who had looked sideways at me at the Jockeys' Fund dance now slapped me familiarly on the back and said they were delighted to see me. Oh yeah, I thought ungratefully. Never kick a man once he's up.

Lord Ferth was standing outside the weighing-room in a knot of people from which he detached himself when he saw me coming.

"Come along to the Stewards' dining-room," he said. "We can find a quiet corner there."

"Can we postpone it until after the third race?" I asked. "I want my cousin Tony to be there as well, and he has some runners . . ."

"Of course," he agreed. "Later would be best for me too, as it happens. After the third, then."

I watched the first three races with the hunger of an exile returned. Tony's horse, my sometime mount, finished a fast fourth, which augured well for next time out, and Byler's horse won the third. As I hurried round to see how Jack Roxford would make out in the winner's enclosure I almost crashed into Kessel. He looked me over, took in the plaster and crutches, and said nothing at all. I watched his cold expressionless face with one to match. After ramming home the point that he had no intention of apologizing he turned brusquely on his heel and walked away.

"Get that," Tony said in my ear. "You could sue him for defamation."

"He's not worth the effort."

From Charlie West, too, I'd had much the same reaction. Defiance, slightly sullen variety. I shrugged resignedly. That was my own fault, and only time would tell.

Tony walked with me to the winner's enclosure. Byler was there, beaming. Jack Roxford still looked lost. We watched Byler suggest a celebration drink, and Jack shake his head vaguely as if he hadn't understood.

"Go and fish Jack out," I said to Tony. "Tell him you're still looking after him."

"If you say so, pal." He obligingly edged through the crowd, took Jack by the elbow, said a few explanatory words to Byler, and steered Jack out.

I joined them and said neutrally, "This way," and led them along towards the Stewards' dining-room. They both went through the door taking off their hats and hanging them on the pegs inside.

The long tables in the Stewards' dining-room had been cleared from lunch and laid for tea, but there was no one in there except Lord Ferth. He shook hands with Tony and Jack and invited them to sit down around one end of a table.

"Kelly? . . ." he suggested.

"I'll stand," I said. "Easier."

"Well now," Ferth said, glancing curiously at Tony and Jack, "you told me, Kelly, that you knew who had framed you and Dexter Cranfield."

I nodded.

Tony said regretfully, "Grace Roxford. Jack's wife."

Jack looked vaguely down at the tablecloth and said nothing at all.

Tony explained to Lord Ferth just what had happened at Cranfield's and he looked more and more upset.

"My dear Roxford," he said uncomfortably, "I'm so sorry. So very sorry." He looked up at me. "One could never have imagined that she . . . that Grace Roxford of all people . . . could have framed you."

"That's right," I said mildly. "She didn't."

XVI

Both Tony and Jack sat up as if electrified.

Lord Ferth said, "But you said . . ." And Tony answered, "I thought there was no doubt . . . She tried to kill Kelly . . . she was going to kill Cranfield too."

"She tried to kill me this time," I agreed. "But not the time before. It wasn't she who fiddled with my car."

"Then *who?*" Lord Ferth demanded.

"Her husband."

Jack stood up. He looked a lot less lost.

I poked Tony on the shoulder with my crutch, and he took the hint and stood up too. He was sitting between Jack and the door.

"Sit down, Mr. Roxford," Ferth said authoritatively, and after a pause, slowly, he obeyed.

"That's nonsense," he said protestingly. "I didn't touch Kelly's car. No one could have arranged that accident."

"You couldn't have imagined I would be hit by a train," I agreed. "But some sort of smash, yes, definitely."

"But Grace . . ." began Tony, still bewildered.

"Grace," I said prosaically, "has in most respects displayed exactly opposite qualities to the person who engineered Cranfield's and my suspension. Grace has been wild, accusing, uncontrolled, and emotional. The planning which went into getting us warned off was cool, careful, efficient, and brutal."

"Mad people are very cunning," Tony said doubtfully.

"It wasn't Grace," I said positively. "It was Jack."

There was a pause. Then Jack said in a rising wail, "Why ever did she have to go to Cranfield's this morning? Why ever couldn't she leave things alone?"

"It wouldn't have done any good," I said, "I already knew it was you."

"That's impossible."

Ferth cleared his throat. "I think . . . er . . . you'd better tell us, Kelly, what your grounds are for making this very serious accusation."

"It began," I said, "when Dexter Cranfield persuaded Edwin Byler to take his horses away from Roxford and send them to him. Cranfield did no doubt persuade Byler, as Grace maintained, that he was a more highly regarded trainer socially than Roxford. Social standing means a great deal to Mr. Cranfield, and he is apt to expect that it does to everyone else. And in Edwin Byler's case, he was very likely right. But Jack had trained Byler's horses from the day he bought his first, and as Byler's fortune and string grew, so did Jack's prosperity and prestige. To lose Byler was to him a total disaster. A return to obscurity. The end of everything. Jack isn't a bad trainer, but he hasn't the personality to make the top ranks. Not without an accident . . . a gift from Heaven . . . like Byler. And you don't find two Bylers in your yard in one lifetime. So almost from the start I wondered about Jack; from as soon as Cranfield told me, two days after the Enquiry, that Byler had been going to transfer his horses. Because I felt such a wrench of regret, you see, that I was not going to ride them . . . and I realized that that was nothing compared to what Jack would have felt if he'd lost them."

"I didn't feel so bad as that," said Jack dully.

"I had an open mind," I said, "because Pat Nikita had much the same motive, only the other way round. He and Cranfield detest each other. He had been trying to coax Kessel away from Cranfield for years, and getting Cranfield warned off was one way of clinching things. Then there were various people with smaller motives, like Charlie West, who might have hoped to ride Squelch for Nikita if I were out of the way. And there was a big possibility that it was someone else altogether, someone I hadn't come across, whose motive I couldn't even suspect."

"So why must it be Mr. Roxford?" Ferth said.

I took the paper Teddy Dewar had sent me out of my pocket and handed it to him, explaining what it meant.

"That shows a direct link between Oakley and the people in the circles. One of those people is Jack Roxford. He did, you see, know of Oakley's existence. He knew Oakley would agree to provide faked evidence."

"But . . ." Lord Ferth began.

"Yes, I know," I said. "Circumstantial. Then there's this list of people from George Newtonnards." I gave him the list, and pointed. "These are the people who definitely knew that Cranfield had backed Cherry Pie with Newtonnards. Again this is not conclusive, because other people might have known, who are not on this list. But that man," I pointed to the name in Herbie Subbings' list of contacts, "that man is Grace Roxford's brother. Jack's brother-in-law."

Ferth looked at me levelly. "You've taken a lot of trouble."

"It was taken for me," I said, "by Teddy Dewar and his friend, and by George Newtonnards."

"They acted on your suggestions, though."

"Yes."

"Anything else?"

"Well," I said. "There are those neatly typed sheets of accusations which were sent to Lord Gowery. So untypical, by the way, of Grace. We could compare the typewriter with Jack's . . . Typewriters are about as distinctive as finger prints. I haven't had an opportunity to do that yet."

Jack looked up wildly. The typewriter made sense to him. He hadn't followed the significance of the lists.

Ferth said slowly, "I obtained from the Stewards' Secretaries the letter which pointed out to them that a disqualified person was living in a racing stable. As far as I remember, the typing is the same as in the original accusations."

"Very catty, that," I said. "More like Grace. Revengeful, and without much point."

"I never wrote to the Stewards' Secretaries," Jack said.

"Did Grace?"

He shook his head. I thought perhaps he didn't know. It didn't seem to be of any great importance. I said instead: "I looked inside the boot of Jack's car this morning, while he was in Mr. Cranfield's house. He carries a great big tool kit, including a hand drill."

"No," Jack said.

"Yes, indeed. Also you have an old grey Volkswagen, the one Grace drove today. That car was seen by the mechanic from my garage when you went to pick over the remains of my car. I imagine you were hoping to remove any tell-tale drill holes which might have led the insurance company to suspect attempted murder, but Derek was there before you. And you either followed him or asked the garage whether he'd taken anything from the wreckage, because you sent David Oakley to my flat to get it back. Oakley didn't know the significance of what he was looking for. A chunk of metal with a hole in it. That was all he knew. He was there to earn a fee."

"Did he find it?" Ferth asked.

"No. I still have it. Can one prove that a certain drill made a certain hole?"

Ferth didn't know. Jack didn't speak.

"When you heard, at the dance," I said, "that I was trying to find out who had framed Cranfield and me, you thought you would get rid of me, in case I managed it. Because if I managed it, you'd lose far more than Byler's horses . . . so while I was talking to Lord Ferth and dancing with Roberta, you were out at the back of the car park rigging up your booby trap. Which," I added calmly, remembering the blazing hell of the dislocations, "I find hard to forgive."

"I'll strangle him," Tony said forcefully.

"What happens to him," I shook my head, "depends on Lord Ferth."

Ferth regarded me squarely. "You find him. I deal with him."

"That was the agreement."

"To your satisfaction."

"Yes."

"And what *is* your satisfaction?"

I didn't know.

Tony moved restlessly, looking at his watch. "Lord Ferth, Kelly, look, I'm sorry, but I've got a horse to saddle for the last race . . . I'll have to go now."

"Yes, of course," said Lord Ferth. "But we'd all be obliged if you wouldn't talk about what you've learned in here."

Tony looked startled. "Sure. If you say so. Not a word." He stood up and went over to the door. "See you after," he said to me. "You secretive so-and-so."

As he went out a bunch of Stewards and their wives came in chattering for their tea. Lord Ferth went over to them and exerted the flashing eyes, and they all went into reverse. A waiter who had materialized behind them was stationed outside the door with instructions to send all customers along to the members' tea room.

While this was going on Jack looked steadfastly down at the tablecloth and said not a word. I didn't feel like chatting to him idly either. He'd cost me too much.

Lord Ferth came briskly back and sat down.

"Now then, Roxford," he said in his most businesslike way, "we've heard Kelly's accusations. It's your turn now to speak up in your defence."

Jack slowly lifted his head. The deep habitual lines of worry were running with sweat.

"It was someone else." His voice was dead.

"It certainly wasn't Grace," I said, "because Lord Gowery was quite clear that the person who tried to blackmail him on the telephone was a man." So was the person who had got at Charlie West a man, or so he'd said.

Jack Roxford jerked.

"Yes, Roxford, we know about Lord Gowery," Ferth said.

"You *can't* . . ."

"You belong to the same club," I said assertively, as if I knew.

For Jack Roxford, too, the thought of that club was the lever which opened the floodgates. Like Gowery before him he broke into wretched pieces.

"You don't understand . . ."

"Tell us then," Ferth said. "And we'll try."

"Grace . . . we . . . I . . . Grace didn't like . . ." He petered out.

I gave him a shove. "Grace liked her sex natural and wouldn't stand for what you wanted."

He gulped. "Soon after we were married we were having rows all the time, and I hated that. I loved her, really I did. I've always loved her. And I felt . . . all tangled up . . . she didn't understand that when I beat her it was because of love . . . she said she'd leave me and divorce me for cruelty . . . so I asked a girl I'd known . . . a street girl, who didn't mind . . . I mean . . . she let you, if you paid well enough . . . if I could go on seeing her . . . but she said she'd given that up now . . . but there was a club in London . . . and I went there . . . and it was a terrific relief . . . and then I was all right with Grace . . . but of course we didn't . . . well, hardly ever . . . but somehow . . . we could go on being married."

Lord Ferth looked revolted.

"I couldn't believe it at first," Jack said more coherently, "when I saw Lord Gowery there. I saw him in the street, just outside. I thought it was just a coincidence. But then, one night, inside the club, I was sure it was him, and I saw him again in the street another time . . . but I didn't say anything. I mean, how could I? And anyway, I knew how he felt . . . you don't go there unless you must . . . and you can't keep away."

"How long have you known that Lord Gowery went to the same club?" I asked.

"Oh . . . two or three years. A long time. I don't know exactly."

"Did he know you were a member?"

"No. He hadn't a clue. I spoke to him once or twice on the racecourse about official things . . . He didn't have any idea."

"And then," Ferth said thoughtfully, "you read that he had been appointed in Colonel Midgely's place to officiate at the Cranfield-Hughes Enquiry, and you saw what you thought was a good chance of getting Cranfield out of racing, and keeping Byler's horses yourself."

Jack sat huddled in his chair, not denying it.

"And when Lord Gowery declined to be blackmailed, you couldn't bear to give up the idea, and you set about faking evidence that would achieve your ends."

A long silence. Then Jack said in a thick disjointed voice, "Grace minded so much . . . about Cranfield taking our horses. She went on and on about it . . . morning, noon, and night. Couldn't stop. Talk, talk, talk. All the time. Saying she'd like to kill Cranfield . . . and things like that. I mean . . . she's always been a bit nervy . . . a bit strung up . . . but Cranfield was upsetting her . . . I got a bit frightened for her sometimes, she was that violent about him . . . Well, it was really because of that that I tried to get Cranfield warned off . . . I mean, he was better warned off than Grace trying to kill him."

"Did you truly believe she would?" I asked.

"She was ranting about it all the time . . . I didn't know if she really would . . . but I was so afraid . . . I didn't want her to get into trouble . . . dear dear Grace . . . I wanted to help her . . . and make things right again . . . so I set about it . . . and it wasn't too difficult really, not once I'd set my mind to it."

Ferth gave me a twisted smile. I gave him a similar one back and reflected that marriage could be a deadly institution. Grace's strung-up state would have been aggravated by the strain of living with a sexually odd man, and Jack would have felt guilty about it and wanted to make it up to her. Neither of them had been rationally inclined, and the whole situation had boiled up claustrophobically inside their agonized private world. Having dear Grace harping on endlessly would have driven many a stronger man to explosive action: but Jack couldn't desert her, because he had to stay with his horses, and he couldn't drive her away because he loved her. The only way he'd seen of silencing his wife had been to ruin Cranfield.

"Why me?" I said, trying to keep out the bitterness. "Why me too?"

"Eh?" He squinted at me, half focussing. "You . . . well . . . I haven't anything against you personally . . . But I thought it was the only way to make it a certainty . . . Cranfield couldn't have swindled that race without Squelch's jockey being in the know."

"That race was no swindle," I said.

"Oh . . . I know that. Those stupid Oxford Stewards . . . still, they gave me such an opportunity . . . when I heard about Lord Gowery being in charge. And then, when I'd fixed up with Charlie West and Oakley . . . Grace's brother told me, just told me casually, mind you, that his bookmaker had told him that Cranfield had backed Cherry Pie, and do you know what, I couldn't stop laughing. Just like Grace, I felt . . . dead funny, it was, that he really had backed Cherry Pie . . . ."

"What was that about Charlie West?" Ferth said sharply.

"I paid him . . . to say Kelly pulled Squelch back. I telephoned and asked him . . . if Kelly ever did anything like that . . . and he said once, in a novice 'chase, Kelly had said, 'OK. Brakes on, chaps,' and I told him to say Kelly had said that in the Lemonfizz Cup, because it sounded so convincing, didn't it, saying something Kelly really had said . . . ."

Ferth looked at me accusingly. "You shielded West."

I shrugged ruefully. Jack paid no attention: didn't hear.

He went on miserably: "Grace was all right before the dance. She was wonderfully calm again, after Cranfield was warned off. And then Edwin Byler said that we would be keeping his horses for always . . . and we were happy . . . in our way . . . and then we heard . . . that Kelly was at the dance . . . saying he'd been framed . . . and was just on the point of finding out who . . . and Grace saw Cranfield's daughter and just boiled over all over again, nearly as bad as before . . . and I thought . . . if Kelly was dead . . . it would be all right again . . ."

Ferth slowly shook his head. The reasoning which had led Jack Roxford step by step from misfortune to crime defeated him.

"I thought he wouldn't feel anything," Jack said. "I thought that you just blacked out suddenly from carbon monoxide. I thought it would be like going to sleep . . . he wouldn't know about it. Just wouldn't wake up."

"You didn't drill a big enough hole," I said without irony. "Not enough gas came through at once to knock me out."

"I couldn't find a large enough tube," he said with macabre sense. "Had to use a piece I had. It was a bit narrow. That was why."

"I see," I said gravely. So close. Not a few inches from the express train. One eighth of an inch extra in the tube's diameter would have done it.

"And you went to look for the pieces of manifold, afterwards?"

"Yes . . . but you know about that. I was furious with Oakley for not finding it . . . he said he tried to make you tell, but you wouldn't . . . and I said it didn't surprise me . . ."

"Why didn't you ask *him* to kill me?" I said matter-of-factly.

"Oh, I did. He said he didn't kill. He said he would dispose of the body if I did it, but he never did the job himself. Not worth it, he said."

That sounded like the authentic Oakley. Straight from the agent's mouth.

"But you couldn't risk it?" I suggested.

"I didn't have any chance. I mean . . . I didn't like to leave Grace alone much . . . she was so upset . . . and then, you were in hospital . . . and then you went back to your flat . . . and I did try to shift you out into the open somewhere . . ."

"You did write to the Stewards' Secretaries," Ferth exclaimed. "After all."

"Yes . . . but it was too late . . . wasn't it . . . She really meant it . . . poor Grace, poor Grace . . . why did I let her go out . . . But she seemed so much better this morning . . . and now . . . and now . . ." His face screwed up and turned red as he tried not to cry. The thought of Grace as he'd last seen her was too much for him. The tears rolled. He sniffed into a handkerchief.

I wondered how he would have felt if he'd seen Grace as I'd seen her.

But probably the uncritical love he had would have survived even that.

"Just sit here quietly a moment, Roxford," Lord Ferth directed, and he himself stood up and signed for me to walk with him over to the door.

"So what do we do with him?" he said.

"It's gone too far now," I said reluctantly, "to be entirely hushed up. And he's if anything more dangerous than Grace . . . She will live, and he will very likely see everything for ever in terms of her happiness. Anyone who treats her badly in any way could end up as a victim of his scheming. End up ruined . . . or dead. People like nurses . . . or relations . . . or even people like me, who did her no harm at all. Anybody . . ."

Ferth said, "You seem to understand his mind. I must say that I don't. But what you say makes sense. We cannot just take away his licence and leave it at that . . . It isn't a racing matter any more. But Lord Gowery . . ."

"Lord Gowery will have to take his chance," I said without satisfaction. "Very likely you can avoid busting open his reputation . . . but it's much more important to stop Jack Roxford doing the same sort of thing again."

"Yes," he said. "It is." He spread out his hands sideways in a pushing gesture as if wanting to step away from the decision. "All this is so *distressing.*"

I looked down the room at Jack, a huddled defeated figure with nervous eyes and an anxious forehead. He was picking at the tablecloth with his fingers, folding it into senseless little pleats. He didn't look like a villain. No hardened criminal. Just a tenacious little man with a fixed idea, to make up to dear Grace for being what he was.

Nothing was more useless than sending him to prison, and nothing could do him more harm: yet that, I imagined, was where he would go. Putting his body in a little cage wouldn't straighten the kinks in his mind. The system, for men like him, was screwy.

He stood up slowly and walked unsteadily towards us.

"I suppose," he said without much emotion, "that you are going to get the police. I was wondering . . . please . . . don't tell them about the club . . . I won't say Lord Gowery goes there . . . I won't tell anybody ever . . . I never really wanted to . . . it wouldn't have done any good, would it? I mean, it wouldn't have kept those horses in my yard . . . wouldn't have made a scrap of difference . . . So do you think anyone need know about . . . the club?"

"No," said Ferth with well-disguised relief. "They need not."

A faint smile set up a rival set of creases to the lines of anxiety. "Thank you." The smile faded away. The lost look deepened. "How long . . . do you think I'll get?"

Ferth moved uncomfortably. "No point in worrying about that until you have to."

"You could probably halve it," I said.

"How?" He was pathetically hopeful. I flung him the rope.

"By giving evidence at another trial I have in mind, and taking David Oakley down with you."

Part Three: March Epilogue

Yesterday I rode Breadwinner in the Cheltenham Gold Cup.

A horse of raw talent with more future than past. A shambling washy chestnut carrying his head low. No one's idea of equine beauty.

Old Strepson watched him slop around the parade ring and said with a sigh, "He looks half asleep."

"Hughes will wake him up," Cranfield said condescendingly.

Cranfield stood in the chill March sunshine making his usual good stab at arrogance. The mean calculating lines round his mouth seemed to have deepened during the past month, and his manner to me was if anything more distant, more master-servant, than ever before. Roberta said she had told him that I had in some way managed to get our licences back, but he saw no reason to believe her and preferred the thought of divine intervention.

Old Strepson said conversationally, "Kelly says Breadwinner was a late foal and a late developer, and won't reach his true strength until about this time next year."

Cranfield gave me a mouth-tightening mind-your-own-business glare, and didn't seem to realize that I'd given him an alibi if the horse didn't win and built him up into one heck of a good trainer if it did. Whatever low opinion Cranfield held of me, I reciprocated it in full.

Farther along the parade ring stood a silent little group of Kessel, Pat Nikita, and their stable jockey, Al Roach. They were engaged in running poor old Squelch, and their interest lay not so fiercely in winning as in finishing at all costs in front of Breadwinner. Kessel himself radiated so much hatred that I thought it was probably giving him a headache. Hating did that. The day I found it out, I gave up hating.

Grace's hatred-headache must have been unbearable . . .

Grace's recovery was still uncertain. Ferth had somehow wangled the best available psychiatrist on to her case, and had also arranged for him to see Jack. Outside the weighing-room when I had arrived, he had jerked his head for me to join him, and told me what the psychiatrist had reported.

"He says Jack is sane according to legal standards, and will have to stand trial. He wouldn't commit himself about Grace's chances. He did say, though, that from all points of view their enforced separation was a godsend. He said he thought their only chance of leading fairly normal lives in the future was to make the separation total and permanent. He said a return to the same circumstances could mean a repeat of the whole cycle."

I looked at Ferth gloomily. "What a cold, sad, depressing solution."

"You never know," he said optimistically, "once they get over it, they might both feel . . . well . . . released."

I smiled at him. He said abruptly, "Your outlook is catching, dammit . . . How about that dinner?"

"Any time," I said.

"Tomorrow, then? Eight o'clock. The Caprice, round the corner from the Ritz . . . The food's better there than at my club."

"Fine," I said.

"And you can tell me how the police are getting on with David Oakley . . ."

I'd had the Birmingham police on my telephone and doorstep for much of the past week. They had almost fallen on my neck and sobbed when I first went to them with enough to make an accusation stick, and had later promised to deliver to me, framed, one of the first fruits of their search warrant: a note from Cranfield to Jack Roxford dated two years earlier, thanking him for not bidding him up at an auction after a selling race and enclosing a cheque for fifty pounds. Across the bottom of the page Cranfield had written:

As agreed. Thanks. D.C.

It was the note Oakley had photographed in my flat. Supplied by Roxford, who had suggested the photograph.

Kept by Oakley, as a hold over Roxford.

The police also told me that Jack Roxford had drawn six hundred pounds in new notes out of his bank during the two weeks before the Enquiry, and David Oakley had paid three hundred of the same notes into his own account five days later.

Clever, slippery Mr. Oakley had been heard to remark that he regretted not having slaughtered Kelly Hughes.

The bell rang for the jockeys to mount, and Cranfield and old Strepson and I walked over to where Breadwinner waited.

The one jockey missing from the day's proceedings was Charlie West, whose licence had been suspended for the rest of the season. And it was only thanks to Hughes' intervention, Ferth had told him forcefully, that he hadn't got his deserts and been warned off for life. Whether Charlie

West would feel an atom of gratitude was another matter.

I swung up easily on to Breadwinner and fitted my right foot carefully into the stirrup. A compromise between me and the orthopod had seen the plaster off seven days previously, but the great surgeon's kind parting words had been, "You haven't given that leg enough time and if it dislocates again it's your own bloody fault."

I had told him that I couldn't afford to have Cranfield engage another jockey for Breadwinner with all the horse's future races at stake. Old Strepson was the grateful type who didn't dislodge a jockey who had won for him, and if some other jockey won the Gold Cup on Breadwinner I would lose the mount for life; and it was only this argument which had grudgingly brought out the saw.

I gathered up the reins and walked the horse quietly round the ring while everyone sorted themselves out into the right order for the parade down the course. Apart from the Grand National, the Cheltenham Gold Cup was the biggest steeplechase of the year. In prestige, probably the greatest of all. All the stars turned out for it, meeting each other in level terms. Bad horses hadn't a hope.

There were nine runners. Breadwinner was the youngest, Squelch the most experienced, and a bad-tempered grey called Ironclad, the favourite.

Al Roach, uninfected by Kessel, lined up beside me at the start and gave me his usual wide friendly Irish grin. "Now Kelly me bhoy," he said, "tell me how you ride this little fellow, now."

"You want to be warned off?" I said.

He chuckled. "What's the owner got against you, Kelly me bhoy?"

"I was right and he was wrong, and he can't forgive that."

"Peculiar fellow, he is, that Kessel . . . "

The tapes went up and we were away. Three and a quarter miles, twenty-one jumps, two whole circuits of the course.

Nothing much happened on the first circuit. No horses fell and no jockeys got excited, and going past the stands and outward bound for the second time a fair-sized sheet would have covered the lot. The next mile sorted the men from the boys, and the bunch flattened out into a relentless, thundering, muscle-straining procession in which hope and sweat and tactics merged into a rushing private world of conflict. Speed . . . jumping at near-disaster rate . . . gambling on the horse's coordination . . . stretching your own . . . a race like the Gold Cup showed you what you were made of . . .

Coming to the second last fence, Ironclad was leading Squelch by three lengths which could have been ten, and he set himself right with all the time in the world. Squelch followed him over, and four lengths behind Breadwinner strained forwards to be third.

Between the last two fences the status quo was unchanged, Breadwinner making no impression on Squelch, nor Squelch on Ironclad. Oh well, I thought resignedly. Third. That wasn't really too bad for such a young horse. One couldn't have everything. And there was always Pound Postage in the Grand National, two weeks on Saturday . . .

Ironclad set himself right for the last fence, launched himself muscularly into the air, crossed the birch with a good foot of air beneath him . . . and pitched forwards on to his nose on landing.

I couldn't believe it. Shook up Breadwinner with a bang of renewed hope and drove him into the last fence for the jump of his young life.

Squelch was over it first, of course. Squelch the sure-footed trained-to-the-minute familiar old rascal . . . Irony of ironies, to be beaten to the Gold Cup by Squelch.

Breadwinner did the best he could to catch him, and I saw that as in the Lemonfizz, Squelch was dying from tiredness. Length by length my gangling chestnut pegged back the gap, straining, stretching, quivering to get past . . . but the winning post was too near . . . it was no good . . . there wasn't time . . .

Al Roach looked round to see who was pressing him. Saw me. Knew that Breadwinner was of all others the one he had to beat. Was seized with panic. If he had sat still, he would have won by two lengths. Instead, he picked up his whip and hit Squelch twice down the flank.

You stupid ass, I thought breathlessly. He hates that. He'll stop. He always stops if you hit him . . .

Squelch's tail swished in fury. His rhythmic stride broke up into bumps. He shook his head violently from side to side.

I saw Al's desperate face as Breadwinner caught him . . . and the winning post was there and gone in a flash . . . and neither of us knew even then which had won.

The photograph gave it to Breadwinner by a nostril. And if I got booed by the crowd after the Lemonfizz they made up for it after the Gold Cup.

Kessel, predictably, was purple with fury, and he seemed on the brink of explosion when someone remarked loudly that Squelch would have won if Hughes had been riding him. I laughed. Kessel looked almost as murderous as Grace.

Old Strepson was pale with emotion but even the Gold Cup did not raise much observable joy in Cranfield; and I found out later that Edwin Byler had just told him he wouldn't be sending him his horses after all. Grace's psychiatrist had written to say that Grace's ultimate sanity might depend on Cranfield not having the horses, and Byler said he felt he owed the Roxfords something . . . sorry and all that, but there it was.

Roberta with her mother had been there patting Breadwinner in the winner's enclosure, and when I came out of the weighing-room twenty minutes later after changing into street clothes, she was leaning against the rails there, waiting.

"You're limping," she said calmly.

"Unfit, that's all."

"Coffee?" she suggested.

"Yes," I said.

She walked sedately ahead of me into the coffee room. Her copper hair still shone after she'd stepped out of the sunshine, and I liked the simple string-coloured coat which went underneath it.

I bought her some coffee and sat at a little plastic-topped table and looked at the litter left by the last occupants; empty coffee cups, plates with crumbs, cigarette butts, and a froth-lined beer glass. Roberta packed them coolly to one side and ignored them.

"Winning and losing," she said. "That's what it's all about."

"Racing?"

"Life."

I looked at her.

She said, "Today is marvellous, and being warned off was terrible. I suppose everything goes on like that . . . up and down . . . always."

"I suppose so," I agreed.

"I've learned a lot, since the Enquiry."

"So have I . . . about you."

"Father says I must remember your background . . ."

"That's true," I said. "You must."

"Father's mind has chains on. Iron bars in his soul. His head's chock-a-block with ideas half a century out of date." She mimicked my own words with pompous mischief.

I laughed. "Roberta . . ."

"Please tell me . . ." She hesitated. ". . . At the level crossing . . . when you called me Rosalind . . . was it her you wanted?"

"No," I said slowly, "it was you . . . In her place."

She sighed contentedly.

"That's all right, then," she said. "Isn't it?"

THE FAR SIDE
OF THE DOLLAR

by

ROSS MACDONALD

1

It was August, and it shouldn't have been raining. Perhaps rain was too strong a word for the drizzle that blurred the landscape and kept my windshield wipers going. I was driving south, about halfway between Los Angeles and San Diego.

The school lay off the highway to my right, in large grounds of its own which stretched along the seashore. Toward the sea I caught the dull sheen of the slough that gave the place its name, Laguna Perdida. A blue heron, tiny in the distance, stood like a figurine at the edge of the ruffled water.

I entered the grounds through automatic gates which lifted when my car passed over a treadle. A gray-headed man in a blue serge uniform came out of a kiosk and limped in my direction.

"You got a pass?"

"Dr. Sponti wants to see me. My name is Archer."

"That's right, I got your name here." He took a typewritten list out of the inside breast pocket of his jacket and brandished it as if he was proud of his literacy. "You can park in the lot in front of the administration building. Sponti's office is right inside." He gestured toward a stucco building a hundred yards down the road.

I thanked him. He started to limp back to his kiosk, then paused and turned and struck himself on the leg. "Bad knee. World War I."

"You don't look that old."

"I'm not. I was fifteen when I enlisted, told them I was eighteen. Some of the boys in here," he said with a sudden flashing look around him, "could do with a taste of fire."

There were no boys anywhere in sight. The buildings of the school, widely distributed among bare fields and dripping eucalyptus groves, lay under the gray sky like scattered components of an unbuilt city.

"Do you know the Hillman boy?" I said to the guard.

"I heard about him. He's a troublemaker. He had East Hall all stirred up before he took off. Patch was fit to be tied."

"Who's Patch?"

"Mr. Patch," he said without affection, "is the supervisor for East Hall. He lives in with the boys, and it plays hell with his nerves."

"What did the Hillman boy do?"

"Tried to start a rebellion, according to Patch. Said the boys in the school had civil rights like anybody else. Which ain't so. They're all minors, and most of them are crazy in the head, besides. You wouldn't believe some of the things I've seen in my fourteen years on this gate."

"Did Tommy Hillman go out through the gate?"

"Naw. He went over the fence. Cut a screen in the boys' dorm and sneaked out in the middle of the night."

"Night before last?"

"That's right. He's probably home by now."

He wasn't or I wouldn't have been there.

Dr. Sponti must have seen me parking my car. He was waiting for me in the secretary's enclosure outside the door of his office. He had a glass of buttermilk in his left hand and a dietetic wafer in his right. He popped the wafer into his mouth and shook my hand, munching. "I'm glad to see you."

He was dark and florid and stout, with the slightly desperate look of a man who had to lose weight. I guessed that he was an emotional man —he had that liquid tremor of the eye—but one who had learned to keep his feelings under control. He was expensively and conservatively dressed in a dark pinstripe suit which hung on him a little loosely. His hand was soft and chilly.

Dr. Sponti reminded me of undertakers I had known. Even his office, with its dark mahogany furniture and the gray light at the window, had a funereal look, as if the school and its director were in continuous mourning for its students.

"Sit down," he said with a melancholy flourish. "We have a little problem, as I told you on the long-distance telephone. Ordinarily we don't employ private detectives to—ah—persuade our lost boys to come home. But this is a rather special case, I'm afraid."

"What makes it special?"

Sponti sipped his buttermilk, and licked his upper lip with the tip of his tongue. "Forgive me. Can I offer you some lunch?"

"No thanks."

"I don't mean this." Irritably, he jiggled the sluggish liquid in his glass. "I can have something hot sent over from dining commons. Veal scallopini is on the menu today."

"No thanks. I'd rather you gave me the information I need and let me get to work. Why did you call me in to pick up a runaway? You must have a lot of runaways."

"Not as many as you might think. Most of our boys become quite school-centered in time. We have a rich and varied program for them. But Thomas Hillman had been here less than a week, and he showed very little promise of becoming group-oriented. He's quite a difficult young man."

"And that's what makes him special?"

"I'll be frank with you, Mr. Archer," he said, and hesitated. "This is rather a prickly situation for the school. I accepted Tom Hillman against my better judgment, actually without full knowledge of his history, simply because his father insisted upon it. And now Ralph Hillman blames us for his son's esca—that is, his surreptitious leavetaking. Hillman has threatened to sue if any harm comes to the boy. The suit wouldn't stand up in court—we've had such lawsuits before—but it could do us a great deal of public harm." He added, almost to himself: "Patch really was at fault."

"What did Patch do?"

"I'm afraid he was unnecessarily violent. Not that I blame him as man to man. But you'd better talk to Mr. Patch yourself. He can give you all the details of Tom's—ah—departure."

"Later, I'd like to talk to him. But you can tell me more about the boy's background."

"Not as much as I'd like. We ask the families, or their doctors, to give us a detailed history of our entering students. Mr. Hillman promised to write one, but he hasn't as yet. And I've had great difficulty in getting any facts out of him. He's a very proud and very angry man."

"And a wealthy one?"

"I don't know his Dun and Bradstreet rating. Most of our parents are comfortably fixed," he added with a quick little smug smile.

"I'd like to see Hillman. Does he live in town?"

"Yes, but please don't try to see him, at least not today. He's just been on the phone to me again, and it would only stir him up further."

Sponti rose from his desk and moved to the window that overlooked the parking lot. I followed him. The fine rain outside hung like a visible depression in the air.

"I still need a detailed description of the boy, and everything I can find out about his habits."

"Patch can give you that, better than I. He's been in daily contact with him. And you can talk to his housemother, Mrs. Mallow. She's a trained observer."

"Let's hope somebody is." I was getting impatient with Sponti. He seemed to feel that the less he told me about the missing boy, the less real his disappearance was. "How old is he, or is that classified material?"

Sponti's eyes crossed slightly, and his rather pendulous cheeks became faintly mottled. "I object to your tone."

"That's your privilege. How old is Tom Hillman?"

"Seventeen."

"Do you have a picture of him?"

"None was provided by the family, though we ask for one as a matter of routine. I can tell you briefly what he looks like. He's quite a decent-looking young chap, if you overlook the sullen expression he wears habitually. He's quite big, around six feet, he looks older than his age."

"Eyes?"

"Dark blue, I think. His hair is dark blond. He has what might be called aquiline features, like his father."

"Identifying marks?"

He shrugged his shoulders. "I know of none."

"Why was he brought here?"

"For treatment, of course. But he didn't stay long enough to benefit."

"Exactly what's the matter with him? You said he was difficult, but that's a pretty general description."

"It was meant to be. It's hard to tell what ails these boys in adolescent storm. Often we help them without knowing how or why. I'm not a medical doctor, in any case."

"I thought you were."

"No. We have medical doctors associated with our staff, of course, both physicians and psychiatrists. There wouldn't be much point in talking to them. I doubt if Tom was here long enough even to meet his therapist. But there's no doubt he was high."

"High?"

"Emotionally high, running out of control. He was in a bad way when his father brought him here. We gave him tranquillizers, but they don't always work in the same way on different subjects."

"Did he cause you a lot of trouble?"

"He did indeed. Frankly, I doubt if we'll readmit him even if he does come back."

"But you're hiring me to find him."

"I have no choice."

We discussed money matters, and he gave me a check. Then I walked down the road to East Hall. Before I went in to see Mr. Patch, I turned and looked at the mountains on the far side of the valley. They loomed like half-forgotten faces through the overcast. The lonely blue heron rose from the edge of the slough and sailed toward them.

2

East Hall was a sprawling one-story stucco building which somehow didn't belong on that expansive landscape. Its mean and unprepossessing air had something to do with the high little windows, all of them heavily screened. Or with the related fact that it was a kind of prison which pretended not to be. The spiky pyracantha shrubs bordering the lawn in front of the building were more like barriers than ornaments. The grass looked dispirited even in the rain.

So did the line of boys who were marching in the front door as I came up. Boys of all ages from twelve to twenty, boys of all shapes and sizes, with only one thing in common: they marched like members of a defeated army. They reminded me of the very young soldiers we captured on the Rhine in the last stages of the last war.

Two student leaders kept them in some sort of line. I followed them, into a big lounge furnished with rather dilapidated furniture. The two leaders went straight to a Ping-Pong table that stood in one corner, picked up paddles, and began to play a rapid intense game with a ball that one of them produced from his windbreaker pocket. Six or seven boys began to watch them. Four or five settled down with comic books. Most of the rest of them stood around and watched me.

A hairy-faced young fellow who ought to have started to shave came up to me smiling. His smile was brilliant, but it faded like an optical illusion. He came so close that his shoulder nudged my arm. Some dogs will nudge you like that, to test your friendliness.

"Are you the new supervisor?"

"No. I thought Mr. Patch was the supervisor."

"He won't last." A few of the younger boys giggled. The hairy one responded like a successful comedian. "This is the violent ward. They never last."

"It doesn't look so violent to me. Where is Mr. Patch?"

"Over at dining commons. He'll be here in a minute. Then we have organized fun."

"You sound pretty cynical for your age. How old are you?"

"Ninety-nine." His audience murmured encouragingly. "Mr. Patch is only forty-nine. It makes it hard for him to be my father-image."

"Maybe I could talk to Mrs. Mallow."

"She's in her room drinking her lunch. Mrs. Mallow always drinks her lunch." The bright malice in his eyes alternated with a darker feeling. "Are you a father?"

"No."

In the background the Ping-Pong ball was clicking back and forth like mindless conversation.

A member of the audience spoke up. "He's not a father."

"Maybe he's a mother," said the hairy boy. "Are you a mother?"

"He doesn't look like a mother. He has no bosoms."

"My mother has no bosoms," said a third one. "That's why I feel rejected."

"Come off it, boys." The hell of it was, they wished I was a father, or even a mother, one of theirs, and the wish stood in their eyes. "You don't want me to feel rejected, do you?"

Nobody answered. The hairy boy smiled up at me. It lasted a little longer than his first smile. "What's your name? I'm Frederick Tyndal the Third."

"I'm Lew Archer the First."

I drew the boy away from his audience. He pulled back from my touch, but he came along and sat down with me on a cracked leather couch. Some of the younger boys had put an overplayed record on a player. Two of them began to dance together to the raucous self-parodying song. "Surfin' ain't no sin," was the refrain.

"Did you know Tom Hillman, Fred?"

"A little. Are you his father?"

"No. I said I wasn't a father."

"Adults don't necessarily tell you the truth." He plucked at the hairs on his chin as if he hated the signs of growing up. "My father said he was sending me away to military school. He's a big shot in the government," he added flatly, without pride, and then, in a different tone: "Tom Hillman didn't get along with his father, either. So he got railroaded here. The Monorail to the Magic Kingdom." He produced a fierce ecstatic hopeless grin.

"Did Tom talk to you about it?"

"A little. He wasn't here long. Five days. Six. He came in Sunday night and took off Saturday night." He squirmed uneasily on the creaking leather. "Are you a cop?"

"No."

"I just wondered. You ask questions like a cop."

"Did Tom do something that would interest the cops?"

"We all do, don't we?" His hot and cold running glance went around the room, pausing on the forlorn antics of the dancing boys. "You don't qualify for East Hall unless you're a juvie. I was a criminal mastermind myself. I forged the big shot's name on a fifty-dollar check and went to San Francisco for the weekend."

"What did Tom do?"

"Stole a car, I guess. It was a first offense, he said, and he would of got probation easy. But his father didn't want the publicity, so he put him in here. Also, I guess Tom had a fight with his father."

"I see."

"Why are you so fascinated in Tom?"

"I'm supposed to find him, Fred."

"And bring him back here?"

"I doubt that they'll readmit him."

"He's lucky." More or less unconsciously, he moved against me again. I could smell the untended odor of his hair and body, and sense his desolation. "I'd break out of here myself if I had a place to go. But the big shot would turn me over to the Youth Authority. It would save him money, besides."

"Did Tom have a place to go?"

He jerked upright and looked at my eyes from the corners of his. "I didn't say that."

"I'm asking you."

"He wouldn't tell me if he had."

"Who was closest to him in the school?"

"He wasn't close to anybody. He was so upset when he came in, they put him in a room by himself. I went in and talked to him one night, but he didn't say much to me."

"Nothing about where he planned to go?"

"He didn't *plan* anything. He tried to start a riot Saturday night but the rest of us were chicken. So he took off. He seemed to be very excited."

"Was he emotionally disturbed?"

"Aren't we all?" He tapped his own temple and made an insane face. "You ought to see my Rorschach."

"Some other time."

"Be my guest."

"This is important, Fred. Tom is very young, and excited, as you said. He's been missing for two nights now, and he could get into very serious trouble."

"Worse than this?"

"You know it, or you'd be over the fence yourself. Did Tom say anything about where he was going?"

The boy didn't answer.

"Then I assume he did tell you something?"

"No." But he wouldn't meet my eyes.

Mr. Patch came into the room and changed its carefree atmosphere. The dancing boys pretended to be wrestling. Comic books disappeared like bundles of hot money. The Ping-Pong players put away their ball.

Patch was a middle-aged man with thinning hair and thickening jowls. His double-breasted tan gabardine suit was creased across his rather corpulent front. His face was creased, too, into a sneer of power which didn't go with his sensitive small mouth. As he looked around the room, I could see that the whites of his eyes were tinted with red.

He strode to the record player and turned it off, insinuating his voice into the silence:

"Lunch time isn't music time, boys. Music time is after dinner, from seven to seven-thirty." He addressed one of the Ping-Pong players: "Bear that in mind, Deering. No music in the daytime. I'll hold you responsible."

"Yessir."

"And weren't you playing Ping-Pong?"

"We were just rallying, sir."

"Where did you get the ball? I understood the balls were locked up in my desk."

"They are, sir."

"Where did you get the one you were playing with?"

"I don't know, sir." Deering fumbled at his windbreaker. He was a gawky youth with an Adam's apple that looked like a hidden Ping-Pong ball. "I think I must of found it."

"Where did you find it? In my desk?"

"No sir. On the grounds, I think it was."

Mr. Patch walked toward him with a kind of melodramatic stealth. As he moved across the room, the boys behind him made faces, waved their arms, did bumps and grinds. One boy, one of the dancers, fell silently to the floor with a throat-slitting gesture, held the pose of a dying gladiator for a single frozen second, then got back onto his feet.

Patch was saying in a long-suffering tone: "You bought it, didn't you, Deering? You know that regulations forbid you fellows to bring in private Ping-Pong balls of your own. You know that, don't you? You're president of the East Hall Legislative Assembly, you helped to frame those regulations yourself. Didn't you?"

"Yessir."

"Then give it to me, Deering."

The boy handed Patch the ball. Patch stooped to place it on the floor —while a boy behind him pretended to kick him—and squashed it under his heel. He gave Deering the misshapen ball.

"I'm sorry, Deering. I have to obey the regulations just as you do." He turned to the roomful of boys, who snapped into conformity under his eyes, and said mildly: "Well, fellows, what's on the agenda—?"

"I think I am," I said, getting up from the couch. I gave him my name and asked if I could talk to him in private.

"I suppose so," he said with a worried smile, as if I might in fact be his successor. "Come into my office, such as it is. Deering and Bronson, I'm leaving you in charge."

His office was a windowless cubicle containing a cluttered desk and two straight chairs. He closed the door on the noise that drifted down the corridor from the lounge, turned on a desk lamp, and sat down sighing.

"You've got to stay on top of them." He sounded like a man saying his prayers. "You wanted to discuss one of my boys?"

"Tom Hillman."

The name depressed him. "You represent his father?"

"No. Dr. Sponti sent me to talk to you. I'm a private detective."

"I see." He pushed out his lips in a kind of pout. "I suppose Sponti's been blaming me, as usual."

"He did say something about unnecessary violence."

"That's nonsense!" He pounded the desk between us with his clenched fist. His face became congested with blood. Then it went starkly pale, like a raw photograph. Only the reddish whites of his eyes held their color. "Sponti doesn't work down here with the animals. I ought to know when physical discipline is necessary. I've been in juvenile work for twenty-five years."

"It seems to be getting you down."

With an effort that crumpled up his face, he brought himself under control. "Oh no, I love the work, I really do. Anyway, it's the only thing I'm trained for. I love the boys. And they love me."

"I could see that."

He wasn't listening for my irony. "I'd have been pals with Tom Hillman if he'd lasted."

"Why didn't he?"

"He ran away. You know that. He stole a pair of shears from the gardener and used it to cut the screen on his bedroom window."

"Exactly when was this?"

"Sometime Saturday night, between my eleven-o'clock bedcheck and my early-morning one."

"And what happened before that?"

"Saturday night, you mean? He was stirring up the other boys, inciting them to attack the resident staff. I'd left the common room after dinner, and I heard him from in here, making a speech. He was trying to convince the boys that they had been deprived of their rights and should fight for them. Some of the more excitable ones were affected. But when I ordered Hillman to shut up, he was the only one who rushed me."

"Did he hit you?"

"I hit him first," Patch said. "I'm not ashamed of it. I had to preserve my authority with the others." He rubbed his fist. "I knocked him cold. You have to make a show of manliness. When I hit them, they go down for the count. You have to give them an image to respect."

I said to stop him: "What happened after that?"

"I helped him to his room, and then I reported the incident to Sponti. I thought the boy should be put in the padded room. But Sponti countermanded my advice. Hillman would never have broken out if Sponti had let me put him in the padded room. Just between you and me, it's Sponti's fault." He brought himself up short and said in a smaller voice: "Don't quote me to him."

"All right."

I was beginning to despair of getting anything useful out of Patch. He was a little dilapidated, like the furniture in the common room. The noise coming from that direction was becoming louder. Patch rose wearily to his feet.

"I'd better get back there before they tear the place down."

"I just wanted to ask you, do you have any thoughts on where Tom Hillman went after he left here?"

Patch considered my question. He seemed to be having difficulty in imagining the outside world into which the boy had vanished. "L.A.," he said finally. "They usually head for L.A. Or else they head south for San Diego and the border."

"Or east?"

"If their parents live east, they sometimes go that way."

"Or west across the ocean?" I was baiting him.

"That's true. One boy stole a thirty-foot launch and headed for the islands."

"You seem to have a lot of runaways."

"Over the years, we have quite a turnover. Sponti's opposed to strict security measures, like we used to have at Juvenile Hall. With all the breakouts we've had, I'm surprised he wants to make such a production out of this one. The boy'll turn up, they nearly always do."

Patch sounded as if he wasn't looking forward to the prospect.

Somebody tapped at the door behind me. "Mr. Patch?" a woman said through the panels.

"Yes, Mrs. Mallow."

"The boys are getting out of hand. They won't listen to me. What are you doing in there?"

"Conferring. Dr. Sponti sent a man."

"Good. We need a man."

"Is that so?" He brushed past me and opened the door. "Keep your cracks to yourself, please, Mrs. Mallow. I know one or two things that Dr. Sponti would dearly love to know."

"So do I," the woman said.

She was heavily rouged, with dyed red hair arranged in bangs on her forehead. She had on a dark formal dress, about ten years out of fashion, and several loops of imitation pearls. Her face was pleasant enough, in spite of eyes that had been bleared by horrors inner and outer.

She brightened up when she saw me. "Hello."

"My name is Archer," I said. "Dr. Sponti brought me in to look into Tom Hillman's disappearance."

"He's a nice-looking boy," she said. "At least he was until our local Marquis de Sade gave him a working-over."

"I acted in self-defense," Patch cried. "I don't enjoy hurting people. I'm the authority figure in East Hall, and when I'm attacked it's just like killing their father."

"You better go and make with the authority, Father. But if you hurt anybody this week I'll carve the living heart out of your body."

Patch looked at her as if he believed she might do it. Then he turned on his heel and strode away toward the roaring room. The roaring subsided abruptly, as if he had closed a soundproof door behind him.

"Poor old Patch," said Mrs. Mallow. "He's been around too long. Poor old all of us. Too many years of contact with the adolescent mind, if mind is the word, and eventually we all go blah."

"Why stay?"

"We get so we can't live in the outside world. Like old convicts. That's the real hell of it."

"People around here are extraordinarily ready to spill their problems—"

"It's the psychiatric atmosphere."

"But," I went on, "they don't tell me much I want to know. Can *you* give me a clear impression of Tom Hillman?"

"I can give you my own impression."

She had a little difficulty with the word, and it seemed to affect her balance. She walked into Patch's office and leaned on his desk facing me. Her face, half-shadowed in the upward light from the lamp, reminded me of a sibyl's.

"Tom Hillman is a pretty nice boy. He didn't belong here. He found that out in a hurry. And so he left."

"Why didn't he belong here?"

"You want me to go into detail? East Hall is essentially a place for boys with personality and character problems, or with a sociopathic tendency. We keep the more disturbed youngsters, boys and girls, in West Hall."

"And Tom belonged there?"

"Hardly. He shouldn't have been sent to Laguna Perdida at all. This is just my opinion, but it ought to be worth something. I used to be a pretty good clinical psychologist." She looked down into the light.

"Dr. Sponti seems to think Tom was disturbed."

"Dr. Sponti never thinks otherwise, about any prospect. Do you know what these kids' parents pay? A thousand dollars a month, plus extras. Music lessons. Group therapy." She laughed harshly. "When half the time it's the parents who should be here. Or in some worse place.

"A thousand dollars a month," she repeated. "So Dr. Sponti so-called can draw his twenty-five thousand a year. Which is more than six times what he pays me for holding the kids' hands."

She was a woman with a grievance. Sometimes grievances made for truth-telling, but not always. "What do you mean, Dr. Sponti so-called?"

"He's not a medical doctor, or any other kind of real doctor. He took his degree in educational administration, at one of the diploma mills down south. Do you know what he wrote his dissertation on? The kitchen logistics of the medium-sized boarding school."

"Getting back to Tom," I said, "why would his father bring him here if he didn't need psychiatric treatment?"

"I don't know. I don't know his father. Probably because he wanted him out of his sight."

"Why?" I insisted.

"The boy was in some kind of trouble."

"Did Tom tell you that?"

"He wouldn't talk about it. But I can read the signs."

"Have you heard the story that he stole a car?"

"No, but it would help to explain him. He's a very unhappy young man, and a guilty one. He isn't one of your hardened j.d.'s. Not that any of them *really* are."

"You seem to have liked Tom Hillman."

"What little I saw of him. He didn't want to talk last week, and I try never to force myself on the boys. Except for class hours, he spent most of the time in his room. I think he was trying to work something out."

"Like a plan for revolution?"

Her eyes glinted with amusement. "You heard about that, did you? The boy had more gumption than I gave him credit for. Don't look so surprised. I'm on the boys' side. Why else would I be here?"

I was beginning to like Mrs. Mallow. Sensing this, she moved toward me and touched my arm. "I hope that you are, too. On Tom's side, I mean."

"I'll wait until I know him. It isn't important, anyway."

"Yes it is. It's always important."

"Just what happened between Tom and Mr. Patch Saturday night?"

"I wouldn't know, really. Saturday night is my night off. You can make a note of that if you like, Mr. Archer."

She smiled, and I caught a glimpse of her life's meaning. She cared for other people. Nobody cared for her.

3

She let me out through a side door which had to be unlocked. The rain was just heavy enough to wet my face. Dense-looking clouds were gathering over the mountains, which probably meant that the rain was going to persist.

I started back toward the administration building. Sponti was going to have to be told that I must see Tom Hillman's parents, whether he approved or not. The varying accounts of Tom I'd had, from people who liked or disliked him, gave me no distinct impression of his habits or personality. He could be a persecuted teen-ager, or a psychopath who knew how to appeal to older women, or something in between, like Fred the Third.

I wasn't looking where I was going, and a yellow cab almost ran me down in the parking lot. A man in tweeds got out of the back seat. I thought he was going to apologize to me, but he didn't appear to see me.

He was a tall, silver-haired man, well fed, well cared for, probably good-looking under normal conditions. At the moment he looked haggard. He ran into the administration building. I walked in after him, and found him arguing with Sponti's secretary.

"I'm very sorry, Mr. Hillman," she intoned. "Dr. Sponti is in conference. I can't possibly interrupt him."

"I think you'd better," Hillman said in a rough voice.

"I'm sorry. You'll have to wait."

"But I can't wait. My son is in the hands of criminals. They're trying to extort money from me."

"Is that true?" Her voice was unprofessional and sharp.

"I'm not in the habit of lying."

The girl excused herself and went into Sponti's office, closing the door carefully behind her. I spoke to Hillman, telling him my name and occupation:

"Dr. Sponti called me in to look for your son. I've been wanting to talk to you. It seems to be time I did."

"Yes. By all means."

He took my hand. He was a large, impressive-looking man. His face had the kind of patrician bony structure that doesn't necessarily imply brains or ability, or even decency, but that generally goes with money. He was deep in the chest and heavy in the shoulders. But there was no force in his grasp. He was trembling all over, like a frightened dog.

"You said something about criminals and extortion."

"Yes." But his steel-gray eyes kept shifting away to the door of Sponti's office. He wanted to talk to somebody he could blame. "What are they doing in there?" he said a little wildly.

"It hardly matters. If your son's been kidnapped, Sponti can't help you much. It's a matter for the police."

"No! The police stay out. I've been instructed to keep them out." His eyes focused on me for the first time, hard with suspicion. "You're not a policeman, are you?"

"I told you I was a private detective. I just came down from Los Angeles an hour ago. How did you find out about Tom, and who gave you your instructions?"

"One of the gang. He telephoned my house when we were just sitting down to lunch. He warned me to keep the matter quiet. Otherwise Tom will never come back."

"Did he say that?"

"Yes."

"What else did he say?"

"They want to sell me information about Tom's whereabouts. It was just a euphemism for ransom money."

"How much?"

"Twenty-five thousand dollars."

"Do you have it?"

"I'll have it by the middle of the afternoon. I'm selling some stock. I went into town to my broker's before I came here."

"You move fast, Mr. Hillman." He needed some mark of respect. "But I don't quite understand why you came out here."

"I don't trust these people," he said in a lowered voice. Apparently he had forgotten, or hadn't heard, that I was working for Sponti. "I believe that Tom was lured away from here, perhaps with inside help, and they're covering up."

"I doubt that very much. I've talked to the staff member involved. He and Tom had a fight Saturday night, and later Tom cut a screen and went over the fence. One of the students confirmed this, more or less."

"A student would be afraid to deny the official story."

"Not this student, Mr. Hillman. If your son's been kidnapped, it happened after he left here. Tell me this, did he have any criminal connections?"

"Tom? You must be out of your mind."

"I heard he stole a car."

"Did Sponti tell you that? He had no right to."

"I got it from other sources. Boys don't usually steal cars unless they've had some experience outside the law, perhaps with a juvenile gang—"

"He didn't steal it." Hillman's eyes were evasive. "He borrowed it from a neighbor. The fact that he wrecked it was pure accident. He was emotionally upset—"

Hillman was, too. He ran out of breath and words. He opened and closed his mouth like a big handsome fish hooked by circumstance and yanked into alien air. I said:

"What are you supposed to do with the twenty-five thousand? Hold it for further instructions?"

Hillman nodded, and sat down despondently in a chair. Dr. Sponti's door had opened, and he had been listening, I didn't know for how long. He came out into the anteroom now, flanked by his secretary and followed by a man with a long cadaverous face.

"What's this about kidnapping?" Sponti said in a high voice. He forced his voice down into a more soothing register: "I'm sorry, Mr. Hillman."

Hillman's sitting position changed to a kind of crouch. "You're going to be sorrier. I want to know who took my son out of here, and under what circumstances, and with whose connivance."

"Your son left here of his own free will, Mr. Hillman."

"And you wash your hands of him, do you?"

"We never do that with any of our charges, however short their stay. I've hired Mr. Archer here to help you out. And I've just been talking to Mr. Squerry here, our comptroller."

The cadaverous man bowed solemnly. Black stripes of hair were pasted flat across the crown of his almost naked head. He said in a precise voice:

"Dr. Sponti and I have decided to refund in full the money you paid us last week. We've just written out a check, and here it is."

He handed over a slip of yellow paper. Hillman crumpled it into a ball and threw it back at Mr. Squerry. It bounced off his thin chest and fell to the floor. I picked it up. It was for two thousand dollars.

Hillman ran out of the room. I walked out after him, before Sponti could terminate my services, and caught Hillman as he was getting into the cab.

"Where are you going?"

"Home. My wife's in poor shape."

"Let me drive you."

"Not if you're Sponti's man."

"I'm nobody's man but my own. Sponti hired me to find your son. I'm going to do that if it's humanly possible. But I'll need some cooperation from you and Mrs. Hillman."

"What can we do?" He spread his large helpless hands.

"Tell me what kind of a boy he is, who his friends are, where he hangs out—"

"What's the point of all that? He's in the hands of gangsters. They want money. I'm willing to pay them."

The cab driver, who had got out of his seat to open the door for Hillman, stood listening with widening mouth and eyes.

"It may not be as simple as that," I said. "But we won't talk about it here."

"You can trust me," the driver said huskily. "I got a brother-in-law on the Highway Patrol. Besides, I never blab about my fares."

"You better not," Hillman said.

He paid the man, and came along with me to my car.

"Speaking of money," I said when we were together in the front seat, "you didn't really want to throw away two thousand dollars, did you?" I smoothed out the yellow check and handed it to him.

There's no way to tell what will make a man break down. A long silence, or a telephone ringing, or the wrong note in a woman's voice. In Hillman's case, it was a check for two thousand dollars. He put it away in his alligator wallet, and then he groaned loudly. He covered his eyes with his hands and leaned his forehead on the dash. Cawing sounds came out of his mouth as if an angry crow was tearing at his vitals.

After a while he said: "I should never have put him in this place." His voice was more human than it had been, as if he had broken through into a deeper level of self-knowledge.

"Don't cry over spilt milk."

He straightened up. "I wasn't crying." It was true his eyes were dry.

"We won't argue, Mr. Hillman. Where do you live?"

"In El Rancho. It's between here and the city. I'll tell you how to get there by the shortest route."

The guard limped out of his kiosk, and we exchanged half-salutes. He activated the gates. Following Hillman's instructions, I drove out along a road which passed through a reedy wasteland where blackbirds were chittering, then through a suburban wasteland jammed with new apartments, and around the perimeter of a college campus. We passed an airport, where a plane was taking off. Hillman looked as if he wished he were on it.

"Why did you put your son in Laguna Perdida School?"

His answer came slowly, in bits and snatches. "I was afraid. He seemed to be headed for trouble. I felt I had to prevent it somehow. I was hoping they could straighten him out so that he could go back to regular school next month. He's supposed to be starting his senior year in high school."

"Would you mind being specific about the trouble he was in? Do you mean car theft?"

"That was one of the things. But it wasn't a true case of theft, as I explained."

"You didn't explain, though."

"It was Rhea Carlson's automobile he took. Rhea and Jay Carlson are our next-door neighbors. When you leave a new Dart in an open carport all night with the key in the ignition, it's practically an invitation to a joy ride. I told them that. Jay would've admitted it, too, if he hadn't had a bit of a down on Tom. Or if Tom hadn't wrecked the car. It was fully covered, by my insurance as well as theirs, but they had to take the emotional approach."

"The car was wrecked?"

"It's a total loss. I don't know how he managed to turn it over, but he did. Fortunately he came out of it without a scratch."

"Where was he going?"

"He was on his way home. The accident happened practically at our door. I'll show you the place."

"Then where had he been?"

"He wouldn't say. He'd been gone all night, but he wouldn't tell me anything about it."

"What night was that?"

"Saturday night. A week ago Saturday night. The police brought him home about six o'clock in the morning, and told me I better have our doctor go over him, which I did. He wasn't hurt physically, but his mind seemed to be affected. He went into a rage when I tried to ask him where he had spent the night. I'd never seen him like that before. He'd always been a quiet-spoken boy. He said I had no right to know about him, that I wasn't really his father, and so on and so forth. I'm afraid I lost my temper and slapped him when he said that. Then he turned his back on me and wouldn't talk at all, about anything."

"Had he been drinking?"

"I don't think so. No. I would have smelled it on him."

"What about drugs?"

I could see his face turn toward me, large and vague in my side vision. "That's out of the question."

"I hope so. Dr. Sponti told me your son had a peculiar reaction to tranquillizers. That sometimes happens with habitual users."

"My son was not a drug user."

"A lot of young people are, nowadays, and their parents are the last to know about it."

"No. It wasn't anything like that," he said urgently. "The shock of the accident affected his mind."

"Did the doctor think so?"

"Dr. Shanley is an orthopedic surgeon. He wouldn't know about psychiatric disturbance. Anyway, he didn't know what happened that morning, when I went to the judge's house to arrange for bail. I haven't told anyone about it."

I waited, and listened to the windshield wipers. A green and white sign on the shoulder of the road announced: "El Rancho." Hillman said, as if he was glad to have something neutral to say:

"You turn off in another quarter mile."

I slowed down. "You were going to tell me what happened that Sunday morning."

"No. I don't believe I will. It has no bearing on the present situation."

"How do we know that?"

He didn't answer me. Perhaps the thought of home and neighbors had silenced him.

"Did you say the Carlsons had a down on Tom?"

"I said that, and it's true."

"Do you know the reason for it?"

"They have a daughter, Stella. Tom and Stella Carlson were very close. Jay and Rhea disapproved, at least Rhea did. So did Elaine, my wife, for that matter."

I turned off the main road. The access road passed between tall stone gateposts and became the palm-lined central road bisecting El Rancho. It was one of those rich developments whose inhabitants couldn't possibly have troubles. Their big houses sat far back behind enormous lawns. Their private golf course lay across the road we were traveling on. The diving tower of their beach club gleamed with fresh aluminum paint in the wet distance.

But like the drizzle, troubles fall in or out of season on everybody.

The road bent around one corner of the golf course. Hillman pointed ahead to a deep gouge in the bank, where the earth was still raw. Above it a pine tree with a damaged trunk was turning brown in places.

"This is where he turned the car over."

I stopped the car. "Did he explain how the accident happened?"

Hillman pretended not to hear me. We got out of the car. There was no traffic in sight, except for a foursome of die-hard golfers approaching in two carts along the fairway.

"I don't see any brake- or skid-marks," I said. "Was your son an experienced driver?"

"Yes. I taught him to drive myself. I spent a great deal of time with him. In fact, I deliberately reduced my work load at the firm several years ago, partly so that I could enjoy Tom's growing up."

His phrasing was a little strange, as if growing up was something a boy did for his parents' entertainment. It made me wonder. If Hillman had been really close to Tom, why had he clapped him into Laguna Perdida School at the first sign of delinquency? Or had there been earlier signs which he was suppressing?

One of the golfers waved from his cart as he went by. Hillman gave him a cold flick of the hand and got into my car. He seemed embarrassed to be found at the scene of the accident.

"I'll be frank with you," I said as we drove away. "I wish you'd be frank with me. Laguna Perdida is a school for disturbed and delinquent minors. I can't get it clear why Tom deserved, or needed, to be put there."

"I did it for his own protection. Good-neighbor Carlson was threatening to prosecute him for car theft."

"That's nothing so terrible. He'd have rated probation, if this was a first offense. Was it?"

"Of course it was."

"Then what were you afraid of?"

"I wasn't—" he started to say. But he was too honest, or too completely conscious of his fear, to finish the sentence.

"What did he do Sunday morning, when you went to see the judge?"

"He didn't do anything, really. Nothing happened."

"But that nothing hit you so hard you won't discuss it."

"That's correct. I won't discuss it, with you or anyone. Whatever happened last Sunday, or might have happened, has been completely outdated by recent events. My son has been kidnapped. He's a passive victim, don't you understand?"

I wondered about that, too. Twenty-five thousand dollars was a lot of money in my book, but it didn't seem to be in Hillman's. If Tom was really in the hands of professional criminals, they would be asking for all that the traffic would bear.

"How much money could you raise if you had to, Mr. Hillman?"

He gave me a swift look. "I don't see the point."

"Kidnappers usually go the limit in their demands. I'm trying to find out if they have in this case. I gather you could raise a good deal more than twenty-five thousand."

"I could, with my wife's help."

"Let's hope it won't be necessary."

4

The Hillmans' private drive meandered up an oak-covered rise and circled around a lawn in front of their house. It was a big old Spanish mansion, with white stucco walls, wrought-iron ornamentation at the windows, red tile roof gleaming dully in the wet. A bright black Cadillac was parked in the circle ahead of us.

"I meant to drive myself this morning," Hillman said. "But then I didn't trust myself to drive. Thanks for the lift."

It sounded like a dismissal. He started up the front steps, and I felt a keen disappointment. I swallowed it and went after him, slipping inside the front door before he closed it.

It was his wife he was preoccupied with. She was waiting for him in the reception hall, bowed forward in a high-backed Spanish chair which made her look tinier than she was. Her snakeskin shoes hung clear of the polished tile floor. She was a beautifully made thin blonde woman in her forties. An aura of desolation hung about her, a sense of uselessness, as if she was in fact the faded doll she resembled. Her green dress went poorly with her almost greenish pallor.

"Elaine?"

She had been sitting perfectly still, with her knees and fists together. She looked up at her husband, and then over his head at the huge Spanish chandelier suspended on a chain from the beamed ceiling two stories up. Its bulbs protruded like dubious fruit from clusters of wrought-iron leaves.

"Don't stand under it," she said. "I'm always afraid it's going to fall. I wish you'd have it taken down, Ralph."

"It was your idea to bring it back and put it there."

"That was a long time ago," she said. "I thought the space needed filling."

"It still does, and it's still perfectly safe." He moved toward her and touched her head. "You're wet. You shouldn't have gone out in your condition."

"I just walked down the drive to see if you were coming. You were gone a long time."

"I couldn't help it."

She took his hand as it slid away from her head, and held it against her breast. "Did you hear anything?"

"We can't expect to hear anything yet a while. I made arrangements for the money. Dick Leandro will bring it out later this afternoon. In the meantime we wait for a phone call."

"It's hideous, waiting."

"I know. You should try to think about something else."

"What else is there?"

"Lots of things." I think he tried to name one, and gave up. "Anyway, it isn't good for you to be sitting out here in the cold hall. You'll give yourself pneumonia again."

"People don't give it to *themselves*, Ralph."

"We won't argue. Come into the sitting room and I'll make you a drink."

He remembered me and included me in the invitation, but he didn't introduce me to his wife. Perhaps he considered me unworthy, or perhaps he wanted to discourage communication between us. Feeling rather left out, I followed them up three tile steps into a smaller room where a fire was burning. Elaine Hillman stood with her back to it. Her husband went to the bar, which was in an alcove decorated with Spanish bullfight posters.

She held out her hand to me. It was ice cold. "I don't mean to monopolize the heat. Are you a policeman? I thought we weren't to use them."

"I'm a private detective. Lew Archer is my name."

Her husband called from the alcove: "What will you drink, darling?"

"Absinthe."

"Is that such a good idea?"

"It has wormwood in it, which suits my mood. But I'll settle for a short Scotch."

"What about you, Mr. Archer?"

I asked for the same. I needed it. While I rather liked both of the Hillmans, they were getting on my nerves. Their joint handling of their anxiety was almost professional, as if they were actors improvising a tragedy before an audience of one. I don't mean the anxiety wasn't sincere. They were close to dying of it.

Hillman came back across the room with three lowball glasses on a tray. He set it down on a long table in front of the fireplace and handed each of us a glass. Then he shook up the wood fire with a poker. Flames hissed up the chimney. Their reflection changed his face for a moment to a red savage mask.

His wife's face hung like a dead moon over her drink. "Our son is very dear to us, Mr. Archer. Can you help us get him back?"

"I can try. I'm not sure it's wise to keep the police out of this. I'm only one man, and this isn't my normal stamping ground."

"Does that make a difference?"

"I have no informers here."

"Do you hear him, Ralph?" she said to her crouching husband. "Mr. Archer thinks we should have the police in."

"I hear him. But it isn't possible." He straightened up with a sigh, as if the whole weight of the house was on his shoulders. "I'm not going to endanger Tom's life by anything I do."

"I feel the same way," she said. "I'm willing to pay through the nose to get him back. What use is money without a son to spend it on?"

That was another phrase that was faintly strange. I was getting the impression that Tom was the center of the household, but a fairly unknown center, like a god they made sacrifices to and expected benefits from, and maybe punishments, too. I was beginning to sympathize with Tom.

"Tell me about him, Mrs. Hillman."

Some life came up into her dead face. But before she could open her mouth Hillman said: "No. You're not going to put Elaine through that now."

"But Tom's a pretty shadowy figure to me. I'm trying to get some idea of where he might have gone yesterday, how he got tangled up with extortionists."

"*I* don't know where he went," the woman said.

"Neither do I. If I had," Hillman said, "I'd have gone to him yesterday."

"Then I'm going to have to go out and do some legwork. You can let me have a picture, I suppose."

Hillman went into an adjoining room, twilit behind pulled drapes, where the open top of a grand piano leaned up out of the shadows. He came back with a silver-framed studio photograph of a boy whose features resembled his own. The boy's dark eyes were rebellious, unless I was projecting my own sense of the household into them. They were also intelligent and imaginative. His mouth was spoiled.

"Can I take this out of the frame? Or if you have a smaller one, it would be better to show around."

"To show around?"

"That's what I said, Mr. Hillman. It's not for my memory book."

Elaine Hillman said: "I have a smaller one upstairs on my dressing table. I'll get it."

"Why don't I go up with you? It might help if I went through his room."

"You can look at his room," Hillman said, "but I don't want you searching it."

"Why?"

"I just don't like the idea. Tom has the right to some privacy, even now."

The three of us went upstairs, keeping an eye on each other. I wondered what Hillman was afraid I might find, but I hesitated to ask him. While everything seemed to be under control, Hillman could flare up at any moment and order me out of his house.

He stood at the door while I gave the room a quick once-over. It was a front bedroom, very large, furnished with plain chests of drawers and chairs and a table and a bed which all looked hand-finished and expensive. A bright red telephone sat on the bedside table. There were engravings of sailing ships and Audubon prints hung with geometric precision around the walls, Navajo rugs on the floor, and a wool bedspread matching one of them.

I turned to Hillman. "Was he interested in boats and sailing?"

"Not particularly. He used to come out and crew for me occasionally, on the sloop, when I couldn't get anyone else. Does it matter?"

"I was just wondering if he hung around the harbor much."

"No. He didn't."

"Was he interested in birds?"

"I don't think so."

"Who chose the pictures?"

"I did," Elaine Hillman said from the hallway. "I decorated the room for Tom. He liked it, didn't he, Ralph?"

Hillman mumbled something. I crossed the room to the deeply set front windows, which overlooked the semicircular driveway. I could see down the wooded slope, across the golf course, all the way to the highway, where cars rolled back and forth like children's toys out of reach. I could imagine Tom sitting here in the alcove and watching the highway lights at night.

A thick volume of music lay open on the leather seat. I looked at the cover. It was a well-used copy of *The Well-Tempered Clavier.*

"Did Tom play the piano, Mr. Hillman?"

"Very well. He had ten years of lessons. But then he wanted—"

His wife made a small dismayed sound at his shoulder. "Why go into all that?"

"All what?" I said. "Trying to get information out of you people is like getting blood out of a stone."

"I *feel* like a bloodless stone," she said with a little grimace. "This hardly seems the time to rake up old family quarrels."

"We didn't quarrel," her husband said. "It was the one thing Tom and I ever disagreed on. And he went along with me on it. End of subject."

"All right. Where did he spend his time away from home?"

The Hillmans looked at each other, as if the secret of Tom's whereabouts was somehow hidden in each other's faces. The red telephone interrupted their dumb communion, like a loud thought. Elaine Hillman gasped. The photograph in her hand fell to the floor. She wilted against her husband.

He held her up. "It wouldn't be for us. That's Tom's private telephone."

"You want me to take it?" I said through the second ring.

"Please do."

I sat on the bed and picked up the receiver. "Hello."

"Tom?" said a high, girlish voice. "Is that you, Tommy?"

"Who is this calling?" I tried to sound like a boy.

The girl said something like "Augh" and hung up on me.

I set down the receiver: "It was a girl or a young woman. She wanted Tom."

The woman spoke with a touch of malice that seemed to renew her strength: "That's nothing unusual. I'm sure it was Stella Carlson. She's been calling all week."

"Does she always hang up like that?"

"No. I talked to her yesterday. She was full of questions, which of course I refused to answer. But I wanted to make sure that she hadn't seen Tom. She hadn't."

"Does she know anything about what's happened?"

"I hope not," Hillman said. "We've got to keep it in the family. The more people know, the worse—" He left another sentence dangling in the air.

I moved away from the telephone and picked up the fallen photograph. In a kind of staggering march step, Elaine Hillman went to the bed and straightened out the bedspread where I had been sitting. Everything had to be perfect in the room, I thought, or the god would not be appeased and would never return to them. When she had finished smoothing the bed, she flung herself face down on it and lay still.

Hillman and I withdrew quietly and went downstairs to wait for the call that mattered. There was a phone in the bar alcove off the sitting room, and another in the butler's pantry, which I could use to listen in. To get to the butler's pantry we had to go through the music room, where the grand piano loomed, and across a formal dining room which had a dismal air, like a reconstructed room in a museum.

The past was very strong here, like an odor you couldn't quite place. It seemed to be built into the very shape of the house, with its heavy dark beams and thick walls and deep windows; it would almost force the owner of the house to feel like a feudal lord. But the role of hidalgo hung loosely on Hillman, like something borrowed for a costume party. He and his wife must have rattled around in the great house, even when the boy was there.

Back in the sitting room, in front of the uncertain fire, I had a chance to ask Hillman some more questions. The Hillmans had two servants, a Spanish couple named Perez who had looked after Tom from infancy. Mrs. Perez was probably out in the kitchen. Her husband was in Mexico, visiting his family.

"You *know* he's in Mexico?"

"Well," Hillman said, "his wife has had a card from Sinaloa. Anyway, the Perezes are devoted to us, and to Tom. We've had them with us ever since we moved here and bought this house."

"How long ago was that?"

"Over sixteen years. We moved here, the three of us, after I was separated from the Navy. Another engineer and I founded our own firm here, Technological Enterprises. We've had very gratifying success, supplying components to the military and then NASA. I was able to go into semiretirement not long ago."

"You're young to retire, Mr. Hillman."

"Perhaps." He looked around a little restlessly, as if he disliked talking about himself. "I'm still the chairman of the board, of course. I go down to the office several mornings a week. I play a lot of golf, do a lot of hunting and sailing." He sounded weary of his life. "This summer I've been teaching Tom calculus. It isn't available in his high school. I thought it would come in handy if he made it to Cal Tech or M.I.T. I went to M.I.T. myself. Elaine was a student at Radcliffe. She was born on Beacon Street, you know."

We're prosperous and educated people, he seemed to be saying, first-class citizens: how can the world have aimed such a dirty blow at us? He leaned his large face forward until his hands supported it again.

The telephone rang in the alcove. I heard it ring a second time as I skidded around the end of the dining-room table. At the door of the butler's pantry I almost knocked down a small round woman who was wiping her hands on her apron. Her emotional dark eyes recoiled from my face.

"*I* was going to answer it," she said.

"I will, Mrs. Perez."

She retreated into the kitchen and I closed the door after her. The only light in the pantry came through the semicircular hatch to the dining room. The telephone was on the counter inside it, no longer ringing. Gently I raised the receiver.

"What was that?" a man's voice said. "You got the FBI on the line or something?" The voice was a western drawl with a faint whine in it.

"Certainly not. I've followed your instructions to the letter."

"I hope I can believe you, Mr. Hillman. If I thought you were having this call traced I'd hang up and goodbye Tom." The threat came easily, with a kind of flourish, as if the man enjoyed this kind of work.

"Don't hang up." Hillman's voice was both pleading and loathing. "I have the money for you, at least I'll have it here in a very short while. I'll be ready to deliver it whenever you say."

"Twenty-five thousand in small bills?"

"There will be nothing larger than a twenty."

"All unmarked?"

"I told you I've obeyed you to the letter. My son's safety is all I care about."

"I'm glad you get the picture, Mr. Hillman. You pick up fast, and I like that. Matter of fact, I hate to do this to you. And I'd certainly hate to do anything to this fine boy of yours."

"Is Tom with you now?" Hillman said.

"More or less. He's nearby."

"Could I possibly talk to him?"

"No."

"How do I know he's alive?"

The man was silent for a long moment. "You don't trust me, Mr. Hillman. I don't like that."

"How can I trust—?" Hillman bit the sentence in half.

"I know what you were going to say. How can you trust a lousy creep like me? That isn't our problem, Hillman. Our problem is can I trust a creep like you. I know more about you than you think I do, Hillman."

Silence, in which breath wheezed.

"Well, can I?"

"Can you what?" Hillman said in near-despair.

"Can I trust you, Hillman?"

"You can trust me."

Wheezing silence. The wheeze was in the man's voice when he spoke again: "I guess I'll have to take your word for it, Hillman. Okay. You'd probably like to talk all day about what a creep I am, but it's time to get down to brass tacks. I want my money, and this isn't ransom money, get that straight. Your son wasn't kidnapped, he came to us of his own free will—"

"I don't—" Hillman strangled the words in his throat.

"You don't believe me? Ask him, if you ever have a chance. You're throwing away your chances, you realize that? I'm trying to help you pay me the money—the information money, that's all it is—but you keep calling me names, liar and creep and God knows what else."

"No. There's nothing personal."

"That's what you think."

"Look here," Hillman said. "You said it's time to get down to brass tacks. Simply tell me where and when you want the money delivered. It will be delivered. I guarantee it."

Hillman's voice was sharp. The man at the other end of the line reacted to the sharpness perversely:

"Don't be in such a hurry. I'm calling the shots, you better not forget it."

"Then call them," Hillman said.

"In my own good time. I think I better give you a chance to think this over, Hillman. Get down off your high horse and down on your knees. That's where you belong." He hung up.

Hillman was standing in the alcove with the receiver still in his hand when I got back to the sitting room. Absently he replaced it on its brackets and came toward me, shaking his silver head.

"He wouldn't give me any guarantees about Tom."

"I heard him. They never do. You have to depend on his mercy."

"His *mercy!* He was talking like a maniac. He seemed to revel in the —in the pain."

"I agree, he was getting his kicks. Let's hope he's satisfied with the kicks he's already got, and the money."

Hillman's head went down. "You think Tom is in danger, don't you?"

"Yes. I don't think you're dealing with an outright maniac, but the man didn't sound too well-balanced. I think he's an amateur, or possibly a petty thief who saw his chance to move in on the heavy stuff. More likely a gifted amateur. Is he the same man who called this morning?"

"Yes."

"He may be working alone. Is there any chance that you could recognize his voice? There was some hint of a personal connection, maybe a grievance. Could he be a former employee of yours, for example?"

"I very much doubt it. We only employ skilled workers. This fellow sounded practically subhuman." His face became gaunter. "And you tell me I'm at his mercy."

"Your son is. Could there be any truth in what he said about Tom going to him voluntarily?"

"Of course not. Tom is a good boy."

"How is his judgment?"

Hillman didn't answer me, except by implication. He went to the bar, poured himself a stiff drink out of a bourbon bottle, and knocked it back. I followed him to the bar.

"Is there any possible chance that Tom cooked up this extortion deal himself, with the help of one of his buddies, or maybe with hired help?"

He hefted the glass in his hand, as if he was thinking of throwing it at my head. I caught a glimpse of his red angry mask before he turned away. "It's quite impossible. Why do you have to torment me with these ideas?"

"I don't know your son. You ought to."

"He'd never do a thing like that to me."

"You put him in Laguna Perdida School."

"I had to."

"Why?"

He turned on me furiously. "You keep hammering away at the same stupid question. What has it got to do with anything?"

"I'm trying to find out just how far gone Tom is. If there was reason to think that he kidnapped himself, to punish you or raise money, we'd want to turn the police loose—"

"You're crazy!"

"Is Tom?"

"Of course not. Frankly, Mr. Archer, I'm getting sick of you and your questions. If you want to stay in my house, it's got to be on my terms."

I was tempted to walk out, but something held me. The case was getting its hooks into my mind.

Hillman filled his glass with whisky and drank half of it down.

"If I were you, I'd lay off the sauce," I said. "You have decisions to make. This could be the most important day of your life."

He nodded slowly. "You're right." He reached across the bar and poured the rest of his whisky into the metal sink. Then he excused himself, and went upstairs to see to his wife.

5

I let myself out the front door, quietly, got a hat and raincoat out of the trunk of my car, and walked down the winding driveway. In the dead leaves under the oak trees the drip made rustling noises, releasing smells and memories. When I was seventeen I spent a summer working on a dude ranch in the foothills of the Sierra. Toward the end of August, when the air was beginning to sharpen, I found a girl, and before the summer was over we met in the woods. Everything since had been slightly anticlimactic.

Growing up seemed to be getting harder. The young people were certainly getting harder to figure out. Maybe Stella Carlson, if I could get to her, could help me understand Tom.

The Carlsons' mailbox was a couple of hundred yards down the road. It was a miniature replica, complete with shutters, of their green-shuttered white colonial house, and it rubbed me the wrong way, like a tasteless advertisement. I went up the drive to the brick stoop and knocked on the door.

A handsome redheaded woman in a linen dress opened the door and gave me a cool green look. "Yes?"

I didn't think I could get past her without lying. "I'm in the insurance—"

"Soliciting is not allowed in El Rancho."

"I'm not selling, Mrs. Carlson, I'm a claims adjuster." I got an old card out of my wallet which supported the statement. I had worked for insurance companies in my time.

"If it's about my wrecked car," she said, "I thought that was all settled last week."

"We're interested in the cause of the accident. We keep statistics, you know."

"I'm not particularly interested in becoming a statistic."

"Your car already is. I understand it was stolen."

She hesitated, and glanced behind her, as if there was a witness in the hallway. "Yes," she said finally. "It was stolen."

"By some young punk in the neighborhood, is that right?"

She flushed in response to my incitement. "Yes, and I doubt very much that it was an accident. He took my car and wrecked it out of sheer spite." The words boiled out as if they had been simmering in her mind for days.

"That's an interesting hypothesis, Mrs. Carlson. May I come in and talk it over with you?"

"I suppose so."

She let me into the hallway. I sat at a telephone table and took out my black notebook. She stood over me with one hand on the newel post at the foot of the stairs.

"Do you have anything to support that hypothesis?" I said with my pencil poised.

"You mean that he wrecked the car deliberately?"

"Yes."

Her white teeth closed on her full red lower lip, and left a brief dent in it. "It's something you couldn't make a statistic out of. The boy—his name is Tom Hillman—was interested in our daughter. He used to be a much nicer boy than he is now. As a matter of fact, he used to spend most of his free time over here. We treated him as if he were our own son. But the relationship went sour. Very sour." She sounded both angry and regretful.

"What soured it?"

She made a violent sideways gesture. "I prefer not to discuss it. It's something an insurance company doesn't have to know. Or anybody else."

"Perhaps I could talk to the boy. He lives next door, doesn't he?"

"His parents do, the Hillmans. I believe they've sent him away some-where. We no longer speak to the Hillmans," she said stiffly. "They're decent enough people, I suppose, but they've made awful fools of them-selves over that boy."

"Where did they send him?"

"To some kind of reform school, probably. He needed it. He was running out of control."

"In what way?"

"Every way. He smashed up my car, which probably means he was drinking. I know he was spending time in the bars on lower Main Street."

"The night before he wrecked your car?"

"All summer. He even tried to teach his bad habits to Stella. That's what soured the relationship, if you want to know."

I made a note. "Could you be a little more specific, Mrs. Carlson? We're interested in the whole social background of these accidents."

"Well, he actually dragged Stella with him to one of those awful dives. Can you imagine, taking an innocent sixteen-year-old girl to a wino joint on lower Main? That was the end of Tom Hillman, as far as we were concerned."

"What about Stella?"

"She's a sensible girl." She glanced up toward the head of the stairs. "Her father and I made her see that it wasn't a profitable relationship."

"So she wasn't involved in the borrowing of your car?"

"Certainly not."

A small clear voice said from the head of the stairs: "That isn't true, Mother, and you know it. I told you—"

"Be quiet, Stella. Go back to bed. If you're ill enough to stay home from camp, you're ill enough to stay in bed."

As she was talking, Mrs. Carlson surged halfway up the stairs. She had very good calves, a trifle muscular. Her daughter came down toward her, a slender girl with lovely eyes that seemed to take up most of her face below the forehead. Her brown hair was pulled back tight. She had on slacks and a high-necked blue wool sweater which revealed the bud-sharp outlines of her breasts.

"I'm feeling better, thank you," she said with adolescent iciness. "At least I was, until I heard you lying about Tommy."

"How dare you? Go to your room."

"I will if you'll stop telling lies about Tommy."

"You shut up."

Mrs. Carlson ran up the three or four steps that separated them, grabbed Stella by the shoulders, turned her forcibly, and marched her up out of sight. Stella kept repeating the word "Liar," until a door slammed on her thin clear voice.

Five minutes later Mrs. Carlson came down wearing fresh make-up, a green hat with a feather in it, a plaid coat, and gloves. She walked straight to the door and opened it wide.

"I'm afraid I have to rush now. My hairdresser gets very angry with me when I'm late. We were getting pretty far afield from what you wanted, anyway."

"On the contrary. I was very interested in your daughter's remarks."

She smiled with fierce politeness. "Pay no attention to Stella. She's feverish and hysterical. The poor child's been upset ever since the accident."

"Because she was involved in it?"

"Don't be silly." She rattled the doorknob. "I really have to go now."

I stepped outside. She followed, and slammed the door hard behind me. She'd probably had a lot of practice slamming doors.

"Where's your car?" she called after me.

"I parachuted in."

She stood and watched me until I reached the foot of the driveway. Then she went back into her house. I plodded back to the Hillmans' mailbox and turned up their private lane. The rustlings in the woods were getting louder. I thought it was a towhee scratching in the undergrowth. But it was Stella.

She appeared suddenly beside the trunk of a tree, wearing a blue ski jacket with the hood pulled up over her head and tied under her chin. She looked about twelve. She beckoned me with the dignity of a full-grown woman, ending the motion with her finger at her lips.

"I better stay out of sight. Mother will be looking for me."

"I thought she had an appointment with the hairdresser."

"That was just another lie," she said crisply. "She's always lying these days."

"Why?"

"I guess people get in the habit of it or something. Mother always used to be a very straight talker. So did Dad. But this business about Tommy has sort of thrown them. It's thrown me, too," she added, and coughed into her hand.

"You shouldn't be out in the wet," I said. "You're sick."

"No, really, I mean not physically. I just don't feel like facing the kids at camp and having to answer their questions."

"About Tommy?"

She nodded. "I don't even know where he is. Do you?"

"No, I don't."

"Are you a policeman, or what?"

"I used to be a policeman. Now I'm a what."

She wrinkled her nose and let out a little giggle. Then she tensed in a listening attitude, like a yearling fawn. She threw off her hood.

"Do you hear her? That's mother calling me."

Far off through the trees I heard a voice calling: "Stella."

"She'll kill me," the girl said. "But somebody has to tell the truth some time. *I* know. Tommy has a tree house up the slope, I mean he used to have when he was younger. We can talk there."

I followed her up a half-overgrown foot trail. A little redwood shack with a tar-paper roof sat on a low platform among the spreading branches of an oak. A homemade ladder, weathered gray like the tree house, slanted up to the platform. Stella climbed up first and went inside. A red-capped woodpecker flew out of an unglazed window into the next tree, where he sat and harangued us. Mrs. Carlson's voice floated up from the foot of the slope. She had a powerful voice, but it was getting hoarse.

"Swiss Family Robinson," Stella said when I went in. She was sitting on the edge of a built-in cot which had a mattress but no blankets. "Tommy and I used to spend whole days up here, when we were children." At sixteen, there was nostalgia in her voice. "Of course when we reached puberty it had to stop. It wouldn't have been proper."

"You're fond of Tommy."

"Yes. I love him. We're going to be married. But don't get the wrong idea about us. We're not even *going* steady. We're not making out and we're not soldered." She wrinkled her nose, as if she didn't like the smell of the words. "We'll be married when the time is right, when Tommy's through college or at least has a good start. We won't have any money problems, you see."

I thought she was using me to comfort herself a little with a story, a simple story with a happy ending. "How is that?"

"Tommy's parents have lots of money."

"What about your parents? Will they let you marry him?"

"They won't be able to stop me."

I believed her, if Tommy survived. She must have seen the "if " cross my eyes like a shadow. She was a perceptive girl.

"Is Tommy all right?" she said in a different tone.

"I hope so."

She reached up and plucked at my sleeve. "Where is he, Mister—?"

"I don't know, Stella. My name is Lew Archer. I'm a private detective working on Tommy's side. And you were going to tell me the truth about the accident."

"Yes. It was my fault. Mother and Dad seem to think they have to cover up for me, but it only makes things worse for Tommy. I was the one responsible, really." Her direct upward look, her earnest candor, reminded me of a child saying her prayers.

"Were you driving the car?"

"No. I don't mean I was with him. But I told him he could take it and

I got the key for him out of Mother's room. It's really my car, too—I mean, to use."

"She knows this?"

"Yes. I told her and Dad on Sunday. But they had already talked to the police, and after that they wouldn't change their story, or let me. They said it didn't alter the fact that he took it."

"Why did you let him take it?"

"I admit it wasn't such a good idea. But he had to go some place to see somebody and his father wouldn't let him use one of their cars. He was grounded. Mother and Dad were gone for the evening, and Tommy said he'd be back in a couple of hours. It was only about eight o'clock, and I thought it would be okay. I didn't know he was going to be out all night." She closed her eyes and hugged herself. "I was awake all night, listening for him."

"Where did he go?"

"I don't know."

"What was he after?"

"I don't know that, either. He said it was the most important thing in his life."

"Could he have been talking about alcohol?"

"Tommy doesn't drink. It was somebody he had to see, somebody very important."

"Like a drug pusher?"

She opened her wonderful eyes. "You're twisting meanings, the way Dad does when he's mad at me. Are you mad at me, Mr. Archer?"

"No. I'm grateful to you for being honest."

"Then why do you keep dragging in crummy meanings?"

"I'm used to questioning crummy people, I guess. And sometimes an addict's own mother, or own girl, doesn't know he's using drugs."

"I'm sure Tommy wasn't. He was dead against it. He knew what it had done to some—" She covered her mouth with her hand. Her nails were bitten.

"You were going to say?"

"Nothing."

Our rapport was breaking down. I did my best to save it. "Listen to me, Stella, I'm not digging dirt for the fun of it. Tommy's in real danger. If he had contacts with drug users, you should tell me."

"They were just some of his musician friends," she mumbled. "They wouldn't do anything to hurt him."

"They may have friends who would. Who are these people?"

"Just some people he played the piano with this summer, till his father made him quit. Tommy used to sit in on their jam sessions on Sunday afternoon at The Barroom Floor."

"Is that one of the dives your mother mentioned?"

"It isn't a dive. He didn't take me to dives. It was merely a place where they could get together and play their instruments. He wanted me to hear them play."

"And Tommy played with them?"

She nodded brightly. "He's a very good pianist, good enough to make his living at it. They even offered him a weekend job."

"Who did?"

"The combo at The Barroom Floor. His father wouldn't let him take it, naturally."

"Tell me about the people in the combo."

"Sam Jackman is the only one I know. He used to be a locker boy at the beach club. He plays the trombone. Then there was a saxophonist and a trumpeter and a drummer. I don't remember their names."

"What did you think of them?"

"I didn't think they were very good. But Tommy said they were planning to make an album."

"Every combo is. I mean, what kind of people were they?"

"They were just musicians. Tommy seemed to like them."

"How much time had he been spending with them?"

"Just Sunday afternoons. And I guess he used to drop in to hear them some nights. He called it his other life."

"His other life?"

"Uh-huh. *You* know, at home he had to hit the books and make his parents feel good and all that stuff. The same way I have to do when I'm at home. But it hasn't been working too well since the accident. Nobody feels good."

She shivered. A cold wet wind was blowing through the windows of the tree house. Mrs. Carlson's voice could no longer be heard. I felt uneasy about keeping the girl away from her mother. But I didn't want to let her go until she had told me everything she could.

I squatted on my heels in front of her. "Stella, do you think Tommy's appointment that Saturday night had to do with his musician friends?"

"No. He would have told me if it had. It was more of a secret than that."

"Did he say so?"

"He didn't have to. It was something secret and terribly important. He was terribly excited."

"In a good way or a bad way?"

"I don't know how you tell the difference. He wasn't afraid, if that's what you mean."

"I'm trying to ask you if he was sick."

"Sick?"

"Emotionally sick."

"No. I— That's foolish."

"Then why did his father have him put away?"

"You mean, put away in a mental hospital?" She leaned toward me, so close I could feel her breath on my face.

"Something like that—Laguna Perdida School. I didn't mean to tell you, and I'm going to ask you not to tell your parents."

"Don't worry, I'll never tell them anything. So that's where he is! Those hypocrites!" Her eyes were fixed and wet. "You said he was in danger. Are they trying to cut out his frontal lobe like in Tennessee Williams?"

"No. He was in no danger where he was. But he escaped from the place, the night before last, and fell into the hands of thieves. Now, I'm not going to load your mind with any more of this. I'm sorry it came out."

"Don't be." She gave me a second glimpse of the woman she was on her way to becoming. "If it's happening to Tommy, it's just like it was happening to me." Her forefinger tapped through nylon at the bone between her little breasts. "You said he fell into the hands of thieves. Who are they?"

"I'm trying to answer that question, in a hurry. Could they be his friends from The Barroom Floor?"

She shook her head. "Are they holding him prisoner or something?"

"Yes. I'm trying to get to them before they do something worse. If you know of any other contacts he had in his other life, particularly under-world contacts—"

"No. He didn't have any. He didn't have another life, really. It was just talk, talk and music."

Her lips were turning blue. I had a sudden evil image of myself: a heavy hunched figure seen from above in the act of tormenting a child who was already tormented. A sense went through me of the appalling ease with which the things you do in a good cause can slip over into bad.

"You'd better go home, Stella."

She folded her arms. "Not until you tell me everything. I'm not a child."

"But this is confidential information. I didn't intend to let any of it out. If it got to the wrong people, it would only make things worse."

She said with some scorn: "You keep beating around the bush, like Dad. Is Tommy being held for ransom?"

"Yes, but I'm pretty sure it's no ordinary kidnapping. He's supposed to have gone to these people of his own free will."

"Who said so?"

"One of them."

Her clear brow puckered. "Then why would Tommy be in any danger from them?"

"If he knows them," I said, "they're not likely to let him come home. He could identify them."

"I see." Her eyes were enormous, taking in all at once the horror of the world and growing dark with it. "I was *afraid* he was in some awful jam. His mother wouldn't tell me anything. I thought maybe he'd killed himself and they were keeping it quiet."

"What made you think that?"

"Tommy did. He called me up and I met him here in the tree house the morning after the accident. I wasn't supposed to tell anyone. But you've been honest with me. He wanted to see me one more time—just as friends, you know—and say goodbye forever. I asked him if he was going away, or what he planned to do. He wouldn't tell me."

"Was he suicidal?"

"I don't know. I was afraid that that was what it all meant. Not hearing from him since, I got more and more worried. I'm not as worried now as I was before you told me all those things." She did a mental double take on one of them. "But why would he deliberately go and stay with criminals?"

"It isn't clear. He may not have known they were criminals. If you can think of anyone—"

"I'm trying." She screwed up her face, and finally shook her head again. "I can't, unless they were the same people he had to see that other Saturday night. When he borrowed our car."

"Did he tell you anything at all about those people?"

"Just that he was terribly keen about seeing them."

"Were they men or women?"

"I don't even know that."

"What about the Sunday morning, when you met him here? Did he tell you anything at all about the night before?"

"No. He was feeling really low, after the accident and all, and the terrible row with his parents. I didn't ask him any questions. I guess I should have, shouldn't I? I always do the wrong thing, either by commission or omission."

"I think you do the right thing more often than most."

"Mother doesn't think so. Neither does Dad."

"Parents can be mistaken."

"Are you a parent?" The question reminded me of the sad boys in Laguna Perdida School.

"No, I never have been. My hands are clean."

"You're making fun of me," she said with a glum face.

"Never. Hardly ever."

She gave me a quick smile. "Gilbert and Sullivan. I didn't know detectives were like you."

"Neither do most of the other detectives." Our rapport, which came and went, was flourishing again. "There's one other thing I've been meaning to ask you, Stella. Your mother seems to believe that Tommy wrecked her car on purpose."

"I know she does."

"Could there be any truth in it?"

She considered the question. "I don't see how. He wouldn't do it to me, *or* her, unless—" She looked up in dark surmise.

"Go on."

"Unless he was trying to kill himself, and didn't care about anything any more."

"Was he?"

"He may have been. He didn't want to come home, he told me that much. But he didn't tell me why."

"I might learn something from examining the car. Do you know where it is?"

"It's down in Ringo's wrecking yard. Mother went to see it the other day."

"Why?"

"It helps her to stay mad, I guess. Mother's really crazy about Tommy, at least she used to be, and so was Dad. This business has been terribly hard on them. And I'm not making it any easier staying away from home now." She got to her feet, stamping them rapidly. "Mother will be calling out the gendarmes. Also she'll kill me."

"No she won't."

"Yes she will." But she wasn't basically afraid for herself. "If you find out anything about Tommy, will you let me know?"

"That might be a little tough to do, in view of your mother's attitude. Why don't you get in touch with me when you can? This number will always get me, through my answering service." I gave her a card.

She climbed down the ladder and flitted away through the trees, one of those youngsters who make you feel like apologizing for the world.

6

I made my way back to the Hillmans' house. It resembled a grim white fortress under the lowering sky. I didn't feel like going in just now and grappling with the heavy, smothering fear that hung in the rooms. Any-

way, I finally had a lead. Which Hillman could have given me if he'd
wanted to.

Before I got into my car I looked up at the front window of Tom's
room. The Hillmans were sitting close together in the niche of the window, looking out. Hillman shook his head curtly: no phone call.

I drove into town and turned right off the highway onto the main
street. The stucco and frame buildings in this segment of town, between
the highway and the railroad tracks, had been here a long time and been
allowed to deteriorate. There were tamale parlors and pool halls and
rummage stores and bars. The wet pavements were almost empty of
people, as they always were when it rained in California.

I parked and locked my car in front of a surplus and sporting goods
store and asked the proprietor where The Barroom Floor was. He
pointed west, toward the ocean:

"I don't think they're open, in the daytime. There's lots of other places
open."

"What about Ringo's auto yard?"

"Three blocks south on Sanger Street, that's the first stoplight below
the railroad tracks."

I thanked him.

"You're welcome, I'm sure." He was a middle-aged man with a sandy
moustache, cheerfully carrying a burden of unsuccess. "I can sell you a
rainproof cover for your hat."

"How much?"

"Ninety-eight cents. A dollar-two with tax."

I bought one. He put it on my hat. "It doesn't do much for the appearance, but—"

"Beauty is functional."

He smiled and nodded. "You took the words out of my mouth. I
figured you were a smart man. My name's Botkin, by the way, Joseph
Botkin."

"Lew Archer." We shook hands.

"My pleasure, Mr. Archer. If I'm not getting too personal, why
would a man like you want to do your drinking at The Barroom
Floor?"

"What's the matter with The Barroom Floor?"

"I don't like the way they handle their business, that's all. It lowers the
whole neighborhood. Which is low enough already, God knows."

"How do they handle their business?"

"They let young kids hang out there, for one thing—I'm not saying
they serve them liquor. But they shouldn't let them in at all."

"What do they do for another thing?"

"I'm talking too much." He squinted at me shrewdly. "And you ask a lot of questions. You wouldn't be from the Board of Equalization by any chance?"

"No, but I probably wouldn't tell you if I was. Is The Barroom Floor under investigation?"

"I wouldn't be surprised. I heard there was a complaint put in on them."

"From a man named Hillman?"

"Yeah. You are from the Board of Equalization, eh? If you want to look the place over for yourself, it opens at five."

It was twenty past four. I wandered along the street, looking through the windows of pawnshops at the loot of wrecked lives. The Barroom Floor was closed all right. It looked as if it was never going to reopen. Over the red-checked half-curtains at the windows, I peered into the dim interior. Red-checked tables and chairs were grouped around a dime-size dance floor; and farther back in the shadows was a bandstand decorated with gaudy paper. It looked so deserted you'd have thought all the members of the band had hocked their instruments and left town years ago.

I went back to my car and drove down Sanger Street to Ringo's yard. It was surrounded by a high board fence on which his name was painted in six-foot white letters. I pushed in through the gate. A black German shepherd glided out of the open door of a shack and delicately grasped my right wrist between his large yellow teeth. He didn't growl or anything. He merely held me, looking up brightly at my face.

A wide fat man, with a medicine ball of stomach badly concealed under his plaid shirt, came to the door of the shack.

"That's all right, Lion."

The dog let go of me and went to the fat man.

"His teeth are dirty," I said. "You should give him bones to chew. I don't mean wristbones."

"Sorry. We weren't expecting any customers. But he won't hurt you, will you, Lion?"

Lion rolled his eyes and let his tongue hang out about a foot.

"Go ahead, pet him."

"I'm a dog lover," I said, "but is he a man lover?"

"Sure. Go ahead and pet him."

I went ahead and petted him. Lion lay down on his back with his feet in the air, grinning up at me with his fangs.

"What can I do you for, mister?" Ringo said.

"I want to look at a car."

He waved his hand toward the yard. "I got hundreds of them. But there isn't a one of them you could drive away. You want one to cannibalize?"

"This is a particular car I want to examine." I produced my adjuster's card. "It's a fairly new Dodge, I think, belonged to a Mrs. Carlson, wrecked a week or so ago."

"Yeah. I'll show it to you."

He put on a black rubber raincoat. Lion and I followed him down a narrow aisle between two lines of wrecked cars. With their crumpled grilles and hoods, shattered windshields, torn fenders, collapsed roofs, disemboweled seats, and blown-out tires, they made me think of some ultimate freeway disaster. Somebody with an eye for detail should make a study of automobile graveyards, I thought, the way they study the ruins and potsherds of vanished civilizations. It could provide a clue as to why our civilization is vanishing.

"All the ones in this line are totaled out," Ringo said. "This is the Carlson job, second from the end. That Pontiac came in since. Head-on collision, two dead." He shuddered. "I never go on the highway when I can help it."

"What caused the accident to the Carlson car?"

"It was taken for a joy ride by one of the neighbors' kids, a boy name of Hillman. You know how these young squirts are—if it isn't theirs, they don't care what happens to it. According to the traffic detail, he missed a curve and went off the road and probably turned it over trying to get back on. He must of rolled over several times and ended up against a tree."

I walked around the end of the line and looked over the Dart from all sides. There were deep dents in the roof and hood and all four fenders, as if it had been hit with random sledgehammers. The windshield was gone. The doors were sprung.

Leaning in through the left-hand door, I noticed an oval piece of white plastic, stamped with printing, protruding from the space between the driver's seat and the back. I reached in and pulled it out. It was a brass door key. The printing on the plastic tab said: DACK'S AUTO COURT 7.

"Watch the glass in there," Ringo said behind me. "What are you looking for?"

I put the key in my pocket before I turned around. "I can't figure out why the boy didn't get hurt."

"He had the wheel to hang on to, remember. Lucky for him it didn't break."

"Is there any chance he wrecked the car on purpose?"

"Naw. He'd have to be off his rocker to do that. Course you can't put anything past these kids nowadays. Can you, Lion?" He stooped to touch the dog's head and went on talking, either to it or to me. "My own son that I brought up in the business went off to college and now he don't even come home for Christmas some years. I got nobody to take over the business." He straightened up and looked around at his wrecks with stern affection, like the emperor of a wasteland.

"Could there have been anybody with him in the car?"

"Naw. They would of been really banged up, with no seat belts and nothing to hang on to." He looked at the sky, and added impatiently: "I don't mind standing around answering your questions, mister. But if you really want the dope on the accident, talk to the traffic detail. I'm closing up."

It was ten minutes to five. I made my way back to The Barroom Floor. Somebody had turned on a few lights inside. The front door was still locked. I went back to my car and waited. I took out the Dack's Auto Court key and looked at it, wondering if it meant anything. It could have meant, among other farfetched possibilities, that the handsome Mrs. Carlson was unfaithful to her husband.

Shortly after five a short dark man in a red jacket unlocked the front door of The Barroom Floor and took up his position behind the bar. I went in and sat down on a stool opposite him. He seemed much taller behind the bar. I looked over it and saw that he was standing on a wooden platform about a foot off the floor.

"Yeah," he said, "it keeps me on the level. Without it I can barely see over the bar." He grinned. "My wife, now, is five foot six and built in proportion. She ought to be here now," he added in a disciplinary tone, and looked at the wristwatch on his miniature wrist. "What will you have?"

"Whisky sour. You own this place?"

"Me and the wife, we have an interest in it."

"Nice place," I said, though it wasn't particularly nice. It was no cleaner and no more cheerful than the average bar and grill with cabaret pretensions. The old waiter leaning against the wall beside the kitchen door seemed to be sleeping on his feet.

"Thank you. We have plans for it." As he talked, he made my drink with expert fingers. "You haven't been in before. I don't remember your face."

"I'm from Hollywood. I hear you have a pretty fair jazz combo."

"Yeah."

"Will they be playing tonight?"

"They only play Friday and Saturday nights. We don't get the weekday trade to justify 'em."

"What about the Sunday jam sessions? Are they still on?"

"Yeah. We had one yesterday. The boys were in great form. Too bad you missed them." He slid my drink across the bar. "You in the music business?"

"I represent musicians from time to time. I have an office on the Strip."

"Sam would want to talk to you. He's the leader."

"Where can I get in touch with him?"

"I have his address somewhere. Just a minute, please."

A couple of young men in business suits with rain-sprinkled shoulders had taken seats at the far end of the bar. They were talking in carrying voices about a million-dollar real-estate deal. Apparently it was somebody else's deal, not theirs, but they seemed to enjoy talking about it.

The small man served them short whiskies without being asked. A lavishly built young woman came in and struggled out of a transparent raincoat which she rolled up and tossed under the bar. She had a Sicilian nose. Her neck was hung with jewelry like a bandit princess's.

The small man looked at her sternly. "You're late. I can't operate without a hostess."

"I'm sorry, Tony. Rachel was late again."

"Hire another baby sitter."

"But she's so good with the baby. You wouldn't want just anybody feeding him."

"We won't talk about it now. You know where you're supposed to be."

"Yes, Mr. Napoleon."

With a rebellious swing of the hip, she took up her post by the door. Customers were beginning to drift in by twos and fours. Most of them were young or young middle-aged. They looked respectable enough. Talking and laughing vivaciously, clinking her jewelry, the hostess guided them to the red-checked tables.

Her husband remembered me after a while. "Here's Sam Jackman's address. He has no phone, but it isn't far from here."

He handed me a sheet from a memo pad on which he had written in pencil: "169 Mimosa, apt. 2."

It was near the railroad tracks, an old frame house with Victorian gingerbread on the façade half chewed away by time. The heavy carved front door was standing open, and I went into the hallway, feeling warped parquetry under my feet. On a closed door to my right, a number 2 stamped from metal hung upside down by a single nail. It rattled when I knocked.

A yellow-faced man in shirt sleeves looked out. "Who is it you want?"

"Sam Jackman."

"That's me." He seemed surprised that anybody should want him. "Is it about a job?" He asked the question with a kind of hollow hopefulness that answered itself in the negative.

"No, but I want to talk to you about something important, Mr. Jackman."

He caught the "mister" and inclined his head in acknowledgement. "All right."

"May I come in? My name is Lew Archer. I'm a private detective."

"I dunno, the place is a mess. With the wife working all day—but come on in."

He backed into his apartment, as if he was afraid to expose his flank. It consisted of one large room which might once have been the drawing room of the house. It still had its fine proportions, but the lofty ceiling was scabbed and watermarked, the windows hung with torn curtains. A cardboard wardrobe, a gas plate behind a screen, stood against the inner wall. Run-down furniture, including an unmade double bed in one corner, cluttered the bare wooden floor. On a table beside the bed, a small television set was reeling off the disasters of the day in crisp elocutionary sentences.

Jackman switched it off, picked up a smoking cigarette from the lid of a coffee can on the table, and sat on the edge of the bed. It wasn't a marihuana cigarette. He was completely still and silent, waiting for me to explain myself. I sat down facing him.

"I'm looking for Tom Hillman."

He gave me a swift glance that had fear in it, then busied himself putting out his cigarette. He dropped the butt into the pocket of his shirt.

"I didn't know he was missing."

"He is."

"That's too bad. What would make you think that he was here?" He looked around the room with wide unblinking eyes. "Did Mr. Hillman send you?"

"No."

He didn't believe me. "I just wondered. Mr. Hillman has been on my back."

"Why?"

"I interested myself in his boy," he said carefully.

"In what way?"

"Personally." He turned his hands palms upward on his knees. "I heard him doodling on the piano at the beach club. That was one day last spring. I did a little doodling of my own. Piano isn't my instrument, but he got interested in some chords I showed him. That made me a bad influence."

"Were you?"

"Mr. Hillman thought so. He got me fired from the beach club. He didn't want his precious boy messing with the likes of me." His upturned hands lay like helpless pink-bellied animals on their backs. "If Mr. Hillman didn't send you, who did?"

"A man named Dr. Sponti."

I thought the name would mean nothing to him, but he gave me another of his quick fearful looks. "Sponti? You mean—?" He fell silent.

"Go on, Mr. Jackman. Tell me what I mean."

He huddled down into himself, like a man slumping into sudden old age. He let his speech deteriorate: "I wouldn't know nothin' about nothin', mister." He opened his mouth in an idiotic smile that showed no teeth.

"I think you know a good deal. I think I'll sit here until you tell me some of it."

"That's your privilege," he said, although it wasn't.

He took the butt out of his shirt pocket and lit it with a kitchen match. He dropped the distorted black match-end into the coffee lid. We looked at each other through smoke that drifted like ectoplasm from his mouth.

"You know Dr. Sponti, do you?"

"I've heard the name," Jackman said.

"Have you seen Tom Hillman in the last two days?"

He shook his head, but his eyes stayed on my face in a certain way, as if he was expecting to be challenged.

"Where have you heard Sponti's name?"

"A relative of mine. She used to work in the kitchen at L. P. S." He said with irony: "That makes me an accessory, I guess."

"Accessory to what?"

"Any crime in the book. I wouldn't even have to know what happened, would I?" He doused his butt in a carefully restricted show of anger.

"That sort of talk gets us nowhere."

"Where does your sort of talk get us? Anything I tell you is evidence against me, isn't it?"

"You talk like a man with a record."

"I've had my troubles." He added after a long silence: "I'm sorry Tommy Hillman is having his."

"You seem to be fond of him."

"We took to each other." He threw the line away.

"I wish you'd tell me more about him. That's really what I came here for."

My words sounded slightly false. I was suspicious of Jackman, and he knew it. He was a watcher and a subtle listener.

"Now I got a different idea," he said. "I got the idea you're after Tommy to put him back in the L. P. School. Correct me if I'm wrong."

"You're wrong."

"I don't believe you." He was watching my hands to see if I might hit him. There were marks on his face where he had been hit before. "No offense, but I don't believe you, mister—"

I repeated my name. "Do you know where Tommy is?"

"No. I do know this. If Mr. Hillman put him in the L. P. School, he's better off on the loose than going home. His father had no right to do it to him."

"So I've been told."

"Who told you?"

"One of the women on the staff there. She said Tom wasn't disturbed in her opinion, and didn't belong in the school. Tom seemed to agree with her. He broke out Saturday night."

"Good."

"Not so good. At least he was safe there."

"He's safe," Jackman said, and quickly regretted saying it. He opened his mouth in its senseless toothless smile, a tragic mask pretending to be comic.

"Where is he then?"

Jackman shrugged his thin shoulders. "I told you before and I'll tell you again, I don't know."

"How did you know that he was on the loose?"

"Sponti wouldn't send you to me otherwise."

"You're quick on the uptake."

"I have to pick up what I can," he said. "You talk a lot without saying much."

"You say even less. But you'll talk, Sam."

He rose in a quick jerky movement and went to the door. I thought he was going to tell me to leave, but he didn't. He stood against the closed door in the attitude of a man facing a rifle squad.

"What do you expect me to do?" he cried. "Put my neck in the noose so Hillman can hang me?"

I walked toward him.

"Stay away from me!" The fear in his eyes was burning brightly, feeding on a long fuse of experience. He lifted one crooked arm to shield his head. "Don't touch me!"

"Calm down. That's hysterical talk, about a noose."

"It's a hysterical world. I lost my job for teaching his kid some music. Now Hillman is raising the ante. What's the rap this time?"

"There is no rap if the boy is safe. You said he was. Didn't you?"

No answer, but he looked at me under his arm. He had tears in his eyes.

"For God's sake, Sam, we ought to be able to get together on this. You like the boy, you don't want anything bad to happen to him. That's all I have in mind."

"There's bad and bad." But he lowered his defensive arm and kept on studying my face.

"I know there's bad and bad," I said. "The line between them isn't straight and narrow. The difference between them isn't black and white. I know you favor Tom against his father. You don't want him cut off from you or your kind of music. And you think I want to drag him back to a school where he doesn't belong."

"Aren't you?"

"I'm trying to save his life. I think you can help me."

"How?"

"Let's sit down again and talk quietly the way we were. Come on. And stop seeing Hillman when you look at me."

Jackman returned to the bed and I sat near him.

"Well, Sam, have you seen him in the last two days?"

"Seen who? Mr. Hillman?"

"Don't go into the idiot act again. You're an intelligent man. Just answer my question."

"Before I do, will you answer one of mine?"

"If I possibly can."

"When you say you're trying to save his life, you mean save him from bad influences, don't you, put him back in Squaresville with all the other squares?"

"Worse things can happen to a boy."

"You didn't answer my question."

"You could have asked a better one. I mean save him from death. He's in the hands of people who may or may not decide to kill him, depending on how the impulse takes them. Am I telling you anything you don't know?"

"You sure are, man." His voice was sincere, and his eyes filled up with compunction. But he and I could talk for a year, and he would still be holding something back. Among the things he was holding back was the fact that he didn't believe me.

"Why don't you believe me, Sam?"

"I didn't say that."

"You don't have to. You're acting it out, by sitting on the information you have."

"I ain't sittin' on nothin', 'ceptin' this here old raunchy bed," he said in broad angry parody.

"Now I know you are. I've got an ear for certain things, the way you've got an ear for music. You play the trombone, don't you?"

"Yeah." He looked surprised.

"I hear you blow well."

"Don't flatter me. I ain't no J. C. Higginbotham."

"And I ain't no Sherlock Holmes. But sooner or later you're going to tell me when you saw Tommy Hillman last. You're not going to sit on your raunchy ole bed and wait for the television to inform you that they found Tommy's body in a ditch."

"Did they?"

"Not yet. It could happen tonight. When did you see him?"

He drew a deep breath. "Yesterday. He was okay."

"Did he come here?"

"No sir. He never has. He stopped in at The Barroom Floor yesterday afternoon. He came in the back way and only stayed five minutes."

"What was he wearing?"

"Slacks and a black sweater. He told me once his mother knitted that sweater for him."

"Did you talk to him yesterday afternoon?"

"I played him a special riff and he came up and thanked me. That was all. I didn't know he was on the run. Shucks, he even had his girl friend with him."

"Stella?"

"The other one. The older one."

"What's her name?"

"He never told me. I only seen her once or twice before that. Tommy knew I wouldn't approve of him squiring her around. She's practically old enough to be his mother."

"Can you describe her?"

"She's a bottle blonde, with a lot of hair, you know how they're wearing it now." He swept his hand up from his wrinkled forehead. "Blue eyes, with a lot of eye shadow. It's hard to tell what she looks like under all that makeup."

I got out my notebook and made some notes. "What's her background?"

"Show business, maybe. Like I say, I never talked to her. But she has the looks."

"I gather she's attractive."

"She appears to be to Tom. I guess she's his first. A lot of young boys start out with an older woman. But," he added under his breath, "he could do better than that."

"How old is she?"

"Thirty, anyway. She didn't show me her birth certificate. She dresses younger—skirts up over her knees. She isn't a big girl, and maybe in some lights she can get away with the youth act."

"What was she wearing yesterday?"

"A dark dress, blue satin or something like that, with sequins on it, a neckline down to here." He touched his solar plexus. "It grieved me to see Tom with his arm around her."

"How did she seem to feel about him?"

"You're asking me more than I can answer. He's a good-looking boy, and she makes a show of affection. But I don't need X-ray eyes to know what is in her mind."

"Would she be a hustler?"

"Could be."

"Did you ever see her with any other man?"

"I never did. I only saw her once or twice with Tom."

"Once, or twice?"

He ruminated. "Twice before yesterday. The first time was two weeks ago yesterday. That was a Sunday, he brought her to our jam session that afternoon. The woman had been drinking and first she wanted to sing and then she wanted to dance. We don't allow dancing at these sessions, you have to pay cabaret tax. Somebody told her that and she got mad and towed the boy away."

"Who told her not to dance?"

"I disremember. One of the cats sitting around, I guess, they object to dancing. The music we play Sundays isn't to dance to, anyway. It's more to the glory of God," he said surprisingly.

"What about the second time you saw her?"

He hesitated, thinking. "That was ten nights ago, on a Friday. They came in around midnight and had a sandwich. I drifted by their table, at the break, but Tom didn't introduce me or ask me to sit down. Which was all right with me. They seemed to have things to talk about."

"Did you overhear any part of their conversation?"

"I did." His face hardened. "She needed money, she was telling him, money to get away from her husband."

"You're sure you heard that?"

"Sure as I'm sitting here."

"What was Tom's attitude?"

"Looked to me like he was fascinated."

"Had he been drinking?"

"*She* was. He didn't drink. They don't serve drinks to minors at the Floor. No sir. She had him hyped on something worse than drink."

"Drugs?"

"You know what I mean." His hands moulded a woman's figure in the air.

"You used the word 'hyped.' "

"It was just a manner of speaking," he said nervously, rubbing his upper arm through the shirt sleeve.

"Are you on the needle?"

"No sir. I'm on the TV," he said with a sudden downward smile.

"Show me your arms."

"I don't have to. You got no right."

"I want to test your veracity. Okay?"

He unbuttoned his cuffs and pushed his sleeves up his thin yellow arms. The pitted scars in them were old and dry.

"I got out of Lexington seven years ago," he said, "and I haven't fallen since, I thank the good Lord."

He touched his scars with a kind of reverence. They were like tiny extinct volcanoes in his flesh. He covered them up.

"You're doing all right, Mr. Jackman. With your background, you'd probably know if Tom was on drugs."

"I probably would. He wasn't. More than once I lectured him on the subject. Musicians have their temptations. But he took my lectures to heart." He shifted his hand to the region of his heart. "I ought to of lectured him on the subject of women."

"I never heard that it did much good. Did you ever see Tom and the blonde with anyone else?"

"No."

"Did he introduce her to anyone?"

"I doubt it. He was keeping her to himself. Showing her off, but keeping her to himself."

"You don't have any idea what her name is?"

"No. I don't."

I got up and thanked him. "I'm sorry if I gave you a rough time."

"I've had rougher."

———⌇———

7

Dack's Auto Court was on the edge of the city, in a rather rundown suburb named Ocean View. The twelve or fifteen cottages of the court lay on the flat top of a bluff, below the highway and above the sea. They were made of concrete block and painted an unnatural green. Three or four cars, none of them recent models, were parked on the muddy gravel.

The rain had let up and fresh yellow light slanted in from a hole in the west, as if to provide a special revelation of the ugliness of Dack's Auto Court. Above the hutch marked "Office," a single ragged palm tree leaned against the light. I parked beside it and went in.

A hand-painted card taped to the counter instructed me to "Ring for Proprietor." I punched the handbell beside it. It didn't work.

Leaning across the counter, I noticed on the shelf below it a telephone and a metal filing box divided into fifteen numbered sections. The registration card for number seven was dated three weeks before, and indicated that "Mr. and Mrs. Robt. Brown" were paying sixteen dollars a week for that cottage. The spaces provided on the card for home address and license number were empty.

The screen door creaked behind me. A big old man with a naked condor head came flapping into the office. He snatched the card from my fingers and looked at me with hot eyes. "What do you think you're doing?"

"I was only checking."

"Checking what?"

"To see if some people I know are here. Bob Brown and his wife."

He held the card up to the light and read it, moving his lips laboriously around the easy words. "They're here," he said without joy. "Leastways, they were this morning."

He gave me a doubtful look. My claim of acquaintanceship with the Browns had done nothing for my status. I tried to improve it. "Do you have a cottage vacant?"

"Ten of them. Take your pick."

"How much?"

"Depends on if you rent by the day or the week. They're three-fifty a day, sixteen a week."

"I'd better check with the Browns first, see if they're planning to stay."

"I wouldn't know about that. They been here three weeks." He had a flexible worried mouth in conflict with a stupid stubborn chin. He stroked his chin as if to educate it. "I can let you have number eight for twelve a week single. That's right next door to the Browns' place."

"I'll check with them."

"I don't believe they're there. You can always try."

I went outside and down the dreary line of cottages. The door of number seven was locked. Nobody answered my repeated rapping.

When I turned away, the old man was standing in front of number eight. He beckoned to me and opened the door with a flourish:

"Take a look. I can let you have it for ten if you really like it."

I stepped inside. The room was cold and cheerless. The inside walls were concrete block, and the same unnatural green as the outside. Through a crack in the drawn blind, yellow light slashed at the hollow bed, the threadbare carpet. I'd spent too many nights in places like it to want to spend another.

"It's clean," the old man said.

"I'm sure it is, Mr. Dack."

"I cleaned it myself. But I'm not Dack, I'm Stanislaus. Dack sold out to me years ago. I just never got around to having the signs changed. What's the use? They'll be tearing everything down and putting up high-rise apartments pretty soon." He smiled and stroked his bald skull as if it was a kind of golden egg. "Well, you want the cottage?"

"It really depends on Brown's plans."

"If I was you," he said, "I wouldn't let too much depend on him."

"How is that, Mr. Stanislaus?"

"He's kind of a blowtop, ain't he? I mean, the way he treats that little blonde wife. I always say these things are between a man *and* his wife. But it rankles me," he said. "I got a deep respect for women."

"So have I. I've never liked the way he treated women."

"I'm glad to hear that. A man should treat his wife with love and friendship. I lost my own wife several years ago, and I know what I'm talking about. I tried to tell him that, he told me to mind my own business. I know he's a friend of yours—"

"He's not exactly a friend. Is he getting worse?"

"Depends what you mean, *worse.* This very day he was slapping her around. I felt like kicking him out of my place. Only, how would that help *her?* And all she did was make a little phone call. He tries to keep her cooped up like she was in jail." He paused, listening, as if the word *jail* had associations for him. "How long have you known this Brown?"

"Not so long," I said vaguely. "I ran into him in Los Angeles."

"In Hollywood?"

"Yeah. In Hollywood."

"Is it true she was in the movies? She mentioned one day she used to be in the movies. He told her to shut up."

"Their marriage seems to be deteriorating."

"You can say that again." He leaned toward me in the doorway. "I bet you she's the one you're interested in. I see a lot of couples, one way and another, and I'm willing to bet you she's just about had her fill of him. If I was a young fellow like you, I'd be tempted to make her an offer." He nudged me; the friction seemed to warm him. "She's a red-hot little bundle."

"I'm not young enough."

"Sure you are." He handled my arm, and chuckled. "It's true she likes 'em young. I been seeing her off and on with a teen-ager, even."

I produced the photograph of Tom that Elaine Hillman had given me. "This one?"

The old man lifted it to the daylight, at arm's length. "Yeah. That's a mighty good picture of him. He's a good-looking boy." He handed the photograph back to me, and fondled his chin. "How do you come to have a picture of him?"

I told him the truth, or part of it: "He's a runaway from a boarding school. I'm a private detective representing the school."

The moist gleam of lechery faded out of Stanislaus's eyes. Something bleaker took its place, a fantasy of punishment perhaps. His whole face underwent a transformation, like quick-setting concrete.

"You can't make me responsible for what the renters do."

"Nobody said I could."

He didn't seem to hear me. "Let's see that picture again." I showed it to him. He shook his head over it. "I made a mistake. My eyes ain't what they used to be. I never seen him before."

"You made a positive identification."

"I take it back. You were talking to me under false pretenses, trying to suck me in and get something on me. Well, you got nothing on me. It's been tried before," he said darkly. "And you can march yourself off my property."

"Aren't you going to rent me the cottage?"

He hesitated a moment, saying a silent goodbye to the ten dollars. "No sir, I want no spies and peepers in my place."

"You may be harboring something worse."

I think he suspected it, and the suspicion was the source of his anger.

"I'll take my chances. Now you git. If you're not off my property in one minute, I'm going to call the sheriff."

That was the last thing I wanted. I'd already done enough to endanger the ransom payment and Tom's return. I got.

8

A blue sports car stood in the drive behind the Hillman Cadillac. An athletic-looking young man who looked as if he belonged in the sports car came out of the house and confronted me on the front steps. He wore an Ivy League suit and had an alligator coat slung over his arm and hand, with something bulky and gun-shaped under it.

"Point that thing away from me. I'm not armed."

"I w-want to know who you are." He had a faint stammer.

"Lew Archer. Who are you?"

"I'm Dick Leandro." He spoke the words almost questioningly, as if he didn't quite know what it meant to be Dick Leandro.

"Lower that gun," I reminded him. "Try pointing it at your leg."

He dropped his arm. The alligator coat slid off it, onto the flagstone steps, and I saw that he was holding a heavy old revolver. He picked up the coat and looked at me in a rather confused way. He was a handsome boy in his early twenties, with brown eyes and dark curly hair. A certain little dancing light in his eyes told me that he was aware of being handsome.

"Since you're here," I said, "I take it the money's here, too."

"Yes. I brought it out from the office several hours ago."

"Has Hillman been given instructions for delivering it?"

He shook his head. "We're still waiting."

I found Ralph and Elaine Hillman in the downstairs room where the telephone was. They were sitting close together as if for warmth, on a chesterfield near the front window. The waiting had aged them both.

The evening light fell like gray paint across their faces. She was knitting something out of red wool. Her hands moved rapidly and precisely as if they had independent life.

Hillman got to his feet. He had been holding a newspaper-wrapped parcel in his lap, and he laid it down on the chesterfield, gently, like a father handling an infant.

"Hello, Archer," he said in a monotone.

I moved toward him with some idea of comforting him. But the expression in his eyes, hurt and proud and lonely, discouraged me from touching him or saying anything very personal.

"You've had a long hard day."

He nodded slowly, once. His wife let out a sound like a dry sob. "Why haven't we heard anything from that man?"

"It's hard to say. He seems to be putting on the screws deliberately."

She pushed her knitting to one side, and it fell on the floor unnoticed. Her faded pretty face wrinkled up as if she could feel the physical pressure of torture instruments. "He's keeping us in hell, in absolute hell. But why?"

"He's probably waiting for dark," I said. "I'm sure you'll be hearing from him soon. Twenty-five thousand dollars is a powerful attraction."

"He's welcome to the money, five times over. Why doesn't he simply take it and give us back our boy?" Her hand flung itself out, rattling the newspaper parcel beside her.

"Don't fret yourself, Ellie." Hillman leaned over her and touched her pale gold hair. "There's no use asking questions that can't be answered. Remember, this will pass." His words of comfort sounded hollow and forced.

"So will I," she said wryly and bitterly, "if this keeps up much longer."

She smoothed her face with both hands and stayed with her hands in a prayerful position at her chin. She was trembling. I was afraid she might snap like a violin string. I said to Hillman:

"May I speak to you in private? I've uncovered some facts you should know."

"You can tell me in front of Elaine, and Dick for that matter."

I noticed that Leandro was standing just inside the door.

"I prefer not to."

"You're not calling the shots, however." It was a curious echo of the man on the telephone. "Let's have your facts."

I let him have them: "Your son has been seen consorting with a married woman named Brown. She's a blonde, show-business type, a good deal older than he is, and she seems to have been after him for money. The chances are better than even that Mrs. Brown and her husband are involved in this extortion bid. They seem to be on their uppers—"

Elaine raised her open hands in front of her face, as if too many words were confusing her. "What do you mean, consorting?"

"He's been hanging around with the woman, publicly and privately. They were seen together yesterday afternoon."

"Where?" Hillman said.

"At The Barroom Floor."

"Who says so?"

"One of their employees. He's seen them before, and he referred to Mrs. Brown as 'Tom's girl friend, the older one.' I've had corroborating evidence from the man who owns the court where the Browns are living. Tom has been hanging around there, too."

"How old is this woman?"

"Thirty or more. She's quite an attractive dish, apparently."

Elaine Hillman lifted her eyes. There seemed to be real horror in them. "Are you implying that Tom has been having an affair with her?"

"I'm simply reporting facts."

"I don't believe your facts, not any of them."

"Do you think I'm lying to you?"

"Maybe not deliberately. But there must be some ghastly mistake."

"I agree," Dick Leandro said from the doorway. "Tom has always been a very clean-living boy."

Hillman was silent. Perhaps he knew something about his son that the others didn't. He sat down beside his wife and hugged the paper parcel defensively.

"His virtue isn't the main thing right now," I said. "The question is what kind of people he's mixed up with and what they're doing to him. Or possibly what they're doing to you with his cooperation."

"What is that supposed to mean?" Hillman said.

"We have to reconsider the possibility that Tom is in on the extortion deal. He was with Mrs. Brown yesterday. The man on the telephone, who may be Brown, said Tom came to them voluntarily."

Elaine Hillman peered up into my face as if she was trying to grasp such a possibility. It seemed to be too much for her to accept. She closed her eyes and shook her head so hard that her hair fell untidily over her forehead. Pushing it back with spread fingers, she said in a small voice that sent chills through me:

"You're lying, I know my son, he's an innocent victim. You're trying to do something terrible, coming to us in our affliction with such a filthy rotten smear."

Her husband tried to quiet her against his shoulder. "Hush now, Elaine. Mr. Archer is only trying to help."

She pushed him away from her. "We don't want that kind of help. He has no right. Tom is an innocent victim, and God knows what is happening to him." Her hand was still at her head, with her pale hair sprouting up between her fingers. "I can't take any more of this, Ralph—this dreadful man with his dreadful stories."

"I'm sorry, Mrs. Hillman. I didn't want you to hear them."

"I know. You wanted to malign my son without anyone to defend him."

"That's nonsense, Ellie," Hillman said. "I think you better come upstairs and let me give you a sedative."

He helped her to her feet and walked her out past me, looking at me sorrowfully across her rumpled head. She moved like an invalid leaning on his strength.

Dick Leandro drifted into the room after they had left it, and sat on the chesterfield to keep the money company. He said in a slightly nagging way:

"You hit Elaine pretty hard with all that stuff. She's a sensitive woman, very puritanical about sex and such. And incidentally she's crazy about Tommy. She won't listen to a word against him."

"*Are* there words against him?"

"Not that I know about. But he has been getting into trouble lately. *You* know, with the car wreck and all. And now you t-tell me he's been dipping into the fleshpots."

"I didn't say that."

"Yeah, but I got the message. Where does the g-girl live, anyway? Somebody ought to go and question her."

"You're full of ideas."

He had a tin ear for tone. "Well, how about it? I'm game."

"You're doing more good here, guarding the money. How did Hillman happen to pick you to bring the money, by the way? Are you an old family friend?"

"I guess you could say that. I've been crewing for Mr. Hillman since I was yay-high." He held out his hand at knee level. "Mr. Hillman is a terrific guy. Did you know he made Captain in the Navy? But he won't let anybody call him Captain except when we're at sea.

"And generous," the young man said. "As a matter of fact, he helped me through college and got me a job at his broker's. I owe him a lot. He's treated me like a father." He spoke with some emotion, real but intended, like an actor's. "I'm an orphan, you might say. My family broke

up when I was yay-high, and my father left town. He used to work for
Mr. Hillman at the plant."

"Do you know Tom Hillman well?"

"Sure. He's a pretty good kid. But a little too much of an egghead in
my book. Which keeps him from being popular. No wonder he has his
troubles." Leandro tapped his temple with his knuckles. "Is it true that
Mr. Hillman put him in the booby—I mean, in a sanatorium?"

"Ask him yourself."

The young man bored me. I went into the alcove and made myself a
drink. Night was closing in. The garish bullfight posters on the walls had
faded into darkness like long-forgotten *corridas*. There were shadows
huddling with shadows behind the bar. I raised my glass to them in a
gesture I didn't quite understand, except that there was relief in darkness
and silence and whisky.

I could hear Hillman's footsteps dragging down the stairs. The telephone on the bar went off like an alarm. Hillman's descending footsteps
became louder. He came trotting into the room as the telephone rang
a second time. He elbowed me out of his way.

I started for the extension phone in the pantry. He called after me:
"No! I'll handle this myself."

There was command in his voice. I stood and watched him pick up the
receiver, hold it to his head like a black scorpion, and listen to what it
said.

"Yes, this is Mr. Hillman. Just a minute." He brought a business envelope and a ballpoint pen out of his inside pocket, turned on an overhead light, and got ready to write on the bar. "Go ahead."

For about half a minute he listened and wrote. Then he said: "I think
so. Aren't there steps going down to the beach?"

He listened and wrote. "Where shall I walk to?" He turned the envelope over and wrote some more. "Yes," he said. "I park two blocks
away, at Seneca, and approach the steps on foot. I put the money under
the right side of the top step. Then I go down to the beach for half an
hour. Is that all?"

There was a little more. He listened to it. Finally he said: "Yes. But the
deal is very much on as far as I'm concerned. I'll be there at nine sharp."

There was a pathetic note in his voice, the note of a salesman trying
to nail down an appointment with a refractory client.

"Wait," he said, and groaned into the dead receiver.

Dick Leandro, moving like a cat, was in the alcove ahead of me. "What
is it, Mr. Hillman? What's the trouble?"

"I wanted to ask about Tom. He didn't give me a chance." He lifted
his face to the plaster ceiling. "I don't know if he's alive or dead."

"They wouldn't *kill* him, would they?" the young man said. He sounded as though he'd had a first frightening hint of his own mortality.

"I don't know, Dick. I don't know." Hillman's head rolled from one side to the other.

The young man put his arm around his shoulder. "Take it easy now, Skipper. We'll get him back."

Hillman poured himself a heavy slug of bourbon and tossed it down. It brought a little color into his face. I said:

"Same man?"

"Yes."

"And he told you where to make the money-drop."

"Yes."

"Do you want company?"

"I have to go there alone. He said he'd be watching."

"Where are you to go?"

Hillman looked at each of our faces in turn, lingeringly, as if he was saying goodbye. "I'll keep that to myself. I don't want anything to wreck the arrangements."

"Somebody should know about them, though, in case anything does go wrong. You're taking a chance."

"I'd rather take a chance with my own life than my son's." He said it as if he meant it, and the words seemed to renew his courage. He glanced at his wristwatch. "It's twenty-five to nine. It will take me up to twenty minutes to get there. He didn't give me much leeway."

"Can you drive okay?" Leandro said.

"Yes. I'm all right. I'll just go up and tell Ellie that I'm leaving. You stay in the house with her, won't you, Dick?"

"I'll be glad to."

Hillman went upstairs, still clutching his scribbled-over envelope. I said to Leandro: "Where is Seneca Street?"

"Seneca Road. In Ocean View."

"Are there steps going down to the beach anywhere near there?"

"Yeah, but you're not supposed to go there. You heard Mr. Hillman."

"I heard him."

Hillman came down and took the parcel of money out of Leandro's hands. He thanked the young man, and his voice was deep and gentle as well as melancholy.

We stood on the flagstone steps and watched him drive away into the darkness under the trees. In the hole in the dark west a little light still persisted, like the last light there was ever going to be.

9

I went through the house to the kitchen and asked Mrs. Perez to make me a plain cheese sandwich. She grumbled, but she made it. I ate it leaning against the refrigerator. Mrs. Perez wouldn't talk about the trouble in the family. She seemed to have a superstitious feeling that trouble was only amplified by words. When I tried to question her about Tom's habits, she gradually lost her ability to understand my English.

Dick Leandro had gone upstairs to sit with Elaine. He seemed more at home than Tom appeared to have been with his own family. I went out through the reception hall. It was nine o'clock, and I couldn't wait any longer.

Driving along the highway to Ocean View, I argued jesuitically with myself that I had stayed clear of the money-drop, I wasn't double-dealing with Hillman, who wasn't my client in any case, and besides I had no proof that Mrs. Brown and her husband were connected with the extortion attempt.

It was deep night over the sea, moonless and starless. I left my car at a view-point near Dack's Auto Court. The sea was a hollow presence with a voice. I hiked down the access road to the court, not using the flashlight that I carried with me.

The office was lighted and had a neon "Vacancy" sign above the door. Avoiding the spill of light from it, I went straight to cottage number seven. It was dark. I knocked, and got no answer. I let myself in with the key I had and closed the self-locking door behind me.

Mrs. Brown was waiting. I stumbled over her foot and almost fell on top of her before I switched on my flashlight. She lay in her winking sequined gown under the jittery beam. Blood was tangled like tar in her bright hair. Her face was mottled with bruises, and misshapen. She looked as though she had been beaten to death.

I touched her hand. She was cold. I turned the light away from her lopsided grin.

The beam jumped around the green walls, the newspaper-littered floor. It found a large strapped canvas suitcase standing at the foot of the bed with two paper bags beside it. One of the bags contained a bottle of cheap wine, the other sandwiches that were drying out.

I unstrapped the suitcase and opened it. An odor rose from its contents like sour regret. Men's and women's things were bundled indiscriminately together, dirty shirts and soiled slips, a rusting safety razor and a dabbled jar of cold cream and a bottle of mascara, a couple of dresses and some lingerie, a man's worn blue suit with a chain-store label and nothing in the pockets but tobacco powder and, tucked far down in the outer breast pocket, a creased yellow business card poorly printed on cheap paper:

HAROLD "HAR" HARLEY
Application Photos Our Specialty

I found the woman's imitation snakeskin purse on a chair by the side window. It contained a jumble of cosmetics and some frayed blue chip stamps. No wallet, no identification, no money except for a single silver dollar in the bottom of the bag. There were also a pack of cards, slick with the oil of human hands, and a dice which came up six all three times I rolled it.

I heard a car approaching, and headlights swept the window on the far side. I switched off my flashlight. The wheels of the car crunched in the gravel and came to a halt directly in front of the cottage. Someone got out of the car and turned the cottage doorknob. When the door refused to open, a man's voice said:

"Let me in."

It was the slightly wheezing, whining voice I'd heard that afternoon on Hillman's phone. I moved toward the door with the dark flashlight raised in my hand. The man outside rattled the knob.

"I know you're in there, I saw the light. This is no time to carry a grudge, hon."

The woman lay in her deep waiting silence. I stepped around her and stood against the wall beside the door. I shifted the flash to my left hand and fumbled for the spring lock with my right.

"I hear you, damn you. You want another taste of what you had today?" He waited, and then said: "If you won't open the door, I'll shoot the lock out."

I heard the click of a hammer. I stayed where I was beside the door, holding the flashlight like a club. But he didn't fire.

"On the other hand," he said, "there's nothing in there I need, including you. You can stay here on your can if you want to. Make up your mind right now."

He waited. He couldn't outwait her.

"This is your last chance. I'll count to three. If you don't open up, I'm traveling alone." He counted, one, two, three, but it would take bigger magic to reach her. "Good riddance to bad rubbish," he said.

His footsteps moved away on the stones. The car door creaked. I couldn't let him go.

I snapped back the lock and opened the door and rushed him. His shadowy hatted figure was halfway into his car, with one foot on the ground. He whirled. The gun was still in his hand. It gave out a hot little flame. I could feel it sear me.

I staggered across the gravel and got hold of his twisting body. He hammered my hands loose with the butt of his gun. I had blood in my eyes, and I couldn't avoid the gun butt when it smashed into my skull. A kind of chandelier lit up in my head and then crashed down into darkness.

Next thing I was a V. I. P. traveling with a police guard in the back of a chauffered car. The turban I could feel on my head suggested to the joggled brain under it that I was a rajah or a maharajah. We turned into a driveway under a red light, which excited me. Perhaps I was being taken to see one of my various concubines.

I raised the question with the uniformed men sitting on either side of me. Gently but firmly, they helped me out of the patrol car and walked me through swinging doors, which a man in white held open, into a glaring place that smelled of disinfectants.

They persuaded me to sit down on a padded table and then to lie down. My head hurt. I felt it with my hands. It had a towel around it, sticky with blood.

A large young face with a moustache leaned over me upside down. Large hairy hands removed the towel and did some probing and scouring in my scalp. It stung.

"You're a lucky man. It parted your hair for you, kind of permanently."

"How bad is it, Doctor?"

"The bullet wound isn't serious, just a crease. As I said, you're lucky. This other lesion is going to take longer to heal. What did you get hit with?"

"Gun butt. I think."

"More fun and games," he said.

"Did they catch him?"

"You'll have to ask them. They haven't told me a thing."

He clipped parts of my head and put some clamps in it and gave me a drink of water and an aspirin. Then he left me lying alone in the white-partitioned cubicle. My two guards moved rapidly into the vacuum.

They were sheriff's men, wearing peaked hats and tan uniforms. They were young and hearty, with fine animal bodies and rather animal, not so fine, faces. Good earnest boys, but a little dull. They said they wanted to help me.

"Why did you kill her?" the dark one said.

"I didn't. She'd been dead for some time when I found her."

"That doesn't let you out. Mr. Stanislaus said you were there earlier in the day."

"He was with me all the time."

"That's what you say," the fair one said.

This repartee went on for some time, like a recording of an old vaudeville act which some collector had unwisely preserved. I tried to question them. They wouldn't tell me anything. My head was feeling worse, but oddly enough I began to think better with it. I even managed to get up on my elbows and look at them on the level.

"I'm a licensed private detective from Los Angeles."

"We know that," the dark one said.

I felt for my wallet. It was missing. "Give me my wallet."

"You'll get it back all in good time. Nobody's going to steal it."

"I want to talk to the sheriff."

"He's in bed asleep."

"Is there a captain or lieutenant on duty?"

"The lieutenant is busy at the scene of the crime. You can talk to him in the morning. The doctor says you stay here overnight. Concussion. What did the woman hit you with, anyway?"

"Her husband hit me, with a gun butt."

"I hardly blame him," the fair one said emotionally, "after what you did to his wife."

"Were you shacked up with her?" the dark one said.

I looked from one healthy smooth face to the other. They didn't look sadistic, or sound corrupt, and I wasn't afraid for myself. Sooner or later the mess would be straightened out. But I was afraid.

"Listen," I said, "you're wasting time on me. I had legitimate business at the court. I was investigating—" The fear came up in my throat and choked off the rest of the sentence. It was fear for the boy.

"Investigating what?" the dark one said.

"Law enforcement in this county. It stinks." I wasn't feeling too articulate.

"We'll law-enforcement you," the dark one said. He was broad, with muscular shoulders. He moved them around in the air a little bit and pretended to catch a fly just in front of my face.

"Lay off, muscle," I said.

The large, moustached face of the doctor appeared in the entrance to the cubicle. "Everything okay in here?"

I said above the deputies' smiling assurances: "I want to make a phone call."

The doctor looked doubtfully from me to the officers. "I don't know about that."

"I'm a private detective investigating a crime. I'm not free to talk about it without the permission of my principal. I want to call him."

"There's no facilities for that," the dark deputy said.

"How about it, Doctor? You're in charge here, and I have a legal right to make a phone call."

He was a very young man behind his moustache. "I don't know. There's a telephone booth down the hall. Do you think you can make it?"

"I never felt better in my life."

But when I swung my legs down, the floor seemed distant and undulant. The deputies had to help me to the booth and prop me up on the stool inside of it. I pulled the folding door shut. Their faces floated outside the wired glass like bulbous fishes, a dark one and a fair one, nosing around a bathyscaphe on the deep ocean floor.

Technically Dr. Sponti was my principal, but it was Ralph Hillman's number I asked Information for. I had a dime in my pocket, fortunately, and Hillman was there. He answered the phone himself on the first ring:

"Yes?"

"This is Archer."

He groaned.

"Have you heard anything from Tom?" I said.

"No. I followed instructions to the letter, and when I came up from the beach the money was gone. He's double-crossed me," he said bitterly.

"Did you see him?"

"No. I made no attempt to."

"I did." I told Hillman what had happened, to me and to Mrs. Brown.

His voice came thin and bleak over the wire. "And you think these are the same people?"

"I think Brown's your man. Brown is probably an alias. Does the name Harold Harley mean anything to you?"

"What was that again?"

"Harold or 'Har' Harley. He's a photographer."

"I never heard of him."

I wasn't surprised. Harley's yellow card was the kind that businessmen distributed by the hundred, and had no necessary connection with Brown.

"Is that all you wanted?" Hillman said. "I'm trying to keep this line open."

"I haven't got to the main thing. The police are on my back. I can't explain what I was doing at the auto court without dragging in the extortion bit, and your son."

"Can't you give them a story?"

"It wouldn't be wise. This is a capital case, a double one."

"Are you trying to tell me that Tom is dead?"

"I meant that kidnapping is a capital crime. But you are dealing with a killer. I think at this point you should level with the police, and get their help. Sooner or later I'm going to have to level with them."

"I forbid—" He changed his tone, and started the sentence over: "I beg of you, please hold off. Give him until morning to come home. He's my only son."

"All right. Till morning. We can't bottle it up any longer than that, and we shouldn't."

I hung up and stepped out into the corridor. Instead of taking me back to the emergency ward, my escort took me up in an elevator to a special room with heavy screens on the windows. They let me lie down on the bed, and took turns questioning me. It would be tedious to recount the dialogue. It was tedious at the time, and I didn't listen to all of it.

Some time around midnight a sheriff's lieutenant named Bastian came into the room and ordered the deputies out into the hall. He was a tall man, with iron-gray hair clipped short. The vertical grooves in his cheeks looked like the scars inflicted by a personal discipline harsher than saber cuts.

He stood over me frowning. "Dr. Murphy says you're feeling critical of law enforcement in this county."

"I've had reason."

"It isn't easy recruiting men at the salaries the supervisors are willing to pay. We can hardly compete with the wages for unskilled labor. And this is a *tough* job."

"It has its little extra compensations."

"What does that mean?"

"I seem to be missing my wallet."

Bastian's face went grim. He marched out into the hall, made some remarks in a voice that buzzed like a hornet, and came back carrying my wallet. I counted the money in it, rather obtrusively.

"It was used to check you out," Bastian said. "L. A. County gives you a good rating, and I'm sorry if you weren't treated right."

"Think nothing of it. I'm used to being pushed around by unskilled labor."

"You heard me apologize," he said, in a tone that closed the subject.

Bastian asked me a number of questions about Mrs. Brown and the reason for my interest in her. I told him I'd have to check with my client in the morning, before I could open up. Then he wanted everything I could give him about Brown's appearance and car.

The moments before and after the shot were vague in my memory. I dredged up what I could. Brown was a man of better than medium size, physically powerful, not young, not old. He was wearing a dark gray or blue jacket and a wide-brimmed grayish hat which shadowed his eyes. The lower part of his face was heavy-jawed. His voice was rough, with a slight wheeze in it. The car was a dirty white or tan two-door sedan, probably a Ford, about eight years old.

I learned two facts from Lieutenant Bastian: the car had an Idaho license, according to other tenants of the court, and Stanislaus was in trouble for keeping no record of the license number. I think Bastian gave me these facts in the hope of loosening my tongue. But he finally agreed to wait till morning.

They shifted me to another room on the same floor, unguarded. I spent a good part of the night, waking and sleeping, watching a turning wheel of faces. The faces were interspersed from time to time with brilliant visions of Dack's Auto Court. Its green ugliness was held in the selective sunset glare, as if it was under a judgment, and so was I.

10

Morning was welcome, in spite of the pain in my head. I couldn't remember eating anything but Mrs. Perez's cheese sandwich since the previous morning. The tepid breakfast coffee and overscrambled eggs tasted like nectar and ambrosia.

I was finishing breakfast when Dr. Sponti arrived, breathing rapidly and audibly. His plump face bore the marks of a bad night. He had sleepless bruises around the eyes, and a gash in his upper lip where his razor had slipped. The chilly hand he offered me reminded me of the dead woman's, and I dropped it.

"I'm surprised you knew I was here."

"I found out in a rather circuitous way. A Lieutenant Bastian phoned me in the middle of the night. Evidently he saw the check I gave you yesterday morning. He asked me a great many questions."

"About me?"

"About the whole situation involving you and Tom Hillman."

"You told him about Tom Hillman?"

"I had no choice, really." He picked at the fresh scab on his lip. "A woman has been murdered in Ocean View. I was honor bound to provide the authorities with all the information I could. After all—"

"Does this include the business of the ransom money?"

"Naturally it does. Lieutenant Bastian considered it highly important. He thanked me effusively, and promised that the name of the school would be kept out of the papers."

"Which is the main thing."

"It is to me," Sponti said. "I'm in the school business."

It was frustrating to have held out for nothing, and to have no secrets to trade with Bastian. But it was relieving, too, that the thing was out in the open. Hillman's imposition of silence had made it hard for me to do my job. I said:

"Have you had any repercussions from Ralph Hillman?"

"He phoned early this morning. The boy is still on the missing list." Sponti's voice was lugubrious, and his eyes rolled heavily toward me. "The parents are naturally quite frantic by this time. Mr. Hillman said things I'm sure he'll regret later."

"Is he still blaming you for the kidnapping?"

"Yes, and he blames me for bringing you into the case. He seems to feel you broke faith with him, shall we say."

"By going to the auto court and getting myself shot?"

"You frightened off the kidnappers, in his opinion, and prevented them from returning his son to him. I'm very much afraid he wants nothing more to do with you, Mr. Archer."

"And neither do you?"

Dr. Sponti pursed his lips and brought his ten fingers together in the air. They made a Norman arch and then a Gothic one. "I'm sure you understand the pressures I'm under. I'm virtually obliged to do as Mr. Hillman wishes in his extremity."

"Sure."

"And I'm not going to ask you to refund any part of your check. The entire two hundred and fifty dollars is yours, even though you've been in my employ"—he looked at his watch—"considerably less than twenty-four hours. The unearned surplus will take care of your medical expenses, I'm sure." He was backing toward the door. "Well, I have to run."

"Go to hell," I said as he went out.

He poked his head in again: "You may regret saying that. I'm tempted to stop payment on that check after all."

I made an obscene suggestion as to the disposition of the check. Dr. Sponti turned as blue as a Santa Clara plum and went away. I lay and enjoyed my anger for a while. It went so nicely with the reciprocating ache in my head. And it helped to cover over the fact that I had let myself in for this. I shouldn't have gone the second time to Dack's Auto Court, at least not when I did.

A nurse's aide came in and took away my tray. Later a doctor palpated my skull, looked into my eyes with a tiny light, and told me I probably had a slight concussion but so had a lot of other people walking around. I borrowed a safety razor from an orderly, shaved and dressed, and went down to the cashier's window and paid my bill with Sponti's check.

I got over two hundred dollars change. Riding downtown in a taxi, I decided I could afford to spend another day on the case, whether Dr. Sponti liked it or not. I told the driver to let me off at the telephone company.

"You said the courthouse."

"The telephone company. We've had a change of plan."

"You should have said so in the first place."

"Forgive my failure of leadership."

I was feeling bitter and bright. It had to do with the weather, which had turned sunny, but more to do with my decision to spend my own time on a boy I'd never seen. I didn't tip the driver.

One end of the main public room in the telephone building was lined with long-distance booths and shelves of out-of-town directories. Only the main cities in Idaho, like Boise and Pocatello and Idaho Falls, were represented. I looked through their directories for a photographer named Harold Harley. He wasn't listed. Robert Brown was, by the legion, but the name was almost certainly an alias.

I installed myself in one of the booths and placed a long-distance call to Arnie Walters, a Reno detective who often worked with me. I had no Idaho contact, and Reno was on the fastest route to Idaho. Reno itself had a powerful attraction for thieves with sudden money.

"Walters Agency," Arnie said.

"This is Lew." I told him where I was calling from, and why.

"You come up with some dillies. Murder and kidnapping, eh?"

"The kidnapping may be a phony. Tom Hillman, the supposed victim, has been palling around with the murdered woman for a couple of weeks."

"How old did you say he was?"

"Seventeen. He's big for his age." I described Tom Hillman in detail. "He may be traveling with Brown either voluntarily or involuntarily."

"Or not traveling at all?" Arnie said.

"Or not traveling at all."

"You know this boy?"

"No."

"I thought maybe you knew him. Okay. Where does this photographer Harold Harley come in?"

"Harley may be Brown himself, or he may know Brown. His card is the only real lead I have so far. That and the Idaho license. I want you to do two things. Check Idaho and adjoining states for Harley. You have the business directories, don't you?"

"Yeah, I'll get Phyllis on them." She was his wife and partner.

"The other thing, I want you to look out for Brown and the boy, you and your informers in Tahoe and Vegas."

"What makes you think they're headed in this direction?"

"It's a hunch. The woman had a silver dollar and a loaded dice in her purse."

"And no identification?"

"Whoever did her in got rid of everything she had in that line. But we'll identify her. We have *her.*"

"Let me know when you do."

I walked across town to the courthouse, under a sky that yesterday's rain had washed clean. I asked the deputy on duty in the sheriff's department where to find Lieutenant Bastian. He directed me to the identification laboratory on the second floor.

It was more office than laboratory, a spacious room with pigeons murmuring on the window ledges. The walls were crowded with filing cabinets and hung with maps of the city and county and state. A large adjacent closet was fitted out as a darkroom, with drying racks and a long metal sink.

Bastian got up smiling. His smile wasn't greatly different from last night's frown. He laid down a rectangular magnifying glass on top of the photograph he had been studying. Leaning across the desk to take his outstretched hand, I could see that it was a picture of Mrs. Brown in death.

"What killed her, Lieutenant?" I said when we were seated.

"This." He held up his right hand and clenched it. His face clenched with it. "The human hand."

"Robert Brown's?"

"It looks like it. He gave her a beating early yesterday afternoon, according to Stanislaus. The deputy coroner says she's been dead that long."

"Stanislaus told me they quarreled over a telephone call she made."

"That's right. We haven't been able to trace the call, which means it was probably local. She used the phone in Stanislaus's office, but he claims to know nothing more about it."

"How does he know Brown gave her a beating?" I said.

"He says a neighbor woman told him. That checks out." Bastian wiped his left hand across his tense angry face, without really changing his expression. "It's terrible the way some people live, that a woman could be killed within a neighbor's hearing and nobody knows or cares."

"Not even Brown," I said. "He thought she was alive at nine-thirty last night. He talked to her through the door, trying to get her to open up. Or he may have been trying to con himself into thinking he hadn't killed her after all. I don't think he's too stable."

Bastian looked up sharply. "Were you in the cottage when Brown was talking through the door?"

"I was. Incidentally, I recognized his voice. He's the same man who extorted twenty-five thousand dollars from Ralph Hillman last night. I listened in on a phone call he made to Hillman yesterday."

Bastian's right fist was still clenched. He used it to strike the desk top, savagely. The pigeons on the window ledge flew away.

"It's too damn bad," he said, "you didn't bring us in on this yesterday. You might have saved a life, not to mention twenty-five thousand dollars."

"Tell that to Hillman."

"I intend to. This morning. Right now I'm telling you."

"The decision wasn't mine. I tried to change it. Anyway, I entered the case after the woman was killed."

"That's a good place to begin," Bastian said after a pause. "Go on from there. I want the full record."

He reached down beside his desk and turned on a recorder. For an hour or more the tape slithered quietly from wheel to wheel as I talked into it. I was clientless and free and I didn't suppress anything. Not even the possibility that Tom Hillman had cooperated with Brown in extorting money from his father.

"I'd almost like to think that that was true," Bastian said. "It would mean that the kid is still alive, anyway. But it isn't likely."

"Which isn't likely?"

"Both things. I doubt that he hoaxed his old man, and I doubt that he's still alive. It looks as if the woman was used as a decoy to get him in position for the kill. We'll probably find his body in the ocean week after next."

His words had the weight of experience behind them. Kidnap victims were poor actuarial risks. But I said:

"I'm working on the assumption that he's alive."

Bastian raised his eyebrows. "I thought Dr. Sponti took you off the case."

"I still have some of his money."

Bastian gave me a long cool appraising look. "L. A. was right. You're not the usual peeper."

"I hope not."

"If you're staying with it, you can do something for me, as well as for yourself. Help me to get this woman identified." He slid the picture of Mrs. Brown out from under the magnifying glass. "This postmortem photo is too rough to circularize. But you could show it around in the right circles. I'm having a police artist make a composite portrait, but that takes time."

"What about fingerprints?"

"We're trying that, too, but a lot of women have never been fingerprinted. Meantime, will you try and get an identification? You're a Holly-wood man, and the woman claimed that she was in pictures at one time."

"That doesn't mean a thing."

"It might."

"But I was planning to try and pick up Brown's trail in Nevada. If the boy's alive, Brown knows where to find him."

"The Nevada police already have our APB on Brown. And you have a private operative on the spot. Frankly, I'd appreciate it if you'll take this picture to Hollywood with you. I don't have a man I can spare. By the way, I had your car brought into the county garage."

Cooperation breeds cooperation. Besides, the woman's identity was important, if only because the killer had tried to hide it. I accepted the picture, along with several others taken from various angles, and put them in the same pocket as my picture of Tom.

"You can reverse any telephone charges," Bastian said in farewell.

Halfway down the stairs I ran into Ralph Hillman. At first glance he looked fresher than he had the previous evening. But it was an illusory freshness. The color in his cheeks was hectic, and the sparkle in his eyes was the glint of desperation. He sort of reared back when he saw me, like a spooked horse.

"Can you give me a minute, Mr. Hillman?"

"Sorry. I have an appointment."

"The lieutenant can wait. I want to say this. I admit I made a mistake last night. But you made a mistake in getting Sponti to drop me."

He looked at me down his patrician nose. "*You'd* naturally think so. It's costing you money."

"Look, I'm sorry about last night. I was overeager. That's the defect of a virtue. I want to carry on with the search for your son."

"What's the use? He's probably dead. Thanks to you."

"That's a fairly massive accusation, Mr. Hillman."

"Take it. It's yours. And please get out of my way." He looked compulsively at his wristwatch. "I'm already late."

He brushed past me and ran upstairs as if I might pursue him. It wasn't a pleasant interview. The unpleasantness stuck in my crop all the way to Los Angeles.

11

I bought a hat a size too large, to accommodate my bandages, and paid a brief visit to the Hollywood division of the L. A. P. D. None of the detective-sergeants in the upstairs offices recognized Mrs. Brown in her deathly disguise. I went from the station to the news room of the Hollywood *Reporter.* Most of the people at work there resented being shown such pictures. The ones who gave them an honest examination failed to identify Mrs. Brown.

I tried a number of flesh peddlers along the Strip, with the same lack of success and the same effect. The photographs made me unpopular. These guys and dolls pursuing the rapid buck hated to be reminded of what was waiting on the far side of the last dollar. The violence of the woman's death only made it worse. It could happen to anybody, any time.

I started back to my office. I intended to call Bastian and ask him to rush me a Xerox copy of the composite sketch as soon as his artist had completed it. Then I thought of Joey Sylvester.

Joey was an old agent who maintained an office of sorts two blocks off Sunset and two flights up. He hadn't been able to adapt to the shift of economic power from the major studios to the independent producers. He lived mainly on his share of residuals from old television movies, and on his memories.

I knocked on the door of his cubbyhole and heard him hiding his bottle, as if I might be the ghost of Louis B. Mayer or an emissary from J. Arthur Rank. Joey looked a little disappointed when he opened the door and it was only me. But he resurrected the bottle and offered me a drink in a paper cup. He had a glass tumbler for his own use, and I happened to know that nearly every day he sat at his desk and absorbed a quart of bourbon and sometimes a quart and a half.

He was a baby-faced old man with innocent white hair and crafty eyes. His mind was like an old-fashioned lamp with its wick in alcohol, focused so as to light up the past and its chauffeur-driven Packard, and cast the third-floor-walkup present into cool shadow.

It wasn't long past noon, and Joey was still in fair shape. "It's good to see you, Lew boy. I drink to your health." He did so, with one fatherly hand on my shoulder.

"I drink to yours."

The hand on my shoulder reached up and took my hat off. "What did you do to your head?"

"I was slightly shot last night."

"You mean you got drunk and fell down?"

"Shot with a gun," I said.

He clucked. "You shouldn't expose yourself the way you do. Know what you ought to do, Lew boy? Retire and write your memoirs. The unvarnished sensational truth about Hollywood."

"It's been done a thousand times, Joey. Now they're even doing it in the fan mags."

"Not the way you could do it. Give 'em the worm's-eye view. There's a title!" He snapped his fingers. "I bet I could sell your story for twenty-five G's, make it part of a package with Steve McQueen. Give some thought to it, Lew boy. I could open up a lovely jar of olives for you."

"I just opened a can of peas, Joey, and I wonder if you can help me with it. How is your tolerance for pictures of dead people?"

"I've seen a lot of them die." His free hand fluttered toward the wall above his desk. It was papered with inscribed photographs of vanished players. His other hand raised his tumbler. "I drink to them."

I cluttered his desk top with the angry pictures. He looked them over mournfully. "Ach!" he said. "What the human animal does to itself! Am I supposed to know her?"

"She's supposed to have worked in pictures. You know more actors than anybody."

"I did at one time. No more."

"I doubt that she's done any acting recently. She was on the skids."

"It can happen overnight." In a sense, it had happened to him. He put on his glasses, turned on a desk lamp, and studied the pictures intensively. After a while he said: "Carol?"

"You know her."

He looked at me over his glasses. "I couldn't swear to it in court. I once knew a little blonde girl, natural blonde, with ears like that. Notice that they're small and close to the head and rather pointed. Unusual ears for a girl."

"Carol who?"

"I can't remember. It was a long time ago, back in the forties. I don't think she was using her own name, anyway."

"Why not?"

"She had a very stuffy family back in Podunk. They disapproved of the acting bit. I seem to remember she told me she ran away from home."

"In Podunk?"

"I didn't mean that literally. Matter of fact, I think she came from some place in Idaho."

"Say that again."

"Idaho. Is your dead lady from Idaho?"

"Her husband drives a car with an Idaho license. Tell me more about Carol. When and where did you know her?"

"Right here in Hollywood. A friend of mine took an interest in the girl and brought her to me. She was a lovely child. Untouched." His hands flew apart in the air, untouching her. "All she had was high-school acting experience, but I got her a little work. It wasn't hard in those days, with the war still going on. And I had a personal in with all the casting directors on all the lots."

"What year was it, Joey?"

He took off his glasses and squinted into the past. "She came to me in the spring of '45, the last year of the war."

Mrs. Brown, if she was Carol, had been around longer than I'd thought. "How old was she then?"

"Very young. Just a child, like I said. Maybe sixteen."

"And who was the friend who took an interest in her?"

"It isn't like you think. It was a woman, one of the girls in the story department at Warner's. She's producing a series now at Television City. But she was just a script girl back in the days I'm talking about."

"You wouldn't be talking about Susanna Drew?"

"Yeah. Do you know Susanna?"

"Thanks to you. I met her at a party at your house, when you were living in Beverly Hills."

Joey looked startled, as though the shift from one level of the past to another had caught him unawares. "I remember. That must have been ten years ago."

He sat and thought about ten years ago, and so did I. I had taken Susanna home from Joey's party, and we met at other parties, by agreement. We had things to talk about. She picked my brains for what I knew about people, and I picked hers for what she knew about books. I was crazy about her insane sense of humor.

The physical thing came more slowly, as it often does when it promises to be real. I think we tried to force it. We'd both been drinking, and a lot of stuff boiled up from Susanna's childhood. Her father had been a professor at UCLA, who lost his wife young, and he had supervised Susanna's studies. Her father was dead, but she could still feel his breath on the back of her neck.

We had a bad passage, and Susanna stopped going to parties, at least the ones I went to. I heard she had a marriage which didn't take. Then she had a career, which took.

"How did she happen to know Carol?" I said to Joey.

"You'll have to ask her yourself. She told me at the time, but I don't remember. My memory isn't what it was." The present was depressing him. He poured himself a drink.

I refused the offer of one. "What happened to Carol?"

"She dropped out of sight. I think she ran off with a sailor, or something like that. She didn't have what it takes, anyway, after the first bloom." Joey sighed deeply. "If you see Susanna, mention my name, will you, Lew? I mean, if you can do it gracefully." He moved one hand in an undulating horizontal curve. "She acts like she thought I was dead."

I used Joey's phone to make a call to Susanna Drew's office. Her secretary let me talk to her:

"This is Lew Archer, Susanna."

"How nice to hear from you."

"The occasion isn't so nice," I said bluntly. "I'm investigating a murder. The victim may or may not be a girl you knew back in the forties, named Carol."

"Not Carol Harley?"

"I'm afraid she's the one."

Her voice roughened. "And you say she's dead?"

"Yes. She was murdered yesterday in a place called Ocean View."

She was silent for a moment. When she spoke again, her voice was softer and younger. "What can I do?"

"Tell me about your friend Carol."

"Not on the telephone, *please*. The telephone dehumanizes everything."

"A personal meeting would suit me much better," I said rather formally. "I have some pictures to show you, to make the identification positive. It should be soon. We're twenty-four hours behind—"

"Come over now. I'll send your name out front."

I thanked Joey and drove to Television City. A guard from the front office escorted me through the building to Susanna Drew's office. It was large and bright, with flowers on the desk and explosive-looking abstract expressionist paintings on the walls. Susanna was standing at the window, crying. She was a slim woman with short straight hair so black the eye stayed on it. She kept her back to me for some time after her secretary went out and closed the door. Finally she turned to face me, still dabbing at her wet cheeks with a piece of yellow Kleenex.

She was fortyish now, and not exactly pretty, but neither did she look like anybody else. Her black eyes, even in sorrow, were furiously alive. She had style, and intelligence in the lines and contours of her face. Legs still good. Mouth still good. It said:

"I don't know why I'm carrying on like this. I haven't seen or heard from Carol in seventeen or eighteen years." She paused. "I really do know, though. 'It is Margaret I mourn for.' Do you know Hopkins's poem?"

"You know I don't. Who's Margaret?"

"The girl in the poem," she said. "She's grieving over the fallen autumn leaves. And Hopkins tells her she's grieving for herself. Which is what I'm doing." She breathed deeply. "I used to be so *young.*"

"You're not exactly over the hill now."

"Don't flatter me. I'm old old old. I was twenty in 1945 when I knew Carol. Back in the pre-atomic era." On the way to her desk she paused in front of one of the abstract paintings, as if it represented what had happened to the world since. She sat down with an air of great efficiency. "Well, let me look at your pictures."

"You won't like them. She was beaten to death."

"God. Who would do that?"

"Her husband is the prime suspect."

"Harley? Is she—was she still with that *schmo?*"

"Evidently she still was."

"I knew he'd do her in sooner or later."

I leaned on the end of her desk. "How did you know that?"

"It was one of those fated things. Elective affinities with a reverse twist. She was a really nice child, as tender as a soft-boiled egg, and he was a psychopathic personality. He just couldn't leave her alone."

"How do you know he was a psychopathic personality?"

"I know a psychopathic personality when I see one," she said, lifting her chin. "I was married to one, briefly, back in the fabulous fifties. Which constitutes me an authority. If you want a definition, a psychopathic personality is a man you can't depend on for anything except trouble."

"And that's the way Harley was?"

"Oh yes."

"What was his first name?"

"Mike. He was a sailor, a sailor in the Navy."

"And what was the name of his ship?"

She opened her mouth to tell me, I believe. But something shifted rapidly and heavily in her mind, and closed off communication. "I'm afraid I don't remember." She looked up at me with black opaque eyes.

"What did he do before he went into the Navy? Was he a photographer?"

She looked back over the years. "I think he had been a boxer, a professional boxer, not a very successful one. He may have been a photographer, too. He was the sort of person who had been a number of things, none of them successfully."

"Are you sure his name wasn't Harold?"

"Everybody *called* him Mike. It may have been a *nom de guerre.*"

"A what?"

"A fighting name. You know." She breathed deeply. "You were going to show me some pictures, Lew."

"They can wait. You could help me most right now by telling me what you can remember about Carol and Harley and how you got to know them."

Tensely, she looked at her watch. "I'm due in a story conference in one minute."

"This is a more important story conference."

She breathed in and out. "I suppose it is. Well, I'll make it short and simple. It's a simple story, anyway, so simple I couldn't use it in my series. Carol was a country girl from Idaho. She ran away from home with an awol sailor. Mike Harley came from the same hick town, I think, but he'd already been in the Navy for a couple of years and seen the world. He promised to take her out to the coast and get her into the movies. She was about sixteen and so naïve it made you want to weep or burst out laughing."

"I can hear you laughing. When and where did you happen to meet her?"

"In the early spring of 1945. I was working at Warner's in Burbank and spending weekends in various places. You know the old Barcelona Hotel near Santa Monica? Carol and Harley were staying there, and it's where I—well, I got interested in her."

"Were they married?"

"Carol and Harley? I think they'd gone through some sort of ceremony in Tia Juana. At least Carol thought they were married. She also thought Harley was on extended leave, until the Shore Patrol picked him up. They whisked him back to his ship and Carol was left with nothing to live on, literally nothing. Harley hadn't bothered to make an allotment or anything. So I took her under my wing."

"And brought her to see Joe Sylvester."

"Why not? She was pretty enough, and she wasn't a stupid girl. Joey got her a couple of jobs, and I spent a lot of time with her on grooming and diction and posture. I'd just been through an unhappy love affair, in my blue period, and I was glad to have somebody to occupy my mind with. I let Carol share my apartment, and I actually think I could have made something out of her. A really wholesome Marilyn, perhaps." She caught herself going into Hollywood patter, and stopped abruptly. "But it all went blah."

"What happened?"

"Harley had left her pregnant, and it began to show. Instead of grooming a starlet, I found myself nursing a pregnant teen-ager with a bad case of homesickness. But she refused to go home. She said her father would kill her."

"Do you remember her father's name?"

"I'm afraid not. She was using the name Carol Cooper for professional purposes, but that wasn't her true surname. I *think* her father lived in Pocatello, if that's any help."

"It may be. You say she was pregnant. What happened to the baby?"

"I don't know. Harley turned up before the baby was born—the Navy had finally kicked him out, I believe—and she went back to him. This was in spite of everything I could say or do. They were elective affinities, as I said. The Patient Griselda and the nothing man. So seventeen years later he had to kill her."

"Was he violent when you knew him?"

"Was he not." She crossed her arms over her breast. "He knocked me down when I tried to prevent her from going back to him. I went out to find help. When I got back to my apartment with a policeman they were both gone, with all the money in my purse. I didn't press charges, and that was the last I saw of them."

"But you still care about Carol."

"She was nice to have around. I never had a sister, or a daughter. In fact, when I think back, *feel* back, I never had a happier time than that spring and summer in Burbank when Carol was pregnant. We didn't know how lucky we were."

"How so?"

"Well, it was a terribly hot summer and the refrigerator kept breaking down and we only had the one bedroom and Carol got bigger and bigger and we had no men in our lives. We thought we were suffering many deprivations. Actually all the deprivations came later." She looked around her fairly lavish office as if it was a jail cell, then at her watch. "I really have to go now. My writers and director will be committing mayhem on each other."

"Speaking of mayhem," I said, "I'll ask you to look at these pictures if you can stand it. The identification should be nailed down."

"Yes."

I spread the photographs out for her. She looked them over carefully.

"Yes. It's Carol. The poor child."

She had become very pale. Her black eyes stood out like the coal eyes of a snowgirl. She got to her feet and walked rather blindly into an adjoining room, shutting the door behind her.

I sat at her desk, pinched by her contour chair, and used the phone to ask her secretary to get me Lieutenant Bastian. He was on the line in less than a minute. I told him everything Susanna Drew had told me.

She came out of the next room and listened to the end of the conversation. "You don't waste any time," she said when I hung up.

"Your evidence is important."

"That's good. I'm afraid it's taken all I've got." She was still very pale.

She moved toward me as if the floor under her feet was teetering. "Will you drive me home?"

Home was an apartment on Beverly Glen Boulevard. It had a mezzanine and a patio and African masks on the walls. She invited me to make us both a drink, and we sat and talked about Carol and then about Tom Hillman. She seemed to be very interested in Tom Hillman.

I was becoming interested in Susanna. Something about her dark intensity bit into me as deep as memory. Sitting close beside her, looking into her face, I began to ask myself whether, in my present physical and financial and moral condition, I could take on a woman with all those African masks.

The damn telephone rang in the next room. She got up, using my knee as a place to rest her hand. I heard her say:

"So it's you. What do you want from me now?"

That was all I heard. She closed the door. Five minutes later, when she came out, her face had changed again. A kind of angry fear had taken the place of sorrow in her eyes, as if they had learned of something worse than death.

"Who was that, Susanna?"

"You'll never know."

I drove downtown in a bitter mood and bullyragged my friend Colton, the D. A.'s investigator, into asking Sacramento for Harold or Mike Harley's record, if any. While I was waiting for an answer I went downstairs to the newsstand and bought an early evening paper.

The murder and the kidnapping were front-page news, but there was nothing in the newspaper story I didn't already know, except that Ralph Hillman had had a distinguished combat record as a naval aviator and later (after Newport Line School) as a line officer. He was also described as a millionaire.

I sat in Colton's outer office trying to argue away my feeling that Bastian had shoved me onto the fringes of the case. The feeling deepened when the word came back from Sacramento that neither a Harold nor a Mike Harley had a California record, not even for a traffic violation. I began to wonder if I was on the track of the right man.

I drove back to the Strip through late afternoon traffic. It was nearly dusk when I reached my office. I didn't bother turning on the light for a while, but sat and watched the green sky at the window lose its color. Stars and neons came out. A plane like a moving group of stars circled far out beyond Santa Monica.

I closed the Venetian blind, to foil snipers, and turned on the desk lamp and went through the day's mail. It consisted of three bills, and a proposition from the Motel Institute of St. Louis. The Institute offered me, in effect, a job at twenty thousand a year managing a million-dollar convention motel. All I had to do was fill out a registration form for the Institute's mail-order course in motel management and send it to the Institute's registrar. If I had a wife, we could register as a couple.

I sat toying with the idea of filling out the form, but decided to go out for dinner first. I was making very incisive decisions. I decided to call Susanna Drew and ask her to have dinner with me, telling myself that it was in line of business. I could even deduct the tab from my income tax.

She wasn't in the telephone book. I tried Information. Unlisted number. I couldn't afford her anyway.

Before I went out for dinner by myself, I checked my answering service. Susanna Drew had left her number for me.

"I've been trying to get you," I said to her.

"I've been right here in my apartment."

"I mean before I knew you left your number."

"Oh? What did you have in mind?"

"The Motel Institute of St. Louis is making a very nice offer to couples who want to register for their course in motel management."

"It sounds inviting. I've always wanted to go out to sunny California and manage a motel."

"Good. We'll have dinner and talk strategy. Television won't last, you know that in your heart. None of these avant-garde movements last."

"Sorry, Lew. I'd love dinner, another night. Tonight I'm not up to it. But I did want to thank you for looking after me this afternoon. I was in a bad way for a while."

"I'm afraid I did it to you."

"No. My whole lousy life reared up and did it to me. You and your pictures were just the catalytic agent."

"Could you stand a visit from a slightly catalytic agent? I'll bring dinner from the delicatessen. I'll buy you a gardenia."

"No. I don't want to see you tonight."

"And you haven't changed your mind about that telephone call you wouldn't tell me about?"

"No. There are things about me you needn't know."

"I suppose that's encouraging in a way. Why did you leave your number for me, then?"

"I found something that might help you—a picture of Carol taken in 1945."

"I'll come and get it. You haven't really told me how you met her, you know."

"Please don't come. I'll send a messenger with it."

"If you insist. I'll wait in my office." I gave her the address.

"Lew?" Her voice was lighter and sweeter, almost poignant. "You're

not just putting on an act, are you? To try and pry out my personal
secrets, I mean?"

"It's no act," I said.

"Likewise," she said. "Thank you."

I sat in the echoing silence thinking that she had been badly treated
by a man or men. It made me angry to think of it. I didn't go out for
dinner after all. I sat and nursed my anger until Susanna's messenger
arrived.

He was a young Negro in uniform who talked like a college graduate.
He handed me a sealed Manila envelope, which I ripped open.

It contained a single glossy print, preserved between two sheets of
corrugated cardboard, of a young blonde girl wearing a pageboy bob and
a bathing suit. You couldn't pin down the reason for her beauty. It was
partly in her clear low forehead, the high curve of her cheek, her perfect
round chin; partly in the absolute femaleness that looked out of her eyes
and informed her body.

Wondering idly who had taken the photograph, I turned it over. Rub-
ber-stamped in purple ink on the back was the legend: "Photo Credit:
Harold 'Har' Harley, Barcelona Hotel."

"Will that be all?" the messenger said at the door.

"No." I gave him ten dollars.

"This is too much, sir. I've already been paid."

"I know. But I want you to buy a gardenia and deliver it back to Miss
Drew."

He said he would.

12

1945 was a long time ago, as time went in California. The Barcelona
Hotel was still standing, but I seemed to remember hearing that it was
closed. I took the long drive down Sunset to the coastal highway on the
off-chance of developing my lead to Harold Harley. Also I wanted to take
another look at the building where Harley and Carol had lived.

It was a huge old building, Early Hollywood Byzantine, with stucco
domes and minarets, and curved verandahs where famous faces of the
silent days had sipped their bootleg rum. Now it stood abandoned under
the bluff. The bright lights of a service station across the highway showed

that its white paint was flaking off and some of the windows were broken.

I parked on the weed-ruptured concrete of the driveway and walked up to the front door. Taped to the glass was a notice of bankruptcy, with an announcement that the building was going to be sold at public auction in September.

I flashed my light through the glass into the lobby. It was still completely furnished, but the furnishings looked as though they hadn't been replaced in a generation. The carpet was worn threadbare, the chairs were gutted. But the place still had atmosphere, enough of it to summon up a flock of ghosts.

I moved along the curving verandah, picking my way among the rain-warped wicker furniture, and shone my light through a French window into the dining room. The tables were set, complete with cocked-hat napkins, but there was dust lying thick on the napery. A good place for ghosts to feed, I thought, but not for me.

Just for the hell of it, though, and as a way of asserting myself against the numerous past, I went back to the front door and tapped loudly with my flashlight on the glass. Deep inside the building, at the far end of a corridor, a light showed itself. It was a moving light, which came toward me.

The man who was carrying it was big, and he walked as if he had sore feet or legs. I could see his face now in the upward glow of his electric lantern. A crude upturned nose, a bulging forehead, a thirsty mouth. It was the face of a horribly ravaged baby who had never been weaned from the bottle. I could also see that he had a revolver in his other hand.

He pointed it at me and flashed the light in my eyes. "This place is closed. Can't you read?" he shouted through the glass.

"I want to talk to you."

"I don't want to talk to you. Beat it. Amscray."

He waved the gun at me. I could tell from his voice and look that he had been drinking hard. A drunk with a gun and an excuse to use it can be murder, literally. I made one more attempt:

"Do you know a photographer named Harold Harley who used to be here?"

"Never heard of him. Now you get out of here before I blow a hole in you. You're trespashing."

He lifted the heavy revolver. I withdrew, as far as the service station across the street. A quick-moving man in stained white coveralls came out from under a car on a hoist and offered to sell me gas.

"It ought to take ten," I said. "Who's the character in the Barcelona Hotel? He acts like he was bitten by a bear."

The man gave me a one-sided smile. "You run into Otto Sipe?"

"If that's the watchman's name."

"Yeah. He worked there so long he thinks he owns the place."

"How long?"

"Twenty years or more. I been here since the war myself, and he goes back before me. He was their dick."

"Hotel detective?"

"Yeah. He told me once he used to be an officer of the law. If he was, he didn't learn much. Check your oil?"

"Don't bother, I just had it changed. Were you here in 1945?"

"That's the year I opened. I went into the service early and got out early. Why?"

"I'm a private detective. The name is Archer." I offered him my hand. He wiped his on his coveralls before he took it. "Daly. Ben Daly."

"A man named Harold Harley used to stay at the Barcelona in 1945. He was a photographer."

Daly's face opened. "Yeah. I remember him. He took a picture of me and the wife to pay for his gas bill once. We still have it in the house."

"You wouldn't know where he is now?"

"Sorry, I haven't seen him in ten years."

"What was the last you saw of him?"

"He had a little studio in Pacific Palisades. I dropped in once or twice to say hello. I don't think he's there any more."

"I gather you liked him."

"Sure. There's no harm in Harold."

Men could change. I showed Carol's picture to Daly. He didn't know her.

"You couldn't pin down the address in Pacific Palisades for me?"

He rubbed the side of his face. It needed retreading, but it was a good face. "I can tell you where it is."

He told me where it was, on a side street just off Sunset, next door to a short-order restaurant. I thanked him, and paid him for the gas.

The short-order restaurant was easy to find, but the building next door to it was occupied by a paperback bookstore. A young woman wearing pink stockings and a ponytail presided over the cash register. She looked at me pensively through her eye make-up when I asked her about Harold Harley.

"It seems to me I heard there was a photographer in here at one time."

"Where would he be now?"

"I haven't the slightest idea, honestly. We've only been here less than a year ourselves—a year in September."

"How are you doing?"

"We're making the rent, at least."

"Who do you pay it to?"

"The man who runs the lunch counter. Mr. Vernon. He ought to give us free meals for what he charges. Only don't quote me if you talk to him. We're a month behind now on the rent."

I bought a book and went next door for dinner. It was a place where I could eat with my hat on. While I was waiting for my steak, I asked the waitress for Mr. Vernon. She turned to the white-hatted short-order cook who had just tossed my steak onto the grill.

"Mr. Vernon, gentleman wants to speak to you."

He came over to the counter, an unsmiling thin-faced man with glints of gray beard showing on his chin. "You said you wanted it bloody. You'll get it bloody." He brandished his spatula.

"Good. I understand you own the store next door."

"That and the next one to it." The thought encouraged him a little. "You looking for a place to rent?"

"I'm looking for a man, a photographer named Harold Harley."

"He rented that store for a long time. But he couldn't quite make a go of it. There's too many photographers in this town. He held on for seven or eight years after the war and then gave up on it."

"You don't know where he is now?"

"No sir, I do not."

The sizzling of my steak reached a certain intensity, and he heard it. He went and flipped it with his spatula and came back to me. "You want French frieds?"

"All right. What's the last you saw of Harley?"

"The last I heard of him he moved out to the Valley. That was a good ten years ago. He was trying to run his business out of the front room of his house in Van Nuys. He's a pretty good photographer—he took a fine picture of my boy's christening party—but he's got no head for business. I ought to know, he still owes me three months' rent."

Six young people came in and lined up along the counter. They had wind in their hair, sand in their ears, and the word "Surfbirds" stenciled across the backs of their identical yellow sweatshirts. All of them, girls and boys, ordered two hamburgers apiece.

One of the boys put a quarter in the jukebox and played "Surfin' ain't no sin." Mr. Vernon got twelve hamburger patties out of the refrigerator and lined them up on the grill. He put my steak on a plate with a handful of fried potatoes and brought it to me personally.

"I could look up that Van Nuys address if it's important. I kept it on account of the rent he owed me."

"It's important." I showed him Carol's picture, the young one Harley had taken. "Do you recognize his wife?"

"I didn't even know he had a wife. I didn't think he'd rate a girl like that."

"Why not?"

"He's no ladies' man. He never was. Harold's the quiet type."

Doubt was slipping in again that I was on the right track. It made my head ache. "Can you describe him to me?"

"He's just an ordinary-looking fellow, about my size, five foot ten. Kind of a long nose. Blue eyes. Sandy hair. There's nothing special about him. Of course he'd be older now."

"How old?"

"Fifty at least. I'm fifty-nine myself, due to retire next year. Excuse me, mister."

He flipped the twelve hamburger patties over, distributed twelve half-buns on top of them and went out through a swinging door at the back. I ate at my steak. Mr. Vernon returned with a slip of paper on which he had written Harley's Van Nuys address: 956 Elmhurst.

The waitress delivered the hamburgers to the surfbirds. They munched them in time to the music. The song the jukebox was playing as I went out had a refrain about "the day that I caught the big wave and made you my slave." I drove up Sunset and onto the San Diego Freeway headed north.

Elmhurst was a working-class street of prewar bungalows built too close together. It was a warm night in the Valley, and some people were still out on their porches and lawns. A fat man drinking beer on the porch of 956 told me that Harley had sold him the house in 1960. He had his present address because he was still paying Harley monthly installments on a second trust deed.

That didn't sound like the Harley I knew. I asked him for a description.

"He's kind of a sad character," the fat man said. "One of these guys that wouldn't say 'boo' to a goose. He's had his troubles, I guess."

"What kind of troubles?"

"Search me. I don't know him well. I only saw him the twice when I bought the house from him. He wanted out in a hurry, and he gave me a good buy. He had this chance for a job in Long Beach, developing film, and he didn't want to commute."

He gave me Harley's address in Long Beach, which is a long way from Van Nuys. It was close to midnight when I found the house, a tract house near Long Beach Boulevard. It had brown weeds in the front yard, and was lightless, like most of the houses in the street.

I drove past a street light to the end of the block and walked back. The all-night traffic on the boulevard filled the air with a kind of excitement, rough and forlorn. I was raised in Long Beach, and I used to cruise its boulevards in a model-A Ford. Their sound, whining, threatening, rising, fading, spoke to something deep in my mind which I loved and hated. I didn't want to knock on Harley's door. I was almost certain I had the wrong man.

The overhead door of the attached garage was closed but not locked. I opened it quietly. The street light down the block shone on the rear of a dirty white Ford sedan with an Idaho license plate.

I went to the lefthand door of the car and opened it. The dome light came on. The car was registered in the name of Robert Brown, with an address in Pocatello. My heart was pounding so hard I could scarcely breathe.

The door from the garage into the house was suddenly outlined by light. The door sprung open. The light slapped me across the eyes and drenched me.

"Mike?" said the voice of a man I didn't know. He looked around the corner of the door frame. "Is that you, Mike?"

"I saw Mike yesterday."

"Who are you?"

"A friend." I didn't say whose friend. "He left his car for you, I see."

"That's between him and I."

His defensive tone encouraged me. I moved across the lighted space between us and stepped up into his kitchen, closing the door behind me. He didn't try to keep me out. He stood barefoot in his pajamas facing me, gray-haired and haggard-faced, with drooping hound eyes.

"My brother didn't tell me about a partner."

"Oh? What did he tell you?"

"Nothing. I mean—" He tried to bite his lower lip. His teeth were false, and slipped. Until he sucked them back into place he looked as if I had scared him literally to death. "He didn't tell me a thing about you or anything. I don't know why you come to me. That car is mine. I traded him my crate for it."

"Was that wise?"

"I dunno, maybe not." He glanced at the unwashed dishes piled in the sink as if they shared responsibility for his lack of wisdom. "Anyway, it's none of your business."

"It's everybody's business, Harold. You must know that by now."

His lips formed the word "Yes" without quite saying it. Tears came into his eyes. It was Harold he mourned for. He named the most terrible fear he could conjure up:

"Are you from the FBI?"

"I'm a police agent. We need to have a talk."

"Here?"

"This is as good a place as any."

He looked around the dingy little room as if he was seeing it with new eyes. We sat on opposite sides of the kitchen table. The checkered oil-cloth that covered it was threadbare in places.

"I didn't want any part of this," he said.

"Who would?"

"And it isn't the first time he got me into trouble, not by a long shot. This has been going on for the last thirty-five years, ever since Mike got old enough to walk and talk. I kid you not."

"Just what do you mean when you say he's got you into trouble? This time."

He shrugged crookedly and raised his open hands as if I should plainly be able to see the stigmata in his palms. "He's mixed up in a kidnapping, isn't he?"

"Did he tell you that?"

"He never told me anything straight in his life. But I can read. Since I saw the papers today I've been scared to go out of the house. And you know what my wife did? She left me. She took a taxi to the bus station and went back to her mother in Oxnard. She didn't even wash last night's dishes."

"When was your brother here?"

"Last night. He got here around ten-thirty. We were on our way to bed but I got up again. I talked to him right here where we're sitting. I thought there was something screwy going on—he had that wild look in his eye—but I didn't know what. He gave me one of his stories, that he won a lot of money in a poker game from some sailors in Dago, and they were after him to take the money back. That's why he wanted to change cars with me. He said."

"Why did you agree to it?"

"I dunno. It's hard to say no when Mike wants something."

"Did he threaten you?"

"Not in so many words. I knew he had a gun with him. I saw him take it out of his car." He lifted his eyes to mine. "You always feel sort of under a threat when Mike has something going. Stand in his way and he'll clobber you soon as look at you."

I had reason to believe him. "What was the make and model and license number of your car?"

"1958 Plymouth two-door, license IKT 449."

"Color?"

"Two-tone blue."

I made some notes. "I'm going to ask you a very important question. Was the boy with Mike? This boy?"

I showed him Tom's picture. He shook his head over it. "No sir."

"Did he say where the boy was?"

"He didn't mention any boy, and I didn't know about it, then."

"Did you know he was coming here last night?"

"In a way. He phoned me from Los Angeles yesterday afternoon. He said he might be dropping by but I wasn't to tell anybody."

"Did he say anything about changing cars when he phoned you?"

"No *sir.*"

"Did you and your brother have any previous agreement to change cars?"

"*No* sir."

"And you didn't know about the kidnapping until you read about it in the paper today?"

"That's correct. Or the murder either."

"Do you know who was murdered?"

His head hung forward, moving up and down slightly on the cords of his neck. He covered the back of his neck with his hand as if he feared a blow there from behind. "I guess—it sounded like Carol."

"It was Carol."

"I'm sorry to hear about that. She was a good kid, a lot better than he deserved."

"You should have come forward with information, Harold."

"I know that. Lila said so. It's why she left me. She said I was setting myself up for a patsy again."

"I gather it's happened before."

"Not this bad, though. The worst he ever did to me before was when he sold me a camera he stole from the Navy. He turned around and claimed I stole it when I visited him on his ship on visiting day."

"What was the name of the ship?"

"The *Perry Bay.* It was one of those jeep carriers. I went aboard her in Dago the last year of the war, but I wisht I never set foot on her. The way they talked to me, I thought I was gonna end up in the federal pen. But they finally took my word that I didn't know the camera was hot."

"I'm taking your word now about several things, or have you noticed?"

"I didn't know what to think."

"I believe you're an honest man in a bind, Harold."

My spoken sympathy was too much for him. It made his eyes water again. He removed his hand from the back of his neck and wiped his eyes with his fingers.

"I'm not the only one you have to convince, of course. But I think you can probably work your way out of this bind by telling the whole truth."

"You mean in court?"

"Right now."

"I want to tell the truth," he said earnestly. "I would have come forward, only I was ascared to. I was ascared they'd send me up for life."

"And Mike too?"

"It wasn't him I was worried about," he said. "I'm through with my brother. When I found out about Carol—" He shook his head.

"Were you fond of her?"

"Sure I was. I didn't see much of her these last years when they were in Nevada. But Carol and me, we always got along."

"They were living in Nevada?"

"Yeah. Mike had a job bartending in one of the clubs on the South Shore. Only he lost it. I had to—" His slow mind overtook his words and stopped them.

"You had to—?"

"Nothing. I mean, I had to help them out a little these last few months since he lost his job."

"How much money did you give them?"

"I dunno. What I could spare. A couple of hundred dollars." He looked up guiltily.

"Did Mike pay you back last night by any chance?"

He hung his head. The old refrigerator in the corner behind him woke up and started to throb. Above it I could still hear the sound of the boulevard rising and falling, coming and going.

"No he didn't," Harold said.

"How much did he give you?"

"He didn't *give* me anything."

"You mean he was only paying you back?"

"That's right."

"How much?"

"He gave me five hundred dollars," he said in horror.

"Where is it?"

"Under my mattress. You're welcome *to* it. I don't want any part of it."

I followed him into the bedroom. The room was in disarray, with bureau drawers pulled out, hangers scattered on the floor.

"Lila took off in a hurry," he said, "soon as she saw the paper. She probably filed suit for divorce already. It wouldn't be the first time she got a divorce."

"From you?"

"From the other ones."

Lila's picture stood on top of the bureau. Her face was dark and plump and stubborn-looking, and it supported an insubstantial dome of upswept black hair.

Harold stood disconsolately by the unmade bed. I helped him to lift up the mattress. Flattened under it was an oilskin tobacco pouch containing paper money visible through the oilskin. He handed it to me.

"Did you see where this came from, Harold?"

"He got it out of the car. I heard him unwrapping some paper."

I put the pouch in my pocket without opening it. "And you honestly didn't know it was hot?"

He sat on the bed. "I guess I knew there was something the matter with it. He couldn't win that much in a poker game, I mean, and keep it. He always keeps trying for the one more pot until he loses his wad. But I didn't think about *kidnapping,* for gosh sake." He struck himself rather feebly on the knee. "Or murder."

"Do you think he murdered the boy?"

"I meant poor little Carol."

"I meant the boy."

"He wouldn't do that to a young kid," Harold said in a small hushed voice. He seemed not to want the statement to be heard, for fear it would be denied.

"Have you searched the car?"

"No sir. Why would I do that?"

"For blood or money. You haven't opened the trunk?"

"No. I never went near the lousy car." He looked sick, as if its mere presence in his garage had infected him with criminality.

"Give me the keys to it."

He picked up his limp trousers, groped in the pockets, and handed me an old leather holder containing the keys to the car. I advised him to put on his clothes while I went out to the garage.

I found the garage light and turned it on, unlocked the trunk, and with some trepidation, lifted the turtleback. The space inside was empty, except for a rusty jack and a balding spare tire. No body.

But before I closed the trunk I found something in it that I didn't like. A raveled piece of black yarn was caught in the lock. I remembered Sam Jackman telling me that Tom had been wearing a black sweater on Sunday. I jerked the yarn loose, angrily, and put it away in an envelope in my pocket. I slammed the turtleback down on the possibility which the black yarn suggested to my mind.

13

I went back into the house. The bedroom door was closed. I knocked and got no answer and flung it open. Harold was sitting on the edge of the bed in his underwear and socks. He was holding a .22 rifle upright between his knees. He didn't point it at me. I took it away from him and unloaded the single shell.

"I don't have the nerve to kill myself," he said.

"You're lucky."

"Yeah, very lucky."

"I mean it, Harold. When I was a kid I knew a man who lost his undertaking business in the depression. He decided to blow out his brains with a twenty-two. But all it did was blind him. He's been sitting around in the dark for the last thirty years. And his sons have the biggest mortuary in town."

"So I should be in the mortuary business." He sighed. "Or anything but the brother business. I know what I have to go through."

"It's like a sickness. It'll pass."

"My brother," he said, "is a sickness that never passes."

"He's going to, this time, Harold. He'll be taken care of for the rest of his life."

"If you catch him."

"We'll catch him. Where did he head from here?"

"He didn't tell me."

"Where do you think?"

"Nevada, I guess. It's always been his favorite hangout. When he has money he can't stay away from the tables."

"Where did he live when he worked on the South Shore of Tahoe?"

"They were buying a trailer but he lost that when he lost his barkeep job. His boss said he got too rough with the drunks. After that they moved from one place to another, mostly motels and lodges around the lake. I couldn't give you any definite address."

"What was the name of the club he worked at?"

"The Jet. Carol worked there, too, off and on. She was sort of a singing waitress. We went to hear her sing there once. Lila thought she was lousy, but I thought she was okay. She sang pretty sexy songs, and that's why Lila—"

I interrupted him. "Do you have a phone? I want to make a couple of collect calls."

"It's in the front room."

I took the rifle with me, in case he got further ideas about shooting himself, or me. The walls of the front room were as crowded as the walls of a picture gallery with Harold's photographs. Old Man, Old Woman, Young Woman, Sunset, Wildflowers, Mountain, Seascape; and Lila. Most of them had been hand-tinted, and three portraits of Lila smiled at me from various angles, so that I felt surrounded by toothy, flesh-colored face.

I went back to the bedroom. Harold was putting on his shoes. He looked up rather resentfully.

"I'm okay. You don't have to keep checking up on me."

"I was wondering if you had a picture of Mike."

"I have one. It's nearly twenty years old. After he got into trouble he never let me take him."

"Let's see it."

"I wouldn't know where to find it. Anyway, it was done when he was a kid and he doesn't look like that anymore. It's an art study, like, of his muscles, in boxing trunks."

"What does he look like now?"

"I thought you saw him."

"It was dark at the time."

"Well, he's still a fairly nice-looking man, I mean his features. He quit fighting before he got banged up too bad. He has brown hair—no gray —he parts it on the side. Mike always did have a fine head of hair." He scratched at his own thin hair. "Greenish-gray eyes, with kind of a wild look in them when he's got something going. Thin mouth. I always thought it was kind of a cruel mouth. Teeth not so good. But I dunno, he's still a nice-looking fellow, and well set-up. He keeps himself in pretty good physical shape."

"Height and weight?"

"He's an inch or so under six feet. He used to fight light-heavy, but he must be heavier now. Maybe one eighty-five."

"Any scars or distinguishing marks?"

Harold jerked his head up. "Yeah. He's got scars on his back where Dad used to beat him. I got some of my own." He pulled up his undershirt and showed me the white scars all up and down his back, like hieroglyphs recording history. Harold seemed to take his scars as a matter of course.

"Are your parents still living?"

"Sure. Dad's still running the farm. It's on the Snake River," he said without nostalgia. "Pocatello Rural Route 7. But Mike wouldn't be going there. He hates Idaho."

"You never can tell, though," I said as I made some notes.

"Take my word. He broke with Dad over twenty years ago." As an afterthought, he said: "There's a portrait I did of Dad in the front room. I call it 'Old Man.'."

Before I sat down with the telephone I looked more closely at the portrait: a grizzled farmer with flat angry eyes and a mouth like a bear trap. Then I called Arnie Walters in Reno and gave him a rundown on the old man's son, Mike Harley, ex-sailor, ex-fighter, ex-bartender, gambler, kidnapper, wife-beater, putative murderer and driver of a 1958 Plymouth two-door, California license number IKT 449.

"You've been busy," Arnie said when he finished recording my facts. "We have, too, but we haven't come up with anything. We will now." He hesitated. "Just how much muscle do you want put into the operation?"

"You mean how much can I pay for?"

"Your client."

"I lost my client. I'm hoping this stuff I've uncovered will get me another one, but it hasn't yet."

Arnie whistled. "What you're doing isn't ethical."

"Yes it is. I'm temporarily an investigator for the local sheriff's office."

"Now I know you've flipped. I hate to bring this up, Lew, but you owe me three hundred dollars and that's a charity price for what we've done. Tomorrow at this time it'll be six hundred anyway, if we stay with it. With our overhead we just can't work for nothing."

"I know that. You'll be paid."

"When?"

"Soon. I'll talk to you in the morning."

"What do we do in the meantime?"

"Carry on."

"If you say so."

Arnie hung up on me and left me feeling a little shaky. Six hundred dollars was what I got for working a full week, and I didn't work every week. I had about three hundred dollars in the bank, about two hundred in cash. I owned an equity in the car and some clothes and furniture. My total net worth, after nearly twenty years in the detective business, was in the neighborhood of thirty-five hundred dollars. And Ralph Hillman, with his money, was letting me finance my own search for his son.

On the other hand, I answered my self-pity, I was doing what I wanted to be doing. I wanted to take the man who had taken me. I wanted to find Tom. I couldn't drop the case just as it was breaking. And I needed Arnie to backstop me in Nevada. Carry on.

I made a second collect call, to Lieutenant Bastian. It was long past midnight, but he was still on duty in his office. I told him I was bringing in a witness, and I gave him a capsule summary of what the witness was going to say. Bastian expressed a proper degree of surprise and delight.

Harold was still in the bedroom, standing pensively beside the tie rack attached to the closet door. He was fully dressed except for a tie.

"What kind of a tie do you think I ought to wear? Lila always picks out the tie I wear."

"You don't need a tie."

"They'll be taking my picture, won't they? I've got to be properly dressed." He fingered the tie rack distraughtly.

I chose one for him, a dark blue tie with a conservative pattern, the kind you wear to the funerals of friends. We closed up the house and garage and drove south out of Long Beach.

It was less than an hour's drive to Pacific Point. Harold was intermittently talkative, but his silences grew longer. I asked him about his and his brother's early life in Idaho. It had been a hard life, in an area subject to blizzards in the winter and floods in the spring and extreme heat in the summer. Their father believed that boys were a kind of domestic animal that ought to be put to work soon after weaning. They were hoeing corn and digging potatoes when they were six, and milking the cows at eight or nine.

They could have stood the work, if it hadn't been for the punishment that went with it. I'd seen Harold's scars. The old man used a piece of knotted wire on them. Mike was the first to run away. He lived in Pocatello for a couple of years with a man named Robert Brown, a high-school coach and counselor who took him in and tried to give him a chance.

Robert Brown was Carol's father. Mike paid him back for his kindness eventually by running away with his daughter.

"How old was Mike then?"

"Twenty or so. Let's see, it was about a year after they drafted him into the Navy. Yeah, he'd be about twenty. Carol was only sixteen."

"Where were you at the time?"

"Working here in Los Angeles. I was 4–F. I had a job taking pictures for a hotel."

"The Barcelona Hotel," I said.

"That's right." He sounded a little startled by my knowledge of his life. "It wasn't much of a job, but it gave me a chance to freelance on the side."

"I understand that Carol and your brother stayed there, too."

"For a little. That was when he was awol and hiding out. I let them use my room for a couple of weeks."

"You've done a lot for your brother in your time."

"Yeah. He paid me back by trying to frame me for stealing a Navy camera. There's one extra thing I could have done for him."

"What was that?"

"I could have drowned him in the river when he was a kid. That's all the use he's been to anybody. Especially Carol."

"Why did she stick to him?"

He groaned. "She wanted to, I guess."

"Were they married?"

He answered slowly. "I think so. She thought so. But I never saw any papers to prove it."

"Lately," I said, "they've been calling themselves Mr. and Mrs. Robert Brown. The car he left with you is registered to Robert Brown."

"I wondered where he got it. Now I suppose I'll have to give it back to the old guy."

"First the police will be wanting it."

"Yeah. I guess they will at that."

The thought of the police seemed to depress him profoundly. He sat without speaking for a while. I caught a glimpse of him in the headlights of a passing car. He was sitting with his chin on his chest. His body appeared to be resisting the movement which was carrying him toward his meeting with the police.

"Do you know Carol's father?" I asked him finally.

"I've met Mr. Brown. Naturally he holds Mike against me. God knows what he'll think of me now, with Carol dead and all."

"You're not your brother, Harold. You can't go on blaming yourself for what he's done."

"It's my fault, though."

"Carol's death?"

"That, too, but I meant the kidnapping. I set it up for Mike without meaning to. I gave him the idea of the whole thing."

"How did you do that?"

"I don't want to talk about it."

"You brought it up, Harold. You seem to want to get it off your chest."

"I've changed my mind."

I couldn't get him to change it back. He had a passive stubbornness which wouldn't be moved. We drove in complete silence the rest of the way.

I delivered Harold and the five hundred dollars to Lieutenant Bastian, who was waiting in his office in the courthouse, and checked in at the first hotel I came to.

14

At nine o'clock in the morning, with the taste of coffee still fresh in my mouth, I was back at the door of the lieutenant's office. He was waiting for me.

"Did you get any sleep at all?" I said.

"Not much." The loss of sleep had affected him hardly at all, except that his voice and bearing were less personal and more official. "You've had an active twenty-four hours. I have to thank you for turning up the brother. His evidence is important, especially if this case ever gets into court."

"I have some other evidence to show you."

But Bastian hadn't finished what he was saying: "I talked the sheriff into paying you twenty-five dollars per diem plus ten cents a mile, if you will submit a statement."

"Thanks, but it can wait. You could do me a bigger favor by talking Ralph Hillman into bankrolling me."

"I can't do that, Archer."

"You could tell him the facts. I've spent several hundred dollars of my own money, and I've been getting results."

"Maybe, if I have an opportunity." He changed the subject abruptly: "The pathologist who did the autopsy on Mrs. Brown has come up with something that will interest you. Actual cause of death was a stab wound in the heart. It wasn't noticed at first because it was under the breast."

"That does interest me. It could let Harley out."

"I don't see it that way. He beat her and then stabbed her."

"Do you have the weapon?"

"No. The doctor says it was a good-sized blade, thin but quite broad, and very sharp, with a sharp point. It went into her like butter, the doctor says." He took no pleasure in the image. His face was saturnine. "Now what was the evidence you referred to just now?"

I showed Bastian the piece of black yarn and told him where I had found it. He picked up the implication right away:

"The trunk, eh? I'm afraid it doesn't look too promising for the boy. He was last seen wearing a black sweater. I believe his mother knitted it for him." He studied the scrap of wool under his magnifying glass. "This looks like knitting yarn to me, too. Mrs. Hillman ought to be shown this."

He put the piece of yarn under glass on an evidence board. Then he picked up the phone and made an appointment with the Hillmans at their house in El Rancho, an appointment for both of us. We drove out through morning fog in two cars. At the foot of the Hillmans' driveway a man in plain clothes came out of the fog-webbed bushes and waved us on.

Mrs. Perez, wearing black shiny Sunday clothes, admitted us to the reception hall. Hillman came out of the room where the bar was. His movements were somnambulistic and precise, as if they were controlled by some external power. His eyes were still too bright.

He shook hands with Bastian and, after some hesitation, with me. "Come into the sitting room, gentlemen. It's good of you to make the trip out here. Elaine simply wasn't up to going downtown. If I could only get her to eat," he said.

She was sitting on the chesterfield near the front window. The morning light was unkind to her parched blonde face. It was two full days and nights since the first telephone call on Monday morning. She looked as if all the minutes in those forty-eight hours had passed through her body like knots in wire. The red piece of knitting on the seat beside her hadn't grown since I'd seen it last.

She managed a rather wizened smile and extended her hand to Bastian. "Ralph says you have something to show me."

"Yes. It's a piece of yarn which may or may not have come off your boy's sweater."

"The black one I knitted for him?"

"It may be. We want to know if you recognize the yarn." Bastian handed her the evidence board. She put on reading glasses and examined it. Then she put it aside, rose abruptly, and left the room. Hillman made a move to follow her. He stopped with his hands out in a helpless pose which he was still in when she returned.

She was carrying a large, figured linen knitting bag. Crouching on the chesterfield, she rummaged among its contents and tossed out balls of wool of various colors. Her furiously active hand came to rest holding a half-used ball of black wool.

"This is what I had left over from Tom's sweater. I think it's the same. Can you tell?"

Bastian broke off a piece of yarn from the ball and compared it under a glass with my piece. He turned from the window:

"The specimens appear identical to me. If they are, we can establish it under the microscope."

"What does it mean if they are identical?" Ralph Hillman said.

"I prefer not to say until we have microscopic confirmation."

Hillman took hold of Bastian's arm and shook him. "Don't double-talk me, Lieutenant."

Bastian broke loose and stepped back. There were white frozen-looking patches around his nose and mouth. His eyes were somber.

"Very well, I'll tell you what I know. This piece of yarn was found by Mr. Archer here, caught in the lock of a car trunk. The car was one driven by the alleged kidnapper, Harley."

"You mean that Tom was riding in the trunk?"

"He may have been, yes."

"But he wouldn't do that if—" Hillman's mouth worked. "You mean Tom is dead?"

"He may be. We won't jump to any conclusions."

Elaine Hillman produced a noise, a strangled gasp, which made her the center of attention. She spoke in a thin voice, halfway between a child's and an old woman's: "I wish I had never recognized the yarn."

"It wouldn't change the facts, Mrs. Hillman."

"Well, I don't want any more of your dreadful facts. The waiting is bad enough, without these refinements of torment."

Hillman bent over and tried to quiet her. "That isn't fair, Elaine. Lieutenant Bastian is trying to help us." He had said the same thing about me. It gave me the queer feeling that time was repeating itself and would go on endlessly repeating itself, as it does in hell.

She said: "He's going about it in a strange way. Look what he's made me do. All my balls of yarn are spilled on the floor." She kicked at them with her tiny slippered feet.

Hillman got down on his knees to pick them up. She kicked at him, without quite touching him. "Get away, you're no help, either. If you'd been a decent father, this would never have happened."

Bastian picked up the evidence board and turned to me. "We'd better go."

Nobody asked us not to. But Hillman followed us out into the hall.

"Please forgive us, we're not ourselves. You haven't really *told* me anything."

Bastian answered him coolly: "We have no definite conclusions to report."

"But you think Tom's dead."

"I'm afraid he may be. We'll learn more from an analysis of the contents of that car trunk. If you'll excuse me, Mr. Hillman, I don't have time for further explanations now."

"I do," I said.

For the first time that morning Hillman looked at me as if I might be good for something more than a scapegoat. "Are you willing to tell me what's been going on?"

"So far as I understand it."

"I'll leave you men together then," Bastian said. He went out, and a minute later I heard his car go down the drive.

Hillman deputed Mrs. Perez to stay with his wife. He led me into a wing of the house I hadn't visited, down an arching corridor like a tunnel carved through chalk, to a spacious study. Two of the oak-paneled walls were lined with books, most of them in calfbound sets, as if Hillman had bought or inherited a library. A third wall was broken by a large deep window overlooking the distant sea.

The fourth wall was hung with a number of framed photographs. One was a blownup snapshot of Dick Leandro crouching in the cockpit of a racing yacht with his hand on the helm and the white wake boiling at his back. One showed a group of Navy fliers posing together on a flight deck. I recognized a younger Hillman on the far right of the group. There were other similar pictures, taken ashore and afloat; one of a torpedo-bomber squadron flying formation in old World War II Devastators; one of an escort carrier photographed from far overhead, so that it lay like a shingle on the bright, scarified water.

It seemed to me that Hillman had brought me to this specific room, this wall, for a purpose. The somnambulistic precision of his movements was probably controlled by the deep unconscious. At any rate, we were developing the same idea at the same time, and the photograph of the escort carrier was the catalyst.

"That was my last ship," Hillman said. "The fact is, for a few weeks at the end I commanded her."

"A few weeks at the end of the war?"

"A few weeks at *her* end. The war was long since over. We took her from Dago through the Canal to Boston and put her in mothballs." His voice was tender and regretful. He might have been talking about the death of a woman.

"She wasn't the *Perry Bay* by any chance?"

"Yes." He swung around to look at me. "You've heard of her?"

"Just last night. This whole thing is coming together, Mr. Hillman. Does the name Mike Harley mean anything to you?"

His eyes blurred. "I'm afraid you're confusing me. The name you mentioned earlier was Harold Harley."

"I had the wrong name. Harold is Mike's brother, and he's the one I talked to last night. He told me Mike served on the *Perry Bay.*"

Hillman nodded slowly. "I remember Mike Harley. I have reason to. He caused me a lot of trouble. In the end I had to recommend an undesirable discharge."

"For stealing a Navy camera."

He gave me a swift responsive look. "You do your homework thoroughly, Mr. Archer. Actually we let him off easy, because he wasn't quite responsible. He could have been sent to Portsmouth for stealing that expensive camera." He backed up into a chair and sat down suddenly, as if he'd been struck by the full impact of the past. "So eighteen years later he has to steal my son."

I stood by the window and waited for him to master the immense coincidence. It was no coincidence in the usual sense, of course. Hillman had been in authority over Harley, and had given Harley reason to hate him. I had heard the hatred speak on the telephone Monday.

The fog over the sea was burning off. Ragged blue holes opened and closed in the grayness. Hillman came to the window and stood beside me. His face was more composed, except for the fierce glitter of his eyes.

"When I think of what that man has done to me," he said. "Tell me the rest of it, Archer. All you know."

I told him the rest of it. He listened as if I was an oracle telling him the story of his future life. He seemed particularly interested in the murdered woman, Carol, and I asked him if he had ever met her.

He shook his head. "I didn't know Harley was married."

"The marriage may not have been legal. But it lasted."

"Did Harley have children?"

"One at least."

"How could a man with a child of his own—?" He didn't finish the thought. Another thought rushed in on his excited mind: "At any rate this disposes of the notion that Tom was mixed up with the woman."

"Not necessarily. Harley could have been using her as bait."

"But that's fantastic. The woman must be—have been old enough to be his mother."

"Still, she wasn't an old woman. She was born about 1930."

"And you're seriously suggesting that Tom had an affair with her?"

"It's an academic question under the circumstances, Mr. Hillman."

His patrician head turned slowly toward me, catching the light on its flat handsome planes. The days were carving him like sculpture. "You mean the fact that Tom is dead."

"It isn't a fact yet. It is a strong possibility."

"If my boy were alive, wouldn't he have come home by now?"

"Not if he's deliberately staying away."

"Do you have reason to believe that he is?"

"Nothing conclusive, but several facts suggest the possibility. He was seen with the woman on Sunday, under his own power. And he did run away in the first place."

"From Laguna Perdida School. Not from us."

"He may expect to be clapped back into the school if he returns."

"Good Lord, I'd never do that."

"You did it once."

"I was forced to by circumstances."

"What were the circumstances, Mr. Hillman?"

"There's no need to go into them. As you would say, the question is academic."

"Did he attempt suicide?"

"No."

"Homicide?"

His eyes flickered. "Certainly not." He changed the subject hurriedly: "We shouldn't be standing here talking. If Thomas is alive, he's got to be found. Harley is the one man who must know where he is, and you tell me Harley is probably on his way to Nevada."

"He's probably there by now."

"Why aren't you? I'd fly you myself if I could leave my wife. But you can charter a plane."

I explained that this took money, of which I'd already spent a fair amount in his behalf.

"I'm sorry, I didn't realize."

He produced the two-thousand-dollar check that Dr. Sponti and Mr. Squerry had given him on Monday, and endorsed it to me. I was back in business.

15

Stella, in her hooded blue jacket, was waiting for me part way down the driveway. The girl had a heavy pair of binoculars hung around her neck on a strap. Her face was bloodless and thin, as if it had provided sustenance for her eyes.

When I stopped the car, she climbed uninvited into the seat beside me. "I've been watching for you."

"Is that what the field glasses are for?"

She nodded gravely. "I watch everybody who comes in or goes out of Tommy's house. Mother thinks I'm bird-watching, which she lets me do because it's a status-symbol activity. Actually I am doing a bird study for next year's biology class, on the nesting habits of the acorn woodpeckers. Only they all look so much alike they're hard to keep track of."

"So are people."

"I'm finding that out." She leaned toward me. Her small breast brushed my shoulder like a gift of trust. "But you know what, Mr. Archer? Tommy tried to call me this morning, I'm almost certain."

"Tell me about it."

"There isn't much to tell, really. It was one of those calls with nobody on the other end of the line. My mother answered the phone, and that's why Tommy didn't speak. He wanted me to answer it." Her eyes were luminous with hope.

"What makes you think it was Tommy?"

"I just know it was. Besides, he called at five to eight, which is the exact same time he always used to call me in the morning. He used to pick me up and drive me to school."

"That isn't too much to go on, Stella. More likely it was a wrong number."

"No. I believe it was Tommy. And he'll be trying again."

"Why would he call you instead of his parents?"

"He's probably afraid to call them. He must be in serious trouble."

"You can be sure of that, one way or another."

I was only trying to moderate her hopefulness, but I frightened her. She said in a hushed voice: "You've found out something."

"Nothing definite. We're on the track of the kidnapper. And incidentally, I have to be on my way."

She held me with her eyes. "He really was kidnapped then? He didn't go to them of his own accord or anything like that?"

"He may have in the first place. After that, I don't know. Did Tommy ever mention a woman named Carol?"

"The woman who was killed?"

"Yes."

"He never did. Why? Did he know her?"

"He knew her very well."

She caught my implication and shook her head. "I don't believe it."

"That doesn't prevent it from being true, Stella. Didn't you ever see them together?"

I got out my collection of pictures and selected the one that Harold Harley had taken of Carol in 1945. The girl studied it. She said with something like awe in her voice:

"She's—she was very beautiful. She couldn't have been much older than I am."

"She wasn't, when the picture was taken. But that was a long time ago, and you should make allowances for that."

"I've never seen her. I'm sure. And Tommy never said a word about her." She looked at me glumly. "People *are* hard to keep track of." She handed me the picture as if it was heavy and hot and would spill if it was tilted.

At this point a female moose deprived of her calf, or something closely resembling her, came crashing through the oak woods. It was Stella's mother. Her handsome red head was tousled and her face was brutalized by anxiety. She spotted Stella and charged around to her side of the car. Stella turned up the window and snapped the lock.

Rhea Carlson rapped on the glass with her fist. "Come out of there. What do you think you're doing?"

"Talking to Mr. Archer."

"You must be crazy. Are you trying to ruin yourself?"

"I don't care what happens to me, that's true."

"You have no right to talk like that. You're ungrateful!"

"Ungrateful for what?"

"I gave you life, didn't I? Your father and I have given you everything."

"I don't want everything. I just want to be let alone, Mother."

"No! You come out of there."

"I don't have to."

"Yes you do," I said.

Stella looked at me as if I had betrayed her to the enemy.

"She's your mother," I said, "and you're a minor, and if you don't obey her you're out of control, and I'm contributing to the delinquency of a minor."

"*You* are?"

"Reluctantly," I said.

The word persuaded her. She even gave me a little half-smile. Then she unlocked the door and climbed out of the car. I got out and walked around to their side. Rhea Carlson looked at me as if I might be on the point of assaulting her.

"Calm down, Mrs. Carlson. Nothing's happened."

"Oh? Would you know?"

"I know that no harm will ever come to Stella if I'm around. May I ask you a question?"

She hesitated. "I won't promise to answer it."

"You received a phone call this morning at five to eight. Was it local or long distance?"

"I don't know. Most of our long-distance calls are dialed direct."

"Was anything said?"

"I said hello."

"I mean on the other end of the line."

"No. Not a word."

"Did whoever it was hang up?"

"Yes, and I'm sure it wasn't the Hillman boy. It was just another stupid mistake in dialing. We get them all the time."

"It was so Tommy," Stella said. "I *know* it."

"Don't believe her. She's always making things up."

"I am not." Stella looked ready to cry.

"Don't contradict me, Stella. Why do you always have to contradict me?"

"I don't."

"You do."

I stepped between them. "Your daughter's a good girl, and she's almost a woman. Please try to bear that in mind, and treat her gently."

Mrs. Carlson said in scornful desperation: "What do you know about mothers and daughters? Who are you, anyway?"

"I've been a private detective since the war. In the course of time you pick up a few primitive ideas about people, and you develop an instinct for the good ones. Like Stella."

Stella blushed. Her mother peered at me without understanding. In my rear-view mirror, as I started away, I saw them walking down the driveway, far apart. It seemed a pity. For all I knew, Rhea Carlson was a good girl, too.

I drove downtown and took Sponti's two-thousand-dollar check to the bank it was drawn on. I endorsed it, under Ralph Hillman's signature: "With many thanks, Lew Archer." It was a weak riposte for being fired, but it gave me some satisfaction to think that it might bring out the purple in Dr. Sponti's face.

The transfusion of cash made me feel mobile and imaginative. Just on a hunch, I drove back to Harold Harley's place in Long Beach. It was a good hunch. Lila answered the door.

She had on an apron and a dusting cap, and she pushed a strand of black hair up under the cap. Her breast rose with the gesture. Lila wasn't a pretty woman, but she had vitality.

"Are you another one of them?" she said.

"Yes. I thought you left Harold."

"So did I. But I decided to come back."

"I'm glad you did. He needs your support."

"Yeah." Her voice softened. "What's going to happen to Harold? Are they going to lock him up and throw the key away?"

"Not if I can help it."

"Are you with the FBI?"

"I'm more of a free lance."

"I was wondering. They came this morning and took the car away. No Harold. Now no car. Next they'll be taking the house from over my head. All on account of that lousy brother of his. It isn't fair."

"It'll be straightened out. I'll tell you the same thing I told Harold. His best chance of getting free and clear is to tell the truth."

"The truth is, he let his brother take advantage of him. He always has. Mike is still—" She clapped her hand to her mouth and looked at me over it with alarm in her brown eyes.

"What is Mike still doing, Mrs. Harley?"

She glanced up and down the dingy street. A few young children were playing in the yards, with their mothers watching them. Lila plucked at my sleeve.

"Come inside, will you? Maybe we can make some kind of a deal."

The front door opened directly into the living room. I stepped over a vacuum-cleaner hose just inside the door.

"I've been cleaning the house," she said. "I had to do something and that was all I could think of."

"I hope Harold will be coming home to appreciate it soon."

"Yeah. It would help him, wouldn't it, if I helped you to nail his brother?"

"It certainly would."

"Would you let him go if you got Mike in his place?"

"I can't promise that. I think it would probably happen."

"Why can't you promise?"

"I'm just a local investigator. But Mike is the one we really want. Do you know where he is, Mrs. Harley?"

For a long moment she stood perfectly still, her face as unchanging as one of her photographs hanging on the wall. Then she nodded slightly.

"I know where he was at three A.M. this morning." She jabbed a thumb toward the telephone. "He called here from Las Vegas at three A.M. He wanted Harold. I told him I didn't know where Harold was—he was gone when I came home last night."

"You're sure it was Mike who called?"

"It couldn't have been anybody else. I know his voice. And it isn't the first time he called here, whining and wheedling for some of our hard-earned money."

"He wanted money?"

"That's right. I was to wire him five hundred dollars to the Western Union office in Las Vegas."

"But he was carrying over twenty thousand."

Her face closed, and became impassive. "I wouldn't know about that. All I know is what he said. He needed money bad, and I was to wire him five hundred, which he would pay back double in twenty-four hours. I told him I'd see him in the hot place first. He was gambling."

"It sounds like it, doesn't it?"

"He's a crazy gambler," she said. "I hate a gambler."

I called the Walters Agency in Reno. Arnie's wife and partner Phyllis told me that Arnie had taken an early plane to Vegas. Harold Harley's two-tone Plymouth had been spotted at a motel on the Vegas Strip.

Not more than two hours later, after a plane ride of my own, I was sitting in a room of the motel talking with Arnie and the Plymouth's new owner. He was a man named Fletcher who said he was from Phoenix, Arizona, although his accent sounded more like Texas. He was dressed up in a western dude costume, with high-heeled boots, a matching belt with a fancy silver buckle, and an amethyst instead of a tie. His Stetson lay on one of the twin beds, some women's clothes on the other. The woman was in the bathroom taking a bath, Arnie told me, and I never did see her.

Mr. Fletcher was large and self-assured and very rough-looking. His face had been chopped rather carelessly from granite, then put out to weather for fifty or fifty-five years.

"I didn't want to buy his heap," he said. "I have a new Cadillac in Phoenix, you can check that. He didn't even have a pink slip for it. I paid him five hundred for the heap because he was broke, desperate to stay in the game."

"What game was that?" I asked him.

"Poker."

"It was a floating game," Arnie said, "in one of the big hotels. Mr. Fletcher refuses to name the hotel, or the other players. It went on all day yesterday and most of last night. There's no telling how much Harley lost, but he lost everything he had."

"Over twenty thousand, probably. Was the game rigged?"

Fletcher turned his head and looked at me the way a statue looks at a man. "It was an honest game, friend. It had to be. I was the big winner."

"I wasn't questioning your honesty."

"No sir. Some of the finest people in Phoenix visit the little woman and I in our residence and we visit them in their residences. Honest Jack Fletcher, they call me."

There was a silence in which the three of us sat and listened to the air-conditioner. I said: "That's fine, Mr. Fletcher. How much did you win?"

"That's between I and the tax collector, friend. I won a bundle. Which is why I gave him five hundred for his heap. I have no use for the heap. You can take it away." He lifted his arm in an imperial gesture.

"We'll be doing just that," Arnie said.

"You're welcome to it. Anything I can do to cooperate."

"You can answer a few more questions, Mr. Fletcher." I got out my picture of Tom. "Did you see this boy with Harley at any time?"

He examined the picture as if it was a card he had drawn, then passed it back to me. "I did not."

"Hear any mention of him?"

"I never did. Harley came and went by himself and he didn't talk. You could see he didn't belong in a high-stakes game, but he had the money, and he wanted to lose it."

"He wanted to lose it?" Arnie said.

"That's right, the same way I wanted to win. He's a born loser, I'm a born winner."

Fletcher got up and strutted back and forth across the room. He lit a Brazilian cigar, not offering any around. As fast as he blew it out, the smoke disappeared in the draft from the air-conditioner. "What time did the game break up this morning?" I said.

"Around three, when I took my last big pot." His mouth savored the recollection. "I was willing to stay, but the other people weren't. Harley wanted to stay, naturally, but he didn't have the money to back it up. He isn't much of a poker player, frankly."

"Did he give you any trouble?"

"No sir. The gentleman who runs the game discourages that sort of thing. No trouble. Harley did put the bite on me at the end. I gave him a hundred dollars ding money to get home."

"Home where?"

"He said he came from Idaho."

I took a taxi back to the airport and made a reservation on a plane that stopped in Pocatello. Before sundown I was driving a rented car out of Pocatello along Rural Route Seven, where the elder Harleys lived.

16

Their farm, green and golden in the slanting light, lay in a curve of the river. I drove down a dusty lane to the farmhouse. It was built of white brick, without ornament of any kind. The barn, unpainted, was weathered gray and in poor repair.

The late afternoon was windless. The trees surrounding the fenced yard were as still as watercolors. The heat was oppressive, in spite of the river nearby, even worse than it had been in Vegas.

It was a far cry from Vegas to here, and difficult to believe that Harley had come home, or ever would. But the possibility had to be checked out.

A black and white farm collie with just one eye barked at me through the yard fence when I stepped out of the car. I tried to calm him down by talking to him, but he was afraid of me and he wouldn't be calmed. Eventually an old woman wearing an apron came out of the house and silenced the dog with a word. She called to me:

"Mr. Harley's in the barn."

I let myself in through the wire gate. "May I talk to you?"

"That depends what the talk's about."

"Family matters."

"If that's another way to sell insurance, Mr. Harley doesn't believe in insurance."

"I'm not selling anything. Are you Mrs. Harley?"

"I am."

She was a gaunt woman of seventy, square-shouldered in a long-sleeved, striped shirtwaist. Her gray hair was drawn back severely from her face. I liked her face, in spite of the brokenness in and around the eyes. There was humor in it, and suffering half transformed into understanding.

"Who are you?" she said.

"A friend of your son Harold's. My name is Archer."

"Isn't that nice? We're going to sit down to supper as soon as Mr. Harley finishes up the milking. Why don't you stay and have some supper with us?"

"You're very kind." But I didn't want to eat with them.

"How is Harold?" she said. "We don't hear from him so often since he married his wife. Lila."

Evidently she hadn't heard about the trouble her sons were in. I hesitated to tell her, and she noticed my hesitation.

"Is something the matter with Harold?" she said sharply.

"The matter is with Mike. Have you seen him?"

Her large rough hands began to wipe themselves over and over on the front of her apron. "We haven't seen Mike in twenty years. We don't expect to see him again in this life."

"You may, though. He told a man he was coming home."

"This is not his home. It hasn't been since he was a boy. He turned his back on us then. He went off to Pocatello to live with a man named Brown, and that was his downfall."

"How so?"

"That daughter of Brown was a Jezebel. She ruined my son. She taught him all the filthy ways of the world."

Her voice had changed. It sounded as if the voice of somebody slightly crazy was ranting ventriloquially through her. I said with deliberate intent to stop it:

"Carol's been paid back for whatever she did to him. She was murdered in California on Monday."

Her hands stopped wiping themselves and flew up in front of her. She looked at their raw ugliness with her broken eyes.

"Did Mike do it to her?"

"We think so. We're not sure."

"And you're a policeman," she stated.

"More or less."

"Why do you come to us? We did our best, but we couldn't control him. He passed out of our control long ago." Her hands dropped to her sides.

"If he gets desperate enough, he may head this way."

"No, he never will. Mr. Harley said he would kill him if he ever set foot on our property again. That was twenty years ago, when he ran away from the Navy. Mr. Harley meant it, too. Mr. Harley never could abide a lawbreaker. It isn't true that Mr. Harley treated him cruelly. Mr. Harley was only trying to save him from the Devil."

The ranting, ventriloquial note had entered her voice again. Apparently she knew nothing about her son, and if she did she couldn't talk about him in realistic terms. It was beginning to look like a dry run.

I left her and went to the barn to find her husband. He was in the stable under the barn, sitting on a milking stool with his forehead against the black and white flank of a Holstein cow. His hands were busy at her teats, and her milk surged in the pail between his knees. Its sweet fresh smell penetrated the smell of dung that hung like corruption in the heated air.

"Mr. Harley?"

"I'm busy," he said morosely. "This is the last one, if you want to wait."

I backed away and looked at the other cows. There were ten or twelve of them, moving uneasily in their stanchions as I moved. Somewhere out of sight a horse blew and stamped.

"You're disturbing the livestock," Mr. Harley said. "Stand still if you want to stay."

I stood still for about five minutes. The one-eyed collie drifted into the stable and did a thorough job of smelling my shoes. But he still wouldn't let me touch him. When I reached down, he moved back.

Mr. Harley got up and emptied his pail into a ten-gallon can; the foaming milk almost overflowed. He was a tall old man wearing overalls and a straw hat which almost brushed the low rafters. His eyes were as flat and angry and his mouth as sternly righteous as in Harold's portrait of him. The dog retreated whining as he came near.

"You're not from around here. Are you on the road?"

"No." I told him who I was. "And I'll get to the point right away. Your son Mike's in very serious trouble."

"Mike is not my son," he intoned solemnly, "and I have no wish to hear about him or his trouble."

"But he may be coming here. He said he was. If he does, you'll have to inform the police."

"You don't have to instruct me in what I ought to do. I get my instructions from a higher power. He gives me my instructions direct in my heart." He thumped his chest with a gnarled fist.

"That must be convenient."

"Don't blaspheme or make mock, or you'll regret it. I can call down the punishment."

He reached for a pitchfork leaning against the wall. The dog ran out of the stable with his tail down. I became aware suddenly that my shirt was sticking to my back and I was intensely uncomfortable. The three tines of the pitchfork were sharp and gleaming, and they were pointed at my stomach.

"Get out of here," the old man said. "I've been fighting the Devil all my life, and I know one of his cohorts when I see one."

So do I, I said, but not out loud. I backed as far as the door, stumbled on the high threshold, and went out. Mrs. Harley was standing near my car, just inside the wire gate. Her hands were quiet on her meager breast.

"I'm sorry," she said to me. "I'm sorry for Carol Brown. She wasn't a bad little girl, but I hardened my heart against her."

"It doesn't matter now. She's dead."

"It matters in the sight of heaven."

She raised her eyes to the arching sky as if she imagined a literal heaven like a second story above it. Just now it was easier for me to imagine a literal hell, just over the horizon, where the sunset fires were burning.

"I've done so many wrong things," she said, "and closed my eyes to so many others. But don't you see, I had to make a choice."

"I don't understand you."

"A choice between Mr. Harley and my sons. I knew that he was a hard man. A cruel man, maybe not quite right in the head. But what could I do? I had to stick with my husband. And I wasn't strong enough to stand up to him. Nobody is. I had to stand by while he drove our sons out of our home. Harold was the soft one, he forgave us in the end. But Mike never did. He's like his father. I never even got to see my grandson."

Tears ran in the gullies of her face. Her husband came out of the barn carrying the ten-gallon can in his left hand and the pitchfork in his right.

"Go in the house, Martha. This man is a cohort of the Devil. I won't allow you to talk to him."

"Don't hurt him. Please."

"Go in the house," he repeated.

She went, with her gray head down and her feet dragging.

"As for you, cohort," he said, "you get off my farm or I'll call down the punishment on you."

He shook his pitchfork at the reddening sky. I was already in the car and turning up the windows.

I turned them down again as soon as I got a few hundred yards up the lane. My shirt was wet through now, and I could feel sweat running down my legs. Looking back, I caught a glimpse of the river, flowing sleek and solid in the failing light, and it refreshed me.

17

Before driving out to the Harley farm, I had made an evening appointment with Robert Brown and his wife. They already knew what had happened to their daughter. I didn't have to tell them.

I found their house in the north end of the city, on a pleasant, tree-lined street parallel to Arthur Street. Night had fallen almost completely, and the street lights were shining under the clotted masses of the trees. It was still very warm. The earth itself seemed to exude heat like a hot-blooded animal.

Robert Brown had been watching for me. He hailed me from his front porch and came out to the curb. A big man with short gray hair, vigorous in his movements, he still seemed to be wading in some invisible substance, age or sorrow. We shook hands solemnly.

He spoke with more apparent gentleness than force: "I was planning to fly out to California tomorrow. It might have saved you a trip if you had known."

"I wanted to talk to the Harleys, anyway."

"I see." He cocked his head on one side in a birdlike movement which seemed odd in such a big man. "Did you get any sense out of them?"

"Mrs. Harley made a good deal of sense. Harley didn't."

"I'm not surprised. He's a pretty good farmer, they say, but he's been in and out of the mental hospital. I took—my wife and I took care of his son Mike during one of his bouts. We took him into our home." He sounded ashamed of the act.

"That was a generous thing to do."

"I'm afraid it was misguided generosity. But who can prophesy the future? Anyway, it's over now. All over." He forgot about me completely for a moment, then came to himself with a start. "Come in, Mr. Archer. My wife will want to talk to you."

He took me into the living room. It had group and family photos on the walls, and a claustrophobic wallpaper, which lent it some of the stuffiness of an old-fashioned country parlor. The room was sedately furnished with well-cared-for maple pieces. Across the mantel marched a phalanx of sports trophies gleaming gold and silver in the harsh overhead light.

Mrs. Brown was sitting in an armchair under the light. She was a strikingly handsome woman a few years younger than her husband, maybe fifty-five. She had chosen to disguise herself in a stiff and rather dowdy black dress. Her too precisely marcelled brown hair had specks of gray in it. Her fine eyes were confused, and surrounded by dark patches. When she gave me her hand, the gesture seemed less like a greeting than a bid for help.

She made me sit down on a footstool near her. "Tell us all about poor Carol, Mr. Archer."

All about Carol. I glanced around the safe, middle-class room, with the pictures of Carol's ancestors on the walls, and back at her parents' living faces. Where did Carol come in? I could see the source of her beauty in her mother's undisguisable good looks. But I couldn't see how one life led to the other, or why Carol's life had ended as it had.

Brown said: "We know she's dead, murdered, and that Mike probably did it, and that's about all." His face was like a Roman general's, a late Roman general's, after a long series of defeats by barbarian hordes.

"It's about all I know. Mike seems to have been using her as a decoy in an extortion attempt. You know about the Hillman boy?"

He nodded. "I read about it before I knew that my daughter—" His voice receded.

"They say he may be dead, too," his wife said.

"He may be, Mrs. Brown."

"And Mike did these things? I knew he was far gone, but I didn't know he was a monster."

"He's not a monster," Brown said wearily. "He's a sick man. His father was a sick man. He still is, after all the mental hospital could do for him."

"If Mike was so sick, why did you bring him into this house and expose your daughter to him?"

"She's your daughter, too."

"I know that. I'm not allowed to forget it. But I'm not the one that ruined her for life."

"You certainly had a hand in it. You were the one, for instance, who encouraged her to enter that beauty contest."

"She didn't win, did she?"

"That was the trouble."

"Was it? The trouble was the way you felt about that Harley boy."

"I wanted to help him. He needed help, and he had talent."

"Talent?"

"As an athlete. I thought I could develop him."

"You developed him all right."

They were talking across me, not really oblivious of me, using me as a fulcrum for leverage, or a kind of stand-in for reality. I guessed that the argument had been going on for twenty years.

"I wanted a son," Brown said.

"Well, you got a son. A fine upstanding son."

He looked as if he was about to strike her. He didn't, though. He turned to me:

"Forgive us. We shouldn't do this. It's embarrassing."

His wife stared at him in unforgiving silence. I tried to think of something that would break or at least soften the tension between them:

"I didn't come here to start a quarrel."

"You didn't start it, let me assure you." Brown snickered remorsefully. "It started the day Carol ran off with Mike. It was something I didn't foresee—"

His wife's bitter voice cut in: "It started when she was born, Rob. You wanted a son. You didn't want a daughter. You rejected her and you rejected me."

"I did nothing of the sort."

"He doesn't remember," she said to me. "He has one of these convenient memories that men have. You blot out anything that doesn't suit your upright idea of yourself. My husband is a very dishonest man." She had a peculiar angry gnawing smile.

"That's nonsense," he protested. "I've been faithful to you all my life."

"Except in ways I couldn't cope with. Like when you brought the Harley boy into our home. The great altruist. The noble counselor."

"You have no right to jeer at me," he said. "I wanted to help him. I had no way of knowing that he couldn't be reached."

"Go on. You wanted a son any way you could get one."

He said stubbornly: "You don't understand. A man gets natural pleasure from raising a boy, teaching him what he knows."

"All you succeeded in teaching Mike was your dishonesty."

He turned to me with a helpless gesture, his hands swinging out. "She blames me for everything." Walking rather aimlessly, he went out to the back part of the house.

I felt as if I'd been left alone with a far from toothless lioness. She stirred in her chair.

"I blame myself as well for being a fool. I married a man who has the feelings of a little boy. He still gets excited about his high-school football teams. The boys adore him. Everybody adores him. They talk about him as if he was some kind of a plaster saint. And he couldn't even keep his own daughter out of trouble."

"You and your husband should be pulling together."

"It's a little late to start, isn't it?"

Her glance came up to my face, probed at it for a moment, moved restlessly from side to side.

"It may be that you'll kill him if you go on like this."

"No. He'll live to be eighty, like his father."

She jerked her marcelled head toward one of the pictures on the wall. Seen from varying angles, her head was such a handsome object I could hardly take my eyes off it. It was hard to believe that such a finely shaped container could be full of cold boiling trouble.

I said, partly because I wanted to, and partly to appease her: "You must have been a very beautiful girl."

"Yes. I was."

She seemed to take no pleasure even from her vanity. I began to suspect that she didn't relate to men. It happened sometimes to girls who were too good-looking. They were treated as beautiful objects until they felt like that and nothing more.

"I could have married anybody," she said, "any man I went to college with. Some of them are bank presidents and big corporation executives now. But I had to fall in love with a football player."

"Your husband is a little more than that."

"Don't *sell* him to me," she said. "I know what he is, and I know what my life has been. I've been defrauded. I gave everything I had to marriage and motherhood, and what have I got to show for it? Do you know I never even saw my grandson?"

Mrs. Harley had said the same thing. I didn't mention the coincidence.

"What happened to your grandson?"

"Carol put him out for adoption, can you imagine? Actually I know why she did it. She didn't trust her husband not to harm the baby. That's the kind of a man she married."

"Did she tell you this?"

"More or less. Mike is a sadist, among other things. He used to swing cats by their tails. He lived in this house for over a year and all the time I was afraid of him. He was terribly strong, and I never was certain what he was going to do."

"Did he ever attack you?"

"No. He never dared to."

"How old was he when he left?"

"Let me see, Carol was fifteen at the time. That would make him seventeen or eighteen."

"And he left to join the Navy, is that correct?"

"He didn't go into the Navy right away. He left town with an older man, a policeman who used to be on the local force. I forget his name. Anyway, this man lost his position on the force through bribery, and left town, taking Mike with him. He said he was going to make a boxer out of him. They went out to the west coast. I think Mike joined the Navy a few months later. Carol could—" She stopped in dismay.

"What about Carol?"

"I was going to say that Carol could tell you." The angry smile twisted and insulted her mouth. "I must be losing my mind."

"I doubt that, Mrs. Brown. It takes time to get used to these shocks and changes."

"More time than I have. More time than I'll ever have." She rose impatiently and went to the mantelpiece. One of the trophies standing on it was out of line with the others. She reached up and adjusted its position. "I wonder what Rob thinks he's doing in the kitchen."

She didn't go and find out what he was doing. She stood in an awkward position, one hip out, in front of the empty fireplace. Under her dowdy black dress, the slopes and masses of her body were angry. But nothing that she could do with her body, or her face, could change the essential beauty of the structure. She was trapped in it, as her daughter had been.

"I wish you'd go on with your story, Mrs. Brown."

"It hardly qualifies as a story."

"Whatever you want to call it, then. I'm very grateful for the chance to talk to you. It's the first decent chance I've had to get any information about the background of this case."

"The background hardly matters now, or the foreground either."

"It does, though. You may tell me something that will help me to find Harley. I take it you've seen him and Carol from time to time over the years."

"I saw *him* just once more—after that, I wouldn't give him house room—when he came home from the Navy in the winter of 1944-45. He claimed to be on leave. Actually he was absent without leave. He talked himself back into Rob's good graces. Rob had been terribly let down when he left town with that ex-policeman, the bribery artist. But my gullible husband fell for his line all over again. He even gave him money. Which Mike used to elope with my only daughter."

"Why did Carol go with him?"

She scratched at her forehead, leaving faint weals in the clear skin. "I asked her that, the last time she was home, just a couple of months ago. I asked her why she went and why she stuck with him. She didn't really know. Of course she wanted to get out of Pocatello. She hated Pocatello. She wanted to go out to the coast and break into the movies. I'm afraid my daughter had very childish dreams."

"Girls of fifteen do." With a pang, I thought of Stella. The pang became a vaguely formed idea in an unattended area of my mind. Generation after generation had to start from scratch and learn the world over again. It changed so rapidly that children couldn't learn from their parents or parents from their children. The generations were like alien tribes islanded in time.

"The fact is," I said, "Carol did make it into the movies."

"Really? She told me that once, but I didn't believe her."

"Was she a chronic liar?"

"No. Mike was the chronic liar. I simply didn't believe that she could succeed at anything. She never had."

The woman's bitterness was getting me down. She seemed to have an inexhaustible reservoir of the stuff. If she had been like this twenty years before, I could understand why Carol had left home at the first opportunity, and stayed away.

"You say you saw Carol just a couple of months ago."

"Yes. She rode the bus from Lake Tahoe in June. I hadn't seen her for quite a long time. She was looking pretty bedraggled. God knows what kind of a life he was leading her. She didn't talk much."

"It was a chancy life. Harley seems to have lost his job, and they were on their uppers."

"So she told me. There was the usual plea for money. I guess Rob gave her money. He always did. He tried to pretend afterwards, to me, that he gave her the car, too, but I know better. She took it. Apparently their old car had broken down, and they couldn't live at Tahoe without a car."

"How do you know she took it if your husband says she didn't?"

She showed signs of embarrassment. "It doesn't matter. They were welcome to the car." It was her first generous word. She half-spoiled it: "We needed a new one, anyway, and I'm sure she did it on the spur of the moment. Carol always was a very impulsive girl.

"The point is," she said, "she left without saying goodbye. She took the car to go downtown to the movies and simply never came back. She even left her suitcase in her room."

"Had there been trouble?"

"No more than the usual trouble. We did have an argument at supper."

"What about?"

"My grandson. She had no right to put him out for adoption. She said he was her baby to do with as she pleased. But she had no right. If she couldn't keep him, she should have brought him to us. We could have given him opportunities, an education." She breathed heavily and audibly. "She said an unforgivable thing to me that evening. She said, did I mean the kind of opportunities she had? And she walked out. I never saw her again. Neither did her father." Her head jerked forward in emphatic affirmation: "We *did* give her opportunities. It's not our fault if she didn't take advantage of them. It isn't fair to blame us."

"You blame each other," I said. "You're tearing each other to pieces."

"Don't give me that sort of talk. I've had enough of it from my husband."

"I'm merely calling your attention to an obvious fact. You need some kind of an intermediary, a third party, to help straighten out your thinking."

"And you're electing yourself, are you?"

"Far from it. You need an expert counselor."

"My husband *is* a counselor," she said. "What good has it done him? Anyway, I don't believe in seeking that kind of help. People should be able to handle their own problems."

She composed her face and sat down in the armchair again, with great calm, to show me how well she was handling hers.

"But what if they can't, Mrs. Brown?"

"Then they can't, that's all."

I made one more attempt. "Do you go to church?"

"Naturally I do."

"You could talk these problems over with your minister."

"What problems? I'm not aware of any outstanding problems." She was in despair so deep that she wouldn't even look up toward the light. I think she was afraid it would reveal her to herself.

I turned to other matters. "You mentioned a suitcase that your daughter left behind. Is it still here in the house?"

"It's up in her room. There isn't much in it. I almost threw it out with the trash, but there was always the chance that she would come back for it."

"May I see it?"

"I'll go and get it."

"If you don't mind, I'd sooner go up to her room."

"I don't mind."

We went upstairs together, with Mrs. Brown leading the way. She turned on the light in a rear bedroom and stood back to let me enter.

The room provided the first clear evidence that she had been hit very hard by Carol's running away. It was the bedroom of a high-school girl. The flouncy yellow cover on the French provincial bed matched the yellow flounces on the dressing table, where a pair of Kewpie-doll lamps smiled vacantly at each other. A floppy cloth dog with his red felt tongue hanging out watched me from the yellow lamb's wool rug. A little bookcase, painted white like the bed, was filled with high-school texts and hospital novels and juvenile mysteries. There were college pennants tacked around the walls.

"I kept her room as she left it," Mrs. Brown said behind me.

"Why?"

"I don't know. I guess I always thought that she'd come home in the end. Well, she did a few times. The suitcase is in the closet."

The closet smelled faintly of sachet. It was full of skirts and dresses, the kind girls wore in high school a half-generation before. I began to suspect that the room and its contents had less to do with Carol than with some secret fantasy of her mother's. Her mother said, as if in answer to my thought:

"I spend a lot of time here in this room. I feel very close to her here. We really were quite close at one time. She used to tell me everything, all about the boys she dated and so on. It was like living my own high-school days over again."

"Is that good?"

"I don't know." Her lips gnawed at each other. "I guess not, because she suddenly turned against me. Suddenly she closed up completely. I didn't know what went on in her life, but I could see her changing, coarsening. She was such a pretty girl, such a pure-looking girl." Her mouth was wrenched far off center and it remained that way, as if the knowledge of her loss had fallen on her like a cerebral stroke.

The suitcase was an old scuffed cowhide one with Rob Brown's initials on it. I pulled it out into the middle of the floor and opened it. Suddenly I was back in Dack's Auto Court opening Carol's other suitcase. The same sour odor of regret rose from the contents of this one and seemed to permeate the room.

There was the same tangle of clothes, this time all of them women's, skirts and dresses and underthings and stockings, a few cosmetics, a paperback book on the divination of dreams. A hand-scrawled piece of paper was stuck in this as a bookmark. I pulled it out and looked at it. It was signed "Your Brother 'Har.' "

Dear Mike,

I'm sorry you and Carole are haveing a "tough time" and I enclose a money order for fifty which I hope will help out you have to cash it at a postoffice. I would send more but things are a little "tight" since I got married to Lila shes a good girl but does not believe that blood is thicker than water which it is. You asked me do I like bing married well in some ways I really like it in other ways I dont Lila has very strong ideas of her own. Shes no "sinsational" beauty like Carole is but we get long.

Im sorry you lost your job Mike unskilled jobs are hard to come by in these times I know you are a good bartender and that is a skill you should be able to pick up something in that line even if they are prejudiced like you say. I did look up Mr. Sipe like you asked me to but he is in no position to do anything for anybody hes on the skids himself the Barcelona went bankrupt last winter and now old Sipe is just watchman on the place but he sent his best regards for old time sake he wanted to know if you ever developed a left.

I saw another "freind" of yours last week I mean Captain Hillman I know you bear a grudge there but after all he treated you pretty good he could have sent you to prison for ten years. No Im not rakeing up old recrimations because Hillman could do something for you if he wanted you ought to see the raceing yacht he has thats how I saw him went down to Newport to take some sailing pictures. I bet he has twenty-five thousand in that yacht the guy is loaded. I found out he lives with his wife and boy in Pacific Point if you want to try him for a job hes head of some kind of "smogless industry."

Well thats about all for now if you deside to come out to "sunny Cal" you know where we live and dont worry Lila will make you welcome shes a good soul "at heart."

Sincerely yours

Mrs. Brown had come out of her trance and moved toward me with a curious look. "What is that?"

"A letter to Mike from his brother Harold. May I have it?"

"You're welcome to it."

"Thank you. I believe it's evidence. It seems to have started Mike thinking about the possibility of bleeding the Hillmans for money." And it explained, I thought, why Harold had blamed himself for instigating the crime.

"May I read it?"

I handed it to her. She held it at arm's length, squinting.

"I'm afraid I need my glasses."

We went downstairs to the living room, where she put on horn-rimmed reading glasses and sat in her armchair with the letter. "Sipe," she said when she finished reading it. "That's the name I was trying to think of before." She raised her voice and called: "Robert! Come in here."

Rob Brown answered from the back of the house: "I was just coming."

He appeared in the doorway carrying a clinking pitcher and three glasses on a tray. He said with a placatory look at his wife: "I thought I'd make some fresh lemonade for the three of us. It's a warm night."

"That was thoughtful, Robert. Put it down on the coffee table. Now, what was the name of the ex-policeman that Mike left town with, the first time?"

"Sipe. Otto Sipe." He flushed slightly. "That man was a bad influence, I can tell you."

I wondered if he still was. The question seemed so urgent that I drove right back to the airport and caught the first plane out, to Salt Lake City. A late jet from Minneapolis rescued me from a night in the Salt Lake City airport and deposited me at Los Angeles International, not many miles from the Barcelona Hotel, where a man named Sipe was watchman.

18

I had a gun in a locked desk drawer in my apartment, and one in my office. The apartment in West Los Angeles was nearer. I went there.

It was in a fairly new, two-story building with a long roofed gallery on which the second-floor apartments opened directly. Mine was the second-floor back. I parked in the street and climbed the outside stairs.

It was the dead dull middle of the night, the static hour when yesterday ended and tomorrow gathered its forces to begin. My own forces were running rather low, but I wasn't tired. I had slept on the planes. And my case was breaking, my beautiful terrible mess of a case was breaking.

A light shone dimly behind my draped front window, and when I tried the door it was unlocked. I had no family, no wife, no girl. I turned the knob quietly, and slowly and tentatively opened the door.

It seemed I had a girl after all. She was curled up on the studio couch under a blanket which came from my bed. The light from a standing lamp shone down on her sleeping face. She looked so young I felt a hundred years old.

I closed the door. "Hey, Stella."

Her body jerked under the blanket. Throwing it off, she sat up. She was wearing a blue sweater and a skirt. "Oh," she said, "it's you."

"Who were you expecting?"

"I don't know. But don't be cross with me. I was just dreaming something, I forget what, but it was depressing." Her eyes were still dark with the dream.

"How in the world did you get in here?"

"The manager let me in. I told him I was a witness. He understood."

"I don't. A witness to what?"

"Quite a few things," she said with some spirit. "If you want me to tell you, you can stop treating me like a mentally retarded delinquent. Nobody else does, except my parents."

I sat on the edge of the studio couch beside her. I liked the girl but at the moment she was an obstruction, and could turn into a serious embarrassment. "Do your parents know you're here?"

"Of course not. How could I tell them? They wouldn't have let me come, and I had to come. You *ordered* me to get in touch with you if I ever heard from Tommy. Your answering service couldn't find you and finally they gave me your home address."

"Are you telling me you've heard from him?"

She nodded. Her eyes held steady on my face. They were brimming with complex feelings, more womanly than girlish. "He phoned around four o'clock this afternoon. Mother was at the store, and I had a chance to answer the phone myself."

"Where was he, did he say?"

"Here in—" She hesitated. "He made me promise not to tell anyone. And I've already broken my promise once."

"How did you do that?"

"I put a little note in Mr. Hillman's mailbox, before I left El Rancho. I couldn't just leave him dangling, when I *knew.*"

"What did you tell him?"

"Just that I'd heard from Tommy, and he was alive."

"It was a kind thing to do."

"But it broke my promise. He said I wasn't to tell anyone, especially not his parents."

"Promises have to be broken sometimes, when there are higher considerations."

"What do you mean?"

"His safety. I've been afraid that Tom was dead. Are you absolutely certain you talked to him?"

"I'm not telling a lie."

"I mean, you're sure it wasn't an impostor, or a tape recording?"

"I'm sure. We talked back and forth."

"Where was he calling from?"

"I don't know, but I think it was long distance."

"What did he say?"

She hesitated again, with her finger raised. "Is it all right for me to tell you, even after I promised?"

"It would be all wrong if you didn't. You know that, don't you? You didn't come all the way here to hold it back."

"No." She smiled a little. "He didn't tell me too much. He didn't say a word about the kidnappers. Anyway, the fact that he's alive is the important thing. He said he was sorry I'd been worried about him, but he couldn't help it. Then he asked me to meet him and bring some money."

I was relieved. Tom's need for money implied that he had no part of the payoff. "How much money?"

"As much as I could get hold of in a hurry. He knew it wouldn't amount to a great deal. I borrowed some from the people at the beach club. The secretary of the club gave me a hundred dollars of her own money—she knows I'm honest. I took a taxi to the bus station. You know, I never rode on a bus before, except the school bus."

I cut in impatiently: "Did you meet him here in Los Angeles?"

"No. I was supposed to meet him in the Santa Monica bus station at nine o'clock. The bus was a few minutes late, and I may have missed him. He did say on the phone that he mightn't be able to make it tonight. In which case I was to meet him tomorrow night. He said he generally only goes out at night."

"Did he tell you where he's staying?"

"No. That's the trouble. I hung around the bus station for about an hour and then I tried to phone you and when I couldn't I took a taxi here. I had to spend the night somewhere."

"So you did. It's too bad Tom didn't think of that."

"He probably has other things on his mind," she said in a defensive tone. "He's been having a terrible time."

"Did he say so?"

"I could tell by the way he talked to me. He sounded—I don't know —so upset."

"Emotionally upset, or just plain scared?"

Her brow knit. "More worried than scared. But he wouldn't say what about. He wouldn't tell me anything that happened. I asked him if he was okay, you know, physically okay, and he said he was. So I asked him why he didn't come home. He said on account of his parents, only he didn't call them his parents. He called them his anti-parents. He said they could probably hardly wait to put him back in Laguna Perdida School."

Her eyes were very dark. "I remember now what I was dreaming before you woke me up. Tommy was in that school and they wouldn't let him out and they wouldn't let me see him. I went around to all the doors and windows, trying to get in. All I could see was the terrible faces leering at me through the windows."

"The faces aren't so terrible. I was there."

"Yes, but you weren't locked up there. Tommy says it's a terrible place. His parents had no right to put him there. I don't blame him for staying away."

"Neither do I, Stella. But, under the circumstances, he has to be brought in. You understand that, don't you?"

"I guess I do."

"It would be a rotten anticlimax if something happened to him now. You don't want that."

She shook her head.

"Then will you help me get him?"

"It's why I came here, really. I couldn't sic the police on him. But you're different." She touched the back of my hand. "You won't let them put him back in Laguna Perdida."

"It won't happen if I can possibly help it. I think I can. If Tom needs treatment, he should be able to get it as an outpatient."

"He isn't sick!"

"His father must have had a reason for putting him there. Something happened that Sunday, he wouldn't tell me what."

"It happened long before that Sunday," she said. "His father turned against him, that's what happened. Tommy isn't the hairy-chested type, and he preferred music to trapshooting and sailing and such things. So his father turned against him. It's as simple as that."

"Nothing ever is, but we won't argue. If you'll excuse me for a minute, Stella, I have to make a phone call."

The phone was on the desk under the window. I sat down there and dialed Susanna Drew's unlisted number. She answered on the first ring:

"Hello."

"Lew Archer. You sound very alert for three o'clock in the morning."

"I've been lying awake thinking, about you among other things and people. Somebody said—I think it was Scott Fitzgerald—something to the effect that in the real dark night of the soul it's always three o'clock in the morning. I have a reverse twist on that. At three o'clock in the morning it's always the real dark night of the soul."

"The thought of me depresses you?"

"In certain contexts it does. In others, not."

"You're talking in riddles, Sphinx."

"I mean to be, Oedipus. But you're not the source of my depression. That goes back a long way."

"Do you want to tell me about it?"

"Another time, Doctor." Her footwork was very skittish. "You didn't call me at this hour for snatches of autobiography."

"No, though I'd still like to know who that telephone call was from the other day."

"And that's why you called me?" There was disappointment in her voice, ready to turn into anger.

"It isn't why I called you. I need your help."

"Really?" She sounded surprised, and rather pleased. But she said guardedly: "You mean by telling you all I know and like that?"

"We don't have time. I think this case is breaking. Anyway I have to make a move, now. A very nice high-school girl named Stella has turned up on my doorstep." I was speaking to the girl in the room as well as to the woman on the line; as I did so, I realized that they were rapidly becoming my favorite girl and woman. "I need a safe place to keep her for the rest of the night."

"I'm not that safe." A rough note in her voice suggested that she meant it.

Stella said quickly behind me: "I could stay here."

"She can't stay here. Her parents would probably try to hang a child-stealing rap on me."

"Are you serious?"

"The situation is serious, yes."

"All right. Where do you live?"

"Stella and I will come there. We're less than half an hour from you at this time of night."

Stella said when I hung up: "You didn't have to do it behind my back."

"I did it right in front of your face. And I don't have time to argue."

To underline the urgency I took off my jacket, got my gun and its harness out of the drawer, and put it on in front of her. She watched me with wide eyes. The ugly ritual didn't quite silence her.

"But I didn't want to *meet* anybody tonight."

"You'll like Susanna Drew. She's very stylish and hep."

"But I never *do* like people when adults tell me I will."

After the big effort of the night, she was relapsing into childishness. I said, to buck her up:

"Forget your war with the adults. You're going to be an adult pretty soon yourself. Then who will you have to blame for everything?"

"That isn't fair."

It wasn't, but it held her all the way to the apartment house on Beverly Glen. Susanna came to the door in silk pajamas, not the kind anyone slept in. Her hair was brushed. She hadn't bothered with makeup. Her face was extraordinarily and nakedly handsome, with eyes as real and dark as any night.

"Come in, Lew. It's nice to see you, Stella. I'm Susanna. I have a bed made up for you upstairs." She indicated the indoor balcony which hung halfway up the wall of the big central studio, and on which an upstairs room opened. "Do you want something to eat?"

"No, thank you," Stella said. "I had a hamburger at the bus station."

"I'll be glad to make you a sandwich."

"No. Really. I'm not hungry." The girl looked pale and a little sick.

"Would you like to go to bed then?"

"I have no choice." Stella heard herself, and added: "That was rude, wasn't it? I didn't mean it to be. It's awfully kind of you to take me in. It was Mr. Archer who gave me no choice."

"I had no choice, either," I said. "What would you do if you had one?"

"I'd be with Tommy, wherever he is."

Her mouth began to work, and so did the delicate flesh around her eyes and mouth. The mask of a crying child seemed to be struggling for possession of her face. She ran away from it, or from our eyes, up the circular stairs to the balcony.

Susanna called after her before she closed the door: "Pajamas on the bed, new toothbrush in the bathroom."

"You're an efficient hostess," I said.

"Thank you. Have a drink before you go."

"It wouldn't do anything for me."

"Do you want to go into where you're going and what you have to do?"

"I'm on my way to the Barcelona Hotel, but I keep running into detours."

She reacted more sharply than she had any apparent reason to. "Is that what I am, a detour?"

"Stella was the detour. You're the United States Cavalry."

"I love your imagery." She made a face. "What on earth are you planning to do at the old Barcelona? Isn't it closed down?"

"There's at least one man living there, a watchman who used to be the hotel detective, named Otto Sipe."

"Good Lord, I think I know him. Is he a big red-faced character with a whisky breath?"

"That's probably the man. How do you happen to know him?"

She hesitated before she answered, in a careful voice: "I sort of fre-

quented the Barcelona at one time, way back at the end of the war. That
was where I met Carol."

"And Mr. Sipe."

"And Mr. Sipe."

She wouldn't tell me any more.

"You have no right to cross-question me," she said finally. "Leave me
alone."

"I'll be glad to."

She followed me to the door. "Don't leave on that note. Please. I'm not
holding back for the fun of it. Why do you think I've been lying awake
all night?"

"Guilt?"

"Nonsense. I'm not ashamed of anything." But there was shame in her
eyes, deeper than her knowledge of herself. "Anyway, the little I know
can't be of any importance."

"Which is why it keeps you awake."

"You're not being fair. You're trying to use my personal feeling for
you—"

"I didn't know it existed. If it does, I ought to have a right to use it any
way I need to."

"You don't have that right, though. My privacy is a very precious thing
to me, and you have no right to violate it."

"Even to save a life?"

Stella opened her door and came out on the balcony. She looked a little
like a young, pajamaed saint in a very large niche.

"If you *adults*," she said, "will lower your voices a few decibels, it
might be possible to get a little sleep."

"Sorry," I said to both of them.

Stella retreated. Susanna said: "Whose life is in danger, Lew?"

"Tom Hillman's for one. Possibly others, including mine."

She touched the front of my jacket. "You're wearing a shoulder holster.
Is Otto Sipe one of the kidnappers?"

I countered with a question: "Was he a man in your life?"

She was offended. "Of course not. Go away now." She pushed me out.
"Take care."

The night air was chilly on my face.

19

Traffic was sparse on the coastal highway. Occasional night-crawling trucks went by, blazing with red and yellow lights. This stretch of highway was an ugly oil-stained place, fouled by petroleum fumes and rubbed barren by tires. Even the sea below it had a used-dishwater odor.

Ben Daly's service station was dark, except for an inside bulb left on to discourage burglars. I left my car in his lot, beside an outside telephone booth, and crossed the highway to the Barcelona Hotel.

It was as dead as Nineveh. In the gardens behind the main building a mockingbird tried a few throbbing notes, like a tiny heart of sound attempting to beat, and then subsided. The intermittent mechanical movement of the highway was the only life in the inert black night.

I went up to the front door where the bankruptcy notice was posted and knocked on the glass with my flashlight. I knocked repeatedly, and got no answer. I was about to punch out a pane of glass and let myself in. Then I noticed that the door was unlocked. It opened under my hand.

I entered the lobby, jostling a couple of ghosts. They were Susanna, twenty years old, and a man without a face. I told them to get the hell out of my way.

I went down the corridor where Mr. Sipe had first appeared with his light, past the closed, numbered doors, to a door at the end which was standing slightly ajar. I could hear breathing inside the dark room, the heavy sighing breathing of a man in sleep or stupor. The odor of whisky was strong.

I reached inside the door and found the light switch with my right hand. I turned it on and shifted my hand to my gun butt. There was no need. Sipe was lying on the bed, fully clothed, with his ugly nostrils glaring and his loose mouth sighing at the ceiling. He was alone.

There was hardly space for anyone else. The room had never been large, and it was jammed with stuff which looked as if it had been accumulating for decades. Cartons and packing cases, piles of rugs, magazines and newspapers, suitcases and foot lockers, were heaped at the back of the room almost to the ceiling. On the visible parts of the walls were pictures of young men in boxing stance, interspersed with a few girlie pictures.

Empty whisky bottles were ranged along the wall beside the door. A half-full bottle stood by the bed where Sipe was lying. I turned the key that was in the lock of the door and took a closer look at the sleeping man.

He wasn't just sleeping. He was out, far out and possibly far gone. If I had put a match to his lips, his breath would have ignited like an alcohol burner. Even the front of his shirt seemed to be saturated with whisky, as though he'd poured it over himself in one last wild libation before he passed out.

His gun was stuck in the greasy waistband of his trousers. I transferred it to my jacket pocket before I tried to rouse him. He wouldn't wake up. I shook him. He was inert as a side of beef, and his big head rolled loosely on the pillow. I slapped his pitted red cheeks. He didn't even groan.

I went into the adjoining bathroom—it was also a kind of kitchen fitted out with an electric plate and a percolator that smelled of burned coffee —and filled the percolator with cold water from the bathtub faucet. This I poured over Sipe's head and face, being careful not to drown him. He didn't wake up.

I was getting a little worried, not so much about Sipe as about the possibility that he might never be able to give me his story. There was no way of telling how many of the bottles in the room had been emptied recently. I felt his pulse: laboriously slow. I lifted one of his eyelids. It was like looking down into a red oyster.

I had noticed that the bathroom was one of those with two doors, serving two rooms, that you find in older hotels. I went through it into the adjoining bedroom and shone my light around. It was a room similar in shape and size to the other, but almost bare. A brass double bed with a single blanket covering the mattress was just about the only furniture. The blanket lay in the tumbled folds that a man, or a boy, leaves behind when he gets up.

Hung over the head of the bed, like the limp truncated shadow of a boy, was a black sweater. It was a knitted sweater, and it had a raveled sleeve. Where the yarn was snarled and broken I could see traces of light-colored grease, the kind they use on the locks of automobile trunks. In the wastebasket I found several cardboard baskets containing the remains of hamburgers and French frieds.

My heart was beating in my ears. The sweater was pretty good physical evidence that Stella had not been conned. Tom was alive.

I found Sipe's keys and locked him up in his room and went through every other room in the building. There were nearly a hundred guest and service rooms, and it took a long time. I felt like an archaeologist exploring the interior of a pyramid. The Barcelona's palmy days seemed that long ago.

All I got for my efforts was a noseful of dust. If Tom was in the building, he was hiding. I had a feeling that he wasn't there, that he had left the Barcelona for good. Anybody would if he had the chance.

I went back across the highway to Daly's station. My flashlight found a notice pasted to the lower righthand corner of the front door: "In case of emergency call owner," with Daly's home number. I called it from the outside booth, and after a while got an answer:

"Daly here."

"Lew Archer. I'm the detective who was looking for Harold Harley."

"This is a heck of a time to be looking for anybody."

"I found Harley, thanks to you. Now I need your help in some more important business."

"What's the business?"

"I'll tell you when you get here. I'm at your station."

Daly had the habit of serviceability. "Okay. I'll be there in fifteen minutes."

I waited for him in my car, trying to put the case together in my mind. It was fairly clear that Sipe and Mike Harley had been working together, and had used the Barcelona as a hideout. It didn't look as if Tom had been a prisoner; more likely a willing guest, as Harley had said from the start. Even with Laguna Perdida School in the background, it was hard to figure out why a boy would do this to his parents and himself.

Daly came off the highway with a flourish and parked his pickup beside me. He got out and slammed the door, which had his name on it. He gave me a frowzy sardonic pre-dawn look.

"What's on your mind, Mr. Archer?"

"Get in. I'll show you a picture."

He climbed in beside me. I turned on the dome light and got out Tom's photograph. Every time I looked at it it had changed, gathering ambiguities on the mouth and in the eyes.

I put it in Daly's oil-grained hands. "Have you seen him?"

"Yeah. I have. I saw him two or three times over the last couple of days. He made some telephone calls from the booth there. He made one yesterday afternoon."

"What time?"

"I didn't notice, I was busy. It was along toward the end of the afternoon. Then I saw him again last night waiting for the bus." He pointed down the road toward Santa Monica. "The bus stops at the intersection if you flag it down. Otherwise it don't."

"Which bus is that?"

"Any of the intercity buses, excepting the express ones."

"Did you see him get on a bus?"

"No. I was getting ready to close up. Next time I looked he was gone."

"What time was this?"

"Around eight-thirty last night."

"What was he wearing?"

"White shirt, dark slacks."

"What made you interested enough to watch him?"

Daly fidgeted. "I dunno. I didn't *watch* him exactly. I saw him come out of the grounds of the Barcelona and I wondered what he was doing there, naturally. I'd hate to see such a nice-looking boy mixed up with a man like Sipe." He glanced at the photograph and handed it back to me, as if to relieve himself of the responsibility of explaining Tom.

"What's the matter with Sipe?"

"What isn't? I've got boys of my own, and I hate to see a man like Sipe teaching boys to drink and—other things. He ought to be in jail, if you want my opinion."

"I agree. Let's put him there."

"You're kidding."

"I'm serious, Ben. Right now Sipe is in his hotel room, passed out. He probably won't wake up for a long time. Just in case he does, will you stay here and watch for him to come out?"

"What do I do if he *comes* out?"

"Call the police and tell them to arrest him."

"I can't do that," he said uneasily. "I know he's a bad actor, but I got nothing definite to go on."

"I have. If you're forced to call the police, tell them Sipe is wanted in Pacific Point on suspicion of kidnapping. But don't call them unless you have to. Sipe is my best witness, and once he's arrested I'll never see him again."

"Where are you going?"

"To see if I can trace the boy."

His eyes brightened. "Is he the one that's been in all the papers? What's his name? Hillman?"

"He's the one."

"I should have recognized him. I dunno, I don't pay too much attention to people's faces. But I can tell you what kind of a car they drive."

"Does Sipe have a car?"

"Yeah. It's a '53 Ford with a cracked engine. I put some goop in it for him, but it's due to die any day."

Before I left, I asked Daly if he had seen anyone else around the hotel. He had, and he remembered. Mike Harley had been there Monday morning, driving the car with the Idaho license. I guessed that Tom had been riding in the trunk.

"And just last night," he said, "there was this other young fellow driving a brand-new Chevvy. I think he had a girl with him, or maybe a smaller fellow. I was just closed up, and my bright lights were off."

"Did you get a good look at the driver?"

"Not so good, no. I think he was dark-haired, a nice-looking boy. What he was doing with that crumb-bum—" Shaking his head some more, Ben started to get out of my car. He froze in mid-action: "Come to think of it, what's the Hillman boy been doing walking around? I thought he was a prisoner and everybody in Southern California was looking for him."

"We are."

It took me a couple of hours, with the help of several bus-company employees, to sort out the driver who had picked Tom up last night. His name was Albertson and he lived far out La Cienaga in an apartment over a bakery. The sweet yeasty smell of freshly made bread permeated his small front room.

It was still very early in the morning. Albertson had pulled on trousers over his pajamas. He was a square-shouldered man of about forty, with alert eyes. He nodded briskly over the picture:

"Yessir. I remember him. He got on my bus at the Barcelona intersection and bought a ticket into Santa Monica. He didn't get off at Santa Monica, though."

"Why not?"

He rubbed his heavily bearded chin. The sound rasped on my nerves. "Would he be wanted for something?" Albertson said.

"He would."

"That's what I thought at the time. He started to get off and then he saw somebody inside the station and the kid went back to his seat. I got off for a rest stop and it turned out there was a cop inside. When I came back the boy was still on the bus. I told him this was as far as his fare would take him. So he asked me to sell him a ticket to L. A. I was all set to go and I didn't make an issue. If the kid was in trouble, it wasn't up to me to turn him in. I've been in trouble myself. Did I do wrong?"

"You'll find out on Judgment Day."

He smiled. "That's a long time to wait. What's the pitch on the kid?"

"Read it in the papers, Mr. Albertson. Did he ride all the way down-town?"

"Yeah. I'm sure he did. He was one of the last ones to get off the bus."

I went downtown and did some bird-dogging in and around the bus station. Nobody remembered seeing the boy. Of course, the wrong people were on duty at this time in the morning. I'd stand a better chance if I tried again in the evening. And it was time I got back to Otto Sipe.

Ben Daly said he hadn't come out of the hotel. But when we went to Sipe's room the door was standing open and he was gone. Before he left he had finished the bottle of whisky by his bed.

"He must have had a master key, Ben. Is there any way out of here except the front?"

"No sir. He has to be on the grounds some place."

We went around to the back of the sprawling building, past a dry swimming pool with a drift of brown leaves in the deep end. Under the raw bluff which rose a couple of hundred feet behind the hotel were the employees' dormitories, garages, and other outbuildings. The two rear wings of the hotel contained a formal garden whose clipped shrubs and box hedges were growing back into natural shapes. Swaying on the topmost spray of a blue plumbago bush, a mockingbird was scolding like a jay.

I stood still and made a silencing gesture to Daly. Someone was digging on the far side of the bush. I could see some of his movements and hear the scrape of the spade, the thump of earth. I took out my gun and showed myself.

Otto Sipe looked up from his work. He was standing in a shallow hole about five feet long and two feet wide. There was dirt on his clothes. His face was muddy with sweat.

In the grass beside the hole a man in a gray jacket was lying on his back. The striped handle of a knife protruded from his chest. The man looked like Mike Harley, and he lay as if the knife had nailed him permanently to the earth.

"What are you doing, Otto?"

"Planting petunias." He bared his teeth in a doggish grin. The man seemed to be in that detached state of drunkenness where everything appears surreal or funny.

"Planting dead men, you mean."

He turned and looked at Harley's body as if it had just fallen from the sky. "Did he come with you?"

"You know who he is. You and Mike have been buddies ever since he left Pocatello with you in the early forties."

"All right, I got a right to give a buddy a decent burial. You just can't leave them lying around in the open for the vultures."

"The only vultures I see around here are human ones. Did you kill him?"

"Naw. Why would I kill my buddy?"

"Who did?"

Leaning on his spade, he gave me a queer cunning look.

"Where's Tom Hillman, Otto?"

"I'm gonna save my talk for when it counts."

I turned to Ben Daly. "Can you handle a gun?"

"Hell no, I was only at Guadal."

"Hold this on him."

I handed him my revolver and went to look at Harley. His face when I touched it was cold as the night had been. This and the advanced coagulation of the blood that stained his shirt front told me he had been dead for many hours, probably all night.

I didn't try to pull the knife out of his ribs. I examined it closely without touching it. The handle was padded with rubber, striped black and white, and moulded to fit the hand. It looked new and fairly expensive.

The knife was the only thing of any value that had attached itself to Mike Harley. I went through his pockets and found the stub of a Las Vegas to Los Angeles plane ticket issued the day before, and three dollars and forty-two cents.

Ben Daly let out a yell. Several things happened at once. At the edge of my vision metal flashed and the mockingbird flew up out of the bush. The gun went off. A gash opened in the side of Daly's head where Otto Sipe had hit him with the spade. Otto Sipe's face became contorted. He clutched at his abdomen and fell forward, with the lower part of his body in the grave.

Ben Daly said: "I didn't mean to shoot him. The gun went off when he swung the spade at me. After the war I never wanted to shoot anything."

The gash in the side of his head was beginning to bleed. I tied my handkerchief around it and told him to go and call the police and an ambulance. He ran. He was surprisingly light on his feet for a man of middle age.

I was feeling suprisingly heavy on mine. I went to Sipe and turned him onto his back and opened his clothes. The wound in his belly was just below the umbilicus. It wasn't bleeding much, externally, but he must have been bleeding inside. The life was draining visibly from his face.

It was Archer I mourned for. It had been a hard three days. All I had to show for them was a dead man and a man who was probably dying. The fact that the bullet in Sipe had come from my gun made it worse.

Compunction didn't prevent me from going through Sipe's pockets. His wallet was fat with bills, all of them twenties. But his share of the Hillman payoff wasn't going to do him any good. He was dead before the ambulance came shrieking down the highway.

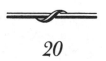

20

A lot of talking was done, some on the scene and some in the sheriff's office. With my support, and a phone call from Lieutenant Bastian, and the fairly nasty cut in the side of his head, Ben was able to convince the sheriff's and the D. A.'s men that he had committed justifiable homicide.

But they weren't happy about it. Neither was I. I had let him kill my witness.

There was still another witness, if she would talk. By the middle of the morning I was back at the door of Susanna Drew's apartment. Stella said through the door:

"Who is it, please?"

"Lew Archer."

She let me in. The girl had bluish patches under her eyes, as if their color had run. There was hardly any other color in her face.

"You look scared," I said. "Has anything happened?"

"No. It's one of the things that scares me. And I have to call my parents and I don't want to. They'll make me go home."

"You have to go home."

"No."

"Yes. Think of them for a minute. You're putting them through a bad time for no good reason."

"But I do have a good reason. I want to try and meet Tommy again tonight. He said if he didn't make it last night he'd be at the bus station tonight."

"What time?"

"The same time. Nine o'clock."

"I'll meet him for you."

She didn't argue, but her look was evasive.

"Where's Miss Drew, Stella?"

"She went out for breakfast. I was still in bed, and she left me a note. She said she'd be back soon, but she's been gone for at least two hours." She clenched her fists and rapped her knuckles together in front of her. "I'm worried."

"About Susanna Drew?"

"About everything. About me. Things keep getting worse. I keep expecting it to end, but it keeps getting worse. I'm changing, too. There's hardly anybody I like any more."

"The thing will end, Stella, and you'll change back."

"Will I? It doesn't feel like a reversible change. I don't see how Tommy and I are ever going to be happy."

"Survival is the main thing." It was a hard saying to offer a young girl. "Happiness comes in fits and snatches. I'm having more of it as I get older. The teens were my worst time."

"Really?" Her brow puckered. "Do you mind if I ask you a personal question, Mr. Archer?"

"Go ahead."

"Are you interested in Miss Drew? You know what I mean. Seriously."

"I think I am. Why?"

"I don't know whether I should tell you this or not. She went out for breakfast with another man."

"That's legitimate."

"I don't know. I didn't actually see him but I heard his voice and I'm very good on voices. I think it was a married man."

"How can you tell that from a man's voice?"

"It was Tommy's father," she said. "Mr. Hillman."

I sat down. For a minute I couldn't think of anything to say. The African masks on the sunlit wall seemed to be making faces at me.

Stella approached me with an anxious expression. "Shouldn't I have told you? Ordinarily I'm not a tattletale. I feel like a spy in her house."

"You should have told me. But don't tell anyone else, please."

"I won't." Having passed the information on to me, she seemed relieved.

"Did the two of them seem friendly, Stella?"

"Not exactly. I didn't see them together. I stayed in my room because I didn't want him to see *me*. She wasn't glad to have him come here, I could tell. But they did sound kind of—intimate."

"Just what do you mean by 'intimate'?"

She thought about her answer. "It was something about the way they talked, as if they were used to talking back and forth. There wasn't any politeness or formality."

"What did they say to each other?"

"Do you want me to try and tell you word for word?"

"Exactly, from the moment he came to the door."

"I didn't hear all of it. Anyway, when he came in, she said: 'I thought you had more discretion than this, Ralph.' She called him Ralph. He said: 'Don't give me that. The situation is getting desperate.' I don't know what he meant by that."

"What do you think he meant?"

"Tommy and all, but there may have been more to it. They didn't say. He said: 'I thought I could expect a little sympathy from you.' She said she was all out of sympathy, and he said she was a hard woman and then he did something—I think he tried to kiss her—and she said: 'Don't do that!' "

"Did she sound angry?"

Stella assumed a listening attitude and looked at the high ceiling. "Not so very. Just not interested. He said: 'You don't seem to like me very much.' She said that the question was a complicated one and she didn't think now was the time to go into it, especially with somebody in the guest room, meaning me. He said: 'Why didn't you say so in the first place? Is it a man?' After that they lowered their voices. I don't know what she told him. They went out for breakfast in a few minutes."

"You have a very good memory," I said.

She nodded, without self-consciousness. "It helps me in school, but in other ways it isn't so fabulous. I remember all the bad things along with the good things."

"And the conversation you heard this morning was one of the bad things?"

"Yes, it was. It frightened me. I don't know why."

It frightened me, too, to learn that Hillman might have been the faceless man with Susanna when she was twenty. In different degrees I cared about them both. They were people with enough feeling to be hurt, and enough complexity to do wrong. Susanna I cared about in ways I hadn't even begun to explore.

Now the case was taking hold of her skirt like the cogs of an automated machine that nobody knew how to stop. I have to admit that I wouldn't have stopped it even if I knew how. Which is the peculiar hell of being a pro.

"Let's see the note she left you."

Stella fetched it from the kitchen, a penciled note scrawled on an interoffice memo form: "Dear Stella: I am going out for breakfast and will be back soon. Help yourself to the contents of the refrig. S. Drew."

"Did you have anything to eat?" I said to Stella.

"I drank a glass of milk."

"And a hamburger last night for dinner. No wonder you look pinched. Come on, I'll take you out for breakfast. It's the going thing."

"All right. Thank you. But then what?"

"I drive you home."

She turned and walked to the sliding glass doors that opened onto the patio, as far away in the room as she could get from me. A little wind was blowing, and I could hear it rustling in the fronds of a miniature palm. Stella turned back to me decisively, as if the wind and the sunlight had influenced her through the glass.

"I guess I have to go home. I can't go on *scaring* my mother."

"Good girl. Now call her and tell her you're on your way."

She considered my suggestion, standing in the sunlight with her head down, the white straight part of her hair bisecting her brown head. "I will if you won't listen."

"How will I know you've done it?"

"I never lied to you yet," she said with feeling. "That's because you don't tell lies to me. Not even for my own good." She produced her first smile of the morning.

I think I produced mine. It had been a bad morning.

I immured myself in a large elaborate bathroom with fuzzy blue carpeting and did some washing, ritual and otherwise. I found a safety razor among the cosmetics and sleeping pills in the medicine cabinet, and used it to shave with. I was planning an important interview, a series of them if I could set them up.

Stella's cheeks were flushed when I came out. "I called home. We better not stop for breakfast on the way."

"Your mother's pretty excited, is she?"

"Dad was the one I talked to. He blames you. I'm sorry."

"It was my bad judgment," I said. "I should have taken you home last night. But I had something else to do." Get a man killed.

"It was *my* bad judgment," she said. "I was *punishing* them for lying about Tommy and me and the car."

"I'm glad you know that. How upset is your father?"

"Very upset. He even said something about Laguna Perdida School. He didn't really mean it, though." But a shadow crossed her face.

About an hour later, driving south with Stella toward El Rancho, I caught a distant glimpse of the school. The rising wind had blown away all trace of the overcast, but even in unobstructed sunlight its buildings had a desolate look about them. I found myself straining my eyes for the lonely blue heron. He wasn't on the water or in the sky.

On impulse, I turned off the highway and took the access road to Laguna Perdida. My car passed over the treadle. The automatic gates rose.

Stella said in a tiny voice: "You're not going to put me in here?"

"Of course not. I want to ask a certain person a question. I won't be long."

"They better not try to put me in here," she said. "I'll run away for good."

"You've had more mature ideas."

"What else can I do?" she said a little wildly.

"Stay inside the safety ropes, with your own kind of people. You're much too young to step outside, and I don't think your parents are so bad. They're probably better than average."

"You don't know them."

"I know you. You didn't just happen."

The old guard came out of his kiosk and limped up to my side of the car. "Dr. Sponti isn't here just now."

"How about Mrs. Mallow?"

"Yeah. You'll find her down the line in East Hall." He pointed toward the building with the ungenerous windows.

Leaving Stella in the car, I knocked on the front door of East Hall. After what seemed a long time, Mrs. Mallow answered. She was wearing the same dark formal costume that she had been wearing on Monday, and the same rather informal smell of gin.

She smiled at me, at the same time flinching away from the daylight. "Mr. Archer, isn't it?"

"How are you, Mrs. Mallow?"

"Don't even ask me that question in the morning. Or any other time, now that I come to think of it. I'm surviving."

"Good."

"But you didn't come here to inquire after my health."

"I'd like to have a few minutes with Fred Tyndal."

"I'm sorry," she said, "the boys are all in class."

"It could be important."

"You want to ask Fred some questions, is that it?"

"Just one, really. It wouldn't have to take long."

"And it won't be anything disturbing?"

"I don't think so."

She left me in the lounge and went into Patch's office to make a telephone call. I wandered around the big battered homeless room, imagining how it would feel to be a boy whose parents had left him here. Mrs. Mallow came back into the room:

"Fred will be right over."

While I was waiting, I listened to the story of her marriages, including the one that had lasted, her marriage to the bottle. Then Fred came in out of the sunlight, none of which adhered to him. He sort of loitered just inside the door, pulling at the hairs on his chin and waiting to be told what he had done wrong this time.

I got up and moved toward him, not too quickly. "Hello, Fred."

"Hello."

"You remember the talk we had the other day?"

"There's nothing the matter with my memory." He added with his quick evanescent smile: "You're Lew Archer the First. Did you find Tom yet?"

"Not yet. I think you can help me find him."

He scuffed the door frame with the side of his shoe. "I don't see how."

"By telling me everything you know. One thing I can promise—they won't put him back in here."

"What good will that do me?" he said forlornly.

I had no answer ready. After a moment the boy said: "What do you want me to tell you?"

"I think you were holding back a little the other day. I don't blame you. You didn't know me from Adam. You still don't, but it's three days later now, and Tom is still missing."

His face reflected the seriousness of this. He couldn't stand such seriousness for very long. He said with a touch of parody:

"Okay, I'll talk, I'll spill everything."

"I want to ask you this. When Tom broke out of here Saturday night, did he have any definite person or place in mind that he intended to go to?"

He ducked his head quickly in the affirmative. "Yeah, I think so."

"Do you know where he was going?"

"Tom didn't say. He did say something else, though, something about finding his true father." The boy's voice broke through into feeling he couldn't handle. He said: "Big deal."

"What did he mean by that, Fred?"

"He said he was adopted."

"Was he really?"

"I don't know. A lot of the kids here want to think they're adopted. My therapist calls it a typical Freudian family romance."

"Do you think Tom was serious?"

"Sure he was." Once again the boy's face reflected seriousness, and I caught a glimpse there of the maturity that he might reach yet. "He said he couldn't know who he was until he knew for sure who his father was." He grinned wryly. "I'm trying to forget who my father is."

"You can't."

"I can try."

"Get interested in something else."

"There isn't anything else."

"There will be."

"When?" he said.

Mrs. Mallow interrupted us. "Have you found out what you need to know, Mr. Archer? Fred really should be going back to class now."

I said to him: "Is there anything else you can tell me?"

"No, sir. Honestly. We didn't talk much."

The boy started out. He turned in the doorway suddenly, and spoke to me in a voice different from the one he had been using, a voice more deep and measured:

"I wish you were my father."

He turned away into the bleak sunlight.

Back in the car, I said to Stella: "Did Tom ever tell you that he was adopted?"

"Adopted? He can't be."

"Why not?"

"He can't be, that's all." The road curved around a reedy marsh where the red-winged blackbirds sounded like woodwinds tuning up, and violins. Stella added after a while: "For one thing, he looks like his father."

"Adopted children often do. They're picked to match the parents."

"How awful. How *commercial*. Who *told* you he was adopted?"

"He told a friend at the school."

"A girl?"

"A boy."

"I'm sure he was making it up."

"Did he often make things up?"

"Not often. But he did—he does have some funny ideas about some things. He told me just this summer that he was probably a changeling, you know? That they got him mixed up with some other baby in the hospital, and Mr. and Mrs. Hillman weren't his real parents." She turned toward me, crouching on the seat with her legs under her. "Do you think that could be true?"

"It could be. Almost anything can happen."

"But you don't believe it."

"I don't know what I believe, Stella."

"You're an adult," she said with a hint of mockery. "You're supposed to know."

I let it drop. We rode in silence to the gate of El Rancho. Stella said:

"I wonder what my father is going to do to me." She hesitated. "I apologize for getting you into this."

"It's all right. You've been the best help I've had."

Jay Carlson, whom I hadn't met and wasn't looking forward to meeting, was standing out in front of his house when we got there. He was a well-fed, youngish man with sensitive blue eyes resembling Stella's. At the moment he looked sick with anger, gray and shuddering with it.

Rhea Carlson, her red hair flaring like a danger signal, came out of the house and rushed up to the car, with her husband trudging behind her. He acted like a man who disliked trouble and couldn't handle it well. The woman spoke first:

"What have you been doing with my daughter?"

"Protecting her as well as I could. She spent the night with a woman friend of mine. This morning I talked her into coming home."

"I intend to check that story very carefully," Carlson said. "What was the name of this alleged woman friend?"

"Susanna Drew."

"Is he telling the truth, Stella?"

She nodded.

"Can't you talk?" he cried. "You've been gone all night and you won't even speak to us."

"Don't get so excited, Daddy. He's telling the truth. I'm sorry I went to Los Angeles but—"

He couldn't wait for her to finish. "I've got a right to get excited, after what you've done. We didn't even know if you were alive."

Stella bowed her head. "I'm sorry, Daddy."

"You're a cruel, unfeeling girl," her mother said. "And I'll never be able to believe you again. Never."

"You know better than that, Mrs. Carlson."

Her husband turned on me fiercely. "You stay out of it." He probably wanted to hit me. In lieu of this, he grasped Stella by the shoulders and shook her. "Are you out of your mind, to do a thing like this?"

"Lay off her, Carlson."

"She's my daughter!"

"Treat her like one. Stella's had a rough night—"

"She's had a rough night, has she? What happened?"

"She's been trying to grow up, under difficulties, and you're not giving her much help."

"What she needs is discipline. And I know where she can get it."

"If you're thinking of Laguna Perdida, your thinking is way out of line. Stella is one of the good ones, one of the best—"

"I'm not interested in your opinion. I suggest you get off my place before I call the police."

I left them together, three well-intentioned people who couldn't seem to stop hurting each other. Stella had the courage to lift her hand to me in farewell.

21

I went next door to the Hillmans'. Turning in past their mailbox, I heard the noise of a sports car coming down the driveway. I stopped in the middle of the narrow blacktop so that Dick Leandro had to stop, too.

He sat there looking at me rather sulkily from under his hair, as if I'd halted him in the middle of a Grand Prix. I got out and walked over to the side of his car and patted the hood.

"Nice car."

"I like it."

"You have any other cars?"

"Just this one," he said. "Listen, I hear they f-found Tom, is that the true word?"

"He hasn't been found yet, but he is running free."

"Hey, that's great," he said without enthusiasm. "Listen, do you know where Skipper is? Mrs. Hillman says he hasn't been home all night." He looked up at me with puzzled anxiety.

"I wouldn't worry about him. He can look after himself."

"Yeah, sure, but do you know where he *is?* I want to ta-talk to him."

"What about?"

"That's between him and I. It's a personal matter."

I said unpleasantly: "Do you and Mr. Hillman share a lot of secrets?"

"I w-wouldn't say that. He *advises* me. He gives me g-good advice."

The young man was almost babbling with fear and hostility. I let him go and drove up to the house. Elaine Hillman was the one I wanted to see, and she let me in herself.

She looked better than she had the last time I'd seen her. She was well groomed and well dressed, in a tailored sharkskin suit which concealed the shrinkage of her body. She was even able to smile at me.

"I got your good news, Mr. Archer."

"Good news?" I couldn't think of any.

"That Tom is definitely alive. Lieutenant Bastian passed the word to me. Come in and tell me more."

She led me across the reception hall, making a detour to avoid the area under the chandelier, and into the sitting room. She said almost brightly, as if she was determined to be cheerful:

"I call this the waiting room. It's like a dentist's waiting room. But the waiting is almost over, don't you think?" Her voice curled up thinly at the end, betraying her tension.

"Yes. I really think so."

"Good. I couldn't stand much more of this. None of us could. These days have been very difficult."

"I know. I'm sorry."

"Don't be sorry. You've brought us good news." She perched on the chesterfield. "Now sit down and tell me the rest of it."

I sat beside her. "There isn't much more, and not all of it is good. But Tom is alive, and free, and very likely still in Los Angeles. I traced him from the Barcelona Hotel, where he was hiding, to downtown Los Angeles. He was seen getting off a bus in the main station around ten o'clock last night. I'm going back there this afternoon to see if I can find him."

"I wish my husband was here to share this," she said. "I'm a little worried about him. He left the house early last evening and hasn't been back since." She looked around the room as if it felt strange without him.

I said: "He probably got word that Tom was alive."

"From whom?"

I left the question unanswered.

"But he wouldn't go without telling me."

"Not unless he had a reason."

"What possible reason could he have for keeping me in the dark?"

"I don't know, Mrs. Hillman."

"Is he going out of his mind, do you think?"

"I doubt it. He probably spent the night in Los Angeles searching for

Tom. I know he had breakfast this morning with Susanna Drew."

I'd dropped the name deliberately, without preparation, and got the reaction I was looking for. Elaine's delicate blonde face crumpled like tissue paper. "Good Lord," she said, "is that still going on? Even in the midst of these horrors?"

"I don't know exactly what *is* going on."

"They're lovers," she said bitterly, "for twenty years. He swore to me it was over long ago. He begged me to stay with him, and gave me his word of honor that he would never go near her again. But he has no honor." She raised her eyes to mine. "My husband is a man without honor."

"He didn't strike me that way."

"Perhaps men can trust him. I know a woman can't. I'm rather an expert on the subject. I've been married to him for over twenty-five years. It wasn't loyalty that kept him with me. I know that. It was my family's money, which has been useful to him in his business, and in his hobbies. Including," she added in a disgusted tone, "his dirty little bed-hopping hobby."

She covered her mouth with her hand, as if to hide the anguish twisting it. "I shouldn't be talking this way. It isn't like me. It's very much against my New England grain. My mother, who had a similar problem with my father, taught me by precept and example always to suffer in silence. And I have. Except for Ralph himself, you're the only person I've spoken to about it."

"You haven't told me much. It might be a good idea to ventilate it."

"Do you believe it may be connected in some way with—all this?" She flung out her arm, with the fingers spread at the end of it.

"Very likely it is. I think that's why your husband and Miss Drew got together this morning. He probably phoned her early in the week. Tuesday afternoon."

"He did! I remember now. He was phoning from the bar, and I came into the room. He cut it short. But I heard him say something to the effect that they must absolutely keep quiet. It must have been that Drew woman he was talking to."

The scornful phrase made me wince. It was a painful, strange colloquy, but we were both engrossed in it. The intimacy of the people we were talking about forced intimacy on us.

"It probably was her," I said. "I'd just told Lieutenant Bastian that she was a witness, and Bastian must have passed it on to your husband."

"You're right again, Mr. Archer. My husband had just heard from the lieutenant. How can you possibly know so much about the details of other people's lives?"

"Other people's lives are my business."

"And your passion?"

"And my passion. And my obsession, too, I guess. I've never been able to see much in the world besides the people in it."

"But how could you possibly find out about that phone call? You weren't here. My husband wouldn't tell you."

"I was in Miss Drew's apartment when the call came. I didn't hear what was said, but it shook her up."

"I hope so." She glanced at my face, and her eyes softened. She reached out and touched my arm with gentle fingers. "She isn't a friend of yours?"

"She is, in a way."

"You're not in love with her?"

"Not if I can help it."

"That's a puzzling answer."

"It puzzles me, too. If she's still in love with your husband it would tend to chill one's interest. But I don't think she is."

"Then what are they trying to conceal?"

"Something in the past." I hoped it was entirely in the past. Susanna, I had learned in the course of the morning, could still hurt me where I lived. "It would help if you'd go into it a little deeper. I know it will also hurt," I said to myself and her.

"I can stand pain if there's any purpose in it. It's the meaningless pain I can't stand. The pain of Tom, for instance." She didn't explain what she meant, but she touched her blue-veined temple with her fingertips.

"I'll try to make it short, Mrs. Hillman. You said the affair has been going on for twenty years. That would take it back to around the end of the war."

"Yes. The spring of 1945. I was living alone, or rather with a woman companion, in a house in Brentwood. My husband was in the Navy. He had been a squadron commander, but at the time I'm talking about he was executive officer of an escort carrier. Later they made him Captain of the same ship." She spoke with a kind of forlorn pride, and very carefully, as if the precise facts of the past were all she had to hold on to.

"In January or February of 1945 my husband's ship was damaged by a kamikaze plane. They had to bring it back to San Diego for repairs. Ralph had some days of leave, of course, and of course he visited me. But I didn't see as much of him as I wanted to, or expected to. I found out later why. He was spending some of his nights, whole weekends, with Susanna Drew."

"In the Barcelona Hotel?"

"Did she tell you?"

"In a way." She had given me Harold Harley's picture of Carol, and the printing on the back of the picture had sent me to the Barcelona Hotel. "About herself she told me, not about your husband. She's a loyal girl, anyway."

"I don't want to hear her praised. She's caused me too much suffering."

"I'm sorry. But she was only twenty, remember."

"She's closer to forty now. The fact that she was twenty then only made it worse. I was still in my twenties myself, but my husband had already discarded me. Do you have any idea how a woman feels when her husband leaves her for a younger woman? Can you imagine the crawling of the flesh?"

She was suffering intense remembered pain. Her eyes were bright and dry, as if there was fire behind them. The cheerfullest thing I could think of to say was:

"But he didn't leave you."

"No. He came back. It wasn't me he cared for. There was the money, you see, and his postwar plans for his engineering firm. He was quite frank on the subject, and quite impenitent. In fact, he seemed to feel that he was doing me an enormous favor. He felt that any couple who couldn't have a child—" Her hand went to her mouth again.

I prompted her: "But you had Tom."

"Tom came later," she said, "too late to save us." Her voice broke into a deeper range. "Too late to save my husband. He's a tragically unhappy man. But I can't find it in my heart to pity him." Her hand touched her thin breast and lingered there.

"What's the source of the trouble between him and Tom?"

"The falsity," she said in her deeper voice.

"The falsity?"

"I might as well tell you, Mr. Archer. You're going to find out about it sooner or later, anyway. And it may be important. Certainly it's psychologically important."

"Was Tom—is Tom an adopted son?"

She nodded slowly. "It may have to come out publicly, I don't know. For the present I'll ask you not to divulge it to anyone. No one in town here knows it. Tom doesn't know it himself. We adopted him in Los Angeles shortly after my husband left the Navy and before we moved here."

"But he resembles your husband."

"Ralph chose him for that reason. He's a very vain man, Mr. Archer. He's ashamed to admit even to our friends that we were incapable of producing a child of our own. Actually Ralph is the one who is sterile. I'm telling you this so you'll understand why he has insisted from the beginning on the great pretense. His desire to have a son was so powerful, I think he has actually believed at times that Tom is his own flesh and blood."

"And he hasn't told Tom he isn't?"

"No. Neither have I. Ralph wouldn't let me."

"Isn't that supposed to be a poor idea, with an adopted child?"

"I told my husband that from the beginning. He had to be honest with Tom, or Tom would not be honest with him. There would be falsity at the center of the household." Her voice trembled, and she looked down at the carpet as if there was no floor under it. "Well, you see what the consequence has been. A ruined boyhood for Tom and a breakdown of the family and now this tragedy."

"This almost-tragedy. He's still alive and we're going to get him back."

"But can we ever put the family back together?"

"That will depend on all three of you. I've seen worse fractures mended, but not without competent help. I don't mean Laguna Perdida. And I don't mean just help for Tom."

"I know. I've been wretchedly unhappy, and my husband has been quite—quite irrational on this subject for many years. Actually I think it goes back to Midway. Ralph's squadron was virtually massacred in that dreadful battle. Of course he blamed himself, since he was leading them. He felt as though he had lost a dozen sons."

"How do you know?"

"He was still writing to me then," she said, "freely and fully, as one human being to another. He wrote me a number of very poignant letters about our having children, sons of our own. I *know* the thought was connected with his lost fliers, although he never said so. And when he found out he couldn't have a son of his own, and decided to adopt Tom, well—" She dropped her hands in her lap. Her hands seemed restless without knitting to occupy them.

"What were you going to say, Mrs. Hillman?"

"I hardly know. I'm not a psychologist, though I once had some training in philosophy. I've felt that Ralph was trying to live out some sort of a fantasy with Tom—perhaps relive those terrible war years and make good his losses somehow. But you can't use people in that way, as figures in a fantasy. The whole thing broke down between Tom and his father."

"And Tom caught on that your husband wasn't his father."

She looked at me nervously. "You think he did?"

"I'm reasonably certain of it," I said, remembering what Fred Tyndal had told me. "Mrs. Hillman, what happened on the Sunday morning that you put Tom in Laguna Perdida?"

She said quickly: "It was Ralph's doing, not mine."

"Had they quarreled?"

"Yes. Ralph was horribly angry with him."

"What about?"

She bowed her head. "My husband has forbidden me to speak of it."

"Did Tom say something or do something very wrong?"

She sat with her head bowed and wouldn't answer me. "I've told you more than I should have," she said eventually, "in the hope of getting to the bottom of this mess. Now will you tell me something? You mentioned a hotel called the Barcelona, and you said that Tom had been hiding there. You used the word 'hiding.'"

"Yes."

"Wasn't he being held?"

"I don't know. There may have been some duress, possibly psychological duress. But I doubt that he was held in the ordinary sense."

She looked at me with distaste. I'd brought her some very tough pieces of information to chew on, and probably this was the hardest one of all. "You've hinted from the beginning that Tom cooperated willingly with the kidnappers."

"It was a possibility that had to be considered. It still is."

"Please don't sidestep the question. I can stand a direct answer." She smiled dimly. "At this point I couldn't stand anything else."

"All right. I think Tom went with Harley of his own free will, rode in the trunk of Harley's car to the Barcelona Hotel, and stayed there without anybody having to hold a gun on him. I don't understand his reasons, and I won't until I talk to him. But he probably didn't know about the extortion angle. There's no evidence that he profited from it, anyway. He's broke."

"How do you know? Have you seen him?"

"I've talked to somebody who talked to him. Tom said he needed money."

"I suppose that's good news in a way."

"I thought it was."

I made a move to go, but she detained me. There was more on her mind:

"This Barcelona Hotel you speak of, is it the big old rundown place on the coast highway?"

"Yes. It's closed up now."

"And Tom hid, or was hidden, there?"

I nodded. "The watchman at the hotel, a man named Sipe, was a partner in the extortion. He may have been the brains behind it, to the extent that it took any brains. He was shot to death this morning. The other partner, Harley, was stabbed to death last night."

Her face was open, uncomprehending, as if she couldn't quite take in these terrible events.

"How extraordinary," she breathed.

"Not so very. They were heavy thieves, and they came to a heavy end."

"I don't mean those violent deaths, although they're part of it. I mean the deep connections you get in life, the coming together of the past and the present."

"What do you have in mind?"

She grimaced. "Something ugly, but I'm afraid it has to be said. You see, the Barcelona Hotel, where my son, my adopted son, has been staying with criminals, apparently"—she took a shuddering breath—"that very place was the scene of Ralph's affair with Susanna Drew. And did you say that the watchman's name was Sipe, the one who was shot?"

"Yes. Otto Sipe."

"Did he once work as a detective in the hotel?"

"Yes. He was the kind of detective who gives our trade a bad name."

"I have reason to know that," she said. "I knew Mr. Sipe. That is, I talked to him once, and he left an impression that I haven't been able to wipe out of my memory. He was a gross, corrupt man. He came to my house in Brentwood in the spring of 1945. He was the one who told me about Ralph's affair with Miss Drew."

"He wanted money, of course."

"Yes, and I gave him money. Two hundred dollars, he asked for, and when he saw that I was willing to pay he raised it to five hundred, all the cash I had on hand. Well, the money part is unimportant. It always is," she said, reminding me that she had never needed money.

"What did Sipe have to say to you?"

"That my husband was committing adultery—he had a snapshot to prove it—and it was his duty under the law to arrest him. I don't know now if there was ever such a law on the books—"

"There was. I don't think it's been enforced lately, or an awful lot of people would be in jail."

"He mentioned jail, and the effect it would have on my husband's reputation. This was just about the time when Ralph began to believe he could make Captain. I know from this height and distance it sounds childish, but it was the biggest thing in his life at that time. He came from an undistinguished family, you see—his father was just an unsuccessful small businessman—and he felt he had to shine in so many ways to match my family's distinction." She looked at me with sad intelligence. "We all need something to buttress our pride, don't we, fragments to shore against our ruins."

"You were telling me about your interview with Otto Sipe."

"So I was. My mind tends to veer away from scenes like that. In spite of the pain and shock I felt—it was my first inkling that Ralph was unfaithful to me—I didn't want to see all his bright ambitions wrecked. So I paid the dreadful man his dirty money—and he gave me his filthy snapshot."

"Did you hear from him again?"

"No."

"I'm surprised he didn't attach himself to you for life."

"Perhaps he intended to. But Ralph stopped him. I told Ralph about his visit, naturally." She added: "I didn't show him the snapshot. That I destroyed."

"How did Ralph stop him?"

"I believe he knocked him down and frightened him off. I didn't get a very clear account from Ralph. By then we weren't communicating freely. I went home to Boston and I didn't see Ralph again until the end of the year, when he brought his ship to Boston harbor. We had a reconciliation of sorts. It was then we decided to adopt a child."

I wasn't listening too closely. The meanings of the case were emerging. Ralph Hillman had had earlier transactions with both of the extortionists. He had been Mike Harley's superior officer, and had thrown him out of the Navy. He had knocked down Otto Sipe. And they had made him pay for his superiority and his power.

Elaine was thinking along the same lines. She said in a soft, despondent voice:

"Mr. Sipe would never have entered our lives if Ralph hadn't used that crummy hotel for his crummy little purposes."

"You mustn't blame your husband for everything. No doubt he did wrong. We all do. But the things he did nineteen or twenty years ago aren't solely responsible for this kidnapping, or whatever it was. It isn't that simple."

"I know. I don't blame him for everything."

"Sipe, for instance, would probably have been involved anyway. His partner Mike Harley knew your husband and had a grievance against him."

"But why did Tom, my poor dear Tom, end up at that same hotel? Isn't there a fatality in it?"

"Maybe there is. To Sipe and Harley it was simply a convenient place to keep him."

"Why would Tom stay with them? They must be—have been outrageous creatures."

"Teen-age boys sometimes go for the outrageous."

"Do they not," she said. "But I can't really blame Tom for anything he's done. Ralph and I have given him little enough reality to hold on to. Tom's a sensitive, artistic, introverted boy. My husband didn't want him to be those things—perhaps they reminded Ralph that he wasn't our son, really. So he kept trying to change him. And when he couldn't, he withdrew his interest. Not his love, I'm sure. He's still profoundly concerned with Tom."

"But he spends his time with Dick Leandro."

One corner of her mouth lifted, wrinkling her cheek and eye, as if age and disillusion had taken sudden possession of that side of her face. "You're quite a noticer, Mr. Archer."

"You have to be, in my job. Not that Dick Leandro makes any secret of his role. I met him coming out of your driveway."

"Yes. He was looking for Ralph. He's very dependent on Ralph," she added dryly.

"How would you describe the relationship, Mrs. Hillman? Substitute son?"

"I suppose I would. Dick's mother and father broke up some years ago. His father left town, and of course his mother got custody of Dick. He needed a substitute father. And Ralph needed someone to crew for him on the sloop—I sometimes think it's the most urgent need he has, or had. Someone to share the lusty gusty things he likes to do, and would like a son to do."

"He could do better than Dick, couldn't he?"

She was silent for a while. "Perhaps he could. But when you have an urgent need, you tend to hook up with people who have urgent needs of their own. Poor Dick has a great many urgent needs."

"Some of which have been met. He told me that your husband put him through college."

"He did. But don't forget that Dick's father used to work for Ralph's firm. Ralph is very strong on loyalty up and down."

"Is Dick?"

"He's fanatically loyal to Ralph," she said with emphasis.

"Let me ask you a hypothetical question, without prejudice, as they say in court. If your husband disinherited Tom, would Dick be a likely heir?"

"That's excessively hypothetical, isn't it?"

"But the answer might have practical consequences. What's your answer?"

"Dick might be left something. He probably will be in any case. But please don't imagine that poor stupid Dick, with his curly hair and his muscles, is capable of plotting—"

"I wasn't suggesting that."

"And you mustn't embarrass Dick. He's come through nobly in this crisis. Both of us have leaned on him."

"I know. I'll leave him alone." I got up to go. "Thank you for being frank with me."

"There's not much point in pretending at this late date. If there's anything else you need to know—"

"There is one thing that might help. If you could give me the name of the agency through which you adopted Tom?"

"It wasn't done through an agency. It was handled privately."

"Through a lawyer, or a doctor?"

"A doctor," she said. "I don't recall his name, but he delivered Tom at Cedars of Lebanon. We paid the expenses, you understand, as part of the bargain that we made with the mother."

"Who was she?"

"Some poor woman who'd got herself in trouble. I didn't actually meet her, nor did I want to. I wanted to feel that Tom was my own son."

"I understand."

"Does it matter who his parents were? I mean, in the current situation?"

"It does if he's wandering around Los Angeles looking for them. Which I have reason to think he may be doing. You should have a record somewhere of that doctor's name."

"My husband could tell you."

"But he isn't available."

"It may be in his desk in the library."

I followed her to the library and while she rummaged in the desk I looked at the pictures on the wall again. The group photo taken on the flight deck must have been Hillman's squadron. I looked closely at their faces, wondering which of the young men had died at Midway.

Next I studied the yachting picture of Dick Leandro. His handsome, healthy, empty face told me nothing. Perhaps it would have meaning for somebody else. I took it off the wall and slipped it into the side pocket of my jacket.

Elaine Hillman didn't notice. She had found the name she was looking for.

"Elijah Weintraub," she said, "was the doctor's name."

22

I phoned Dr. Weintraub long-distance. He confirmed the fact that he had arranged for Thomas Hillman's adoption, but he refused to discuss it over the phone. I made an appointment to see him in his office that afternoon.

Before I drove back to Los Angeles I checked in with Lieutenant Bastian. He'd been working on the case for nearly three days, and the experience hadn't improved his disposition. The scarlike lines in his face seemed to have deepened. His voice was hoarse and harsh, made harsher by irony:

"It's nice of you to drop by every few days."

"I'm working for Ralph Hillman now."

"I know that, and it gives you certain advantages. Which you seize. But you and I are working on the same case, and we're supposed to be cooperating. That means periodic exchanges of information."

"Why do you think I'm here?"

His eyes flared down. "Fine. What have you found out about the Hillman boy?"

I told Bastian nearly all of it, enough to satisfy both him and my conscience. I left out the adoption and Dr. Weintraub, and the possibility that Tom might turn up at the Santa Monica bus station at nine that night. About his other movements, and the fact that he had probably been a voluntary captive in the Barcelona Hotel, I was quite frank.

"It's too bad Otto Sipe had to die," Bastian grumbled. "He could have cleared up a lot of things."

I agreed.

"Exactly what happened to Sipe? You were a witness."

"He attacked Ben Daly with a spade. Daly was holding my gun while I examined Harley's body. The gun went off."

Bastian made a disgusted noise with his lips. "What do you know about Daly?"

"Not much. He has a service station across from the Barcelona. He struck me as dependable. He's a war veteran—"

"So was Hitler. L. A. says Daly had previous dealings with Sipe. Sipe bought secondhand cars through him, for instance."

"That would be natural enough. Daly ran the nearest service station to where Sipe worked."

"So you don't think Daly killed him to shut him up?"

"No, but I'll bear it in mind. I'm more interested in the other killing. Have you seen the knife that Harley was stabbed with?"

"Not yet. I have a description." Bastian moved some papers around on top of his desk. "It's what they call a hunting knife, made by the Oregon firm of Forstmann, with their name on it. It has a broad blade about six inches long, is very sharp and pointed, has a striped rubber handle, black and white, with finger mouldings on it. Practically brand new. Is that an accurate description?"

"I only saw the striped rubber handle. The fact that the blade is quite broad, sharp, and pointed suggests that it's the same knife that stabbed Carol."

"So I told L. A. They're going to send me the knife for identification work."

"That's what I was going to suggest."

Bastian leaned forward, bringing his arms down heavily among the papers on his desk top. "You think somebody in town here stabbed him?"

"It's an idea worth considering."

"Why? For his share of the money?"

"It couldn't have been that. Harley had nothing left by the time he left Las Vegas. I talked to the high-roller who cleaned him out."

"I'm surprised Harley didn't shoot him."

"I gather there were professional guns around. Harley was never more than a semi-pro."

"Why then?" Bastian said, his eyebrows arched. "Why was Harley killed if it wasn't for money?"

"I don't think we'll know until we put our finger on the killer."

"Do you have any nominations?" he said.

"No. Do you?"

"I have some thoughts on the subject, but I'd better not think them out loud."

"Because I'm working for Hillman?"

"I didn't say that." His dark eyes veiled themselves, and he changed the subject. "A man named Robert Brown, the victim's father, was here asking for you. He's at the City Hotel."

"I'll look him up tomorrow. Treat him gently, eh?"

"I treat 'em all gently. Harold Harley called me a few minutes ago. He's taking his brother's death hard."

"He would. When did you let him go?"

"Yesterday. We had no good reason to hold him in custody. There's no law that says you have to inform on your own brother."

"Is he back home in Long Beach?"

"Yes. He'll be available for the trial, if there's anybody left to prosecute."

He was needling me about the death of Otto Sipe. On that note I left.

I made a detour up the coast highway on the way to my appointment with Dr. Weintraub, and stopped at Ben Daly's service station. Ben was there by the pump, with a bandage around his head. When he saw me he went into the office and didn't come out. A boy who looked like a teen-aged version of Ben emerged after a while. He asked in an unfriendly way if there was anything he could do for me.

"I'd like to talk to Mr. Daly for a minute."

"I'm sorry, Dad doesn't want to talk to you. He's very upset, about this morning."

"So am I. Tell him that. And ask him if he'll look at a picture for identification purposes."

The boy went into the office, closing the door behind him. Across the roaring highway, the Barcelona Hotel asserted itself in the sunlight like a monument of a dead civilization. In the driveway I could see a number of county cars, and a man in deputy's uniform keeping back a crowd of onlookers.

Daly's boy came back with a grim look on his face. "Dad says he doesn't want to look at any more of your pictures. He says you and your pictures brought him bad luck."

"Tell him I'm sorry."

The boy retreated formally, like an emissary. He didn't show himself again, and neither did his father. I gave up on Daly for the present.

Dr. Weintraub's office was in one of the new medical buildings on Wilshire, near Cedars of Lebanon Hospital. I went up in a self-service elevator to a waiting room on the fifth floor. This was handsomely furnished in California Danish and had soothing music piped in, which got on my nerves before I had time to sit down. Two pregnant women on opposite sides of the room caught me, a mere man, in a crossfire of pitying glances.

The highly made-up girl behind the counter in one corner said:

"Mr. Archer?"

"Yes."

"Dr. Weintraub will see you in a few minutes. You're not a patient, are you? So we needn't bother taking your history, need we?"

"It would give you the horrors, honey."

She moved her eyelashes up and down a few times, to indicate shocked surprise. Her eyelashes were long and thick and phony, and they waved clumsily in the air like tarantula legs.

Dr. Weintraub opened a door and beckoned me into his consulting room. He was a man about my age, perhaps a few years older. Like a lot of other doctors, he hadn't looked after himself. His shoulders were stooped under his white smock, and he was putting on weight. The curly black hair was retreating from his forehead.

But the dark eyes behind his glasses were extraordinarily alive. I could practically feel their impact as we shook hands. I recognized his face, but I couldn't place it.

"You look as though you could use a rest," he said. "That's free advice."

"Thanks. It will have to come later." I didn't tell him he needed exercise.

He sat down rather heavily at his desk, and I took the patient's chair facing him. One whole wall of the room was occupied by bookshelves. The books seemed to cover several branches of medicine, with special emphasis on psychiatry and gynecology.

"Are you a psychiatrist, doctor?"

"No, I am not." His eyes were melancholy. "I studied for the Boards at one time but then the war came along. Afterwards I chose another specialty, delivering babies." He smiled, and his eyes lit up. "It's so very satisfying, and the incidence of success is so very much higher. I mean, I seldom lose a baby."

"You delivered Thomas Hillman."

"Yes. I told you so on the telephone."

"Have you refreshed your memory about the date?"

"I had my secretary look it up. Thomas was born on December 12, 1945. A week later, on December 20 to be exact, I arranged for the baby's adoption by Captain and Mrs. Ralph Hillman. He made a wonderful Christmas present for them," he said warmly.

"How did his real mother feel about it?"

"She didn't want him," he said.

"Wasn't she married?"

"As a matter of fact, she was a young married woman. Neither she nor her husband wanted a child at that time."

"Are you willing to tell me their name?"

"It wouldn't be professional, Mr. Archer."

"Not even to help solve a crime, or find a missing boy?"

"I'd have to know all the facts, and then have time to consider them. I don't have time. I'm stealing time from my other—from my patients now."

"You haven't heard from Thomas Hillman this week?"

"Neither this week nor any other time." He got up bulkily and moved past me to the door, where he waited with courteous impatience till I went out past him.

23

With its portico supported by fluted columns, the front of Susanna's apartment house was a cross between a Greek temple and a Southern plantation mansion. It was painted blue instead of white. Diminished by the columns, I went into the cold marble lobby. Miss Drew was out. She had been out all day.

I looked at my watch. It was nearly five. The chances were she had gone to work after her breakfast with Hillman. I went out and sat in my car at the curb and watched the rush-hour traffic crawling by.

Shortly after five a yellow cab veered out of the traffic stream and pulled up behind my car. Susanna got out. I went up to her as she was paying the driver. She dropped a five-dollar bill when she saw me. The driver scooped it up.

"I've been hoping you'd come to see me, Lew," she said without much conviction. "Do come in."

She had trouble fitting her key into the lock. I helped her. Her handsome central room appeared a little shabby to my eyes, like a stage set where too many scenes had been enacted. Even the natural light at the windows, the fading afternoon light, seemed stale and secondhand.

She flung herself down on a sofa, her fine long legs sprawling. "I'm bushed. Make yourself a drink."

"I couldn't use one. There's a long night ahead."

"That sounds ominous. Make me one then. Make me a Journey to the End of the Night cocktail, with a dash of henbane. Or just dip me a cup of Lethe, that will do."

"You're tired."

"I've been working all day. For men must weep and women must work, though the harbor bar be moaning."

"If you'll be quiet for a bit, I want to talk to you seriously."

"What fun."

"Shut up."

I made her a drink and brought it to her. She sipped it. "Thank you, Lew. You're really a dear man."

"Stop talking like a phony."

She looked up at me with hurt dark eyes. "Nothing I say is right. You're mad at me. Maybe I shouldn't have left Stella by herself, but she was still sleeping and I had to go to work. Anyway, she got home all right. Her father called, to thank me, just before I left the office."

"To thank you?"

"And to cross-examine me about you and a few other things. Stella seems to have left home again. Mr. Carlson asked me to get in touch with him if she comes here. Should I?"

"I don't care. Stella isn't the problem."

"And I am?"

"You're part of it. You didn't leave Stella this morning because you had to go to work. You had breakfast with Ralph Hillman, and you ought to know that I know it."

"It was in a public place," she said irrelevantly.

"That's not the point. I wouldn't care if it was breakfast in bed. The point is you tried to slur over the fact, and it's a damned important fact."

The hurt in her eyes tried to erupt into anger, but didn't quite succeed. Anger was just another evasion, and she probably knew that she was coming to the end of her evasions. She finished her drink and said in a very poignant female voice:

"Do you mean important to you personally, or for other reasons?"

"Both. I talked to Mrs. Hillman today. Actually she did most of the talking."

"About Ralph and me?"

"Yes. It wasn't a very pleasant conversation, for either of us. I'd rather have heard it from you."

She averted her face. Her black head absorbed the light almost completely. It was like looking into a small head-shaped area of almost total darkness.

"It's a passage in my life that I'm not proud of."

"Because he was so much older?"

"That's one reason. Also, now that I'm older myself, I know how wretchedly mean it is to try and steal another woman's husband."

"Then why go on doing it?"

"I'm not!" she cried in resentment. "It was over almost as soon as it started. If Mrs. Hillman thinks otherwise, she's imagining things."

"I'm the one who thinks otherwise," I said. "You had breakfast with him this morning. You had a phone call from him the other day, which you refused to discuss."

Slowly she turned and looked up at my face. "But it doesn't *mean* anything. I didn't *ask* him to phone me. I only went out with him this morning because he was desperate to talk to someone and I didn't want to disturb Stella. Also, if you want the truth, so he couldn't make a pass at me."

"Does he go in rather heavily for that?"

"I don't know. I hadn't seen him in about eighteen years. Honestly. I was appalled by the change in him. He was in a bad way this morning. He'd been drinking, and he said he'd been up all night, wandering around Los Angeles, searching for his son."

"I've been doing a little searching myself, but nobody goes out to breakfast with me and holds my hand."

"Are you really jealous of him, Lew? You can't be. He's *old*. He's a broken-down old man."

"You're protesting too much."

"I mean it, though. I had an enormous sense of revulsion this morning. Not just against Ralph Hillman. Against my whole misguided little life." She looked around the room as if she perceived the shabbiness I had seen. "I'm liable to spill over into autobiography at any moment."

"That's what I've been waiting for, Susanna. How did you meet him?"

"Make me another drink."

I made it and brought it to her. "When and how did you meet him?"

"It was in March of 1945, when I was working at Warner's. A group of Navy officers came out to the studio to see a preview of a war movie. They were planning a party afterwards, and I went along. Ralph got me drunk and took me to the Barcelona Hotel, where he introduced me to the stolen delights of illicit romance. It was my first time on both counts. First time drunk, first time bedded." Her voice was harsh. "If you wouldn't stand over me, Lew, it would be easier."

I pulled up a hassock to her feet. "But it didn't go on, you say?"

"It went on for a few weeks. I'll be honest with you. I was in love with Ralph. He was handsome and brave and all the other things."

"And married."

"That's why I quit him," she said, "essentially. Mrs. Hillman—Elaine Hillman got wind of the affair and came to my apartment in Burbank. We had quite a scene. I don't know what would have happened if Carol hadn't been there. But she got the two of us quieted down, and even talking sensibly to each other." She paused, and added elegiacally: "Carol had troubles of her own, but she was always good at easing situations."

"What was Carol doing in that situation?"

"She was living with me, didn't I tell you that? I took her into my home. Anyway, Carol sat there like a little doll while Elaine Hillman laid out for me in detail just what I was doing to her and her marriage. The ugliness of it. I saw I couldn't go on doing it to her. I told her so, and she was satisfied. She's quite an impressive woman, you know, at least she was then."

"She still is, when you get under the surface. And Ralph Hillman is an impressive man."

"He was in those days, anyway."

I said to test her honesty: "Didn't you have any other reason for dropping him, besides Elaine Hillman's visit?"

"I don't know what you mean," she said, failing the honesty test, or perhaps the memory test.

"How did Elaine Hillman find out about you?"

"Oh. That." The shame that lay beneath her knowledge of herself came up into her face and took possession of it. She whispered: "Mrs. Hillman told you, I suppose?"

"She mentioned a picture."

"Did she show it to you?"

"She's too much of a lady."

"That was a nasty crack!"

"It wasn't intended to be. You're getting paranoid."

"Yes, Doctor. Shall I stretch out on this convenient couch and tell you a dream?"

"I can think of better uses for a couch."

"Not now," she said quickly.

"No. Not now." But in the darkest part of our transaction we had reached a point of intimacy, understanding at least. "I'm sorry I have to drag all this stuff out."

"I know. I know that much about you. I also know you haven't finished."

"Who took the picture? Otto Sipe?"

"He was there. I heard his voice."

"You didn't see him?"

"I hid my face," she said. "A flashbulb popped. It was like reality exploding." She passed her hand over her eyes. "I think it was another man in the doorway who took the picture."

"Harold Harley?"

"It may have been. I didn't see him."

"What was the date?"

"It's in my memory book. April 14, 1945. Why does it matter?"

"Because you can't explode reality. Life hangs together in one piece. Everything is connected with everything else. The problem is to find the connections."

She said with some irony: "That's your mission in life, isn't it? You're not interested in people, you're only interested in the connections between them. Like a—" she searched for an insulting word—"a plumber."

I laughed at her. She smiled a little. Her eyes remained somber.

"There's another connection we have to go into," I said. "This one involves the telephone, not the plumbing."

"You mean Ralph's call the other day."

"Yes. He wanted you to keep quiet about something. What was it?"

She squirmed a little, and gathered her feet under her. "I don't want to get him into trouble. I owe him that much."

"Spare me the warmed-over sentiment. This is for real."

"You needn't sound so insulting."

"I apologize. Now let's have it."

"Well, he knew you had seen me, and he said we had to keep our stories straight. It seems there was a discrepancy in the story he told you. He told you he hadn't met Carol, but actually he had. After Mike Harley was arrested, she made an appeal to him and he did what he could. I wasn't to tell you about his interest in Carol."

"He was interested in Carol?"

"Not in the way you mean," she said with a lift of her head. "I was his girl. He simply didn't like the idea of leaving a child bride like Carol alone in the Barcelona Hotel. He asked me to take her under my wing. My slightly broken wing. Which I did, as you know."

"It all sounds very innocent."

"It was. I swear it. Besides, I liked Carol. I loved her, that summer in Burbank. I felt as if the baby in her womb belonged to both of us."

"Have you ever had a child?"

She shook her head rather sadly. "I never will have now. I was sure I was pregnant once, that very spring we've been talking about, but the doctor said it was false, caused by wishful thinking."

"Was Carol seeing a doctor when she lived with you?"

"Yes, I made her go. She went to the same doctor, actually. Weintraub, his name was."

"Did he deliver her baby?"

"I wouldn't know. She'd already left me, remember, and gone off with Mike Harley. And I didn't go back to Dr. Weintraub on account of the unpleasant associations."

"Was he unpleasant to you?"

"I mean the association with Ralph Hillman. Ralph sent me to Dr. Weintraub. I think they were buddies in the Navy."

Dr. Weintraub's plump face came into my mind. At the same time I remembered where I had seen a younger version of it, stripped of excess flesh, that very day. Weintraub was a member of the group on the flight deck, in the picture hanging on Hillman's library wall.

"It's funny," Susanna was saying, "how a name you haven't heard for seventeen or eighteen years will crop up, and then a couple of hours or a couple of days later, it will crop up again. Like Weintraub."

"Has the name been cropping up in other contexts?"

"Just this afternoon at the office. I had a rather peculiar caller whom I meant to tell you about, but all these other matters pushed him out of my mind. He was interested in Dr. Weintraub, too."

"Who was he?"

"He didn't want to say. When I pressed him, he said his name was Jackman."

"Sam Jackman?"

"He didn't mention his first name."

"Sam Jackman is a middle-aged Negro with very light skin who looks and talks like a jazz musician on his uppers, which he is."

"This boy seemed to be on his uppers, all right, but he certainly isn't Sam. Maybe he's Sam's son. He can't be more than eighteen or nineteen."

"Describe him."

"Thin-faced, very good features, very intense dark eyes, so intense he scared me a little. He seemed intelligent, but he was too excited to make much sense."

"What was he excited about?" I said with a mounting excitement of my own.

"Carol's death, I think. He didn't refer to it directly, but he asked me if I had known Carol in 1945. Apparently he'd been all the way out to Burbank trying to find me. He came across an old secretary at Warner's whom I still keep in touch with, and used her name to get past my secretary. He wanted to know what I could tell him about the Harley baby, and when I couldn't tell him anything he asked me what doctor

Carol had gone to. I dredged up Weintraub's name—Elijah Weintraub isn't exactly a forgettable name—and it satisfied him. I was quite relieved to get rid of him."

"I'm sorry you did."

She looked at me curiously. "Do you suppose he could be the Harley baby himself?"

I didn't answer her. I got out my collection of photographs and shuffled them. There was an electric tremor in my hands, as if time was short-circuiting through me.

Susanna whispered fearfully: "He isn't dead, is he, Lew? I couldn't bear to look at another dead picture."

"He's alive. At least, I hope he is."

I showed her Tom Hillman's face. She said: "That's the boy I talked to. But he's very much the worse for wear now. *Is* he the Harley baby?"

"I think so. He's also the baby that Ralph and Elaine Hillman adopted through Dr. Weintraub. Did you get the impression that he was on his way to see Weintraub?"

"Yes. I did." She was getting excited, too. "It's like an ancient identity myth. He's searching for his lost parentage."

"The hell of it is, both of his parents are dead. What time did you see him?"

"Around four o'clock."

It was nearly six now. I went to the phone and called Weintraub's office. His answering service said it was closed for the night. The switchboard girl wouldn't give me Weintraub's home address or his unlisted number, and neither would the manager of the answering service. I had to settle for leaving my name and Susanna's number and waiting for Weintraub to call me, if he was willing.

An hour went by. Susanna broiled me a steak, and chewed unhungrily on a piece of it. We sat at a marble table in the patio and she told me all about identity myths and how they grew. Oedipus. Hamlet. Stephen Dedalus. Her father had taught courses in such subjects. It passed the time, but it didn't relieve my anxiety for the boy. Hamlet came to a bloody end. Oedipus killed his father and married his mother, and then blinded himself.

"Thomas Harley," I said aloud. "Thomas Harley Hillman Jackman. He knew he wasn't the Hillmans' son. He thought he was a changeling."

"You get that in the myths, too."

"I'm talking about real life. He turned on his foster parents and went for his real parents. It's too bloody bad they had to be the Harleys."

"You're very certain that he is the Harley child."

"It fits in with everything I know about him. Incidentally, it explains why Ralph Hillman tried to hush up the fact that he'd taken an interest in Carol. He didn't want the facts of the adoption to come out."

"Why, though?"

"He's kept it a secret all these years, even from Tom. He seems to be a little crazy on the subject."

"I got that impression this morning." She leaned across the corner of the table and touched my fingers. "Lew? You don't think he went off his rocker and murdered Carol himself?"

"It's a possibility, but a remote one. What was on his mind at breakfast?"

"Him, mostly. He felt his life was collapsing around his ears. He thought I might be interested in helping him to pick up the pieces. After eighteen years he was offering me my second big break." Her scorn touched herself as well as Hillman.

"I don't quite understand."

"He asked me to marry him, Lew. I suppose that's in line with contemporary *mores*. You get your future set up ahead of time, before you terminate your present marriage."

"I don't like that word 'terminate.' Did he say what he intended to do with Elaine?"

"No." She looked quite pale and haunted.

"I hope divorce was all he had in mind. What was your answer?"

"My answer?"

"Your response to his proposal."

"Oh. I told him I was waiting for a better offer."

Her dark meaningful eyes were on my face. I sat there trying to frame a balanced answer. The telephone rang inside before I had a chance to deliver it.

I went in through the door we had left open and picked up the receiver. "Archer speaking."

"This is Dr. Weintraub." His voice had lost its calmness. "I've just had a thoroughly upsetting experience—"

"Have you seen the Hillman boy?"

"Yes. He came to me just as I was leaving. He asked me essentially the same question you did."

"What did you tell him, Doctor?"

"I told him the truth. He already knew it, anyway. He wanted to know if Mike and Carol Harley were his parents. They were."

"How did he react to the information?"

"Violently, I'm afraid. He hit me and broke my glasses. I'm practically blind without them. He got away from me."

"Have you told the police?"

"No."

"Tell them, now. And tell them who he is."

"But his father—his adoptive father wouldn't want me—"

"I know how it is when you're dealing with an old commander, Doctor. He was your commander at one time, wasn't he?"

"Yes. I was his flight surgeon."

"You aren't any more, and you can't let Hillman do your thinking for you. Do you tell the police, or do I?"

"I will. I realize we can't let the boy run loose in his condition."

"Just what is his condition?"

"He's very upset and, as I said, violently acting out."

With his heredity, I thought, that was hardly surprising.

24

I kissed Susanna goodbye and drove down Wilshire through Westwood. I wanted to be at the Santa Monica bus station at nine, just in case Tom showed up, but there was still time for another crack at Ben Daly. I turned down San Vicente toward the coastal highway.

The sun was half down on the horizon, bleeding color into the sea and the sky. Even the front of the Barcelona Hotel was touched with factitious Mediterranean pink. The crowd of onlookers in the driveway had changed and dwindled. There were still a few waiting for something more interesting than their lives to happen.

It was a warm night, and most of them were in beach costume. One man was dressed formally in a dark gray business suit and dark gray felt hat. He looked familiar.

I pulled up the drive on impulse and got out. The man in the dark gray suit was Harold Harley. He was wearing a black tie, which Lila had doubtless chosen for him, and a woebegone expression.

It deepened when he saw me. "Mr. Archer?"

"You can't have forgotten me, Harold."

"No. It's just that everything looks different, even people's faces. Or that hotel there. It's just a caved-in old dump, and I used to think it was a pretty ritzy place. Even the sky looks different." He raised his eyes to the red-streaked sky. "It looks hand-tinted, phony, like there was nothing behind it."

The little man talked like an artist. He might have become one, I thought, with a different childhood.

"I didn't realize you were so fond of your brother."

"Neither did I. But it isn't just that. I hate California. Nothing really good ever happened to me here in California. Or Mike either. " He gestured vaguely toward the cluster of official cars. "I wisht I was back in Idaho."

I drew him away from the little group of onlookers, from the women in slacks and halters which their flesh overflowed, the younger girls with haystacks of hair slipping down their foreheads into their blue-shadowed eyes, the tanned alert-looking boys with bleached heads and bleached futures. We stood under a magnolia tree that needed water.

"What happened to your brother started in Idaho, Harold." And also what happened to you, or failed to happen.

"You think I don't know that? The old man always said Mike would die on the gallows. Anyway, he cheated the gallows."

"I talked to your father yesterday."

Harold started violently, and glanced behind him. "Is he in town?"

"I was in Pocatello yesterday."

He looked both relieved and anxious. "How is he?"

"Much the same, I gather. You didn't tell me he was one step ahead of the butterfly nets."

"You didn't ask me. Anyway, he isn't like that all the time."

"But he had to be committed more than once."

"Yeah." He hung his head. In the final glare of day I could see the old closet dust in the groove of his hat, and the new sweat staining the hatband.

"It's nothing to blame yourself for," I said. "It explains a lot about Mike."

"I know. The old man was a terror when Mike was a kid. Maw finally had him committed for what he did to Mike and her. Mike left home and never came back, and who could blame him?"

"But you stayed."

"For a while. I had a trick of pretending I was some place else, like here in California. I finally came out here and went to photography school."

I returned to the question that interested me. It was really a series of questions about the interlinked lives that brought Mike Harley and Carol Brown from their beginnings in Idaho to their ends in California. Their beginnings and ends had become clear enough. The middle still puzzled me, as well as the ultimate end that lay ahead in darkness.

"I talked to Carol's parents, too," I said. "Carol was there earlier in the summer, and she left a suitcase in her room. A letter in it explained to me why you blamed yourself for the Hillman extortion."

"You saw my letter, eh? I should never have written a letter like that to Mike. I should have known better." He was hanging his head again.

"It's hard to see ahead and figure what the little things we do will lead to. And you weren't intending to suggest anything wrong."

"Gosh, no."

"Anyway, your letter helped me. It led me back here to Otto Sipe, and I hope eventually to the Hillman boy. The boy was holed up here with Sipe from Monday morning till Wednesday night, last night."

"No kidding."

"How well did you know Otto Sipe?"

Harold winced away from the question. If he could, he would have disappeared entirely, leaving his dark business suit and black tie and dusty hat suspended between the crisp brown grass and the dry leaves of the magnolia. He said in a voice that didn't want to be heard:

"He was Mike's friend. I got to know him that way. He trained Mike for a boxing career."

"What kind of a career did he train you for, Harold?"

"Me?"

"You. Didn't Sipe get you the job as hotel photographer here?"

"On account of—I was Mike's brother."

"I'm sure that had something to do with it. But didn't Sipe want you to help him with his sideline?"

"What sideline was that?"

"Blackmail."

He shook his head so vehemently that his hat almost fell off. "I never had any part of the rake-off, honest. He paid me standard rates to take those pictures, a measly buck a throw, and if I didn't do it I'd lose my job. I quit anyway, as soon as I had the chance. It was a dirty business." He peered up the driveway at the bland decaying face of the hotel. It was stark white now in the twilight. "I never took any benefit from it. I never even knew who the people were."

"Not even once?"

"I don't know what you mean."

"Didn't you take a picture of Captain Hillman and his girl?"

His face was pale and wet. "I don't know. I never knew their names."

"Last spring at Newport you recognized Hillman."

"Sure, he was the exec of Mike's ship. I met him when I went aboard that time."

"And no other time?"

"No sir."

"When were you and Mike arrested? In the spring of 1945?"

He nodded. "The fifth of March. I'm not likely to forget it. It was the only time I ever got arrested. After they let me go I never came back here. Until now." He looked around at the place as if it had betrayed him a second time.

"If you're telling the truth about the date, you didn't take the picture I'm interested in. It was taken in April."

"I'm not lying. By that time Otto Sipe had another boy."

"What gave him so much power around the hotel?"

"I think he had something on the management. He hushed up something for them, long ago, something about a movie star who stayed here."

"Was Mike staying here at the time he was picked up?"

"Yeah. I let him and Carol use my room, the one that went with the job. I slept in the employees' dormitory. I think Otto Sipe let Carol stay on in the room for a while after me and Mike were arrested."

"Was it the room next door to his, at the end of the corridor?"

"Yeah."

"Did it have a brass bed in it?"

"Yeah. Why?"

"I was just wondering. They haven't changed the furnishings since the war. That interconnecting bathroom would have been handy for Sipe, if he liked Carol."

He shook his head. "Not him. He had no use for women. And Carol had no use for him. She got out of there as soon as she could make other arrangements. She went to live with a woman friend in Burbank."

"Susanna."

Harold blinked. "Yeah. That was her name, Susanna. I never met her, but she must have been a nice person."

"What kind of a girl was Carol?"

"Carol? She was a beauty. When a girl has her looks, you don't think much about going deeper. I mean, there she *was*. I always thought she was an innocent young girl. But Lila says you could fill a book with what I don't know about women."

I looked at my watch. It was past eight, and Harold had probably taken me as far as he could. Partly to make sure of this, I asked him to come across the highway and see his old acquaintance, Ben Daly. He didn't hang back.

Daly scowled at us from the doorway of his lighted office. Then he recognized Harold, and his brow cleared. He came out and shook hands with him, disregarding me.

"Long time no see, Har."

"You can say that again."

They talked to each other across a distance of years, with some warmth and without embarrassment. There was no sign of guilty involvement between them. It didn't follow necessarily, but I pretty well gave up on the idea that either of them was involved in any way with the recent crimes.

I broke in on their conversation: "Will you give me one minute, Ben?

You may be able to help me solve that murder."

"How? By killing somebody else?"

"By making another identification, if you can." I brought out Dick Leandro's picture and forced it into his hand. "Have you ever seen this man?"

He studied the picture for a minute. His hand was unsteady. "I may have. I'm not sure."

"When?"

"Last night. He may be the one who came to the hotel last night."

"The one with the girl, in the new blue Chevvy?"

"Yeah. He could be the one. But I wouldn't want to swear to it in court."

25

The Santa Monica bus station is on a side street off lower Wilshire. At a quarter to nine I left my car at the curb and went in. Stella, that incredible child, was there. She was sitting at the lunch counter at the rear in a position from which she could watch all the doors.

She saw me, of course, and swung around to hide her face in a cup of coffee. I sat beside her. She put down her cup with an impatient rap. The coffee in it looked cold, and had a grayish film on it.

She spoke without looking directly at me, like somebody in a spy movie. "Go away. You'll frighten Tommy off."

"He doesn't know me."

"But I'm supposed to be alone. Besides, you look like a policeman or something."

"Why is Tommy allergic to policemen?"

"You would be, too, if they locked you up the way they locked him up."

"If you keep running away, they'll be locking you up, Stella."

"They're not going to get the chance," she said, with a sharp sideways glance at me. "My father took me to a psychiatrist today, to see if I needed to be sent to Laguna Perdida. I told her everything, just as I've told you. She said there was nothing the matter with me at all. So when my father went in to talk to her I walked out the front door and took a taxi to the bus station, and there was a bus just leaving."

"I'm going to have to drive you home again."

She said in a very young voice: "Don't teen-agers have any rights?"

"Yes, including the right to adult protection."

"I won't go without Tommy!"

Her voice rose and broke on his name. Half the people in the small station were looking at us. The woman behind the lunch counter came over to Stella.

"Is he bothering you, miss?"

She shook her head. "He's a very good friend."

This only deepened the woman's suspicions, but it silenced her. I ordered a cup of coffee. When she went to draw it, I said to Stella:

"I won't go without Tommy, either. What did your psychiatrist friend think about him, by the way?"

"She didn't tell me. Why?"

"I was just wondering."

The waitress brought my coffee. I carried it to the far end of the counter and drank it slowly. It was eight minutes to nine. People were lining up at the loading door, which meant that a bus was expected.

I went out the front, and almost walked into Tommy. He had on slacks and a dirty white shirt. His face was a dirty white, except where a fuzz of beard showed.

"Excuse me, sir," he said, and stepped around me.

I didn't want to let him get inside, where taking him would create a public scene that would bring in the police. I needed a chance to talk to him before anyone else did. There wasn't much use in trying to persuade him to come with me. He was lean and quick and could certainly outrun me.

These thoughts went through my head in the second before he reached the door of the station. I put both arms around his waist from behind, lifted him off his feet, and carried him wildly struggling to my car. I pushed him into the front seat and got in beside him. Other cars were going by in the road, but nobody stopped to ask me any questions. They never do any more.

Tom let out a single dry sob or whimper, high in his nose. He must have known that this was the end of running.

"My name is Lew Archer," I said. "I'm a private detective employed by your father."

"He isn't my father."

"An adoptive father is a father, too."

"Not to me he isn't. I don't want any part of Captain Hillman," he said with the cold distance of injured youth. "Or you either."

I noticed a cut on the knuckle of his right hand. It had been bleeding. He put the knuckle in his mouth and sucked it, looking at me over it. It was hard to take him seriously at that moment. But he was a very serious young man.

"I'm not going back to my cruddy so-called parents."

"You have nobody else."

"I have myself."

"You haven't been handling yourself too well."

"Another lecture."

"I'm pointing out a fact. If you could look after yourself decently, you might make out a case for independence. But you've been rampaging around clobbering middle-aged doctors—"

"He tried to make me go home."

"You're going home. The alternative seems to be a life with bums and criminals."

"You're talking about my parents, my real parents." He spoke with conscious drama, but there was also a kind of bitter awe in his voice. "My mother wasn't a bum and she wasn't a criminal. She was—nice."

"I didn't mean her."

"And my father wasn't so bad, either," he said without conviction.

"Who killed them, Tom?"

His face became blank and tight. It looked like a wooden mask used to fend off suffering.

"I don't know anything about it," he said in a monotone. "I didn't know Carol was dead, even, till I saw the papers last night. I didn't know Mike was dead till I saw the papers today. Next question."

"Don't be like that, Tom. I'm not a cop, and I'm not your enemy."

"With the so-called parents I've got, who needs enemies? All my—all Captain Hillman ever wanted was a pet boy around the house, somebody to do tricks. I'm tired of doing tricks for him."

"You *should* be tired, after this last trick. It was a honey of a trick."

He gave me his first direct look, half in anger and half in fear. "I had a right to go with my real parents."

"Maybe. We won't argue about that. But you certainly had no right to help them extort money from your father."

"He's not my father."

"I know that. Do you have to keep saying it?"

"Do you have to keep calling him my father?"

He was a difficult boy. I felt good, anyway. I had him.

"Okay," I said. "We'll call him Mr. X and we'll call your mother Madam X and we'll call you the Lost Dauphin of France."

"That isn't so funny."

He was right. It wasn't.

"Getting back to the twenty-five thousand dollars you helped to take them for, I suppose you know you're an accomplice in a major felony."

"I didn't know about the money. They didn't tell me. I don't think Carol knew about it, either."

"That's hard to believe, Tom."

"It's true. Mike didn't tell us. He just said he had a deal cooking."

"If you didn't know about the extortion, why did you ride away in the trunk of his car?"

"So I wouldn't be seen. Mike said my dad—" he swallowed the word, with disgust—"he said that Captain Hillman had all the police looking for me, to put me back in Laguna—"

He became aware of his present situation. He peered around furtively, scrambled under the wheel to the far door. I pulled him back into the middle of the seat and put an armlock on him.

"You're staying with me, Tom, if I have to use handcuffs."

"Fuzz!"

The jeering word came strangely from him, like a foreign word he was trying to make his own. It bothered me. Boys, like men, have to belong to something. Tom had felt betrayed by one world, the plush deceptive world of Ralph Hillman, with schools like Laguna Perdida on the underside of the weave. He had plunged blindly into another world, and now he had lost that. His mind must be desperate for a place to rest, I thought, and I wasn't doing much of a job of providing one.

A bus came down the street. As it turned into the loading area, I caught a glimpse of passengers at the windows, travel-drugged and blasé. California here we come, right back where we started from.

I relaxed my grip on Tom. "I couldn't let you go," I said, "even if I wanted to. You're not stupid. Try for once to figure out how this looks to other people."

"This?"

"The whole charade. Your running away from school—for which I certainly don't blame you—"

"Thanks a lot."

I disregarded his irony. "And the phony kidnapping and all the rest of it. An adopted son is just as important as a real one to his parents. Yours have been worried sick about you."

"I bet."

"Neither one of them gave a damn about the money, incidentally. It's you they cared about, and care about."

"There's something missing," he said.

"What?"

"The violin accompaniment."

"You're a hard boy to talk to, Tom."

"My *friends* don't think so."

"What's a friend? Somebody who lets you run wild?"

"Somebody who doesn't want to throw me into the Black Hole of Calcutta, otherwise known as Laguna Perdida School."

"I don't."

"You say you don't. But you're working for Captain Hillman, and he does."

"Not any more."

The boy shook his head. "I don't believe you, and I don't believe him. After a few things *happen* to you, you start to believe what people do, not what they say. People like the Hillmans would think that a person like Carol was a nothing, a nothing woman. But she wasn't to me. She liked me. She treated me well. Even my real father never raised his hand to me. The only trouble we had was about the way he treated Carol."

He had dropped his brittle sardonic front and was talking to me in a human voice. Stella chose this moment to come out of the loading area onto the sidewalk. Her face was pinched with disappointment.

Tom caught sight of her almost as soon as I did. His eyes lit up as if she was an angel from some lost paradise. He leaned across me.

"Hey! Stell!"

She came running. I got out of the car and let her take my place beside the boy. They didn't embrace or kiss. Perhaps their hands met briefly. I got in behind the wheel.

Stella was saying: "It *feels* as though you've been gone for ages."

"It does to me, too."

"You should have called me sooner."

"I did."

"I mean, right away."

"I`was afraid you'd—do what you did." He jerked his chin in my direction.

"I didn't, though. Not really. It was his idea. Anyway, you have to go home. We both do."

"I have no home."

"Neither have I, then. Mine's just as bad as yours."

"No, it isn't."

"Yes, it is. Anyway," she said to clinch the argument, "you need a bath. I can smell you. And a shave."

I glanced at his face. It had a pleased, silly, embarrassed expression.

The street was empty of traffic at the moment. I started the car and made a U-turn toward the south. Tom offered no objection.

Once on the freeway, in that anonymous world of rushing lights and darkness, he began to talk in his human voice to Stella. Carol had phoned him, using his personal number, several weeks before. She wanted to arrange a meeting with him. That night, driving Ralph Hillman's Cadillac, he picked her up at the view-point overlooking the sea near Dack's Auto Court.

He parked in an orange grove that smelled of weddings and listened to the story of her life. Even though he'd often doubted that he belonged to the Hillmans, it was hard for him to believe that he was Carol's son. But he was strongly drawn to her. The relationship was like an escape hatch in Captain Hillman's tight little ship. He kept going back to Carol, and eventually he believed her. He even began to love her in a way.

"Why didn't you tell me about her?" Stella said. "I would have liked to know her."

"No, you wouldn't." His voice was rough. "Anyway, I had to get to know her myself first. I had to get adjusted to the whole idea of my mother. And then I had to decide what to do. You see, she wanted to leave my father. He gave her a hard time, he always had. She said if she didn't get away from him soon, she'd never be able to. She wasn't good at standing up for herself, and she wanted my help. Besides, I think she knew he was up to something."

"You mean the kidnapping and all?" she said.

"I think she knew it and she didn't know it. You know how women are."

"I know my mother," she answered sagely.

They had forgotten me. I was the friendly chauffeur, good old graying Lew Archer, and we would go on driving like this forever through a night so dangerous that it had to feel secure. I remembered a kind of poem or parable that Susanna had quoted to me years before. A bird came in through a window at one end of a lighted hall, flew the length of the hall, and out through another window into darkness: that was the span of a human life. The headlights that rose in the distance and swooped by and fell away behind us reminded me of Susanna's briefly lighted bird. I wished that she was with me.

Tom was telling Stella how he first met his father. Mike had been kept in the background the first week; he was supposed to be in Los Angeles looking for work. Finally, on the Saturday night, Tom met him at the auto court.

"That was the night you borrowed our car, wasn't it?"

"Yeah. My fa—Ralph had me grounded, you know. Carol spilled some wine on the front seat of the car and he smelled it. He thought I was driving and drinking."

"Did Carol drink much?"

"Quite a bit. She drank a lot that Saturday night. So did he. I had some wine, too."

"You're not old enough."

"It was with dinner," he said. "Carol cooked spaghetti. Spaghetti à la Pocatello, she called it. She sang some of the old songs for me, like 'Sentimental Journey.' It was kind of fun," he said doubtfully.

"Is that why you didn't come home?"

"No. I—" The word caught in his throat. "I—" His face, which I could

see in the rear-view mirror, became contorted with effort. He couldn't
finish the sentence.

"Did you want to stay with them?" Stella said after a while.

"No. I don't know."

"How did you like your father?"

"He was all right, I guess, until he got drunk. We played some gin
rummy and he didn't win, so he broke up the game. He started to take
it out on Carol. I almost had a fight with him. He said he used to be a
boxer and I'd be crazy to try it, that his fists could kill."

"It sounds like a terrible evening."

"That part of it wasn't so good."

"What part of it was?"

"When she sang the old songs. And she told me about my grandfather
in Pocatello."

"Did that take all night?" she said a little tartly.

"I didn't *stay* with them all night. I left around ten o'clock, when
we almost had the fight. I—" The same word stuck in his throat again,
as if it was involved with secret meanings that wouldn't let it be spoken.

"What did you do?"

"I went and parked on the view-point where I picked her up the first
time. I sat there until nearly two o'clock, watching the stars and listening,
you know, to the sea. The sea and the highway. I was trying to figure out
what I should do, where I belonged. I still haven't got it figured out." He
added, in a voice that was conscious of me: "Now I guess I don't have any
choice. They'll put me back in the Black Hole of Calcutta."

"Me too," she said with a nervous giggle. "We can send each other
secret notes. Tap out messages on the bars and stuff."

"It isn't funny, Stell. Everybody out there is crazy, even some of the
staff. They get that way."

"You're changing the subject," she said. "What did you do at two
A.M.?"

"I went to see Sam Jackman when he got off work. I thought I could
ask him what to do, but I found out that I couldn't. I just couldn't tell him
that they were my parents. So I went out in the country and drove
around for a few hours. I didn't want to go home, and I didn't want to
go back to the auto court."

"So you turned the car over and tried to kill yourself."

"I—" Silence set in again, and this time it lasted. He sat bolt upright,
staring ahead, watching the headlights rise out of the darkness. After a
time I noticed that Stella's arm was across his shoulders. His face was
streaked with tears.

26

I dropped Stella off first. She refused to get out of the car until Tom promised that he wouldn't go away again, ever, without telling her.

Her father came out of the house, walking on his heels. He put his arms around her. With a kind of resigned affection, she laid her head neatly against his shoulder. Maybe they had learned something, or were learning. People sometimes do.

They went inside, and I turned down the driveway.

"He's just a fake," Tom said. "Stella lent me the car, and then he turned around and told the police I stole it."

"I believe he thought so at the time."

"But he found out the truth later, from Stella, and went right on claiming I stole it."

"Dishonesty keeps creeping in," I said. "We all have to watch it."

He thought this over, and decided that I had insulted him. "Is that supposed to be a crack at me?"

"No. I think you're honest, so far as you understand what you're talking about. But you only see one side, your own, and it seems to consist mainly of grievances."

"I have a lot of them," he admitted. After a moment he said: "You're wrong about me only seeing one side, though. I know how my—my adoptive parents are supposed to feel, but I know how I feel, too. I can't go on being split down the middle. That's how I felt, you know, these last few nights, like somebody took a cleaver and split me down the middle. I lay awake on that old brass bed, where Mike and Carol, you know, conceived me—with old Sipe snoring in the other room, and I was there and I wasn't there. You know? I mean I couldn't believe that I was me and this was my life and those people were my parents. I never believed the Hillmans were, either. They always seemed to be putting on an act. Maybe," he said half-seriously, "I was dropped from another planet."

"You've been reading too much science fiction."

"I don't *really* believe that. I *know* who my parents were. Carol told me. Mike told me. The doctor told me, and that made it official. But I still have a hard time telling my*self.*"

"Stop trying to force it. It doesn't matter so much who your parents were."

"It does to me," he said earnestly. "It's the most important thing in my life."

We were approaching the Hillmans' mailbox. I had been driving slowly, immersed in the conversation, and now I pulled into the driveway and stopped entirely.

"I sometimes think children should be anonymous."

"How do you mean, Mr. Archer?" It was the first time he had called me by my name.

"I have no plan. I'd just like to change the emphasis slightly. People are trying so hard to live through their children. And the children keep trying so hard to live up to their parents, or live them down. Everybody's living through or for or against somebody else. It doesn't make too much sense, and it isn't working too well."

I was trying to free his mind a little, before he had to face the next big change. I didn't succeed. "It doesn't work when they lie to you," he said. "They lied to me. They pretended I was their own flesh and blood. I thought there was something missing in me when I couldn't feel like their son."

"I've talked to your mother about this—Elaine—and she bitterly regrets it."

"I bet."

"Let's not get off on that routine, Tom."

He was silent for a while. "I suppose I have to go and talk to them, but I don't want to live with them, and I'm not going to put on any phony feelings."

No phoniness, I thought, was the code of the new generation, at least the ones who were worth anything. It was a fairly decent ideal, but it sometimes worked out cruelly in practice.

"You can't forgive them for Laguna Perdida."

"Could you?"

I had to think about my answer. "It would depend on their reasons. I imagine some pretty desperate parents end up there as a last resort with some pretty wild sons and daughters."

"They're desperate, all right," he said. "Ralph and Elaine get desperate very easily. They can't stand trouble. Sweep it under the rug. All they wanted to do was get me out of sight, when I stopped being their performing boy. And I had all these terrible things on my mind." He put his hands to his head, to calm the terrible things. He was close to breaking down.

"I'm sorry, Tom. But didn't something crucial happen that Sunday morning?"

He peered at me under his raised arm. "They told you, eh?"

"No. I'm asking you to tell me."

"Ask them."

It was all he would say.

I drove up the winding blacktop lane to the top of the knoll. Lights were blazing outside and inside the house. The harsh white floods made the stucco walls look ugly and unreal. Black shadows lurked under the melodramatic Moorish arches.

There was something a little melodramatic in the way Ralph Hillman stepped out from one of the arches into the light. He wasn't the wreck Susanna had described, at least not superficially. His handsome silver head was sleekly brushed. His face was tightly composed. He held himself erect, and even trotted a few steps as he came toward my side of the car. He was wearing a wine-colored jacket with a rolled collar.

"Prodigal son returneth," Tom was saying beside me in scared bravado. "But they didn't kill the fatted calf, they killed the prodigal son."

Hillman said: "I thought you were Lieutenant Bastian."

"Are you expecting him?"

"Yes. He says he has something to show me."

He stooped to look in the window and saw Tom. His eyes dilated.

"My boy!" His hoarse, whisky-laden voice hardly dared to believe what it was saying. "You've come back."

"Yeah. I'm here."

Hillman trotted around to the other side of the car and opened the door. "Come out and let me look at you."

With a brief, noncommittal glance in my direction, Tom climbed out. His movements were stiff and tentative, like a much older man's. Hillman put his hands on the boy's shoulders and held him at arm's length, turning him so that his face was in the light.

"How *are* you, Tom?"

"I'm okay. How are you?"

"Wonderful, now that you're here." I didn't doubt that Hillman's feeling was sincere, but his expression of it was somehow wrong. Phony. And I could see Tom wince under his hands.

Elaine Hillman came out of the house. I went to meet her. The floodlights multiplied the lines in her face and leached it of any color it might have had. She was pared so thin that she reminded me vaguely of concentration camps. Her eyes were brilliantly alive.

"You've brought him back, Mr. Archer. Bless you."

She slipped her hand through my arm and let me take her to him. He stood like a dutiful son while she stood on her toes and kissed him on his grimy tear-runneled cheek.

Then he backed away from both of them. He stood leaning against the side of my car with his thumbs in the waistband of his slacks. I'd seen a hundred boys standing as he was standing against cars both hot and cold, on the curb of a street or the shoulder of a highway, while men in uniform questioned them. The sound of the distant highway faintly disturbed the edges of the silence I was listening to now.

Tom said: "I don't want to hurt anybody. I never did. Or maybe I did, I don't know. Anyway, there's no use going on pretending. You see, I know who I am. Mike and Carol Harley were my father and mother. You knew it, too, didn't you?"

"I didn't," Elaine said quickly.

"But you knew *you* weren't my mother."

"Yes. Of course I knew that."

She glanced down at her body and then, almost wistfully, at her husband. He turned away from both of them. His face had momentarily come apart. He seemed to be in pain, which he wanted to hide.

"One of you must have known who I really was." Tom said to Hillman: "You knew, didn't you?"

Hillman didn't answer. Tom said in a high desperate voice: "I can't stay here. You're both a couple of phonies. You put on a big act for all these years, and as soon as I step out of line you give me the shaft."

Hillman found his voice. "I should think it was the other way around."

"Okay, so I did wrong. Stand me up against a wall and shoot me."

The boy's voice was slightly hysterical, but it wasn't that that bothered me so much. He seemed to be shifting from attitude to attitude, even from class to class, trying to find a place where he could stand. I went and stood beside him.

"Nobody's talking about punishing you," Hillman said. "But a homicidal attack is something that can't be laughed off."

"You're talking crap," the boy said.

Hillman's chin came up. "Don't *speak* to me like that!"

"Or what will you do? Lock me up with a bunch of psychos and throw away the key?"

"I didn't *say* that."

"No. You just went ahead and did it."

"Perhaps I acted hastily."

"Yes," Elaine put in. "Your father acted hastily. Now let's forget the whole thing and go inside and be friends."

"He isn't my father," Tom said stubbornly.

"But we can all be friends, anyway. Can't we, Tom?" Her voice and look were imploring. "Can't we forget the bad things and simply be glad they're over and that we're all together?"

"I don't know. I'd like to go away for a while and live by myself and think things through. What would be wrong with it? I'm old enough."

"That's nonsense." Hillman shouldn't have said it. A second later his eyes showed that he knew he shouldn't have. He stepped forward and put his hand on the boy's shoulder. "Maybe that isn't such a bad idea, after all. We're intelligent people, we ought to be able to work something out between us. There's the lodge in Oregon, for example, where you and I were planning to go next month. We could step up our schedule and synch our watches, eh?"

The performance was forced. Tom listened to it without interest or hope. After a bit Elaine put her hand inside her husband's arm and drew him toward the house. Tom and I followed along.

Mrs. Perez was waiting at the door. There was warmth in her greeting, and even some in Tom's response. They had a discussion about food. Tom said he would like a hamburger sandwich with pea soup. Mrs. Perez darted jouncily away.

Hillman surveyed the boy in the light of the chandelier. "You'd better go up and bathe and change your clothes."

"Now?"

"It's just a suggestion," Hillman said placatingly. "Lieutenant Bastian of the sheriff's department is on his way over. I'd like you—you should be looking more like yourself."

"Is he going to take me away? Is that the idea?"

"Not if I can help it," Hillman said. "Look, I'll come up with you."

"I can dress myself, Dad!" The word slipped out, irretrievable and undeniable.

"But we ought to go over what you're going to say to him. There's no use putting your neck in a noose—I mean—"

"I'll just tell him the truth."

The boy walked away from him toward the stairs. Ralph and Elaine Hillman followed him with their eyes until he was out of sight, and then they followed his footsteps with their ears. The difficult god of the household had returned and the household was functioning again, in its difficult way.

We went into the sitting room. Hillman continued across it into the bar alcove. He made himself a drink, absently, as if he was simply trying to find something to do with his hands and then with his mouth.

When he came out with the drink in his hand, he reminded me of an actor stepping out through a proscenium arch to join the audience.

"Ungrateful sons are like a serpent's tooth," he said, not very conversationally.

Elaine spoke up distinctly from the chesterfield: "If you're attempting to quote from *King Lear*, the correct quotation is: 'How sharper than a serpent's tooth it is to have a thankless child!' But it isn't terribly appropriate, since Tom is not your child. A more apt quotation from the same work would be Edmund's line, 'Now, gods, stand up for bastards!' "

He knocked back his drink and moved toward her, lurching just a little. "I resent your saying that."

"That's your privilege, and your habit."

"Tom is not a bastard. His parents were legally married."

"It hardly matters, considering their background. Did you and your precious Dr. Weintraub have to choose the offspring of criminals?"

Her voice was cold and bitter. She seemed, after years of silence, to be speaking out and striking back at him.

"Look," he said, "he's back. I'm glad he's back. You are, too. And we want him to stay with us, don't we?"

"I want what's best for him."

"I *know* what's best for him." He spread his arms, swinging them a little from side to side, as if he was making Tom a gift of the house and the life that went on inside it.

"You don't know what's best for anybody, Ralph. Having men under you, you got into the habit of thinking you knew. But you really don't. I'm interested in Mr. Archer's opinion. Come and sit here beside me," she said to me, "and tell me what you think."

"What exactly is the subject?" I said as I sat down.

"Tom. What kind of a future should we plan for him?"

"I don't think you can do it for him. Let him do his own planning."

Hillman said across the room: "But all he wants to do is go away by himself."

"I admit that isn't such a good idea. We should be able to persuade him to tone it down. Let him live with another family for a year. Or send him to prep school. After that, he'll be going away to college, anyway."

"Good Lord, do you think he'll make it to college?"

"Of course he will, Ralph." She turned to me. "But is he ready now for an ordinary prep school? Could he survive it?"

"He survived the last two weeks."

"Yes. We have to thank God for that. And you."

Hillman came and stood over me, shaking the ice in his glass. "Just what was the situation with those people? Was Tom in league with them against us? Understand me, I don't intend to punish him or do anything at all about it. I just want to know."

I answered him slowly and carefully. "You can hardly talk about a boy being in league with his mother and father. He was confused. He still is. He believed you had turned against him when you put him in Laguna Perdida School. You don't have to be a psychiatrist to know that that isn't the kind of school he needs."

"I'm afraid you aren't conversant with all the facts."

"What are they?"

He shook his head. "Go on with what you were saying. Was he in cahoots with those people?"

"Not in the way you mean. But they offered him an out, physically and emotionally, and he took it. Apparently his mother was kind to him."

"*I* was always kind to him," Elaine said. She shot a fierce upward glance at her husband. "But there was falsity in the house, undermining everything."

I said: "There was falseness in the other house, too, at Dack's Auto Court. There's no doubt that Mike Harley was conning him, setting him up for the phony kidnapping. He didn't let his paternal feelings interfere. Carol was another matter. If she was conning Tom, she was conning herself, too. Tom put it something like this: she knew Harley was up to something, but she didn't let herself know. You get that way after twenty years of living with a man like Harley."

Elaine nodded slightly. I think it was a comment on her own marriage. She said: "I'm worried about Tom's heredity, with such parents."

The blood rushed into Hillman's face. "For God's sake, that's really reaching for trouble."

"I hardly need to reach for it," she said quietly. "It's in my lap." She looked at him as if he had placed it there.

He turned and walked the length of the room, returned part way, and went into the bar. He poured more whisky over the ice in his glass, and drank it down. Elaine watched him with critical eyes, which he was aware of.

"It settles my nerves," he said.

"I hadn't noticed."

He looked at his watch and paced up and down the room. He lost his balance once and had to make a side step.

"Why doesn't Bastian come and get it over with?" he said. "It's getting late. I was expecting Dick tonight, but I guess he found something more interesting to do." He burst out at his wife: "This is a dismal household, you know that?"

"I've been aware of it for many years. I tried to keep it together for Tom's sake. That's rather funny, isn't it?"

"I don't see anything funny about it."

I didn't, either. The broken edges of their marriage were rubbing together like the unset ends of a bone that had been fractured but was still living.

Bastian arrived at last. He came into the reception hall carrying a black metal evidence case, and he was dark-faced and grim. Even the news that Tom was safe at home failed to cheer him much.

"Where is he?"

"Taking a bath," Hillman said.

"I've got to talk to him. I want a full statement."

"Not tonight, Lieutenant. The boy's been through the wringer."

"But he's the most important witness we have."

"I know that. He'll give you his full story tomorrow."

Bastian glanced from him to me. We were just inside the front door, and Hillman seemed unwilling to let him come in any farther.

"I expected better cooperation, Mr. Hillman. You've had cooperation from us. But come to think of it, we haven't had it from you at any time."

"Don't give me any lectures, Lieutenant. My son is home, and it wasn't thanks to you that we got him back."

"A lot of police work went into it," I said. "Lieutenant Bastian and I have been working closely together. We still are, I hope."

Hillman transferred his glare to me. He looked ready to order us both out. I said to Bastian:

"You've got something to show us, Lieutenant, is that right?"

"Yes." He held up his evidence case. "You've already seen it, Archer. I'm not sure if Mr. Hillman has or not."

"What is it?"

"I'll show you. I prefer not to describe it beforehand. Could we sit down at a table?"

Hillman led us to the library and seated us at a table with a green-shaded reading lamp in the middle, which he switched on. It lit up the tabletop brilliantly and cast the rest of the room, including our faces, into greenish shadow. Bastian opened the evidence box. It contained the hunting knife with the striped handle which I had found stuck in Mike Harley's ribs.

Hillman drew in his breath sharply.

"You recognize it, do you?" Bastian said.

"No. I do not."

"Pick it up and examine it more closely. It's quite all right to handle it. It's already been processed for fingerprints and blood."

Hillman didn't move. "Blood?"

"This is the knife that was used to kill Mike Harley. We're almost certain that it was also used to kill the other decedent, Carol Harley. Blood of her type was found on it, as well as her husband's type. Also it fits her wound, the autopsist tells me. Pick it up, Mr. Hillman."

In a gingerly movement Hillman reached out and took it from the box. He turned it over and read the maker's name on the broad shining blade.

"It looks like a good knife," he said. "But I'm afraid I don't recognize it."

"Would you say that under oath?"

"I'd have to. I never saw it before."

Bastian, with the air of a parent removing a dangerous toy, lifted the knife from his hands. "I don't want to say you're lying, Mr. Hillman. I do have a witness who contradicts you on this. Mr. Botkin, who owns the surplus goods store on lower Main, says that he sold you this knife." He shook the knife, point foremost, at Hillman's face.

Hillman looked scared and sick and obstinate. "It must have been somebody else. He must be mistaken."

"No. He knows you personally."

"I don't know him."

"You're a very well known man, sir, and Mr. Botkin is certain that you were in his store early this month. Perhaps I can refresh your recollection. You mentioned to Mr. Botkin, in connection with the purchase of this knife, that you were planning a little trip to Oregon with your son. You also complained to Botkin, as a lower Main Street businessman, about an alleged laxness at The Barroom Floor. It had to do with selling liquor to minors, I believe. Do you remember the conversation now?"

"No," Hillman said. "I do not. The man is lying."

"Why would he be lying?"

"I have no idea. Go and find out. It's not my job to do your police work for you."

He stood up, dismissing Bastian. Bastian was unwilling to be dismissed. "I don't think you're well advised to take this attitude, Mr. Hillman. If you purchased this knife from Mr. Botkin, now is the time to say so. Your previous denial need never go out of this room."

Bastian looked to me for support. I remembered what Botkin had said to me about The Barroom Floor. It was practically certain that his conversation with Hillman had taken place. It didn't follow necessarily that Hillman had bought the knife, but he probably had.

I said: "It's time all the facts were laid out on the table, Mr. Hillman."

"I can't tell him what isn't so, can I?"

"No. I wouldn't advise that. Have you thought of talking this over with your attorney?"

"I'm thinking about it now." Hillman had sobered. Droplets of clear liquid stood on his forehead as if the press of the situation had squeezed the alcohol out of him. He said to Bastian: "I gather you're more or less accusing me of murder."

"No, I am not." Bastian added in a formal tone: "You can, of course, stand on your constitutional rights."

Hillman shook his head angrily. Some of his fine light hair fell over his forehead. Under it his eyes glittered like metal triangles. He was an extraordinarily handsome man. His unremitting knowledge of this showed in the caressive movement of the hand with which he pushed his hair back into place.

"Look," he said, "could we continue this séance in the morning? I've had a hard week, and I'd like a chance to sleep on this business. I've had no real sleep since Monday."

"Neither have I," Bastian said.

"Maybe you need some sleep, too. This harassing approach isn't really such a good idea."

"There was no harassment."

"I'll be the judge of that." Hillman's voice rose. "You brought that knife into my home and shook it in my face. I have a witness to that," he added, meaning me.

I said: "Let's not get bogged down in petty arguments. Lieutenant Bastian and I have some business to discuss."

"Anything you say to him you'll have to say in front of me."

"All right."

"After I talk to the boy," Bastian said.

Hillman made a curt gesture with his hand. "You're not talking to him. I don't believe I'll let you talk to him tomorrow, either. There are, after all, medical considerations."

"Are you a medical man?"

"I have medical men at my disposal."

"I'm sure you do. So do we."

The two men faced each other in quiet fury. They were opposites in many ways. Bastian was a saturnine Puritan, absolutely honest, a stickler for detail, a policeman before he was a man. Hillman's personality was less clear. It had romantic and actorish elements, which often mask deep evasions. His career had been meteoric, but it was the kind of career that sometimes left a man empty-handed in middle life.

"Do you have something to say to the lieutenant?" Hillman asked me. "Before he leaves?"

"Yes. You may not like this, Mr. Hillman. I don't. Last night a young man driving a late-model blue Chevrolet was seen in the driveway of the Barcelona Hotel. It's where Mike Harley was found stabbed, with that knife." I pointed to the evidence box on the table. "The young man has been tentatively identified as Dick Leandro."

"Who made the identification?" Bastian said.

"Ben Daly, the service-station operator."

"The man who killed Sipe."

"Yes."

"He's either mistaken or lying," Hillman said. "Dick drives a blue car, but it's a small sports car, a Triumph."

"Does he have access to a blue Chevrolet?"

"Not to my knowledge. You're surely not trying to involve Dick in this mess."

"If he's involved, we have to know about it." I said to Bastian: "Maybe you can determine whether he borrowed or rented a blue Chevrolet last night. Or it's barely possible that he stole one."

"Will do," Bastian said.

Hillman said nothing.

27

Bastian picked up his evidence case and shut it with a click. He walked out without a sign to either of us. He was treating Hillman as if he no longer existed. He was treating me in such a way that I could stay with Hillman.

Hillman watched him from the entrance to the library until he was safely across the reception hall and out the front door. Then he came back into the room. Instead of returning to the table where I was, he went to the wall of photographs where the squadron on the flight deck hung in green deep-sea light.

"What goes on around here?" he said. "Somebody took down Dick's picture."

"I did, for identification purposes."

I got it out of my pocket. Hillman came and took it away from me. The glass was smudged by fingers, and he rubbed it with the sleeve of his jacket.

"You had no right to take it. What are you trying to do to Dick, anyway?"

"Get at the truth about him."

"There *is* no mysterious truth about him. He's a perfectly nice ordinary kid."

"I hope so."

"Look here," he said, "you've accomplished what I hired you to do. Don't think I'm ungrateful—I'm planning to give you a substantial bonus. But I didn't hire you to investigate those murders."

"And I don't get the bonus unless I stop?"

"I didn't say that."

"You didn't have to."

He spread his hands on the table and leaned above me, heavy-faced and powerful. "Just how do you get to talk to your betters the way you've been talking to me?"

"By my betters you mean people with more money?"

"Roughly, yes."

"I'll tell you, Mr. Hillman. I rather like you. I'm trying to talk straight to you because somebody has to. You're headed on a collision course with the law. If you stay on it, you're going to get hurt."

His face stiffened and his eyes narrowed. He didn't like to be told anything. He liked to do the telling.

"I could buy and sell Bastian."

"You can't if he's not for sale. You know damn well he isn't."

He straightened, raising his head out of the light into the greenish shadow. His face resembled old bronze, except that it was working. After a time he said:

"What do you think I ought to do?"

"Start telling the truth."

"Dammit, you imply I haven't been."

"I'm doing more than imply it, Mr. Hillman."

He turned on me with his fists clenched, ready to hit me. I remained sitting. He walked away and came back. Without whisky, he was getting very jumpy.

"I suppose you think I killed them."

"I'm not doing any speculating. I am morally certain you bought that knife from Botkin."

"How can you be certain?"

"I've talked to the man."

"Who authorized you to? I'm not paying you to gather evidence against me."

I said, rather wearily: "Couldn't we forget about your wonderful money for a while, and just sit here and talk like a couple of human beings? A couple of human beings in a bind?"

He considered this. Eventually he said: "You're not in a bind. I am."

"Tell me about it. Unless you actually did commit those murders. In which case you should tell your lawyer and nobody else."

"I didn't. I almost wish I had." He sat down across from me, slumping forward a little, with his arms resting on the tabletop. "I admit I bought the knife. I don't intend to admit it to anyone else. Botkin will have to be persuaded to change his story."

"How?"

"He can't make anything out of that store of his. I ought to know, my father owned one like it in South Boston. I can give Botkin enough money to retire to Mexico."

I was a bit appalled, not so much by the suggestion of crude subornation—I'd often heard it before—as by the fact that Hillman was making it. In the decades since he commanded a squadron at Midway, he must have bumped down quite a few moral steps.

I said: "You better forget about that approach, Mr. Hillman. It's part of the collision course with the law I was talking about. And you'll end up sunk."

"I'm sunk now," he said in an even voice.

He laid his head down on his arms. His hair spilled forward like a broken white sheaf. I could see the naked pink circle on the crown which was ordinarily hidden. It was like a tonsure of mortality.

"What did you do with the knife?" I said to him. "Did you give it to Dick Leandro?"

"No." Spreading his hands on the tabletop, he pushed himself upright. His moist palms slipped and squeaked on the polished surface. "I wish I had."

"Was Tom the one you gave it to?"

He groaned. "I not only gave it to him. I told Botkin I was buying the bloody thing as a gift for him. Bastian must be aware of that, but he's holding it back."

"Bastian would," I said. "It still doesn't follow that Tom used it on his father and mother. He certainly had no reason to kill his mother."

"He doesn't need a rational motive. You don't know Tom."

"You keep telling me that. At the same time you keep refusing to fill in the picture."

"It's a fairly ugly picture."

"Something was said tonight about a homicidal attack."

"I didn't mean to let that slip out."

"Who attacked whom and why?"

"Tom threatened Elaine with a loaded gun. He wasn't kidding, either."

"Was this the Sunday-morning episode you've been suppressing?"

He nodded. "I think the accident must have affected his mind. When I got home from the judge's house, he had her in his room. He was holding my revolver with the muzzle against her head"—Hillman pressed his fingertip into his temple—"and he had her down on her knees, begging for mercy. Literally begging. I didn't know whether he was going to give me the gun, either. For a minute he held it on me. I half expected him to shoot me."

I could feel the hairs prickling at the nape of my neck. It was an ugly picture, all right. What was worse, it was a classic one: the schizophrenic execution killer.

"Did he say anything when you took the gun?"

"Not a word. He handed it over in a rather formal way. He acted like a kind of automaton. He didn't seem to realize what he'd done, or tried to do."

"Had he said anything to your wife?"

"Yes. He said he would kill her if she didn't leave him alone. She'd simply gone to his room to offer him some food, and he went into this silent white rage of his."

"He had a lot of things on his mind," I said, "and he'd been up all night. He told me something about it. You might say it was the crucial night of his young life. He met his real father for the first time"—Hillman grimaced—"which must have been a fairly shattering experience. You might say he was lost between two worlds, and blaming you and your wife for not preparing him. You should have, you know. You had no right to cheat him of the facts, whether you liked them or not. When the facts finally hit him, it was more than he could handle. He deliberately turned the car over that morning."

"You mean he attempted suicide?" Hillman said.

"He made a stab at it. I think it was more a signal that his life was out of control. He didn't let go of the steering wheel, and he wasn't badly hurt. Nobody got hurt in the gun incident, either."

"You've got to take it seriously, though. He was in dead earnest."

"Maybe. I'm not trying to brush it off. Have you talked it over with a psychiatrist?"

"I have not. There are certain things you don't let out of the family."

"That depends on the family."

"Look," he said, "I was afraid they wouldn't admit him to the school if they knew he was that violent."

"Would that have been such a tragedy?"

"I had to do something with him. I don't know what I'm going to do with him now." He bowed his disheveled head.

"You need better advice than I can give you, legal and psychiatric."

"You're assuming he killed those two people."

"Not necessarily. Why don't you ask Dr. Weintraub to recommend somebody?"

Hillman jerked himself upright. "That old woman?"

"I understood he was an old friend of yours, and he knows something about psychiatry."

"Weinie has a worm's-eye knowledge, I suppose." His voice rasped with contempt. "He had a nervous breakdown after Midway. We had to send him stateside to recuperate, while men were dying. While men were dying," Hillman repeated. Then he seemed to surround himself with silence.

He sat in a listening attitude. I waited. His angry face became smooth and his voice changed with it. "Jesus, that was a day. We lost more than half of our T. B. D.'s. The Zekes took them like sitting ducks. I couldn't bring them back. I don't blame Weinie for breaking down, so many men died on him."

His voice was hushed. His eyes were distant. He didn't even seem aware of my presence. His mind was over the edge of the world where his men had died, and he had died more than a little.

"The hell of it is," he was saying, "I love Tom. We haven't been close for years, and he's been hard to handle. But he's my son, and I love him."

"I'm sure you do. But maybe you want more than Tom can give you. He can't give you back your dead pilots."

Hillman didn't understand me. He seemed bewildered. His gray eyes were clouded.

"What did you say?"

"Perhaps you were expecting too much from the boy."

"In what way?"

"Forget it," I said.

Hillman was hurt. "You think I expect too much? I've been getting damn little. And look what I'm willing to give him." He spread his arms again, to embrace the house and everything he owned. "Why, he can have every nickel I possess for his defense. We'll get him off and go to another country to live."

"You're way ahead of yourself, Mr. Hillman. He hasn't been charged with anything yet."

"He will be." His voice sounded both fatalistic and defiant.

"Maybe. Let's consider the possibilities. The only evidence against him is the knife, and that's pretty dubious if you think about it. He didn't take it with him, surely, when you put him in Laguna Perdida."

"He may have. I didn't search him."

"I'm willing to bet they did."

Hillman narrowed his eyes until they were just a glitter between the folded lids. "You're right, Archer. He didn't have the knife when he left the house. I remember seeing it afterwards, that same day."

"Where was it?"

"In his room, in one of the chests of drawers."

"And you left it in the drawer?"

"There was no reason not to."

"Then anybody with access to the house could have got hold of it?"

"Yes. Unfortunately that includes Tom. He could have sneaked in after he escaped from the school."

"It also includes Dick Leandro, who wouldn't have had to sneak in. He's in and out of the house all the time, isn't he?"

"I suppose he is. That doesn't prove anything."

"No, but when you put it together with the fact that Dick was probably seen at the Barcelona Hotel last night, it starts you thinking about him. There's still something missing in this case, you know. The equations don't balance."

"Dick isn't your missing quantity," he said hastily.

"You're quite protective about Dick."

"I'm fond of him. Why shouldn't I be? He's a nice boy, and I've been able to help him. Dammit, Archer." His voice deepened. "When a fellow reaches a certain age, he needs to pass on what he knows, or part of it, to a younger fellow."

"Are you thinking of passing on some money, too?"

"We may eventually. It will depend on Elaine. She controls the main money. But I can assure you it couldn't matter to Dick."

"It matters to everybody. I think it matters very much to Dick. He's a pleaser."

"What is that supposed to mean?"

"You know what it means. He lives by pleasing people, mainly you. Tell me this. Does Dick know about the gun incident in Tom's room?"

"Yes. He was with me that Sunday morning. He drove me to the judge's house and home again."

"He gets in on a lot of things," I said.

"That's natural. He's virtually a member of the family. As a matter of fact, I expected him tonight. He said he had something he wanted to talk over with me." He looked at his watch. "But it's too late now. It's past eleven o'clock."

"Get him out here anyway, will you?"

"Not tonight. I've had it. I don't want to have to pull my face together and put on a front for Dick now."

He looked at me a little sheepishly. He had revealed himself to me, a vain man who couldn't forget his face, a secret man who lived behind a front. He pushed his silver mane back and patted it in place.

"Tonight is all the time we have," I said. "In the morning you can expect Bastian and the sheriff and probably the D. A. pounding on your door. You won't be able to put them off by simply denying that you bought that knife. You're going to have to explain it."

"Do you really think Dick took it?"

"He's a better suspect than Tom, in my opinion."

"Very well, I'll call him." He rose and went to the telephone on the desk.

"Don't tell him what you want him for. He might break and run."

"Naturally I won't." He dialed a number from memory, and waited. When he spoke, his voice had changed again. It was lighter and younger. "Dick? You said something to Elaine about dropping by tonight. I was wondering if I was to expect you . . . I know it's late. I'm sorry you're not too well. What's the trouble? . . . I'm sorry. Look, why don't you come out anyway, just for a minute? Tom came home tonight, isn't that great? He'll want to see you. And I particularly want to see you . . . Yep, it's an order. . . . Fine, I'll look for you then." He hung up.

"What's the matter with him?" I asked.

"He says he doesn't feel well."

"Sick?"

"Depressed. But he cheered up when I told him Tom was home. He'll be out shortly."

"Good. In the meantime I want to talk to Tom."

Hillman came and stood over me. His face was rather obscure in the green penumbra. "Before you talk to him again, there's something you ought to know."

I waited for him to go on. Finally I asked him: "Is it about Tom?"

"It has to do with both of us." He hesitated, his eyes intent on my face. "On second thought, I don't think I'll let my back hair down any further tonight."

"You may never have another chance," I said, "before it gets let down for you, the hard way."

"That's where you're wrong. Nobody knows this particular thing but me."

"And it has to do with you and Tom?"

"That's right. Now let's forget it."

He didn't want to forget it, though. He wanted to share his secret, without taking the responsibility of speaking out. He lingered by the table, looking down at my face with his stainless-steel eyes.

I thought of the feeling in Hillman's voice when he spoke of his love for Tom. Perhaps that feeling was the element which would balance the equation.

"Is Tom your natural son?" I said.

He didn't hesitate in answering. "Yes. He's my own flesh and blood."

"And you're the only one who knows?"

"Carol knew, of course, and Mike Harley knew. He agreed to the arrangement in exchange for certain favors I was able to do him."

"You kept him out of Portsmouth."

"I helped to. You mustn't imagine I was trying to mastermind some kind of plot. It all happened quite naturally. Carol came to me after Mike and his brother were arrested. She begged me to intervene on their behalf. I said I would. She was a lovely girl, and she expressed her gratitude in a natural way."

"By going to bed with you."

"Yes. She gave me one night. I went to her room in the Barcelona Hotel. You should have seen her, Archer, when she took off her clothes for me. She lit up that shabby room with the brass bed—"

I cut in on his excitement: "The brass bed is still there, and so was Otto Sipe, until last night. Did Sipe know about your big night on the brass bed?"

"Sipe?"

"The hotel detective."

"Carol said he was gone that night."

"And you say you only went there once."

"Only once with Carol. I spent some nights in the Barcelona later with another girl. I suppose I was trying to recapture the rapture or something. She was a willing girl, but she was no substitute for Carol."

I got up. He saw the look on my face and backed away. "What's the matter with you, is something wrong?"

"Susanna Drew is a friend of mine. A good friend."

"How could I know that?" he said with his mouth lifted on one side.

"You don't know much," I said. "You don't know how sick it makes me to sit here and listen to you while you dabble around in your dirty little warmed-over affairs."

He was astonished. I was astonished myself. Angry shouting at witnesses is something reserved for second-rate prosecutors in courtrooms.

"Nobody talks to me like that," Hillman said in a shaking voice. "Get out of my house and stay out."

"I'll be delighted to."

I got as far as the front door. It was like walking through deep, clinging mud. Then Hillman spoke behind me from the far side of the reception hall.

"Look here." It was his favorite phrase.

I looked there. He walked toward me under the perilous chandelier. He said with his hands slightly lifted and turned outward:

"I can't go on by myself, Archer. I'm sorry if I stepped on your personal toes."

"It's all right."

"No, it isn't. Are you in love with Susanna?"

I didn't answer him.

"In case you're wondering," he said, "I haven't touched her since 1945. I ran into some trouble with that house detective, Sipe—"

I said impatiently: "I know. You knocked him down."

"I gave him the beating of his life," he said with a kind of naïve pride. "It was the last time he tried to pry any money out of me."

"Until this week."

He was jolted into temporary silence. "Anyway, Susanna lost interest—"

"I don't want to talk about Susanna."

"That suits me."

We had moved back into the corridor that led to the library, out of hearing of the room where Elaine was. Hillman leaned on the wall like a bystander in an alley. His posture made me realize how transient and insecure he felt in his own house.

"There are one or two things I don't understand," I said. "You tell me you spent one night with Carol, and yet you're certain that you fathered her son."

"He was born just nine months later, December the twelfth."

"That doesn't prove you're his father. Pregnancies often last longer, especially first ones. Mike Harley could have fathered him before the Shore Patrol took him. Or any other man."

"There was no other man. She was a virgin."

"You're kidding."

"I am not. Her marriage to Mike Harley was never consummated. Mike was impotent, which was one reason he was willing to have the boy pass as his."

"Why was that so necessary, Hillman? Why didn't you take the boy and raise him yourself?"

"I did that."

"I mean, raise him openly as your own son."

"I couldn't. I had other commitments. I was already married to Elaine. She's a New Englander, a Puritan of the first water."

"With a fortune of the first water."

"I admit I needed her help to start my business. A man has to make choices."

He looked up at the chandelier. Its light fell starkly on his hollow bronze face. He turned his face away from the light.

"Who told you Mike Harley was impotent?"

"Carol did, and she wasn't lying. She was a virgin, I tell you. She did a lot of talking in the course of the night. Her whole life. She told me Mike got what sex he got by being spanked, or beaten with a strap."

"By her?"

"Yes. She didn't enjoy it, of course, but she did it for him willingly enough. She seemed to feel that it was less dangerous than sex, than normal sex."

A wave of sickness went through me. It wasn't physical. But I could smell the old man's cow barn and hear the whining of his one-eyed dog.

"I thought you were the one who was supposed to be impotent," I said, "or sterile."

He glanced at me sharply. "Who have you been talking to?"

"Your wife. She did the talking."

"And she still thinks I'm sterile?"

"Yes."

"Good." He turned his face away from the light again and let out a little chuckle of relief. "Maybe we can pull this out yet. I told Elaine at the time we adopted Tom that Weintraub gave me a test and found that I was sterile. I was afraid she'd catch on to the fact of my paternity."

"You may be sterile at that."

He didn't know what I meant. "No. It's Elaine who is. I didn't need to take any test. I have Tom to prove I'm a man."

He didn't have Tom.

28

We went into the sitting room, the waiting room. Though Tom was in the house the waiting seemed to go on, as if it had somehow coalesced with time. Elaine was in her place on the chesterfield. She had taken up her knitting, and her stainless-steel needles glinted along the edge of the red wool. She looked up brightly at her husband.

"Where's Tom?" he said. "Is he still upstairs?"

"I heard him go down the back stairs. I imagine Mrs. Perez is feeding him in the kitchen. He seems to prefer the kitchen to the sitting room. I suppose that's natural, considering his heredity."

"We won't go into the subject of that, eh?"

Hillman went into the bar alcove and made himself a very dark-looking highball. He remembered to offer me one, which I declined.

"What did that policeman want?" Elaine asked him.

"He had some stupid questions on his mind. I prefer not to go into them."

"So you've been telling me for the past twenty-five years. You prefer not to go into things. Save the surface. Never mind the dry rot at the heart."

"Could we dispense with the melodrama?"

"The word is tragedy, not melodrama. A tragedy has gone through this house and you don't have the mind to grasp it. You live in a world of appearances, like a fool."

"I know. I know." His voice was light, but he looked ready to throw his drink in her face. "I'm an ignorant engineer, and I never studied philosophy."

Her needles went on clicking. "I could stand your ignorance, but I can't stand your evasions any longer."

He drank part of his drink, and waved his free hand loosely over his head. "Good heavens, Elaine, how much do I have to take from you? This isn't the time or place for one of those."

"There never is a time or place," she said. "If there's a time, you change the clocks—this is known as crossing the International Ralph Line—and suddenly it's six o'clock in the morning, in Tokyo. If there's a place, you find an escape hatch. I see your wriggling legs and then you're off and away, into the wild Ralph yonder. You never faced up to anything in your life."

He winced under her bitter broken eloquence. "That isn't true," he said uneasily. "Archer and I have been really dredging tonight."

"Dredging in the warm shallows of your nature? I thought you reserved that pastime for your women. Like Susanna Drew."

Her name sent a pang through me. It was a nice name, innocent and bold and slightly absurd, and it didn't deserve to be bandied about by these people. If the Hillmans had ever been innocent, their innocence had been frittered away in a marriage of pretenses. It struck me suddenly that Hillman's affair with Susanna had also been one of pretenses. He had persuaded her to take care of Carol without any hint that he was the father of the child she was carrying.

"Good Lord," he was saying now, "are we back on the Drew girl again after all these years?"

"Well, are we?" Elaine said.

Fortunately the telephone rang. Hillman went into the alcove to answer it, and turned to me with his hand clapped over the mouthpiece.

"It's Bastian, for you. You can take the call in the pantry. I'm going to listen on this line."

There wasn't much use arguing. I crossed the music room and the dining room to the butler's pantry and fumbled around in the dark for the telephone. I could hear Mrs. Perez in the kitchen, talking to Tom in musical sentences about her native province of Sinaloa. Bastian's voice in the receiver sounded harsh and inhuman by comparison:

"Archer?"

"I'm here."

"Good. I checked the matter of Dick Leandro's transportation, in fact I've just been talking to a girl friend of his. She's a senior at the college, named Katie Ogilvie, and she owns a Chevrolet sedan, this year's model, blue in color. She finally admitted she lent it to him last night. He put over a hundred miles on the odometer."

"Are you sure she wasn't with him? He had a girl with him, or another boy, Daly wasn't quite sure."

"It wasn't Miss Ogilvie," Bastian said. "She was peeved about the fact that he used her car to take another girl for a long ride."

"How does she know it was a girl?"

"The lady dropped a lipstick in the front seat. A very nice white gold lipstick, fourteen carat. I don't think," he added dryly, "that Miss Ogilvie would have testified so readily if it wasn't for that lipstick. Apparently Leandro impressed the need for secrecy on her."

"Did he say why?"

"It had something to do with the Hillman kidnapping. That was all she knew. Well, do we pick up Leandro? You seem to be calling the shots."

"He's on his way out here. Maybe you better follow along."

"You sound as if things are building up to a climax."

"Yeah."

I could see its outlines. They burned on my eyeballs like the lights of Dack's Auto Court. I sat in the dark after Bastian hung up, and tried to blink them away. But they spread out into the darkness around me and became integrated with the actual world.

Sinaloa, Mrs. Perez was saying or kind of singing to Tom in the kitchen, Sinaloa was a land of many rivers. There were eleven rivers in all, and she and her family lived so close to one of them that her brothers would put on their bathing suits and run down for a swim every day. Her father used to go down to the river on Sunday and catch fish with a net and distribute them to the neighbors. All the neighbors had fish for Sunday lunch.

Tom said it sounded like fun.

Ah yes, it was like Paradise, she said, and her father was a highly regarded man in their *barrio*. Of course it was hot in summer, that was the chief drawback, a hundred and twenty degrees in the shade sometimes. Then big black clouds would pile up along the Sierra Madre Occidental, and it would rain so hard, inches in just two hours. Then it would be sunny again. Sunny, sunny, sunny! That was how life went in Sinaloa.

Tom wanted to know if her father was still alive. She replied with joy that her father lived on, past eighty now, in good health. Perez was visiting him on his present trip to Mexico.

"I'd like to visit your father."

"Maybe you will some day."

I opened the door. Tom was at the kitchen table, eating the last of his soup. Mrs. Perez was leaning over him with a smiling maternal mouth and faraway eyes. She looked distrustfully at me. I was an alien in their land of Sinaloa.

"What do you want?"

"A word with Tom. I'll have to ask you to leave for a bit."

She stiffened.

"On second thought, there won't be any more secrets in this house. You might as well stay, Mrs. Perez."

"*Thank* you."

She picked up the soup bowl and walked switching to the sink, where she turned the hot water full on. Tom regarded me across the table with the infinite boredom of the young. He was very clean and pale.

"I hate to drag you back over the details," I said, "but you're the only one who can answer some of these questions."

"It's okay."

"I'm not clear about yesterday, especially last night. Were you still at the Barcelona Hotel when Mike Harley got back from Vegas?"

"Yes. He was in a very mean mood. He told me to beat it before he killed me. I was intending to leave, anyway."

"And nobody stopped you?"

"He wanted to get rid of me."

"What about Sipe?"

"He was so drunk he hardly knew what he was doing. He passed out before I left."

"What time did you leave?"

"A little after eight. It wasn't dark yet. I caught a bus at the corner."

"You weren't there when Dick Leandro arrived?"

"No sir." His eyes widened. "Was he at the hotel?"

"Evidently he was. Did Sipe or Harley ever mention him?"

"No sir."

"Do you know what he might have been doing there?"

"No sir. I don't know much about him. He's *their* friend." He shrugged one shoulder and arm toward the front of the house.

"Whose friend in particular? His or hers?"

"His. But she uses him, too."

"To drive her places?"

"For anything she wants." He spoke with the hurt ineffectual anger of a displaced son. "When he does something she wants, she says she'll leave him money in her will. If he doesn't, like when he has a date, she says she'll cut him out. So usually he breaks the date."

"Would he kill someone for her?"

Mrs. Perez had turned off the hot water. In the steamy silence at her end of the kitchen, she made an explosive noise that sounded like "Chuh!"

"I don't know what he'd do," Tom said deliberately. "He's a yacht bum and they're all the same, but they're all different, too. It would depend on how much risk there was in it. And how much money."

"Harley," I said, "was stabbed with the knife your father gave you, the hunting knife with the striped handle."

"I didn't stab him."

"Where did you last see the knife?"

He considered the question. "It was in my room, in the top drawer with the handkerchiefs and stuff."

"Did Dick Leandro know where it was?"

"*I* never showed him. He never came to my room."

"Did your mother—did Elaine Hillman know where it was?"

"I guess so. She's always—she was always coming into my room, and checking on my things."

"That's true," Mrs. Perez said.

I acknowledged her comment with a look which discouraged further comment.

"I understand on a certain Sunday morning she came into your room once too often. You threatened to shoot her with your father's gun."

Mrs. Perez made her explosive noise. Tom bit hard on the tip of his right thumb. His look was slanting, over my head and to one side, as if there was someone behind me.

"Is that the story they're telling?" he said.

Mrs. Perez burst out: "It isn't true. I heard her yelling up there. She came downstairs and got the gun out of the library desk and went up-stairs with it."

"Why didn't you stop her?"

"I was afraid," she said. "Anyway, Mr. Hillman was coming—I heard his car—and I went outside and told him there was trouble upstairs. What else could I do, with Perez away in Mexico?"

"It doesn't matter," Tom said. "Nothing happened. I took the gun away from her."

"Did she try to shoot you?"

"She said she would if I didn't take back what I said."

"And what did you say?"

"That I'd rather live in an auto court with my real mother than in this house with her. She blew her top and ran downstairs and got the gun."

"Why didn't you tell your father about this?"

"He isn't my father."

I didn't argue. It took more than genes to establish fatherhood. "Why didn't you tell him, Tom?"

He made an impatient gesture with his hand. "What was the use? He wouldn't have believed me. Anyway, I *was* mad at her, for lying to me about who I was. I did take the gun and point it at her head."

"And want to kill her?"

He nodded. His head seemed very heavy on his neck. Mrs. Perez invented a sudden errand and bustled past him, pressing his shoulder with her hand as she went. As if to signalize this gesture, an electric bell rang over the pantry door.

"That's the front door," she said to nobody in particular.

I got there in a dead heat with Ralph Hillman. He let Dick Leandro in. The week's accelerated aging process was working in Leandro now. Only his dark hair seemed lively. His face was drawn and slightly yellow-ish. He gave me a lackluster glance, and appealed to Hillman:

"Could I talk to you alone, Skipper? It's important." He was almost chattering.

Elaine spoke from the doorway of the sitting room: "It can't be so important that you'd forget your manners. Come in and be sociable, Dick. I've been alone all evening, or so it seems."

"We'll join you later," Hillman said.

"It's very late already." Her voice was edgy.

Leandro's dim brown glance moved back and forth between them like a spectator's at a tennis game on which he had bet everything he owned.

"If you're not nice to me," she said lightly, "I won't be nice to you, Dick."

"I do-don't care about that." There was strained defiance in his voice.

"You will." Stiff-backed, she retreated into the sitting room.

I said to Leandro: "We won't waste any more time. Did you do some driving for Mrs. Hillman last night?"

He turned away from me and almost leaned on Hillman, speaking in a hushed rapid voice. "I've *got* to talk to you alone. Something's come up that you don't know about."

"We'll go into the library," Hillman said.

"If you do, I go along," I said. "But we might as well talk here. I don't want to get too far from Mrs. Hillman."

The young man turned and looked at me in a different way, both lost and relieved. He knew I knew.

Hillman also knew, I thought. His proposal to Susanna tended to prove it; his confession that Tom was his natural son had provided me with evidence of motive. He leaned now on the wall beside the door, heavy and mysterious as a statue, with half-closed eyes.

I said to the younger man: "Did you drive her to the Barcelona Hotel, Dick?"

"Yessir." With one shoulder high and his head on one side, he held himself in an awkward pose which gave the effect of writhing. "I had no w-way of knowing what was on her mind. I *still* don't know."

"But you have a pretty good idea. Why all the secrecy?"

"She said I should borrow a car, that they had phoned for more money and Skipper wasn't here so we would have to deliver it. Or else they'd kill him. We were to keep it secret from the police, and afterwards she said I must never tell anyone."

"And you believed her story?"

"I c-certainly did."

"When did you start to doubt it?"

"Well, I couldn't figure out how she could get hold of all that c-cash."

"How much?"

"Another twenty-five thousand, she said. She said it was in her bag—she was carrying her big knitting bag—but I didn't actually see the money."

"What did you see?"

"I didn't actually *see* anything." Like a stealthy animal that would eventually take over his entire forehead, his hair was creeping down toward his eyes. "I mean, I saw this character, the one she—I saw this character come out of the hotel and they went around to the back and I heard this scream." He scratched the front of his throat.

"What did you do?"

"I stayed in the car. She told me to stay in the car. When she came back, she said it was an owl."

"And you believed her?"

"I don't know much about birds. Do I, Skipper?"

Elaine cried out very brightly from her doorway: "What under heaven are you men talking about?"

I walked toward her. "You. The owl you heard last night in the hotel garden. What kind of an owl was it?"

"A screech—" Her hand flew up and pressed against her lips.

"He looked human to me. He wasn't a very good specimen, but he was human."

She stopped breathing, and then gasped for breath. "He was a devil," she said, "the scum of the earth."

"Because he wanted more money?"

"It would have gone on and on. I had to stop him." She stood shuddering in the doorway. With a fierce effort of will, she brought her emotions under control. "Speaking of money, I can take care of you. I'm sure the police would understand my position, but there's no need to connect me with this—this—" She couldn't think of a noun. "I can take care of you and I can take care of Dick."

"How much are you offering?"

She looked at me imperiously, from the moral stilts of inherited wealth. "Come into the sitting room," she said, "and we'll talk about it."

The three of us followed her into the room and took up positions around her chesterfield. Hillman looked at me curiously. He was very silent and subdued, but the calculator behind his eyes was still working. Dick Leandro was coming back to life. His eyes had brightened. Perhaps he still imagined that somehow, somewhere, sometime, there would be Hillman money coming to him.

"How much?" I said to her.

"Twenty-five thousand."

"That's better than a knife between the ribs. Does that mean twenty-five thousand overall or twenty-five thousand for each murder?"

"Each murder?"

"There were two, done with the same knife, almost certainly by the same person. You."

She moved her head away from my pointing finger, like a stage-shy girl. A stage-shy girl playing the role of an aging woman with monkey wrinkles and fading fine blonde hair.

"Fifty thousand then," she said.

"He's playing with you," Hillman said. "You can't buy him."

She turned toward him. "My late father once said that you can buy anyone, anyone at all. I proved that when I bought you." She made a gesture of repugnance. "I wish I hadn't. You turned out to be a bad bargain."

"You didn't buy me. You merely leased my services."

They faced each other as implacably as two skulls. She said:

"Did you have to palm her bastard off on me?"

"I wanted a son. I didn't plan it. It happened."

"You made it happen. You connived to bring her baby into my house. You let me feed and nurture him and call him mine. How could you be such a living falsity?"

"Don't talk to me about falsity, Elaine. It seemed the best way to handle the problem."

"Stallion," she said. "Filth."

I heard a faint movement in the adjoining room. Straining my eyes into the darkness, I could see Tom sitting on the bench in front of the grand piano. I was tempted to shut the door, but it was too late, really. He might as well hear it all.

Hillman said in a surprisingly calm voice: "I never could understand the Puritan mind, Ellie. You think a little fun in bed is the ultimate sin, worse than murder. Christ, I remember our wedding night. You'd have thought I was murdering you."

"I wish you had."

"I almost wish I had. You murdered Carol, didn't you, Ellie?"

"Of course I did. She phoned here Monday morning, after you left. Tom had given her his telephone number. I took the call in his room, and she spilled out everything. She *said* she had just caught on to her husband's plans, and she was afraid he would harm Tom, who wasn't really his son. I'm sure it was just an excuse she used to get her knife into me."

"Her knife?" I said.

"That was a badly chosen image, wasn't it? I mean that she was glorying over me, annulling the whole meaning of my existence."

"I think she was simply trying to save her son."

"*Her* son, not mine. Her son and Ralph's. That was the point, don't you see? I felt as if she had killed me. I was just a fading ghost in the world, with only enough life left to strike back. Walking from where I left the Cadillac, I could feel the rain fall through me. I was no solider than the rain.

"Apparently her husband had caught her phoning me. He took her back to their cottage and beat her and left her unconscious on the floor. She was easy for me to kill. The knife slipped in and out. I hadn't realized how easy it would be.

"But the second time wasn't easy," she said. "The knife caught in his ribs. I couldn't pull it out of him."

Her voice was high and childish in complaint. The little girl behind her wrinkles had been caught in a malign world where even things no longer cooperated and even men could not be bought.

"Why did you have to stick it into him?" I said.

"He suspected that I killed Carol. He used Tom's number to call me and accuse me. Of course he wanted *money."* She spoke as if her possession of money had given her a special contemptuous insight into other people's hunger for it. "It would have gone on and on."

It was going on and on. Tom came blinking out of the darkness. He looked around in pity and confusion. Elaine turned her face away from him, as if she had an unprepossessing disease.

The boy said to Hillman: "Why didn't you tell me? It could have made a difference."

"It still can," Hillman said with a hopefulness more grinding than despair. "Son?"

He moved toward Tom, who evaded his outstretched hands and left the room. Walking rather unsteadily, Hillman followed him. I could hear them mounting the stairs, on different levels, out of step.

Dick Leandro got up from his place, rather tentatively, as if he had been liberated from an obscure bondage. He went into the alcove, where I heard him making himself a drink.

Elaine Hillman was still thinking about money. "What about it, Mr. Archer? Can you be bought?" Her voice was quite calm. The engines of her anger had run down.

"I can't be bought with anything you've offered."

"Will you have mercy on me, then?"

"I don't have that much mercy."

"I'm not asking for a great deal. Just let me sleep one more night in my own house."

"What good would that do you?"

"This good. I'll be frank with you. I've been saving sleeping pills for a considerable time—"

"How long?"

"Nearly a year, actually. I've been in despair for at least that long—"

"You should have taken your pills sooner."

"Before all this, you mean?" She waved her hand at the empty room as if it was a tragic stage littered with corpses.

"Before all this," I said.

"But I couldn't die without knowing. I knew my life was empty and meaningless. I had to find out why."

"And now it's full and meaningful?"

"It's over," she said. "Look, Mr. Archer, I was frank with you today. Give me a *quid pro quo*. All I'm asking for is time to use my pills."

"No."

"You owe me something. I helped you as much as I dared this afternoon."

"You weren't trying to help me, Mrs. Hillman. You only told me what I already knew, or what I was about to find out. You gave me the fact that Tom was adopted in such a way that it would conceal the more important fact that he was your husband's natural son. You kept alive the lie that your husband was sterile because it hid your motive for murdering Carol Harley."

"I'm afraid your reasoning is much too subtle for me."

"I hardly think so. You're a subtle woman."

"I? Subtle? I'm a ninny, a poor booby. The people in the streets, the scum of the earth knew more about my life than I—" She broke off. "So you won't help me."

"I can't. I'm sorry. The police are on their way now."

She regarded me thoughtfully. "There would still be time for me to use the gun."

"No."

"You're very hard."

"It isn't me, really, Mrs. Hillman. It's just reality catching up."

The sheriff's car was in the driveway now. I rose and went as far as the sitting-room door and called out to Bastian to come in. Elaine sighed behind me like a woman in passion.

Her passion was a solitary one. She had picked up her knitting in both hands and pressed both steel needles into her breast. She struck them into herself again before I reached her. By the middle of the following day she had succeeded in dying.

THE COMFORTS OF HOME

by

FLANNERY O'CONNOR

Thomas withdrew to the side of the window and with his head between the wall and the curtain he looked down on the driveway where
the car had stopped. His mother and the little slut were getting out of
it. His mother emerged slowly, stolid and awkward, and then the little
slut's long slightly bowed legs slid out, the dress pulled above the knees.
With a shriek of laughter she ran to meet the dog, who bounded, over-
joyed, shaking with pleasure, to welcome her. Rage gathered throughout
Thomas's large frame with a silent ominous intensity, like a mob assem-
bling.

It was now up to him to pack a suitcase, go to the hotel, and stay there
until the house should be cleared.

He did not know where a suitcase was, he disliked to pack, he needed
his books, his typewriter was not portable, he was used to an electric
blanket, he could not bear to eat in restaurants. His mother, with her
daredevil charity, was about to wreck the peace of the house.

The back door slammed and the girl's laugh shot up from the kitchen,
through the back hall, up the stairwell and into his room, making for him
like a bolt of electricity. He jumped to the side and stood glaring about
him. His words of the morning had been unequivocal: "If you bring that

girl back into this house, I leave. You can choose—her or me."

She had made her choice. An intense pain gripped his throat. It was the first time in his thirty-five years . . . He felt a sudden burning moisture behind his eyes. Then he steadied himself, overcome by rage. On the contrary: she had not made any choice. She was counting on his attachment to his electric blanket. She would have to be shown.

The girl's laughter rang upward a second time and Thomas winced. He saw again her look of the night before. She had invaded his room. He had waked to find his door open and her in it. There was enough light from the hall to make her visible as she turned toward him. The face was like a comedienne's in a musical comedy—a pointed chin, wide apple cheeks and feline empty eyes. He had sprung out of his bed and snatched a straight chair and then he had backed her out the door, holding the chair in front of him like an animal trainer driving out a dangerous cat. He had driven her silently down the hall, pausing when he reached it to beat on his mother's door. The girl, with a gasp, turned and fled into the guest room.

In a moment his mother had opened her door and peered out apprehensively. Her face, greasy with whatever she put on it at night, was framed in pink rubber curlers. She looked down the hall where the girl had disappeared. Thomas stood before her, the chair still lifted in front of him as if he were about to quell another beast. "She tried to get in my room," he hissed, pushing in. "I woke up and she was trying to get in my room." He closed the door behind him and his voice rose in outrage. "I won't put up with this! I won't put up with it another day!"

His mother, backed by him to her bed, sat down on the edge of it. She had a heavy body on which sat a thin, mysteriously gaunt and incongruous head.

"I'm telling you for the last time," Thomas said, "I won't put up with this another day." There was an observable tendency in all of her actions. This was, with the best intentions in the world, to make a mockery of virtue, to pursue it with such a mindless intensity that everyone involved was made a fool of and virtue itself became ridiculous. "Not another day," he repeated.

His mother shook her head emphatically, her eyes still on the door.

Thomas put the chair on the floor in front of her and sat down on it. He leaned forward as if he were about to explain something to a defective child.

"That's just another way she's unfortunate," his mother said. "So awful, so awful. She told me the name of it but I forget what it is but it's something she can't help. Something she was born with. Thomas," she said and put her hand to her jaw, "suppose it were you?"

Exasperation blocked his windpipe. "Can't I make you see," he croaked, "that if she can't help herself you can't help her?"

His mother's eyes, intimate but untouchable, were the blue of great distances after sunset. "Nimpermaniac," she murmured.

"Nymphomaniac," he said fiercely. "She doesn't need to supply you with any fancy names. She's a moral moron. That's all you need to know. Born without the moral faculty—like somebody else would be born without a kidney or a leg. Do you understand?"

"I keep thinking it might be you," she said, her hand still on her jaw. "If it were you, how do you think I'd feel if nobody took you in? What if you were a nimpermaniac and not a brilliant smart person and you did what you couldn't help and . . ."

Thomas felt a deep unbearable loathing for himself as if he were turning slowly into the girl.

"What did she have on?" she asked abruptly, her eyes narrowing.

"Nothing!" he roared. "Now will you get her out of here!"

"How can I turn her out in the cold?" she said. "This morning she was threatening to kill herself again."

"Send her back to jail," Thomas said.

"I would not send *you* back to jail, Thomas," she said.

He got up and snatched the chair and fled the room while he was still able to control himself.

Thomas loved his mother. He loved her because it was his nature to do so, but there were times when he could not endure her love for him. There were times when it became nothing but pure idiot mystery and he sensed about him forces, invisible currents entirely out of his control. She proceeded always from the tritest of considerations—it was the *nice thing to do*—into the most foolhardy engagements with the devil, whom, of course, she never recognized.

The devil for Thomas was only a manner of speaking, but it was a manner appropriate to the situations his mother got into. Had she been in any degree intellectual, he could have proved to her from early Christian history that no excess of virtue is justified, that a moderation of good produces likewise a moderation in evil, that if Antony of Egypt had stayed at home and attended to his sister, no devils would have plagued him.

Thomas was not cynical and so far from being opposed to virtue, he saw it as the principle of order and the only thing that makes life bearable. His own life was made bearable by the fruits of his mother's saner virtues—by the well-regulated house she kept and the excellent meals she served. But when virtue got out of hand with her, as now, a sense of devils grew upon him, and these were not mental quirks in himself or the old lady, they were denizens with personalities, present though not visible, who might any moment be expected to shriek or rattle a pot.

The girl had landed in the county jail a month ago on a bad check charge and his mother had seen her picture in the paper. At the breakfast table she had gazed at it for a long time and then had passed it over the coffee pot to him. "Imagine," she said, "only nineteen years old and in that filthy jail. And she doesn't look like a bad girl."

Thomas glanced at the picture. It showed the face of a shrewd ragamuffin. He observed that the average age for criminality was steadily lowering.

"She looks like a wholesome girl," his mother said.

"Wholesome people don't pass bad checks," Thomas said.

"You don't know what you'd do in a pinch."

"I wouldn't pass a bad check," Thomas said.

"I think," his mother said, "I'll take her a little box of candy."

If then and there he had put his foot down, nothing else would have happened. His father, had he been living, would have put his foot down at that point. Taking a box of candy was her favorite nice thing to do. When anyone within her social station moved to town, she called and took a box of candy; when any of her friends' children had babies or won a scholarship, she called and took a box of candy; when an old person broke his hip, she was at his bedside with a box of candy. He had been amused at the idea of her taking a box of candy to the jail.

He stood now in his room with the girl's laugh rocketing away in his head and cursed his amusement.

When his mother returned from the visit to the jail, she had burst into his study without knocking and had collapsed full-length on his couch, lifting her small swollen feet up on the arm of it. After a moment, she recovered herself enough to sit up and put a newspaper under them. Then she fell back again. "We don't know how the other half lives," she said.

Thomas knew that though her conversation moved from cliché to cliché there were real experiences behind them. He was less sorry for the girl's being in jail than for his mother having to see her there. He would have spared her all unpleasant sights. "Well," he said and put away his journal, "you had better forget it now. The girl has ample reason to be in jail."

"You can't imagine what all she's been through," she said, sitting up again, "listen." The poor girl, Star, had been brought up by a stepmother with three children of her own, one an almost grown boy who had taken advantage of her in such dreadful ways that she had been forced to run away and find her real mother. Once found, her real mother had sent her to various boarding schools to get rid of her. At each of these she had been forced to run away by the presence of perverts and sadists so monstrous that their acts defied description. Thomas could tell that his mother had not been spared the details that she was sparing him. Now and again when she spoke vaguely, her voice shook and he could tell that she was remembering some horror that had been put to her graphically. He had hoped that in a few days the memory of all this would wear off, but it did not. The next day she returned to the jail with Kleenex and cold-cream and a few days later, she announced that she had consulted a lawyer.

It was at these times that Thomas truly mourned the death of his father though he had not been able to endure him in life. The old man would have had none of this foolishness. Untouched by useless compassion, he would (behind her back) have pulled the necessary strings with his crony, the sheriff, and the girl would have been packed off to the state penitentiary to serve her time. He had always been engaged in some enraged action until one morning when (with an angry glance at his wife as if she alone were responsible) he had dropped dead at the breakfast table. Thomas had inherited his father's reason without his ruthlessness and his mother's love of good without her tendency to pursue it. His plan for all practical action was to wait and see what developed.

The lawyer found that the story of the repeated atrocities was for the most part untrue, but when he explained to her that the girl was a psychopathic personality, not insane enough for the asylum, not criminal enough for the jail, not stable enough for society, Thomas's mother was more deeply affected than ever. The girl readily admitted that her story was untrue on account of her being a congenital liar; she lied, she said, because she was insecure. She had passed through the hands of several psychiatrists who had put the finishing touches to her education. She knew there was no hope for her. In the presence of such an affliction as this, his mother seemed bowed down by some painful mystery that nothing would make endurable but a redoubling of effort. To his annoyance, she appeared to look on *him* with compassion, as if her hazy charity no longer made distinctions.

A few days later she burst in and said that the lawyer had got the girl paroled—to her.

Thomas rose from his Morris chair, dropping the review he had been reading. His large bland face contracted in anticipated pain. "You are not," he said, "going to bring that girl here!"

"No, no," she said, "calm yourself, Thomas." She had managed with difficulty to get the girl a job in a pet shop in town and a place to board with a crotchety old lady of her acquaintance. People were not kind. They did not put themselves in the place of someone like Star who had everything against her.

Thomas sat down again and retrieved his review. He seemed just to have escaped some danger which he did not care to make clear to himself. "Nobody can tell you anything," he said, "but in a few days that girl will have left town, having got what she could out of you. You'll never hear from her again."

Two nights later he came home and opened the parlor door and was speared by a shrill depthless laugh. His mother and the girl sat close to the fireplace where the gas logs were lit. The girl gave the immediate impression of being physically crooked. Her hair was cut like a dog's or an elf's and she was dressed in the latest fashion. She was training on him a long familiar sparkling stare that turned after a second into an intimate grin.

"Thomas!" his mother said, her voice firm with the injunction not to bolt, "this is Star you've heard so much about. Star is going to have supper with us."

The girl called herself Star Drake. The lawyer had found that her real name was Sarah Ham.

Thomas neither moved nor spoke but hung in the door in what seemed a savage perplexity. Finally he said, "How do you do, Sarah," in a tone of such loathing that he was shocked at the sound of it. He reddened, feeling it beneath him to show contempt for any creature so pathetic. He advanced into the room, determined at least on a decent politeness and sat down heavily in a straight chair.

"Thomas writes history," his mother said with a threatening look at him. "He's president of the local Historical Society this year."

The girl leaned forward and gave Thomas an even more pointed attention. "Fabulous!" she said in a throaty voice.

"Right now Thomas is writing about the first settlers in this country," his mother said.

"Fabulous!" the girl repeated.

Thomas by an effort of will managed to look as if he were alone in the room.

"Say, you know who he looks like?" Star asked, her head on one side, taking him in at an angle.

"Oh some one very distinguished!" his mother said archly.

"This cop I saw in the movie I went to last night," Star said.

"Star," his mother said, "I think you ought to be careful about the kind of movies you go to. I think you ought to see only the best ones. I don't think crime stories would be good for you."

"Oh this was a crime-does-not-pay," Star said, "and I swear this cop looked exactly like him. They were always putting something over on the guy. He would look like he couldn't stand it a minute longer or he would blow up. He was a riot. And not bad looking," she added with an appreciative leer at Thomas.

"Star," his mother said, "I think it would be grand if you developed a taste for music."

Thomas sighed. His mother rattled on and the girl, paying no attention to her, let her eyes play over him. The quality of her look was such that it might have been her hands, resting now on his knees, now on his neck. Her eyes had a mocking glitter and he knew that she was well aware he could not stand the sight of her. He needed nothing to tell him he was in the presence of the very stuff of corruption, but blameless corruption because there was no responsible faculty behind it. He was looking at the most unendurable form of innocence. Absently he asked himself what the attitude of God was to this, meaning if possible to adopt it.

His mother's behavior throughout the meal was so idiotic that he could barely stand to look at her and since he could less stand to look at Sarah Ham, he fixed on the sideboard across the room a continuous gaze of disapproval and disgust. Every remark of the girl's his mother met as if it deserved serious attention. She advanced several plans for the wholesome use of Star's spare time. Sarah Ham paid no more attention to this advice than if it came from a parrot. Once when Thomas inadvertently looked in her direction, she winked. As soon as he had swallowed the last spoonful of dessert, he rose and muttered, "I have to go, I have a meeting."

"Thomas," his mother said, "I want you to take Star home on your way. I don't want her riding in taxis by herself at night."

For a moment Thomas remained furiously silent. Then he turned and left the room. Presently he came back with a look of obscure determination on his face. The girl was ready, meekly waiting at the parlor door. She cast up at him a great look of admiration and confidence. Thomas did not offer his arm but she took it anyway and moved out of the house and down the steps, attached to what might have been a miraculosly moving monument.

"Be good!" his mother called.

Sarah Ham snickered and poked him in the ribs.

While getting his coat he had decided that this would be his opportunity to tell the girl that unless she ceased to be a parasite on his mother, he would see to it, personally, that she was returned to jail. He would let her know that he understood what she was up to, that he was not an innocent and that there were certain things he would not put up with. At his desk, pen in hand, none was more articulate than Thomas. As soon as he found himself shut into the car with Sarah Ham, terror seized his tongue.

She curled her feet up under her and said, "Alone at last," and giggled.

Thomas swerved the car away from the house and drove fast toward the gate. Once on the highway, he shot forward as if he were being pursued.

"Jesus!" Sarah Ham said, swinging her feet off the seat, "where's the fire?"

Thomas did not answer. In a few seconds he could feel her edging closer. She stretched, eased nearer, and finally hung her hand limply over his shoulder. "Tomsee doesn't like me," she said, "but I think he's fabulously cute."

Thomas covered the three and a half miles into town in a little over four minutes. The light at the first intersection was red but he ignored it. The old woman lived three blocks beyond. When the car screeched to a halt at the place, he jumped out and ran around to the girl's door and opened it. She did not move from the car and Thomas was obliged to wait. After a moment one leg emerged, then her small white crooked face appeared and stared up at him. There was something about the look of it that suggested blindness but it was the blindness of those who don't know that they cannot see. Thomas was curiously sickened. The empty eyes moved over him. "Nobody likes me," she said in a sullen tone. "What if you were me and I couldn't stand to ride you three miles?"

"My mother likes you," he muttered.

"Her!" the girl said. "She's just about seventy-five years behind the times!"

Breathlessly Thomas said, "If I find you bothering her again, I'll have you put back in jail." There was a dull force behind his voice though it came out barely above a whisper.

"You and who else?" she said and drew back in the car as if now she did not intend to get out at all. Thomas reached into it, blindly grasped the front of her coat, pulled her out by it and released her. Then he lunged back to the car and sped off. The other door was still hanging open and her laugh, bodiless but real, bounded up the street as if it were about to jump in the open side of the car and ride away with him. He reached over and slammed the door and then drove toward home, too angry to attend his meeting. He intended to make his mother well-aware of his displeasure. He intended to leave no doubt in her mind. The voice of his father rasped in his head.

Numbskull, the old man said, put your foot down now. Show her who's boss before she shows you.

But when Thomas reached home, his mother, wisely, had gone to bed.

The next morning he appeared at the breakfast table, his brow lowered and the thrust of his jaw indicating that he was in a dangerous humor. When he intended to be determined, Thomas began like a bull that, before charging, backs with his head lowered and paws the ground. "All right now listen," he began, yanking out his chair and sitting down, "I have something to say to you about that girl and I don't intend to say it but once." He drew breath. "She's nothing but a little slut. She makes fun of you behind your back. She means to get everything she can out of you and you are nothing to her."

His mother looked as if she too had spent a restless night. She did not dress in the morning but wore her bathrobe and a grey turban around her head, which gave her face a disconcerting omniscient look. He might have been breakfasting with a sibyl.

"You'll have to use canned cream this morning," she said, pouring his coffee. "I forgot the other."

"All right, did you hear me?" Thomas growled.

"I'm not deaf," his mother said and put the pot back on the trivet. "I know I'm nothing but an old bag of wind to her."

"Then why do you persist in this foolhardy . . ."

"Thomas," she said, and put her hand to the side of her face, "it might be . . ."

"It is not me!" Thomas said, grasping the table leg at his knee.

She continued to hold her face, shaking her head slightly. "Think of all you have," she began. "All the comforts of home. And morals, Thomas. No bad inclinations, nothing bad you were born with."

Thomas began to breathe like someone who feels the onset of asthma. "You are not logical," he said in a limp voice. *"He* would have put his foot down."

The old lady stiffened. "You," she said, "are not like him."

Thomas opened his mouth silently.

"However," his mother said, in a tone of such subtle accusation that she might have been taking back the compliment, "I won't invite her back again since you're so dead set against her."

"I am not set against her," Thomas said. "I am set against your making a fool of yourself."

As soon as he left the table and closed the door of his study on himself, his father took up a squatting position in his mind. The old man had had the countryman's ability to converse squatting, though he was no countryman but had been born and brought up in the city and only moved to a smaller place later to exploit his talents. With steady skill he had made them think him one of them. In the midst of a conversation on the courthouse lawn, he would squat and his two or three companions would squat with him with no break in the surface of the talk. By gesture he had lived his lie; he had never deigned to tell one.

Let her run over you, he said. You ain't like me. Not enough to be a man.

Thomas began vigorously to read and presently the image faded. The girl had caused a disturbance in the depths of his being, somewhere out of the reach of his power of analysis. He felt as if he had seen a tornado pass a hundred yards away and had an intimation that it would turn again and head directly for him. He did not get his mind firmly on his work until mid-morning.

Two nights later, his mother and he were sitting in the den after their supper, each reading a section of the evening paper, when the telephone began to ring with the brassy intensity of a fire alarm. Thomas reached for it. As soon as the receiver was in his hand, a shrill female voice screamed into the room, "Come get this girl! Come get her! Drunk! Drunk in my parlor and I won't have it! Lost her job and come back here drunk! I won't have it!"

His mother leapt up and snatched the receiver.

The ghost of Thomas's father rose before him. Call the sheriff, the old man prompted. "Call the sheriff," Thomas said in a loud voice. "Call the sheriff to go there and pick her up."

"We'll be right there," his mother was saying. "We'll come and get her right away. Tell her to get her things together."

"She ain't in no condition to get nothing together," the voice screamed. "You shouldn't have put something like her off on me! My house is respectable!"

"Tell her to call the sheriff," Thomas shouted.

His mother put the receiver down and looked at him. "I wouldn't turn a dog over to that man," she said.

Thomas sat in the chair with his arms folded and looked fixedly at the wall.

"Think of the poor girl, Thomas," his mother said, "with nothing. Nothing. And we have everything."

When they arrived, Sarah Ham was slumped spraddle-legged against the banister on the boarding house front-steps. Her tam was down on her forehead where the old woman had slammed it and her clothes were bulging out of her suitcase where the old woman had thrown them in. She was carrying on a drunken conversation with herself in a low personal tone. A streak of lipstick ran up one side of her face. She allowed herself to be guided by his mother to the car and put in the back seat without seeming to know who the rescuer was. "Nothing to talk to all day but a pack of goddamned parakeets," she said in a furious whisper.

Thomas, who had not got out of the car at all, or looked at her after the first revolted glance, said, "I'm telling you, once and for all, the place to take her is the jail."

His mother, sitting on the back seat, holding the girl's hand, did not answer.

"All right, take her to the hotel," he said.

"I cannot take a drunk girl to a hotel, Thomas," she said. "You know that."

"Then take her to a hospital."

"She doesn't need a jail or a hotel or a hospital," his mother said, "she needs a home."

"She does not need mine," Thomas said.

"Only for tonight, Thomas," the old lady sighed. "Only for tonight."

Since then eight days had passed. The little slut was established in the guest room. Every day his mother set out to find her a job and a place to board, and failed, for the old woman had broadcast a warning. Thomas kept to his room or the den. His home was to him home, workshop, church, as personal as the shell of a turtle and as necessary. He could not believe that it could be violated in this way. His flushed face had a constant look of stunned outrage.

As soon as the girl was up in the morning, her voice throbbed out in a blues song that would rise and waver, then plunge low with insinuations of passion about to be satisfied and Thomas, at his desk, would lunge up and begin frantically stuffing his ears with Kleenex. Each time he started from one room to another, one floor to another, she would be certain to appear. Each time he was half way up or down the stairs, she would either meet him and pass, cringing coyly, or go up or down behind him, breathing small tragic spearmint-flavored sighs. She appeared to adore Thomas's repugnance to her and to draw it out of him every chance she got as if it added delectably to her martyrdom.

The old man—small, wasp-like, in his yellowed Panama hat, his seersucker suit, his pink carefully-soiled shirt, his small string tie—appeared to have taken up his station in Thomas's mind and from there, usually squatting, he shot out the same rasping suggestion every time the boy paused from his forced studies. Put your foot down. Go to see the sheriff.

The sheriff was another edition of Thomas's father except that he wore a checkered shirt and a Texas type hat and was ten years younger. He was as easily dishonest, and he had genuinely admired the old man. Thomas, like his mother, would have gone far out of his way to avoid his glassy pale blue gaze. He kept hoping for another solution, for a miracle.

With Sarah Ham in the house, meals were unbearable.

"Tomsee doesn't like me," she said the third or fourth night at the supper table and cast her pouting gaze across at the large rigid figure of Thomas, whose face was set with the look of a man trapped by insufferable odors. "He doesn't want me here. Nobody wants me anywhere."

"Thomas's name is Thomas," his mother interrupted. "Not Tomsee."

"I made Tomsee up," she said. "I think it's cute. He hates me."

"Thomas does not hate you," his mother said. "We are not the kind of people who hate," she added, as if this were an imperfection that had been bred out of them generations ago.

"Oh, I know when I'm not wanted," Sarah Ham continued. "They didn't even want me in jail. If I killed myself I wonder would God want me?"

"Try it and see," Thomas muttered.

The girl screamed with laughter. Then she stopped abruptly, her face puckered and she began to shake. "The best thing to do," she said, her teeth clattering, "is to kill myself. Then I'll be out of everybody's way. I'll go to hell and be out of God's way. And even the devil won't want me. He'll kick me out of hell, not even in hell . . ." she wailed.

Thomas rose, picked up his plate and knife and fork and carried them to the den to finish his supper. After that, he had not eaten another meal at the table but had had his mother serve him at his desk. At these meals, the old man was intensely present to him. He appeared to be tipping backwards in his chair, his thumbs beneath his galluses, while he said such things as, She never ran me away from my own table.

A few nights later, Sarah Ham slashed her wrists with a paring knife and had hysterics. From the den where he was closeted after supper, Thomas heard a shriek, then a series of screams, then his mother's scurrying footsteps through the house. He did not move. His first instant of hope that the girl had cut her throat faded as he realized she could not have done it and continue to scream the way she was doing. He returned to his journal and presently the screams subsided. In a moment his mother burst in with his coat and hat. "We have to take her to the hospital," she said. "She tried to do away with herself. I have a tourniquet on her arm. Oh Lord, Thomas," she said, "imagine being so low you'd do a thing like that!"

Thomas rose woodenly and put on his hat and coat. "We will take her to the hospital," he said, "and we will leave her there."

"And drive her to despair again?" the old lady cried. "Thomas!"

Standing in the center of his room now, realizing that he had reached the point where action was inevitable, that he must pack, that he must leave, that he must go, Thomas remained immovable.

His fury was directed not at the little slut but at his mother. Even though the doctor had found that she had barely damaged herself and had raised the girl's wrath by laughing at the tourniquet and putting only a streak of iodine on the cut, his mother could not get over the incident. Some new weight of sorrow seemed to have been thrown across her shoulders, and not only Thomas, but Sarah Ham was infuriated by this, for it appeared to be a general sorrow that would have found another object no matter what good fortune came to either of them. The experience of Sarah Ham had plunged the old lady into mourning for the world.

The morning after the attempted suicide, she had gone through the house and collected all the knives and scissors and locked them in a drawer. She emptied a bottle of rat poison down the toilet and took up the roach tablets from the kitchen floor. Then she came to Thomas's study and said in a whisper, "Where is that gun of his? I want you to lock it up."

"The gun is in my drawer," Thomas roared, "and I will not lock it up. If she shoots herself, so much the better!"

"Thomas," his mother said, "she'll hear you!"

"Let her hear me!" Thomas yelled. "Don't you know she has no intention of killing herself? Don't you know her kind never kill themselves? Don't you . . ."

His mother slipped out the door and closed it to silence him and Sarah Ham's laugh, quite close in the hall, came rattling into his room. "Tomsee'll find out. I'll kill myself and then he'll be sorry he wasn't nice to me. I'll use his own lil gun, his own lil ol' pearl-handled revol-lervuh!" she shouted and let out a loud tormented-sounding laugh in imitation of a movie monster.

Thomas ground his teeth. He pulled out his desk drawer and felt for the pistol. It was an inheritance from the old man, whose opinion it had been that every house should contain a loaded gun. He had discharged two bullets one night into the side of a prowler, but Thomas had never shot anything. He had no fear that the girl would use the gun on herself and he closed the drawer. Her kind clung tenaciously to life and were able to wrest some histrionic advantage from every moment.

Several ideas for getting rid of her had entered his head but each of these had been suggestions whose moral tone indicated that they had come from a mind akin to his father's, and Thomas had rejected them. He could not get the girl locked up again until she did something illegal. The old man would have been able with no qualms at all to get her drunk and send her out on the highway in his car, meanwhile notifying the highway patrol of her presence on the road, but Thomas considered this below his moral stature. Suggestions continued to come to him, each more outrageous than the last.

He had not the vaguest hope that the girl would get the gun and shoot herself, but that afternoon when he looked in the drawer, the gun was gone. His study locked from the inside, not the out. He cared nothing about the gun, but the thought of Sarah Ham's hands sliding among his papers infuriated him. Now even his study was contaminated. The only place left untouched by her was his bedroom.

That night she entered it.

In the morning at breakfast, he did not eat and did not sit down. He stood beside his chair and delivered his ultimatum while his mother sipped her coffee as if she were both alone in the room and in great pain. "I have stood this," he said, "for as long as I am able. Since I see plainly that you care nothing about me, about my peace or comfort or working conditions, I am about to take the only step open to me. I will give you one more day. If you bring the girl back into this house this afternoon, I leave. You can choose—her or me." He had more to say but at that point his voice cracked and he left.

At ten o'clock his mother and Sarah Ham left the house.

At four he heard the car wheels on the gravel and rushed to the window. As the car stopped, the dog stood up, alert, shaking.

He seemed unable to take the first step that would set him walking to the closet in the hall to look for the suitcase. He was like a man handed a knife and told to operate on himself if he wished to live. His huge hands clenched helplessly. His expression was a turmoil of indecision and outrage. His pale blue eyes seemed to sweat in his broiling face. He closed them for a moment and on the back of his lids, his father's image leered at him. Idiot! the old man hissed, idiot! The criminal slut stole your gun! See the sheriff! See the sheriff!

It was a moment before Thomas opened his eyes. He seemed newly stunned. He stood where he was for at least three minutes, then he turned slowly like a large vessel reversing its direction and faced the door. He stood there a moment longer, then he left, his face set to see the ordeal through.

He did not know where he would find the sheriff. The man made his own rules and kept his own hours. Thomas stopped first at the jail, where his office was, but he was not in it. He went to the courthouse and was told by a clerk that the sheriff had gone to the barber-shop across the street. "Yonder's the deppity," the clerk said and pointed out the window to the large figure of a man in a checkered shirt, who was leaning against the side of a police car, looking into space.

"It has to be the sheriff," Thomas said and left for the barber-shop. As little as he wanted anything to do with the sheriff, he realized that the man was at least intelligent and not simply a mound of sweating flesh.

The barber said the sheriff had just left. Thomas started back to the courthouse and as he stepped on to the sidewalk from the street, he saw a lean, slightly stooped figure gesticulating angrily at the deputy.

Thomas approached with an aggressiveness brought on by nervous agitation. He stopped abruptly three feet away and said in an over-loud voice, "Can I have a word with you?" without adding the sheriff's name, which was Farebrother.

Farebrother turned his sharp creased face just enough to take Thomas in, and the deputy did likewise, but neither spoke. The sheriff removed a very small piece of cigaret from his lip and dropped it at his feet. "I told you what to do," he said to the deputy. Then he moved off with a slight nod that indicated Thomas could follow him if he wanted to see him. The deputy slunk around the front of the police car and got inside.

Farebrother, with Thomas following, headed across the courthouse square and stopped beneath a tree that shaded a quarter of the front lawn. He waited, leaning slightly forward, and lit another cigaret.

Thomas began to blurt out his business. As he had not had time to prepare his words, he was barely coherent. By repeating the same thing over several times, he managed at length to get out what he wanted to say. When he finished, the sheriff was still leaning slightly forward, at an angle to him, his eyes on nothing in particular. He remained that way without speaking.

Thomas began again, slower and in a lamer voice, and Farebrother let him continue for some time before he said, "We had her oncet." He then allowed himself a slow, creased, all-knowing, quarter smile.

"I had nothing to do with that," Thomas said. "That was my mother."

Farebrother squatted.

"She was trying to help the girl," Thomas said. "She didn't know she couldn't be helped."

"Bit off more than she could chew, I reckon," the voice below him mused.

"She has nothing to do with this," Thomas said. "She doesn't know I'm here. The girl is dangerous with that gun."

"He," the sheriff said, "never let anything grow under his feet. Particularly nothing a woman planted."

"She might kill somebody with that gun," Thomas said weakly, looking down at the round top of the Texas type hat.

There was a long time of silence.

"Where's she got it?" Farebrother asked.

"I don't know. She sleeps in the guest room. It must be in there, in her suitcase probably," Thomas said.

Farebrother lapsed into silence again.

"You could come search the guest room," Thomas said in a strained voice. "I can go home and leave the latch off the front door and you can come in quietly and go upstairs and search her room."

Farebrother turned his head so that his eyes looked boldly at Thomas's knees. "You seem to know how it ought to be done," he said. "Want to swap jobs?"

Thomas said nothing because he could not think of anything to say, but he waited doggedly. Farebrother removed the cigaret butt from his lips and dropped it on the grass. Beyond him on the courthouse porch a group of loiterers who had been leaning at the left of the door moved over to the right where a patch of sunlight had settled. From one of the upper windows a crumpled piece of paper blew out and drifted down.

"I'll come along about six," Farebrother said. "Leave the latch off the door and keep out of my way—yourself and them two women too."

Thomas let out a rasping sound of relief meant to be "Thanks," and struck off across the grass like someone released. The phrase, "them two women," stuck like a burr in his brain—the subtlety of the insult to his mother hurting him more than any of Farebrother's references to his own incompetence. As he got into his car, his face suddenly flushed. Had he delivered his mother over to the sheriff—to be a butt for the man's tongue? Was he betraying her to get rid of the little slut? He saw at once that this was not the case. He was doing what he was doing for her own good, to rid her of a parasite that would ruin their peace. He started his car and drove quickly home but once he had turned in the driveway, he decided it would be better to park some distance from the house and go quietly in by the back door. He parked on the grass and on the grass walked in a circle toward the rear of the house. The sky was lined with mustard-colored streaks. The dog was asleep on the back doormat. At the approach of his master's step, he opened one yellow eye, took him in, and closed it again.

Thomas let himself into the kitchen. It was empty and the house was quiet enough for him to be aware of the loud ticking of the kitchen clock. It was a quarter to six. He tiptoed hurriedly through the hall to the front door and took the latch off it. Then he stood for a moment listening. From behind the closed parlor door, he heard his mother snoring softly and presumed that she had gone to sleep while reading. On the other side of the hall, not three feet from his study, the little slut's black coat and red pocketbook were slung on a chair. He heard water running upstairs and decided she was taking a bath.

He went into his study and sat down at his desk to wait, noting with distaste that every few moments a tremor ran through him. He sat for a minute or two doing nothing. Then he picked up a pen and began to draw squares on the back of an envelope that lay before him. He looked at his watch. It was eleven minutes to six. After a moment he idly drew the center drawer of the desk out over his lap. For a moment he stared at the gun without recognition. Then he gave a yelp and leaped up. She had put it back!

Idiot! his father hissed, idiot! Go plant it in her pocketbook. Don't just stand there. Go plant it in her pocketbook!

Thomas stood staring at the drawer.

Moron! the old man fumed. Quick while there's time! Go plant it in her pocketbook.

Thomas did not move.

Imbecile! his father cried.

Thomas picked up the gun.

Make haste, the old man ordered.

Thomas started forward, holding the gun away from him. He opened the door and looked at the chair. The black coat and red pocketbook were lying on it almost within reach.

Hurry up, you fool, his father said.

From behind the parlor door the almost inaudible snores of his mother rose and fell. They seemed to mark an order of time that had nothing to do with the instants left to Thomas. There was no other sound.

Quick, you imbecile, before she wakes up, the old man said.

The snores stopped and Thomas heard the sofa springs groan. He grabbed the red pocketbook. It had a skin-like feel to his touch and as it opened, he caught an unmistakable odor of the girl. Wincing, he thrust in the gun and then drew back. His face burned an ugly dull red.

"What is Tomsee putting in my purse?" she called and her pleased laugh bounced down the staircase. Thomas whirled.

She was at the top of the stair, coming down in the manner of a fashion model, one bare leg and then the other thrusting out the front of her kimona in a definite rhythm. "Tomsee is being naughty," she said in a throaty voice. She reached the bottom and cast a possessive leer at Thomas whose face was now more grey than red. She reached out, pulled the bag open with her finger and peered at the gun.

His mother opened the parlor door and looked out.

"Tomsee put his pistol in my bag!" the girl shrieked.

"Ridiculous," his mother said, yawning. "What would Thomas want to put his pistol in your bag for?"

Thomas stood slightly hunched, his hands hanging helplessly at the wrists as if he had just pulled them up out of a pool of blood.

"I don't know what for," the girl said, "but he sure did it," and she proceeded to walk around Thomas, her hands on her hips, her neck thrust forward and her intimate grin fixed on him fiercely. All at once her expression seemed to open as the purse had opened when Thomas touched it. She stood with her head cocked on one side in an attitude of disbelief. "Oh boy," she said slowly, "is he a case."

At that instant Thomas damned not only the girl but the entire order of the universe that made her possible.

"Thomas wouldn't put a gun in your bag," his mother said. "Thomas is a gentleman."

The girl made a chortling noise. "You can see it in there," she said and pointed to the open purse.

You *found* it in her bag, you dimwit! the old man hissed.

"I found it in her bag!" Thomas shouted. "The dirty criminal slut stole my gun!"

His mother gasped at the sound of the other presence in his voice. The old lady's sybil-like face turned pale.

"Found it my eye!" Sarah Ham shrieked and started for the pocketbook, but Thomas, as if his arm were guided by his father, caught it first and snatched the gun. The girl in a frenzy lunged at Thomas's throat and would actually have caught him around the neck had not his mother thrown herself forward to protect her.

Fire! the old man yelled.

Thomas fired. The blast was like a sound meant to bring an end to evil in the world. Thomas heard it as a sound that would shatter the laughter of sluts until all shrieks were stilled and nothing was left to disturb the peace of perfect order.

The echo died away in waves. Before the last one had faded, Farebrother opened the door and put his head inside the hall. His nose wrinkled. His expression for some few seconds was that of a man unwilling to admit surprise. His eyes were clear as glass, reflecting the scene. The old lady lay on the floor between the girl and Thomas.

The sheriff's brain worked instantly like a calculating machine. He saw the facts as if they were already in print: the fellow had intended all along to kill his mother and pin it on the girl. But Farebrother had been too quick for him. They were not yet aware of his head in the door. As he scrutinized the scene, further insights were flashed to him. Over her body, the killer and the slut were about to collapse into each other's arms. The sheriff knew a nasty bit when he saw it. He was accustomed to enter upon scenes that were not as bad as he had hoped to find them, but this one met his expectations.

A Note About the Editor

Ross Macdonald was born near San Francisco in 1915. He was educated in Canadian schools, traveled widely in Europe, and acquired advanced degrees and a Phi Beta Kappa key at the University of Michigan. In 1938 he married a Canadian who is now well known as the novelist Margaret Millar. Mr. Macdonald (Kenneth Millar in private life) taught school and later college, and served as communications officer aboard an escort carrier in the Pacific. For over twenty years he has lived in Santa Barbara and written mystery novels about the fascinating and changing society of his native state. Among his leading interests are conservation and politics. He is a past president of the Mystery Writers of America. In 1964 his novel *The Chill* was given a Silver Dagger award by the Crime Writers' Association of Great Britain. Mr. Macdonald's *The Far Side of the Dollar* was named the best crime novel of 1965 by the same organization. *The Moving Target* was made into the highly successful movie *Harper* (1966). And *The Goodbye Look* (1969), *The Underground Man* (1971), and *Sleeping Beauty* (1973) were all national best sellers.

A Note on the Type

The text of this book is set in Caledonia, a type face designed by William Addison Dwiggins for the Mergenthaler Linotype Company in 1939. Dwiggins chose to call his new type face Caledonia, the Roman name for Scotland, because it was inspired by the Scotch types cast about 1833 by Alexander Wilson & Son, Glasgow type founders. However, there is a calligraphic quality about Caledonia that is totally lacking in the Wilson types. Dwiggins referred to an even earlier type face for this "liveliness of action"—one cut around 1790 by William Martin for the printer William Bulmer. Caledonia has more weight than the Martin letters, and the bottom finishing strokes (serifs) of the letters are cut straight across, without brackets, to make sharp angles with the upright stems, thus giving a "modern face" appearance.

W. A. Dwiggins (1880–1956) began an association with the Mergenthaler Linotype Company in 1929 and over the next twenty-seven years designed a number of book types, the most interesting of which are the Metro series, Electra, Caledonia, Eldorado, and Falcon.